Praise for
James A. Michener

"A book about oil and water, rangers and outlaws, frontier and settlement, money and power . . . James Michener is something rare and valuable: an honorable craftsman doing honorable work. . . . He manages to make history vivid."
—The Boston Globe, on Texas

"Fascinating . . . a wonderful rampage through history."
—The New York Times, on The Source

"Alaska takes the reader on a journey through one of the bleakest, richest, most foreboding, and highly inviting territories in our Republic, if not the world. . . . The characters that Michener creates are bigger than life. . . . Colorful, informative, and historically accurate."
—Los Angeles Times Book Review, on Alaska

"[A] mammoth epic of the islands, [a] vast paranormal . . . wonderful."
—Baltimore Sun, on Hawaii

"The severity, the vastness and the poetry of a faraway land . . . a slam-bang success."
—New York Herald Tribune, on Caravans

"Michener's most ambitious work of fiction in theme and scope."
—The Philadelphia Inquirer, on Chesapeake

BY JAMES A. MICHENER

CARIBBEAN

CARIBBEAN

A NOVEL

JAMES A. MICHENER

DIAL PRESS TRADE PAPERBACKS

NEW YORK

2014 Dial Press Trade Paperback Edition

Copyright © 1989 by James A. Michener
Cartography copyright © 1989 by Jean Paul Tremblay
Illustrations copyright © 1989 by Franca Nucci Haynes
Introduction copyright © 2014 by Steve Berry

Published in the United States by Dial Press Trade Paperbacks, an imprint of Random House, a division of Random House LLC, a Penguin Random House Company, New York.

DIAL PRESS and the HOUSE colophon are registered trademarks of Random House LLC.

Originally published in hardcover in the United States by Random House, an imprint of The Random House Publishing Group, a division of Random House LLC, in 1989.

LIBRARY OF CONGRESS CATALOGING-IN-PUBLICATION DATA
Michener, James A. (James Albert)
Caribbean / James A. Michener
p.   cm.
ISBN 978-0-8129-7492-8
eBook ISBN 978-0-8041-5153-5
I. Caribbean Area—History—Fiction. I. Title
PS3525:I19C38 1989 813.'54-dc20 89-42785

Printed in Canada on acid-free paper

www.dialpress.com

Book design by Carole Lowenstein

12th Printing

This book is dedicated
to the gentle memory
of

ALEC WAUGH

who told me when we were working
together in Hawaii in 1959
"Someday you must write about my
Caribbean."

INTRODUCTION

Steve Berry

I grew up in the 1960s, a time when the extent of reading material for kids was, to say the least, limited. R. L. Stine, J. K. Rowling, Suzanne Collins, and so many others had yet to come along. In fact, what we now know as the young adult genre had yet to be invented. Back then, at least for me, it was Hardy Boys and Nancy Drew. A limited selection, but what gems those tales were— each loaded with action, adventure, secrets, and conspiracies. Wondrous stories to fuel young imaginations. I devoured them.

Then one day when I was sixteen years old, a friend handed me a dog-eared paperback copy of *Hawaii* by James Michener. Its thousand pages immediately intimidated me, as did the small print. I'd never seen so much information packed into one book. The opening sentence alone contained thirty-six words—monstrous in comparison to the prose of Franklin W. Dixon.

But what a sentence: *Millions upon millions of years ago, when the continents were already formed and the principal features of the earth had been decided, there existed, then as now, one aspect of the world that dwarfed all others.*

I kept reading.

What unfolded was a saga spanning many centuries that described how a tiny group of islands in the Pacific Ocean were formed by nature and then settled by man. The epic involved Polynesians, Chinese, Japanese, Europeans, and Americans. Its massive chapters, hundreds of pages long, featured one expansive episode after another—each intertwined—forming a chronicle that defined both the land and its culture. I read it cover to cover. Then I found more books by this guy Michener and read every one. Eventually, I started collecting them, and now, more than forty years later, I own a first edition of each, save one—*Tales of the South Pacific*. That book is hard to find. Only a few thousand were printed and, if by some miracle one of those 1947 first editions can be found, the price is through the roof. I keep every one of my Michener books prominently displayed, wrapped in plastic. I see them every day. They are a source of pride and comfort. Today, I write modern-day thrillers in which history plays a central role. Without question, the seed for that technique was planted the day I discovered *Hawaii*.

James Michener led an incredible life. Born in 1907, he was orphaned but was soon adopted by a woman named Mabel Michener, who was already raising two other children. Some of his biographers have hypothesized that he was actually Mabel's natural son, the adoption story used to protect both of their reputations. No one knows the truth, and as an adult Michener refused to comment on the subject.

By the time he turned ten, the family had moved to Bucks County, Pennsylvania. They were poor, barely able to put food on the table. His classmates, and even a teacher or two, tormented Michener about the secondhand clothes and toeless sneakers he wore every day. Later in life he recounted that taunting with a sly smile and a twinkle in his eye. He would say that those early years instilled in him an appreciation for life that he never forgot. They taught him about living simply and not attaching too much value to material things. And though he eventually earned hundreds of millions of dollars from writing, he always feared ending up poor.

Before he'd even reached twenty years of age, Michener had traveled across the country in boxcars, by thumbing rides, or simply by walking. He worked in carnival shows and other odd jobs, and he visited all but three states. Of that time, he wrote in his 1991 autobiography, *The World Is My Home,* "Those were years of wonder and enchantment. Some of the best years I would know. I kept meeting American citizens of all levels who took me into their cars, their confidence and often their homes." He would also say that those wandering years spurred inside him an insatiable curiosity about people, cultures, and faraway lands.

In 1925 he entered Swarthmore College, a prestigious Quaker institution, on a four-year scholarship, graduating with highest honors. He attended graduate school in Scotland, then returned home and taught at a school in Bucks County. He eventually ended up in New York City, editing textbooks at Macmillan Publishing.

World War II changed everything. At age forty Michener enlisted in the navy, where he discovered the enchanting South Pacific. He earned the rank of lieutenant commander and was made a naval historian, assigned to investigate cultural problems on the various islands. A near-fatal crash landing in French New Caledonia altered the course of his life. He wrote in his autobiography, "As the stars came out and I could see the low mountains I had escaped, I swore: 'I'm going to live the rest of my life as if I were a great man.' And despite the terrible braggadocio of those words, I understood precisely what I meant."

That brush with death also made him realize what every soldier was experiencing during the war, and that one day, when the danger had passed, people might want to recall those things. So each night he began writing down observations, recording comments, describing people and places. Fifty years later, in 1991, he said:

> Sitting there in the darkness, illuminated only by the flickering lamplight, I visualized the aviation scenes in which I had participated, the landing beaches I'd seen, the remote outposts, the exquisite islands with bending palms, and especially the valiant people I'd known: the French planters, the Australian coast watchers, the Navy nurses, the Tonkinese laborers, the ordinary sailors and soldiers who were doing the work, and the primitive natives to whose jungle fastnesses I had traveled.

All of that became *Tales of the South Pacific*.

The story of how that first manuscript made it to print is typical Michener—an unexpected combination of skill, determination, and luck. Using a pseudonym, he submitted the work to Macmillan, the publisher he'd worked for before enlisting. He omitted his name because he knew the company had a strict policy against publishing anything by an employee. Once the war was over he definitely intended to return to work there, but at the time of the submission he was technically a naval officer and not an employee. So the company bought the book, which was published in 1947. One year later *Tales of the South Pacific* won the Pulitzer Prize for fiction.

Michener changed publishers in 1949, moving to Random House, where he stayed for the rest of his life. More books followed—*The Fires of Spring, Return to Paradise, The Bridges at Toko-Ri,* and *Sayonara*. Also in 1949 he moved to Honolulu and soon began work on his most ambitious project to date. Four years of research and three years of writing were needed to produce *Hawaii*. Its epic scope, length, and breadth proved to be the stamp of Michener's trademark style, one he would master over the next forty years. Legend has it that he finished *Hawaii* on March 18, 1959, the day Congress voted to accept the islands as the fiftieth state.

In 1962 Michener ran for Congress as a liberal Democrat but lost. Then, in 1968, he worked as secretary of the Pennsylvania Constitutional Convention. Outer space was a lifelong interest, and he served on NASA's advisory council, an experience that led to his novel *Space*.

Honors were something Michener shied away from, but in 1977 Gerald Ford bestowed upon him the Presidential Medal of Freedom, the nation's highest civilian award. Eventually, he wrote nearly fifty books, including five on Japanese art. His work has been translated into multiple languages, and there are more than 75 million copies of his books in print. These latest editions, being rereleased with new covers, will only add to that already staggering inventory.

A myth associated with Michener speaks of his cadre of researchers, used to gather the enormous amount of historical detail included in each of his epics. The reality was quite different. Most of the work was accomplished with the help of only three secretaries. He was a disciplined writer, establishing a routine early in his career and maintaining it his entire life. An early riser, he would go straight to work, where he wrote using a manual typewriter. He then had a light breakfast, maybe a meeting or two, and went back to work until around one P.M. Evenings were a time to be by himself. In the final year of his life, at age ninety, he still kept to his daily routine, except he spent three days a week at a renal treatment center, undergoing kidney dialysis.

The treatment proved painful in a multitude of ways, perhaps the most difficult being that it prevented him from straying far from home. The man who'd visited nearly every country could no longer travel. He told an interviewer at the time, "I sit in the TV room and see shows on the big ships I used to travel or areas that I used to wander, and a tear comes to my eye. It's not easy."

And that explains his death—he simply decided there would be no more dialysis. Instead, he welcomed the end.

Michener died on October 16, 1997.

I recall the day vividly. A segment on the evening news reported that he was gone. A sadness came over me, as if I'd lost a close friend—which, in a sense, I had.

In preparation for writing this introduction, I reviewed many articles written just after Michener passed. Most came from folks who'd had some personal contact with him through the years—an experience that had clearly stuck in their memory. All of them recounted what happened as if they had been in the presence of a king or head of state. It seemed a privilege to have spent just a little time with James Michener.

And that legacy lives on.

Though he was known to be fanatically frugal, he gave away more than $100 million. Recipients of his generosity included libraries, museums, and universities. He donated $30 million to the University of Texas for the establishment of a creative writing program. Several million more went to the creation of the James A. Michener Art Museum in Pennsylvania. One wing of that building was named for his third wife, Mari Sabusawa Michener, who died before him, in 1994.

He never really liked talking about himself, and he could frustrate interviewers. "Famous is a word I never use," he would say. "I'm well known. I've written thirty or forty books. I've done a great deal. I let it go at that." He was extremely generous with his autograph, so much so that he once noted, "The most valuable books are those that aren't signed."

Of my own collection, only one bears his signature.

To the frequently asked question, "Which book are you most proud of?" he would just smile and say, "The one I'm working on next."

By no means was he perfect. He could be a difficult man to know. He wasn't the type to start conversations with strangers, and he detested small talk. He had few close friends, and those who counted themselves in that number knew to tread lightly. He could be abrupt, even rude, and quite aloof. After his death we learned that he utilized collaborators on some of the big books, a fact he refused to acknowledge in life. He was married three times and at one point maintained a mistress. He was a multimillionaire, yet he would constantly fret about not having enough money to pay his bills. And though he was an orphan himself and a co-founder of an adoption agency, in the 1950s he gave up his claim to an adopted child when he divorced his second wife.

All of which shows that he was human.

But still, what a remarkable man.

Michener possessed an incomparable ability to simultaneously enthrall, entertain, and inform. Nobody else could write a two-hundred-word sentence with such grace and style. And he chose his subjects with great care: the South Pacific (*Tales of the South Pacific, Return to Paradise*), Judaism (*The Source*), South Africa (*The Covenant*), the West Indies (*Caribbean*), the American West (*Centennial*), the Chesapeake Bay (*Chesapeake*), *Texas, Alaska,* Spain (*Iberia*), *Mexico, Poland,* the Far East.

Like millions of other readers, I loved them all.

I never met James Michener. I would have loved to tell him how he sparked the imagination of a sixteen-year-old boy, which led first to a lifelong love of reading, then to a career as a writer. When, in 1990, I decided to write my first novel, it was Michener who influenced me most. By the end of that decade, though, changes had firmly begun to take hold. Today you won't encounter many two-hundred-word sentences or millennia-long sagas involving hundreds of characters. Instead, in the twenty-first century, story, prose, and purpose are expected to be tight. In the Internet age—with video games, twenty-four-hour news, streaming movies, you name it—there is just little time for thousand-page epics. Toward the end of his life Michener gave an interview in which he doubted he would have ever been published if he'd first started in that environment.

Thank goodness he came along when he did.

Now his stories can live forever.

FACT AND FICTION

Though it is based on fact, this novel uses fictional events, places and characters. The following paragraphs endeavor to clarify which is which.

I. Croton. The peaceful Arawaks were overrun by the warrior Caribs at about the time indicated. There is historical evidence for the life of the two tribes as portrayed. All characters are fictional.

II. Maya. Tulúm, Cozumel, Chichén Itzá and Palenque are historic sites accurately portrayed. All characters are fictional.

III. Columbus. Cristóbal Colón, King Ferdinand, Francisco de Bobadilla and the heroic canoeist Diego Méndez are historic characters; all others are fictional. Colón was heavily investigated and was sent home a prisoner.

IV. Spanish Lake. Sir John Hawkins and Sir Francis Drake are historic, as is Viceroy Martín Enriquez, their Spanish adversary at San Juan de Ulúa. All other Spanish characters are fictional. The exploits of Drake are accurately summarized.

V. Barbados. Lord Francis Willoughby, Sir George Ayscue and Prince Rupert are historic, all others are fictional. The various events are historic and are accurately presented.

VI. Buccaneers. Henry Morgan and his various raids are historic and are accurately portrayed. All other characters are fictional. The circumnavigation of South America occurred, but with real buccaneers and in about the same route and elapsed time as given.

VII. Sugar. Admiral Edward Vernon, General Thomas Wentworth and the Spanish naval hero Don Blas de Lezo are historic, and their confrontation at Cartagena is accurately portrayed. The great Beckford and Dawkins planter families are accurately depicted. William Pitt (the Elder) is historic, as were the Danish rules for disciplining slaves. All other characters are fictional.

VIII. Nelson. Horatio Nelson, Admiral Sir Edward Hughes and Mrs. Nisbet are historic. All others are fictional, but everything said about Nelson and his frantic search for a wealthy wife is based on fact.

IX. Guadeloupe. Victor Hugues was a real man, but while sources agree on his behavior during the French Revolution, both in France and in the islands, they vary as to his early years. Some deny that he had ever been a barber in Haiti. All other characters are fictional, but the grisly events in Guadeloupe are historic and Hugues did die a strong reactionary in responsible office.

X. Haiti. The black General Toussaint L'Ouverture, Napoleon's General Charles Le Clerc and his wife Pauline Bonaparte, the English General Thomas Maitland and the black voodoo leader Boukman are all historic, as was the ill-fated Polish battalion. All other characters are fictional, but the various swings of war and the ultimate black victory are accurately described.

XI. Martial Law in Jamaica. Only the two plantation owners, Jason Pembroke and Oliver Croome, are fictional. Governor Edward John Eyre and all others are historic, especially the leaders of the debate in London: Tennyson and Carlyle of the pro-Eyre forces, Mill of the antis. Their attitudes are reported accurately. The actions of the two murderous martial-law enforcers, Hobbs and Ramsay, are historic, including their suicides. The ugly opinions of Carlyle can be found in his writings.

XII. Letters at All Saints. The island itself is purely fictional, a composite of several real places. All characters are fictional, except that the great black cricketer Sir Benny Castain is based upon four real black athletes of considerable fame.

XIII. Trinidad Scholar. The events and the characters who participate in them are totally fictional, but the two universities, West Indies and Miami, are faithfully presented. Events relating to the fraudulent marriage were verified by Immigration authorities and represent common practice.

XIV. Rasta Man. All events and characters are fictional, but the characteristics of the Rastafarian and his religion are based on careful study and interviews.

XV. Cuba. Fidel Castro is historic. All other characters are fictional, but none are exaggerated. Data on life in Miami and Havana are authentic, but the interview with Castro is based on reports of others.

XVI. Final Tour. Thérèse Vaval is totally fictional, as are her ship the *Galante* and the cruise it makes and the characters she encounters. But some ten or a dozen ships like hers leave Miami or San Juan weekly for island routes that are markedly similar except that they do not visit Trinidad. The general conditions she finds can be easily duplicated and her conclusions are shared by many.

CONTENTS

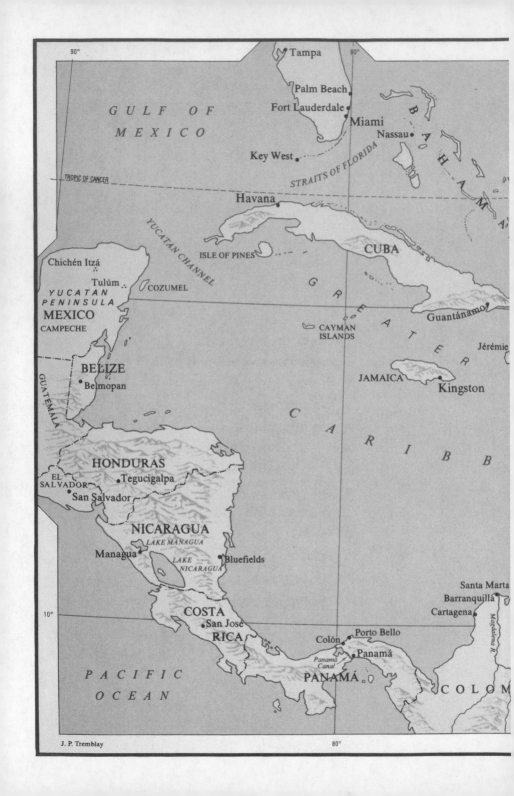

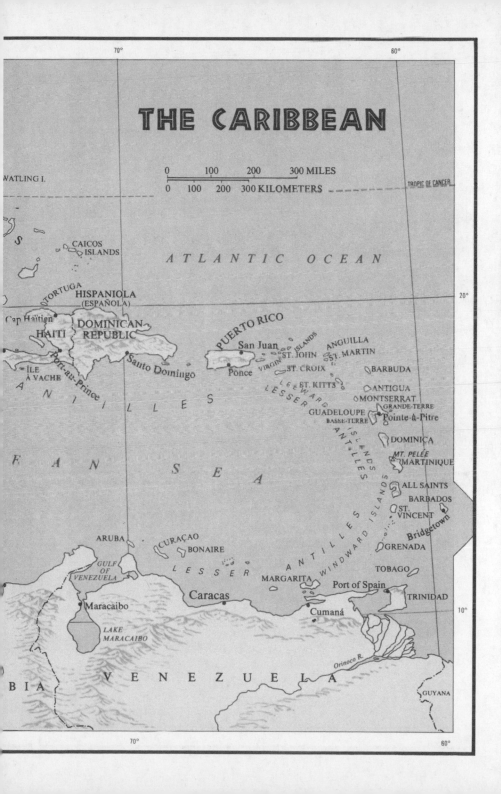

THE CARIBBEAN

0   100   200   300 MILES

0   100   200   300 KILOMETERS

TROPIC OF CANCER

WATLING I.

CAICOS ISLANDS

ATLANTIC OCEAN

20°

TORTUGA

HISPANIOLA
(ESPAÑOLA)

Cap Haïtien

DOMINICAN REPUBLIC

HAITI

ÎLE À VACHE

Port-au-Prince

Santo Domingo

PUERTO RICO

San Juan

Ponce

VIRGIN ISLANDS

ST. JOHN

ST. CROIX

ANGUILLA

ST. MARTIN

BARBUDA

ST. KITTS

ANTIGUA

MONTSERRAT

GRANDE-TERRE

GUADELOUPE

BASSE-TERRE

Pointe-à-Pitre

DOMINICA

MT. PELÉE

MARTINIQUE

ALL SAINTS

BARBADOS

ST. VINCENT

Bridgetown

GRENADA

TOBAGO

Port of Spain

TRINIDAD

10°

LEEWARD ANTILLES

WINDWARD ISLANDS

LESSER ANTILLES

ANTILLES

GREATER ANTILLES

CARIBBEAN SEA

ARUBA

CURAÇAO

BONAIRE

GULF OF VENEZUELA

LESSER

MARGARITA

Caracas

Cumaná

Maracaibo

LAKE MARACAIBO

COLOMBIA

VENEZUELA

Orinoco R.

GUYANA

70°

60°

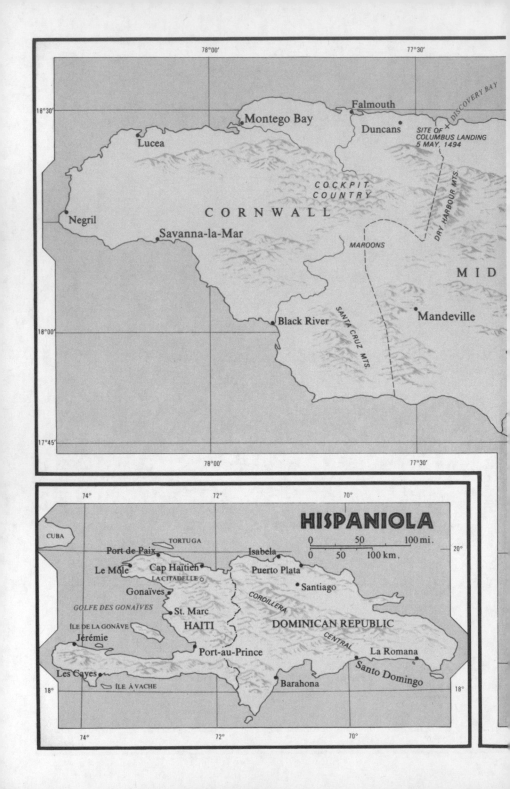

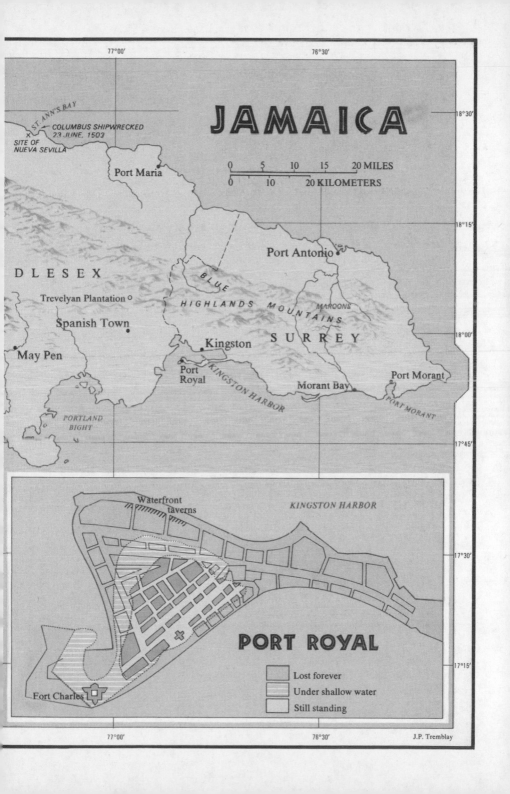

JAMAICA

ST. ANN'S BAY

× COLUMBUS SHIPWRECKED
23 JUNE, 1503

SITE OF
NUEVA SEVILLA

Port Maria

| 0 | 5 | 10 | 15 | 20 MILES |

| 0 | 10 | 20 KILOMETERS |

18°30'

18°15'

Port Antonio

D L E S E X

Trevelyan Plantation ○

BLUE

HIGHLANDS MOUNTAINS

MAROONS

Spanish Town

Kingston

S U R R E Y

18°00'

May Pen

Port
Royal

KINGSTON HARBOR

Port Morant

Morant Bay

PORT MORANT

PORTLAND
BIGHT

17°45'

Port Royal inset

Waterfront
taverns

KINGSTON HARBOR

17°30'

PORT ROYAL

Fort Charles

17°15'

	Lost forever
	Under shallow water
	Still standing

77°00'

76°30'

J.P. Tremblay

CARIBBEAN

I

A HEDGE
OF CROTON

THE CHIEF CHARACTER IN THIS NARRATIVE IS THE CARIBBEAN
Sea, one of the world's most alluring bodies of water, a rare gem
among the oceans, defined by the islands that form a chain of lovely
jewels to the north and east. Although bounded on the south and
west by continental land masses, it is the islands that give the Caribbean its unique charm. On the north lies the large and important
trio: Puerto Rico, Hispaniola (Haiti and the Dominican Republic)
and great Cuba. On the east are those heavenly small islands that so
artistically dot the blue waves: Antigua, Guadeloupe, Martinique, All
Saints, Trinidad and remote Barbados among them. The southern
shore is formed by the South American countries of Venezuela and
Colombia and the Central American nation of Panamá. The western
shore is often overlooked, but it contains both the exciting republics
of Central America—Costa Rica, Nicaragua and Honduras—and
the wonderful, mysterious peninsula of Yucatán where the ancient
Maya flourished.

The Caribbean, nearly nineteen hundred miles wide from Barbados to Yucatán, does not include either the Bahama Islands or Florida, but does contain near its center an island which at intervals
assumed an importance greater than most of the others, Jamaica
with its turbulent history.

In the centuries following its discovery by Columbus in 1492, the Caribbean was dominated by European nations fascinated by its wealth, its inviting charm and its strategic importance in naval warfare. Spain, Holland, England, France and, at brief intervals, Denmark and Sweden all became embroiled in Caribbean affairs, until it seemed that the area's destiny was determined not by actions in the Caribbean but by what transpired in Europe. Conversely, and this became a crucial factor in world history, European destinies were frequently determined by great sea battles in the Caribbean, especially those fought among the fleets of Spain, Holland, England and France.

But one must always keep in mind the salient fact about this sea and its islands: the dominant settlers of the area would become the black slaves who arrived in such droves from Africa that in time they outnumbered and eventually outpowered all other groups combined. Many islands would ultimately become black republics with blacks holding all major offices like governor general, prime minister and chief of police.

In the nineteenth century a heavy influx of Hindus and Muslims from India introduced unique influences, making certain islands and regions even more colorful, while in recent decades businessmen predominantly from Canada and the United States have streamed down to invest their intelligence and money in efforts to make the islands tourist havens and international banking centers.

The Caribbean is often referred to erroneously as the Mediterranean of America. In a strictly geographical sense the comparison is apt: both seas are landbound, they are almost identical in size (Mediterranean, 969,100 square miles; Caribbean, 971,400). Both have been important historically, but there the similarities between the two great seas end. The lands bordering the Mediterranean gave rise to many outstanding civilizations and the three great religions, while the only great indigenous civilization that operated in the Caribbean area was the Maya in Yucatán, and even it was dying out before the explorers arrived from Europe.

But what the Caribbean did provide, and generously, was a sea of heavenly beauty, a cluster of unmatched islands and a varied series of national occupiers; it certainly has never lacked for either variety or excitement. Above all, it was the theater for one of nature's most violent manifestations, the vast hurricanes that were spawned mysteriously off the shores of Africa and came roaring across the South

Atlantic with demonic fury. Each summer a gathering of these monsters rampaged among the islands, sometimes missing land entirely, in other years devastating everything, flattening palm trees, tearing houses apart, and killing thousands. The hurricanes kept to a preordained swath, rarely striking as far south as Trinidad or Cartagena, occasionally as far north as Bermuda, but Barbados and Jamaica could expect to be visited at least once in a decade, and some smaller islands were ravaged with even greater frequency. Sunny beaches of white sand and crystal-blue water were the glory of the Caribbean, hurricanes the hell.

But however magnificent the sea is, the stories of human endeavor must focus on the scattered islands, just as in the larger world, history concentrates on the settled continents. We have neither the time nor space to deal with all the islands, each worthy of its own treatment, but we shall visit in close detail more than a dozen, and in the process observe many diverse civilizations dominated by a wide variety of mother nations: Spain, Holland, England, France, Denmark, the United States, and the societies unrelated to Europe: Arawak, Carib, Maya, African, East Indian. It is a rich tapestry we shall be inspecting.

The story begins in the year 1310 on an island —which would later be named Dominica—lying in the middle of the eastern arc.

Tiwánee suspected there might be trouble as soon as she heard that strangers had settled on the other side of the island. She learned this disturbing news from the most reliable man in the Arawak settlement, her mate Bakámu, who on one of his constant roamings had espied the three strange canoes from the top of a hill where he was digging for an agouti. The canoes were much larger than those familiar to the island, and the people taller and darker-skinned.

Forgetting his pursuit of the agouti, which had burrowed deeper than usual, he ran back across the island, beneath the branches of the tall clustering trees that covered the hills, to shout to his woman: "They have come."

These words summarized a world of mystery and apprehension, for never before had strangers come to the island, nor was there any conceivable way in which Bakámu could have known that they were coming, or even that they existed elsewhere. But Bakámu was not an ordinary man, as his name testified—it meant *he has struggled back—*

and it was well earned, for as a young fellow, still bearing his birth name Marabul, he had hollowed out a huge log, made himself a stout canoe, and in it had paddled bravely to other islands not seen before. To the north he went over open seas to the island that would centuries after his death be named Guadeloupe and to the south he visited Martinique, discovering that his smaller island lay between two larger ones which seemed to be uninhabited.

He had pondered the mystery of why his small island contained people, while its larger neighbors had none, but could find no answer, and talked with no one about it. He kept his silence even after he took Tiwánee as his wife to live with him in the shelter he had built for them. She has great wisdom, he thought, and someday I will tell her. But now Bakámu was caught up in the discovery that his wife had accumulated rare knowledge, and better than other women, she knew when to plant manioc and sweet potato, how to cultivate corn, and where in the forest she could find star apples, guava and especially the rich, sweet cashew nut. And when her man brought home an iguana, once or twice a year, she knew how to prepare the first joyous feast and then dry the rest of the meat and save it for later.

Tiwánee's skills were respected by all in the village, and they formed one of the most attractive couples on the sunset side, he a man of robust build and somewhat ponderous, she a darting little brown bird looking into everything. Since he demonstrated unusual ability in whatever physical activity he attempted—running, leaping, swimming, games—he commanded the respect of his fellows and in public his words carried weight, but everyone knew that in the home he listened to and obeyed his wife. Although men did not consider her beautiful, the wonderful animation of her pert little face when she talked or smiled attracted special attention. And when they walked together along the beach or through the village, Tiwánee in her brightly colored garment, Bakámu in a dun-colored breechclout, she invariably stayed in front, as if she with her rapidly scanning eyes and natural inquisitiveness was scouting the way for him. But regardless of where they were or what they were doing, they laughed a lot, and it was clear to all that they were happily mated.

It was easy to determine where Bakámu and his wife lived, for although their round hut built of wooden poles, wattles and mud resembled all others clustered in friendly circles, the plot of land on which it stood was outlined by a remarkable hedge which glowed when sunlight reflected from it.

When planting it, Tiwánee had used only the croton, a tropic plant which produced in its big, broad leaves a variety of colors that was bedazzling. There were reds, yellows, blues, purple, deep brown and four or five other colors, all dusted with iridescent specks of gold. Some plants, for no discernible reason, had leaves of all one color, others displayed the wildest variations, and occasionally, as if to prove its versatility, the same plant would produce one bright color topside of each leaf, a much darker color on the underside.

A hedge of croton was a perpetual bewilderment and joy, because the individual plants were a rowdy lot; they grew in wild profusion, obedient to none of the sensible laws that governed ordinary plants. Had Tiwánee used in her hedge any of the glorious red flowers her village produced—those that would later be called poinsettias, anthuriums or hibiscus—she would have had a known quantity; those flowering shrubs grew to a preordained height, behaved themselves, and clung together as if ruled by only one benelovent spirit: "You were intended to be thus and so you will remain, to gladden men's eyes."

But croton was an outlaw. Again and again Tiwánee would trim her hedge all of a level and then one morning she would find that two of her plants had taken off like seabirds leaving the bay to soar aloft. They would grow like determined little trees, until they were so out of proportion that she had to eliminate them, for they ruined her hedge. Or again, she would have in one section of her planting crotons of one color, perhaps all yellow, a gorgeous plant, when out of nowhere would spring up one that became a dark purple, and again her design was destroyed.

No one could make a bunch of croton behave, not in size, or color, or general appearance. The most irritating behavior of all was when some especially beautiful plant, showing perhaps a combination of four colors, would suddenly stop growing upward and decide to grow with great proliferation sideways, its leaves becoming ever more glorious as its form degenerated.

One evening as Tiwánee sat with her husband in the sunset glow, surveying her lovely but unruly croton hedge, she told Bakámu: "This is the plant closest to people. It can be anything, tall or short, this color or that, bright or dark. You can't make it obey, for it lives by its own rules, but if you let it have its own way, it can be glorious. Look over there!" And they studied a splendid stretch of hedge in which all the plants were of the same size and color, a scintillating red, all that is except one in the middle which ruined the whole display: it was a garish purple, two times taller than any other and determined to grow higher.

"That one reminds me of you," she said, "going your own way."

She was right in thinking that Bakámu acted according to his own rules, and when he finally shared with her his knowledge of the other islands he had discovered, she snapped: "You should have told me sooner. Doesn't it stand to reason? If we're here, won't someone else be there?" Most earnestly she wanted to go back with him to inspect those lands more closely, but that, of course, was impossible, for if any woman touched Bakámu's special canoe, which had the form of a man's genitals, he believed she would destroy its magic, and were she actually to get into the canoe for a voyage, that exploration would surely end in disaster.

But that did not keep her agile mind from traveling even further than he had gone, and she reasoned: "Remember the legends, Bakámu? That we came from a great water to the south, down there, and that when we came here we first settled on the sunrise side where the waves are intolerable? There all bad things happened to us till we came around in our canoes to the sunset side. Then we prospered."

Bakámu nodded, for that was the accepted truth of his people, and his own experience confirmed the old stories, for when he had first started exploring in his canoe he had paddled and sailed around the island, and on the sunrise side had encountered only trouble and destructive waves and forbidding cliffs, and he had been wise enough to detect that the ocean, the one to be called the Atlantic, controlled a far more powerful type of magic than the sea which would come to be known as the Caribbean: "No protection over there. Powerful waves. Darker, too," and then he added the fact which really condemned the sunrise side: "No fish."

He was widely admired in his village, and in other villages along the sunset coast, as a prodigious fisherman who knew the secrets of the deep. He would remain for hours in his canoe, long spear at the ready, awaiting the arrival of fish in the waters below, and usually he had anticipated where they would come. Now he paddled far to the west trailing a huge manatee that had strayed into these waters, and he stayed with the great sea animal even when he lost sight of the coast, for he knew that if he could somehow bring that huge beast to land, all the villages along the sunset side would have enough meat for feasts untold.

As Bakámu chased the ponderous creature, almost as big as a small whale, one of the raging storms that hammered at the island from time to time, a dreaded hurricane, swept in, and for three terrible days the waves were so tumultuous that even the manatee had to find refuge, while Bakámu's canoe spun and wallowed in the cavernous waves. Shipping his paddle and lying prone in the bottom of his canoe, he gave thanks to the Great Spirit who had commanded him: "Make your canoe more sturdy than the others, against the storms," but even so at several moments when the waves were stupendous, he thought he was doomed. He did not cry out in despair, nor did he quake with fear; instead, facedown, he clung tightly to the canoe he had built and muttered: "Man comes, man goes. On sea same as on land." And then he thought of his woman alone in their hut, and his worry was for her, because in a hurricane at sea, men died swiftly in one shattering destruction of their canoe; on land, death was slower and more painful as dwellings flew apart and great trees fell, often pinning the people to the ground and holding them there until they died.

While he was having these agitated thoughts at sea, Tiwánee was in their hut, protected by her croton hedge and wondering in terror what might be happening to her man, and like others in the village when the hurricane abated she looked out to the empty but still turbulent sea and concluded: Oimé! The great fisherman, the daring explorer, is dead. And the villagers, after burying those who had died on land, helped organize a mourners' ceremony for Bakámu who had died at sea.

When two boys playing along the shore spotted a canoe approaching two days after the great storm had subsided they began to shout, and everyone streamed down to the water's edge to see this amazing sight, their man Bakámu bringing his canoe back through the waves and towing behind the body of the manatee he had tracked again when the storm subsided. It was then, in that moment of joy, that an old man cried: "He has struggled back!" and the name Bakámu gained even greater honor.

Now, as they talked about the strangers in the big canoes and he reminded Tiwánee of how desolate the sunrise side was, she asked thoughtfully: "Is it as bad over there as our legends say?"

"Worse."

"But if our early ones found it unkind, won't the newcomers want to leave?"

"Maybe so."

"And won't they do what our people did? Come over here to the better side?"

"They might."

At this point she began the kind of intense interrogation she engaged in when her suspicious mind felt the need for more specific knowledge: "You say they were darker in face than we are?" Yes. "And their women crept about like frightened animals?" Yes.

Continuing with her questions, her inquisitive face close to his, she uncovered two facts about which Bakámu wanted to talk in greater detail, for he too was eager to understand the newcomers and fathom their intentions. Accordingly, he volunteered this information: "Their leader, a bigger and rougher man, carried a huge club which he often swung about his head, driving everyone back. And once I saw him so angered that he struck a man with it, knocking him flat."

"Killing him?"

"I think so. Others carried him away."

Now came a painful pause, for Bakámu wanted to share with his wife a fearful doubt he had been unwilling to admit even to himself: "Tiwánee, I must say this. Soon after, the ones who took the dead man away came back with large pieces of meat. Not agouti, not manatee, and they threw the meat into a pot and prepared for a feast."

Tiwánee listened to the awesome words, sucked in her breath, and asked quietly: "You think they ate their own brother?" When Bakámu remained silent, she broke into a wail, crying: "These are evil times," and terror fell upon them both.

Her questioning had been so orderly and its revelations so conclusive that she began that afternoon to take those prudent steps which would enable her to protect her family and herself against the brutal newcomers when they came over the mountains, which she was certain they would.

That phrase—"when they came over the mountains"—dominated all her thinking in the days ahead. She said it as she broke branches to mask the obvious approaches to their hut, and she repeated it when she asked Bakámu to fetch her a branch of very hard wood from the forest. "What are you going to do with it?" he asked, and watched in amazement as she cut an arm's length of the wood, then sharpened one end to a fine point, which she hardened in her cooking coals. When she did this, the delicate tip burned away, but then she whittled the remaining end to a new and harder tip until at last she had a short, fire-hardened, deadly dagger.

Bakámu was astonished to see her do this. The Arawaks on this and other islands were one of the most peaceful peoples in the world: they had no word for *war,* for none was needed, and they reared their children in abounding love. They revered their old people and eased them along their journey through the years, bringing them portions of maize and collecting taro roots for them, and even sometimes sharing with them a succulent little coney if they caught one sunning itself beside its burrow. They lived in harmony with their small universe, reveling in the abundance and beauty of the island and accepting the hurricanes when they roared in to remind them that nature was omnipotent, not man.

Indeed, their lives were measured principally by the sunset. At the end of each long day it was customary for them to sit along the shore in the evening and watch the glorious orb of the sun as it dipped swiftly toward the distant waves; then mothers assured their children: "It will come back." When the sun disappeared the Arawaks renewed their faith, and in the following darkness retired in peace to their small circular dwellings and an evening meal.

Tiwánee, as the mother of a lively baby girl, named Iorótto after the hummingbird, realized that she had a special responsibility for protecting and cultivating the child's promised beauty. The Arawaks were one of several tribes throughout the world who believed that the human face was most attractive when the forehead sloped sharply backward from the eyebrows; a head which rose directly upward from the nose bridge was considered gross and somehow offensive. So, each night, in a patient effort to make Iorótto more beautiful, her mother bound against her forehead a wide, flat board which would press the frontal part of the skull slowly backward until the desired slant was attained. In this position the little girl slept, for among the Arawaks beauty was both prized and desired.

As the sun set and little Iorótto went peacefully to sleep, the strangers on the sunrise side of the island were settling in. They were the Carib Indians, who had come north from the great rivers of what would be called South America, a wildly different lot from the peaceful Arawaks. They gloried in war and organized their society solely for its conduct. A fierce, terrible people, they were cannibals who fought any strangers, not only to subdue them but also to eat them.

Precisely as Tiwánee had predicted, they had been on the ocean side of the island only briefly when their leader, one Karúku, a violent man in his mid-twenties, with black hair shorn so that it fell down toward his eyes, decided that his clan must move across the island toward what he was sure would be a gentler climate with food and fish more abundant. But he was impelled equally by the fact that this sunrise side was unpopulated and therefore provided no targets for the warfare in which he excelled. He longed to have his warriors intermingled with people against whom they could exercise their martial arts and from whom they could take prisoners, but he also had a strong personal motive: on the voyage north from the jungles of the Orinoco River his wife had died, and since all the women in the three canoes were taken, he was left without a wife and was not happy about it. Guessing that the other side of the island must be more clement and possibly inhabited, he directed his Carib warriors to prepare for scouting expeditions into the mountains in search of settlements from which he might capture a wife.

This tactic of stealing women was an important part of Carib culture, one that had been practiced for hundreds of years; the warriors might eat the men they captured in battle, and they castrated young boys to fatten them like capons for later feasts; but they did not eat women, they were too valuable for breeding and as the creators of future warriors.

So with varied purposes Karúku the Carib laid plans to conquer whatever he might find on the island, and the end of the battle was clear in his mind: the extermination of the others.

In many corners of the world at this time similar expeditions were being launched with similar goals, as groups of human beings, finding it impossible to coexist with those of a different color or religion, were concluding that extermination was the only solution. This conviction would continue to scar the world for the next eight hundred years and probably long after that.

Karúku was a formidable foe, for he had demonstrated in forays along the Orinoco his skill in warfare and had left that amiable river primarily to find a new area which he could dominate. He was not only skilled in face-to-face battle, wielding a huge war club violently and cracking any skulls that came in the way, but he also had a keen sense of tactics and strategy taught him by his father and grand-father, who had also been awesome warriors.

The heritage of the Caribs was brutality, warfare and little else. They would bequeath to the world words originating in force and terror: *cannibal, hurricane,* the war *canoe,* the manly *cigar,* the *barbecue,* in which they roasted their captives. As they marched they had war drums but only a few songs of battle and none of love. Their food habits were totally primitive and graced with none of the refinements that the Arawaks and other tribes had developed; the Caribs ate by grabbing with dirty fingers scraps of meat from the common platter, the men invariably snatching theirs before the women, who were allowed the leftovers. Their canoes were heavy and crude, not the flying things of delicate line created by others, and even their personal adornment was invariably of a warlike nature, and it was the men, never the women, who were decorated with the whitened bones of their victims.

But like the military Spartans of ancient Greece, who also seemed brutal when compared to the more cultured Athenians, the Caribs were very good at what they chose to do, and were the terrors in any area into which they wandered. They believed that by eating the most powerful of their enemies they inherited their prowess, and that by taking the most beautiful and healthy of their women they enhanced the vitality of their own group; in this latter belief they were, of course, correct. They were a hybrid group of people, constantly reinforced by fresh blood, and they profited from the brutal strength that such hybridism often produces.

When Karúku and three others left the sunrise side one morning to explore their newfound island, they moved stealthily and with intense purpose, and after they had probed through the forests for some hours without spotting any signs of habitation, they began to ascend the high mountains that filled the center of the island. Night overtook them before they had seen anything, but this did not distress them, for they were accustomed to sleeping in the open, and for food, they carried with them fragments of fish and meal of which they would eat sparingly, for they could not anticipate who or what they might encounter before they returned to their own people.

On the afternoon of the second day they came upon a sight that delighted them: it was a clearing in the forest and they concluded that it must have been made purposefully by human beings, for there grew in a consciously designed pattern the tuberous manioc, a major source of food. "They're here!" Karúku cried, and the way in which he uttered the words betrayed not joy in finding that other humans were on the island, but grim satisfaction that his group would soon once more be in combat with a new foe for the possession of a new land.

For the rest of the day the spies moved cautiously, always westward, until they reached a high spot from which they could look down upon the village they had been seeking. There it lay in the sunlight of late afternoon, a collection of well-made huts to be occupied when the present owners were dispossessed, canoes already built, fields close at hand in which foodstuffs could be grown. But there was also the placid sea, so much gentler than the wild ocean to the east, and as the sun set on that first evening, the Caribs were convinced that they had come upon a paradise much more desirable than any they had known along the Orinoco or elsewhere on their journey north.

"We shall go back," Karúku said, "collect our men and return to take this village." As he uttered these commands he was looking down at the hut surrounded by varicolored croton, and to himself he said: That one for me, and with purposeful strides, as if he could hardly wait to assault the sleeping village, he led his men back to their dark side of the island.

Bakámu and his wife, because of the valuable skills they possessed, enjoyed special positions in their village, he as an athlete of unusual ability and strength, she as the keeper of a secret that accounted for much of the tribe's good fortune.

Tiwánee understood the ways of manioc, source of four-fifths of the stuff her people ate, and one of the world's most remarkable good-evil foods. Like potatoes, yams and beets, manioc produced under the surface of the earth a bulbous growth which when rooted out and shredded yielded a potatolike food that looked and smelled most inviting. However, in this stage of its existence, it contained among its fibers a thick, deadly poisonous juice, and manioc culture required that this juice be extracted, and totally, before the residue could be processed into an excellent flour from which a nutritious and highly satisfying bread could be baked.

Long before Tiwánee was born the ancient ones sought a solution to the problem: How can the poisonous juices of the manioc be removed and their deadly power exorcised? The answer came from a clever Arawak woman, who while huddling in the jungle had seen a boa constrictor grasp a shrieking rodent in its cavernous jaws and slowly swallow it, still kicking. She then saw the great snake digest its heavy burden by tightening and relaxing its powerful belly muscles until all bones were broken and absorption could begin. Cried she: "If I had the help of that powerful snake, I could squeeze the poison from my manioc," and this idea so possessed her that she brooded for weeks and months as to how she might make herself a snake, and finally she found the solution: I'll gather the best and strongest palm fronds and the thinnest vines and weave me a long, thin, narrow snake whose sides will compress and relax like his, and by that means I'll expel the poisons.

She did this, fabricating an imitation snake called a matapi, some ten feet long, very narrow, very strong, and into its insatiable maw she crammed all the manioc she and her neighbors had grated that day. And now her genius manifested itself, for after she had squeezed the snake by hand for some time she discovered two facts: the plan worked, for the poisonous juice did spew forth; but it was murderously difficult work: I'd go mad squeezing like this all day!

So she constructed a device which enabled her to apply such extreme pressure on the snake that she could extract the poisonous juice with relative ease. First she attached the top of her ten-foot snake to a rafter some dozen feet above her. Then, using a pile of rocks for a fulcrum, she converted a long plank into a child's seesaw, with two little girls at one end, a heavy woman perched on the other. To the seesaw she attached the tail end of the snake, placing a large wooden bowl below to catch the liquid. When the woman weighed down her end of the plank, the tension on the woven sides of the snake expelled the poisons, then the woman ran forward toward the fulcrum, and the two girls were able to pull down their end and the snake relaxed. And so it went.

When the game ended, the dried contents of the imitation snake were ready for baking. This manioc flour was called cassava; from it, big, flat breadlike pancakes were made, and on it the Arawaks thrived.

In Tiwánee's village she was one of the women responsible for processing the manioc, and it was thanks to her ever-inquisitive mind as she performed this menial task that a bold innovation was introduced. In all the ages before she was born, the poisonous liquor expelled from the make-believe snake had been discarded as both useless and dangerous, but one day she noticed that when she inadvertently left some of the liquid in a clay bowl standing in bright sunlight, the intense heat caused it to change color to a rich golden brown, which looked so inviting that she told her husband: "Anything that looks so good ought to taste good, too."

"Tiwánee!" he shouted. "Don't be foolish!" but despite his pleading she dipped a finger into the altered substance and gingerly brought it to her mouth. As she had expected, that first exploratory taste was reassuring: salty, sharp, with an invitation to try more, which she did, without apparent danger to herself. In succeeding days she kept tasting her brew, finding it increasingly good, and at last, without advising her husband of the bold step she was about to take, she gulped down such a generous amount of her new substance that had it been the original poison, she would surely have died. She didn't. In fact, she felt extremely well, and after two days had passed without ill effect she told Bakámu: "It's safe and tastes good."

Soon all the women in the village were keeping pots of the once-poisonous liquor quietly bubbling at the back of their fires and tossing into the brew bits of vegetable and fish and even agouti meat on the rare occasions when one of those succulent little animals was caught. When sharp and biting peppers were added to the mixture, a fine, tasty and nourishing stew resulted, all thanks to Tiwánee, who by popular acclaim became the seer of the community, not in competition with the old shaman who propitiated the spirits but as the protector of the hearth where men and women were fed and revived.

When this accolade was bestowed upon her, she became a changed woman. She grew noticeably wiser, as if powers long dormant were suddenly codified and whipped into shape, as if knowledge which she had been quietly accumulating mysteriously blossomed to produce new and totally unexpected fruit, and she was recognized as a leader. Throughout the known world this miracle was duplicated: an ordinary man or woman would be elected to some office, and during the conduct of its business would mysteriously become able enough to discharge the duties of that office, so that in the end someone who might originally have been a rather common person developed into a genius.

Having undergone such a metamorphosis, Tiwánee now found little pleasure in her exalted position, for although she was pleased that she had brought her village wise leadership, she realized that with her new position came new responsibilities, and she continued to brood about the possible dangers that might ensue if strangers had indeed settled upon the opposite side of her island.

One of her duties as a leader in the village was to make the decision as to when it was time to plant the manioc. But because this was of such extreme importance to the village, a matter of life and death, that decision could not be left to her alone; responsibility was shared with the old shaman whose counsel had kept the spirits of the other world favorably inclined toward this village. Fortunately, Tiwánee and the old man cooperated easily, he taking charge of all in the other world, she of the sun, the rainfall and the coming of summer in this, and between them they kept the manioc maturing just when it was most needed. Had they in any way been at odds, their people would have suffered, and they knew it.

On a propitious day before the very hot spell arrived with its threat of hurricanes, the two protectors of the village agreed that the time had come when manioc cuttings should be planted, and as soon as the shaman cried: "The planting can begin!" Bakámu took over the leadership of everything. Dashing along the waterfront, he shouted

joyously: "Ball game! To celebrate the manioc!" and everyone hastened to the flat playing field whose boundaries were defined by large
boulders with flattish faces planted like an informal wall around the
edges of a rectangular field with clearly marked goal lines at each
far end. Mysteriously, these ball courts of the ancient Arawaks and
their cousins the Maya to the west were similar in size to the fields
that Europeans and Americans centuries later would choose for their
soccer, football, rugby and lacrosse fields, some eighty yards long by
thirty wide, as if some inner measuring system of the human body
had cried through all the centuries: "A man can run, when others are
hammering at him, about this far and no farther," and the fields in all
these heavy sports conformed to these dimensions.

The one at Bakámu's village was located on a majestic spot parallel to the seashore, so carefully oriented that neither team would
enjoy any advantage from the changing positions of the sun. It was a
splendid green field, with grass chopped low and protected to the east
by mountains clothed in purple. It had witnessed games of great excitement and notable performance, games that lived in memory, and
some of the best had occurred at times like this, when the entire village came out to celebrate the replenishment of human life. In this
village, at least, the great ball game was a thing of zest and wild
cheering and victory for everyone, even the vanquished, who knew
they had suffered defeat in a joyous cause.

The game required a large rubber ball, but the islands had no rubber trees, and communication between them by canoe was almost
unheard of, except for Bakámu's tentative explorations north and
south. Rubber trees grew only in the jungles on lands of continental
magnitude, but yet rubber balls on which the near-religious sport of
the region depended did circulate even to the most remote islands. It
was as if these Arawaks knew what was important in their lives and
cherished as national treasures any rubber balls which came their
way. At any rate, this village had had a series of such balls, each arriving as its predecessor was about to expire, and each was kept in the
protection of the shaman, for it was a treasure beyond mere value: it
was almost the soul of the village, for without it the wild games could
not proceed, and in their absence the manioc plants might die, and
the people, too.

In Bakámu's village the game was played by two teams of four
men each; in other villages with somewhat larger fields there might be
as many as six, but on this smaller field four seemed about right.

Each team had a goal to defend, but every member was free to roam the entire field, so long as he was always ready to scamper back to defend his own goal. The aim was to drive the ball across the other team's goal line, and whenever play approached one of the goals, the screams of the spectators lining the fields grew intense.

Hands could not be used. If one touched the ball, the player was sent to the sidelines, for the ball must be struck primarily off the shoulder or the hip; not even elbows could be used, nor heads nor heels, but even under these limitations the players became wonderfully adept in moving the ball around. Since the strategies of the game demanded that players be prepared to throw themselves on the ground to obstruct opponents or dive for the ball, men wore knee and elbow guards, always on the right joints, but the captain of each team wore in addition a remarkable piece of equipment. It was a huge stone ring, unbroken in its circle but with an opening just wide enough for him to step into it, then bring it up over his knees and wide hips until it rested easily about his middle. Since it weighed twenty-four pounds, it gave extraordinary power when he struck the ball either with it directly or with his weighted hip.

When the teams lined up, the two captains, each with a stone circle about his waist, obviously located themselves as goalkeepers, sending any ball which came their way far back in the opposite direction with a tremendous blow.

On this day of special significance the spectators crowded the platforms behind the two goals and lined the spaces between the big upright stones. Flowers festooned the perimeters of the field, and boys with drums made a lively racket. In the interval before the game started, women sang and men danced stately measures intended to placate the spirits who determined the growth of manioc. When the excitement was at its height, an older man serving as a referee sounded a horn made from a big conch shell, the revelers cleared the field, and the play began.

Deftly tossing the rubber ball so that it bounced between two opposing players in the middle of the field, the referee started the game, and the movements of the two men were so brilliant, one striking the ball with his hip, the other rejecting it with his shoulder, that the game got off to a noisy start. Back and forth the ball sped, with the two goal tenders sending it down the field whenever it came their way, but the most exciting moments came when some daring player in midfield threw himself with abandon onto the hard earth, skidded along on his protecting pads, and gave the ball a sharp thrust with either shoulder or hip. Then the crowd roared.

As the game progressed, it looked as if Bakámu's team would be defeated, because for each time his team had a shot at the far goal, the other team had three or four at his. But he was so agile that he deflected them when the situation looked least promising, and thus kept his team in the game.

Then, suddenly, he took one enemy shot on his hip, struck it with his big stone girdle, and sent it adroitly into the face of one of the standing stones, from which it reflected in such a way that he was in the right spot to give it another shot onto the face of another upright. In this remarkable manner Bakámu ricocheted the ball five times from stone to stone until he had it clear down the field, where, with a mighty swing of his heavy girdle, he smashed it home for a score.

It had been a prodigious feat, a one-man gallop through the entire opposition made possible only by the exquisite skill with which he used those upright stones for his carom shots. There could not have been many young men in the world that day who could have duplicated his amazing combination of agility, skill, precision and endurance, and when he completed his tour de force, the crowd broke into ecstatic cheers, with the old shaman coming down onto the court to congratulate him: "This year the manioc will grow."

In the ancient days among the Arawaks, at such a moment of triumph it was customary for the captain of the losing team, the guardian of the far goal with his own heavy stone belt at his waist, to be decapitated and his blood to be scattered over the playing area to ensure that the grass there would remain green for the next ritual game, but after some centuries of such sacrifices the practical-minded Arawaks had reasoned among themselves: "Isn't it rather ridiculous and lacking in profit to kill off each planting season the second-best player we have?" And when it was found further that grass outside the playing area grew just as green without the constant application of human blood, it was decided to halt the decapitations. Henceforth, the losing captain bore the pain of having lost an important game but not the greater pain of losing his head, and everyone in the village applauded the new rule, for it was certainly more sensible in that they preserved good players for later games.

However, there was a shaman, in the year when the sacrifices following the games ended, who was a powerful man who had the welfare of his community at heart, and whereas he was more or less forced to approve the cessation of decapitations after games, he insisted that the bloody ritual continue on the eve of the winter solstice, that tremulous day when the sun reached its farthest dip to the south, leaving the world uncertain whether it would ever return north to bring its bounty with it: "We must sacrifice something precious to the sun to lure it back. That's obligatory."

But Tiwánee's great-great-grandmother many generations back had been a woman of powerful reasoning, and she argued: "Some say we must behead people to solve two important problems. To ensure the growth of manioc and to ensure that the sun comes back. Sometimes manioc does not grow well, so maybe sacrifice is needed to make the choice. But there has never been a time when the sun did not come back, so maybe that sacrifice is unnecessary. Then again, we've already proved that manioc can grow whether there's sacrifice or not—even if you do sacrifice and it doesn't rain, no manioc—so why continue sacrificing good men when we know the sun always comes back?"

She carried the day, whereupon the outraged shaman predicted that she would die within the year that the sun sacrifice ended –but she lived for another sixty.

So this year the glorious day of the ball game in honor of manioc ended in near-perfection. After Bakámu's unparalleled feat of bouncing the ball five times against the upright slabs and catching it each time on a dead run, two more games were played, with Bakámu's side winning two goals to one. A feast ensued, at which Tiwánee supervised the distribution of cassava cakes and small bowls of her pepperpot stew made from what had once been poison. There was dancing, and lovemaking for the young, and singing far into the night. These eminently practical people who had long ago dispensed with human sacrifice loved the joyousness of living. They revered the wonderful mysteries that came with the setting of a blood-red sun and the ending of a perfect game and the soft approach of night with its own triumphs, like the golden moon which rose to irradiate the beach and the sea and the watching mountains.

The day of the game there was another spectator—hiding in the mountains behind the town and watching with increasing bewilderment all that unfolded on the plain beside the sea. It was Karúku the Carib, and what his dark, scowling eyes beheld astounded him:

Grown men playing a game! No warriors anywhere. No barriers protecting the approaches to the village. Everyone seems to be in attendance, but I see no weapons of any kind. The men in the game look strong, but even they carry no weapons that I can see. What is this?

It was incomprehensible to him that men of fighting age should not be constantly ready to fight and that a village with obvious advantages had taken no steps to protect itself from possible invaders: What kind of people are they, down there? No army? No weapons? No defenses? What do they think life is? And he reached the only conclusion that concerned him: Properly led, my men could capture that village and everyone in it without the loss of a man. And then he ticked off on the fingers of his left hand the unprotected booty that awaited him: Women for breeding. Boys for fattening. Men for feasting. And as the sun set over the peaceful and even benevolent scene he smiled grimly, and started planning how to prepare his people for the task that confronted them, a task of extreme simplicity, it seemed to him.

When Karúku returned to his temporary ill-constructed village on the Atlantic shoreline north of the cliffs, he shared with his people the results of his spying, and with cunning and skill outlined a clever three-pronged assault on the unsuspecting village: "I'll lead my men in from the north and make a noise. But then you, Narivet, make a big attack in the middle, and when they're confused, running this way and that, Ukalé from the south will start the real assault. I'll wait till they run to that side, then I'll rush in, no stopping, and kill them from the rear."

Three times he drilled his cadres, arranging signals and making it clear that he intended his men to sweep forward into the center of the village regardless of what belated defensive steps the Arawaks might take: "If any man on our side falls back, he is dead. Even if they start fires to hamper us, we run right through them. Everyone!" And he indicated by the fury with which he spoke that he included himself in that command.

During the third rehearsal he carried in his right hand the wand of office. It was a long bludgeon fashioned from a very hard gray-green wood into which had been imbedded with a powerful forest gum sharp slivers of rock and conch shell, so that no matter from what direction the club came, it tore any flesh it struck and thrust into the wound the manioc poison that tipped the sharp cutting edges. It was a dreadful instrument and an appropriate treasure for the Caribs, for they had brought with them in their canoes from the Orinoco no household deities or ancient treasures which defined the tribe, but only this dreadful war club which had been perfected into a superb tool for killing. It symbolized the difference between the two peoples: the Arawaks treasured the golden conch shell as the source of tools and adornments for their women, the Caribs for the lethal spikes it gave their clubs; the Arawaks had adapted manioc liquid to enhance their food, the Caribs used it as a fatal poison against enemies; the Arawaks had a rubber ball as their totem, the Caribs this murderous club. But most significant, the Arawaks had progressed to the point in civilization in which they respected, defended and adored women, while the Caribs treated them only as beasts of burden and breeders of new warriors. The impending struggle between these two contrasting groups was bound to be unequal, for in the short run brutality always wins; it takes longer for amity to prevail.

This first battle would foreshadow many more that would scar the islands of this beautiful sea. In far western reaches, brutal warriors from central Mexico would crush the kindlier civilizations of the Maya. Exploring newcomers from Spain would decimate the peaceful Indians they found. Englishmen on far western Barbados would harry peaceful cargo ships and put all to the sword. And in island after island white owners would treat black slaves with a sickening barbarity. The assault of the warlike Caribs upon the peaceful Arawaks was merely the first in an unbroken chain of brutalities.

On the day of attack the Caribs struck according to plan, with the first group under Karúku rushing in from the north and making a considerable clamor, which drew the frightened Arawaks to that quarter to protect their village. But when they ran in that direction, the second group of Carib warriors rushed toward the middle with even greater noise, and all became confusion.

Then the third contingent, brandishing war clubs and shouting wildly, swept in from the south, and any defense of the village collapsed. But Karúku's victory was not going to be as uncontested as he had hoped, for in the final moments of the attack, the big man he had watched admiringly in the game, the one with the stone belt about his waist, summoned young men who had been on his team, and these four, joined by men from the team that had lost, gathered at the playing court on which they had performed so well, and there, with sticks and improvised clubs, defended themselves as good athletes would.

Led by Bakámu's fierce determination and encouraged by his shouts, they gave such a strong account of themselves that they drove some of the attackers from the fight, an event which infuriated Karúku, who directed four of his men to seize Bakámu and immobilize him. When this was done, at great risk to the assailants who felt the power of the Arawak's resistance, Karúku rushed up, spat in the face of the prisoner whose arms were pinioned, then swung his deadly club in full circle over his head and brought it down with bone-crushing force on Bakámu's skull, killing him on the spot.

Then, in Carib battle ritual, he called for branches from a tree, and when these were provided he gently placed them over the dead hero's chest and cried: "This one was the bravest. On him will we feast!"

Next he ordered his warriors to parade before him, as he sat on the edge of the playing field, the entire group of Arawak prisoners, and he delivered his judgments: "Those three boys, to be castrated and fattened. Those four little girls, too young for any good, kill them. Those older women, no good. Kill them. These women, yes, save them." And then his eyes fell on Tiwánee, pale and weeping over the slaughter of her husband, and she was most desirable, so he cried: "That one for me!" and she was thrust aside.

On and on he went, ordering his men to kill the old ones, men and women alike, and the very small girl children who would require years of care before they could breed, but saving young women for his men. Most of the Arawak men were slain on the spot, there on the playing field which they had once graced, but some sixteen of the hardiest were saved for later feasts. The young boys were castrated, also on the spot.

Tiwánee, forced to sit by Karúku, watched with growing horror as his orders were carried out. But the strangulation of her beautiful daughter Iorótto, her forehead already sloping backward, was more than she could bear, and she started to faint. In that moment she felt beneath her thin garment the fire-hardened wooden dagger she had concealed there at the beginning of the attack. "I will never allow them to use me," she muttered as the slaughter continued. "Either they kill me, or I kill myself."

In those moments when grief had driven her close to insanity, a chain of things happened which suddenly cleared her mind, allowing her to see not only today's horror but also the dreadful future of this hideous new society.

The first was a desecration, for Karúku strode in triumph to the middle of the playing field and shouted: "Knock down those silly stones!" and brawny Caribs threw down the upright stones defining the field on which the lovely, spirited game had taken place. "This will be a training place for warriors," he cried, and Tiwánee wept as the site where so much good had occurred was obliterated. Here young men had proved themselves without harm to others; here contests had been held in which all were winners; and now the field was converted to death. She felt a dull numbness, as if the world had gone mad. And when the blood-red sun started to drop toward the west, Karúku waved his deadly club and Carib warriors lugged to the middle of the field great burdens of wood, which they stacked so as to ensure a roaring fire when set ablaze.

At this moment Karúku saw something which irritated him mightily, the rubber ball used by the Arawak men in their game, and he shouted scornfully: "Destroy that plaything of children! This village is now occupied by men!" Carib warriors hacked the precious ball into halves and then quarters, which they threw upon the rising fire. Flames leaped at the segments, dark smoke swirled from the pyre, and the ball which had appeared on the island so mysteriously vanished forever.

But it was the third obscenity that was in some ways the worst, for it not only destroyed a thing of robust beauty but also foreshadowed what the new world would be like. When Karúku chose for himself the hut once occupied by Bakámu and Tiwánee, some of his men, acting on their own, began to knock down the croton plants, both those in front and those in back, and when Karúku himself protested, shouting: "Keep them!" one of his lieutenants explained: "Assailants might hide in those bushes in a plot to murder you," and Karúku, acknowledging the advisability of clearing the area, nodded: "Clear the space!" and the crotons were slashed to the roots.

As they fell, Tiwánee realized that the tyrant Karúku had acted not through strength but through fear, and she felt contempt for him: Despite his great power, he has not found courage. He is driven by demons. He does not move like a hero, but like a coward. And scorning the frenzied acts of Karúku, Tiwánee whispered: "He has to be afraid of his own men! He's frightened of shadows! But Bakámu, living freely, was afraid of nothing."

She watched with sorrow as the hedge she had so lovingly tended disappeared, and as she watched she spoke to her plants in a kind of trance, for she knew they would revive:

"Grow, croton, to the highest reach of heaven,
Undisciplined, determined to be free.
Red, yellow, blue, dark purple, lively green
Spattered with gold and iridescent all.
Allow no man to master you, stand free,
Hold to your roots. Surrender never! Grow!"

As she bade her farewell to the croton, she realized that the three hideous events which had repelled her so violently had not involved the killing of human beings, but the assassination of benevolent ideas, and when she saw the destruction of these great good things, she felt herself so outraged that she was prepared to fight even the spirits of hell to resist the new order.

The formalities of the victory feast began. Four women specially designated to honor heroes slain in battle reverently lifted Bakámu's corpse and bore it to the edge of the flames, where they recovered the branches which had been placed across his breast. These they delivered to Karúku, who accepted them, carried them solemnly back to the pyre, and tossed them as votive offerings into the flames. Then, whirling about with arms upraised, he shouted: "Victory! Victory! Our new home!"

The fire roared, the human flesh was roasted, and the feast began, but Karúku would not be allowed to enjoy it. For when Tiwánee saw the leaping flames, she uttered a sigh of tragic resignation, as if she could no longer absorb what she had been forced to witness this day. Quickly her ancient courage reasserted itself, and she cried out: "I can bear this outrage no longer!" And from the folds of her garment she took the fire-hardened dagger, intending to kill herself rather than submit to the brutality that now controlled her village. But then she saw Karúku reveling with the victors, and she was so mortally offended that with a strength she had never known before she broke from her captors, dashed up behind the Carib leader, and plunged her dagger through the middle of his back and deep into his heart.

II

DEATH
OF
GREATNESS

O N JULY NINTH OF THE YEAR 1489 ACCORDING TO THE CHRIS-
tian calendar—a day noted as 11:13.8:15.6. in the much more
accurate Maya rendering—on the remote island of Cozumel at the
extreme western end of the Caribbean, the thirty-seven-year-old
widow of the High Priest who served the local Temple of Fertility
faced a grievous crisis.

She was Ix Zubin—the first name signifying *female*—and she was
admirably qualified for what loomed ahead. She was robust in health,
just under five feet tall, and built as if constructed of three sturdy
globes: buttock, breast and dark round head. Her very black hair
met her eyebrows in a straight bobbed line, creating the effect of a
permanent scowl, except that her face could suddenly break into a
generous, warm-hearted smile, as if some bit of fortunate news had
made her feel good all over. But her sharp, penetrating eyes were
dominant, darting here and there, demanding to know everything
that happened about her, for she was a woman of unusual intellect.

The crisis stemmed from the unfortunate condition in which her
island and her temple found themselves. Cozumel was a handsome
island, but it was small and it did lie at the extreme edge of the once-
great Maya empire that spread over the southern part of what would
later be known as Mexico. The capital city of the fragment of empire

that still existed, Mayapán, lay far to the west and was so involved in its own crumbling affairs that it had neither time nor wealth to waste on Cozumel.

Left to govern their own affairs, the islanders became increasingly pessimistic: "With things falling apart on the mainland, pregnant women no longer flock here for our services. The temple is expensive to maintain. The world is different now, and old centers like this no longer serve any useful purpose." A rumor circulated that no new High Priest would be appointed and the building would be abandoned to the salt winds blowing in from the sea. But some perceived another problem: "Boatmen have grown lazy and no longer care to ferry travelers to us from the mainland." One cynic summarized the situation: "We've been forgotten. Not enough pilgrims coming to keep us alive. Desolation is upon us."

If the rumor was true, Ix Zubin would face a double loss, for she not only loved the ritual which ensured the birth of strong children but she also had nurtured a plan whereby her son Bolón might one day ascend to the position of High Priest. Thus both her religion and her family were in jeopardy.

This little bundle of energy was no ordinary woman. Because of the extraordinary position she had held in Cozumel during the lifetimes of her grandfather and her husband, she had during the past three years convinced herself that Bolón was the ideal person to inherit the priesthood. Had the boy's father lived another four years, till the boy was twenty, she was certain she could have maneuvered him into the office of High Priest, thus ensuring the continuation of the valuable temple and its records, but her husband's premature death had put a tragic end to that plan.

The unique position she enjoyed in Cozumel society had begun when her grandfather, Cimi Xoc, a noble man of wisdom who knew the stars as brothers and was one of the greatest High Priests, famed even among the rulers at Mayapán for his mastery of the calendar and the orderly procession of the stars, realized that his only son, Ix Zubin's father, was not capable of mastering the intricacies of Maya astronomy upon which the welfare of the world depended. Grieved by his son's deficiency, he found solace in the fact that his granddaughter, the amazing child Ix Zubin, did have that peculiar gift, awarded to only a few in each generation, of being able to comprehend almost intuitively the mysteries of numbers and calendars, the moon's motion and the wanderings of planets.

She was only five when her grandfather had cried with delight: "This child has much wisdom!" and he began to allow Ix Zubin to help him plot the movements of the brilliant morning-evening star long named Venus by scholars elsewhere in the world. Indeed, except for her lack of outstanding physical beauty, she understood the planet so well that she herself might have been called Venus: "Grandfather! When she hides between morning star and evening, she's like the women who hide when they're going to have babies," and from that moment she appreciated the close identification the planet had with Cozumel's Temple of Fertility, whose fortunes the male members of her family directed.

That insight led to her unprecedented education, for normally women in Maya culture were prevented from any contact with the sacred learning that enabled civilization to move forward. The mysteries of astronomy were kept hidden from them; they were never allowed to participate in the sacred propitiatory rites that ensured the benevolence of the gods; and there were a score of secret places in any temple into which women would never be admitted. A hundred rules were enforced to keep them obedient.

So when Cimi Xoc decided that his genius of a granddaughter should be instructed in the mathematical mysteries, it was a decision of tremendous significance, for it flouted the ancient belief that women should not be involved in such sacred matters. But like all keepers of treasured knowledge, he was determined that the lore he had accumulated during a long lifetime be preserved for later generations, realizing that it constituted an emotional bridge between past, present and future.

Ix Zubin had inherited this passionate respect for the history of her people and made repeated efforts to instill in her son a regard for his ancestry: "Our people are the wisest," she told him. "Others are better at warfare, obviously, since strangers from the west did overrun us and install their gods in place of ours, but in all else we are supreme." Her comments on history invariably referred to migration from the west, sometimes to relationships with the south, and occasionally to influences drifting down from the north, but the east where the great sea rolled was never mentioned.

Yet the Maya must have been known there. The green jade adornments so beloved by the Arawak and Carib women and the rubber balls so cherished by their men must have been transported from Maya lands, since there were no rubber trees or jade deposits on the little islands far out in the Caribbean. And there was the custom of applying heavy boards to make the foreheads of children, especially those of female babies, slant backward from the bridge of the nose. But how these things had reached those distant specks of land, neither Ix Zubin nor her learned grandfather nor any other chronicler of Maya history could say.

In other respects, Maya knowledge was prodigious in both volume and precision. Two thousand years before the old man made his calculations, Maya astronomers, always seeking to refine their measurements, had determined that the year was not 365 days long but 365:24. Europeans, who failed to achieve this precise computation, stumbled along with their calendar falling each year into deeper error. Not until 1582, nearly two centuries after Cimi Xoc's death, did European astronomers catch up with the Maya, who had also determined that the journey of Venus through the heavens required exactly 583:92 days.

Such basic facts had for centuries been recorded in tables inscribed on papyruslike sheets and jealously guarded by the priests who perfected them by making minute adjustments. But the intellectual accomplishment of Cimi Xoc and his peers that would amaze subsequent civilizations was their ability to forecast eclipses of the sun: When the old man first showed his granddaughter the tables, he chanced to point to a date five hundred years in the future which indicated that on Sunday 29 March 1987 a total eclipse of the sun would occur. To Ix Zubin's astonishment, her grandfather's table of predictions continued through two hundred years beyond that.

Long before the birth of Christ the Maya had devised a multipart numerizing system which enabled them to calculate with the most elegant exactitude dates going back ten thousand years or more, and, for an equal span, into the future. In their five-number system the first figure represented a very large number, the second a somewhat smaller, the third a portion comparable to one year, the fourth the number of units close to a month, and the fifth the number of days.

When European scholars in the early twentieth century unlocked the secret of the Maya calendar system, they found that the precise day of the week for any date reaching back three thousand years could be correlated, as could dates probing far into the future. Each group of five Maya numbers meant a specific day in a certain month of a given year. But more significantly, they formed a throbbing tie to the ancestors.

These records were preserved in a beguiling way. In front of temples and public buildings were erected groups of stelae, squared stone pillars four feet wide and sometimes as tall as three men, but more often shorter. On each of the long, slim faces thus provided, sculptors of rare skill had carved intricate hieroglyphics—faces of gods, officials in regal and ornate costumes, animals and arcane symbols to remind the worshipers that mysterious powers influence daily life. But for Cimi Xoc and his granddaughter the most valuable segment of each stela was the inscription of dates of the period. Ix Zubin would never forget the first day when her grandfather, in defiance of custom, had taken her to the nearby mainland city of Cobá, where he showed her, a mere girl, the magnificent scatter of stelae summarizing that site's resplendent history.

"This one speaks of things that happened more than a thousand years ago," he said reverently. "A priest of our line helped this ruler," and here he indicated the specific king reigning in that distant period, "to consolidate his power. You can see the slaves kneeling before him."

He then showed her symbols dating the stela's events to Friday 9 May 755—9:16.4:1.17 7 Imix 14 Tzec—and it was with this clearly defined time that she began her involvement with the Maya numbering system. Soon she was able to read other stelae, one recording events from November 939, another more recent, in February 1188.

From that simple start with the reading of the Cobá stelae, which she accomplished with ease, he taught her the intricate systems which his son, her father, would have to master were he to take charge of the temple's calculations, but which the young man had proved too limited intellectually to learn. Gradually Ix Zubin began to perform her father's calculations, and in a surprisingly short time she was working in astronomy, then in the calculations for Venus, and finally in formulae for predicting eclipses. "There are very few parts of our priestly art," her grandfather said, "more useful to us and more awesome to the people, including our rulers, than our ability to warn: 'Next month the sun will disappear, and unless you help us build that new room in the temple, the sun will not reappear and we shall all die.' The threat is useful, because when the sun actually disappears as we predicted, they listen, even the rulers. And the house is completed."

For fifteen years, 1474 through the first months of 1489, Ix Zubin remained in the shadows, performing the sacred calculations required by her father in the conduct of his duties, and his reports became so treasured because of their accuracy that he became renowned on the island, one who had to be listened to. They were a family tandem—the High Priest performing before the crowds, and his sharp little daughter working her magical numbers in the shadows. The pair filled an honored role in Cozumel, and when she married a young priest in the temple, she helped prepare him for the day when he would take over the role of High Priest.

In those early years when Ix Zubin first became aware that great changes threatened to engulf and modify the Maya empire, she was—though completely unknown—one of the most effective astronomers in the far-flung realm and much superior to any then working in Europe or Asia, for her subtle knowledge of the passage of the earth through its seasons and the movement of the stars through their heavens was unsurpassed, while her mastery of numbers and the calculation of time were equaled in no other part of the world.

Those were years of contentment. Often she thought that her father, her husband and she were the happiest trio in Cozumel, and when her son Bolón was born life seemed complete. Later, when her father died and her husband inherited the outward trappings of High Priest, she continued to provide that office with its astronomical calculations. But she also strove to perfect her knowledge, grasping secretly for the crumbs of other experiments being conducted in other parts of the Maya lands, but the time came when both she and her husband realized that she ought to be passing along to their son the lore she had accumulated, and from this impulse, more scientific than motherly, she began to instruct Bolón in her mysteries.

He had been fourteen at the time, and she quickly saw that he had none of the insights she had had at five, for even then she had been a genius, one of those miracle children born attuned to the universe and its arcane movements, and that kind of knowledge no mother could automatically impart to her son; such geniuses arrive in the world at broken intervals and their coming is inexplicable. But if she could not bestow on Bolón her veiled power, she could teach him to be a solid mathematician and to use the tables her predecessors had compiled over thirty centuries, and this she did.

As the boy learned the manipulative secrets of the priesthood, his father became satisfied that his son had the qualifications to follow him as High Priest of the Cozumel temple, and he began to instruct him in the practical aspects of that role: "Your mother has taught you to read the principles on which our temple rests. It's ancient, powerful, and worthy of the respect the women pilgrims give it. But to protect it you must be attentive to every shift in power among those who rule, for we exist at their pleasure? And for the first time the boy heard the two powerful names which summarized so much of Maya history—Palenque and Chichén Itzá.

"Very long ago, in a place I've never seen, Palenque, far to the west," and he pointed vaguely to where the sun sank, "the learned priests and powerful rulers uncovered the secrets which made it the most glorious city of our people. Much, much later, enemy aliens from valleys far to the west* invaded our peaceful lands and thrust upon us a cruel new religion, which they established at Chichén Itzá and later at great Mayapán."

Here Ix Zubin interrupted her husband in order to make a most disturbing observation: "It was not until those horrible strangers came with their bloodthirsty gods that our people began human sacrifices. The rain god Chac Mool is insatiable. He demands sacrifices of many slaves, and what is worse, he must have our young too. In the old days our benevolent Maya gods helped us to tend the fields, and give birth to strong sons, and maintain a quiet home. We never sacrificed any human being to a stone statue . . ."

"Zubin! No!" her husband cried in terror. "Never speak against the sacrifices. I've warned you a hundred times." Then, turning to his son, he added. "Forget that your mother said that. If the priests who conduct the sacrifices heard you . . ." He paused ominously. "Cleanse your mind and keep it clean, or you won't live to be a priest."

But when Ix Zubin was alone with her son she whispered: "My grandfather, wisest of them all and the only one on this island who personally had been to Palenque, told me quite forcefully: 'Before the intruders came, there was no sacrifice of our best young people. Without such bloody help the sun returned each morning and started its northward journey at the appointed time each year. But new rulers bring new rules, and those who are sensible obey them.' "

It was here that Bolón betrayed the fact that he might not prove a fervent follower of the adopted religion from the west based at Chichén Itzá, for he asked: "Was our temple here before the new religion arrived?" and his mother said: "Yes," and that was all that passed between them on the subject, but she remembered well the day on

*From Tula in central Mexico, during the years 920–1205.

which she had asked her grandfather that same question and had received the same one-word answer: "Yes."

In the two months following the death of his father, the High Priest, Bolón, then sixteen, and Ix Zubin faced a series of difficult problems, for it became evident that the rulers of Cozumel, having received no orders from Mayapán about the Temple of Fertility, were determined to shut it down, but were prevented from doing so immediately by the continued influx of women from the mainland coming to seek assurance from the gods that they would become pregnant. Deciding to wait until steps could be taken to halt this flow, they turned their attention to a great ritual ceremony which was being planned to terminate worship at the temple.

The affair was to have a dual purpose: a dismissal of the old gods of the ancient Maya and a showy confirmation of the new gods of the newer religion. To accomplish this most effectively, the civil authorities decreed that an offering be made to Chac Mool, the powerful rain god, whose benevolence assured proper amounts during the growing season. When Ix Zubin heard of this decision, she was sickened, for there was no god in the pantheon that she detested more than Chac Mool. With ample reason she felt that his savage rites debased the fine temple whose high quality had been protected and enhanced by the men of her family.

Chac Mool, in both appearance and function, was one of the ugliest gods which the conquering strangers from the west had imposed upon the Maya, a deity from strange lands demanding strange sacrifices. He appeared in hundreds of massive stone statues throughout Maya lands, a fierce warrior shown lying flat on his back, his chest propped up by his elbows, his knees flexed, his feet resting firmly on the ground. This unnatural posture meant that his cramped stomach area provided a broad flat space into which was carved a big saucer held in place by the idol's two stone hands. Obviously, the waiting receptacle was intended to be filled by donations from women who came to seek help from the gods, and on festive days it overflowed with flowers and bits of jade and even pieces of gold, a form of worship to which Ix Zubin did not object.

But the civil authorities, not the priests, ordained that on certain great days, Chac Mool, this brutal figure lying uncomfortably on his back, must receive rather more important gifts than bits of jade.

When this edict was made known, male slaves on Cozumel and all young men of the island grew apprehensive, for they knew that what the empty saucer resting on the god's belly wanted now was a human heart, ripped out of a living body, and that nothing else would satisfy.

When Ix Zubin heard news of the impending festival of rain, she quietly took her son to the temple, being careful not to step in any areas forbidden to women, and led him to the statue. "Look!" she whispered. "Have you ever seen a more terrifying face?" With her customary insight she had identified the real horror of Chac Mool, for in an already awkward position his stone head was turned ninety degrees to the left, so that his warrior face, topped by a big stone helmet covering his hair and with protuberances jutting out from his ears, glared malevolently, the corners of the mouth drawn into a ferocious grimace at whoever might be approaching.

It was a brutal, deformed depiction of the human body, but she had to admit that it was powerful: the figure of a vindictive god demanding his sacrifices, and wherever he appeared throughout the land he was instantly recognizable, for his curious posture was invariable, except that occasionally his ugly stone face was turned to the right rather than to the left. Chac Mool was a god calculated to produce terror in the heart of any beholder, and that had been the purpose of those who had inflicted him on the people.

"He's waiting for a human heart," Ix Zubin whispered. "That was never intended in this temple. He's an impostor."

"When did he arrive?"

"In my grandfather's day. They placed two Chac Mools on the island, but not in our temple, and sacrifices became quite common, slaves usually but our own sons when required, and Grandfather spoke out against the practice."

"What happened?" Bolón asked, staring at Chac Mool.

"Something Grandfather never anticipated. When an unseasonal drought came, they decided that an additional Chac Mool must be installed in our temple, and over my grandfather's objections this beastly thing was hauled in here and placed as you see it," and now she, too, stared at the implacable stone visage. "And on the day it was finally set in place, more than fifty men edging that huge rock into position, the other priests suddenly grabbed Grandfather, dragged him to that stone altar over there, bent him backward across it, and with a sharp obsidian dagger, slashed open his chest like this." With a trembling forefinger she indicated the passage of a knife across her son's belly, then added in a voice choking with remembered grief: "The priest holding the knife dropped it, reached his hand into the opened gash, fumbled for the still-beating heart, ripped it from Grandfather's body, and threw it in there."

Pointing to the stone saucer held by the statue, ugly in every perspective, she shuddered and led her son from the temple, with Chac Mool's evil gaze following them as they left.

Ix Zubin spent the month prior to the impending sacrifice adding two pages to the papyrus record of Cozumel, and in them she summarized the achievements of her renowned grandfather and the lesser accomplishments of his son. With Bolón watching and confirming the accuracy of her symbols, she added the specific dates during which each had exercised power, and when she had finished, mother and son looked at the scrolls with pride. "There the record will be," she said. "Your forebears were men to be remembered." Then she pressed her son's hand: "And so shall you be. To guide us through the stormy days ahead."

She had barely made this prediction when the clouds began to gather, for three burly messengers from the island leaders came to confiscate the scrolls: "These are to be kept by those in charge," and for the first time in centuries the scrolls left the confines of the temple. As the messengers disappeared she called after them: "Why?" and one called back: "They believe all that your grandfather did was wrong. That's why they want to close down what they call 'his temple.'"

Stunned by this desecration of the sacred scrolls, Ix Zubin wandered for two days about her lovely island, nodding to the pregnant women climbing out of the canoes after their long journeys. Then from a hilltop she studied the endless sea as it came to the eastern shore, but always she came back to that handsome assembly of nine buildings at the shrine, with their white-pebbled walkways, tall trees and flowered nooks. They formed a noble scene, one to gladden the heart, and she was not prepared to surrender it to mean men who lacked vision or appreciation. Her mind was made up.

Returning to her quarters at the rear of the main temple, she told her son: "We must leave at once and make our plea in person at Mayapán," and Bolón had been so startled by recent developments on the island and so aware of their significance that he did not have to ask his mother why. But he was not prepared for what she said next: "We shall set forth on a mission of extreme importance—to you . . . to me . . . to Cozumel. If you are to save our temple and serve in it, you must understand the glory of our accomplishment. You must see what we were and what we might become again." And a new sense of gravity was introduced into their pilgrimage.

But now Ix Zubin was confronted by an almost insurmountable problem, for according to Maya custom it would be unthinkable for a lone woman accompanied only by a sixteen-year-old to make a journey of any distance, and to make one of protest to the faltering power of Mayapán would be preposterous. It was obligatory that she find some man older than herself to serve as head of her expedition; she might be the most capable woman in all of Yucatán, but tradition insisted that for her to make such a journey, she must have a man to lead her.

She spent the next two days discussing the situation with Bolón, reviewing and discarding candidates: "Too frightened. If a fox jumped, he'd cry for help." "Too stupid. I'd never be able to explain." "Too indebted to the rulers, whoever they might be at any time." Irritated by her inability to visualize a trustworthy man, she fell silent. Just then, as they sat quietly under a tree near the temple, she saw, picking his way among the flowers, the answer to her needs: her aged uncle Ah Nic (Ah indicating *male*) —a minor priest at the Cozumel temple who had few interests in life save for his love of flowers and his tender concern for orphaned children. A man who minced when he walked and smiled when things went poorly, he was easily dismissed by better men but tolerated by them for his gentleness. Ah Nic's going would occasion no comment, so as he moved toward her she called "Uncle! Please, I need your help," and when she outlined her plan to approach the authorities at Mayapán, he said quietly: "If you are willing to waste your time going to that powerless place, I will accompany you. But first I think we should show your son a real monument—Chichén Itzá."

At the mention of this once-great city she drew back, for it had been believed in her family that when the alien invaders from the west established their new religion there, they destroyed much of the greatness of the Maya people. "It's a harsh place," she said. But her uncle remained firm: "Its gods are cruel, its temples sublime," and with these words the old man struck a responsive chord, and she turned to her son: "When I was a girl your age, Bolón, my grandfather took me on a journey to see Chichén Itzá, and when I saw the deep well into which they threw young girls to appease the gods, I was terrified."

"Then why would you go back?" her son asked, and she explained: "But I also saw greatness, and long after the hideous gods retreated from my dreams, I remembered the noble temples and the beautiful courts. You are entitled to see them, Bolón, so that you'll know what greatness is."

So, in the dark of night, without a light to guide them lest it attract attention, the three gathered the clothes and goods they would require: the good cotton tunics Ix Zubin had woven and sewed, the extra pair of boots shod with heavy skins, the rain covers made from tightly woven reeds and slender lianas, and most important, the three types of money they would need for the purchase of food along the way: jade, gold and cacao beans.

Ix Zubin produced from various hidden places the bits of green jade she had sequestered through the years; some of them, she knew, belonged to the temple, not to her, but she justified what amounted to theft by telling Bolón: "Your father and I worked for this jade. It's only proper." Bolón had gathered up wealth of a radically different kind, and in this case he was certainly entitled to it, for he spread before her the precious cacao beans, each one worth a meal, that the Maya used for money. It was, perhaps, the most interesting kind of coinage used anywhere in the world, for after it had passed as currency for a year or two, it finally gravitated into the hands of some man already wealthy who ground up the beans to make the delicious chocolate drink which Maya people craved. Bolón, treasuring the bag in which he had accumulated such beans by doing small jobs for important families, assured his mother: "This takes us there and back." Both Ix Zubin and Bolón were surprised when Ah Nic brought forth a small horde of gold pieces which through the years he had hidden from offerings made to the temple, and in the middle of the night they set forth.

The men who owned the big canoe they would be using for the important first leg of their journey were not happy about venturing south in darkness, but since they had taken such trips twice before they knew that disaster was not inevitable, so when Bolón took from his bag four cacao beans, the canoe men grabbed them and started paddling.

As the rowers strained at their oars through the quiet night, with gentle water from the Caribbean lapping at the sides of their canoe,

Ix Zubin revealed her plan: "There is something of importance you must see at Tulúm," and she explained how they would go south to Tulúm, then to Chichén Itzá before going to Mayapán.

Bolón was not really listening, for her reasoning was so personal and mystifying that he could not follow it; his attention was on the musical, mysterious sea, that strange body of water that he had never before ventured upon, and it captivated him: "Why don't we build really big canoes and explore this great body of water?" and Ah Nic gave the answer that had been given for the past thousand years: "We're land people. We know nothing of water like this," and he told Bolón of how adventurous it had been, many generations ago, for the Maya to quit the land which was their home and make the bold leap across water to Cozumel, a distance of not much more than eleven miles, with land visible at all times: "It was a brave act, and many of those first people died still convinced that catastrophe must overtake them because they had broken with tradition by crossing water to an island." Ah Nic enjoyed giving such explanations.

"Would you have that same fear about venturing into that sea out there?" and the way in which Bolón phrased his question revealed that he thought of the waters they were traversing as safe, because land was visible throughout the starry night, while that "other water" would be terrifying beyond belief once the reassuring land had become invisible.

His mother confirmed this fear: "When Grandfather first took me down to Tulúm in a canoe like this, four big men paddling, I was sure we were heading for the end of the world. And I can tell you, I was relieved when we climbed back onto safe land." Chuckling at her fears, she added: "As for venturing out there, I'd be terrified."

"So would I," Ah Nic agreed.

It was only about forty miles from the departure point at Cozumel to Tulúm, and since waves could be high and progress slow, it was not until dawn of the second day that they approached the temple area. As the two sailors beached their canoe, the occupants could look up and see some forty feet above them the grim outlines of a fortress tower unlike anything on Cozumel. Poised on the edge of the sea, it appeared to shout a warning to those down below: "Do not attempt to assault the city I guard, for we are impregnable!"

When they had bade their paddlers farewell and climbed the steep slope to the town they found the impression of defense intensified. Once more they faced something Bolón had not seen before: the entire central area of forts and temples also was enclosed within a massive unbroken stone wall twice as high as a man and unbelievably thick. It did contain several portals, and when the pilgrims passed through the one nearest the landing, they saw a collection of many temples lined along a main street running east to west, the whole creating a strong sense of order, with the homes of ordinary citizens scattered far outside the walls.

But the three had inspected only one temple when Ix Zubin expressed her disgust at the sloppy, inartistic manner in which the edifices had been built: "They're as gross and brutal as our Chac Mool."

Tulúm had been built in the days when Maya glory was fading, when architects were content to use rude chunks of rock on which no attempt had been made to achieve a finish. The buildings showed façades that were inherently ugly and were so oriented that no lovely vistas resulted. A few apertures did look out upon the Caribbean but they were very small, as if the priests inside had been afraid to face the frightening sea, preferring instead the scrub woodland which attacked from the west and with which they were familiar. The principal temple did serve one useful purpose: it was convenient as a pilgrimage center for those who could not afford the longer journeys to Cozumel or Chichén Itzá, but the men who served it were as uncouth as their building. The temple had as its prized adornment an exceptionally hideous Chac Mool whose reclining body was so cramped and distorted that it seemed hardly human and whose brutal scowl was terrifying. There was little else that might awaken spiritual understanding, and Ix Zubin was harsh when she helped her son evaluate what he was seeing: "It's a hodgepodge. No beauty. No lifting of the spirit. No inner sense of majesty inspired these architects and sculptors. No reason, really, for the temples at all, except maybe to serve a population that couldn't afford the trip to a real one."

Her son, acquainted only with the temples on Cozumel, could not agree: "Tulúm's twice as big as anything we have. I like the way it overlooks the sea. It's high, too, up on this cliff, much higher than any of ours."

Ix Zubin was impatient with such limited reasoning: "Big is no measure, Bolón. Look at that Chac Mool. Horrible though ours is, in comparison to this it's a work of art. Ours is well carved, properly finished, and the boots and headdresses are handsomely done. It's a real statue, and if you can tolerate Chac Mool, which I can't, ours must be considered effective. But this one!" and she scorned its manifold defects. "What's most irritating, Bolón, it doesn't do what it's supposed to do."

"What is that?"

"Create a sense of awe . . . a feeling of mystical power."

"When I see that stone saucer resting on his belly and imagine what's to go in it, I feel awe," Bolón said, but she would not accept this: "Bolón, look at the hideous thing. It offers nothing but shock," and she elaborated on the principle that had guided both her grandfather and her in their service to their island: "Whenever you do a job, do it right in its essentials, but then add something to make it more important than it would otherwise be. I hate our Chac Mool, you know that, but I admire the way the sculptor took pains to make the boots so perfect, the helmet so right. Let that be your guide when you become High Priest of our temple."

As they prepared to leave Tulúm for the journey to Chichén Itzá, Ix Zubin had an opportunity to study her son, and the more she saw of him as he stood on the verge of manhood, the more pleased she was. "Look at him!" she whispered to herself as he marched ahead. "What a handsome body, what a quick mind in its own way." And she saw with motherly satisfaction that the countless nights she had spent binding boards against his forehead had borne fruit, for his face sloped backward in a perfect unbroken line from the tip of his nose to the top of his head in the way a Maya head was supposed to. No forehead bone interrupted that unblemished sweep, and with such a profile her son was assured of being judged one of the most handsome young men in any community. She could not understand why some mothers, and she could name a few in the better families of Cozumel, failed to train their son's heads properly, for all it took was patience and the application of pressure every night for the first six years.

There was a haphazard, poorly tended trail from the temple at Tulúm to the congregation of great buildings at Chichén Itzá, but it could not be called a proper road. However, along it did come, now and then, some important personage riding in a chair covered like a tent with woven mats and carried on the shoulders of four slaves. Bolón, watching one such entourage sweep hurriedly by, with those behind the chair following at a run, told his mother: "That's the way I'd like to go," and she reprimanded him: "What a lofty ambition! To ride on the backs of others," and he blushed at having been so presumptuous.

The narrow path received enough shade from the low trees to

protect the travelers from the blinding sun, but the humidity was so great that they did perspire profusely; Ix Zubin's thin garment was damp most of the time, and although Bolón traveled bare to the waist, his scanty breechclout was soaked. Whenever they reached one or another small village in a clearing, they were more than eager to stop for whatever refreshment the place provided. Gingerly and only after the most cautious calculations and the careful counting of Bolón's cacao beans did Ix Zubin decide that she could risk a small piece of jade or fragment of Ah Nic's gold from her horde to pay for the food they needed. But she was gratified when her son scouted to find things they could eat without surrendering further treasure: a monkey killed with a sharp spear and roasted, a turkey trapped in a net, succulent buds of familiar trees, a fish which Ah Nic caught from a sluggish stream, roots of proven nutritional value and even young, carefully selected leaves of bushes. At night they slept under trees, using leaves and extra clothing as their bedding.

When they broke out of the low woodland they saw stretching far before them the great, flat plains of Yucatán, broken only occasionally by forlorn groups of scraggly trees. Now the sun beat so relentlessly upon them that they feared they might faint. But their good luck persisted, for one day when they fell exhausted beneath a tree that offered meager shade, they were joined by a group of pilgrims who had come from another part of the forest. These men and women carried with them light woven mats which they attached to pairs of forked branches, to form a comfortable protection above their heads, and since they were taking surplus mats to a trading center near Chichén Itzá, they allowed Ix Zubin and her companions to borrow some to make their own head coverings.

The strangers, having no interest in Chichén Itzá, broke away well before the ancient site, but Ah Nic, loath to lose the protection of his head covering, cried like a little child: "I want to keep mine!" and when Ix Zubin offered the traders a small piece of jade for the three mats, the purchase was completed. The strangers gone, Ix Zubin said: "I'm glad we're alone, for these are solemn moments," and when Bolón asked why, she explained: "When you travel you must not only look but also think," and as they sat in their newly purchased shade she talked with her son regarding the glories of their people. She was delighted when she saw that he was following carefully what she said, and that night when she lay stretched upon the ground she thought: He's becoming a priest. Given enough time, he'll make it.

The next day Ix Zubin continued to discuss issues with her son: "Whoever becomes the High Priest at our temple, and I'm sure it will be you, must be strong in defense of old beliefs. He must know the great traditions of our people, or he won't be able to fulfill his responsibilities," and she spoke of her introduction to the grandeur of Maya life: "When my grandfather realized that at five I could handle counting and the mysteries of numbers better than most men of twenty striving to be priests, he said: 'Cozumel isn't big enough for your dreams,' and he stopped everything he was doing to cross the water to the big land and take me down the jungle paths to Tulúm, where he showed me how miserable that temple was, then through the dark paths we followed to just about this spot, where he told me: 'Now you shall see the greatness of our people.' When I asked why we had walked so far, he said: 'Unless you've seen what greatness is, you can never achieve it in your own life. When you study the papyrus in our temple, I want you to read it not as a singular thing, but as one among thousands, found in a hundred temples across this broad land, and each confirming all the others. That's what we travel to Chichén Itzá for,' and that's why you and I have come, so many years later."

As they approached the vast collection of buildings, now empty because leadership of the Maya had passed to Mayapán, Ix Zubin saw that temples she had so vividly remembered, and with such frightening memories, were now even more awesome, for they had been captured by crawling vines which passed over them like clutching fingers. Confronted by this mystery of the land reclaiming the temples, she became a different woman, a priestess self-ordained and inspired by her memories of dreams and nightmares. She was again that child of dazzling brilliance, the adventurous young woman who had preserved the long memories of her Maya people. Her first visit to Chichén Itzá had so awakened her to the terror and glories of Maya life that she now became hungry to instill in her son an equal appreciation. With that resolve, she strode past the Chac Mool and plunged her son into the grandeur of the Chichén Itzá ruins.

Bolón was staggered by the vastness of the buildings, their architectural brilliance, their variation and the manner in which they linked one with the other, providing large open spaces for the assembling of people, ball courts for games with rubber balls and deep, mysterious wells called cenotes into which, after the strangers came with their new religion, maidens were thrown, throats slashed, so that the gods might be appeased. Even though the invaders from the west had reached this spot a full five hundred years earlier, Ix Zubin still thought of them, because of the cruel religious customs they had imposed, as strangers.

But it was a trial of a different order that she wanted to impress upon her son, and as she stood over one of the cenotes, she told Bolón: "Whenever the city faced a crisis that required immediate instruction from the gods, the priests brought twelve naked maidens here at dawn and tossed them one by one into the deep water down there. At noon they came back with long poles to fish out as many girls as had survived, and these lucky ones were supposed to bring with them specific instructions from the gods."

"What if none survived?"

"That meant the city was in trouble."

"I think it was the twelve girls who were in trouble," Ah Nic ventured, but his niece reproved him for making light of a religious tradition, horrible though it was.

It was two quite different features which Bolón would remember longest: the noble pyramids falling into ruin but with high temples still atop their pinnacles, and the artistic excellence of the Chac Mools who, with their gaping saucers on their bellies, seemed better carved than the ones he had known at Cozumel and seen briefly at Tulúm.

But his mother now called his attention to something else: "Look at how these temples were built, the perfection of their stones, the magical way in which one blends with the other," and as he studied these details she continued in an almost mystical monotone: "These temples were built by men who talked with the gods, who had seen a vision of a more perfect world." At one point, when the three stood together sharing a view of four temples whose façades seemed to intertwine, each serving its prescribed purpose, Ix Zubin grasped Bolón's hands and cried: "In spite of the horrors I saw here, if I'd never seen the glories of Chichén, I would have died blind," and she continued in an unbroken litany to describe its wonders.

For three days they remained among the ruined temples but seemed barely to have touched the richness of the place, for when Bolón believed that he had exhausted the things he wanted to inspect, he came upon a ball court much smaller than the imposing one he had first seen, and this lesser court was so handsomely set down among larger buildings that they seemed to protect it and the two stelae that marked its end lines. It was a gem, a practice court no doubt, and he was led to dash into the middle of its playing area and leap and twist as if he were engaged in a vigorous game, and soon he was shouting as if to unseen teammates. His mother, watching as she waited beside one of the handsomely carved markers, said to herself: He's caught the spirit. He's prepared to be a priest. And that night, as they camped near the little court, she told him: "You're ready to be a priest, perhaps even a great one like Grandfather, but in your own way. The problem now is, are you ready to be a man? Let's move on to Mayapán to see how you do battle against the powers there," and they went to bed hungry yet satisfied, for the richness of the temples had satiated them.

In the morning Bolón was up early, eager to resume the journey to Mayapán and test his will against the rules of that city, but before they could get started they were surprised by the arrival at the temple of a group of eleven somber men and women, obviously dispirited and without a leader. When Bolón ran forward to interrogate them, one said sullenly: "We're from Mayapán," and he cried: "That's where we're going!" whereupon all spoke at once: "Don't do it!" and "No reason to go!" and "We've just left and all is confusion."

Ix Zubin hurried up to ask: "What happened there?" and a man with a black spade beard said almost tearfully: "When our leaders saw their power slipping away, great Mayapán sliding into the dust, they became frantic and did all the wrong things. Stupid laws, beheading citizens who disobeyed those laws, riots everywhere. Flames, houses gone and temples too. The end of the world."

When the Cozumel people moved among the newcomers they heard ample confirmation: "Yes, Mayapán was in turmoil for many years. When all was chaos, new invaders swarmed from the south with new gods and new laws. Many loud promises . . ." The speaker, a workingman, shrugged his shoulders, and his wife, gathering her daughter to her, completed his observation: "Promises . . . and now . . . who knows?"

"Even to attempt to go there," the man with the beard warned, "would be to risk life and reason."

"Where, then, are you going?" Ah Nic broke in, and a very old man with white hair gave a long evasive reply, punctuated with lamentations: "Ah me, when the heavens fall in tempest, wise ones huddle close to the earth so that lightning does not strike them."

"Good counsel," Ix Zubin said impatiently. "But where will you find that protective earth?" for she was concerned about her son's safety, and the old man, after more expressions of grief, started another aimless answer: "In these days we seek consolation . . . courage . . . the wisdom of those who went before," and a woman who showed irritation at these ramblings broke in with a solid statement: "We're going to Palenque, where the gods first took us under their protection," and at the mention of this almost sacred name, both Ix Zubin and her uncle gasped, for that ancient site was strong in their minds, and this sudden opportunity to see it was compelling. Without consulting her two companions, and abandoning any thought of visiting moribund Mayapán, Ix Zubin cried: "Can we go with you?" and before anyone could respond, Bolón cried with equal pleading: "Can we? Can we?"

The verbose old man smiled, and said with condescension: "It's many days travel, west and south. As a woman, you couldn't possibly—"

Boldly Ix Zubin interrupted: "I'm the granddaughter of Cimi Xoc," and when the man with the spade beard heard that august name he held out both hands to greet Ix Zubin, but then he posed certain sensible questions whose answers would prove or disprove her relationship with the revered astronomer. She responded properly, going far beyond expectations and revealing herself as one who had some knowledge of the secrets of the planets and even considerable information about how the Maya people had governed themselves in ancient times.

Her questioner was a prudent man who did not want his group to be saddled with weaklings, so before he gave his answer he pointed to the heavens where a waning moon still showed visible in daylight, and said: "Palenque is far. Before we reach there, that moon will stand once more where it stands today. Before we are able to return, it will have stood there twice."

Turning to her men, Ix Zubin started to query them to see if they deemed themselves equal to the task of continuing on to Palenque, and when Ah Nic, whom she questioned first, displayed the reticence which she expected, she heard the people from Mayapán murmuring against admitting him to their group. This distressed her, for she could see animosities festering which would destroy their expedition, so with great force she challenged her uncle: "You are a priest of the Temple of Fertility in Cozumel. These women from Mayapán would travel a far distance to receive your blessing. You are the conscience of our people, the custodian of good things. Brace yourself and assume the leadership to which your rank entitles you."

Her words had a double effect. The women among the newcomers, realizing how indebted they were to the rites at Cozumel, and to any priest who supervised them, began to whisper, while Ah Nic himself acknowledged the truth of what his niece had said. Mustering his courage and assuming a proper demeanor, he spoke quietly: "I am your priest and it is my duty to see that all of you reach Palenque, that holy place, in good stead. Of course Bolón and I can stand the rigors, and as for Ix Zubin, she's stronger of heart than any of us. Let us move forward," and the long trek to Palenque began.

Although the Mayapán men were impressed by the old man's willingness to assume command, they needed two more assurances. "This could well be the last journey any of us will ever make," they said, "so we must be sure. When you walk from here to Palenque, you travel through jungle, swamps, streams overflowing suddenly . . . Days without seeing the sun . . . A million insects, snakes . . . Few villages . . ." Staring at the would-be voyagers, the spokesman asked: "Can you face that?" and Ah Nic said grandly: "Yes."

Then came the crucial question: "We'll have to buy many things along the way . . . whenever we have a chance. Do you carry anything of value?"

Bolón started to tell them that yes, they had . . . but Ah Nic gently placed his hand on the young fellow's arm, smiled at the Mayapán people, and assured them: "We do," and they, approving of his reluctance to disclose the exact level of their wealth, nodded and said: "In that case, off we go," and the company of fourteen started the thirty-three-day walk to Palenque.

It was a magical journey, and, sooner than Ix Zubin expected, the narrow roadway, used only occasionally by the most intrepid wanderers, dived into dense jungle where the upper limbs of towering trees interlocked to form a canopy which obscured the sun and sky. Then the travelers moved in perpetual twilight, with parasite lianas, thick as a man's leg, drooping down from the trees like writhing snakes seeking to entrap them. Birds screeched as the men struggled to push aside the vines before taking their next steps, and the air was so heavy that bodies glistened with perspiration. Now Uncle Ah Nic came into his own, for as a man devoted to the natural world, he knew immediately which leaves and roots were edible, in which direction the hunters from Mayapán should venture if they wished to catch some animal whose meat would provide food, and which trees might be hiding combs of honey which Bolón could collect. As soon as the boy shouted "Bees!" Ah Nic was first there to light the fires that would smoke them out and allow others to grab the honey. And it was he who distributed the food supplies to the women cooks, with instructions as to how they should prepare them. He was a fussbudget and the brains of the expedition.

Bolón was amazed that a major road to a place as important as Palenque had been should now be only this grudging track through jungle. But Ix Zubin knew that this experience with the power of the jungle to smother land would be the best preparation for what he would probably see at Palenque, if it remained as it had been when her grandfather described it; she doubted that the ancient city could provide anything equal to what Bolón had already seen in the dry-lands of Chichén Itzá.

There were, of course, a few small villages in clearings where the pilgrims could find food and water, but they were such mean affairs that Bolón asked the white-haired man: "How could Chichén be so grand and these places so miserable?" and the old fellow replied in sorrow: "People and places know greatness for a while, then decline."

"Why are you making this long journey?"

"To see, once again before I die, the greatness our people knew in the old days, and to mourn its passing."

The man was so patient with Bolón that the boy stayed close to him, discussing ideas relating to temples and proudly explaining the important role played by his family in the Temple of Fertility at Cozumel. The old man listened attentively, but what really intrigued him was Bolón's insistence that his mother really did know the secrets of astronomy and the manipulation of numbers, for he had never known a woman conversant in such matters. When he had heard Ix Zubin say earlier that she understood something about astronomy, he had assumed that she knew where the starry figures stood in the sky. Real astronomy? Never. But now, discovering that she really was learned, he sought her out.

The two conducted long talks, both as they traveled and when they rested, and the Mayapán man marveled at this woman's facility. Once, when they came upon a small temple left in ruins, he led her to a broken stela whose bottom third remained upright and asked her to decipher its glyphs and carvings, and she did so with ease, evoking for him the long-dead events which had once so excited the people supporting this temple that they had carved this stela to commemorate them.

"I wonder what the missing part would have told us?" the man mused, but not even Ix Zubin was clever enough to reconstruct that.

On the long days when nothing happened except dull plodding through jungle, Ix Zubin and her son pursued different interests, the boy heading off with the other hunters to see what food he might find or catch, and Ix Zubin talking with the two women who had accompanied their husbands from Mayapán. One interested her especially. This strong-minded woman had a daughter of fourteen, Ix Bacal by name, who was especially beautiful by Maya standards in that her mother had carefully trained her to be conspicuously cross-eyed: "When she was four days old I kept a feather dangling before her eyes on a length of grass, and as she stared at it, day after day, her eyes began to cross rather nicely. Then, when she was older, I asked her father to get us a piece of bright shell, and this was hung so that light from the sun reflected into her eyes, and this too helped to train them inward, the way a mother wants them. Finally, when she could walk, I would stand before her and bring my finger from way back here straight to the point of her nose, and in time her eyes locked properly, the way you see them today."

Then the mother apologized for her own inadequate eyes: "My parents did not take such pains, and you can see that my eyes barely cross, and for certain they're not locked. Eyes that wander get a woman into trouble. Eyes that turn in bring illumination to her soul, and you can see that Ix Bacal has such eyes." So the two Maya women, as they rested in the jungle, congratulated themselves on the proofs of their maternal care—Bolón's nicely sloping head and Ix Bacal's lovely crossed eyes.

To Ix Zubin's dismay, her son seemed unaware of the beautiful girl, and since he was soon to be seventeen, she was beginning to wonder if he was ever going to discover the other sex, for to have an unmarried priest in charge of a fertility temple would be unacceptable if not preposterous.

When they were about two-thirds of the way to Palenque, with the tropic moon verifying their progress each night, they came upon a clearing occupied by a gang of ugly, dirty men who were tapping a grove of wild rubber trees to collect the precious sap which could be used in so many ways. Bolón saw that the blackness on their hands and faces came not from ordinary dirt but from the soot that accumulated when they heated the sap over slow fires to cure it and convert it into the rubber he had known when playing the ball game.

He noticed also that the Mayapán travelers treated these workmen with considerable deference, but even this recognition of their power did not prevent the ugly fellows from trying to grab at Ix Zubin, for they had not seen women for many days. When this happened, Ah Nic cried out in protest and Bolón leaped forward to defend his mother. But the men's gestures had been a ruse, for what they really wanted was the young girl of fourteen, Ix Bacal, but when they tried to drag her away, Bolón heard her screams, and he and two of the travelers leaped at her attackers and drove them off while Ah Nic tried to hit them with a switch. Hurriedly, Ix Zubin and the man with the spade beard collected the pilgrims and fled the area of the malevolent rubber gatherers, who jeered at them as they left.

Back in the safety of the arched-over jungle trail, Bolón found himself trapped in an enticing mental problem: What would the ugly men have done with Ix Bacal if they had made away with her? and he now looked at the girl in a new way. No more long conversations with the old man, no more consultations with his mother. In his spontaneous leaping to the defense first of his mother and then of the girl, he had unknowingly taken the subtle step from boyhood to young manhood, and it was a development that Ix Zubin approved. She knew that her son's ultimate effectiveness as a priest at their temple would depend in part upon the kind of young woman he would have as his partner. Her famous grandfather had been helped in many subtle ways by his good wife, and she herself had been of inestimable value to her husband, therefore, there was good reason to hope that Bolón would find himself a worthy mate.

So she took as much interest in this young girl as did her son. In appearance Ix Bacal was already a superior girl and gave promise of becoming an even finer-looking woman, but when Ix Zubin attempted to engage her in conversation, she quickly learned that the girl was ignorant and not interested in any aspect of Maya life, not even in her potential role as a mother. She was a pretty nothing, and for a young man as promising as Bolón, that was not enough.

But Ix Zubin was a wise woman—this astronomer who understood not only the heavens but the human heart—and she realized that she must not in any way openly oppose young Ix Bacal, for Bolón had reached the age when he must begin to make his own decisions, and when she saw her son lead the girl into the darker edges of the forest she was sensible enough to leave them alone. But she did wonder how, when she and Bolón returned to Cozumel, she could help him find a proper wife.

After many days the pilgrims reached the edge of the once-great religious and political center of Palenque, and both Ah Nic and Ix Zubin, knowing the disappointment the others in the group were about to experience, prepared to soften the blow. Ix Zubin moved close to her son, but this did no good, for when he looked at Palenque, all he could see were trees, in a jungle of such profusion that nothing was visible more than six lengths in any direction. "Where is Palenque?" he asked fretfully, for this had been a long journey to end in so little, and his mother said: "Climb that tree and look about you," but when he did he called down: "I still see nothing," and she cried: "Bolón, look at the clotted mounds!" and when he did he began slowly to see that the area was covered with spots where the trees leaped upward as if they were hiding something below, and he called down: "It's like the waves on the sea at Tulúm," and indeed it was. There were great temples below him and scores of revealing stelae and beautiful palaces too, but none were visible, for human beings had left the area nearly a thousand years earlier, leaving the jungle free to confiscate the place, and it had.

Palenque, as Bolón saw it from his tree that October day in 1489, was nothing but a vast collection of mounds buried under a sea of trees, twisted roots and creeping lianas. Not even a vestige of the grandeur that once characterized the site was discernible, and as he climbed down to rejoin the other pilgrims waiting amid the jungled mounds, the site of one lost building rarely visible from another, all were overcome with a sense of mourning for past glories.

Then the man with the spade beard began, in whispering voice, to explain what had happened: "In its time, thousands of moons ago, this was a place of noble range, but it lived its day. Its people lost their enthusiasms. Its proud message was moved to other centers, and it perished.

" 'Why, then, do we come here?' you ask. To remind ourselves of what we stem from, and to uncover our past. Yes, to uncover." And he explained that when he had been here, years ago, he and his group had fixed upon one mound and had torn away the trees and matted vines to reveal the treasure hidden below, and that in the morning this group would do the same. Pointing to two of the men and Bolón, he said: "Choose the mound and we'll see what it hides," and the committee of three spent some hours prowling among the mounds that hid the monuments. But as they were about to settle upon an imposing one that seemed certain to hide something of merit, the man with the spade beard came to them with a caution: "Not something too big. There'll be too much digging before we come to the walls," so they chose a small, clearly formed mound not overburdened with tall trees.

In the morning they hurried to their exciting task, but they had worked for only an hour when everyone realized that it would be impossible to clear the entire mound; that would take a moon of effort, but they could, as others had done on visits past, clear a tunnel of sufficient size to allow reasonable inspection of some portion of what lay hidden below, and to this more limited task the diggers applied themselves.

On the second day Bolón was deep in the tunnel, ripping away roots that clung avariciously to some hidden object, when, with a mighty pull of his arms, he tore the last roots free and cried: "It's here!" and the others rushed up behind him to finish enlarging the passageway so that their companions could stoop and walk through to see at least this remnant of Palenque's greatness. Then, when a substantial surface of the buried temple had been cleared, all could examine the exquisite workmanship that had characterized Maya building at its zenith.

"Look!" the bearded man cried, his eyes alight with wonder. "See how each stone fits exactly every other, on all sides. And how the surfaces are polished. And if we could locate a carved stela, we'd see real wonders."

This challenge so excited Bolón and the two other diggers that they scrambled about among the debris, shoving and hauling, until they uncovered not a traditional stela but a carved portion of wall, and when it had been cleaned, the pilgrims saw revealed what their man had promised: a piece of carving so fine that the figure of an ancient chieftain who had accomplished something of merit seemed to leap off the wall to resume command. "Why did they always dress themselves in those tremendous head adornments?" Bolón asked as he stared at the fantastic crown composed of serpents, leaves, flowers and the head of a snarling jaguar with teeth bared.

"Our ancestors knew that a man was a limited creature," the bearded man explained, as if he were living at that time, "so they adopted a headdress that made them taller, that brought all mystical powers to their support." Then he smiled and added: "Also, it impressed and even frightened the ordinary people." Turning to the others, he asked: "Can you imagine standing before that judge, with those snakes and jaguar teeth staring down at you, and admitting that you'd done something wrong?" The headdress of the life-size figure was three feet high.

Only a corner of the little temple had been cleared by the diggers, but now Bolón and another man decided to probe just a bit farther, and in doing so, came upon the blocked entrance to an inner room. When this was opened and torches brought, Ah Nic led them inside to the true miracle of Palenque, for there in the dim and gloom, protected by thick outer walls from the inquisitive roots, rose an inner wall some seven feet high and twelve feet long, covered completely with glyphs and scripts and figures of the most beautiful composition, some carved, some painted, summarizing an account of what must have been a heroic action in times long past.

It was a work of majestic art, a communication from the heartland of the Maya composed in the days before the new religion came in from the west, and Ix Zubin especially was staggered by its size and magnificence, but when her son asked: "What does it say?" she had to confess that neither she nor Ah Nic nor anyone living that day could read the old writing. This was tantalizing, because obviously it conveyed a specific message about events of consequence which the writers wanted to record for posterity. "It's infuriating," Ix Zubin grumbled, "that not one of us is able to read that message,"* but though she was frustrated, she did find satisfaction in solving the date, comparable to Thursday 14 June A.D. 512.

While she was doing this, Bolón was mesmerized by the carvings, for they were so grand in their gray-white purity, with colors applied

---

*When in the summer of 1959, I came upon this newly discovered wall, its glyphs were still undecipherable, for the Rosetta stone which would unlock the secrets of Maya writing has not yet been found. Recently, however, scholars in various countries, aided by computers, have begun to make translations.

sparingly here and there, that he could not fathom how they had been made. "What is this?" he appealed to the others, knocking his knuckles against what he took to be a stone, but unlike any he had known.

Ah Nic knew the answer. "The hills near here gave them a remarkable stone, easy to crush, easy to mix with sand and broken pebbles and lime and just enough water. It formed a plaster, not solid, not liquid, and it was easily worked. As it dried it could be carved, but when it hardened . . ." Picking from the floor a small rock, he banged it mightily against the carved face of a ferocious god, and the pebble cracked while the god's cheek remained unscarred. "We call it stucco," Ah Nic said, "and it accounts for the beauty of Palenque."

When Bolón inspected this little treasure room he saw that the walls, the ceiling, the decorations and the statues were all of stucco, and when he left, reluctantly, looking back till the last flare died, he realized that the first figure he had admired had been constructed in the same way: a pillar had been covered with wet stucco which, when hardened, could be carved into fantastic configurations.

As the time approached to start the return journey, Ah Nic led the group through a jungle morass to the edge of a massive mound reaching high into the air and covered by a literal forest of trees: "If that little corner of such a minor temple revealed such wonders, can you imagine what grandeur will be seen when great mounds like this are uncovered?" Then he allowed his voice to fall to a whisper: "And as we have seen, there are scores of such mounds, scores of temples lying hidden all around us," and in the silence that followed, Bolón understood why his mother had insisted on this pilgrimage, for he knew that knowledge of the past gave men courage to face the future.

When Ix Zubin led her son, now a proven man, back to the point on the mainland where they would catch the ferry to Cozumel, they found confusion, for the men who customarily sailed the large canoes were nowhere to be seen, nor were their craft. Instead, a group of catch-as-catch-can little craft were swarming around in the hands of men who knew little about them. When the three travelers chose one in which they had scant faith, the young fellow in charge told them a doleful story: "Much bad this year. Nobody in Mayapán to give orders. Nobody in Cozumel to set rules."

"What's happened?" Ah Nic asked, sensing that it would not look right for a woman to be seen asking political questions, and the doleful young man said as he propelled them inexpertly homeward: "Much burning in Cozumel. Many old buildings gone in the fighting." None of the three wanted to query the fate of the Temple of Fertility, but without being asked, the man volunteered: "No more pilgrims coming to our temples. Too much trouble in Mayapán. No more big canoes here to carry them." He paused, studied Ah Nic, whom he did not want to offend, then added tentatively: "Maybe all people . . . not believe priests anymore."

When they landed, ignoring people who might want to interrogate them about having been absent for more than half a year, they walked benumbed toward their temple, and wherever they looked they saw scars and things torn away. Then Bolón, running ahead, stopped aghast, for the Temple of Fertility which he should have inherited had been wantonly destroyed, its walls torn down, its cluster of supporting buildings burned. Even its detestable Chac Mool had been carried off to a more exposed site where human sacrifices could be staged with greater spectacular effect.

But what appalled Ix Zubin beyond consolation was that the precious papers on which her grandfather had computed his calculations on the planet Venus had been burned, along with his predictions of eclipses for centuries to come. She was enraged when she learned of this savagery, but she did not confide her feelings to Bolón lest he react spontaneously as he had when the rubber tappers assaulted her. She did, however, caution him: "We may have caused the destruction of our own temple . . . going on pilgrimage without their permission . . . Beware, son. They may have other punishments awaiting us. Beware." And she monitored whatever he did, trying to keep him away from his superiors in hopes of protecting him.

But very soon attention was diverted from them by the arrival of a long canoe, unprecedented in width and construction, whose rowers indicated in sign language that they had come from a big land far to the east containing tall mountains and fine rivers.* The legends of Cozumel held that a huge island lay well to the east, occupied by savages of a totally different breed. With these mysterious islanders men of olden times had sometimes traded Maya rubber balls and bits of green jade in return for cruder items, and Bolón assumed that these rowers were the very men his elders had sometimes spoken of.

*Cuba.

It was obvious to him that they had traversed the same sea that he had speculated upon when gazing out from the towers of Tulúm. He therefore became one of the eager young men who conversed with the strangers; they knew no Cozumel words, but like all traders, were able to convey their needs and explain what goods they had to offer in exchange.

To his superiors, Bolón explained: "They are like the long-ago people you spoke about. They want from us only two things. Pieces of jade and rubber balls for their games."

"What have they to offer?"

"Beautiful mats, best ever seen," Bolón said with enthusiasm, betraying the fact that he had become excited by the mysteriousness of their sudden appearance. "Seashells, beautifully carved. Rowing paddles of a strong new wood."

When the rude men who now ruled Cozumel growled: "We have no need of paddles," Bolón unwisely protested this decision, pointing out that the time could very well come when the men of Cozumel might want to venture out upon the sea which these strangers had apparently crossed with ease.

"No!" the new rulers snarled. "The sea is not for us. We're people of the land."

But Bolón found himself opposed to them, for he had fallen under the spell of the sea that rolled in such majesty onto the eastern shore of his island, and he began to speculate upon its significance: If these men have come to us in their large canoe, perhaps others will arrive in much larger ones? Cherishing his thoughts, he began walking for hours along the shore, staring eastward as if striving to glimpse the lands which he suspected might rest invisibly in the distance. At electrifying moments during his speculations he began to comprehend secrets of the sea, and it seemed as if bolts of lightning struck his imagination: Is it not possible that the future of Cozumel will lie not with the mainland to the west where all things seem to be crumbling, but rather somewhere in this unknown sea to the east where things seem fresh and new? At the conclusion of one such vision he strode into the waves and cried: "Waters of the world, I embrace you," and from that moment his decision was made.

He associated constantly with the rowers of the canoe, taking them bits of jade from his mother's store and rubber balls from his friends, and these items he used to trade for mats and carved seashells. Significantly, he did not keep these for himself, for he had conceived the idea that he might be going with the men when they left Cozumel, and if he did accompany them to their homeland, it would be foolish to carry with him the things they made. But he would pay a terrible penalty for this generosity, because one of his friends had turned informer, whispering to the authorities: "Bolón trades with the strangers despite your instructions, and he may even be considering sailing away with them."

Both charges were true. Bolón had been so awed by his visit to Palenque that he had returned to Cozumel yearning to do something that would re-create the grandeur lost in that buried city. But now, with his temple destroyed and any possibility of his becoming a priest erased, he was casting about for other areas in which he could exercise his energy, and the idea of carrying Maya concepts of life to new lands became inviting. So one morning, without carefully exploring what such an emigration would entail, he hurried down to where the canoe was loading and indicated to the rowers: "I'd like to go with you," and they replied that he'd be welcome.

That night, after sunset, still unaware that the Cozumel authorities were closely watching his behavior, he told his mother: "I've been thinking. With the loss of everything here, maybe it would be better if I sailed with the strangers when they leave in the morning."

For some moments Ix Zubin did not reply, for since their departure from Palenque she had been worried about her son's future. Some of the signs she detected were ominous, like his constant association with the newcomers; others reassuring, like his increased maturity and willingness to discuss important matters with her. But what really disturbed her were his frequent wanderings along the shore, for she guessed that he had become infatuated with the sea. Recalling how profoundly it had affected him during their trip to Tulúm, she warned: "Bolón, do not fall in love with a stranger. Keep your feet dry."

Trying desperately to determine whether her son was still a boy or had truly become a man, one night she shared her assessment with him: "At Tulúm you said you liked it better because it was bigger than Cozumel. Remember that foolish statement? Also, when the official in the palanquin passed us on the road, you said your ambition was to ride in one when you grew up. How silly. And on the ball court at Chichén you were a mere boy, playing with dreams."

Then she reassured him: "But in seeking out honeybees on the trip, you were better than the men. In fighting off the rubber tappers, you were strongest of all. And with lovely, cross-eyed Ix Bacal you behaved as a proud and proper young man should. But it was in the explorations at Palenque that you really led the way—in uncovering the treasures . . . in understanding what you found."

For some moments she rocked back and forth, bending from the waist, then she leaned sideways and embraced her son: "I took you away from Cozumel a boy. I brought you back a man." Then, taking his hands, she whispered: "You say you may be going away with the strangers in their canoe. That's the kind of decision only a grown man is eligible to make. Well, you're a man now. Think carefully, son," and she drew his hands to her lips and kissed them in a kind of benediction.

The realization that he might be leaving Ix Zubin forever overwhelmed him and he fell silent, not knowing what to say. Ill at ease about revealing the love he felt for her, he made a totally different observation: "It's difficult when the world's changing . . . when the old dies but you can't yet see the new."

In the hours that followed, these two good people who saw so clearly that their world was disintegrating, with nothing better to take its place, sat in a darkness alleviated only by the stars which they had studied so faithfully, and they became mourners for the death of Palenque and Chichén Itzá and even huge Mayapán that had served a useful purpose during its good days. They had been great cities motivated by worthy purposes, but they had either vanished or were in the process of doing so. Cozumel, too, was doomed, as fatally wounded as Tulúm, and soon there would be no need for astronomers or mathematicians or men who knew how to make and use stucco. "Everywhere the jungle will reclaim the land," Ix Zubin said, but she refused to lament. Straightening her little shoulders as if to muster new resolve, she said: "New worlds, new tasks," but she could not envision what purpose either she or Bolón, trained as they had been, could serve in the new order.

The long night ended strangely, with mother and son sitting in silence, he desolate because he could not fathom his future, she even more anguished because she saw that with the destruction of her records her past too might be lost,* and each convinced that the present must continue bleak.

*She was justified in her fear, because on 12 July 1562 well-meaning Diego de Landa, Fourth Bishop of Yucatán, seeking to protect Catholicism from Maya heresy, gathered all known copies of scrolls like the ones Ix Zubin and her grand-

A few days later Bolón had to make his crucial decision, for the newcomers had warned him: "On the morrow, we row back to our island." Upon rising, he ate nervously, kissed his mother, and wandered almost aimlessly down to where the canoe was being loaded, still undecided whether to jump into it for the great adventure or merely wave them an affectionate farewell. When he reached the water's edge the men shouted: "Hola! Hola!" indicating that he was invited to join them, but at the last moment he drew back and allowed them to depart.

Ix Zubin, watching from a distance, felt a surge of joy in knowing that he would stay with her, but this euphoria vanished when she asked herself the question that would haunt her remaining days: Should I have encouraged him, even driven him, to leave this doomed place and find a better life? Her fears that she might have acted improperly were temporarily assuaged when her son strode back from the sea with a decisive step, spotted her watching, and came to her, saying in a voice from which irresolution had been cleansed: "My life is here. To help you rebuild our temple. To save this island from a terrible error," and he led her off to launch their first steps in that effort. Following behind, her heart sang: He has become the man we needed.

But as they approached their shack seven guards leaped upon Bolón lest he try to run down to the departing canoe, pinioned his arms, stripped him of his clothing, and informed him in loud voices: "You're for the next sacrifice to Chac Mool. At the feast, three days hence," and they rushed him away to the wicker cage in which the human sacrifices were imprisoned while awaiting the feast day.

In wild panic Ix Zubin tried to rescue her son from this terrible end, but she was powerless; the rulers had lodged such serious charges against her that her pleas were nullified. She had gone on pilgrimage without permission. She had encouraged her son to have dealings with the strangers. And worst of all, she had kept in her possession pages of papyrus containing mystic calculations which ought to be administered only by men. Had custom allowed women to be sacrificed to the rain god, she would surely have volunteered to take her son's place in the waiting pen. Instead, she had to suffer her grief and outrage alone.

In her lonely shack she reviewed the horror of the situation and

---

father Cimi Xoc had collected and burned them in a great bonfire. Only three in all Mayaland survived and it is from them that we know the history of this great civilization.

her role in it: I took such pains to rear a worthy son . . . applied the boards to give him a noble appearance to his head . . . taught him the rituals of our temple . . . instructed him in the stars . . . trained him to be responsible . . . encouraged him when he met that lovely girl. What more could I have done?

She knew the answer: I could have demanded that he flee this dreadful island with those men in the canoe. He knew that his destiny lay in the sea to the east, but I intruded. Then came the most terrible recrimination of all: I helped to strike him down in the very moment when he became a full man, and to her mind's eye came that final vision of him as he strode back from the seashore, his body bronzed by the sun, his mind and courage forged in the fires of his generation. Wailing to herself, she cried: "He was the best man on this island, and I helped destroy him," and she cursed the gods.

Bolón, held tightly in his cage, knew neither rage nor fear. His recent experiences at majestic Chichén Itzá and sacred Palenque had given him a new understanding. He realized that civilizations waxed and waned and that he was unfortunate in having been born into an era when old values were dying, dying beyond recall. He was glad that his mother had rejected her original plan of going to Mayapán, for he sensed that such a visit to a moribund center would have been not only unproductive but also depressing. Palenque, on the other hand, had been like a flame in a dark night, throwing beautiful shadows in corners that would otherwise have been completely dark. He was proud to be the inheritor of the men and women who had built Palenque.

Also, he remembered his sudden courage in fighting off the rubber tappers, for it had made him aware, now that he was seventeen, that a world of women waited with their own mysteries; life was twice as complicated and interesting as he had perceived it earlier. This thought did bring flashes of regret; he did not want to die before those other avenues were explored; he was unwilling to go before he knew from what lands to the east the strangers had come.

But above all, he was a Maya, profoundly indoctrinated in the lore of his people, and he truly believed that if he behaved poorly at his execution, he would bring shame upon his mother and a punishing drought to his island, and this he would not do. So he huddled in his cage, erased all fear, and awaited the moment when he would be taken to the stone altar beside which Chac Mool waited with the stone saucer resting on his belly.

At the appointed time the guards came to the cage, unlocked it and pulled him out, but this required no effort, for Bolón was in a hypnotic state. He saw the ruins of his temple as he was dragged along, but they signified nothing. He saw the waiting Chac Mool, but its hateful features no longer terrified him. He saw his weeping mother, but he was so self-benumbed that he could not even make a gesture of farewell.

Now the guards threw him roughly, face up, on the big stone altar, whereupon four young acolytes leaped forward to grab his arms and legs and pull them tightly backward so as to force his chest upward. Bolón actually watched with personal concern as the high priest, wearing a robe covered with arcane symbols painted in gold and blood and a tremendous headdress two feet high crawling with snakes and jaguars, lifted his obsidian knife, plunged it into the left side of the rib cage, drew it deeply across, and while Bolón was still alive, reached in and grabbed the beating heart, ripping it from its hiding place. Bolón remained alive just long enough to see his own heart placed reverently in the waiting saucer of Chac Mool.

On the very day that Bolón died on the island of Cozumel, a council of some importance was meeting in the Spanish city of Sevilla, where King Ferdinand and Queen Isabella listened attentively as a team of three learned savants cited six reasons why the Italian navigator Cristoforo Colombo, now converted into the Spanish supplicant Cristóbal Colón, was egregiously wrong in his preposterous theory that Asia could be reached by sailing westward out of a port in southern Spain:

"First, we already know that the Western Ocean is infinite. Second, since the voyage he proposes would require at least three years, it would be impossible for him to get there and back. Third, if he did reach the Antipodes on the other side of the globe, how could he sail back up against the slope? Fourth, St. Augustine has clearly said: 'There can be no Antipodes because there is no land down there.' Fifth, of the five zones into which the earth is divided, the ancients have assured us that only three can be inhabited. Sixth, and most important, if so many centuries have passed since Creation, is it reasonable that any lands can still wait undiscovered?"

When everyone present finished acclaiming the irrefutable reasoning of the wise men, Colón stepped forward, and like a tough-spirited bulldog refusing to surrender a bone held in its teeth, growled: "I know Asia lies where I say it does. I know I can get to it by sailing westward. And before I die, with God's help I shall do so."

The courtiers laughed. The royal couple looked at him in dismay and shook their heads. The wise men congratulated themselves on having helped Spain avoid error. But Colón marched out of the court still determined to pursue the great adventure in which he had unfaltering faith.

III

CHRISTOPHER COLUMBUS IN HISPANIOLA

I N THE SPRING OF 1509 THE COURTIERS ATTENDING THE KING OF
Spain in his temporary headquarters at Segovia just north of Madrid awaited anxiously the arrival of a caped horseman who had
been expected some hours earlier. When he came clattering into the
paved courtyard they rushed to help him dismount, but he vaulted
from his horse, ignoring the offers of help.

"How dare you keep the king waiting!" they cried.

"Gypsies camping under a bridge," he said curtly. "Set it afire
cooking their stolen meats."

"Three times the king has summoned you."

"And I wasn't here to answer, was I?" he snapped, but then as he
brushed himself and discarded his cape, throwing it across his saddle,
his momentary brusqueness dissolved into a gracious smile: "He'll
understand," and he headed for the palace door.

He was a tall man, with a small patch of red and gold brocade
covering his left eye and a long-healed scar crossing his weathered
cheek. He was Don Hernán Ocampo, forty-seven years old and a
veteran of the triumphant wars Spain had recently waged to expel
the Moors from Europe. His protracted military service in battle had
been unusual in that as a young man he had been trained in law,
not warfare. Following his military successes, he had proved so able

at his chosen profession that he had become a *licenciado* practicing in Sevilla, where he had met and married a granddaughter of the Duke of Alba, and he had helped Ferdinand of Aragon consolidate so much scattered power that the latter ultimately became King of Spain. Since Ocampo had also helped arrange Ferdinand's masterful marriage to Isabella of Castille he had reason to trust that the king would forgive his tardiness today. But when he was ushered into Ferdinand's presence, he found the handsome monarch, a year older than himself and much more corpulent, in an ugly mood: "I've needed you, Ocampo. You must perform a major task on my behalf."

Ocampo bowed with the lean grace of a gallant courtier and waved his left hand toward the king: "As always, Majesty." The familiar manner in which he moved and spoke, avoiding the word *king* as improper to be used among two men who had long worked together, almost said in words what each knew: Did I not lose this eye and gain this scar in your behalf?

Ferdinand nodded slightly to acknowledge his friendship but he did not relax his sense of irritation and urgency. Throwing his arms about Ocampo's shoulder, he led him to a divan covered with gold and purple embroidery and pulled him down beside him: "It's those damned Colón heirs. They're driving me crazy with petitions and noisy claims."

"Still? I thought that had long been settled."

"No. When their father died three years ago they began pestering me in earnest. Said that since he had discovered the New World for Isabella and me, I owed them, as his heirs, huge amounts of gold. More than the treasury has!"

"I am a lawyer, Majesty, but I do not bemire myself in family inheritances. In such battles honest men always lose."

"That's my problem, Ocampo. Yours is to sail out to Española and ascertain the truth as to how Cristóbal Colón discharged his duties there in my behalf."

Ocampo moved away from the king, and placing his left thumb under his chin, he began, with the forefinger of that hand, to stroke his right cheek, closing his good eye; in this posture which he often used when trying to delay a decision, he gave the strong impression of a man immersed in deep thought. The king, seeing this, allowed him time to reflect, and when Ocampo finally spoke he surprised the monarch: "But didn't you send an inquisitor out there eight or ten years ago to do the very thing you're now asking me to do?"

The shrewdness of this response pleased the king and caused him to relax. Clapping Ocampo on the knee, he said: "You have a long memory. Yes, nine years ago I dispatched Francisco de Bobadilla to Española to check on Colón. Gave him five extraordinary powers."

"Didn't he do a good job?"

"That's what this problem is about. Isabella and I accepted his report, and we thought that finished the matter. But now the Colón heirs are claiming that Bobadilla was both prejudiced against their relative and a liar. If so, their pleas for more rewards might be justified."

"What kind of man was Bobadilla?"

In answer the king rose, took Ocampo by the arm, and walked with him out into the garden of the palace, and there, among the spring flowers and budding trees, he gave a sharp summary of his onetime secret agent: "As different from you, Ocampo, as a man could be. Where you are slim, he was so fat he was almost ridiculous. Where you have a cautious, well-trained mind, he was impetuous. And where you bear the scars of honorable service to your country, he was terrified of a mouse, and the sound of a cannon sometimes unhinged him."

"Why did you give such a man an important job?" and the king said: "Isabella favored him, and I could deny her nothing."

These words produced an astonishing result, for as the king walked beside a line of tall, thin cypress trees, reminding him of those that had marked the cemetery where funeral rites for the great Isabella had been held, he broke into tears. Turning to Ocampo, he clutched his trusted friend to him and sobbed: "I have been desolate since her death. Ocampo, she was the finest queen the world has produced. None ever served their king more graciously . . ." He stopped abruptly, then said in a much different voice: "She was in many ways more brilliant than I am. I work hard, keep my eye on the task, adjust to the storms about me. She was calm and steady, like a flower-filled meadow when the wild storm passes."

They had reached a point in their walk from which, across fields, the famous Roman aqueduct of Segovia could be seen, and this notable structure, now almost fifteen hundred years old and still delivering water to the city, reminded them of empire and government and the powerful things they themselves had helped create in Spain. Sitting on a wooden bench, the king said: "We united this country. No one thought it could be done, all those warring principalities. But we triumphed."

"What I have always admired about you, Majesty, was your willingness to make bold moves. To do vast things that others would have shied away from."

"You mean like throwing the Muhammadans out of Spain and Europe?"

"But also evicting the Jews."

"That was a strong move," the king agreed. "But you must remember, we did give them a fair chance. If they converted to our religion, we allowed them to stay. If not . . ." He hesitated ominously, then fingered a gold medallion that hung suspended upon his chest by a silver chain: "I am as proud of this medal as anything I have in the world. The pope gave it to me when he awarded me the title El Católico. Said I was the premier Catholic in the world, because I strive to see that all my realms—Castille, Aragon, Sicily and New Spain across the seas—are as Catholic as I am."

The two friends were particularly proud of their role in establishing the Holy Inquisition to defend the church. Its task, under the directions Ferdinand had spelled out when instituting the office, was to root out heresy wherever found in the world: "The priests have been doing a splendid job, Ocampo, and when you reach Española you must harass the infidels there—atheists, pagans, Jews, stamp them out!"

Before Ocampo could affirm his determination to support the faith in the New World as he had in the Old, the two men were joined by a sprightly Frenchwoman, Germaine de Foix, niece of the King of France and Ferdinand's new wife. He seemed pleased to see her, but after she had led the men into a salon where a tasty repast awaited—meat, cheese, chewy bread and strong Spanish wine—she left them, and when Ocampo asked: "Has she adjusted to Spain comfortably?" the king said brightly: "Oh yes! Better than any of us could have expected. And our friendship with France is stronger, thanks to her." Then he paused, looked toward the door to be sure she was out of earshot, and said: "But she does not compare with Isabella."

Ocampo saw that the great man, who had accomplished so much good in Europe, was about to break into tears again, so he started to turn away, but Ferdinand, seizing control of himself, caught Ocampo by the arm and swung him around: "Please, trusted friend, uncover the truth about Colón."

"I shall, I promise you. But before I leave, can we not agree that Colón did the major things he promised? Did he not find new lands of enormous value? Did he not complete successfully three later voyages, in 1493, in 1498 and in 1502, to demonstrate to others how easy it was to cross the ocean?"

"We know what he did at sea. I want to know what he did on land."

"Which land? If we can believe him, he touched on many lands, perhaps China, Japan, India, but for sure, the islands he named, Cuba, Puerto Rico, Jamaica . . ."

"We're interested only in Española. He served us there as our viceroy, and it's from there the charges against him came." As the king bade Ocampo farewell and God's speed he said with great warmth: "Solve this problem for me, Hernán, and any position in the kingdom is yours, any title you choose," and they embraced.

When the lookout called "Land!" to the ship's captain, the mariner hesitated briefly to assure himself that Española* did lie ahead, then summoned his important passenger to his side: "There lies your island!" and for the next hour Hernán Ocampo stood spread-legged in the prow of the ship, watching the miracle of an island rising slowly from the sea. The captain, noting with approval the one-eyed man scanning the horizon, said to the sailor at the wheel: "He's making believe he's Colón, arriving to take command of that island and this sea."

"Why's he wear that eye patch?"

"Lost his eye fighting the Moors."

"I know. But why red and gold?"

"I've wondered myself."

"Ask him."

"You don't ask a man like him a question like that."

"I would."

"Then give me the wheel, because I'd like to know too," and the young fellow went directly to Ocampo, coughed to make his presence known, and asked, deferentially: "Excellency, can I ask you a question?"

"I'm not an excellency. Just another *licenciado.*"

"Why is your eye patch that mix of red and gold?"

---

*Historically known to the world as Hispaniola. Later the western one-third became Haiti, the eastern two-thirds, the Dominican Republic.

Ocampo took no offense; instead, he smiled at the sailor: "Don't you know?"

"I'm completely lost."

"When an army fights, it must have a banner that all can recognize, a signal of our side against theirs. Have you never seen the banner we Spaniards used against the Moors? A red and gold flag, two magnificent colors, don't you think?"

"I do."

"So when I lost my eye in the siege of Granada, I swore: 'I shall proclaim the colors of Spain until I die.' And here I am." With that he resumed his watch on the waiting land.

Española was a big island offering a hilly profile, and as it grew clearer Ocampo detected an appealing aspect: it contained numerous white-sand beaches edged by palm trees dancing in the breeze. He would always remember that first poetic image: a curving beach, inviting and clean, with a ballet of swaying palms.

When the captain cried: "That's your town, Santo Domingo," Ocampo saw the first organized settlement of the New World, capital not only of this island but of all Spain's possessions in the lands Colón had discovered. As Ocampo watched the city emerge from the sea he saw that it was still only a collection of one-storied wooden structures, dominated by one obviously important stone building of two floors.

"Whose is that?" he asked, and the captain replied: "One Pimentel, the lieutenant governor. Man of high family. Seems to dominate the place."

When a small fleet of canoes manned by Indians swarmed out from the shore, Ocampo noticed that the men were savage in appearance—low foreheads, very dark hair, brownish skin, wearing no more than a loincloth—but sharp-eyed and eager to conduct their simple commerce with the ship. Then he looked above their clamoring hands and waving paddles, and he caught a remarkably clear impression of the town itself.

It contained, he calculated from imperfect evidence, about nine hundred people, a chain of rude houses along the beach and a central square of sorts from whose northern side rose a wooden church with a proud steeple topped by a sturdy cross. It was in all respects, he judged, the kind of solid Spanish town he had seen so often in the hill country south of Madrid, and he felt reassured by its comforting appearance: In this town I will not feel a stranger.

As soon as the watchers who had lined the shore to greet the incoming ship saw Ocampo stride ashore, sternly dressed, cavalier's hat cocked on his head, imperial in every motion, with that red and gold patch gleaming in the sun, they realized that an important force had come amongst them on a mission of some moment. Those who had been stealing from the king began to shiver, fearing that he might find them out, but in the next moment they were astonished by a sudden change in his manner: he smiled at the silent watchers, bowed as if paying them honor, and even relaxed his rigid stride, for he wanted to give them a message: "I come among you as a friend."

They were impressed when he signaled back to the ship, from which two scribes now descended, men in their twenties carrying bundles of papers. No sooner had they hit land than they began to scurry about, looking for an appropriate building to commandeer for headquarters. Rather quickly they focused on the two-story stone house which the captain had said was occupied by a man named Pimentel, but when they asked to inspect the place, the owner, anticipating their mission, coldly informed them: "This house would not be appropriate. My wife's family occupies more than half, and grandchildren romp everywhere."

When Ocampo joined his scribes he asked: "What's the matter here?" but before his men could explain, the owner stepped forward and introduced himself: "Alejandro Pimentel y Fraganza, representative of the king," and Ocampo bowed, for the man's last two names were distinguished in Spanish history.

"I am Hernán Ocampo of Sevilla, personal emissary of the king and eager to find headquarters for the work he ordered me to do on his behalf." In this courteous manner each informed the other that he was a man of some importance, not to be treated lightly.

Pimentel, an austere man in his sixties, bowed stiffly and assured the newcomer: "I shall do everything to assist you, but as I have explained to your men, this house would not be convenient for you. My wife's family— —" His sentence was interrupted by the appearance in the doorway of Señora Pimentel, an attractive woman in her thirties accompanied by an older woman who had probably been her *dueña* in the years before marriage and who now served as a kind of confidential maid, for she moved close to her mistress as soon as she saw that strange men were present. "I have been explaining to the king's special emissary that since your family occupies much of our house . . ."

His wife spoke softly but with an obvious desire to settle the problem: "The Escobar house in the square, facing the sea, is hardly being used," and walking beside her husband, with her former *dueña* two steps behind in her traditional place, she showed Ocampo a simple but commodious frame building with two large windows, one looking out to sea, the other into the heart of the square facing the church, which the citizens were already calling "our cathedral."

As soon as Ocampo and his men satisfied themselves that the house suited their purpose and was available, the two scribes sprang into action, requisitioning furnishings in the king's name and directing sailors how to unload and place the items Ocampo had brought with him from Sevilla. The principal piece was a magisterial oak chair, with a heavily carved back and two massive arms, which caused anyone who occupied it to appear aloof and formidable.

"Place it so that I face the shaded wall," Ocampo directed, "and put the chair for the person I'm interrogating facing the bright light from the window. Your two tables can go wherever you find it most convenient." But when the four chairs were in position, he studied them, readjusted them slightly, them demanded a saw.

After some searching through the town the saw arrived, and Ocampo revealed his strategy: "Cut a meager fraction from each front leg of the witnesses' chair. I want to be relaxed and comfortable as I lean back in my big chair, them to be nervous and slipping forward in the small one."

In those first days the citizens of the island looked with quiet awe at the newcomer, seeing a man whom they could not easily characterize: "Look! Tall and straight like any grandee, with the piercing eyes and pointed beard of a gentleman, but he didn't get that scar and eye patch playing cards in a garden. If you move forward to speak with him, he smiles and welcomes you." One of the scribes, hearing such comments, warned listeners: "Suave like a turtle dove, tenacious like .a hawk," and this epigram circulated. Before the week was out Ocampo and his men were listening to a flood of testimony relating to the behavior and performance ashore of the Admiral of the Ocean Sea, the late Cristóbal Colón, né Cristoforo Colombo.

Ocampo accepted the testifiers as they came, not trying to keep them in chronological order; he wanted to hear the natural flood of complaints with all the contradictions, lies and verifiable charges as they spewed forth. However, each night when the two scribes were finished with their scratching pens, they arranged their sheets in logical order, and it is in this sequence that Ocampo's report was submitted to the king.

The opening statement in that final report was made by one Vicente Céspedes, a rough seaman thirty-nine years old from the famous seaport of Sanlúcar de Barrameda at the mouth of the Guadalquivir from which the galleons of Sevilla regularly set sail. Growling pugnaciously, he said: "If they've told you about me, which I'm sure they have, because there's some as wants to silence me, you already know that I don't think much of the admiral, seein' that he stole money from me."

"If this concerns the withholding of your pay, we already know about that."

"It does not. It concerns what happened on a Thursday, the eleventh of October in 1492."

When Ocampo heard this notorious date he cringed, remembering the king's orders: "We know what he did at sea. I want to know what he did on land." Staring sternly with his good eye, he told the sailor: "I warned you. We're interested only in what happened on Española."

"But that's what this is about, if you'll listen, excusin' my roughness as I can't read or write or speak like a gentleman . . ."

Seeing that he could not halt this torrent of words, Ocampo said: "Do proceed."

"That afternoon the captain general summoned all hands to the afterdeck, very nervous he was, and he said: 'What did I promise yesterday when you were near mutiny?' and a man near me bellows: 'That if we don't see land in three days, back we go safe to our homes in Spain.' And he said: 'That's still the promise,' and we cheered.

"But then his jaw firmed, real mad like, and he told us: 'I am positive, I swear on the grave of my mother, that Asia lies just ahead. It must,' and I whispered to the man next to me: 'He's tryin' to convince himself,' but then he reminded us: 'What did the queen promise when we left Palos?' and it was me who answered, for I sore wanted that prize: 'Ten thousand maravedis* a year for life,' and he said: 'True, and today I add that I shall also give the lucky man a silken doublet,' and I could fair feel that silk makin' love to me back.

---

*About $70 U.S. at today's rate, but enough to mean luxury for a sailor of that time.

"Well, about this time a fresh wind blew up from the east and fairly whisked us along to the shores of China, and Colón had been so convincin' in his speech that all of us believed that before we reached the end of the third day, when otherwise we would turn back, we would see China, and I was sure as I had so often dreamed, that it would be me who first saw it."

"Why were you so sure there would be land?"

"I'd studied the sea, every day. I could tell by the look of the water, its feel maybe, that we were passing into a new area. The big waves had disappeared and the quiet sea looked like some precious jewel that women wear."

"So your dream came true?"

"It did. Sometime toward midnight I spotted a light on what had to be a shore, it had to be, so I called out: 'Land ahead!' and prepared to don my silken doublet and pocket those lifelong maravedis, but can you guess what actually happened, Excellency?"

"I'm not an excellency. What did happen?"

"Captain General Colón refused to honor my discovery and pay me my rewards. And do you know what he did that was much worse? Next mornin' he suddenly shouts: 'Land ahead!' and he claims the maravedis and gives himself the silken doublet."

"What has this to do with Española?" Ocampo asked, being careful not to sound too impatient, for he had learned long since that it was the most wandering testimony that sometimes produced the most valuable kernels of truth.

"I'm comin' to that, and when you hear you'll have to admit it does small credit to Colón. On the fifth of December, after explorin' south and west near the island that the captain general later named Cuba, our three caravels landed for the first time on this island." With a kind of mock salute, he told Ocampo: "So you now have me on this island of Española, where you wanted me."

Ocampo, ignoring the familiarity, merely nodded: "Go on."

"Bleak shore, nothing to tempt us, and when some of the sailors asked: 'Can this be the China of Marco Polo?' the captain general grew furious and would not speak further with us. So we sailed around this island on Christmas Eve, a Monday, I believe it was, for I had the watch and you remember those things. We come to a fine bay on the north shore of this selfsame island as we're on now, and all was peaceful, and the men off duty—there was forty of us altogether in the crew, countin' officers—began to hum songs of Christmas, and at midnight, me bein' off duty, I fell asleep to dream of the Christmases I'd known in Spain.

"Where was General Colón? Fast asleep. Second in command? Third? All sound asleep. And in that condition the *Santa Maria* gently, silently slipped onto a sandy reef and before the men runnin' wildly about the deck could break her free, big waves setting in from the northwest drove her ever higher onto what you might call the land. It was horrible. Colón should have been ashamed of himself, for in the hour before sunrise it was clear to us that our ship was a total loss and we shifted over to the little *Niña,* which could ill afford to accept us, seein' that her regular crew of twenty-two had already used up all space available and we would be forty more."

"And then?"

"The captain general said: 'We'll take the plankin' from the *Santa Maria* and build the first Spanish city in China,' for he insisted that that was where we were. We built two shacks and Colón and the priest, or the man who passed as one, held a service and dedicated the place as La Navidad, out of memory for the day, Christmas, when we landed there. And when the time came for the little *Niña* to carry us back to Spain, Colón saw that twenty-two of her men plus forty of ours was far too many to make the trip, so he appointed thirty-nine men to man the new town, and I was one of them. Then off he sailed to save his own skin."

As soon as these words were spoken, Ocampo knew them to be false, for earlier testimony had established without question that everyone left at La Navidad in January of 1493 had perished: there had been no survivors; and thus Vicente Céspedes had revealed himself as one more romancer with a grudge to settle against Colón.

Leaning forward, Ocampo asked harshly: "Why do you come to me with such lies? You know all the men at La Navidad died?"

Céspedes, almost sliding from his sloping chair, said, with almost boyish eagerness to clear himself: "It was a miracle, Excellency, I've never been able to fathom it. But as the *Niña* was about to sail, one of the men aboard, a friend of mine from Cádiz, shouted: 'Céspedes! I'd like to stay . . . see the natives,' and we exchanged. He died and I didn't."

Ocampo was enormously interested in the sailor's simple statement. It touched directly upon Colón's sense of responsibility toward his men: "What steps were taken to protect the lives of the thirty-nine left behind?"

"Damned little." As soon as he uttered the words he drew back and looked apprehensively at Ocampo, remembering that some authorities considered the word *damn* a serious blasphemy punishable in New Spain by a visit to the chambers of the Inquisition, but Ocampo as a former soldier did not. Swallowing, Céspedes resumed: "In fairness to Colón, there was very little we could have given them, but when we sailed away, good houses had not yet been built, we couldn't give them much powder for the few guns we could spare, not much lead for bullets, and no food."

"None?"

"Maybe one half-barrel of flour, some scraps of pork." Céspedes shook his head, then added brightly: "But my friend from Cádiz, the one who traded with me because he wanted to stay, said: 'We can fish and hunt game and depend on help from the natives.'"

"There were natives?"

"Many. And since we'd had good relations with them, we supposed the thirty-nine would depend on them for assistance."

"But General Colón did leave the men in a kind of settlement? I mean, there were paths and latrines and places to sleep?"

"Oh yes! It was the beginnings of a town. After all, it did have a name, La Navidad."

"But no real houses? No women?"

Céspedes laughed nervously: "The men thought of that. A year, maybe two years with no women. My friend from Cádiz said: 'Maybe we'll take the women we need from the natives.'"

"When you sailed, you ordinary sailors, did you expect the thirty-nine to survive?"

"Yes! Just as we parted I loaned my friend my good knife. 'I'll be back to claim it,' I told him. But as I said, he died and I didn't." He dropped his head, brought his hands to his lips, and stared at Ocampo, then whispered: "The natives killed them all, but even though I don't like Colón, I don't think you can blame him for that."

"How did you get back to Española?"

"On the next trip with Colón in 1493. He was an admiral by then. He didn't like me, for I reminded him that he had stolen my prize, but he knew me for a good sailor. And what a difference between the two trips! First time, three little ships, only a few men, feeling our way across an unknown ocean and terrified we'd fall off the edge of the world. Second trip, near two dozen fine ships, hundred of men, swift passage across a friendly ocean, and as soon as we passed through that chain of islands guarding the eastern edge of this inner sea we recognized the beauty of what the men were beginning to call 'our Spanish lake.' It was becoming home to us, the more so when we spotted this island we already knew. Our hearts expanded and it should have been a triumph. But when we reached La Navidad we found nothin' . . . houses torn down . . . skeletons where the natives had attacked. I found one body that could have been my friend, head severed. And I said a prayer as I buried it: 'You gave your life for me. I'll live on this island and make it a decent place in your honor,' and here I am."

One important question remained, but it was Céspedes who brought it up: "Sir, will you give sailors like me the money the admiral stole from us?"

"You still believe he did that?"

"Not only from me, from all those poor men who died at La Navidad." When he saw Ocampo glaring at him for repeating such rumors, he ended lamely: "Maybe he felt their money would be safer that way. Besides, what could they have used it for in a place like La Navidad?"

An old sailor, a widow and an abandoned son each came forward to relate how men had been paid only a portion of their wages or none at all, when it was clear that funds were available for this purpose.

A local resident named Alonso Peraza, whose manner and speech indicated that he had profited from the education his priest in Salamanca had given him, offered a partial explanation of why Colón may have acted in this miserly way: "The admiral was insane about money. He said the king and queen wouldn't pay him what they promised. He said they owed him a tenth, an eighth and a third."

"What do those terms mean? I'm unfamiliar with them."

"When Colón returned from his first trip it was some time before he was recognized as a great hero. Then King Ferdinand and his Queen Isabella agreed to a document written on parchment and sealed by notaries which formalized a preposterous proposal, put forth by Colón, that he receive in perpetuity one-tenth of all the wealth generated by the new lands he discovered."

"In that document, did *perpetuity* mean what I think it does?"

"Yes, for Colón during his lifetime, and his heirs forever after."

"A fortune, eh?"

And Peraza replied: "No ships large enough to carry it home." He then explained that the eighth referred to the portion of wealth that might be generated during the voyages by bartering trade goods with the local settlers, whoever they might be. "That made sense," Peraza said, "but Colón found it difficult to collect his share because accounts were too complex to keep."

"What was left?" Ocampo asked sardonically. "A third part of anything is apt to be substantial."

Peraza broke into disrespectful laughter: "Colón seriously demanded the right to levy a tax in that amount on every business transaction carried out in the Indies. Yes, one-third of everything."

Ocampo leaned back and studied his thin fingers as he made a calculation: "Those three taken together—tenth, eighth, third—would have added up to more than half the total wealth developed in the entire New World. It would have made him the richest man in Christendom, and no king could permit that." Leaning forward, he asked: "Yet you say he demanded it?"

"He did, and his heirs still press those ridiculous claims. They seek to be richer than the king."

Ocampo's attention now began to focus on one of the most serious charges against the admiral. The testifier who broached the subject was an ordinary sailor, one Salvador Soriano, who had served on the famous *Niña* and returned to Santo Domingo to live out his life: "It's a miracle I'm here to answer your questions, Excellency."

"I'm not really an excellency, you know. What do you wish to tell me?"

"We called him Colón the Killer because when he was viceroy in charge of this island he had a passion for ordering men to be hanged. There were gibbets all over the place . . . six . . . eight, all bearing fruit, men dancing without their toes touching the ground. And the hangings would have continued if Special Emissary Bobadilla had not had the courage to halt them."

"What were the charges? Mutiny?"

"Anything that irritated him at the moment. Hiding gold from the appointed collector. Speaking poorly about the admiral or one of his family. He kept going back and forth to Spain and bringing more and more of his family and they were sacred here. Two men were hanged for using a fishing boat without permission."

"That sounds incredible," Ocampo said, but the man surprised him by saying with great force: "I was sentenced to be hanged, with my nephew Bartolomeo, and for what? Eating fruit that was reserved for some other purpose and then arguing with one of Colón's men about it when we were reprimanded. Mutiny, he called that mutiny, and we were led to the gallows."

"I see you're still here. Did the admiral relent?"

"Not him. He hanged a score of us. Fearful temper."

"Then who saved you?"

"Bobadilla. You might say he saved the whole island. Because the way Colón was going, there'd have been revolution for sure."

Since this was the fourth time Ocampo had heard the name Bobadilla, the first having been when the king himself referred to him, it became clear that he must fix firmly in his mind who this shadowy figure Bobadilla was, for regardless in what direction Ocampo turned, he found himself face-to-face with this elusive man who seemed to have played a major role in Colón's life. Setting aside an entire afternoon, he sat with his scribes and asked: "Now what do we know about this Bobadilla? The king told me several things. Bobadilla was Queen Isabella's choice, not his. He was a man of distinguished background, overly fat, an errant coward."

"Doesn't sound appealing," one of the scribes remarked.

"Very intelligent. And most important, he arrived on this island to track down Colón's misbehavior armed with five different letters empowering him in ways far beyond my commission. In fact, the king told me: 'Because Bobadilla abused his five letters, I'm giving you only one.'"

"You mean you have no power to arrest? To force a man to give evidence? The rack if necessary?"

"I do not have such powers, nor would I want them." He concluded the meeting with an order: "Let us direct all our attention to learning as much about Bobadilla as possible, for if we first understand him, we may understand Colón."

Two days later the senior scribe informed him: "I've found a man whose life was saved by Bobadilla," and Ocampo said: "Fetch him." Within minutes one Elpidio Díaz, sailor from Huelva, was seated uneasily in the tilted chair eager to testify: "Bobadilla was a gentleman, a splendid man. He knew how to govern. Stepped off the ship that brought him from Spain, first thing he saw on the island was me and my cousin waiting to be hanged, rope ready and all. And he cried in a loud voice, I can still hear the words, believe me: 'Release those men!' Colón's people were furious. Refused to obey. And I thought:

Here we go. But Bobadilla whipped out some papers which showed he'd been sent by the king to clean up the mess on Española, and the hangings were stopped."

"You say hangings? Plural?"

"There was a score of condemned like me waiting in this area or that. In the little town of Xaraguá far west of here, sixteen of us prisoners were held in a deep well, all sentenced to be hanged. It was Bobadilla who saved our lives: 'Get those men out of there. Set them all free.'"

"You have a high opinion of him?"

"The finest. A man of common sense and order."

Ocampo began to acquire a balanced assessment of a man whom neither he nor the king liked. He might have been cowardly in battle, but he was certainly not afraid to confront ugly messes. He seemed to have exercised solid judgment and was certainly not a cruel man. He was honest, so far as could be seen. But there the list of positive aspects stopped, for again and again he emerged from the testimony as an obese, gluttonous, self-important functionary who used his five royal letters in an obscene way, like a cat using her claws to play with a mouse.

Supporters of Colón, and there were many, especially those who owed their jobs to the admiral, excoriated Bobadilla as an unfeeling, vengeful man who delighted in bringing the great explorer down, but more sober citizens assured Ocampo that Bobadilla had done a masterful job in a humane way, and it was almost impossible to discern who was telling the truth. And so the questioning about both Colón and Bobadilla continued.

In the late afternoons, when the interrogations ended, Ocampo liked to leave his office and take an evening walk along the beautiful waterfront of Santo Domingo; he preferred to walk three paces in the lead, with his two scribes trailing behind him. In this way, the three Spaniards from the homeland formed an elegant trio: Ocampo in front, tall and rigidly erect, with his conspicuous eye patch and scar attesting to his valor, the two scribes dressed in black marching behind in orderly fashion, and all comporting themselves like grandees from earlier centuries.

When they encountered citizens they knew, Ocampo would bow graciously and inquire as to their welfare. His scribes noticed that it was he who always bowed first, and when asked about this, he said: "A soldier carries his dignity in his heart. He can afford to be generous to others, especially if they have no dignity whatever."

When his oldest scribe said: "But you're a *licenciado*," he replied: "Once a Spaniard has borne arms, he's a soldier forever."

In his walks Ocampo learned much about this tropical capital, not yet twenty years old, for to its harbor came all the ships traversing the Caribbean or putting in to islands like Puerto Rico and still-unsettled Cuba. Watching these daring ships, he saw clearly that it was Spain's destiny to rule this inland sea, but he was equally interested in the natives, whom men were calling Indians, a name Colón had proposed when he finally had to admit that he had not reached China. In his obstinacy he had said: "Then it must have been India," and thus the natives, offspring of those early Arawaks who had escaped annihilation by the Caribs, received a name totally inappropriate and erroneous.

Sometimes as he took his evening stroll he would meet Alejandro Pimentel y Fraganza, the lieutenant governor, and the two proud men, each suspicious of what hidden powers from the king the other might have, would bow formally, say nothing, and pass on. It was obvious to Ocampo that Pimentel feared that he, Ocampo, had arrived on the island to investigate Pimentel's behavior. Once Ocampo told his men: "I am so relieved we're getting on well with that fellow. I'm sure he is suspicious of us, but I like him."

On two occasions when the strollers met Pimentel, they saw with pleasure that his young wife was with him, but she was so closely guarded by her onetime *dueña* that they had no opportunity to speak with her.

Occasionally the evening walks bore unexpected fruit, for strangers would approach Ocampo and whisper furtive hints regarding questions he might want to raise, but a more important consequence was that the women of Santo Domingo became accustomed to seeing the man they had supposed to be so austere coming toward them with a gracious smile and a gentlemanly bow. So when the town felt at ease with him, he surprised certain citizens, especially those from good families who adhered to the old patterns of Spanish life, by inviting to his interrogations several women, as if the time had come when they, too, should be listened to, and from them he obtained those unusual insights which so often illuminate major concerns. For example, when he interrogated Señora Bermudez he listened patiently while she outlined the distinguished heritage from which she came. It was much more exalted than her husband's, she claimed, and Ocampo learned several interesting facts: Francisco de Bobadilla was exactly the right man for the job, for he was of ancient lineage, had served the king in many positions of honor, and was a caballero in the military Order of Calatrava, than which there was no higher. A most excellent man, wise in the ways of the world and more than able to penetrate the effronteries of a peasant like Colón and the insufferable members of the admiral's family working here, who only wanted to enrich themselves at the expense of others.

Ocampo felt that he must correct such a gross misstatement lest it find its way into his official report: "But certainly, Señora Bermudez, there could not have been seven Colóns here, because there weren't that many in Spain. His brother Bartolomé, his brother Diego, and his own son Diego and maybe one of his brother's sons. Counting him, that's only five, and it's not unusual for the head of a Spanish family to find jobs in his retinue for five family members."

Señora Bermudez, once started, was not one to surrender easily: "You're right in your count, as far as it goes, but you're forgetting men related to his wife, or his brother's wives, or associated in other ways. Seven?" and her voice rose. "More like a dozen." Then she became conciliatory: "But Colón did discover this island . . . and all the others. He alone kept his ships from turning back. He alone persevered."

But as she rose to leave Ocampo's office she stopped, sat down again, and began speaking as if her interview had just begun: "The worrisome thing about Colón and his endless relatives, all of them absorbing money that should have come to us, was that he was an Italian. Not Spanish at all. And to think of him as lording it over good Spaniards like my husband and me, who come from the great families of Spain, was intolerable. It was simply intolerable!"

It was a woman of much different character who provided Ocampo with his most valuable information about Colón. As Ocampo had been about to sail from Sevilla to take up his duties in Española, a grandee from a noble family had come secretly to deliver a bottle of perfume distilled by Arab experts working in Venice. And it was so valuable that the nobleman begged: "Protect it with your life, Don Hernán, and when you reach Española deliver it privately to Señora Pimentel. Her going desolated me."

For this subtle reason, Ocampo had been more than casually interested to meet the Pimentels on his evening walks. He had spent many hours when alone wondering what kind of woman the young señora was, and from the meager information he had and having observed her quiet dignity, her obvious reserve, he suspected that she might be the kind of intense woman who would tell her husband nothing about the presence of an admirer in Sevilla. He decided to follow the nobleman's advice and deliver the perfume in strictest secrecy.

He therefore dispatched one of his scribes to the Pimentel house to inform Señora Pimentel that he would like to question her about the Great Admiral, and in due course she appeared, attended as always by her remorseless watchdog. Displaying no irritation, Ocampo started to question his visitor about Colón, engineering it so that he could block out the *dueña's* view, whereupon he slipped the señora the vial of perfume. Then he returned to his desk and looked at her meaningfully for a moment. "In Sevilla," he said casually, "I met many who remember you and your husband with pleasure," and he made arrangements then to interrogate her further at another time.

On the next visit, with the hawklike servant still in evidence, Ocampo noted that Señora Pimentel had deposited somewhere about her face or neck a drop or two of the rare perfume, for its soft aroma permeated his office in a most alluring way. It was then that she started talking about the Great Admiral, and her shrewd conclusions made more sense than those of any of the other testifiers: "Cristóbal Colón has fascinated me from the first day that I arrived here, when he was hanging men by the dozens. I saw him then as a monster, and when I learned how he had mismanaged his first two settlements, La Navidad and Isabela, a forlorn, doomed town on the north shore, far away from the first one, I could not understand how their majesties tolerated him. My husband and I visited there in its last days, a miserable boat trip, smooth as glass here in our sea, turbulent beyond words when we reached the ocean. It was a heartbreaking place to have been named after our great queen. No decent port for ships. Not a stone house in the place. Fields had been chopped from the woods but had not been tended, and I'm told the last settlers there nearly starved, because the Indians would not bring them food. That was Colón at his worst, incapable of launching any village and sustaining it.

"I knew him only briefly in that period, his worst you could say, and I viewed him principally as a boorish Italian adventurer. But then he began to take his meals with us. Even though my husband was a personal representative of the king, like all the others, we lived in those early days in nothing more than a shack, but Colón filled it with his extraordinary vitality, his imagination, his quest always for something new and challenging, and I came to admire him as a genius, difficult but standing at the edge of the known world. To hear him explain his dreams in his accented Spanish was to witness greatness in action, and I was awed by his volcanic power.

"But my husband and I also saw his flaws, and they were monstrous, almost disqualifying. He rarely followed through on what he started. He could not govern for the simple reason that he could not keep his eyes on the task at hand . . . always looking to the future. He was a brutal man at times, arbitrary to the point of hanging anyone who disagreed with him, and he was certainly avaricious, mean, untruthful and petty, even when dealing with his own men. And his greatest fault was his almost insane nepotism and favoritism.

"However, when the grand balance is struck, Colón was the man who gave us this New World, and I doubt I shall ever see his like again."

She had permitted no interruptions, and when she finished she indicated to her companion that they must go, but as Señora Pimental left the room, the aroma of her presence hanging in the air like a memory of flowers, she told Ocampo: "I was interested to hear that you were once in Sevilla." And then she was gone.

Ocampo had supposed that this was the last he would see of Señora Pimentel, so he was surprised when only a few days later one of his scribes came into the interrogation room to announce an unexpected visitor. "A woman to see you. I think she's the one that comes with Señora Pimentel." Into the room came the *dueña,* with bows and apologies: "Excellency, Lieutenant Governor Pimentel and his lady seek the honor of your presence at the evening meal tomorrow night, and he apologizes for the lateness of this invitation."

Ocampo showed unseemly haste in accepting, but next evening when he was ready to set out for the stone house of the Pimentels, he stopped at the door of his quarters and reflected on what he was about to do, and the caution he displayed was an indication of how colonial Spain was governed: It could be most imprudent for me to go to that house alone. Pimentel might have discovered the perfume and supposed it came from me and concluded that I was in love with his wife, or he could be suspicious about my motives in coming to Española. In either case, he might want to dispose of me, so it would be better if I didn't go alone. Calling for his scribes, he asked them to form the customary parade group and thus they marched to the Pimentel home, where he said casually: "I brought my men, of course," to which the Pimentels replied: "They can dine with the rest of the family," and the scribes were seen no more.

The house which the señora had modestly described as being "nothing more than a shack" was now a colonial mansion as fine as a visitor might have found in a rural town in Spain. The stone masonry was strong and well joined; the floor of the main room was of some hard tropical wood, neatly polished, those of the lesser rooms of tile brought from Sevilla. The entire home bespoke the quiet dignity of a Spanish gentleman's residence. The Pimentels had obviously imported many things from home, including first-rate carpenters and stoneworkers, but there was no garish display of rich fabric or precious metal. If anything, the rooms were underfurnished, though Ocampo was pleased to note that the best of Spain had reached this capital of the New World.

"This house will stand forever," he predicted, to which Pimentel replied: "It must. Spain must seek deep roots here, because soon envious others will appear in this golden sea to wrest the islands from us. Or try to."

The dinner was impeccable, with at least four different servants appearing at intervals to serve it. "My wife's cousins," Pimentel said offhandedly, but Ocampo observed that at least one was an Indian and the others were from peasant stock.

Since Señora Pimentel took no part in the conversation, Ocampo was bewildered as to the purpose of his being there, but when the rich wine of Cádiz passed at the end of the meal, the lieutenant governor said: "We delayed so long to invite you to our modest home because, frankly, we could not guess why you had really been sent to our island. Now we have cause to believe that what you said from the start was true. You came here to investigate the dead Colón, not us."

Ocampo, struggling for some pleasantry with which to acknowledge this gracious concession, happened to be facing the room's only major piece of decoration, a rather large ironbound chest which must have been imported from Toledo, considering its careful metalwork and two large, intricate locks: "Spain is as securely founded in this special sea as that chest is secured against theft," and, without looking at the chest, the Pimentels nodded.

Thus the remarkable dinner with the distinguished family ended, with no word having been spoken regarding either Colón or Bobadilla, for which Ocampo was grateful: "I've been hearing so much about those two adversaries that tonight was a pleasant respite. Thank you."

On the walk back to quarters, he told his scribes: "It's time we restrict our summons to those older men of good judgment who can tell us truthfully about Colón as a business administrator, for we must remember that he had for quite a few years been the all-powerful viceroy of our holdings in this part of the world."

The first witness Ocampo summoned was Gonsalvo Pérez, an older man who had held high office under Viceroy Colón and who had that sagacious approach to problems that sometimes comes with increasing years. He was a handsome man, the deep lines in his face attesting to a maturing character and a detached, amused attitude toward life, for on the frequent occasions when he smiled at some injudicious act of his own about which he was forced to confess, his entire face lit up, the lines becoming frames for flashing eyes which had seen so much of the world's nonsense and had understood it all.

"It seems to me," he said, nodding to the scribes as he tried to relax in the witness chair, "that one should judge a viceroy on how successfully he performed those certain tasks which form the very base of any viceroy's job, whoever he might be. Did he settle the new lands placed under his control? Did he protect the king's money? Was he just in dealing with men under him? When he left were things better or worse than when he came?"

"The very questions I've been trying to find answers to."

"Let's first clean up the crucial points. Was he honest in dealing with the king's funds? Scrupulously, and I was in a position to know. He never diverted the smallest coin to his own use, not one maravedi, and would allow none of us to do so, either. So on that basic point, you can halt your investigation right now."

"Second fundamental, did he leave things better or worse than when he took command?"

"Neither. Our island had not deteriorated, but neither had it progressed the way it might have. But the fault was not Colón's. It was Spain's."

"You mean . . . the king's?"

"No, I mean Spain's. The Spanish nature. The inborn arrogance of Spanish men, especially those of good family."

"I cannot follow you."

"We should have brought to this island, twelve years ago, carpenters and weavers and shipbuilders and sixteen or seventeen men of middle age who knew how to run things like shops and bakeries and ironmongeries, men who could *do* things." He accented this word heavily, then added with a touch of regret: "Instead, we brought out the sons of rich families, young fellows who'd never in their lives done a day's work at anything constructive and whom Colón was simply unable to discipline. He set them a good example. He worked, believe me. I worked on his accounts because I knew my numbers and how to write. His brother Bartolomé worked because he had a position to defend. But the vast majority of the dandies worked at nothing. They had come across the Atlantic to fight, collect gold in buckets from the streams, and go home rich.

"And that leads us to the first of Colón's great failures as viceroy. He was unable, with the kinds of men he had at his disposal, to build settlements. All failed. When he found La Navidad had been destroyed in his absence, he started a second settlement—Isabela he called it out of his love for the queen who had done so much to spur his career. It was a disaster, a place of infinite sadness, and I think you should enclose in your report some account of what happened there, for I heard it firsthand from my cousin to whom it happened." And he interrupted his comments to recount this true adventure:

"His name was Girolamo, son of my uncle, and he told me that when he visited the ruins of Isabela two years ago he was walking along the empty street, looking at the deserted buildings, when, upon turning a corner, he came upon two caballeros — swords, long capes, plumed hats—men of obvious distinction. Astonished at finding such settlers still there, my cousin approached them and said in a friendly voice: 'Gentlemen, how fare you?' and they answered silently by putting their hands to their hats to return his courtesy, but when they doffed their plumed hats their heads came off, too, and for a moment they stood there headless. Then two heartbreaking sighs came from the heads as if the burden of living in Isabela had been too great, and before my cousin could interrogate them, they vanished, he could not say how."

"Very interesting," Ocampo said, "but if Colón failed in his first two attempts at settlement, he certainly succeeded here in Santo Domingo."

"False. He did get the place started on the right track, the south side of any island is always better, but real progress came only when Bobadilla took over with those plenary powers the king had given him."

"You say he wrested control from Colón?"

"And not a moment too soon. Now the growth of the city is ensured. Bobadilla also saw to its protection, and when I concede that, it means something, because I was always a Colón man. I never really liked Bobadilla, especially not after I watched how he treated Colón."

Ocampo interrupted: "You just said something most interesting—'I was a Colón man.' Were you one of those who represented the admiral's weakness for nepotism?"

Pérez smiled most engagingly, held his two hands palms up as if crying "*Mea culpa,*" and confessed: "I was the perfect example. You see, my wife's brother, a real ne'er-do-well, married a sister . . ." He broke into self-deprecating laughter and concluded: "It's too long a story and not a happy one, but you're right. Colón knew we Spaniards resented him for being an Italian upstart, so he felt he had to surround himself with men who were completely loyal, and how better than to give the crucial jobs to his relatives . . . and in my case, to relatives of his relatives?" He shrugged: "So in the case of the Pérez relatives, he got one total failure, my wife's brother, and one very hardworking expert who helped hold things together, my wife's husband."

"I'm told you were exceptional," Ocampo said with a slight bow. "And now about the other criteria of a good viceroy?"

"Did he extend the king's landholdings? He certainly did. Did he subdue the rebellious natives and bring order where chaos had been? He did, he did. And most important of all, I think, he was always attentive to bringing Christianity to them. Yes, that was foremost in his mind, for he often reminded me: 'Pérez, Queen Isabella personally begged me to make sure that the natives became Christian, and that I've done.'"

"So if I accept your testimony, the Great Admiral was a success in things that mattered, not so in certain minor concerns?"

"Exactly what I intended to convey."

Ocampo received his most intriguing testimony during an evening party at the governor's house when a woman guest with a hoarse voice and a gleaming eye led him aside into a hallway where no one could overhear, and confided: "I wonder if you're missing the most important point of all, Excellency."

"I'm not an excellency, ma'am. Just an honest scholar trying to do his best."

"Where I'm concerned, anyone who comes with your powers from the king is an excellency. Now, what I want to remind you of is something that the others may be too delicate to speak of, but did you know that Cristóbal Colón was a Jew?"

No, Ocampo did not know, and he was offended by the intimation, but the woman continued in her confidential, raspy whisper: "Yes, unquestionably a Jew. A *converso*. Made a false show of converting to Christianity but continued to practice the Jewish rituals, and if you and I reported him to the Inquisition, he'd be burned at the stake."

"Ma'am, I find it impossible to believe that a man who has been so amiably accepted at court . . ."

"The court! It's infested with Jews, and many of them ought to be burned, too."

Striving to discover how this woman had penetrated the secret of Colón's Jewishness, he asked her various questions there in the hallway, but she always retreated to her first justification, that "everyone knows his ugly secret." But later, when questioning through the town, Ocampo learned that only this woman and a few other malcontents mentioned anything of Colón's supposed Jewishness, and even though he remembered the king's determination to stamp out the Jewish religion wherever it appeared in his realms, he now concluded that there was no substance to the charge against Colón.

Ocampo's attitude was that of most sensible educated Spanish gentlemen of the time: He respected those Jews who, recognizing the superiority of Christianity, had converted to that faith, and he welcomed them without reserve to the core of Spanish life; he had extended his friendship to converts many times in the years since the great expulsion of the Jews in 1492. But he was repelled by those Jews who made a public gesture of converting but who then continued to practice their ugly rites in secret; they were beyond the pale and deserved the harsh treatment the Inquisition handed them. He had attended several big public burnings in Sevilla and had seen God's hand in them.

He was therefore pleased to hear reassurance from many islanders that whereas there were many things wrong with Cristóbal Colón, principally that he and his brothers were Italians, it was good to know he wasn't also Jewish, and one afternoon he gave his scribes forthright instructions: "We will say nothing in our report regarding the scandalous rumors that the viceroy was a secret Jew, still practicing and warranting the attention of the Inquisition." And no notes on that delicate subject were transcribed.

But there was another matter regarding Colón which involved a question of somewhat similar moral gravity for which Ocampo was quite unprepared. It was presented to him by a most unusual visitor who came unannounced to his office, a young priest of twenty-six named Father Gaspar, a nervous sort of fellow, with stringy hair, a bad complexion and fidgety hands, whose awkward behavior betrayed the fact that he knew he was stepping outside his field of responsibility. But there he was, sitting in the witness chair, showing every indication of staying there until he had said his piece: "With your permission, Excellency . . ."

As always, Ocampo declined that title: "I'm like you, Father, a worker in the vineyard." The disclaimer reassured the young priest, and he said with a rush of words: "Sir, everyone is aware by now of what you're doing, and what I have to relate is important in the completion of your portrait of the Great Admiral."

"That's well said, Father. Very aptly phrased. That's what I'm trying to do, paint a portrait of the viceroy as he conducted his important office on this island." Leaning forward, he added: "So what are the brush strokes you think I might have missed?"

"The natives."

"You mean the Indians?" Ocampo asked.

"Indians, if you wish, Excellency."

"It's not important," Ocampo said as he leaned back.

The priest continued: "We in the church have been told that a principal mission, especially insofar as Queen Isabella of sacred memory was concerned, of any Spanish activity in our New World is the conversion of Indians to Christianity . . ."

"No higher mission on earth, Father. Why do you raise the subject?"

"Because the admiral did not try to convert the Indians . . ."

"That's not true, young man, and I hope you'll withdraw such an accusation. Everyone tells me how devout Colón was and how assiduous in bringing Indian souls to Christ. The testimony's unanimous."

"Not from members of the church," the young man said stoutly, and when Ocampo started to reprimand him again, the priest astonished him by interrupting: "Please let me finish my statement." The *licenciado,* slowly awakening to the fact that he had a rather difficult situation on his hands, nodded to the young man as if the latter were a cardinal: "Please continue."

"I was saying that Colón was supposed to convert the Indians but instead he slaughtered them."

"An appalling statement."

"I have made bold to bring before you the figures which none of your other people would dare even to discuss." And the young priest unwrapped a silken cloth tied at the corners and brought forth a carefully prepared summary of what had happened to the Taino Indians* in the years since Admiral Colón's arrival in 1492. And he proceeded to recite the dismal figures: "In 1492 this island seems to have had about three hundred thousand Tainos."

"How can anyone state a fact like that?"

"Church records. Our priests went everywhere. Four years later, in 1496, the population and this figure we know for sure, because as a very young priest I helped assemble it the population had dropped by a third to two hundred thousand."

"What do you mean by the word *dropped?* Who dropped what?"

"I mean senseless slaughter." The ugly word struck the placid witness room like the explosion of a carelessly piled sack of black powder, and Ocampo was singed. From this moment forward, the interview took on entirely different dimensions, with young Father Gaspar assuming the role of accuser and Ocampo that of the Great Admiral's defender.

The *licenciado* coughed, adjusted uneasily in his chair, and asked: "Now what do you mean by the words *senseless slaughter?*"

Undaunted, the priest said: "Unnecessary, barbarous killing." And Ocampo snapped: "But if our frontiers had to be protected, certainly the viceroy had every right to defend the king's lands?"

"Were they the king's?" Father Gaspar asked with an almost boyish simplicity. "The Tainos had occupied them for centuries."

---

*Taino was the name used in several large western Caribbean islands for those peaceful Arawaks who had sought refuge in these islands after the arrival in the small eastern islands of the cannibalistic Caribs in or about the early 1300s.

The question was difficult, and Ocampo knew it, but he had strong and reassuring doctrine to fall back upon: "The pope has decreed that all savages who know not God or the salvation of Jesus Christ are to be civilized by us and brought into the safety and sanctity of the church."

"Yes. That's why I'm here, and the others, and we labor mightily to achieve that salvation."

"And so did Colón. Everyone says so."

"Not those of us who work in true conversion."

"And what do you mean by that?"

"Conversion of men's souls. The bringing of light to dark places so that even the Indians can know the love of Jesus Christ."

"Isn't that what we all work toward? Isn't that the mission of Spain in the New World?"

Father Gaspar, only twenty-seven that year, made bold to smile at this idealistic version of Spanish goals: "I would rather say that our mission in the New World is fourfold: finding new lands, conquering them, finding gold, and Christianizing the savages, in that exact order. The hundred thousand Indians missing in this first four violent years were needlessly slaughtered under the orders of Admiral Colón."

Profoundly agitated, Licenciado Ocampo rose from his heavily ornamented chair, strode about the room, and returned to stand over the priest: "I cannot accept that word *needlessly*. Surely Colón chastised the Indians for their own good." He stopped abruptly, realizing the essential foolishness of that statement, and as a man of good sense he altered his argument: "I mean, weren't the savages threatening our settlement?"

Father Gaspar broke into a nervous laugh: "Excellency, did your ship stop at Dominica on the way here? Did the sailors tell you of how those fierce Carib Indians, cannibals all, killed every Spaniard who tried to land on their island? That's what the word *savage* means. Our Tainos are not like that at all. They fled the Caribs. Gentlest people in the islands. At no time did Colón have any excuse for destroying them."

"Now just a minute, Father. I've sat here for days listening to how your gentle Indians killed every one of the thirty-nine men Colón left at La Navidad in 1493. And how they killed so many of our men at Isabela in those bad years around 1496. Don't tell me that your precious Indians were gentle—"

To Ocampo's astonishment, the young priest broke in unceremoniously to make a point he deemed so relevant it could not wait: "But your men stole their food, for one thing. Their women, for another."

Ocampo recalled that memorable phrase of the sailor Céspedes reporting what his friend from Cádiz had said: "Maybe we'll take the women we need from the natives . . ." but he said: "I would hope that self-respecting Spanish men would not have—"

But again the fiery young priest interrupted: "Let me complete my figures. Last year, in 1508, we took another census, this time very accurate, seventy-eight thousand Tainos left. Down from three hundred thousand only a few years ago. Soon, at the rate we're going, there will probably be less than a thousand."*

"I cannot accept those figures," Ocampo said, and suddenly Father Gaspar became all humility: "Excellency, forgive me. I've been most rude and I'm ashamed. But you're preparing an important document and the truth really must be respected."

"Thank you, young man. I shall pray that what you've been telling me isn't the truth."

"With your permission, Excellency. Could I recite the details of an incident, a typical one, I believe? I served as chaplain to an expeditionary force sent out from this capital and I was a witness to it myself."

"Proceed," and the *licenciado,* a somewhat chastened man, leaned forward once more to hear what this ardent young fellow had to say, for what he'd heard so far was certainly disturbing but also curiously convincing:

"In the summer of 1503, I was ordered by my superiors to report to Governor Nicolás de Ovando, who was about to launch an expedition of many soldiers to discipline the Tainos on the far western tip of Española. We marched for many days before we reached that distant and dangerous part of our realm, but when we arrived there we began a systematic punishment of those caciques, or native rulers, who had hitherto refused to obey orders issued by our governor, the said Ovando.

"In every instance, before the killings started, I begged the governor for permission to visit the Tainos, because I was certain

---

*Father Gaspar's estimate was too generous. An exhaustive census in 1548 could turn up only 490 Arawaks, and in certain other of the western islands the total extinction was complete long before that.

I could resolve their worries, explain the new laws, and pacify them as I had done so often before. But always the governor said: 'They've disobeyed my pronouncements and must be punished.'

"So without war ever having been either declared or conducted we rampaged through Xaraguá Province, burning villages and slaying inhabitants. In all we killed eighty-three of the caciques, and when I say *killed* I mean we racked them, garroted them slowly, dismembered them, and slowly burned them alive. When we wanted to show our benevolence, we hanged them swiftly and properly. Besides the important caciques, we must have slain forty thousand.

"Among the caciques there was a most beautiful lady leader, Anacoana, not yet thirty, I judged, with long and graceful hair which flowed over her body that was otherwise naked. When she scorned Governor Ovando and refused to pledge obedience to his future pronouncements, he, in a rage, ordered her to be burned alive, but while he was attending other matters I ordered three soldiers to strangle her quickly and as painlessly as possible, and when she felt their merciful hands about her neck, she smiled at me, and it was I who wept, not she."

The *licenciado* had listened to this narrative with close attention, then sent for local officials, whom he questioned on the spot with Father Gaspar listening: "Was there an expedition against Xaraguá Province?" Yes. "Did Governor Ovando lead it?" He did. "Were many caciques slain?" There had to be. "Was a beautiful lady cacique burned alive?" That was the order, but this good priest here signaled to me and two others to strangle her, which we did.

Ocampo sat silent for some moments, forefingers propping his chin as he tried to visualize what had happened, but then he coughed and leaned forward as if to say: Now let's get to the facts in this case. "Tell me, Father Gaspar, are you one of those who hold that black men and Indians have souls?"

"I am."

"What justification for such belief have you heard?"

"That all men who live are human, all equal in God's love and the care of Jesus."

"Even savage Indians who know not God . . . or Jesus?"

"Jesus instructed us to teach them the truth, show them the light, so they could know."

"Then you hold that white men are wrong in making blacks their slaves?"

"Yes. It would be better if they treated them as brothers."

"Then you condemn our king and queen for having slaves?"

"I do."

"But if by making these savages slaves, we are able to bring them into the sheepfold of the Good Shepherd Jesus, is that not a path to salvation?"

Father Gaspar studied this neat dilemma for some moments, then conceded: "If that is the only avenue to salvation, yes, it would be justified. But I would think that as soon as the black man or the Indian became a Christian, he would have to be released from his bondage."

"To get back to my original question. Do you really believe that black men and Indians have souls, like you and me?"

"I do. Else, by what means could they see the light of Christianity? Through their eyes? Their ears? Their stomachs? It can only be apprehended through their souls."

This gave Ocampo trouble, and after a while he asked, almost tentatively: "You know, I suppose, that many learned doctors of theology deny that savages have souls?"

"I've heard that argument, and all who make it have a lot to explain."

"I make it. I have tried incessantly since landing on this island to understand how the savage Indians I see, the ones our Great Admiral had to chastise so harshly, could possibly have souls. Nor can they be classified as human." He said this forcefully, then asked: "I suppose, then, you consider them human beings?"

"I do," and before Ocampo could respond, he added: "And I do for this reason. I cannot believe that the uninstructed Indian standing over there under his tree has no soul, but if he comes over here and listens to my instruction and accepts baptism that somehow I confer a soul upon him. How? In the water I pour over him? I think not."

"What do you think?"

Very humbly Father Gaspar said: "Excellency, I do honestly believe that at birth every human being on earth arrives with a God-bestowed soul which can remain hidden in darkness until someone like our noble Queen Isabella, may God grant her peace in heaven, sends someone like Admiral Colón aided by men like you and me to explain Christianity and salvation to them."

"But at the beginning of our talk, you were very harsh with Colón."

"He lost sight of his primary mission. He was satisfied to become a killer, not a savior."

"Are you still as harsh . . . after this exploration we've had?"

When the young man nodded, unwilling to yield an iota to his superior, Ocampo rose in some agitation, walked about his office, and stopped at a window that looked out upon the busy street, where his eyes fell upon an unfamiliar and startling sight—a big, handsome black man, his sweaty skin glistening in the sunlight as he strode along behind his master. The slave had come to Española on a Spanish trading ship, having been bought in a Portuguese port on the African coast since at this time only the Portuguese were engaged in that trade. From his viewpoint Ocampo had a sudden vision of what was to come—turbulent days when the streets of the town and the roadways of this island would be crowded with such black men and their women, and he was both fascinated and disturbed by this prospect.

In real perplexity he summoned Father Gaspar to stand beside him, and when he pointed to the black man, he asked: "Father, do you really believe that that one, the big black fellow . . . does he have a soul like you and me?"

"Yes," Father Gaspar answered, and then the gift of prophecy came upon him, for he had brooded upon this matter since the day Admiral Colón started massacring the Tainos because they did not conform to his idea of what a subservient people should be, and he predicted: "The history of this island, and all of the islands Spain has captured in this lovely sea, will involve the slow and even reluctant admission that the big black man down there has a soul."

Ocampo, in no way convinced by the young priest, now turned his attention to the most difficult part of the investigation, this matter of the great indignity Francisco de Bobadilla, his distinguished predecessor as special investigator, had visited upon Admiral Colón. As he started his intensive study, he felt like Bobadilla—both had been dispatched with roughly the same kind of commission—but Bobadilla's task had been much the more difficult, and Ocampo realized that, so he started gingerly, and the testimony of the early witnesses was reported succinctly by the scribes:

Melchior Sánchez, an unpleasant man and an avowed enemy of Colón, gave it as his opinion that Bobadilla had arrived three years too late, had performed brilliantly in clearing up the mess, and had treated Colón justly and even mercifully. Sánchez thought that Bobadilla would have been justified in hanging the admiral, but this evidence was neutralized by Ocampo's discovery that Colón had justly hanged the oldest Sánchez boy for repeated theft.

Alvaro Abarbanel, a responsible merchant in goods imported from Spain, whose trade the admiral had assisted by bringing in merchandise in government ships, said briefly and harshly: "Bobadilla should have been horse-whipped for treating a great man as he did. The admiral would have been justified in shooting him, and I came close to doing so."

And so it went, back and forth. After some sixteen witnesses had split about nine in favor of Bobadilla, seven supporting Colón, Ocampo told his scribes: "We had now better get some rational statements, no opinions, no heated animosities, as to what actually happened," and an official who had served each of the viceroys of the island, one Paolo Carvajal of good family and better reputation, laid out the facts: "Francisco de Bobadilla arrived here on 23 August 1500, bringing with him a complete set of papers from the king awarding him plenipotentiary powers, but the important thing was, none of us knew the extent of these powers, and Bobadilla conducted himself, I must say, brilliantly. No general, master of strategy, ever did better.

"First he called us together and had the notary read out what one might call a standard commission to look into things generally. Men like that with letters like that visit Spanish territories, here and at home, frequently, so we thought little of it, and we helped him as he made routine examinations, which did not focus on the admiral at all. In fact, Colón showed his disgust for the whole affair by stalking out of town in the middle of the investigation. 'I'm off to chase down Tainos,' he said with an insolence that infuriated Bobadilla.

"What did he do? Nothing vengeful, but he did summon the people again to hear the reading of his second letter, and I remember standing in the sunlight beside him as citizens gathered in the square before the church, all three hundred of them. The fat fellow climbed onto the church steps, a rickety affair, for we didn't even have a steeple in those days, and in a surprisingly strong voice, read words which shocked us all. They came from Ferdinand and Isabella: 'Our good and faithful servant, Francisco de Bobadilla, is herewith appointed governor of Española.'

"Well, that created a storm, but the arrogant Colón brothers, and they were Italians, mind you, refused to obey him, and again Bobadilla was all patience, but on the next day he had the notary read his third letter, which gave him power over all military establishments in the island, and under this edict he began to assemble power about him. But it was the reading of his fourth letter, on the next day, that gave him the power to strangle the three Colóns. Again I hear the notary's voice, for its message affected me personally: 'Our loyal and trusted friend and brother, Francisco de Bobadilla, shall have the power to pay all loyal subjects who have wages coming to them but have had them sequestered.' You can see what this meant. Men like me would now get, immediately that we applied to Bobadilla, all the money that the Great Admiral had kept from us. Naturally, we became outspoken supporters of Bobadilla, and when Colón finally returned to the town, all were against him.

"And then came the crushing blow, for with this support behind him, Bobadilla revealed the most powerful letter of all, the one which gave him complete power to make whatever changes in administration and arrests he saw fit. And before its words had died in the tropic air, the three Colón brothers were grabbed by Bobadilla's police, thrown into jail, and forced to undergo the indignity of holding out their arms and ankles while the blacksmith fastened iron fetters about their extremities, with heavy chains linking wrist to wrist, leg to leg."

At this point the *licenciado* interrupted: "You mean like common criminals? Like robbers or smugglers or murderers?"

"The same."

"Not the admiral?"

"Especially the admiral, and in that condition the three were unceremoniously dragged down to the waterfront, tossed onto a small ship, and sent off to trial in Spain."

Here Carvajal paused, looked at his interrogator and made a cruel and telling point: "I was commissioned by Bobadilla to accompany the Colóns to Spain and see that they were delivered over to the proper authorities, and on my own responsibility, as soon as the ship had left the shadow of Española, I took into the hold, where the Great Admiral huddled against the rough planking, my blacksmith, and I said: 'Admiral, it's not proper that a man of your dignity, a viceroy no less, should remain in chains during this long voyage. Pedro here will strike them off and we'll replace them just as we arrive in Sevilla.' But with difficulty Colón rose and said: 'These chains were thrown upon me by the king and queen, and I shall wear them until they personally give the order to have them removed,' and he refused to allow Pedro to touch them. When he sank once more onto the floor, his chains clanking as he did so, tears came to my eyes, and when he saw them he told me: 'You do well to weep, Don Paolo, for you see the man whose courage alone gave Spain all of Japan and China, wealth unmeasured for all time. And his reward?' He held up his manacled arms and cried: 'These chains! This great indignity!'

"I visited with him often on that long trip and in time I became accustomed to seeing him in his bondage, for he wore the chains as a badge of honor, and I developed immense respect for this fighting hero. One thing, however, perplexed me, and still does."

Ocampo, much moved by this portrait of a stubborn hero fighting the world, said: "Don Paolo, you speak of him as if you loved him." And Carvajal reflected on this before answering, which he did in slow, carefully chosen words: "Love is not the word you'd use for him, because lovable he was not." He stopped, then started brightly, as if opening a wholly new conversation: "One noon when I took him his bowl of gruel he pushed it away and said almost pleadingly, as if eager to convince me who needed no convincing: 'They never understood, Carvajal. They didn't send me to serve as viceroy in Sicily, settled for a thousand years with roads and men who could reason. No! I was sent to where no man had ever been before.' And I protested: 'The Indians were here, of course,' and he snapped: 'I was speaking of Christians.'"

When this revealing narrative ended, Ocampo and Carvajal sat in silence, staring at the floor as if afraid to look at each other and acknowledge the terrible wrong that had been done Cristóbal Colón, discoverer of new worlds, new opportunities and new ideas. After a while, Ocampo said: "Strange how fate teases us. As I prepared the final pages of my report last night I was haunted by what had happened to Bobadilla when he finished *his* report back in 1500. It was voluminous and supported by sheaves of documents and individual statements. They tell me that it took three men to carry the whole affair onto the ship bound for Spain. But the ship had barely left harbor, when it sank, taking Bobadilla and all his papers to the bottom of the sea. That might have been God's judgment on the whole sad affair."

Before Ocampo left Española with his amazingly even-handed report on the behaviors and misbehaviors of the Great Admiral, he had two additional interviews, each accidental, each compelling. The first involved an ordinary sailor, an illiterate, who brought with him his priest, who could read, a man Ocampo had not seen before. And the sailor said: "I heard people were telling you bad things about the admiral and I was afraid you might take them as truth. I wanted you to hear the real truth. Colón was a sailor, first and last, and a better never sailed. I was with him on two voyages, but the one I'll never forget, nor none of us, was the last, after he got out of his chains, that was."

"No one has told me of that," the *licenciado* said, leaning forward as he always did when he suspected that something he was about to hear might be of more than usual interest, and the sailor said: "It was a disappointing sail. Nothing new in the little islands, but when we reached the shores of Asia* we did find some gold but hardly worth the trip, and we lost a lot of men in the fighting."

It was a dreary tale of meaningless forays and repeated disappointments, and Ocampo, losing interest, began to fidget and seek some way to get the sailor out of there, but then the narrative caught fire, and in its blaze the *licenciado* saw the ghostly figure of the real admiral: "On the way back to this island, with little to show for our troubles, we were seized by violent storms that seemed never to relent and that punished our two old and creaking ships, driving their timbers apart and allowing great waves to wash aboard. Only by the most diligent effort did the admiral keep us afloat and together, and in this pitiful condition we staggered onto the north shore of Jamaica, an island we had discovered years earlier on his second trip, but still settled only by Indians. There we beached the two ships and built over them a kind of roof to protect us from sun and storms. Dreadful situation, for we now had no means of sailing on, since the ships were beyond

---

*In Central America, really, especially parts of the future Nicaragua and Honduras.

repair. What made it worse, there was no way by which anyone on Española could know that we had been marooned or where we were, and each morning when we woke someone would lament: 'How will we ever get out of here?' and we could think of no way.

"To tell the truth, Excellency, I thought we'd perish there and that no one would ever know how we died, for no ships would come to Jamaica."

"How did you escape?" Ocampo asked, and the sailor said: "Only through the courage of the admiral. He never flagged. Each new day he'd assure us: 'Somehow we'll be rescued,' and when we were starving, he promised: 'Somehow we'll find food,' and he led us in making clever traps for catching fish. Also, he himself tested new kinds of fruit to determine which were safe to eat. He was tireless in driving us to build better huts."

"Huts! How many days were you marooned on Jamaica?"

Aghast, the sailor simply stared at his interrogator: "Days? Excellency, it was months, June of one year to March of another. Excellency, we were at the end of the world. Nobody could know where we were. In Española they thought we were dead, and some said 'Good riddance,' because the admiral could be a difficult man, especially where young nobles were concerned." Wiping his nose with his left forefinger, he leaned close to Ocampo and said: "Excellency, we were all dead. The last months was special hell."

"How?"

The sailor hesitated, uncertain as to how to explain that terrible isolation and loss of hope. Then he cleared his throat: "If ever you get into trouble, you'll need no friend more trustworthy than Diego Méndez," and he spoke the name with such reverence that Ocampo was driven to ask: "And who was he?" and the sailor said: "Our savior," and Ocampo said: "Tell me."

The sailor did not answer directly, for he had important things to say about Méndez and did not propose to be diverted: "Most young noblemen who shipped with us were swine, especially when handing out orders to the likes of me, but Méndez once said to me: 'Those leaks have to be caulked, so let's caulk them,' and in the worst days, when we seemed about to sink, he worked the pumps as long as any of us."

Ocampo nodded in respect for an unknown young nobleman who seemed to have been a paragon, and what the seaman said next proved that he was.

"Méndez was a man without fear. When the rest of us failed to invent some way of escape, he built a canoe. You wouldn't cross a river in it. And he told us: 'I will sail it to Española and bring back a ship to save you,' and in this little craft he did just that. Storms, waves, bad luck on the first try, threatened by Indians, this man Méndez paddled on in his little canoe." The sailor stopped, crossed himself, and said: 'With God's aid he saved us after our nine months on Jamaica, where we had been sure we would die unknown and unmissed." He paused again, wiped his eyes, and concluded: "The Great Admiral, saved from an unmarked grave by the heroism of one man. Because Méndez did paddle all the way to this island and he did find a big ship and he did sail back to Jamaica, where, when he landed, Admiral Colón and the rest of us embraced him."

In the silence that followed, Ocampo looked not at the sailor, whose emotions overwhelmed him, but at the priest the sailor had brought with him: "And what brings you here, Father?"

"While the Great Admiral was marooned on Jamaica, convinced that he would die there without ever reporting on his last voyage, he wrote a very long letter to the king and queen, telling them of his adventures and reviewing the high points of his later life. It was the kind of testimonial a good man imagines writing when he is dying and wants his children to know the outlines of his career, a truly remarkable document."

"Why do you tell me?" Ocampo asked, and the priest said: "Because a copy of that letter, signed 7 July 1503, was left by Colón when he returned to this island from Jamaica, and I think that before you write your report you ought to know what Colón at the door of death thought about himself. When all the brawling about his errors here and there are forgotten, this is the Cristóbal Colón who will live."

The priest took a breath and began by giving in his own words an account of an unbelievable affront thrown in Colón's face by the governor of Santo Domingo, the port at which he himself had once been viceroy: "Seeing that a storm we call the *hurricano* was brewing, Colón sent a message ashore advising two actions: 'Let me come into your harbor and anchor. Do not dispatch to Spain the fleet that appears ready to sail.' Both suggestions were denied, probably because the acting viceroy feared he might lose his sinecure if Colón came ashore. The result? Listen to the Great Admiral's report of that hurricane."

The document the priest read covered many pages, and in reading, he skipped long portions, but the words of certain passages reverberated in the air of Ocampo's office like the ringing of some fine bronze bell:

> "The tempest was terrible throughout the night, all the ships were separated, and each one driven to the last extremity, without hope of anything but death; each of them also looked upon the loss of the rest as a matter of certainty. What man was ever born, excepting not even Job, who would not have been ready to die of despair at finding himself as I then was, yet refused permission either to land or put into the harbor which I by God's mercy had gained for Spain . . .

> "The distress of my son grieved me to the soul, and the more when I considered his tender age, for he was but thirteen years old, and he enduring so much for so long a time. Our Lord, however, gave him such strength that he encouraged the others, and he worked as if he had been at sea for eighty years . . .

> "My brother was also in the ship that was in the worst condition and the most exposed to danger; and my grief on this account was the greater because I had brought him with me against his will. I have gained no profit from my twenty years of service and toil and danger, and at this moment I do not possess a roof in Spain that I can call my own; if I wish to eat or sleep, I have nowhere to go but some inn or tavern, and most times lack wherewithal to pay the bill . . .

> "Let those who are accustomed to slander and aspersion ask, while they sit in the security of their home: 'Why didst thou do so-and-so under such circumstances?' I wish they were now embarked upon this voyage. Verily I believe that another journey of another kind awaits them, if there is any reliance to be placed upon our Holy Faith . . .

> "When I discovered the Indies, I said that they composed the richest lordship in the world. I told you of gold and pearls and precious stones, of spices and the traffic that might be carried on in them. But because these riches were not forth-

coming at once I was abused. That punishment now causes me to refrain from relating anything but what the natives tell me. But in this land of Veraguas* I have seen more signs of gold in the first two days than in Española in four years, and that the lands of this country cannot be more beautiful or better tilled . . .

"For seven years I was at your royal court, and everyone to whom my enterprise was mentioned treated it as ridiculous, but now there is not a man, including even tailors, who does not beg you to be allowed to go discovering. There is reason to believe that they make the voyage only for plunder, and the licenses they get are to the great disparagement of my honor and the detriment to the undertaking itself . . ."

At the phrase about even tailors begging for licenses to explore, Ocampo snapped his fingers and said: "He's right, I've seen them. A score of ne'er-do-wells who couldn't sail a ship or build a shed presuming when they got here to follow in Colón's footsteps." And the priest waited before reading the solemn, pleading close to this remarkable document written at the edge of the grave:

"I was twenty-eight years old when I came to Your Highnesses' service, and now I have not a hair upon me that is not gray; my body is infirm and all that was left to me, as well as my brothers, has been taken away and sold, even to the cloak that I wore, to my great dishonor. I hope that was done without your Royal knowledge . . .

"I am ruined. Hitherto I have wept for others. May Heaven now have mercy upon me, and may the earth weep. With regard to temporal things, I have not even a blanca† to offer for prayers, and here in the Indies, I am unable to follow the prescribed forms of religion. Solitary in my troubles, sick and in daily expectation of death, surrounded by millions of hostile savages full of cruelty, I fear my soul will be forgotten if it be separated from my body in this alien land. Weep for me, whoever has charity, truth and justice . . .

*The Caribbean coast of the modern nation of Panamá.
†About one-third of a penny.

"I did not come out on this voyage to gain to myself honor or wealth; all hope for such was dead. I came to Your Highnesses with honest purpose of heart and zeal in Your cause. I humbly beseech You that if it please God to rescue me from this place, you will graciously sanction my pilgrimage to Rome and other Holy Places . . . ."*

With that cry from the depths, the priest finished, and for a while no one spoke, for the words so clearly evoked the embattled spirit of Cristóbal Colón that his presence seemed to have entered the room, but then Ocampo broke into a quiet laugh: "Extraordinary, really! Here is the poor man, marooned, facing death, but he still writes first about his brother and a son. He was Colón to the end." Then, abruptly, he reached for the letter and read aloud the reference to the pilgrimage: "Here he is, not home from one disastrous trip and already planning another." He tapped the letter, leaned back, and looked up at the ceiling: "I can see him now. Him and his two brothers and his two sons and six or seven nephews, trailing as pilgrims all over Europe and the Holy Lands and complaining about everything." And he handed back the letter and thanked both the sailor and the priest.

On the night before he left Española, with his documents in order and his conclusions about the Great Admiral carefully phrased, Ocampo was visited in his quarters once again by Señora Pimentel, whom he hurried forward to greet: "This is an elegant way to end my long visit. You do me honor, but if I'm any judge, you want to confide some last-minute revelation."

"Yes. I perceive that your report and the welfare of the numerous Colón hangers-on who are laying claims to whatever fortune he left and his titles will depend on what you say about Bobadilla, so I think you should know two additional facts. When Colón arrived here in 1502 at the start of his final voyage, he arrived with his four little

---

*Numerous translations of this long and famous document known as *Léttera Rarissima* exist in English. Madariaga offered a fine one in 1936. Morrison gives a sparkling vernacular version done especially for him in 1963 by Dr. Milton Anastos. One of the best occurs in the Penguin *Four Voyages of Columbus* by J. M. Cohen in 1969. Wishing to preserve a more archaic mode, this account uses with certain clarifications the fine translation done in 1849 by R. H. Major.

ships off our anchorage out there, and Bobadilla, eager to keep Colón from coming ashore to contest his authority, refused to allow him entrance to our harbor.

"My husband, a stalwart man, protested: 'Excellency, a storm is brewing, and if it develops into a hurricane, his ships really must be allowed entrance.' But the viceroy was adamant, and poor Colón was forced to remain outside, and that very night, as my husband had warned, a tremendous hurricane struck. Have you ever seen one of our hurricanes? They can be terrifying.

"And what do you suppose happened? A major fleet headed for Spain, for which Bobadilla was responsible, was torn apart by the storm—thirty vessels in peril and thirteen lost with five hundred sailors and all their cargoes."

"What happened to Colón's little four?"

"Great navigator that he was, he maneuvered his ships majestically, right in the teeth of the hurricane, and saved every one. But even after that display, Bobadilla refused to allow him entrance, so off Colón sailed to his final burst of exploration. He found nothing, and ended on the beach in Jamaica, no gold, no ships, no hopes, no assignments in the future, with death staring him in the face each day for nearly a year."

Ocampo, awed by her sagacity and mature judgment, asked if he might seek her guidance on two nagging questions, and she, grateful for his treating her as an intellectual equal, nodded, so he asked: "Did the petty nobles accuse him because he was Italian?" and she replied with vigor: "Yes, a few presumptuous idiots. But that was ridiculous, for he wasn't really an Italian any longer. Pure Spanish all the way. So far as we know, he never wrote one word in Italian, because Spanish was his only language, Spain his only home, and good men like my husband were proud to serve under him as their leader."

"Was he a Jew?"

"Not when I knew him."

"Was he, perhaps, a renegade *converso,* living in danger of the stake?"

"When he lived with us after his rescue from the shipwreck in Jamaica, he went to Mass every day to give thanks."

That was all she cared to say, but after the *licenciado* offered her a final cup of coffee from beans grown and roasted on the island, she said: "He was truly great, that one." And then, as they were about to part, she stood in the doorway and said: "One of your misunderstandings really must be corrected. You've been completely misled about Bobadilla. What they told you was popular legend. He wasn't a nobleman. He was never a member of the military Order of Calatrava. That was another man, same name, who died in 1496, four years before our Bobadilla got here."

"Even so," Ocampo said, "it's rather pleasant in a gruesome way to know that your Bobadilla did drown right out there in the harbor from which he had barred the admiral during that hurricane."

"More local legend. The ship did sink, as we all remember, but he wasn't on it."

"Where is he?"

"Back in Spain. One of my cousins saw him in Sevilla, large as life and awaiting a new assignment from the king."

After Señora Pimentel left the room and Ocampo could see her walking sedately along the waterfront on her way home, he said to his scribes: "There goes the soul of Spain. A woman who brings the best of our land to the Colonies. Her home, the one you saw, is a beacon of civilization in this sea." Before he finished speaking, his scribes began to laugh, and when he asked, visibly irritated, what they thought amusing about his reflections, the senior one explained: "That night while you were feasting with the Pimentels in the big room, we were talking with his people in the kitchen, and we began to hear hints—no accusations, you understand—that his finances would not stand scrutiny. His fine house seems to have been built solely with money belonging to the king. His stonemasons were supposed to work for the government, not for him. He uses the king's ships for carrying on his own trading, and when we asked a few quiet questions we began to discern that he is completely corrupt."

Ocampo was appalled by these facts, which he should himself have uncovered, but before he could say anything, his junior scribe struck a hard blow: "Pimentel is a thief, but the members of his wife's family are worse. Real bandits, and she encourages them."

Ocampo gasped, but the most serious revelation was still to come: "It is believed that the big chest they keep locked, there in the room where you were, is filled with silver belonging to the king. Three different men have seen Señora Pimentel place money they've given her for the right to do business on the island in that chest. It must contain a fortune, and we think you ought to report this to the king."

Ocampo was furious: "Why didn't you tell me this before?"

"We wanted to be sure."

"Well, are you?"

"Yes! We've written it here!"

Ocampo accepted their papers, studied one, and pushed them back: "Burn them." And when they had lit a fire on the tile floor and destroyed the accusations, he said: "I'm a soldier. I have but one commission from the king. To inquire into Colón. You and I have done that properly, and now it's time for us to take our report and sail home."

"Leaving the Pimentels free to continue their abuses?"

"If they don't do the stealing, someone else will," and he stomped from the room, going for the first time out into the streets alone, while his honor guard remained behind.

He walked toward the sea, and the first building he saw was the fine stone house of the Pimentels, and he laughed at himself: I saw the chest of silver but neglected to investigate what was inside.

Ocampo walked for several hours, reflecting on the confused data he had uncovered, and his straightforward judgment was: Colón, Bobadilla, Pimentel. All honorable men, as Spanish gentlemen are required to be, but also rascals and thieves, as Spanish gentlemen are prone to be. Colón earned his honors, no man on earth more honorably than he, and the king must let his heirs have their rewards, within reason. Bobadilla, if he is really alive, does little harm in pretending to be a knight. And Pimentel, with his silver, will become a marquis or better.

He had a sense of frustration that a simple soldier would feel whose tests of honesty had always been on the battlefield, where a man either did his duty with courage or shirked it in cowardice, and he felt repelled by the complexities and nuances of political life. As he stared out at the sea he cried: "That town behind me. Everything in it is for sale or prey to thieves . . . or already stolen. I would like to be with King Ferdinand on a ship out there, sailing to Sicily for an honest battle. Friend here, foe over there." But then he wondered: Ferdinand could trust *me,* but could I trust *him*?

Stepping toward the water, he ventured a short distance, even though his Cordoba shoes might be damaged, and he looked westward to the island of Jamaica: In all this testimony the only man I would feel I could trust was one I never saw. That fellow Diego Méndez who sailed his canoe across the sea to rescue Colón and his men. Shaking his head in sorrow, he cried with regret: "Spain! Spain! I wish you could create a thousand such men."

When Ocampo had calmed down he felt ready to return to his quarters, but as he began walking back he could not resist turning around one more time to gaze out upon this beautiful sea, which would one day be called the Caribbean, and he had a powerful intimation of what the coming centuries portended: I see the men of Spain who come to these islands repeating in perpetuity the behavior of Colón and Pimentel—steal, abuse the natives, place relatives on the king's payroll, think always of self and family, never of the general weal. It's a bad precedent we've established here in Española.

IV

THE SPANISH LAKE

I N THE LATTER YEARS OF THE SIXTEENTH CENTURY, 1567–1597, two fabled mariners, one Spanish, one English, waged an incessant duel throughout the Caribbean. The two men fought at the extreme western end at Nombre de Dios, and beyond the northern limits at Vera Cruz in Mexico. They fought on the isthmus, the approaches to Panamá, at little ports on the coast of South America and at the huge harbor of San Juan in Puerto Rico. But most often they faced each other at Cartagena, the walled city that became in the early 1500s the capital of Spain's empire in the Caribbean. In heritage, training, religion, manner and personal appearance, these men differed conspicuously, but in personal heroism and eagerness to defend their honor they were identical.

The Spaniard was a tall, thin, beardless aristocrat with the hollow-cheeked austerity that El Greco liked to depict in his scowling portraits of Spanish noblemen and church authorities; he usually wore a Toledo blade with an elegant, filigreed hilt, a deadly instrument he was ever ready to wield in defense of King Philip and his Catholic church.

The Englishman was a short, muscular fellow of undistinguished parentage, the owner-master of a small trading ship which he sailed to ports in France and the embattled Netherlands, always keen to protect the interests of Queen Elizabeth and her new Protestant religion. Men under his command said of him: "He's all gristle and nerves."

The Spaniard carried the insolent and resonant name of Don Diego Ledesma Paredes y Guzman Orvantes. If he had been a proper Englishman, his name would have been a simple James Ledesma and let it go at that, but the Spanish style had a grace that gave it added attraction. The various names evoked memories for any Spaniard hearing them; for example, on the father's side the Ledesmas had always been notable defenders of the king and to have Ledesma in one's name signified honor. The male branch also sprang from the Paredes family of northern Spain, and its contribution to the last defeat of the Moors in 1492 had been heroic; this was a name worth preserving.

The letter *y* indicated that whatever names followed belonged to the maternal side of the family, and here the Guzmans were as distinguished as either of the paternal ancestors, while the Orvantes men were considered, at least in the little region from which they came, the most outstanding of the four because of their bravery in helping expel the Moors from Spain. To make things more complex, at his birth adoring and important members of his family had to be honored, so that his full name became Juan Tomas Diego Sebastian Leandro Ledesma Paredes y Guzman Orvantes. But this occasioned no trouble, for everyone called him just Don Diego, omitting the other eight names, laden with honor though they were.

Don Diego was inordinately proud of his family's ancient fame and saw in his three unmarried daughters—Juana, María and Isabella—an opportunity to enhance it if he could find acceptable young men to marry them, but he never lost sight of his primary obligation: augmenting his family's present power. As a young naval officer of unusual daring, he had won an enviable reputation for defending against pirates the Spanish armadas which carried Peruvian gold and Panamanian silver across the Caribbean on its way to Sevilla in southern Spain. His bold successes enabled him to rise swiftly to the rank of captain, and in 1556, at the age of only twenty-four, he had been appointed governor at Cartagena. During his first day on the job he issued the order which would characterize his long tenure: "The Caribbean is a Spanish lake, from which all intruders will be expelled." The first step he took to enforce this boast was to make his home city of Cartagena so impregnable that no enemy would dare attack it.

Nature assisted him in this effort, for it had made the city easy to defend: Cartagena stood in the middle of a strange island. Stretching some seven and a half miles along the coast of South America, with one shore beautiful, straight and smooth, and the other resembling an octopus with many arm- and leg-like peninsulas, with vast impenetrable swamps and unscalable cliffs, this island was designed by nature gone mad. To invade its one settlement, Cartagena, was almost impossible. Of course, when an adversary came at Cartagena from the Caribbean he found an approach that appeared both easy and promising, for at the southern tip of the octopus island waited a broad, beautiful entrance into the harbor leading to the city; Boca Grande it was called, Big Mouth. But its allure was deceptive, for it was extremely shallow; and what was worse, to keep out any enemy, Don Diego had commanded that ships be scuttled in the middle of the passage, which meant that not even an alien rowboat could penetrate.

And if the arriving enemy continued some easy miles to the south, he came upon Boca Chica, Little Mouth, a deep entrance but treacherous because of its extreme narrowness and certain intruding islands. Should a determined ship captain work his way through, he would find himself lost in the first of four distinct bays: big Southern leading into smaller Middle, which led into small Northern, which debouched into tiny Harbor atop which rose the battlements of the city. Cartagena was well-nigh impregnable.

In the late summer of 1566, King Philip of Spain dispatched to Cartagena the kind of investigating ambassador who had tormented Cristóbal Colón at Española eighty years earlier. But unlike Bobadilla, this man, after the most inquisitive probing, uncovered no malfeasance, though his shrewd report anticipated weaknesses that might cause trouble in future years:

> Don Diego is a brave, honest man who serves Your Majesty admirably. He protects your treasure ships. He rebuffs pirates. He does not steal. And the word *cowardice* is unknown to him. You would profit if you had many such governors.
>
> I found only two weaknesses. Don Diego is so vain of his slim, regal appearance that he has taken to calling himself Admiral, even though he is not entitled to that rank, but since he fights his ships more resolutely than any of Your Majesty's real admirals, I recommend that this presumption be overlooked.

His other weakness is more troublesome. Having only daughters, he is distressed that the Ledesma name might not be perpetuated, so he brings to Cartagena any male bearing the name and promotes him instantly to some position of power, whether capable or not. I fear that if Your Majesty leaves him long as governor, every position in the city will be occupied by some Ledesma.

My final judgment of the man is one I heard one of his juniors recite late one night: "Don Diego is an austere nobleman who loves to posture as a military man, but God help the English pirate who ventures into his lake, for then he charges out, all flags flying to destroy the insolent invader." I heard him boast: "My city of Cartagena cannot be invaded by any power on earth." I agree with him.

Yet even as King Philip read this reassuring statement, there was on the cold east coast of England a tough seafarer, twenty-three years old, with his one small ship, who was swearing in blind fury: "I shall fight the King of Spain until I die. And I shall exact full recompense for every slave the Dons stole from me. When I'm through, Cartagena will lie in ruins."

The sailor who made this fiery boast was not a large, aggressive man; only five feet four, of a stocky build and with a bulletlike round head and a jutting chin already covered with a closely trimmed beard, his dominant feature was a pair of sharp blue eyes which could flash fire. Much older seamen had learned to avoid him if trouble brewed, for in any argument he was accustomed to have his way. A difficult, capable young man, he was not only eager to be sailing back to the Caribbean; he was lusting to do so. His reasons for this burning hunger were manifold, involving religion and slaves.

His name was Francis Drake, eldest son of a retired seaman who had fathered eleven other children and who, back on land in a Devon village near Plymouth, became a vigorous Protestant clergyman. These were troubled years when England was trying to decide whether it was old Catholic or new Protestant, and on a Whitsunday in 1549 the Catholics of Devon rose in rebellion against the new religion that was being forced upon them. Reverend Drake and his family barely escaped with their lives, and young Francis never forgot the terror he felt that night.

Afraid to return to their old home, the fourteen Drakes scuttled off to a naval base near the mouth of the Thames, and there the family lived miserably in the hulk of a discarded ship. Here again they were made to pay heavily for being Protestants, for when Queen Mary ascended the throne, determined to take all England back to Catholicism, family friends who resisted Mary's order were hanged, and the Drakes themselves barely escaped execution. After this unfortunate second brush with Catholicism, young Francis generated that intense hatred which would dominate his wildly active life.

Toward the end of 1567 he suffered intensely from an additional reason for despising Spaniards—the dreadful thing they had done to his friend Christopher Weed—and, burning for revenge, he hurried out to Plymouth to consult with one of England's greatest sea captains, John Hawkins—whom he called Uncle, although what the precise blood relationship between them was nobody knew. Most called the two *kinsmen* and let it go at that.

Hawkins was a remarkable seaman, one of the greatest the world would know, for in a day when compasses were uncertain and there were no means of determining longitude, no powerful guns or reliable medicines or any of the appurtenances which later captains would take for granted, he drove his ships far and wide through storm and enemy action, always bringing them to safe and profitable harbor.

Thirty-five years old, he was of medium stature, with small head, steel-gray eyes that did not blink, big mustache and small beard to make him look more impressive; he had oversized ears of which he was ashamed and a bulldog determination which never flared into excessive posturing. He was a man's man, and from those who served under him he exacted a loyalty that verged on fanaticism. To sail with John Hawkins was the ultimate challenge for a seafaring man.

Curiously, he was not by nature a warrior; he thought of himself as a merchant and a navigator who would go to any lengths to avoid a battle at sea. When he drifted from one Spanish-held island to the next, selling his slaves, officials he encountered had no cause for fear, for they had learned that he did not sack cities or burn towns.

Now, as he sat with Francis Drake in a building used as naval headquarters overlooking Plymouth Sound, he suspected that once more he might have to dampen his nephew's headstrong energy, but before he could issue words of caution, Drake's seething fury exploded: "Uncle, I must sail with you on your next voyage to the Caribbean. Now more than ever."

Hawkins placed a restraining hand on Drake's knee: "Mad desire for revenge is never a sound base for action, Francis. I'm almost afraid to take you with me."

"But I have cause, Uncle. The Spaniards . . ." and a great hatred burned through his words.

"Must I remind you? If you do sail with me, it's so we can sell our slaves to the Spaniards, not fight against them."

"I'll trade with them all right . . . at the point of a gun . . . my gun."

"I would like to take you with me. I need men of your courage when we're on the Slave Coast. Pirates, Portuguese adventurers trying to steal our slaves, the flotsam of the world always attacking English ships."

"That's the kind of action I seek," Drake said eagerly, but again his uncle reproved him: "To fight off pirates in Africa, yes. To fight our peaceful Spanish customers in the Caribbean, no."

"Peaceful Spanish customers?! Let me tell you about those peaceful Spanish customers. Early this year, at Río de la Hacha," and Drake spat out the Spanish name as if he loathed it, "the governor lured me ashore with my ninety slaves, which he offered to buy. But when the time came to pay me, he whistled for his soldiers. They drove me back to my ship, and he kept my slaves. Paid me nothing."

"It happens, Francis. My slaves have often been stolen by corrupt officials. But the slaves I have left I sell to honest officials at strong prices. In your battle with the Dons, you came home a winner, did you not?"

Drake leaped to his feet: "Uncle! Forty of those slaves were mine! Not the queen's! I paid for them in Africa with my own money. Those Dons stole my profits from *me,* personally. And I've sworn I'll get them back."

Hawkins, growing impatient, snapped: "Don't be a fool. Never allow revenge to get in your way of earning a decent profit."

"You don't understand," Drake blurted out. Then he whistled for a young sailor of nineteen to join them: "Tell Captain Hawkins what happened to Christopher Weed." Then, turning to his uncle, he explained: "You remember young Weed? Son of Fleet Preacher Timothy Weed?" and Hawkins said: "I know him."

"No more," Drake said with iron grating against his words. Then, to the sailor: "Tell my uncle what happened to my friend Weed."

"We sailed from Plymouth," the young sailor said, "to trade our goods for those of Venice. But as we passed the Spanish coast our little ship was captured and we were thrown in prison. They announced that since we were Englishmen, we had to be heretics and must be duly punished."

"Then what?" Drake asked, eyes flashing.

"Half our crew recanted—said they'd always been faithful Catholics and were still. They were lashed for having ventured into Spanish waters, then released. The other half, and I was one, refused to recant, so we were sentenced to the galleys. Six years . . . ten years . . . life."

"And you? How many years?"

"Ten, but our ship was attacked by pirates and I escaped."

"God was watching over you. But what of Christopher Weed and the other two?"

"Somehow the Spaniards learned that they were the sons of Protestant ministers—"

"But so were you," Hawkins interrupted, and the young sailor said: "Yes, but no one revealed that to the Spaniards."

"Tell him what happened to the three ministers' sons," Drake said, his hands clasped so tightly that no blood showed beneath his fair skin.

"All of us, we who were headed for the hulks, even those to be released, were led to the great square in Sevilla. There, before the cathedral and the beautiful tower—I shall always remember them—stakes were driven into the ground, bonfires were built about them, and Weed and his two fellows were lashed to the stakes and burned alive. One of our men standing near me shouted: 'For love of Christ, shoot them!' but they let them burn. To teach the rest of us a lesson."

Grimly, Drake said: "You may leave us!"

When the two seamen were alone again, Hawkins said harshly: "Francis, when I see the blazing hatred in your eyes I have no wish to take you with me." Then he sighed, and said reluctantly: "But I think for various reasons I may have to. The ships I'll be taking belong to the queen and must be protected. Two-thirds of the slaves we capture will belong to her, and two-thirds of our profits, all hers. This is her expedition and she has ordered me to take along only the most trusted men, for she cannot afford to lose the great wealth this adventure might bring. Desperately she needs the money."

"Why?"

In reply, Hawkins, trusted friend of the queen, gave an explanation which revealed the curious state of affairs in Europe: "You remember that our Queen Mary of sacred memory," and he crossed himself, "took as her husband King Philip of Spain, and even though Mary is dead, Philip still wants to be King of England. He begs Elizabeth to marry him . . . bring England back to Catholicism. She needs money to fend him off, every penny we can earn on this slaving voyage." He paused, broke into a mischievous smile, and added: "Do you see the humor, Francis? You and I stealing from King Philip in order to do him harm . . . with his own money?"

"And if we return to Río Hacha, will I have your permission to bombard that wretch who stole my slaves?"

"No! And now I want to show you why I need you."

Leaving the naval headquarters, the two men walked to an anchorage where Drake saw for the first time the great vessel Queen Elizabeth had recently purchased with her own money to serve as flagship for her slaving ventures. It was the *Jesus of Lübeck,* a ship to gladden the heart of any sailor, especially one who might have to be aboard as she sailed into battle. Built in Germany some thirty years earlier, she had been intended from the start to be a mighty man-of-war.

"Look at her!" Hawkins said as Drake's eyes widened. "More than seven hundred tons, those four masts each twice as thick as any you've known. That long bowsprit, the great fortresslike towers soaring high into the air, fore and aft. And the flags!"

From various protuberances eight flags of England flew and at the deck level another ten, but Drake was noticing other aspects: "Look at these monster guns and the hoard of smaller ones . . . the room below for sleeping soldiers as well as sailors . . . that clean deck space for swordplay if we have to repel raiders. That's a ship that's crying to be fought properly, and we can do it."

He then indicated to Hawkins that he would be honored to sail in her, but his kinsman shook his head: "No, Francis, you're not to sail in the *Jesus,*" and when Drake scowled, Hawkins added: "I want you always on my starboard, in your own ship, as captain," and he pointed to a handsome little fighting ship, the *Judith,* in which Drake, after he had purchased her, would sail to both glory and shame.

Hawkins, placing his arm about Drake's shoulder, said: "From the start I knew I had to take you. The queen is so eager that her expensive new toy be protected that she gave me orders: 'Hire your nephew Drake, a real fighting man I'm told, to sail at your elbow to safeguard my purchase.' So you sail at her command and my wish," and it was agreed.

In the weeks that followed, Drake was busy visiting ship's chandlers in Plymouth and ordering supplies for the long voyage. A list in his handwriting of purchases indicated the level of his rough education and his freedom to spell as he wished: "vi pynazzes, bysket, beare, bieff, chiese, rieze, vyneger, sweete oyle, hamars" (6 pinnaces, biscuit, beer, beef, cheese, rice, vinegar, sweet oil, hammers), but purchase was also made of "Caste ordenanunce, forged same, and divers munytions mownts," for Drake insisted that his little *Judith* be prepared for battle.

On 2 October 1567, Hawkins headed his little flotilla for the coast of Africa, where it would pick up some five hundred slaves to be carried into the heart of the Caribbean, where they would be peddled from one Spanish island to another. But wherever Hawkins and Drake sailed as partners, one vast difference would separate them: Hawkins, the cautious older man, wanted peace; Drake, the impetuous younger, sought vengeance against Spaniards wherever and however he met them.

In the spring of 1568, while Hawkins was heading westward from the African coast, the holds of his vessel crammed with slaves, Governor Ledesma of Cartagena was listening to an ugly report from the captain of a small Spanish trading vessel out of Sevilla: "Esteemed Excellency, when I left Spain I was directed to enter the Indies by the extreme southern route to report on conditions on our island of Trinidad, and as you well know, for it lies within your territory, there has been no serious Spanish settlement there, nor any other that I could detect. Trinidad was empty and safe.

"But some seven leagues after we had sailed west along the coast of America, we came to our great salt pans of Cumaná, and it was fortunate for me and my crew that we were comfortably out to sea, because a horde of some dozen ships, which I took from their build to be Dutch renegades, had deposited their teams of thieves onto our salt beds and were stealing a fortune."

When Don Diego heard this distressing news, he did not reveal his dismay. Controlling his emotions, which were in turmoil, he asked quietly: "And what did you do when you saw the Dutch thieves?" and the captain said honestly: "Glad that my ship was fast and theirs slow, I fled," and Don Diego said with equal candor: "Wise man. Even two Dutch ships would be an overmatch if their crews were determined to get salt—and you say there were at least a dozen working there?" When the captain nodded, Don Diego said: "I think we must drink a toast to your successful trip . . . and your prudence."

The apparent ease with which Ledesma received this report of Dutch incursions into the salt flats masked the considerable fright the news had caused, and after the captain left, Don Diego hurried to his wife, his face flushed: "Darling, walk with me on the battlements. I want no one to hear," and they paced for some time atop the defensive wall that protected the center of their city.

"Ugly news. The Dutch have trespassed on our salt flats again."

"Cumaná?"

"Yes. This time they've come in force."

"How do you know?"

"A ship captain, just out from Sevilla. He saw them robbing us. And if he's warned me, he'll certainly warn the king, and Philip will expect me to act . . . to drive the scoundrels off."

"Isn't Cumaná a long way from here?"

"It is. More the reason why we must keep the Dutch away," and as they walked he spoke briefly of this treasure spot, so important to Spanish trade: "A long hook of land starting east and running west cuts off a shallow bay. This happens often along seacoasts. Remember the handsome one we saw when we laid over in the island of Jamaica, southern shore?" And Doña Leonora nodded.

"The gulf at Cumaná looks the same, but is different. It's shallow, and every summer when the sun is high the water evaporates, leaving an enormous deposit of salt. There's so much salt there, you can scrape it up with shovels."

"But don't we station soldiers to protect the flats?"

"Because it is so hot, no one can stay around Cumaná for long. The heat beating back from the white salt is incredible, not like any other known, and the saline air corrodes nostrils and makes breathing difficult. Men work with huge flat-bottomed shoes tied to their feet so as not to break up the salt deposits on which they walk, and a merciless glare shines back from the intensely white surface. A season in Cumaná is a season in hell. But the Dutch sea captains who creep onto the flats enjoy an unusual advantage. Judges in Holland tell criminals: 'Death or work in Cumaná,' so the salt is collected by men who have to work there, the ships are loaded, and salted herring is made available to large parts of Europe.

"What I must do," Ledesma told his wife, "is take a fleet out there before the king orders me to do so."

"Can't you send one of your captains?" she asked, and he replied honestly: "I suppose I could, but would it not look better . . ." He hesitated, because as the father of three unmarried daughters and the uncle of two nephews with limited futures, he faced what could be called "The Spanish Problem": "How can I protect and extend the interests of my family?"

In the Spanish society a man like Don Diego acknowledged tremendous obligations to four entities: God, God's church, the king, his own family, though in reverse order if he was a prudent Spaniard. One could argue as to whose claims were greater, God's, the church's or the king's, but any sensible man would have to admit that first came his family's. And Don Diego had a most demanding one. His three daughters needed husbands of wealth and importance and his wife's two able nephews deserved jobs. Then there were his three brothers, who had no titles but did have ravenous appetites for good things, and Doña Leonora's inexhaustible array of cousins. If he played his cards cleverly and retained his governorship for another fifteen or twenty years, he would have a reasonable chance of placing all his relatives in profitable positions, and no man could discharge his family obligations more honorably than that.

So it was advisable that he conduct in person this campaign against the Dutch interlopers, for in doing so he might be able to connive two promotions for his wife's nephews and at the same time ingratiate himself with a young captain of troops, a man of excellent family in Saragossa whom Doña Leonora had settled upon as a proper husband for their eldest, Juana. If, during action, Don Diego could find an opportunity to promote the young man, and then commend him in his report to the king, a marriage might very well be attainable. Getting the nephews started young in the naval service could mean that he might later be justified in placing them in command of one of the treasure galleons that sailed each spring from Cartagena for Havana and Sevilla. In fact, the more Don Diego thought of this expedition to the salt flats, the more attractive it became. A man could kill a chain of doves with one arrow well shot.

It was for these personal reasons, plus a desire to knock the insufferable Dutch renegades in the head, that Governor Ledesma assembled in late February 1568 a fleet of seven ships, well armed and manned, and set sail for distant Cumaná, a town most governors would never see but to which they would send troops on occasion to monitor the valuable salt flats. As self-appointed admiral of the fleet, he rode in the largest vessel, one with the biggest guns, and after the ships had sailed for some days on a northeast heading so as to clear the jutting peninsula protecting Maracaibo, he turned them due east for the long run to Cumaná. And he placed his nephews in charge of the port and starboard wings of the fleet.

These assignments were shocking, for as one of the captains who had to surrender his post grumbled: "Those whelps aren't past the age of twenty-five and know nothing of the sea." But the answer from another old sea dog touched reality: "True, but you must remember they're his wife's nephews, and that does count."

Satisfied that he had made two judicious moves, Don Diego now attended to the young nobleman who had been courting Juana Ledesma, and for him he created a wholly new position, vice-regent to the admiral; no one knew what it entailed, but it did evoke in the young man a feeling of great warmth toward Don Diego and his entire family. When one of the old-line captains asked: "What are the vice-regent's duties?" Don Diego replied without hesitation: "He relays my orders to my vice-admirals." When he went to sleep that night, with three more members of his family taken care of, he felt not even a wisp of shame at having abused his position so blatantly. If the truth were known, the long-dead bearers of the distinguished names he bore had probably gained their high places in history by similar attention to the promotions of their sons, nephews and cousins, for that was the Spanish way.

Toward the end of March, the fleet approached Cumaná from the west, and found at the mouth of the salt lagoon a group of three big renegade Dutch traders, each protected by heavy guns. Without the least hint of indecision Don Diego attacked, and in forty minutes the Battle of Cumaná, as the Spanish scribes would name it in their enthusiastic reports, was over, with one enemy ship sunk, one smoldering on a reef, and the middle one a captured prize.

Aware, even in the heat of battle, that he was a Spanish gentleman bound by the rules of honor, Don Diego directed his interpreter to shout in Dutch to the survivors: "You may keep that ship you have and seek what port you can. But we'll chop down your masts so you can't chase after us in the night." But as his own men watched the defeated Dutchmen begin to climb aboard the surviving ship, a stout one, they protested: "Why give them that fine ship, while we must do with this poor one of ours?" and he called to his men who were about to destroy the masts: "Stop! Don't touch that mast!" And without a moment's reflection he directed his men to cut down the mast of one of his own ships and turn it over to the Dutchmen.

When his crew climbed aboard their prize and all the Dutchmen had been crammed into the leaky old craft, Don Diego called down: "What's the name of this ship?" and they pointed to the stern where the words had been neatly carved in oak: STADHOUDER MAURITZ. While the Dutchmen argued about which way to head, a horde of bright yellow butterflies seeking land saw the captured ship and alighted upon her rigging, clothing it in gold.

"An omen!" Don Diego cried, and before nightfall carpenters had fashioned a new board with the lovely new name MARIPOSA. When it was in place, each member of the crew was issued a bottle of captured Dutch beer with which he toasted the admiral when he poured his bottle over the new name and shouted: "We christen thee *Mariposa!*"

That night, flushed with victory, Don Diego directed his scribe to compose a letter informing King Philip of the capture of the Dutch ship, adding in his own handwriting: "Without the exceptional bravery and shrewd military judgment of the vice-regent and the two vice-admirals, this victory over three huge Dutch ships would not have been possible. They did their fighting on the decks of the enemy and deserve both commendation and promotion."

During a spell of fine weather on the homeward voyage, when the Caribbean rolled in those long, graceful swells which made it famous, Don Diego told his future son-in-law: "Notice what a fine ship we got for ourselves. When she rolls to port or starboard, doesn't matter which, she always returns to the upright position and holds it for a long moment. Doesn't wallow continuously from side to side like a drunken Frenchman." He pointed out another feature of even greater significance: "Look at the structure. Clinker-built with her strakes overlapping for strength. Not like so many Spanish ships, carvel-built with the boards abutting against each other and liable to split apart in a storm." But the feature he seemed to like best was one rarely seen in Spanish ships: "Her hull is double-planked." Clicking his tongue, he said with great warmth: "When you and I captured this one, we got ourselves a real ship."

Suffused with this euphoria, Ledesma completed his long run westward, then headed south for home, and as he coasted down the western edge of Cartagena's island and saw on the cliffs above him the safe, solid town which he commanded, he was inspired to discharge seven salvos to inform the citizens of his victory.

But as he was luxuriating in his defeat of the Dutch and the capture of their fine ship, his future son-in-law, the vice-regent, showed what a perceptive young man he was by asking permission to address the admiral, and when Don Diego gave assent, the young man said: "You know, Excellency, that my great-uncle was once governor of Peru?"

"Of course! That's one reason why Doña Leonora and I have been so proud to think of you as a possible member of our family. Don Pedro, one of the finest."

"Then you also know what happened to him?"

Don Diego's easy smile turned into a frown: "Terribly unfair. Enemies brought all sorts of base charges against him. Reports to the king were biased . . ."

"And he was hanged." There was silence in the cabin, after which Don Diego asked: "Why do you remind me of that sad affair?" and the young man said: "Because you must not boast about your victory at Cumaná. Neither in your report to Spain nor in your comments here in Cartagena."

"What would be the peril . . . if I did . . . which I certainly won't?"

"Envy. The envy that your enemies here and in Spain will feel." In the silence that followed, the young man mustered his courage, then continued: "You have promoted me to high office. Same with your two nephews. And before we sailed you did likewise with two of your brothers. Tongues will wag. Spies, even aboard this ship, will begin framing their secret reports to the king."

How well Don Diego knew and appreciated the truth of this warning. Any Spanish governor in charge of a territory far from home ran the constant risk of being summoned back to Spain to refute charges of the basest sort, and the nature of his commission made this inevitable, for he was assigned a position of enormous authority, in charge of riches beyond the imagination even of rapacious men, but given almost no remuneration. The kings of Spain were a penurious lot, grasping for every gold or silver piece their colonies produced but unwilling to pay a decent wage to their overseers. The Spanish viceroys and governors were *expected* to steal, allowed ten or fifteen years to enrich themselves, and it was supposed that they would return to Spain with wealth great enough to last them and their voluminous families the rest of their lives.

But at the same time the suspicious kings encouraged a constant chain of spies to report on the misbehaviors of their viceroys and governors, with the result that after a man—like, say, Columbus— had been in one of those offices for a dozen years, he was almost certain to be visited by an official audiencia whose members might spend two years looking into his behavior and inviting his enemies to testify in secret against him, with the result that repeatedly an official who had enjoyed extraordinary powers in some far place like Mexico, Panamá or Peru finished his illustrious career by sailing home in chains, to languish in jail after he got there. The unlucky ones were hanged.

Don Diego felt driven to recall the mournful list of Spain's great conquistadores who had met bitter ends, and as he recited their fates, his son-in-law nodded grimly: "Cristóbal Colón? Home in chains. Cortés in Mexico? Chains. Nuñez de Balboa? One of our finest. Beheaded. The great Pizarro of Peru? Slain by jealous underlings."

These two good men, one a governor who kept his stealing within reason, the other the scion of a splendid family and himself destined to become a colonial governor, had identified the fundamental reasons why Spanish lands in the New World would fail, during the next four hundred years, to achieve any simple, responsible system of governance, democratic or not, in which good men could rule without stealing and alienating the riches of their countries.

A fatal tradition had already been codified during the rule of Diego Ledesma in Cartagena: provide reasonably good government for the time being, steal as much as decency and the envy of others will allow, and then, because your own position is tenuous, place every relative in the richest position possible so that he, too, can accumulate a fortune. This will mean that even if you are dragged home in disgrace, the members of your family will be left in positions of power, and after a few years they can ease their way back into Spain laden with wealth and titles, to become the new viceroys and governors or to marry into the families who do, and thus find new opportunities to steal new fortunes.

It was a system that provided swings of the pendulum so wide that men became dizzy, and a form of government that wasted the tremendous resources of the New World. With far fewer natural riches, both France and England would establish more lasting forms of good government than Spain with its superior holdings ever did. On that day in 1568 as Don Diego sailed home in triumph, Spain had already been in control of the New World since 1492, more than three-quarters of a century, whereas both France and England would not start their occupancy until the 1620s and 1630s, another half-century later. But the seeds of Spain's deficiencies had already been sown.

However, neither of these reflective men perceived the lasting damage their philosophy was creating: First, if it was known and condoned that their governor was appropriating public funds, officials on the next tier down were justified in doing the same, although to a more restrained degree. Then those on the third tier were invited to try their luck, and on down to the lowest functionary. All had their hands out and all levels of government proceeded by theft and bribery. Second, and equally destructive, if thousands of men like Don Diego returned each year to Europe with their booty, they left the New World colonies increasingly impoverished.

At about this time a Cartagena poet summarized such rules of conduct in six sardonic lines: "My Spain against all other countries. / Her religion against all other religions. / My part of Spain against all other parts. / My colony against their colony. / My big family against all other big families. / And my wife and children against my brother's wife and children." As one of the most congenial practitioners of this art of personal and familial self-protection, the governor of Cartagena applied nine-tenths of his energies to finding jobs for his family and treasure for himself, one-tenth defending his Caribbean against intruders. But his victory against the Dutch proved that when aroused, he could be valiant. For in the Spanish society a man could be a peculator but not a coward.

On the day that John Hawkins and Francis Drake loaded the *Jesus of Lübeck* with the maximum number of slaves, Don Diego de Guzman, a Spanish spy at Queen Elizabeth's court, drafted a note in code and hurried it to the Thames waterfront, where a swift ship was waiting to depart for Spain. At the Escorial Palace, a monstrous pile of dark rock near Madrid, King Philip's scribes made rushed copies of the orders he had drafted in cold fury, so that six hours after Philip received the news, a horseman was galloping down to Sanlúcar de Barrameda near the mouth of the Guadalquivir River. From there three small boats set sail on the tide for the island of Española, where the messages were delivered to the governor at Santo Domingo. He promptly dispatched a swarm of small, swift coastal frigates to speed the news to seven different Caribbean capitals, so that by 3 February 1568, when Hawkins left Africa, his target islands in the Caribbean were about to receive news that he was coming.

One of the Española frigates put into Cartagena's well-protected harbor, where the messenger hurried to inform Ledesma: "Excellency, I hand you an ominous message. John Hawkins is heading this way, and Guzman in London has heard on the best authority, someone close to the queen, that he is heading for Puerto Rico, Río Hacha and Cartagena, with permission to land and destroy each place if we oppose him."

Don Diego listened, nodded several times, and waited till he himself had read the instructions, then said in a judicial voice that betrayed no fear: "There are ways to handle Englishmen. They're not like French pirates who slay and burn with no questions asked, nor the Dutch who flourish on sheer pillage."

But then the messenger disturbed this tranquillity by revealing privileged information which had come by word of mouth: "Hawkins is sailing in a very powerful ship, the queen's own *Jesus of Lübeck,*" and as the name of the famous warship hung in the air, Admiral Ledesma, as a well-informed navy man, could visualize that terror of the seas. To have the *Jesus* with its many guns bearing down upon smaller and poorly defended Spanish ships was not a happy prospect, but it was what the messenger added as his last bit of information that caused the governor his greatest worry: "Hawkins will bring with him a second major warship, the *Minion,* impossible to sink, and five lesser ships. *Swallow,* one hundred tons; *Judith,* fifty tons; *Angel,* thirty-three tons," and as he ended the recitation he added: "In command of the *Judith* will be young Francis Drake, a kinsman of Captain Hawkins, on whom Hawkins will depend if fighting becomes necessary."

At the mention of this name Ledesma flinched, for he had heard about the threat Drake had uttered when the Spaniards at Río Hacha stole the forty slaves from him the year before: "When I return to these waters I will demand full payment for my slaves and burn Cartagena."

That afternoon Ledesma issued a host of instructions for the further fortification of his capital. In the following days three more ships were sunk across Boca Grande to make it totally impassable and additional guns were emplaced to protect the entrance to Boca Chica. Each headland the Hawkins fleet would have to pass if it were to threaten the small inner harbor was given additional firepower, and troops were trained in tactics for driving English assailants back if they attempted to scale the battlements.

"Cartagena cannot be taken," Ledesma announced when the work was finished, but a few weeks later a small boat scurried in from Río Hacha with the appalling news that not only had Hawkins returned to the Caribbean, but he had indeed brought the tough little fire-eater Drake with him.

"Excellency, my crew of three and I escaped miraculously from under the English guns, and I report only the truth, as these men will testify. On the fifth day of June, this year, Captain Hawkins, with a fleet of seven English vessels and some French acquired along the way, passed the salt flats of Cumaná without stopping, but he did sell some of his slaves at the pearl island of Margarita and at Curaçao, from where he sent ahead two of his smallest ships, the *Angel* and the *Judith,* the last under the command of Captain Francis Drake, to clear the way for his big ship, the *Jesus of Lübeck.*

"Drake was a reasonable choice for this mission, since he had visited Río Hacha last year, as you will remember. Immediately upon arriving he started hostilities, capturing the dispatch boat from Española and making the officials thereon his prisoners, something never done before. He then fired two shots at the town, not over the rooftops as the English are supposed to do when trading, but right at the house occupied by his great enemy, Treasurer Miguel de Castellanos, who took the slaves from him last year. And I am ashamed to say that one of Drake's broadsides ripped right through the treasurer's house and would have killed him had he been dining."

"What did Castellanos do?" Ledesma asked, and the messenger replied: "For five days all he did was glare at those two little ships in his harbor, powerless to do anything against them but also strong enough to prevent Drake from landing with his soldiers."

"You mean the assault on Río ended in such a stalemate? Doesn't sound like Drake."

"Oh no! On the sixth day Captain Hawkins arrived, bringing his great *Jesus of Lübeck* into the harbor. Now all was different. First thing Hawkins did, according to his custom of never making Spain angry, was give back the dispatch boat and its passengers as warrant of his peaceful intention. Then, to prove that he meant business, he marched two hundred armed men ashore, but as you know, the treasurer had long ago decided that if ever the English returned, he would oppose them to the death, and this he did, or rather, tried to do.

"A serious battle ensued, with two English dead, but their attack was so relentless that Castellanos' troops fled, and Hawkins found himself possessor of a town containing no women, no gold, silver, pearls or objects of value. Hawkins gave the obdurate treasurer three days to bring back his people and his treasure, and when the man refused, Hawkins threatened to burn the place. Heroically, Castellanos said: 'Rather than give in to you, I'll see every island in the Indies ablaze,' whereupon Drake, who heard the vain boast, started setting houses afire, but Hawkins stopped him, saying: 'There must be a better way.'

"After five days of patient waiting, an escaped slave showed Hawkins where the treasure was hidden. And so Hawkins won everything he wanted."

"What do you mean, he won everything?"

"He sold us two hundred fifty slaves at fair prices. He made us give him extra money for the families of the two English soldiers who were killed. And then he asked us to produce the women belonging to homes that Francis Drake had burned, and when they stood before him, tired and dirty from their time hiding in the jungle with our treasure, he said: 'Englishmen do not make war against women. I give you each four slaves to recompense you for your loss,' and he turned over sixty additional slaves at no charge."

"Very generous!" the governor said sardonically. "But he did have our treasure, didn't he?" and the messenger said: "Yes. All of it."

"And how did Captain Drake behave when Hawkins did these things?" Ledesma asked, and the man said: "He bit his tongue and obeyed, that's what he did. But I was at the shore when he departed, and he growled at me: 'When I come back as captain of my own fleet, I shall burn every house in this godforsaken town.'"

The governor reviewed the humiliation that had been visited on one of his towns, the great loss of treasure and the peculiar behavior

of his Spaniards: "Our treasurer, he seems to have played the man."
The messenger nodded. "But our soldiers on the scene. Despicable."

"Excellency, when the *Jesus of Lübeck* is in your harbor, assisted
by six other English ships and two French, all guns pointed ashore, it
can be terrifying." He was about to add: "As you will learn in the next
few days when Hawkins and Drake come into your harbor down
there," but he thought better of it and said merely: "As the English
ships left us Drake shouted from the *Judith:* 'On to Cartagena.'"

On 1 August 1568 the English fleet swept down upon Cartagena.
Hawkins wanted only to sell his remaining fifty slaves at customary
profit and trade his ordinary goods for such food and pearls as the
Spaniards might have, but Drake hoped to invade the town and hold
it for ransom. But though the English had a horde of sailors, they
had only three hundred and seventy trained fighting men, while up
on his hillside Governor Ledesma had five hundred Spanish infantry,
two companies of highly skilled cavalry and not less than six thousand trained and armed Indians. So when Captain Drake dispatched
a messenger under a flag of truce to inform Ledesma of the terms
under which the English proposed dealing with Cartagena, the governor refused even to open the letter, advising the messenger to tell
Drake that no one in Cartagena cared a fig what the English did or
did not do, and that the sooner they hied themselves off, the better.

When Drake heard this insulting reply, he sailed as close in as he
could and ordered his guns to pepper the town, but since he was still
not close enough, the cannonballs fell harmlessly and rolled about
the streets. Ledesma, chuckling at the impotence of the braggadocio
Englishman, signaled his heavy guns to fire back, not in salute but in
earnest, but he too missed.

Hawkins, distressed that things were going so badly, landed on
the barren islands south of the city, where nothing was found but
some large casks of wine, which Hawkins ordered his men to leave
untouched, saying: "We're not pirates or thieves." Thereupon
Ledesma sent word that they should feel free to take the wine, since
it was of such poor quality that only Englishmen would drink it.

Actually, the wine was a good vintage from Spain and the English
reveled in it—Drake refused to touch it—and when Hawkins realized
that he must leave Cartagena with nothing accomplished, he ordered
his men to place beside the empty wine casks enough fine English

trade goods to match the value, "to prove that we follow the custom of gentlemen." But as they took the ships back out of the big southern basin, Drake could hear Spaniards in the guard forts laughing at their departure, and his men had to restrain him from firing parting shots at them.

Ledesma and Drake had now had two confrontations without ever seeing each other, and although the rugged little Englishman was bold, the austere Spaniard was resolute and not easily frightened. His fortitude, and that of his agent in Río Hacha, had enabled the Spaniards to rebuff Drake, but the two adversaries knew that the next meeting could be bloody and decisive, though neither could guess where it might occur. Ledesma warned his men: "Drake will be back, of that we can be sure," and Drake told his sailors: "One day I shall humiliate that arrogant Spaniard."

Now that English ships roamed the Caribbean with impunity, trading where and how they willed, this body of water could no longer be considered a Spanish lake. It had become a public thoroughfare, but Don Diego, who had been commissioned to keep it Spanish, believed that if Drake and Hawkins could be lured into some major sea battle, English power might be broken, and he directed his waking hours to that strategy. He was therefore pleased when a dispatch frigate sped in from Sevilla and Española with these orders:

> To Governor Ledesma Paredes y Guzman Orvantes, Greetings. A major fleet of my vessels, twenty in all, will sail from Sevilla to San Juan de Ulúa to load the fall shipment of silver from Mexico. Since Captain Hawkins is known to be in the Caribbean, move the maximum possible fleet from Cartagena to ensure the safe arrival of my fleet at Ulúa, the safe loading of our silver thereon, and the safe departure of my ships for Havana and home. I am aware that you have given yourself the title of Admiral. You should not have done this. But because of your bravery at Cumaná and your good management at Cartagena, I convert your courtesy admiralcy to a permanent appointment as Admiral. King Philip II, his hand at Madrid.

Swiftly assembling nine vessels led by the *Mariposa*, Admiral Ledesma sailed out of Cartagena with sails set to catch the wind that would speed him, he hoped, to Ulúa before Hawkins and Drake reached there, if that was indeed their secret destination. Once again his two Amadór nephews were in charge of the port and starboard wings and his new son-in-law served beside him in the rugged *Mariposa* as vice-regent, a position still undefined. With these reliable aides, Ledesma was confident that he would be able to control the English pirates if they ventured into his lake.

On the voyage north to Mexico the newly empowered admiral assembled his captains and invited an officer acquainted with Ulúa to instruct the men as to what they would find when they reached that vital harbor.

The island of Ulúa, situated about a half-mile from the land-based Vera Cruz, served as protection for the mainland, where the riches of Mexico's silver mines were brought together to wait for the king's galleons from Sevilla to pick them up. Composed of solid rock and defended from the open sea by big reefs, Ulúa was also famous for its dungeon caverns where mutinous sailors and workers were imprisoned.

It was an exciting moment when Admiral Ledesma realized that he had beaten Hawkins north and brought his vessels into the spacious harbor of Ulúa: "There's the great fort, absolutely impregnable. Out there, the protecting reef. Over there, the warehouses of Vera Cruz, crammed with silver bars, and gold ones too. And dead ahead the six ships from Spain always based here to fight off any pirates that might attack." With Ledesma's nine Cartagena vessels, the harbor now contained fifteen ships of war, but anchorages were so plentiful that the harbor seemed almost empty. Even so, innumerable cannon mounted on shore kept the various ships in their sights in case of unexpected trouble. Ulúa was invincible, and Admiral Ledesma, as the senior officer present, would be expected to assume command of its defenses until the empty treasure ships from Sevilla arrived.

Within minutes of anchoring the *Mariposa,* he was in a small boat heading for the fort, and even as he climbed its stone stairway he was giving orders: "These guns to be kept permanently aimed at the entrance to the harbor, in case Hawkins or Drake tries to slip in. And to be manned around the clock, always primed." When he toured the land installations, almost a mile of trenches and protective structures for the guns hidden there, he gave similar orders, and later, when he inspected the three companies stationed permanently in Vera Cruz, he handed them new assignments: "This company to be ready at a moment's notice to run to protect the guns along the shore, this company to rush to the fort, this one to defend the entrance to Vera Cruz itself."

Ledesma went to bed that first night satisfied that as commander in chief of the defenses of San Juan de Ulúa, he had done everything possible to protect the anchorage, so that when he received the surprising news that another Spanish fleet would soon be arriving from Nombre de Dios, a rich depot on the Caribbean side of the Isthmus of Panamá, bringing additional treasure from Peru, he was elated. "When it arrives, this will be the richest port in the world," he boasted to his subordinates, "and the best defended."

Next day a battered Spanish ship limped into port with news of a horrendous hurricane to the south. Its winds had been so violent that everyone assumed that if Hawkins and his English ships had tried to breast the same storm, they must have either sunk or fled home to England badly damaged.

Ledesma was therefore appalled when, two days later, a lookout shouted: "Ships approaching!" and the first vessel into the harbor turned out to be the famous *Jesus of Lübeck,* except that one of her identifying castles was missing. There she came, a misshapen thing though still a formidable warship, followed by the stout *Minion* and five smaller vessels. The invading English ships had so intermingled themselves with the Spanish that the shore batteries dared not fire for fear of sinking their own vessels, and Ledesma's own *Mariposa* was overawed by the powerful guns of the *Jesus of Lübeck,* which pointed directly at it from a distance of yards. Hawkins and Drake, without having had to fire a shot, had occupied the harbor of San Juan de Ulúa, and there was nothing Ledesma could do to eject them.

When he looked out from his headquarters in the fort, Don Diego saw that infuriating *Jesus* riding arrogantly in his anchorage with Drake's insolent *Judith* alongside, and his choler rose to a point that nearly disrupted his reason and certainly obliterated many of the normal compunctions dictated by the sense of honor which is supposed to govern gentlemen in battle. His consuming motivation became "Death to the English invaders," but which tactics would produce the destruction, he did not know, so he played for time until possibilities became clearer.

First, displaying his unquestioned courage, he had himself rowed out to the *Jesus* and climbed onto the deck as she rolled gently despite the fact that she was lacking her towering aft castle. Escorted with due ceremony to Hawkins' cabin, he found the great English captain dressed as if about to attend a court levee: Italian pumps with silver buckles, breeches of finest gray linen, silken shirt with ruffles, heavily brocaded jacket, kerchief also of silk, and cockaded hat.

"We face each other at last," Hawkins said graciously, indicating where his guest might find comfort in a padded chair.

Ledesma wanted to know why the Englishmen had dared to enter into a harbor of such importance to Spain, and Hawkins replied frankly: "Storms drove us here."

"A greater storm will drive you away," Ledesma said, and then, with either exquisite guile or aimless stupidity, he added: "Because very shortly the powerful plate fleet of twenty armed vessels will arrive from Spain to carry Mexico's silver back to Sevilla. They will destroy you in minutes . . . if you are still here."

"English ships can carry silver as easily as Spanish," Hawkins said, to which Ledesma replied sneeringly: "If they can get their hands on it."

The verbal sparring was interrupted by the unannounced appearance of Hawkins' first assistant, a short, stocky mariner with a bullet head and a close-cropped beard. As soon as Don Diego saw him he rose from his chair, pointed a finger, and cried, almost with delight at meeting a man so famous: "You're Drake!" and for the first time the two duelists stood face to face, nodding like gentlemen, each waiting for the other to speak.

Drake broke the silence: "Your people stole forty slaves from me at Río Hacha," at which Ledesma smiled: "But we gave you the free wine at Cartagena . . . when you couldn't get into our city."

Without revealing his anger at this insult, Drake said: "That time we didn't try to force our way in. But next time, beware."

Hawkins broke the tension by saying gently: "That was good wine you let us have at Cartagena, Don Diego, but you must remember that we did pay for it," and at last the three broke into the comradely laughter which often characterized seafaring men. Encouraged by this, Ledesma asked, sailor to sailor: "How did you lose your aft castle?" and Hawkins replied honestly: "These damned top-heavy ships do toss about in a hurricane. We had to chop down the superstructure to keep from capsizing." He added: "When I'm in charge of building ships, no more castles, fore or aft. Low and swift." He paused: "Your *Mariposa* out there is more to my taste," and Ledesma said: "It was Dutch. They know how to build. Your *Jesus* is German. All heavy show."

Now Hawkins laid down the reasonable terms under which he and Drake would leave Ulúa: "I have fifty remaining slaves to sell, and you must buy. Then you must sell us at decent prices adequate food for my seven ships for their return to England. Finally, you must instruct your gunners up in the fort to allow us free passage out of here, and all will be well."

Gently, almost in a whisper, Ledesma said sardonically: "And the scores of my gunners along the shore where you can't see them. I suppose I must instruct them, too." Then he said more firmly: "As my men surely told you at Río Hacha and as I did at Cartagena, my king has forbidden trade with Englishmen. What food we have we require for the incoming plate fleet. And you must realize, Captain Hawkins, no matter how brave you are, our gunners are never going to allow your *Jesus* to leave this harbor. You say she's the property of your queen. Well, Elizabeth will never see her again."

In the silence that followed these words the three seamen bowed, and Ledesma left the ship.

When Ledesma returned to his fort he began to lay his traps. Secretly he moved a hundred shore-based soldiers into positions overlooking the anchored ships, and when they were in place, he imported another hundred to the island to strengthen the fort. He selected one of the big Spanish ships already in the harbor, and instructed her captain: "Convert her secretly into a fire ship," and when the man asked in amazement: "You mean we set her ablaze?" Ledesma said coldly: "We shall, and she must be so filled with inflammables that she will burn herself to the waterline within the hour." He then held long sessions with his two nephews and the vice-regent, during which they laid the most careful plans for assaulting the English vessels when the time came, so that at the end of the plotting each young captain knew the role he must play in destroying the English.

But just as the opening moves of this well-devised plan were to begin, a fleet of thirteen huge Spanish ships arrived from the south, bringing not only a vast cargo of gold and silver from the depot at Nombre de Dios, but also the incoming viceroy of Mexico, Don Martín Enriquez, a devious man always ready to take charge of any complex predicament, which was why the king had appointed him to Mexico where bold talents were needed.

Enriquez now found himself in a most delicate situation. Three fleets contested the occupancy of Ulúa: fifteen Spanish warships, including Admiral Ledesma's inside, thirteen other big Spanish ships outside, and John Hawkins' seven English ships blocking entrance and exit. Cool nerves were required in this impasse, and the three commanders had them.

Hawkins initiated maneuvers by sending his longboat to Viceroy Enriquez's ship with a formal invitation to dinner, and when the Spaniard entered the Englishman's cabin, he was astounded to find Hawkins dressed in his customary well-tailored costume. The Englishman's words were blunt: "Honorable Viceroy, instruct Admiral Ledesma's men ashore to meet the demands I made, and I'll depart in peace . . . no guns fired."

"Now, isn't that ridiculous!" the viceroy replied, almost contemptuously. "You're not in a position to demand anything." Hawkins did not flinch. Instead, he pointed out: "Excellency, your thirteen ships carry treasure and many lives, none so precious as your own but still of some value to King Philip. Your ships lie out there unprotected. If a storm like the one which tore away my aft castle blows up, your ships will be smashed to pieces on those rocks we can see even from here. You know you're in mortal peril and must do something."

Calmly the viceroy began to count aloud: "One, two, three   " When he reached sixty, he shifted his chair and continued: "Sixty-one, sixty-two . . ." on to a hundred. Then he turned again till he faced the spit of land, and the count came to more than a hundred and thirty. "That's how many Spanish guns are pointed at you right now, Admiral Hawkins."

"It's Captain Hawkins. I shall resist the guns, most of which are too far away to reach me, block this harbor entrance, and watch your ships break to pieces in the coming storm."

Since it was clear that no agreement of any kind could be reached that day, the viceroy returned in anger to his fleet, but in the late afternoon he had his boatmen quietly slip him ashore to the fort for a meeting with Admiral Ledesma, and the plan he proposed so shocked Don Diego that he listened aghast and for some moments did not respond: "I have waiting outside a young officer of extraordinary bravery and skill. You will insert him in the negotiating party you are sending to parley with Hawkins, and as the meeting progresses . . ."

He brought his young assassin into the room, and the rogue showed Ledesma how a poisoned stiletto had been hidden in the left sleeve of his jacket in a way that no one could detect. With a flash of his right hand, so swift that Ledesma could not follow, the stiletto was out and poised at Don Diego's heart. "Hawkins is dead," the murderer cried.

"The other members of the team will protect our man," Enriquez explained, "and our little boats will dart in to rescue all when they leap into the bay."

For a long breathless moment Don Diego reflected on the plot, and he recalled that only a few days past in this very room he had said in anger: "I will adopt any stratagem to destroy that pirate." But now he was being presented with one that his sense of family honor would not allow him to consider, and he felt he must, as a gentleman, reject it: "Assassination? Under a flag of truce? A Ledesma flag of truce? Oh no!"

The viceroy, without raising his voice, pointed out in silky tones: "The king has sent me to protect his empire, his gold and his ships. Can you imagine what he might do if I had to tell him that you prevented me from ending the life of that pirate Hawkins?" Then, with the harsh cry "Seize him!" he directed his men to pinion Ledesma: "Shoot him if he tries to hinder us in any way."

Immobilized in a corner, Ledesma heard the young assassin ask: "If I have but one try, which of the two pirates?" and after some hesitation the viceroy said: "Drake's our perpetual enemy. Hawkins we know how to deal with," and the killer said with confidence: "Drake it shall be."

Ledesma, straining against his captors, cried: "No! Let us deal with him decently . . . in battle," but he was silenced.

The young officer, posing as a member of the admiral's negotiating team, was rowed to the *Jesus of Lübeck* under a white flag, and participated in the discussions with Hawkins. The latter, always alert, had noticed that when the young stranger was introduced to him, the arrogant fellow paid no attention, but when Drake joined the company, the Spaniard became all attention and continued to hover near him. Thus it was that when the young man with a cry of *"Muerte!"* whipped out his poisoned stiletto and leaped at Drake, Hawkins was prepared to grab his arm before he could strike.

Ashen-faced, Hawkins now spoke: "They came to us under a flag of truce. Return them so, to the perpetual shame of those who sent them."

With the sham formalities ended, the three fleet leaders, Ledesma, Enriquez and Hawkins, realized that this was now a duel to the death.

No more negotiations, no more naval pleasantries conducted by supposed gentlemen, only heavy gunfire and ships maneuvering for their lives. On the afternoon of 23 September 1568, Ledesma and Enriquez unleashed a furious barrage which sank three English ships— *Grace of God, Swallow, Angel*—while Ledesma's nephews braved English muskets to board the fire ship, set it ablaze, and hoist the sails so that it bore down directly on the *Jesus of Lübeck*. Blazing like an angry volcano, the ship crashed into the *Jesus* and within a minute set ablaze the dried timbers of the stunted castle.

Soon the great vessel, proud flagship of the queen's navy and her personal possession, was ablaze in all quarters and burning uncontrollably toward the waterline. Still she might have fought her way out of the harbor had not Admiral Ledesma, once more in command of the *Mariposa*, dogged the burning *Jesus* and poured in a shattering broadside which penetrated the waterline. With no chance of saving his flagship, Hawkins shouted to his loyal sailors: *"Sauve-que-peut!"* the time-honored French cry "Save yourself if you can." Over the side of the historic ship piled the sailors, dropping onto the deck of an English ship maneuvering alongside. The last sailor leaping down shouted: "Captain Hawkins! Jump!" and as the rescue ship drew away, Hawkins made a wild leap from the *Jesus*, barely reaching the deck of the other ship, from which he would have slipped into the water had not alert seamen seen his plight and grabbed him just as he started to fall backward.

In the lurid light provided by the flames, the few surviving Englishmen who had made it to their two ships still afloat, the big *Minion* now commanded by Hawkins, and the little *Judith* with Drake as captain, watched in anger and futility as the *Mariposa* stood off and continued to pound their *Jesus*, noblest ship ever to have ventured into the Caribbean. It burned until all its timber vanished in smoke. Then, almost as if issuing a final sigh of despair, the flames hissed as they met the sea and the remains of the hulk slipped beneath the waves.

What happened next remains a mystery to English sailors and a permanent blot on the history of the English navy, for Francis Drake, commanding the still-seaworthy little *Judith* with its usual complement of men and adequate supplies, took the phrase *"Sauve-que-peut"* too literally and fled the scene of battle. John Hawkins was left unprotected in his savagely overcrowded, bigger ship, lacking even minimum supplies. In the slang of that day, Drake, the future hero of

English seamanship and as notable a hero as Nelson, cut and ran, leaving his uncle to the mercy of the Spaniard.

Under Drake's able guidance, the *Judith* completed an uneventful passage home to Plymouth, arriving unscathed on 20 January 1569 with mournful news of the defeat at San Juan de Ulúa and the loss of Captain Hawkins and all his other ships. There was deep mourning, for England could not easily absorb such a total defeat and the death of a captain like Hawkins and so many of his men. Queen Elizabeth, still suffering relentless pressure from Spain, had neither ships nor mariners to waste.

And then, five days later, on 25 January, an outlook on a headland near Plymouth sighted an English ship, battered and barely moving, striving to approach land, with no success. Hastening to Plymouth, the watchman alerted the town, and rescue ships were sent out to intercept the *Minion,* whose crew was in such pitiful condition that they could no longer man the yards. When the rugged ship, veteran of a score of battles, finally limped into harbor, John Hawkins, without ever naming his kinsman, gave his report on the defeat at Ulúa, concluding with the bitter condemnation which still rankles in the English navy when men speak of Drake: "So with the *Minion* only and the *Judith* (a small barke of fifty tunne) we escaped, which barke that same night forsooke us in our great miserie."

Of the hundred who had left Ulúa that flaming night in the *Minion,* only fifteen survived the terrible, starving passage back to Plymouth, but in Drake's *Judith,* with its adequate supplies, all made it. Of the fifty slaves that Hawkins took with him to Ulúa, half drowned, for they were in chains in the hold of the *Jesus* and went down with her as the sailors were leaping to safety. The remaining twenty-five reached England in the surviving ships and were sold at considerable profit to householders in Devon.

When Admiral Ledesma brought his seven ships home to Cartagena he announced erroneously that both Hawkins and Drake had perished in the tremendous Spanish victory at Vera Cruz, and that the Caribbean was once again a Spanish lake. He even sent a boastful dispatch to the king:

> *Imperial Majesty, with the death of the two principal English pirates, Hawkins and Drake, your Caribbean is now visited only by Spanish ships, and your treasure armadas from*

*Nombre de Dios now sail to Havana and across to Sevilla
without fear of attack.*

He was crestfallen when the king replied acidly that "apparently the
ghosts of men as daring as Hawkins and Drake must be feared, for
they have been spotted by our spies in Plymouth, Medway and London," and later information reached Cartagena that Drake had been
seen prowling the Caribbean, but since he landed nowhere, attacked
no land settlements, and bothered no Spanish shipping, the rumors
were discounted.

In 1571 these rumors were repeated, but if Drake actually did
visit his favorite sea, he did not behave characteristically, for again he
attacked nothing Spanish. This shadowy behavior did have one curious effect upon the Ledesma household, whose three daughters had
provided the family with several grandchildren, and when their play
became rowdy their nurses disciplined them by warning: "If you
don't behave, El Draque will snatch you and take you away on his big
black ship." And Ledesma noted that even adults mentioned El
Draque in their ordinary conversation: "That is, if El Draque doesn't
come" or "I think the season's past for El Draque."

This nebulous period of "He's still alive, he's definitely dead" confused even Don Diego, who found himself telling the vice-regent: "I
almost hope he is alive! To grapple with him once more. To drive him
from our sea forever." And then, in June 1572, the king sent Ledesma
intelligence which provoked a surge of excitement:

> *On 24 May inst. Captain Francis Drake, who is very much
> alive, supported by his brother John sailed from Plymouth with
> the warship* Pasha, *80 tons, as his admiral and the* Swan, *30
> tons, as his vice-admiral. An ugly whisper current in London
> says that he may be planning to march across the isthmus and
> burn Panamá, hoping thereby to capture our silver coming up
> from Peru and our gold coming down from Mexico. To accom-
> plish this, Drake is taking with him a crew of seventy-three,
> only one of them past the age of thirty.*
>
> *Do you therefore hasten to La Ciudad de Panamá and ensure
> safe passage of our gold and silver to our collection port at
> Nombre de Dios.*

If Drake's ships were not large, they were extraordinarily sturdy and
they must have provided more cargo space than was apparent, for the

king added a postscript about a detail which obviously fascinated him:

> *One English sailor, when put to the torture, confided that Captain Drake had built, on shore at Plymouth, three complete pinnaces of some size, numbered each board, then taken them apart and stowed them in the bowels of the admiral, to be reassembled upon reaching the target area. Be warned.*

Each item of the king's intelligence was correct, for after a swift passage of only five weeks, the two little ships reached Dominica again and entered quickly into the Caribbean, where they sped swiftly to the far western shore at a spot not far from their target town of Nombre de Dios. Here they intended capturing King Philip's gold and silver awaiting shipment to Sevilla.

But a skilled mariner other than Drake had also been laying careful plans, for when the king's directive reached Admiral Ledesma, he sprang into action, and now the value of having members of one's own family in positions of importance proved itself, for when he rasped out orders to his many relatives, he could trust they would be followed. To his son-in-law the vice-regent he said crisply: "Fly you to Nombre de Dios and put everything in readiness." To his two Amadór nephews he said: "Plunge into the jungle and erect barricades to block the route between Panamá and Nombre." To a trusted brother he said: "Hasten to Río Hacha and man its defenses. He might stop there for sheer revenge." To another brother and three cousins he handed over the defenses of Cartagena itself, while he, in obedience to the king's commands, hastened to the city of Panamá, where he assumed overall management of the defense system. When Drake reached the western Caribbean, his purported target, he would find not less than sixteen members of Ledesma's immediate family defending the Spanish interest.

On 12 July 1572, Drake was ready to strike. At a safe harbor some distance from Nombre de Dios, a name that would forever be associated with him, he brought the stacks and spars up from the hold of the *Pasha* and reassembled the three pinnaces he had built back in Plymouth. That night he convened ashore a council of the men who would attempt the great adventure. When one of the young sailors—a boy, really—asked timorously: "How will we know what to do when we reach Nombre?" he turned to the lad and asked softly: "What do you think I've been doing the last two summers when I scouted the Caribbean? Wasting my time?"

And with a stick he outlined in the white sand on which the three pinnaces rested a diagram of the treasure town he had spied upon during his two secret trips: "We row to here, ignore the big ships staring down at us . . . they'll be asleep. We come ashore here, speed directly to the governor's house here. We'll capture silver bars for all . . . and take the governor prisoner. Then rush down here to the Treasure House, strongly built and guarded, which holds what we're really after—great stores of gold and precious stones."

"And then?" a small voice asked, and without pausing to discern who had spoken, Drake said: "Then we throw our treasure aboard our pinnaces, and row back here to the protection of our big guns on the *Pashu* and the *Swan*." He paused, chuckled, then added: "We row *very* fast."

It was, like any Drake enterprise, perfectly planned and resolutely carried out. In fact, during the first stages of the assault on Nombre de Dios it seemed as if the Spaniards were playing parts in which they had been rehearsed by Drake. The sailors in the big ships guarding the port were asleep. Citizens in the plaza did step aside to let the English raiders pass. And the first part of the strategy worked, for at the governor's house, Drake's men did find well over a million pesos' worth of silver bars awaiting transshipment.

But they also found something they did not expect. In the bedroom above the fortune had been sleeping Admiral Ledesma's valiant vice-regent. Awakened by the noise below, he leaped from bed, strapped on his sword, grabbed two pistols, and walked calmly down the stairs, asking in easy tones: "What goes on here?" Then he recognized Drake from events at Ulúa: "Ah, Captain Drake! You survived the great defeat at Vera Cruz?"

"I always survive," Drake said, pointing his pistol directly at the young intruder. The vice-regent displayed no fear, keeping his two pistols aimed directly at the Englishman's heart, so the confrontation was a stand-off. With each man comporting himself with extreme courtesy, Drake said: "I've come to collect payment for the slaves your people stole from me at Río Hacha," and pointed to the stacked silver ingots.

"The king would be most unhappy if you touched his silver," the vice-regent said, and Drake responded by telling his men: "Each free to carry as many ingots as you can manage, then we're off to the Treasure House, where real riches await," but all became so engrossed in stealing samples from the great hoard that they allowed the vice-regent to dash off to freedom.

Irritated, Drake shouted: "Forget this minor booty! Capture the Treasure House, now!" But as the Englishmen sought to rejoin their companions in the plaza, the vice-regent, running ahead at great speed, shouted: "Fire! Fire!" and a bullet cut into Drake's left leg, bringing much blood, which he stanched by keeping his hand in his pocket and pressing its cloth against the wound.

In this way he reached the Treasure House, where another group of his men attempted to blow off the doors. Meanwhile, the vice-regent had rallied his troops and launched a counterattack, which might have annihilated the small English force had not a sailor seen that Drake was bleeding profusely from the leg, and urged him to abandon the scheme.

When Drake hesitated, infuriated by being so close to untold wealth but unable to touch it, four of his soldiers dragged him bodily away from the attacking Spaniards and took him to the safety of the pinnaces.

To the astonishment of the Spaniards in Nombre de Dios, the arrogant Englishmen retreated slowly to an island in the middle of the bay, where they established headquarters with the implied challenge: "Dislodge us if you dare."

The Spaniards then dispatched one of their small boats to the island under a white flag. It bore the vice-regent, who came ashore and addressed Drake as if they were diplomats meeting in formal session at some court. "And when will you be departing, Captain?" the Spaniard asked, and Drake replied: "Not until we capture the gold and precious stones in your Treasure House," and the Spaniard said without changing his tone: "I'm afraid that will be a long time coming, since our guns will destroy you if you move in that direction."

"Only a lucky shot prevented me from ransacking your Treasure House yesterday," said Drake. And the Spaniard replied: "Our men are given to lucky shots."

Then, to rub salt into Drake's wound, the vice-regent said: "I am, as you may remember, son-in-law to Don Diego, governor of Cartagena. He sent me here to forestall you, which I have done, and I'm sure he would want you to know that if you had taken with you the silver you had already captured at my house, you would have had ten million pesos at least, and if you'd broken open our Treasure House, you'd have another hundred million." When Drake did not flinch, the vice-regent added: "Four times now Governor Ledesma and I have frustrated you. Why don't you sail back to England and leave us alone?" and Drake replied without rancor: "I shall accept your counsel and sail back soon, but you and your father will be astonished at what my men do before we go."

The visit ended in such apparent amiability that one English sailor who had waited on them whispered: "You'd think they were cousins," and when the vice-regent reached shore he told the people awaiting him: "A splendid meeting. I was never treated with more civility in my life."

What Drake did as a first step in achieving his revenge was as amazing to his own men as to the Spaniards, for he left Nombre de Dios with its treasure intact, regained his two ships, and with the three little pinnaces trailing behind, crossed back to Cartagena, fired a few insolent shots over the city walls, and came brazenly in through Boca Chica, where he captured several trading ships carrying just the supplies he needed.

Then, in a daring gesture unequaled at the time, he himself sank his little English ship as too small to bother with, assuring his men: "We'll find a better." And he did, capturing a big, fine Spanish merchant ship which promptly became his vice-admiral for the incredible feat he was about to try.

Throwing a few final farewell shots into Cartagena, whose citizens sighed with relief to see him go, he escaped just in time to avoid meeting a very strong Spanish fleet coming in from Spain with hundreds of well-armed soldiers. Once free of that danger, he headed west toward the Isthmus of Panamá, where he revealed his hitherto secret plans to his astonished men: "We're going to march across the isthmus to the city of Panamá, intercept the mule train laden with gold and silver, and earn each man his fortune." There were sixty-nine young men and boys on whom he would depend to accomplish this bold attack against a city of thousands.

The isthmus was a terrible place to cross, filled with mortal vapors, unknown animals, deadly snakes, polluted water, and some of the most obdurate Indians in the New World, armed with poisoned arrows. They were a breed apart, not Caribs from the east, nor Arawaks from Hispaniola, nor Incas from Peru, nor Aztecs from Mexico; they were formidable and made their isthmus one of the most perilous stretches of land in the known world, but it was the link between the silver mines of Peru and the safe harbor of Nombre de Dios. It was this lifeline that Drake now proposed to sever.

But in the months since he had received the latest intelligence on Panamá, a significant change had taken place: Governor Ledesma of Cartagena had arrived to take personal responsibility for the accumulation of treasure in Panamá and its safe transfer by mule train to Nombre de Dios, where his son-in-law was awaiting it.

He had taken all practical steps, having his nephew install forts along the jungle path and training both the muleteers and their protecting soldiers in procedures for frustrating English attacks. The mule train that Governor Ledesma would be leading might be assaulted but it would not be surprised.

On the dark night of 14 February 1573, Drake, having hacked his way through uncharted jungle to avoid the blockades guarding the normal path, secreted his pitifully small contingent at the western outskirts of a little jungle village only a few miles from Panamá, each man dressed in white to avoid confusion in the night fight ahead. His orders were strict: "No man to move until the mule train has passed well beyond us. So that when we attack, it cannot scamper back to Panamá but must stand and fight us. Remember—if we take it, thousands for all!"

His daring plan would have worked except for the wise foresight of Governor Ledesma, who himself was in the lead, tall and silent and resolute.

Just before his mules started into the jungle he had a brilliant idea: "Commander! Move six of our reserve mules bearing nothing to the front, with three peons who will look like soldiers." A stop was made to accomplish this, but as the decoy mules were about to move out, he had a second good thought: "Place bells about their necks," and when this was done the six mules sounded like sixty.

The name of the Englishman they fooled, Robert Pike, has come down in infamy through the annals of the English navy. He heard the spurious mules approaching with their bells tinkling and their attendant soldiers marching cautiously ahead. Eager to play the hero, Pike leaped up as the mules reached him and began assaulting the three peons with loud cries of: "For St. George and England!"

Ledesma heard the strange cry, heard the mules twist in confusion, and heard a shot fired either by Pike or one of the terrified peons. In less than three seconds he uttered his command: "About! Flee!" And there in the darkness Robert Pike's intemperate action and Governor Ledesma's judicious one deprived Captain Francis Drake of more than fifteen million pesos.

There was nothing he could do. By the time he regrouped his men, Ledesma and his mule train were galloping back to Panamá, with swift horsemen spurring ahead to mobilize a force so large and well trained that it would have annihilated the Englishmen had the latter tried to follow. In despair at having been defrauded yet again by Ledesma and his team, Drake could do nothing but retreat through that steaming jungle to find refuge in his waiting ships.

And then, in the depth of a self-inflicted misery over his failure, he proved himself to be one of the most remarkable men of his age. He had not yet performed those feats which would make him immortal—his circumnavigation of the globe, his raid on Cádiz, and his humbling of the Spanish Armada—and so, what he did now in this remote corner of the world with only a handful of men seems all the more incredible.

First, he returned to Nombre de Dios, not boldly as before but creeping like an animal through the jungle. Then, so close to town that his men could hear its citizens at work, he waylaid the next mule train from Panamá, gaining his men a small fortune. But now he had to get his men many miles back to their ships, through that pathless jungle beset by snakes and swamps and insects and hunger, and when he returned to his ships—the original *Pasha* and the one captured earlier from the Spaniards—he realized that they were not seaworthy enough to get him back to Plymouth with his treasure. So, with a defiance that was unbelievable, he sailed back to Cartagena, where a great Spanish fleet rested in the tight inner harbor. Trusting that none of the larger ships could maneuver in time, he sailed right into the large southern harbor, negotiating the narrows of Boca Chica in full sail, spotted the kind of huge ship he needed, boarded it, fought off its sailors, and sailed insolently out of Cartagena—in one fine new ship in place of his two leaky old craft. Firing a final salute at the city which had tormented his dreams, he repeated the oath he had taken long ago at Río Hacha: "I'll be back, Cartagena." And off he sailed for England and the great adventures that awaited.

But when Diego Ledesma Paredes y Guzman Orvantes returned to Cartagena, he could claim the greater victory, for as he reported to his king:

> By following the instructions Your Majesty prudently issued, we have been able to frustrate Captain Francis Drake at every turn. He stole no gold at Nombre de Dios. He did not reach Panamá. He did not capture the richly laden mule train that I organized. And he failed three times to assault Cartagena. Furthermore, we caused him to lose both his Pasha and his Swan, forcing him to flee home in whatever mean ships he could muster.

Admiral Ledesma was not obligated to tell his king the whole truth—that Drake himself had sunk the *Swan* because her smallness was holding him back and, as a gesture of extreme decency, had given his *Pasha* to a group of Spanish prisoners he had been forced to detain. Nor did he explain that what he dismissed as "whatever mean ships he could muster" was really one of His Majesty's finest galleons.

But Ledesma was careful in his letter to point out that the notable victories over Drake had been made possible only by the remarkable performances of several members of the Ledesma family. The king in his next instructions to Cartagena promoted seven of them.

Now came those watershed years when in the lives of great nations some begin to ascend, others to decline. At first none is aware that the shift in power is under way, for the signals are so slight that only a speculative genius could detect their significance. Six men in a small town in the Netherlands finally dare to oppose their Spanish governor and are executed. In the distant Celebes a sultan acquires unexpected power and decides to trade with whatever European ships struggle into his domain. In a small German town a man devises a better way to cut type, and at his press books are printed faster.

In the 1580s, Spain and England were involved in this shift of power, for in the dark, gloomy rooms of the Escorial, King Philip II slowly, patiently conceives and perfects a massive operation which he calls only "The Enterprise of England." By it he intends to settle once and for all his decades-long competition with his sister-in-law, Queen Elizabeth.

But she is not idling away her time, waiting for the enemy to strike.

Under the inspired direction of John Hawkins, she is assembling a fleet of swift, small ships of a radical new design, and assembling the great heroes of England to man them: Howard, Frobisher, Hawkins and, above all, Drake. Every nation in Europe who had spies in either Spain or England knew that an immense confrontation between Spain and England, between Philip and Elizabeth, was imminent.

Governor Ledesma, safe within his walled capital of Cartagena, received news of crucial events that were about to determine the fate of Europe via two ways: reports from Spain alerting him to this possible danger, or warning him about real ones, or simply conveying empire gossip; he also entertained travelers making their way from one Spanish possession to another, and often these men and women provided insights that not even the king in Madrid would have had, or would have listened to if he did have them.

In early January 1578, one of King Philip's swift postal frigates arrived in Cartagena with a copy of the somewhat confused instructions which were being delivered to all Caribbean cities:

> *Some things we know for certain, others are obscure. On 15 November 1577, Captain Francis Drake sailed from Plymouth with five ships, the* Pelican, *100 tons as admiral, the* Elizabeth, *80 tons as vice-admiral. Exact complements are unknown, but among his five ships he can have no more than 160 men, sailors and all.*

> *Where he is heading and what his mission is we have been unable to determine. Our men in Plymouth trapped one of his sailors and shipped him to Cádiz, but protracted tortures revealed nothing and his jailers believe he and the other sailors were not instructed as to their destination. But from the size and care with which the fleet was put together we must assume that he is heading for some major target in your domain. Española? Puerto Rico? Cuba? Cartagena? Panamá? Beware.*

The timetable of reaction was identical in all the sites mentioned. First month: keen apprehension. Second month: some relief in knowing that if Drake was in the Caribbean, at least he wasn't attacking *our* city. Third month: total perplexity, with everyone asking: "Where can that El Draque be?"

It was almost a year before intelligence from Spain finally dispelled the mystery:

We now know for certain that Captain Francis Drake has taken his fleet into the Pacific Ocean, but in passing the Strait of Magellan he seems to have lost all but one of his ships, his admiral originally christened Pelican *but now renamed the* Golden Hind.

Drake caused considerable disruption along the coasts of Chile and Peru but seems to have spared Panamá. No man knows where he will head next, but several of our loyal servants he took prisoner and then released say that while he held them in his power he talked much and freely of sailing either far north to find the lost passage, or far west to China and the Spice Islands, or back through Magellan for a major attack upon the Caribbean. Be alert.

But in early 1579 there came to Cartagena from Panamá via one of the treasure ships sailing from Nombre de Dios, a Señora Cristóbal, sister-in-law of the famous shipowner San Juan de Anton, merchant and government official of Lima in Peru, and she was talkative. As a friend of Don Diego's wife, she naturally stayed at the residence of the Ledesmas, and while there, she spoke incessantly of great events along the west coast of South America, reporting on diverse incidents about which King Philip apparently did not know.

"Contradictions! Contradictions! You, Admiral Ledesma, know better than most what a cruel monster El Draque is supposed to be, how he burns and slays, so that Spanish children are warned to be obedient lest El Draque come for them. A thousand tales are told at night about his evil acts. But I can tell you as a principal authority, for I was there and I met scores who had dealings with him, that in neither Chile nor Peru did he burn or slay. Two hundred sailors and merchants will testify that when they and their ships were captured on the high seas or while dozing in some hidden port, he gave them back their ships after valuables had been transferred to his and saw to it that they had ample food to reach home. Of course, he sometimes chopped down their masts, and on one occasion he wrapped all their sails around their anchor chains and tossed the whole to the bottom of the sea lest they try to follow him or speed ahead to warn others of his coming. He is a terror, no question about that, but he is not a brutal savage like a Frenchman and he does obey the established laws of the sea."

Prompted by Don Diego, she went on to relate her version of

what happened at Santiago in Chile: "All official reports about what happened there are filled with lies. Out of the blue, Drake in his *Golden Hind* arrived at Valparaíso, the port city near Santiago, and within a few minutes had captured the place, which is not surprising, since at the first sight of the strange English ship, everyone in the harbor town, and I do mean everyone, for later I talked with many of these people, fled into the hills. Valparaíso was completely sacked but not burned, and no lives were lost. But what has been kept secret so far is that from Valparaíso, and the settlements leading to Santiago, Drake took a fortune in wealth of all kinds. One English sailor told my brother-in-law while he was a captive on Drake's ship: 'We took so much loot at Valparaíso that we could have turned back at that spot and gone home wealthy men, all of us,' and as a joke Drake allowed Don San Juan to go down into the hold of the *Golden Hind* and see for himself the great bales of stolen wealth loaded at that port. My brother-in-law said it was tremendous, enough, as he expressed it, 'to adorn a dozen cathedrals.' And remember, Valparaíso was only one of his many stops along the coast. Heaven knows what he stole at other towns I haven't even heard of."

Admiral Ledesma, leaning forward in his chair, was mesmerized by what his visitor was saying, for he could not hear enough about the behavior of his mortal enemy: "Tell me, what happened when Drake captured your family's ship, the *Cacafuego*?" At the mention of this famous vessel, Señora Cristóbal threw up her hands and chortled: "It was, as I'm sure you know better than me, properly christened *Señora de la Concepción,* a name singing with piety and grace. It was a noble ship, still is, because although Drake captured it, he handed it back to Don San Juan. It was known, still is, I believe, as the Glory of the Pacific, none bigger, none grander. I sailed on it several times, Lima to Panamá and back, and my cabin was better equipped than my bedroom at home. The name by which it became vulgarly known, *Cacafuego,* is such a terrible embarrassment that I am ashamed even to say it. Who knows how it got such a disgraceful name, I'm sure I don't. Our beautiful ship, besmeared so horribly.* But that's what they call it and that's what Drake called it when he dogged it for five days on its way to Panamá with riches . . ."

Here Señora Cristóbal broke down, but after sniffling for a while, resumed with this information: "A fair portion of what that damned

*Shitfire.

Drake stole from the *Cacafuego* . . . I mean, it took him three full days to move the stuff from our ship to his . . . I call it our ship because certainly a fair part does belong to my husband and me. Our sailors have told me, because as you may know, Drake set them all free to sail the *Cacafuego* back to Panamá after the cargo was transferred from our ship to his. One sailor told me that when the *Golden Hind* broke away to resume its exploration for the Northwest Passage, its cargo of stolen treasure was so great that the ship rode perilously low, and that he had heard one of Drake's sailors remark: 'If we manage to get this leaky basket back to Plymouth, we can all buy estates in Devon'—because the tremendous treasure would be shared by less than a hundred and thirty men. That's all there were on Drake's ship, and to think that these few stormed so many of our seaports, captured so many of our ships, stole so much of our wealth!"

When she composed herself Señora Cristóbal continued: "Did you know, Don Diego, that when Drake captured the *Cacafuego* he first gave its owner, my brother-in-law, a fine cabin aboard the *Golden Hind,* with instructions to his crew that Don San Juan was to be given exactly the same amenities that they would give Drake? And that later he allowed him to return to his more spacious quarters on the *Cacafuego,* where the two men conversed, night after night? Did the reports say that? And when the time came for the two ships to part, Drake gave every sailor on the *Cacafuego* a present of some kind, and he was thoughtful enough to take the presents from the loot he had taken at Valparaíso and not from what he had stolen from their own ship. Some of the presents were quite valuable, tools and things like that which men prize. When he gave Don San Juan three lovely pieces of jewelry for his wife, my brother-in-law said: 'I have a sister-in-law, part owner of this ship you could say, and she adores pretty things,' and Drake sent me these two emerald brooches, also from Valparaíso."

Señora Cristóbal's prolonged monologue had contradictory effects upon Don Diego. On the one hand he was relieved that Drake was demonstrating his demonic power in other parts of the Spanish empire: "Now maybe those governors will appreciate what we had to put up with. Maybe they'll recognize what we did in holding him within bounds."

But then, perversely, he felt a sense of deprivation to think that Drake was performing these daring raids and gigantic thefts in a new area, and he felt deprived of an additional opportunity to frustrate this greatest of the English pirates: "In our ocean we never allowed him to steal a *Cacafuego.*" It was as if he and Drake had been destined to duel in the Caribbean, and to change suddenly the definitions of the contest was unfair. Sometimes, when caught in these confusions, he visualized Drake and himself as medieval jousters, himself the designated hero of a great king, Drake the champion of a beautiful queen, but such imaginings fell apart when he remembered what a mean-spirited king Philip was and how epically ugly Elizabeth was to be a queen.

Don Diego was fascinated when he learned from Madrid that Drake had completed his journey around the world. "Proves he's as obdurate a man as I said in my dispatches," he told members of his government. And to himself he said: I must be the only man in the world who has defeated Drake four times.

He was further pleased in 1581 when broadsheets from Europe arrived in the Caribbean, showing Queen Elizabeth in great lace ruffs about her neck standing on the deck of the *Golden Hind* while Drake knelt before her to receive his knighthood. That flamboyant act, a thumbing of the English nose at the Spanish king, as if she were saying: "See, Philip, how I honor your principal enemy!" seemed to make Drake and Ledesma equal, the former now an English knight, the latter a Spanish admiral.

But Don Diego was not altogether happy when the lisping grandchildren in his family began chanting in the gardens of Cartagena the Spanish version of a new nursery rhyme honoring Drake's promotion:

> *"This man will make*
> *The oceans quake*
> *When he comes to take*
> *Our Spanish Lake . . ."*

At this point one of the children would shout: "What man?" and the others would reply in screaming unison: "SIR FRANCIS DRAKE!"

And then, in late August 1585, King Philip's postal frigates again darted through the Caribbean with ominous dispatches:

Admiral Drake in command of twenty-one ships, nine above 200 tons, including two owned by the queen and manned by practiced seamen like Frobisher, Fenner and Knollys, preparing for some great adventure, we know not what. But from what our spies inform us about the provisioning of said ships, we conclude they must be headed for your seas and your capital cities.

The guess was a shrewd one, for at the end of January 1586 a young Spanish officer arrived with an incredible tale, which he revealed in stammering syllables as he sat with Don Diego in the governor's quarters: "On the first day of the New Year, Drake's fleet sailed arrogantly into our harbor at Santo Domingo on Española, and this time everything was different, for he landed not adventurous sailors but a real army clad in armor. I'm ashamed to report that time and again our troops took one look at those fierce Englishmen, fired their muskets, mostly in the air, and fled, the leaders of our city having done so earlier. By nightfall, Santo Domingo lay completely open to Drake, who came ashore on 3 January to stake his claim to the town and everything in it."

Ledesma was shaken by this appalling news concerning a city he had often visited and with whose governor he had cooperated: "It was no meager town of wooden buildings and grass shacks that Colón and Ocampo knew at the beginning of the century. This was a city of carved stone, broad avenues. If Drake could subdue it, what might he do here at Cartagena?" His lips dry, he asked the messenger: "You mean that after only one day of fighting . . ."

"More like one morning, Excellency."

"And Drake was in control of everything—buildings, homes, churches?"

"Everything. He was especially hard on the churches. Carted away anything of value, and raged when he learned that the priests had sequestered the jewels and other treasures deep in the surrounding woods."

"But why? I know this man. He's not like that." Ledesma was not so much protecting Drake's reputation as he was striving to escape the painful realization that Drake, if he was so changed, represented a much graver danger than before, and the stuttering messenger added fuel to that thought: "To a group of military officers engaged in negotiation with him, he sent his reply in the hands of a little black boy, but one of our officers shouted scornfully: 'I do not accept communications from niggers,' and in his rage he ran his sword clean through the boy's body. The wound was fatal, but the boy did not die before crawling back to Drake, where he gave the officer's answer and died."

"And what did Drake do?"

"On the spur of the moment he grabbed from a holding cell filled with Spanish prisoners two of our monks and had them hanged on the spot. He then sent a prisoner to inform the officers that unless they produced the man who had slain the black boy, he would hang two more monks every morning and afternoon."

"Did you produce him?" Ledesma asked, and the young man said: "We did, and Drake refused to hang him. He threw the culprit back at us officers and said: 'You hang him,' and we did."

"But why is he suddenly so bitter against our church?" Ledesma asked, and the officer said: "I heard Drake say: 'Your Inquisition burns alive any English sailor they catch, if he admits he respects the new faith in England. Many of my men have perished that way.'"

"What did he do with Santo Domingo? If there was no treasure from the churches, no ransom money?"

"He said he would wait three days, and when no money came back from the people who had fled, he began to burn down the city . . . one area each day. The stone buildings that would not easily burn he destroyed by pulling down the walls."

"How did you escape?"

"We have always kept our frigates hidden in estuaries, far from town."

"So Santo Domingo is destroyed?"

"No. After three weeks, even Drake tired. The burning had stopped before I left. About half the city still stands."

"Get some rest. Tomorrow I want you to go fast to Nombre de Dios. To warn them to prepare."

On the afternoon of 9 February 1586, Admiral Sir Francis Drake led his twenty-one ships smartly past the western walls of Cartagena, and disappeared to the south as if ignoring the city and the futile shots fired at him from its forts. But just when Governor Ledesma and his military leaders were congratulating themselves that they had escaped the fearful El Draque, he turned sharply to port and entered

Boca Chica, whose narrow entrance he had forced before. Without slowing his speed, he came into the big Southern Bay, where he anchored in familiar waters, just as if he were back home at Plymouth. Soon his twenty companions were anchored near him and it was obvious that the great siege of Cartagena had begun.

Governor Ledesma asked those about him: "Will he be able to force his way into the city?" and they assured him that the only causeway into the town was much too narrow to permit the entry of soldiers, especially when guns upon the walls would be aimed directly at them. "We're safe," his men repeated, "and since we have adequate food inside the walls and deep wells, there's nothing Drake can do."

But there was. Placing his army troops under the direction of the forceful general who had subdued Santo Domingo so easily, he moved his ships first into the spacious Middle Bay and then into the close-in Northern Bay, from where a few foot soldiers could be put ashore for a flanking attack on the causeway. Then, with great daring, he moved some of his larger ships boldly into the small Inner Bay that gave directly on the approaches to the city.

Never before had Cartagena been attacked by so many troops so capably led, and before Ledesma's generals had time to shift their troops to more favorable positions, Drake's men were upon them. The fighting was unexpectedly fierce, because when Ledesma led the defense of a city the result was quite different from the pusillanimous surrender at Santo Domingo. English soldiers fell, scores of them, and with Ledesma and his three sons-in-law rallying their troops now here, now there, the battle's outcome seemed to hang in the balance, favoring first the English, then the Spanish.

But in the end Drake's superior firepower told, and gradually Ledesma's men were driven back to the central plaza. There, under Don Diego's personal leadership, they fought with extraordinary bravery. But the English smelled blood, principally from their own dead, and with unparalleled fury they literally shoved the Spaniards back, yard by yard, until the assault filled the marketplace, and there the Spaniards, including the fifteen men from the Ledesma clan who had borne arms, surrendered.

Early next morning Drake brought all his ships into the tight little Inner Bay, in which position his gunners could command the city, and only then did he come ashore to savor his capture of Cartagena, a city which the Spaniards had boasted could never be taken. Asking directions to the governor's house, where he could dictate the terms of surrender, he was led to Ledesma's fine residence facing the cathedral, and there he met the sixteen men of the family that had given him so much trouble.

"Admiral Ledesma," he said in the excellent Spanish he had been taught by Spanish captives on his voyage around the world, "your men fought with commendable bravery," but before Ledesma could respond, General Carleill, leader of the English troops, added: "Not only his troops, Drake. He himself," and Drake saluted.

The simple negotiations for a surrender required a frustrating five weeks, for if Ledesma was obdurate in battle, he was a brazen lion when it came to frustrating the English conquerors, regardless of what reasonable demands they made. Backed by no soldiers, fortified by no fleet, and not even supported by the dignitaries of his church, all of whom had fled with their valuables to the mainland hills, tall, composed Don Diego could rely only upon the shrewd counsel of a few of his family members and the solid support of his conquered people.

Drake opened negotiations with a straightforward request, such as he had used with success in dealing with other captured Spanish cities: "I will leave in peace, not one house having so much as a door broken, for a modest ransom, let's say one million ducats* loaded by your men on my waiting ships."

Don Diego said quietly: "But, Admiral, you can see there's simply no money in the city. None."

Without raising his voice, Drake said: "Then you must know from what recently happened at Santo Domingo that if the ransom is not paid, I shall start tomorrow morning to burn a different section of your city each day until Cartagena is no more."

Maintaining the same level of discourse, Don Diego asked: "Admiral, do you wish to be remembered as the Tamerlane of the West, the forever hated scourge of the West Indies?"

During the first four agonizing weeks, when every Spaniard he spoke to, including some members of his own family, advised him to surrender to Drake's demands, at least as far as possible, Ledesma resisted Drake's considerable pressure, and at the same time persuaded the Englishman not to burn the city. In the later stages of negotiations he was supported only by his three sons-in-law, whose

---

*A ducat was worth five shillings sixpence, so Drake was asking for £275,000, which in today's values would be not less than $13,000,000.

wives hiding in the hills slipped messages into the city: "Husband, do not give in," and with this comforting assistance he persisted.

These were four of the strangest weeks in the history of Cartagena, because Drake and Ledesma shared the same house, the governor's residence, and in the evenings they invited whatever leading citizens still remained in the city to lavish dinners at which Drake and the governor tried to outdo each other in courtesies extended to the guests. With Drake speaking in Spanish, Ledesma in English, they discussed subjects of grave importance to their two nations and to the Caribbean in general, each man and his supporters feeling free to express his convictions and defend them.

On one March evening, with spring peering over the mountains to the east, the talk turned to religion, and Don Diego said: "How simple things would be if your Catholic Queen Mary had lived longer in England, with our Philip as her husband, and one great religion binding our nations together. Then we could as allies terminate that damnable apostasy in the Netherlands and wipe out Lutheranism in Germany and live together with France and Italy as our Catholic cousins, one citizenship, one faith."

"I'm afraid differences have grown too great in Europe," Drake said, but then he told the guests: "On my trip around the world, and on all trips, I have prayers nightly and hold services on Sunday, with my own Protestant chaplain, whom I take with me. But never did I demand that any of my men attend my worship if their allegiance was to the faith of Queen Mary and King Philip, and whenever we captured a priest we invited him to conduct prayers for such of our sailors who wished to listen."

This encouraged Ledesma to offer an interesting proposal, which he had often contemplated: "Would it not be best for all if the nations would agree to leave the lands of the Caribbean in Spain's hands and Catholic, as Columbus intended them to be when he found them? But invite Englishmen and Frenchmen and Dutchmen to trade freely wherever they wished?"

Drake asked: "Are you not somewhat hesitant to make such a suggestion, knowing that I sit here with complete power over you, and your city?" and Ledesma said: "I'm not, because I know that whereas you may burn my city, you will not harm me."

Drake laughed: "Even though you tried to have that one with the hidden dagger kill me at Ulúa?" and Don Diego replied: "We had to kill you to get your ships. You don't have to kill me to get my city."

Then, to the surprise of the guests, including Drake, Don Diego said: "Sir Francis, could we perhaps walk upon the battlements, alone?" "No," Drake said. "You tried to kill me once, you'll try again." Ledesma, humbled by this reply of a cautious fighting man, started to apologize, when Drake stopped him: "But I will walk with you if ten soldiers, five Spanish to protect you from me, five English vice versa come along," and the two adversaries, opponents in so many frays, walked out into the starry night—a rigid, imperial Spaniard with a clean-shaven hawklike face, and the short, nervously twitching Englishman with his carefully trimmed beard.

The first words spoken were by Drake as he looked down upon the four bays of Cartagena and their amazing collection of protective islands: "You have here, Don Diego, one of the best anchorages in the world."

But Ledesma felt compelled to speak of more portentous matters, ones that had to be clarified: "You know, Drake, that I did not send the assassin at you," and the Englishman replied: "I knew you did not, could not do it."

"How did you know?"

"From the way you behaved in our past struggles . . . and because my men interrogated that infamous rogue before they let him go. He told us they silenced you in your protests by clapping you in arrest."

The two men walked to diverse parts of Ledesma's uncompleted battlements, always coming to rest at some spot overlooking the Caribbean, that noble body of now placid, now hurricane-driven water for which each of the admirals felt responsible.

"We conduct our battles on a splendid sea, Don Diego."

"Sometimes it seems our fine North Sea was made for battle—a Spanish lake protected on all sides by either islands or great land masses."

"We were made for this sea, Don Diego. We've contested it with honor and bravery. But let me warn you. It is no longer what you call your Spanish Lake. It's now the English Lake, too."

The soldiers who guarded them saw a curiously matched pair, each the best of his race, each touched with greatness. But if the soldiers had overheard the next exchange between these two giants of the North Sea, they would have been bewildered, for Ledesma was singing a nursery rhyme to the Englishman: "My granddaughters . . . goodness, the little ones are *great*-granddaughters . . . they sing it in your honor and to my disgust:

"This man will make
The oceans quake
When he comes to take
Our Spanish Lake . . .
Sir Francis Drake."

"I'll have that engraved on my tomb," said Drake, and the two men rejoined their guests.

At the beginning of the fifth week of this gentlemanly sparring, a plan evolved, not wholly satisfactory to either side. Don Diego, after consulting with his sons-in-law, conceded that he could accumulate not one million ducats in ransom but something like one hundred thousand, and Drake countered: "I want extra for not touching the monastery and an additional bounty for not sacking your churches," and each of his ship captains and his general of troops also had minor demands, so that in the end Ledesma produced far more than he had intended while Drake had to accept far less than he wanted.

It was an honorable peace, grudgingly accepted by each side, but applauded by all Spaniards who had been hiding in the woods and by the English sailors who yearned to get home and claim their share of the diminished booty. During the last days of March, Drake loaded his ships and one bright morning raised anchor and sailed out through Boca Chica. Governor Ledesma, profoundly relieved to see him go, for only he and Drake appreciated how arduous their bargaining had been, ordered the fortress guns to fire a parting salute, which was done to the wild congratulatory cheering of the Cartagenians. Don Diego's courage had saved their city.

And then, to the horror of everyone, Drake's fleet wheeled in the morning sunlight and came sailing right back through Boca Chica and into the Northern Bay, from where it could, if it wished, resume bombarding the city. "Merciful God," Don Diego prayed, "don't do this to me," and his son-in-law the vice-regent had to catch him lest he fall in a faint.

Drake's demands were simple this time: "That big French ship we captured. Badly sprung. I'll need some of your men to help me shift the cargo."

"Yes, yes!" Don Diego cried, nominating his sons-in-law to supervise the work, and during the eight days required for this heavy work—for the French prize was laden to the waterline with goods captured from Spanish ships and towns in the Caribbean—Drake,

Ledesma, the generals of both sides and the clergymen back from their hiding in the hills, met at the governor's house for good talk and the fine wine the priests had hidden from the invaders.

At one such dinner Ledesma introduced his daughters, telling Drake: "It was these three who defeated you. They sent me notes each night from the hills: 'Father, do not give in!' " and Drake, kissing the hand of each, told the group: "The sorrow of my life? I've been married . . . but no sons . . . not even any daughters." Those were the last words he said in Cartagena, but as he returned to his ship to prepare the true departure in the morning, Ledesma, from the ramparts, watched him go, and swore an oath: "I know the kind of man you are, Francis Drake. You'll come back, of that I'm sure, and when you do, I'm fated to dig your grave."

During the various periods of peace, these two adversaries, so different in all aspects, were amazingly similar in the way they diverted their surging energies when not called upon to do battle at sea. Indeed, they seemed almost like twins, so nearly identical were their actions.

Drake served as mayor of Plymouth, Ledesma as governor of Cartagena; Drake on his own initiative provided Plymouth with a reliable water supply, Ledesma gave his city a great wall that enclosed it; Drake served terms in Parliament, Ledesma on the informal Council of the Indies; Drake spent much energy in finding himself an heiress as his second wife, Ledesma had to find wealthy husbands for his granddaughters; and Drake issued an unending stream of advice as to how England could gain control of the Caribbean, while Ledesma counseled King Philip as to how that sea could be made even more completely Spanish.

But since both remained essentially superb naval captains, each read with intense attention a report made by a French spy working in London and circulated to outlying Spanish posts like Cartagena, but also acquired by English spies, who sent a copy to Drake:

> It is believed by all leaders in London that King Philip of Spain is collecting a vast concentration of ships, sailors and armament in the ports of his country in order to make a major attack on England in the latter months of 1587. Queen Elizabeth, when captured, is to be dragged off to Rome to be burned

alive in a public square already identified for that purpose,
Philip will try to become King of England, and the followers of
Luther are to be exterminated. Steps to frustrate Philip's plan
are under way throughout England.

Don Diego found all parts of this remarkable account preposterous,
for as he told the members of his family: "Spain doesn't have enough
ships for such a venture. They would never burn a queen like a common criminal. And Philip has enough trouble ruling Spain, the Netherlands and bits of Austria." But within a week after he delivered this
judgment, the courier from what remained of Santo Domingo
brought an official report from Madrid which clarified much:

In Spanish court circles it is called The Enterprise of England
and it consists of three parts which will be put into operation in
the latter part of 1587. A huge fleet of hundreds of vessels will
leave Spain and sail to the English coast. Meanwhile, a very
large army of Spanish troops will have been assembled in the
Netherlands for transport into England. When Elizabeth is
caught, she will be disposed of; and when Philip assumes the
throne, Lutheranism will be exterminated.

Since these plans are already known in England, extreme se-
crecy is not required, but in speaking of these matters, refer to
them only as The Enterprise of England *and let others guess*
what it consists of.

Before Don Diego had much time for reveling in anticipation of England's humiliation, a correction of the timetable was dispatched
from Madrid, and like many of King Philip's communications, it said
much while explaining little:

The Enterprise of England *has had to be delayed. It will not*
occur in 1587 but will in 1588.

That left the Caribbean governors trying to guess what kind of disaster the cryptic words "has had to be delayed" masked, and Don
Diego had a sinking feeling: I'll wager Drake had something to do
with this. His suspicions were confirmed when a mature, tightly controlled man in his thirties arrived from Spain with shocking news:
"I'm Roque Ortega, Excellency, son of your cousin Euphemia. Fortune did not smile on her, as you probably know. Married to a sea
captain who lost both his ship and his life. One good thing, my father

kept his home at Sanlúcar de Barrameda at the mouth of the Guadalquivir, so I learned about ships."

Ortega was so handsome and compelling in his quiet speech that
Doña Leonora remained in the reception room, contrary to her usual
deportment when her husband had political or military guests.
"What brings you to our city?" she asked, and he gave a remarkable
answer: "Despair and hope." Then he added: "Despair because I
captained one of the king's ships in the disaster at Cádiz . . ."

"What disaster?" Don Diego asked, almost leaping forward, and
Captain Ortega revealed the dimensions of that tragic affair: "In
February of this year the king began to assemble in various ports his
ships intended for *The Enterprise of England.*" Stopping in midflight,
he asked: "You know of the *Enterprise?*" and both Ledesmas nodded.

"I was ordered to take my *Infanta Luisa* down to Cádiz, where I
moored her between two large men-of-war. Throughout March other
important ships drifted in, until by the first of April we had a congregation of at least sixty-six ships—Dutch, French, Turkish, four
English—all of which we had captured in recent months, plus our
own heavily armed warships, more than enough to invade England.
We had the right to be called an armada.

"On the late afternoon of the nineteenth of April, a date I wish I
could forget, an additional twenty-five major ships which I could not
immediately identify sailed boldly into the harbor. But when a pilot
boat went out to welcome them, it learned to its horror that they were
English! Yes, Admiral Drake had sailed right into our strongest harbor."

"What did you do?" Doña Leonora asked, moving closer to catch
details, and Captain Ortega said with modesty: "Like other captains,
I tried to break my *Infanta* from her moorings so I could fight effectively, but before my men loosened one rope, an English ship bore
down upon me, rammed my stern and those of the big ships alongside
me, and then poured cannon fire into our waterlines until we settled
on the bottom without having fired a salvo. It was humiliating."

In obvious disgust with himself, Ortega said: "Lost my ship before the battle started." For some moments he sat shaking his head,
thus providing Doña Leonora with an opportunity to study his
manly features and the way his lean face seemed to announce quietly: "I am ready for any challenge." But then he added details that
were even more infuriating: "As night fell, Drake's ships played havoc
with our vessels, chopping and snarling and setting fires, and we were

powerless to halt him. Our shore batteries, on which we depended, could not shoot at his ships without hitting ours. In the morning Cádiz Bay was littered with sunken ships, all ours, and the bodies of Spanish sailors."

Ortega stopped, looked at Governor Ledesma, and said, with his hands raised upward: "Not one of our anchored ships was able to break loose and give him battle, and those that tried he sank. Night fell, but not darkness, for the flames of our stricken ships made the carnage visible, and when dawn came, Drake finished off the cripples, sending more of our good men to their graves in the harbor."

Recollection of the tremendous losses was so painful that for some moments he could not speak, but when he did he summarized the tragedy in a few words: "On the morning of the nineteenth we were the most powerful fleet in Europe. At midnight of the same day, practically destroyed."

Don Diego, as a fellow seafaring man, felt no embarrassment in probing: "How many ships did we lose?" and Ortega said: "So many that the *Enterprise* cannot go forward."

In the lull that followed, Doña Leonora asked: "That was obviously the disaster. What was the hope?" and Ortega said quietly: "When I reached home, far from Cádiz, my mother wept: 'Like your father, you lost your ship; you were lucky you didn't lose your life.' Seeing that there were few prospects for me, she said: 'You have an uncle of sorts who's governor in Cartagena. Try your luck there,' and here I am. You are my hope."

At this honest disclosure, Doña Leonora looked at her husband and raised her eyebrows in a secret gesture which meant "Why not?" and he nodded slightly to indicate "Go ahead," so she said brightly: "Captain Ortega, you must remain with us till you find quarters," and he did not engage in mock humility: "That would be most generous. But a captain with no ship has little to offer in return."

In the days that followed, Doña Leonora saw with approval that her husband and Ortega got along handsomely, for they were both active men who required few words to belabor attitudes on which they agreed. On many evenings they walked together along the battlements, staring down at the landlocked harbor: "Was Cádiz much like this?" and Ortega would place the Spanish ships among the islands, then show Drake sweeping in to create his havoc: "My ship? I never got her away from her mooring!"

Don Diego said: "The loss of a ship like yours is no worry, really.

To you, yes. To the king, no. What really hurts is the rumor that the wily John Hawkins is building a score of ships to bring against us. Men like Drake will devise ways to protect themselves when we strike. More English ships, more English sailors."

Ortega added: "And more ammunition when the fighting begins," and Don Diego concluded: "As a seaman who has fought Drake many times, winning and losing, I know how tenacious he can be."

They studied the sea in silence, then Don Diego asked: "Will you be going back to fight him?" and Ortega said: "I'd swim back to have the chance."

But other important matters in Cartagena intruded, and *The Enterprise of England* was temporarily forgotten, because if Don Diego was constantly striving to enhance his family's fortunes, his wife was equally determined to improve hers. Her campaign began one evening at supper when she asked bluntly: "Captain Ortega, are you married?" and he replied: "Was once. She's dead," and no more was said.

Señora Ledesma had on the island of Española a cousin her age who had a daughter with a lovely name, Beatrix, but no face to match. With Santo Domingo, the capital of Española, having been recently sacked by El Draque, ordinary social life had been disrupted, so that poor Beatrix had slimmer chances than ever of catching a husband, and Doña Leonora decided to do something about it.

As swiftly as the dispatch frigate could get to Santo Domingo and back, it deposited on the docks of Cartagena a young woman twenty-two years old and extremely seasick from a rough crossing. Her whole intention was to climb into bed at her cousin's house and feel sorry for herself, but Leonora would have none of that, for it was important that Captain Ortega see Beatrix soon and in the best possible light. So Leonora summoned two of her married daughters to the bedroom where Beatrix supposed she would be resting, and with the seasick girl listening, the three Ledesma women surveyed their problem.

"First thing, fetch her some salts," Leonora said, and when these were waved under her nose the two younger women sorted out the newcomer's clothes and expressed disgust with what they saw: "Have you nothing decent, nothing whatever?" and when Beatrix broke into tears, Leonora slapped her: "Your whole future is at stake, girl. You don't find a man like Captain Ortega very often," and together the three women worked a miracle on their distressed cousin.

Borrowing one of Juana's fine dresses, they called to the kitchen for a seamstress to pinch in the waist, and María, the middle Ledesma daughter, gave her a pair of shoes and a lovely fawn-colored shawl for her shoulders. Then, squeezing her forcefully into the dress until she cried "I can't breathe!" they told her: "You don't have to. Until after you meet him."

When the transformation was complete, with her hair exquisitely done and cosmetics applied to her pallid face, she was what she had always been, had she but known it: a lovely young Spanish woman, not dazzling in beauty but adorable in her vulnerability, the beauty of her posture and the quivering about her mouth as she whispered to herself: "I will not get sick. I will not get sick."

Indeed, when Doña Leonora and her daughters propelled her into the main hall where Captain Ortega waited, Beatrix was truly the finest-looking of the lot, her wan face, perfectly powdered, giving her the appearance of a princess in a fairy tale. Small wonder that Ortega was taken with her immediately, but he had to wait for a dance because others reached her first.

The courtship progressed at a reassuring pace, orchestrated by Doña Leonora, and she would surely have had her cousin married had not imperative news reached Cartagena in January of 1588:

Admiral Ledesma, Greetings! The Enterprise of England re-*sumes. Assemble all available heavy ships, crews and repair materials and report immediately to Lisbon. There you will form part of the train carrying supplies for the Duke of Parma's troops, whom you will transport from the Netherlands across the Channel for their invasion of England.*

To seafaring men like Ledesma and Ortega the message brought both joy and irritation—joy for having another chance to fight Hawkins and Drake, irritation that their ships would carry not the invading army but only cargo to Spanish soldiers already waiting in the Netherlands. "Of course," Ledesma said reassuringly, "as soon as we deliver the goods, we'll ferry them across the Channel and land them in England. We'll still see a lot of the fighting."

Despite his disappointment in not being part of the battle fleet, he told his wife: "It's great for a man my age to be back on the deck of his ship. It takes a steady hand to manage the *Mariposa* and I can do it."

She thought him surprisingly old for such adventures and was downright disgusted when she learned that Captain Ortega was leaving too. She realized that this ended any hope of an immediate marriage for Cousin Beatrix, but she had faced such disappointments before, and surprisingly often they worked out well when years were used as the measuring stick instead of days.

She and Beatrix found solace in the fact that their men would be participating in this great adventure in a ship as sturdy as the *Mariposa,* for they had been assured: "That one will get us there and back." There were tearful farewells as the odd assortment of ships weighed anchor and headed out into the Caribbean, firing salutes as they passed through Boca Chica and coasted under the battlements of Cartagena.

Now came the months of tension. Since all available ships had been requisitioned by King Philip for his vast Armada, the mightiest invasion fleet ever to have been assembled, none were available to carry news to Spanish possessions in the Caribbean. The citizens of Cartagena remained in darkness while their home country fought great battles in its quest for domination of the known world.

Doña Leonora and her daughters met regularly with their priest, who preached but one message to the citizens of his walled city: "Since our men are fighting to protect God's true religion, He will never allow heretics to win," and these words gave Doña Leonora comfort.

But when months passed with no news, she reasoned with her daughters: "If the news was good, surely the king would have spared at least one small ship to speed to us. No ship? No news? Disaster." Gradually this conclusion was reached by so many that even the priest's reassurances began to sound hollow, and many whispered: "Who cares about victory? Will our ships return? Have our sons and husbands been lost in wintry seas?" and gloom prevailed.

Then one morning a lookout cried the joyous news: "Sail on the horizon!" and all ran to the ramparts to see the sturdy old *Mariposa* come down from the north as if arriving from a routine trip to Cuba, and as it came parallel to the city and continued down to Boca Chica and the entrance home, watchers swore that they could identify this man or that, and word passed that Admiral Ledesma was among those returning, but others denied that anyone could be recognized from such a distance.

It was a most painful hour and a half as the lumbering Dutch ship sailed far south to make the turn, then disappeared behind the forts at Boca Chica, only to reappear in the lower bay in what looked to be excellent condition—"She has her masts. No holes in her sides"—and as the ship grew larger coming up the bay, watchers could accurately pick out this man and that. Then came a triumphant cry: "Ledesma! Ledesma!" and the governor's white hair could be clearly seen.

When the ship gave no triumphant signal, Doña Leonora whispered: "It did not go well," and as she watched the close approach of the *Mariposa* she saw something which caused her heart to stumble. Don Diego, having brought his ship home from the wars with at least some of its crew, was so grateful to provident God who had guided him through terrible battles in the English Channel and fearsome struggles with his ancient adversary Drake that he fell upon the deck of his ship as it touched the wharf and kissed the planking. It was obvious to his wife that he was overcome with emotion, but she also saw that he was too weak to regain his feet without assistance from Captain Ortega, and she thought: The old man has suffered some terrible defeat, and her heart ached with love for him.

But as she watched him steady himself against Ortega's arm, she saw him stiffen in the old way, throw back his shoulders as if facing one more enemy, and come ashore, where with a raised arm he silenced the cheers which would be deserved only by returning conquerors. Walking directly to where the assistant governors of the city stood, the ones who had protected Cartagena in his absence, he stood before them, nodded gravely, and announced in a clear voice: "Spain has suffered a terrible defeat. Let the bells be tolled," and all that mournful day the bells of Cartagena struck the slow, heavy notes that signaled grief.

In the afternoon, while the bells were still mourning, Ledesma had the courage to assemble the leaders of the city, and in subdued tones he and Ortega reported on the encounter of the big, slow ships of the Armada with the smaller, swifter ships of the English.

"It started with a monstrous humiliation," Ledesma said, and Ortega confirmed: "We were not allowed to be a fighting ship. Nor did we even carry fighting weapons. When we reported to Spain to take our place in the fleet, we were sent to the rear." He was too ashamed to reveal what happened next, but Ledesma was not.

"In the holds of our ship where we expected to carry guns and ammunition, what do you suppose we loaded? Hay. And in the holds where we could have managed heavy field guns and cannonballs, what did we get? Horses." He looked at the floor, then said softly: "You remember how we sailed out of here. Flags, salutes, men ready to die for the glory of God and King Philip. What we were asked to do, instead, was feed horses."

"But you did deliver them to the troops?" a counselor asked.

"We never found the troops," Ortega said. "They were supposed to be with Parma, a great general, somewhere in the Netherlands. He never appeared."

"You didn't invade England?" several men asked at once, and Ledesma said with a bitterness which had been growing for months: "We never got close to England. We never even got close to her ships."

"But the great battle? Our fleet against theirs?" men asked in amazement, and Ledesma allowed his captain to explain: "We sailed right up the Channel, in splendid formation. Every one of our captains knew just what to do."

"And then? In the battle?"

"We never had a battle. The English refused to come at us from the front, where they were supposed to. We'd have destroyed them. Instead, they came pecking at us from the rear . . , sending fireboats among our ships to disrupt us."

The officials, appalled at what they were hearing, looked to Ledesma for explanations, and he said: "He speaks the truth. We never had a battle. We sailed up the Channel, fighting off the gnats that buzzed around us, and never made contact with our land troops. Sailed right past, and before long we were so far beyond England that their ships stopped chasing us. We escaped."

"But your duel with Drake, the one you told us about when you left . . . the one you were burning to fight?"

"We never saw Drake, nor Hawkins either. They darted in and out among us like falling stars at night."

"They were there," Ortega said. "We could tell by the way the English fought, but we never saw them."

"But your fleet did escape?" a local leader asked, and Ledesma nodded: "We lost a few ships, but most escaped," and Ortega said: "Our admiral here received honors for what he accomplished. He started the invasion in command of twenty-three cargo ships and brought twenty of them safely through battles and attacks of fire and the heaviest gunfire Drake and the others could throw against us. Cartagena can be proud of its governor."

"But the horses?" asked a man who had a country estate outside the walls. "What did you do with the horses?" and Ledesma turned away and refused to say it, indicating with his left hand that Ortega should: "When we couldn't find the cavalry that was supposed to get them, we thought we would carry them back to their farms in Spain, but the order came: 'As we start on our long sail around Ireland, all ships must be lightened.'"

"And the horses?"

"We threw them overboard. In the middle of the Channel."

"Were they able to swim to shore?" the countryman asked, and Ledesma had to say: "No one knows."

At this point the listeners shifted in their chairs, obviously eager to hear more details about the fighting, and one asked: "But if you escaped up the Channel, and fled around Scotland and Ireland, most of your ships must have made it back to Spain. So the defeat couldn't have been as bad as you made it sound at first," and Doña Leonora, who had been listening intently to this broken narrative, saw her husband's shoulders sag and his face pale.

"Too much for one day, my dear friends. We're home and six of the other ships from Cartagena will be coming in too, I trust. We'll talk later," and without further amenities he left them with Ortega, who continued the dismal story, except that he also avoided any discussion of the passage of the ships back to Spain.

When Doña Leonora led her husband to bed she saw how exhausted he was, not from the sea voyage home, for he loved his old *Mariposa* as one of the sturdiest ships in the ocean, but from the anguish of being forced to report on the humiliations and disasters that had overtaken the little fleet he had taken from Cartagena. As soon as she observed his response to her first questions she knew she must stop and allow him to sleep. She asked: "Did your other ships carry horses too?" and he groaned. Then she asked: "If you saved twenty of your ships in the battle, how many did you get back home to Spain?" and he turned his face to the wall, indicating that he could accept no further conversation. He was one more valiant warrior, the same in all centuries, who had come home from battle unable to explain to his wife what had happened.

Next day, however, when he again met with the elders of his city he was prepared, with Ortega's help, to speak frankly about the catastrophes in which he had participated: "We were led by a complete ninny, the Duke of Medina-Sidonia, a man who hated the sea, who got violently sick when a ship rolled, and who had warned the king: 'Since I do not know how to fight ships, I will do poorly,' and he did. The English outsmarted him at every turning of the tide."

"Was he a coward?"

"Spaniards are never cowards . . . but they can be stupid."

But the men kept asking: "You sailed that great fleet to England and never fought a battle?" and Ledesma said: "Not in the old style, no. Great ships lunging at each other? No. More like trained dogs worrying a bull till he staggers."

"And you never saw Drake or his ship?"

Very slowly Ledesma said: "I never . . . saw . . . Drake," but Ortega voiced what he had intimated the day before: "But we knew he was out there," and when someone asked how, he said: "By the results."

"Now tell us . . . what happened to the fleet as it passed Ireland?" and bracing his shoulders, Ledesma turned to his captain: "Ortega, what happened to our sanity at Ireland? Why did we Spaniards throw the whole thing away?"

The question was one that would haunt naval historians for the next half-millennium, and even then no sensible answers would be produced. However, Ortega, as one of the few captains who had brought his ship safely through the disaster, did know certain basic facts: "We had no proper charts. They failed to show how far Ireland jutted out into the Atlantic. When our ships turned south prematurely they ran into headlands that shouldn't have been there, and driven by the gale blowing so strong from the west, they couldn't tack to escape those terrible rocks."

The tale having been properly launched, Ledesma, always willing as the commander of an operation to assume his share of the blame when things went wrong, said quietly: "We should have had a safe run home to our Spanish ports. No English ships were harassing us. But we lost twenty-six of our largest Armada vessels . . . an entire navy . . . not one ship down as a result of enemy action. In the wild storms of the North Atlantic, sheathing came apart. In mournful darkness they collided and sank. But most of them, running before the fierce winds of approaching winter, crashed head-on into those dreadful headlands of western Ireland, drowning half the crew, depositing the others near naked on the inhospitable shore . . ."

Shaking his head at the magnitude of the disaster he had escaped because of his own superior seamanship, he indicated that Ortega should continue: "Tell them of what happened when our shipwrecked men were lucky enough to make it to land," and the captain revealed an incredible tale: "By the time we left Spain for here, all we had were rumors, but I questioned three of our sailors who escaped the terrors of Ireland, and they told a story of such horror that it flashed through the fleet. It seems that whenever a Spanish crew reached shore, one of three things happened. Some were stripped naked by the wild Irish peasants and most killed on the spot. Those who survived fell into the hands of Irish landlords who sought favor with the English and were either slaughtered or turned over to them. And those who surrendered honorably to English officials were murdered one by one, and in public, to teach them a lesson."

Later, when rumor could be hardened into demonstrable fact, it would be determined that six thousand of Spain's finest sons landed on Irish beaches after their ships sank, and all but seven hundred were murdered.

Ledesma, looking at his fellow Cartagenians, said: "The brave young men who sailed with me from this city . . . so valiant . . . so indestructible. We brought them through a hell that few men ever know, and we held them together . . ." He clenched his hands and pounded at air: "We brought them through everything Drake could throw at us. And then to lose them to English murderers in Ireland. Oh my God . . . my God."

The listeners could see his fists tighten and the muscles in his neck stand out: "Yes, the English murdered our men, shamelessly, but we'll be avenged. I'm certain that before I die, El Draque will return to these waters. He must . . . And when he comes, if God allows me strength, I shall do battle with him once more, and I shall hound him to his grave." And from that moment Ledesma manifested the kind of blood hatred of the Englishmen who had murdered his sailors that Francis Drake had always had for Spaniards who had burned his sailors. On neither side would the passionate enmity be allowed to wane.

The tragedy that overtook Admiral Ledesma in his futile confrontation in Europe was so harrowing that in an effort to forget it, he turned his remaining energy to more humane concerns, and day after day he roamed his city, identifying projects that must now go forward: "I want to finish the battlements to enclose the entire city. We need better wells . . . a fort to protect Boca Chica . . ." And once when he was inspecting a section of wall he stopped suddenly and turned to face Ortega: "I've watched you carefully, Roque." This was the first time in this chaotic year that he had ever called his kinsman anything but Captain. "And I've seen that you're a man of honor. We'd not have brought the *Mariposa* back with any lesser captain." Ortega saluted. "And I'm growing old, sixty-one this year, very old I find, and have no son to carry on my name. Why don't you become Roque Ledesma, and plan to take my place when I'm gone?" And Ortega saluted again, speechless.

Then a happy idea struck: "Look, you're already entitled to the name Ortega y Ledesma. Change it to Roque Ledesma y Ledesma and let people guess if it represents some kind of incest." He laughed at his joke, but still Ortega did not speak, so the admiral left his suggestion hanging.

He soon learned that his widowed captain was attending to a very serious matter pushed upon him by Doña Leonora, who had resumed her determined campaign to find a proper husband for Señorita Beatrix, her niece from Española. "I want you to give Captain Ortega a week of rest, Diego," she said, and during those relaxing days she kept Beatrix constantly before Ortega, and whereas in the first two days he was still preoccupied with Spanish defeats, on the third he began to notice how charming Beatrix was, but the girl remained too shy to press her attention upon him. So Doña Leonora knew it was incumbent upon her to intervene. "Captain Ortega," she said boldly, "surely you've noticed that Beatrix is quite taken with you . . . your manly ways and all." He coughed modestly.

"She's a dear girl, really she is. While you were away at war I had a chance to see what a splendid wife she'd make." When Ortega hesitated, she added: "You're not getting any younger, Roque . . ." and with her unprecedented use of his first name he recalled that the admiral had done the same when speaking to him about the name change, and all of a sudden he could see the shattered fragments of his life—his impoverished mother, the loss of his wife, the defeat in England, the uncertainty in the New World—mending themselves in a grand coalescence with the Ledesmas of Cartagena. He would marry their niece, adopt their name, and enter the grand alliance they were building for themselves in this rich and famous city.

In a low voice he asked: "Doña Leonora, would I have your permission to ask your husband for Señorita Beatrix's hand in marriage?" and she reacted with opened mouth and arched eyebrows as if the idea were his alone and somewhat startling: "I think he would listen," and she left with the satisfaction of knowing that she had solved the problems of yet another of her numerous relatives.

But when the vice-regent, now a senior official, heard of the proposal to give Ortega a new name, he lodged serious objections: "Don Diego, where is your sanity? People are already whispering: 'This town isn't Cartagena, it's Carta-Ledesma.' If you make this name change, you'll be throwing your nepotism in their faces."

Don Diego promised that he would think about the danger, but that night as he strolled upon his battlements he thought: The most permanent goal a man can achieve is to use members of his family to weave a network of influence and stability. Look at Drake. In shadows, for fame is transient. Look at what happened to Cortés. The favor of a king is a fragile reed to lean upon. But to have your daughters' husbands in positions of power, to see your sister's sons with good salaries, that's permanent. That you can depend on. What did Drake say that last night? He grieved that he had no sons? Well, I too have none, but I'm going to get one, Roque Ledesma y Ledesma, fine name, and those who don't like it can go to hell! So the name change took place.

The seven years following the disaster of the Armada produced little excitement in the Caribbean, primarily because Drake left it alone, and without him to duel, the place seemed unimportant. Mule trains crossed the isthmus from Panamá to Nombre de Dios and off-loaded their treasure onto ships which Cartagena's flotilla escorted to Havana, where bullion fleets were organized for the passage home to Sevilla, and in these years not a ship was lost.

Word did filter through that Drake had taken as his second wife an heiress of good family and had been elected as the Plymouth Member of Parliament, where he occasionally spoke on naval and military matters. Lured out of retirement to command an attack on the northwest coast of Spain and Portugal, he made a hash of the effort and was rebuked by being forced into what everyone supposed was a permanent retirement. After that the Caribbean heard nothing of him and people began to suppose that both he and his older companion, Hawkins, now Sir John, were dead.

And then, in late February 1596, came the revitalizing news that Don Diego had been awaiting for so many years. It came not from King Philip in the Escorial but from one of his ministers in Madrid:

> Our trusted spies inform us that on 25 January of this year that infamous heretic, Elizabeth of England, commissioned her two knights, Drake and Hawkins, to lead a fleet of 27 war vessels to assault our cities in the West Indies. King Philip is old and ailing. Give him the heads of these two pirates before he dies.

The average Spanish governor experienced a moment of dizziness when he learned that both Drake and Hawkins were coming to assail him, but not Don Diego, who reveled in the realization that both his mortal enemies would be coming into his predilected waters at the same time. "God is being good to me," he told the men of his family, and they reassembled their team to frustrate this final challenge of the English sea dogs.

With maps spread on tables, the Ledesmas concerted their strategies, guided always by Don Diego, who had a sixth sense as to what Queen Elizabeth would instruct her admirals to do and what precise steps they would take to do it. In their planning, the men referred invariably to Drake first and Hawkins second, it having been agreed in all European fleets that now the old uncle took orders from the younger and bolder nephew. Don Diego, in framing his strategies, thought only of Drake, and directed the vice-regent: "Since you beat him back at Nombre de Dios that other time, go back and do it again." When the young man demurred: "I doubt Drake will bother with so small a town," Don Diego snapped: "He's Drake. He'll be drawn to that spot the way a shark is drawn to the smell of a wounded body. He seeks revenge."

Convinced that Drake would make another attempt to sack Panamá, Don Diego assigned his two other sons-in-law to build a dozen barricades along the jungle trail the Englishmen would be attempting to follow, and to poison all available springs. Then he looked at his most recent bright hope, Roque Ledesma, and with that good sailor he pored over the charts of the Caribbean and decided: "He will not come to Española, for he destroyed it last time. Where will he come?"

After considerable speculation the two plotters decided that Drake would invade Puerto Rico, where the rich capital of San Juan would offer the kind of treasure he had taken last time at Santo Domingo: "You and I will go there, Roque, to make his life miserable."

"You never take Hawkins into your calculations," one of his nephews pointed out, and Don Diego explained: "Hawkins is like me, predictable. We fight him as we find him. But with Drake, you have to be guessing all the time, for his brain is like a hummingbird. His wings never rest."

In conclusion, he made an arbitrary assignment. To the Amadór brothers, his loyal supporters for decades, he said: "Go back to Río Hacha. He's sure to strike there at some point in this rampage," and when the brothers argued truthfully that Río was now a desolate place with very little to attract the avarice of a pirate, Don Diego replied: "His memories are there because it was there he suffered his first defeat. He'll be back."

But then Roque voiced the greatest objection of all to this dispersal of the Ledesma forces: "You're leaving Cartagena unprotected," and Don Diego said: "He'll not come here again. Because he conquered this city once, no need to repeat. Puerto Rico's a new target. All the others are defeats that have to be avenged."

"Then why won't he go back to San Juan de Ulúa? His greatest defeat of all?"

This was a penetrating question which the old warrior had to weigh carefully, but in the end he gave the answer of a very tired man: "If he goes to Ulúa, and with Hawkins present, there would be reason . . . well, then the job of fighting him is Mexico's." He pondered this and added: "Our job—protecting the Caribbean—is demanding enough."

Spring dragged on, with no substantial news of Drake's movements, but in mid-April news of an entirely different kind was rushed to Cartagena. It came from San Juan in Puerto Rico and was substantial indeed:

On 9 April there limped into the harbor of this city the king's great galleon *Begoña,* flagship of the treasure fleet. Demasted in a violent storm and carrying 300 souls and more than 2,000,000 pesos in gold and silver, it had no possibility of resuming its homeward journey and is now safe in our sanctuary. Its cargo of bullion has been hidden properly ashore where it will be retained until we learn of Sir Francis Drake's plans. In the meantime, other cities should rush all spare force to Puerto Rico to protect this great treasure so badly needed by the king for his ventures.

Now came anxious moments for Don Diego. He wanted to rush to Puerto Rico to help defend that great treasure and was inwardly gratified that he had some months ago deduced that Drake would be heading there, but he did not care to make any move until he was certain that Drake's fleet had actually sailed. In the third week of September word flashed through the islands and the Main: "Drake has sailed!" but shortly thereafter came the perplexing news that Drake and Hawkins had stopped along the way to lay a nonproductive siege at the Grand Canary. "Ah ha!" Don Diego cried when he heard the news. "If he's come by way of the Canaries, he's heading for Puerto Rico," and next day he dispatched the nineteen men of his family to their various posts.

When Don Diego approached San Juan in the *Mariposa* and saw the setting of roadstead and harbor in which he would be fighting what would surely be his last great duel with these two intrepid Englishmen, he was struck by a disarming thought: Good God! We're all old men, fighting as if we were boys! Drake was fifty-two that summer, Hawkins sixty-three, and himself an ancient sixty-seven: But we're still the best on the oceans.

As he entered the harbor Don Diego saw that reports about the loss of the *Begoña* had been accurate: demasted in a fierce Caribbean storm, she had no chance of proceeding to Spain, and sailors in the escort boat shouted: "We have her two million deep in the fortress over there. Drake'll never touch it." When he landed he found surprises awaiting, for the local commander informed him: "We've decided there's no hope of fighting those two on the open seas. All ships inside the harbor." Much as he disliked such restriction, he had to obey, so against his better judgment, he berthed his stalwart flagship inside. But when the last of his incoming fleet was safely tucked away, the commander startled him by announcing: "Tomorrow we bottle up the harbor by sinking what's left of the *Begoña* right in the middle, and four smaller ships on either side," and although both Ledesma and the captain of the big galleon protested, this was done.

Since Don Diego's little fleet was now imprisoned so it could not get out, nor Drake get in, he asked the local authorities: "What am I supposed to do?" and they told him curtly: "Help install the extra shore batteries," so he and Roque removed all guns from the impounded ships and placed them at strategic points atop hills overlooking the approaches to the harbor.

While the Spaniards worked with belated speed to ready their defenses, they supposed they would be allowed three or four weeks for the task, but that was not to be. However, two items of extraordinary good luck now occurred to give them an advantage. As the English fleet sailed into the Caribbean, two of its ships lagged and alert Spanish frigates captured one of them, learning that Drake and Hawkins would arrive shortly at Puerto Rico. Armed with this precious knowledge, the scouting ships sped to San Juan, shouting the news as they arrived, so that when the English ships appeared every Spanish gun would be ready to fire directly in their teeth.

The other happening was one the Spaniards could not be aware of at the time, but no sooner had this English fleet left Plymouth back in August than its two admirals fell into violent dispute. Hawkins, as the older and more prudent, had wanted to cross the Atlantic at top speed and strike Puerto Rico before its defenses could be strengthened. Drake, however, insisted upon fighting a chain of fruitless battles on the way out, and thus wasted weeks.

Even now, on the eve of battle when every second was going to count, Drake demanded another useless layover in the Virgin Islands, hardly a day's sail to Puerto Rico. Hawkins protested vehemently, failed once more to convince his impulsive associate, and realizing that their final adventure in the Caribbean was doomed because of Drake's intransigence, he retired to his cabin, turned his weary body to the wall, and died.

After the burial of Hawkins in the sea on whose glorious surfaces he had gained renown, Drake arrived tardily at San Juan, where the stout land defenses organized by the Spanish generals easily repulsed him. Never did he get close to forcing his way into San Juan harbor, nor did he ever learn where the *Begoña*'s two million pesos were hidden, let alone capture the treasure.

Infuriated by the Spaniards' refusal to fight in the open sea, he tried to force a landing party ashore, but succeeded only in losing many men. Lashing about like a wounded animal, Drake behaved exactly as Don Diego had predicted: in blind fury he roared south across the Caribbean to vent his rage on the undefended town of Río Hacha, where he captured not one gold piece but did waste nineteen futile days, at the end of which in almost diabolical fury he burned everything in revenge for those slaves stolen from him nearly thirty years before. From there he stormed on to Santa Marta, another defenseless town, where again he found no treasure, and again wrecked the place.

Ledesma, learning upon his own return to Cartagena of Drake's irrational behavior, paused only long enough to gather about the *Mariposa* a small, tight fleet with which he was determined to harry Drake to his death, and on the night before he sailed for the showdown at Nombre de Dios, he walked the battlements with his still-beautiful white-haired Leonora, and told her: "In a way, I pity him. Raging about like a wounded bull, attacking anything that moves, whether it's part of his design or not."

"Take care," his wife warned "A wounded bull is the most dangerous," but he told her as they went up to bed: "Drake's always dangerous, wounded or not, and now we have him."

In the morning Ledesma weighed anchor and led his family forces on their final chase. As he had predicted, Drake did not bother with Cartagena this time, so with a sense of relief Don Diego and Roque trailed him at a respectful distance as he headed yet again for that little town which held such a stranglehold on his imagination, Nombre de Dios, where he found literally nothing but a collection of rotting houses, most of them long since abandoned: the terminus of the treasure trains from Panamá had been moved a short eighteen miles westward to a more favorable anchorage at a site called Porto Bello. Enraged at finding no treasure in Nombre de Dios, he burned the ruins. The vice-regent said as his soldiers watched from a safe lookout, "It's not our town he's burning. It's his."

Enmeshed in an increasing fury, Drake sailed the few miles to unfamiliar Porto Bello, found no treasure there, and burned that town too, as if personally insulted that it should have presumed to supplant his Nombre de Dios. Then, in an act of shocking irresponsibility, he dispatched a small body of heavily armed foot soldiers onto that dreadful footpath through the jungle to loot Panamá and perhaps destroy it—sixty against six thousand—but after the English soldiers had struggled hopelessly against the swamps, the mosquitoes and the repeated roadblocks erected by Diego's other sons-in-law, where Indians lurked with poisoned arrows, the men sensibly revolted, shouted at their officers: "We'll tolerate no more of this," and trailed back empty-handed to their ships.

Now Drake, disheartened by this unbroken chain of disasters, conceived the insane idea of invading the rich cities that were supposed to rest on the highlands of Nicaragua, but when a Spaniard he captured from a small coasting vessel convinced him that there were no such golden cities and that the little ones which did exist had not a spare coin among them, he abandoned that diversion. Instead, he sailed back to Nombre de Dios as if lured there by the same mysterious challenge that had attracted him years before. In his despair, with Don Diego's hounding ships lurking on the horizon like vultures, he took counsel with himself as to what grandiose action he might accomplish to humiliate King Philip—I'll capture some vast treasure as I did at Valparaíso. I'll destroy Havana the way I did San Domingo—but all he actually did was lash out halfheartedly against Don Diego's fleet, like a great whale tormented by a host of worrisome foes he could not reach.

He was ending his days as Don Diego had foreseen "thrashing around but accomplishing nothing," and when the dreadful fevers of Nombre de Dios assailed his ship, causing the deaths of many of his stout English sailors without their having struck one meaningful blow against Philip, he railed against the unlucky fate which had overtaken him. And then one evening the fever which had always lurked in these fetid areas, killing with a grand impartiality both the Spaniards who lugged silver across the isthmus and the Englishmen who tried to wrest it from them, struck Drake with malignant fury. When he looked up helplessly at his companions they saw terror in his eyes. "Is it to end like this?" he asked feebly, and in the morning he was dead.

To protect his body from the stalking Spaniards who might, his men feared, defile it in their hatred, they wrapped his corpse in canvas, weighted his shoulders and legs with lead, and pitched him into the waters of the Caribbean, which would forever carry echoes of his greatness.

Don Diego, whose persistence had hounded both Hawkins and Drake to their deaths, was not allowed to relish his victory for long, because when he returned to Cartagena to reassemble his scattered family he found a small flotilla in the spacious anchorage, and he feared for a moment that some contingent of Drake's forces had slipped away to torment his walled city once again. But as he drew closer he saw that the ships were Spanish, and when he reached his house he learned that it was indeed men who had come to torment him as he had tormented Drake, but they were from Spain, not England.

They were a three-man audiencia sent by King Philip to assess the numerous accusations that had been accumulating against him, thirty-one charges in number, ranging from gross theft of the king's funds to suspected heresy in that someone had heard him say after a battle: "Let Drake worship in his way, I'll worship in mine." One of the most telling charges against him was that "he placed some nineteen of his family in positions from which they could steal vast sums belonging to the king, his most arrogant act being that of persuading a fine Cádiz ship captain, one Roque Ortega, to be rebaptized as Roque Ledesma y Ledesma in order to gain additional distinction for the family name."

In the four months following Drake's death, when the Ledesmas should have been celebrating with all other Spaniards in the Caribbean, the leader of their family sat at his desk trying to respond to these accusations, some so grave as to warrant the death sentence if proved, most so trivial that a magistrate would have dismissed them before lunch. But in the end the severe unblinking master of the commission persuaded his two associates to join him in finding Don Diego indictable on all counts, whereupon the savior of Cartagena was clapped into irons, hand and foot, and ordered back to Spain for trial in one of King Philip's courts not famous for finding accused colonial officials innocent.

On his last night ashore, he begged his captors to allow him to walk once more on the battlements overlooking the Spanish Lake he had defended with such valor, but they would not permit this, afraid lest citizens rally to the defense of their hero and steal him from them. Instead, he sat bound in the noble hall in which he had met with the rulers of New Spain, with admirals returning from victories, with that wonderfully garrulous woman who had told of El Draque's "heroic exploits in Chile and Peru"—yes, and with Drake himself when they wrestled for the salvation of the city.

When his wife, so loyal through the decades, came to sit with him and slipped cool rags between the fetters and his skin to ease the pain, he said: "Perhaps it is God reminding me: 'You and Hawkins and Drake were brothers-in-arms. It's time you rejoined them.' I'm ready."

In his extremity Don Diego found one saving grace: he could look at his extensive family and know that they were in place; they possessed the positions, the power and the treasure which would enable them to control Cartagena and its environs long after he was gone. As a man of honor he had fulfilled his duty to his God, his king and his family, and clothed in that assurance he should have felt no shame in returning to Spain in shackles. But he did have a moment of burning resentment when, for his trip home, he was dragged aboard his own ship, the *Mariposa,* and thrown in chains into her hold: I fought this ship, captured her, led her against the *Jesus of Lübeck* and resisted Drake in the Armada. He raised his manacled hands to cover his face and the degradation he felt.

But he did not reach Spain, for as the *Mariposa* approached the famous Windward Passage between Cuba and Española, a vast storm blew up, and when disaster seemed imminent he called up from the hold: "Run to the captain. Tell him I know how to handle this ship in a storm," but after some tempestuous tossing about, a voice shouted down: "He says you're to stay in chains, king's orders." And so Don Diego lay in the hold, feeling his beloved ship being driven into one fatal mistake after another, until at last she plunged in agony to the bottom of the Caribbean.

Traveler, you who sail into the Caribbean in silvered yacht or gilded cruise ship, pause as you enter these waters to remember that deep below rest three men of honor who helped determine the history of this onetime Spanish Lake: Sir John Hawkins, builder of the English navy; Sir Francis Drake, conqueror of all known seas; and Admiral Ledesma, stubborn enhancer of his king's prerogatives and the interests of his own strong family.

V

BIG STORMS IN LITTLE ENGLAND

BECAUSE THE ISLAND OF BARBADOS, A PLACE OF HEAVENLY beauty, lay so far to the east of that chain of islands which mark the boundary of the Caribbean, and so far south of the ocean currents that ships naturally followed when setting out from Europe and Africa, Columbus did not discover the island on any of his voyages in 1492–1502, and it remained unknown for decades. A few Arawak Indians reached there, finding refuge when the terrible Caribs ravaged the other islands, but long before the white man arrived, they appear to have died out.

It was not till very late, 1625, that the waiting island, unpopulated but extremely rich in soil, was seriously taken note of by a chance English trader, and two more years passed before an orderly settlement began. Because this paradise waited so long for the white man to arrive, many believed that the best of the Caribbean had been saved till last. Although lying some hundred miles to the east and not actually a part of that magical sea, it was, nevertheless, widely regarded as one of the loveliest of the Caribbean sisterhood.

Like the Arawaks before them on Dominica, the English settlers shied away from the violent waves and storms of the windward, or Atlantic, side, clinging by preference to the warm and congenial western side facing the glorious sunsets. There, along the shores of a small and not too well protected bay, a collection of rude houses took shape, eventually to be called Bridgetown, soon to be famed for having one of the most civilized sites in the Caribbean: a curving beach marked by swaying palms, tidy little streets lined with low white houses built in the Dutch style, an industrious population, a small church topped by a tiny steeple, and in the background, a rise of low hills, brilliantly green after a rain. It was even in those early years a village that made the heart expand with a warm assurance when one saw it for the first time from the sea: "Here's a town in which a family can be happy."

In the early 1630s a small group of hardy emigrants from England toiled in the fields back of town to raise enough crops to feed themselves yet be able to ship an excess back to England in exchange for the goods they needed: cloth, medicines, books, and such. The cultivation of the three crops that were wanted by traders in England—cotton, tobacco and indigo for the dyeing of cloth—involved such brutal work that the early colonists quickly devised a plan whereby they could supervise their plantations with some ease while others did the work. They imported penniless young men, often from southwest England or Scotland, to serve as bondsmen for five years, after which the young fellows would be given a small amount of cash plus title to whichever five acres of unoccupied land caught their fancy.

In the first group of indentured laborers, as they were legally termed, appeared a surly young chap from the north of England, John Tatum by name, whose passage from Bristol had been paid, as was the custom, by the wealthiest of the Barbados tobacco planters, Thomas Oldmixon. The relationship between the two was never a happy one. Oldmixon was a rotund, hearty man, with a booming voice, red face and the habit of clapping his equals on the back and regaling them with stories that he considered rib-tickling but whose point his listeners usually failed to catch; with his inferiors, and he had so categorized his indentured servant Tatum, he could be brusque and even insulting.

During the five years that Tatum was required to serve—no pay, a dank room, miserable food and not even the work clothes that other masters provided their servants—Oldmixon was vigorously engaged in acquiring additional fields, which meant that Tatum had to fell trees, pull stumps, and till new fields for planting. It was such harsh work for no visible return that he generated a bitter hatred of Oldmixon, and one Englishman in Bridgetown, who treated his indentured men more humanely, predicted: "Before Tatum finishes his stint, we could see a murder at Oldmixon's."

But the next year, when Tatum's servitude ended and he had selected a choice five acres east of Bridgetown, one of those trivial accidents occurred which alter the history of islands. An English ship on the way to Barbados with a fresh supply of white indentured laborers came upon a Portuguese vessel whose crew was engaged in selling Negro slaves from island to island, in the same way that farmers' wives in Europe peddled their husbands' vegetables in town from one dwelling to the next.

The Englishmen, always looking for a chance to earn an honest shilling, attacked the Portuguese slaver, won the sea battle, and found themselves with a cargo of slaves that had to be disposed of. The first available port was Bridgetown in Barbados, and there they off-loaded not only the indentured workers intended for the island, but also eight black Africans. An auction was held on the steps of the church in the town square, with Thomas Oldmixon purchasing three of the slaves, and his recently freed bondsman, John Tatum, spending the first money he ever had in Barbados to acquire one for himself. Each of these canny men realized at the first sight of these powerful black men that money could be made from their services. Thus did slavery begin on this exquisite island.

In these years Bridgetown was becoming an increasingly delightful place in which to live: the white Dutch houses now had roofs of red tile surreptitiously imported from Spain; new streets were being opened, some with spacious parks set among the houses; mahogany benches had been installed in the church; and even a small shop had been opened by a widow who sold goods "imported" from all parts of Europe. The Dutch architecture and the smuggling were easily explained, and appreciated by everyone in Bridgetown: the settlers had turned to the Dutch when avaricious English traders, hungry for every shilling they could squeeze from their colonies, persuaded their Parliament to pass laws obligating the settlers to trade only with English firms and at whatever prices those firms decided to establish. Those same preposterous mercantile laws were already beginning to rouse protests in other colonies like Massachusetts and Virginia. Lucrative trade with suppliers in France, Holland, Italy and Spain was forbidden as was trade among the different colonies themselves; a would-be merchant on Barbados was not allowed to deal directly with a manufacturer in Massachusetts, much to the disgust of established men like Oldmixon or those just starting out like Tatum. To aggravate matters further, the English firms frequently failed to deliver their expensive goods, thus leaving the settlers doubly frustrated.

The solution was simple. Dutch trading ships, captained by men of extreme daring and commercial competence, ignored the English laws, sailed where they pleased, became remarkably skilled in evading English patrol ships, and conducted their smuggling operations on a vast scale. Barbados survived for two reasons: sensible English government abetted by capable Dutch semipirates. Whenever the settlers in Bridgetown saw the Dutch ship *Stadhouder* edge surreptitiously into port under the expert guidance of Captain Piet Brongersma, smuggler extraordinary, they knew that goods they needed would now become available, and they applauded his coming, even going so far as to post sentries on the headlands to alert him in case a British warship approached unexpectedly. Then all the Dutchmen on Brongersma's ship would leap into action, weighing anchor and hoisting sail, and sometimes within minutes the speedy *Stadhouder* would be safely out to sea before the English warship arrived.

In this easy manner, without any shots being fired, honest men thrown into jail, or bitterness engendered, life proceeded: Thomas Oldmixon gathered new fields year after year; to his five acres John Tatum brought a sturdy English lass, who gave him a daughter, Nell, and two fine sons, a very sober-sided Isaac and a rambunctious Will; governors came from England, some sagacious, some pathetic, as in all colonies; and the slave population increased because numerous babies were born to those already on the island, and Dutch smugglers kept slipping in more slaves from Africa.

There were two developments which worried thoughtful men in both Barbados and England: with the slow depletion of the soil, it became more difficult each year to grow the basic crops, tobacco being especially destructive. In London traders affiliated with Barbados saw with dismay that year by year tobacco from the island was becoming inferior to that grown in competing colonies like Virginia and Carolina, while Barbados cotton simply could not compare with that grown in the more easily cultivated fields of Georgia. In 1645, when Oldmixon saw how little his factors in London had remitted from the sale of his tobacco and cotton, he told his fellow planters:

"We're sliding downward. Worse every year. We must find some new crop, or we sink beneath the waves."

All agreed that Barbados would find a new crop to prolong its prosperity. This general optimism was well voiced by Oldmixon one day when he went to the harbor to greet a new settler who had come from Sir Francis Drake's old bowling ground, Devon. As he walked the newcomer through the clean streets of Bridgetown, pointing out the red-roofed Dutch houses, he recited a litany: "Have you seen a better island than ours? A finer town? Here you can feel the peace and ease. You'll see the little churches that mark our crossroads. My friend, this is Little England, and some of us believe it's better than the big one."

This phrase was remembered, and in time it became the accepted description of Barbados: "Little England, forever loyal to the homeland."

There had been one ugly moment in 1636 when the authorities clarified a matter which had been causing some concern. At that time the nature of slavery had not been clearly defined: neither the slave nor the master knew for sure how long the term of servitude was intended to last, and a few generous-hearted Englishmen argued that it was for a limited period only and some went so far as to claim that any child born to slaves on the island should be free from birth.

Authorities put a quick halt to that heresy: they passed an ordinance stating that slaves, whether local Indian or African, served for life, as did their offspring. Only a few slaves were aware that the new law had been passed, household servants mostly, so it did not occasion any island-wide protest, but those who did understand chafed under the realization that their servitude would never end.

Gradually, these few dissidents began to infect many of the island blacks, and by 1649, a vague subterranean sense of unease had spread through the entire community without the white masters being aware of the change. The racial composition of the island had altered radically in recent years, for when the law of 1636 was passed, Barbados had few slaves and mostly white indentured workers in a total population of only six thousand. But by 1649, there were thirty thousand slaves on the island as against almost the same number of whites, so that the slaves judged they had a chance for victory.

Among them was one of the Tatum slaves, a clever Yoruba named in his homeland Naxee and by his classically trained Barbadian owner, Hamilcar. In both Africa and Barbados he had shown a marked capacity for leadership, and had he been a white man emigrating from Europe to a colony like Massachusetts, he would surely have played a significant role in the political development of his colony. On Barbados, because he was black, he had no opportunity to contribute his skills, so in despair he began secretly to organize a rebellion against the irrational deprivations he suffered.

He was a tall, robust man with sparkling eyes and commanding voice, and so persuasive that he quickly enlisted a dozen supporters, each of whom enrolled four or five others who could be trusted, and the night came when he revealed his gruesome plan.

Obviously, the fifty-odd blacks never convened as a group, for from the earliest days of slavery, island rules had forbidden meetings of slaves from different plantations; there was to be no midnight plotting in Barbados. The message was spread in the English of the slave fields, since his followers had come from widely varied parts of Africa with different languages: "Three nights from now, sun goes down, wait two hours, then each man kills all the white men in three different houses close by. Then we spread out, all the island." It was not a tidy plan, but if the slaves could immobilize the principal white families of Bridgetown, they would stand a good chance of taking over the island. And because of the subtle skill with which Hamilcar had maneuvered the exchange of information and strategies, three nights from the terrible rebellion no white men were aware of the danger.

On the first night after having set the timetable, Hamilcar could not sleep, for he could visualize a wide scatter of things that might go wrong, but on the second night, tired from hurried meetings with his major lieutenants, he slept easily, assured that his plan would work, and next morning he rose prepared to execute the massacre.

On the eastern edge of Bridgetown, well in from the sea, stood a small cottage occupied by the two sons of Thomas Oldmixon's former servant, John Tatum. The father had died young, having worked himself to death clearing Oldmixon's many fields, and then his own, but he did leave his widow this cottage and ten acres—five he had been given as his right at the end of his indenture, and five on which he had spent his first savings, for he loved land and taught his sons to do the same. His widow had died soon thereafter, and so the boys, cautious Isaac and free-spirited Will, inherited the small holding. The former had a wife who reminded him repeatedly: "This cottage is too small for three. Your brother should find work elsewhere," but Will showed no sign of wanting to leave.

Their plantation was small, big enough to provide work for only three slaves, but Isaac was so furiously ambitious that he did not propose to remain a minor planter long. "Soon," Isaac told his wife, Clarissa, and his brother, "the Tatum name will be of some importance on this island," and he confided that the only route to the eminence for which he thirsted was "more land each year, more slaves each half-year, and this family will scrimp and save until those goals are reached."

Will was an undisciplined lad of fourteen, whose nature was already unpredictable and whose ready, beguiling smile betrayed the fact that he could well develop into a scoundrel. The two Tatums differed greatly in appearance. Isaac was almost unnaturally short, a disability he tried to overcome with manly posturing, wedges in his shoes and a cultivated rumble to make his voice deeper. He had pale, sandy hair and shifty eyes, as if always calculating the main chance, and to spur himself into manhood as quickly as possible he had married early, locating a young woman two years older than himself and twice as ambitious. As a pair, he and Clarissa were formidable.

The two brothers, so different in appearance and character, worked well together, with Will aiding his brother's ambitions in an original way: he treated the three Tatum slaves so generously that they did the work of six. When there was a muddy task to be completed in a hurry, he leaped in beside them and helped, something his more austere brother would never do. "Gentlemen have their place," Isaac pontificated, "slaves theirs, and the distances must be preserved."

The two black men worked in the fields, while the woman, Naomi, served as maid and general household assistant to Clarissa. When she was growing up along the Volta River of the Gold Coast, Naomi had enjoyed a carefree existence before her capture by Portuguese slavers; she had rebelled furiously when first dumped onto the shore of Barbados, and was so cruelly abused by her first master, she had come close to killing herself in despair. Sold off, she fell into the hands of the Tatums, who treated her justly. She had adopted the younger brother as her own, giving him kitchen lectures on how to behave as a young man should and receiving from him instruction in the alphabet, which may have been contributory to the tragedy about to engulf Barbados.

From the first days of slavery, the rulers of the island had foreseen that if they educated their slaves, sooner or later there would have to be insubordination or worse, so they forbade the learning of the alphabet and absolutely outlawed any instruction in Christianity; blacks were never allowed in churches. Naomi knew this, and she delighted in the forbidden lessons Will gave her. Early on she recognized that he was like her; Will, too, was a rebel. She felt responsible for him, and as he grew older she took pride in his manly developments and his willingness to oppose anyone who trespassed on his right. "That Will," she told the two men slaves, "he worth six of his brother."

On the night before the slaughter of whites was to begin, Naomi felt pangs of regret, for she could not bear to think of her fine young man with his throat cut, so she sought Will out and whispered: "Tomorrow doan' go to de field," and when he asked why, she said: "And doan' stay in de house." Then, in some confusion as to what she was saying, she added: "Blood promise me, doan' tell no one."

Will Tatum was a bright lad, and when he went to bed he tried to sort out what Naomi's cryptic messages had really signified, and when the ugly possibilities became clear, he wakened his brother and they rapidly deduced what Naomi had known but had been afraid to spell out, and in a rush they alerted the neighboring white families, then galloped off to surrounding plantations.

When the two Tatums rushed to the outskirts of Bridgetown to spread the alarm, Isaac first headed east for the plantation of Henry Saltonstall, a respected planter but not one of the richest, while Will started north to alert Thomas Oldmixon, the most powerful planter on one of the largest plantations. But the two young riders were hardly out of the gate when Isaac shouted: "Halloo, Will! I'll ride to Oldmixon's," and without stopping, they switched directions, for Isaac, as always calculating the advantage, believed he might gain some if he were the one to save the big man's life.

When he reached the impressive Oldmixon estate in the northern part of the island, a pillared mansion at the end of a lane edged by tall trees, he started shouting: "Sir! Sir!" and was gratified to see how quickly a light appeared.

"Who are you?" old Oldmixon asked as he opened the door in his nightclothes, complete with tasseled cap, and when Isaac revealed his last name, the florid-faced master growled: "So you're John Tatum's boy. Never liked your father. Skimped on the work he owed me." He was about to turn the young man away when his essential decency manifested itself: "I respect the way you've taken hold after your father's death, Tatum, picking up new land whenever you can. That's the way I started." Then he noticed Isaac's extreme nervousness: "Why did you gallop up here from Bridgetown? Fire or somethin'?"

"Worse," and seeking to make the most of this opportunity to assist the great man, he whispered: "Better inside," and when he had Oldmixon's attention, Isaac gave the dreadful news: "Slave uprising, sir." Now Oldmixon, though in his early sixties but still capable of quick action when required, first grabbed for his two pistols, then shouted in stumbling words: "By gad, Tatum, we must be off and movin', off and movin' I say," and he actually started for the door in his nightclothes, when he stopped suddenly to utter a loud cry: "Rebecca! Don't let me make a fool of meself!" and to Tatum he said apologetically: "Man mustn't ride to hounds in his nightcap." While Isaac waited, the big man, with his wife's help, drew on his cotton britches, his leather boots with their wide turned-down tops, his undershirt and brocaded weskit, and then donned his badge of position and honor, a big, broad-brimmed bonnet with the left side tucked up and displaying a bright turkey feather. His uniform in place, he ran to his horse, leaped easily astride and dashed down the lane, shouting back over his shoulder: "Off to the wars, Tatum, off to the wars!"

Will Tatum rode the much shorter distance due east of Bridgetown to the substantial plantation of Henry Saltonstall, a slim, straight, beardless man of forty-two, who was still in his working clothes, for he had been reading by candlelight: "What is it, young man?"

"I'm Will Tatum, from the edge of town."

"Ah yes, and what could bring you here so late?"

"We'd better step inside, sir," and when the two had done so, Will said quietly: "Slave uprising, sir."

At the mention of these terrible words, ones that every white man in the Caribbean feared more than any others, Saltonstall leaned against a corner of his desk, steadied himself, and asked: "How can you be sure?" and when Will explained, the tall gentleman reached for his long gun, handed Will two more to carry, and said quietly: "I must inform my wife. Wait for me outside." Within minutes he was back, and as he mounted his horse, he cried: "We must alert the western planters," and off they rode to spread the dreadful news.

As happened so often before in history, when masters were alerted by some loving slave, black rebels were frustrated. In this case, eighteen of the leaders, including Hamilcar and the other Tatum male slave, were hanged. The accounts penned at the time and later endlessly reprinted said only: "The Tatum slave Hamilcar and seventeen of his criminal accomplices were hanged." These brave men, some of whom had held positions of power in Africa, died without even their names being recorded, but their dark bodies were left swaying in the wind as warning.

When it became known through the loose-lipped talk of the white leaders who ordered and supervised the hangings that it had been the Tatum slave girl Naomi who had betrayed the plot, no surviving slaves would tolerate her, and one night when the Tatum brothers came home from work, they saw suspicious signs in the little slave hut, and when they looked inside they found Naomi with her throat cut. The authorities preferred to ask no questions, and in this quick, harsh way the first major slave insurrection on Barbados was extinguished, and the principle was established that slaves were chattels with no rights other than those a benevolent master elected to give them. As a result of the hangings and murder, the Tatums were left with no field hands, and Isaac's dream of acquiring more fields until he became a big planter evaporated. The fact that it was he who had alerted the island to the tragedy that was about to overwhelm it did not impress his wealthy neighbors, for on Barbados there were only three classes of people: white men who owned big plantations, white men who owned small or none, and black slaves, and the first group did not encourage any members of the second to climb upward.

With no slaves, the Tatum brothers had to do the work on their plantation themselves, and it was remarkable to watch Clarissa pitch in as if she were a third man. Never complaining, she kept the Tatum house cleaned and her two men fed and neatly clothed, and if occasion demanded, she volunteered to help in the tobacco and cotton fields, but she did not allow her husband to think that she intended continuing that pattern. "When is a new ship coming in?" she demanded day after day. "We've saved enough to buy us three or four good slaves, and we must do so."

"When the ship arrives," her husband promised, "I'll be first to greet the slave master," and in her prayers, which she said night and morning, he heard her whispering: "Please, God, bring us a ship," but England knew trouble in those years, with the result that ships from London or Bristol to Barbados were not common, and no new slaves arrived.

Many now prayed for the good old days when everything the islanders needed, from needles to medicines, reached Barbados in these ships, which in exchange carried back to England bales of cotton, tobacco, indigo and in recent years casks of a new experimental crop, sugar. But loyal as the islanders were to their mother country, they were also attentive to their own commercial interests, and when no English ships came, even vocal patriots like Thomas Oldmixon evaded the laws which forbade trade with ships of any nation other than Britain. They were especially bold in welcoming the well-known Captain Brongersma and his *Stadhouder.*

"Hmmm," Oldmixon had grumbled when told that he ought to wait for legal English ships. "We wait for those tardies, we'd starve," and then he added the more pertinent comment: "And we'd get none of the slaves we need. I say, 'God bless the Dutchmen.'"

On a crisp morning in early March 1649, Will Tatum, up at five and staring out to sea, saw the dim outline of a sailing ship whose silhouette he thought he knew, and as day brightened and the ship moved close to shore, he leaped in the air, let out a yell, and sped through the streets, shouting "*Stadhouder* coming!" And every merchant who hoped to have his stock replenished hurried to the shore.

When Will carried the exciting news home, Clarissa stopped preparing breakfast, wiped her hands on her apron, and raised her face in prayer: "God, let there be on that ship the things we need!" but her husband, always eager to curry favor with Thomas Oldmixon, called for his horse and galloped north to inform the important planter that the Dutch ship was in, almost surely with a fresh supply of slaves.

He found Oldmixon already out of bed, supervising his slaves in the care of the sugar crop he had experimented with that year. Tatum hurried toward him, bursting to tell him the good news, but Oldmixon spoke first: "Glad to see you, Isaac. Been wantin' to talk with you," and although Tatum tried to interrupt him, the big fellow barged ahead: "If you're the smart feller I take you for, and I believe you are, you'll quit your present crops and switch to sugar. Sure to be a bright future for it. A bright future, I say."

Isaac, not listening and eager to deliver his news, cried: "Sir!

Tremendous! Brother Will spotted the *Stadhouder* in the bay. Bringing slaves."

As soon as he heard this, Oldmixon became a different man, for slaves had played a major role in his life. He had been one of the first planters to use them in goodly number, and his reputation as one of the leaders on the island stemmed from an ingenious solution he had crafted for an irritating problem. A clergyman reported the affair in a letter to his brother in England:

> *As I informed you in my last letter, I have been much concerned about a regrettable rumor circulating amongst our slaves. Tired of working in our fields and convinced that they would never again see their homeland, they whispered among themselves: "If you commit suicide, you cheat the owner and your spirit returns to Africa." So one fine strong slave after another killed himself, to the detriment of his master, who had paid good money for him and who was entitled to his services.*

> *Planters asked me to move among their slaves, telling them that this belief is false, but I accomplished nothing, and the suicides continued. At this point, Thomas Oldmixon, a leader on the island, lost a fine Ashanti man, value of eleven pounds, and cried: "Enough! This foul practice must be stopped!" and he devised a simple remedy. Going to the grave of his dead slave, he had the body dug up, whereupon he cut off the head of the corpse, carried it to his slave quarters, and posted it atop a tall pole.*

> *"See!" he shouted to his Africans. "Caesar did not go back to Africa. How could he, without a head? And you won't go back, either, so halt this silly business of killing yourselves." We have had no more suicides, and from that day on, Oldmixon has been recognized as a man of good sense.*

Now, at Tatum's fine news that a new slave ship had arrived, Oldmixon cried: "Capital! But we've got to get there before the sale starts," and with his turkey feather flowing in the breeze he kicked his horse in the ribs and the two men galloped off for Bridgetown.

At the halfway point the horses fell back to an easy canter, and Isaac felt that the time had come when he could best reveal the complications which beset his personal life: "Clarissa and I lost our three slaves in the uprising. But we've saved what money we've been able to get our hands on and we face a ticklish problem, one we don't know how to resolve."

"Such as?" Oldmixon asked, turning in his saddle.

"I'm torn by two desires. Spend it on more slaves? Or more land?"

Oldmixon took so long to reply that Tatum wondered if the big man had heard, but then the planter surprised him with an answer of remarkable probity: "Young feller, I think you're preparin' to broach me for a loan, and I don't make loans. Too many complications. So you'll have to make up your own mind about how you want to apply your funds, and I'm pleased to learn that you have some. You must be thrifty."

To hide his disappointment, Isaac said: "It's my wife who tends the money, and she is thrifty, I can assure you."

"Excellent. More I hear about you, Tatum, more I like you. Your father wasn't really a bad sort. Just lazy. So here's my proposal. I'm convertin' to sugar in a big way, three-fourths of my fields. Now, it would help me mightily if some of you other men would plant cane and make sugar too, 'cause then we could combine our yield and send it to England as a full cargo."

"But doesn't sugar require slaves . . . absolute necessity?"

"It does. So what I want you to do, buy up as much land as your funds allow, and borrow on it to buy more and plant it all in sugar."

"How can I raise sugar with no slaves?"

"You can't, and that's why I'm going to buy you seven. Keep the title in my name until you can pay me with your first crop. You board and feed them and use them in your fields like they were your own."

Isaac dropped his head, almost in prayer, for an offer like this exceeded even his most extravagant hopes, and when he looked sideways at Oldmixon and saw the big man nod and then wink as if to say: "That's what I promised," he cried out: "It's help I never expected," and Oldmixon corrected him: "No, you'll be the one helpin' me if we can get sugar started on Barbados."

Having said this, he looked over Tatum's shoulder and cried out in a petulant voice: "Well, here comes Saltonstall with his damned beasts," and Isaac turned to see a sight which never ceased to amaze him. From the plantation of Henry Saltonstall came that tall, dour man perched atop a huge camel, behind which lumbered in an orderly fashion six others, all laden with produce from the Saltonstall lands and headed to Captain Brongersma's *Stadhouder* for transport to European markets. It was a dramatic caravan, which children cheered as they ran behind the huge-footed beasts, so well suited to heavy work on plantations.

But Oldmixon and Tatum were concerned not with camels but with what for them was a much more important matter: the auction of the forty-seven slaves Captain Piet Brongersma had brought in cages belowdecks from Africa. The captain had not come ashore to conduct the sale, but his first mate, an able Dutchman who spoke English, was ready to start the auction, when he saw Oldmixon approaching. Bowing low, he asked, from former experience: "Do you wish to buy the entire lot, Mr. Oldmixon?" and smaller planters who had hoped to acquire a few slaves groaned, but Oldmixon said: "No, my friend here wants seven, and I want fifteen. More than enough left for you men," and he indicated the others, who cheered.

Oldmixon, impressed with the crafty manner in which young Tatum chose his seven, said: "You know slaves, young feller," but Isaac said: "I know which men and women will be able to work," at which Oldmixon said: "Pick my fifteen," and with equal skill Isaac passed among the frightened slaves, trying to select for Oldmixon fifteen as good as the seven he had chosen for himself.

Then came the shocking moment of this bright March day. Captain Brongersma was rowed ashore, and when he landed he came forward gravely, his big bulletlike head and square face creating an ominous impression. He moved directly and silently to Thomas Oldmixon, whom he had known favorably as a planter to be trusted. Not greeting Oldmixon in his accustomed way, he came close and whispered in a heavy Dutch accent: "Assemble the other leaders," and when this was done, he announced, as if informing each man of the death of a brother: "On the thirtieth day of January past, Cromwell's men beheaded your King Charles."

"No, by heavens! It can't be," shouted Oldmixon, grabbing Brongersma by the jacket, and the other leading planters whom Oldmixon had brought into the shed joined him in averring that no loyal Englishmen, not even cravens like Oliver Cromwell, would dare to strike their king, let alone behead him.

"What proof have you?" one planter cried, and Brongersma had to admit: "None. I was already in the Channel . . . no chance to buy a newssheet."

"Then how do you know, if you weren't even on land?" Oldmixon demanded, and the Dutchman replied: "An English ship spoke me and over the horn gave me the news." Others began to pester him, but even though he lacked visible proof, he stuck to the report as he had heard it: "On thirty January last, Cromwell's men beheaded your king. All is chaos."

And then Henry Saltonstall joined the crowd to which he had not been invited. "You were busy unloading your camels," Oldmixon said as if apologizing, and Saltonstall, a man of sharp wisdom, perceived from the faces of his friends that something devastating had happened, and he asked bluntly: "What is it? War again with the Dutch?" and Brongersma replied: "Those days are past. Your King Charles has been beheaded," and Saltonstall said instantly: "It was bound to happen." The other planters in the shed looked at him with abhorrence, their manner foretelling the angry days that were about to engulf Barbados.

The next few days were the finest in Will Tatum's life so far, for now that his brother had seven slaves, he, Will, often sneaked away from the fields, and he spent the time aboard the *Stadhouder,* mostly in Captain Brongersma's cabin, for the Dutchman not only enjoyed talking with the boy but also found him useful as a source of information about doings on Barbados.

In turn, Brongersma threw out fascinating bits of information: "Our hold is filled with salt we collected after a running fight at the great flats of Cumaná on the Spanish Main."

"Where's the Spanish Main?"

"The coastline of Central and South America, where the Caribbean touches the mainland."

"Why did you have to fight for the salt?"

"The Spaniards never want us to take it away. It's theirs, they say."

"Then why do you take it?"

"To salt our herring. And you know what herring is to a Dutchman? The same as a shilling is to an Englishman."

"Do you fight the Spanish often?"

Brongersma reflected for some moments before answering this ticklish question, then said: "I suppose it's time you knew, Will. We make our living three ways. Capturing salt at Cumaná, running contraband into Barbados and the other English islands, and best of all, tracking down some rich Spanish ship, boarding her and winning ourselves a fortune."

"Are you pirates, then?"

"That's not a word we fancy. We're legal pirates, you may say, freebooters with papers giving us the right to attack Spanish ships wherever we meet them."

"Don't the Spaniards ever fight back?" Will asked, and Brongersma burst into laughter: "Do they ever fight back! Look at that scar on my wrist—from a handsome Spanish ship laden with Potosí silver out of Havana on her way to Sevilla. Part of a great armada she was, protected by four warships of the line, but we cut her out, boarded her, and would have won ourselves a fortune except . . ."

"What happened?" Will was on the edge of his chair as the Dutchman said glumly in recollection of that sad day: "One of their warships spotted us, what we were doing, came roaring back, and we were lucky to escape with our skins."

"Are the Spaniards good fighters?"

"Never believe the English fairy tale that one Englishman is better than three Spaniards. The well-armed Don from Sevilla with a sharp Toledo blade is a match for any fighting man on any ship. Halloo, Franz! Show us your face," he shouted as into the cabin came a big Dutchman with a long scar, scarcely healed, across his right chin. "He's our best swordsman, none better," the captain said, "but a Spaniard with a Toledo would have killed him for sure, except one of our men shot the Spaniard dead as he was about to do so."

The next time Will returned to the ship, Brongersma said: "I wish I'd had a son like you," and Will asked: "Would you have taken me to sea with you? To fight the Spaniards?"

"Now, that's a difficult question, lad. As a father I'd agree with your mother, that you ought to stay in Amsterdam and learn your letters. But as captain of the *Stadhouder,* I'd want you at my side when we took on the Spaniards, for there's nothing nobler in this world that a Dutchman can do than wage sea war against those swine."

"Why do you call them that?" and the captain became quite grave, there in the hot cabin, and spoke with an intensity Will had not heard before: "My grandfather, his grandfather before him were hanged by Spaniards ruling the Low Countries, and no man like me can ever forget that."

"Why were they hanged?"

"They were Protestants . . , followers of Luther. But the Duke of Alva . . . the Duke of Parma . . . they were strong Catholics, and the quarrel between the two religions could be settled only by hangings, endless hangings." He looked at the floor as he said quietly: "So if you sailed with me as my son, we'd have eight or nine Spanish ships to burn before my rage was quenched."

On their last day together Brongersma was in a more relaxed mood: "This was a profitable stop, lad. We bought our slaves from the Portuguese at nine pounds and sold them at thirty. We bought six new camels for Mr. Saltonstall at eleven each and sold them at thirty-three. We sail home with a ballast of pure salt and casks topside with brown sugar, which will bring a fortune." He tapped his pipe against his left hand, and said: "On a day like this, with a calm sea out there, and a fast run home, and always the chance of catching a Spaniard laden with gold or silver . . ." He paused, not knowing how to end his sentence, then concluded quietly: "A man could sail on forever . . . forever till the final darkness comes."

"You love sailing your ship, don't you?" and Brongersma said: "I'll sail the *Stadhouder* till her bottom is eaten through by the worms and my bottom is ready for its return to dust."

Will asked: "Why do you get angry when someone calls you a pirate? Are you not one?" and Brongersma replied: "There's a difference, I'm an honorable Dutch captain who fights the Spaniard. I shall be unhappy if you call me pirate." And next morning at dawn, when Will scouted the sea, the *Stadhouder* was gone.

For the next eleven days the men and women of Barbados had no solid information about their king, only those rumors brought by Captain Brongersma, but then a trading ship arrived from Bristol with printed confirmation. King Charles I, beloved of the island's Royalists, had actually been beheaded at Whitehall by a common axeman who executed ordinary criminals.

The shock was profound, and in the days of tension that followed, the islanders divided into the two camps that would contest for the right to govern. On Barbados, as in England, each side adopted a name for itself: the conservatives elected to be called *Cavaliers,* which implied men of breeding, substance and unquestioned loyalty to the king, while liberals elected to be called *Roundheads,* which described sturdy men of middle position socially possessed with business acumen, common sense and a preference for rule by Parliament.

Derivations for the two names were interesting: the *Cavaliers* took theirs from the gaudily dressed, bewigged and flamboyant cavalry officers who fought so bravely in defense of the king, and *Roundheads* came from men with a preference for an austere haircut that made their heads seem like ugly round pumpkins when compared to the elaborate locks of their opponents.

A contemporary, who knew members of both sides well, described them in this way: "Cavaliers comprise the gentry, the Church of England clergy and the loyal peasants. Your Roundheads are apt to be men from the middle class, the rich merchants and a surprising number of great nobles; you might say, all who can read and write."

The archetypal Cavalier was dashing Prince Rupert, nephew of the king and probably the greatest cavalry officer who ever fought one major battle after another, winning most; the quintessential Roundhead was the blind poet John Milton, austere in person but with a pen that scattered fiery diamonds, especially in his prose essays dealing with politics.

On Barbados the Cavaliers were led by robust Thomas Oldmixon, who announced: "I've always been loyal only to the king and shall remain so, and if Charles I is truly dead, his son Charles II is my king and I'll fight to protect his claim," and men of similar loyalties began to cluster about Oldmixon and look to him for leadership.

Control of the Roundheads, fewer in number but equally dedicated to their cause, devolved naturally upon Henry Saltonstall, who approved of the deposition of the king though not his murder, and who believed that Parliament could rule England more effectively than royalty had done.

The effect of all this on the Tatum brothers was especially divisive. Isaac was a young man who intuitively liked royalty and its attendant nobility; secretly he hoped that one day he would, through increase in the size of his plantation, his slave holdings and the consequent amount of sugar produced, amass a fortune. Then he planned to donate large sums to enterprises in which the king was interested and thus win attention in London, and who knows, perhaps even a title.

Roustabout Will would not have known what to do with a title had it been offered him. In fact, he had already shown certain tendencies which greatly disturbed Isaac and Clarissa: he had been overly familiar with the slaves; he sometimes ridiculed Thomas Oldmixon's pompous ways; twice he had absented himself on Sundays from the parish church, when everyone knew that attendance was required by law; and most distressing, he had frequented the waterfront, palling around with Captain Brongersma, who only a few years before had been at war with England.

As the political debate intensified, Clarissa warned Isaac: "Your brother isn't a person to be trusted. Next thing you know, he'll be announcing that he's siding with Saltonstall." She proved a good prophet, because a few nights later at supper Will made bold to say, even though he knew the loyalties of the older Tatums: "I think Saltonstall and his Roundheads make a lot of sense. Does England really need a king?" The question was so bluntly asked that Isaac and Clarissa were too stunned to respond.

As the turmoil on the island spread, Isaac became increasingly concerned that his favorable start with Oldmixon might grind to a halt. As he explained to his wife: "With the execution of the king, anything can happen," but she advised steadiness: "Don't falter now. All's at chance." When she learned that Oldmixon had declared for the king, she told Isaac, leading him to his horse and spurring him on: "Now's the time to strike. Ride up there and tell him you're with him."

Bursting into Oldmixon's hall, Isaac cried in the deep voice he cultivated: "I'm for the new king," and the wealthy owner clasped him warmly: "You're a welcome volunteer to the Cavaliers, Tatum." Then he drew back, studied the man he had only recently come to know, and cried: "Egad, Tatum! You have done me three favors. Forestalling the slave rebellion, planting sugar, and now joining me for the king. I have a feeling we'll be seeing a lot of each other." Even in his enthusiasm, Oldmixon took care to say *egad,* because blasphemy was severely punished on this island, which led men to use old, safe forms like *egad* as a substitute for *ah God, "sblood* for *by God's blood* and *zounds* for *God's wounds.*

When Isaac Tatum returned home he told Clarissa: "I did what you said. We're in this together now." They did not say anything to Will, but that evening the Tatums had a serious conversation, started by the wife: "If Will persists in his sentiments, I can't be happy having him share quarters with us."

"Half the house is his, my love. Half the fields."

"Can we buy him out?"

"With what?"

After a long silence Clarissa said: "Will's a hothead, we've seen that. He's a rebel, and if this island remains loyal to the new king, as I'm sure it will, he'll do something that will drive him from Barbados. His land will be forfeit . . ."

"My love, there's no way we can ask him to leave now. I need his help with the new slaves and the sugar."

Petulantly she said: "Isaac! I'm not happy with him around. Answer me this. Why did that Naomi tell him about the plot? Why didn't she tell us? What was there between them?"

Isaac had to lay down the law: "We need him. We need his share of the land. And we must have his share of the work." When she began to cry, he promised: "As soon as things are steady, we'll ask him to leave. He can always stay with the Pennyfeathers," referring to the Tatum sister, Nell, who had married a fairly worthless shopkeeper, Timothy Pennyfeather. The thought set Isaac's mind to working: "On one thing you're right, Clarissa. Will's share of the land must come to us, because the secret of wealth on this island is control of land, and I aim to accumulate a great deal of it."

And then, as the year closed with the island divided into two almost warring factions and with the split in families like the Tatums, an event transpired which demonstrated the unique quality of Barbados, for when it was announced in the various churches that a hunting party would be setting forth for the island of All Saints, one hundred and fifty miles to the west, men of every persuasion flocked to the little ship that would convey them there. Thomas Oldmixon, head of the Cavaliers and a master shot, had nineteen of his supporters at his side, while Henry Saltonstall, armed with two fine guns, led the Roundheads. Isaac Tatum stood with Oldmixon, brother Will with Saltonstall.

When the ship hove to on the western side of the glorious bay of All Saints, its small boat ferried the hunters ashore, with leaders Oldmixon and Saltonstall sharing the same small craft and the Tatum brothers riding side by side on a later trip. When the party was assembled, Oldmixon issued instructions in his hearty voice: "Men, Saltonstall, a fine shot, will lead his half in that direction, rest come with me—and we'll see if we can finish with these buggers."

What would they be hunting? Carib Indians who had fanned out from their original home on Dominica to the neighboring islands of All Saints and St. Vincent, where the cannibals had proved murderously dangerous to any English or French sailors shipwrecked on their shores. They were an implacable foe who so belligerently refused any overtures for peaceful sharing of their islands that European settlers deemed extermination to be the only policy. This was not the first hunting party sent after them, but it was the largest, and the Englishmen with their long muskets set out at a merry clip, with many cries of self-encouragement to battle with the savages. It was by no means a one-sided fight. Venal Dutch and French and English traders—pirates, really, of whom Brongersma of the *Stadhouder* was one of the worst—had provided the Caribs with guns fabricated in the American colonies and ample shot and shell to go with them, so the Barbadian hunting party and its intended prey started about even; the English shooters knew they were going to be shot at.

Thus, in only a few centuries, the fierce Caribs who had uttered wild war cries as they swept down to annihilate the Arawaks, now heard those same cries shouted against themselves.

In the first half-hour Thomas Oldmixon, with Isaac Tatum at his side as kind of gun-bearer, killed two Caribs and dodged Indian bullets as they rattled back at him. Saltonstall's team, containing many Roundheads who tended to be fine shots, also killed its share of Caribs, and for about two hours the hunt continued, with Barbadians shouting in triumph whenever they brought down an Indian and keeping score as they might have done at a pigeon shoot, for it was wildly exciting to see a brown form scuttling through the low brush and to hit him dead-on and see him turn and twist as he fell. Of course, sometimes the running figure was a woman or a child, but the shooting continued, and during the entire hunt not one Barbadian expressed concern about gunning down the savages, male or female, and certainly no remorse.

At the end of the third hour, when light was beginning to fade, both teams put on an extra drive, and because they were attacking from different directions, they forced the Indians into a defensive position at the far end of the beautiful bay that gave this island its distinctive character, and there they hammered at the Caribs with a deadly crossfire until some nineteen men and women, plus a handful of children, were exterminated. That night the Barbadians returned temporarily to their ship, and there was considerable celebration in which Cavaliers and Roundheads toasted each other with good English ale.

During the second day, as the group was surrounding another Carib camp, one Carib marksman who had mastered his fine New England musket, hid in a tree, drew a bead on young Will Tatum, and would have killed him had not the boy moved at the last second. The bullet ripped through Will's left arm but missed the bone, and when Isaac bound the wound with a bit of torn shirttail, all members of the hunting party congratulated Will as the hero of the expedition. In that congenial frame of mind the Barbadians sailed away from All Saints satisfied that they had "taught the damned Caribs a lesson."

When the hunting party returned to Barbados, the almost-forgotten factionalism revived: at times debate between the two parties grew heated, and men with any sense of history anticipated the day when angry words would be replaced by ugly deeds. But it was to be a characteristic of Barbados in those troubled years that both sides, Cavalier and Roundhead, carefully, almost passionately, avoided overt actions of a hostile kind or the bloodshed that might have been expected to accompany such basic and emotional differences. Credit for this common-sense approach was due to the two leaders, Oldmixon and Saltonstall, for neither man was the kind who might encourage his followers to drastic action; each believed in legal procedures and the avoidance of either riot or rebellion. Oldmixon might talk louder than Saltonstall but never to the point of incitation, and although Saltonstall seemed to have beliefs more profoundly grounded than Oldmixon's, he never saw civil disturbance or attack upon his adversary's property or person as a proper means for advancing them.

In short, and this was the highest praise that could be bestowed on Barbados at this crossroads in Caribbean history, the islanders were behaving like properly disciplined English gentlemen and proving that they merited the enviable title "Little England."

The same courteousness prevailed in the Tatum household, though Clarissa clearly wanted to rid the place of her disreputable brother-in-law and Isaac considered him an embarrassment, especially when Thomas Oldmixon asked one day: "What's this I hear about your brother Will? Is he with us or not?"

"He's been contaminated by Saltonstall."

"Cut him off, Isaac. No good ever comes from brothers in contention."

"He owns half my land."

Oldmixon, who delighted in making immediate decisions, growled: "Time may be at hand, Isaac, when men like your brother will be gone from this island . . . forever. Prepare for that day."

When Isaac told his wife that Oldmixon had agreed with her attitude about Will, she said: "We won't blemish Christmas and let's celebrate New Year's together, but after that, out he goes, land or no land."

It was a tense holiday season, despite the fact that Barbados never seemed lovelier. Palm trees bowed in that heaven-sent wind, blowing always hard from the east, and on Christmas Day the three Tatums carried their dinner to a hill on the edge of Bridgetown, where Isaac, in a burst of brotherly affection which he knew would soon be terminated, said: "That divine easterly wind, it never fails us. It protects our independence, Will, and our freedom." When Clarissa asked how that could be, he said in a dreamlike voice: "Why was Barbados, of all the Caribee islands, unpopulated when Columbus passed through to the north? Why did the Spanish never conquer this island? Why have the French and the Dutch and the others captured one island after another, but never Barbados? Why are we so special, as if God looks over us?"

"You mean the wind?" Will asked, and his brother clapped him on the shoulder: "That I do. The wind from the east that bends those trees, as it has unfailingly for a thousand years. All the nations I've mentioned have *wanted* to conquer Barbados. They've known it was the choicest island in the Caribees, with the best land, the best crops. But to conquer us, they would have to sail their ships from the west where the other islands are, to the east where we are, and they cannot breast that furious wind."

Clarissa asked: "Then how did the English land?"

"Because they came as friends. They could take their time and ease their way in. No one on shore shooting at them." And he directed his wife and brother to study an incoming Dutch merchant ship that had been trying for two exasperating days to beat against the wind and make the harbor.

"Imagine it a warship," Isaac almost chortled, "coming to do us damage. It would stand out there almost motionless, caught in the wind, and our guns would pound it to pieces," and the others could see that what he said was true. "But if we want to capture All Saints, which we may have to do before long, we load up our ships, move them into the stream, and ride right down that furious wind, landing on All Saints forty minutes after they first see us."

For some minutes they contemplated the beneficence that the easterly wind provided and felt themselves enveloped in a warm family companionship, but then Will broke the spell by asking: "Why would we want to invade All Saints? Nobody there but Indians," and Isaac said sharply: "The time of testing may be at hand. We cannot risk leaving any island unguarded . . . to fall under control of the king's enemies."

"Do you think we could capture it?" Will asked, almost innocently, and his brother snapped: "We're more powerful than you might think. These islands may prove to be the salvation of England." He rose, moved about nervously, then came to stand over his brother: "You might be interested to know that secret messengers from Virginia and Carolina, two of the strongest American colonies, have crept into Barbados recently to assure us that they'll join us if we make a stroke for the king. The Bahamas, too."

Will, who had been talking geography and maritime affairs with Captain Brongersma and his Dutch pirates, laughed at his brother's pretensions: "Do you know how big the Bahamas are? How many people there are in Virginia? Parliament would muster a fleet in three weeks . . ."

"Don't talk treason," Clarissa snapped, and Will shot back: "Don't you talk sheer nonsense," and before they could retreat to the calming influence of their house, half owned by Isaac, half by Will, Clarissa had shouted in a loud voice: "You better leave us, Will. Today. You're headed for the gallows."

Will, not one to point out that she was dismissing him from a house that was half his, stalked back to their dwelling in silence, grabbed together such belongings as he had, and departed for his sister's home above the drapery shop run by her husband, Timothy Pennyfeather.

In 1650 the various political storms in Little England accelerated into hurricanes, for on the third of May the men like Thomas Oldmixon governing the island in a de facto manner declared the entire island loyal to King Charles II, the uncrowned claimant who was still in protective exile in France. But all of England remained under the control of the Roundhead Parliament and most of the North American colonies were obedient to its rule. Even the majority of the British islands of the Caribbean had turned against the Royalists, but here was stout little Barbados defying overwhelming adverse power and declaring that it would remain loyal to the new king until the rest of the world regained its senses. The Bahamas and certain Royalists in the southern American colonies let it be known that they, too, sympathized with the action of Barbados, which made the distribution of power about ten for Barbados, ten thousand for Parliament.

But Oldmixon and his optimistic Cavalier planters never wavered. As soon as news spread through the island that the decision had been made, noisy support came from every corner, and thoughtful Royalists began to collect guns and ammunition against the day when an enemy fleet might appear off Bridgetown and attempt a landing and an occupation. Oldmixon, supported by his eager aide Isaac Tatum, started drilling troops; small fortresses were erected; watches were maintained.

Open warfare was avoided principally because sensible Roundheads like Saltonstall kept their tempers under control, convincing themselves that Cromwell's men in London would not let them down, but four days after Oldmixon's decision to deliver Barbados to the king's defense, his Cavaliers received exhilarating support, for a ship arrived with news that excited Oldmixon and his supporters: "Cromwell's government is sending out a new governor. Named Willoughby and said to be a secret Royalist."

But an ordinary seaman, a surly fellow with his hair cut Roundhead style, quietly warned such islanders as he met: "Careful of Lord Willoughby. He changes sides so fast that watchin' him makes you dizzy. Cavalier? Roundhead? Who can say which he is today or will be tomorrow?"

Three weeks later, when Francis, Fifth Baron Willoughby of Parham was rowed ashore from an incoming ship, the waterfront was lined to watch his imperial arrival, and they saw in the prow of the little craft a handsome man standing very erect, sword at his side, sash across his breast, exuding an air of "Here I come to take command," and in the fast-paced days that followed, the islanders learned that their noble lord had indeed been three times a fanatic Cavalier, three times an equally determined Roundhead. In his latter incarnation he had once commanded troops obedient to the Parliament; in his former, he had been Speaker of the House of Lords and vociferously supportive of the king. Finally trapped in his contradictions, he had been sentenced to the Tower for hanging, but escaped by fleeing to Holland, where he loudly proclaimed that he had always been Royalist at heart. Incredible as it seemed at the time, after the beheading of Charles he once again served Cromwell, and it was a tribute to his flexibility in big affairs of state and his integrity in the little affairs of daily living that both Cavalier and Roundhead not only liked him, but actually trusted him in whatever position they gave him. He was a miracle of his age and exactly the kind of level-headed pragmatist Barbados needed at this time.

As soon as he had established headquarters he summoned Oldmixon, and let it be known that he, Lord Willoughby, intended pursuing exactly the course that Oldmixon had initiated. Then, on the latter's advice, he selected Isaac Tatum as his principal aide, and thus began Isaac's rise to power. Soon, he and Clarissa acquired from a sugar planter who was in disfavor because of his troublesome defense of Parliament a batch of eleven more slaves . . . at a thieving price which Isaac was able to enforce because he had arranged for the man to be sent into exile.

With that lucky boost, Isaac appropriated in rapid succession three small plantations adjacent to his by the simple expedient of continuing to initiate moves which ended in the owners' deportation. With these forced departures he gained more slaves, until Oldmixon told him one evening as he and the Tatums were dining in the former's big house: "Isaac, you're well started. But I must warn you— take steps to consolidate your holdings, for otherwise you might lose 'em all if Lord Willoughby is ever forced to leave the island and conditions revert. They have a way of doing that, you know."

When Isaac asked: "How do you protect yourself?" Oldmixon said from experience: "Get papers which prove the lands are legally yours." And taking that advice, the Tatums spent the summer of 1650 maneuvering so that Lord Willoughby was practically forced to issue papers which confirmed the Tatums in their ownership of the lands they had acquired in various questionable ways. In October of that year everyone among the leadership on Barbados and especially the Tatums thanked their good fortune that Lord Willoughby had organized the island according to Royalist principles and issued land titles which clarified who owned what.

And then the Barbadian peace was shattered. Cromwell's men, having grown tired of the travesty of allowing this little island to ignore the rules that governed the rest of Great Britain, had issued orders to one of its finest admirals, Sir George Ayscue: "Assemble a great fleet, sail to Barbados and reduce it to obedience. You are both authorized and commanded to land troops, surprise their forts, force the islanders to submission, beat down their castles and places of strength, and seize all ships and vessels belonging to them or any other ships trading there."

When word of these draconian orders reached Barbados they did not, strangely enough, cause panic, for the islanders were secure in their belief that even though small and alone, they could stand against the entire British force of arms and send Admiral Ayscue scuttling back to England. At a dinner the host, Lord Willoughby, the week after the news arrived, told Oldmixon and Tatum: "Sir George is an able seaman, and he'll get his fleet into the harbor down there, proper enough. But how will he land his troops? And if we deny him landing, what will his men eat? Where will they get their water? Mark my words, he'll wait here four or five months, then hurry on to Virginia and try to discipline them. Hold on! That's all we have to do, hold on, till England recovers her senses."

After this strategy had been refined, and heartily approved, a toast was drunk to "King Charles II, absent for the moment in France but soon to rule," and then Milord said: "I do despise that name they're trying to foist on us. Great Britain. Started in my father's time when James Stuart ascended to the joint throne. 'First and Sixt' we always called him—King James First of England, Sixth of Scotland. But out of deference to Scotland, Wales and Ireland, the new name had to be Great Britain. What an ugly, formless pair of words, meaning nothing. We're English, and our land is England, and I make bold to propose another toast: 'To England. May she soon return to her senses.' In the meantime, thank God for Little England." And to that fine toast all raised their glasses.

When conversation resumed, Willoughby asked Isaac: "How's your brother doing? Oldmixon here warns me he's become a bit of a problem," and Tatum replied: "He has, Milord. Fallen under the spell of Saltonstall. I see little of him, and would like to see less."

"We must sort such relationships out, Tatum. Now then, this man Ayscue they're sending is no fool. We'll need all our wits to fend him off. But we shall do it," and with this stern resolve he finished the report he had been working on before dinner. An exact transcription of his words illustrates the curious orthography of those times:

I assure ye Lord^{shps} that ye siergy^{nt} Majjor hath taken a verry great deal of Paines getting ye troopes inn fiteing Trimm. He hath binn up early and Downe late inn devizing how to pro-

tekt his Maj^{ties} interests agaynst ye allegations and Clames w^{ch}
ye Planters of th^s Ile hath lodged.

Some days later, a small ship put into Bridgetown with tremendous
news, and desiring to inspirit his forces, Willoughby directed Oldmixon and Tatum to gather as many of the Cavalier planters as possible, and when the leading men of the island were assembled, he
informed them: "Prince Rupert, the king's nephew and the strategist
behind all the battles the Royalists won, has been made Admiral of
the Fleet, loyal to our new king in France, and he's heading here to
save us from Ayscue and his Roundheads."

Rousing cheers greeted this information, for no military man
then alive, regardless of his nation, had the exalted reputation enjoyed by this handsome, dashing prince upon whom destiny obviously smiled. His presence in the Caribbean could mean an enormous
difference, and as the meeting continued the Cavaliers became more
certain with each glass of ale consumed that Rupert would punish
Ayscue and end the forthcoming war before it began. "It'll be all over
by Christmas," Oldmixon predicted loudly, and with others making
even more extravagant interpretations of what Rupert's coming
might mean, the heartened Cavaliers dispersed.

When Willoughby was alone, he mused: I may well die on this
island, but I will never surrender it. Ayscue will have to fight his way
ashore inch by inch. Oh! How shameful it would be if I were the man
to lose this heavenly isle! Not me, not me!

His mind now turned to Prince Rupert and he desperately wished
he had some local Cavalier he could trust, because he wanted to disclose the suspicions that haunted him. He certainly could not discuss
sensitive issues with Thomas Oldmixon: Too blatant, too conceited,
too lacking in judicious knowledge. And he had no taste whatever for
any talk of serious matters with Isaac Tatum: Too sycophantic, too
grasping . . . He considered these two adjectives, and shook his head:
How damning. Could one speak worse of a friend?

He was thus forced to evaluate the coming tests without counsel,
and his conclusions were bleak: Prince Rupert is a gallant man. I
headed his ground troops twice during his great cavalry charges and
once served afloat with him. He was a real man, as handsome as his
uniforms. But Admiral Rupert! Dear God, I doubt if he knows one
end of a ship from t'other. On a horse, a genius. On a ship, in charge

of a dozen other ships, a complete ass. We're in deep trouble this night. Gods of war, pray for me.

His predictions concerning Rupert's naval abilities proved accurate, for after an unconscionable waste of time, when the cavalry genius did finally head to the rescue of Barbados, he ran into minor troubles, as his navigator reported later:

> When we were about fifty leagues east of Barbados on what I took to be a perfect heading, some outlook spied a small ship which looked as if she might be Dutch and richly laden, so we set sail after her, but she proved faster and we never caught her. During said chase Admiral Rupert's ship sprang such a great leak that we had sore trouble trying to keep her afloat, and when the chase ended we found we had overrun our reckonings and had passed Barbados in the night without seeing it. We doubled back but never did find it, and the troops we carried for the islands' defense were wasted.

What was worse, Rupert, while searching for Barbados, sailed his squadron headlong into the tail of a Caribbean hurricane off Martinique, and in the violent tossing about of his ships lost much of his force, including his gallant brother Maurice, also a land fighter. Ignominiously, he crept back to Europe, leaving Barbados in worse condition than when he started out to save it.

Admiral Ayscue was considerably more efficient than Prince Rupert, but even so, he required exactly one full year—October 1650 to October 1651—to organize, assemble, and train his fleet of seven vessels plus its two thousand troops and get them across the ocean to Barbados. In the meantime, the islanders appeared to be going about their business ignorant of the fact that beneath them rested a keg of black powder to which was attached a very long fuse slowly but resolutely burning toward the explosion point. Lord Willoughby continued to give entertainments at his rude mansion, where wealthy planters, who sold their new crops of sugar surreptitiously to ships sneaking in from Holland, assured one another that "this idiot Ayscue will never get his ships into the bay down there," and increasing pressure was placed on Roundheads like Saltonstall.

But the apparent levity of these Cavaliers could not hide the fact that they, too, felt increasing uncertainty as months passed and no Roundhead ships appeared on the horizon, while Roundheads asked with noticeable irritation: "Will the damned ships never arrive?" Meanwhile, both groups went to their chosen churches on Sundays as required by law, with ten times more worshipers attending the Church of England services than were gathered in the scattered chapels serving such dissidents as the Methodists and Quakers. Barbados continued to be a beautiful island, one of the most beautiful, but it was not a relaxed one.

The tension did not affect young Will Tatum, sixteen years old and enjoying his small room above the Pennyfeather shop on the main street of Bridgetown. Many reasons accounted for this: his sister was a gentle soul who tolerated his peculiarities in a way that his more proper sister-in-law never could; he found excitement and freedom in life along the waterfront; he appreciated for the first time the orderly Dutch quality of Bridgetown's buildings, some of them squat stone affairs of great dignity, topped by red roofs, others, like the one the Pennyfeather shop occupied, built of dark wood properly joined; but mostly because of the delightful fact that in James Bigsby's neat butcher-baker-kitchenware shop across the street there was a fourteen-year-old daughter Betsy, whose quiet smile and carefully attended braids set the hearts of several young men beating at a faster pace. She was a sober girl, reserved in public, soft-spoken with friends. She was never a blatant flirt like some of the other Barbados girls of the middle class, and she created a sense of well-being wherever she moved. Not so tall as Will, she complemented him perfectly, he thought, on the few occasions when he was able to stand beside her or speak with her by chance in the street; and frequently that year he had the warm fantasy of having her with him in four rooms above a little shop, like Nell and Timothy in theirs.

There is little in nature more lovely to watch, more reassuring to the human spirit, than the behavior of a pretty fourteen-year-old girl, newly aware of her powers, who wants to attract the approval of a sixteen-year-old boy. Softly she dances along the village street, in a dozen subtle ways she makes herself more attractive, her voice drops to a lower level, and her eyes run riot, sending new messages and startling promises never even dreamt of before. This year the knowing citizens of Bridgetown watched with amused approval as the proper daughter of their storekeeper took notice of the Tatum boy and practiced on him her yet-tentative arts of coquetry.

Will, himself awakened by the experience, was encouraged to speculate on such matters by the fact that his sister was big with child that autumn, and he marveled that she could move about and tend customers when so heavily burdened, and the more he studied Nell, the more he appreciated Betsy, imagining her going about in the same manner with his child. It was a confusing, instructive period in his life, made more perplexing by the arrival in the harbor of Captain Brongersma's *Stadhouder,* and when he grabbed a rowboat to be first aboard the intrepid trader, he found its captain a much-sobered man.

"Lad, we had a sorry chase after we left you last. Saw this rich Spanish prize, overtook her easily, boarded as usual, and I was leading our men when suddenly a company of well-armed soldiers that had been kept in hiding leaped at us from nowhere—and I want you to see what happened." Taking Will out onto the deck, he showed him the sun-bleached stains where Dutch blood was spilled after the Spanish soldiers reversed tables and boarded the *Stadhouder,* with deadly effect.

"We might have lost our ship," Brongersma said sadly when he returned to his cabin, "but when that threatened, our men proved valiant. Cut . . . slash . . . fire the gun down his throat . . . back we drove them to their own ship. And off it sailed to Sevilla, off we limped back to Amsterdam."

This conversation had a profound effect on Will Tatum, and during the next days people in Bridgetown saw the boy suddenly stop in the middle of a path to engage in imaginary warfare against the Spanish: "Cut, slash, fire the gun down his throat, back we drove them." He never visualized the Dutch defeat, nor the dead men on the *Stadhouder's* deck; he could think only of the glory. But so obsessed did he become with this story that one day he quietly arranged for Betsy Bigsby to accompany him out to the ship, and Captain Brongersma fell in love with her: "What a tidy little mistress . . . those golden braids! Ah, that I had a daughter like you!"

He spent the better part of an hour showing her the mementos he had acquired in sailing the various seas, and when she asked about running blockades, he told her: "See that man aloft? He watches for the arrival of English warships, and when he sees one he shouts out 'Danger west!'—and off we hurry, because we can sail faster than your English ships can."

"But if you're unlawful," she asked in her small, inquisitive voice, "why do the Englishmen ashore welcome you so heartily?" and he asked: "What's your father do, missy?" and she said: "The store on the big street that sells everything." He laughed: "Ah, yes! You ask your father why he's so happy to see me come," and she looked at him bewitchingly and whispered: "Don't you think I know?"

Will had questions of his own about fighting against Spaniards, and in sharp, brief responses the Dutch freebooter summarized what life aboard the *Stadhouder* was like: "Fifteen days' run in the sun, nothing but work. Ten days in calm, row like hell. Three days in a storm, bail and pray. Then you spot a Spanish ship, but you can't catch her. Then you do catch one, but she's guarded by troops. Then you flee an English patrol boat. Finally, if God smiles, you come upon an unprotected Spaniard loaded with silver, and the long trip's been worth the effort." He dropped his voice: "But only if you're brave when boarding time comes."

Betsy Bigsby, listening intently, shivered at the thought of bloodshed, but from the corner of her eye she saw that Will was leaning forward eagerly, his eyes ablaze, and as they left the ship she said: "Captain, I think you may have found a new hand," and Brongersma threw his arm about Will.

In mid-1651 the tempo on Barbados accelerated, and apprehension about when Ayscue's fleet might arrive goaded the Cavaliers surrounding Lord Willoughby to pass harsh measures which he would never have proposed if left to his own decisions. All known Roundheads were removed from positions of influence; Cavaliers were organized into regiments and trained in tactics for repelling landing forces; and in a move which shocked the island, the principal Roundhead leaders were stuffed onto a boat and shipped back to England. Will Tatum halted his quiet courtship of Betsy Bigsby long enough to ride out to Henry Saltonstall's plantation on the hill east of town to say farewell to that honorable man as he vacated the stone house his father had built, and both men were close to showing tears when they parted.

"Look after the plantation," Saltonstall said before he mounted his horse and rode down to the waterfront and exile.

The ship had not left harbor before Isaac Tatum had come to claim Saltonstall's property, and he had with him, in Clarissa's care, papers certifying that "the property once known as Saltonstall Manor, owned by the notorious traitor Henry of said name, is attainted and turned over to the ownership of Isaac Tatum, loyal servant of King Charles II and officer in the Leeward Regiment, said ownership to be perpetual to said Tatum and heirs." The Tatums slept in their new home that night, and each had dreams of endless honors in the years ahead, for when the Saltonstall lands were added to those he and Clarissa had already acquired, the Tatums were going to have one of the top three or four Barbados plantations, every field laden with sugarcane.

But when Roundhead friends alerted Will Tatum, asleep in his little room above the drapery store, to the ominous news that his brother had appropriated the Saltonstall house and lands, he borrowed a horse, rode out to the estate, and banged on the door till his brother appeared: "What have you done, Isaac?"

"Only what the law provides. Henry Saltonstall is a proved enemy of the king and has been banished forever. His lands have been attainted and passed on to me, as a loyal servant."

Will was so outraged by his brother's arrogant behavior that he sprang at him, and there would have been a serious altercation had not Clarissa appeared in her nightgown, with a peremptory shout: "Will, what are you doing?" and when tempers cooled she gave her young brother-in-law sober advice: "I've been watching you, Will. You're headed for trouble, the most serious trouble. Barbados is to be Cavalier, now and forever, and there'll be no place for you. Why don't you leave the way Saltonstall and those others did?"

Will's jaw tightened: "You stole my land from me, and the other little pieces from men who couldn't protect themselves. But by God, you'll not steal Mr. Saltonstall's land. I'll not allow it." But as he stomped off to his borrowed horse he heard Clarissa's sharp threat: "Will, you used the Lord's name in vain. You'll hear from the church authorities."

In the days that followed, while Will sought in vain for some way to reverse the usurpation of his friend's property, he forgot his sister-in-law's threat, for Nell was about to give birth. It was he who ran for the midwife and tended the shop until the baby was born, and it was he who stood by the bed when the baby was nestled in his sister's loving arms. "He's to be called Ned, and if anything happens to Timothy, you're to look after him." Hands were shaken across the bed, and Will even stooped down to shake the infant's tiny hand as if to confirm that now his nephew was his responsibility.

That night, in a confusion of happy and tense emotions, he

roamed the streets of Bridgetown, looking at the trim houses, the prosperous shops and the reassuring English ships idling with their copious goods coming into Barbados and their holds heavy with sugar heading out, for despite the threats of naval warfare, commerce had to move. Talking aloud to himself, he tried to sort out the thoughts swirling in his head: "I don't want to go into exile like Mr. Saltonstall, I like this island. And I don't want to leave Betsy. And if the promised ships ever arrive out there, certain Cavaliers are going to be knocked in the head." He was almost determined at that moment to move to the windward side of the island where a number of Roundhead adherents were forming a regiment to oppose the Cavaliers if fighting began, which it threatened to do. But he remembered his discussions aboard the Dutch freebooter: Now, that's a life! A man with spirit could have excitement on such a ship. Then common sense took over: I promised Nell I'd look after Ned, and I certainly want to look after Betsy, if she'll have me. And now the overriding question which was tormenting far more Barbadians these days than merely Will: But what to do when the Roundhead ships arrive?

The suspense ended on 10 October 1651, when Admiral Ayscue's fleet of seven ships and two thousand fighting men hove to, some in the bay off Bridgetown, others well down the coast where the troops had a chance of landing unopposed. The great battle between land-based Cavaliers and shipbound Roundheads was about to begin.

While the rulers of Parliament were extremely desirous of humiliating Barbados to prevent the lingering sore of Royalist sympathy from spreading, they did not send to do this job some harebrained fire-eater who would storm ashore and shoot up everything in sight. With commendable English caution they nominated a remarkably stable man, veteran of peaceable negotiation rather than military bombast, and from the first moment Sir George Ayscue drew within sight of Barbados, he acted with exemplary restraint. Indeed, he stood offshore during most of October, all of November and much of December, hoping to gain a peaceful settlement of differences. His patience worn by Willoughby's sturdy defiance, he finally came ashore with his two thousand men, and desultory engagements ensued without much loss of life—poor bumbling Timothy Pennyfeather being among the few casualties.

In them, Thomas Oldmixon behaved gallantly for the Cavaliers, as did Isaac Tatum, but with only just enough courage to allow himself to be seen in the fighting but never close enough to the Roundheads to be damaged by them. Will Tatum, on the other hand, took heroic steps to make contact with the invading force and fight along with it. He gave such a good account of himself that when the Roundheads returned to their ships for safety and supplies, they took him with them as a valued guide, and in that capacity he informed them about the confiscation of Henry Saltonstall's plantation. "That will soon be corrected," Ayscue's men promised. However, the gentlemanly fighting did not resume, for both Willoughby and Ayscue realized that each could do great damage to the other, but that neither was going to win an outright military victory. Accordingly, as early as the second week in January 1652, the two sides met in a historic series of sessions in the Mermaid Tavern at the port town of Oistins, where they contrived one of the most sensible and just documents ever to end a war. In grave, conciliatory terms the governor and the admiral stated the principles on which Little England, too beautiful an island to destroy, would henceforth be governed, and some of the terms would resound in British history:

ARTICLE 1. That a liberty of conscience shall be allowed to all . . .

ARTICLE 4. That no man shall be imprisoned or put out of his possession without due proceedings according to the known laws of England . . .

ARTICLE 9. That the people of this island shall be free to trade with England and with any nations that do trade with and are in amity with England . . .

ARTICLE 11. That all persons shall be free at any time to transport themselves and their estates when and where they think fit . . .

ARTICLE 12. That all persons on both sides be discharged and set free, and that all horses, cattle, servants, Negroes and other goods be returned to their right owners . . .

ARTICLE 15. That the three small vessels now on ground before Bridgetown do remain the property of their owners with liberty to sail to any port laden . . .

ARTICLE 17. That all such persons of this island whose estates have been sequestered or detained from them be forthwith restored to their plantations . . .

ARTICLE 19. That the government of this island be by a
Governor, Council and Assembly, according to the ancient
and usual custom here . . .

Article 20 contained an unusual provision: That since most of the
island's troubles had been caused by "loose, base and uncivil language," a law be passed "with a heavy penalty" forbidding "any revil-
ing speeches remembering or raveling into former differences and
reproaching any man with the cause that he formerly defended."

In other words, let peace return to Little England and let past
animosities be buried deep in memory. The strategy of these two just
leaders worked; citizens of Barbados were still Cavalier or Roundhead but they did not flaunt their differences, and certainly no man
abused the other for his past preferences. But it must not be thought
that all deviousness of human nature was either purified or suppressed, for when Will Tatum, clutching in his left hand a copy of
Article 17, hurried out to Henry Saltonstall's forfeited estate, demanding that it be returned to his custodianship, Isaac and Clarissa
primly informed him that the Saltonstall case was different and that
a secret agreement between Willoughby and Ayscue had exempted
from the general amnesty that estate and two others that Isaac had
seized. When Will, now a husky young fellow, threatened his brother,
Clarissa warned him that Article 20, which forbade rough speech
against former enemies, would be a cause for jailing, and he could do
nothing but retreat, leaving his brother in possession of the plantations he had stolen.

During the next few years Will, taking the place of his brother-in-
law, assumed responsibility for Tim's family and business, and though
he still hoped one day to marry Betsy, could make no plans toward
that end.

Then, in 1658, joyous word arrived. Oliver Cromwell was dead, and
although the island's Cavaliers were infuriated to learn that their remorseless enemy had been buried in Westminster Abbey, they rejoiced that this menace was at last removed. Feasts were held, and
Thomas Oldmixon invited as many of his neighbors as could borrow
a horse to come and dine at his expense from long wooden tables set
up under his trees. An improvised band played marches, and selected
friends, the Isaac Tatums among them, gathered with him in the

quiet of a back room to toast an event which now seemed not far removed: "To King Charles II in France, soon to be in England!" and there was levity on Barbados.

In fact, the resurgence of the Cavaliers gave Isaac Tatum such confidence that when he and Clarissa returned to the former Salton-stall big house, he asked her to sit with him in the spacious garden overlooking the distant sea: "Cromwell's dead. The king is surely on his way back to London. We have the land we needed and sixty-nine slaves to tend the cane. The price of sugar was never higher. All's in order, except one thing."

"What worries you?"

"Will. Nell told me the other day when I took a present to her son that Will was finally to marry that pretty little girl from across the street, father runs that strange shop where you can buy anything the last ship smuggled in. I forget her name."

"What's wrong with that?"

"I'm afraid of Will. He becomes stronger in the community. People respect him. He could become a danger to us if he's listened to."

"But what can he do?"

"He'll never surrender on this house, these lands. I'm sure he's been in contact with Saltonstall, wherever he is."

"That's been settled, Isaac. We have more than enough papers."

"Never enough if Saltonstall should gain the ear of the new king."

"Not likely. He was too strong a Roundhead."

"Look at the Roundheads here in Barbados. You'd think they won the war."

"I believe I know a way to get rid of Will," and some days later she rode into Bridgetown to accost her brother-in-law at the drapery shop. After paying respects to Nell and her well-behaved seven-year old, Clarissa took Will aside and told him bluntly: "Will, there's no future for you on this island. You really should move on to London. There's more of your kind there." When he scorned this suggestion, she said ominously: "All right, Will, you've had your chance," and off she flounced.

She did not return to the plantation, storming instead to the parish church, where she sought the clergyman already subservient to her because of her wealth: "I have grievous news, Father, which I'm most loath to report, but my husband's brother, Will . . ."

"I know him, a most uncertain fellow."

"He's taken to blasphemy. Abuses the Lord's name most wantonly."

"That's a grave charge, ma'am. Do you wish to lodge it formally?"

"I do," she said sternly, and after reflection the clergyman replied hesitantly: "You appreciate that this will mean the pillory for your brother?" She shocked him by adding with an obvious lust for vengeance: "I think he should be stigmatized, too, to make him mind his manners."

At the utterance of the terrible word the churchman actually shuddered, for he could not support it: "No, ma'am, that would be too harsh." But when she insisted, the clergyman had to bethink her position in the community as well as his own, and supinely he consented: "I will propose it to the authorities."

When she reached home that evening she assured her husband: "I'm sure we've scotched that snake. Never again will your brother be able to show his face in Barbados."

The established church in the English islands enjoyed a special and important role. It was the guardian of both orthodoxy and propriety; it supported the government, especially when it involved royalty; since none of the islands had a press, it served as the disseminator of official news decisions, which is why the phrase "Ordered to be read for three Sundays in all Parish Churches" appeared at the foot of documents; and in an age when blasphemy was a major sin, it was the protector of public morals.

So when Clarissa Tatum accused her brother-in-law of blasphemy, the elders of the church in St. Michael's Parish had to listen, and when they had accumulated enough evidence against the young man they presented it to the magistrates, who sentenced him to "stigmatism and two hours in the public pillory where the main roads cross in Bridgetown." There, on a hot Wednesday at ten in the morning, a bonfire was prepared with so many short sticks of kindling that it would be sure to form a lively blaze, and when the flames were reassuringly high, Will Tatum was led to the nearby pillory and his head and wrists were thrust into the frame that would keep his face immovable. Then, while the townspeople watched, some in horror, some with grim satisfaction, an officer of the church thrust the iron brand B, for blasphemer, into the flames, waited till it became red hot, then pressed it strongly into Will's left cheek, where it hissed until it drew blood and produced the permanent scar of the stigmata.

Will fainted as some cried out in horror, and others in celebration of virtue's triumph.

Will remained unconscious for half an hour, but then the flies tormenting his wound and eyes revived him, and the throbbing pain resumed. Forced to listen to the scorn of the public and see his own brother Isaac and sister-in-law Clarissa riding past at a distance to mock him, he remained in the sun, head exposed, and suffered a public agony that had not been intended for minor dissidents like him. His wretchedness was alleviated by Nell and Betsy, two brave women who dared public censure by attending to him, bringing cloths to wipe his face and unguents to soothe the scar. They also brought drafts of cold water to ease his parched lips. Nell was at his side first, and after she was gone, with protests sounding in her ears, Betsy came by with salves and a look of tenderness to let him know she loved him.

At two in the afternoon he was released by a verger of the parish church, and some watchers wondered what he might do. On certain memorable occasions men punished like this had gone straight to the church officials who had consigned them to the pillory and thumped them roundly, and in one case a man had struck the person responsible for denouncing him so viciously that death resulted. Then there had to be a hanging, and as that doomed man approached the gallows he shouted for all to hear: "May this whole island rot in hell," and he would have cursed more had not the black hood been drawn tight about his head.

Will Tatum did nothing like that. With a tight, fixed smile on his scarred and aching face he stalked through the silent crowd to his sister's shop, climbed the stairs, kissed Nell and thanked her, then shook hands with young Ned, and said: "I'll be back to watch over you," and disappeared down the stairs, walking straight down the street to the waterfront without having the courage to say farewell to Betsy Bigsby. With his cheek marked forever with the hideous B, he called for rowers from the *Stadhouder* still in the harbor, climbed aboard, and reported to Captain Brongersma: "I want to fight Spaniards," and he was seen no more on Barbados.

In the long years ahead he would sometimes think of Betsy before attacking a Spanish treasure ship, or in a jail in Spain, or even when slogging through a swamp-ridden jungle, and in his mind's eye she would be forever a beautiful girl of twenty with slim waist, braided hair and sparkling eyes. She would be with him in a hundred different scenes, always the same, always a burning memory, and for him she would never age. He would cherish her as the purest memory of an island which had not treated him well, perhaps because he did not treat it with the respect his brother did. He realized that night as he left Barbados that he was making a decision of profound importance. He was losing Betsy Bigsby, and might never see her again.

In 1660 the news that Barbados longed for arrived. Charles II was anointed King of England while perched upon the Stone of Scone, symbolizing the fact that he was also King of Scotland. Great celebrations were held which even reluctant Roundheads joined and there was general relief that things in Little England were back to normal.

As proof of everyone's desire to forget old animosities, a document arrived in Bridgetown in the latter part of 1661 that gave great joy to the island: "His Majesty King Charles II has been pleased to award his faithful servants in Barbados seven baronetcies and six knighthoods," and people clustered about Government House to learn who would henceforth be called "Sir," with older citizens explaining to younger: "A baronetcy can be passed in the family from generation to generation forever; but a knighthood expires at the death of the recipient."

The seven baronetcies caused quite a stir, because four of them honored Cavaliers who had from the first moment been loyal to the king, while the last three went to Roundheads who had served their parliamentary cause honorably, bowing at last to the popular will. If any gesture in this troubled period gave evidence of England's desire to bind up old wounds, it was this bestowing of honors equally between victors and losers.

First on the list of baronets was, of course, Sir Thomas Oldmixon, who had never wavered in his loyalty, never drawn back from defense of his king's name, whether in debate or war. His selection was loudly applauded, as was that of Sir Geoffrey Wrentham, another valiant defender of the king, but there was almost equal praise for the first of the Roundheads, Sir Henry Saltonstall, present whereabouts unknown.

When the reading of the six ordinary knights began, Isaac Tatum and his wife stood transfixed. They knew they had been stalwart defenders of the king, and both their social and economic position on the island entitled them to recognition. Their plantation was one of the biggest, and their yearly shipment of clayed sugar to England was surpassed by that of no other Caribbean planter. In the war they had fought bravely though briefly for the king, so it was not preposterous for them to hope, but they knew that things did sometimes go awry.

The first two names were those of well-known Cavaliers: "Sir John Witham, Sir Robert Le Gard." No surprises there, but the next two were of former Roundheads, and the Tatums' brows began to show perspiration. But then came the clear voice of the clerk: "Sir Isaac Tatum," and he might have swooned had not his wife held him upright with a firm grip on his arm.

Some weeks later another bit of news arrived from London to gladden the hearts of Cavalier Barbadians: "The mob's fury could not be contained. Shouting 'The Abbey is contaminated!' the people rushed into Westminster Abbey, uprooted the grave of Oliver Cromwell, dug out his corpse, and dragged it through the streets until they came to a gibbet, where they hanged it for the crimes its former owner had committed." When the news was confirmed and it was learned that the tale of vengeance was accurate, church bells rang and in certain parishes prayers of deliverance were offered.

It is difficult to explain how this little island, so fraught with differing loyalties, had been able to escape civil war, but a local official did suggest some interesting hints: "From the start we wanted Barbados to be a refuge for people offering new ideas, whether in religion or business, so we welcomed the Dutch traders, and the Quakers, a contentious lot, and invited Huguenots, an industrious people when France expelled them. Saltonstall before he left us was responsible for the law which admitted even Catholics and Jews, although he did add the warning, 'providing they did not commit public scandal on our days of worship.'" Proof of this compatibility occurred at a gala dinner held shortly after the hanging of Cromwell's corpse.

For years the island had faced war and invasion, and its citizens were at each other's throats, with all suffering real privation, yet it was possible, only a short time after hostilities, to hold this dazzling feast. It was best described by a French visitor, who, being neither Cavalier nor Roundhead, submitted a report which can be accepted as accurate:

It was fortunate that I had met the newly knighted Sir Thomas Oldmixon, for he told me that tomorrow afternoon a fellow knight, Sir Isaac Tatum, is offering his admirers what he assured me would be a "master celebration," and when I asked what was being celebrated he said: "The hanging of Oliver Cromwell," and he explained how the corpse had been removed from Westminster Abbey and desecrated, very un-English I thought.

Last night we rode out to the plantation of Sir Isaac, who had invited some fifty of his friends to a celebration of the honors list. He and his wife had arranged tables at which some thirty slaves in uniform served the guests a variety of dishes that would have made Lucullus twitch with envy. At the end of the ninth or tenth dish, when it became obvious that many more were to come, I asked permission of our host to make a list, and I was afraid this might be resented as an intrusion, but I think he was proud of the variety he was offering.

For the occasion he had killed a young ox and now served its meats in fourteen diverse ways: rump boiled, chine roasted, breast roasted, cheeks baked; tongue, tripe and odds minced for pies seasoned with suet, spice and currants; and a dish of marrow bones. Next came a potato pudding, collops of pork, a dish of boiled chickens, a shoulder of young goat, a kid with pudding in his belly, a suckling pig, a shoulder of mutton, a pasty of young goat, a young shoat, a loin of veal with a sauce made of oranges, lemons and limes, three young turkeys, two capons, four ducklings, eight turtle doves, three rabbits.

For cold meats we had two Muscovy ducks, Westphalian bacon, dried tongue, pickled oysters, caviar, anchovies, and the best of fruits: platanos, bananas, guavas, melons, prickled pear, custard apple and water millions. For drinks we had mobbie, brandy, kill-devil, claret wine, white wine, Rhenish wine, sherry, canary, red sack, wine of Fiall, and other spirits come from England which I did not recognize.

The host gave all as cheerful and as hearty a welcome as any man in these islands can give to his closest friends. What astonished me was that in this case his "friends" included all his past enemies, including especially those Roundheads who had received knighthoods at the time he did. I am told they call this island Little England, but when you are in the care of Sir Isaac it becomes Big England.

That night, after the guests were gone and the Tatum slaves, including the cook, had more or less put the remainders of the food away, Sir Isaac and Lady Clarissa sat in their handsome front garden and looked down upon the roofs of Bridgetown as they glistened in the moonlight. Several ships rode easily in the bay, two showing lights which made silvery paths across the water, and a sense of ease came over the master and mistress of this fine plantation. At one point Clarissa did say reflectively: "I sometimes wonder what Will's doing on a night like this," and had she been told that he was at that moment in a Spanish prison waiting to be burned alive, she would have had no comprehension of how he could have reached such a conclusion to his life or what it signified.

Sir Isaac did not care to speculate on the whereabouts of his feckless brother: "Forget him. He was worthless when we knew him, and he's sure to be worthless now. Besides, just before the dinner I received excellent news." His wife leaned forward, for she enjoyed her husband's triumphs and often felt that she had been of some help in achieving them: "The clerks who tracked down Henry Saltonstall to alert him to his knighthood and the fact that the agreement ending our war entitled him to reclaim his old plantation were told by him: 'To hell with Barbados. Boston's better, even with snow.'"

The two sat in silence for some time, reflecting on the turbulent storms their island had experienced in recent years, and finally, as Sir Isaac led his wife to bed, he said with justifiable pride: "With the price of sugar so high, and our slaves multiplying as they do, these lands for which we paid not over ninety pounds are now worth more than ninety thousand, thanks to our husbandry," and when his wife clasped his arm to show her approval, he added: "No matter what the turmoil, we kept our balance, preserving the old virtues and proving to all witnesses that we truly are Little England."

VI

THE BUCCANEER

BY THE SEVENTEENTH CENTURY THE MOUNTAIN-GIRT INLAND city of Potosí in eastern Peru was one of the most opulent settlements in the Americas, North or South. Its fabled wealth derived from the lucky chance that one of the nearby mountains was practically solid silver; there was nothing comparable in the world, and the city's coat of arms justly boasted: "The king of all mountains, and the envy of all kings."

On the morning of 6 October 1661 overseer Alonso Esquivel, in charge at the largest of the silver refining mills, directed his Inca slaves to break away the sides of the mold in which he had formed his final silver ingot. When the ironwood sides were removed, the precious ingot, a cone some nine inches high, stood in the sun.

It did not glisten, for the silver was not totally pure, and the wooden mold in which it had been formed did not have smooth sides, but in the bright sunlight its handsome roughened surface bore the unquestioned appearance of wealth. When purified in the smelters of Spain or the Netherlands, the ingots would be highly polished to form objects of great value or silver coinage to pay for the king's adventures on the battlefields of Europe.

Proud of his accomplishment in meeting the strict requirements of the viceroy of Peru, with each ingot of his quota filled, all hundred and nineteen of them at verified weight, Esquivel took a brush charged with heavy black ink and marked this last ingot P-663, a code number which would identify it as completion of the total Potosí contractual obligation for 1661.

When the fifty mules were loaded, muleteers stood ready at the heads of their beasts and thirty armed soldiers, helmets shining, awaited the commands of the captain-in-charge. Esquivel saluted, a bugle sounded, and the precious cargo started on its long mountainous journey down the slopes to the important Pacific Ocean seaport of Arica more than 340 miles distant.

At first, the ancient roadway, wide enough for two such caravans, passed through fairly open fields where the danger of assault by robbers was minimal and the military guards could relax and carry their heavy guns in any fashion, but for the last thirty miles the terrain roughened and a heavy growth of trees impeded progress. Now the caravan passed through tunnels of matted branches of trees, and the file became so strung out that one mule could scarcely see the tail of another. Here the danger of attack by robbers was great, so each soldier diligently guarded two mules, the one beside him and the one ahead.

On 10 November 1661 the captain-in-charge sighed with relief as his fifty mules brought their treasure safely to the dockside at the port of Arica, where it was quickly loaded onto the exquisite little Spanish galleon *La Giralda de Sevilla*, which set sail immediately for Callao, the seaport serving Peru's nearby capital of Lima. This 750-mile stage of the journey was an uneventful run to the north, but at Callao many important things happened: the viceroy came down to inspect the galleon, the number and quality of the silver ingots were certified, officials headed home to Spain embarked, gold bars from the mines of northern Peru were added to the cargo, and a contingent of soldiers marched aboard to guard the increasingly precious cargo and the equally important official passengers.

Seven days were wasted at Callao, but on 2 December 1661 the *Giralda* set sail for the great Pacific Ocean city of Panamá. This 1,600-mile leg of the voyage was very dangerous, because in these waters French or English pirates sometimes struck, knowing that galleons from Lima were apt to be heavily laden. To capture one northbound galleon would justify ten years of fruitless prowling, so the Spanish soldiers remained alert, even titled passengers served as volunteer lookouts, and the captain reminded each watch: "It was in these waters that Francis Drake captured the great *Cacafuego* in 1578."

Again, the passage was uneventful, and after fifty-six days at sea, Ingot P-663 rested safely off the crucial port of Panamá, where the vast wealth of Spanish America became concentrated. Panamá was a city to enflame the imagination, where entire warehouses were crammed with gold and silver bars, where every household could accumulate its share of coins, and where rich goods imported from Spain, France and the Netherlands were stored before onward passage to the towns and cities of Peru. It should not, in those rich days, have been called an entrepôt—a port city into which goods came and out of which they quickly went—because Panamá was more a kingdom of its own, center of an incredibly wealthy empire, feeding goods east and west, north and south, as deemed best. It was also one of the largest cities in the New World, and one of the best defended, for as the governor boasted: "If Drake was unable to capture it in 1572 when it had only meager fortifications, what chance could an invader have today?"

A week was required for the *Giralda* to disgorge its holds, and it should have taken two, but the governor himself came to the dock to urge speed: the mule caravan which would carry the treasure across the isthmus had to depart early in February in order to meet the alleons from Spain that would be arriving at Porto Bello on the Caribbean side. So on 8 February 1661, after a stop far too short to appreciate the wonders of Panamá, the officials from Peru supervised the loading of the large caravan and sent it on its way across the isthmus. The trail from the Pacific to the Caribbean was only sixty miles long, but it was still as formidable as when Drake struggled to negotiate it. Rotting trunks of fallen trees still barred the way, wild animals and snakes proliferated, and if a soldier broke the skin on his leg, the wound might never heal, so infected with putrid material would it become.

When the perilous journey ended with beautiful Porto Bello in sight, even more danger was present, for the town itself was as pestilential as ever. Soldiers coming out of the jungle and seeing the place for the first time often stopped on the hillside to gape at the numerous ships clustered in the great harbor, each awaiting its cargo of gold and silver, at the huge warehouses lining the shore, and at the row of protective cannon jutting out from the surrounding heights. Often they would reassure one another: "No damned English pirates would come near this port," and they would feel great security.

But the captain of the mule train, who had made this journey three times before, uttered more sensible words: "Dear God in whom we find our salvation, let me be among those who will survive," for he knew that of the ninety men in his mule train, not less than forty could be expected to die from the fevers lurking in the charnel house below. Crossing himself, he muttered to his lieutenant: "Sometimes the Spanish cannot be understood except by fellow idiots. They left famous old Nombre de Dios because it was unhealthy, moved a few miles west to this hellhole, which is five times worse." When his aide, who had never crossed the isthmus before, asked: "What's wrong with Porto Bello?" he snapped: "I'll show you!"

As he led the mules down into the seaport, he pointed out the tragic weaknesses of the place: "This stream should be covered. Left open, it becomes a sewer, spreading disease everywhere. That rotting shed should have been burned years ago, only rats infest it now. That house seems fine, but look at its well. Stands right beside the latrine. The people who live there will drink themselves to death, and not on Spanish wine. Look at those carcasses rotting in the sun. They'll account for a dozen deaths. And the shacks, crowded so close that what causes a death in one immediately migrates to all the others. And the air is heavy, the jungle so close."

He concluded his indoctrination with sage advice: "I'll tell you how to be one of the lucky few who stay alive in Porto Bello. Don't eat the meat, it's putrefying. Don't eat the fish, they're poisoned. Don't breathe the air, it's filled with jungle fever. And don't fool with the Porto Bello girls, for their lovers will cut your throat."

"You said you've been here three times before. How did you survive?"

"By following my rules."

But even this observant visitor to Porto Bello failed to identify the mystery of the place. The chameleon town took its lethal coloring from whoever was the last to visit it. If an armada of ships lay in the harbor to collect silver, whatever diseases the sailors brought with them flourished. If no ships were in, the town caught such diseases as the latest mule train carried from the Pacific side of the isthmus. And when the streets lay empty, local diseases festered in the nearby swamps and gathered strength so as to strike whoever ventured within their reach.

The reason for this deadliness was complex: nearness to the rotting vegetation of the jungle, lack of movement in the air because the town lay in a pocket into which breezes did not come, and a water supply that simply could not be purified. A Catholic priest who served the town throughout the year and who witnessed one plague after another said: "Porto Bello is like a beautiful woman who carries a deadly disease, fatal not to herself but to any who comes in contact. And, my friend, she is beautiful—the endless flowers, the wonder of that flawless anchorage, the surrounding hills burdened with great trees, the little streets with their inviting houses . . . and the noble forts to protect the charm. When people visit our town on the edge of the jungle they leave remembering two things: beauty and death."

It was the custom for the townfolk to cluster about the dock when the mule trains arrived to unload their burden of silver, and although the precious metal could not actually be seen, the crates in which the heavy ingots were packed intensified the mystery of wealth. They looked like gifts intended for a distant king, and not until the silver was safely aboard and under the protection of the armed guards did the celebrations begin.

It was like a village play in some remote German hamlet in the year 900 when death stalked the celebrations, picking off this one and that while scrannel pipes played and dances continued on the green. This year the captain's prayer was not answered; despite three earlier successful journeys and his studious care not to drink contaminated water, the fever caught him and a thousand others, and when the galleons hoisted anchor for the return trip to Cartagena, the ranks of their sailors and soldiers were also depleted by about half. For six frantic weeks Porto Bello had been the richest little town in the world, but also the most dangerous.

In these years, Our Noble and Powerful City of Cartagena, as it was often called in official documents, was still a majestically located settlement on the southwestern coast of the Spanish Main. The famous hook protecting the inner bay still functioned, but the scores of little islands were now fortified with castles and gun emplacements and batteries of cannon. Drake had once subdued it and some daring French pirates had held it for ransom, but no more. It was unassailable, and in its broad outer and inner harbors the great ships of Spain collected to wait for the gold and silver of Peru.

On 6 April 1662 the silver-laden galleons from Porto Bello sailed into Cartagena, and after provisioning from the copious stores assembled there, were ready for the 1,300-mile run north to Havana. As soon as Governor Alfonso Ledesma, lineal descendant of that notable second governor of Cartagena, Roque Ledesma y Ledesma, stepped aboard, the fleet headed out.

On 7 May, Ledesma anchored his treasure ships in Havana's ample harbor, where the local governor rushed out in a small boat to deliver exciting news: "Don Alfonso! The king, in honor of your past braveries and your undoubted courage this time, has invested you with the position of Admiral of the Combined Fleets on their Atlantic voyage to Spain. Admiral Ledesma, I salute you."

The other half of this great armada—hundreds of ships of all sizes—would arrive from the port of Vera Cruz bringing vast stores of silver from the mines at the Mexican city of San Luis Potosí, named after the more famous site in Peru, and when these huge galleons started coming into the harbor, Ledesma appreciated what a responsibility had been given him: "The wealth of Spain for the next ten years rides out there."

When all ships were accounted for, the governor of Cuba gave a dinner for the departing captain, at which he asked: "Don Alfonso, you may be absent from Cartagena for several years, perhaps five . . . six. What arrangements have you made for your government, your family?" and Ledesma raised his glass: "To Don Victorio Orvantes, son of my cousin, who will guard Cartagena for me. And to my wife, Doña Ana, who is at this moment on her way with our child Inés to stay with her sister in Panamá till I return . . . with glory, I pray."

They drank to his health, asked that prayers be said for him and his fleet, and in the morning fired many salutes as the magnificent assembly of great galleons and little fighting ships sailed forth. It took all day for the tail-end members of the armada to catch enough wind and get under way, but when they were properly formed up outside the Havana harbor, the governor cried to those standing with him on the turrets of the fort: "No English pirates will dare attack that mighty flotilla!"

It was a vain boast, for in November 1662, just as the armada was approaching the coast of Spain, "Right in the king's featherbed," an Englishman later boasted, "seven of our swiftest raiders swept down upon the Spaniards, and would have cut out a galleon had not their admiral executed a sudden maneuver which left us bewildered. We accomplished nothing and instead lost one of our own ships, the *Pride of Devon,* with all hands."

Flushed with the victory caused by his quick thinking, Admiral Ledesma led his fleet to the mouth of the Guadalquivir River and to the customs port of Sanlúcar de Barrameda, where officials properly registered the fact that on this day, 20 December 1662, the galleons from Cartagena and Vera Cruz arrived without the loss of even one of the small protecting ships, thanks to the courage and skill of the admiral, Don Alfonso Ledesma Amadór y Espiñal."

The treasure which he had delivered so expeditiously despite all dangers did not remain in Spain; it was forwarded swiftly to foreign battlefronts where Spanish troops were fighting insurgency in their empire.

Potosí silver bar P-663 and many like it were rushed a thousand miles farther north to the Netherlands, where a last-minute, futile attempt was being made to regain control of that rebellious colony. There the silver was minted, and the new coins were distributed as wages to soldiers, as profit to the agents of foreign countries, and as interest to the powerful Fugger banking firm which seemed at times to hold half of Spain in fee because of past royal borrowings. So this tremendous fortune which required such effort to move—more than 11,000 miles in 526 days—accomplished nothing. But even as this was being conceded by the Spanish captains still struggling to hold on to the Netherlands, new ingots of silver were being cast in Potosí, and new galleons were gathering at Cartagena like a flock of hungry sea birds to collect the bullion at Porto Bello after it had crossed the deadly isthmus.

Erroneously the king and his advisers believed that the prosperity of a nation rested in its control of bullion; the more gold and silver the galleons brought to Sevilla, the richer the nation would be. This philosophy overlooked one timeless truth: the wealth of a nation derives from the hard work of its citizens at home, the farmers, the leather workers, the carpenters, the shipbuilders and the weavers at their looms; they create the usable goods which measure whether a nation is prospering or not.

In Spain in these critical years, when its entire future hung in the balance, her galleons continued to bring in untold wealth while her artisans and shopkeepers languished. Up the Channel, English ships brought little or no gold, but did bring the produce of the new lands and took back to them the surplus goods produced by England's shrewd and industrious citizens. Year by year Spain imported only bullion while the English exported and imported the goods by which men and nations live, and although that year English watchers must have envied the enormous fortune which Don Alfonso delivered to Madrid, had they been all-wise they would have realized that their small trading ships were bringing to England the more important treasure.

On a bright January day in 1665 in the Spanish city of Cádiz, a grisly event occurred which, some years later, would have violent repercussions in the Caribbean.

During Admiral Ledesma's resolute defense of his armada in the battle off the coast of Spain, nineteen English sailors from the *Pride of Devon* were captured. It had been the intention of the captain of the galleon under attack to hang the lot, but Admiral Ledesma was a political opportunist as well as a brave seaman, and he saw in these prisoners an opportunity to ingratiate himself with the religious authorities who played such an important role in Spanish life. Accordingly, he delivered these orders: "These men are heretics. Take them to Cádiz and turn them over to the Inquisition. But be sure to tell the authorities that it was I who sent them." And this was done.

For more than two long years, from November 1662 to January 1665, the Englishmen wasted away in the dungeons of Cádiz without light or exercise or adequate food, for if the creaking wheels of the Inquisition ground with inexorable force, they did so with aggravating slowness. During spells of activity the Englishmen might be interrogated five days in a row by their austere black-robed judges and then ignored in silence for five months.

During their questioning the sailors were reminded that many years ago the headquarters of the Inquisition in Toledo had handed down an extraordinary three-part edict: in the early days of King Henry VIII all Englishmen had been loyal Catholics; but following his lead in 1536, in a final act of dissolution, they were forced to become Protestants; which meant that they turned their backs on Catholicism and the one and only true church of Christ. Thus, any sailors from England who were shipwrecked on Spanish shores or captured from English ships at sea were ipso facto guilty of heresy, for which the inevitable sentence was to be burned alive at the stake.

Of course, the Inquisition itself did not carry out this cruel sentence. It merely judged the men guilty, then turned them over to the secular government for the burning, so on this January day, with no members of the inquisitorial board present, soldiers herded out three Englishmen in black robes and with shaven heads, and led them to the stakes, where the other sixteen prisoners would be lined up to watch the punishment that would be repeated on them in the weeks ahead.

As they marched to their doom, the three unfortunates cried out to their brethren: "Resist! Cromwell and a free religion!"

They could have chosen no other words so guaranteed to infuriate the Spanish officials, who looked upon Oliver Cromwell, long dead, as an archfiend and the murderer of England's King Charles I, a splendid ruler then on his way to leading England back to the pope. Cromwell had installed what they saw as a fierce atheistical Protestantism, and anyone who invoked his name in Spain deserved to die. So the fires were lit, and through the smoke and the screams came the defiant voice of one victim who would not be stifled: "England and freedom!"

When the fires died down and the ashes were scattered along the open road, the officials in charge passed among the surviving sailors, marking the men to be burned at the next auto-da-fé: "You and you and you," the last designation falling upon a stocky sailor with a deep scar showing the letter B on his left cheek. Thirty years old, he came from the remote island of Barbados in the Caribbean. He had reached Europe on a Dutch trading ship, the *Stadhouder,* and after it had discharged its cargo of brown sugar called muscovado and casks of rich golden rum, he had transferred to an English ship, the *Pride of Devon,* which had joined a group of other English vessels attacking a Spanish bullion fleet, and been sunk off the Spanish coast.

His name was Will Tatum, and the news that he was soon to be burned at the stake aroused in him such a fury that when he was returned to his cell he beat upon the walls in blind rage at prolonged intervals for two whole days. But on the third his frenzy subsided, and he looked at his bloodied hands in disgust: Fool! Fool! You have a few days to live. Think of something! Spurred thus by a fierce desire to remain alive, he considered even the most improbable opportunities for escape. The walls were too thick to be breached. The ceiling was too high. The door to his cell was never opened. But his feverish mind continued to leap from one impossibility to another, leading him always closer to the fiery stake.

Three days before he was to be executed, the door did open, and two armed guards entered, their guns pointed at his head, while behind them came an official of the Inquisition to plead with him to recant his Protestantism so that he could be mercifully hanged and thus escape the horror of the flames. Tatum, restraining his desire to leap at the man and kill him bare-handed, explained for the tenth time: "You have it wrong. Oliver Cromwell is long dead and his son fled. England has a king again and Catholics do not suffer."

The austere official would not listen. Working so far from the capital, his knowledge was decades old, and all he knew was that Englishmen had expelled Catholic priests and denied the true religion. Heretics they were and as heretics they must die. Making one last appeal, he begged: "Sailor, will you admit error and rejoin the Mother Church so that you may die the easy way?"

With a look of hatred that could never be extinguished, Tatum cried: "No!" The two guards, their guns still pointed at his head, withdrew and the door to his cell clanged shut, to be opened again only when he would go to his death.

Then, the next day, when he could hear carpenters adding seats to the platform from which the officials would watch him die, the miracle for which he had hoped occurred. One of the other condemned men caught a guard by the throat as the man appeared with the evening meal of bread and gruel, strangled him, and grabbed from his dead body the keys to the cells. Realizing that with others to help he would have a better chance, he rushed to the nearest cells, opened them, and whispered: "No turning back. It's sure torture if they take us." Thus, the five men, Will Tatum among them, moved stealthily down the stone corridor, surprised the two Spaniards guarding it, and broke their way to freedom.

Outside the jail, they kept close to the walls so that night shadows protected them, and in this manner covered some distance before a wild alarm was sounded and guards began fanning out in pursuit. In the first melee three of the men were caught and clubbed to death, but Tatum and the man who had made the flight possible, a fiery Welshman named Burton, managed to find their way to an impoverished part of town and spent the night hiding between two shacks.

Shortly before dawn they broke into a house, smothered the occupants in their beds, and stole new clothing and food to sustain them in the perilous days ahead. They felt no compunction over the murders, because, as Burton said when they were headed out of Cádiz: "It was them or us."

They now set themselves a hazardous task, for their only chance of escape lay in reaching Portugal, which was well to the west, and many obstacles impeded that path. They would have to cross first the Guadalquivir River, where the treasure ships entered on their way from Mexico to Sevilla. Then the great empty Marismas plain blocked their way to Huelva, from where Columbus had left to find the New World. At Huelva, there would be another river, and then a short, dangerous run into Portugal. It was dangerous because in these troubled years Spain and Portugal were engaged in what amounted to an undeclared war, so the border was well guarded. But in another sense that would be helpful, for certainly no Portuguese would send them back to Spain.

They survived through days of terror and nights of starvation, and at Sanlúcar they crossed the Guadalquivir in a stolen rowboat that passed almost under the creaking prow of a caravel coming home from Havana laden with silver and gold, and when light from the ship's lantern fell across Tatum's face, Burton whispered: "Where'd you get that scar?" and Will replied: "Protestant clergyman burned me in Barbados. Catholic priests going to burn me here in Spain. Who wins in this game?"

Transit of the Marismas, that vast semidesert fronting on the Golfo de Cádiz, proved more difficult, for during the first half of their journey they had no food; then, after Burton, a most resourceful man, stopped two exit holes from a burrow and dug out a pair of rabbits which the fugitives chewed raw, they spent the second half with no water. Near Huelva they came upon a small stream, of which they drank to near-explosion, and again feeling no compunction, they robbed two houses in succession, murdered the occupants of one, crossed the river north of the town, and made their way into Portugal.

The deprivations of their trip intensified in each man his consuming hatred of all things Spanish, so that when the Portuguese authorities welcomed them and wanted to place them on a ship running a Spanish blockade, they leaped at the opportunity, and spurred their fellow sailors whenever a chance presented itself to board and capture a Spanish ship. Where fighting ensued, for Spanish sailors had grown accustomed to warding off English, French and Dutch ships trying to steal their treasures, Tatum and Burton were remorseless. They killed when there was no necessity, when the outcome of battle had already been decided, and they did so with glee. For as they warned their fellow sailors: "If the Spaniards capture you, they burn you alive."

In this fearful lusting for revenge, the two iron-hard sailors spent most of 1665 on Portuguese ships prowling the Spanish coast, intercepting Spanish vessels, and spreading terror. Once when they put into Lisbon they learned that their homeland was again on the way to becoming Catholic and they wondered if it would be safe for them to head back to London.

One spring morning in 1666 they sailed out of Lisbon on one of the many English ships that slipped in to trade at that port, and during the run north, as they neared the English coast, the sailors informed Will and Burton of the tragedy that had afflicted London during the past year: "It's over now, mostly. But while it lasted, it was terrifying. The Black Plague they called it, and death was so common they couldn't even bury the victims proper. Threw them in ditches at the edge of town and had horses drag earth over them."

"What is this plague, as you call it?" Tatum asked, and one of the men explained: "Nothin' you can see. Nothin' that causes it. You get up in the mornin', feel dizzy, feel tight in your lungs, so you lie down and never get back up. End of three days, always three, they cart you off."

Another sailor added: "When we was last in port, fierce, ragin' sweep. Thousands died. We fled without a full cargo. Captain shouted one afternoon: 'We leave this hell port!' and off we went, untouched."

"But we're going back," Tatum protested, and the sailors assured him: "Safe now. The plague ran its course, a ship told us in Lisbon."

It had, but not quite, for when Tatum and Burton went ashore, deeply moved to be in England again, they used some of their pirate gains for lodgings in the mean quarter close to the wharfs, and there the brave Welshman Burton woke one morning with a racking fever. Unable to leave his bed, he told Tatum: "It's the plague. See I have a proper grave," and in the foreordained three days, he was dead.

At some danger to himself, Tatum buried the man who had saved him from burning, and at the lonely graveside, attended only by himself, the clergyman and the gravedigger, Burton, whose first name Will had never known, was laid to rest. The gravedigger, a man whose occupation kept him apart from people, wanted to talk as he started to shovel in the echoing earth: "We couldn't dig enough graves last week; same, two weeks before. This may be the last of the lot. Plague's over, they keep tellin' us, but it wasn't over for him, was it?"

Tatum spent the next five months trying in vain to find a cargo ship headed for the Caribbean. Fear of the plague had halted traffic into London, so he was still in his foul quarters on the wharf on the second of September when, as the devout claimed, "God sent a fiery furnace to cleanse London of sin and the plague." It started innocuously, a fire among some old houses so unimportant that on that first day Tatum was not even aware that a conflagration was under way. But on the next day, he and the vagrants living in the mean shacks around his gathered to watch the columns of smoke rising from the center of the city, and that morning soldiers ran through the wharf area, shouting: "All men report immediately. Bring axes and shovels." At sunset the sky was lighted by flames, and on the fourth of September it seemed as if the entire city was ablaze. Three-fourths of it was.

Tatum worked without rest for two days and two nights, sometimes rescuing people from houses soon to explode in flames, at other times trying to chop down old structures to form a break in the incessant spread. On the evening of the fourth day of the fire, when the flames had subsided, leaving the once-proud city of London a smoking ruin, Tatum fell asleep at the edge of the roadway, exhausted, but well before dawn he was awakened by a military officer, who said sharply: "On your feet! Carry these papers," and he spent that day trudging along behind the officer as the latter compiled his dismal census: "Every church we've seen, completely destroyed. Put it down as seventy churches."

The burned-out private residences, the officer calculated, must number in the tens of thousands, for when subalterns ran up to him with their reports, they were identical: "All houses in my area gone." The only good news Tatum heard that long day was that the fires were out, because on the day before, scores had still been raging unchecked. Toward three in the afternoon a group of women got together some food within the walls of a warehouse that had been built of stone, and Tatum ate like a glutton. The officer, smiling at his voracious appetite, commended him: "You've earned the right to be a pig."

The next week a ship reached the Thames with a cargo of sugar and molasses from the Caribbean, and after helping unload it into the arms of people who wept to see sugar again after the fire, Tatum found passage home on the return trip. Like most ships of that time, this one made its first stop at the lovely island of Barbados, and when Will saw the familiar green fields and the reassuring sight of sugar-cane growing, tears came to his eyes. He had left this tender, gracious island on a Dutch ship, in 1659, a disgraced and branded exile in

search of adventure, and during his years of wandering had participated in pirate battles between great ships at sea, had watched his
companions burn, had tried to console the Welshman Burton as the
plague reached out to make him one of its last victims, and had
rubbed smoke from his eyes as London burned. He had come home
with no money, no prospects of work at any known job, but he did
have what many lesser men would never have: a burning compulsion,
more unquenchable than life itself—someday he would wreak vengeance on Spaniards.

In the fall of 1666, when Will came ashore at Bridgetown and realized that within minutes he would be back in familiar haunts, he experienced a pressing desire to see four people: the adorable Betsy
Bigsby with her golden braids, Nell and Ned and, perversely, his
pompous brother, Isaac: I can't wait to see what that one's up to.

Landing at the familiar waterfront with one small bag containing
the rewards from five years of adventuring, he almost ran to the Bigs-
bys' store, only to find that it was now operated by new owners, and
when he asked what had become of Betsy, for he was most eager to
see her again in hopes that she might still marry him, he received a
curt ending to that dream: "Met a soldier, went to England."

His luck was a bit better when he crossed the street to his sister's
shop. Nell looked painfully worn, but as always she put up a bold
front: "Ned and I live upstairs, as always, and he's a boy a mother can
be proud of. Isaac? He's let his knighthood and his plantations go to
his head."

"He got knighted, eh?" Will whistled softly. "And he's a great
plantation owner now?"

"Yes. And judged by some to be an even bigger man than Oldmixon. I can say this. Between the two, they run the island."

Will took to young Ned the moment he met him, for he was a
fine-looking lad of fifteen, with curly red hair, freckles, and the kind
of frank, open face that instills confidence in other boys who would
want him on their side in games and in girls who would speculate:
"Could he swing me in a dance!"

He had quit the village school at fourteen, having mastered the
alphabet, his numbers, the easier theorems of Euclid and a smattering of Greek and Roman history. His early association with Cavaliers
at school and church had made him an ardent Royalist, a fact that

might have endeared him to his uncle, Sir Isaac, except that the latter wanted little to do with the shopkeeping Pennyfeathers and rarely saw his nephew. Ned spent most of his time helping his mother at the shop, a duty for which he had no inclination, and some in town wondered what the lad would be when he matured, but his lively ways and rambling mind gave no hint that he ever would.

Uncle Will saw at once that the boy was much as he had been at that age, and to Nell's surprise, told him one night at supper: "Always remember this scar on my face, Ned. I needn't have put it there. Don't pick up scars by accident. Earn them in doing something big!"

Easily, almost without making a conscious decision, Will settled in with his sister, helped with the store, and did odd jobs about the waterfront, where he kept close watch on various ships coming from England or moving westward through the Caribbean to other islands. He told no one what he was looking for, but when the townspeople learned that he had for some years after his earlier departure been a pirate on ships of various nations, they supposed that he might be tending in that direction again: "We won't be seein' Will for long. Not a solid man like his brother."

Will speculated on when he might run into Sir Isaac, and when Nell suggested that in decency he ought to walk out to the old Saltonstall plantation and make himself known, Will said: "He knows I'm back. His move." Thus, more than a month passed without his having seen Isaac or his wife, Lady Clarissa, but he did not care.

If he experienced any disappointment equal to his loss of Betsy Bigsby, it was learning that his Dutch friend, Captain Brongersma, no longer brought the *Stadhouder* to Barbados. "And well he shouldn't," a sailor told him, "seein' he lost her and his life in a battle with Spaniards at Cumaná salt flats."

"What happened?"

"Killed when the Spaniards boarded. Tried to fight them off, but their blades were longer and sharper."

This knowledge so pained Will that on Sunday he accompanied his sister and Ned to the parish church, where he said prayers for Brongersma's turbulent soul, and when he opened his eyes he saw Sir Isaac and Lady Clarissa across the aisle staring at him, and next he saw that the clergyman who would be conducting the service was the sniveling fellow who had branded him. It was not a happy Sunday morning, nor were his thoughts of a highly religious nature; they concerned imaginative things he would like to do to the clergyman, Sir Isaac and Lady Clarissa.

At close of service he led Nell from the church, and they both hoped to avoid their brother and his unpleasant wife, but unfortunately, they all met at the church door, where Sir Isaac said with proper aloofness: "Good to see you, Will. Hope things go better this time," and as he spoke, Lady Clarissa offered the thinnest smile seen in many months. Then they were gone.

At supper that night, after Ned had left the table, Will asked the question which had been bothering him: "Nell, doesn't Isaac share any of his wealth with you? To help with you and the boy?"

"Never. He's ashamed of us, and he must be mortified to have you back."

Will, who had given his sister whatever funds he had got hold of for work along the waterfront, was so outraged by his brother's selfishness that he walked out to Saltonstall Manor, as he still called it in hopes that the sturdy Roundhead would one day return to claim it, entered the now-palatial residence without knocking, and confronted his brother in his office. Isaac, afraid that Will had come to chastise him for the stigmatization, reached for an andiron, but Will laughed: "Put it down, Isaac. I'm not here to talk about me. It's about Nell."

"What about her?"

"It's indecent, you living here like this while she struggles in town to keep the store open and her son clothed."

"He's a big boy now. He can soon find work as an overseer on one of the plantations." Isaac, who in his prosperity seemed taller than Will remembered, added rather haughtily: "As a matter of fact, Will, you could too. We need overseers. Have to send to Scotland to get a good one." Then he smiled coldly and added: "But of course, I suppose you'd rather go pirating," and when he showed Will the door it was clear that no money for the Pennyfeathers would be forthcoming from him.

Sir Isaac's reference to the difficulty that plantations were having in finding overseers for their sugar fields alerted Will to the many changes that had overtaken Barbados in recent years. Nell filled him in further: "Wealthy men like Thomas Oldmixon and Isaac have gobbled up so many plantations that farmers of modest means can find none to purchase. Many of them have moved west to the open lands of Jamaica."

"What has that to do with Isaac's plantation?"

"With the white men who would normally serve as overseers gone, Oldmixon and Isaac and their like have to import them—just like it was done in our father's time. Indentured servants they still call them, fine lads who work their hearts out for seven years, for board and keep but no wages, with hopes that at the end of their seven years they'll be able to buy themselves a plot of land and become plantation owners themselves."

"But you say that Isaac and others have grabbed all the available lands. So what do the young Scotsmen do?" Will asked, and his sister said: "Look up young Mr. McFee, who sailed here to work for your brother. He has the story."

When Will found Angus McFee, he heard a doleful tale: "I lived in a Highland hamlet west of Inverness and sailed here under a misunderstanding. In Scotland the agent promised: 'Sir Isaac Tatum will pay your passage out to Barbados, and in gratitude you're legally bound to give him seven years of honest help. At the end he hands you the wages he's been saving for you plus fifty pounds thank-you money. Then you'll be free to buy your own plantation, and you're on your way . . .'"

"I've heard that's how many come."

"Yes, but when we get here we find it's all work, horrible hut and worse food, no pay accumulating, no thank-you payment at the end, and no land to buy if you had the money."

"What do you do?"

"What can we do? As free men, we go back to work for your brother or men like him for whatever wages they choose to pay." He leaned against a fence post, and said bitterly: "Any chance I had of bringing my lassie out from Inverness to build a plantation and a family is lost."

"Haven't you protested?" Will asked, and McFee spat: "I did. Appealed to the courts, but who are the justices? Oldmixon and your brother, and they invariably side with the other plantation owners. An ordinary overseer has almost no rights, a laborer none whatsoever."

When Will heard these details of life on the new Barbados he told McFee: "I'd like to learn more," and as he moved about the island he saw many things that perplexed him. The next time he saw McFee, he said: "Far more than half the faces I meet are black. Didn't used to be that way," and McFee explained: "When one white man like Old-mixon owns land that sixteen white men used to work, he has to have slaves . . . always more slaves—'Get me slaves at the auction when the Dutch ships bring them in'—so now the island has many blacks. In another ten years, fifty rich white men will own all the land and oper-ate it with fifty young Scotsmen like me, one to each plantation su-pervising forty thousand slaves."

"The slaves I've known," Will said, "aren't stupid. Get enough of them in one place, they'll begin to fight for their rights." Anticipating what that would mean, he told McFee one afternoon: "I'd not want to live on a Barbados like that," and McFee, looking about before he spoke, said: "I'm not so happy living on this one."

That exchange of two short sentences set in motion a chain of events which would carry the two conspirators far beyond what they contemplated when the more-or-less careless words were spoken, for McFee began to study carefully the operation of the Tatum estates and Will began hanging around the Bridgetown waterfront, noticing with a practiced mariner's eye all sorts of developments and particu-larly which ships were coming from where, and it was as a result of this process that he renewed his knowledge of the Tortuga that Cap-tain Brongersma had spoken about with such enthusiasm. It was a unique island, sailors said, lying close to the northwest shore of the great Spanish island Hispaniola, which Columbus had settled and ruled.

"It's practically French," said one grizzled veteran who knew it well. "Not half as large as Barbados. Supposed to belong to Spain, which tried to recapture it from time to time. But the French, they're pirates, really . . . call themselves buccaneers. *Buccaneer* is how we English pronounce it. The French word is *boucanier.* Four years I served with them in Tortuga. Very excitin' I can tell you. But as I was sayin', these wild men, and they're wilder than anything you see on Barbados . . . believe me, they live on two things. Huntin' down small Spanish ships, killin' the crew and stealin' the vessel and whatever's inside. And goin' over to the forests on Hispaniola and killin' wild hogs. They bring the meat back, cut it in strips, rub in salt and spices and roast it very slowly over a low fire . . . maybe four days. *Boucan* they call it, so that makes 'em *boucaniers.* They sell the meat for a tidy profit to Dutch and English privateers workin' those waters against the Spaniards."

"Do they really capture Spanish ships?" Tatum asked, and his ears pricked up when the old man said: "Many. You see, the hatred the buccaneers have for Spain and anything Spanish goes back to 1638 when there was a big *boucanier* settlement on Tortuga." (He used the two versions of the word interchangeably, but he obviously preferred the latter.) "Spanish officials in Cartagena sent a big force up to Tortuga, and their savage soldiers killed every *boucanier* on the little island—men, women, children, even the dogs. And as I may have told you, the one thing in this world a *boucanier* loves is his huntin' dogs. They can smell a wild boar at two miles. But hundreds of us were absent, huntin' on Hispaniola, and when we sailed back the few miles to Tortuga and saw our friends' bodies still unburied, we swore that before we died . . ."

"How do you join the buccaneers?" Will asked, and the old fellow said: "You just go there. Steal yourself a ship of some kind, sail to Hispaniola, avoid the Spanish on the south side of the island, and coast around to the northwest. You don't need no papers to join. Frenchmen come, Indians from Honduras, Dutchmen who've fought with their captains and maybe murdered them and taken their ships, Englishmen, half a dozen from the American colonies . . ." The man would have said a great deal more, but Will had heard enough, and that night he began talking seriously with Angus McFee.

In daytime he did his best to look after the interests of his sister, noting with anxiety that her health was failing rapidly, and he discussed the matter with Ned, who said: "Mum knows. Told me she wasn't long for this world."

"Why didn't you tell me?" and the boy said: "She swore me to secrecy. Said you had your own problems."

"We must do something for her," and in a series of swift, loving moves he sold the store to a young couple just out from England, placed the money in the care of a trustworthy local businessman, added to it all his own savings, moved Nell into the home of a neighbor who could care for her, and even went to see Isaac to beg him to contribute to his sister's upkeep. But with Lady Clarissa sitting primly beside him, Sir Isaac said: "She went her way, I went mine," implying by his smug look that Will, too, seemed to have gone his own way, a dreadfully wrong way.

"But, Isaac, she's dying. I can see it in her eyes. She's worked herself to death," and Isaac said: "That rambunctious boy of hers should get a job and not fool around that silly store."

"The store's been sold," and Clarissa said: "Well, then she does have some money," and Will simply looked at the two misers, the skin around his scar flushing with the hatred he felt for them, and there was nothing more he cared to say. Stopping by McFee's hut as he started back to town, he said with unhesitating resolve: "The plan we talked about the other night is right. We go."

Sir Isaac, like many of the wealthier plantation owners, had a ship called *Loyal Forever,* in boastful memory of the defense of King Charles during the Barbadian troubles of 1649–1652. It was not large, for it was intended merely for the interisland trade with places like Antigua and for Carib hunting on All Saints, but it was sturdy, having been built by the best shipwrights in Amsterdam and brought by Dutch sailors to Barbados with a hold full of slaves. Sir Isaac had bought the ship, its charts and slaves in one big deal on which he had already made a huge profit, and this would double when he sold the *Loyal Forever* to some other planter about to enlarge his plantation.

In a series of secret meetings, McFee, Tatum, two other abused indentured servants, three trusted slaves of great ability and the boy Ned discussed plans for capturing the *Loyal Forever,* persuading as many of the crew as possible to remain on the ship, and sailing it to Tortuga to join the buccaneers. With a sharp needle Will punctured the left forefingers of his seven co-conspirators and made them dab a sheet of paper on which nothing had been written: "Your oath. If you betray us with even one word . . ." and he drew his own bloody forefinger across his throat.

When Will and Ned saw from their room ashore a signal that the ship had been taken with no gunfire, they walked down to the wharf to board her, moving slowly lest they attract attention. But at the last moment Ned broke away and ran back to the neighbor's house in which Nell was staying. Rushing into the small room, he embraced his rapidly failing mother and whispered: "Mum, I'm off for a buccaneer! Me and Uncle Will." Looking up at her son, so bright and promising, she said softly: "Maybe it's better. Not much here for you two." And she kissed him for the last time. "Be careful." Leaving the house with never a backward glance, the young fellow strolled nonchalantly down to the stolen ship, trying to look like an indifferent old seaman.

It was more than a thousand miles from Barbados to Tortuga, and the would-be buccaneers chose what they judged to be the route least likely to throw them into contact with other ships: through the St. Vincent passage and into the Caribbean proper, then northwest to Mona Passage between the Spanish islands of Puerto Rico and Hispaniola, then along the north coast of the latter island, and into the channel that separated it from Tortuga.

During the first days of the trip, which took about three weeks, it was obvious that whereas McFee was a brave man and intelligent, he was no sea captain, but no one else wanted the job. Fortunately, Tatum and others aboard were seasoned sailors, and in Ned Pennyfeather, Will had an aide who had learned from a Dutchman how to use a remarkable but still primitive instrument, the astrolabe, for checking latitude whenever the sun was visible at noon or the North Star at night. They had left Barbados at near thirteen degrees and climbed the ladder of the latitudes to past twenty, and Ned delighted in telling Captain McFee the ship's position twice each day: "Sixteen degrees latitude North and on course," and so on. But since no ship at that time had a reliable way of determining longitude, he never really knew exactly where the *Loyal Forever* was. When they had made their way far enough north to be reasonably sure they had passed Hispaniola, they headed due west toward Tortuga.

As they entered the channel and Will saw how small Tortuga was, how low and unimpressive its hills, he had a moment of disbelief: How could this place be the wonderful center Brongersma told me about? And as McFee brought the *Loyal Forever* to its anchorage among nine or ten other ships, Ned said: "None of these ships are as big as even the small Dutch traders that sneak into Barbados."

But when they went ashore, they saw a strange sight. This vital center of the Caribbean was not a town but a haphazard collection of houses, each duplicating the owner's memories of his homeland: a famous Dutch pirate had used his enormous wealth to create a replica of his childhood home in Holland, complete with dormer windows and a windmill; an Englishman who would later hang at Tyburn had built himself a Devon cottage with a fenced-in garden and a flower bed; a Spaniard had a house of tile; but it was the French, who predominated, who contributed the wildest assortment of miniature chalets and country cottages.

But most of the living places were shacks of the meanest sort, with many tents and canvas lean-tos propped against trees, and there were trading spots but no real stores. Wherever one looked, there was an easy juxtaposition of considerable wealth and abject poverty.

Since a pirate's standing depended upon his most recent capture at sea, and since most had gone months or even years without having taken a prize, Tortuga was not a handsome place.

But every dwelling did have two features: an open hearth topped by an iron spit for the slow smoking of *boucan,* and at least one dog, more often two or three. Those were the hallmarks of Tortuga.

When Captain McFee's mutineers from Barbados anchored their *Loyal Forever* close to the shore of this small, wild island, none realized that this had once been part of the area governed by Christopher Columbus, for Tortuga had always been an appendage to Hispaniola and still was. Santo Domingo, the ancient capital and still a major city, lay far away, two hundred and thirty miles, but it faced the Caribbean while Tortuga had to battle Atlantic storms. That was fitting, for it was a tempestuous, unruly place, its chaotic appearance explained by the fact that at irregular intervals some Spanish governor in Cartagena would bellow: "Enough of those damned pirates in Tortuga preying on our ships. Destroy the place." Then Spanish soldiers in helmets, brought north by a small fleet, would storm ashore, burn all the houses to the ground, kill everyone including the children and dogs, and leave only ashes. Tortuga would then lie desolated for a while, but soon a new gang of pirates would come ashore, sort through the still-warm ashes, and start to build their own preposterous dwellings.

When the Barbados men got there they found the island jammed with outlaws who had grudgingly conceded that they lived most easily if they submitted themselves to a rough form of government. They had even agreed upon a governor, of sorts, a Frenchman elected by his fellow buccaneers.

Tortuga, the island shaped like a turtle, hence its name, was a place of excitement and promise, and Ned was proud to be one of the youngest buccaneers. And because his uncle Will had insisted that Ned learn French and Spanish, he was enlisted in important negotiations regarding the *Loyal Forever.*

Two big and terrifying French pirates had services to offer which McFee and his Englishmen could not ignore, for as the two Frenchmen explained: "If you stole your ship standing out there, English patrols will be looking for you. If they catch you, the noose. Because you are now technically pirates."

As McFee and Tatum listened to this blunt statement, Ned saw them wince, but then the Frenchmen made their offer: "We'll take your ship and have our carpenters . . ."

McFee broke in: "Don't you do the work?" and the Frenchmen laughed: "We arrange. Last Spanish ship we captured, we got ourselves eight experienced carpenters. We keep them as our slaves, you might say, but we do feed them well." He summoned the carpenters, who exploded in a flurry of Spanish as they described how they would tear the *Loyal Forever* apart and rebuild it so it could never be identified.

"And," said the Frenchmen, like thoughtful bankers concluding a loan, "we take your boat and give you ours, the one you see anchored over there. Not quite as big as yours, but not so vulnerable, either."

The deal was arranged, and by midafternoon the Spanish carpenters were destroying practically everything on the *Loyal Forever* that might betray its origin, and building in its place a superstructure which created a new silhouette. After a week of intense labor the new ship looked longer, narrower, and had two masts instead of one. The ship they were receiving in exchange had also been sharply modified, and Ned wondered who had owned it before. As to its name, McFee asked the Spanish workmen to carve him a board to attach to the stern, and when it was in place, Ned asked: "What's *Glen Affric?*" McFee told him: "A glen in Scotland where the angels sing." Ned noted with satisfaction that their new ship had portholes for eight small cannon. "This *Glen Affric* will do some singing, too," he predicted.

But the dream of a quick dash north to intercept a lone Spanish bullion ship on its way to Sevilla was rudely ended when McFee brought disappointing news: "No action till the Spanish ships go past in May. They want us to go ashore on Hispaniola to hunt wild boar," and Ned was given a very long gun with a spadelike butt to jam against his shoulder, a high pointed cap to protect him from the blazing sun, a ration of tobacco and a big, rangy black female hunting dog that had belonged to a French buccaneer killed during a boarding fight. With this gear, plus a bowl made from half a coconut and a blanket rolled into a tube whose ends he tied about his waist, he was ready for the forests of Hispaniola, and when a small boat placed him and ten others on the shore opposite Tortuga, he was prepared for his initiation into the arcane rites of the buccaneer.

Although they were now on the historic island of Hispaniola, the one from which the entire Caribbean had been settled by the probing Spanish, the part they were in was untamed wilderness of low trees, savannah, wild hogs and no settlers at all. But it remained a part of the Spanish empire, even though few in command remembered that it existed.*

In this strange but captivating mixture of wilderness and prairie, Ned was taken from his uncle's group and thrown in with a group of six, headed by a bright young fellow of twenty-seven or so who had been hunting in Hispaniola for some years during those spells when seaborne filibustering was not under way. "My name Mompox," he said, just that, nothing more, and in the days that followed, Ned learned that he was half-Spanish, quarter-Meskito Indian from Honduras and quarter-Negro from the Isthmus of Panamá. "Because my color, Spaniards make me slave, work in building fort at Cartagena."

"How did you break free?" Ned asked, and the big man with roguish eyes replied: "Like him, like that one, like you maybe," and he let it go at that. However, from things he said hunting on Hispaniola, Ned deduced that he had been a Tortuga buccaneer for some years.

Of all the group that had been assigned to hunt under him, Mompox seemed to like Ned the best, for he took special pains to instruct him in how to handle his big gun and utilize his trained dog in tracking down wild boar. And when Ned finally shot two in succession, after having missed two, Mompox showed him how to gut the animals, skin them, and cut their rich meat into strips.

When enough hogs had been slain to justify building a big fire, Mompox instructed Ned in the art of barbecuing, and for several days the boy had the job of tending the fire and watching to see that the pork strips did not burn; he also applied salt to the meat and rubbed it with a handful of aromatic leaves that Mompox provided. "This meat," Mompox assured him in a wild mix of many languages, "will keep for months. Many ships stop by to buy it from us. It fights scurvy."

When the older man felt that Ned now knew the basic principles of *boucan*, he led him on a long foray into the interior, and they penetrated to a point so far from shore that along with three others, they

---

*In 1697, because the French pirates had taken effective control of this western portion of Hispaniola, the Treaty of Ryswick, which ended a European war, awarded it to France, who held it until 1804, when rebellious blacks expelled Napoleon's armies and established the republic of Haiti. Tortuga, too, is now a part of Haiti.

reached a spot often visited by patrols from the Spanish part of the big island. On this day they had the bad luck to encounter one, and Ned might have been killed by a sharpshooter had not Mompox seen the Spaniard and shot him. At the end of the tangled fight which ensued, the buccaneers took the man prisoner, but Mompox cut his throat, leaving his corpse propped against a tree.

When the various hunting parties were ready to return to Tortuga, they gathered on the shore and waited two days with their huge bundles of dried meat for ships to come for them, and in that time Will observed with some apprehension the interest Mompox was taking in Ned. When they ate, Mompox slipped the boy better pieces of meat, and when they camped beside the channel, Mompox gathered twigs for Ned's sleeping place. Tatum also noticed that even when the two were separated, Mompox's sharp eyes frequently came to rest on Ned, regardless of where the boy was sitting.

During the waiting time Will said nothing to his nephew, but when the ships came to collect the cured meat and the hunting teams, Will interposed himself onto a bench so that Mompox could not sit beside Ned, but the big chief hunter forestalled him by saying boldly: "Sit over here, Ned." Will ignored the move as if it were of no concern; however, when they returned to Tortuga and were off by themselves, he took his nephew aside for some fatherly talk.

"Have you noticed, Ned, how each buccaneer seems to pick out some one person to work with? Sort of look out for each other?"

"Yes. If Mompox hadn't come back for me that time, I'd be dead."

"You didn't tell me. What happened?" and when Ned explained the incident with the Spanish sharpshooter, Will said approvingly: "You were lucky Mompox was there," but then he changed his approach: "Were you there the night before we went to Hispaniola? The night one of the men suddenly leaped up and stabbed that other fellow?"

"Yes."

"Why do you suppose he did that?"

"Maybe money?" Ned really did not know and had not the experience to make a sensible guess, so very quietly Will said: "I doubt it was money. When a lot of men gather together, with no women around . . . haven't seen one for months and even years . . . Well, men behave in strange ways . . . fight each other for strange reasons."

He stopped there, but Ned was quick-witted enough to know that this conversation had not ended: "What are you trying to tell me?"

And Will said simply: "Don't get too close to Mompox. No, I don't mean that. Don't let him get too close to you."

"But he saved my life."

"That he did, and you owe him a great deal. But not too much."

Both Will and Ned, and Mompox too, were disappointed when, on their return to Tortuga, they found no plans under way for either an attack on a Spanish treasure galleon or a land assault on a city in Cuba or Campeachy, and they were appalled at what was proposed. McFee explained as best he could: "We've sold all the *barbacoa* we can, and there's no money coming in from any raids. But those two big ships out there, one English, one Dutch, have promised they'll buy all the logwood we can cut . . ."

At even the mention of logwood the older buccaneers groaned, for there was no job in the Seven Seas worse than cutting logwood. As one old sailor who had once been forced to work the salt pans at Cumaná said: "Logwood is worse. At Cumaná you at least worked on land. Logwood? Up to your bum in water eighteen hours a day."

But with Spanish treasure nonexistent, McFee's men had no choice but to sail due westward to the distant shores of Honduras, with the two big ships trailing behind to purchase such logwood as the buccaneers felled. When Ned saw the forlorn tangle of sea and swamp in which the many-branched trees grew, and imagined the insects and snakes and panthers infesting that jungle, he lost heart, but his uncle, who had been two days from death in that Cádiz cell, encouraged him: "Six months of hell, Ned, but they do pass. And for years after, we'll tell others how bad it was."

It was exactly what Will had predicted, six months of the most torturous work men could do, up to their thighs in slimy water, beset by cruel insects, attacked now and then by deadly watersnakes, and arms tense from chopping at the tangled logwood trees. It was difficult to believe that these ugly trees were valuable, but one old fellow told Ned: "Pound for pound, about as valuable as silver," and a fight broke out when someone else shouted: "Horse manure!"

Ned would have had a difficult time in the logwood forest had not Mompox been at hand to look after him, tend the horrendous insect bites when they festered, and see that he received adequate food. Once when Ned nearly fainted from a fever caused by bites and constant immersion, Mompox persuaded the Dutch ship to take Ned aboard so that he could at least catch some uninterrupted sleep, and while there the weakened lad asked the captain: "What do people do with this damned logwood?" and the Dutchman explained: "Look at the core of that exposed piece. Have you ever seen such a beautiful deep, dark purple-brown . . . maybe even a touch of gold?" And when Ned looked, he saw how magnificent the corewood was that he had been harvesting.

"I still don't see what you do with it."

"A dye, son. One of the strongest and most beautiful in the world."

"I thought dyes were yellow and blue and red. Bright handsome colors that women like."

"Those are showy, yes, but this . . . this is imperial."

When Ned was able to go back to work he chopped at his trees with more respect, but as for the occupation of logwood cutter, he had to agree with the men who had described it before he came to Honduras: "It's hellish."

On the voyage back to Tortuga he asked in some irritation: "When do we strike the Spanish?" and a longtime member of the force on the island reminded him: "We wait for the right year with the right wind and the right advantages for our side. Remember that in 1628, Piet Heyn, the great Dutch pirate, waited two years for the moment—but he caught the whole silver armada on its way home to Sevilla. In a daring move never to be repeated, he captured not three treasure galleons, not four, but the whole fleet. Yes, fifteen million guilders in one shot, and a guilder was worth more than a pound. That year his company paid a fifty-percent dividend. I sailed with Heyn, and we got so much prize money I could have bought a farm. But I didn't."

In the tedious months of 1667 and early 1668, Captain McFee's buccaneers in their perky little *Glen Affric* participated in no such lucky assaults, but they did manage to engage in two rather sharp fights in which, in tandem with three other small ships, they attacked two isolated Spanish galleons, losing one and taking the other after a difficult boarding fight. The galleon yielded gratifying prize money for the four crews, and Ned had a chance to watch how his uncle and Mompox treated Spanish prisoners—they shot all of them and pitched their bodies overboard.

That January, when McFee told his crew that during the forthcoming quiet season, when no Spanish ships could be expected, they had two choices: "Hunt wild boar on Hispaniola or go back to Honduras for more logwood," they rebelled: "No. We took great risks to come here to fight Spanish ships, and that we shall do."

"Brave speech!" McFee said as if applauding their courage, but then he became scornful: "And what will you eat for the next ten months? Choose. Hunting or chopping."

It was Mompox who solved the dilemma, for he was an adroit man who listened to whatever rumors circulated: "They say there's a captain who's very lucky over in Jamaica. And I like to sail with lucky captains, because we share in whatever he captures."

And for the first time Will Tatum and his nephew heard more than the general rumors that had been filtering through the Caribbean. The captain was Henry Morgan, a thirty-three-year-old Welshman who had come out to Barbados some years before as an indentured servant and who had graduated, like McFee, to a life of buccaneering, a trade in which he had known spectacular successes. He was widely regarded as a lucky captain, one to whom rich target ships were drawn as if by magnets. He had not yet enjoyed feats like the great Piet Heyn, or sacked Spanish cities the way the cruel Frenchman L'Ollonais did so effectively, but he had proved his mettle by driving his little ships against huge adversaries and coming away victorious. As Mompox told the men on the *Glen Affric*: "They say. 'When you sail with Morgan, you come home with money.'" And off they sailed to Port Royal.

Ned would never forget the day of their arrival. Standing in the prow of the *Glen Affric,* he watched as they approached from the south the big island of Jamaica, and as if he might have to bring his own ship into port at some future time, he excitedly rattled on, though Will was barely paying attention to him: "From this distance it's impossible to see there's a port anywhere on that coast. Just Jamaica, big and looming. But look! There seems to be a chain of pinpoint islets sweeping westward, parallel to the land. They can't be far offshore, but I can see they must shelter a bay behind them. But to enter it, I'd have to sail far to the west, turn, and then sail back east. That's just what we're doing."

He had no sooner made this deduction than he gasped, for the bay subtended by his arc of little islands was enormous: "All the warships of England could find safe harboring in here. Uncle Will! This is stupendous!" But Will was looking at the real miracle of this anchorage. What young Ned had assumed was a chain of islets was in reality a long, low sandspit curving from the mainland, and at its end stood a town.

"That must be Port Royal!" Will whispered, and the sense of awe with which he clothed the words forced Ned to study more closely the famous buccaneers' capital: "It has a fort, so they mean to protect it. Hundreds of houses, so people live here. That's a church. A place for hauling out ships to scrape the bottoms. And those must be shops. But look at that sign! It's a wine shop . . . and that one . . . and that."

Only then did he look eastward to inspect the great bay itself: "More than two dozen huge ships! They can't all belong to buccaneers! There wouldn't be enough Spanish ships for that many to attack."

As Captain McFee edged the *Glen Affric* toward its anchorage, his crew caught the full impact of this fabled seaport, the most savage and uncontrolled anywhere in the western world that ships dropped anchor. From where the *Glen Affric* came to rest, its sailors were close to a most inviting town, with white houses in a row, big shore establishments for the holding of goods, four or five churches and a small cathedral of sorts. What they could not see, but which they took for granted from the stories Mompox had told, were the forty taverns and fifty entertainment houses that accounted for the town's evil reputation.

It was not exaggerated, for when they went ashore they quickly saw that Port Royal was special. It had no police, no restraints of any kind, and the soldiers stationed in the fort seemed as undisciplined as the pirates who roared ashore to take over the place, night after night. They were of all breeds and certainly all colors, and all with nefarious occupations. In some hectic months Port Royal averaged a dozen killings a night, and prominent on the waterfront was a rude gallows from whose yardarm, "dancing in Port Royal sunshine," was the corpse of some pirate who had attacked the wrong ship at the wrong time.

How different it was, Ned thought during his first few days, from Tortuga. The latter had been dour and barren, the food monotonous and the beer rotten. Port Royal, on the other hand, was a rollicking place. The food was excellent, with fresh fruits from inland Jamaica, beef from the plantations and fish from the sea. Whole casks of wine arrived from Europe and a rough beer from local brewers. But better than those amenities, most pirates thought, were the women of all colors who streamed in from lands in or touching upon the Caribbean. They were wild and wonderful, addicted like the men to strong drink and riotous living, and men who came down from the womanless world of Tortuga eagerly sought the diversion these lively women could provide.

Curiously, on Sundays the churches on the spit were just as crowded as the taverns had been during the week, and clergymen did not hesitate to remind their bleary-eyed congregations that if they continued piracy and debauchery as their way of life, retribution was sure to follow. Church of England rectors, who appreciated a nip now and then, did not inveigh against drinking, but ministers from the more rigorous sects did, and there was usually some traveling missionary from either England or the American colonies who preached fire and brimstone as the likely termination of Port Royal's dissolute ways.

Ned, who had promised his mother that he would attend church, was faithful to his vow, and it was after a particularly thunderous sermon, which he had listened to with Mompox at his side, that the minister, seeing him among the known buccaneers and marking his youth, stopped him as he was leaving the church and invited him to the rectory for Sunday dinner. Ned said that Mompox would have to come too, and the minister laughed: "Enough for three, it'll stretch to four."

The dinner combined tasty food, a fine wine and a fascinating history of Jamaica by a man who had participated in it: "In 1655, Oliver Cromwell sent into the Caribbean two gloriously incompetent men, buffoons, really, Admiral Penn in charge of only God knows how many ships, and General Venables leading an army of men. Their chaplain? Me. We had simple orders: 'Capture Hispaniola from the Spaniards.' But when we tried, Penn landed thirty miles from our target and Venables forgot to take along food or water. When we finally reached the walls of Santo Domingo, we were so exhausted that three hundred Spanish soldiers defeated three thousand of ours, and we ran like the devil back to our ships, dropping our arms as we ran."

Ned, aghast at this tale of incompetence, said: "A terrible defeat," but with a wide smile the clergyman corrected: "Not at all! A glorious victory!"

"How could that be?" Ned asked. "Did you go back and take the city?"

"Not at all!" the ruddy-faced minister repeated in the same exultant accents. "A crisis meeting was held aboard ship, and Penn said: 'If we sail home now, Cromwell will chop off our heads,' and Venables asked: 'What shall we do?' Neither could think of an escape, but a very young lieutenant named Pembroke, hardly more than a boy, asked brightly: 'Since we're already in these waters, why don't we capture Jamaica?' When Penn studied his chart he saw that it was only four hundred and sixty miles to the west, and cried out: 'On to Jamaica!'

"Well, I expected another disaster, because I could see that Penn knew nothing about ships and Venables less about armies, but Pembroke guided our fleet into this harbor, and this time our thousands of soldiers went ashore within walking distance of the Spanish, who had only a handful of men to oppose us. We won, and took possession of this magnificent island. When Penn and Venables returned to England, they said little to the newspapers or Parliament about their defeat at Hispaniola but a good deal about their capture of Jamaica. They talked themselves into heroes.

"Both Penn and Venables wanted me to return to England with them. Promised me a good church in Cromwell's new religion. But having seen Jamaica, I didn't want to leave." He smiled at his guests, and added: "So you see, young men, you can sometimes lose a big battle but go on to win a bigger one. Jamaica is the jewel of the Caribbean."

On the following Monday, Ned was lounging in a tavern when several old-timers gathered round in hopes that he was buying, and after he treated, they instructed him in the niceties of maritime warfare as conducted by Englishmen: "You mustn't never call us pirates. A pirate is a sailor who storms about the seas, obeyin' no laws, no rules of decency. He'll attack anything that floats, even a sea gull if he can't spy no Spanish galleon. Frenchmen can be pirates, and Dutchmen too, but never a proper Englishman." They warned Ned that if he wished to get his skull cracked, all he had to do was call a Port Royal man a pirate.

"You can't use corsair, neither. Just a fancy name for pirate. Freebooter, neither. Nor even buccaneer, which is only a shade better. Unruly, stuck away on Tortuga with his long gun and dog. Never washes. Lashes out now and then, captures a little ship with little cargo, then scuttles back to Tortuga to celebrate with his filthy cronies." The man speaking spat in a corner: "And what do you think this here buccaneer does when he can't catch a Spaniard? Cuts log-wood in Honduras."

The mere mention of such labor sickened Ned. "What do you want to be called?" he asked.

"What are we? We're privateers. We sail under Letters of Marque and Reprisal issued by the king and we act obedient to his law. You might say we're part of his navy, informal like."

At this point the gathering was electrified by a shout from Mom-pox, who appeared in the doorway: "Henry Morgan's sailing for the Main!" and he had hardly begun to explain that this meant the main-land of South America when others ran in, crying out and adding to the general confusion: "Henry Morgan for Cartagena!" and "Cap-tain Morgan for Havana!"

In seconds the tavern was emptied as men of all character rushed to a small government building in whose main room the great priva-teer waited to instruct the captains whose ships would comprise his fleet, and both Ned and his uncle were delighted when one of Mor-gan's aides announced that among those chosen to participate was Angus McFee and his *Glen Affric*. Then Morgan rose, a husky man of medium height with strange mustaches that started thin under his nose and bloomed into little round bulbs on his sun-darkened cheeks. Beneath his lower lip sprouted a small goatee, and about his shoul-ders hung a heavy brocaded coat. His most impressive feature was the sternness of his eyes, for when he glared at a man and issued an order, it was clear that it would be impossible to disobey.

Asking the eleven captains who would join him to step forward, he told them in a low voice: "It's to be Porto Bello," and before they could respond to the striking news, for that well-fortified harbor was sup-posed to be impregnable, he spoke as if its capture would be nothing more than an ordinary land operation. But later, when Captain McFee assembled his crew aboard the *Glen Affric*, Ned heard with surprise how strict the rules would be: "Upon pain of instant death, never attack an English ship. Nor any ships of a nation enjoying a treaty of peace with us, and for the time being that includes the Dutch."

Concerning injuries, the usual rules would apply: "Lose a right arm, you get six hundred pieces of eight, or six slaves; loss of a left, five hundred, or five slaves. Same if you lose a right leg or a left. If you lose an eye, one hundred pieces, or one slave; and for the loss of a finger, the same."

A captain was allowed to include in his crew men of any nationality, and McFee's would ultimately have Englishmen, Portuguese, Dutch, Indians from the Meskito coast, many Frenchmen and even a few disgruntled Spaniards who had been ill treated in Cartagena or Panamá. The rule governing slaves was complicated: "We can take slaves aboard to do heavy work, but only such as we find on the vessels we capture. Severe penalties if we accept any slaves who have run away from Jamaica plantations. Owners there need them for the sugar crop."

And then came two curious rules which determined certain odd behaviors of the privateers: "If we capture a foreign ship at sea, we must sail it back to Port Royal so the crown can catalogue its contents and skim off its share of our prize. But if we sack a Spanish town on land, the entire spoil belongs to us. That's why Captain Morgan is going to ignore the big Spanish ships and head right for Porto Bello, where the land treasure is."

Morgan himself came before the captains to recite ominously the final rule, handed down by the king, which governed English pirates, corsairs, buccaneers and privateers alike; its harsh terms would explain much of the barbaric behavior Ned would engage in during the years ahead: "If you capture Spanish prisoners, treat them exactly as our subjects are treated when the Spaniards capture them."

Then the twelve captains signed receipts indicating that they had received from the Jamaican government Letters of Marque which bestowed legality on their enterprise, but such niceties did not influence Tatum or his nephew. "We're not privateers," Will said. "We're plain buccaneers, and that's what I want to be called." Ned agreed; he had not run away from home, experienced the wild life on Tortuga and the slavery of the logwood jungles to find refuge in the legal refinements of privateering. He would sail with Morgan and proudly obey his orders, but at heart he would still be a buccaneer.

As Henry Morgan's armada of twelve nondescript vessels crept secretly along the coast of Nicaragua on their approach to the rich target of Porto Bello, they were blessed with two strokes of good luck: they captured the Spanish lookout vessel which was supposed to speed back to Porto Bello with news of any approaching pirates; and spotted in dark waters a small boat being paddled by six Indians who signaled to the big ships as if calling for help. When brought aboard, the Indians turned out to be Englishmen, with a gruesome story:

"We're ordinary prisoners taken from English ships by Spaniards. How were we treated? Chained hand and foot to the ground of a prison cell that contained thirty-three of us, so close that each unwashed man offended the nose of the man chained next to him. At dawn we were unchained and taken into salt water up to our bellies, where we worked all day in the blazing sun. Look at our bodies. Leather. Some days no food at all. Others meat with worms. Legs torn, feet bleeding, and at night, the same chains on the same cold ground in the same crowded cell."

Captain Morgan asked: "How did you escape?" and they said: "We killed two guards, so if they ever catch us, it's torture and death." Then Morgan asked: "Will you guide us in our attack on Porto Bello?" and the chief spokesman said: "If necessary, on our hands and knees," and when Morgan promised: "You will have your revenge," the man revealed news which caused gasps:

"Remember when Prince Rupert, the glorious cavalryman, lost one of his ships in that hurricane off Martinique? And everyone believed that his brother, Prince Maurice, drowned? Not at all! In a small boat he and others reached the coast of Puerto Rico, where the Dons arrested him. And he's one of those languishing in the bowels of that castle."

Morgan, realizing that if his buccaneers could rescue the prince and restore him to the royal family in England, great honor would come to him and his men, saw to it that the sun-blackened Englishmen were passed from ship to ship so that all could hear their report of what was sure to happen if they were captured during the attack. When the men reached McFee's *Glen Affric*, Will Tatum asked to serve as their custodian, and at the conclusion of their report, he asked for a few minutes to relate his experiences in the jail at Cádiz where English sailors were burned alive, and the crowded quarters in which he spoke became silent as the sailors grimly listened.

When the big ships had sneaked as far down the coast as they dared without being prematurely detected, twenty-three large canoes were dropped into the water, each capable of carrying a score of fighting men. For three days and nights oarsmen rowed and paddled eastward, until, on the dark night of 10 July 1668, Will Tatum, steering in the lead canoe, passed the word to those following: "The guides say this is the last safe place." Silently, the sailors dragged their canoes ashore, and every man checked his three weapons: gun, sword, dagger. Only then did Morgan give the order: "We take the town first and then the big fort."

Since Porto Bello contained three powerful forts—two at strategic points along the bay, one commanding the city—the Spaniards were sure that no seaborne force could successfully attack their fortress city, but they had never been assaulted on land by men like Morgan's privateers. Stealth and the accurate spy work by the leather-skinned former prisoners enabled the attackers to reach the western outskirts of the city undetected. There in the hours before dawn they assembled, and suddenly, with wild yells and the firing of guns at anything that moved, they created havoc, in the midst of which they were able to capture the heart of the city without the loss of a single man. But Morgan knew that this was a hollow victory so long as the Spaniards held the three forts, so without stopping for meaningless celebration, he cried: "To the big castle!" and he personally led the attack.

This fortress-castle had been so strategically placed and solidly constructed, its massive guns commanding both the streets of the city and the anchorages in the harbor, that it looked impregnable, but it was afflicted with that indolent rot which doomed so many Spanish ventures in the steamy climates of the New World. The officer in charge, the castellan, was a man of such flawed character that his ineptness was comical. For example, his constable of artillery, who should have been able to man his considerable cannons with lethal effect against a storming party, did not even have his cannon loaded, so with almost shameful haste the great fortress was surrendered. In the final assault the castellan was mercifully slain, releasing him from the painful obligation of explaining his deficiencies to the king.

The ineffective constable suffered a more bizarre fate. Surrounded by Englishmen to whom he wanted to surrender his guns, his fort and his honor, he looked about for some officer among the invaders and saw Captain McFee. Falling before him on one knee, he threw his arms wide, exposed his chest, and cried in broken English: "Dishonored . . . failure to my king . . . no life ahead . . . shoot me!" McFee was staggered by such a plea, but not Tatum, who stood beside him. With a sudden grab for his pistol, Will thrust it against the man's chest and pressed the trigger.

Now came Ned Pennyfeather's harsh introduction to the life and morals of buccaneering, for the victorious Englishmen herded all the castle's Spanish officers and men into a room as small as the cell in which the English prisoners said they had once been kept. When they were in place, Ned was sent down into the cellar to haul barrels of gunpowder into position under the room, and when he returned to where Will was guarding the prisoners, he saw to his horror that his uncle had laid a trail of heavy black powder from that room and down the stairs to the barrels.

"Smell this," Will cried bitterly to an imprisoned Spanish captain. "What is it?"

"Gunpowder."

"Run for your lives," Will shouted to Ned and the other sailors, and when they were gone, he ignited the powder trail in the room, watched it start down the stairs, and dashed to safety. Before the prisoners could break free, a tremendous explosion destroyed their corner of the castle and all were blown to bits.

Morgan had eliminated one of the castles, but another of significant strength remained, and it was commanded by a most valiant man, the governor himself, supported by soldiers of merit who repulsed one English attack after another, until even Morgan had to admit: "If we don't do something powerful, they'll prevail."

What he did was teach even the Spaniards a lesson in the brutalities of pirating, for he halted his attack on the castle, turning instead to raid a monastery, from which he collected a group of monks, and a convent, from which he took many nuns. While this was being done, his carpenters were assembling extremely wide ladders, "so broad that four men could climb side by side to scale a wall."

When all was ready he gave simple orders to the monks and nuns: "You and you, lift those ladders and carry them to the wall of that castle." And behind the religious he marched the mayor of the city, the businessmen and the elders to help bear the weight of the ladders: "If anyone falters, man or woman, you'll be shot in the back." To ensure that the ladders went forward, he intermixed sailors with the group, and Ned was assigned the job of goading forward the nuns.

As this tragic procession started toward the walls, the men around Morgan said: "But the Spaniards will never dare fire at their own people, and religious ones at that," and he said: "You don't know Spaniards."

Slowly the heavy ladders inched toward the walls. Nervously Ned bent double to hide behind the nuns. Urgently Morgan drove the column forward. And on the parapets the governor waited, deliberating. He saw that the ladders were of such dimension that once planted, scaling his walls would be possible, and if that happened, all was lost. But he also realized that he could halt the progress of the deadly ladders only by firing directly at the best citizens of his city.

Now from the ladder-bearers rose pitiful cries directed at the governor: "Do not fire on us! Save us, we are your people!" Some called him by name. Others reminded him of past relationships, and all looked upward into the barrels of his guns.

"Fire!" he shouted, and the guns blazed into the mass of his friends. After the dead nuns and the shattered monks had fallen aside, Ned and the others goaded the survivors to keep plodding ahead with their ladders.*

"Fire!" Others fell, but then the ladders were tilted against the walls and a hundred sailors led by remorseless Will Tatum were up and over.

The fighting was wild and close in, and marked by great heroism on both sides. This was no easy victory like that at the first fort, no Spanish officer asking the English to shoot him. The Spanish governor in particular conducted himself with such outstanding bravery that even Tatum had to admire him: "Sir, yield with honor! Your life will be spared!"

Thinking that the governor did not hear him, for he fought on incredibly, Will called for Ned to interpret for him, and his nephew shouted: *"Honorable Gobernador, rindase con honor."* This time the noble fighting machine heard the words, saluted, and half lunged at three assailants, who had no course but to cut him down.

To Ned, the next two days would always remain a blur, days that happened but which he preferred to erase from memory. The privateers, having won an incredible victory against one of Spain's main cities, a key link in the Peru-Sevilla chain, felt themselves entitled to a victory debauch, and they launched one with no regard to the rights of the

---

*In 1678 one of Morgan's buccaneers, a Dutchman of questionable background known as Exquemelin or Esquemeling, published in Amsterdam the sensationally popular *De Americaensche Zee-Rovers.* When it appeared in London in 1684 in English, Morgan started legal action, claiming that this story, among others, was libelous. Two different publishers recanted and settled for £200 each, but other buccaneers who had participated in the attack averred that the accounts of Morgan's brutality were true.

defeated or the rules of decency. Rape and pillage, maiming and burning, turned proud Porto Bello into a charnel house, and many a Spanish man seeking to protect his woman ended with a saber through his chest. Ned, watching the saturnalia, thought: When I left Barbados, I wasn't seeking this.

It was not a Spanish survivor who reported the bestiality of these two days, but a Dutchman who had served as one of Morgan's captains. Many years after, when an old man in retirement at The Hague, he wrote:

What the English did at Porto Bello leaves a scar on my soul, for I did not believe that men who were such decent companions afloat could be such fiends ashore. After we captured the two castles we gathered all the citizens into the public square and told them: "Show us where you hid the money, or we will make you tell."

This brought forth some money from people who knew what to expect from English pirates, because that's what they were despite calling themselves privateers. Having gained the easy money, they now set about searching for the hard, and they did this by applying to men and women alike the most hellish tortures that man has devised. Racks were set up in various spots to tear limbs apart. Fire was applied to all parts of the body. They used a most terrible torture they called *woolding*, whereby a broad cord was placed around the head at the middle forehead. Then, with sticks knotted into the cord at the back, they drew the cord ever tighter, causing the worst pain a man could know, for even his brains were addled, his eyes began popping out of his head, until at last he fainted and often died from a crushed brain.

I saw them cut people apart, slowly and with repeated shouts "Where's it hidden?" until body and soul fragmented at the same instant. I saw them do things to women that are best forgotten, but what haunts me to this day are the indecencies visited upon Catholic nuns who could not have had even one peso.

In this Dutchman's horrified recollection of the sack of Porto Bello appeared a passage which threw oblique light on how these extravagances affected young Pennyfeather on his first serious privateering adventure:

> Each morning Captain Morgan sent scouting parties to search the woods for men and women who had fled at first gunfire: "If they were clever enough to flee, they were also smart enough to have gathered riches in years past. We must find where the jewels and silver are hidden." These people, when caught, were subjected to the worst tortures, and on the fourth morning, when I was sent out at the head of a detachment to capture the last groups that had remained in hiding, I had in my command a fine English lad called Ned, and together we found three families of refugees, but as we were bringing them in, roped together, I saw Ned watch carefully the other pirates, and when they were not looking he untied the women and set them free. He caught me looking at him, but, not wishing to see acts I would have to report, I turned away.

When the tortures were concluded, emissaries were sent across the isthmus to the capital city of Panamá to demand a ransom of 350,000 pesos in silver, failing which, the entire city of Porto Bello would be burned to the ground. Officials in Panamá replied that they could not raise such a sum, but they did offer to give Morgan a promissory note on a bank in Genoa; he replied, sensibly: "Privateers feel safer with hard bullion." In the end, 100,000 pesos were paid, and twenty-four days after the initial assault the privateering fleet weighed anchor and started the swift run back to Port Royal, where Will Tatum, Ned Pennyfeather and each of the other participants received at least a hundred and fifty English pounds, in those days a tremendous sum. Ned sent his share back to his mother.

If Ned Pennyfeather at the sack of Porto Bello in 1668 saw Henry Morgan at his brutal worst, in 1669 at the attack on Maracaibo he saw him at his strategic best. The story of how Morgan came to attack the nearly impregnable site is one of the dramatic tales of the Caribbean.

After his reverberating victory at Porto Bello the British government gave him, as their *soi-disant* Admiral of the Spanish Main, a powerful new ship, the *Oxford,* a 34-gun frigate with a crew of a hundred and sixty. Naval warfare in the Caribbean was about to be drastically modified.

To a convocation held aboard his new ship anchored at Isla Vaca, a small Jamaican island halfway between the pirate strongholds of Tortuga and Port Royal, Morgan invited any captains who might be interested in a major privateering foray, and a cutthroat gang of desperadoes met to decide what rich city along the Main to attack next. As always, they would be guided by the rule: "If we capture a ship, the king gets his share, but if we sack a city, we get it all." Before the discussion began, Morgan, in a show of schoolboy pride, wanted to display his new ship: "Look at the stoutness of this cabin, the heaviness of the holds. This is a fighting ship." And then he added: "Gentlemen, in a few minutes we shall select our next target, and remember that for the first time we will have at the core of our fleet this powerful ship, stronger than anything the Spanish can muster against us." And then, in his enchanting Welsh way, he could not refrain from adding a comic touch: "The *Oxford* was sent out here for one purpose only, to suppress piracy. So if you sight any pirates, let me be the first to know."

Because of the *Oxford,* discussion of possible targets was animated, and lesser towns like those serving the logwood trade were not even considered. "Any profit in heading back to Porto Bello?"

"None," Morgan said. "We picked that chicken clean."

"What chances at Vera Cruz?"

"If Drake and Hawkins failed, how could we succeed? We've proved we're good, and with this new one, we'll be very good. But not invincible."

"Campeche?"

"Not rich enough."

"Havana?"

"Those new forts? No!"

And then Captain McFee named the target that all had been thinking of but none had been brave enough to mention: "Cartagena?"

This magical name evoked a flood of memories. Drake had gained much booty there. Dutch pirates had attacked it. The fierce French pirate, L'Ollonais, cruelest man ever to sail the Caribbean, had tried Cartagena, and many others had attempted investing it for its almost limitless wealth, only to be thrown back by its formidable defenses. One who had been defeated there described it as "a bay within a bay whose forts protect a smaller, tighter bay rimmed with guns. It can be taken, but not by mortals."

"Drake took it," someone said, and another captain replied: "A century ago, before the new forts were built." Before anyone could comment, he reminded them: "Spanish engineers can build a lot of forts in a hundred years."

Then Morgan spoke: "The thirty-four big guns of our *Oxford* can silence whatever guns the Spanish have. It's Cartagena!"

The more timorous captains would surely have advised against such boldness had not, at this precise moment, a careless spark from some source never identified fallen into the powder magazines, igniting an explosion of such enormous magnitude that it blew the *Oxford* completely apart, causing it to founder immediately and sink with more than two hundred men. Miraculously, Morgan and his senior captains were saved by the stout construction of the room in which they met, and as he said nonchalantly when fished from the water: "The Morgan luck held again."

When the sea-drenched survivors huddled ashore, Morgan did not allow them even a minute to lament their great loss, for while the few members of the crew who had escaped built fires to dry off, he told the captains: "As we were saying a few minutes ago, we're not strong enough to attack Vera Cruz, and now without the *Oxford* we can't assault Cartagena. Well, men, what city is available?"

A French captain who had probed all corners of the Caribbean, and fiercely, said: "Admiral Morgan, there's one no man has mentioned. Maracaibo," and the English captains looked hesitantly, one at the other, and for good reason.

On the northern coast of Venezuela, nearly five hundred miles west of the great salt flats at Cumaná but only four hundred miles east of Cartagena, lay the huge gulf of Venezuela, at whose southern end a very narrow channel led to an inland fresh-water lake nearly as big as the gulf itself. It was called La Laguna de Maracaibo, to be famous in later centuries for its large deposits of oil, and it measured eighty-six miles north to south, sixty east to west, more than five thousand square miles. It was a world to itself, practically cut off from the sea and rimmed by fruitful fields, prosperous villages and, at the end of the channel, by the substantial town bearing the same name as the laguna.

Maracaibo was thus both a tempting target because of its wealth and a very dangerous one because of the risk of getting one's ships trapped inside the lake if a squadron of Spanish warships could be summoned while a raid was under way. Even well-armed privateers with ample gunfire thought twice about trying to sack the Maracaibo area: "The spoils would be vast, but there's always that terrible risk of getting trapped in the channel. What happens then?"

Morgan, reflecting on the dangers involved in attempting this ticklish target, said: "Let's get some sleep, if we can," and in the morning he gathered his captains: "It's got to be Maracaibo." And that was how, on the morning of 9 March 1669, Ned Pennyfeather stood in the prow of the *Glen Affric* with a sounding line checking the depths of the tortuous entrance into the laguna. At times the passageway was so narrow, he felt he could reach out and touch the shore, but he was so busy attending to his job that he almost failed to see looming ahead on a prominent point a Spanish fort whose guns might destroy the ship. It was prodigious, a huge mass of stone wall and iron battlement with heavy guns pointed directly at the ten approaching ships.

"Guns!" he shouted belatedly, just as a shot, poorly aimed and elevated, screamed overhead, far wide of the invading ships. It was the Spanish tragedy repeated: a fine castle-fortress, perfectly placed and properly armed, but undermanned by troops lacking in either determination or skill. Ned was almost ashamed at how easily Morgan's men took this excellent fort without the loss of a single sailor.

But his uncle Will voiced the apprehension of all old-timers: "It was easy getting in, but will we get out?" and in subsequent days, while the fleet stormed through the great lagoon, achieving victory after victory, the older sailors kept wondering: "How do we get our booty out of this trap?"

The booty was enormous, for the smaller towns perched on the banks of the lagoon were rich indeed, but the citizens had cleverly hidden their gold and jewels, so that Ned was confronted with a grave moral crisis, realizing that if the buccaneers hoped to collect the great wealth, someone must capture rich citizens who had fled into the hills, bring them back in shackles, and somehow force them into revealing their secret hiding places. Doing the latter was horrible, involving as it did the rack, the fire and the terrible *woolding*. But he never participated in the tortures. He did track down and deliver the people to the quarters in which the questioning took place, and when the hiding places were revealed, he did hurry there and dig up the jewels.

During a drinking celebration when the buccaneers were celebrating the success of their raid, a lookout who had been stationed at the entrance to the lagoon arrived with the news all had feared: "Spanish warships have moved in to block the escape route." Instantly men hovering on the edge of drunkenness sobered and all faces turned to watch Morgan, who showed that he was not surprised by this unlucky turn. He asked the messenger to sit down, take a drink of ale, and answer questions.

"How many ships?" One big and six or seven smaller, about the size of Captain McFee's.

"Any attempt to reactivate the fort we partially destroyed?" Oh yes! Heavy rebuilding, new cannons, first-class troops moving in.

"Any attempt to move the Spanish ships into the laguna?" None. They're bunched in the channel, waiting for you to try to break through.

At this point Morgan took an apparently unrelated tack: "The big ship? Has it high sides?" . . . "Is there an area near the fort where a canoa could land and discharge men?" . . . "Any forest in the vicinity?" When he had heard enough, he calmly told his captains: "Problem is simple, gentlemen. We break through their blockade, sail back to Port Royal, and distribute our prize money," and none of the captains dared ask him "How?"

He had only one option: to run the gauntlet even though the forces arrayed against him seemed overpowering, and on 27 April 1669 he prepared to do just this. Ned, who now served aboard the flagship, had an opportunity to observe at close hand the brilliant manner in which Morgan prepared to make his dash for freedom. Moving his ten-ship flotilla toward the contested exit, he addressed his sailors: "We don't have to do it the way they expect. We'll do it our way." And he assigned the men diverse tasks. Some cut lengths of wood from which to make a host of imaginary men, others dressed them in improvised hats, while still others armed them with sticks. Having learned that Will Tatum was a man to trust with important tasks, Morgan summoned him from another ship: "Will, I want you to bury this deck with everything you can find that burns. Especially tar, pitch and loose gunpowder. Then cover the mess with dry leaves and sticks." Will asked quietly: "You're not going to sacrifice your own flagship?" and Morgan replied: "No Spanish admiral would do it, but I shall." And while Will and Ned prepared the ship for the flames,

Morgan directed his blacksmiths: "Forge me six huge grappling hooks, twice as big as any you've made before," and when they were done, great clawing monsters, Morgan himself helped reeve heavy ropes to them.

When all was ready, with three smaller ships pared to the gunwales so they could fly over the water, Morgan gave the signal, and his fearfully overmatched fleet set sail as if trying to break through the cordon, but when the fire ship, controlled only by Tatum, Pennyfeather and eight daring men, plus the wooden sailors who stood ferocious along the deck, drew abreast of the big Spanish ship that formed the heart of their defense, the pirate craft did not try to steal past, but turned suddenly to head straight for the midquarter of the enemy ship, while two of the smaller English vessels attacked fore and aft. The three English ships smashed simultaneously the great Spanish warship, grappled themselves to her, and caused the Spanish defenders to break into three groups. They would have done better by opposing only the big ship in the middle, for once the hooks were set and separating made impossible, Tatum and Pennyfeather shouted to the other Englishmen: "Flee! We fire the powder!" and the men leaped overboard to be rescued by a trailing ship while Will did what gave him pleasure: setting fire to the chain of powder which, even before he and Ned leaped into the sea, exploded in a vast fireball that ignited all the inflammables on deck, leaving the huge Spanish warship prey to the roaring flames.

In one gigantic blaze the two ships intermingled their fates, iron grapples binding them together as they burned to the water line and sank as one. The major Spanish plug in the escape route had been removed.

Meanwhile, the second largest Spanish ship had fled toward the fort in an attempt to beach itself so that its crew could get ashore and help man the fort, but one of the swift English vessels trailed it and with fireballs set it ablaze, leaving it a smoking hulk. The third big Spanish ship was chased right out of the laguna and into the narrows, where it was captured and where Morgan adopted it as his flagship to replace the one he had sacrificed to the burning. The lagoon was cleared of Spanish ships and the first of the impediments to freedom had been removed.

In the morning Captain Morgan addressed himself to the problem of how to get past that menacing fort whose restored guns could destroy any enemy trying to sneak by. The task looked impossible.

But on that morning more than a month ago when he had sailed his ships past the fort, he had seen a way to get them back out, and now he put it into effect. Gathering about him all the big canoas his men had captured within the laguna, he placed in each twenty well-armed men, clearly visible, and directed the steersman to head for shore near the approaches to the castle but to land in the midst of tangled trees. There the canoas ostensibly unloaded what would become an assault force on the fort, but when they returned to the pirate ships, with only two rowers visible, the other eighteen were stretched flat in the bottom with leaves covering their bare arms, lest they glisten and betray the trick.

In this clever manner, Morgan appeared to have landed at the foot of the fort an immense assault party, whereas in reality all his men were back aboard their ships, but hidden belowdecks. The occupants of the fort, determined not to be taken by surprise, switched their heavy guns away from the seafront and pointed them directly at the spot where the sailors had landed and from where they could be expected to launch their attack.

It never came. Instead, a lone lookout attending the sea passage shouted: "They're escaping!" And when the defenders rushed to that side of their fort, armed only with pistols and swords, their guns having been pointed the wrong way, they saw Henry Morgan and his fleet of ten heading serenely into the narrow channel that would lead them to freedom. One Spanish officer who had a navigator's glass studied the lead ship, and cried to his fellows: "That swine! He's using our *Soledad* as his flagship and he's sitting there drinking what has to be rum." Morgan was free and on his way back to Port Royal.

The deadly trio, Captain McFee with his *Glen Affric*, Will Tatum as his first mate and Ned Pennyfeather as a hanger-on, wasted the year 1670 in diverse and unproductive ways: loafing around the inns of Port Royal, drinking and carousing. A Quaker missionary, come down from Philadelphia to serve on Barbados, was laid over in Port Royal when his ship lost a spar, but after one horrendous day ashore he retreated to his cabin, from which he would not budge so long as his ship remained in that hellhole: I often read about Sodom and Gomorrah, and I thought: They could not have been real, just symbols of evil. But Port Royal is very real, and if this were the old days, God would sweep this place off the face of the earth.

Grown irritable in their idleness, the *Glen Affric* men set out to sea with no sensible plan in mind. "The logwood jungles we don't want," the sailors insisted, and they kept hoping to intercept a Spanish treasure ship, but none appeared. So they wandered first toward Porto Bello, but the unexpected arrival of an entire Spanish convoy from Cartagena scared them away from certain disaster.

In their random wandering, they never called the sea upon which they were traveling the Caribbean. That word had in those years not yet come into common usage. Because of the curious way in which the Isthmus of Panamá ran—west to east and not, as one might have expected, north to south—the Caribbean was always referred to as the North Sea, which it was, and the Pacific as the South. So Drake fought the Spanish in the North Sea, then crept through the Strait of Magellan to come home by way of the South Sea, not the Pacific. And Sir Harry Morgan ravaged the North Sea, not the Caribbean.

One sailor kept telling McFee: "Mexico is where the silver is," so for want of anything better, the *Affric* sailed northwest to the first Mexican land they could find. It turned out to be the historic island of Cozumel, but when they stormed ashore, guns ready, they found nothing but a collection of decaying temple ruins from some ancient period. Will, studying the fallen rocks, announced them to be Egyptian and the others accepted his opinion, but there was much discussion as to how the Egyptians had reached this forlorn spot.

At Cozumel they found not one peso, but Ned did come across a small carved head which must have been broken from a larger statue, and this he carried back to the ship with him, but when his uncle saw it on the boy's hammock he threw it overboard: "We don't want no heathen idols on this Christian ship. Bad luck."

In the last days of 1670, Captain Morgan himself let it be known that he had in mind "to try one of the vastest enterprises ever attempted in these seas," and as the rumor spread, captains like Angus McFee with his small tough *Glen Affric* swarmed back into Port Royal, to hear the official confirmation: "Captain Henry Morgan, with official papers from the king and from the governor of Jamaica, has been appointed admiral and commander in chief of all forces arranged against the Spanish, and he invites any ships and crews interested to meet with him at Isla Vaca off the southwest corner of Hispaniola to lay plans." Within a few days the roadstead at Port Royal was deserted as a small armada converged upon the little island off whose shore the great warship *Oxford* had exploded two years before, and Morgan was delighted to see that nearly a dozen battle-scarred French ships were among them, for he had high regard for the fighting ability of the French buccaneers. "Best in the Caribbean," he frequently said, adding: "If properly led," and he intended leading them to gold and glory. When Morgan as admiral addressed his assembled captains, he stunned them with the boldness of his vision: "Gentlemen, we have assembled here thirty-eight ships and nigh three thousand fighting men." Morgan halted the cheers which greeted this with a warning finger: "But we have just learned that England is now formally at peace with Spain." Loud groans. "All is not lost, for we have further instructions that if we uncover any Spanish plot to invade Jamaica or any other English possession, we are commanded to attack Spain wherever vulnerable in order to render said attack impossible." More cheers. Then the sober news: "Gentlemen, we have no proof of any such Spanish plan, and I would be most grateful if you could find me some."

What happened next is best described in a memorial which Ned Pennyfeather composed to Admiral Morgan when the latter was long since dead:

To capture proof of Spanish duplicity, several small ships ranged far and wide to take prisoners who would testify that Spanish forces in Cartagena were planning to mount a major effort to retake Jamaica. I judge there was no such plan, for we captured two Spanish ships, one after the other, and despite the most prolonged interrogations at which I served as translator, we learned nothing, whereupon the obstinate Spaniards were loaded with weights and thrown into the sea.

However, one of our sister scouting ships did capture two prisoners who were willing to betray Spanish secrets, and I was moved to that ship to ensure the accuracy of their reports. The two were not Spaniards, really, but Canary Islanders of a base sort and I was never convinced that they told the truth or that, indeed, they knew anything at all about which they testified, but after they saw three of their companions, who had refused to talk, well weighted and tossed overboard, they were willing to swear on the Bible I provided that in Cartagena a massive fleet of many vessels and untold soldiers was preparing for an assault on Jamaica. And when I handed my copy of their statements to Admiral Morgan, he crunched them in his right hand, raised them high in the air, and shouted: "This is all we need!" and that very afternoon he informed the assembled captains: "We sail for the isthmus, march across it, and sack the great and rich city of Panamá." When I heard these words I trembled, and so did many of the captains.

There were two routes across the isthmus, leading from the Caribbean on the east to the Pacific on the west. The first was by land, the infamous one traversed by Drake and the mule trains from Peru. The second, a route utilizing the Chagres River some miles to the north and fearsomely protected by a stupendous fort at its mouth, so ingeniously located and fortified that one of Morgan's men would later require two closely packed pages to describe its frightening armaments: "Built upon a high mountain . . . surrounding ditch thirty feet deep . . . supported by a smaller fort with eight great guns commanding the river." And finally: "Besides all this, there lies in the entrance to the river a great rock, scarce to be perceived unless at low tide."

The attack on the fort by four hundred of Morgan's men against the same number of resolute Spanish defenders was long and terrible. Dusk fell with no resolution, and it looked to Ned, fighting with the grenadiers whose perilous job it was to run close to the walls and throw in grenades and lighted brands, as if the defenders might repulse the raiders and throw them back to their waiting ships. But, as light faded, one of those unforeseen events occurred which determine the outcome of battles: a skilled Indian marksman fighting with the Spaniards sent an arrow that passed completely through the shoulder of a grenadier standing beside Ned. Cursing, the Englishman ripped it out of the wound, tipped it with a mixture of cotton and powder, set it ablaze, and shot it back into the fort, where it landed on a dry roof. Within minutes that portion of the fort was aflame, and through the long night daring forays of other grenadiers including Ned lobbed additional fireballs into the fort, so that by morning most of the wooden portions blazed.

Then followed a day of horror. More than a hundred privateers, a number never matched before, died in their attempt to subdue this stubborn fort, whose Spanish defenders lost all but a few of their force. And never in Ned's prior experience had so many Spanish soldiers fought with such valor, especially the castellan, who was driven back by concentrated fire first to a corner of his fort, then from room to room, fighting with cutlass all the way, until he was at last forced into a corner, where he held off three buccaneers until a fourth rushed in to administer the *coup de grâce*. Ned, who had been one of the three and nearly slain by this heroic man, knelt over the corpse, retrieved the Spaniard's sword, and placed it over his fallen body with the handle serving as a cross. There the castellan lay as flames embraced him and his fort.

On 19 January 1671, when Admiral Morgan and his near two thousand men started their trip up the Chagres River in their fleet of canoes, none were aware, Admiral Morgan least of all, that they were engaged in what would turn out to be one of the most ill-prepared expeditions in military history. For when one of his sailors, seeing that he had left behind all their food supplies in order to carry weapons needed for the assault on Panamá, asked: "What are we going to eat on our march?" he said lightly, as had many other generals in history: "We'll live off the land."

Unfortunately, there was no land. The Chagres River did not drain into fine farmlands populated by Indians in little grass huts tending cattle, harvesting fruit trees, and growing vegetables. It drained only into swamps that contained no huts, no cattle, and to the amazement of the sailors, not even any fruit trees. So this huge army of men went three days without one bite to eat. On the fourth day there was a perverse kind of joy among the troops, for scouts cried: "Ambush ahead!" To the starving marchers it did not mean danger, but a chance to fight a devil-may-care battle and capture some food. However, when they reached the site of the supposed ambush, they found to their horror that the Spaniards had fled, leaving behind not a morsel of food. All they left was a half-score of leather field bags such as soldiers in all countries prefer for the safekeeping of their valuables, and these the famished sailors ate. One of them wrote later:

> You ask how men can eat leather? Simple. Scrape off the hair, cut it into strips, beat it between two rocks as you soak it in river water, then boil it to make it tender and roast it to make

it tasty. You still can't bite it, but you can cut it in very small bits and roll them around in your mouth for the delicious taste, and finally swallow them. They carry no nourishment to your belly, but they do give it something to work on, and this ends for a while the terrible gripe when a belly works but finds nothing.

Ned almost missed this feast, such as it was, because he was scouting up the river when the leather was distributed, but when he returned and saw the men chewing on what he assumed was food, he cried in panic: "Where's mine?" and Mompox took him by the arm, sat him down, hushed the protest, and explained what the sailors were trying to eat. Then he separated his apportionment of roasted leather and gave his friend half. Ned later told Will Tatum: "It saved my life. I couldn't have gone another day."

The ninth day was one never to be forgotten, for after an excruciating climb to the top of a sizable hill, the starving men looked south and saw a sight which stunned them with its beauty and significance, as Ned Pennyfeather wrote when he recalled it:

Mompox and I rose early, sought the Lord's blessing on what we feared might be our last day on this earth, and started up a steep hill while we still had remnants of energy. As I struggled with my head bent forward to keep my empty belly snug in its growling pain, Mompox cried: "Ned! Oh, Ned!" And when I looked up I saw the immense expanse of the South Sea stretching infinitely out to where the sky became almost black. Gentle waves no higher, it seemed, than a few inches broke onto the beach in endless dimension and glory. There was no sign of the Panamá that Morgan had described to us, only this vast ocean stretching onward beyond the imagination.

Then from behind me came a cry: "Look! Panamá!" and I turned toward a direction I had not attended, where I saw the gleaming city that was going to make us rich. I could detect many churches and the stately tower of a cathedral, and houses innumerable crammed with the things we sought. And in the bay before the city, more than a dozen ships, some of them galleons of enormous size bringing north the silvery riches of Peru. Mompox and I knelt to give thanks, for in that city there would have to be food.

As they descended they came upon a valley containing a quantity of cows, bulls, horses, goats and asses. Butchering the animals hastily, they started great fires for barbecuing, but many, including Mompox and Ned, could not wait for the meat to cook. As soon as it began to smoke they grabbed it from the brands and began eating, the blood spilling down their fronts as they gorged themselves.

On the tenth day since their capture of the fort at the Chagres, Admiral Morgan and his replenished men were ready to launch their attack on Panamá, whose numerous defenders awaited them in battle order on a flat plain before their city. In addition to trained troops, able cavalry and strong leadership, the Spaniards had a secret weapon in which they placed much reliance: two immense herds of wild bulls to be released simultaneously against the pirates at a propitious moment. With a cry of *"Viva el Rey!"* the cavalry started the charge, reinforced by valiant foot soldiers, and for two hours the battle raged, with the Spaniards unable to break the dogged ranks of the invaders, who knew that if they lost this fight, their days in Spanish prisons would be hellish and short.

At the start of the third hour the Spaniards released their wild bulls, twelve hundred in each herd, left flank and right. They rushed straight at the pirates, heard the noise of battle, stampeded, and doubled back right into the Spaniards, who, in total confusion, retreated pell-mell toward the city, with Morgan's men roaring after them.

Morgan's entry into Panamá was bitterly contested, and so many of his men lost their lives that a rage began to consume him. When he found that fleeing soldiers and civilians had taken refuge in ditches, hoping to surrender after the fury had passed, he ordered his men to shoot them all, men and women alike, and not a prisoner was taken. Inside the gates he came upon a large group of nuns and monks, and in his blind fury, he shouted: "They're about to attack!" and he led his men in a charge which slaughtered them indiscriminately.

His rage intensified even more when he gained the city and found that from the huge warehouses along the seafront all silver had been evacuated, and from the fabulously rich monasteries and churches all embellishments had vanished. Morgan had won a tremendous victory against huge odds, but he gained only the shell of a city. Its treasures had escaped him.

In a fury that now knew no bounds and recognized none of the limits of decency, he turned Panamá over to the pillage of his sailors, and after they had rampaged for several days he ordered his men to set the city afire. During the four weeks he and his men remained there the endless flames raged, until everything was consumed. Churches, monasteries, homes, warehouses—all were destroyed in one consuming blaze. Only the rock-built tower of the cathedral remained to mark where this splendid crossroads city had been.

In the meantime, Morgan's men, enraged by the absence of the wealth they had suffered so much to get, went about capturing as many citizens as they could find and putting them to the torture to make them reveal their hiding places. Both Will Tatum and Mompox participated in seeking out the fugitives and then subjecting them to the refined tortures the pirates had perfected in earlier raids. They used the rack, fire, the horrible *woolding,* dismemberment, rape, and when their patience ran out, murder. The sack of Panamá accounted for some four hundred soldiers dead on the battlefield, many times that number of civilians slain in the interrogations.

This time Ned did not participate in chasing down those in hiding; instead, he was given charge of the interrogations. It became his duty to attempt to ferret out where the riches of Panamá were hidden, and because he shared in the disappointment of his mates, and knowing that if they did not uncover the hidden treasures they would return to Port Royal with little reward for their days of battle and starvation, he became a ruthless interrogator. When women refused to reveal family secrets, he had no compunction in shouting to his assistants: "Ask her again," and the torture would be escalated until the prisoner sometimes died there in the improvised room in which Ned worked.

Among those captured was a man of obvious importance and considerable wealth, found by Tatum and Mompox during a raid far from the city. When he delivered him for questioning, Will said: "He had three menservants who gave their lives protecting him. Mompox and me, we had to kill them. This one knows something."

No one ever learned who he was, and Ned began to think that he might be a member of some religious order. Finally, after torments that few could have withstood, the man broke into demonic laughter: "You damned fools! You idiots! Bring Morgan here and I'll reveal everything," and when Morgan hurried to the questioning room, the prisoner, lashed to the rack, looked at him with the infinite contempt of a dying man: "You great ass! You posturing general without a grain of sense!"

"Ask him where it's hidden!" Morgan shrieked, and when Ned

repeated the question, the Spaniard said: "You had it in your grasp, Morgan. It was all there, two boat lengths from shore when you roared into our city . . . our beautiful city." For a moment it seemed that the man was going to weep, not from pain but from sorrow over the burning of his city, so Morgan told the men working the rack: "Tighten it," and after the man screamed involuntarily, he said with infuriating calm: "Before you came I ordered all the treasures in Panamá—plate from the churches, bullion from the warehouses, great treasures from the monasteries and official buildings, everything, a pirate's dream of wealth . . . I placed it in that little galleon you saw when you stormed our city." He gasped, for speaking was a painful effort with death so near. "But you, Morgan, you utter fool, you jackass. When you came in you allowed your men to revel and get drunk and rape and burn churches. What a pitiful general. And all the while the tremendous treasure you sought was within your reach . . ." Taut ropes prevented him from raising his head, so he dropped his voice to a whisper, causing Morgan to bend forward to hear where the treasure had fled, whereupon the dying man spat full in his face.

"Tighten the ropes!" Morgan shouted, and slowly the man was torn apart.

The rape and burning of Panamá occupied Morgan from 28 January to 24 February, exactly four weeks, and when he and his men were satiated with the desolation they had caused, they marched almost empty-handed back to the headwaters of the Chagres River, down which they sped in the canoes they had left behind a month earlier. During the trip Ned had ample opportunity to study his commander, for Morgan rode in his canoe and Ned had several occasions to talk with him. Morgan never deviated from the conclusion he had reached when first alerted to the fact that somehow the riches of Panamá had eluded him: "It was a noble effort. If we'd done nothing but reduce that fearful fort, it would have been a triumph. English vessels can use this river in the campaigns ahead. And the sacking of their great silver port! When the King of Spain hears what we did these weeks he'll tremble in his bed." Actually, the new king was a ten-year-old near-idiot whose inadequacy marked the end of Hapsburg rule in Spain, the substitution of the French Bourbons, and the decline of

Spanish power throughout the world and especially in the Caribbean.

Morgan, of course, knew nothing of these European matters: "A man does what he can, Ned, and there'll be spoils enough. Not lavish, but enough." As to his carelessness in allowing the treasure ship to escape when he had it almost within his fingers: "At Porto Bello and Maracaibo, we had good luck we didn't deserve; at Panamá, bad luck we did deserve. Did you say you took part in all three raids? If you saved your shares, the average won't be trivial."

As their boat passed the place where they had found the leather bags which they ate, Morgan laughed: "A couple of days without meat never hurt any man. Tightens up his belly." But Ned had to speak: "It was ten days, sir," and the famous admiral grew sober: "Yes, and at seven or eight I wondered if I could go on, but at nine and ten when I began to smell the sea . . ." He stared at the banks of the river that had been so inhospitable: "I'd not like to make that trip again . . . well, not that way. But you and I'll be making other good trips in our day, that we will."

Ned treasured these conversations with Morgan, for in them the great admiral displayed a warmth and understanding of his people that was otherwise not visible. In action he seemed a remorseless man willing to sacrifice anything, any human life, to achieve his brutal aims, and the Spaniards he had caused to die on his three culminating trips were uncountable, many as a result of fair and open military action, about the same number during interrogations regarding their hidden wealth, real or supposed. But in the closing days of this extraordinary expedition he proved himself to be a most extraordinary man whose fame, Ned thought, would reverberate throughout the Caribbean as long as men loved the sea and the heroic actions possible thereon.

As San Lorenzo became visible, that remnant whose reduction had cost so many lives, Ned felt driven to let Morgan know how much he admired him: "Admiral, my father died when I was too young to know him. After these adventures with you, I'll always think of you as the kind of father I wish I'd known," and Morgan, only thirty-six years old at the time, said gruffly: "I've watched you, Ned. You're a real man. I'd be proud to have a son like you."

But Ned was to change his opinion of Admiral Morgan; his assessment came in the opening pages of an extensive log he kept of events which transpired after the expedition returned to the fort at San Lorenzo and the sailors prepared to reboard their ships for the return to Port Royal. Rendered into acceptable English, with its arbitrary spellings clarified, it reads:

LOG OF A BUCCANEER

TUE 14 MARCH 1671: One of the darkest days of my life. For all these months my uncle Will Tatum and I have been following Captain Morgan like puppy dogs, listening to him boast how he would bring us home "not hundreds but thousands." Well, this morning he gathered his crew under three big trees and cried: "Search all!" and we stripped to nothing, and each man searched the clothing of someone else, every pocket and seam, so that coins and jewels, even the tiniest pieces of value were thrown into the common pot. The trunks of what little treasure we had carried from Panamá were unloaded so that all could see, and when every item stood before us, Captain Morgan started the division: "This to you and you, and two shares to the ship captains and four shares to me." On he went till the last Spanish peso had been distributed, and then he did a bold thing. Throwing off all his garments but his small clothes, he cried: "Search me too!" and nothing was found secreted. "Is this all we get?" Will cried, and the disappointment in his voice encouraged Mompox and the others to cry: "Where is the wealth you promised?" until there was a general commotion which might have turned into a riot, except that Captain Morgan bellowed: "Be quiet, you sheep! We missed the big treasure at Panamá but each of you has his fair share of what we did get." It was a pitiful eleven pounds, seven shillings each. "You've robbed us!" men began to shout, and if Captain Morgan had not signaled the captains to gather about him, he might have been injured.

WED 15 MARCH: All last night Captain Morgan slept in his tent with men guarding him, and he was wise to do so, because I for one wanted to kill him. Sailors who had sailed and fought with him for more than three years had little for their pains, and in their bitterness started rumors that he had stolen much gold and great boxes of coins, but where he had hidden them no man could say. As for me, I think he smuggled them aboard his ship that stands offshore. I told Will about this, and he said: "Let's search it now," but Captain Morgan's men, well armed, kept us away from the small boats we would need to sail out to the ship.

THU 16 MARCH: Damn his dirty eyes, damn his fat mustaches,

damn his goatee, and damn his flowered jacket. Today, before most of us on shore were awake, Captain Henry Morgan rowed secretly to his ship, upped anchor, and slipped away from us before we could prevent him. He sneaked out with thousands or even millions of our pesos and untold quantities of gold bars which he had withheld from an honest sharing. When I shouted to Will: "There he goes!" Will ran down to the shore and screamed: "I hope your magazine explodes! I hope a great whale overturns you!" Mompox and some sailors jumped into their boats and tried to overtake him, but Captain Morgan, knowing chase was futile, stood on the stern of the vessel, laughed at them, and ordered his gunner to fire two parting salutes, which rattled the branches over our heads. In this infuriating way I finished my buccaneering duty with Captain Henry Morgan and his Letters of Marque and Reprisal.

FRI 17 MARCH: When our furies cooled, Uncle Will collected some forty men he trusted, and reasoned: "Let's forget this morning. We've been tricked by a master. I say let's be real buccaneers. Let's march back across the isthmus, capture a treasure ship, sack what's left of Panamá, and return home as God allows." Every man he approached was in a mood to try this venture, for we all knew that we had the force and courage to do as Will proposed: "Buccaneers like to have a captain they can trust, and I think we should all vote for McFee." When we cheered the suggestion, Will and Mompox fired a salute and announced "election unanimous," and forty-six fighting men shouted "Halloo." Fifteen Indians, including a Meskito named David who had proved his skill at both fishing and carpentering, begged us to let them come along, as did nineteen black slaves who did not want to sail back to harsh masters in the sugar fields of Jamaica. And of course I insisted that Mompox join us. So we have a party of eighty-one, every man a killer if required.

SAT 18 MARCH: I am writing this on the trail back to the South Sea. Never have I witnessed as much effort as I did yesterday. Some of our men collected a group of Indian canoes, long and spacious, into which we piled all the guns, pikes and powder we could gather from the ships that had chosen to return to Jamaica. And since we remembered how we had starved on the first trip, we wanted to take all the food we could, but some of the sailors who were afraid to join us tried to keep food from us, so Will shot one of them and we had no more trouble. I took from one of our ships two lengths of hollowed bamboo, sealed at the ends, in which I would keep my pens and papers, for I wanted to keep an honest account of how we performed without Captain Morgan. On this first day we did well, coming at least fifteen English miles up the river.

TUE 28 MARCH: We rose early, sought the Lord's blessing on His day, and marched only a few miles, with me and Mompox in the lead, when I saw once more the immense expanse of the South Sea. How different it looked this time! When I saw it last from this hilltop we were going to sack Panamá, turn around, and go home rich men. This time we intend capturing us a ship and setting forth upon that vast ocean to seek the opposite shore, if there is one. And when I turned to look at the ruins of where Panamá City used to be, I saw two things, one promising, the other not. The Spaniards had reclustered about their cathedral, so they were conveniently gathered for plucking, and this time we plan to catch their wealth before they hide it. But anchored in the bay were some of the biggest warships I had ever seen. I began to tremble.

WED 5 APRIL: One of the most exciting days of my life, because I proved that I am a true buccaneer. We rose early and set forth in our eight strongest canoes to do or die in our attempt to break through the cordon of Spanish ships and capture one of the big galleons riding in the harbor. As we approached the fleet, the Spaniards thought to oppose us by throwing many of their sailors and fighting men into three small, fast vessels they call *barcas,* and these made for us as if they would devour us, which I thought they might. But as they bore down on us, Captain McFee, a true fighting man, shouted: "Let them draw nigh!" and for what I considered a most dangerous waiting period, we withheld our fire. Then, when we could see their faces plainly, we let loose a fusillade of such magnitude and careful aim that we stunned them. They did try to fire back but by now we were upon them, and with great dexterity we leaped from our canoes, boarded their *barcas,* and began fighting hand-to-hand. In the excitement of battle I forgot my fears and gave a rather good account of myself, but when only two of us tried to force five of them backward into the stern of their *barca,* they proved too much, and they might have slain me with their brutal pikes had not Mompox leaped to my defense with sword and dagger, killing one of the Spaniards and badly wounding his partner. Before the sun reached the meridian we had become masters of two of the *barcas* and had sent the third scudding back to safety in the harbor.

Our victory left us with some eighty Spanish prisoners, almost two for every Englishman, far more than we knew what to do with. My uncle, who had conducted himself with a special bravery which gave him the right to speak, wanted to kill them all, and when Captain McFee asked why, he growled: "They're Spaniards, aren't they?" McFee would have none of this, so three canoas were brought alongside the *barcas* which were now ours, and into them the Spaniards were loaded. But as this was being done, my uncle and Mompox went among them, shot those that were badly wounded and tossed their bodies into the sea. The rest could row their way home.

By capturing the two *barcas* we gained an immense replenishment of cutlasses, guns, powder and balls, so that we had suddenly become not a group of Indian canoas but two small, swift men-of-war, capable, because of our superior English fighting ability, of menacing even the biggest galleons could we get close to them. And I too was changed, because I now knew that I was capable of leaping out of my boat onto the deck of a larger ship and sweeping the deck of Spaniards. I think my companions gained the same assurance, for in this battle we forty-six defeated four times that number, with only two killed and three seriously wounded. Our dead Indians and blacks who had helped us we did not count.

Captain McFee replenished our losses in a curious manner, for as we were preparing to send our prisoners ashore, he stood by the railing of the *barca* into which I had leaped for the battle and there he peered into the faces of all the Spaniards, and by this device alone, selected five that seemed most intelligent and strong and held them back. Since he does not speak Spanish, it fell to me to serve as translator, and I learned several valuable facts. The richly laden galleon which comes across the Pacific from Manila never puts in to Panamá. It goes only to Acapulco. The galleon that fled Panamá during Morgan's raid on the city stayed at sea until we were gone and then came back, so that a huge treasure is now ashore, awaiting us if we can get there. And the galleon that brings the silver from Peru has not yet arrived, but when it does, it will be attended by numerous fighting ships. With that intelligence I go to sleep tonight in a new ship, a new hammock, and inspired by new dreams.

FRI 7 APRIL: One of the most disappointing days of my life. We have tried in vain to penetrate the defenses of Panamá, lured passionately by the knowledge that the great treasure Morgan missed awaits us. I would like to meet the scoundrel who started the rumor that Spaniards are cowards. Not when they have treasure to defend.

We tried every way to best them and failed. At sea they fended us off with a battery of great guns and by land they overwhelmed us with numbers. I felt we were no more than a flight of pestiferous gnats trying to attack a lion, for no matter where we headed we got slapped. At sea we lost two Englishmen killed by gunfire, on land two more, so that our original forty-six are now no more than forty, and I see that buccaneering can be triumphant when things go well, perilous when they don't. Beaten and bested, we are heading home, but whether by Cape Horn or Good Hope, we have not yet decided. At Panamá the Spanish were too much for us.

MON 10 APRIL: Day of glory, day of mystery! Yesterday when we stood at 6° 40' North of the equator by my reckoning on the crude forestaff we have with us, our lookout shouted: "Lima galleon two points east of south!" and when all in my *barca* crowded forward, we saw the most gallant sight our eyes have ever beheld, a small, trim Spanish galleon, aft tower riding high in the air, gilded ornaments glistening in the morning sunlight. It rolled majestically, like some enormously wealthy grandee out for a morning stroll, now to port, then gently to starboard, and at each roll proclaiming: "Gaze upon me, heavy with treasure."

The sight of this galleon so inflamed our hunger that as we closed upon her, there was no man amongst us who was not prepared to capture her or die in the attempt. Captain McFee, drawing our two *barcas* together, addressed us: "This is the target we dreamed of. We shall go at her from their port side, midships. Our best men will scale her with pistol and cutlass, no quarter. Our slaves we leave tied up in our *barcas* under guard. All men on the boarding party follow me, for I shall lead."

These were stern orders, and all of us who heard knew that on this day we proved our worth or went to perpetual sleep at the bottom of the sea. I was not frightened at the prospect, but my breath came uneasy and my mouth was very dry. My uncle, who rode with me, said only: "Well, lad, this is what you came seeking. There she rides." And when I looked at that huge Spanish ship towering above us, I must confess that I wondered to myself: Can she be taken by forty men? But as immediately as the thought came, I corrected it: By forty Englishmen? And I answered myself in words shouted aloud to sustain my bravery: "Yes, by St. George and England, we can do it!" and men about me took up the cry: "George and England!" and even though our captain was a Scot, he joined us in the shouting.

The Spanish captain, seeing us coming and well aware that this would be a fight to the finish, adopted the same tactics as the galleons had done at Panamá. He launched three *barcas,* each larger than ours, in an attempt to keep us away from his sides. When the vessels approached us, we tore into them as if they were sheep sent out to pasture and we ravenous lions.

"Leave them drown!" my uncle shouted as the Spanish *barcas* foundered, throwing their sailors into the water, and then occurred one of those vast mysteries of fate, for as we regrouped and sped toward the galleon, whose officers must have been terrified to see how quickly we disposed of their first line of defense, a stupendous fire swept the deck above us. Some careless act aboard the galleon must have thrown a fire of some kind into a barrel of powder, killing far more Spaniards than we did when we climbed up to take command.

Once in control, my uncle and I rampaged through the lower decks, finally locating the huge stores of silver, each bar marked with its Potosí number, and we realized that we had taken a prize of immeasurable value. Will cried in joy: "No division this time of eleven pounds each!" And we knew, there in the dark hold, that we would be wealthy men if we could but sail this great ship back to Port Royal in Jamaica.

While we were in the bowels of the galleon we heard a confused shouting on deck, and fearing that a sortie of armed Spaniards might have hidden against the moment they could spring out upon us and retake their ship, we rushed aloft, our faces grimed from the hold, our guns and swords at the ready. Instead, I found myself standing face-to-face with the most beautiful young woman I had ever seen. She was, I judged, about seventeen, fair of skin as if the sun had never touched her pretty face, dressed in fine fabrics more suited to a ball than to a galleon, with perfect figure, dark hair and eyes of an exquisite quality that danced with excitement, even in these uncertain surroundings.

She was accompanied by a woman I took to be her mother, a stately creature of some forty years perhaps, or more, for I am no judge past the age of twenty, and of an austere character which disapproved of all that had happened this morning and especially of the black-faced English rogues who were now taking control of her and her daughter.

Later that afternoon, when we found out who they were, we were astounded at our great good fortune, for the tall, solemn priest who had accompanied them told us in polished Spanish: "They are the wife and daughter of the governor of Cartagena, the most honorable Don Alfonso Ledesma Amadór y Espĩnal. They've been visiting in Peru, and if you mar either of them in any way, the wrath of the entire Spanish empire will hound you to your graves." And with that he introduced us to Doña Ana Ledesma y Paredes, and her beautiful daughter Inez. He informed us further that he was Fray Baltazar Arévalo of the town of that name in the province of Ávila on the borders of Segovia. He rattled off these names as if each bestowed a special grandeur upon his family heritage.

He was a tall man with dark visage, and he looked as if the burden of leading a flock of Catholic Spaniards in the New World was a dismal business, which I have no doubt it was, but he obviously intended defending his two present charges with his life. When my uncle saw him, he whispered in my ear: "That one looks just like the Inquisition man who sentenced me to death in Cádiz," and I think he would have thrust a poniard into the gloomy priest right then had I not restrained him.

I have not gone to sleep as yet, because Captain McFee assigned me to the duty of guarding the hundred-odd prisoners we took during the battle, and I can hear them now as I write, battened down below hatches and wondering what fate awaits them. My uncle is for killing them, but others say: "Put them in the boats and head them for shore. Let them find their own way." I would be most unhappy if Señorita Inez were treated thus.

TUE 11 APRIL: When we learned that the name of our fine little galleon was *La Giralda de Sevilla* we wanted to know what the words meant, and the gloomy priest told us: "In Sevilla, loveliest city in Spain, there is a majestic cathedral so big you would not believe me if I told you. Attached to it is the most beautiful tower, the Giralda, in itself a thing of grace, built by the Moors."

"What is a *giralda*?" I asked, and he snapped impatiently: "Weather vane." For some crazy reason the dumb Spaniards named a tower after a weather vane. So our ship is *The Weather Vane of Sevilla.* Some men did not like sailing in a ship with a Spanish name, but when they proposed changing it to a decent, clean English name like the *Castle,* because we did have a castlelike structure aft, there was loud protest from others who knew of ships that had changed their names and had encountered only bad luck as a result: "We capturcd a *St. Peter* and changed it to the *Master of Deal* and within four weeks it caught fire and burned." After five other dismal stories had been recited, one man gave contrary testimony: "We captured a Dutch ship *Frau Rosalinde,* and our captain, who had much trouble with his wife, vowed: 'I'll not sail in a ship named after a woman,' and we changed it to *Robin Hood,* and before the month was out we had captured a Spanish craft with stores of bullion." But the bad cases outnumbered the good nine to two, so we voted to keep *Giralda* and when I told the priest, he said grudgingly: "Good omen. Every sailor needs a weather vane."

SUN 16 APRIL: First prayers, at which we gave thanks that God had delivered into our hands this rich prize, then big decisions, I can tell you. Captain McFee and the group of five who counsel him have agreed to crowd all the prisoners into *barcas* with allowances of food and water and let them get home as best they can, but only after the masts have been sawed off to prevent them taking action against us. They further decided to keep aboard the *Giralda* the Spanish chirurgeon, who certainly knows his pills and ointments better than we, but my uncle cautioned: "Search his bottles and remove all poisons, or he will mix one for us." They decided to keep also a Master Rodrigo, a learned man who had served the Spanish captain as navigator and who told me in excellent English: "I know these waters, Acapulco to Cape Horn, so inform your captain that I might be of some service." When I asked why he might want to serve with us, he said: "A sailor's life is to sail, and as for those in the little *barcas,* who knows what will happen?" We also kept seven black men who had served as slaves on the *Giralda* and who would continue in the same duties with us. Our new navigator asked us to allow him his assistant, but Uncle Will growled: "My nephew knows navigating. He can be your assistant," and it was done.

Now came the weighty problem of what to do about the two Ledesma women and their priest. My uncle was about to throw them into one of the *barcas* and to God's mercy, for he visualized only trouble if we kept them with us, but Fray Baltazar stopped him with an anguished plea: "Save these women, you fools! Governor Ledesma will pay a noble ransom," and I stepped forward to bring the ladies back, but Uncle Will said: "He'll offer the ransom, but how are we going to collect it?" McFee silenced him with the reminder: "No man ever has enough siller," and when I asked what *siller* was, my uncle said gruffly: "It's how them Scots say *silver,* and he may be right."

However, I could see that he was not happy this afternoon when the *barcas* started drifting toward some distant shore without the Ledesma women aboard. And as for the dark priest, my uncle still wanted to knife him and may do so before this trip is over.

I was given the task of finding quarters for the two women and their priest, and I arranged for them to keep the cabins they had occupied atop the stern castle, what they call the poopdeck, but when Captain McFee heard of my decision, he growled: "They can't stay there," and when I asked why not, he astonished me: "Because four days from now that castle won't be there," and so I had to find smaller and less-polished cabins below. When Fray Baltazar objected, I told him, making my voice sound official: "Because four days from now that castle won't be there," and I let him explain that to his women.

MON 17 APRIL: *Giralda* may not have been a major Manila galleon, but it is sumptuously equipped with the most modern instruments required in navigation, and when Master Rodrigo satisfied himself that I had a certain skill in using the forestaff to take shots of the sun in order to determine latitude, he accepted me fully as his assistant: "You must put aside your forestaff, for it is little better than a guessing game," and he showed me for the first time a beautiful new instrument called a backstaff fashioned of bleached pearwood and ivory and of such an ingenious purpose that I could not believe it. "When taking a sight, do not point it at the sun," he explained, "for then the eye grows weary. This one you point *away* from the sun, catch the shadow it throws here, and bring it together with the horizon you see through this peephole." When I followed his instructions I caught a perfect sighting on my first effort.

TUE 18 APRIL: Today when I handed Master Rodrigo the latitude from my noon shot made with his backstaff, I asked: "How did you learn to speak English?" and he told me: "A Dutch navigator told me, and they're the best, to get myself a copy of Eduardo Wright's *Errors in Navigation,* which, he said, would make all things clear. When I found a copy I had to learn English to read it, and well worth the effort it was." He handed me his precious book to study, and when I did so to the level that I could understand, I told him: "Now I'm ready to be a navigator," and he said: "Maybe in ten years."

TUE 28 APRIL: Big fight with Master Rodrigo. When he found that I had dated the above entry *Tue 18 April,* which was correct, he screamed: "The entire civilized world uses Catholic dating. Your crazy Protestant calendar lags ten days behind. Change it right now or you can no longer be my assistant." So I changed it, as you can see, but I do believe Rodrigo must be wrong, for I cannot think that people in England could ever make such a mistake.

THU 30 APRIL: So when we anchored off the island which we face tonight, I took my sighting and found that we were 3° 01' North latitude and the mariner told us: "This is Gorgona Island, not a bad spot for your purpose," so we warped the *Giralda* inland as far as possible into a small stream, and when we had nearly grounded at high tide, we threw lines from the ship to trees ashore, and after we were well secured, Captain McFee informed us: "Here we shall remain about a month to accomplish the things that must be done if we hope to get our ship safely back to Port Royal." And before the sun went down he started the tremendous job of converting this fancy little galleon into a good fighting ship worthy of a buccaneer. I was astonished at all he proposed: "Off comes that castle aft." When some protested that this would deprive us of all the good cabins, he growled: "Ships are for fighting, not for siestas." The two masts would be lowered by half, ridding us of all those high and fashionable sails which look so pretty when they're pushing some heavy galleon ahead in fair weather and good wind, but which are so useless when we are trying to fight another ship and have to maneuver quickly to gain advantage. One mast far aft is to be discarded entirely, so at least half our sails will be of no further use. The very thick and heavy ropes will be stowed below, never to be used again aboard our ship, but to be sold at some future port to great ships that may still need them. The clutter on deck is to be what he called "cleansed entirely" for as Captain McFee pointed out: "If the Spanish captain had had his powder barrels below, he'd never have lost this ship to a boarding party." In almost every other detail of this fine galleon, he sees something that can be chopped away or otherwise disposed of and he urges Mompox with his ax to get at it.

TUE 5 MAY: This morning when Fray Baltazar and Señora Ledesma saw that we really intended chopping off the two top decks aft, he made an angry protest, and she a tearful one, claiming that Captain McFee was destroying a beautiful ship, but he was firm, jutting out his Scottish jaw: "We're building a fast fighting ship to carry you and our hoard of silver safely to Jamaica. All else is nothing," and we continued the destruction.

MON 25 MAY: Well, the rebuilding is finished, and Master Rodrigo, looking at the rubbish left ashore, said: "We must weigh half of what we did before," but Captain McFee, looking at the same graveyard of overtall masts, unnecessary cabins and even whole decks that were only for show, told our crew: "Now we have a ship that can cut through the waves and outmatch any Spanish ship." Tomorrow we break loose the lines tying us to shore and set forth . . . for where? We know we want to get to Jamaica, but we cannot make up our minds exactly how to get there. Whether to take the shortest course around Cape Horn, not a pleasant trip they tell me, or clear around the world across the Pacific to Asia, and then around Good Hope and home across the Atlantic. A frightening course either way, but Uncle Will says: "Take either. It's always good to see new lands."

THU 28 MAY: I have never lived as satisfying a day at sea. This morning Señorita Inez, who has been kept away from me by her mother and Fray Baltazar, escaped from their watch and walked with me far forward where they could not spy on us. She allowed me to take her hand, and I do believe she wanted to let me know that she thought me a decent fellow, even though an Englishman. I know enough Spanish to understand when she told me: "My name is not Inez like you say. It's Inés," and she pronounced this in such a soft, lovely manner, that I much preferred her version: "Eee-*ness*."

She then shared with me the history of what she called "Our Famous Family," and I was not too pleased to learn that her great-grandfather had hounded our Sir Francis Drake to a watery death. Seeing me frown, she assured me that her grandfather, who had the curious name of Roque Ledesma y Ledesma, had been the governor of Cartagena who allowed trading relations with England, so he must have been a good man. Our pleasant visit was interrupted by my uncle, who shooed us out from our hiding place so that Fray Baltazar could spy us and come running. When I asked Will why he had done this, he said: "There's a proper English girl waiting for you in Barbados," and when I asked who, he snapped: "You know damn well who, somebody . . ." and off he stomped cursing at Spaniards in general.

FRI 29 MAY: Went walking on the deck with Señorita Inés, but when Uncle Will saw us he scurried like a tattletale to Fray Baltazar, who rushed out to whisk her away. Later my uncle apologized: "I suppose she's better than that Mompox. But you've got to remember she's papist and will cheer when her priest burns you as a heretic . . . if he gets the chance."

THU 25 JUNE: At sea, 2° 13' South off the renowned city of

Guayaquil, we captured a big Spanish ship heading north to Panamá, with no loss of life to us and only three of them. Same as before. Everyone into small boats with the masts chopped off. Head for the mainland and good luck while we transfer all goods to the *Giralda,* set fire to the Spaniard and continue south. While rejoicing at this good luck, I found myself once more alone with Señorita Inés, and she said she was most grieved to see those good men who had done no harm set adrift with no mast or sails, and although I agreed with her, I suddenly found myself defensive, for I could not tolerate any Spaniard criticizing English sailors: "You must ask my uncle. When your Spaniards captured his ship they burned our sailors alive and were about to do the same to him, when he escaped." She could not believe that her people had so behaved, and when the ever-watchful Fray Baltazar came as usual to rescue her from me, she asked: "Good priest, tell me if it is true that we have in Spain an Inquisition that burns Englishmen?" and it was then that he began his effort to educate me. "Yes," he told us, "the Holy Church had to establish a group to protect it from the heretic and the infidel, and yes, sometimes the punishments had to be cruel, but no more so than what your uncle does when you Englishmen take a ship and shoot the wounded or drown those who fought with extra vigor against you. The spirit of man is rude, and it requires constant taming."

He told us that on the Spanish Main the Inquisition did not burn people, for which he was grateful, but that the fight against heretics had to continue lest the one True Church be what he called "contaminated." And he added: "We protect it for your interest as well as ours." This I could not understand, so he explained: "Less than a hundred and twenty years ago you Englishmen were all Catholics, and one of these days, when a proper king occupies your throne, you'll be so again." Before I could protest, he asked: "You've seen most of the North Sea, Ned. Wouldn't it be simpler and better if we were all one group of islands, all Catholic and subject to one king in Spain and one pope in Rome?"

I was so astounded by such an idea that when he took Inés away I sought my uncle, and said: "Fray Baltazar says that a hundred years ago all Englishmen were Catholics," and he growled: "Not my people. Back to the time of Jesus Christ himself, we was always Church of England," and I did not know who to believe.

MON 13 JULY: On this day I gained much respect for our captain, because at latitude 12° 05' South we stood off Lima's great port of

Callao in Peru, and when I saw the multitude of ships there, with fleet war vessels among them bristling with guns, I thought: Dear God, protect us if we try anything here. They know that one Englishman is worth ten Spaniards, but those ships are too many, even for us. And to my eternal thanks, Captain McFee must have had the same idea, for when he dropped the glass from his eye he turned to Master Rodrigo and said: "Carry as she goes," and the navigator saluted and replied: "A very good decision, sir."

I am confused about this Rodrigo. He's a loyal Spaniard and must hope to see us taken by some warship of his country, but he is first of all a responsible seaman and as such he wants to preserve his vessel and put her into safe waters. I saw how he was hurt, terribly, when we chopped his proud galleon to pieces, but now he is equally proud of her performance as a sleek ship that performs wondrously in our battle actions. We in turn trust him, for as Captain McFee says: "What else can we do? He knows these waters and we don't."

WED 22 JULY: Of Arica, I can say only this. Richest port in Peru, for all the silver of Potosí ships from here. Defended by the best Spanish troops. Crafty swine, allowed us to storm ashore like we were going to capture Madrid. Waited till we were far from our ship, then sent cavalry at us, knocked us galley-west. When we regained our ship, Uncle Will told me: "See! You can never trust a Spaniard."

TUE 28 JULY: We gained our revenge for the loss of three good men at Arica, but I was not much impressed with our triumph. At a good distance south of that port we anchored off the town of Hilo and stormed ashore to capture a sugar mill, where we held the plantation manager hostage. Sending a sharp message to the owners out in the country, which I delivered under the protection of a white flag, we said we would burn the sugar mill to the ground unless a ransom of one hundred thousand pesos was paid within two days. The owners assured us they had the money in Arica, but it would require two days' travel time. I told them: "Two days, you bring us the money or we burn your mill," and two days later they came to us under their white flag and we were overjoyed that we would be getting the hundred thousand pesos. But they brought us nothing, said that the messenger from Arica had been delayed, but please don't burn our mill because two days hence we will be back with the money. Two days passed, no money, so back I went with my white flag, and they told me that since the money had reached the next village it would be delivered tomorrow, so please don't burn our mill, and I promised. But when yesterday came and went with still no money, Captain McFee said in anger: "They've been toying with you, Ned. Burn everything." And we rushed to all corners of the plantation, burning houses and barns and destroying machinery until there was nothing standing over six inches high. As we retired from the place my uncle told me: "Well, you've seen how untrustworthy the Spaniards are. Have nothing more to do with that girl and her priest."

FRI 28 AUGUST: My magical backstaff tells me we're now well below the equator at 26° 21' South, and I've been having a fine time on land hunting wild pigs along the shores of the bay and catching sea turtles. We've eaten well on this buccaneering trip. We're now careening the *Giralda,* which means that stout ropes have been attached to our mast so that the ship can be pulled over on its beam ends one side at a time, which allows us to work with bars and axes, chopping away the barnacles that cover the bottom, some as big as a man's hand, and then scrape off the seaweed that clings like wavy hair. These things slow a ship tremendously, as if big hands held us back in the water, and old sailors tell me that if the barnacles are allowed to grow undisturbed, the day will come when the ship won't be able to move forward at all.

But the most important part of careening is not merely clearing the bottom, but scraping off the worms that multiply in warm waters and dig into wood so fast they can eat away a bottom in one year. We dug out a small mountain of worms and chopped in half as many again, providing food for a hundred gulls who swarmed about us without saying thanks.

During the two weeks we spent at this necessary job, with our cabins tilted this way and that, we slept ashore, and several times I was able to take long walks with Señorita Inés. We spent such happy moments at the edge of the bay, watching the fish and the turtles, that I became convinced she had developed an interest in me. After all, every time I had seen her aboard ship, she had also seen me, and if I grew mightily attached to her, is it not reasonable I asked myself, that she might feel the same about me?

One afternoon when I was hard at work scraping the bottom and preparing it for the metal sheathing we had found in the hold, I saw Inés walking by the shore without the customary protection of her mother or the priest, that careful watchdog, and as I continued looking after the girl I had grown to love during our long passages, I spied one of our rascally hands, a gross fellow of filthy tongue named

Quinton, trailing her, and as she passed from sight I heard her scream. Rushing pell-mell to where I had last seen her, without hesitation or thought I unlimbered my pistol and shot him dead. The noise attracted both Señora Ledesma and Fray Baltazar, who wrapped the fainting girl in their arms and bore her to the tent they were occupying during the careening.

There had to be a meeting of the crew, for one of their members had been slain, and I was quickly absolved, but my uncle took the occasion to reprove me: "You should not waste a bullet killing an Englishman who is assaulting a Spaniard. Save it to kill a Spaniard who affronts an Englishman."

Now that our crew was already gathered at one place, someone remembered the tradition: "Buccaneers have always elected their captains," and soon many were complaining of the way McFee had behaved at various points, and so many others voiced their displeasure that the first man made a motion, like we were in Parliament: "I move to elect a new captain," and before I knew what was happening, we had deposed Captain McFee and elected a sailor who spoke loud but did little.

THU 3 SEPTEMBER: Today my uncle, in a show of temper, bawled me out: "You give me nothing but headaches, Ned. Stay away from that Inés. She'll bring you only trouble." And when I started to protest, he actually roared: "And stay away from that Mompox, too. He'll bring you even greater trouble." When I asked why this sudden outburst, he said almost plaintively: "You were intended for some fine English girl in Barbados, and by the horns of hell, I'm going to see you delivered safely home."

MON 14 SEPTEMBER: Our new captain has made the big decision: "We shall return home by way of China, India and Good Hope," and in pursuit of that goal we have sailed far to the west on latitude 34° 07' South and have come to an island called Juan Fernández, in whose principal bay we rest tonight, and for me, who aspires to become a skilled navigator, the visit to this lonely island has been a kind of gift, because in the heavens, which have magically cleared of storms as if in my favor, I saw tonight for the first time those great concentrations of stars which mariners have named the Clouds of Magellan, for he was the first civilized man to see them. How mysterious, how wonderful they were, hung in the southern skies like a collection of celestial flowers. But while I stood gazing in awe Master Rodrigo came to stand by me, and said glumly: "Beautiful, yes, but not one-tenth the value of our North Star which tells us where we are." And then he showed me how, using the Southern Cross, which is certainly as beautiful as any constellation we have in our northern seas, a sailor can construct in his imagination a southern substitution for the North Star. It was a clever mental exercise and I thanked him.

When he was gone a much different night wanderer took his place and I felt my hand gently held in hers. It was Señorita Inés, come to see the Clouds of Magellan, and as she joined me she whispered: "Ned, I'm glad to be with you," and before I really knew what was happening we kissed, and it was more pleasant than any kiss I had known in Port Royal. We remained thus for the better part of an hour, looking at Magellan and kissing, and then we heard a vast commotion on the deck below, and here comes Señora Ledesma and Fray Baltazar, running here and there, now together, now with her in one direction, him in another, and each shouting: "She's not here. Is she over there?" As they ran, Inés stood always closer to me, holding my arms about her waist, until we seemed one person, and then she would kiss me again and laugh at the noises her mother and the priest were making. Finally Fray Baltazar spotted us on the high deck. "Just as we suspected! She's with him!" And together the two wild searchers rushed up the ladders to rescue Inés, who remained in my arms until they arrived.

"You naughty child!" her mother cried as she tore Inés from me. "You ugly boy!" Fray Baltazar added, elbowing me away from the two women. But after Inés had been safely stowed below, Baltazar returned to stand with me and watch the stars. We talked most of the night away as he told me of his boyhood in Arévalo and of how he had been permitted in his life to watch a dozen marriages between couples who were not suited and of how each had ended in misery at least and sometimes tragedy. There was always a lot of human tragedy when Fray Baltazar talked.

"What do you mean, *not suited*?" I asked, and he had a dozen examples: "A lady of noble bearing married a Moor, different color, different religion, very bad. She stabbed him with a dagger. A lady in our town of some quality married a Portuguese of low estate. Strangled her for her money. I accompanied him to the scaffold and am glad to say he died in repentance." He gave three instances in which Spanish ladies of what he called "some repute" married Protestants, and their experiences were downright pitiful. So at the end of this narration I asked: "Who should marry who?" and he said firmly:

"A fine Catholic girl like Inés of notable family must marry only a young man of equally good family, who is also Catholic. What you do, as a heretic, is of little matter." When he left me alone, staring at the stars, it was almost dawn and I could still feel the arms of Inés about me and I went to bed satisfied that she loved me.

WED 30 SEPTEMBER: Amazing events. During our long stay on Juan Fernández our crew tired of the silly ways in which our new captain gave orders exhibiting his power over us, and there was also serious criticism of his decision to take us home by way of China, so last night a meeting was held and we told him he was no longer our captain, and when he asked: "Well, who is?" we had an election, and our old captain, Mister McFee, was restored to office. I don't like this. Ordinary sailors should not go around discharging and rehiring captains. The English way is a lot better. Appoint a man captain and keep him there until he sinks his ship. Of course, if he goes down with her, as he is supposed to, that ends that.

Captain McFee's first decision was not a happy one. He decided, with our approval, not to pursue our course across the South Sea but to head for Cape Horn and home. However, he left Juan Fernández so quickly, we had no time to search the beach for members of our crew who might be still ashore, and when we were at sea some hours, my uncle came crying: "Go back! The Miskito David is still ashore!" but Captain McFee would not listen: "We're too far on our way," and we plunged toward the Strait of Magellan. I spent many hours brooding about David and what his fate might be. Imagine, alone, all by himself on that forlorn island. How will he eat? What if he gets sick? Poor David, poor Indian, I weep for him.*

The next excitement on this memorable day came when we sighted a Spanish ship heading north and decided to give chase. Many sailors, including me, argued against capturing another ship and one so far south that it could not have carried gold or silver, but Captain McFee said: "A sailor on a long voyage can never have enough food or gunpowder," so we closed upon her, boarded without the loss of

---

*The Miskito Indian known as David was rescued years later by the legendary pirate-naturalist-writer William Dampier and carried to freedom. Curiously, in 1704 the famous Scottish sailor Alexander Selkirk marooned himself on this same island, where he lived in total solitude for four and a half years before being found by this same Dampier on a return visit to Juan Fernández. Daniel Defoe, who knew Dampier, later borrowed the story, unacknowledged, as the basis for his novel *Robinson Crusoe*.

any of our men, put nine of theirs to the sword, pillaged their ship of all goods worth taking, saved her longboats, and set her afire. We loaded most of our Spanish captives and all of hers into the long-boats, threw away their masts, and sent them on their way to the mainland, which is by my reckoning a long way off. I asked my uncle: "Do you think they'll ever reach shore?" and he said: "I hope not." I have risen from my hammock to add these sentences. I could not sleep from thinking of David the Miskito marooned on that island and the Spanish sailors trying to reach shore with no sails and little food or water. I find that I am tired of killing. I am weary of shooting unarmed Spanish prisoners or setting them adrift to perish. Capture their ships, yes, and fight valiantly if we have to, swords and pistols, but this continued slaughter? No. I shall participate no further. Of course, such regrets do not bother Uncle Will, who is asleep in the hammock above me and snoring.

TUE 13 OCTOBER: Day after day of dull nothing heading south for Cape Horn. No fish to catch, no birds to follow, no Spanish ships to chase, nothing. These must be the loneliest seas in the world. But today things livened when Master Rodrigo challenged me to a test: "Well, *muchacho*, to be a navigator, let's see if you can take a proper sight," and he gave me a slip of paper, himself another, and he said: "It's about noon. We'll both shoot the sun, tell no one our reading, and figure our latitude on these papers, then compare them." He al-lowed me to go first, and with feet steady and arms firm, my back to the sun and the magical staff held tight, I calculated a latitude of 39° 40' South and wrote this on my slip. Then he took his sighting, much more rapidly than me, and wrote it down. "Now we'll com-pare," he said, and when my slip was laid beside his they both read 39 degrees and were only twelve minutes apart: "*Muchacho,* you're a budding navigator. Nine more years."

I then asked: "Master Rodrigo, if we can tell so accurately where we are north and south, why can't we do so east and west?" and he stopped whatever he had been doing and gave me a long lesson in which he compared the two problems: "For latitude, we have two fixed marks, the sun at noon, the North Star at night. God hung those two for us, steady forever. One shot of either, you know exactly how far you are north or south of the equator." He then said some-thing that Fray Baltazar would not have approved: "But God was careless about His east and west. We have no fixed beacons. As to our longitude, the best we can do is guess." And he spent more than an hour instructing me in the secrets whereby practiced navigators guess where they are. "Suppose I know where Cádiz is as we start to sail, and I know how fast my ship is traveling and in what direction. At the end of twenty-four hours I can make a pretty good guess as to where we are. From there we make new calculations of tide, wind, drift, supposed speed, and twenty-four hours later we again guess where we are then. And so it goes. We guess our way around the world. Right now, because we have charts and know what we've been doing, I'd say we were about sixty-nine degrees of longitude west of Cádiz." At the end of his lecture he frowned: "It's infuriating to have no reliable system. Maybe someone will invent a chain we'll drag in the water and it will tick off the miles. Or a new way to shoot the sun sideways instead of up and down. Or a clock which tells you always what time it is in Cádiz so you can compare noon there with noon here." Pointing to the ivory backstaff, he told me: "If men can invent this so late in the day, they can invent other useful devices too." And by making shrewd guesses together about tides and winds and whether our charts were reliable or not, we calculated that on some of these tedious days south we covered as many as ninety miles, which would be about four English miles an hour, and on one day we made well over a hundred, but on others when winds were adverse, only twenty or even less.

SAT 21 NOVEMBER: 56° 10' South. Yes, that's right. I've checked it with my backstaff every time the sun has peeked through the frozen clouds and my numbers confirm a miserable story of lost channels, frustration, despair and freezing fingers. Since Master Rodrigo has never sailed through the Strait of Magellan connecting the South Sea of the Pacific to the Atlantic Ocean, and since heavy cloud has enveloped us almost from the time we captured our last Spanish ship, no one aboard really knew what we were doing, and several sailors told me: "Lucky you know how to work that astrolabe, else we'd be totally lost." If my sightings are right and if our charts do not lie, which they may, we have missed Magellan completely and are well down toward the South Pole. But at least we've found open water, so tomorrow the navigator and I will advise Captain McFee to head north, for I'm convinced we have rounded Cape Horn and are now in the Atlantic Ocean, but I'm not much impressed with my company of buccaneers who do not even know what ocean we're in.

SUN 29 NOVEMBER: Day of miracles! Lost in the bitter cold of wherever we are, I calculated from my sighting of the sun that we must be about 52° 10' South and that the nest of feathery clouds I had kept watching for the last two days to the northeast must be hanging over some island not shown on our maps. Presenting my conclusions to Captain McFee, I recommended that he sail in that direction, but he said: "Go to hell. No boy tells me where to sail," and he refused. Now the sailors, convening a meeting, elected to throw him from command yet again "for that he missed Magellan and the whole end of South America," but their arrogance did not hide their fear at being lost in an unknown ocean.

So for some minutes we were without a captain, and then the miracle happened, for my uncle cried in a loud voice: "The islands! Just where the lad said they'd be!"* And when the frightened men looked, they saw the fine green islands promising fresh water and fresh deer meat, and Will shouted again: "Damn me, only one seems to know where we are is the lad," and the men cheered and elected me their captain, with the firm orders: "Take us home, son."

So here I am at age twenty, nigh onto twenty-one, in command of the Spanish galleon, later English fighting ship *Giralda,* with a crew of forty-one battle-tested Englishmen, nine Spanish sailors who chose to stay with us and seventeen slaves, fourteen Indians, Mompox, Master Rodrigo, Fray Baltazar and the two Ledesma women, plus a hold heavy in silver bars.

Where are we? I know only that we have come safely into the Atlantic and that our home refuge of Port Royal lies some six thousand seven hundred miles to the north, if our captured charts are correct. As captain responsible for the safe passage of my ship, I have to suppose that sooner or later we must encounter some big Spanish warship that can outman, outgun and outfight us, and that I want to avoid. In the few hours since I was given command, I have thought not of the easy way we captured small Spanish ships but of the way we fled before big Spanish ships at Panamá, Lima and Arica, and of how Spanish soldiers, when in good supply, punished us at the silver port. I have decided that to be a proper buccaneer, a man does not have to be a fool.

SAT 12 DECEMBER: 34° 40' South off the coast at Buenos Aires, where an entirely new event has occurred, to my enormous surprise. As captain of our ship I now take my meals in the cabin where the Ledesma women and their priest eat, and this has put me face-to-

---

*The Falklands in English. In Spanish, Las Islas Malvinas.

face, three times each day, with the adorable Señorita Inés, and I think I can speak for us both, certainly for me, when I write with trembling hand and beating heart that we have fallen wonderfully, magnificently in love. She has proved highly skilled in slipping away from both her mother and her priest and finding me where they cannot. The other evening we had near to three hours alone, and it was, well, sort of overwhelming. When she slipped away she whispered: "Ned, I feel it in my heart that at the end of this cruising we shall be married," and I assured her: "That becomes my whole aim."

This noon, after I had shot the sun, with the results penned above, I asked at the table: "Where's Señorita Inés?" and her mother said smugly: "Locked in her cabin," and when I gasped, the priest asked with a slight sneer: "And who do you think's guarding the door?" and when I said I couldn't guess, he said: "Your uncle."

Yes, the sternest enemy of my love for Inés is my own uncle, who said, when I stormed out to challenge him: "Boy, your life could be . . ." I tried to brush him aside: "I'm not a boy. I'm the captain of this ship," but I could not budge him. He was siding with the priest and Señora Ledesma for the good of my soul, he said, and because no Englishman with Tatum blood in his veins should marry a Spaniard.

So three determined people, two Spanish, one English, have banded together to prevent headstrong Señorita Inés and determined me from a pledge of our love. Last night, I can tell you, they failed, not because of anything bold that I did but because Inés escaped while Fray Baltazar was guarding her, ran swiftly into the cabin where I was sleeping, and barred the door from the inside. With sweet abandon she threw herself into my arms, crying: "Ned, I cannot live without you . . . so brave . . . captain of your own ship . . . so much desired." Well, I can tell you I was overwhelmed by her bold action, and especially what she kept saying as she poured kisses on my trembling lips: "We shall be married." This was exactly what I had dreamed about on the long passages south to the Cape, and I began to think that marriage with this delectable girl was possible, regardless of how vigorously her mother and my uncle might object.

But even as she made her professions of love, which I accepted as the kind of miracle that occurs when a man became captain of a fine ship, a great knocking came at my cabin door, and we could hear Señora Ledesma and Fray Baltazar, the one voice high, the other low, pleading with Inés to open the door and behave like a proper Spanish young lady. She refused, crying repeatedly: "I shall not open till you agree that Ned and I can move about his ship as we decide," and it seemed to me, listening to their knocking and her response, that a great scandal must be under way, with my crew aware of everything, and I wondered what the effect would be.

The problem faded into insignificance in view of what happened next, for I heard my uncle shouting in the early dawn: "Spanish ship! Attack!" and such a clatter arose that I had to know that our *Giralda* was rushing full speed ahead and girding her decks for an assault. It was, I saw, pretty ridiculous for me to be locked in my cabin, prisoner of a Spanish lass, when the ship I was supposed to be commanding was bearing down on an enemy who might prove to be well armed.

"I must go!" I cried to Inés, striving to break free, but she stood by the barred door and refused to let me open it, and I spent the next minutes in a frenzy of indecision, with Señora Ledesma banging on my door, Fray Baltazar thundering anathemas, and my uncle speeding my ship into battle against an enemy I could not see and whose strength I could not estimate. I realized it was a sad position for a captain to be in, but I saw no escape, and with Inés in my arms I awaited the clash of arms that would come when the sailors of the *Giralda* tried to board the fleeing Spanish ship.

It was a frightening two hours, locked in that cabin with the girl I loved. We could hear the ships collide, the swift movement of feet on the deck, the play of swords so far distant that it must come from the deck of the other ship, the echoes of salute guns being fired, and eventually the cries of victory. Only then did Inés let me go.

When I came onto the deck I found Will about to make eleven Spanish prisoners, weighted with chains, walk the plank to instant death. "No!" I shouted. "Let them have a small boat. Better yet, let them have their own ship with the masts cut away."

When my uncle and the usual hotheads who could be depended upon to support his piratical deeds refused to obey my commands, I shouted: "Stop it! I'm your captain," and two of the men shouted back in the same breath: "Not anymore, hiding in your cabin while we fight," and a meeting was held then and there which deposed me and once again restored Mister McFee to his original command.

When buccaneers try to run ships, they can be damned fools. Imagine electing the same man to be captain three different times. But in a way I was glad he now had the command, because the first order he gave was: "Stop leading those prisoners to the gangplank," and because he was older, the men had to obey him. He then ordered the captured ship to be stripped of everything we might need on the final rush to Port Royal, especially the casks of fresh water and the food. Our sailors were invited to take control of as much powder and ball as they thought they might need, and the masts were chopped down to deck level. The defeated Spaniards were allowed to climb back aboard their ship and head it for the mainland, while our men fired salutes to speed them on their way.

I had been captain for fifteen days, during which time I moved our ship homeward from 56° South to 34°. It could be said that during my captaincy we captured this Spanish vessel without the loss of an English life and that I received a proposal of marriage from a most wonderful Spanish girl. A lot of buccaneer captains take a longer time to achieve less.

But with the new order of things I was no longer allowed to take my meals with the Ledesma women and the priest, so I must devise some trick to see once more the girl who loves me.

FRI 25 DECEMBER: Well off the coast at 22° 53' South, opposite Rio de Janeiro in Brazil. This afternoon all the bitterness I have harbored against Fray Baltazar vanished, for when the entire ship's company had gathered on the afterdeck during a fine spring afternoon for holy services honoring the birthday of Our Lord Jesus Christ, the tall, dark priest said, following his prayers: "Let there be harmony on this blessed day. I have prayed in Catholic Spanish for my countrymen, will you pray in Protestant English for yours," and to my amazement he placed his Spanish Bible in my hands, and I was so moved that for some moments I could not speak, but then I heard my uncle's voice growling: "Get on with it, lad," and a torrent of words sprang from my lips:

> "Almighty God, we have come a long voyage in our sturdy ship, and we have helped one another. We could not have navigated the coast of the Spanish Main without the guidance of Master Rodrigo, and for his good work we give thanks. We have been aided by the prayers and guidance of Fray Baltazar, a worthy priest. Three times we've called upon Captain McFee to command this ship, and may he get us home safely at last with our treasure intact."

It was simply impossible for me to close a Christmas prayer without mention of the girl I had come to love, so to the astonishment of the crew I added:

"Dear God, I in particular thank Thee for having let me know on this long voyage a blessed young woman whose courage never faltered on dangerous days or failed to inspire on good. She has been one of our best sailors, so protect her wherever her voyaging takes her."

As I said these words she broke away from her mother and came to stand by me, and no one sought to take her away. And as she stood there I thought of the remarkable adventures my band of buccaneers has known: the hasty decision to go our own way after Captain Morgan stole our just rewards; the long march and sail across the isthmus; the battles; the soaring victories against vast odds; the defeats at Panamá and Arica; the little ships we captured and the big ones from which we ran; the Clouds of Magellan at night; the Strait of Magellan that we never found . . . And then a hand of ice seemed to grip my heart, and in a low voice I ended my prayer:

"Merciful God who protects sailors and brings them home after long voyages, send Thy special love on this holy day to the Indian David, castaway on Juan Fernández, alone. Send a ship to rescue him and bring us all safely back to our home ports."

FRI 8 JANUARY IN THE NEW YEAR 1672: On this day when nothing of significance happened, not even a good meal or a fight among the men, we crossed the equator and all began to breathe with more excitement, for we are nearing Port Royal.

FRI 29 JANUARY: Day of victory, day of despair! For some days Captain McFee, Uncle Will, Fray Baltazar and I have held urgent meetings to devise a plan for delivering the Ledesma women and our prisoners into proper Spanish hands, and to collect a ransom if it could be arranged. No one, not even my uncle, wants to kill or otherwise harm them, but to sail boldly into Cartagena with them would be too risky. They do not want us to land them in Port Royal, where they would have no assurance of ever making their way back to Cartagena, where their families await them.

Captain McFee and my uncle were determined to get rid of them, because to keep them might involve too many problems, but how to do this they did not know. So it was left to Fray Baltazar and me to plan some procedure, and as we began talking on a corner of the afterdeck I asked if I could invite Mompox to join us, since he as a man

of color had so much to gain or lose by what we did, and Fray Baltazar countered: "And I should like to have the assistance of Master
Rodrigo, our navigator," to which I agreed.

When we were assembled, the priest said gravely: "We're talking
about life and death. A mistake, and we could all die. So let us seek
the right conclusions."

Mompox said with admirable clarity: "Considering my color,
I must not go wherever men of ill will can throw me into slavery.
Not Cartagena. Not Barbados. Not Jamaica. And not the southern
American colonies."

"What's left?" Baltazar asked and Mompox said: "Put me on
some trading ship to Boston," and we agreed that if possible we would
do so.

"Now, how do we get the Ledesmas back to Cartagena?" Baltazar asked, and I broke in: "Inés stays with me," and he said in that
grave voice I had come to respect: "My son, it cannot be. She is of
one world, you of another." Very firmly he added: "It will not work.
It will never happen." When he saw my dismay he added: "My son,
you've had great triumphs on this voyage. Captain of your own ship.
Successful in battle. Courage that no man can challenge. Leave it at
that." Seeing that I was still distraught, close to tears, really, he said:
"My son, the voyage ends. The ship sails into its harbor and new lives
begin, lives of honor and dignity, and proper loves. Believe me, believe me, she to her haven, you to yours. That's the better way."

I was unwilling to accept such a decision, but then I heard a sailor
ask apprehensively: "How do you make such an exchange?" and
Master Rodrigo said: "When we pass the isle of Trinidad we sail west
along the Spanish Main until we meet a Spanish ship. We signal our
peaceful intentions, we meet, and we Spaniards transfer over to the
other ship."

"How can we send such a signal?" I asked, and Fray Baltazar replied: "I don't know, but we must."

When we gathered all hands to explain what our tactics were
going to be, both the Spanish side and the English immediately saw
the danger, as Captain McFee said: "They'll think we're pirates and
run. And if we chase after them, they'll fire upon us, and then by
God, we'll sink them."

"I would trust no Spanish ship," Will rumbled, and many of our
men supported him, but Master Rodrigo said: "There is no other
way," and my uncle said grudgingly: "We'll try, but I and my men will

have our guns trained on them every minute," and Master Rodrigo said: "And I am sure they'll have their guns on us. In the meantime, make us two big white flags, very big, with the word PAX painted in blue letters on each."

For the rest of that day we coasted along the northern line of Trinidad, and five days later we passed the great salt pans at Cumaná where the battles with the Dutch fleets had occurred. Then, this morning, when we had almost given up any chance of encountering a Spanish vessel, we came upon one, and a ridiculous affair developed.

They, seeing us and our rakish form with cannon, decided that we were buccaneers about to board them, and fled, while we, with our two white flags aloft, chased after them. But the harder we tried to overtake them, the faster they scampered away, and it looked as if our plan would end in disruption, when Captain McFee made a clever maneuver which put the *Giralda* directly ahead of the Spanish ship, whereupon it had to slow down. Then he ordered a small boat to be lowered, and into it climbed Master Rodrigo, Fray Baltazar, my uncle and me, and with our own small white flag showing, we rowed over to the startled Spaniard. With my uncle pointing his gun directly at the heart of the Spanish captain and Spaniards pointing their guns at us, Master Rodrigo called in a loud voice: "We have Spanish prisoners for Cartagena!" and Fray Baltazar called out the more significant message: "We have aboard the wife and daughter of Governor Ledesma. I am their priest, Fray Baltazar."

The two messages, especially the latter, had a volcanic effect. Two boats were lowered, white flags were hastily improvised and the captain himself, after concluding that we were telling the truth, leaped down, followed by three other officers, and rowed almost frantically to our ship. When we four climbed aboard with them, we witnessed a most unusual scene. The captain, spotting Señora Ledesma and her daughter, ran forward, bent down on one knee, and kissed the mother's hand, saying in a loud voice: "I greet you, Condesa de Cartagena!" and when Inés' mother showed surprise, the other officers crowded about to tell the good news: "Yes! The king has made your husband Conde de Cartagena!"

It was then that my despair began, for it was obvious that both the Spaniards and the Englishmen were eager to get the prisoners off our ship and onto theirs, and as the first small boats pulled away filled with sailors and common prisoners, the four important Spaniards— Rodrigo, Baltazar and the two Ledesma women, now the wife and daughter of a count—prepared to leave us. Our sailors helped the two men to gather the rude possessions they had acquired during our voyage together, and Mompox and I helped the women, but when I had Señorita Inés' baskets packed and I started toward the rough ladder with them, anguish choked me, and I could not bear to think that I was bidding farewell to this precious young woman who loved me and who I loved with all my heart. It was an anguish I could not bear, and when she ran to kiss me goodbye, I thought: I can never let her go. But then Fray Baltazar put his arm about me and drew me away: "Remember, lad, all ships come home to harbor. Ours heads west, yours east," and he embraced me, adding as he climbed down into the waiting boats: "You've played the man, Ned, and you can be proud."

But the departure was not to be peaceful, for to the surprise of the Spaniards, young Lady Inés flatly refused to leave the *Giralda*. Clasping her arms across her chest, she said in sharp, clear tones: "We love each other. We have been ordained by God to be man and wife and you cannot tear us apart." Well, they landed on her as if they were an army attacking a fort. The captain of the Spanish ship said solemnly: "Senorita Inés, you are the daughter of a *conde*. You represent the honor of Spain. You simply must . . ."

The *condesa* broke in: "You are a silly headstrong child. How can you possibly know . . . ?"

But it was Fray Baltazar who uttered the sensible words: "Sweet child, it is marvelous in spring when flowers bloom for the first time. But the real meaning of the tree comes later, when it is laden with fruit, as God intended. You've had a wonderful introduction to love, none finer, but the great years lie ahead. Kiss this fine young man farewell, and let us head for those other, better years."

I bit my lip when I heard him say those words, and I swore I would not allow my tears to be the last thing she saw of me, but my attempt at courage was not needed, for now Uncle Will stormed forward, shouting: "What about our ransom money?" and other sailors took up the cry, and there might have been a riot spoiling everything, for the Spanish captain shouted in broken English: "No! No! Ransom nobody." But again Fray Baltazar assumed command, and as the men from the Spanish ships listened attentively, he reminded all of us of forgotten days: "When these Englishmen captured us, they could have killed us all, shot us, drowned us. I informed them that these two lovely women were from an important family that would pay a ransom for their safe return."

He stopped and looked at us: "I cannot say what drove these men to save our lives, mine and Master Rodrigo included. I would like to think it was Christian charity. But if it was only the lure of money, I can assure you that they earned it. Here we are, all of us, unscarred. Captain, if you have any funds aboard your ship, you owe it to these men," and when there were murmurs against this decision, he said: "Captain McFee and I will row over to your ship to collect whatever you have." Some of us went along, of course, well armed, and a surprising number of coins was collected. When we brought them back to the *Giralda*, the priest delivered them with only four words: "A debt of honor," and the exchange was concluded, women for silver.

I wanted to ride in the boat with Inés to her ship, but that was not possible, for she rode in one of the Spanish boats, and it would be hoisted aboard as soon as its four passengers were discharged. So I stood by our rail, where my uncle and his gunners kept their aim on the Spanish ship in case treacherous moves developed, and as her boat moved farther and farther away I saw with aching heart that one of the young Spanish officers was tending Inés and wrapping a robe about her feet. Once aboard her deck, so many things happened that she had no chance to wave back at me, and slowly our two ships drew apart. We had sailed together for two hundred and ninety-five days, during which she captured my heart forever.

Then suddenly into one of the Spanish boats that had been left in the water leaped an officer, and the boat came speeding back to ours and voices cried in both Spanish and English: "Señor Ned! Mr. Ned!" and when I rushed to the railing where the boat would touch ours, the young officer who had tended Inés with the robe shouted: "She says this is her present to you," and he handed up Master Rodrigo's precious pearwood-and-ivory backstaff, to which a message had been tied: *"Para Eduardo, mi querido navegante que nos traja a casa."*

SUN 21 JANUARY: On that final day, while I was attending to Señorita Inés, Captain McFee was acquiring important news from the Spanish captain. Spain and England were officially at peace, and the English king, to make happy his Spanish cousins, as he called them, had issued orders that all pirates, English or not, and especially those operating in the Caribbean, should be hanged: "There have been several dancing in the air at Port Royal, so beware." His warning was an act of kindness in our favor because of the decent way we had treated the Spanish prisoners.

So it took no prolonged debate for us to decide that we would not head northwest for Port Royal but due east for Barbados, and when this was announced, Captain McFee told us: "I do not know those waters." What happened next made me think that buccaneers weren't too bad as sailors, after all, for as soon as we decided to head not for Port Royal but back to Barbados, the men cried: "That's where Pennyfeather lives!" and they elected me captain again, and for the past nine days I've been in sole command of the *Giralda,* and because Master Rodrigo was no longer on hand to harry me about his damned calendar, the first thing I did was move dates back, as this entry proves, to the real calendar as intended by God. However, I did use Rodrigo's pearwood backstaff for navigating past St. Vincent and the Grenadines, coming at dawn this morning to Barbados itself, with the red sun rising behind its beautiful hills.

How excellent it was to reach home and find waiting in our harbor a ship from our Massachusetts colony which will carry my trusted friend Mompox—Spaniard-Indian-Negro—to Boston and freedom. As we parted for the last time he reminded me: "You must tell any ship headed that way to look out for David the Miskito," and then he asked quietly: "Ned, may I kiss you farewell?" and out of regard for all that he had done for me, I said yes, to my uncle's disgust.

We were now free to dock our ship and present our Letter of Marque and Reprisal proving that we had authority from the king to protect his interests at sea. The question then arose: "But have you conducted yourself in a worthy way and not as pirates?" and now I handed over the letter from the Spanish captain which certified that "the officers and crew of the captured Spanish galleon *Giralda* did pay gentlemen's respect to the Conde de Cartagena's women during a long sea voyage," and we were thus doubly saved from hanging. This being Sunday, we thought it irreverent to distribute our prize money.

FRI 26 JANUARY 1672: Our voyage has officially ended, but it required all day for the king's officials to determine and claim their legal share of our prize money, and several hours for us to divide the remainder among our men. After the spoils had been separated into fifty-six equal piles, we distributed them in this fashion: Captain McFee received three shares for his careful service, the first man who relieved him two, and me two for having brought us away from Cape

Horn and onward toward Barbados. The thirty-eight sailors one full share each, the fourteen Indians each a half-share for their faithful help, and the sixteen slaves a quarter-share each, adding up to the proper total, less, of course, the fistful of coins we had given Mompox when he boarded his Boston ship. The slaves, to their delight, ended up with enough to buy their freedoms, and we wished them well.

So we returned to Bridgetown, me having lost Inés but, as Uncle Will reminded me, with Spanish gold aplenty to heal my wounds, and on that confusing note, here ends this *Log of a Buccaneer.*

NED PENNYFEATHER

When Will saw the lassitude into which his nephew had fallen over the loss of Inés, he challenged him: "You commanded a ship, surely you can command your own life," but Ned insisted: "Inés, I can't forget her," and Will said: "You better. She's in another part of the world," but Ned continued to mope, keeping to the small room that his uncle had rented in Bridgetown.

To distract his attention, Will suggested a daring excursion—they would visit Sir Isaac. And one morning, having no horses, they walked out to Saltonstall Manor, now even more resplendent with its lane bordered by young trees and hedges of croton. Banging on the door, they attracted several of the slaves working inside and could hear a woman calling. "Tell Pompey men he come," and promptly a black man in golden-yellow livery with big white cuffs opened the door and asked in a polite voice: "Gem'mum, what your pleasure?"

When Will snapped: "We want to see Sir Isaac," the slave said: "Well, now . . ." but Will pushed him aside, strode into the reception area, and bellowed: "Isaac, come out!" and when both Sir Isaac and his lady appeared, Will said, with a bow: "We've come back."

Icily, Clarissa said: "We heard. You've been pirating they tell us," and since neither she nor her husband made any gesture toward welcoming their relatives, Will asked: "Aren't you going to ask us to stay?" and after a grudging invitation was extended, Pompey was sent to fetch some refreshments.

In the interval, the older Tatums, now approaching their prosperous fifties, stared uneasily at the intruders, seeing in Will a battle-scarred veteran of naval brawling and in Ned a youth just entering his twenties whose life was surely already ruined from his years as a buccaneer. They were a sorry pair, and Lady Clarissa could feel no regrets at having been responsible for the branding of her brother-in-law: Let the world see him for what he is.

The visit was extremely unpleasant, and even before the first cup of tea was passed, it was painfully obvious that Sir Isaac was already wondering how he could get rid of these unwelcome relatives. Leaning back and speaking as if from a distance, he asked: "And what do you two propose doing on Barbados this time?" and Will replied, as he reached for his tea: "We'll be looking around. By the way, pass me one of those little cakes?" and Ned thought: He actually wants Uncle Isaac to lose his temper. But the plantation owner refused to rise to the bait. Turning to Ned, he asked, still from a great distance: "Where will you be looking? Several plantations seek overseers, but I suppose you'll be off adventuring again?"

"With mother gone . . ."

"She died shortly after you left the last time. Lady Clarissa and I attended to her funeral."

"Thank you."

"She left a small fund for you. Mr. Clapton the banker has it in his care, and it's growing, he tells me. Honorable man, Clapton."

"I'm glad to hear about the money. I've been thinking I ought to make my home in Bridgetown. I've seen the oceans."

This statement, which implied so much, awakened no interest in the older Tatums, for whom the sea was no more than a highway from Barbados to London. The rest of the world's oceans were superfluous, and Will, sensing that this was the case, said solemnly: "The boy was navigator of a great ship at nineteen, captain at twenty, fighting off the Spaniards."

"We've been warned," Clarissa said, "that those who fight Spaniards these days are to be hanged. New rules for new times."

And so the frigid meeting ended, with no invitation to return, no inquiry as to what assistance the master and his lady might extend, and when Sir Isaac told Pompey in haughty syllables: "Direct the groom to saddle three horses and lead these men back to town," Will said crisply: "No thanks. We'll walk," and down the long avenue of trees they trudged.

But when they reached their quarters Will said: "Ned, we've got to get serious about your future," and he suggested that they dip into their *Giralda* prize money, rent two horses, and ride straight eastward across the island to the wild Atlantic shore where he knew a sailor recluse named Frakes who had an unusual treasure.

It was a journey Ned would never forget, as exciting in its way as trying to negotiate the Magellan, for it carried him through parts of Barbados he had not seen before: lovely hills from whose crests he saw endless fields sweeping eastward; lanes through the heart of great plantations with green sugarcane stalks crowded like trees in a forest; little vales filled with multitudes of flowers; and clusters of brown shacks in which lived the slaves who made the prosperity possible. The ride, under a warm sun that peeped from behind white clouds sweeping from the unseen ocean, was an adventure into the heart of the splendid island, and as each new vista revealed itself he felt increasingly attached to this land. He knew then that he did not wish ever to leave Barbados. The buccaneer had become the settler.

Even at this late hour in their day's journey, Ned still had no intimation of what the attraction of this old seaman Frakes could be. Now they reached the western edge of the central plateau which comprised most of Barbados and found themselves at the edge of a considerable cliff down whose face a narrow path led to the seashore below, and there surged the great Atlantic, a wild ocean whose waves beat upon a desolate shore completely different from that provided by the gentler Caribbean.

Reining in to savor the grand panorama, Ned cried: "It's been hiding all these years," and his uncle replied: "Only the strong ones dared to come over here," and with his long right arm extended, he pointed to the remarkable feature which differentiated this shore from all others, and Ned saw for the first time that haunting collection of gigantic reddish boulders which at certain spots clustered along the edge of the sea, their feet deep in the water, their jagged faces tilted to catch the sun. At some locations they stood four or five together, like huge judges trying to reach a verdict, at others a lone giant defied the ocean, but at a spot that caught Will's eye, a parade of nearly a dozen left the shore and marched out to sea, forming a peril to navigation attested to by the wrecked timbers of a cargo vessel that had strayed too close.

"Where did they come from?" Ned asked, and Will explained: "Either God dropped them accidentally when He was building the earth, or giants used them to play marbles."

Inland, from where the procession started, stood a small, rudely built house whose lone doorway revealed how enormously thick were the stone walls into which it had been set. "Frakes?" Ned asked, and his uncle nodded, whereupon the travelers descended to the plain below. On their arrival at the stone cottage with heavy moss growing across the roof, Ned still had no inkling of why the journey had been made. When Tom Frakes came to the door, Ned saw a tall lanky man with a wild head of hair and a scraggly beard which looked as if he trimmed it with dull scissors, but only occasionally. He wore tattered trousers and shirt, the former held about his nonexistent waist by a rope whose ends were frayed. His face was as timeworn as his clothes, for he had few teeth, a badly broken nose and eyes that watered sadly. He appeared to be in his late sixties, but that might have been deceptive, for he had lived a hard life which was now approaching its battered end.

Recognizing Will as a former shipmate, he left the doorway to clasp him about the shoulders: "Dear Will, come in, come in!" But then he stopped, stared at Ned, and asked: "Who's the lad?" and when Will replied: "My nephew," the old man shouted: "Twice welcome!" and into the cottage they went.

Ned expected the interior to resemble its owner, an unholy mess. Instead, it was a revelation—neat, with furniture, some of it elegant, properly disposed against walls that were decorated with fine paintings expensively framed. The floor was covered by two rugs, probably from Persia or some similar country, and the three chests which stood in corners were finished with heavy brass trimmings.

"This is a treasure trove!" Ned cried admiringly, and Will explained: "Frakes salvages wrecks that pile up on his rocks out there," and the ships that went astray must have been preciously laden, for the old sailor owned some items of great value.

And then from the small inner room came his greatest possession, his daughter Nancy, a lovely girl of sixteen, dark, lithe and unusually beautiful. In that first moment, within seconds, really, it was clear to everyone that Will Tatum had brought his nephew Ned on this long trip in hopes that he would find this child of the storms attractive and perhaps want to marry her. Old Frakes, his time running out, was delighted, and Nancy was breathing deeply, for she had begun to wonder if she was ever going to meet a young man. Ned was spellbound.

The visit lasted three wonderful days, during which Frakes led explorations of storm-beaten wrecks while Ned and Nancy trailed behind, kicking at rocks and speculating as to how those gigantic boulders had found their way to the shore. Later, when the visitors were alone, Will confided: "Government suspects that on stormy nights he keeps a bright light showing on his cottage to confuse captains into thinking it's a lighthouse. Next morning he combs the wreck," and that afternoon Frakes, in what was obviously an encouragement to Ned, showed his guests a storeroom attached to the back of the cottage in which he had amassed a treasure in baled carpets, fine furniture, silver settings and an endless number of practical tools and small machines, all salvaged from ships which had crashed onto the rocks at his doorstep.

"A young couple could do wonders with these things," Frakes said, and when Will asked "What?" the old sailor said: "Depends on the couple."

Next day Will suggested that the young people have a picnic by themselves, and when Nancy led the way to a height from which they could watch the surging Atlantic thunder upon the boulders, Ned asked: "How did your father get here?" and she explained that he had gone buccaneering with Will Tatum, had heard from him about Barbados, and had come here at the end of their cruise to inspect: "When he returned to England he asked Mother and me one foggy November day: 'Who's for Barbados and the sun?' and he didn't have to ask twice."

"Was it your mother who taught you to be a lady?" and she replied, eyes lowered: "Yes, that was always Mother's dream," and Ned, bursting with sentiment, blurted out: "She taught you well."

On their last day Will said abruptly: "Time we got down to business," and as the four sat on grassy mounds among the boulders he broached the subject that had preoccupied everyone: "Frakes, you're an old man. You have a splendid daughter who ought to be getting married. I'm not so young anymore, and I have a nephew here who also ought to be finding himself a mate. What do you young people say?"

For some moments everyone looked out to sea where the Atlantic was delivering great waves, and then Nancy quietly slipped her hand into Ned's, felt the warm pressure of his response, and exclaimed: "What a wonderful day!" Then she further surprised Ned by giving him an ardent kiss.

That night as they sat at supper, she said: "When Father was away at sea, Mum worked as a barmaid and . . ." Ned broke in: "But she always wanted to be a lady?" and Nancy replied, laughing: "Her? She wouldn't have known a lady if she saw one, but she did try to teach me: 'If you want to catch a proper young man, act like a lady, however that would be.' She loved it here, and it was she who insisted on neatness, everything in its place. She was a good one."

Once the marriage was agreed upon, Nancy took charge, and in doing so, displayed that wild joyousness that many would comment upon in the years ahead: "We have a wealth of stuff here, if we can only figure out what to do with it," and sometimes she would suddenly stop her planning, run to her father, and kiss him: "Oh, I do love you so much, Father, and you mustn't leave us, ever." And then she would pout: "But I do so want to live in Bridgetown with its shops and ships," and she asked Uncle Will, as she had been asked to call him: "But what could we do in Bridgetown to earn a living?"

Will and Ned decided to remain an extra day to explore the possibilities, and they sat among the boulders as one idea after another was proposed and rejected, until finally Will said: "Wherever I've gone—Port Royal, Tortuga, Lisbon—I've noticed that men need inns and taverns. Places to talk, to learn what ships are sailing where, to drink with old friends and remember battles. Bridgetown's growing. It could use another inn. A proper one."

When this was agreed upon, with Nancy lilting about as if she were already mistress of the place and teasing the customers, Frakes said: "Capital idea for you youngsters. You can have everything in the cottage, and the storeroom. Make it a handsome inn, a lively one, but I, I'll stay here by the sea."

This decision dampened the discussion, but then Will said: "He's right. Might as well spend it where he's happy," but Nancy argued: "You know, there's a sea at Bridgetown, too," and he replied: "I mean the real sea."

Talk then turned to what name the proposed inn should have, and Will warned: "The right name means everything. Men grow to cherish it," and he suggested copies of the type so popular in England: "Cavalier & Roundhead, or maybe Pig & Thistle." Nancy offered The Carib or perhaps Rest & Riot, but Ned volunteered nothing until the others had exhausted their wits. Then he said quietly: "It'll be The Giralda Inn," and when each of the others protested, he explained: "That's why I'm here today. It's the ship I helped capture, the one I captained, the one that brought us safely home," and Will thought: And the one in which you discovered love with Inés, and it's proper that a man should honor such a ship.

When the time came for Will and Ned to leave, Frakes surprised them by announcing: "Nancy and I'll be comin' with you. Sooner married, sooner bedded," and he suggested that Will and Ned scour the eastern shore to find carters who would carry the treasures of his cottage into Bridgetown for the furnishing of the inn, and the others were astonished when he told the draymen: "Clean out everything," and when the place was bare, Nancy asked: "Now what will you live with?" and he said: "I'll make do." He must have been receiving signals, for two days after he attended the wedding in Bridgetown and saw to the installation of his furniture and paintings in the building Ned had purchased with the money left him by his mother, he died, but not before issuing orders to a woodcarver for a rather large sign which would proclaim The Giralda Inn.

The inn quickly became noted for three features: the red-haired keeper who had served as a buccaneer with Henry Morgan, the beautiful and vivacious black-haired girl who tended bar, and the older fellow, now forty-one, with a deep scar on his left cheek, who occupied a chair at a corner table, telling dubious but interesting stories of his supposed adventures at the sack of Panamá, the wild days at Tortuga and his escape from a Spanish prison. He had a host of tales and became one of the reasons why sailors hurried to the Giralda as soon as their ships anchored. Rarely did they mention a port at which he had not touched: Maracaibo, Havana, Porto Bello, Cádiz, Lisbon, he'd seen them all, and then he'd add, with a touch of true disappointment: "Cartagena, I never reached. We tried, but the Dons were too strong for us. Maybe if I ever go out again . . ."

However, it was Nancy who established the spirit of the place, with her constant smile and bright laughter and the little tricks she had developed to keep the customers happy. When one sailor made bold with her after a long trip at sea, she did not take offense. Shouting to all in the bar, she would cry: "Did you hear what he just said?" and she would repeat word for word the man's improper proposal, but then, when everyone was jeering, she would chuck the sailor under the chin, plant a kiss on his forehead, and say, equally loudly: "But he didn't mean a word of it."

Her lively ways fathered the rumor that The Giralda Inn was a place of assignation, with Nancy being little better than an ordinary prostitute, and when this reached the ears of Sir Isaac and Lady Clarissa, they became outraged—Isaac, because it demeaned the exalted position he occupied in the island; Clarissa, because it was an offense against morals—and once again she visited her obsequious clergyman with a demand that he make his churchmen do something about the scandal. A vigorous drive was launched to close down the Giralda as a menace to the proprieties of Little England. Sermons were preached and discussions held, with Sir Isaac leading the assault under his wife's sharp supervision, and it looked for a while as if Will Tatum and his ugly breed would once again be thrown off the island.

But by this time things had changed, for many of the planters—certainly the smaller ones—were fed up with the domination of outworn Cavaliers like Oldmixon and Tatum, so that when the time came for a showdown, the islanders discovered that they loved honest Will Tatum, scar and all, and disdained his pompous brother, Sir Isaac.

This showdown came in a public meeting which Isaac and Clarissa had goaded their toadies into convening. "We shall kill two birds if we manage it properly," Isaac predicted. "We'll outlaw the Giralda as a public menace, and without that anchor to cling to, Will can be run out of town."

The plot was faulty, for unexpected speakers preempted the platform, launching such a barrage against the petty tyrannies of the older Tatums that unruly listeners began to cheer each accusation. Sir Isaac stood revealed as a would-be dictator, and an insufferable prude as well. When it was clear that his plans, whatever they might have been, had been frustrated, a farmer with a modest number of acres took the floor. "I think we've uncovered this man's plot," he said, and pointed contemptuously toward Sir Isaac. "He wants to run his brother out of Barbados, as he and his wife once did long ago. I'd like to hear what the man involved thinks about this, and so would we all. Tell us, Will."

Gratified that old wrongs were being righted, Will rose, coughed to clear his voice, then said quietly, turning his back on his brother: "When I first fled the island, I went with this scar across my face. You know who gave it to me. I played the pirate. I fought the Don, and when he won I was an inch from being burned alive. I cut logwood in Honduras, and fought with Sir Harry Morgan at Panamá. I rounded the Horn, and no man should be forced to do that. Now I've made it back home, and you ask me what I think of my brother. After such adventures, do you think I would bother my head over that silly ass?"

The crowd roared. Will was carried back on shoulders to the Giralda. And when the lights were dimmed and night regained the town, Sir Isaac and his wife slipped away through the side streets.

Two nights later, Will decided that the victory of honest men over tyrants should be celebrated, so he organized an affair at which he paid for drinks and refreshments for all who came from the waterfront. "A late feast for my nephew and his bride," he called it, and Ned wondered why his uncle was creating such a fuss, singing old songs and telling wild stories, but as midnight approached, Will banged a glass for attention and asked quietly: "How many of you saw that Dutch ship dropping anchor out there this morning?" and when two men indicated they had, he addressed them: "They've spent all day unloading cargo, and in the morning they sail westward to Port Royal."

Nancy looked at her husband as if to ask: "What is this?" and Will said: "When she sails, I'll be aboard. I still have old scores to settle with Spain," and all in the room gathered about to see if he meant what he said. He did, and when some asked why he should leave his good life, he replied with solemn emphasis: "Time comes when a man wants to go back to what he does best," and because Ned and Nancy realized that their uncle's violent life meant they might never see him again, they stayed close as he sat in his corner, regaling younger sailors with his tales of far places. When the night was late Nancy heard him tell a sailor: "I should never have picked up this scar. Carelessness. If you get one, young feller, and you will, get it for trying something big." And in the morning he was gone.

The Dutch ship put into Port Royal, where Will saw once more the wild activity of that Caribbean hellhole: the small boats scurrying among British ships of the line to bring sailors ashore for the grog shops and the girls, pickpockets plying their silent trade, interrupted now and then by cries of "Stop that thief!" but most of all, the movement of people of every color, every tongue, in and out of the hundreds of shops and greasy eating places. Port Royal on a bright January morning was a striking relief from the English aloofness of Barbados, and he looked forward to being back in the business of hauling captured Spanish vessels and crews and silver into its turmoil.

To his surprise, he had difficulty finding a berth on a privateer, for despite his acknowledged bravery when boarding a Spanish ship with pistol and cutlass, there were few privateers scouring the seas these days. As one old French sailor explained: "Henry Morgan, he's Sir Henry now. Lieutenant governor. Seeks to make his English king happy. Arrests all pirates."

"You mean . . ." Tatum could not believe that this old Welsh pirate had allowed himself to be seduced by a big title and a little salary, but the Frenchman corrected him: "Not one title, many," and he ticked off Morgan's new glories: "Acting governor, lieutenant general, vice-admiral, colonel commandant of the Port Royal regiment, judge of the Admiralty Court, justice of the peace and Custos Rotulorum." Seeing Will gaping, he added with a leering wink: "The old rule. Set a thief to catch a thief."

"I've got to see him," Will interrupted. "If I can just talk to him man to man . . ." But when he tried to visit his shipmate at his office inland in Spanish Town, he was bluntly told by the young officer guarding access: "Sir Henry refuses to see old privateers. He has one message for them: 'Go home and leave Spain alone.'"

Tatum would not accept this, and when he persisted in wanting an explanation, the young man said: "Our king has promised the King of Spain: 'No more pirates will be allowed in Port Royal. No more attacks on your Spanish ships.' Sir Henry obeys the king."

Appalled by this shameless twisting in the wind, Tatum went back to Port Royal without seeing Morgan, and after much thrashing about, found a berth on a Dutch pirate ship whose captain did not feel bound by any agreements made in Europe: "In the Caribbean, we decide," and he decided, to Tatum's delight, to prowl the Main once more for Spanish prizes.

Whenever in the years that followed he succeeded in taking a ship from the King of Spain, Tatum was first aboard the stricken vessel, and while Dutch sailors fought among themselves for the booty, he raged with cutlass and pistol, slaying any Spaniards who gave even a hint they might oppose him, until his Dutch captain had to cry: "Tatum! Stop!"

As the Dutch buccaneer prowled the Caribbean, word of Tatum's wild behavior trickled back to Port Royal, and British officers warned Lieutenant Governor Morgan: "You've got to discipline this damned fool. If the Spanish king complains to our king, hell's to pay."

So once when the Dutch ship was spotted returning laden with prize money to Port Royal, Acting Governor Morgan, racked with pain from the gout in his left big toe occasioned by his excessive drinking, hobbled into his office and growled out an ugly set of orders: "Intercept that ship. Fetch me that crazy Will Tatum," and when the old pirate was brought before him, he said simply: "You're a menace to the king. You're living many years too late."

Will was appalled at the appearance of his former captain, immense in girth, red of face, his foot in bandages, his voice a beer-heavy rasp. And then he heard the brutal decision: "Tatum, to prove we're trying to maintain the peace, I've got to deliver you as prisoner to the Spanish governor at Cartagena."

"No!" Will shouted.

"King's orders."

"Spaniards hate me. They'll kill me." When Morgan smiled, Will pleaded: "But I was your right-hand man at Porto Bello . . . Panamá."

This particular plea amused Morgan, for he remembered Tatum well: a hero once when he blew up the Spanish soldiery at Porto Bello, again when he led the storming of the defenses at Panamá, but an arrant knave when he organized the loud protests at the division of spoils on the beach. And the last offense obliterated the two contributions. He owed this old buccaneer nothing.

"Different times, different problems," he said curtly as he limped from the office.

As the English ship bearing the prisoner Tatum approached Cartagena, that fatal port where so many English lives had been lost, Will could not believe the fatal twists of history. Years ago in Cádiz he had been within two days of being burned at the stake, but he had escaped to serve Portugal, England, and Henry Morgan, always against the immortal enemy Spain. Now he was being delivered, wrists bound, back into the Spanish captivity he had escaped thirty years before, and to a punishment equally barbaric.

His trial before the Inquisition opened with his soulful protestations that he had been an ordinary sailor, no better, no worse than others, but the prosecuter brought forward six Spaniards who testified that this man, Will Tatum, infamously known on the Main, had led assaults on their ships, killed their mates, and sent them and others adrift in small boats with no sails and little water. His guilt was unquestioned, and when the senior judge intoned: "You have offended God and Spain," Will supposed that he was about to receive another sentence of death. But since the Inquisition in Cartagena was notoriously loath to order executions, he heard a more lenient sentence: "Life imprisonment as a rower in the galleys," and in the moments after the words were spoken he thought it sardonic that he who had been such a menace to Spanish shipping would now spend the rest of his life rowing it across the seven seas.

But now a sharp-eyed junior priest noticed the faded B on Will's left cheek, a most unusual mark, and recalled that an English prisoner marked like that had not only escaped from the Inquisition in Cádiz but had murdered guards in doing so, and Will was brought back to the black-robed judges to hear his new sentence: "Judgment passed in Spain on the heretical criminal Tatum will be executed here. By hanging."

Back in his cell, Will reflected on his tumultuous life as a buccaneer: nights of wild celebration in Port Royal, cutting logwood in Honduras, sacking Panamá, getting lost in rounding Cape Horn, capturing a Spanish galleon off Cuba, losing the *Pride of Devon* off Cádiz, in jail and out, and four days from now . . . a gibbet in Cartagena. He shrugged his shoulders and went to sleep.

On the third morning he was visited by two distinguished citizens of Cartagena who knew him well, the *condesa* and her spiritual adviser, Fray Baltazar, who spoke first: "Will Tatum, the sentence against you is just and you deserve to die for your crimes in the Old World as well as the New. However, the *condesa* wishes to speak." And she said in those crisp tones that Will remembered so well: "Tatum, despite our long ordeal, you helped bring my daughter Inés home a virgin. I do not forget, and have prevailed upon the *conde* to spare your life."

He was released that day, and as soon as he was free he hurried unrepentant to the seafront to sign on with any ship that might carry him back to Port Royal, but when he appeared near the water he was apprehended by three policemen under the control of Fray Baltazar: "You have been such an implacable enemy of Spain that you must remain here in Cartagena for the rest of your life. We dare not risk having you play pirate against our shipping."

Submitting to this more lenient sentence, Will became a laborer on public roads away from the seafront, and after seven months of tiring work he accepted the dismal prospect of spending the remainder of his life in such toil, when, on a day in late 1692, gloomy Fray

Baltazar hurried his mule to where Will labored, shouting: "Tatum! They need you at the wharf!" and Tatum made a comical sight as he rode behind the priest, clinging to his robes.

The problem was perplexing, for a Dutch trading ship had limped into port, where it had no right to be, with its spars and decks a shambles. Its crew had a tale so preposterous that the captain was forced to repeat it at least six times in his broken Spanish, and still the Cartagena officials could not believe him. When Tatum arrived he was shoved forward: "You speak English and you know Port Royal. What can sensible men make of what he is saying?" And it was Will's careful rendition that was entered into the chronicles of Cartagena:

> On the morning of 7 June 1692, a day never to be forgotten, our ship was riding peacefully at anchor in the roads at Port Royal in Jamaica when of a sudden we saw the land in town begin to heave, break into large fragments and writhe in violent contortion. Great cavities appeared in the earth, sucking entire churches into them, never again to be seen. Lesser openings engulfed large groups of unsuspecting people, and soon tidal waves swept in to cleanse the ruins and sink more than half of the former land area beneath the sea. Two thousand citizens lost their lives within the first trembling minutes, and huge waves punished ships in the harbor, sweeping our decks and smashing everything.
>
> Sailors from the ships, those who had saved themselves from drowning, helped rescue victims left floating in the sea where their homes had been, and one old man told us: "The ancient gods must have grown disgusted with the debauchery of the buccaneers who had made our town a cesspool, and decided to bury it deep within the waves."

In this manner, Port Royal, capital of the buccaneers and the wildest haven in the Seven Seas, vanished from the earth in less than twenty-five minutes.

Will received small thanks for translating the tragic news about Port Royal, for next day he was back laboring on the roads, but on the day after, he received an unexpected reward, for Fray Baltazar reappeared on his little mule: "Tatum, the *conde* appreciated your help the other day. He tells me you've been an upstanding prisoner, obedient and good at your job. He gave permission to grant you a boon. Lay down your shovel and share with me a stew and a bottle of red wine . . . at my sister's."

Every Spanish man, whether priest or scoundrel, trusted old adviser or conniving clerk in a government office, was subservient to the ironclad rule that had always dictated behavior in Cartagena: "Look after your family," and not even Baltazar was exempt from that stern edict. His sister was a presentable widow with forty-four acres of productive land who had for a dozen years been trying to find a new husband. On this day when her brother brought yet another unmarried man for one of her fine stews, she served such a splendid meal that Will was encouraged to return frequently, without Fray Baltazar's urging. Then one day the priest rode his mule to Will's workplace, bringing an unexpected proposition for this Englishman he had grown to trust: "Will, you must have observed that my sister needs someone to help work her land. I will explain to the *conde*. I know he will release you . . . and you could live there . . ."

"Oh, you want me to marry your sister? But I'm not Catholic and . . ."

"Who said marry?" the priest shouted. "For me to marry a Protestant like you to a good Catholic like her would be a mortal sin. I'd roast in hell. But I've had a small hut built . . . on a corner of her land . . . I'm not talking about marriage!"

Before Will could respond to this amazing suggestion, the priest said almost in a whisper: "She's a good woman, Will, a dear woman whom I love. I'm past sixty and I must see to it that she has help on her little farm."

In this manner, Will Tatum, mortal enemy of things Spanish, became caretaker for a Spanish widow with forty-four acres and marvelous skill in the kitchen, and as the years passed, and he took his meals increasingly at her table, he discovered that "When a man understands the Spanish, they aren't all that bad."

VII

THE SUGAR INTEREST

ENGLISH SETTLERS IN JAMAICA KNEW THEM AS MAROONS, black slaves of fierce character whose ancestors had escaped when their Spanish owners were driven from the island by the British in the 1650s. These slaves had fled to remote mountain glens in the center of the island, and there they had survived and prospered for more than eighty years, repelling all English efforts to dislodge them. Year by year their numbers had grown as new slaves, imported into Jamaica at great expense, worked a few years on the sugar plantations, then disappeared into the mountains to form the new stock of Maroons.

In 1731 the situation grew so grave, with daring Maroons actually mounting formal assaults on sugar plantations, that the white planters decided on a drastic counterattack, and launched a major campaign against the mountain robbers. Each plantation was required to contribute arms, money and especially white men or trusted blacks to a militia formed to chastise the renegades. As expected, the distinguished Trevelyan Plantation north of the capital, Spanish Town, contributed many arms, much ammunition and a captain for the force, Sir Hugh Pembroke. He was forty-six that year, military in bearing, his slim form showing to good advantage in the uniform of an English regiment. A descendant of that bold young Officer Pembroke who had suggested to Admiral Penn in 1655 "Since the Spanish have thrown us out of Hispaniola, why don't we throw them out of Jamaica?"—thus adding this fine island to the empire—Sir Hugh loved politics and was an important member of Parliament in London.

The large contingent of more than a hundred from Spanish Town and its attendant plantations marched north to Trevelyan, where the troop was joined by an extraordinary planter, Pentheny Croome, two hundred and forty pounds, a shape like a newly patted butterball, and a flaming red face. Like Sir Hugh, he was a member of the British Parliament, famed in that body as "the only man in either House who has never read a book." Indeed, some members said behind his back: "We doubt he even knows his alphabet, but for sure he knows how to calculate fifteen percent per annum on his investments."

Pentheny's investments, like those of all the senior leaders of this improvised expeditionary force, were in sugar, for he had, through natural cunning, avarice and theft, acquired not only a huge working plantation, twice as large as Sir Hugh's, but also several thousand acres which he was about to bring into cultivation. He was a giant man with giant appetites, and when the troops were ready to start their chase through the hills, he told them: "We're goin' to rout out them Maroons and kill the lot! No quarter!"

Sir Hugh, with superior military experience, corrected him: "No, Pentheny, my good friend, the governor's orders are quite different. We've tried to shoot the Maroons for the past three decades. One excursion after another. The tally? Six of us dead, for sure. Four of them dead, maybe."

"Then why're we goin'?"

"A truce. Men, we're not going to fire at a single Maroon. We're going to offer them a truce. No more war . . . ever . . . if they'll pledge to bring back our slaves who try to run away."

"Can we trust them?" Croome asked, and Sir Hugh retorted: "What other choice do we have?"

Pentheny Croome muscled his way to the front, thrust his face close to Sir Hugh's, and asked: "Was that your recommendation, Pembroke?" And Sir Hugh said loud enough for all the troops to hear: "Back in 1717 when they passed that law, difficult slaves could be mutilated at your and my decision. Even dismembered and burned if the offense was grave enough. I warned you then it wouldn't work. And it hasn't." He stared at each of the other plantation owners:

"Well, now we're going to try something better, at least in our part of Jamaica." And he led his troops into the hills.

After four days of climbing up and down the backbreaking cock-pit country, they had seen no sign of the Maroons they knew to be in the area, despite the fact that they had sent scouts ahead to call out the name of the Maroon leader: "Cuffee! Cuffee! Come out! We want to talk." There was no response, but toward sunset on the fifth day, Maroon fire came from a tangle of banyan roots, and Croome shouted: "Over here!" and into the matted jungle he crashed, firing his gun and killing one of the Maroons.

"That's how we'll handle this," he said as he sat on a log cleaning his gun, the dead black at his feet. But Sir Hugh would have none of it. Tying a big white kerchief to the tip of his rifle, he called to his son Roger to do the same, and together they walked toward the banyan thicket, crying: "Cuffee! Cuffee! It's Sir Hugh here. Come talk with me." And as darkness fell the famous leader of the Maroons, a man of forty whose forefathers had been hauled from the Gulf of Guinea in 1529, came cautiously out to parley with the enemy, as if he were a head of state.

When the expeditionary force returned to civilization, Sir Hugh did not stop off at Trevelyan, but accompanied by Pentheny Croome, rode on to Spanish Town, where he reported to the governor, General Hunter: "Brief skirmish. Croome here reacted with extreme bravery in one tight squeeze. Had to kill a Maroon."

"Excellent man, Croome. And what did you accomplish?"

"Met with Cuffee. Saw his men. Saw their huge cache of stolen guns, bullets. Concluded the agreement you and I spoke of. No more killing on his part. No more fires in the night. On our part, we'll give him additional ammunition against the chance of a Spanish inva-sion."

The governor exploded: "Good God, man! You mean you shied away from the real topic?"

"I did not, with all respect, sir. Cuffee and his lieutenants, all of them, agreed to harbor no more runaway slaves. He'll bring them back. Ten pounds alive, five dead."

"Good work, Pembroke." He saluted, left, then returned with good news for Croome: "That cleared land? Papers have been certi-fied, just as you said they would be. It's yours." With a gesture of real affection, for Pentheny Croome was the kind of man he understood, he gripped the huge fellow by the shoulder and ushered him out.

Next morning Sir Hugh was up well before dawn and rode off with Roger without even saying farewell to Pentheny, for he was homesick for the one secure refuge he knew in this world, superior even to his safe seat in Parliament, the glorious green fields of Trevelyan Plantation. When he saw the outer boundaries enclosing land that was neat and clean, he cried to his son: "Maintain it this way, Roger! A place like this is something to gladden a man's heart."

Since the sun was well up, he was not surprised to see his slaves marching to the slightly rolling fields where the myriad little rectangles had been lined out with severe exactitude, their four sides carefully delineated by hoeing up loose earth, inside which the ratoons of sugarcane would be planted, each with its own irrigation system ensured by the low earthen walls.

He did not expect the slaves to show any pleasure from the fact that he was once more among them, but had he inspected closely, he would have detected signs that they would rather have him here in Jamaica than in London: "When de boss foot touch de soil, things grow."

Then Hugh's heart beat faster, for he was approaching the slight rise at which he always stopped when returning home after any prolonged absence from his plantation, and when he reached the top he reined in his horse, leaned back in the saddle, and gazed once more upon one of the finest sights in Jamaica and perhaps the entire Caribbean.

Atop a hill in the distance rose a handsomely constructed stone cylindrical building, shining in the morning sunlight and displaying as its crown the four big canvas sails which proclaimed it to be a working windmill. Near its foot on a large flat area stood a somewhat similar stone building that boasted no windmill, but it resembled the first in that the interior of each contained a vertical crushing mechanism into which raw sugarcane was fed so that the rich juice could be extracted.

These two handsome buildings, each as well built as a cathedral, were the laboring heart of the plantation, for when the wind blew, as it did at least half the days during the harvesting season, the tall building did the work, obtaining power from its windmill. But when the winds ceased, as they sometimes did at inopportune moments, shouting black boys in the smaller building drove pairs of heavy oxen endlessly around a tight circular path to activate the heavy rollers. As long as either of the two buildings was prepared to operate, the plantation was ready for work.

Near the foot of the windmill came a meandering stream, not big enough to be called a river or even a rivulet, but nevertheless a reliable flowing stream that sometimes sang as it tumbled down the hillside to pass under a handsome stone bridge consisting of two arches. This bridge, a structure of elegant proportions, was the center of the sugar-processing area.

From the two crushers on the hill flowed down the freshly extracted juice by way of an uncovered Roman stone aqueduct which ran right across the bridge, forming one of its parapets and delivering its precious liquid to the vats where the juice was collected, the copper kettles in which it was boiled, the pans in which it turned magically into brown crystals called muscovado, the pots in which the muscovado was treated with white clay imported from Barbados to produce the white crystals that merchants and housewives wanted, all contained within a cluster of trimly built small stone buildings which also housed the enclosure for the mules and the stills where the wastage of the process, the rich, dark molasses, was converted into rum.

Trevelyan Plantation enjoyed an enviable reputation in the sugar-molasses-rum trade because of the intelligent decision of one of the first owners. He told his family back in the 1670s: "Cotton and tobacco are fools' crops in Jamaica. The American colonies outproduce us in both cost and quality. But I'm told there's a canny fellow over on Barbados, Thomas Oldmixon, they say, who's beginning to earn real money by growing sugarcane smuggled in from the Guyanas. I'm sailing over to see how he does it." He did, and found Oldmixon making a huge profit from his canes, but the man was a suspicious lot despite his air of being a friend to all: "Why should I give you my secrets and watch Jamaican sugar outdistancing my own?" and he would tell his visitor nothing and show him less. When he caught Samuel Trevelyan creeping back at dusk to see how the canes grew, he ordered him off his plantation and let loose two dogs to ensure that he stayed off.

The visit would have been fruitless had Trevelyan not encountered a likable chap called Ned Pennyfeather—owner of The Giralda

Inn along the waterfront in Bridgetown—who, after listening to the tale of defeated hopes, said: "Stands to reason, doesn't it? Oldmixon smuggled his canes in from Brazil, I think it was, and they were furious down there when they discovered what he'd done. He doesn't want to share with you the advantage he's gained."

"I've come a far distance for this. What am I to do?"

Pennyfeather considered this for a moment, then gave an answer which would account for Jamaica's future prosperity: "There's a mean-spirited man atop that slight rise to the east. If you were dying of thirst, he wouldn't give you a drink, but for a handful of coins he'd sell you anything. Name's Sir Isaac Tatum."

"Oldmixon said it was against the interest of Barbados."

"Sir Isaac recognizes no interests but his own. You'll get your canes if you have the money." Isaac Tatum did drive a hard bargain, but Trevelyan did get his canes, and in Jamaica they prospered, as he said in his thank-you note to Pennyfeather, "wondrous well."

Of course, when he knew more about sugarcane he discovered that Sir Isaac had cheated him outrageously. He had sold him not honest root cuttings which remained viable for years, but only ratoons, accidental suckers from the roots which looked like the real thing but which produced usable cane for little more than two seasons. However, the ratoons did get Samuel Trevelyan launched, and two years later he was able to buy real roots from an honest planter— and the great Jamaican plantation was on its way to the huge fortune he and his family eventually accumulated.

An accidental discovery accounted for much of the Trevelyan wealth. One of the plantation's slaves, a careless fellow, threw into the still in which molasses was being converted into rum a mess of old molasses whose sugar content had been caramelized in the sun. When he saw how much darker than usual the resulting rum was, he hid it in a special cask which happened to have been made of charred oak, and when Trevelyan finally discovered this mistake, he found not the light-golden liquid produced on the ordinary plantation, but a heavy dark rum, magnificent in flavor, now called by some "a golden black." Trevelyan became the recognized name for this rum, sought by connoisseurs who relished the best, and the money flowed in from its sale in Europe and New England, because no other plantation had yet mastered the trick of producing its equal.

• • •

On the right side of the bridge clustered the little cabins of the slaves, masonry walls halfway up, then wooden poles at the corners, with woven wattle and mud, well hardened in the sun, in between, and thatched roofs of palm fronds. The floors were hard and dry, a mixture of mud, pebbles and lime, well pounded and swept. Sir Hugh, inspecting them casually as he rode by, found them in reasonable order.

On the hill, not far from the windmill, rose the great house, a three-storied manor with mansard roof and projecting wings, called Golden Hall because of the row of trees whose bright yellow blossoms made the place joyous. Lady Beth Pembroke had loved these trees, and their brilliant blooming reminded both Sir Hugh and his three sons of her onetime presence.

Safe at last on the veranda of Golden Hall, Sir Hugh, home from the wars, could look down upon a scene whose elements were so perfectly disposed—arched bridge, stone buildings, slave quarters, rum still, tilled fields, woods—that it might have been created for the brush of some medieval artist. It was a little kingdom of which any prince of that bygone age would have been proud.

By no means the largest of the Jamaican plantations—Pentheny Croome's was more than twice as big even without the lands recently acquired—it did have seven hundred acres, of which seventy-seven were in mature canes, one hundred and fifty-four in ratoons and another seventy-seven in young plants. It was worked by two hundred and twenty slaves, forty mules and sixty-four oxen, and their joint efforts produced just under three hundred tons of sugar, about half of it clayed, the other half brown muscovado which would be shipped to England for refining. And, pride of the plantation, each year it barreled more than a hundred puncheons of Trevelyan rum, or about ten thousand gallons, at a masterful price when delivered abroad.

Sir Hugh, a good man with a pencil, figured his costs carefully: "Each slave, two hundred and five American dollars; each mule a hundred and eighty; total cost of replacing the stone buildings and the windmills, two hundred thousand American; out-of-pocket expenses each year, about thirty thousand dollars; average income per year, fifty-five thousand; average profit per year, twenty-five thousand American." He also kept his accounts in pounds sterling and Spanish currencies, but however he calculated his profits, they were immense in the money values of that time and enabled him and his family to live in what was called "the grand style of a Jamaican planter." This meant that Golden Hall had some dozen house servants, six yard boys, grooms for the horses, a plantation doctor, a clergyman for the little church beyond the bridge, and numerous other helpers.

As Sir Hugh studied the excellence of his plantation he reflected on what a superior island his Jamaica was. The last rough census had shown some 2,200 whites of the master-mistress category, about 4,000 whites of lower category, and 79,000 slaves. As he had told a recent visitor from England: "We never forget that we whites, counting every one, are outnumbered six to seventy-nine. It makes us careful how we act, very careful how we manage our slaves, who could rise up and slay us all if so minded." But he also confessed that he himself earned substantial profits from the slave trade: "Last year in Jamaica we were able to import some seven thousand slaves from Africa, and we could have sold twice that many: we immediately forwarded more than five thousand of the newcomers on to Cuba and South Carolina, and on their sale we made a tremendous profit."

He told every stranger who asked, either in Jamaica or England, that his island was a haven of refuge for all kinds of people: "We accept Spaniards who flee harsh governments in South America, slaves who escape cruel masters in Georgia, artisans from New England who want to start a new life, and last year the governor issued a proclamation that henceforth he would admit even Catholics and Jews if they promised not to create public scandals."

But the life of the Pembrokes was not limited to Golden Hall by any means, because each of the three boys had been educated in England at Rugby School in Warwickshire and had spent much of his youth at either the Pembroke townhouse on Cavendish Square near London's Hyde Park, or in the small and lovely Cotswold cottage in Upper Swathling, Gloucestershire, some fifty miles west of London, where Lady Pembroke—known to all as Lady Beth—had supervised the creation of one of the finer small flower gardens in the south of England.

The Pembrokes were like most of the West Indies sugar planters, legally domiciled on the island where their plantation lay but emotionally always tied to England. Their sons were educated in England; they maintained family homes in England; and they served in Parliament so as to protect what was recognized throughout the empire as "the Sugar Interest." In these years, some two dozen planters like Sir Hugh held seats in the House of Commons, where they formed an ironclad bloc monitoring all legislation to ensure that sugar received the protection they felt it deserved.

But how did an almost illiterate planter like Pentheny Croome in remote Jamaica gain a seat in Parliament? Simple. He, like the others, bought it. There were in those years in England a handful of what were called "rotten boroughs," the remnants of towns which had been of some importance when seats in Parliament were originally distributed but which had declined or in some cases actually disappeared. Still, each of those shadowy areas retained the right to send a man to Parliament and it became the custom for a landowner who held title to a rotten borough to sell his seat to the highest bidder. Pentheny had paid £1,100 for his borough; Sir Hugh, £1,500 each for his two, one for himself and one for his oldest son, Roger. The other West Indians had made their own deals, and all agreed with Pentheny: "Some of the best money I've ever spent. Helps protect us against the rascals," a rascal being anyone who wanted a fair price on sugar.

And that was the significant difference between Great Britain's West Indian colonies and her North American ones. Maturing colonies like Massachusetts, Pennsylvania and Virginia controlled not a single seat in Parliament; they were unprotected against the taxes and rules so arbitrarily imposed; they kept their politicians at home, where they mastered those intricacies of rural American politics that would carry them to freedom. The West Indies islands, infinitely more favored in those decades, would never master the local lessons, for their best men were always absent in London.

Of equal importance, when bright young lads from Jamaica and Barbados were away at school in England, their contemporaries from Boston and New York were attending Harvard and King's College in their hometowns and forming the intercolonial friendships that would be so important when their colonies decided to strike for freedom. In retrospect, it would become clear that the West Indies paid a frightful penalty for the ephemeral advantages they enjoyed in the period from 1710 through the 1770s.

But now, in 1731, Sir Hugh was quite content to be in residence at Golden Hall prior to returning to London for the coming session of Parliament, when matters of grave concern to the sugar planters would be discussed. It was pleasant to have his three sons at home. Roger at twenty-six would one day inherit the baronetcy and become

Sir Roger; for the present he owned the second rotten borough that the Pembrokes controlled and was making his way slowly and quietly in Parliament, in accordance with the instructions handed down by his father: "For the first two sessions, say nothing, attract no attention, but be there to vote whenever a sugar item comes up." Roger gave strong promise of becoming, with maturity, a leader of the sugar delegation.

But in many ways it was the second son who made the exalted position of the Pembrokes secure, because Greville stayed in Jamaica and ran the plantation. At twenty-four he had proved himself a genius in scheduling work for the slaves in such a way as to keep them reasonably happy and more than reasonably productive. He was also good at figures and had a sharp judgment as to whether it was more profitable to ship his surplus molasses to England or to Boston. As the Jamaica planters said: "Massachusetts citizens must drink more rum per person than people anywhere else in the world. They have seven distilleries up there and their appetite for our molasses is insatiable." He had engineered a profitable deal with Pentheny Croome's brother Marcus, who operated two small ships carrying cargo out of Jamaica, and it seemed that whatever Greville turned his hand to earned money for the Pembrokes.

To have a son occupy the position of plantation manager was a boon that most families missed. Because many of the owners preferred to spend most of their time in England, they had to leave the running of their plantations to untested young Scotsmen or Irishmen who came to Jamaica for that purpose. Or, if lucky, they found a trusted local lawyer who would serve as manager; if unlucky, they fell into the clutches of some dishonest man who stole half their profits while they were not looking. Of the two dozen West Indian planters who formed the Sugar Interest in Parliament in the year 1731, only two had been fortunate enough to find honest members of their own families to run their plantations, whereas an appalling thirteen had gone to England as young men and had never once returned to their home island to supervise the on-site production of sugar. They were concerned only when they had to defend the islands against competing interests in England, in France, and especially in North America.

Sir Hugh's third son was something of a problem. A young man of twenty-two, John Pembroke was as fine a fellow as Jamaica produced and had he been firstborn, he would have been a worthy inheritor of his father's title and his seat in Parliament. Had he been the second son, he might well have filled Greville's place as manager of the plantation, but there was no opening in that direction, and John himself told his father one night: "I doubt I could ever do the job that Greville does." So the question kept arising: "What are we going to do about John?" and no one had an answer. He had done well at Rugby, and traditionally third sons either went into the army or clergy, but John showed no disposition for either. John assured his father nevertheless: "I'm all right. I'll find something."

In the meantime, he was engaged in a battle which his two brothers had waged successfully. Pentheny Croome's daughter Hester was a big, brassy young woman with prospects of inheriting an income of not less than twenty thousand pounds a year, a prodigious sum in the England of those days and certainly enough to ensure her a choice of husbands. But early in life she had set her cap for a Pembroke and had jammed it down so securely on her red head that only one of the famous island hurricanes would have been able to dislodge it. At sixteen she had made strong overtures to the future Sir Roger, but he had eluded her by marrying a planter's daughter from Barbados. At eighteen, bereft at her loss of Roger, she had settled on Greville, and would have brought him to the altar had not a lively lass from a plantation near Spanish Town ensnared him.

She was now, at age twenty, much attracted to John Pembroke, whom she described to her father as "probably the best of the Golden Hall lot." Brazen in her attempts to allure him, she rode her gray mare to his home to invite him to dances, and insisted that he attend the play the local young people were putting on for the officers of the British warship stationed at Kingston: "It's a French farce, John. Very naughty. And I'm the leading lady, you might say, in the role of the maid."

Reluctantly, he agreed, and found that he enjoyed himself immensely. The young officers were such fun to talk with that he wondered briefly whether he might not try to join the navy; and during the play his attention was fixed on Hester, who was more than satisfactory as the rowdy maid. She displayed a robust sense of humor, a capacity for laughing at herself, and a surprising tenderness in the love scenes.

In that two-and-a-half-hour period she promoted herself from rather objectionable to almost acceptable, and when he drove her home, the plaudits of her audience still ringing in his ears, he came close to expressing his interest, for he had seen that several of the navy men had been attracted to her lively ways. But the next day he participated in a strategy meeting attended by Hester's fat father, a crude and overbearing man, and John, seeing the daughter in the father, shied away.

The meeting was attended by Sir Hugh Pembroke and his two sons, Roger and John, Pentheny Croome and a big planter from Spanish Town who was almost as gross as Hester's father. The topic for debate was crucial to the welfare of the Sugar Interest, as Sir Hugh explained: "Already they're calling it the Molasses Act, as if it were already passed. It's bound to determine our profits for the next twenty years, so firm action is obligatory. If we let them have their way, our income plummets. If we force them to write it our way, unlimited profits."

He explained that the West Indies planters faced three determined enemies: "Those pitiful rascals in Boston and New York who will want to buy our molasses at bottom price so they can earn fortunes with the sorry rum they make." Here the meeting diverted for a frosty assault on the British colonies on the North American mainland, with special opprobrium for Boston and Philadelphia, two trading centers whose rapacious Puritans and Quakers sought to steal their trading partners blind. All present agreed that in the long run, the natural enemy of the West Indian planters was that collection of ill-mannered American colonies, but the Jamaican members of Parliament knew tricks with which to frustrate them.

"Our second enemy is closer at hand," Sir Hugh warned. "I mean the French Islands of Guadeloupe and Martinique. The problem's this. Our sugar plantations of Jamaica are blessed with reliable winds. The French islands have none. And since they're denied windmills, they must use horses and mules. And where do they get them? From Massachusetts and New York. Hundreds of little ships a year load up with animals in Boston and run down to Martinique and sell at a fantastic profit."

"How does that hurt us?" the planter from Spanish Town asked, and Croome growled: "Because when they unload at Martinique, they fill their ship with French molasses and run it as contraband back to Boston. Totally illegal both ways, but very profitable."

"Croome should know," Sir Hugh said caustically, "because there's rumor that his brother Marcus is engaged in the trade," and the big man replied harshly: "He better not be."

"And if we discipline Boston and Martinique," Sir Hugh continued, "we then face our permanent enemy, the housewife in England who screams constantly for a lower price on sugar." He made a distasteful grimace as he visualized the unfair pressures brought by these women who were so eager to buy sugar at a slightly reduced price that they would imperil the wealth of the Sugar Interest.

His son Roger introduced the ugly fact they had to face: "Word circulates. In France the best grade of clayed white sugar is eight pence a pound. In England the housewife has to pay ten a pound. The outcry is becoming stentorian."

"What's that mean?" Pentheny asked, and Roger explained: "Very loud. Named after the loud-voiced herald in the *Iliad*."

"And what's that?"

"The poem by Homer. Greece at war with Troy."

"I've heard of them. But Greece and Troy have nothing to do with the price of sugar in England." It was his opinion that the controlled monopoly price should be raised, not lowered, and as for the complaints of English homemakers who knew nothing of the problems of a plantation—"the niggers and the Maroons up the hills and French competition"—the women could go to hell.

Sir Hugh advised his friend not to make that speech in public, at least not in England, and the conspirators planned to meet six weeks hence in London with a rigid plan, to which all planters would be bound, to attain three ends as Sir Hugh summarized them: "Make Boston buy her molasses from us at our price. Halt the shipment of mules and horses into Martinique. And raise the sale price of West Indian sugar in England while rigorously keeping out foreign supplies which would sell at half our price if allowed entry." The men felt hopeful that if they could get the island members of Parliament to stick together, they could attain those desirable ends.

As the meeting broke up, Pentheny asked where John Pembroke, who had left the room, went, and his brother, who could guess what was coming, said: "I don't really know," but Sir Hugh, wanting always to have Pentheny on his side, said: "I think he's in the library," and when Pentheny found John, he said: "Hester wondered if you'd be free for dinner tonight," and John was about to say "No," when his father broke in: "He'd be delighted."

An observer who was acquainted with the powerful sugar planters of the Caribbean only in their rather rude country homes on Jamaica or

Antigua or St. Kitts might catch an occasional hint as to how the planters spent their huge fortunes, but to appreciate how they used their wealth to achieve their political and social power, the onlooker would have had to visit England, and see how members of the Sugar Interest lived. Each maintained year-round a luxurious mansion in one of the popular London squares, plus a beautifully appointed country place in some rural village not too far from the capital. If a planter controlled three seats in Parliament, as several did, that family would probably have six English homes, three in London, three outside. As one witty observer remarked: "In Jamaica these men are insufferable boors; in London, polished gentlemen who invite the Prince of Wales to tea."

In London, Sir Hugh and his son Roger had houses on opposite sides of Cavendish Square, the father's being somewhat larger but not more ostentatious than the son's. It was four stories high, with a handsome entryway and sets of three carefully matched windows on each floor. Protected by a modest iron railing low enough to be stepped over by a gentleman, it showed no outward display of wealth except for the heavily carved door. Inside, the rooms were spacious and handsomely furnished with an abundance of paintings in heavy gilt frames. If one looked at them casually, one had the impression that the owner displayed good taste and a nice sense of which painting went well on what wall, but upon closer inspection, one was startled by the artists represented, each name being displayed on a small, neatly engraved brass plate.

The landscape that one saw first was a Rembrandt, selected by Sir Hugh himself in Dresden. The mother and child in beautiful red and gold and green was a Raphael, the personal purchase of Lady Beth just before she died. The man on horseback was a Van Dyck and the scene with wood nymphs a Rubens. But the canvas that Sir Hugh loved above all others was a landscape, not overly large, by the Dutch painter Meindert Hobbema. It showed a country scene in Holland, with a bridge much like the one at Trevelyan, and whenever Sir Hugh chanced to come upon it by accident, as it were, he felt the presence of his plantation in Jamaica.

There were nine other paintings, including a Bellini Madonna and an attractive portrait of Lady Beth Pembroke by a fashionable court painter. In a back room there was a matched set of six English paintings, but they were of such scandalous character that Sir Hugh displayed them only to close friends who were known to have a ribald sense of humor.

The upper floors were decorated in a restrained style reflecting the taste of Lady Beth Pembroke, née Trevelyan. One knowledgeable visitor, seeking to flatter Sir Hugh, said: "I can see that whereas your wife had good judgment in art, it must have been you who encouraged her to make the purchases."

"Not so," snapped Sir Hugh. "It was her money. Her good taste." And if pressed, he would confess that on his own he had bought only the two landscapes, the Rembrandt and the Hobbema.

Many strategy meetings, formal and informal, of the Sugar Interest had been held in this house, but leaders like the elder Pitt and Robert Walpole also came here to beg the West Indies contingent to support bills that were to the benefit of the nation at large. They usually got the votes they sought, provided they promised to allow passage of other bills of interest to the sugar men.

But Pembroke House in Cavendish Square was not the London headquarters of the Sugar Interest. That function was filled by Pentheny Croome's grand mansion in Grosvenor Square. It was really two fine Palladian houses erected originally side by side, but Mrs Croome, brash daughter of a Jamaican sugar man, had knocked out the dividing walls, so that the interior became a vast exhibition hall for the curios she had acquired on her three rambles with her daughter Hester through Germany, France and Italy. The two women were bedazzled by German carvings in translucent limestone, paintings whipped up by Italian artists depicting Lake Como or the French ship which had brought them to Italy. And although they were stout Church of England members, they had been captivated by a painting of one of the popes, whose stern portrait, the dealer vowed, was among the world's most remarkable works of art.

The big double room was really a museum of travelers' art, with seven statues on plinths, depicting near-nude women with marble silks draped miraculously about them to satisfy any prudes who might enter the room. Here the members of the Sugar Interest convened most often, for the Croomes were generous hosts. Their income from their huge plantation and other interests totaled nearly £70,000 a year, and after Pentheny allowed funds for the management of his plantations, for allowances to his illegitimate mulatto children in the islands, for the expensive tastes of his wife and daughter, he still had more than enough left over to entertain handsomely during the London season.

His parties were lavish, with six or seven kinds of meat, three kinds of fowl and desserts of intricate imagination. Much drink was supplied, but out of deference to his colleagues, he always served a light rum made on his plantation and the heavy, dark rum of his neighboring plantation, Trevelyan.

In 1732, Pentheny Croome spent upward of £20,000 to ensure the passage of the proper Molasses Act, but he was clever enough to allow his friend Sir Hugh to deal with the real leaders of Parliament, for as he told his wife after one of his own grandiose parties which the leadership had ignored: "Sometimes mere money ain't enough. But you and I can get votes that Sir Hugh could never muster. We're a strong pair."

He had touched upon a salient factor in the way the Sugar Interest controlled so many critical votes in Parliament. Pembroke and Croome had once been humorously described in the volatile English press as "the Two Peas in a Pod," and the name was picked up by the furious pamphleteers who conducted the wars that raged regarding the sugar question. But the two men were not at all that, though they were two clever manipulators. Sir Hugh used his inherent taste, with his Raphael Madonna and his Rembrandt, to lure one kind of voter, while Pentheny Croome wooed the others, his burlesque display of wealth proving that hard currency backed his claims.

When the vote came on the Molasses Act of 1733, the "Two Peas in a Pod" won a smashing victory. The pusillanimous American colonies, with no voice in Parliament, got nothing but a slap in the face. The rum distillers in Boston would be forced to buy their molasses from Jamaica and her sister islands at ridiculously high prices; the lucrative trade in horses and mules to Martinique was halted, and no more cheap French molasses would be carried on the return trips. In fact, the American colonies were treated with such blatant inconsideration that hitherto loyal citizens in Massachusetts, Pennsylvania and Virginia began to mutter: "Each decision made in London favors the West Indies and damages us." And of greatest importance to the Sugar Interest, every household in Great Britain would pay a yearly tribute to planters like Pembroke and Croome, who would grow constantly richer.

After the vote was tallied, Sir Hugh left the Houses of Parliament with Roger, rode home to their square, and bade him goodnight:

"There's not another father and son who have done as much for England this day as you and I." He then repaired to that little private room which not many were allowed to enter, and chuckled as he surveyed the walls. The paintings had been done by the English artist William Hogarth, whose popularity was rising after his sardonic series *A Harlot's Progress* had been engraved and widely sold.

Sir Hugh was amused as he affectionately studied the paintings: Good God! To think I paid him to do them! Even suggested the subjects . . . that is, the Jamaica part.

The set of paintings, which was already receiving attention from the engraver, was entitled: *The Sugar Planter, at Home and Abroad.* The central figure, a planter whom everyone in Parliament would have to recognize as Pentheny Croome, was shown in Jamaica in the first three scenes: a brute whipping a slave, a miser hoarding his gains, a father surrounded by his black concubines and their four mulattoes. In the three London scenes Croome was dressed in lavish city finery: entertaining in a huge mansion, manipulating a vote in Parliament, nodding approvingly as lines of impoverished housewives paid exorbitant prices for his sugar. It was Hogarth at his most savage, and Sir Hugh trembled to think of how his friend Pentheny might react.

No need to worry. When the engravings appeared in the shops in late 1733, Pentheny Croome proudly buttonholed his fellow members of Parliament: "I say, old chap! D'ja happen to see them engravings by this fellow Hogarth? That's me in the pictures." He became the rage of London, with everyone wanting to meet him: "Tell us, Croome? You really have four pickaninny bastards in the islands?" And many, awakened by the engravings to the fact that Pentheny Croome was very rich, clustered about in hopes of catching a share of that wealth. At the height of his notoriety he gave a thousand pounds to a school for poor boys and a subscription of five hundred to a hospital in a poor section of London. He appeared in full and majestic dress at a concert by two Italian singers, man and woman, and helped open three country fairs.

He also purchased six sets of Hogarth's engravings for his friends in the islands, but when he returned to Jamaica he found that his brother Marcus with his two small ships was engaged in a most nefarious business. Loading the *Carthaginian* at Kingston with the maximum number of choice empty Jamaican barrels intended for the shipping of island molasses to Boston, Marcus had forged his papers to show that the barrels had been filled with Jamaican molasses.

Then, weighing anchor, he had sneaked over to Martinique and filled his casks with a cheap French product. Running it quickly to Boston, he had papers to prove to customs that he was bringing in choice Jamaica stuff, and his profits were enormous.

When Pentheny heard of this deception, he laid a trap for Marcus, and satisfied on all points, rode over to Golden Hall to show Pembroke proof of this criminal behavior. Sir Hugh made only one response: "He's stealing from us. It's money out of your pocket and mine, Croome, and he's got to be stopped."

Pentheny, outraged by his brother's behavior, swore to put an end to it. Along the waterfront where the sunken Port Royal had once flourished with its hordes of pirates, he chartered a small, swift vessel crewed by an unruly lot of characters who assured him they were ready for anything, and after he was certain that his brother in the *Carthaginian* had set sail for Boston, he swept in, overtook her and joined his sailors as they forcibly boarded the smuggler.

The confrontation was terse. "What's this?" Marcus cried, and Pentheny roared: "You're defrauding honest men!"

"I'm not," his brother shouted—and there would be much debate as to what happened next, but those who stood close to the two men agreed that having said this in an ugly mood, Marcus Croome reached for a pistol. Pentheny, who had come aboard anticipating such an act, had his pistol out seconds before Marcus, and he fired point-blank at his brother, blowing a hole in his chest.

When word reached London that Pentheny Croome had frustrated an act of piracy in this dramatic fashion, with the dead pirate being his own brother, his fame increased, and several patrons of Hogarth suggested that the artist add a seventh panel to his famous series on the sugar planters, and when he protested—"A set's a set"— a hack artist, copying the frame of Hogarth's series, rushed to the streets with Panel Seven, "The Pirate Trapped by His Own Brother," which sold famously.

It required no less than considerable turbulence in Europe for John Pembroke to escape the entangling toils of Hester Croome. In these years, that continent seemed to be in constant turmoil, and, fortunately for John, an appropriate event presented itself when needed.

This was the sequence. The King of Poland died. Tradition required that the Polish nobles, a headstrong lot, elect some European prince, not a Pole, to rule the country. France and Spain backed one contestant, Russia and Austria another, and before long most of Europe was embroiled in the famous War of the Polish Succession.

Lorenz Poggenberg, a minor nobleman of the Danish court, left Copenhagen on a secret mission to London, hoping to enroll Great Britain in some naval schemes that Denmark fancied in this time of trouble, and in London he was advised to present his appeal to Sir Hugh Pembroke, leader of a major faction in Parliament.

The Danish tactic accomplished nothing, but during the protracted discussions, Poggenberg learned that Sir Hugh controlled large sugar estates in Jamaica, and this awakened such considerable interest that joint British-Danish naval adventures in the Caribbean were forgotten: "Did you say sugar, Sir Hugh?"

"I did, and a tricky business it is."

"I know. Slaves, muscovado, rum, finding the right markets."

Sir Hugh's interest was piqued: "Now how would you know about such things, Baron?"

"My family has a large plantation on St. John. We simply cannot find a manager to run it properly. I can't go out, business at court, and I have no sons to handle the messy task."

Later Sir Hugh told his wife: "When Poggenberg said that, I did not reply for at least five minutes, for my mind was whirling like a top. But then everything cleared, like sunlight after a storm. And I thought: John is just the man they're seeking."

He made the proposal cautiously: "Baron, I may have the answer to your problem." When Poggenberg leaned forward, Pembroke said: "My son John. Twenty-four years old. Wonderfully skilled in sugar. Looking for a plantation he can whip into shape." He paused, then added a clause that any European head of family would appreciate: "Third son, you know. Prospects in Jamaica not too bright." And before that day ended in London, it was agreed that John Pembroke of Trevelyan, Jamaica, would sail to St. John in the Danish islands to bring some order to the sugar plantation of the Poggenbergs.

When word of his new assignment reached Jamaica in the summer of 1732, it brought both relief and joy to John Pembroke, for he saw in his removal to St. John a heaven-sent device for avoiding the entrapment of Hester Croome, and he was able to assume a mask of near-sadness when he informed her that reluctant though he might be, he must leave Jamaica to take up the duties his family had arranged for him in the Danish isles.

Hester said promptly: "I'll sail with you. Running a sugar planta-tion requires a mistress of the big house, you know," but John's older brother assured her that St. John was so primitive, et cetera, et cetera, that she tearfully withdrew her offer. But at the sailing of the cargo ship she promised to wait for him, and he called from the deck: "It may be ten years before I get back to Jamaica," at which she uttered a barely repeatable oath.

When he arrived at the Poggenberg plantation on the Danish Vir-gin Islands in late December, John found it much more beautiful than any he had known in Jamaica, for it shared a fine rise at the north end of St. John with two other plantations. From the big house in which he would live he could see far vistas of the Atlantic to the north and the Caribbean to the west, and each body of water was festooned with crowds of little tree-lined islets. Lunaberg Plantation it was called, and when the first full moon rose over the peaceful scene, with the waves drifting silently below, he had to agree that it had been aptly named.

It was much smaller, of course, than Trevelyan—only four hun-dred acres—but the land looked promising, and John was thoroughly pleased when he found that in addition to its beauties, Lunaberg had fine neighbors on its western boundary, a Danish chap, Magnus Lemvig, and his most beautiful wife, Elzabet. "We'll help you get started," Lemvig said in good English, and his wife, her blond hair neatly plaited in two strands bound about her head, volunteered to send her personal slaves to bring some order to the plantation house. She warned: "Since you've brought no wife, you must be attentive to which slaves serve in your house. You can be kind to them, but don't let them dominate you."

The plantation owner to the east was a much different sort, Jor-gen Rostgaard, a disillusioned Dane in his forties with a grumpy wife: "Watch the niggers! They'll steal your socks while you sleep!" He had a dozen suggestions for keeping slaves obedient, all of them brutal: "You have two choices, Pembroke. You can baby your slaves the way Lemvig does or keep them in line the way I do. You'll learn my way's best." Then he said, almost insultingly: "We don't spoil our niggers the way you English do in Jamaica. The important thing, get started right. Let your niggers know who's boss."

John Pembroke took up his position as director of the Lunaberg Plantation on St. John on the first day of January 1733, and spent that month acquainting himself with both the land and the slaves he would be supervising, and the more he saw of each, the more satisfied he was that with the proper mix of kindness and firmness, he could whip both into shape and ensure his employers in Copenhagen a gratifying profit.

The land was first class and its situation atop a rise assured drainage so that the canefields did not sour because of swampiness. And since the slaves seemed as strong and healthy as those he had known on his family estates in Jamaica, he assumed he would be able to weld them into a responsible team. By the end of the month he had shown that he meant for them to work hard, but that when they did they would receive such valued concessions as larger rations of food and extra supplies of cane juice for their midday meals. As February began he judged that he had got things off to a solid start. But on the fourth, a tall sergeant in the Danish armed forces rode into Lunaberg accompanied by a drummer, and when all the whites from the hilltop establishments were assembled, the sergeant nodded to the drummer, who beat a long tattoo, whereupon a scroll was unrolled displaying an official seal, and the eighteen new rules for treatment of slaves were proclaimed:

Given by Governor Phillip Gardelin, may God grant him long life, St. Thomas, the Danish Isles, 31 January 1733, the new rules for the governance of slaves:

1. The leader of runaway slaves shall be pinched three times with a red hot iron and then hanged

2. Each of the other runaway slaves shall receive one hundred and fifty lashes and then lose one leg

5. A slave who runs away for eight days, one hundred and fifty stripes; twelve weeks, lose a leg; six months, hanged

6. Slaves who steal to the value of four dollars, pinched and hanged

8. A slave who lifts his hand to strike a white person shall be pinched and hanged

13. A slave who shall attempt to poison his master shall be pinched three times with a red-hot iron, then broken on a wheel till dead

15. All slave dances, feasts and plays are forbidden unless permission be obtained from the master

When Pembroke listened to the last of these draconian measures and heard the concluding drum roll, he told himself: If the blacks on St. John are as strong-minded as those we have on Jamaica, the consequences of this day will be hideous. And that night he began to hide away in his big house supplies of powder and balls. When the slaves learned of the new rules as they stood at attention on the various plantations, they too began to bring together such guns and ammunition, and long knives from the cane fields, as they had been able to steal over the years. And a careful observer could detect anxiety in the conversations of whites and a growing surliness in the behavior of blacks.

John, eager to keep abreast of developments during his first months on the island, sought advice from both Lemvig on his west and Rostgaard on his east. The former frankly admitted: "Trouble threatens, but I do believe the new laws can be enforced in a Christian way." Elzabet, daughter of a clergyman in rural Denmark and a devout Lutheran, fortified her husband's hopes: "I see no possibility that we, or you, would ever enforce the cruelest provisions of the new code. Breaking one of our men on the wheel? I would almost give my own life to prevent that."

But John heard quite a different story from Rostgaard. "Pembroke," he said in his heavy accent, "we have two niggers on this hill that bear watchin', one on your place, one on mine. Before long each of them will be hanged . . . or worse."

"On my plantation?"

"Yes. Mine's the worst of the pair. Cudjoe, a bad one from the Guinea coast. Very bold. Yours is more sly. That big fellow, Vavak."

John knew the man, a leader among the blacks but restrained in the presence of whites: "Where'd he find such a name?"

"Jungle drums. They're all heathens, you know. His former owner told me a crazy story."

"I'd like to hear it . . . since he's one of my men."

"On the Dutch slaver that brought him here he was chained belowdecks where something clacked incessantly against the ship's side—right at his head: 'Vavak! Vavak!' To keep from going mad, he took the sound into himself. Day and night, *he* repeated Vavak, Vavak, as if he was in charge, not the ship. So when he staggered off the ship muttering 'Vavak, Vavak,' they thought that was his name."

"He must have a real name."

"Who knows? But this we do know, Pembroke. If he keeps talkin' to my niggers, I'll see him hanged . . . or worse."

Twice Rostgaard had used that ominous phrase "or worse," and John was content not to know what particular barbarity was implied, but that Rostgaard intended enforcing it if either his Cudjoe or John's Vavak misbehaved, he had no doubt.

The two slaves identified by Rostgaard as troublemakers were of contrasting backgrounds. Both had been born in Africa, captured by Portuguese slavers, and deposited in barracoons of the big Danish fort, Fredericksborg, located near where the famed Gold Coast (to the east) met the Ivory Coast (to the west). But Cudjoe, Rostgaard's slave, was an Ashanti, from a nearby tribe famed for its warriors who gave infinite trouble when forced into slavery, while Vavak had been captured by black slavers from a far distant tribe, the peaceful and superior Mandingos, and sold to the Portuguese. Each in his own way rotted in slavery and lusted for freedom. Cudjoe collected arms and prepared to lead a violent rebellion against the outnumbered whites—208 Danes, Frenchmen, Englishmen and Spaniards versus 1,087 Ashanti, Fante, Denkyira and one Mandingo—while Vavak moved quietly to inspirit his fellow slaves and prepare them for peaceful and in time irresistible pressure against the owners.

Since their plantations were side by side, the two slaves conspired to meet, but the rules against what the owners called "wandering" were so severe that whenever Rostgaard heard that Cudjoe had strayed even a short distance, he tied him to a tree and gave him twenty lashes. And once in June when he caught Vavak talking among the slaves on his plantation, he took it upon himself to give Pembroke's slave a thorough beating.

When John heard of this he rode over to Rostgaard's big house, a sorry affair kept in permanent disarray, to protest, but the older man was not about to tolerate a lecture from an English intruder: "If you refuse to discipline your slaves, I'll have to do it for you," and he vowed to repeat the lashings if Vavak ever again set foot across the borderline between the two plantations.

John, in some confusion, visited the Lemvigs to try to unravel the problems he was having with Rostgaard, but was given little consolation: "The reason there was a vacancy for you at Lunaberg,

Pembroke, was that Rostgaard had terrified all of the young men Poggenberg sent out to run the plantation. The chaps couldn't suffer that man's overbearing ways and fled."

"What can I do?"

"I'll tell you one thing not to do. Don't intercede on behalf of your slaves. If you do, Rostgaard will turn all the whites on the island against you. After all, he does have the law on his side. The new rules make that clear." And Elzabet reinforced this counsel: "Leave him alone. He's a monster."

The truth of what the Lemvigs had advised was demonstrated in July when Rostgaard captured one of his own slaves who had run away and remained hidden for twelve weeks and one day. Since this rendered the slave guilty under new Rule 5, Rostgaard decided to teach the other slaves in his region a lesson, so a sergeant accompanied by a soldier with a drum went to the two other plantations on the hill, summoning the slaves and their owners to an assembly in front of Rostgaard's house, and there the bearded owner prepared his punishment.

A small platform built of logs freshly cut was flanked on one side by the sergeant, on the other by the drummer, who kept up a lively tattoo. Up an improvised stairway climbed Rostgaard, accompanied by a slave who carried in his arms for all to see a huge knife, a coil of rope and a saw. When the owner was in position, the runaway was dragged from a hut, brought before the platform, and lashed to a pole, where a white assistant produced a huge bullwhip, well knotted, with which he applied a hundred and fifty lashes. With each fall of the whip, the drummer beat a flourish on his drum while Rostgaard, from above, counted. Well before the hundredth stroke, the runaway fainted, but the punishment continued.

Finally, the drum halted, and the inert slave was dragged onto the platform, where cold water was thrown over him so that he would be awake for the next and worst portion of his discipline. When he was revived and tied by ropes in a prostrate position, Rostgaard signaled the sergeant, who produced a copy of the new rules, which he read in entirety. "Listen to that," Rostgaard bellowed from the platform. "That's how things are going to be from now on." And he saluted the soldier, who saluted back, signifying that the Crown of Denmark approved what he was about to do.

From the platform Rostgaard shouted so that all of Lemvig's and Pembroke's slaves could hear: "This one runaway, stayed away twelve weeks, law says he loses a leg." And with that, he grabbed the big knife, felt its keenness, and began sawing away on the slave's right leg above the knee. When that cut was made, with blood gushing forth, the slave was turned face up so that the front cut could be made. Almost without stopping, Rostgaard reached for the saw and began screeching through the bone. When the leg was detached, Rostgaard held it aloft for the other slaves to see: "This is what happens if you ever run away." And then, to Pembroke's horror, the big Dane launched into a sermonlike speech about how wrong it was for a slave to run away and deprive his master, who really cared for him like a father, of his property: "When you run away, you steal from your owner what is rightfully his, your work in helping him to make sugar so that he can clothe and feed you."

The dismembered slave was dragged away and the platform torn down. The sergeant saluted, and the soldier kept beating his drum as they left the field. In the heavy silence Lemvig whispered to Pembroke: "What in the name of God can the slaves think who were made to watch that hideousness?"

The two black leaders, each so different from the other, had asked the same question even before the cutting of the leg had begun. While the lashes were still falling, Cudjoe, the wild Ashanti, and Vavak, the patient Mandingo, moved slowly and almost imperceptibly not into contact with each other but close enough to flash eye signals. With extreme self-control, Vavak nodded his head ever so slightly; and Pembroke, who had turned away, unable to watch the grisly sawing, chanced to see the look of horror on his slave's face and the fleeting nod of acquiescence to a signal from elsewhere. Looking quickly in the direction of Vavak's eyes, he saw a dark visage of someone he assumed to be Rostgaard's troublesome slave Cudjoe.

It was then that the Englishman Pembroke, surrounded by Danish planters, deduced that a slave insurrection of some kind must soon erupt. The scene he had just witnessed was so far from what might have happened at Trevelyan had a runaway been captured that he knew there would have to be some response, and given the hatred he saw on the faces of his own well-treated slaves who had been marched some distance to witness the punishment, he supposed that Rostgaard's brutalized ones must be even more tormented and vengeful.

It was then, in late July, that he launched upon a program of doing everything possible to ameliorate the lot of his Lunaberg slaves. He instituted more sensible work routines, fed them a little better, and took special pains to conciliate Vavak, who betrayed no sign that he knew what the master was doing. Not a single reflex indicated that a kind of bond had been established between the two, and when John tried to talk with the slave, Vavak feigned inability to understand the Englishman when he spoke Danish. Nevertheless, John continued trying to communicate, and from time to time caught a fugitive spark of understanding. In this way the critical months of August and September passed.

But in October 1733, Rostgaard caught another runaway and preparations were made for one more public dismemberment, with the sergeant and drummer passing from one plantation to another, assembling the slaves to watch the gruesome exhibition. But when the runaway was being hauled to the ugly platform from which he would soon leave a beaten cripple, he suddenly broke away from his captors, ran with fierce speed to the edge of the promontory on which the three plantations rested, and pitched himself in screaming defiance down the great height onto the rocks below, where his corpse, crushed and bleeding, was seen by those crowding the edge.

Rostgaard, deprived of both a mature slave and his revenge, grabbed the bullwhip from the man who was to have administered the hundred and fifty lashings and roared through the crowd of slaves, Lemvig's and Pembroke's as well as his own, flailing at them with the knotted lash and screaming: "Away, you beasts! Don't look at him! He's dead, and you'll be too if you don't mind!"

He had struck some dozen of Pembroke's men when he saw Vavak, whom he despised, and although the black man stood perfectly still, simply watching this obscene display, Rostgaard lunged at him with special fury, preparing to lash him about the head. John quickly interceded, saying in his broken Danish: "Not that one, he's mine."

This obvious interruption by a white man of what Rostgaard considered his justified chastisement of a slave, an intrusion seen by all, so infuriated the Dane that he turned his fury on the Englishman, and would have thrashed him with his whip had not John anticipated the assault and grasped the bullwhip near the handle. For a moment the two men were immobilized, each by the other's force, and then slowly Pembroke forced the whip down. Snarling and cursing, Rostgaard moved off to thrash indiscriminately at the other slaves, seeking Cudjoe in particular but not finding him.

During the rest of October and the first two weeks of November, Jorgen Rostgaard circulated among the other Danish plantation owners, warning them that "this damned Englishman won't be trustworthy when the trouble comes." He did not carry this message to the Lemvigs because he suspected that they had been contaminated by Pembroke's views on handling slaves, but he did not need to try to frighten Magnus and Elzabet, because, like Pembroke, they were already horrified by what might happen in the weeks ahead. They saw the looks of hatred in the eyes of their slaves; they heard the mutterings; and they knew that Rostgaard's lead slave, Cudjoe, had disappeared, and if that intractable man was plotting something, they expected Pembroke's man Vavak to join him before long.

But October waned and Vavak still labored in Lunaberg's cane fields. Pembroke went out of his way to speak reassuringly to the obviously troubled man, but Vavak did not respond. Nevertheless, John felt certain that his gestures of conciliation were noticed and appreciated, for when a special law came down from the governor's headquarters on St. Thomas, only a few miles distant across placid water, Vavak volunteered to help Pembroke in its enforcement. The new instructions were simple:

> Every plantation manager, on pain of fine and imprisonment, is to padlock to some tree near the shore any small ship or boat or canoe belonging to his plantation when such vessel is not in use by him. Such action will prevent runaway slaves, when reaching the shore, from stealing a vessel and fleeing over the sea to Spanish Puerto Rico or French St.-Domingue.

Pembroke faced a difficult situation. He had two rowboats and two padlocks, but he did not have enough chains long enough to go around trees, so he instructed Vavak to mind the locks while he rode off to see if Lemvig, who had no boats, might be able to lend him some chain. He found Magnus gone, but Elzabet was there, pretty as ever in her flaxen braids, and they discussed the new law.

"It's prudent," John said. "Boats are an invitation to the runaways."

"Do you think there'll be trouble? The way the others talk?"

"Cudjoe's gone to the woods. One of my men is missing."

"Magnus said . . ." But now the young Dane appeared to speak for himself, and when he heard that Pembroke had left his locks with Vavak, he showed real fright: "John! Two of my slaves have gone to the woods. Your man could run off with the locks." But when the two men galloped their horses down to the seafront, there stood Vavak guarding the boats and holding the precious locks at his side. He watched with interest as the two men prepared the boats for their chains and helped them drag the craft ashore, where Pembroke attached the chains in such a way that slaves might tear the boats from their moorings, but if they did, the shell would be broken and the boat would sink. Vavak understood what was being done and why.

At the end of the second week in November, Jorgen Rostgaard, accompanied by two planters like him, toured the island to satisfy themselves that the boat law had been complied with, and they were almost surprised to find that the Englishman had lashed his securely. "Good job," Rostgaard said in Danish. "Keep an eye on things. That Cudjoe is still somewhere in the woods. And Schilderop here has lost two of his slaves."

One of the other men vowed: "We'll catch them," and Rostgaard said: "When we do, that's it for Cudjoe." And with his forefinger extended, he made a twirling gesture upward, imitating rising smoke and indicating that this time the slave would be burned alive.

On the night of 23 November 1733, John Pembroke was awakened at a quarter past midnight by distraught horsemen shouting: "Slaves in rebellion! Plantations burning! Men and women slain!" And before he could question them, they had galloped eastward to alert Rostgaard and others in that direction, but as they left Lunaberg, one shouted back: "Better look in at Lemvig's. We had no response there."

After John had armed himself with all the firepower he had sequestered plus a long knife, he ran first to inspect the little shacks occupied by his slaves, and found that every one was empty and that all the knives used for slashing cane were missing too.

With increasing anxiety he ran to the Lemvig plantation, but its slave quarters were also vacant, and he was about to assume that the two Lemvigs had taken flight when he heard a moan coming from the house. Dashing in, he found only darkness, then a weak whisper from a corner: "Is that you, John?"

It was Elzabet, and when he made a light he found her crouched behind a table, holding in her bloodied arms the body of her young husband, whose throat had been slashed to the neckbone. "Oh, Elzabet!" he cried, and when he dragged her away from the corpse she whimpered: "Our own slaves did it. They'd have killed me too, but your Vavak saved me."

And down in the lowlands they could see aflame in the night the various plantations in which the white owners lay dead.

The history of the great slave rebellion on St. John in the winter of 1733–1734 was one of constantly increasing terror. On the first dreadful night, slaves killed all the plantation families they could reach. They made an assault on Rostgaard's place but were driven off, and for some reason they neither tried to kill Pembroke nor burn his plantation.

Intensive questioning of those slaves who remained loyal to their masters, and there were more than a few, proved what Rostgaard had surmised. "Cudjoe's in command. Vavak and that other from the east are his lieutenants. It will be hell routing them out of those forests."

He was more than right, because the slaves, with an adroitness and skill their white masters had always predicted they did not have and could not have, mounted an offensive-defensive war of remarkable subtlety. At the end of five days of hit-and-run they had burned some two dozen plantations and ridiculed attempts by their white masters to subdue them or even locate them.

On 29 November, the sixth day of the fighting, an English man-of-war which happened to be in the islands to take on water landed a large contingent of trained soldiers to subdue the rebels, and after marching here and there in fine order, they finally stumbled into a contingent of blacks led by Cudjoe. There was a brief skirmish. The Englishmen were routed after twenty minutes of firing at an enemy they never saw, and they retreated, leaving their wounded to trail along after them.

Rostgaard and his planters were not so easily subdued, though in their rampage they found few of Cudjoe's and Vavak's men. Instead they slaughtered thirty-two noncombatants "to teach the others a lesson."

As word flashed throughout the other islands that a rebellion had occurred on St. John, planters and their families were terrified: "Is this the beginning of the end? Will there be general uprisings on all the islands?" To prevent that, a major expedition was mounted from St. Kitts under an officer named Maddox, who led his men ashore on St. John with drums and fife, but after a gallant chase clear across the island during heavy rainstorms, these volunteers had encountered not a single slave they could see but had ended up with three Englishmen dead and eight wounded. The St. Kitts men had had more than enough, and when they retreated to their ship, no drums sounded and the fife was silent.

In the weeks that followed, Pembroke lost any understanding of how the battle against the slaves was going, because his attention was focused on trying to comfort and protect the Widow Lemvig. With her slaves vanished and no white hands to help her maintain her home, she was left terribly alone, and John could not decide how best to assist her. He visited her daily, took her food which he had prepared himself, for his slaves were gone too, and after much negotiation, arranged for a black woman who had remained faithful to her master on a plantation to the west to stay on the hill with Elzabet, the two of them rattling around in the big house.

The sensible thing would have been for Elzabet to flee by small boat to St. Thomas, where the revolt had not spread, but she refused to quit the only property her husband had left her, their plantation. It would also have been reasonable for her and her black helper to move over to the relative safety of Lunaberg, but her sense of propriety would not permit this. Despite the great crisis, her upbringing as the daughter of a Lutheran clergyman asserted itself, and she asked Pembroke when he suggested the move: "What would the islanders say?"

He replied harshly: "What'll they say when they find you one morning with your throat cut?" but this did not relax her attitude, and he had to content himself with aiding her from a distance.

But now the terror in which St. John was gripped spread to the other islands. The French in Martinique, who owned the important island of St. Croix a few leagues to the south of St. John, decided that the black revolt had run rampant too long, so on 23 April 1734 they dispatched a competent, well-armed contingent of more than two hundred local creoles, four trained officers from France and seventy-four colored and black West Indians. The Frenchmen marched with great vigor here and there, but it was many days before they located Cudjoe's men, who had, in the meantime, continued to burn and ravish the Danish plantations. Finally, on 29 April the French pinned the blacks into a defile from which they could not retreat, and a real battle was enjoined. Since the French had every advantage, plus determined leadership, they prevailed, and after chasing the remnants of the slaves for an additional two weeks, they finally captured the black general Cudjoe of the Rostgaard plantation.

Many of the last-ditch rebels were shot during the battle, but some eleven were set aside for what the local officials called "special attention." The details of their prolonged deaths at public exhibitions were not recorded, but when Jorgen Rostgaard stormed French headquarters to demand the right to take care of his rebellious slave Cudjoe, the invaders, out of respect for the remorseless fury with which Rostgaard had helped them track the rebels, acceded to his request.

Cudjoe's execution took place on the platform which Rostgaard had used before. The same sergeant stood at one side to read the death warrant, the same drummer marked the hundred and fifty lashes, but now there would be a difference, for the warrant had said "Racked and Burned," and Rostgaard was eager to supervise both.

On the platform, enlarged to accommodate the machinery, wheels and levers had been installed, with lengths of thick rope attached, their free ends awaiting their victim. After the lashings, Cudjoe was revived, hauled onto the platform, and stretched out while ropes were attached to his ankles, his wrists and his shoulders and, at a signal from Rostgaard, these ropes were tightened by slow and painful degrees until the joints began to tear apart.

Pembroke, watching the execution with most of the other two hundred surviving whites who were required by rules governing the emergency to be present with such of their slaves as could be assembled in that area, was outraged by the prolonged cruelty of the rack, but that was only a preamble to the horror that was about to occur, for as the ropes were pulled almost to the breaking point, with the black man insensate from the pain, Rostgaard signaled that slaves should set afire the timbers and shavings assembled below the platform. Pembroke looked away, unable to watch as the inert body was carried to the fire, but as he gazed at the placid Atlantic, he heard a gasp, and when he looked back he saw the most sickening sight of all. A triumphant Jorgen Rostgaard had taken up a long knife and was approaching the taut body of his slave. With swift cuts through the distended joints he severed arms and legs, throwing them onto the growing fire. "Now take him down!" he shouted, pouring water as he did so in an attempt to revive the still-living torso, which was thrown into the swirling flames. Cudjoe, the resolute Ashanti, had been taught not to rebel.

When John Pembroke walked with staggering steps back toward the big house he no longer cared to occupy, he realized that Elzabet Lemvig had not been made to attend the execution, so he walked right past his temporary home and kept going till he reached the Lemvig plantation. Eager for the solace of another human being like himself, and not some vengeful monster like Rostgaard who had brought this terror to his community, he shouted: "Elzabet, where are you?" and when she appeared, wan and thin, he rushed to her, took her in his arms, and cried out: "Elzabet, for God's sake, let us quit this hideous place. Start a new life with hope, not despair."

She tried to respond to what was in effect a marriage proposal, but it came so unexpectedly and on such a wretched day that sensible words were beyond her. Instead, she fell limp in his arms, which was itself a signal that she would now rely only on him.

When he revived her, he led her outside the lonely house and perched her beside him on the porch overlooking the cluster of islands to the west. When she was calm enough to ask in a whisper: "What did you say in there?" he repeated: "You and I must leave this blood-soaked place and start a better life elsewhere."

"I think you are right," she said, and for the first time since that day sixteen months ago when they became neighbors, he kissed her.

But because life on the islands always seemed urgent, he proceeded immediately to give her strange news: "Did you ever wonder why those French volunteers from Martinique were so eager to rush their troops over here to help us put down our slave rebellion?" When she said no, he continued: "They've been wanting for years to sell the island of St. Croix to the Danes. Thanks to their gesture of good will, helping us against our slaves . . . well, the sale's gone through."

"What would that mean to us?"

"The Danish government wants me to move down and establish a big sugar plantation on English principles."

Very firmly but quietly she said: "I would not want to live on any plantation where our new rules were in effect. I'll not go with you, John."

Her words caused him not disappointment but joy: "Oh, Elzabet!

I explained in the minute they made the offer that I'd be returning to Jamaica. I'm taking you to Trevelyan. You'll love it there."

This time she kissed him, and as the sun sank lower, he said gravely: "I've one thing more to do on this terrible day."

With her holding on to his arm, he led the way to where his two boats were padlocked to trees, and when she asked what this was about, he said: "I've seen signs that Vavak is somewhere in our forest. They've never caught him, you know."

"He saved my life that night."

"And mine too, I think. No other reason why they didn't kill me."

When they reached the boats, John took from his trouser pocket the large key that worked the locks, and while Elzabet watched he carefully unlocked the boats, setting them free for the use of any slaves still hiding in the woods who might want to try the long sail to Spanish Puerto Rico or French St.-Domingue.

As he and Elzabet started back up the path to the house, they heard a rustling in the trees, and from the shadows emerged Vavak and a woman, and it was a fearful moment, because the slave was armed and the master was not. The path was narrow, so narrow that only one person could occupy it, and as the two men walking in front met, each stepped aside to let the other pass, and the Englishman thought ruefully of another of the new rules: A slave meeting a white person shall step aside and wait until he passes; if not, he may be flogged.

They passed, and no one spoke, but all knew why Pembroke had released his boats.

John and Elzabet remained hidden by trees as they watched Vavak and his woman test the two boats, choose the better, and set forth on the long and dangerous voyage to the land to be known as Haiti, where their descendants would continue their quiet fight for freedom.

When John Pembroke surprised Trevelyan Plantation by bringing home a Danish wife, reactions were varied. Sir Hugh, at ease now that all his sons were safely married, welcomed Elzabet heartily and assigned the couple a suite of three rooms on the second floor of Golden Hall. John's brothers, Roger and Greville, were relieved that he had escaped the entrapments of Hester Croome, but that young woman, when she learned of the marriage, came running to

Trevelyan, rushed up to Elzabet, enclosed her in wide-sweeping arms, and said: "We welcome you to Jamaica!" after which she broke into uncontrolled sobbing.

John would give his wife no explanation for Hester's amazing behavior, but Roger confided: "She's a dear girl, Hester. Worth a triple fortune, and she set her lure for landing one of us Pembroke boys. Although heaven knows she didn't need us." Embarrassed by the unintended frankness of his revelation about a good neighbor, he added: "She's a grand girl and she'll have no trouble finding herself a husband." Then, as if compelled to describe Hester accurately, he said: "When Greville and I married, she adopted our wives. Warmly and honestly. And she'll do the same with you. Not a mean streak in her body."

And that's what happened. At the big dinners given on the various plantations, the three Pembroke boys, as they were called despite their years, sat with their pretty wives while Hester Croome, big and awkward and ebullient, cried: "Aren't they the pride of Jamaica, that trio?" And she was especially kind to Elzabet the Dane: "John brought back a beauty, didn't he?"

The family decided that John and Elzabet should remain at Trevelyan, at least for the first years of their marriage, helping Greville and getting to know the whole of Jamaica and the other British islands. It was a happy time, for it seemed that Jamaica and the Caribbean then stood at the apex of their joint history. Governments were stable. Sugar prices were never higher. And although war seemed always to be raging somewhere, it did not often manifest itself in the islands. John and Elzabet shared in the general euphoria when she became pregnant.

There was, however, one persistent problem across the Caribbean: the proper management of slaves. In later centuries scholars and writers would frequently ask: "Why were the slaves so passive? If they outnumbered the whites six and eight to one, why didn't they rebel?" The truth is they did rebel, constantly, violently, on all the islands, as the chronicle of those years shows: Jamaica, 15 rebellions in all; Barbados, 5; Virgin Islands, 6; Hispaniola, 8; Cuba, 16; every island experienced at least one major rebellion.

In 1737 a shocking affair occurred in a remote corner of Jamaica and it projected the Pembrokes into the middle of the slavery problem. A clergyman of the Church of England sent by foot messenger two reports, one to the capital now at the new town of Kingston, the other to the king in London:

> It is my grievous duty to inform you that Thomas Job, a member of my church in Glebe Quarter, has by solemn count been responsible for the deaths of more than ninety of his slaves. The facts, widely known among his neighbors, were kept secret from me, but when rumors reached me I confirmed each word of what I am about to report.
>
> Job, this inhuman monster, delighted in stretching his slaves upon the ground, tying down wrists and ankles and beating them constantly for upward of an hour till they expired. He disciplined his female servants by forcing their mouths open with sticks and pouring large amounts of boiling water down their throats. All died. I personally know of one slave who was sent to the woods to recapture some runaways. When he failed, a red-hot iron was jammed down his throat and, of course, he died.
>
> It will, I know, be difficult for you to believe, but on numerous occasions Job grew irritated with pickaninnies and stuck their heads under water till they drowned. Others were tossed into kettles of boiling water. Please, please, do something to restrain this monster.

When news of this appeal reached the governor, he called upon Greville Pembroke, known to be a sensible planter, to take the long trip to Glebe Quarter to investigate the charges, and if they were found to be accurate, to institute legal proceedings against Job. "But," the governor warned, "I must remind you that not one bad word has been spoken against Job since I took office. This could be a canard."

Greville nodded, then suggested: "Excellency, my duties at the plantation are heavy, but my younger brother John has had more experience than me in slave affairs. I would recommend that he be dispatched." It was done, and ten minutes after his arrival at Glebe Quarter, John had Thomas Job in the town's improvised jail. Acting upon the governor's written orders, he ordered a jury to be convened, and listened in astonishment as the men, all white, all part of the Sugar Interest, found Job not guilty on the grounds that "it's difficult to control niggers without stern measures, and in our judgment Thomas did not exceed to any degree the customs of this island."

When John heard the verdict he was so infuriated that he wanted to organize a hanging party to dispose of Job on the spot, but the clergyman advised against this, and Job went free. Next morning, assuming himself to have not only been vindicated but also authorized to resume his old ways, Job spotted a slave doing some trivial thing that he, Job, did not approve of and beat him to death in the customary manner.

A young Scotsman working for Job had had enough, and when he reported the death to the reverend, the latter summoned Pembroke to hear the details, and by a curious chance the dead slave's name happened to be one commonly used in the islands, Cudjoe. As soon as the name was uttered, John recalled the hideous time when he had been forced to watch when Rostgaard's Cudjoe was "racked and burned," and he knew what course he must take.

This trial, a new one dealing with an entirely new case, was going to be different, because now John would have a white man to testify to Job's brutal behavior. The trial was a sensation, but when the young Scot rose to testify, a plantation man in the rear of the court shouted: "Shoot that bastard!" and there were many similar displays of support for Job, but the jury, unable to ignore the solid evidence, had to bring in a verdict of guilty.

That afternoon John Pembroke, on his own recognizance, caused a gallows to be erected, and before the sun sank, Thomas Job, master fiend of Jamaica, was hanged.

Late that night Pembroke's small boat slipped out of Glebe Quarter's harbor and made its way homeward with the young Scot as passenger; it could have been fatal to leave him among the sugar planters, who were seething to think that one of their kind had been hanged for merely disciplining his niggers.

But when Pembroke and the Scot reached Kingston to report on the happenings at Glebe Quarter, they found that a swift horseman had beat them to the capital with a monstrously distorted account of what had transpired. Tempers were high among members of the Sugar Interest, and Pentheny Croome was organizing a gang to thrash the Scot, or worse, but John intercepted him: "Pentheny, what in the world are you doing?"

"If we let one planter be disciplined for doin' what we all do, revolution's upon us. The slaves'll cut our throats in the night."

"Pentheny, you said 'Doing what we all do.' Do you want to hear what he really did? Sit still and listen," and in dispassionate tones he recited the hideous behavior at Glebe Quarter. When he had finished recounting the barbarities against the male slaves, the indecent tortures inflicted on the females and the incredible cruelty to the children, he asked quietly: "Longtime friend of my father's, are you Two Peas in a Pod not well respected in London? Do you not occupy important positions in Parliament? Do you want Thomas Job's behavior to cloud your reputations? And drag down the whole Sugar Interest?"

Pentheny was shaken, even more so when John bored in: "A copy of my report has gone to the king. When he asks 'How did you handle this matter?' are you going to say 'We saw nothing wrong in what he did?' Are you going to befoul your own nest?"

Pentheny swallowed hard, and said in a very small voice: "I'd like to hear from that Scot we were goin' to hang," and when the tales of horror were elaborated upon, Pentheny rose, moved toward the young man, and embraced him: "I need a feller like you to mind my plantation while I'm in London," and a week later Hester Croome was back at Trevelyan, bubbling to the wives: "Wonderful young man started working for my father. I'm sort of sorry we sail for London on Friday."

In 1738 young John Pembroke attracted his first favorable attention in London. There had been trouble with a nest of Maroons on the eastern end of Jamaica, and instead of sending an army against them, the governor dispatched Pembroke and a guard of sixteen from the Gibraltar regiment now stationed on the island. "What we hope for," the governor said as the men marched off, "is a repetition of that lasting peace your father made with the Maroons in his district. Same assurances from us, same promises from them."

It was a long trek across difficult terrain, and when Pembroke reached the Maroon area the former slaves did not wish to talk, but an adroit mixture of patience and pressure accomplished wonders and finally a truce was agreed upon. In 1739, John was dispatched to western Jamaica with the same commission, and again he achieved what none had been able to accomplish before, a lasting truce. The island was now pacified, and officials in London sent a dispatch to Kingston: "Advise John Pembroke, well done."

• • •

This led to a surprising assignment, for when a fighting squadron of immense size, some hundred ships in all, anchored in Port Royal Roads under the command of a senior admiral, Edward Vernon, everyone connected with government could see that the British had at last decided to drive the Spanish from the Caribbean.

Already many of the holdings had been lost, Jamaica to the British, the future Haiti to the French, and nowhere in the eastern chain of islands did Spain regain control. At the southern tip of that string, Trinidad was nominally still Spanish, but it was being settled mostly by the French and would soon pass into British hands. However, rich Mexico and richer Peru were still Spanish, as was the Main, but to protect its hold on even these vital areas, Spain simply had to retain the key port of Cartagena, so naturally the English decided to capture it, and thus imperil all the rest of Spain's holdings in the New World. As so often before, again the fate of the European nations would be settled in the Caribbean.

Excitement rose when English officials revealed the target: "Vernon will be off to capture Cartagena! Erase the humiliations we've suffered there," and when the admiral came ashore to complete the last-minute preparations, he boasted: "This time we blast that city off the map."

He was a colorful sea dog, fifty-seven years old, who was invariably seen in a battered green overcoat made of grogram, a rough fabric woven of silk, mohair and wool. From this he took the name "Old Grog," and when in an effort to instill sobriety among his sailors he diluted their traditional rum ration with two quarts of water to one pint of rum, his name entered the dictionary, but in a perverse way, since originally *grog* meant *watered down* and not *rum*.

He had gained a frenzied popularity in 1739 when he boasted that Porto Bello was not invulnerable: "Give me six good ships and I guarantee I'll capture it." The government gave him the ships, and he won such a smashing victory, not losing a ship or any men, that bonfires were lit across England and medals struck in his honor. But sailors who had participated in "the Great Victory" whispered to anyone who would listen: "The Spanish didn't try to defend. A few troops, an empty fort."

Nevertheless, he was the hero of the moment, and immediately he proposed to vanquish Cartagena.

Since he would need officers to assist him when dictating the terms of peace after the enemy surrendered, he asked the governor of Jamaica for any likely candidates, and John Pembroke's recent heroics commended him. In the capacity of an arbiter he sailed south on 26 January 1742, and shortly found himself facing that formidable collection of islands, fortified headlands, fortress-lined narrows and inland harbor rimmed with cannon that comprised Cartagena. The story was that when King Philip II learned that the equivalent of fifty million dollars had been spent on these fortifications, he went out onto the terrace of his Escorial and looked in the direction of Cartagena: "With that much money spent, I should be able to see the fortifications from here."

The siege and battle, one of the most crucial in the Western Hemisphere, was an unfair struggle. Admiral Vernon had collected 170 ships in all, 28,000 men, including large forced levies from ten different American colonies, and innumerable cannon. The Spaniards had only a few small ships—quickly immobilized—and perhaps 3,000 men. But they also had on their side a man known as "two-thirds of an admiral."

Don Blas de Lezo, one of the great fighting men of history, had spent a long life battling the British navy, and always losing more than just the battle. At Gibraltar in 1704 he had lost his left leg to an English cannonball; at Toulouse, his left eye to an English sharpshooter; and in a fight off Spain, his right arm. Now, when yet one more battle against the ancient enemy loomed, he jumped about the forts without the assistance of an aide, inspecting defenses, and he lay awake at night trying to guess what Admiral Vernon with his tremendous superiority might try next. And as he tossed sleepless he sometimes chuckled as if laughing at the extremity in which he found himself: At Gibraltar, years ago when we were both young, Admiral Vernon and I faced each other in battle, and that time he won. But this is another day, another battleground, and this time I have a powerful ally, General Yellow Fever.

Even before the battle started, the fever struck, killing the valiant British general who was to have led the ground forces as they left Vernon's ships. In the dead man's place the admiral received one of the most inept generals in history: Brigadier General Thomas Wentworth, a flunky and a totally inept vacillator propelled into a command he did not want and could not exercise. The consequence was reported by Pembroke:

I was liaison aboard Admiral Vernon's flagship, and each morning it was the same. "Has General Wentworth started to attack the fort?" he would ask me, and I would reply "No," and he would turn to ask the others: "Why not?" and they would reply "Nobody knows."

Time was wasted. Rains began. Fever struck our men with terrible force, and still Wentworth did not move forward. In the end, our great armada, more powerful than the one which attacked England from Spain, had to withdraw, having accomplished nothing. Not even a major battle. Not a single wall thrown down. Nothing.

And why did we fail? Because at every turn that damned one-leg Spanish admiral outguessed us. He proved a genius.

If the combined British navy and army achieved nothing but disaster, John Pembroke did somewhat better, for he attained what the English fighting man always aspired to, "a mention in dispatches," as Admiral Vernon reported to London:

When we sought to lay the small ship *Galicia* close to the Spanish fort to test the range and ability of our guns, we asked for volunteers, for the task was extremely dangerous. John Pembroke, civilian guide, sprang forward, and when the ship got into trouble, in the teeth of enemy batteries and rifle fire, he leaped into the water among the bullets to break her loose. His was an act of heroism of the highest order.

It accomplished nothing, because when General Wentworth still refused to attack, his inescapable enemy General Yellow Fever, aided by Admiral Cholera, struck his huddled troops, and the almost instantaneous loss of life was fearful. Men would fall sick as if with a mere cold, catch at their throats, and strangle. A soldier would be cleaning his rifle; the weapon would fall from his hands; he would look up in horror and fall to the ground atop it. Fifty-percent deaths in a unit was common, with the levies from the American colonies suffering up to seventy.

The sad, disgraceful day came when Admiral Vernon, still unable to budge Wentworth, who now had justification in not attacking, had to pass the order: "All troops back aboard ships. All ships back to Jamaica." England's mighty thrust to drive Spain from the Caribbean had been frustrated by a courageous admiral who was only two-thirds of a man.

On the mournful sail back to Port Royal, John Pembroke moved among officers and men, gathering the firsthand information which he would later include in his well-regarded pamphlet *True Account of Admiral Vernon's Conduct at Cartagena,* whose most often quoted paragraphs were these:

> By honest count we lost 18,000 men dead, and according to a Spanish soldier we captured, they lost at most 200. Admiral One-Leg with his excellent leadership and fire killed 9,000 of our men, General Fever killed a like number. When I last saw the harbor of Cartagena its surface was gray with the rotting bodies of our men, who died so rapidly that we could not bury them. The poor, weak farmers from our North American colonies died four men in five.
>
> But the greater loss was that had we won we would have brought all the Caribbean under English rule. It would have become a unified world, with all the opportunity for growth that unity provides. One rule, one language, one religion. Now that chance is gone and it may never come again.

The reward that John Pembroke received for his heroism at Cartagena was unexpected; it came in the form of a letter from his father in London:

> *We are all proud of your heroic deportment. I wish I could tell my friends: "It's how we Pembrokes have always responded when our nation calls." Alas, we Pembrokes have no such record of gallantry in battle, so I congratulate you on starting the tradition. I trust that you and Elzabet will hurry over, putting aside any obligations at Trevelyan, as I have three surprises for you, and I assure you they are worthy of your attention.*

So the youngest Pembrokes left Trevelyan in the late summer of 1743, taking their two children with them, and as they sailed past the remnants of Port Royal, John could not even begin to know that he would not see Jamaica again until the turbulent 1790s. For when they reached London, Sir Hugh met them at the dock with the first of his three surprises: "John, you've behaved manfully these past few years. The entire Jamaica contingent is proud of you, especially the Sugar Interest. We agreed unanimously on your reward." He paused dramatically to allow the young couple to try to guess what he would say next, but the blank look on their faces assured him that they had not probed his secret.

"I've bought you a seat in Parliament!" Yes, at the age of thirty-four, with no previous experience in politics, John Pembroke would take up a seat purchased by his father from one of the rotten boroughs; after three years of holding the seat he rode far into the country west of London to see where it was, and found three cottages comprising the ruins of what had once been an important trading town. He met the two old men, the only voters left in his entire district, who would henceforth cast the votes that would elect him unanimously, year after year. "I hope I can continue to be a representative worthy of our district," he said, and the men replied: "Aye."

The Pembroke family now controlled three seats in Parliament, and John, as something of a military hero, added considerable force to his persuasiveness in cloakroom debate. His responsibilities were simple, as explained by his father: "Don't allow the French an inch. Remember, they're our perpetual enemy. And keep those fools in the American colonies in line. And lift the price of sugar."

The Pembrokes were by no means the outstanding Jamaican family in Parliament. In fact, they ranked only third in public esteem, for the Dawkins family also had three of its members in Parliament, while the notable Beckford family of a plantation not far from Trevelyan had three outstanding brothers. William Beckford was twice Lord Mayor of London and won his election to Parliament from that city. Richard Beckford sat for Bristol, while Julius represented Salisbury. Thus three rural families in Jamaica controlled nine seats in Parliament, while eight other Jamaican planters each owned one. Counting those purchased by wealthy planters from the smaller islands like Antigua and St. Kitts, the power of the Sugar Interest was formidable, with one critic claiming: "Those damned islanders will have in this session twenty-four of their own seats plus twenty-six held by men indebted to them."

The pejorative word *islanders* was not entirely justified when describing this phenomenon, because throughout England voters saw the rich West Indian contingent merely as local men who had gone to the islands temporarily to make their fortunes. Indeed, of the seventy island members who would hold seats over the span of years, more than half had never visited the Caribbean, nor would they ever. They were the famous absentee landholders whose forebears had made the adventurous trip to Jamaica, arranged for their fortunes, and sailed back home to stay. Now their homes were in England, but they remembered that their wealth still came from Jamaica and voted accordingly.

At the moment John and Elzabet were concerned with what their father's second surprise was going to be, but Sir Hugh remained silent with growing nervousness as they approached his house on Cavendish Square. But the carriage did not stop there, for the driver had been previously directed to deliver the young people to a fine, handsomely proportioned house on the far side of the square, close to Roger's residence. When they stepped down, Sir Hugh said, almost as if embarrassed: "Your new home," and he led them into rooms that had been tastefully decorated.

"Father Hugh!" Elzabet cried. "What a thoughtful gift," and John echoed her approval: "What possibly could you have hiding as our third gift?"

At the word *hiding* Sir Hugh blushed furiously, coughed, and said in a voice hardly stronger than a whisper: "You can come out now," and from an inner room where she had been waiting, a woman slammed open a door, rushed in like a Jamaican hurricane, and cried in a joyous voice: "John! Elzabet! I'm your new mother!"

It was Hester Croome Pembroke, tall, big, redheaded, and almost splitting her stays with merriment. Rushing across the entrance foyer, she clasped John in her powerful arms and cried: "John, dear boy! I'm a Pembroke at last!" Then, moving to Sir Hugh's side, she stood with him and looked benignly at John and Elzabet. "My God!" she cried. "Are we not a handsome foursome?"

The next two decades represented the apex of West Indian power in London. When Lord Mayor Beckford was not giving a huge party to encourage his supporters, Pentheny Croome was offering an entertainment of staggering munificence, with Italian opera singers and German fiddlers. Occasionally, Sir Hugh, Lady Hester and his two sons would open their houses to a more restrained kind of reception: quiet conversation and music by Handel, who sometimes put in an

appearance to lead a small orchestra himself. The three big families—
Beckford, Dawkins, Pembroke—had between them nineteen children
and grandchildren at good English schools like Eton, Rugby and
Winchester, so the Englishness of the Caribbean grew more pronounced each decade.

In these years Sir Hugh seemed to escalate to a new level of enjoyment in living, and the younger Pembrokes were pleased that he
had remarried. They saw that his step was lighter, his smile more
ready, as if he were quietly amused by his new wife's bubbling vitality.
As John told Elzabet: "Best thing he's done in years is marry that
Jamaican hurricane."

Things were never allowed to remain sober when Lady Hester
was in charge, and the once stately quality of Sir Hugh's big reception room with its sedate Rembrandt and Raphael was somewhat
altered by the insertion of a gigantic marble sculpture that Hester
brought back from a trip on which she had met the artist in Florence.
The lovely Raphael was now partly obscured by *Venus Resisting the
Advances of Mars,* a white tangle of flailing arms and legs. When her
husband first saw it he growled: "Hester, I'm goin' to bring over four
cans of paint. His arms red, hers blue. His legs purple, hers yellow.
Then we'll know who's doin' what to who."

The Rembrandt was also overshadowed by a larger painting she
had brought over from her father's mansion, the one which had been
sold to the Croomes by an enthusiastic dealer, who told them: "One
of the most famous works of art in the world. Look at the pope's
eyes. No matter where you move in the room, he follows you. If
you've done wrong, you can't hide."

Bit by bit Hester's dinners became more rambunctious, until
parliamentary members from all parties grew to prefer her entertainments to any other. She developed a kind of rough Jamaican acceptance of both defeat and victory, and if a group of members tried
to force the Board of Trade to lower the price of sugar and failed, she
jollied them along just as she did when her own three Pembrokes lost
a battle. And this aptitude helped both her and the Sugar Interest in
the turbulent years following 1756, when all the nations of Europe
seemed at war with one another, first in this alignment then in that;
Prussia, Germany, Austria, Russia, France, Spain, Portugal and England were involved at one time or another in various alliances, and
Europe quaked.

With the cleverness that powers sometimes exhibit, France and

England restricted their major land battles to remote North America, and their sea battles to the Caribbean. In 1760, General Louis Joseph Montcalm, leading the French, and General James Wolfe, the British, both died on the same day in the great battle on the Plains of Abraham at Québec, mournful climax of the British conquest of Canada.

At sea Admiral Rodney confused things in 1762 by conquering the French islands of Martinique, St. Vincent, Grenada and All Saints, adding them to the big island of Guadeloupe, which the British already possessed. Rodney's victories were so important to the safety of the empire that when word reached London, bonfires were lit and people danced in the streets, but not the members of the Sugar Interest. They clustered in muted groups and whispered: "My God! What a disaster! How can we neutralize this dreadful mistake?"

The danger was real. If England retained as spoils of war the big French islands of Guadeloupe and Martinique, not to mention the little ones, so much new sugar-producing acreage would become available to compete for the British market that established islands like Jamaica and Barbados would be sorely damaged. "Hell," Pentheny Croome said with keen foresight, "sugar in England could then be as cheap as it now is in France, and that would destroy us."

He was correct, and in the latter part of 1762 and the beginning of 1763 the Sugar Interest, led by Sir Hugh Pembroke, the powerful Beckfords and the very wealthy Pentheny Croome, pulled every secret string it commanded to achieve one purpose: the English negotiators at the peace conference in Paris must be forced to accept Canada in place of the French islands in the Caribbean. If France didn't want them, give them to Spain or set them adrift, but under no circumstances let them join the British union.

Obviously, powerful forces were arranged against the West Indians, who were lampooned in the press and in pamphlets for being concerned only with their selfish interests. Strong French leaders wanted to keep Canada and get rid of the islands, which had been a constant financial burden. British military geniuses, especially the admirals, agreed; they were willing to give Canada away if they could hold on to Martinique and All Saints, two islands which commanded the eastern entrances to the Caribbean: "In any future naval battles in this sea, the nation that commands those islands will have the advantage. Canada? What worth is it except to beavers and Indians?"

But the strongest voice was that of the English housewife, who pled with her government: "Please, please give us the French islands so that we can have sugar at a reasonable price."

In recent years a new factor had entered this debate: the growing popularity of tea, both in the home and in the public tearooms. But to enjoy their tea properly, the English had to add sugar, and plenty of it, so as the demand for tea rose spectacularly, the need for cheaper sugar rose commensurately, and the West Indian sugar planters realized they were threatened by the new French islands.

Meetings in London were continuous, with political leaders dropping in on the Beckfords, members of Parliament who could use a few pounds of his wealth stopping by to consult with Pentheny Croome, while the molders of public opinion, the quiet manipulators of Parliament, convened in hushed tones with Sir Hugh Pembroke and his sons. The meetings were apt to be tense, with men of the Sugar Interest applying strong pressure to win their basic point: "Take Canada. It has a future. Give the islands back to France. For Britain to keep them would be a terrible mistake."

When any member of Parliament countered with the popular refrain "But the public needs sugar at lower prices," the canny sugar men refrained from saying "To hell with the public," which was what men like Pentheny said when they were behind closed doors; instead, they argued with honeyed words: "But, Sir Benjamin, don't you realize that Jamaica is enormous? We have untold fields on which we can grow more sugar . . . twice as much . . . three times as much. Leave this matter to us." Of course, for the last quarter-century they had owned thousands of arable acres which they had stubbornly refused to develop. As Pentheny said, with that profound intuitive knowledge he commanded: "Why should my slaves labor to cultivate a thousand acres, when on five hundred with half the work we can make twice the money . . . if we keep the price of sugar high?"

In 1760 the sugar people suffered a serious blow when a knowledgeable economist named Joseph Massie published at his own expense a pamphlet with the intriguing title: *A computation of the money that hath been exorbitantly raised upon the people of Great Britain by the sugar planters in one year, from January 1759 to January 1760; shewing how much money a family of each rank, degree or class hath lost by that rapacious monopoly having continued so long, after I laid it open, in my State of the British Sugar-Colony Trade, which was published last winter.* With impeccable reasoning and such data as he had available, Massie proved that the West Indian planters had milked the British public, during a stretch of twenty years, of the prodigious sum of "EIGHT MILLIONS OF POUNDS sterling, over and above very good profits."

The attack was frontal and complete. Men of the Sugar Interest were revealed as enemies of the state and ruthless exploiters not only of their black slaves in West Indian Jamaica, but also of white house-wives in Great Britain. The grave injustice could be solved, politi-cians of Massie's persuasion argued, by the simple device of retaining Martinique and Guadeloupe, for as another pamphleteer accurately pointed out: "The great planters of Jamaica have promised us for the last thirty years that one of these days they were going to open up more cane fields on their island, but as my figures shew, Pentheny Croome hath selfishly accumulated thousands of new acres but culti-vated not one."

These new attacks were so factual and so persuasive that one night in 1762 the leading planters met for dinner in Sir Hugh and Lady Hester's grand dining room. The great William Pitt, staunch proponent of holding on to the French islands, had been invited to hear arguments against doing so, but he became engrossed in Lady Hester's account of how her latest monstrous marble masterpiece had been got through the doors of her mansion.

"It's entitled, as you can see, *Victory Rewarding Heroism,* and when it arrived, there was no way to force it through our doors. So Luigi was sent for and he came up from Florence and showed us how simple it really was. With a special saw he cut right through here, Vic-tory left on one side, Heroism on the other, and each manageable half could be moved through the door over there."

"But how did you put the halves back together?" Pitt asked. "I see no betraying mark."

"Ah ha!" Hester cried, moving to the statue. "That's exactly what I asked, Mr. Pitt, and Luigi told me: 'Every artist has his secrets,' and he refused to reveal his. But there it stands . . . and isn't it magnifi-cent?"

She asked this question directly of Pitt, who replied: "Well, it cer-tainly is bigger than most."

Lady Hester's interruption had provided Pitt with time to mar-shal his courage, of which he had an unlimited supply, and after Hes-ter had withdrawn to her own room, he said frankly: "Gentlemen, as you know, I've always been in favor of retaining the big French islands. More trade for England, lower prices for sugar, strategic advantages for our navy." Several planters gasped and tried to dissuade him from including that stipulation regarding Martinique and Guadeloupe in the peace treaty which he was even then negotiating with the French during sessions in Paris.

They made no headway with him, but when the port was passed and the cigars lighted he leaned back, looked at each planter in turn, and confided: "Gentlemen, I have good news for you and bad news for England."

"How could any situation be so described?" Sir Hugh asked gently, but Pitt ignored him: "I am being removed from our negotiating team in Paris. The Earl of Bute is to supersede me, and as you well know, he is far more partial to your cause than I ever could be."

As he departed he threw a parting thought, generous and potentially productive, even though it operated against his own interests: "If I were you, gentlemen, I would have someone on my side rush out a pamphlet to counteract that persuasive affair of Joseph Massie's. It's doing your side real damage, you know." With that, he departed.

As soon as Pitt was gone, Lady Hester, who had read the Massie pamphlet with rising fury, took charge of the meeting: "Pitt's right. Our side has got to answer those false charges. And we'd better do it right now." After only a few minutes of discussion, it was agreed that a broadsheet should be printed and distributed widely, Pentheny Croome would pay for it, but then the problem became more complicated, for none of the planters felt competent to answer the sharp criticism of Massie. Each deferred to others, until Lady Hester cut the Gordian knot: "My husband will write it," and when he blurted out a gasping refusal, she said simply: "I'll help you over the difficult parts, my sweet."

He and Hester spent the next three weeks hammering out a masterful riposte to the anti-planter pamphlets, pointing out their errors, gently ridiculing their pretensions as to international affairs, and bringing forth sharp new points of view and economic inevitables. In the writing, Sir Hugh was invariably conciliatory, Lady Hester always thrusting at the jugular. They formed an invaluable team, an elder statesman in his seventies, a forceful woman in her fifties, and in record time they had their essay scattered across London and in the major cities of Great Britain:

AN UNEMBELLISHED ACCOUNT

ENTITULATED

IMPORTANCE OF THE SUGAR TRADE

TO THE

PERMANENT INTERESTS AND FINANCIAL CONCERNS

OF THE

ENTIRE BRITISH EMPIRE
INCLUDING ESPECIALLY ENGLAND

WITH A SHORT AND TELLING ARGUMENT

WHY THE ISLANDS OF

GUADELOUPE AND MARTINIQUE

MUST NOT BE MADE A

PERMANENT PART OF THE BRITISH EMPIRE

RESPECTFULLY SUBMITTED BY

ONE PEA IN A POD

A JAMAICA PLANTER WHO KNOWS

LONDON: 1762

The pamphlet was a striking success, for it played on British dogged-ness, English heroism, hopes for the future and patriotism in gen-eral, while effectively masking the venality of the Sugar Interest and hiding the heavy tribute the average Briton was paying in order to maintain Jamaican families like the Beckfords, the Dawkinses, the Pembrokes and the Croomes in their lavish pattern of living.

An Unembellished Account provided powerful ammunition for the Earl of Bute as he labored on the peace treaty which would ar-range affairs in Europe, India, North America and the Caribbean, for it anticipated all the ends he desired to accomplish and provided him with fresh and telling justifications. On a return trip to London he sent a signal to Sir Hugh and his planters: "Things look promis-ing. You will have no Guadeloupe around your necks."

This assurance from one so highly placed caused rejoicing among the planters, but not in the household of John Pembroke, for his frail Danish wife, kept to her bed by a series of fainting spells, had grave misgivings when he told her that the French islands were to be given back: "Oh, John! It seems so wrong!"

He was surprised: "But, darling, that's what we've been fighting for. To protect the markets for our sugar crop."

"I know," she said with mild impatience. "But there are other considerations."

"What could possibly be more important to us right now?"

"Surely the destiny of the Caribbean is to have all the islands under one grand government. It's folly the way it is now. Like a sour porridge with raisins. A few Danish islands over here. A couple of Swedish. Some Dutch. A few Spanish, ill-governed. Some French. They could be mostly English, with a chance to invite all the remnants to join."

He said: "But our entire program . . . get rid of Guadeloupe . . ."

"John! Do the right thing now! Give our wonderful sea a united government. Do it when you have what may be your last chance . . . the last chance ever."

She spoke with such vehemence that her husband said: "Elzabet, I never knew you were of such an opinion," and she said: "I've been watching and listening and reading. Nations are given one chance, maybe two, to do the right thing at the right time, and if they refuse . . . I see only tragedy ahead if this wonderful sea we were given is not united . . . now, when we have our last opportunity."

She began to weep, and John asked in trepidation: "Bett, what is it?" and she sobbed: "I'm homesick for the islands. Those beautiful islands . . ."

"Bett, as soon as this is over, back we go. I too want to see Trevelyan again."

"I was so happy there . . ." and within minutes she was dead. When John, in quiet anguish, asked the doctors: "How could you allow such a thing to happen?" they said simply: "She lived intensely and it was her time to go."

After her funeral, which was arranged by Lady Hester on his behalf, for John was too distraught to make decisions, he tried, out of respect for Elzabet's opinions, to withdraw from the final battles on the peace treaty, but neither Sir Hugh nor Lady Hester would permit this; they drew him deeper and deeper into the negotiations prior to the all-important vote in Parliament which would accept or reject the Earl of Bute's handiwork.

Thus, abetted by Lady Hester, who was proving a fierce defender of Jamaican interests, John arranged for an additional printing of eight hundred copies of *An Unembellished Account,* which she distributed personally in areas where they would do the most good. She also organized resplendent dinner parties at which arms were twisted and rural members of Parliament were instructed in the substantial advantages their district would reap if the Bute terms were accepted.

Ponderously the debate continued through December of 1762 and into January and much of February of the new year, with the Sugar Interest taking great abuse because the facts were so uniformly against them, but finally, on 20 February 1763, the vote could no longer be delayed, and the great planters who practically ran Parliament watched smugly as the tally showed 319 for the treaty, with the French islands going back to France, and only 65 against.

That night William Pitt, always bitter in debate but gracious in defeat, accompanied Lady Hester Pembroke to her home from the House of Commons, and as he sat on a velvet chair in front of *Victory Rewarding Heroism* he watched the jubilant planters celebrating their victory. At a break in the festivities he looked back over his shoulder and pointed to the gargantuan statue: "Gentlemen, I must remind you that Lady Victory, immense though she seems in this room tonight, is a fickle dame. In winning, I fear you have lost the American colonies from our empire. They're men of great fortitude over there, a new breed, and they'll not tolerate the cruel disadvantages you have thrown into their teeth this day."

"What do you expect them to do about it?" Croome asked. "They have no power, and we do."

"I expect them to rebel. To rebel against these injustices." With that, he went to Lady Hester, kissed her two hands, and asked her to escort him to the door and his waiting carriage.

Pitt was right, it did prove a costly victory for Sir Hugh. The energy he had expended so unceasingly over the past two years in his battle to defend sugar had exhausted him. He knew that he was wearing out, and found little pleasure when the great planters celebrated what Mr. Pitt had termed "your costly victory." He was also distressed to see his youngest son so dispirited by the loss of his wife, and day by day Sir Hugh weakened.

He did, however, find consolation in the remarkable vitality of his wife, and one evening when he knew his strength was failing, he told her: "Men like me, educated in England, often smiled at Jamaican planters like your father, who knew only what the land had taught them. But now I see that he, and you too, took nourishment from those fields, those forests." Suddenly he broke into sobs: "Jamaica, Jamaica! I shall never see the bridge at Trevelyan again."

Next day he was dead, and most of the members of Parliament who were in residence in London at that time attended his funeral, for he had been the one member of the Sugar Interest that all could respect.

In the seventh week after the funeral, that is, in April when rural England was at its loveliest, a carriage drew up to the country home in Upper Swathling where John Pembroke was mourning his double loss. A woman descended at the door, ignored knocking, and burst into the room where John sat. It was his stepmother, Lady Hester Pembroke, and her message was shocking: "John, listen to me! You cannot fritter away your life like this. My God, you're only fifty-four."

He rose to offer her a chair, but she refused it, preferring to stand until she had her say: "I've loved you for many years, John. My heart was broken when you brought Elzabet home from the Virgins, but I hid it. There's no longer need to hide anything. I'm a Pembroke, always have been, and now that we're both free people . . ."

He was aghast. Stalking from the room, he watched her carriage from an upstairs window, hoping that his rudeness would force her to depart, but she did not, and after half an hour collecting his thoughts, he returned, intending to rebuke her. He failed, for when he reached her she was laughing, a big and hearty woman whose life in London had matured her and polished her into a formidable hostess with graces that women less bold never attained. When she saw his distress she said: "John, it's inevitable. You know I'll never surrender. I allowed you to run away once, and I lost you. Never again." She assured him that his older brother, now Sir Roger, would recognize the good sense of what she was proposing and that his and Elzabet's three children, all safely married and living in London, would surely approve: "They won't want to see you wither like a cut cane stalk left in the sun." The Jamaican simile emboldened her to add a relevant point: "Besides, John, they won't fear that I've grabbed you for your money, which would otherwise come to them in your will."

She made no headway that first day, but since she had taken rooms at a nearby inn, she saw him constantly, and in proper time the numbness of his life relaxed and he gradually saw both the virtue of what Hester was saying and its inevitability. He proposed in a curious way, one day as they walked in the glades: "You know, you'll lose your title *Lady*. I'm not Sir John," and she said: "I'll keep using what once was mine, and to hell with them." She also had an effective answer when he pointed out that the Church of England must have rules against a man marrying his stepmother: "No matter. We'll be married in France. Over there they permit anything."

She also arranged for the honeymoon, dragging him to Florence, where her sculptor friend showed her a really massive piece he had just finished. *Justice Defending the Weak* he called it, and she bought it on sight. Her husband, who was appalled by the monstrosity a near-naked woman protecting six cowering supplicants—was powerless to prevent its purchase, for as he explained to Sir Roger after it had been installed in London: "It was her money."

VIII

A
WEDDING
ON NEVIS

WHEN THE INFAMOUS PIRATE DEN AT PORT ROYAL ON THE southern shore of Jamaica sank beneath the sea during the terrible earthquake of 1692, a long, thin sliver of land escaped oblivion. It formed only a small percent of the former area, but since it contained a stout fortress with thick stone walls properly disposed to withstand attack from the sea, Parliament in London had decreed that additional gun emplacements should be added, making it strong enough to withstand any French assault.

Unlike the days of Queen Elizabeth and Francis Drake when Englishmen grew nervous anytime the Spanish made a warlike gesture, now, two hundred years later, no one took a Spanish threat seriously. It was the French whose misbehavior attracted attention, for the skilled navy of that country was a constant threat to British independence. Curiously, the great battles of this period were fought not in European waters but in the Caribbean, where fleets of the two nations met often in battle, sharing alternating victories and defeats. In one great clash in the waters off the Carib island of Dominica, Britain won a signal victory, but in the years about to be discussed, the French showed every capability and intention of striking back. To be a naval officer in this sea was to be constantly on the alert for the ominous cry from the lookout: "French ships on the horizon!" for then one leaped to his battle station.

It was in such a climate of fear that the remnant of Port Royal left above water after the dreadful earthquake became of crucial importance to the British fleet, for whichever nation controlled Fort Charles, at the tip of Port Royal, controlled huge Jamaica Bay, and the heart of the Caribbean. To keep it secure, the British government in the turbulent year 1777, when the British were still trying to discipline the American colonies, placed in command an amazing young officer not yet twenty and soon to become the youngest captain in the fleet. When hardened veterans, some twice his age, saw this frail figure less than five feet five and weighing not much over eight stone, they muttered: "London's sent us no more than a lad," but even as they said this the young fellow was looking at the vast anchorage and saying to himself: We could anchor all the ships of the world in this safe harbor, and I shall defend it with my life if need be.

He was Horatio Nelson, an unlikely lad for service at a post so distant from England: unimpressive figure, washed-out blond hair, high-pitched voice, and the sometimes unintelligible country accent of easternmost England. In fact, as he stepped forward to assume command he looked much like a newly ordained clergyman applying to some rich relative for an appointment to one of the churches on the family estates, and this would have been logical, since his father, both grandfathers and numerous great-uncles had been ministers, in the Church of England, of course.

The force under his youthful command was as frail as he, for he had seven thousand fighting men at most, while it was well known that the French commander in the Caribbean was prowling the sea with at least twenty-five thousand tough veterans in a fleet of ships bristling with heavy guns. So on his first evening in the fort he ate a hasty meal, then walked back and forth upon the battlements of his new command, giving himself orders: You're to install additional guns at this point. You're to organize musters to see how rapidly the men can reach their posts when the bugle sounds. You're to clean away the rubble on the foreshore—we want no French spies hiding there.

As he made his rounds he became aware that a young midshipman who had sailed with him from England, a red-headed lad of thirteen, was trailing along, so without warning he stopped, whirled about, and demanded: "What brings you so close behind?" and the boy said in a high voice: "Please, sir. I want to see our new fort too. To pick my spot when the Frenchies come."

"And who are you, lad?"

"I served in the *Dolphin* with you."

"I remember, but who are you?" and the boy gave a surprising answer: "Alistair Wrentham. My grandfather is the Earl of Gore and my father was an officer on the Indian Station, but he died in battle."

Nelson, superior and aloof in manner, was excited by this information, for if the boy was in line to inherit the earldom, he might prove of enormous value to Nelson's ambitions, but the boy disappointed him: "My father was the fourth son and I'm the fourth son, so I'm far removed." Still, recalling that on the voyage the lad had demonstrated intelligence and valor, Nelson said: "I shall want you close to me. To mind the little things," and they walked the battlements together.

Soon the soldiers and seamen stationed at Port Royal had acquired a solid understanding of their young leader. They found that he possessed a backbone of unyielding oak, an insatiable lust for fame and a devotion to heroic behavior and rectitude that was enviable. During the long night watches when no French invaders could be seen in the tropical moonlight, he revealed, never boastfully, incidents of his amazing career, for at twenty he'd had more experiences than most seagoing men had accumulated at forty.

"My older brother became the clergyman our family wanted, so I was free to become a sailor. I went to sea at thirteen and first sailed in this Caribbean at fourteen. I came back later, so I know these waters. When I was fifteen, or maybe still fourteen, I went to the Arctic. Great exploration, that one."

"Is that when you fought the polar bear?" Alistair Wrentham asked, for drawings of Nelson in mortal combat with a huge white bear had circulated. Since he was often asked about this incident, Nelson was meticulous in his answer: "Thomas Flood and I, he was fourteen too, we'd left the *Cargass* to go exploring on our own. We were on an ice pack not too far from the ship when a huge polar bear roared up behind us, and he might have killed me had not Captain Lutwidge shouted a warning."

"Is that when you turned to fight the bear?" Alistair asked.

"Fight? I wouldn't say that. I'd been walking with an oar, a piece of wood maybe, and I did try to fend him off. But fight? No."

"How were you saved?"

"The captain of our ship saw the peril we were in and ordered a cannon to be fired. The noise terrified Flood and me, but it also frightened the bear, and off he ran."

"What did the captain say when you came aboard?"

To this question, Nelson would always reply honestly: "Never again were we to go exploring on our own."

At other times he told how, while still only a lad of seventeen, he had sailed to India: "The great ports, the strange people, we saw them all. We fought the pirates and protected the merchant ships." Then he would grow silent, and after a while tell his listeners: "The fever trapped me and I would have died had not a wonderful man, Captain Pigot, James Pigot, and remember that name, taken me under his protective wing and saved my life." Here, when talking with fellow sailors, he would invariably stop, look at each one, and say, "There is nothing on earth or sea that is finer than the tested friendship of comrades in arms. On the battlefield, in political fighting and especially at sea, we are propped up by the bravery of the man who shares our dangers. I'm here today only because of Captain James Pigot."

At night, especially when a tropic moon flooded the old fort with a silvery light and mysterious shadows, the young captain liked to gather about him a group of established officers and young midshipmen, plus any ordinary sailors who showed an interest, and instruct them in military matters, especially the handling of ships in times of war. But he was insistent that they first appreciate the significance of their present work in the Caribbean:

"This elegant sea has always lain close to the heart of Europe, because whatever happens in one arena determines what happens in the other. Suppose a war is fought only on land in Europe, when the peace treaty is written, its terms decide whether Spain, France, Holland or England will own this Caribbean island or that, and nothing we can do out here changes the matter.

"But also, when our navies clash at sea out here, they determine what happens on land in Europe. Why, you ask, when our islands are so small and their countries so large? Because we grow sugar, one of the most valuable substances on earth, and Europe waxes rich when we ship our sugar and molasses and rum to the homelands. Jamaica, that brooding island over there which we protect with this fort, provides the money which keeps England alive. The ships we sail in are built with Jamaican money.

"France the same way. Their small island of St.-Domingue just a few days' sail north of that mountain is the richest land in the world. If we could cut navigation between St.-Domingue and Rochefort, we'd strangle the French fleet, because it's the sugar riches of the Caribbean that keeps the homeland functioning. Gentlemen, you are serving in a sea of tremendous importance to England."

But in these night meetings, which many men would remember in later years, Nelson also spoke of naval strategy, for his agile brain was perpetually speculating on new procedures which might give English ships even a slight advantage in the battle against the French:

"Always remember that just a few years ago, in 1782, the fate of England was decided off the island of All Saints, when our Admiral Rodney met the entire French battle fleet under De Grasse. Always before in such an engagement, the two fleets disposed themselves in line ahead, broadside on, with cannon blazing all the while. Do you know what Rodney did?"

Midshipman Wrentham did know, but before he could speak, Nelson placed a restraining hand on his knee, because he did not want the effect of his narration to be spoiled:

"He opened the engagement with his fleet in line ahead, as always, like dancers in a set formation, but halfway down he turned the line ninety degrees and dashed boldly right at the middle of the French line, smashed the French ships head-on, broke through their line, and caused havoc. He created a whole new method of war at sea.

"Let us suppose that you nine men are the French ships, we'll be the English. Form lines as in the old days. Pass, pass, guns booming. Bang, bang, bang! Now here we break the rules and smash! Right into the middle of the French line. See the confusion. See how we can chop and chivvy the bewildered French ships. Another victory for England."

"Please, sir," Midshipman Wrentham said. "My father taught me that now we must always say Great Britain," to which Nelson replied:

"Your father's right. Scotland and Wales and Ireland are fine lands with stout sons, but remember that our ships are built by English workmen using English oak and are manned by English sailors, none better in the world, and if we ever fail our duty, the less important parts of Great Britain sink with us. We are England, the heart of Great Britain, and never forget it."

There was one revealing incident in Nelson's career about which he never spoke himself, and he refrained, not through modesty, a virtue he did not have, but rather because when Midshipman Wrentham told the story in his boyish enthusiasm, Nelson came off the greater hero:

> "Last year we sailed out of Port Royal to punish the privateers from the rebellious American colonies . . . they were trying to trade with our islands . . . Captain Nelson called them 'arrogant swine.' We had many great chases and sank two of them.

> "But the last time we didn't have to sink their ship, because our gunners really hammered them and they were glad to surrender, I can tell you, and bring their insolent flag down. But now a problem. The seas were so choppy that sailors near me asked: 'Can we possibly row a small boat from our ship to theirs and deliver a boarding crew to take possession?'

> "I was sure it could be done, so I jumped in early, and I expected the first lieutenant to jump down beside me, but when he saw the violence of the sea and the waters so high, he became timid and cried: 'No small boat can get to there from here,' and he refused to join us.

> "Now Captain Locker dashed up: 'Why aren't you boarding her?' and he became so angry, seeing us down there in our small boat without a leader that he shouted scornfully: 'Have I no officer brave enough to board that prize?' and he made as if to jump down with us, but at that moment Lieutenant Nelson, he wasn't captain yet, leaped forward, restrained the captain, and cried: 'It's my turn now. And if I fail, then it will be yours.' And down he leaped, and off we went through the great seas that tossed us about like a cork in an agitated basin. Finally we reached the American and Nelson climbed aboard, with me right behind, and I heard him shout: 'Lieutenant Horatio Nelson, officer of His Majesty King George

Third and commander of this vessel.' And let me tell you, when the cargo from that capture was sold in Jamaica, we all profited richly."

Other stories were told, there in the fort as the Englishmen awaited the attack that never came, and all attested to the bravery of Nelson but also to his stubbornness and his determination to do things his way, but always clearly within the rules of the British navy and obedient to the time-honored laws of the sea. Poor performance he would not tolerate in men serving under him, even though they might often be twenty years older than himself, nor would he silently suffer incompetence in his superiors. If the latter flagged in their duty, he was quick to reprimand them.

For the moment, in the old fort at Port Royal he bided his time, preoccupied with other concerns. As a young man entering his twenties he was of course interested in women. Avidly he sought a wife who would support him emotionally in his naval career, so with his fellow officers, all junior to himself and like him unmarried, he conducted long and amazingly frank discussions regarding the type of young woman who might be suitable. And often in these discussions he would lay out his two basic rules for a navy marriage: "First, an officer is only half a man if he lacks a wife and children, so get married. Second, he must pick that wife with extreme caution, for she must be his firm support and not the cause of his downfall." He was sometimes reluctant, when speaking in public, about revealing his two final rules, for he applied them particularly to himself: "Third, the woman I pick must be rich, so that I can cut a responsible figure among my equals. Fourth, she must come from an important family whose members can help me gain promotions. And I'm sure that somewhere in this world there is a young woman who fulfills those requirements." Then he quickly added: "And it would help if she hates the French, as we must do when engaging them in battle."

When a listener asked if he expected to be fighting the French for the rest of his life, he snapped: "What other enemy could there be?" Quickly he corrected himself: "Enemies we have aplenty, but none so valiant at sea as the French. They're the immortal foe." As he uttered these words he was looking out upon the sea in which his great predecessor Drake had said precisely the same about the Spanish and in which his successors would affirm their undying enmity to the Germans. Same sea, same ships of oak and iron and steel, same men of

Devon and Sussex and Norfolk, same enemy under different names, same islands to defend, and same young fellows wondering in the long watches of the night whom they would marry.

Of his four requirements, it was the third which gave him the most difficulty—that his wife be rich. As the sixth of eleven children born to an impecunious Norfolk clergyman, he was inordinately afraid of poverty and obsessively concerned with money. This made him a shameful fortune hunter, willing to marry almost anyone if she brought him both a sufficient dowry and relatives who would give a forward push to his naval career, so he refrained from telling his young associates the real reason why he had avoided marriage with the various young charmers he had tentatively wooed.

In each case he tormented himself with ugly questions: How much will her parents give her? Will she inherit their wealth when they die? How soon could one expect them to die? Will she prove a careful custodian of the few funds we will have? And the most terrifying question of all: Suppose when this appointment ends I am not given a ship and am left ashore with only a hundred pounds a year? Could she possibly live with a naval officer on half-pay and with no prospects? And when the answers to this barrage of rhetorical questions proved adverse, as they always did, he fled the young woman, grieved over their separation, and stumbled like the amorous sailor he was into another infatuation doomed to a similar end.

This terrible preoccupation with money revealed itself only when he was thinking of his matrimonial problems. When free to think about himself in his role as a fighting man, he invariably ignored personal gain, as Admiral Digby reported on Nelson's having been offered the New York Station: "I greeted him with 'Good fortune, Lieutenant Nelson. You are come on a fine station for capturing prize money,' and he astounded me by snapping: 'Yes, sir, but the Caribbean is the station for gaining honor.'"

And it was honor, fame, glory that Horatio Nelson sought. Indeed, he was so hungry for these accoutrements to a naval career that as a boy he pleaded, badgered and groveled for assignments to fighting ships, and as a man, suffered untold humiliations in begging his superiors for an appointment to this or that larger ship. And if he was finally given one with 28 guns, he connived to get one with 64 and as soon as he boarded that ship he started machinations to get one with 74. But he was no fool chasing only greater size, for when he dined aboard the Spanish monster *Concepción* with her 112 guns, he was not overawed, for he saw quickly that whereas "the Dons may make fine ships, they cannot seem to make the men to staff them. Long may they remain in their present state!"

As Nelson grew older he also grew more bold, and occasionally statements came tumbling out revealing his positive lust for glory. One night at the fortress in Port Royal he thought, while staring at the marvelous bay where the old town had vanished beneath the waves: How awful it would be to die before one had had his chance at glory! And next day he began writing a torrent of letters to his superiors, begging them for promotions, assignments to better posts, commands of this fine ship or that. Shameless in his ambition, he was also honing himself mercilessly in those attributes of leadership which would entitle him to command, if opportunity ever came.

Since he could find no white heiress to fit his requirements on Jamaica, he was forced to seek temporary companionship from among the lively beauties of no means who clustered about Fort Charles, and Jamaican legend would always insist that in his loneliness he found warm consolation in the arms of three different girls of high color. Their names are not recorded, for they were not deemed worthy of remembrance, being half-breeds, as the local gentry called them contemptuously, but the little houses near the fort in which they lived could be pointed out, especially in those later years when the name Nelson was engraved in golden letters in the hearts of Englishmen.

"That's the wee house where Captain Nelson lived with his dark beauty," the locals would say, and in time the three little houses lent a touch of humanity to the stories about the austere young captain who fretted in idleness awaiting a French attack on Port Royal.

Among the troops who monitored their captain's amatory behavior with closest attention was Midshipman Alistair Wrentham, sixteen at the time and just beginning to experience the compelling fascination that a pretty girl can exert upon a young sailor. He was not yet brave enough to consider approaching one of the half-caste girls, and since he knew no other, he spent his time wandering about the ruins of Port Royal and standing on the inner shore of the island, trying to catch a glimpse of the houses that had sunk beneath the waves when the earthquake struck. Others could see them, or so they claimed, but not he; however, one afternoon when he commandeered a small boat and went prowling offshore, he did spot the battered remains of a ship that had sunk at that distant time, and when he hurried back to the fort to announce his discovery, Captain Nelson himself wanted to be taken out to see the marvel, and in a kind of celebration he asked his dark lady friend to pack a basket of bread and cheese and dried meat, and he brought along a bottle of wine.

It was a gala afternoon, with Wrentham proud to be showing Nelson a matter connected with the sea, but the young fellow was deflated when Nelson peered closely below the waves and said: "That ship, that style of ship I mean, can't be more than a dozen years old," and when they rowed ashore to ascertain when the sinking had taken place, old-timers who had been watching them chuckled: "We know what you was thinkin', the earthquake and all. That'n sunk ten years ago, caught in one of our hurricanes with her caulkin' already worked loose. Went down like that." So instead of receiving praise for his acuity as a sailor, even Nelson laughed at Alistair, not insultingly but with the implied caution: Look more carefully next time.

Wrentham's attention was diverted from such matters when two servants from Trevelyan, the famous sugar plantation in the center of the island, came with a carriage to the spot on the big island opposite Port Royal, launched a small skiff and sailed over to the fort: "We bring a message to Midshipman Wrentham," the men said, one white, one black, and when he stepped forward they turned to address Captain Nelson: "The Pembrokes who own our plantation are close friends of the Wrenthams on All Saints, and our master seeks permission to entertain the young man for six or seven days." When they looked inquiringly at Nelson, he nodded briskly and said: "Fine young man. Ready for promotion soon. On your way." But as Alistair was about to leave the fort, Nelson overtook him and cautioned: "Not seven days, five, because I may soon be moved to another station and I'd like to see you again before I leave."

The servants sailed their skiff westward the short distance to where their carriage waited and then drove at a steady gait northwestward to Spanish Town, the stately capital of the island which still retained reminders of when Spain owned Jamaica. Wrentham, charmed by his first view of the interior of the island he had speculated upon so often while serving guard duty at the fort, hoped that the men would halt there for the night, but they pressed on, taking a narrow but colorful road that led north along the banks of a tumbling stream, first with the stream on the left, then a ford and the stream on the right. Tall trees lined the way, with birds weaving in and out of the lower branches and calling to one another as if to proclaim the coming of Alistair Wrentham into the realm of the great sugar plantations.

When they broke out of the leafy trail and into the broad expanse of handsome fields where the sugarcanes grew, the men explained: "Trevelyan ain't the biggest plantation. The one we're passin' now is, off to the right. Croome it's called, and it's enormous. But ours is richer . . . better soil . . . better kept, too." And when they reached that spot at which, years ago, Sir Hugh Pembroke used to stop to survey his principality, they saw roughly the same: "Yonder atop the hill, the windmills, sails flappin'. Below, the crusher where the oxen take the place of the breeze. See the little stone ribbon comin' down the hill to them small buildin's? Thass the channel brings the juice down to be cooked into sugar. And over there the most precious spot of all. Thass where we makes the black rum folks like so well, Trevelyan, and when you're a man, don't drink nothin' else. 'Cause real men drinks Trevelyan."

Urging the horses on, the men brought Alistair down from the rise and onto the handsome stone bridge with its two arches and the stone aqueduct forming one of the parapets, then across it and up a slight rise toward the imposing great house: "Golden Hall we calls it. Thass where the Pembrokes lives." As they approached, the driver held the reins between his knees, brought his hands to his mouth, and uttered a powerful "Halloo!" and to the front door came not one of the older Pembrokes but the most ravishingly beautiful young woman Alistair had ever seen, blond hair neatly braided, very white skin, flashing dark eyes, a hint of dimples at the chin and mysterious hollows in the cheeks. She wore, that day when he first saw her, a simple white dress, gathered high above her waist and held in place by a pink ribbon whose carefully tied bow streamed in front. He even noticed her shoes, delicate slippers with no heels, but then he noticed something disheartening: she seemed, in that first glance, strangely older than he, perhaps even nineteen or twenty, and he supposed, with a sense almost of terror, that she was either married or engaged to some young man of the district.

"My name's Prudence," she said lightly as she came forward to extend her hand as he dropped off the carriage, and when he took it he felt quivering shocks run up his arm.

The five days he spent at Golden Hall with Prudence Pembroke and her family were an awakening to young Alistair, for even though his family, the Wrenthams of All Saints, was affiliated in some way with the Earls of Gore back in England, they had no sugar plantation nor the tremendous wealth that stemmed from the astute sale of muscovado and rum to hungry factors in London. He had never seen such a well-run plantation, nor a mansion like Golden Hall, nor a family like the Pembrokes: great tables of highly polished wood, framed oil paintings on the wall, portraits of both Sir Hugh and his powerful friend in Parliament, William Pitt, servants in military-type uniforms, and signs of luxury everywhere. The conversation, too, was what he called "elegant," for it dealt half with Jamaican problems, half with those in London, and he learned with dismay that fairly soon the Pembrokes, including Prudence, would be returning to their London home.

On that first full day at Golden Hall his embarrassment began, because, as he had anticipated, Prudence did turn out to be nineteen, more than three years older than he, but eight or nine years older in sophistication and her interest in the opposite sex. She was a kind girl and not boastful about her reception by men, but she could not help dropping intimations that in both Jamaica and London young men had found her attractive, or that they had taken her to this ball and that, and the more she said, the more clear it became that he at a callow sixteen would have no chance at all to engage her attention.

But as a well-bred young lady she knew it was her responsibility to help entertain this friend of her family, so she took him on an exploration of the plantation, an inspection of the building from which the dark rum of Trevelyan issued, and even an excursion back to Croome Plantation, where he met one of the owner's sons, a young man in his late twenties. Is he the one she's engaged to? he wondered in a flush of jealousy, but he was relieved later when she whispered: "He's such a bore. All he thinks of are horses and hunting."

On the third day, when he was helping her over a stile that bridged a fence, she stumbled on one of the descending steps and fell inescapably into his arms, and he felt an enormous urge to hold her there and embrace her and even kiss her, but he could do none of these things. Instead, to his astonishment, she kissed him, crying: "You're a perfect gentleman, Midshipman Wrentham, and the girl who gets you will be mighty lucky." And off they went to watch the slaves tending the still-unharvested canes.

It was that kiss which set his mind to thinking seriously about her, and although he realized that she could never be interested in him, he was increasingly interested in her, and late that night he was projected bolt upright in bed: My God! I do believe she's the kind of young woman Captain Nelson's been looking for. And he ticked off the requirements he had heard Nelson expound so often: Loyal she would be, of that I'm convinced. Her parents have brought her up right. And she comes from an important family. They'd help him gain promotions. She'd look good, too, as an officer's wife. Know what to do ashore. But then he thought: Is she rich? Obviously the family has money, but will any of it come to her?

He could not return to sleep, so convinced was he that if Prudence Pembroke was assured of funds, she was the ideal wife for his captain, and when day broke he was down early, awaiting her. In her absence he tried, with awkwardly self-revealing silences, to question his hosts regarding their plans for their daughter: "What happens to a huge place like this when . . . ?" He could not say the phrase *you die*?

Mr. Pembroke had obviously contemplated this problem, for he said easily: "That's always been a problem with us sugar planters, all of us. How to pass the plantation along without allowing it to be broken up."

"How do you do that?"

"We always hand it on to the oldest son. That's the English way, the safe way."

"But if you have no son?"

"Then the family can fall into difficulties. Avaricious sons-in-law and all that. But fortunately, we do have a fine son—in England now, working in the office of our factors to learn how the sugar trade is controlled."

"You are fortunate," and the conversation ended as Prudence came in, wearing bright red ribbons in her hair and about her waist. She announced that she was taking Alistair out to the far field to see cattle recently imported from England, and when they stood together, leaning on the rails that fenced the small holding pen in which the imported animals were being kept till they acclimatized, Alistair asked, audaciously: "Prudence, are you rich?"

"What a silly question, Alistair. That's impudent!"

"I mean it. Would your parents allow you enough funds to pave the way for a naval officer . . . that is, if you married one?"

She turned to face him, and said gently, almost tenderly: "Alistair, you're a dear boy. Really you are. Handsome and well-mannered. But you are just a boy and I couldn't possibly . . ."

"I don't mean me!" he blurted out, astonished rather than hurt.

"Who then?"

"Captain Nelson!" And in the agitated moments that followed he painted such a magnificent word portrait of Horatio Nelson, twenty-two years old, able, good family, brave beyond imagination, destined for high command, and seriously seeking a wife if she met his requirements, that she had to listen. Encouraged by her willingness to follow what he was saying, he told her of Nelson's heroic fight with the polar bear, of his leaping down into the small boat to take the surrender of the American pirate, and of how his men adored him as the finest young officer of his time.

They spent all that morning talking of nothing but Nelson and of what life with him would be like. "He would," said Alistair, "be faithful unto death." He spoke so persuasively that she finally said, very quietly: "I have many young men, here and in London, but never one young man. Your Captain Nelson sounds like . . . I mean, you make him out to be a hero."

"He is." And then a clever idea exploded between them, each entertaining it at the same moment, but he voiced it first: "Ride back with me to Port Royal and let me introduce . . ."

"Yes. Yes, I should like to meet your Captain Nelson."

"We mustn't tarry, you know. He's due to be shipped out and we could miss him."

Of course, when they proposed such a trip to the older Pembrokes, the latter were amused: "Young women do not go traipsing off to meet young men to whom they've not been introduced."

"But I would introduce them," Alistair cried. "Nelson's a fine man. You'd like him."

"I'm sure we would," Mr. Pembroke said. "England exists because of her navy, none better in the world."

"It would be unthinkable for you to go to Port Royal, Prudence," her mother said firmly, and Alistair replied: "But if I hurry back and tell Nelson what a marvelous daughter you have . . ."

"Alistair!" Mrs. Pembroke said. "We're not trying to get rid of Prudence. We're very happy with her, and in due course . . . She knows scores of eligible young men."

"But not Horatio Nelson." He said this with such force that the three Pembrokes had to pay attention, and each thought: This boy is no fool. And if he says that Nelson is such a catch, perhaps we should listen.

Mrs. Pembroke said quietly: "Every planter in Jamaica owes the Royal Navy a substantial debt. They keep us free. Protect our lifeline to London. We would be honored to have your Captain Nelson spend a week with us, providing he can break away from his duties," and forthwith Mrs. Pembroke went to her desk and wrote out a courteous and encouraging note to Horatio Nelson, inviting him to visit Trevelyan Plantation as the guest of a family who appreciated the fine services provided by the navy.

"Please deliver this to your captain," she told Alistair as she handed it to him, and he said enthusiastically as he accepted: "We will all remember this day."

But when Alistair Wrentham reached the end of the road and took the skiff over to Port Royal and hurried back to the fort, he was shattered by a fierce disappointment: "Captain Nelson received orders yesterday and sailed for his new assignment this morning." Numbed, young Wrentham moved along the familiar corridors of the fort, bemoaning the fact that he had arranged the fateful meeting between Nelson and Prudence Pembroke one day too late, for he believed that such a marriage had been ordained by the gods of history. And when the final irony reached him he shuddered with regret, for the last task Nelson performed before sailing was to leave a note for Wrentham: "As of this date, I have officially recommended, in recognition of your exemplary record, that you be promoted to the rank of master's mate in the Royal Navy. Horatio Nelson, Captain."

Tears came to Wrentham's eyes as he held the paper, of special value not only because the promotion was a stepping stone to full lieutenancy but because it contained Nelson's signature. "Too late," he muttered, fighting back dismay. "Too late. She was the wife he sought, I know it."

At that moment, Nelson, aboard the ship that was taking him from Jamaica forever, had reached the point in the Caribbean at which the ramparts of the fort he had commanded so ably began to sink below the horizon. Saluting the rugged old building as it disappeared, he reflected on his continuing bad luck: Here I am at twenty-two years old heading home without a wife and without a command of my own. A mere passenger on this tedious boat, carrying bags of sugar and casks of rum instead of guns. His final judgment on Port Royal as it faded from view was a bitter one: That famous earthquake they keep talking about, better it had submerged the entire town.

The next four years were not the most disappointing that Nelson would know—we'll shortly see him in worse—but they were agonizing. He had no occupation but sailor, and here he was ashore with no ship and no promise of any. He was on half-pay of only a hundred pounds a year—charwoman's wages he called it—which he knew was inadequate to support a wife and the children he wanted.

It was during this spell of idleness that he crystallized his vision of himself. "I am a seaman," he wrote in his diary. "I was born to command some great ship in battle. There is no man in England, or France either, who has a better knowledge of seamanship and naval tactics. I must find me a ship, or my life is cut in half, useless and to no purpose."

At twenty-four, pledging that the rest of his life would be spent in conflict with the French, he decided to spend his idle hours learning that language, so on his meager allowance he hied himself to France to study both the language and French customs against the day when he would profit from both. But alas! When he reached the house in the small provincial town where he had decided to settle, he found it occupied by an extraordinary English gentleman, a preacher with a hospitable wife and many children, including two remarkable daughters in their early twenties. They dressed well, spoke French without an accent, played the piano like virtuosos, and talked intelligently on any subject thrown before them.

In addition, they were beautiful, flirtatious and amusing, but best of all, to Nelson's thinking, it was rumored that they would have substantial dowries, so it was not long before he abandoned his French lessons—he would try four times later to master that difficult language, and fail—and started a serious courtship. To a friend he wrote: "I am at last in love with a young woman admirably suited to be a naval officer's wife," but curiously, he never in any of his letters identified which of the sisters he had settled upon. And then the love-stricken letters ceased; he had learned that whereas his Miss Andrews did have a dowry, it was a modest one, not nearly so large as he felt entitled to. He broke off his courtship and left France in a pout.

On 14 January 1784 he began a series of extraordinary letters to older acquaintances who might conceivably help him, and one summarizes the rest: "There arrives a time in a man's life when his influential friends must either find him a situation in which he can rest secure for the rest of his life, or give him outright enough money to secure his position in society and the world. For me that critical moment has now arrived."

With appalling frankness he informed a friend that he had lately found in England a young woman worthy in every respect of marriage to an officer, except that she had no fortune. Since he, Nelson, was now receiving no more than a hundred and fifty from his navy half-pay, would his friend please assure him a yearly gift of another hundred? Furthermore, he hoped the friend would do everything possible, knock on all doors, to find him an appointment to a ship or at least "some public office, where I would not have to work? There must be many such jobs if you can but find them."

Since his friend could not promise an annuity or find him a sinecure, the man who was destined to become the greatest naval genius in history considered his career ended at twenty-five, and in early 1784 he decided to abandon the sea and run for Parliament! For several hectic months he threw his considerable energies in that direction, but his slight figure and unruly hair, which he wore in a huge, unkempt pigtail, and his unimpressive voice charmed few, and his try at public office was a miserable failure.

At this low point, one of his friends, responding to his cries for help, prevailed upon the Lords of the Admiralty to give Nelson command of a small 24-gun frigate, the *Boreas,* headed for the West India Station.

Weak with joy at this unexpected reprieve, he informed his naval friends: "A ship again. Aprowl in a sea I know well! Defending islands I love against the French! Never before have I known such exaltation!"

His new assignment, an important one, was not without its temporary drawbacks, because when he reported to the *Boreas,* his first lieutenant, former Midshipman Alistair Wrentham, promoted from watch duty at Port Royal, informed him: "Admiralty has arranged for you to carry with you a dozen young midshipmen from good families, oldest fourteen . . ."

"Youngest?"

"Eleven, my nephew, destined to be the next Earl of Gore." Nelson coughed, and Wrentham continued: "You're also to deliver to Barbados a rather difficult woman, Lady Hughes and her unlovely daughter Rosy."

"What do you mean, unlovely?"

"A big blob of a girl, high giggle, pitiful complexion, and desperate for a husband."

As soon as Nelson saw the unpalatable pair coming down the dock accompanied by three servants, he exercised his captain's prerogatives and snapped: "I will not take them aboard my ship. Tell them scat!"

Lieutenant Wrentham smiled, nodded as if he were about to order the women away, then said: "I think you should know, sir, Lady Hughes is the wife of Sir Edward Hughes, admiral in charge of the West Indies Station, and it was his suggestion that she come out with you."

Nelson rocked back and forth, studied the sky, and said quietly: "Wrentham, bring Lady Hughes and her entourage aboard," and Alistair hurried off to do so.

That night, after the women had retired to their quarters, Wrentham asked Nelson: "What did you think of the daughter, sir?"

"Repulsive."

"Begging your pardon, sir, but isn't it obvious that she's being taken out to the West Indies Station so she can find a husband? All those young officers and no English women."

"What are you saying, Wrentham?"

"Mind your step, Captain, if I may be so bold as to suggest."

"How?"

"Lady Hughes will want you for her son-in-law, of that I'm sure."

It was as painful a cruise as Nelson would ever make, for Lady Hughes was obnoxious, sticking her nose into everything on her husband's behalf, while daughter Rosy grew more impossible each time he saw her. Between the mother's blatant attempts to match Rosy and Nelson, and the girl's porcine behavior—she made noises when she ate, her fat lips slobbering over liquids—Nelson would gladly have surrendered the command he had sought for so long.

"They're horrid," he told Wrentham during one night watch, and that was before he heard the worst. The incredible news was delivered by Wrentham: "Sir, are you aware that according to naval rules, since Lady Hughes, her daughter and her three servants are technically your guests aboard the *Boreas,* you're responsible for their passage?"

"What do you mean by *responsible?*"

"I mean, as the host, you must pay their fare—a hundred and ten pounds, I believe."

"Good God, Wrentham! That's more than half my pay."

"Navy rules, sir." And now whenever Nelson looked at his two ungainly passengers he saw not only the boorishness of the mother and the grossness of the daughter, but also the flight of his pay. Since they were related to Admiral Hughes, he was obliged to be exceptionally polite, so one evening as they dined while the *Boreas* neared Barbados, he feigned courtesy and attention when Lady Hughes asked archly: "Captain Nelson, am I correct in believing that you are not married?"

"As ever, ma'am, you are correct."

"And is there, perhaps, some fortunate young lady waiting ashore? 'A sailor's life, hi-ho! A sailor's wife, hi-ho!'"

"I'm afraid young ladies have scant time for the likes of me."

Lady Hughes betrayed her desperation by her next move: "Rosy, darling, do fetch me that gray-silk kerchief." When the ungainly girl had loped off, her mother told Nelson directly: "Rosy, a dear child, thinks the world of you, Captain. Proximity and all that . . ." She nudged him: "That's what these romantic voyages are famous for, you know: 'Under the stars the world seems vaster. Lulled by the waves, two hearts beat faster.'"

"They tell me that's often the case."

Quickly, before Rosy could return with the kerchief, Lady Hughes said boldly: "You know, Captain Nelson, when Rosy marries she'll bring with her a considerable competence from her grandmother, considerable . . ."

While Nelson mused on this information, Lady Hughes added: "And the admiral and I would be very supportive. She's such a dear girl . . . Very supportive, indeed."

When dinner ended, Nelson took from the table a confusing problem. Lady Hughes had defined the situation so specifically that no listener could have been in doubt as to its possibilities: the fortunate young officer who married Admiral Hughes's daughter Rosy would have a considerable inheritance from the girl's grandmother, a sizable gift from the parents, and career support from the admiral, who had proved himself a canny political fighter where promotions and assignments to good ships were concerned.

Every anxiety that Nelson had voiced in his famous letters now had a favorable resolution—money, a fighting ship, promotions, and a wife already accustomed to naval matters—and as he strolled nervously beneath the stars he could visualize his ready-made career: Given the right ship and the right command and a faltering French opponent, I could soar to the highest realms of glory. Stomping about the deck, he made brave to voice his innermost dreams: "Once I have a fair start, Westminster Abbey for me. Buried among the great ones. My memory respected."

Caught in the grandiloquent euphoria of battles and heroisms ahead, he uttered the final self-assessment: "The day will come when England will need me. I cannot fail. And I shall not fail with her."

But then the awful truth thrust its ugly head over the side of the ship, like some fearful dragon come to slay the sleeping defenders: The key to all this is Rosy, and no man should be expected to pay such a heavy price, not even for immortality. And he continued to stomp the ship, muttering under his breath with each step: "No, no, no, no, no!" By the time the midnight bells sounded, he had made up his mind: if his future was to be determined in the hideous bed of Rosy Hughes, he would have to forgo it. And in the final days of his voyage he provided Lady Hughes with enough negative hints to enable her to guess what his decision had been.

To his surprise, this battle-hardened veteran of the matrimonial wars showed no personal grievance against him for rejecting her daughter, and on their last night at table she said effusively: "Captain Nelson, I predict a great future for you in the navy."

"What have I done to encourage that generous opinion?"

"I've watched you with the young boys who serve on deck."

"Have I been harsh with them? They do require minding."

"On the contrary. You've been kind and understanding."

"Madam," he said with forced gallantry, "you have the advantage of me."

"I mean that twice when some little fellow was too frightened to scramble up the shrouds to the crow's nest, I heard you tell him in a kindly voice: 'Well, sir, I am going to race up the masthead, and believe that I may meet you there,' and when the lad saw you climbing the rigging, out of respect he had to follow, and when you greeted him at the top, all fear was gone."

Her good wishes for his career in her husband's navy were so generous, and delivered with such honest warmth, that this last supper ended in general benevolence, with Nelson even smiling at Round Rosy, as the younger officers called her. "Mistress Rosy, I do believe I've seen some of my men making eyes at you," Nelson said, joking good-naturedly with the girl, and at the end of the meal a bright-eyed officer, who had ambition but no prospects of help from his family, stopped by to ask permission to lead Miss Rosy for a walk around the deck, which both Lady Hughes and Captain Nelson granted almost too eagerly, and as the two departed, Nelson thought: Clever chap. He's heard about the dowry. And he felt so relieved to be free of responsibility for the admiral's ungainly child that he almost forgot that he was paying, out of his meager salary, the costs of her courtship.

Horatio Nelson was twenty-seven when he sailed the *Boreas* into the roadstead at Barbados and took temporary quarters ashore at The Giralda Inn, but his character was already formed, many parts of it not pleasant. Ambitious almost to the point of frenzy, he was intensely jealous of even the slightest prerogative that might accrue to him, and he was so bold in defending his rights that within a few days of his arrival at the station, it was so obvious that he was going to be difficult that one-eyed Admiral Hughes, who was nearing retirement and who had hoped to round off his duty without unpleasantness, warned his wife: "I think we may have trouble on our hands with that young man you seem to like." But she defended Nelson: "He's stern, but he's just, and I doubt you've ever had a better."

The admiral's prediction was the right one, for the moment at least, because his young captain set something of a record by immediately precipitating a series of crises, each stemming from his vanity and obsessive demand for recognition. The first, as might be expected, arose from his mortal distrust of anything French. Upon putting into the island of Guadeloupe to pay a courtesy call at Point-à-Pitre he became so outraged when the proper respect was not paid to the British flag, he initiated protests of such vehemence that they might have led to war, except that the French backed down and fired the proper salutes. Storming ashore, he demanded that the officer who had been delinquent be punished, and only when this was done did his anger subside. "No Frenchman humiliates a ship commanded by Horatio Nelson," he told Lieutenant Wrentham.

But he could also show his fury to English malefactors, for when on the same voyage he approached for the first time the splendid anchorage on the island of Antigua, known then as English Harbour, and later as Nelson's, he studied not the beauty of the place nor the security it would offer a battle fleet, but a military sight which infuriated him.

"Lieutenant!" he shouted in his high-pitched voice. "What do I see hanging from the yardarm of that ship over there?"

"I do believe it's a broad pendant, sir," and when Nelson put his glass upon it his suspicions were confirmed; the English ship riding at anchor did fly a broad pendant, a kind of long flag which indicated that the ship displaying it was personally commanded by the senior officer in the area, and in this case that officer could only be Nelson himself.

In slow, carefully accented words Nelson demanded: "What ship could that possibly be, Lieutenant?"

"A supply ship, based here in Antigua."

"And who would be the captain of such a workhorse ship?"

"Someone appointed by the land-based officer in charge of the base, I presume."

"Send for that someone!" Nelson thundered, and when the unhappy young man stood nervously before him, Nelson asked in tones of ice: "Have you any order from Admiral Hughes to fly a broad pendant?"

"No, sir."

"Then why do you dare to do it when I am the senior officer present?"

"The officer in charge of the base gave me permission."

"Does he command any ship of war?"

"No, sir."

"Then strike it, sir. Immediately. I am the senior officer in Antigua and I demand the respect due my rank." And he watched while Lieutenant Wrentham rowed the frightened young man back to his ship, where the two officers quickly lowered the offending flag. Only then did Nelson raise his own pendant aloft. When Wrentham returned, Nelson told him: "I'm in command in these waters and I intend to let people know it."

He soon had the opportunity to prove his determination, for one calm, sunny afternoon when the 24-gun *Boreas* was on patrol among the small islands north of Antigua, he came by chance upon a trading vessel flying the flag of the newly constituted United States of America. Since the provisions of the famed Navigation Act of 1764 forbade all commerce, no matter how trivial, between the British islands of the Caribbean and the merchants of Boston, New York and Philadelphia, Nelson, obedient to those harsh laws, saw it as his duty to arrest this illegal intruder.

"Lieutenant, be so kind as to put a shot across her bow," and when this was done a second time, the astonished Boston ship hove to and allowed herself to be boarded by the Englishmen. When her captain was brought to the *Boreas,* Nelson demanded: "And why do you trade in these waters when you know it is forbidden?" and the captain almost laughed when offering his reply: "But, sir! We've been trading with your islands since time out of mind. You want our spars and horses. We want your sugar and molasses."

Nelson's jaw dropped: "You mean other of your ships are engaged in this unlawful trade?"

"Many. All your islands are hungry for what we have to sell."

"Such traffic ends today," and he ordered his men to board the American trader and toss overboard the entire cargo. But Wrentham was soon back, reporting: "Sir, he was telling the truth. He has sixteen fine horses aboard."

"Overboard, like all the rest."

"But, sir . . ." And upon reflection, Nelson conceded: "We'll land the horses ashore. Confiscated property." But when he did so he found that no one in Antigua had ordered them or had specific use for them, and this perplexed him, until the young officer who had flown the broad pendant improperly suggested in a whisper: "We could take them to the French islands, where the lack of a reliable breeze makes it necessary for them to import horses to work their sugar mills. In Guadeloupe those sixteen horses will be worth a fortune."

Drawing himself to his full height, which was not great, Nelson stormed: "Me, Horatio Nelson? Trading with the French to their advantage? Never!" and he ordered that the captured horses be distributed free among the farmers of Antigua.

But this act of generosity did not make him a hero to the Antiguans, nor to the English planters in nearby St. Kitts and Nevis, either, for the well-to-do businessmen of all the islands, English and French alike, had grown accustomed to the secret arrival of ships from the United States and dependent upon the profits earned in such trade. They were therefore perturbed when the new commander of the fleet in their waters stated publicly that he intended not only putting a stop to this illegality but also arresting those merchants ashore who connived at it.

When word of his decision circulated in the islands, Nelson found himself confronted first by stern advisers, who warned him: "Captain Nelson, if you interfere with this profitable trade, our islands will suffer grievously," and then by actual revolutionaries, who brazenly announced that they would continue the trade, whether he liked it or not. Fuming in his cabin on the *Boreas,* he threatened to hang any man who did business with the American blockade runners, but be-

fore he could announce his intentions ashore, Wrentham prudently
warned against such a pronouncement, whereupon Nelson turned
his attention away from the Englishmen in Antigua and toward the
insolent Americans on the high seas. In the weeks that followed he
captured one Yankee vessel after another, confiscating and dumping
a fortune in trade goods and putting island commerce in peril. The
outcries of the damaged American sea captains were reinforced by the
wails of the English traders, but Nelson remained impervious to both.

He loathed Americans, seamen or not, on grounds which he expressed forcefully to Wrentham: "Good heavens, man! They were
part of the British Empire, weren't they? What better could happen
to a land than to be an honorable part of our system? Look at those
pitiful French islands compared to the order and sanity of Barbados
and Antigua. Those damned Americans, little better than savages,
should get down on their knees and beg us to take them back . . . to
decency . . . to civilization. And mark my words, Alistair, one of
these days they'll do just that!" He simply could not understand why
the colonies should have battled to be what they called *free* when they
could have remained a part of England.

Infuriated by their ingratitude, he found positive pleasure in sinking or capturing their impertinent ships, not caring about the effect on
the islands' sugar producers, and turning a deaf ear to the plea so well
voiced by their spokesman, one Mr. Herbert of Nevis: "There are not
enough British trading ships to supply our needs, nor do they arrive
often enough to provision us. Without the Americans we'll starve."

Nelson, like most naval officers, especially those who traditionally came from circles of social prominence, held in awe those exalted
families that had inherited fortunes but despised those hardworking
merchants who were in the process of acquiring theirs. The latter
were beneath contempt, necessary perhaps, but hardly people with
whom one would care to associate, and to hear them complaining
against the manner in which their betters ran the empire was intolerable: "Dammit, Wrentham. England sends out what ships she deems
best and at what times she proposes. Let 'em accommodate themselves to us, not us to them."

Navy personnel acquainted with Nelson soon realized that he
never used the words *Britain* or *Great Britain,* nor did he take it
kindly when his officers did so in his presence: "It's an English fleet,
commanded by English officers trained in the great traditions of English seamen, and upstart American pirates invading our waters bet-

ter be careful of their ships . . . and their lives." He never wavered from those simple convictions: Americans were a worrisome lot of ungrateful freebooters. Merchants were a grubby lot who should be ignored. And both should be disciplined by English naval officers, who tended to know what was best for everybody. Some twenty years hence, on the morning of his death at the youthful age of forty-seven, when it came time to utter the most famous phrase of naval history, he did not refer to Great Britain. Instead, he harkened back to his basic belief that it was England which was destined to rule the world: "England expects every man will do his duty."*

On a historic day in January 1785, Captain Nelson sailed the *Boreas* to the beautiful little island of Nevis to discuss matters regarding the sugar trade with that community's leading English planter, the same Mr. Herbert who had lectured him in Antigua about the desirability of allowing American freebooters to continue their illicit trade in the Caribbean. Always fascinated by money, but loath to associate with mere merchants, he told Wrentham prior to the meeting with Herbert: "He is, we must remember, a sugar planter with proper estates and not some hawker of vegetables." And Nelson became excited when Wrentham reported the results of cautious inquiries: "Sir, this Herbert, he's the richest fellow in Nevis, Kitts or Antigua. Has a daughter Martha, but she'll inherit none of his great wealth because she's marrying against his wishes. His great fortune will go to a very attractive niece, a Mrs. Nisbet . . ."

"But if she's already married . . ."

"Widow. Five years younger than you, just right. Has a fine-looking five-year-old son."

At this information, Nelson began daydreaming: An attractive widow, very wealthy, with a fine son already in being—that fits my requirement for a perfect naval marriage. With secured funds and a family safe at home, a man could venture against the French with every feeling of security. To get at one blow a wife, a fortune and a

*As originally phrased by Nelson, it was "Nelson confides every man . . ." in the old sense of *is confident that*. One fellow officer suggested that *expects* was a more idiomatic word, another that the message would be stronger if it said *England* expects . . . and Nelson eagerly accepted each improvement. The word *that* was not included in the final twelve-flag hoist, done in the system devised by Sir Henry Popham in 1803.

great ship of seventy-four guns . . . I hear the stately march of mourners' feet in Westminster Abbey.

He was thus in a frame of mind to fall in love with the Widow Nisbet even before he saw her, and when she first came fluttering into the room of her uncle's mansion in Nevis, she swept Nelson away, for she was delicately beautiful, charming, witty in conversation, and gifted as a musician. Her attributes, which were many, were enhanced by the fine deportment of her son, Josiah, who at age five already wanted to go to sea. But most reassuring of all was the intelligence which his trusted friend Alistair Wrentham quietly collected for Nelson when the latter returned starry-eyed to the *Boreas:* "It's impossible to determine just how much money old Herbert has, but it must be tremendous, because he controls three different sugar plantations, his factors assure me that year after year he ships back to London at least six hundred hogsheads of sugar. I've made my own count of his slaves and they're worth not less than sixty thousand pounds. Can you imagine what the total fortune has to be?"

Nelson could not. But Wrentham, enthusiastic and accustomed to large figures, cried: "With his wealth, Herbert could easily provide his niece with twenty thousand. Now, if you invested that in Consols at five percent, you'd have . . . how much? Wonderful! You'd have a thousand pounds a year!" But upon reflection, Wrentham thought that the old man might want to give as much as £40,000 outright, which would yield a handsome two thousand a year, and this figure became fixed in Nelson's mind as securely as if Mr. Herbert had promised it in writing; he was going to be a rich man, a condition to which he felt he was entitled.

Despite the fact that Lieutenant Wrentham had assured himself that Nelson was going to be a wealthy man, he frequently caught himself thinking about his exciting days at Trevelyan Plantation, and lamenting: Why couldn't it have been Prudence Pembroke and not this one? Prudence had all the money Nelson needed, and beauty too. Her family could have been even more influential in gaining him promotions. There's something about this affair . . . maybe her having a son . . . that I don't like. Besides, Nelson is not in good health. His constant attention to detail continues to wear him down, and he ought to be thinking about taking a long rest rather than getting married. Then he would visualize Prudence as he had seen her that first day on the steps of Golden Hall, an apparition of delight in her charming dress, her welcoming smile, and he would drop his head and move it slowly from side to side, as if attempting to turn back the clock to those happy days when he was striving to find a wife for the man he revered.

No place for regrets, now, he told himself one day as he watched Nelson launch his tempestuous courtship of Mrs. Nisbet. Frustrated so many times before, and needing money now more than ever, Nelson also felt that he must not allow this dazzling opportunity to escape, and since Fanny Nisbet apparently felt the same way, a love match was under way. But there was one small cloud threatening this dreamy landscape: Mr. Herbert pointed out that his niece had contracted to serve as his housekeeper, and he could not see his way clear to releasing her from those duties for another eighteen months. So the love-smitten couple had to waste all of 1785 and much of the next year in courtship rather than marriage, but since this occurred on the lovely little island of Nevis, the long months acquired a fairy-tale aspect, and that kept Nelson content.

Only one weakness in the marriage plan kept intruding, that Herbert's natural daughter might move back into his affections and thus imperil Mrs. Nisbet's fortune. But Wrentham made discreet inquiries and brought Nelson news that was both reassuring and scandalous: "Martha is stubbornly going ahead with the marriage her father refuses to approve—and who do you think the man is?"

"I've no interest."

"You will. It's a Mr. Hamilton, and he's related to that other Hamilton from Nevis, the famous Alexander who played such a despicable role in America's revolution against us and who now parades as one of the leaders of the new nation."

"I refuse to associate with traitors or friends of traitors," Nelson said angrily, but Alistair soothed him: "No need to see the American scoundrel or the Nevis one, either. Remember, father and daughter don't speak. The fortune is secured to Fanny."

So on 11 March 1787, in a lavish ceremony at Mr. Herbert's Nevis mansion, Nelson, attended by no less a person than Prince William, son of George III and later to be crowned as King William IV, marched beneath a festooned bower to where Fanny Nisbet and her young son waited. It was a gala affair, this wedding of the promising young naval officer and an heiress whose huge fortune would spur his career. But the future king, known to his friends as Silly Billy, took a more cautious view, for in a letter to a friend he made four statements: "I gave the bride away. She is pretty. She has a great deal of money. Nelson is in love with her. But he needs a nurse more than he does a wife." Ominously, he added: "I wish that he may not repent the step he has taken."

Wrentham, suppressing his apprehensions about the marriage, joined the other junior officers that evening at a banquet, and they congratulated themselves on having, in a small way, helped their gifted friend achieve the financial security he had so long and heretofore so fruitlessly pursued. As Wrentham, thinking of his own improved chances for promotion if Nelson prospered in the service, reminded his fellows: "A rising tide lifts all ships in the harbor. When Nelson climbs the ladder of preferment, we climb with him."

Then everything seemed to fall apart. With a shock that threatened to unnerve him, Nelson discovered that his wife was not five years younger than he, but five months older. He then learned that Mr. Herbert, owner of this immense sugar fortune, was by no means disposed to settle upon his niece any sum ensuring her £2,000 a year; he was willing to provide an annuity of £100, which, with the hundred that Nelson had in his own right, meant that the newlyweds could count upon a meager £200 a year until such time as Mr. Herbert died, when the whole fortune would presumably pass to Mrs. Nelson.

But now Lieutenant Wrentham brought appalling news: "Martha Hamilton, Herbert's recently married daughter, has effected a reconciliation with her father, and it's she who will inherit the entire fortune." When Nelson, in a state of trembling agitation, asked Mr. Herbert about this, he was told that "blood is thicker than water," and that furthermore, Nelson would be wise to tend to his own affairs, since the merchants of the Caribbean were about to bring legal charges against him for interfering with their trade with Boston and New York.

Nelson's enemies laid a devious trap. Knowing him to be rigorously honest and an officer devoted to any printed instructions, they used decoys to let him know that two land-based officials of the English navy yards in the Caribbean were stealing governmental funds, and although Wrentham warned against precipitate action, Nelson came out raging like a bull, publicly charged the men with theft, and then recoiled in stunned amazement when they fought back, bringing their own charges against him and suing him for the frightening sum of £40,000.

His last days in the Caribbean, a sea he had grown to love for its opulence, its marvelous islands and their safe harbors, were miserable. Tied to a near-penniless wife five years older than he had been led to believe, saddled with the care of a boy he had not fathered, scorned by the powerful men on the sugar estates, and hounded by lawyers pursuing their lawsuits against him, he felt so badgered from all sides that he cried aloud like Job: "Why did I ever sail into this accursed sea?" In his despair he overlooked the fact that it was in these waters that he identified his true merits—his courage, his fortitude, his inventiveness, his ability to command men—those attributes so essential to military leadership and so often left undeveloped by would-be commanders. It was in the Caribbean that he forged his character, almost terrifying in its single-mindedness, shameful in its willingness to beg and kowtow to authority if one command of a ship could be obtained. He was a product of the Caribbean, as he may have foreseen when as a beginning officer he had rejected that glamorous assignment in the New York fleet in order to take a command in the Caribbean "because that's the station for gaining honour." In his dark days he may have rejected the Caribbean, but when he sailed away from it, he was one of the most resolute men in the world at that time. Great sea battles are often won on shore, where future captains are hardening themselves for the day of test.

But, as always, he felt that others owed him funds for his career and recommendations for promotion to better assignment. "Why," he asked Wrentham plaintively, "doesn't Admiral Hughes over in Barbados do anything to defend me against my enemies or promote me among my friends?" Alistair laughed: "You must know that Hughes is a ninny. Spent all his time doing nothing but trying to find a husband for Rosy."

"What's happened to the little pudding?"

"Didn't you hear? He offered young Lieutenant Kelly who sailed with us five thousand pounds if he'd marry Rosy. But Kelly was no fool. Married that lively cousin of your wife's."

"And Rosy?"

Wrentham laughed, and said with great warmth: "It made me feel good when it happened. Lady Hughes and the admiral combed the entire fleet but could press-gang no one. However, an impecunious major in the 67th Infantry Regiment, a nobody named John Browne, finally took the bait, picked up the whole five thousand and Rosy as well. I attended the wedding, and you never saw a happier pair—

Rosy, who never expected to find a husband, and good old Browne, grinning with upper teeth not meeting the lower, because he'd never expected to have a fortune. And off to one side Admiral Hughes, looking as if he'd just won a battle against the French."

Nelson was forgiving: "Hughes can't be as bad as everyone says. After all, he did lose his eye in combat and I respect him for it."

"Have you never heard how he really lost it?"

"In battle with Rodney against the French, I presumed."

"No. He was in his kitchen in Barbados trying to kill a giant cockroach with a fork. Missed the dirty beast but stabbed himself in the eye."

Now came the terrible years which would have destroyed a lesser man. Most men did not realize how terrible they were, because they were accompanied by no hurricanes, no exploding fires at night, no sudden deaths, no incarceration, no dismemberment, no imbecility. What the years did bring were fierce storms that did not ruffle the surface of a country lake but that tore at a human soul, and left it so ravaged that the visible outer shell might have disintegrated had not the owner firmed his courage and his will and cried: "No! It cannot be so! I will not let this happen!"

When Nelson brought H.M.S. *Boreas* home to the Thames in England he was handed the instructions he feared: "Your ship is to be decommissioned and your crew paid off." The words *paid off* had a sinister ring, for they meant that the ordinary sailors who had served long and faithfully would be thrown ashore with a few pounds— in some cases, only four or five—and no promise of employment or money for medical bills in case they had lost an arm or a leg. Midshipmen received nothing, and even the officers left the ship they had tended so faithfully without enough pay to enable them to live decently in the empty years ahead.

Of course, if France kicked up her heels, and ominous rumors kept coming out of that unfortunate country, the *Boreas* would be expected to sail staffed by a group of Englishmen like the ones who were now being tossed aside. So Horatio Nelson left his first senior command with only half-pay and some assurance that he would be recalled to active service "if and when the need arises."

What was he to do at age twenty-nine—with a new wife, a young son, no fortune, and not even a house into which he might move? He did what other officers like himself did in peacetime: he moved back into his father's home at Norfolk. There he tended the garden, planting vegetables in the spring, flowers in the summer, and "neating up the place" throughout the year.

Nelson's neighbors, watching him occupied with rural tasks and seeing him in attendance at fairs where vegetables were judged and loaves of bread compared, accepted him as one of themselves, and when this happened a curious shift occurred: everyone began calling him familiarly by his boyhood name, Horace. Weeks would go by without his ever hearing his real name, and before long he started thinking of himself as Farmer Horace.

But he never lost that other side of his nature, for often after attending some rural festival, he would return to his father's rectory and sit at a desk long into the night, writing innumerable long and pleading letters to his wealthy friends, imploring them to find him an assignment with the navy, and in a shocking number of cases, beseeching them not to lend him money but to "settle upon me that degree of money you can well afford and which I need so desperately if I am to maintain my position as one of the king's naval captains."

His pleas, and there were scores of them each year, went unanswered; he was given no ship; he was the recipient of a miserable amount of half-pay; and for five desperate years he continued to live by begging from his father's meager largesse, all the while depriving his faithful but tedious wife of new dresses and the other small enjoyments to which she was entitled. The Horace Nelsons were living in genteel poverty, for their £200 a year allowed them no frivolities and not too many essentials.

However, the couple did scrimp so that Horace could, at intervals, make the journey to London, where he trudged from one government office to another, begging for a ship. He told the Lords of the Admiralty: "I'm trained to be a naval officer. I know how to command a ship, ensure the courage of my crew, and fight the enemy as he has never been fought before. Sirs, I must have a ship." Never given a logical reason, he was consistently rebuffed.

And then late one afternoon in 1792, after he had dragged himself from one insulting interview to another, he chanced upon an old naval friend coming out of one of the Admiralty offices. It was his former first lieutenant, Alistair Wrentham, very handsome in the braid of a navy captain. Greeting each other with embraces, they repaired to a coffeehouse, where Wrentham reported with obvious pleasure that he had recently been given command of a 64-gun vessel headed for a patrol of the French coast, but as soon as he said these words he saw Nelson stiffen, and from this he deduced that his friend, six years older than himself and with a vastly superior understanding of ships, was "on the beach," with scant prospects of getting off.

"I'm so sorry, Nelson. It's so dashed unfair."

"What has caused this embargo against me? If you know, tell me."

Wrentham drew back, studied his old captain, and asked: "Do you really want to know?"

"I do, I do!"

Before speaking, Wrentham leaned forward and placed his two hands on those of his friend, as if to prevent him from taking violent action when he learned the explanation: "Nelson, you must know that word has circulated through the Admiralty condemning you as a very difficult man."

Withdrawing his hands with a fierce tug, Nelson cried in great pain: "Difficult? I run my ship in proper style. I bring dignity and efficiency to the navy."

Having launched this unpleasant discussion, Wrentham did not propose halting in midflight, and in firm tones he ticked off the accumulated complaints: "On your first day in Antigua, remember, you made that other fellow lower his broad pendant, forcibly, as the situation demanded."

"He had no right to it, Alistair. It was totally against the rules."

"You also provoked the French at Guadeloupe . . . could have been an international incident."

"No Frenchman fails to pay proper respect to a ship I command."

"Then you continued your warfare against the American smugglers."

"The Navigation Acts demanded that I chastise them."

"And chastise you did. Their captains are bringing suit against you in the London courts."

"Who circulated these charges against me at Admiralty?"

"Admiral Hughes of the Barbados Station. He tells everyone that you are headstrong and difficult."

"You mean Ninny Hughes? Father of Rosy that he peddled through the fleet? The one who knocked out his own eye while trying to kill a cockroach?"

"The same. I was informed by a friend in high office, Nelson, that you're never to be given a ship unless the revolutionaries in France stir up trouble."

Nelson heard this cynical strategy in silence, then, to Wrentham's surprise, he lifted his coffee cup and held it delicately in the fingers of his right hand, twisting it this way and that. Only then did he control his anger sufficiently to permit speech: "Alistair, it's been the same in all the navies of the world. In peacetime, what the high command wants is the polished gentleman who can manage a teacup in a lady's salon, one who can meet the Turkish ambassador, who can keep his decks trim and whitestoned. And never, never do they want a true sailor like me who can command a ship and fight her with the total loyalty of my men. To hell with teacups," and he dashed the one he held to the floor with a great clatter that brought one of the serving maids running.

"I am so sorry, my girl," he apologized. "It slipped."

After the girl returned with another cup, he resumed: "But when the guns begin to roar and the coastline is endangered by some Spanish armada or French expeditionary force, then the navies of the world shout for men like me: 'Come, save us . . . Drake, or Hawkins, or Rodney!' And always we respond, for we have no other occupation but to save the homeland."

Afraid that he had revealed far more of himself than he intended, he looked rather sheepishly at Wrentham, then placed his hands on those of the young captain: "Alistair, it's obvious that I envy you your command. I wish it were mine . . . to have a ship again . . ." He hesitated, then pressed his hands more tightly: "But you must understand, dear friend, although I envy you, I do not resent you. You have your own career to make, and you're off to a fine start." He was quiet for a moment before he concluded: "When France strikes and they call me back to command . . . maybe the entire battle fleet, I shall want you in charge of my starboard line. I can trust you, because I know you are not concerned only with teacups."

If Nelson had said generously in London that he did not resent young Wrentham's good fortune in getting a ship of sixty-four guns, on the lonely ride back to Norfolk he could not prevent a terrible indignation from overwhelming him: Boys! They're placing boys in command, and we men in our thirties rust in idleness. While the coach bumped along, he reviewed his miserable situation: Saddled with a wife who grows more complaining each day, responsible for the education of a son not my own, defrauded by her uncle of a legacy I had every right to expect, and deprived of a ship by rumors . . . Grinding his fist into his knees, he concluded: My life's in tatters and there's no hope.

He was therefore in dismal condition when he reached home to find his wife distraught: "Oh, Horace! Two of the most dreadful men banged their way through our front door, demanded to know if I was the wife of the naval officer Nelson, and when I said yes, they thrust these papers at me."

"What papers?"

"That lawsuit in Antigua. They've moved it to London and are demanding forty thousand pounds. Said that if you didn't pay, you'd rot in prison for the rest of your life."

In the rage that followed, Nelson did so many seemingly irrational things that his wife and father conspired to send a messenger to London to Captain Alistair Wrentham, whom Nelson had spoken of as the only friend he could trust, and when they learned that the young officer was a lineal member of the Earl of Gore's family, they had hopes that he might help clear away the confusion that possessed Horace. With a promptness that surprised them, young Wrentham arrived in Norfolk to find that his old commander had packed his belongings and was preparing for a hasty flight to France.

"My God, Horatio! What are you doing?"

To his surprise, Nelson fell upon him with an ardent embrace: "It's so good to hear that name again, Alistair. Up here they call me Horace. And I really began to think of myself as Horace. But dammit, I'm a sea captain named Horatio, and a good one!"

"But why the packing?"

"Flight."

"To where?"

"I don't know. Those scoundrels in Antigua have moved their lawsuit against me to London . . . forty thousand pounds . . . prison for life if I don't pay up." In a gesture of despair and futility, he cried in his high-pitched voice: "Where would I get forty thousand pounds?"

"Horatio! Be sensible. Government have already promised they'll defend your suit. You acted in their behalf, even Admiral Hughes admits that."

"But I face another suit. Remember those men I caught stealing Admiralty funds? Oliver, did you know that I found them in default of more than two million pounds?"

"Governments are never happy with an underling who points out mistakes, even if they run to two million. But you really have no cause to flee."

"I'm heading for France. I'll finally master that despicable language against the day I capture some great French ship of war and have to deliver terms to her captain."

At this bizarre reasoning, Wrentham exploded: "Horatio, you'll never be happy in France. Let me lay your case before the Admiralty. My grandfather, the earl, does command a hearing."

Nelson did not seem to hear this assurance as he continued: "What I shall really do, Alistair, is pass through France to St. Petersburg, where I shall offer my services to Catherine of Russia and her fleet."

This statement was so shocking that Wrentham was rendered speechless, and Nelson continued, with great excitement and much movement of his hands: "Remember that damned Scotsman John Paul, who turned his back on us in the American war, added the name Jones and became their naval hero? Well, when they wouldn't make him an admiral, which I must say he deserved, for he knew how to fight his ship, he hied himself off to Russia and received a top assignment from the czarina, and so far as I know, is still there. I'd enjoy fighting alongside a man with spirit like that."

Now Wrentham became angry: "Horatio, you're no John Paul Jones. The man was as fickle as a spring breeze. Born a Scot, should have fought on our side, offered his services to France, then the American colonies, now Russia . . . and God knows where next. Maybe Turkey, maybe France again." He came to stand over Nelson as he delivered his ultimatum: "You're English, Nelson. Could never be anything else. The lawsuits? I'll attend to them. For the present, I want you to unpack . . . and please accept this small gift to help you restore your sense of propriety."

Having anticipated that Nelson might be in pitiful straits, he had brought with him from his bank in London £200, which he now gave to his former commander. For some moments Nelson just stood there, both hands thrust forward with the notes resting in them. Then he spoke: "The humiliations I've known. The endless letters which receive no responses. The appeals to the Admiralty which go unanswered. The crawling, the scraping, the inability to buy your wife the dresses she merits, the constant taking of money from an old father, the impotence when your married sister needs a little help. I've lived in hell these past years, none worse on earth, and if war comes and I get a ship, God help the Frenchman that I go up against, for I shall be all fire and black powder."

But then his mood changed completely, for he waved the notes in the air and cried: "Ever since they've remade me into Farmer Horace, I've wanted to buy myself a pony. Never had the money. But if I'm destined to be a farmer and not a naval officer, I want that pony!" Almost joyously he led Wrentham into the village where he had long ago spotted the fine little animal he craved. To the owner's surprise he cried: "Jacko, me boy, I'll take her. Here's a hundred and you can bring me the change when convenient." And with a satisfaction he had not known for years, he led the beast home, saying truthfully: "If I'm to be a farmer, Alistair, I shall be a good one."

The prospect of this potentially great sea captain wasting his life as a farmer disgusted Wrentham, and when he further saw the miserable condition in which Nelson lived subservient to his father, and the whining character of Mrs. Nelson, suddenly so much older in appearance and manner, and the ever-present penury, he became so agitated that he was tempted to reveal something about which he should never have spoken and which he would later regret: "Nelson, when you allowed me to visit that great plantation in Jamaica, I met the lovely daughter of the place, nineteen she was and too old for me. But I kept talking about you so much that she said: 'I'd like to meet your Captain Nelson,' and it was arranged. I would hurry back to Port Royal with an invitation from her family. They were rich. They loved the navy. And you would visit Trevelyan. But when I reached the fort, you had sailed away . . . only hours before."

He bowed his head over the kitchen table, then said: "It all could have been so different. That one would have followed you even into battle."

Nelson coughed to catch Wrentham's attention, then said: "Alistair, it is infamous that you should tell me such a story . . . at such a time," and he was about to order the young officer from his father's house when his eye fell upon a chance mix of vegetables left upon the kitchen table in preparation for tomorrow's stew, and their juxtaposition captivated him.

"Supposing that you and I were facing the French fleet, off Antigua, say, or in some other ocean, and they were trying to escape us in this formation . . ." Suddenly the kitchen table was filled with potatoes representing the French fleet and onions the English, and long into the night he revealed the naval strategies he had been devising during his walks through the Norfolk countryside: "You remember what I told you in Port Royal about Admiral Rodney's bold move at The Saints. He wheeled and brought his full force smack into the middle of the French line. Look at the confusion." And now the table was filled with a great melee of French potatoes thrown into confusion by English onions.

"But, Alistair! Suppose in the next battle, and there will be one, of that we can be sure, for the French will never let us rest, nor we them . . . Suppose that this time just as we seem about to repeat Rodney's strategy, for which the French will certainly be prepared, we suddenly break our attacking fleet into two lines, me here to port, you there to starboard, well separated, and in that formation we slam into the French fleet. What terrible confusion in two quarters. Pairs of ships fighting each other across the entire ocean."

When Wrentham saw the vast mix of potatoes and onions, he asked: "But how will our two forces maintain contact—for signals, for battle orders?" and Nelson looked at him aghast: "Alistair! On that day of battle when I send you off to starboard, you get no further orders from me. Each ship in your line becomes its own command. You fight your battle, I fight mine."

"It sounds like chaos."

"Planned chaos, in which I would expect you and every captain under you to do his duty . . . his sensible duty." He ended with a conviction that had grown upon him in recent months: "The French like to lay off and fire at our masts and sails. We like to move in close and rake their decks. In close, Alistair! Always in close!"

Through the long night they moved their fleets back and forth, and when dawn broke they were still at their imaginary battles, the seas red with blood and filled with sinking ships. And before breakfast Wrentham helped his old commander unpack the bags that might otherwise have carried him to Russia.

Captain Alistair Wrentham, in fulfilling every promise he had made at Norfolk, preserved the naval career of his friend. Government did step forward to defend him against the spurious lawsuits; Admiralty did listen to Wrentham's impassioned defense of Nelson; and even the French came to his assistance, for in Paris the madmen of the French Revolution kept making such threatening moves that war obviously loomed. Toward the end of January 1793, when spies hurried to London with irrefutable proof that "the entire French fleet seems to be assembling for an attack on our coast," the Admiralty behaved exactly as Nelson had predicted that day in the coffeehouse: they sent messengers galloping north to inform Captain Horatio Nelson that they wanted him to take immediate command of a major ship of the line.

When the messengers departed, he stood alone in the rectory, not gloating over the triumph he had foreseen nor railing against the injustices he had suffered, but steeling himself for darkened storms he saw ahead: Now comes the test of greatness. I escape from the vale of despond and sail into the clash of battle, and may God strengthen me in my resolve.

It would be popular in later decades to claim that Admiral Horatio Nelson had forged his revolutionary strategies and imperturbable character during his varied experiences at sea, especially in the Caribbean, but that was not the case; they were painfully annealed in those four dismal years when he was "on the beach" in his father's rectory in Norfolk. There, humiliated, impoverished and ignored, he had hammered out his principles and devised those stratagems which would make him perhaps the finest officer ever to command a battle fleet. Aware of the miracle that had been wrought within him, he said farewell to his self-enforced prison in Norfolk, turned his face toward London, and cried: "Horace no more! Horatio forever!"

On 7 February 1793, when France was ablaze with war, Nelson, once again an active captain in His Majesty's Navy, stepped aboard the trim 64-gun *Agamemnon,* turned aft to salute the quarterdeck, and took immediate steps to whip his handpicked crew into fighting shape.

Some days later, with all the excitement of a midshipman eleven years old hastening forward to inspect his first ship, he shouted to his men: "Cast off!" and to his helmsman: "Steady as she goes!" Feeling the great ship laden with guns rolling beneath his feet, he headed down the Channel for the Mediterranean, where destiny waited to award him victory at sea, scandal in Naples with the bewitching Lady Hamilton, and immortality at Trafalgar.

IX

THE CREOLES

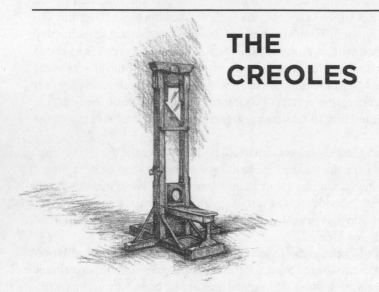

I N 1784 VISITORS TO ONE OF THE LIVELIEST SPOTS OF THE CARIB-
bean, the public square of Point-à-Pitre on the French island of
Guadeloupe, were likely to chance upon three young creoles—clearly
the best of friends, even to a casual observer—who, unbeknownst to
anyone at the time, would be plunged into a drama not of their own
making and culminating in horrid excesses.

The square was a spacious, friendly area, lined with trees and
made hospitable by numerous wooden benches and a central kiosk
where the town band played and from which citizens could purchase
hot coffee and croissants as they relaxed in the sun. At its broad
southern end the square opened upon the sea, where boats clustered,
white sails shining against blue waters. The other three sides were
defined by private homes built in the style of Mediterranean France,
except that where stone would have been used in Marseilles, here the
preferred material was wood, most often a handsome mahogany impervious to insects. Each house had a second-floor veranda adorned
with bright tropical flowers, making the square a garden in which
happy citizens congregated throughout the day.

Off the eastern side of the square ran a small street, and on a
corner thus formed stood a house that was a masterpiece: three stories high, with two verandas, not just one, and cascading from each,

flowers—yellow, red and blue. But what made it unforgettable to those who admired it as they took their coffee from the kiosk below was the delectable latticework, woven with very slender iron strands, which decorated the two extended verandas. "Metallic lace," an approving woman had called the effect, and her description had stuck: *Maison Dentelle*—House of Lace.

On the ground floor, Monsieur Mornaix, one of Point-à-Pitre's leading citizens, kept the office from which he conducted his banking and money-lending business, but the upper levels, the ones with the lacework, were reserved for his family, and often young men idling their time in the square below would gaze longingly at the flower-bedecked house and sigh: "There she is!" and their eyes would follow Eugénie Mornaix, the banker's lovely young daughter, as she strolled one of the verandas. "She's one of the flowers," the young men said.

Their adoration was fruitless, for her affection had been claimed. In the much simpler wooden house on the opposite corner—two stories, one modest veranda, a few flowers—where the town's apothecary, Dr. Lanzerac, kept his small shop, lived his son Paul. He had known Eugénie since birth, and they had now reached the exciting age when they were beginning to realize that each had a special attachment to the other, for he was fourteen and she, much more clever at the moment, was twelve.

Their parents, hardworking shopkeepers of the upper middle class, approved of the special relationship which seemed to be developing between their children, for the two families shared many attributes and interests. Both were devoutly Catholic, finding the church a comforting guide to behavior on earth and later in heaven; both were frugal, believing that God meant for His children to work hard and save their money to ensure protection throughout a long life, and every member of both families loved France with a passion that had never been exhibited by the Spanish colonists for their homeland. Monsieur Lanzerac, the apothecary, liked to tell the young people: "A Spaniard respects his homeland, a Frenchman loves his." In the entire reach of French influence, from the Rhine River to St.-Domingue, there were no Frenchmen more patriotic than those found on the sugar island of Guadeloupe.

It lay only eighty-five miles north of Martinique, but it cherished the differences between the two colonies, for as Lanzerac Père explained to Dutch sea captains who worked their ships through the blockades to sell their contraband goods at Point-à-Pitre: "You ask the difference between the two islands? Simple. Back in France they always speak of 'The Grand Messieurs of Martinique,' because nobody there does a day's work, and of 'The honest *bonnes gens* of Guadeloupe,' because they know that here we do. What does Martinique send the homeland? Polished reports. What do we send? Sugar and money."

There was a greater difference: Martinique was an ordinary kidney-shaped island, a clone of hundreds like it in the world, but Guadeloupe was completely unique, beautiful in fact, mysterious in origin. In shape and color it resembled a green-gold butterfly, drifting lazily to the northwest; the green came from the heavy cover of vegetation, the gold from the constant play of sunlight. It was really two islands with the two butterfly wings separated by a canal so preposterously narrow that a drunk once said: "Give me three beers and I'll jump from one island to the other." The eastern wing of the butterfly was low and flat and composed of tillable farmland; the western, of high and rugged mountains that permitted no cross-island roads. The explanation for this remarkable difference lay in the origins of the two halves: the eastern had risen from the rock base of the Caribbean forty million years ago, and this had provided ample time for its peaks to be eroded away, but the western had achieved its rise to the surface only five million years ago, and its mountains were still young. Born of different impulses at vastly different times, the two halves were now semijoined in one magnificent whole, and the people who lived on Guadeloupe said: "Ours is an island a man can love," and they felt sorry for those who had to live on what they called "that other island," Martinique.

In this green-gold paradise the two creole children developed a passionate attachment to both their native island and their French homeland, so that words like *glory, patriotism* and *the French manner* echoed in their hearts like the Angelus sounding for evening prayer. These were solemn commitments, profound allegiances, and Paul, who attended the school taught by the local priest, often told Eugénie, who stayed at home in her House of Lace learning the secrets of kitchen and laundry: "When I'm older I shall go to France and study in Paris and become a soldier of the king." When he said the awesome word *king* he meant Louis XVI, whose woodcut portrait printed in great numbers graced the main rooms of both homes. To the children, King Louis, with his round face and wig reaching beyond his shoulders, was a person whom they expected to meet personally someday if they ever reached France.

The children were being raised to be good Catholics, loyal patriots and protectors of the king, and as such they represented the aspirations of ninety-nine out of a hundred citizens on their island. Their only enemies were the British, whose nefarious behavior toward their island enraged them. In 1759, long before they were born, a British expeditionary force comprising many ships and thousands of soldiers had invaded Guadeloupe without reason and captured the western half of the butterfly; the British established a strong base and then attempted to conquer the eastern half, where the Lanzeracs and the Mornaixs of that time lived.

"It took them about a year," Lanzerac Père explained to the children, "to accumulate their strength before they felt powerful enough to attack our part of the island, because they knew we Grande-Terre people were fighters, but in due course they came at us, and that was when your great-grandmother earned her place in the pantheon of French heroes." Whenever he reached this point in his narration he would pause dramatically and remind his listeners: "I said heroes, not heroines, for Grandmère Lanzerac was the equal of any man."

What she did was to retreat into the Lanzerac storehouse out on the sugar plantation, bring all her slaves behind its walls, and arm them with guns collected from the other less formidable plantations, and there, as one British general recalled in his memoir of the campaign:

This remarkable old woman, sixty-seven and white-haired, supported only by her three sons and forty-one slaves, held back the entire might of the British invasion force. When I came upon the scene and asked: "What's holding us up?" my white-faced lieutenant replied: "There's a damned old woman who won't let us past her fort," and when I inspected this preposterous thing I saw he was correct. For our troops to get a foothold in Grande-Terre, they had to squeeze through the bottleneck that she commanded. And for two whole days we could not do it.

Don't tell me that black troops can't stand and fight. They were sensational, nothing less, and from time to time we would see the old woman, white hair flying, rushing here and there to encourage her men until, at last, I had to order a bayonet charge against her fortified plantation house, but in doing so, I gave firm orders: "Don't kill the old woman." They had no choice, for she came at them with two pistols, and they cut her down.

Grandmère Lanzerac became the patron saint of the French during the four-year occupation by the British, and her name was revered by Paul and Eugénie as they grew up.

They were a handsome pair of children: Paul with blond hair, bright open face and freckles; Eugénie with dark hair, a beautiful face and a willowy figure that resembled a wisp of marsh grass when she was twelve, the bending of a young tree when she became fourteen. They went through the normal periods of intense association when Paul walked the flowering verandas with Eugénie, sharing secrets and impossible dreams. Then there were months when they drew apart, heading in separate directions, but always they moved back together, for they recognized an affiliation that would never dissolve. They could not know whether it might blossom into normal love experiences, and as for even considering marriage, that would have been ridiculous to think about at their ages.

They were trapped in ambiguities and they knew it, and the cause was the final creole* of their trio, a delightful olive-skinned mulatto girl named Solange Vauclain, daughter of an immigrant from France who had been hired as a plantation manager and had married one of the slave girls. Solange lived with her parents on what was now one of the larger sugar plantations, east of town, and it was, Solange told her friends in Point-à-Pitre, "really a garden of flowers," for all the spaces not utilized for sugar were crowded by a wealth of the varied flowers which made Guadeloupe a wonderland. Birds-of-paradise that looked like golden canoes at sunset, flaming anthuriums, delicate hibiscus and a magnificent red plant that would later be named bougainvillea. Over all, arched stately coconut palms, hundreds of them, as if they were huge green flowers, and about the plantation buildings grew the mysterious crotons which could show any of six or seven different colors. But the one Solange chose as her own was the red ginger, shaped almost like a human heart. "That's the flower

---

*Creole has many different definitions. In Russian Alaska it signified a child born of a white Russian father and an Aleut woman, and it was not pejorative. In Louisiana and other American areas which heard the word, it was often used to denote a person born of a white French father and a black woman, and was pejorative. In the English-speaking islands it was used to imply "a touch of the old tarbrush, doncha know?" but, as one expert explained: "Mulatto is the word we use when referring to that unfortunate condition." In the French islands it meant simply "any locally born persons or thing of whatever color or derivation," and the name bore no adverse connotation. There could, for example, be creole horses or cows.

of Guadeloupe," she told her friends, "big and bold and brash. You won't find it on Martinique. Down there they like roses and lilies."

Although Solange felt wonderfully at home among her flowers, she often visited her mother's black relatives in Point-à-Pitre, taking them gifts of ginger flowers, and since she was the same age as Eugénie, it was inevitable that in this small town the two girls would become friends. Indeed, Solange became so intimate a confidante that she was more like a sister than a friend, sharing with Eugénie whispers and speculations about this boy or that or the goings-on of the young widow near the port.

But the presence of Paul Lanzerac in the house opposite soon made him the focus of their conversation, and it would have been difficult to determine which girl had the greater interest in him, for as Solange confided: "When I grow up, I hope I meet someone like Paul," and in the hot tropic nights when they shared a bedroom she sometimes whispered strange confessions: "Eugénie, I do believe that Paul loves each of us . . . in different ways," and when Eugénie wanted to pursue this striking analysis, dark-eyed Solange said only: "Oh, you know." Had Paul been asked, he would have confessed that he liked Eugénie, because they had shared so many experiences while growing up, but that he loved Solange in a different and more compelling way.

Once, when Eugénie had gone into the country to stay for two days with Solange, the mulatto girl cried in a burst of sisterly confidence: "Oh, Eugénie, whichever of us marries Paul, let's all be friends, forever and ever," and Eugénie drew back, studied her friend, and asked: "Has he been kissing you?" and Solange said: "Yes, and I love him so desperately."

Then all things changed, for the time had come for Paul to return to France for the serious education which he would require if he were to occupy his rightful place in the French system. Before he departed in 1788, at the age of seventeen, he spent a couple of long days with the two girls, then fifteen, sharing with them his hopes and the possibilities he foresaw when he would return three years later: "I don't intend to be an apothecary, like my father."

"A doctor?" Solange asked, flushed with excitement at such serious talk, and he said: "No. I respect my father's life . . . his neat shop . . . and I'd be proud to be a doctor . . . ."

"What then?" Solange pressed, and he looked away from her and spoke to Eugénie: "Like what we talked about. In government, a lawyer maybe, an officer who's sent from island to island."

"But you will be coming back?" Solange asked, and he replied enthusiastically: "Oh yes! This is my home, forever. My Grandmère Lanzerac died defending this island. I could not live anywhere else."

Then Solange, her beautiful dark face aglow, said almost sorrowfully: "But you'll have been in Paris . . ."

"Oh no!" he corrected. "I won't even see Paris," and she cried in astonishment: "Not see Paris!" Then he explained that his ship would land him in Bordeaux in southern France, and from that port he would travel by various rural conveniences straight across to the extreme eastern border: "I'll be going to the little town where the Lanzeracs had started, Barcelonnette, near the Italian border. Mountains and rushing streams. Some of my uncles live there." When Solange asked: "But why would anyone travel across an ocean to find a little mountain town?" he said: "Because my father says it's the best part of France. It's the border, where you have to fight to live." He reminded them: "That fighting old woman who held off the British to save this island, she was from Barcelonnette," and it was clear to the girls that he expected to conduct himself in her glorious tradition, a true-blue Frenchman fighting for France.

If a bright young man from any of the French colonies wished to revitalize his love for his homeland in the tense year of 1788, there could have been few places more appropriate for him to visit than the remote town of Barcelonnette. It was set among mountains and so close to the Italian border that a sense of defending the frontier affected all who lived or visited there; there was also a strong appreciation of the colonies because numerous sons of the town, unable to see much future in the limited opportunities it provided, had emigrated to the New World to find their fortunes there. Decades ago Paul's branch of the prolific Lanzerac family had sent three brothers to the Caribbean—one to Mexico, one to Cuba and the youngest to Guadeloupe—and all had done so well that they could send their sons, or at least the firstborn, back to Barcelonnette for an education. And there, among the quiet mountains, these young fellows met with their uncles and grandfathers and cousins to learn from them the timeless glories of French culture.

It had been arranged that Paul would spend his stay of three years in the household of an Uncle Méderic, who had not left home, and be educated in the school headed by another relative, Père Emile, who had stayed in Barcelonnette to become its priest and its respected scholar.

Paul had been in the care of these two fine men only a few weeks when he realized that in coming to his ancestral homeland, he had escalated to a whole new level of learning and understanding. Coincidentally, in early January of 1789 the French government sent a notice to the six hundred and fifteen districts that comprised the nation, advising them that since a rare and powerful event was about to take place, a convocation of the Etats-Generals—nobles, clergy and third estate or commoners—each district was to send to Paris a traditional *cahiers de doléances,* or notebook of grievances. So just as Paul was settling down to his studies he found two members of his family engaged in composing the grievances of Barcelonnette: Père Emile was contributing to the clergy's report, Uncle Méderic was in charge of the commoners', and as Paul watched these two thoughtful men at work summarizing the views of France, he imbibed from them an appreciation of what made France most distinguished among nations.

Uncle Méderic was the more thoughtful, for he saw France as a radiant beacon whose destiny it was to enlighten the rest of Europe and the world. As he prepared to draft his final version he told members of his family: "The Etats-Generals last met forty years ago. This is a rare opportunity to express our opinions to the king," and he made it clear that his list of grievances would be brief: "There's nothing wrong with France. Radicals from cities like Lyons and Nantes will complain about everything. More voting privileges. More aid to the poor. A stronger police. But what are the facts? This is a noble country and with just a little attention it will remain that way," and in that spirit his list was short: "We must have more troops along the border to protect ourselves from Italian smugglers; there should be better mail service with Paris; and the bridge on the way to Marseilles should be widened to accommodate our carts." Then, to let Paris know what his district thought about government in general, he wrote a fervid passage which would be widely quoted then and in later generations when scholars wondered how, on the very eve of a revolution, this obviously literate little town could state:

If Louis XII, if Henry IV are still today the idols of Frenchmen because of their good deeds, Louis XVI the Beneficent is the god of loyal Frenchmen; history will propose him as the model of kings in all countries and in all centuries. No changes of any kind are necessary.

Père Emile did not actually draft the clergy's list of grievances, but since he did contribute heavily to it, Paul gleaned an insight into the priests' thinking:

As long as France adheres to the teachings of the church and the guidance given by our king, the nation is on secure ground. The genius of France is to be rational in its scientific approach to problems of the military, industry and commerce, but to be spiritual in its interpretation of human life. If we can achieve this balance, and this committee is certain we can, we shall demonstrate to the world our superiority over the principles that govern less able nations like England. No major changes are required, but the bridge to Marseilles should be widened.

Paul found these solid assurances fortified by the instruction he was receiving from Père Emile and his three fellow teachers. Their école, as it was called, was an advanced school for fifteen-year-olds which offered instruction on the first-year level of a good university like Salamanca or Bologna: its students learned specific details as to how France achieved her greatness, and in one subject after another the supremacy of French thought and performance was extolled. While there was no specific class in literature, the teachers referred constantly to works by Racine, Corneille, Rabelais and especially Molière, whose work was judged to be the finest mix yet available of profound thought and comedy. One teacher did admit that Shakespeare of England had merit, especially in his sonnets, but that his plays were apt to be fustian. He also said grudgingly that the German author Goethe was worth studying, but that his *Die Leiden des Jungen Werthers* was far too sentimental for the taste of an educated gentleman. Dante was not dismissed, as Boccaccio was, but he was charged with being abstruse and unable to tell a tale properly.

In all fields it was the same: French kings were superb, French generals without parallel, French admirals the glory of the seas, and the French explorers of America among the bravest men of history, far superior to an Italian like Christopher Columbus who had merely sailed safe ships to islands which philosophers already knew existed.

In similar schools all over France such lessons were being hammered into the heads of young boys, who, conscripted into the army in a few years, would conquer most of Europe and march all the way to Moscow. Had Paul remained in Barcelonnette, this cradle of brave men, he would surely have become one of Napoleon's better officers and disseminators of French values.

But he was to spend only three years on his mountain because on the fourteenth of July, in what the authors of the local Cahiers de Doléances had reported as a land without any need of change, the rabble in Paris, by storming Bastille prison, launched a wave of change that would prove shattering. However, Paul remained largely unaware of the convulsions that were beginning to wrack his beloved France, for he was engaged in a rather difficult battle of his own.

When young men like him returned to Barcelonnette for their education, every effort was made to find them a local wife, on the understandable grounds that women of the region were a known product and most desirable. No one sponsored this belief more strongly than Uncle Méderic, who paraded before his nephew one local beauty after another, and some of them were breathtaking, with flawless complexions produced by mountain air and the firm, steady characters which resulted from protected rural life. One girl in particular, named Brigitte, a distant cousin of sorts, since everyone in the district seemed to be interrelated, was especially charming. The daughter of a wealthy farmer, she was not only a mistress of household arts like cooking, sewing and cleanliness, but was also the possessor of a rich singing voice and a lively pair of heels when a fiddle began to play. Also, Uncle Méderic reminded his nephew, her father could be expected to provide a handsome dowry.

But Paul could not give her serious attention, for a strange malady now attacked him: he was homesick for the tropical splendor of Guadeloupe and the demonstrated charms of Eugénie Mornaix and Solange Vauclain. The simple fact was that Brigitte, by the wealth of her virtues, had reminded him that he was already in love, but with which of the two creole girls, he had not yet decided. When he thought of women in the abstract, it was Solange with her dark beauty who filled his heart, but when he applied himself seriously to the question "Which one?" he found himself thinking always of Eugénie, and for three weeks he mooned about the hills of Barcelonnette so lost in dreams that his uncle saw that bold steps were required.

"What's the matter with you, boy? Can't you see that Brigitte has her cap set for you? Let me tell you, a catch like that doesn't wander across a young man's path more than once." The first two or three of these assaults achieved no results, for Paul ignored them, but when his uncle asked bluntly: "Are you afraid of women?" he started to reveal his secret: "I'm in love with a girl back on the island."

"What kind of girl?" and from the manner in which his nephew fumbled with this question, Méderic concluded that the boy was lying. The truth was, Paul didn't know what to say. Finally he blurted out: "Eugénie Mornaix," whereupon his uncle hit him with a barrage of penetrating questions which so confused Paul that in offering one answer he let slip, by accident, the name Solange.

"And who's she?"

"Another girl, just as pretty as Eugénie."

"Can't make up your mind? You're in trouble if you're caught in that trap. Tell me, is either of them as pretty as Brigitte?"

"They're different. Eugénie is smaller and very sharp of mind. Solange is taller and darker . . . very beautiful."

"Darker? What do you mean?" and in his fumbling reply Paul revealed that Solange had had a slave mother.

There was silence in the farmhouse, then Uncle Méderic stroked his chin and pointed to a timber darkened by the smoke of centuries: "You mean her mother was as dark as that?" and when Paul nodded, his uncle began asking a long series of questions about slaves on the islands, and Paul told him that many of the Frenchmen married women imported from Africa, "very beautiful women whose children are as bright as you or me." Indeed, he told illustrative stories with such skill that on subsequent evenings Uncle Méderic called in other members of his family to hear the young man's report on life in Guadeloupe, and gradually the French attitude on the relations between races manifested itself.

Père Emile said: "We're all God's children," and a cousin agreed: "We have never seen slaves in Barcelonnette, but I'm sure once they've been baptized . . ." and the priest agreed.

But Uncle Méderic, still championing the cause of Brigitte, made a judicial observation: "If a man was going to live his life in the islands, I suppose a black woman would be acceptable, but if he was under consideration for a job in France . . . well, a black wife . . ."

"She's not black!" Paul said defensively. "She's . . . In Point-à-Pitre you can see girls of every color, and some of them are truly beautiful. The men, too." And he was goaded into revealing something which he had up to now kept from everyone. Going to his room, he returned holding in his hand a small sheet of white paper, perhaps seven inches square, onto which had been carefully glued a silhouette which an island artist had skillfully snipped with tiny scissors. It was of Solange from the waist up, and although it was almost the standard silhouette which the artist made of any pretty girl, it had for Paul a very real evocation of his beautiful island friend.

"See," he said shyly, "she's very pretty," but an aunt, holding the paper close to her eyes, pointed out: "She is black," and Père Emile explained that all silhouettes were cut from black paper and pasted onto white: "Gives the required clean outline."

As that particular discussion dragged to a conclusion, no one offered the argument that would have been made in nearby England, that Paul was a white man and therefore the possessor of blood too precious to be melded with black. Not one Frenchman hammered at him: "But such a marriage would be unthinkable. You'd be ostracized from the best society, and your friends and their wives would cut you dead." Even Uncle Méderic, who had pointed out the disadvantages a man might suffer if he brought his black wife to Paris, retreated: "Come to think of it, there was that fellow on the road to Marseilles. Brought back a wife he'd met in Turkey or Algeria. Remarkably dark, but no one seemed to care. If this Solange is as attractive as you say, and you're to make your home in the islands . . ." And in the days that followed he stopped praising the charms of Brigitte, but he did repeat the warning he had once issued: "Seriously, my son, any man who's in love with two girls at the same time and in the same town . . ." He pressed his hands against his head: "Trouble, trouble."

But then the revolution erupted and Cousin Paul's problems were forgotten, for a local man who had gone to Paris to test his fortune had returned breathless with news: "They've forced a new form of government on the king. He tried to flee the country . . ."

"He what?" astonished townsmen cried, and their onetime neighbor said: "Yes, disguised as a woman, they say."

"What happened?" a woman cried. "Was he caught?"

"Yes. Hauled him back to Paris, made him agree to a new form of government they call the Legislative Assembly. King has no power anymore. The rabble runs everything. When I left, the country roads were filled with men and women of quality fleeing Paris."

Avid for news of changes that might affect life in Barcelonnette, the townsmen sent messengers scurrying about, but the news with which they returned was fragmentary: "Paris is in turmoil. No one knows what will happen to our beloved king."

"Is it as serious as that?" Uncle Méderic asked gravely, recalling the praise he had heaped upon the king in his report to the Etats-General, and one of the newsgatherers replied: "Who knows? No one can really say what's happening in Paris."

Clothed in this shadowy uncertainty, Paul Lanzerac left Barcelonnette in the fall of 1791, his heart filled with an understanding and a love for France, and for this benevolent group of Lanzeracs in their mountain town who had made his life there so pleasant and so rewarding: "I shall never forget you. And each of you will have a home in Guadeloupe if you ever choose to come." As he was about to climb into the cart that would start him on his way to a ship at Bordeaux, Brigitte rushed up to him, embraced him, and whispered: "Please come back, Paul. And do take care." It was Père Emile, priest and schoolmaster, who gave the benediction of the entire town, for he said as he ran beside the cart for a short distance: "Paul, you're a young man with a strong education and a strong character. Make something of yourself as a tribute to this town and to France." And the young man, boy no more, rode down the mountain road with a determination to do as the priest instructed.

For a young man of intelligence and promise to cross all of southern France from the Italian border to the Atlantic coast in the closing months of 1791 was to acquire an education in contemporary realities. Along country roads he saw the impoverishment of a once-rich land, and in small villages he was greeted with looks of resentment and even hatred. One stagecoach driver warned: "Young fellow, take off that jacket. It betrays you as one to be despised," and Paul stuffed into his bag the lace-touched jacket his Uncle Méderic had given him as a parting present.

On the ferry which took him across the Rhone, a peasant with twitching hands told a terrible story of what had happened at Lyons just up the river: "It started quiet. People like me askin' for bread. Police said: 'You can't go there,' but we went. Arrests. Heads busted. Turmoil in the streets. Then prisoners led from the jails. Well dressed. They could read and write, you supposed. Sixteen at a time lined up against a wall by ordinary men, not in uniform, with muskets. Then a bang. And down go the sixteen, but one not dead. A pistol was shot right through his face as he was lookin' up pleadin' for mercy. Horrible."

West of the Rhone conditions worsened, and at the entrance to one village a man moderately well dressed halted the stagecoach: "Don't go in there. They're going mad," and everyone in the coach, including the two drivers, were well content to make a wide detour. Even so, that afternoon they entered another village where their horses were stopped by boys of twelve or thirteen, who shouted to their elders: "Nobles fleeing the country!" and there were tense moments when it looked as if the coach might be emptied and its passengers shot, but the drivers, rough countrymen, convinced the mob that these were ordinary folk, some of them headed for the sugar colonies via Bordeaux, and after one dreadful moment in which Paul was afraid that the young rascals who had halted the coach might search his luggage and find the jacket, the stagecoach was waved on. As they passed through the village they could see pockmarks on the walls where victims had been shot.

When they were free of this ugly place smelling of death, Paul asked the man seated next to him: "What's happening to France?" and the man said: "Old scores being settled."

At Bordeaux, just as Paul was about to board the ship heading for Guadeloupe to pick up a cargo of much-needed sugar, he heard astonishing rumors: "The king has been arrested and is in jail. Hundreds of his supporters arrested, so if you're a king's man, keep your mouth shut. Massacres everywhere, and the Prussian army is trying to invade to protect the king, but our brave men are fighting them off." And it was with such inconclusive intelligence that Paul left his homeland, with Père Emile's counsel ringing in his confused ears. "Make something of yourself as a tribute to this town and to France." The achievement of such a goal had already become immensely difficult.

The long trip across the Atlantic was a time of reflection and peace, except for one ominous afternoon when a sail was sighted and the lookout called: "British ship to starboard," causing all passengers to breathe deeply, but the French captain hoisted more sail until the distance between the ships lengthened. At supper that night it was generally agreed that the British were a poor lot, little better than the pirates who used to prey upon these waters, and such horrible tales were told of Captain Kidd and L'Ollonais and Henry Morgan that one lady passenger spoke for the others when she said: "I'll be afraid to go to bed tonight."

In February 1792 the ship reached Basse-Terre, main port of the island on the western wing of the butterfly island called Guadeloupe, without incident, and there several passengers heading for Point-à-Pitre on the eastern wing of the butterfly debated the practicality of hiring coaches to take them directly there. They were soon disabused of this preposterous plan: "Do you know how high the mountains are between here and there? Goats couldn't negotiate them," and one resident of Basse-Terre said simply: "Coach roads? There are no roads of any stripe," so the people headed eastward had to wait while they took aboard the sugar cargo.

But while the ship stayed in port, several smaller craft whisked around to the eastern wing, carrying exciting news to Paul's hometown: "Ship in from Bordeaux. Lanzerac's aboard. All France in an uproar. King's fate uncertain." So by the time the cargo ship had made its way to Point-à-Pitre, the townsfolk were eager for a sight of their returning son and the news that he would be bringing, and they crowded the dock to greet his arrival.

When he appeared at the railing of the ship they saw a fine-looking young man of twenty-one, with erect posture, light hair edging down toward his left eyebrow and a reserved countenance which was capable of breaking into a warm smile, but the lasting impression he created was one of dignity and capability. Many a mother seeing him about to land felt he was the kind of young man she would appreciate having visit her kitchen for a friendly chat and a supper with her daughter.

In the last moments, as the ship eased its way to the dock, Paul could see the two dear friends who stood side by side in the waiting area below, Eugénie Mornaix and Solange Vauclain, and he was struck by what beautiful young women they had become, each in her own way. Eugénie, the smaller and fairer of the two, was a little jewel with a delicate figure totally appropriate to her size, and a lovely smile which she flashed at Paul as he waved. Solange was taller, slimmer and more provocative as she stared at him with her dark, handsome face tilted slightly to one side. She was, he thought, like a Caribbean volcano waiting to explode.

Behind them he saw his patient father, who had provided the money for his stay in France, and to him he shouted special greetings, but when the passengers were allowed to disembark it was to the two girls that he rushed, and for several dazzling moments there on the dock the citizens watched with admiration the tableau of these three handsome young creoles: the white daughter of a respected banker recently demised, the sinewy, dark-skinned child of a well-regarded planter, and between them the reserved son of the apothecary, home from France with a diploma of honor from a French école. It was a moment of restrained elegance that many would remember during the terrible days that awaited.

The troubles revealed themselves gradually. Paul laughed when his father warned: "Two restless young women out there waiting for you, son." He was intent only on reestablishing his warm relationships with his family, and reported twice each item of news from Barcelonnette.

"I met some wonderful girls in France," he said, describing Brigitte and explaining to his parents what family she was related to.

"I know them!" Mme. Lanzerac cried. "Oh, why didn't you bring her home with you?" He said: "I could never get the girls of Point-à-Pitre out of my mind," and forthwith he began his serious dual courtship, with the town aware of what was happening.

Jocular bets were made as to which of the lovely creoles would land Paul in her net, and sometimes the talk grew serious. A woman observant of island life reflected as she sat with a neighbor on a bench in the sun-filled square: "It's such a mysterious moment. Three lives in suspension. A golden moment, really. A choice made that determines a lifetime." The older listener, who was staring at the cargo ships preparing for the run to the offshore islands, nodded: "And most often we choose wrong."

As the first delightful days of reacquaintance passed, the young people became aware that they must get on with their lives. The girls knew they had reached the age of bearing children; Paul knew he was eager to start a family, had, indeed, been ready that last year in Barcelonnette, so the process of choosing became more intense.

He did not cast up the comparative virtues of the two women, with points for this or that, but he was aware of the great basic differences that had existed since his earliest days with Eugénie and Solange: the former was the perfect mate, the latter a woman who exploded the heart, and when he was alone with either he was content. But as the pressure increased he tended to show sympathy for Eugénie, who had lost her father, and then preference, and when this was perceived by everyone in Point-à-Pitre, Solange did something she would later regret. She confronted her friends and said accusingly: "If I'd been white . . ." and she fled to her father's plantation, refusing to participate in the wedding she had foreseen, nor was she present when the young couple set up housekeeping in the House of Lace.

When the excitement over Paul's choice abated, the citizens resumed serious discussion of events in France, and on one memorable evening M. Lanzerac said firmly: "If our king is in danger, he can certainly count on our support," and so much applause greeted this affirmation of loyalty that an informal party of Royalists was founded on the spot. Priests, plantation owners, sugar factors, men who owned trading ships in partnership with others, petty merchants, all loudly voiced their support for the king and the good old ways, while a few men of mean spirit took secret note of their names.

Each new ship arriving at Basse-Terre brought more shocking revelations about the discord that was shattering the homeland— abolition of the monarchy, installation of radical new agencies of government, war against external enemies—and finally the gruesomeness that shocked the island into sullen silence: "King Louis has been executed. All is in turmoil."

In the following days the French island of Guadeloupe reacted precisely as the English island of Barbados had done one hundred and forty-four years before when British revolutionaries had chopped off the head of their king: everyone in any position of dignity declared himself to be an adherent of their dead king and an opponent of radical new patterns, and no one was more committed to this lost cause than Paul and Eugénie. Because they sensed intuitively that the chaos in France must ultimately reach Guadeloupe, with disruptions that could not be defined, they decided, in preparation for the storm, to restore their friendship with Solange. So together they rode out to the plantation, where she greeted them among her wealth of flowers. "Come back with us," Eugénie pleaded. "We're destined to be friends forever," and after gathering bouquets to liven up her room in Point-à-Pitre, Solange saddled her horse and joined them on the return trip.

Her reappearance as a close friend of the Lanzeracs was an embarrassment to no one: she loved Paul, as she had from the age of nine, but after his marriage to Eugénie she seemed to have stored that part of her former life in a closet, with every apparent intention of keeping it there. Both Paul and Eugénie realized that Solange adored him, but they agreed that so long as emotions were kept under control, no one was the loser in the present arrangement, and husband and wife took serious steps to find the beautiful Solange a husband.

In 1793, Guadeloupe was shaken by a series of disasters arriving from two different quarters. From France came the hideous news that a reign of uncontrolled terror had swept the country, with thousands being executed by a new beheading device called the guillotine after the imaginative physician who had sponsored it. From the German border came word that many nations had combined to destroy France's revolution and place a new king on the throne. Finally came the saddest news of all, Queen Marie Antoinette, a frivolous but gracious lady, had also been executed.

This shameful act intensified the emotions of the island Royalists, who held meetings at which they orated . . . while spies listed new names. Paul Lanzerac, already a man of substance although only twenty-three, led the fiery orations, calling upon memories of France's greatness under her distinguished kings, but what really animated him was the arrival in the French islands of a decree announcing that any worship of God or Jesus or the Virgin Mary had been abolished in favor of what was called the Cult of Reason. There was also to be an entirely new calendar, with months named for natural phenomena like Germinal (seed month) and Thermidor (heat month) and Fructidor (fruit/harvest month). A subsidiary note reported that priests and nuns were being exterminated at a lively rate, with a suggestion that patriots in the colonies might like to conduct a similar cleansing.

When Paul heard these revolting stories his anger flared to such a pitch that he led a huge mass meeting in the plaza opposite his father's shop, at which he railed for some minutes against the assassins who had killed the king and queen and now sought to kill Jesus and the Virgin Mother, and it was in the soaring emotions of that afternoon that at least the eastern half of Guadeloupe declared itself unequivocally in support of the old system of government and religion as opposed to the new. And when Paul finished, Solange leaped to the improvised stage and declared that the women of the island felt their own devotion to the dead queen and the church.

Then, in late 1793, the few mulattoes and the many blacks out in Guadeloupe's country areas united for the first time in island history to redress the grievances under which they had long suffered—mulattoes from ostracisms, slaves from physical abuses—and they mounted such a furious attack on white citizens in the town that Paul Lanzerac cried to his cohorts: "It's the madness of Paris come to the New World!" and he organized a tiny defense force to hold off the attackers, who, having heard what the lower classes of Paris had achieved in their rebellion, started to burn plantations and assault their white owners. From his defense group Paul selected a cadre of horsemen, whom he molded into a cavalry unit which launched forays far into the countryside to save the sugar growers.

The dash of these volunteers, plus Lanzerac's excellent leadership, established a perimeter of safety inside which plantation owners could survive the attacks of the dark-skinned rebels, but during one sortie far to the eastern shore of the island where plantations bordered on the Atlantic, a fellow rider asked Paul: "Did you know that Solange Vauclain has gone out to her plantation to help her father save it from burning?" When he asked his troop: "Shall we ride back by way of the Vauclain place to rescue Solange if she's still there?" they demurred: "No concern of ours. She's mulatto and no doubt fighting on their side."

So the detour to help Solange was aborted, but late that night when Paul told his wife: "I'm really frightened. She's out there and she's got to be brought in," she replied without hesitation: "Of course," and she kissed him goodbye as he left to round up three volunteers to aid him on his starlit gallop eastward.

It was not a long ride, just to the safe perimeter and three miles beyond, but the last portion could prove extremely dangerous if the rebels were alert, so at the point where the riders had to leave the protection of the French guns, he cried: "We're heading over there. Any who wish to remain, do so," but none stayed, so with his three men behind him he made a dash for the Vauclain plantation.

It was a sharp ride over rough terrain, but they did avoid the rebels and at dawn approached the Vauclain plantation, but one of the men, knowing of Paul's affection for Solange, galloped ahead and immediately returned, right hand in the air to stop the riders: "Don't go. It's terrible." Brushing past him, Paul sped on to see the fearful desolation that had been wreaked upon one of Guadeloupe's finest sugar settlements. The big house had been leveled; its fine mahogany furnishings were smoldering. The owner, a just man and a fine manager, hung by his neck from a tree that he had planted.

When Paul, near fainting, started to poke among the embers to see what had happened to Solange and her mother, the others tried again to stop him, but when he heard a whimper from a chicken coop, he found the girl and her mother huddled inside, terrified lest the horsemen might be a second round of rebels come to finish the destruction.

When Paul saw the pitiful condition of his beautiful friend, he took her in his arms, and said that she and her mother must mount

behind two of the horsemen for a speedy ride back to the safety of
the town. He was astonished that Mme. Vauclain refused to accompany him, and when he wanted Solange to plead with her mother, the
old woman snarled: "I'm black. The Frenchmen have never wanted
me. I'm with the slaves. And one day we'll drive you from the island."
She stood erect, told her daughter: "Do as you please, but they won't
want you either," and off she strode toward the camps of the very
men who had burned her plantation and killed her husband.

For a moment Solange, the daughter of a murdered father and a
rebellious mother who had deserted her, looked in confusion at the
man she had always loved, and felt near to collapsing. But with the
same strength that her African mother had shown, she calmly shook
the dust from her skirt, and then cried: "We go!" And after Paul
helped her mount and himself eased back into the saddle, she clasped
him about the waist and they headed back for Point-à-Pitre.

Eugénie Lanzerac was not surprised when she saw her husband
ride up with their dear friend mounted behind, nor was she shaken
by the burning of the Vauclain plantation, the murder of its owner
and the decision of the widow to join the rebels. "These are dreadful times," she told Solange consolingly, and in succeeding days each
helped the other during shortages of provisions or attacks by the
enemy. The town was in a state of siege, and on days when Paul led
a detachment of his cavalry out to forage for extra food, the two
women, each twenty-one and mature, stood at the doorway to their
house and bade him farewell and Godspeed. When he returned
safely, it would have been impossible to detect which woman greeted
him with greater affection or uttered the more sincere prayers.

But when one of Paul's three companions was wounded during a
sortie, both Paul and Eugénie were in for a surprise when the next
excursion set forth, because on the wounded man's horse rode Solange, ready for the chase east. No one, not Eugénie or Paul or the
other two horsemen, made comment; she was a creole woman, a
daughter of the island, and her people needed sustenance. When she
rode back with the men in late afternoon, Eugénie helped her down
from her horse and embraced her.

In the difficult days that followed, Solange rode regularly with the
three men, and once as they came over a slight rise and saw a hedge-
row composed of the glorious flowers of Guadeloupe, she cried:
"Paul, this is an island worth saving!" and they swore to do just that.
During such forays, one of the riders, son of a sugar factor, fell obvi-

ously in love with this gallant young woman; he could not take his eyes off her golden-brown face and he spoke admiringly of her daring horsemanship. She knew well what was happening on their long rides, for he rode near her to protect her and lent her his horse when hers tired, but she could not find it in her heart to reciprocate his affection. Her attention was now, as it had ever been, on Paul Lanzerac, and after the other horseman had been rebuffed half a dozen times, he said to her one day: "You're in love with him. Aren't you?" but she made no reply. However, on subsequent days the would-be suitor rode with the other men, and they watched as Solange and Paul galloped across the countryside, taking great risks and escaping danger primarily because they were superb riders.

One afternoon when they came home exhausted, drooping in their saddles, the waning sun on their faces, Eugénie met them at the gate and thought: They are so handsome. As if they had been made for each other. But this obvious fact did not disturb the friendship, because when Eugénie appeared that night at supper with her baby son, Jean-Baptiste, tucked in motherly fashion under her left arm while she ladled up soup with her right, Solange thought: She is so much the mistress of a home, so much the mother. And Solange's own participation in this curious arrangement remained on an even keel.

Then in early 1794, when distant Paris was caught in a vortex of terror, when one after another of the bloody leaders was executed— Hébert, Chaumette, Cloots, Danton, Desmoulins, each dead with a hundred crimes on his hands, a thousand corpses—a minor terror of its own kind was about to strike Guadeloupe, but it appeared first in the guise of salvation from a most unexpected quarter.

When it seemed that the rebellious slaves and their mulatto leaders were about to overwhelm the beleaguered town, a small flotilla of ships appeared in the harbor, and a watchman shouted: "My God! They're British!" Paul Lanzerac and two other daring men leaped into a rowboat, and ignoring the danger that they might be fired upon by the sailors, pulled right under the bow of the lead ship, and cried: "We're Royalists! The slaves are besieging us!"

The admiral in charge of the invasion force was a man from Barbados, a Hector Oldmixon whose great-grandfather had been a Royalist in his day, though in the English cause, and he was not a man to tolerate foolishness from slaves. When Lanzerac was hauled on deck, he listened to the Frenchman's story and growled: "There's nothing more infamous on this earth than the doctrine that niggers have souls. Equality, sir, will be the destruction of great nations. Now, how can we best get ashore on your island?"

Since Paul loved the daughter of a slave and appreciated the qualities mulattoes could have, he was antagonized by Oldmixon's crude dismissal of anyone with color, but could not forget that in the recent rioting, mulattoes had sided with slaves against the whites. Maybe the English rule as exemplified in nearby Barbados was correct— "White with black, a forbidden mix"—while the French willingness to accept if not encourage such liaisons might be a mistaken policy. But he could not abide Oldmixon; the man was insufferable, seeming to take delight in lording it over the French, whom he apparently despised, but he was the potential savior of the island and therefore had to be accepted.

For these tangled reasons, Paul Lanzerac, a Frenchman of such devotion to his native land that he wept when he heard of the disasters overtaking it, was constrained to help a British naval force capture both wings of the Guadeloupe butterfly. The occupation was made without much loss of life, since at Point-à-Pitre, Paul and his associates welcomed the British sailors, while at Basse-Terre the opposition was minimal. Within two weeks the island was secure.

A curious event happened when the British army units that came ashore early in the battle marched inland from Point-à-Pitre to subdue the last of the slaves; when they thought they had the rebels penned into their final redoubt, they found to their astonishment that it was commanded by a ferocious woman whom spies identified as the widow of the murdered French planter Philippe Vauclaín. Hearing of this preposterous affair, Admiral Oldmixon rode up on a horse provided him by Paul Lanzerac and demanded of his men: "What in hell goes on here?" and they explained: "There's an old black woman in there, every time we arrange a truce because they don't have a chance . . . you can see that . . . she starts the fight again."

Oldmixon was outraged. A blustery type to whom everything not authentically English was anathema, even his fortuitous French allies here on the island, he was not about to allow a slave woman, and an elderly one at that, to hold up his occupation of Guadeloupe, so he bellowed at his men: "Storm that plantation and shoot the old bitch," but at this moment young Lanzerac, having heard of the impasse, galloped up, shouting: "No! No!" and when he dismounted before the irate Englishmen he said: "You can't. She's the widow of a white man and the mother of a trusted friend."

"Whatcha sayin', Frenchie?" Oldmixon snapped, and Paul assured him that this was true. "I'll go in and bring her out," and laying aside all arms and extending his two hands, palms open, before him, he walked slowly toward the plantation house, saying in a pleading voice: "I'm Solange's friend. She sent me. I'm your daughter's friend. She sent me," and as he came nearer he thought: She's Grandmère Lanzerac come back to life . . . same thing . . . same courage against the English. And when at last he entered the house and saw her and the few remaining slaves ranged against the wall, their guns lowered, he repeated: "I'm your daughter's friend. The one who rescued Solange that day." From the window where she still stood erect, holding her own gun, she said in a low voice, speaking perfect French: "Then you're Lanzerac? Why didn't you marry her?" He said nothing as he led her to where Admiral Oldmixon waited.

"Throw her into jail," the Barbadian said, and despite the most fervent pleas from Paul and Eugénie and Solange when they had Oldmixon to supper that night, he persisted, because, as he said: "She was once a slave, and she'll never forget it. Can't beat the urge for freedom out of 'em. Rebel once, rebel always." But as the night waned, Paul noticed that Oldmixon kept his eye always on Solange, and when the Englishman left the house to return to his ship he said at the gate: "That girl, if only she was white, what a beauty!"

During the occupation the Lanzeracs repeatedly invited Oldmixon, as leader of the superior force on the island, to dine with them. He rightly suspected that they did this mainly because he could bring rations of scarce meat for their meals, but even so, he enjoyed the companionship of intelligent people and an opportunity to refresh his considerable mastery of French. "My goodness, you do handle the language beautifully," he told Solange one night, and she replied: "Small wonder, seeing that my father was from Calais."

"Indeed! A sailor perhaps?"

"His father was. He feared the sea," and Oldmixon said: "So did I, but me father beat me over the head with a stool and said: 'It's the navy for you, me hearty,' and here I am, commander of an island which I've captured for the king."

During his frequent visits to the Lanzeracs' he was increasingly attracted to Solange but equally determined not to surrender to the girl's pleas that her mother be released from jail: "Sorry, my dear, but we can't run the risk of her runnin' wild again." However, as the weeks passed, while he became lonelier and she more attractive, he intimated that if Solange wished to move into his cabin on the ship, something might be arranged regarding her mother, and to the amazement of the Lanzeracs, he made this proposal not to Solange herself but to them. Paul considered the suggestion indecent, and as soon as Oldmixon left for his ship he told his wife so. But against her better judgment Eugénie, after putting her son to bed, sent Paul from the room and talked frankly with her companion.

"Solange, your mother will die in jail, and I want to see her freed."

"So do I."

"Admiral Oldmixon told us to tell you . . . if you'll . . . if you wanted to stay aboard his ship till the fleet leaves . . ."

Solange was sitting in a chair near the fireplace when Eugénie said this, and for a long time, while light from the fire shone on her handsome face, outlining its bony structure, she said nothing. Then, laughing almost irreverently, she said: "You know the four rules they teach us mulatto girls? First, attract a white man. Second, make him happy enough to marry you. Third, when you have a daughter by him, see that she too marries a white man. Move up, always move up, and make the family whiter."

"But Oldmixon would never marry you," Eugénie said, and Solange burst into laughter: "Then we bring in the fourth rule. Take every franc the poor fool has." But then her face grew grave and she looked long and deep into her friend's eyes. "We never intended the rules to apply to us, did we?" she whispered. For a long time they sat together, sadly silent, until Eugénie went to join her husband.

"Solange won't be going to the admiral's ship," and Paul replied: "I was sure she wouldn't."

During these momentous years when France struggled through the death throes of an ancient regime without finding a way to forge a new, the historic island of Hispaniola, where Columbus once ruled and where he was buried, was divided in curious ways—the result of a decision made almost a century earlier. The rather flat, unproductive eastern portion, Santo Domingo, was Spanish; the mountainous western part, St.-Domingue,* was French. Eastern spoke Spanish, western French; eastern, whose fine, flat lands might have been ex-

*Sahn-*doh*-mong: with the last letter pronounced something between a *g* and a nasal *h*.

pected to produce bounteous crops, yielded little, while the rough and difficult lands of the west produced the world's most valuable sugar crop; and, in some ways most important of all, Santo Domingo was populated with Spanish mulattoes, St.-Domingue with such an abundance of African slaves that at times it seemed an all-black colony.

In the still-orderly year of 1783, in a small town in the French portion of the island a barbershop of mean dimension was operated in a grudging manner by a young Frenchman who seemed designed by both birth and development to be a prototype of the world's average man, for he lacked any outstanding feature that would have distinguished him from the general mob. Victor Hugues (last name OO-geh) was then twenty-one, reputedly the son of petty merchants in Marseilles, but there was some confusion about this because he had an olive complexion, neither white nor mulatto but halfway between, and regardless of where he went, the rumor spread: "Hugues is part African. His mother must have been careless, Marseilles being a port town and all that."

He was of average height or slightly under, and of average weight or just a bit over. He had good teeth except for one missing on the left, a ratty type of hair of no distinct color, and a habit of staying off to one side and watching to see how an argument was proceeding, then suddenly intervening with great vigor and some skill in haranguing those opposed to the side he had arbitrarily taken. He did not read much, but he listened with the acute skill of a preying animal, and one thing was certain above all others: he was brave, always willing to flail about when debate descended into blows, and if he lost one tooth in such brawling, his opponents lost mouthfuls. He was a fearful adversary, and would allow nothing to stand in his way.

How had he wound up in a St.-Domingue barbershop? Early in his life his parents had given up trying to make anything decent of him, and he had responded by slipping down to the Marseilles docks and offering himself to the first ship heading anywhere. Since it was destined for Mexico, he went there, and at age seventeen was doing the waterfront work of a man. Later he drifted to various exotic ports of the Caribbean, but regardless of where he went or in what capacity, he manifested the only characteristic that made those around him take notice: early in life he had developed an insatiable hunger to be with girls, and he had taken the first one to bed when he was eleven. In the Caribbean his appetite reached ravenous proportions: Mexican alley girls, a ship captain's daughter at Porto Bello, a serving girl in Jamaica, a young Englishman's newly wedded wife in Barbados, and others wherever his ship docked.

Despite this fevered activity he was not a traditional roué who treated his conquests with contempt; he adored women, respected them, and let them know that he considered them individually and as a group the best part of life; few women he had known remembered him with animosity. Yet there was a darker side to his passion, one which could produce wildly aberrational behavior at the end of an affair, and some of his women mysteriously disappeared from the community.

His ownership of the barbershop in St. Domingue had come about because of this combination of rhapsodic pleasure and murderous opportunism, for when he arrived in Port-au-Prince a near-penniless youth of nineteen, he chanced to fall in with a mulatto who had both a barbershop and a young wife of exquisite amber coloring. Imploring the barber to teach him the skills of that trade, he spent much time with the barber's wife and, perhaps by coincidence, just as Victor mastered the profession of cutting hair, the barber vanished and after a decent interval Hugues appropriated both the shop and the widow.

This fortuitous disappearance occurred in 1785, and for the next two years Hugues ran a profitable barbering establishment, cutting the hair of white plantation owners who ran St.-Domingue and of the few mulattoes of marked ability who assisted them. Blacks, who comprised nine-tenths of the population, were forbidden entrance to the shop, though some later testified that: "At night, when the whites and mulattoes were not around, Victor invited any free blacks who had the money to come to a back door which led to an inner room, and there Hugues would cut their hair. He always had a great affinity for blacks, especially the former slaves, for he told me once: 'They are the dispossessed of the world and merit our charity.'"

He manifested this concern in dramatic fashion, for in that year he closed his barbershop, rented a large house in Port-au-Prince, and, with the help of the beautiful mulatto he had inherited, opened a first-class brothel, employing six girls of varied color and from four different islands. His clientele was ostensibly restricted to white plantation owners and mulattoes of importance, but again, when no one was looking too closely, he opened a rear door to admit freed black men, and he continued doing so even after he had received warnings to stop, for as he told an official of the government: "I've been in all corners of this sea . . . all the islands . . . and it's destined to be an area in which men and women of every color live together freely."

Outraged by such revolutionary thought, the official dispatched a secret report to powers in the home office, which neatly summarized this dangerous man:

> In the capital city we have a former barber who now runs a fancy house of convenience, one Victor Hugues who says he is from Marseilles and claims to be of white parentage generations back, an assertion which his skin coloring might refute. He is of a rebellious and contentious nature, but what is more potentially dangerous, he advocates the rights of *noirs* and frequently speaks out against slavery. I recommend that you order your people to keep a close watch on this Victor Hugues.

This report reached Paris in November 1788, and a liberal spy in the office to which it was addressed made a copy for a fellow member of a private political club called the Jacobins, and it was in this oblique way that the barber-brothelkeeper came to the attention of Maximilien François Marie Isidore de Robespierre, a member of the French gentry and a revolutionary whose ideas were germinating at a fantastic rate.

In early 1789, when affairs in France were at a boil, Robespierre began thinking about the colonies, especially St.-Domingue, which associates assured him was "the greatest producer of wealth in the entire French system." Appointing a study committee of fellow Jacobins to advise on how the colonies should be handled if a revolutionary form of government ever attained power, he suddenly remembered this barber out in St.-Domingue and sent him a message: "Come to Paris. I require your presence on important matters."

When Hugues arrived in June 1789 he could not locate Robespierre, but one of that leader's friends, knowing of the invitation, introduced the newcomer to a powerful philosophical club, the Société des Amis de Noirs, whose revolutionary thinkers were delighted to find someone who had firsthand knowledge of the colonies and the problems related to slavery. Hugues was lionized, gave a series of explanatory speeches, proved himself to be at least as advanced in his practical thinking as they were in their speculative analyses, and marched with them on 14 July 1789 when they celebrated the fall of the Bastille. Late that night, when he finally went to bed with a young woman who had marched beside him screaming at the police, he told her in tired, almost dreamlike sentences: "It was fated that I should come to Paris. Great things are about to happen and men like me will be needed."

His prediction came true dramatically, for when he finally did meet Robespierre, then on his bloody ladder to ascendancy, the fiery leader embraced him almost as an equal. And when the new government which had replaced King Louis XVI, the Legislative Assembly, decided to send a French army to St.-Domingue to pacify an island disturbance which threatened to interrupt the orderly flow of sugar to European markets, Hugues was asked to brief the commissioner who would be taking the troops to the island. He submitted such a perceptive oral report that the leaders of the government heard about it and marked him for preferment:

"General Commissioner, you'll find three nations in St.-Domingue. The white French, who have all the apparent power; the mulattoes, who hope to inherit it if the French leave; and the blacks, who could possess it if they can ever organize themselves. No matter how large a French army you call in to help you, you'll never have enough soldiers if you ally yourself only with the whites. If you can arrange a union of interest between the whites and mulattoes, you might achieve . . . well, at best perhaps a temporary truce.

"But if you want a long-range peace in that island which I know so intimately, it must be based fundamentally on the blacks, with concessions to both the other groups. Failing that, I see only continued revolution in the years ahead, especially when the island hears about what's happening here in France."

The commissioner asked: "Couldn't a union of white interest, mulattoes and a determined French army preserve peace and keep the sugar flowing?" and Hugues said impatiently: "You'd never have an army big enough . . . or healthy enough. These are hot lands, Commissioner, and fever knocks down more men than bullets do."

The commissioner did not appreciate such advice, and after Hugues had left the room he said to an aide: "What could you expect from a barber who runs a whorehouse? Probably got his ideas about black power from some African slave he'd been sleeping with."

After this rebuff Hugues remained in shadows, living on the few coins he could scrounge from his revolutionary friends, but after January 1793, when the king was beheaded and terror began to grip the boulevards, his peculiar talents were recognized by Robespierre, who assigned him the job of whipping into line the smaller towns surrounding Paris. Then the barber, reinforced by a traveling guillotine which could be disassembled and packed onto a small cart, had the opportunity of revealing a long-dormant aspect of his character: mercilessness. Showing no emotion and indulging in no personal display, this extremely ordinary man marched his grisly entourage from one little town to the next, following identical procedures, which he exhibited first in Brasse, some twenty miles southwest of Paris. Accompanied only by two officials in their tricorn hats, he halted at the edge of town his entourage of cart, two carpenters and the two constables, walked slowly into the rural town of seven hundred, and without making a great fuss, demanded to see the mayor: "Orders of the National Convention. I want everyone in your town assembled in the square immediately." And when this order was obeyed, he indicated that local spies who had been identified long before should aid the two constables in keeping the citizens together.

Then Hugues walked slowly back to where his other men waited, signaled to them, and they brought their creaking cart drawn by two oxen into the center of the square, where he directed them in the fascinating process of reassembling their guillotine. First the two towers were brought upright, the ones that would guide the dreadful knife in its fall, then the supporting structure to keep the towers erect, then the platform on which the condemned would kneel, then the curved part into which the neck would fit and the movable piece that would hold neck and shoulders firm, and lastly the big, shining knife itself, heavy and swift and final. A test drop using a head of cabbage having satisfied Hugues that the miraculous machine was in working order, he signaled for his spies to point out the wealthiest landowner in the district and any others who might be assumed to be enemies of the new regime, and these frightened people, women among them, were immediately segregated and placed under armed guard.

Then, with a speed which seemed incredible to the terrified watchers, Hugues said, in a low voice which only a few of the watchers could hear: "Let the accused be brought forward," and in these opening moments of his performance he always liked it best if the most powerful representative of the old regime was dragged before him, some petty

nobleman who had been ostentatious in the exercise of his prerogatives or some landowner fat from the produce of his many fields. On
this day he was pleased, for when he asked in his low, menacing voice:
"And who is this prisoner?" one of his spies shouted accusingly: "The
Compte Henri de Noailles!" and when Hugues continued: "And what
are the charges against him?" any impartial listener would have been
aghast at the meanness and lack of specificity as the count's accusers
poured forth their accumulation of petty grievances:

"He was always an enemy of the people."

"He let his pigs roam in my garden."

"He made us work on feast days and paid low wages."

Raising aloft both hands to stanch the flow of charges, Hugues
said in a sepulchral voice: "He is condemned!" and the quivering
wretch, too frightened to comprehend fully what was happening, was
dragged by the constables to the guillotine and up its three steps to
the fatal platform. There the carpenters took charge, bound his hands
behind his back, forced him onto his knees, and brought his head
forward so that his neck fitted into the curved portion of the block.
With a noisy creaking of wood against wood, the upper bar was
brought into play, pinning the neck fast. Then, slowly, one of the
carpenters cranked a windlass, dragging the immense slanted knife
high aloft in the twin grooves of the tower. When it was in position,
Hugues addressed the crowd: "This is the punishment that overtakes
all enemies of France," and with an upraising of his right hand he
signaled the carpenters to release the knife, which fell with silent
swiftness onto the exposed neck and with such awful force that the
head rolled away while the severed neck gushed blood.

In each small town he visited, Hugues liked to guillotine three
prominent citizens on the first day; he had learned that this brought
the whole area to attention and made his inquisition of the remainder easier, for each man was eager to testify against his neighbors
before they testified against him. His procedures, swift and remorseless and certain, caused two different reports concerning his work to
be sent to Robespierre:

> Hugues is a tyrant. He makes no pretense at a legal trial. He
> absolutely never finds innocent anyone charged hastily by lo-
> cals. And he leaves behind a sense of shock which may in time
> work against our general aims.

But a second report represented the majority of judgment on his work in the near provinces:

> The great virtue of the way Hugues conducts his raids, for that is what they are, is that he works swiftly, never postures to bring attention to himself, and appears so remorseless and inevitable that he seems to speak with the authority of the entire Convention. He sweeps in and out like some inevitable storm, leaving nothing to be angry at.
>
> He has only one weakness, but in time it could undo him. He seems to have an insatiable desire for women, and in town after town he grabs onto the first one available. He finishes his guillotine at dusk, eats a big dinner, and is in bed with some local lass an hour later. It is rumored that he wins their favors by threatening them with his guillotine if they do not comply, or equally effective, threatening the neck of their husband or son. One day someone may shoot him or pierce him with a rapier.

Robespierre read these reports in September 1793, and thought: How effectively the barber gives his haircuts. I do wish I had a dozen more like him in Lyons and Nantes. These were two strongholds of Royalists where shortly an appalling number of resisters would be slain in ways far less neat and effective than those utilized by Hugues and his traveling guillotine. Ten thousand would die in Lyons in mass murders of the wildest frenzy involving all sorts of excesses, fifteen thousand in Nantes while Hugues plodded along, methodically lopping off the heads of his eight and ten, day after day, with never an uprising in protest. "The man's a genius," Robespierre told his associates, and when in mid-October, Queen Marie Antoinette, that foolish, giddy thing, was to be beheaded, Hugues was invited back to Paris to participate in the celebrations that followed. It was during this holiday that Robespierre intimated to him that a more important assignment was in the offing. Since he did not say what, Hugues returned to his deadly travels and lovemaking, assured that his efforts toward freedom were appreciated in Paris. Then, at the close of that frightful year, came the communication he had been awaiting:

> Citizen Hugues, in the revered name of the Cult of Reason you are ordered to proceed immediately to the Port of Rochefort, assume command of the ships and troops assembled

there and sail to our Island of Guadeloupe, where you will serve as Agent Particulier, our Commissioner in Charge, with one responsibility. See that this island remains in French hands. Your exemplary work in the environs of Paris satisfies us that you are equal to this important promotion.

Repairing at once to Rochefort, a tiny Atlantic harbor on the Atlantic between Nantes in the north and Bordeaux to the south, Hugues learned to his disgust that his supposed fleet consisted of two overage frigates, a corvette, two small vessels and two lumbering cargo ships with exactly 1,153 poorly trained farmers as troops. When he complained, the harbormaster assured him: "Not to worry. Ship arrived last week from Guadeloupe. Island's safe in our hands. All you have to do is reinforce our ships and troops already in command."

The harbormaster was right; so were the officers from the trading ship recently arrived from Guadeloupe, for when they left their island it was still French. What they could not know was that shortly after they sailed, Admiral Oldmixon leading a strong British force had stormed ashore, captured the island, and dug powerful emplacements for his guns and fortifications for his thousands of hardened troops. The St.-Domingue barber and brothelkeeper was heading into a hornet's nest of which he was totally unaware.

Nevertheless, he was nervous, for a cart which he had dispatched from Paris well before he left had not yet arrived, and it looked as if he might have to sail without this precious cargo. "Can we delay two more days?" he pleaded with the captains of his ships, but they said, properly: "Our job is to avoid British warships. We sail as planned." To Hugues' relief, at dawn on the last day the big cart rumbled onto the dock to deliver its seven crudely wrapped packages.

There was much speculation as to what kind of precious cargo might have warranted such concern, and the sailors who struggled to bring the items aboard made many guesses, until one farm boy, more daring than the rest, furtively tore open the end of one package and found himself facing an immense steel blade.

"Mon Dieu!" he whispered. "A guillotine."

It would be difficult to guess who was the more astonished that bright June day—Hugues, who found his island occupied by the enemy, or Oldmixon, who saw this ragtag armada heading his way to do battle.

The odds in favor of the English were overwhelming: at sea, some twenty battle-tested ships against seven nondescripts; on land, 10,000 men against 1,153, plus control of the civil government thanks to the cooperation of Royalists like Paul Lanzerac. Of course, Oldmixon could not summon all his ships at once and many detachments of his troops were scattered among lesser islands, but the force confronting Hugues was not merely intimidating, it was terrifying.

Too uninformed on warfare to realize that he had no chance of winning, Hugues ordered his little ships to clear the harbor, which amazingly they did, whereupon he led his troops ashore in a charge three times as valiant as Oldmixon had ever seen before, and after unbelievable heroics the Hugues forces had recaptured that half of the island. An English colonel said later: "This French barber who had never read a book on tactics was too stupid to know he couldn't win, so he won."

The first thing Hugues did on taking possession of Point-à-Pitre was to draft a report to the Convention back in Paris. In it he described himself as ten times braver than he had been, which was brave enough, and the message was so inspiring that the authorities caused it to be published in a Paris broadsheet illustrated with a fine woodcut showing Hugues, saber in hand, leading a charge into the very muzzles of the British guns. It was entitled: SANGFROID INTRÉPIDE DE VICTOR HUGUES, COMMISSAIRE DU GOUVERNEMENT Á LA GUADELOUPE.

On 16 Floreal of the year 2 of the Revolution the brave Victor Hugues led his valiant Frenchmen against horrendous odds. Though there was no hope of victory, Hugues and his men fought like lions, but they were overwhelmed. At the moment of maximum peril an English voice was heard to shout: "Surrender!" but the ever-brave Victor Hugues cried back immediately: "No! We will defend ourselves to the death!" It was this admirable response that enabled the French under the gallant leadership of the masterful Victor Hugues to recapture Guadeloupe from the English invaders and return it to the Glory of France. Brave Victor Hugues!

Both English and French reporters testified that Hugues actually did these things; with his few Frenchmen he defeated an enormously superior enemy, but in one statement his admirers were wrong: he did not *charge ashore*. When the battle was over he *walked ashore* like some great, detached conqueror humble in victory and weighed down by his responsibilities as Agent Particulier. Retreating quickly to his anonymous look and posture, he represented to the citizens of Point-à-Pitre the picture of an undistinguished Frenchman of thirty-two, slightly overweight, slightly shorter than they might have expected in a conqueror, with a kind of sandy hair, pocked face, very thin legs, long arms and hooded eyes which kept darting about as if to intercept any would-be assassin.

By the time he came ashore, Hugues was overcome by an inner determination of tremendous force to be the revolutionary governor of this precious island that had strayed so far from principles which now governed France. And the citizenry of Point-à-Pitre would have been terrified had they realized what the seven huge packages he had brought with him contained.

His men started unloading the packages at two in the afternoon, lugging each piece to the sunlit square in front of the House of Lace, and while this was being done Hugues was following the routine which had served him so well in the little towns around Paris. Assembling the island's revolutionary spies, he inspected their lists of Royalist names, flicked them with an official tick of his right forefinger, and said: "Arrest them all." But before the men could go about their task, aided by armed sailors, he asked: "And who is the banker? The richest plantation owner?" and when they were identified, he said. "Be sure to fetch them. And who has been the most outstanding Royalist?" and when this was agreed upon among the spies, he said: "That one we want for sure."

At about a quarter to five that first afternoon the guillotine was placed at the center of the square, and when practice drops of the great knife proved its good working order, an awful hush fell over the crowd of watchers, for prior to this they had only heard of this monstrous machine as it operated in distant Paris and had never dreamed that it might one day appear on their island.

"You must hurry," a local spy warned Hugues. "There's no twilight here in the tropics. Six o'clock it's night, just like that."

"I know, I know," Hugues retorted, but added: "You'll see. This will be a twilight to remember. All we need, fifteen, sixteen minutes," and he signaled for the first batch of prisoners to be brought forward. When they were, Solange Vauclain, watching from a spot not far from Hugues, uttered such an agonized cry that he had to turn to see where it came from, and he looked into the eyes of the most dazzling woman he had seen in many months: tall, face like a Raphael Madonna, graceful even in the way she brought her two hands to her chin in horror at what she was seeing, and gifted with that rare quality that makes men hesitate and look a second time.

"Who is that one?" Hugues asked, and a mulatto, who had participated in the earlier riots but who had now turned spy for the revolutionaries, whispered: "Name's Solange. Daughter of a white planter the rebels killed and that black woman you just released from jail."

"And why did this Solange cry out?" and the spy whispered: "Because she grew up with those two," and he pointed to where Paul and Eugénie Lanzerac stood among the first group to be executed, and it seems preposterous to say, but in the very instant when this cold, bloodthirsty man saw the Lanzerac woman, more desirable in her peculiar French way than even Solange, his warped mind devised a battle plan: he would have both these women.

A sailor from the ships beat out a drum roll, an assistant to Commissioner Hugues lifted a sheet of paper closer to his eyes and read: "Plantation owner Philippe Joubert, you have stolen sugar that belonged to the people, you have mistreated your slaves, and you have declared yourself an enemy of the Revolution. You are condemned to death." And the terrified man was dragged to the well-used platform, brought to his knees, and strapped into the neck restraint. The drum sounded, almost softly, the sun sank lower in its own swift descent, and down came the knife in its awful rush, striking the exposed neck with such a powerful slicing force that Joubert's head rolled into the street, where a sailor lifted it from the paving blocks and tossed it into a basket.

"Paul Lanzerac," the man with the list shouted, and two sailors rushed him to the execution area. He was twenty-four that June evening, recipient of the best education that France provided, and possessor of a mind and character and the kind of precious talent that would have proved invaluable to the nation. Yet here he stood, listening to the charges against him: "You have tried to defeat the Revolution by bringing a new and foolish king to the throne. You have mistreated slaves and you have misused public property. You are condemned to death!" And brutal hands dragged him up onto the platform and fixed the wooden frame about his shoulders.

But before the deadly knife could fall, Solange uttered another scream, broke through the ranks of sailors protecting the execution area, and sped to the guillotine, where she threw her arms about the imprisoned head and showered its lips with the kisses she had been denied during the years she had loved the prisoner. The sailors would have dragged her away contemptuously had not Victor Hugues, executioner extraordinary, held up his hand: "Let her say farewell," and the hushed crowd heard her cry: "Paul, we have always loved you." Hugues realized that these were strange words, but he also knew that she spoke for the town and all of Guadeloupe, and that since they loved this brilliant young man, it was even more imperative that he be removed with theatrical effect.

"Take her away," he said without any ugliness in his voice, and when this was done, he gave the signal, the knife fell, and the fairest head in the islands rolled on the cobblestones.

Now came a series of sharp commands, and Eugénie Lanzerac was hauled forth, the list of crimes her dead father was supposed to have committed was read, and she was thrown down upon the boards leading to the neck restraint. But now a real dilemma developed, for Solange, numbed from watching the death of Paul Lanzerac, simply could not allow her dearest and truest friend to be executed, so she broke free, clambered onto the platform, and threw herself upon Eugénie's prostrate body with the cry: "Take me, not her," and she clung so tightly that she could not be dislodged and something drastic had to be done.

The mechanics working the guillotine looked at the chief executioner as if to ask: "Shall we let the knife fall?" and Hugues, almost automatically, said: "Stay the knife. Release them," and the men tending the rope that would free the blade for its terrible descent asked: "Free both of them?" and Hugues said: "Yes."

Before natural darkness possessed the beautiful square, moral darkness obscured the place, for in rapid-fire order the three young horsemen who had accompanied Paul and Solange on their excursions into the countryside were dragged to the execution block and strapped down to greet the fall of the hideous blade. By nightfall, when the five executions of the first round were completed, with the basket of heads left at the foot of the guillotine for the townsmen to see, Hugues complimented the men who had conducted the brief trials and efficient executions, issued orders for the next series on the morrow, and announced quietly, "I'll take that one," and he pointed to the House of Lace, from which Eugénie was summarily evicted, while her husband's executioner moved in with a young white woman who accompanied him in obedience to orders delivered by one of his assistants: "Attend Citizen Hugues or you'll be next on his machine."

The four years of the Hugues dictatorship, 1794–1798, were marked by extreme brutality, excellent statesmanship, liberal social legislation far ahead of its time, and the dictator's incessant chasing after women.

He conducted his extirpation of the upper class rapidly and effectively. He hauled his portable guillotine into all corners of the populous eastern wing of the island, erected it at central points to which he summoned anyone with wealth, land, slaves or suspected Royalist tendencies and chopped off their heads in public displays that became something like sporting events or rural celebrations.

A hundred leaders died in this manner in the first weeks, seven hundred by the end of the first year, and finally, more than a thousand of the island's finest citizens, the ones on whom the future of Guadeloupe would have depended. All vanished, their heads in baskets, and when that mode of execution proved too cumbersome, they were lined up in tens and scores and shot.

Since it was too difficult to lug the guillotine to the western wing of the gold-green butterfly, executions there took not only the form of mass shootings but also public hangings, with the rabble cheering as their so-called betters danced wildly in the air, and there were outbursts of vengeance in which clubs and rakes and pitchforks were utilized. This half of the island also suffered an almost complete depopulation of its leaders, including priests and nuns who had represented and defended the old regime. Never did the killing wane while Hugues was Commissioner.

His lust for savage revenge knew no rational bounds and was sometimes carried to ridiculous extremes, as with the body of General Thomas Dundas. In the months just before Hugues' arrival, when the English captured the island, the ground troops supporting Admiral Oldmixon had been commanded by a gallant officer of illustrious reputation, Major General Thomas Dundas, scion of a Scottish family whose numerous sons had illuminated the history of both Scotland and Ireland. Among members of the family were: Baron Amesbury, Lord Arniston, Viscount Melville, let alone the many generals, lord chief justices and other honored positions that normally fall to the members of a great and distinguished family.

Major General Dundas was no military flunky, but despite his careful upbringing, or perhaps because of it, he had acquired the harrumphing, no-nonsense, teach-'em-their-place superior attitude of a Scottish country gentleman. At any rate, any human being with a drop of color in his blood or skin which betrayed "a touch of the tarbrush" was both beneath contempt and outside the law so far as Dundas was concerned. How ironic it was, therefore, that a few short months after his triumphal conquest of Guadeloupe he fell victim to a disease and died surrounded by black and mulatto nurses who did their best to cool his fevers.

He was buried in the islands, his grave marked by a small stone bearing an inscription in English which informed the world that here rested a gallant British hero, but when Victor Hugues came upon the stone following his occupation of the island, he flew into a blind fury and issued a proclamation, which said:

Liberté, Égalité, Droit et Fraternité. It is resolved that the body of Thomas Dundas, interred in Guadeloupe, be dug up and given as prey to the birds of the air; and upon that spot shall be erected, at the expense of the Republic, a monument having on the one side this decree and on the other an appropriate inscription.

Forthwith, the corpse of the British hero was disinterred, hung up for the birds to pluck, and then thrown into the public sewer. A stonemason from one of the French ships was brought ashore to incise a monument which contained on one side the above condemnation and on the other these words:

This ground, restored to Liberty by the valour of the Republicans, was polluted by the body of Thomas Dundas, Major General and Governor of Guadeloupe for the Bloody King George the Third of England.

Hugues himself had composed the second inscription, for, as he explained to his citizens: "All honest men deplore the cruel acts of the infamous English king."

His worst actions were incomprehensible, explicable neither as acts of revenge nor of sadism; his was dark behavior dredged up from the hidden abysses of the days when humans were emerging from a brutal animal existence. During one heated action when two hundred and fifty British troops were supported by three hundred French Royalists who despised Hugues, the latter demonstrated once again his military genius, for with an inferior force he attacked from three sides, overwhelming the enemy. To the British soldiers he acted with the formality of a great general, allowing them to retreat in honor, sword in hand, to their main army, but for the French Royalists he had much different plans. After throwing them all into a prison camp, along with wives and children, he trundled up his portable guillotine, erected it personally inside the gate of the camp, and started lopping off heads at a rate which stunned those who assisted in the grisly rite. Scarcely had the bleeding trunk of one man been tossed off the platform and into a growing pile than the neck of another was thrust beneath the blade.

But even though he was able at this frantic speed to behead fifty in the space of an hour, he was not satisfied, so he ordered the remaining men, women and children to be fettered together in twos and threes and marched to the edge of a pit, where they were shot by untrained woodsmen firing at random. Some of the Royalists were killed outright, some were wounded, and some escaped the chance firing altogether, but at a signal from Hugues all were pitched alike into the pit, where men shoveled earth upon them, burying alive all who had survived the bullets, their screams for mercy going unheeded.

Despite the sadism, he was sincerely desirous of attaining order at home. As any good politician must, he gave the island an excellent administration, doubling its production of sugar and rum, producing food in abundance where there had been shortages before he arrived, eliminating useless and expensive jobs, and introducing an effective creole police force which served well, once most of the French-born whites had been slain.

He also had what might be called a foreign policy, for, having put his own island in order, he decided to export his revolution to others, and his small, swift boats sneaked past big British warships to invade and capture All Saints, Grenada and Tobago, in each of which he inspired slaves to take arms against their masters. Having accomplished this, he sent his secret agents throughout the Caribbean, fomenting slave rebellions against French, English and Spanish plantation owners.

His most extraordinary international adventure was a kind of declaration of war against the newly born United States, for which he had generated a savage contempt: "Look at them. Ten years ago they were fighting the English, and if it hadn't been for French help, they'd have been crushed. Now they sell supplies to those same British who try to defeat us." He ordered his small but capable navy to capture any American vessel that came into the Caribbean, and succeeded in taking nearly a hundred prizes. One American admiral said of him: "He's a pest, but have you ever tried to rid yourself of those invisible gnats that attack you on warm summer nights?" and he added ruefully: "The dirty bastard knows how to use what he's got."

One of the international moves he made that produced excellent results was his encouragement of Dutch contraband shipping, for, as in centuries past, the Dutch were the imaginative operators in the Caribbean. Having only the smallest islands of their own, they insinuated their ships into the major ones, scorning local laws against them and bringing to places like Barbados, Jamaica, Trinidad and Cartagena the trade goods so badly needed. "An honest Dutch pirate," Hugues said, "is a man of endless value."

One night while he was haranguing a group of junior administrators, mulatto and black, he cried with great enthusiasm: "I dream not of victory here in Guadeloupe or in British Barbados, but of the day when the kind of benevolent French rule we have introduced here will extend to all islands in the Caribbean. Not only in St.-Domingue and on Martinique, which we already have, but on Jamaica too, and Trinidad and all the Virgins. Above all, Cuba. One government, one language, all guided spiritually by our Cult of Reason."

He returned often to explain this vision to others: "This glorious sea—you know I've been in all parts of it—it must be ruled by one power. Spain had her opportunity and threw it away. England might have succeeded but she lost energy. Those American colonies, they'll try someday. But the people who have the best claim, the most appropriate concepts are we French. This ought to be a French sea, and it shall be."

Basic to this idea of a French hegemony was his conviction that the French understood better than any other European nation the fundamental strength of the black man in the Caribbean: "Look what we've accomplished already in Guadeloupe. First thing I did on landing was abolish slavery. It's a dead idea. It wastes human energy. And I've also put an end to social systems which held back mulattoes. If white men are extra intelligent and black men are extra strong, why not unite them? Raise a new race of gods. There'll be no white owner, no black slave on an island I govern."

And he did exactly what he preached, for he told the blacks: "You're no longer slaves. That's ended forever. But you're not wastrels either. You work or you go to jail. And I warn you, there's damned little food to spare for prisoners." Through this enlightened leadership he coaxed the blacks into producing more than they ever had before and without constant exhortation or beatings.

He attended also to lesser problems, erasing those petty restrictions on mulattoes and blacks which were so galling and productive of animosities. He wanted all children to enjoy a free education and he emptied the jails of prisoners who were not white. Eager to prove that former slaves could hold positions formerly held by whites only, he was constantly on the search for capable blacks, and when Solange's mother came out of jail during the dispensation, he spotted her as one with governing ability and installed her as a kind of aide, and from this position she was able to save from the guillotine several Frenchmen who had behaved themselves respectably in the treatment of their slaves.

He was a brilliant politician, no doubt about that, but midway in his commissionership certain of his acts caused observers to ask: "How sincere are the man's beliefs?" When he learned almost a year late that his friend and sponsor Robespierre had himself been guillotined, he immediately softened his revolutionary rantings, and after something called the Directory assumed control in Paris, he, without understanding a word of what it stood for, proclaimed himself a loud supporter. Watchers said: "Look how he's stopped appointing blacks to high positions. Mark my words, any day now, he'll bring slavery back."

Regardless of his successes or failures, Hugues would always be remembered in Guadeloupe for his traveling guillotine and wandering eye, and in the closing months of his regime the entire island watched in amusement as he became even more deeply entangled with the two young creoles, Eugénie Lanzerac and Solange Vauclain. What made his frenzied courtship diverting in a gruesome way was that everyone knew that since these two creoles had been in love with the murdered Paul Lanzerac, they must loathe Hugues and even pose a threat to him in their hunger for revenge.

He, too, was aware of this, but he savored the challenge of bringing them to his bed despite their bitterness, imagining himself to be like the hunch-backed Richard III of England, who found sexual delight in wooing the widow of the young king whom he had just caused to be slain.

His pursuit of the two women could have been played out as one of those delightful European comedies in which a pompous official from the capital swaggers into some Italian or Spanish or French country town, casts his lecherous eye on two comely housewives, and is made a laughingstock by their superior wit. But this master plot could not play in Pointe-à-Pitre because the scrawny Hugues was no fat Falstaff; he was an ogre with his own guillotine.

Finding Eugénie unapproachable, since she was preoccupied with mourning her dead husband and caring for her son, he turned to Solange, who, since the destruction of her family's plantation, lived in town with her freed mother, and the more often he saw her moving about the square, the more desirable she became in his fantasies. She was the epitome of those black and mulatto people he had rescued from oblivion; she represented his vision of the future when all the Caribbean islands would exist under what he interpreted as a benevolent French leadership, the tyrannical whites having been exterminated. Thus she became not only an extremely attractive young woman of beautiful face and exquisite movement, but she was also a kind of spiritual symbol of the new world that he was creating.

Of course, coincident with this growing infatuation with Solange, he was bringing to his bed at night an endless chain of whatever women he could inflict his hungry body upon, and some of the stratagems he devised to accomplish this were so wretched that they seemed antithetical to any normal concept of sexual passion. How could a man who spoke of loving a woman cause her husband to be guillotined on Tuesday and derive pleasure from forcing her into his bed at the House of Lace on Thursday? Hugues found no contradiction in such behavior, and he also applied pressure against children to bring their mothers to him and separated girls of fifteen from boys of sixteen who were striving to protect them. One observant Frenchman, an advocate of the revolution in France insofar as he understood it, wrote in a secret letter to Paris: "In your city they speak of a Reign of Terror. Here we whisper about a Reign of Horror, for all decency seems to have fled."

The recipient of this letter read it, snorted his disgust, and sent it back to Hugues with the notation: "Now you have a spy in your midst," and on the evening of its arrival in Guadeloupe, when the drumbeats rolled, the sender of the complaints was guillotined.

Hugues started his assault on Solange by promoting her black mother from a position as his aide to one which required her to work in his office, and when she was comfortably established, he made it plain that she would retain his favor only if she made it possible for him to see her daughter frequently. "You might invite her to help you here," he suggested, and she replied: "Solange is no longer under my control," and he said in tones that could not be misinterpreted: "She'd better be."

When Mme. Vauclain alerted her daughter, Solange said nothing; because of the barbarous conditions in Guadeloupe she was afraid to confide anything to her. Since her mother had been the recipient of the murderer's favor, she could very well have been enrolled as one of his spies, so she kept her counsel, but sometimes late at night she would slip into Eugénie's house to resume plotting with her only confidante.

"I had the strangest feeling yesterday, Eugénie. I was talking with my mother and she asked me a question . . . can't remember what it was . . . probing, though. And I warned myself: 'Better not tell her anything. She may be one of his spies.' " She looked down at the floor, then looked furtively about, for Hugues' spies were everywhere, but she had to share her bitterness with someone, so she continued: "That horrible man. We must go ahead."

Eugénie said quietly, but with even greater force than Solange had shown: "A knife, poison, a gun . . . but they're difficult to smuggle in. How did the Corday woman finish her tyrant? Drowning him in a bath or stabbing him when he was there?"*

Toward the end of 1797 the two women decided that since their prey was so eager to get Solange into his bed, she should mask her loathing and allow him to do so, but as Eugénie pointed out: "Only if you can do so . . . shall we say . . . on some kind of permanent basis." She hesitated: "So you'll have opportunities to do whatever we decide."

---

*The young women are referring to a case whose drama swept France and the colonies. Marie Anne Charlotte Corday d'Armont was of noble lineage but supportive of the more rational aspects of the Revolution. Appalled by the excesses of Jean Paul Marat, she posed as a news reporter, interviewed him while he was in his bath, gave him a list of suspected Royalists, and when he said: "We'll guillotine them all," she stabbed him to death and went herself to the guillotine.

"Oh no!" Solange protested. "Once I go there, I can never come here again, Eugénie. It would be too dangerous for you." Solange then looked at this precious friend who had been so helpful in their growing up, and said softly: "I could not bear losing you and Paul, both. This I must do by myself, but I shall do it," and she started to go, but Eugénie reached out for her hand, and for some time the two young women stood thus in the shadows of the apothecary's house.

"Did you love him so deeply . . . that you'll risk your life?" Eugénie asked, and Solange replied: "You're willing to risk yours," and Eugénie said sensibly: "Of course, but we were married," and the beautiful mulatto, even lovelier in the shadows, replied: "We were too, in another way. And Hugues must die for the great wrong he did us both." With this confession from the past and commitment to the future, the two creoles embraced for the last time, reconciled to the fact that if things went wrong, they might never see each other again, and as they parted in the darkness Eugénie whispered: "Rest easy, beloved sister. If you don't succeed, I shall."

In December 1797, Solange Vauclain moved into the House of Lace with the man she was determined to murder, and for some six weeks this grotesque love affair progressed. She dissembled her feelings so adeptly that Hugues felt the elation that any thirty-five-year-old man would feel at having won the affections of a beautiful twenty-four-year-old woman, but since he never underestimated his potential enemies, he told his spies: "Find out about this one," and they reported: "She hasn't seen her friend Eugénie Lanzerac since the execution. No danger there. She is, of course, the daughter of a French Royalist, now dead. Her mother could be trustworthy or not. You're the best judge of that."

There was more, but none of it added up to a serious suspicion of Solange except for the one irrefutable fact: "She was, at one time, you must always remember, in love with Lanzerac, but so far as we can determine, nothing came of it."

Lulled by such reports and assured that Solange was not seeing the Lanzerac widow, Hugues continued the affair, congratulating himself on having organized his living arrangements so amicably. One morning following a dinner party at which Solange had proved a radiant hostess, he even admitted to himself as he was shaving: She would grace any salon, that one. I get the feeling sometimes that she was made for Paris.

He spent the rest of that morning at his usual duties, including approval of the next batch of executions, then took his lunch with Solange on the balcony of his quarters, the House of Lace, overlooking the square. In the afternoon he and Solange went riding, and he was again impressed with the way she seemed to be able to do almost anything a gentlewoman should; he felt like an adoring husband as he watched her dismount, and kissed her ardently when inside the house which she had known so intimately when Paul and Eugénie occupied it.

Dusty from his ride, Hugues repaired to an upstairs room, to which former slaves brought buckets of hot water for his bath. When they were gone and he was luxuriating in the tin tub which he had brought from Paris, he heard a rustle at the door, and called out: "Is that you, Solange?" and she came slowly, purposefully into the room, holding extended before her a long, sharp knife. With extraordinary speed and deftness, he sprang from his bath, sidestepped her attack, and knocked the blade from her hand. Screaming in terror "Help! Assassins!" he cowered in a corner.

First into the bathroom was Mme. Vauclain, Solange's mother, who understood instantly what her daughter had attempted. "Ah! Girl!" she cried. "Why did you fail?" And she leaped upon Hugues, trying to wrest the knife from him and finish the job. Before she could do so, guards burst into the room and pinioned both women, while Hugues continued to moan: "They tried to kill me!" But as the women were being led away, Mme. Vauclain broke away from the guard, rushed to Solange, and embraced her: "You did right. Don't fear, the monster will be destroyed."

At high noon next day, his private guillotine having been moved into the lovely square, Victor Hugues watched as the African slave woman Jeanne Vauclain was led forth in chains, her face a mass of bruises from her interrogation by the guards, and dragged onto the execution platform. Thrown to her knees, she was locked into position, and the great knife fell. Moments later her exquisite daughter, slim and graceful as a young palm tree in a tropic breeze, was pushed up the three stairs to the platform and forced down till her neck was properly exposed, and again the knife fell.

This time the blade did not fall instantly, for Hugues felt he must issue a warning to his people: "See what happens when reactionary royalists seduce and mislead our mulattoes and blacks. These women were traitors to the cause of freedom, and for that they must die." Slowly he raised his hand to make this heroic point, held it aloft for a moment, then dropped it dramatically, and the knife roared downward in its sickening fall. Solange Vauclain, loveliest creole in her generation, was dead, and as her head rolled into the square her executioner looked across to the house of the apothecary, where Eugénie now lived, and saw that the Lanzerac widow had been watching.

With Solange out of the way, Hugues' pursuit of Eugénie became more concentrated, and although he could not reasonably expect her to move into his quarters, he did apply ingenious pressures to make her consider an alliance: "Madame Lanzerac, we need a new apothecary in the town, so it becomes inevitable that you must leave your home to others who will put it to better use."

When she asked: "Where shall I live?" he replied hesitantly: "'There's always room in your old home," but she professed not to understand what he was proposing.

Once, in extreme irritation, he reminded her: "You remember, of course, that on the night of our arrival you were sentenced to death? Spared only by my generosity. That sentence still hangs over you."

But still she repelled his suggestion, not masking the fact that she considered it odious. So he adopted harsher methods. One morning as she returned from her marketing at the far end of the square facing the ocean, she was greeted by a screaming woman: "Eugénie! They've stolen your boy!" and when she rushed to the room in which she had left him, she saw that he was gone.

In the anguished days that followed she received a bombardment of bewildering rumors, orchestrated by Hugues but never voiced by him, for he intended to step forward later as her savior: "The boy Jean-Baptiste was found dead!" and "The little Lanzerac boy was found in a marketplace near Basse-Terre." In this cruel broth he would let Eugénie stew until she became, in his words, "ready for my closer attention."

No longer having any woman friend to give her support, and with all the young Royalist men who might otherwise have helped executed, Eugénie had, in her almost paralyzing grief, no one to whom she could turn; even the priests who would have aided her had been guillotined in those first terrible days. She could, of course, do what many young women like her had done, seek assistance from generous-hearted slave women who now possessed power, but Mme. Vauclain was dead and Eugénie knew no one like her, so she huddled alone in her empty house and wondered when she would be dispossessed and forced to accept Hugues' hospitality.

The closer this eventuality came, the more certain she was that within a week of such a move, she would murder this dictator, even if she herself was guillotined the next morning: He must not be allowed to live, wallowing in his crimes, and this curious phrase became her shibboleth, the rubric that defined her. She would allow him to possess her over the dead bodies of her husband and son, but in achieving this triumph, he would be signing his death warrant. She, unlike Solange, would not let him see her coming at him with a knife. She would murder him as he lay beside her in his sleep.

But Hugues, more or less guessing her thoughts, confused the situation by sharing with her astonishing news: "You know, Eugénie," he said in the street one day, "if you shared my quarters, there might be some way of finding your son."

She did not raise her voice or charge him with being an inhuman monster for using a child, supposed to be dead, in this way, for she did not wish anyone to see her anger and remind Hugues of the perilous game he was playing. Instead, she asked quietly: "Commissioner, are you intimating that my son is alive?" and he said, with a carefully composed smile: "What I meant was, that under proper circumstances I could direct my men to search more closely."

As he left her to consider this persuasive offer, she remained in the square, staring after him as he entered her House of Lace, and each item of his ugly appearance she found more repulsive than the others: That grisly hair. That slouching walk. Those ridiculous pipe-stem legs, the shoes that look too big. Those long arms like in the pictures of monkeys, and the hands covered with blood. Comparing him with her memories of Paul, she felt faint to think that one so ill-favored should live and that Paul should be dead.

She was more determined than ever that Hugues must die, but the possibility that her son might be alive, and recoverable, forestalled her, and for some days she wandered Point-à-Pitre trying to resolve her dilemma. There was no solution. If Jean-Baptiste was alive, she too must stay alive to rear him, which meant that she must tolerate the only man who could restore her son, the unspeakable Hugues.

Resigning herself to the prospect of a life with Hugues that must end in murder, she went to him voluntarily: "Commissioner, I live only for my son. If your men can find him . . ."

"They already have," Hugues said, his hooded eyes sparkling with desire, and from an inner room a black maid appeared with Jean-Baptiste, four years old and each day a closer replica of his father. With a cry of "Maman!" he rushed into her arms, and Hugues smiled benevolently at the sight of this reconciliation of a boy who might one day be his adopted son and the mother who would soon be his mistress. Then, as she prepared to take Jean-Baptiste to her home across the square, he warned her: "Remember, Mme. Lanzerac, you are still under sentence of death."

Miraculously, an unexpected event occurred the next day which spared her from Hugues and removed the necessity for her to commit murder; a ship arrived from France with exciting news: "Napoleon's won victory after victory, and he's now heading for Egypt." A much less radical government was in control and its more sober members felt disgusted with Hugues, whom they were replacing with a new commissioner carrying surprising orders: "Send Hugues back to Paris under close arrest." By nightfall he was thrown out of his quarters and into a small cabin aboard the newly arrived ship.

When Hugues, defiant and undaunted, learned that the ship would require seven days to unload its cargo and take on the sugar and foodstuffs that Paris required, he demanded: "Give me pen and paper." And when his captors complied, for they knew him to be an important official, he sat in his cabin scratching unceasingly with his pen and composing a masterpiece. It ran to sixty pages and depicted the many miracles of good government he alone had engineered. He spoke glowingly of his courage in battle, of the economic revolution he had inspired, of the many victories his aggressive little fleet had won against Britain and the United States, of his freeing of slaves, and especially of his overall probity and unmatched insight into the problems of the Caribbean.

His self-written panegyric was so mesmerizing that it would have befitted a Pericles or a Charlemagne, and it achieved its purpose, for when the very officials who had ordered his arrest read it, they cried: "This Hugues must be a genius!" and forthwith they appointed him governor of another colony, from which he wrote similar reports of his achievements in his new post.

He did not remain there long, for when Napoleon assumed power, and said in effect: "No more of this nonsense about outlawing slavery, it's restored," Hugues was brought back to Paris, where he became a principal spokesman for the new order, and was often heard giving harsh instructions to young officers headed for the colonies: "You must be careful to keep those damned *noirs* in their place. They're slaves, and don't you let them forget it."

His most unbelievable switch, however, came in 1816, after the coronation of a new king to replace Napoleon, for he now revealed that he had always been an ardent Royalist, ignoring the fact that on Guadeloupe some years earlier he had beheaded more than a thousand such people without giving one of them a chance to defend himself.

He was allowed to make this amazing volte-face for several reasons: he really was a first-class administrator; in 1794 he had with only eleven hundred troops defeated ten thousand; and in the naval wars his few little ships did capture nearly a hundred American ships and an equal number of British. It is recorded that even in his sixties he was pursuing and often catching beautiful women, and he died in bed . . . covered with honors.

Meanwhile, Eugénie Lanzerac, shed of her oppressor and reunited with her son, became one of the most desirable young creole widows in the French islands, and more than a few officers, refugees from the terrors of Paris, sought her hand, for they were hungry for the tranquillity of Guadeloupe. She finally married a young fellow from the Loire Valley, scion of one of the castled families in that region, and with him worked to restore the quiet beauty of Point-à-Pitre.

After they had been married for some months, she sought the stonecutter who had made the infamous marker for the Dundas gravesite, and gave him a strange commission: "Find me a small, stout stone and fashion it as if it were two headstones in one." When this was done she asked him to inscribe on it the first names of the two she had loved: PAUL ET SOLANGE, and this she embedded in the wall of her House of Lace, where it remained for many decades after her death.

X

THE TORTURED LAND

I N 1789 THE WORLD'S MOST PROFITABLE, AND IN MANY WAYS THE
most beautiful, colony was that portion of Columbus' grand island
of Hispaniola owned by France. The colony formed the western third
of the island—the eastern two-thirds having remained in Spain's
hands—and was called St.-Domingue.

Its terrain was mountainous, covered with a growth of marvelous
tropical trees, and watered by many tumbling streams. Its yearly rainfall was precisely that required for the growing of sugarcane, coffee
and a host of luscious tropical fruits not known in Europe, especially
succulent mangoes and plantain, a kind of banana eaten fried. Inter-
spersed among the low mountains were numerous flat areas ideal for
plantations, of which it had well over a thousand, each one of them
capable of earning its lucky owner a fortune.

How did this colony, once so firmly in the grasp of Spain, happen
now to be French? Its history fit the old saying: "There's nothing so
permanent as a temporary arrangement." In the preceding century
when the buccaneers of Henry Morgan's day flourished on the little
offshore island of Tortuga, French pirates tended to come and go,
using the stronghold for temporary advantage, and some of them
came and stayed. The informal rulers of Tortuga and the pig-hunting
grounds on the west coast of Hispaniola were invariably French,

with the result that in 1697 when a comprehensive treaty among European nations was being formalized, France said: "Since our people already occupy the western coastline of Hispaniola, why not cede it to us?" and it was done. Persistent French pirates had accidentally won their homeland a treasure chest.

St.-Domingue, which would soon be surrendering its French name for the old Indian Haiti, produced so much wealth that one planter said before heading back to Paris with his fortune: "You plant sugarcane and the soil turns to gold." The colony's two main settlements—Cap-Français in the north, Port-au-Prince in the south—each a small city, gave proof of this fact with the profligate way they displayed their wealth.

Of the two, Cap-Français was bigger and more important because it fronted on the Atlantic Ocean, and was thus the first and easiest port of call for ships arriving from France. It had a spacious anchorage, a splendid waterfront and a population of some twenty thousand. Its glory was its huge theater, seating more than fifteen hundred patrons, with an "apron" stage that brought the actors well out into the middle of the audience. Since these players had to come all the way from France, it was good business to hold them in the colony for a three- or four-year stint, and this was practicable because there was an even finer theater in Port-au-Prince, seating seven hundred, plus half a dozen rural theaters in the smaller towns in between. Thus the colony could easily support two or three full-sized companies, and Paris actors passed the word among their colleagues: "St.-Domingue is a fine experience."

The theaters offered four kinds of entertainment: current popular dramas, musical plays, a kind of vaudeville and, from time to time, the great classical dramas of Racine and Molière, so that even a child growing up in a small country town would have an opportunity of seeing plays of high quality in his local theater.

At Le Cap, as it was popularly called, there were scores of shops offering about what one would find in similar establishments in French towns like Nantes or Bordeaux—fine leather goods, silverware, the latest modes in women's and men's wear—and several really excellent French patisseries. There were skilled doctors, eloquent lawyers, horse-drawn cabs and patrolling police. Establishments for boys offered a superficial education at best, since any young fellow of promise was whisked off to France for his schooling, but since most of these lads returned to St.-Domingue, the cultural level of the colony was high. There were no schools for girls, nor any record of a girl having been sent to the metropolitan for her education, but there were books and magazines for ladies, so that literacy among the French residents was universal and the quality of conversation high. Whatever happened in Paris was soon known at Le Cap, although in crossing the Atlantic, it tended to adopt a strong conservative coloring.

Glorious as the colony could be—and on fine days, which were plentiful throughout most of the year, the breezes at evening were pleasant, the scenery majestic and the food an exotic mix of the best French cuisine and Caribbean opulence—it could not have produced the endless wealth it did without human beings who were equal to the task of utilizing this richness. And in this respect St.-Domingue was both blessed and cursed.

The blessing was that some deity seemed to have said: "I've given the colony beauty and riches, now I'll populate it with people to match," and as a consequence the beautiful land was occupied by some of the ablest citizens in the Caribbean. The French settlers were educated, hardworking and of strong fiber, the blacks were positively the best brought out of Africa; so the colony should have been a stable area destined for greatness.

Its curse was that three classes of its citizens hated one another, and the wild upheavals of twenty years—1789 through 1809—not only failed to weld these groups into a reasonable whole; they divided them so thoroughly that tragedy became inevitable. The top group was clearly defined: landowners, skilled professionals and *fonctionnaires* sent out from Paris to govern the place, and they were invariably white, rich and in control of everything. They owned the plantations, operated the expensive shops and contributed funds for the theater so as to monopolize the best seats. They tended to be passionately pro-French, even more passionately conservative and indifferently Catholic; religion did not play a major role in St.-Domingue, but the traditional *blanc* would have looked askance at a Protestant who tried to start a business or build a home at Le Cap.

There were two divisions in this class whose interests sometimes diverged—the *grands blancs,* that is, the big whites of the top financial and social category; and the *petits blancs,* the little whites, some of whom amounted to very little indeed. But in the period starting in 1789 they were more or less united.

At the bottom of the groups, and so far down that from the position occupied by the whites they were well-nigh invisible, were the *noirs*—the blacks, the slaves. Born for the most part in Africa, they were illiterate, untrained in plantation life and rigidly excluded from Christianity by their owners, who feared that the teachings of Jesus might lead to a demand for freedom. They retained many African ways, adhered to religions rooted in the Dark Continent, and adjusted to the heat, food and working conditions in St.-Domingue with an adaptability that was amazing. They contained in their seemingly amorphous mass just about the same proportion of potential artists, fine singers, philosophers, religious and political leaders as any other group of people in the world, and certainly, as we shall see, about the same percentage of military leaders as the whites in their colony. But because they lacked education and opportunity, their skills remained hidden until disruptions of one kind or another revealed them. Then the blacks of St.-Domingue were to display a capacity that astounded the world.

Caught in the middle between the two extremely powerful grinding stones of white plantation owner and black slave writhed a considerable mass of citizens who were neither white nor black. Their racially mixed brothers and sisters appeared on all Caribbean islands and always faced the same impediments, promises, hopes and crushing disadvantages; in those other colonies they might be called *mulattoes, coloreds, half-breeds, half-castes, creoles, criollos* or *bastards,* but in St.-Domingue all those terms were avoided, especially *mulatto,* which was deemed to have a pejorative ring. Here they were called *gens de couleur,* or, in English, *people of color,* or, more simply, *free-coloreds.*

Despised by whites, who saw them as parvenus striving to climb up to a level to which they were not entitled, and hated by blacks, who saw them as constituting a middle layer which would forever prevent the slaves from attaining power, the free-colored were spurned from above and below, and their history in St.-Domingue paralleled the experience of similar mestizo groups in the British Caribbean, in India and in South Africa: They had no real home, no ally whom they could trust, and no ascertainable future. But although there were these similarities to the situation in other world colonies, their role in St.-Domingue was especially frustrating because again and again they would come close to reaching a solution, only to find themselves betrayed and hunted down like animals.

In 1789 the whites in the colony numbered about 40,000, free-coloreds about 22,000, black slaves not less than 450,000, and because the death rate among the overworked and underfed blacks was so appallingly high, some 40,000 replacement slaves had to be imported each year from Africa, and this lucrative trade was in the hands of great slaving companies situated in France's Atlantic seaports like La Rochelle, Bordeaux and, preeminently, Nantes.

In 1770, when it became clear to commercial observers that the English colonies in North America must sooner or later fall into either trouble or rebellion, the great shipping house of Espivent in the French seaport of Nantes saw that its traditional business of running slaves from Africa to the New World would have to be increased dramatically in the frenzied time before war erupted. The major branch of the family, ennobled centuries before, decided to place in command of its nine slave ships the most daring captains available, and to tempt them with large bonuses to move their ships to Virginia and Carolina more rapidly than before in order to maximize their profits while slaving was still possible.

Finding only eight acceptable captains, they looked among the many members of the family who worked for them, and spotted Jerome Espivent, twenty-nine and a man of character who had served on many family ships. He knew the slave coast of Africa, the slave markets in Carolina and the Caribbean, and could be trusted to submit honest reports of his dealings. Assigning him to one of their larger ships, his noble relatives told him: "Make our fortune and yours," and he had applied himself so assiduously that by the time the American rebellion broke out in 1776, he had amassed considerable wealth and a rare knowledge of the Caribbean. In 1780, as the war was waning, and running the English blockades no longer paid huge dividends, Espivent decided to quit Nantes, where he would always be under the thumb of the noble wing of his large family, and settle in the Caribbean. Naturally, he thought first of the French islands, Martinique in particular, for it was a place of high culture and rich social life, but he also considered the more plebeian Guadeloupe. Yet in the end he selected a fine hillside in the town of Cap-Français, for in most criteria it far excelled locations elsewhere.

On this hill he built his residence, a brutish kind of Rhineland stone fortress on the outside, a delicate valley château with spacious rooms and expensive decorations on the inside. It commanded views of both the Atlantic, so that he could see the arrival of ships from

France sooner than anyone else, and of the town which lay obedient at its feet. Here Jerome Espivent ruled as the social and political dictator of the seaport, the epitome of French influence in the Caribbean.

He was now forty-eight, a tall, imperial-looking man, with graying hair, a tightly trimmed mustache and a finely pointed Vandyke goatee. Despite the tropic heat, he favored the flowing capes worn by noble Frenchmen in the past century, so he asked a local shopkeeper to import from India cloths of the sheerest weight, from which seamstresses produced elfin-thin capes in light blue or shimmering black, and when he appeared at the theater in one of these, his cockaded hat at an angle, he seemed to be telling the citizens of Le Cap that he bespoke the ancient glory of France.

He was a Royalist, an admirer of the nobility of which he was a collateral part, and a shrewd investor of his savings, for it seemed that whatever he touched prospered beyond expectations. No longer commanding a ship of his own, he served as a kind of shore agent for those operated by other men, and year after year he appeared to make more profits from these ships than did their owners. He also bought coarse muscovado sugar from other plantations which lacked the facilities his had and refined it himself, importing for that purpose big shipments of clay from Barbados. He was a very rich man, but he was no miser, for he helped support the theater, sent bright lads to France for their education even though they were not his sons, and was available for all contingencies, for he felt that Frenchmen of station were obligated to maintain a public presence.

He had one curious concern that had started as a hobby but which had grown, as hobbies will, into an obsession. Believing as he did that God had put white blood into the world to help Him save it from barbarism, he had become fascinated by what he called "the contamination of the black," and this led to a conviction that dominated his life: Even one drop of black blood mixed with white can be visibly detected through the seventh generation. Since this meant that a child in the seventh generation would have had 128 ancestors, he had devised a table which showed every possible combination from 128 pure white = 0 black, to the disgraceful end of the spectrum, 0 white = 128 black.

And he had codified in orderly form the popular names for these mixes, as he was fond of explaining to anyone who would listen: "Suppose a white man with totally clean blood marries a black woman right out of the African jungle with dirty blood. Their child is a mulatto, half and half. Now, never again does one of the men in our example marry another black, always pure white. Next generation, three parts white, one black, and we call him a quadroon. He marries pure white, his child is an octaroon—seven clean, one dirty. Next generation, fifteen white, one black is a mameluke."

Of course, the actual mixing was more confused than in his ideal example, and some of the names of the 128 possible mixes were fascinating: a child one part white, seven black was a sacatra; three parts white, five colored was a marabou; but he considered one of the most exciting mixes to be the griffe, one white, three colored: "Those girls simply do not know when to stop." His incredible system reached the number 8,192, representing the ancestors a human being would have if one counted back to the thirteenth generation: "Only in that generation can a man win his way back to the respectability of being white from which his ancestor departed in shame." He also warned young men: "Counting an average of twenty-two years to a generation, it will require your descendants two hundred and eighty-six years to correct your dreadful mistake if you marry a woman with black blood. The moral? When it comes time to marry, stay away from the free-coloreds."

With such implacable views it was clear that Espivent would have strong feelings about the non-whites in his colony. He had to do business with them, have his beard trimmed by them, order cakes from their bakeries, and employ them to serve as overseers when men from France were not available. Wherever he moved in St.-Domingue he ran into them, bright young men with bright skins and fine teeth "trying always to be better than they are." But the more he saw of them, the more he despised them, for he was sure he could detect in what he called their shifty eyes signs of the revenge they would one day seek. Everything about them infuriated him: "*Mon Dieu,* some of them speak better French than our own children. Did you know that Prémord, that speechifying menace over in the tailor's shop has had the nerve to send his two sons to Paris for their education? These coloreds buy books, they fill the theaters, they attend our churches, they parade their pretty daughters before our sons and hope to trap them. They're worse than mosquitoes, the curse of our colony."

Sometimes he would walk the streets of Le Cap cataloguing each man or woman of color, reciting to himself: That one has three-quarters black blood, that one only one-eighth, that pretty one'll be trying to pass for white one of these days, but the stain will always be there and sooner or later it'll betray her. The sight of an exquisite free-colored girl gave him pain, not pleasure, for he always visualized her trapping some innocent soldier just out from France, forcing him to marry her, and then slipping into the metropolitan with her ineradicable black blood to contaminate the homeland. He frequently felt that the colony and the homeland were doomed, but he stayed on in St.-Domingue because he had a spacious, cool château in town and a grand plantation in the country. Espivent's racial attitudes were antithetical to those of most of his fellow countrymen, and sometimes he was accused of being worse than the English, but he never gave an inch in his dogma of extremism. In fact, he reveled in it.

Jerome Espivent called his huge plantation Colibri, or Hummingbird, and to cultivate its rich acreage he utilized some three hundred slaves—"the best in the Caribbean," he boasted to his fellow planters. He could claim this because during the years that he supervised his slave ship and those of his family, he invariably anchored each new arrival from Africa first off Cap-Français, where he inspected the newcomers, selecting for his plantation the strongest and those who looked the most intelligent. The rejects he shipped on to the American colonies, where such high standards could not be enforced.

But his best slave, César, had reached him not in his own ships but by a most curious route. When the blacks on the Danish island of St. John rebelled in 1733, most of the rebels were executed in terrible ways, but one of the leaders of the revolt, a slave named Vavak, César's father, had fled the island in a small boat, accompanied by his woman. In furtive rowing, they skirted the larger Danish island of St. Thomas, where certain death awaited any fugitive black, and made their way to the north coast of Puerto Rico, where they hid ashore for seven days before proceeding in their same small rowboat to the eastern end of the big island of Hispaniola. There they fell into the hands of a Spanish plantation owner who, predictably, enslaved them again, but they managed to flee to the French side, where they were once more thrown into slavery on a plantation just north of Port-au-Prince.

When, in 1780, Espivent began stocking Colibri, he heard about a slave for sale—whose owner was going bankrupt—who was considered "one of the finest slaves in these islands, a bright, hardworking fellow, south of here." When he went down to inspect, he found a young married man of twenty-four, named Vavak, after his father. It required only a few minutes for Espivent to decide that although this man was rather short, he was the one he wanted to serve as lead slave on his plantation at the north end of the colony. Having bought him at a bargain price, he listened when Vavak begged him in good French to buy his wife too. "That would make sense," Espivent said. "Man works better with his woman at hand to guide and care for him," and the three started back to Colibri, but on the way Espivent said: "Vavak's not a proper French name." After reflecting for a moment, he snapped his fingers and cried: "Vaval! First name César, your woman's name Marie."

César and Marie first saw the great plantation that would be their home on a stormy afternoon in the spring of 1780, and as they trudged behind their new master on his spirited horse, he suddenly reined in, ordered them to halt, and pointed to a magnificent landscape ahead: "The stone house on the right, that hill to the west, the lands sloping down toward the ocean that hides behind that rise, all mine. All yours to tend."

César's first reaction to the plantation was professional delight in the fact that it looked as if sugarcane would grow easily, then pleasure in seeing it was in fine condition, with roads that had been leveled, small houses with roofs, and land that had been properly tilled. But before he could comment, Espivent rose in his stirrups and pointed to a distant hilltop which he could see but the slaves could not: "That's Château Espivent, my home. Sometimes you'll work there, when the hedges need tending." With that, the plantation owner spurred his horse and rode toward the collection of huts in which his new slaves would make their home.

In the years that followed, César did not see his owner regularly, for Espivent did not come often to his plantation, and when he did, it was to examine the cane fields, not the slaves. When riding inspection through his valuable hectares he could stare imperially down avenues of cane and never see his three hundred slaves. He did not ignore them; he simply looked past them as he did past the trees that edged the fields.

He was reasonably kind to the slaves, but he did subscribe to the theory that it was most profitable to treat them like animals—one pair of pants, one shirt, boughs on the ground for a bed, the cheapest food—and work them to death, replacing them with new bodies bought at a bargain from his family's ships. While they lived he did not abuse them, and whenever he found one of his overseers doing so, he discharged him: "Treat your slaves decently and they not only live longer, but they also work better while they do live." An Espivent slave who started healthy survived about nine years, and since he paid for his cost in five years, he represented a profitable investment.

Since it was impossible for César to imagine any better system of slavery than the one he knew, he accepted the belief voiced so often at Colibri: "Ours the best plantation. I been others where they whip. Nobody as good as Monsieur Espivent." Now as the fateful year 1789 edged toward the middle of summer, tremendous events were convulsing metropolitan France, but the slaves of St.-Domingue were prevented from learning about them. Fearful lest black yearnings for freedom be ignited into conflagrations that could not be controlled, Espivent encouraged the *grands blancs* in a campaign to keep all news from France away from the slaves, and he succeeded.

If the black Vavals knew nothing of the revolutionary fires that swept France in the tumultuous days following the attack on the Bastille, the free-colored Xavier Prémord and his wife, Julie, certainly did, for their two sons in France sent them detailed letters about the changes then under way. "Things won't be the same after this," Xavier told his wife, but the improvements he sought were superficial compared to the root-and-branch alterations Julie dreamed of. "It's all got to be different," she said repeatedly as news filtered in of peasant uprisings in the French countryside, mob action in Paris and proposed new forms of government.

Xavier's reaction to this physical and intellectual violence was: "Now we free-coloreds will get the vote and gain some respect in Cap-Français," but his wife aspired to a complete modification in social patterns: "No more will we coloreds be the despised and trod upon," and she was determined that Espivent in his prosperous château cease serving as arbiter of the political and social life of the northern community. Listening to Xavier, one could visualize a slow but steady transition to new patterns of life, but if one attended to what Julie was saying, one heard echoes of revolution.

Although he detested doing so, when Espivent wanted choice material from India for a new cape, he had to buy it from Xavier Prémord's shop near the theater, and when he needed a new jacket and trousers of a special cut he also had to go there, as did the other dandies of Le Cap, for Prémord had not only arranged with weavers of Bordeaux and Nantes to use him as their exclusive agents for the importation of fine wool and sheerest cotton, but he had also made arrangements with the best local seamstresses and tailors to work only for him. Any Frenchman in Le Cap who wanted to be really well dressed had to do business with Prémord, who was usually dressed more modishly than any of them.

Xavier and his wife were prime examples of why the *grands blancs* feared the free-coloreds. He was a tall, handsome man in his thirties, obviously intelligent and prudent in the management of his business; while she was the type of colored woman against whom Espivent railed—slim, attractive and with an amber skin that enshrined her in a golden glow. In addition to this visible benediction from nature, she was a sharp-minded, canny businesswoman with those instincts of caution and profit which seemed to come easily to Frenchwomen of the middle class.

She did not help her husband in his shop; she assumed responsibility for the small plantation inherited from her father near Meduc, a village opposite the pirate island of Tortuga. In fact, it was to the land now occupied by this plantation that the buccaneers Ned Pennyfeather and his uncle Will Tatum had come hunting wild boar more than a century ago.

Once when Espivent met the Prémords as they emerged from Xavier's shop on the way to the opera, the doyen of Le Cap society explained to white friends standing nearby: "That saucy fellow's about eighty-eight white, forty black, very presumptuous type. She? I'd say ninety-six white, thirty-two black, and it's a good thing she's already married, because young officers just out from France would grab at her." And then he gave her high praise: "She runs her plantation out at Meduc as good as any man."

Like all the other free-coloreds who owned land, the Prémords relied upon some forty slaves to cultivate and press the cane, but Julie had, in her first days of management, differentiated herself from the other owners. They often treated their slaves worse than whites treated theirs. This was caused in part by the visceral fear in which they held their slaves, for they saw them as creatures in the abysmal pit from which they themselves had climbed, and back into which they might someday be pushed by the *grands blancs* like Espivent. Julie, in contrast, saw her slaves as human beings and tried to treat them as such.

Her husband's basic position, the one to which he constantly returned, was clearly stated one night in August: "Each year the black population increases. When the slave ships bring in replacements for those that have died, they drop off a couple of hundred extra new Africans. They must in time overrun us. Our only hope is to ally ourselves—now and strongly—with the whites, to make them see that their only hope of survival is allegiance with us."

"I used to think that," Julie said, choosing her next words carefully. "But recent experiences at the plantation have begun to make me wonder. We have an enormous number of slaves in this colony. They outnumber us fearfully."

"We've always known that."

"And I'm quite sure they aren't always going to remain slaves. The disturbances in France will someday filter down to us."

"They're illiterate. They're savages. They know nothing of France."

"Our grandfathers were too, but they learned."

In response, Xavier retreated to one of the great clichés of social analysis: "That was different."

"When our slaves start to move the way our grandfathers did, hundreds of thousands of them, we'd better surrender your vain hopes of acceptance by the whites and join the slaves, for they will prevail." He started to rebut, but Julie forestalled him: "We must do it quickly and firmly, so they see that we do it of our own free will . . . and that we do it to help them gain their liberation."

"Not in our generation, Julie," her husband said. "We coloreds are civilized, they aren't."

The Prémords had as friends two married couples who were also free-coloreds and who also owned plantations out toward Meduc, so that sometimes discussions of these vital matters involved six concerned people, the division being three who wanted to ally with the whites, Julie who advised joining the blacks, and two who counseled: "Wait and see." But one of these rather destroyed his own argument by adding: "I listen in Le Cap. I've been to Port-au-Prince. And I've never felt tensions so high. Events may do the choosing for us."

"You're contradicting what you've been saying," Julie cried in exasperation. "Say it clear and simple, what should we do?" and the man said petulantly: "That's what I've been trying to say. Do nothing. Go ahead as we are. Don't allow ourselves to be used by either side. And when the smoke clears, because I'm sure there's going to be smoke, we'll be in position to dictate our own terms." And whenever the discussion reached this point the participants looked at each other in silence, for they realized that they were debating the chances of life or death.

The Prémords were accustomed to tension, for the laws of St.-Domingue, as dictated and enforced by Espivent and his *grands blancs*, were infuriating in their pettiness toward the free-coloreds. When Xavier talked with others of his caste during chance meetings in the rear of his shop, the men ventilated their fury at the injustices under which they were forced to live. Said one: "We're forbidden to use the good seats in the theater," but another complained: "What irritates me is that I'm the best shot in this colony. Proved it in a score of competitions, but I'm not allowed to serve in the militia. The French say they can't trust a man like me . . . wrong color."

They were forbidden to copy the dress styles of Paris or play European-type games. But what galled Julie whenever she joined these discussions was the mean spirit of the rules enforced by the white women of the colony: "I am forbidden to entertain six of my free-colored women friends at lunch lest we conspire, and there cannot even be a group celebration when two of our young people marry. 'Free-coloreds may not engage in any activities which might become boisterous,' the law says, and if a spy caught us talking together in secret like this, we could all be thrown in jail."

She and Xavier were delighted, therefore, when on cherished occasions a cadre of gallant free-coloreds in Meduc invited friends from the northern part of the colony to a clandestine dinner-discussion-dance. When Julie whispered: "Xavier, they're doing it again," he knew that the courageous Brugnons were once more assembling the free-coloreds illegally, and so he and Julie quietly joined two other couples at the edge of Le Cap. On horseback, with three slaves attending them on mules to mind the horses and the baggage, they rode west. The air was quite festive, a real vacation from sugar and shop-keeping and daily duties. But Julie grew increasingly apprehensive as they neared Meduc, and warned her husband: "None of that foolishness at the dance this year," and when he reassured her: "I've no taste for it either," she made him promise: "You'll keep an eye on me and grab me for your partner at once." He said he would, and on those terms they entered the beautiful little seaport, found lodging with their free-colored friends, and spent the rest of the afternoon in deep discussion about events in Paris and the future of St.-Domingue.

A stranger of unknown credentials, with a livid scar across his face, attracted considerable attention by whispering to the men: "Vincent Ogé, one of us and well regarded by the revolutionists in Paris, may be calling upon you for help."

"For help on what?" Xavier asked, and the man replied evasively: "Sooner or later, won't you, too, have to strike for freedom, eh? The way we did in Paris?" When Prémord ignored the question, the man shrugged and moved along to others, posing the same question.

An orchestra of six slaves played light theater airs during supper, changing to animated dance music when the chairs were pushed back for the real entertainment. It was a vigorous affair, this lively dancing of the free-coloreds, and as movements became increasingly uninhibited, Julie caught her husband's eye, and he nodded, assuring her that he would be staying close.

In those moments before the riot of the night began, he had strongly mixed feelings. As a young man he had found wild delight in these dances of his people, but now, as an older man with a pretty wife and a position of some importance in the colony, he felt that the untrammeled behavior which he knew was about to begin denigrated the free-coloreds and gave the whites justification for some of the ugly things they said about them. So he felt both a sense of increasing excitement, as in the old days, but also a revulsion when he remembered that the stranger from Paris would see how the free-coloreds misbehaved.

At a signal from the men running the dance the orchestra began playing faster and faster, and both men and women started calling to other dancers and even shouting into the air with no message intended. At a sudden cry from the managers, the music stopped, the lights were blown out, and men and women began groping almost blindly one for the other. A particularly attractive young woman, and many were present, might be grabbed at by three or four men, while a handsome fellow like Prémord would be certain to have several women fighting for him.

When the random pairs were established, with the less aggressive men and women having to accept what was left over, the couples retired upstairs, or to hiding places on the lawn, or to the stables behind the square, or wherever they could find reasonable privacy, and there the lovemaking and the squealing and the oaths began, to last long into the night as partners switched and fights began.

Prémord, as promised, leaped to his wife's side as soon as the music stopped and had her safely under his protection when the pairing began. He led her onto a porch away from the activities, and as she whispered: "Thank you, Xavier," the stranger with the scar on his face joined them, and with a shrug of his shoulder toward the now-silent dance floor, said: "No wonder they say we're not worthy of any higher place in society than we now have."

"It will change when we gain the respect that all men desire," Xavier said.

"Why are you here?" Julie asked in the blunt way that her husband knew so well.

"Visiting."

"And what have you been whispering to our men?"

In the dim light provided by a solitary lamp at the far end of the porch, the visitor looked quizzically at Xavier, who nodded: "She knows all that I know," and the man said approvingly: "Good. My wife, the same. What I'm here for, Madame Prémord, is to inform you people that Vincent Ogé, a free-colored leader of some talent, may be calling upon you for help . . . soon."

"To accomplish what?" Julie asked evenly, and the stranger said: "The freedoms that we must have."

"Is this Ogé talking revolution?" Julie asked, and the man said quickly: "No! No! He knows what you and I know, that your group of *gens de couleur* is the smallest in the colony. You're nothing, except that you attend to the management that keeps your colony surviving, and if under Ogé's leadership you present our demands in the proper style . . ."

"We will be slain," Julie said quietly, and to her surprise the man said quietly: "Then we will be slain, but we can wait no longer." Julie, noticing that in this firm declaration he had switched from the pronoun *you* to *we,* asked: "Are you then one of us?" and he replied: "From the day of my birth."

"Where?" Julie probed, for she feared alien *agents provocateurs,* and he said: "Down south. In the port town of Jérémie," and she asked: "Who owns the big store in the public square?" and he said without hesitation: "The Lossiers," and she said: "They're my cousins." Upon her direct questioning he refused to give his own name, but as he left the saturnalia Julie could see the disgust on his face as he watched two men shedding their clothes as they chased after two almost-naked girls.

· · ·

While César Vaval's parents were still alive they spent much effort in teaching him the things they believed he ought to know: "No slavery is any good. Danish is worst by far. French is best, maybe. But you live for one thing only, to be free." His parents had died at about the same time, worked to death by the owner of their plantation, but before they died they told their son: "Study everything the white man does. Where does he get his power? Where does he hide his guns? How does he sell the sugar we make? And no matter how you do it, learn to read his books. There's where he keeps his secrets, and unless you master them, you'll always be a slave."

They had spent their last days persuading a knowledgeable slave to teach their son the alphabet, and as a result, César had, through the subsequent years, read accounts of what was happening in France and other parts of the world. He knew, for example, that the American colonies not far to the northwest had won their freedom from Great Britain, which also owned Jamaica, a colony much like St.-Domingue not far to the south. But the news in which he would have been most interested, the fiery rebellions in France, was still kept from him, for Espivent preached constantly in his club: "Do not allow the slaves to know anything. Madness seems to have taken over in France, and it would be a good idea to keep papers and journals away from the free-coloreds, too." But from a dozen subtle hints, César deduced that things of moment were happening, either in France or in other areas of St.-Domingue, and he was eager to learn more about them.

At thirty-three César was an intelligent, self-respecting black, but he had one limitation which would diminish him throughout his life: he despised free-coloreds. Because he saw so clearly that the ultimate enemy of the blacks was the white man like Jerome Espivent who controlled all sources of money and power, and because he saw that conflict between the *grands blancs* and the *noirs* was inevitable, he resented the intrusion of a formless middle group which interposed itself between the two contestants. "Who are these free-coloreds?" he asked the wiser slaves who looked to him for guidance. "They're not white, they're not black. They can't be trusted by anybody. What's worse, they take the good jobs we ought to have if we do good work, like caretaker and work fixing things. That means we always gots to be field hands." When, on the occasions he was allowed into Le Cap, he viewed free-coloreds like Xavier Prémord, with his white-man's clothes and uppity manners, with distaste if not actual animosity, assessing him accurately as a barrier cutting the slaves off from any chance of a better life.

Julie Prémord perplexed him, for she was obviously a most lovely woman, but the fact that she managed a plantation which had many slaves made her a kind of enemy, except that he had been told by other blacks: "That one, she the best. Her plantation hard rules but you get enough to eat, you get extra clothes." Once as he was lugging plants to beautify Château Espivent he had come face-to-face with her in the street, and for no reason that he could see she had smiled at him, a warm, human gesture that had both pleased and bewildered him. That night he told his wife back at Colibri: "She seem almost like one of us, more black than white," but as soon as he said this he realized how preposterous it sounded: "No, they're far, far from us, all of them, and in the end they'll be worse than the whites."

Despite these feelings, he and his family did not hate anyone, except for one beastly overseer, but they were all prepared to take whatever steps would be necessary to attain the kind of freedom his father Vavak had spoken of. The word *revolution*, with its attendant burnings and killings, would have been anathema to them, but in recent months a new force had come into their lives, one which brought the concept of revolution right onto their plantation. It came in the form of a man, a runaway slave no longer attached to any specific plantation, a fiery-tempered man named Boukman, who said: "Don't ask me where I come from. Ask me only where I'm goin'."

He was a voodoo priest, a man of powerful insight and oratory, and at night meetings at the various plantations he preached a compelling doctrine, after conducting arcane rituals which reminded the slaves of their African origins. He intoned old chants from the jungle, performed rituals hundreds of years old, and used phrases they had almost forgotten, but mostly he shared with them the pulsating news he had picked up while helping unload cargo ships newly arrived from France: "Big fighting in Paris. That a city in France, bigger than Le Cap. People like you, me, we takin' command. All new, all new. Pretty soon, here in Le Cap, too, big change." When he had the attention of his midnight listeners, he dropped the vernacular and preached in good French: "There must be liberty for all. There must be a true fraternity between master and slave. And there must be equality. Do you know what equality is?" and he would scream: "It means 'You're as good as the white man,' and we all must work together, side by side, to prove that."

He realized that most of the slaves attended his secret meetings to renew their acquaintance with voodoo; he saw that they eagerly joined in the chants, were awed by the trances and spells, and found joyful liberation in the dance, but mostly they yearned to reestablish contact with an almost forgotten past. He himself never lost sight of his main mission, and under his clever manipulation, voodoo became an antechamber to revolution, for he realized better than any of his followers that one would surely lead to the other.

Literate slaves like the Vavals, and there were a few on each plantation, paid little attention to Boukman's voodoo exhortations, but when they spoke with him, as César did one night after a long session at Colibri, they heard words that were almost identical to those spoken by the scar-faced stranger during the debauch at Meduc: "The day is coming . . . there will be freedom . . . justice is at hand . . . I will send a message . . . we will need you." How soon the message would arrive, Boukman could not say, but César and his wife became convinced that it would come, and they prepared themselves for the great challenge. A vibrant spirit was in the air in all the plantations, for the heady arguments of Paris had penetrated at last into St.-Domingue.

In February 1791 a quiet call came for free-coloreds from all parts of the colony to rally to the banner of Vincent Ogé, one of their number who had been trained in France and who preached that the time had come to demand equality with the whites. Leaving their plantation, Xavier and Julie Prémord answered the call, but arrangements were so poor and instructions so inadequate that they wandered far south without making contact with the insurrection. Perhaps this was fortunate, for the affair petered out in confusion, with Ogé and his scar-faced lieutenant barely escaping to sanctuary in nearby Spanish Hispaniola.

The putative uprising was successful in one respect—it aroused in the colony's free-coloreds an unquenchable determination to gain freedom within a liberated France, and in that mix of patriotism, confusion and deepening commitment to their caste, the Prémords crept quietly back to Cap-Français.

In that town the semi-uprising of the free-coloreds had exacerbated hatreds. Espivent was vituperative: "We must catch that infamous Vincent Ogé and make an example of him. No punishment would be too severe," and he roamed through the streets and clubs, preaching his doctrine of savage retaliation and making himself the rallying point for all who feared these first signs of a local revolution. "Can you imagine," he thundered, his graying long hair tangled by the February breeze, "what would happen if they got their way? A man of color eating at the same table with your wife and daughters? Can you visualize a poseur like Prémord swaggering his way into your club? And what really threatens, can you imagine his kind sullying the pure blood of France?"

He was so obsessed by his hatred of the free-coloreds that after Ogé and his leading supporters were extradited from Spanish Hispaniola, he forced his friends in the government to hand down a punishment which alone would have been enough to ignite rebellion throughout the colony. The two Prémords, free-coloreds of education, judgment and unquestioned patriotism, left their shop to stand inconspicuously in the crowd on the day the punishment was carried out, and César Vaval happened to be in town delivering a cartload of plantation produce to Château Espivent.

Had Espivent, Prémord and Vaval—these principal actors in the tragedy about to explode—been able to meet and discourse intelligently, three men of wisdom and impeccable love for their colony, they might have reached understandings which would have permitted St.-Domingue to weather its transformations peacefully. If there are, as the ancient Greeks believed, gods eager to aid mortals at times of crisis, one could imagine such gods pushing them toward an understanding which would save their homeland, for it could have been saved. But on this day the gods were inattentive: the Prémords mingled in silence at the edge of the crowd, Vaval remained with his cart at an opposite edge, and Espivent stood like an avenging fury at the foot of a gallows erected in the center of the plaza, crying "Bring forth the prisoners!"

When they were led forth, the Prémords gasped, for in front was the stranger from that night at Meduc, the *provocateur* with the livid scar, and behind him Vincent Ogé, a handsome man of light color and aristocratic mien that seemed to infuriate his white captors, for two of them knocked him to the ground and kicked at his neat clothes. The stranger remained upright, and in the confusion that followed the fall of Ogé he scanned the crowd and saw the Prémords; without betraying that they might have been part of the conspiracy, he flashed a clear signal: See, it has come to this.

The two revolutionaries were to be hanged for challenging white rule, that was clear, but not immediately, for Ogé's two jailers hauled him to a great wheel from which ropes were attached to his four limbs, and when he was securely lashed down and stretched to the breaking point, a huge man with an iron bar moved about his body, breaking each arm and leg in two places. Then tension on the ropes was increased until the limbs began to tear apart. His cries of anguish were so great they filled the plaza, giving satisfaction to the men whose prerogatives he had threatened, and creating terror in the free-coloreds he had defended and bewilderment in the various slaves who watched. When the ropes were slackened, two big jailers hoisted him, as he was unable to stand on his broken legs, onto the gallows, where he was hanged. Once he ceased twitching, he was dropped to the ground and his head was chopped off. Then the stranger was hauled to the wheel, but as he went to his torture he cried defiantly: "Freedom for all," and the tightening of his limbs began while the brute with the iron bar waited.

Those were the images that the free-colored Prémords and the slave César carried away that night, and as the former returned to their shop they vowed: "After this horror, there can be no retreat," and César, when he got back to his plantation, assembled his wife and children: "It was brutality for the amusement of watchers. Madness is afoot, and we must study how to use it for our purpose when the great riots begin, for they will."

He was right in his prediction, for seething resentments were about to explode, but they came from a totally unexpected quarter. On the dark night of 20 August 1791 the wandering voodoo priest Boukman slipped back to harangue the slaves on Colibri with a fury which Vaval and his wife had not heard before. Now there were no obscure religious overtones, no jungle incantations, there was only the throbbing summons to revolution, and for the first time César heard Boukman actually call for the death of all white men: "They have enslaved us and they must go! They have starved our children and they must be punished!" When César heard this last cry he thought: No one on our plantation ever lacked food. Wrong cry, wrong place to make it. And it was that simple realization that would guide him and his family in the tumultuous days that were at hand: he hated slavery and opposed Espivent, but he did not wish him dead.

On the morning of 22 August, Boukman stopped his preaching

and threw lighted brands into the powder kegs of the north. Rallying a thousand slaves, then ten, then fifty thousand, he started in the far environs of Cap-Français and moved like some all-encompassing conflagration toward the city. Every plantation encountered was set ablaze, every white man was slain, as were any women or children caught in the chaos. The destruction was total, as when a horde of locusts strips a field in autumn. Trees were chopped down, irrigation ditches destroyed, barns burned, and the great houses laid in ashes—a hundred plantations wiped out in the first rush, then two hundred, and finally nearly a thousand; they would produce no more sugar, no more coffee. The wealth of the north was being devastated to a point from which it could never recover.

But the real horror lay in the loss of life, in the extreme hatred the blacks manifested toward the whites. Hundreds upon hundreds of white lives were lost that first wild day: men killed with clubs, women drowned in their own private lakes, children pierced with sticks and carried aloft as banners of the uprising, and there were other savageries too awful to relate. One black woman who had not participated in the orgy of killing said as she passed the piles of dead bodies: "This day, even the earth is killed."

Colibri Plantation, at the very heart of the firestorm, was not destroyed, for César Vaval and his family stood guard, fending off the oncoming rioters with quiet words: "Not here. He is a good boss," and since César was a man who had earned respect, the wave parted and rejoined to burn the next plantations in line.

In the meantime, all the whites who could had thronged to Le Cap, where Jerome Espivent was organizing a defense. His first action was representative of the contradictions of this terrible day: because there were not enough white men to defend the town, he had to call upon free-coloreds to help, and he was not embarrassed to seek assistance from the very men whom he had only recently sought to terrify by his brutal execution of their co-patriot Vincent Ogé. When he hurried to their shop to enroll the aid of the Prémords, it never occurred to him to apologize for his past behavior toward them: "I'm assigning you to the most important posts. It's us against the slaves. If they break through, we're all dead." And the Prémords, having no alternative but to obey him, for they knew that the safety of their town depended on the courage and leadership he would display in the next flaming hours, took positions along the most exposed perimeter where they could kill the most blacks.

Throughout that first terrible night, when word filtered into town of the widespread destruction and loss of life, Espivent went sleepless, marching stiffly from one battle position to the next, encouraging the men and consoling wives whose husbands had been out on their plantations: "Yes, it's painful. I have good men at Colibri, and I must hope that they'll find a way to stay alive. Your husband will, too, I'm sure."

For more than a week the fury raged, with Espivent denying the slaves entry to Le Cap, and César Vaval protecting Colibri. As the raping and burning began to decline, the black leaders of the rioting were grateful to César for having maintained the plantation, for it became an oasis of sanity in a fractured world. Blacks came there for food and water and to find rest among the trees. It was an errant irony that the detested Espivent plantation should have been spared.

It was during this savage period that César became a man so well spoken of by his fellow blacks that his reputation spread afar. "He's a man of stability. He knows what can be done and what can't," they said, and one day in September, as a result of this good report, he was visited by a tall, imposing black man, who said: "It was difficult getting through the lines. New troops arriving from France. They've caught Boukman, you know. Going to rack and hang him."

"What plantation are you from?" César asked, assuming the man to be a slave, and the stranger replied: "Bréda," a well-regarded plantation almost as fine as Colibri. Then he added: "I'm the manager there. From what they tell me, you ought to be manager here."

"Monsieur Espivent would never hear of that," and the big man said: "He would if he were wise."

"But what's your name? And why are you here?"

"Toussaint L'Ouverture. And I'm here to see you. To satisfy myself as to what you're like."

He remained for two nights, during which he met with all the other slaves of whom he'd heard good reports, and at the close of his visit he told César: "You'll be hearing from me. Not now. Too much confusion. But hold yourself ready. Remember my name, Toussaint, and when I call, come."

Terror, murder and betrayal spread to every corner of St.-Domingue. On 15 May 1791 the government in Paris passed a law, long overdue, giving the free-coloreds of St.-Domingue the political liberties they had sought, but the edict was so meanly hedged with property and other qualifications that only some one hundred and forty free-coloreds in all of St.-Domingue were eligible. That alone caused an anguished outcry, but when even that truncated document reached Le Cap, Jerome Espivent, conveniently ignoring the gallant role the free-coloreds had played in defending the town, launched a violent assault on the law, shouting in one gathering after another: "To admit them with their contaminated blood to the governance of this colony would be to destroy the meaning of the word France!" and he was so persuasive that he convinced the local council to deny rights to even the one hundred and forty who were eligible.

This clearly meant that the free-coloreds had no hope of justice, now or in the future, and upon no one did the disillusionment fall harder than on the Prémords, who felt so ostracized and humiliated that Julie cried in despair: "We must fight this out with Espivent . . . now!" She forced her reticent husband to march with her to the château, where at first they were denied entrance. But when the owner heard the ruckus at his door, he came out from his study: "What's going on here?" and when he saw the Prémords he growled: "And what do you want?"

"Justice," Julie snapped, but Espivent, always a proper *grand blanc* and a minor member of the nobility to boot, ignored her, indicating he would not discuss any important matter with a woman. But to Xavier he said: "Come in," and when they were inside, he pointedly kept the handsome couple standing, refusing them even the courtesy of a chair. "Now tell me," he said grudgingly, "what is the matter?"

"Your refusal to allow the laws of France to operate here," Julie said with such force that he had to acknowledge her this time, but his answer had a terrible finality about it: "France is France, and if it runs wild, this colony will pick and choose."

"And you choose to keep us in bondage forever?" Julie asked, and he said: "You have greater freedoms than you merit," and he edged them toward the door, thus informing them that they could expect no improvement of their lot so long as he and his friends remained in control of the island.

Julie could not accept this: "Monsieur Espivent, in the bad days, when it looked as if the slaves would burn all of Le Cap, you called on us free-coloreds for assistance—to save your château, your clubs, your theater. Do you remember assigning Xavier and me to positions of extreme importance?" Standing straight and tall in his blue dressing gown, Espivent replied: "In times of crisis a wise general calls upon all the troops he has under his command." Julie lost control: "We'll not be under your command forever," but as he closed his door upon them he said: "I think you will."

So, with expanding revolution threatening to destroy metropolitan France, her colonies and indeed her civilization, the people of St.-Domingue remained separated into their three stubborn groups, each unwilling or incapable of leading the colony toward rational behavior. It is difficult to visualize the pitiful condition to which their continued brawling brought the colony, but the American first mate on a trading vessel out of Charleston in South Carolina reported what he saw when he left ship at Port-au-Prince to travel overland to rejoin his crew at Cap-Français:

"I passed eight burned-out plantations a day, a hundred in all, and I was only one man on one road. I saw white bodies stretched on the ground with stakes driven through them. I saw innumerable white and black bodies dangling from trees, and I heard of scores of entire white families slain in the rioting. At the edge of settlements where the whites had been able to assemble and defend themselves I would see heaps of slaves who had attacked guns with only sticks and hoes, and by the time I finished my journey and rejoined my ship, I no longer bothered to look at the latest indecency, but I did wonder whether, in this flaming burst of terror and murder, there was no slave who merely killed his master and let it go at that, or no white who had been satisfied merely to shoot the slave without desecrating the corpse. May God preserve us from such horrors."

He concluded with comments which summarized his judgment as an experienced trader in these waters:

"Years ago, when our colonies were still part of England, I was a lad working on a ship out of Boston and as we anchored off St.-Domingue our captain warned: 'Treat this colony with respect, for each year it sends home to France more profit than our thirteen combined send to England.' After the destruction I have seen, that can never be said again."

And in that state of chaos St.-Domingue, once the pearl of the Caribbean, envied by all the other islands, plodded along. But new decisions reached in revolutionary France were about to reconstruct the community. Stern orders came: "Limited equality must be immediately granted to those hundred and forty free-coloreds designated earlier," and when notice of this was delivered to Xavier Prémord in his shop he embraced his wife: "This day the world begins anew," but she asked suspiciously: "For us, yes, but what of the others?" and in his club Jerome Espivent grumbled to his cronies: "Revolution has at last crossed the Atlantic. This is the end of decency as we knew it."

But this was merely the start of the upheaval, for shortly thereafter came startling news: "All free-coloreds to be granted legal, military and social equality," and then: "Complete freedom for any slave who has ever served in the French army, and also for their wives and children."

A bellowing of rage greeted the last decree, and it came not only from an outraged Espivent and his fellow *grands blancs,* but also from Xavier Prémord and his free-coloreds, and it would be difficult to determine which faction detested the new regulations more. Certainly Prémord saw it as the first fearful step in a movement that must ultimately alter his life, for once the slaves were free, the free-coloreds would become superfluous, and in rejecting the new law he used almost the same words as Espivent: "The dam is breaking." But his wife was more hopeful: "We cannot change what has happened and we must be prepared to adjust to whatever comes next," and she let her husband know that in her management of their plantation she would begin to take those steps which would enable them to adjust to freedom for their slaves when it came.

And it did come with startling suddenness, for on 14 June 1794 a packet boat arrived from France with final instructions from the revolutionary government: "All slaves in St.-Domingue are to be granted complete freedom." At last it seemed that this glorious island, so filled with human promise, was about to be restored to sanity, with its three groups working together toward the common purpose of equality and productivity. Optimists calculated that within two years the plantations would recover to the point where they would be delivering as much sugar as before, but Julie, who understood her slaves, assured other owners: "We'll do even better, because when your slaves are free, they'll work harder than before."

Despite that chance for sanity, Espivent and his powerful friends declared war against the new decree and threatened to shoot any owner who tried to implement it. Knowing that he would need a united citizenry if the blacks rebelled at being denied what was now legally theirs, he came to Prémord's shop dressed in his full military regalia, and asked: "Could we meet in your kitchen?" and when they sat about the rough, sturdy table that Julie herself had built, he said persuasively: "Obviously, we must now work together, for once the blacks get their freedom, they'll move against both of us." Xavier nodded in agreement, but Julie cried out in protest: "No! This is wrong! The blacks should be free, and we coloreds should work with them, because you"—and she pointed her finger almost in Espivent's face—"will never grant us acceptance, even if we do help you win this time."

"Madam," Espivent said without raising his voice, "had you uttered those words out in the street, you would have been shot. This is war, war to the death, and you must stand with us or we shall both be swept away in a black hurricane." So that night the free-coloreds of Cap-Français placed themselves once more under the leadership of the *grands blancs* for the defense of the town.

Why did they submit so passively to this repeated humiliation and betrayal? Xavier Prémord had known why from the start: "We have no other option. We're trapped between unyielding whites and vengeful blacks, but since the whites have the guns and the ships, we must ally with them and trust that sooner or later they'll show us generosity." Julie, of course, argued differently: "The blacks are so numerous they'll overcome the guns and ships. We must ally with them," but as a woman, her voice in council mattered little.

When the outlines of the great civil war that would destroy even further the wealth of St.-Domingue were drawn, César Vaval, snug in his leadership of the blacks on Colibri Plantation, told his wife: "We have no quarrel with Espivent and he has none with us. Keep calm and do nothing to create a new frenzy like the one Boukman started." And between them they persuaded the Colibri blacks to remain aloof from the rapidly forming battle lines.

But one night that compelling black leader from Bréda Plantation returned, loomed ominously in the doorway, and told Vaval: "I said I'd be coming back one day to summon you. I am here," and Toussaint L'Ouverture's appearance was so commanding, his dedication to the black revolt so forceful, that Vaval asked but one word: "Battle?"

"Yes."

"Against Le Cap again?" When this question was asked so boldly and so quickly, Toussaint became evasive, but César pressed: "Not Cap? We heading south to Port-au-Prince?" at which the Negro leader blurted out: "No! We've been offered tremendous promises by the Spaniards to fight on their side . . . against the French."

Vaval was stunned. He had always supposed that the slaves' fight for freedom would be a prolonged affair against reluctant French whites like his own master, Espivent. But now to be asked to join a foreign army, to fight against what he considered his own country, that seemed treacherous and unworthy, and he said: "I would not feel easy," and Toussaint reached down and grabbed him by the neck: "Do you trust me or not?" and Vaval looked up: "I do."

"Then come!"

Thus in mid-1793 the great black leader led Vaval and some half-dozen of his other lieutenants across the mountainous border and into camps where the Spaniards were preparing a full-scale attack on St.-Domingue. It was a bold decision, a terrible one, really, but Toussaint, having watched a score of constructive laws passed in Paris but ignored in the colony, saw no way to correct such injustice except to join with the Spaniards, drive out the French, and then make the best deal possible with the new victors.

The strategy worked, at least in the beginning, for the reinforced Spanish armies swept across the border and quickly captured the mountainous eastern third of the French colony. With surging joy Toussaint cried to his black troops: "We'll soon have the whole country!" But cautious Vaval probed when they were alone: "Then what? Spaniards don't like us any better than the French do," and Toussaint, finding strength from being back on familiar terrain, said: "Old friend, you must trust me. I want what you want, but the secret is to keep fluid. If you keep watching, you usually discover what the next step must be." Now César, who was becoming his general's conscience, warned: "Don't be too clever."

He had barely uttered this warning when runners from the seacoast brought frightening information: "Toussaint! The British have declared war on everybody—the French, the Spanish, even us. They see a chance to steal the entire colony. Their warships have captured every port on the Caribbean side."

"Le Cap, too?"

"No, the French still hold that."

When subsequent couriers confirmed the news, other self-styled black generals met one afternoon in their camp atop the middle of three small hills—their Spanish allies were occupying the hill to the east, and at a farther distance, the French army waited on the western hill. As the men joined Toussaint they knew that this would be a meeting of crucial importance, but none of them, Vaval least of all, could have guessed what was to be discussed.

Toussaint started by sketching in the earth a rude map of St.-Domingue: "If the Spaniards, with our help, hold this eastern third of the colony, and the British with their ships hold the western third, the French can control only this narrow strip down the middle," and his generals visualized the enormous areas under foreign control. "But there is an important difference," Toussaint continued. "The part the French own is mostly mountains, the part that's easy to defend. The Spaniards and the English have had it too simple up to now. The real battle is yet to begin."

For three days the black leader, a rugged, finely disciplined man of gigantic courage and imagination, kept his own counsel. He was only two generations out of Africa, where his ancestors had been men of leadership, and for that reason, he had great respect for fellow blacks like Vaval whose parents had also known Africa. On the third night of his lonely vigil he invited César to walk with him, and they climbed to a small rise from which they could look down on the smaller hill held by the Spanish soldiers: "What you said, Vaval, it's been nagging at me: 'The Spaniards don't like us any more than the French do.' What would you do in my place?" The two men spent several hours striving to unravel the future although they were barely able to understand the present. "Let's sleep now and talk further in the morning," Toussaint said abruptly, and off he marched to bed. But at half after three that morning an aide awakened Vaval with a curt message: "General Toussaint's tent, immediately!" and when he and the other generals reported, the black leader unveiled his astonishing plans: "This morning . . . now . . . we rejoin the French. Help them fight off the Spanish on the east and the English on the west."

"Why?" a grizzled old fighter asked, and Toussaint whirled about to face him. "Because, old friend, if either Spain or England captures our colony, it's back to slavery for us. But if we help France win, we have a fighting chance. At least they've given freedom to their own people!"

The same old fellow pointed out: "Yes, they did pass a fine law in Paris giving us freedom, but when it crossed the ocean to St.-Domingue, there was no more law, no more freedom," and Toussaint moved a step forward to clap the old man on the back: "True, you wise old bird, but this time we'll be in charge, and we'll see it's real freedom . . . for everyone."

Then, before the sleeping Spaniards on the other hill became aware of what was happening, Toussaint, Vaval and their complete black army were marching off to unite with the French, and when Vaval whispered to Toussaint: "I never slept an easy night in a Spanish uniform," the leader confessed: "Nor did I . . . I'm French."

Now Toussaint proved that he was just as able a leader of men as he was a strategist, for with a grudging promotion to make-believe general conferred almost comically by the French high command, he launched a series of brilliant thrusts, first to the east against the Spaniards, then boldly to the west to throw the British off balance. In these actions he demonstrated an unusual mastery of not only the spectacular one-time tactical raid on an isolated target but also the long-range strategic operation that moved an entire enemy front back a few precious miles. He had converted himself into a real general and, with reliable lieutenants to execute his orders, he had become a formidable one.

In a series of lightning sorties to the east, he practically liquidated the Spanish, but he still had to come to grips with the British, who had poured a huge number of troops into St.-Domingue in hopes of stealing that weakened colony for their empire. Their success had been spasmodic, now surging forward to wipe out the French, now retreating before Toussaint's inspired blacks. But in 1797 they began a final drive, with a chain of spectacular victories. Toussaint, with remarkable self-discipline, allowed them to rampage among the small targets while keeping them isolated from the big, until it became common in the British mess to refer to their black enemy with grudging praise as "that damned Hannibal," for he, like his famous black counterpart from Carthage, utilized mountains with great skill.

By maintaining remorseless pressure over an extended period, Toussaint, with no help from the French, finally forced the British back against the shore from which they had started four years earlier, and toward the end of summer in 1798, Toussaint had recaptured all the major port towns, leaving the British pinched into the northwest corner of the island.

There the British commander, a Scot from a noble family, offered one of those valiant gestures which make others smile at British gentlemen but also salute their devotion to the honorable act; realizing that the black generals had outsmarted him at every turn, he gathered his staff at a port of debarkation and told them: "Those stubborn beggars have been a gallant foe. Let's give them a real salute. They've earned it." And his soldiers decorated the town, built a triumphal arch laden with flowers, conscripted local musicians to augment the military band, and assembled the local cooks to prepare a feast.

On the appointed day the British officers rose early, dressed in their brightest regimental uniforms laden with braid and medals, and marched behind the band to the edge of town, where they greeted in full panoply the two black generals. As those victors approached, the British had to smile, for tall Toussaint took such big strides that stubby Vaval, a head shorter, had to pump his chubby legs twice as hard to keep up. Joined by the Scot, they formed the front rank of the parade, and entered the town to the wild cheering of the black citizens and the polite applause of whites. At the local church Toussaint was handed a silver cross, which he bore proudly to the banqueting hall, and there he listened in solemn grandeur as the Scottish officer, a gallant adversary, said: "At the start we British had every advantage—controlled all your ports, occupied most of them, drove you inland. Total victory for our side."

The British officers applauded, and the speaker continued: "We overlooked these two—General Toussaint L'Ouverture, who could not be pinned down no matter how hard we tried, and this stubborn little fellow Vaval, whom we could never quite catch but who struck at us again and again."

Here the British officers turned to face the black generals and applauded loudly with cries of "Hear! Hear!" Then the Scotsman asked: "Honestly. How did you do it?" and the two black generals sat silent, tears coming to their eyes.

Toussaint and Vaval stood at the dock until the last British troops withdrew, and as the seven ships left the harbor Toussaint said, almost plaintively: "Vaval, our own French leaders never treated us with half the respect that enemy out there did. It could have been so different if they'd only dealt with us honorably."

"It was never possible," Vaval said, and Toussaint replied: "Now let's take this country for ourselves."

"You mean the slaves? Us?"

"We can tend the land as well as the French."

"But why would you risk fighting a lion like Napoleon?"

Toussaint, a slave who had been allowed no education or access to books or the friendship of learned men, fell silent, for he too was amazed at what he was now proposing—grappling with the foremost military genius of his age.

"Time's at hand, old friend, when we must strike out against the French."

"Wait!" Vaval pleaded, raising his voice to an unaccustomed level. "You can't go on doing this. First we side with the French, then the Spanish, then the French again, and now against them. You make yourself look foolish."

"No man is foolish when he calculates strategies to gain his freedom. Besides, we'll have no choice."

"Why not?"

"Because Napoleon will never let us exercise any control in this colony. Sooner or later he'll send troops against us." Bringing his shoulders forward, as if he were a boxer preparing either to attack or defend, he said grimly: "Now we prepare for whatever Napoleon throws against us, and what a shock we'll have for that one." And off the two black generals went to prepare their troops for the battles that could not be avoided.

Napoleon, during his march through Europe, often found recreation at night by reading reports from his colonies, and insofar as the Caribbean in general was concerned, he was not unhappy: "Guadeloupe back in our hands, slave uprisings under control. Our Martinique does remain in British hands, but in retaliation we've captured three of their richest islands. Now, what is happening on that damned St.-Domingue? What do those slaves think they're doing? Are English officers leading those black troops? Some outsider is." Whenever he voiced that suspicion, he concluded: "We've got to teach those slaves a lesson. About who controls France these days."

An aide, who had recently returned to Europe from St.-Domingue and traveled to Austria to meet Napoleon, reported: "This fellow Toussaint, a kind of homemade military genius. You know, of course, that he came back to our side after fighting for a long time against us . . . with the Spanish."

Napoleon stopped him right there: "He did desert to the Spanish, didn't he?"

"With that able assistant, General Vaval."

"Sounds French."

"Black as midnight, but a manly little fighter. Helped Toussaint kick the British completely out of St.-Domingue, and now there's talk among the slaves that they'll throw us out, too."

"Never!" Napoleon growled. "Time's come to discipline them. Get them back to the sugar plantations . . . all of them."

Once he voiced this decision his aides saw his eyes gleam with conspiratorial delight, and they supposed that he had suddenly imagined some stratagem which would startle and subdue Toussaint and Vaval, but that was not the case. What pleased him was the prospect of finally discovering how to get his obstreperous younger sister Pauline out of Paris. For the past five years she had presented him with one difficult problem after another; only twenty-one, she had already weathered some half-dozen tempestuous and even scandalous love affairs, and seemed quite prepared to add to that list whenever she encountered one of his handsome colonels or married generals.

Some months ago he believed he had solved the problem: he had married her to a fine young officer of good family named Charles Leclerc, medium height, erect carriage, dashing, and with a ready wit. Napoleon had attended their wedding, had given his sister away, and had then rushed the promotion of the bridegroom to senior general. Now he said: "We'll put Leclerc in charge of the St.-Domingue expedition, let him win his spurs and make him a duke or something. That would please Pauline." When the announcement was readied, Napoleon warned his aides: "We won't put it in writing, but most important—Pauline must accompany him. We've got to get her out of Paris."

So an expedition of enormous magnitude was mustered, utilizing at least nine ports from Honfleur in the north to Cádiz in the south, thirty-two thousand battle-tested soldiers and gear enough for a yearlong campaign in the tropics. When Napoleon saw the final report of what was being sent to St.-Domingue—the munitions, the extra uniforms, the medical kits, the presence of small, fast ships to serve as messengers back and forth between the scores of big ones—

he remarked: "Young Leclerc may not be a Marshal Soult or Ney, but he'll have older aides of proven merit to keep him headed in the right direction." It was a massive expedition, a tribute to Napoleon for having been able to assemble it and to France for having the men and equipment to spare. As its components sailed forth from their various ports, Napoleon could be forgiven when he claimed: "We've thought of everything," but not even he could have foreseen what kind of enemy his troops were about to face.

On the evening of 1 February 1802, César Vaval, now forty-six, stood on a breakwater at Cap-Français and looked in awe as eleven big French ships dropped anchor in the roadstead while small boats scurried back and forth bearing messages. General Toussaint stood silent beside him, calculating the number of trained French soldiers the ships must carry. Finally he said, with no emotion: "Maybe twelve thousand," and suddenly springing into action, the wily Toussaint dragged the speechless Vaval back into the town, where he gave him surprising orders.

"Things look perilous tonight. But we shall drive that crowd waiting out there right back to Paris . . . if you do your job right."

"I'll try."

"Don't try. Do it. Tomorrow, the next day too, and for as long as possible, fend them off. Don't let them land. Say there's a plague . . . any trick to hold them aboard ship for two days."

"Where will you be?"

"Bringing our troops down from the mountains. And while I do that, you see to it that every white man or free-colored who remains in this town is driven out . . . out!" Then, to Vaval's surprise, Toussaint started running like a hare through the empty streets, shouting: "Pile stacks of wood here! Stack dried tree branches here! Bring in hay from the barns! We're going to light a fire that will be seen in France!" Showing Vaval which houses to ignite first to ensure a giant conflagration, he said grimly: "No matter what general is waiting out there, when he looks ashore I want him to catch a fiery taste of what's ahead when he puts one toe on our land."

Toussaint's guess that the French troops would take some days to deduce that Vaval, the courteous little local manager, was playing them for a fool proved accurate, and those two days of waiting gave Vaval time to carry out orders. He did drive out the remaining whites and coloreds, most of them, and he did pile the street corners with combustibles, but in two of his major assignments he was forestalled by men as brave and resolute as he. The two-storied stone Château Espivent he was unable to capture from a group of *grands blancs* who had assembled there under the leadership of its owner. They resisted all attacks. Nor could he combat a collection of do-or-die free-coloreds who had fled to the big theater at the summons of Xavier Prémord, and who fired at the blacks with deadly accuracy.

On the second evening, when the rat-a-tat of gunfire ashore echoed through the fleet, Leclerc issued his order: "We land at dawn. All forces in small boats to storm the beach." But about an hour before dawn Pauline awakened him: "Charles! The town's on fire!" and with his other generals Leclerc went up on deck, to see wild flames rising above the town that was to have been his capital.

It was a ghastly day, with houses and buildings burning to their foundations. Most of the handsome town was leveled, but the two centers so stoutly defended by Espivent and the free-coloreds still stood defiant when the embers died. From the walls of the château the *grands blancs* had fired such withering blasts at any blacks who tried to storm the place that the arsonists were kept away, but even so, at one critical moment the defense might have collapsed had not General Vaval himself—as he had once defended Colibri—rushed up with a curt command: "Draw back. That one was decent," and the château was saved.

The lovely theater also survived, for there Prémord's free-coloreds maintained a fusillade so resolute that the rioting slaves had to fall back, the fiery brands in their fists useless against guns.

General Leclerc, who could not from his distant point of observation know that anything of the town had been saved, nevertheless put up a brave front. His eyes reddened from the smoke that drifted across his fleet, he cried: "Men, prepare to storm the beaches! I shall lead!" and the little boats were loaded with fighting men. But before Leclerc himself could leave, Pauline gripped his arm and whispered: "When you're the leader, first appearances are everything," and she made him dress in one of his finest uniforms, with sash and cockaded hat, so that when he stepped gallantly ashore with Pauline on his arm, she also in her best, they were indeed emissaries of the great Napoleon come to command a capital town from which the reconquest of the colony would be launched. Because they came properly dressed and apparently unafraid, they gave the white survivors of Le Cap a courage that would otherwise have been lacking.

As the handsome couple moved through the desolated town, one local resident left his stone château overlooking the sea and came forward, waving aloft a French flag and shouting: "Soldiers of France! Come ashore and save us!" It was Jerome Espivent, who had an amazing story to tell the Leclercs: "The black general who burned the town has kept his men away from my place. He'd been one of my slaves and he respects me for the charity I'd shown him."

"A good omen," Pauline said graciously, whereupon Espivent flourished his blue cape, bowed low, and kissed her hand: "My house is your house," and to the general: "My town in ashes is your capital, for I'm sure you will rebuild it," and on these emotional terms Leclerc took possession of the château and plunged into the maelstrom of the colony he had been sent to subdue and rule. While Pauline remained below directing the four Espivent house slaves how to rearrange what furniture was left, her husband withdrew to a room on the second floor, where, apart from others, he unsealed a secret letter which Napoleon had handed him eight weeks before in Paris.

It was one of the most Machiavellian documents in history, and a treasure for those scholars who would seek to unravel the mystery of how Napoleon's mind worked. Why the great general allowed a copy to survive is a mystery, but there it rests in the harsh glow of history, revealing the immorality and duplicity of the man.

Napoleon gave Leclerc minutely detailed instructions, not knowing that his orders in many ways duplicated the ones with which King Philip of Spain had saddled Medina-Sidonia, his unfortunate admiral general of the Armada; had Napoleon been aware of the similarity, and the pitiful results King Philip obtained, he might have given his brother-in-law and sister more freedom to make their own decisions.

The recapture of St.-Domingue, Napoleon wrote, would be relatively simple if a rigid schedule was followed: fifteen days to occupy all port towns, perhaps another month to strike at the slave armies from many different directions, then not more than half a year to track down isolated units that would no doubt try to take refuge in the mountains—after which, victory would be proclaimed and the troops could come home.

This military strategy was first class, even though the time allowances would have been more practical for an assault on a settled European principality without mountains, but the subsidiary orders were venal. Leclerc was ordered to conduct himself differently in each of the three stages of occupation:

As soon as you have secured the victory you will disarm only the rebel blacks, you will parley with Toussaint, promise him everything he asks until you gain control of all principal points in the colony. During this period all Toussaint's chief agents, white or colored, shall be loaded indiscriminately with honors, attentions and assurances that under the new government they will be retained in their posts. And every black man occupying an office of any kind will be flattered, well treated and given whatever promises you think necessary.

At the end of fifteen days, when the second stage was to begin, the screws were to be tightened, and so much pressure was to be applied to Toussaint that he would see the impossibility of relying upon isolated units in the mountains to continue the struggle:

On that very day, without scandal or injury but with honor and consideration, he must be placed on board a frigate and sent immediately to France. And on that same day throughout the colony you will arrest all suspects whatever their color, and also all black generals no matter what their patriotism or past service.

You will allow no variation in these instructions; and any person talking about the rights of those blacks, who have shed so much white blood, shall, using any pretext whatever, be sent to France, regardless of his rank or services.

The infamous fourth instruction was so shameless that it could not be put into writing, for Napoleon did not want anyone to see the inflammable words *a return to slavery,* but during the final meeting in Paris between the two men, Napoleon had said: "Slavery is a word never to be spoken. But it is a system to be reimposed as soon as conditions permit."

Governed by these duplicitous rules, Leclerc went downstairs for his first meeting with the leaders of the colony and, as in old times, he found waiting for him a group of only white men, and he assured them that with his troops from the home country, he, with assistance and guidance from them, would quickly restore order to the rebellious colony. At the meager dinner, Jerome Espivent gave the toast: "To our saviors from France," after which he offered stern counsel: "Keep your hands clean of the free-coloreds. They can only stain you. And never trust black troops. They're as fickle as the wind. The men and women in this room are the only ones you can rely upon. We stand ready to die for France, if only this disgraceful rioting and destruction of our property can be halted." These were no idle words; at every convulsion since that first horrible uprising in 1791, Espivent had been willing to lay down his life in defense of the principles by which he had been reared, and now in his sixtieth year he felt the same way.

Now began the historic battle for St.-Domingue. In the coastal regions of the north, General Leclerc and his immense French army controlled everything, and enthusiastically supported by *blancs* led by Jerome Espivent, laid careful plans to subdue the slave uprising and capture Toussaint and his main aide Vaval. To accomplish this, the French troops would compress the rebellious slaves into ever-smaller enclaves in the center and southern portions of the colony, and when the noose was so tightened that the *noirs* could no longer obtain arms, supplies or new conscripts, Toussaint and Vaval would have no option but to surrender.

Leclerc handled his task superbly, displaying a talent for military tactics which startled even his own subordinates. He made not a single mistake, and almost on the schedule that Napoleon had dictated, he had Toussaint's men driven completely out of the northern areas and so hedged about in the mountains that he could confidently report to Napoleon in Paris: "We have completely demoralized the slaves, and the surrender of their generals can be expected at any moment."

Toussaint and Vaval refused even to consider surrender. "Trusted friend," the powerful black general said whenever prospects looked bleak, "we grow stronger with every backward step we take . . . more compact on our side . . . more scattered on theirs," but at the close of one day in which Leclerc drove his men six miles deeper into the mountain retreats, Vaval leaned against a tree, exhausted, and asked: "Does Leclerc never give up?" and Toussaint replied: "He will. Time, and the mountains, and events we cannot foresee will force him to get back aboard his ships and return to France."

Meanwhile, Jerome Espivent, still in charge of his château, which served as army headquarters, was perplexed by unsavory incidents occurring there. He noticed one French officer after another coming to his château to take tea or wine with Madame Leclerc when her husband was away with his troops, and when such visitors, one by one, were taken to her quarters on the second floor, he began to suspect that this handsome young woman was going to be more difficult for General Leclerc to handle than the black generals. But he always reminded himself that she was Napoleon's sister, so he kept his counsel. After one scandalous incident he said to himself: After all, she is Italian, and maybe that accounts for it, for as a gentleman of near-noble breeding, he could not believe that the French wife of a commanding general would so conduct herself with junior officers.

Once, when he watched Pauline dallying with a married colonel, he lost his temper and asked a lieutenant: "That one, is she never satisfied?" and the young man replied with a leer: "Not too soon, I hope." Espivent thought that as a member of one of France's noble families, he ought to discuss this matter with General Leclerc, but when he saw the fighting little fellow stagger in exhausted from pursuing Toussaint, he had not the effrontery to badger him with Pauline's behavior: What that man needs is not lecturing, but sleep. And when the two dined together, for Pauline was usually out in the ruined town with someone else, he asked only about Toussaint.

"We have him worried," was all Leclerc would say. "I can see it by the moves he makes."

"How can you tell a thing like that?"

"I've seen it three times. He's had a clear run to the south. Might even do us real damage on the way down. But he refuses the escape we've left him . . . and do you know why?"

"My mind doesn't work like a *noir.*"

Leclerc laid down his napkin: "He's not a *noir,* Espivent, damn him, he's a full-fledged general. And if I didn't have three more armies in the field than he does, I'd never catch him."

In March and April 1802, Toussaint L'Ouverture made military history by conducting a Fabian operation of strategic retreat which lured Leclerc ever farther into the mountains, and won the gasping admiration of not only his French adversaries but also those American ship captains who arrived in Cap-Français with cargoes of powder and ball sent down from arsenals around Boston: "Haven't they caught the nigger yet? No? You better watch out; while he has you trapped in the mountains, he'll slip around and burn this town again." One captain brought a newspaper from Charleston, featuring a story about the evil effect Toussaint's exploits were having on South Carolina slaves: "Napoleon must settle this man's hash permanently, because his example must not be allowed to infect our docile slaves in the southern states."

But despite the brilliance and courage of the black generals, Leclerc proved himself such a bulldog, hanging tenaciously onto the heels of his enemy, that the day came when Toussaint had to face the fact that he could not continue the campaign indefinitely. So on a dark night at the end of April, he asked the one man he could trust to walk with him in the darkness: "Dear friend of battle, I can't continue this fight."

"Toussaint!" Vaval cried. "We have them on the run."

"What nonsense from an old friend."

"I mean it."

"Leclerc has never let up. He's trailing us right now, out there."

"I don't mean the troops he has in the field. I mean the ones in their graves." And he told Toussaint about the information their spies had brought: "That hard fighting unit who saw duty along the Rhine . . . gave us so much trouble at the start? Why don't we still face them? A black woman who helps nurse them explains why. Three months ago they started with about thirteen hundred men."

"How many now?"

"Only six hundred alive, and four hundred of them in hospital, that leaves only two hundred able to fight."

"But they keep bringing in replacements," Toussaint said, and Vaval replied: "They do, but always from the north of Europe."

"What does that signify?"

"They aren't accustomed to the tropics. Watch how many are able to face us at the end of two weeks."

Toussaint, who felt his life and his efforts drawing to a close, could not afford to wait even the two weeks which would have verified Vaval's prediction, and next morning he awakened César before dawn: "Old friend, I have no escape. You must come with me," and together, under a white flag, they approached the French lines to arrange the honorable terms under which Toussaint, Vaval and all others in the vicinity could surrender. French officers, speaking for Leclerc, who was overjoyed to receive the news, offered the black leader the exact terms Napoleon had prepared and on which Leclerc and Toussaint shook hands like honorable generals: "France awards freedom to all your black troops. Never again slavery. You and your other officers, like Vaval here, induction into the imperial forces of Napoleon with no reduction in rank. And if as you say you would prefer to live on your old plantation in retirement, do so, and France will give you an honor guard of four of your staff for life."

This was more generous than the black revolutionaries could have hoped for, and Vaval saw it as a testimony to the integrity of Toussaint, who had rarely killed civilians and who had resolutely clung to one abiding principle: "The slaves must be free." In the entire world since the first efforts of Spartacus, he was the first slave general, and a black one at that, to have attained his goal.

On 6 May 1802, exactly three months after the arrival of General Leclerc, the French army units stationed in Le Cap were given a late and generous breakfast at eight, ordered into their dress uniforms at ten, and mustered at eleven to give the salute to Generals Toussaint L'Ouverture and César Vaval as they surrendered their swords to the superior power of First Consul Napoleon Bonaparte and his able brother-in-law Leclerc. Pauline, watching the ceremony from a small thronelike affair in the square, thought: What a handsome man that Toussaint is. Sixty, they say, and he carries himself like a young stallion.

On 5 June 1802, after a month of idleness at his plantation, Toussaint was invited to a gala dinner at the neighboring headquarters of the local French commandant, a General Brunet, and he looked forward so avidly to an afternoon of relaxed military recollections that he asked his aide, General Vaval, to join him: "Give the French a bottle of wine, they talk better than anyone, and I'd enjoy that," but as they neared the plantation where Brunet waited, Vaval had a blinding apocalyptic vision. Reining in his horse, he ordered the black troops accompanying the two generals to move ahead, and said, with panic in his voice: "Toussaint! Death awaits if you go in there. For God's sake, turn back. For God's sake, don't go!"

"What's the matter, old friend?"

"Terror! I'm shaking with terror," and he held out his trembling hands.

"Fool! Grab your reins and let's get on with our little celebration."

"I cannot! The angel of death hovers above that house," and with that, Vaval turned back and galloped away as if the fiends of hell were at his heels, never to see his hero again.

Toussaint and his nine enlisted attendants rode on, entered the plantation compound, and saluted the French soldiers waiting there. They, in turn, saluted Toussaint, who threw his reins to one of his men: "Rest the horses out here," and, giving the French soldiers orders to feed his people, he went in to join the officers.

He had barely stepped into the room when General Brunet hurried forward, embraced him like a brother, and excused himself for a moment to tend the wine. The moment he left the room, the French officers around Toussaint drew their swords, pointing the sharp ends at his heart and throat. "Citizen Toussaint, you're under arrest," and when Brunet, visibly shaken by the disgraceful thing he had been forced to do, returned to the room, thus able to avow in later questioning "I had nothing to do with the arrest of General Toussaint," he said merely: "You're to be sent back to France . . . bound hand and foot."

Betrayed by a breach of honor so foul that all men in uniform reviled the act, Toussaint was immediately thrown aboard a small French ship, abused as a prisoner who had dishonored France, and taken to Brest, from where he was whisked to a fortress prison on the Swiss border. There, in the care of a sadistic jailer, he was starved and ridiculed as a black who had preposterously aspired to equality with the French.

Often during the days of his degradation he reflected upon the contrasting treatment he had received from his two enemies. "The English, who suffered greatly from me," he told his jailer, "gave me a banquet, toasted me as an honorable foe, and embraced me as they sailed away. You French? You lured me to a meeting, your general betrayed his honor, and you threw me into this filthy dungeon." He stared at the jailer and asked: "How could you do these things to a French citizen who fought for France against the Spanish and the English to protect your rights?"

The jailer understood not one aspect of this moral dilemma, and on a spring day in 1803, when he came to bring General Toussaint L'Ouverture his breakfast, he found the great black general dead of exposure in his ice-cold cell, protected by only one thin blanket.

With the arrest and deportation of Toussaint, General Leclerc felt certain that final victory was near, for as he assured Espivent's associates during a dinner at the château: "I have only to subdue that pestilential Vaval and the pacification of St.-Domingue will be complete. Our troops can then return to France."

Had Leclerc been able to consult at that moment with his last major opponent in the field, General Vaval, he would have found that the black commander had assessed the situation in identical terms, for the general was deep in the mountains with only a handful of black troops, and even that force diminished each week. His fellow generals, the murdering monster Jean-Jacques Dessalines and the mercurial Henri Christophe, had gone over to the French side, while the free-colored leaders, André Rigaud and Alexandre Pétion, had fled to Paris, where men with their cast of skin were safe for the moment.

Only he was in the field with anything that might be called an army, and one night, when defeat and surrender seemed inevitable, he sat with his wife at the edge of a forest and lamented not his fate, for he was prepared for anything, but that of his noble leader, Toussaint: "Marie, he defeated everyone. He was magical, a genius. He beat the Spanish before we joined them. He drove the English back into the sea. He defeated armies of free-coloreds when they came at him, and most of all, he defeated the French before they threw thousands of fresh men at us. And what did he achieve? Nothing. He won all the battles and lost the war."

His wife would not accept that: "He won us our freedom. We're not slaves anymore."

"From what I understand, that was mostly the work of good-hearted men in France."

"But we are free, and even if you have to surrender tomorrow, you can't change that. Even in his jail, Toussaint couldn't take credit for that."

Such a nebulous victory gave little consolation to Vaval, who could foresee only the impending defeat of the last of his army and his own surrender as the black general who had held out to the end, and he slept that night on a rude paillasse under the trees, assailed by this gnawing sense of failure.

But he was awakened at dawn by sentries bringing before him a pitiful black straggler who had tried to infiltrate the lines. He was in his seventies, an emaciated man whose lank, bent body showed the hurt and hunger he had undergone in order to join the rebelling slaves of St.-Domingue. He stood head bowed as his captors pushed him before their general.

"Who are you?" Vaval asked, aware that the shuffling fellow who was afraid to look up could be of little use to an army, and he and the black soldiers standing by were surprised when the man replied in excellent French: "I was a slave on Guadeloupe . . . joy like never before when the people in Paris sent us the wonderful news 'You are slaves no more, freemen forever, just like us in France.' We could buy land, work for wages, marry, and have homes like men and women are supposed to."

"Like we have here," Marie Vaval said. "Slaves no more."

The man turned to look at her, and said: "My wife said the same: 'Slaves no more!' but then he came, that monster Napoleon, and shouted at us: 'You're slaves again, and slaves you will remain forever.' "

"What?" Vaval shouted, and the soldiers who had captured the stranger called for others to move close to hear the appalling news.

"Yes! Slavery crushes us again in Guadeloupe. And it will return here too, unless you fight it to the death. It will come here on the next boat . . . or the one after that. Look at my back," and the man pulled up his flimsy shirt to show a crisscross of welts on his black skin. "They did this when they caught me trying that first time to sneak off the island. 'You're not to tell any of the other islands about slavery coming back. They'll receive word when we think it's proper.' They were desperately afraid some slaves might hear the news at a bad moment for them—like now, on this island—while you still have armies in the field. They're afraid the news might make you fight harder."

Although Vaval was thrown into a sullen rage by this news, he could not be sure that the man was telling the truth; he might well be an agent sent by the French to goad the final black army into precipitate action: "How did you get to us? All the way from Guadeloupe?"

"With difficulty—hiding from the search dogs, beaten near to death on my first try, relying on companions who lost heart when they saw the bigness of the sea they were supposed to cross. No food . . . fight in the cane fields . . . a stolen canoe . . ."

As the refugee spoke, Vaval heard only the first portion of his words, for he was remembering the days in the sugar fields in the southern part of St.-Domingue when his father, the slave Vavak, told his children almost the same story: "A stolen boat . . . a beach in Puerto Rico . . . escaping the chase dogs in Santo Domingo . . ." The story of black refugees seeking freedom never ended, never changed, and sometimes, as in this dawn confrontation, the words and images exploded in terrible fury, blinding men to the risk even of death.

"You are one of us," Vaval broke in. "You are to work with me . . .

close . . . because I need to hear your words: *Napoleon will drive us back to slavery.* No! By God, he will not!" And he gathered about him his wife, the messenger of doom and all his lieutenants, and they swore there at the edge of the forest overlooking a gully that stood between them and the French troops in Le Cap: "We will defy Napoleon to the death! We will never again be slaves!" And from that day on, General Vaval, fighting alone, became a military hurricane comparable to the natural ones that periodically ravaged the Caribbean. In battle after battle he surprised the trained French armies whose troops outnumbered his sixty thousand to ten.

But because Charles Leclerc was also a heroic man who knew how to use his superiority in numbers, he was able to drive Vaval's ragtag army slowly backward into the final valley from which there would be no escape. Vaval, realizing this, grew ever closer to his wife, who had supported him during so many bleak midnights, and they took an oath between them: "We will never again be slaves. The French shall not capture us alive."

Despite the valiant boast of its general, Vaval's collection of former slaves certainly would have been pushed back into the final closed valley had not an ally stormed into St.-Domingue to fight on his side. It was a remorseless antagonist, General Yellow Fever, and the prediction made earlier by Vaval was about to come true in terrible dimension. The disease struck the French troops with such fury that the Europeans were overwhelmed by the assault. Carried by mosquitoes, a fact then unknown, it attacked the liver so that jaundice resulted, but it also produced a debilitating fever which caused unrelieved aching in the head and back; then tiny ruptures occurred in the soft tissues of the throat and lungs, resulting in dreadful hemorrhaging from the mouth.

The speed with which these various manifestations struck, one cascading upon the other, was appalling, death often coming within three days of the first attack, and once the disease started, there was no known cure; sometimes—at least often enough to keep hope alive—the disease dissipated of itself, rest, sleep and good diet aiding the process, and then the patient was immune for the rest of his life. And that was what differentiated old-timers in the colony like General Vaval and his black troops from General Leclerc's French newcomers:

the blacks, having had mild attacks when young, were immune, while Leclerc's men from northern climates were pitifully susceptible.

The fatalities were much worse than Vaval had suggested that night in his talk with Toussaint: of an average thousand-troop unit, eight hundred fifty might die, a hundred might be in a hospital of some kind, leaving fifty, if the commander were lucky, available for limited service, limited because a mild form of the disease might be enervating them. It was a monstrous affliction, and when fresh troops were imported from Europe, they provided not replacements in the line but merely new targets for the mosquitoes.

So the betrayal of General Toussaint accomplished little, for although some black units did defect to the French in hopes of landing decent work when the civil war ended, stubborn patriots like Vaval retreated to forest refuges, emerging stealthily now and then to punish careless French units. And they maintained relentless pressure by initiating their own imaginative responses when the French committed barbarities against them.

At Port-au-Prince, the French defenders of the town—assisted as always by the free-coloreds who still trusted that if they helped the whites when the latter were in trouble, the whites would accept them as equals when the trouble ended—thought to discourage Vaval by erecting a tall gallows at the edge of town where the black troops could see the hangings; there each day at noon they executed a black prisoner. Vaval told his men: "Erect me a tall gallows on that rise and fetch me all the white prisoners we have," and next day at noon, after the whites in the town had hanged a black, the blacks outside did the same to a white. After three days of this, Vaval summoned all his white prisoners and told them: "Write your names on this list, then nominate one of your group to take this message into town: 'We can play this game as long as you. Here are the names of the next to go.'" And the public hangings stopped.

The extent to which St.-Domingue had become a phantasmagoria, without reason or justification, was illustrated in General Vaval's experience with the Polish Second Battalion. Napoleon, deeply worried about the possibility that his Polish troops serving in Europe might turn their energies to establishing a free Poland and stop fighting for France, impulsively decided to ship them all off to St.-Domingue to assist Leclerc. Five thousand Poles, unaccustomed to and fearful of the tropics, debarked at Cap-Français in late 1802 and were thrown immediately into action against the black troops of Toussaint's successors.

After a series of skirmishes in which the Poles fought reasonably well, they found themselves supporting French troops in a beautiful town overlooking the Caribbean, the seaport of St.-Marc, where they, the Poles, were forced to become the villains in a cruel conflict. A black general who had been fighting as a trusted ally of the French suddenly decided that a brighter future awaited him if he and his men switched over to General Vaval's slave army. This was a prudent decision, but in leaving, he abandoned one unit of his army containing over four hundred black troops stationed inside the town of St.-Marc in the midst of the French and Polish units.

When the French general commanding the Polish battalion was apprised of his former colleague's shameful act—his taking more than half the combined army over to the enemy—he gave crisp and secret orders to his subordinates: "The blacks out there don't know yet what's happened. Quick, disarm them and assemble them in the public square."

Quietly, his junior officers, all French, explained to the blacks: "The general wants to talk with us about the forthcoming attack. Stack your guns and follow us." When the trusting blacks obeyed, moving forward to hear the general's plans, they heard him cry to his own men and the Poles: "Close ranks!" and around the perimeter of the beautiful square the armed French and Polish soldiers formed a rigid barrier, bayonets pointed outward. Then came the quiet, dreadful order: "Men, kill them all!"

It was done with bayonets, but only by the Poles, while the French stood, prepared to use their guns if any blacks escaped. It was grisly, horrible, and swift. Unarmed men were gutted with one powerful swipe, or took bayonet thrusts to the heart, or fell wounded to their knees to be clubbed to death. Those few who managed to dash into nearby houses were dragged screaming back into the square, where they were stabbed as they knelt, begging for mercy. Not one black soldier escaped and not one French soldier had to fire his gun. The Polish troops did it all.

When news of the massacre reached General Vaval, who had been waiting to welcome the detachment into his army, he was revolted. "Who did the killing?" he demanded, and when someone said: "The Polish battalion," he remained silent for a long time, then said: "They shouldn't even be here. Yellow fever will kill half of them." Then he took an oath: "I shall hunt them down, man by man," but his informant added: "I was there, sir. It was the French general who gave the order and the French soldiers who lined the square."

"Naturally," Vaval said, but nevertheless, in subsequent months, he sometimes marched far out of his way in hopes of coming to grips with that murderous Polish unit. He did not succeed, but spies informed him from time to time that these Europeans were succumbing to the ravages of yellow fever even faster than he had predicted: "Two out of three Poles are either dead or in the hospital." But his dogged tracking of their movements continued.

More than a year later, when his slave army had been victorious in many battles and when he was considered by the mass of blacks to be their finest general, he was on a drive which carried him to a mountainous corner of his old Colibri Plantation. As his aides were pitching his tent, a spy brought disturbing news: "Troops occupying that high hill. Guns all pointed this way."

Vaval studied the height: "We'd lose lives trying to take that one," and then the spy said: "The soldiers are all Polish. Second Battalion."

When Vaval heard this he was paralyzed with indecision. Those men up there were the vicious crew who at St.-Marc had massacred defenseless black soldiers. Those Poles had outraged decency and the rules of war, and they deserved to die, which they surely would if he surrounded the eminence to prevent escape and then launched an assault upon it. But if he did, he would lose many of his best men, and uselessly. For once he did not know what to do, for he feared that if he ordered a costly assault at dawn, he would be doing so only to settle old grudges, and to lose good men that way would be dishonorable.

So at midnight, with the moon dropping low toward the horizon, the black general asked for three brave volunteers to move ahead of him with torches showing that he was carrying a white flag, and when the party was formed the four marched into the night: "Truce! Truce! We want to save your lives."

As they reached the point where the path started climbing sharply upward, they were challenged by French troops led by a lieutenant who came forward, gun at the ready, to parley. At this point the black soldiers quickly thrust their torches into the ground and leveled their own guns at the Frenchmen.

"I am General Vaval." The torches lit up his grave, determined face. "I come to offer you honorable terms to get off this peak. Who's in command?"

"I'm not allowed to say. But he's a colonel. Good fighting man."

"Tell him he can accomplish a good thing if he'll talk with me . . . an honorable thing."

The lieutenant gave an order to his men waiting behind him in the darkness: "Three step forward. It's a legitimate truce party," and when they appeared, to face the black soldiers, he and one of Vaval's men disappeared up the hill.

"What will happen?" one of the black soldiers asked, and Vaval replied: "Common sense will win out, I hope."

Rather promptly the French lieutenant and the black soldier came down the hill, bringing with them four well-armed white soldiers, in the midst of whom came a Polish officer, who said stiffly: "Colonel Zembrowski, Polish Second Battalion."

Vaval moved forward, extended his hand, grasped the Pole's in a warm clasp, and asked: "May we talk alone?" When they moved to a hill with guns from every direction pointed at them, Vaval remembered the dignity with which the English officers had treated him, and his first thought was: I must do no less. And so he said: "Colonel, as you no doubt saw before sunset, we have enough troops to take this hill."

Very calmly Zembrowski, a man in his late thirties and far from home, said: "And you surely saw that we have the men and ammunition to make that very costly. That must be why you're here."

To the Pole's surprise, Vaval changed the course of the conversation completely: "How is it going?" and Zembrowski, as soldier to soldier in a moment of military frankness, repeated almost to the word what Vaval himself had said months ago: "We should never have been sent here. Napoleon was afraid of us."

"Fever?"

"We came with five thousand. Now we have not quite one thousand."

"The British had the same experience when they tried to defeat us."

"And you? Shall you win a nation for yourselves?"

"We already have."

"We should never have tried to stop you. But in the end, Napoleon will."

Quietly, but with enormous conviction, Vaval replied: "Even he will fail. The whites tried, and we overcame them. The free-coloreds tried, and we drove them into the ground. The Spanish tried, the English too, you Poles and even traitors within our own group tried, and they've all failed." Then the harshness in his voice vanished, and he said with deep regret: "Even the French tried . . . to destroy their own children. Napoleon sent his legions against us, and soon they'll be leaving forever." He stopped in the darkness and looked at his black soldiers with their torches and the Poles with theirs, then said: "I've never understood why the fever kills whites and leaves us alone."

Then Vaval asked: "How is it . . . your soldiers fighting alongside the French?" and Zembrowski replied: "The French don't like Poles, but of course they don't like anybody. The generals, though, they're brilliant. Trained. They know history. They study terrain carefully." He broke into a soft chuckle: "Mind if we sit? My left leg took a small shot."

When they were perched on rocks, he laughed outright: "Sometimes I don't blame the French. One general came to me with a piece of paper: 'What are we going to do about this, Zembrowski?' and I saw that he had written the names of two of my junior officers: Żdźbło and Szczygieł. 'We can't handle names like that,' and I said: 'We'll make the first one Dupont, the second Kessel.'"

After a pause he said: "They can't accept us. Because we don't do things their way, they're quick to call us cowards. Claim we don't do our share of the fighting. When our men hear this, when I hear it, we think our honor has been smeared, and to a Pole honor is everything."

For some moments, as the torches flickered, the two soldiers looked only at moving shadows, then Zembrowski felt compelled to speak honestly out of his respect for this powerful black general: "Perhaps you know that our battalion was at St.-Marc?" and Vaval replied: "Yes, I've been trailing you ever since, hoping to catch you like this."

"You know, of course, that it was French officers who gave the commands? Threatened to bayonet us if we didn't bayonet you."

"I supposed so," Vaval said sternly, at which Zembrowski dropped his head in his hands. "Dishonored. General Vaval, we dishonored ourselves that day and I pray you can forgive us."

"I have . . . tonight . . . meeting you on the battlefield, man to man. But in this colony, as you yourself say, Poles are without honor." He hesitated, then rose and started back to the troops, but as they walked together he said: "In the morning, of course, we shall come up and take this hill," to which Zembrowski made a strange reply:

"General, you're a man who has kept his honor intact. I beg you, do not lead your troops tomorrow. Do not." He said no more, but as they stood under the torches for their farewell, Zembrowski reached out impulsively and embraced his black enemy.

Early next morning when the former slaves, with Vaval in the lead, climbed up the hill to wrest it from the Poles, they were astonished to see two French officers running down toward them, waving white flags and shouting: "We surrender! Flag of surrender!" and they had scarcely reached the bottom, their faces white with fear, when a series of titanic blasts enveloped the top of the hill, shattering it and killing every soldier there, including Zembrowski.

The honor of the Polish troops, whatever that means, had been restored. Rather than surrender, they had blown themselves to eternity.

Despite the stubborn heroism of generals like Vaval and the ravages of General Yellow Fever, Leclerc was painfully carpentering a victory pretty much along the lines Napoleon had laid out; black units, seeing the futility of trying to oppose the entire French empire with its endless resources, were beginning to defect in huge numbers, so that even an improvising genius like Vaval had to realize that defeat was at hand. The French were too strong, Leclerc showed a fortitude no one had expected, and the black cause seemed doomed.

French victory would probably have been attained had not Napoleon, believing that he had unlimited power over men, issued the appalling decree which restored slavery in Guadeloupe. This devastating news, which up to now Leclerc had kept suppressed in his colony, seeped out, and now the blacks could not blind themselves to what lay ahead, especially when refugees from Guadeloupe at the eastern end of the Caribbean arrived with tales of what disruptions had occurred on that island when slavery was reinstated.

Leclerc, still trusting that he could dominate the slaves, assembled all his senior officers at the château to inform them: "I'm sure one more push will do it. I'm heading into the mountains to catch that damned Vaval," but before departing on what he hoped would be his final maneuver, he told Espivent: "Look after Pauline for me," and off he rode.

Espivent, standing in his gateway, watched as the gallant general headed for the mountains where Vaval waited, and was swept by feelings of compassion and remorse: We laughed at him when he landed. Napoleon's brother-in-law, a know-nothing, make-believe general. But by God he drove Toussaint into surrender and he's pinned down that pesky Vaval. And as he rides off to his final battle, he leaves here in my house . . . what? A brothel superintended by its only occupant, his wife.

As soon as Pauline was certain that her husband was securely gone into the hills, she began entertaining a series of his officers, and was so blatant about her upstairs sessions—a different man every three days it seemed—that Espivent felt he had to intervene, for it was his château that was being contaminated and his friend's honor defiled: "Good God, madam! Can't you control your appetites?" But even as he reprimanded her he was uncomfortably aware of her dark Italian beauty. She was twenty two that turbulent year, a gorgeous human being who knew full well her effect on men and her skills of coquetry.

"Now, Seigneur Espivent," she said gently, biting her left thumbnail, "you're certainly not talking about the last century, are you?"

"I'm talking about all centuries. About the dignity of France. About the sister of the chief of state. And especially about the honor of a brave husband who is absent leading his troops into difficult battle." As he thundered these words he was dressed in a red skullcap and one of his blue capes, and with his neatly trimmed Vandyke and flashing eyes, he could have been mistaken for some moralist of a preceding century, but he had little impact on Pauline, who that very afternoon entertained a colonel from Espivent's hometown of Nantes.

During this assignation he remained on the ground floor, pacing in such a growing rage that when the colonel descended, smiling and adjusting his sword, Espivent jumped out to bar his way: "If you ever step into my house again, sir, I shall kill you."

"What are you saying?"

The altercation brought Pauline down from her well-used bedroom, and stepping between the two men, she demanded: "What goes on here?" and Espivent said through clenched teeth: "If he comes here again on such a mission, I shall kill him."

"Are you crazy, old man?" she shouted, and in growing anger he shouted back: "Leave my house. I've protected this château through fire and riot and disorder, and I will not have it dishonored in my final days."

The imbroglio ended with Espivent saying righteously: "I shall inform General Leclerc," at which Pauline and the colonel could not refrain from laughter, but they did have the decency to refrain from sneering as they giggled: "He's always known."

Espivent did fully intend to clear this disgraceful matter with Leclerc when the latter returned, but in the middle of October 1802, a brief eight months after his arrival at Le Cap, the general, while on a chase after Vaval, felt the onset of a virulent fever, and turning to his aide, he gasped: "I think it's got me."

He was rushed from the battlefield to the Espivent château, but by the time he reached there his exhausted body had passed into the second and third stages of the dreaded disease, and everyone who looked at his ravaged face and twitching body knew that recovery was impossible. Now Pauline, confronted with the certainty that this honorable man whom she had so abused was dying, became a true sister of Napoleon, fighting the disease with her constant ministrations and ignoring the warnings of her friends: "But, madam! You may become infected yourself."

"He needs me," she said defiantly, and through the long tropical nights she bathed his fevered body and did what she could to alleviate his pains. But on the fifth morning, when he began to hemorrhage from the mouth, she screamed for Espivent: "Help me!" and together they wiped the blood from his face, but to no avail. Charles Leclerc, who had proved his valor in the most unrelenting corner of the French colonial world, was dead at the age of thirty.

Four officers were assigned to accompany the cadaver and Pauline Buonaparte—she spelled her name the Italian way—back to France, and during the extended voyage, for the French ship had to dodge English prowlers, she found solace with three older officers, each of whom had been her lover at Le Cap. An officer, who was never invited to her cabin, was heard to say to one of the sailors: "Looking at those four, I feel like the fifth wheel on a cart," and when the sailor asked what he meant, he said: "I've never been part of their merry games," and the sailor asked: "Would you like to be?" and the complaining officer laughed: "Who wouldn't?" and the sailor said: "Trip's not over."

When the funeral ship reached France, Leclerc was buried with the honors he had won as a courageous fighting man, and Napoleon paid him respect, but the latter's attention was on other matters, for when he realized that he might lose St.-Domingue, he quickly disposed of the other prospering colony he held in Louisiana, selling it at a shockingly low price to President Jefferson of the new American Republic, for in his opinion, probably correct, Louisiana without St.-Domingue as a way station to support it would be indefensible.

He also attended to his rambunctious sister, finding her with amazing celerity an Italian nobleman, a member of the great Borghese family, as her second husband. As a gesture of appreciation, young Borghese sold Napoleon for pennies the vast Borghese collection of art and supervised its removal to Paris. To reciprocate, Napoleon made Pauline a duchess, but this only served to spur her bedroom activities.

With Leclerc gone and the bulldog Vaval still at large, command of the French troops in St.-Domingue fell into the hands of the son of an illustrious general who had helped the American colonies win their independence. Donatien Rochambeau turned out to be one of the horrors of the Caribbean, known for his disgraceful behavior and his Nero-like propensities.

To strike terror into the hearts of Vaval's black remnants still opposing the French, he imported from Cuba a large number of savage dogs specially trained to attack Negroes, introducing the animals at a gala evening performance attended by eager whites. Three black men, stripped to the waist, were brought into an enclosed space, and while they huddled together, unaware of what was about to happen, hatches were thrown open and the dogs leaped into the arena. But they were quickly greeted by a chorus of booing, for the dogs merely sniffed at the blacks, circled them, and withdrew to fight among themselves.

Rochambeau, infuriated by the cries of derision, shouted to his soldiers: "Draw some blood. That'll get them started," and men with bayonets went out, protecting themselves from the dogs who wanted to attack them and not the blacks, and jabbed at the bellies of the three blacks until blood spurted, whereupon the dogs leaped at the men, tore them apart, and devoured them. The audience applauded.

Like Leclerc before him, Rochambeau was domiciled at Espivent's château, where nightly he was encouraged by the owner to continue his assaults on blacks and free-coloreds: "I must show you my studies, General. How one drop of black blood contaminates a family through thirteen generations, 8,192 descendants. So anything you can do to eliminate blacks and even part-blacks is commendable," and these two patriots, representing not more than 40,000 whites among nearly 500,000 blacks, seriously believed that through terrorism they could control the blacks and force them back into slavery: "Finest thing Napoleon's done so far, General, is the reintroduction of slavery, but we may have to kill off all those who knew freedom under Toussaint and that infamous Vaval. They won't surrender, so don't hold back."

Espivent applauded when his new friend disciplined a fractious black brigade in a manner that General Leclerc could not have approved. The hundred or so black would-be mutineers were marched to the public square, surrounded by French soldiers with rifles at the ready, and forced to watch as their wives were then brought into the square and executed in various ways, one by one. Then the guns were turned on the men, and all were slain.

Espivent himself participated in a general elimination of any Cap-Français blacks who were reported by white informants as "being so badly infected with the disease of freedom that they will never again make good slaves." He set up an open-air office on the docks and from it directed some eight thousand blacks to board ships that would, he promised, "take you to freedom in Cuba." When the ships were loaded, one by one, they sailed about a mile out into the bay, where sailors armed with guns and swords killed the blacks, pitching their dead bodies into the sea at such a rate that the nearby shores were lined with decomposing corpses. Espivent remedied this unfortunate development by instructing the captains: "Sail your ships farther so the currents will carry the bodies out to sea."

Espivent did not personally participate in one of the more ingenious assaults on blacks, but he did provide a slaving ship for the experiment and supervised the engineering details: belowdecks a small furnace was erected in which wet sulfur could be burned, and the prodigious amount of smoke it produced was then conveyed by pipes into a lower hold where the blacks were crammed. One potful of burning sulfur gave off enough gas to suffocate sixty blacks, killing them without the waste of bullets or the construction of gallows.

But these atrocities, and there were others, gained Rochambeau nothing, for whenever a new one was reported to General Vaval in the mountains, he listened, did not interrupt, bowed his head and clenched his fists till the nails bit into his palms—and dedicated himself even more furiously than before to a single task: "We shall evict every Frenchman from this colony. There can be no negotiation, no truce." Ten years before, he had not even known words like *evict* and *negotiation*, but now he was using them fluently to help build a new nation.

Each night before his men launched some paralyzing move against Rochambeau's forces, he moved among them, saying in his soft voice: "Tomorrow we win Toussaint's victory for him," and next day when he struck, his drive was so relentless, so composed of cold fury, that the French could not withstand the waves of destruction that crashed down upon them. Toward the end of 1803 an infuriated Rochambeau told his generals: "Dammit, there's no handling that little fiend," and one afternoon he simply gave up the effort. There was no grandiloquent gesture, no honorable acknowledgment that the blacks had won. He simply called in his ships, then spent a night drafting a report to Napoleon explaining how, through trickery and deceit, Vaval had gained a few unimportant skirmishes but would have been totally defeated had not yellow fever intervened.

At the railing of the last French ship to leave St.-Domingue stood Jerome Espivent, headed for exile from the colony he loved. He was now in his sixties, his hair and Vandyke completely white. He had about his shoulders one of his black capes, and in his eyes there was a mist of profound regret as he watched his stone château growing ever smaller. "We should never have lost that land," he said to a young officer from the Loire Valley. "It was all because of the free coloreds," he added, and when he turned back to see Le Cap, both it and his mansion had disappeared from view.

The attempt to whip the blacks of Toussaint and Vaval back into slavery had failed. The great Napoleon, having lost the richest colony in the world and nearly a hundred thousand of his best European troops, would now turn his attention to his own coronation as emperor and his chain of rampages through Europe, culminating in his retreat from Moscow. In his immortal journey he would humble a dozen kings and humiliate a score of generals, but he managed to outsmart the slave Toussaint only by an act of trickery and dishonor, while General Vaval defied him to the end.

In 1804, César Vaval, like the Roman general Cincinnatus in 458 B.C., retired to his land after a chain of significant victories and the establishment of the only black republic in the world. Since he had been a slave in its fields, he was entitled to claim the entire Colibri Plantation of Espivent, but he took only the western portion, the part that contained the hill on which the Polish troops had chosen mass suicide rather than surrender. There he lived with his wife and three children, and sometimes in the evening he told them not of his own exploits, which he felt had been duplicated or excelled by several of Toussaint's other generals, but of the extraordinary heroism of his father, the slave Vavak on the Danish plantation. And as he did so, the past became very real for his children. They could visualize themselves in Africa, or under the Danish lash on St. John, or in a small boat escaping to Puerto Rico and on to Haiti. Vaval drummed into them that they were descendants of exceptionally heroic people, and they felt obligated to sustain the tradition. Of their father's heroics during the war of liberation they never spoke, nor was there need, for it was assumed that they would behave as he had.

Now, as a man nearing fifty, he was not happy with what he saw in his new nation. One of Toussaint's vindictive generals, Jean-Jacques Dessalines, had recently proclaimed himself Emperor for Life. And what a vicious man, Vaval thought one evening as he sat atop the Polish hill. Last year Dessalines had broadcast an amnesty to all the islands of the Caribbean and even to South Carolina: "You whites who fled Haiti, come home. The past is forgotten. Come back and help us build a great new nation!" They came back, yes they did, white people homesick for the colony they had loved. And what happened when they got here?

Vaval sat for some time, head bowed, as he recalled those terrible scenes. When Dessalines had them all in hand, he proclaimed one morning: "Death to every white man in Haiti!" and the killing began. At Cap-Français, the place they now call Cap-Haïtien, he lined up hundreds of whites. They thought he was going to lecture them about their duties as citizens in the new nation. No, no! He murdered them all, maybe four hundred, maybe five. "Cleansing the nation," he called it, and every white in Haiti was slain.

As night began to fall, Vaval looked toward Cap-Haïtien and wondered: Can horrible betrayals like this ever be cleansed from a land? Are there certain crimes that can never be expiated? And then, because he was a man of honor, he had to acknowledge his own guilt. When the whites had been disposed of, attention turned to the free-coloreds, and now Dessalines decreed: "Every free-colored is to be removed from Haiti," and because it was known that Vaval despised the free-coloreds and had frequently engaged them in battle, he was given the job of hunting them down in the north.

Mortally ashamed of his behavior in those frenzied days, Vaval recalled his siege of Meduc. Under the leadership of the Prémords, the coloreds of the region assembled at their plantation, where the fighting was brutal. Vaval could not subdue them, and one of his men asked scornfully: "Vaval? If you handled Leclerc so easily, why not these few free-coloreds?" and he had no answer. They were heroic.

Now came a kindlier remembrance. At the end of the battles, when Vaval had to retreat without having dislodged them, Julie Prémord came to him, and she suggested a nationwide truce to stop this senseless killing. She'd guarantee adherence of the free-coloreds if Vaval would speak for the blacks. But when he sent a horseman into Cap-Haïtien with her suggestion, Dessalines replied: "No truce. Exterminate them." But that could not be done, because the Prémords, the Toussaints of their race, were defending their plantation most ably. So Vaval had to withdraw, knowing that the last sensible opportunity had been lost.

Then his memory flashed to a village square lined with palm trees. Throughout the nation the free-coloreds were being hunted down and slain. In the north they congregated at last in Meduc—the town in which the free-coloreds had once met secretly for their riotous dances—a remnant so powerless they had to surrender. Because Vaval had grown to respect them, he pleaded with the government that these final few be allowed to live quietly in their corner of the north. And he was listened to. In fact, he was dispatched to arrange the terms of surrender and forgiveness.

So at Meduc on a clear, fine day Vaval assembled the free-coloreds who were surrendering and stood with Prémord and his wife as the final details were arranged. "The war is ended," Prémord cried in a clear, solid voice that commanded respect, and as Vaval turned to look at him he thought: What a handsome man! His color is so much more attractive than I used to think. Prémord continued: "We have a new nation and a new ruler. France is gone forever and with it domination by the whites. On this happy day we begin a lasting friendship between groups that have for too long been separated." With that, he embraced Vaval, shouting to his followers: "See how two old enemies start their new friendship!" and everyone cheered.

Then, from a cottage near the square where they were meeting, the self-proclaimed emperor came out, and he cried in a wild voice: "Kill them all!" and his black troops rushed forth with bayonets and guns and murdered every one of the five hundred who had come to make peace. Prémord and his wife, who were standing with Vaval, clutched at his arms, and Xavier cried in anguish: "Vaval, what's happening?" Before Vaval could intercede, they were torn from him, speared with bayonets a dozen times and thrown into a ditch. Not one free-colored survived, and those few who had hidden in the rest of the north were hunted down like animals and exterminated.*

These memories proved too painful for Vaval. With a wild, gasping sound he clutched at his throat: My God! What a terrible burden we've placed on our land! In 1789 it contained half a million prosperous and well-behaved people; now, probably less than two hundred thousand, they say. Plus all the dead English and Spanish and Polish invaders. Can a land tolerate such brutal abuse? Does the blood spilled upon it not contaminate it? Is our new Haiti condemned to be a ghost that will never be real?

Looking again to the north, he could see the roof of the château at Cap-Haïtien and the multiple massacres its inhabitants had known: 1791, 1793, 1799, 1802 . . . no land could absorb such devastation; the scars would never be erased. He thought of the individuals responsible for this unending tragedy: *grands blancs* like Jerome Espivent, who hated both blacks and free-coloreds. And then he winced: Or blacks like me, who "cleansed the land" of whites and coloreds alike. Well, now we have our black nation, totally black, and what are we going to make of it?

As the dark cloud of night spread over his tormented land, he wondered if it would ever lift.

---

*Dessalines' behavior became so murderously irrational that his two military cohorts, Pétion and Christophe, decided that there was no other course but to murder him, which they did. Thus began that recurring cycle of dictatorship, mismanagement and assassination that would plague Haiti henceforth.

XI

MARTIAL LAW

THE DECADES FOLLOWING THE SLAVE REBELLION IN HAITI SAW vast improvements in the fortunes of blacks throughout the Caribbean. Great Britain abolished slavery everywhere in its empire in 1834; France in 1848. The United States engineered a cynical trick in 1863; President Lincoln abolished slavery in the middle of the Civil War, but only in the southern states, over which he had no control. In those border states which he did control, it continued, but in 1865 it was honestly outlawed everywhere. Spanish holdings in the Caribbean retained a brutal slavery long after other areas had stopped, with Cuba continuing till an unbelievable 1886.

Blacks were technically freed, but it was sometimes difficult, when looking at a specific situation, to realize it. In Jamaica, for example, in 1865 a volatile black Baptist preacher, George Gordon, gave a sermon in which he cried: "God wanted slavery ended, and it was," but even as he spoke, an ominous throwback to the olden days was brewing.

"If God ever comes back to check on things," the young man whispered, "I'm sure he'll look like Governor Eyre." As owner of Trevelyan, the sugar plantation producing the dark rum so highly regarded in Europe, and member of the island's Executive Council, Jason

Pembroke exemplified the best in Jamaica. At twenty-eight he had the slim, crisp appearance of a young man who intended to keep everything around him under control, a neatly trimmed black beard and a cautious approach to his job of providing the governor with studied advice.

The man to whom he whispered his opinion was also a member of the council but entirely different in both character and appearance. He was Pembroke's cousin, Oliver Croome, whose sugar estate was larger and more valuable. A hearty man in his forties, clean-shaven, ruddy-faced, somewhat overweight and given to explosive bursts of laughter, he saw his duties much differently than did Pembroke: "The queen tells us what to do, and we do it." It would be unthinkable for him to utter even one word counter to directives originating from the Colonial Office in London: "And if our buggers think they can ignore the queen's rules, there's always the marines to whip 'em into shape."

They were good friends, these dissimilar cousins—Pembroke austere and cautious, Croome flamboyant and given to wild statements—and although they usually differed in politics, with Pembroke a quiet, thoughtful liberal, Croome a loud-spoken archconservative, they did heartily agree on certain attitudes common to their class: loyalty to the crown, love for England, in which their families had spent more time than in Jamaica; and a fierce determination to protect the welfare of sugar planters. To accomplish these desirable ends, they gave their support to Eyre, a heroic type of man who did indeed look like some all-wise, paternal Jove or Jupiter come down from heaven to straighten out the affairs of Jamaica.

"He's a man who knows what he's doing," Oliver whispered to his cousin, and the two nodded deferentially to the austere man seated at the head of their council table. Edward John Eyre, now fifty years old, was a towering figure, heavily bearded and with a mustache so thick that it obscured his mouth, making his halting speech rumble. Once when listening to him orate, Jason Pembroke had said: "When God spoke through the burning bush, He must have sounded a lot like that."

Eyre was not a traditional colonial governor, no effete son of some notable English family who had gained his position because noble relatives had done his bargaining for him. Third son of an impoverished Church of England clergyman whose ancestors had once been well-to-do church leaders, he found himself at seventeen with a good education but no prospects. In this extremity his prudent father did two things to aid him: he collected from friends enough money to purchase the boy a commission in the army, but just as Edward was about to become a soldier, his father suggested: "Why don't you keep the money and try your fortunes in Australia?"

The idea was bold, unexpected, and in October 1832, Edward John Eyre bought passage to the unknown continent, where he arrived in late March of the next year, a tedious voyage of more than a hundred and forty days. In Sydney, like any thoughtful Englishman of the period, he went from house to house, office to office, presenting the numerous letters of introduction which family friends had provided, but nothing came of these solicitations, and he was left on his own with no friends and only the vast, empty continent at hand to provide a home and an occupation.

By virtue of an iron will and a well-disciplined physique, he began heroic explorations into the loneliest parts of Australia, traveling thousands of miles, often attended by only one companion—the smiling, indefatigable aborigine boy Wylie. Together they penetrated the continent in a manner that later experts would say was impossible, and in the end Eyre was recognized as one of the bravest of all Australian explorers and was honored by having the continent's largest lake named after him. His personal courage was unequaled, his perceptions far more acute than those common at the time, and his love for that land unmatched. Had he chosen to spend his life in Australia, he would have died a revered national hero.

But, hungering after fame, the pomp of office and the prerogatives of command, he quit Australia to join Great Britain's colonial service, determined to win rapid promotion to the governorship of some remote colony which he could rule as emperor. His grand design ran into immediate trouble, for when he was posted to New Zealand in a minor position, he accomplished nothing. He had somewhat better luck on the Caribbean island of St. Vincent, and an almost soporific tour of duty on Antigua, after which, in 1862 at the age of forty-seven, he was posted to the important island of Jamaica as lieutenant governor, a job he discharged with enthusiasm and ability, especially when a great fire threatened the island's principal town, Kingston. Reported a paper at the time:

Governor Eyre sped by horse from his residence in Spanish Town, galloping directly into the heart of our city and fearlessly throwing all his energies into fighting the fire that was creating such havoc. Never before have we seen a queen's representative behave so gallantly in the face of very real danger. All praise to Governor Eyre, a man's man.

There were, however, rumbles of discontent among the landed gentry of the island: "How dare they send us a governor with no decent family background when we've been accustomed to members of the aristocracy?" Others said: "His only qualification for this high office, once held by men of the highest type, often nobility, is that he once ran sheep in the godforsaken barrens of Australia. He's not good enough for this island." One of the more serious charges brought against him was that "he has been seen on several occasions riding not in his private carriage but in a public conveyance. Disgraceful! How lacking in dignity or respect for his position!" When a report of this impropriety reached London, Eyre's immediate superior scribbled on the paper: "As to the charge of going in a public vehicle, I have known even a secretary of state guilty of such indecorum," to which the head of the office, the Duke of Newcastle, replied with his own endorsement: "I've done the same."

At the beginning of 1865, that critical year in which so many events would agitate Jamaica, Governor Eyre was so firmly ensconced that his ardent supporters like Pembroke and Croome had reason to suppose that he would remain in office permanently, although Jason had begun to suspect the man's ability to hold the island's various elements together in harmony. As he watched Eyre stalk out of the chamber in imperial grandeur, he said, tugging reflectively on his beard: "I begin to detect signs of great arrogance in our governor."

"What in blazes do you mean by that?" Oliver asked.

"He's so imbedded in Church of England . . ."

"So am I. So are you. Proper thing to be . . . what else?"

"But as our governor, he really ought to listen more patiently to the adherents of other religions that are growing strong on this island. Especially the Baptists."

"They should all be shot, especially the Baptists."

"Now that's a silly thing to say, Oliver. The Baptists are here and they must be taken seriously."

"Eyre has given these damned dissenters every consideration. More than generous. After all, Church of England is the religion of this island, the law says so. We pay our taxes to support it, and its clergymen support the queen. Baptists? Who knows what they believe?" Before Pembroke could respond, Croome added, his face flushing: "I tell you, Jason, I'm not at all pleased with that ugly Baptist report that's been circulating," and at last Pembroke understood his cousin's uneasiness.

Some years before, a visiting Baptist clergyman named Underhill had published, on his return to London, a favorable book on Jamaica, but he soon began receiving from the island a drumfire of letters from local Baptists lamenting the actual state of conditions there. His correspondents were harshly outspoken about the disadvantages which all nonconformist sects like the Baptists suffered at the hands of an unfeeling, ungenerous Church of England majority: "We must pay taxes to support their church and their hard-drinking clergy, but they offer our chapels not one penny in return, even though our preaching is closer to the spirit of Jesus. And the governor hates anyone with a touch of color."

Tormented by these cries, Underhill had, in late December 1864, submitted a noninflammatory report to British authorities. Copies were promptly forwarded to Jamaica, where Church of England leaders, including of course the governor and his supporters, were outraged to think that a mere Baptist would dare to complain against not only God's chosen church but also, by extension, the queen herself, since she had appointed her local surrogates. "It's close to heresy," Croome grumbled, "or treason." And then, with that forthright, simple character that cut through ambiguities, he said with great force, banging the chair next to him as he spoke: "Those goddamned Baptists are nine-tenths niggers, and they're led by a gang of self-ordained preachers who are nine-tenths half-castes. This report strikes at the core of the empire, and the author should be shot." Croome, like his ancestors, was strong for shooting people.

"Calmly, calmly, Croome. Anyone who charges Governor Eyre with being anti-Negro, whether it's some local Baptist fool or you, is ignorant of the man's past record. I've taken pains to look it up, because I've seen animosities growing between us whites and those blacks, with the half-castes in between shifting now this way, now that."

"What was his record?"

"In Australia he served ably as Protector of the Aborigines. In his great explorations, when he couldn't find any white men brave enough to accompany him he trusted a young aborigine. When he was appointed lieutenant governor of St. Vincent he was a powerful champion of niggers, and in that post in Antigua he was the same. The man is right for Jamaica."

"That's why it would be criminal for us to allow the damned Baptists to smear his character. Who allowed copies of that Underhill letter to reach these shores?" Before Pembroke could reply, his cousin, now red in the face, uttered the freighted words that would dictate so much Jamaican behavior in this troubled year: "Jason, our task as members of the Executive Council is to do everything we can to prevent the terrors of the Indian Mutiny, or the horrors that occurred in Haiti when niggers ran wild."

Those were the images that dominated: Cawnpore, the city on the Ganges River where hundreds of Englishmen, men and women alike, were brutalized, slain and pitched into deep wells; and nearby Haiti, not much over a hundred miles distant, where even worse massacres had occurred.

"We must do everything possible to keep peace," Croome said, with grim lines etched on his shaven face, "and if I could lay my hands on that Underhill or any Baptist agitators, I'd shoot them."

Governor Eyre, returning to the council chamber at this moment, saw the cousins and came to stand before them, tall and godlike with his flowing beard: "You are the men I must rely on to protect me when you next take residence in London," he said with as much emotion as his austere nature would permit. "You're as much at home there as you are on your sugar plantations. A rare breed, you two."

Their council duties over, the two cousins rode together along the magnificent trails that led north from Spanish Town, following vibrant streams which had to be forded from time to time, and as they approached the Croome plantation, Jason bade his energetic cousin farewell. "We did good work for the empire this week," he said as Oliver turned his horse toward his gate.

At Trevelyan, Jason was greeted by a deputation he did not much care to entertain, a motley group of farmers, from St. Ann's Parish to the north, led by one of the most difficult of the half-caste Baptist preachers—a smug, persistent man of forty-seven, one George William Gordon, of a color called by white Jamaicans *bedarkened* and with an almost insolent stare that came from fighting incessant battles on behalf of his colored and black parishioners. His face was framed by a curious part-beard which extended from his full head of curly hair down each side of his face and completely under his chin, leaving the rest of his face unshaven and stern, as if his teeth were permanently clenched. He wore wire-set glasses and clergyman's dress, although whether or not he had been legally ordained no one could say; Pembroke thought so, but his cousin was certain that Gordon had assumed both the title and the dress.

As soon as Pembroke recognized him at the head of the group of St. Ann farmers, most of whom lived just over the border from the parish in which Trevelyan stood, he realized there might be trouble, for Gordon's jaw was fiercely set.

Gordon was a tough man, having come up the tough way. His father had been a sniveling white man who had slipped into an alliance with one of his female slaves, by whom he had seven children. But later in life, when he had accumulated a little money, he threw the slave woman and her brood out of his house, married a white woman, and refused ever to allow any of his half-caste children, George William among them, entrance to his new home. Even so, when the father fell into financial trouble, he came whimpering to his son, begging the money which would allow him to maintain decency. In the meantime, the young man had so prospered in various business enterprises that he was able to finance not only the purchase of a home for his father, but also to assist in the care of the latter's white wife and children. Such a man could not be dismissed with contempt, despite his unfortunate color.

Pembroke sought to be congenial, inviting the black and colored farmers into the mansion, where he called for refreshments as he listened to the mournful reason for their visit. "You are the wisest member of the council, Mr. Pembroke," one of the farmers said, "and you know our land in St. Ann better than anyone else except maybe Parson Gordon, who preaches there now and again. We are hardworking men, but we need land for our crops. Thousands of acres lie fallow there, no one working them. When emancipation came years ago we were supposed to receive that land . . . to buy it if necessary. We've saved. We have the money to buy it if the price is reasonable. But the government will not break it loose for us. They tell us: 'Your role is to work for the white man at whatever wages he chooses to pay you.' Well, there are no white plantation owners in St. Ann to hire us, and no land on which we can grow our own crops."

On and on went the pitiful complaints, which could have been echoed in each of Jamaica's parishes. When emancipation came to the British Caribbean in 1834, the former slaves had been tricked into believing that land would be made available to them, but the Legislative Assembly, composed in large part of white plantation owners and their half-caste employees, refused to cede any land, and the lower classes had no recourse. At one point Jamaica had 450,000 citizens, but only 753 were eligible to vote, and they did not propose to turn land over to the Baptist followers of Preacher Gordon, whom they despised.

Pembroke, understanding these matters, listened attentively to the farmers, and when they finished he suggested that they retire and draft a courteous letter to Queen Victoria, laying out their problems and their views as to how they could be solved. When Gordon volunteered to write the letter, Pembroke said gently: "I think not, sir. You're known as a radical, and I'd be reluctant to submit one of your agitations to the queen, even though I believe you to be right."

So with Pembroke's help the letter was drafted, a sensible, restrained appeal for help in time of drought and a respectful prayer that the queen would release some crown lands, which they would then cultivate with their hearts and hands and remit the required rents. When it was read aloud, the farmers agreed that it represented both their cause and their affection for the queen, and they believed that she would listen favorably. Preacher Gordon felt that it could have been stronger, but Pembroke assured him that this was the proper way to address a queen whose generosity was known to all: "I will forward it through proper channels, and I can assure you she will respond." And the rump meeting dissolved with mutual congratulations.

Two days later Oliver Croome strode into Trevelyan, his face livid: "What in the name of hell have you done, Jason?"

"What do you mean?"

"That petition to the queen. The one that swine Gordon wrote for the St. Ann people."

"But I wrote it. In proper tone, I believe."

"You! God, Pembroke, are you out of your mind? Don't you realize that those people are all Baptists echoing the lies of that Underhill report? Those people are revolutionaries. Do you want another Haiti on your hands?"

When Pembroke tried to remonstrate with him, saying that he had helped them draft their letter for the precise reason of avoiding revolution, Croome cut him short: "Jason, you don't understand the nigger question, and as a member of the council you ought to think about it more clearly. This might help," and he thrust into Jason's hands one of the most amazing products of British intellectualism. It had been written sixteen years earlier, in 1849, the year of great revolutions across Europe, and was obviously influenced by those uprisings of the lower orders. It was entitled "Occasional Discourse on the Nigger Question," and was written by Thomas Carlyle, the Scotsman famous for his advocacy of hero worship as a guide to personal and national life. He was also a strong believer in the British right to rule those he lumped together as lesser breeds. And he thought it proper for men to make decisions and for women and children to obey.

As Jason started to read Carlyle's rantings, Croome said: "I'll inspect how you make your great Trevelyan rum," and left his cousin alone in his study.

Quickly Jason caught on to the author's two code words. All blacks, especially freed slaves, were called Quashee, a euphonious name which one of the African tribes used for any child born on Sunday. Carlyle apparently liked the word for the humorous way it dismissed any black to whom it was applied, for he used it almost ad nauseam in his vitriolic comments. He had also picked up, possibly from some visiting cotton or sugar plantation owner from the Carolinas, the idea that blacks spent all their time lolling in the shade eating watermelon, but since Carlyle had never seen a watermelon, he confused it with a pumpkin and filled his essay with humorous references to Quashee and his pumpkins.

Jason frequently gasped as he continued to read the essay, for he could not believe that an intelligent Briton could write such trash: "Our beautiful Black darlings are at last happy; with little labour except to the teeth, which surely in those excellent horse-jaws of theirs, will not fail!" "With a penny-worth of oil you can make a handsome, glossy thing of Quashee." "No, the gods wish that besides pumpkins, that spices and valuable products be grown in their West Indies. Infinitely more they wish, that manful industrious men occupy their West Indies, not indolent two-legged cattle, however happy over their abundant pumpkins."

Then came the crux of Carlyle's solution to the "nigger question": "Quashee, if he will not help in bringing out the spices, will get himself made a slave again, and with beneficent whip, since other methods avail not, will be compelled to work." In other words, Carlyle, a devotee of the master-race theory, was calling for the reimposition of slavery, at least in the West Indies, where lack of slaves had slowed the sugar industry.

He then rhapsodized over the brave British men who had brought civilization to the islands: "Before the West Indies could grow a pumpkin for any Negro, how much European heroism had to spend itself in obscure battle . . . Under the soil of Jamaica, before it could even produce spices or any pumpkin, the bones of many thousand British men had to be laid. How they would have rejoiced to think that all this was to issue in growing pumpkins to keep Quashee in comfortably idle condition!"

In fiery sentences Carlyle spelled out his vision of the world: "My obscure Black friends, you will have to be servants to those who are born *wiser* than you, that are born lords of you; servants to the Whites, if they are (as what mortal man can doubt that they are?) born wiser than you. That is the Law of the World, to be servants, the more foolish to the more wise."

So sorely was Jason Pembroke shaken when he finished this incredible screed that he went outside and shouted to his cousin: "This is appalling—making fun of human beings, speaking of them as if they were horses, calling for the reinstitution of slavery."

"Wait a minute! Do you want what happened in Haiti to happen here? Or another Indian Mutiny? Carlyle speaks the truth, the hard ugly truth. Niggers are really little better than animals, and if they won't work our fields at the wages we propose, they must be made to work, and if that means bringing slavery back, so be it. They asked for it."

Shocked by Oliver's vehement adoption of all that Carlyle had said, Jason inadvertently stumbled onto the one name that would infuriate his cousin: "No wonder Gordon makes headway with the blacks."

"Gordon!" Oliver bellowed as if stabbed near the kidney. "Are you listening to that ranting fool? People like you say he was kind to his white father. But did you know that he had money only because he stole land and houses from that father? Did you know that he had his workers run down the values of all the father's farms so that the old man had to sell at a great loss? And who bought? Gordon."

His contempt for the troublemaker was fathomless, but he saved till last his harshest condemnations: "Are you aware, Jason, that his wife is a white woman . . . that he married her to improve his position in the community? And have you heard that in his sermons he often ridicules our established church with his Baptist heresies? And are you aware that in his constant agitation he casts aspersions on our beloved queen? That man should be destroyed, and I'm amazed you allowed him in your house."

"But don't you think," Jason asked quietly, in an effort to lower the temperature of his cousin's rhetoric, "that your Thomas Carlyle is just as damaging, preaching his hatred?" and Oliver answered: "But they are niggers, Jason."

When Pembroke delivered the supplication of his St. Ann neighbors to Governor Eyre, that officer thanked him, but as soon as Pembroke was gone, he summoned Oliver Croome, and four like-minded planters who thought like Carlyle, to help frame the Jamaican comment on the farmers' appeal to the queen, and they, drawing heavily on "Occasional Discourse on the Nigger Question," undercut everything the supplicants had said, assuring the queen that all was well in Jamaica and that the protest came almost exclusively from disaffected blacks and half-castes who were Baptists. "Not one gentleman or plantation owner in the entire island would demean himself by signing such an impertinent letter." And off it went.

It would never be known for certain who drafted the reply to the starving farmers, but since it was delivered to Jamaica as Victoria's personal response to their pleas, it became known in history as The Queen's Advice:

> The prosperity of the labouring classes depends in Jamaica upon their working for wages, not uncertainly, or capriciously, but steadily and continuously, at the times when their labour is wanted, and for so long as it is wanted . . . They may be assured that it is from their own industry and prudence, in availing themselves of the means of prosperity before them, and not from any such schemes as have been suggested to them, and they must look for an improvement in their conditions.
>
> Her Majesty will regard with interest and satisfaction their advancement through their own merits and efforts.

Not a word about starvation, never a promise to release land locked in idleness, for the plantation owners argued that if the blacks got hold of land for their own use, they would no longer work the sugar fields and rum distilleries. Only that terribly cruel command: "Work for your white masters when they want you, for as long as they want you, and at whatever wages they graciously offer." Jason Pembroke, on finishing his reading of the letter, muttered: "It could have been written by Thomas Carlyle."

When Governor Eyre showed The Queen's Advice to Croome and some of his more conservative friends, they exulted over the fact that Victoria had adopted much of their phraseology, and they loudly agreed with Eyre when he said: "Well, I think that answers the agitations of Brother Gordon." Eyre approved when Croome suggested: "It's so clear, so fair that we must put copies of it on trees and buildings throughout the island," giving authority to print up fifty thousand broadsheets. Croome and his friends arrogantly rushed to all corners of the island, posting these conspicuously and with a final flourish of the hammer as if to shout: "Well, that takes care of your silly petition!"

But when Pembroke saw what was being done, and the sullen rage with which the farmers, the little people and the undernourished mothers read the letter and sometimes spat upon it, he said to himself: It will be worse than Haiti. And he leaped on his horse and rode to Kingston to seek out Preacher Gordon: "My friend, I have grown to respect what you're trying to do, so for God's sake watch your step in the weeks ahead. Keep your lips sealed."

"Why, in the face of such an insulting message from the queen?"

"Because she is the queen. And because men of great power wish you silent." Then, to ease Gordon's disappointment and disgust, he uttered a fatal sentence, which when quoted by agitated blacks and coloreds would account for two hundred of their deaths: "And you can be sure that the queen did not write that letter." With that, he turned and rode back to his plantation, where he tried to reassure his own workers that the queen could never have written that cruel a reply.

The fifty thousand broadsheets which had been nailed to trees and meeting boards were intended, by the foolish writer who composed the letter, by Governor Eyre, who had provided the outline of the response, and by wealthy men like Oliver Croome who circulated it so enthusiastically, to stifle dissent over the harsh way in which Jamaica was being governed. Croome insisted, after a long excursion into the western parishes: "If they can read, they will applaud the queen's intelligent response, and if they can't read, her words can be explained to them. Either way, there should be an end to fruitless discussion and ridiculous claims for land and the distribution of food that hasn't been properly earned," and even other plantation owners better informed than he believed the famous Advice had solved all problems for the next decade.

It had quite the opposite effect, because the farmers of St. Ann who had helped draft the original petition saw at once that the queen had evaded answering every one of their complaints: "How can we work if no work is offered? How can we be industrious if we're allowed no land on which to prove ourselves?"

Across the beautiful island, along the seacoasts and in the valleys, men of good will who were allowed no advantages began discussing the message, and its insolent, almost cruel, phrases created a great fury. They saw no hope for the future. Most powerful in the voices raised was that of Preacher Gordon, who moved through the island haranguing his Baptists and uttering statements that became increasingly inflammatory. "We shall have another Haiti on this island" and "I shy away from revolution, but if it must come, I hope it solves these terrible problems" and "It's shameful to have a German immigrant as the custos of St. Thomas-in-the-East, the parish I love so dearly." This last protest would, as months passed, have special significance.

Under Jamaican law, the governor appointed parish leaders who exercised considerable authority; their title *custos* and its plural *custodes* suggested the *custodian* role they filled. The custos of Gordon's parish was, as pointed out so often, a German immigrant and a fearfully conservative man to whom any expression of public demand was repugnant. Maximilian Augustus Baron von Ketelhodt had been judicious, upon his arrival in the island, in paying court to a wealthy widow, who brought him in their marriage five rich plantations and acceptance as a member of the island's ruling faction. A man of brilliant maneuvering, he ingratiated himself with the lower classes and was no tyrant, even though Gordon, who fell under his custodianship, deemed him so.

St. Thomas-in-the-East Parish, whose affairs the custos supervised, owned that curious name for two reasons: It lay at the extreme eastern tip of Jamaica, and it was named later than an earlier parish in the center of the island which had already usurped that title. It was unique in other ways: being so far from Kingston and Spanish Town, it believed itself free from restraints which bound the other parishes; it was strongly Baptist, which created numerous problems, especially with Baron von Ketelhodt; and it had an unusual number of educated and headstrong half-caste and black preachers, landowners and quasi-scholars. It seemed inevitable that George William Gordon, in coming from this parish, would be disciplined in one way or another by his custos.

The long summer of 1865 was particularly hot and humid, and watchful sugar men like Oliver Croome became aware that the mood of the lower classes had become sullen, so dangerously so that he sought an audience with Governor Eyre to register a warning: "Governor, if things get any worse, we could have a serious rebellion on this island. The planters who accompanied me on the annual tour of the districts are deeply worried about the conditions we saw at St. Thomas-in-the-East, and we recommend that you summon your custos to give his assessment."

Eyre, always terrified by the names *Haiti* and *Cawnpore,* grabbed at Croome's suggestion, and a few days later Baron von Ketelhodt, tall and rigid and ready to stamp out any incipient uprising in his parish, reported to the governor: "That ass Gordon has been creating a disturbance. Seems to have affected one of his underlings, a clown named Bogle . . ."

"Isn't that one a Baptist preacher, too?"

"He is. Gordon ordained him, just as he ordained himself. And there appears to be contempt for the posters of The Queen's Advice."

"Contempt? How expressed?"

"The broadsheets have been spat upon. And in three instances, torn down."

Eyre's face grew grave, his broad brow wrinkled and his long beard trembled. "The Queen's Advice spat upon! We can't allow that, Ketelhodt. What have you done to halt it?"

"Caution," the baron said in his deep Germanic accent. "Not to raise tempers. But to watch. Careful. Careful."

"And what have you learned?"

"That George Gordon is behind every move. That he is inciting to rebellion. That sooner or later we must throw a net for that one, but taking care to avoid inciting his damned Baptist renegades."

When Eyre called for Croome and Pembroke to join the meeting,

the former supported everything the baron had reported, strengthen-
ing some points: "Gordon is actively preaching rebellion and we
ought to silence him now," but Pembroke recommended patience:
"Governor, the most sensible people on this island judge the queen's
letter to have been insensitive. It's understandable that . . ."

Eyre rose from his chair, stared down at Pembroke, and said
sternly: "Are you daring to denigrate the queen?" and Pembroke said
humbly: "Certainly not, sir, but the people are disappointed in it, for
it fails to . . ."

"The queen has spoken," Eyre thundered, as if the lower classes
were pestering him the way flies pester a noble animal, "and the people have naught but to obey."

"Hear! Hear!" cried Croome and the baron together, and the
meeting ended.

But that did not terminate agitation in Jamaica, because six days
later while Gordon was speaking in Kingston, his associate Bogle in
St. Thomas-in-the-East led a frenzied uprising in which infuriated
blacks, tired of waiting for their complaints to be heard, ran amok,
slaughtering in the most brutal fashion eighteen whites, including officers of the queen, plantation owners, minor officials and, with special vengeance, their custos, Baron von Ketelhodt, whose body they
mutilated, cutting off his fingers. These they circulated as souvenirs
of their successful uprising, and some blacks, participating in the
wild rioting, were heard to shout: "Now we do like Haiti!" and island-
wide rebellion loomed.

The two protagonists in the Jamaican tragedy, Governor Eyre and
Preacher Gordon, were indisputably in Kingston when the deadly
riot broke out in St. Thomas-in-the-East, many miles away.

In this extremity, with his governorship being threatened by widespread massacre, Eyre behaved magnificently. Cool, decisive, looking
always at the strategic situation, he gave few orders but always the
right ones. At dusk on the afternoon when he received word of the
rebellion, he said: "Of myself I cannot declare martial law. That must
be done only by our Council of War," and Croome, who was a member of that council, volunteered to spend the night assembling it,
and, in anticipation of their decision, himself drafted the decree.

In the meantime, with a burst of the old energy he had shown in
Australia, Eyre rode out to Spanish Town to attend to duties there,

then galloped back to Kingston to lead a dawn meeting in which martial law was declared for St. Thomas in-the-East and all parishes contiguous thereto. At this point Eyre displayed both great common sense and firm decision, for when everyone, especially Croome, clamored for the town of Kingston to be put under martial law, he said: "No! Only enough force to handle the situation. Martial law in a crowded place like this might lead to terrible brutalities," and he could not be persuaded.

Alone with Croome and Pembroke, the governor asked Jason: "Did not your ancestor gain fame for having pacified the Maroons . . . a century ago?" Jason nodded. "And was it not he who pacified those at the eastern end of the island?" and again Jason agreed. Making an instant decision of great subsequent importance, Governor Eyre cried: "Pembroke, ride posthaste to the Maroons and implore them not to side with the niggers in this dreadful affair." When Jason snapped: "Yes, sir!" Eyre urged: "Make any concessions. Offer them any inducements. But keep them from joining the rebellion." That was his first use of that fearful word, and during the next four decades it would be one he would constantly employ when he justified his actions: "It was rebellion and I had to put it down."

Before seven that morning Jason was riding hard to the perilous mountain area which his great-great-grandfather had penetrated under comparable conditions to try his hand at peacekeeping.

At eight the Council of War proclaimed martial law for the east, and as soon as this gave him the authority he required, Governor Eyre, accompanied by Oliver Croome, chartered a French packet ship to speed him along the coast to the troubled area, and at ten in the morning he was on his way. Intercepting another ship limping into Kingston crammed with refugees from the rebellion, he heard for the first time the gruesome details of what had happened in one of his most peaceful and prosperous parishes: "Church of England Reverend Herschell, tongue ripped out while still alive, hacked to death, black women tried to skin him. Member of Assembly Price, a black man, belly ripped open, guts pulled out while he still alive. Lieutenant Hall, him brave, pushed into privy, door locked, he burned alive. Eyes scooped out, heads smashed open, brains dripping. German baron, hacked to death but he fight them to the end." Thanking the refugees for their horrifying reports, but sickened at hearing them, he told them to proceed to Kingston, while he headed for St. Thomas-in-the-East.

There he found the military courts-martial already under way, staffed by enthusiastic young officers from army regiments stationed in Jamaica or from ships which had hurried to the area. Proceedings were brusque, with prisoners being stood before the court in batches and sentenced in the same way. Any black man arrested for any unusual behavior whatever, even looking furtively at a soldier, was condemned without a chance to defend himself. "Hang them all," the presiding officer cried, and forthwith half a dozen black men would be suspended from the remaining walls of the burned-out courthouse. It was a hideous way to die, whether guilty or innocent, for a rope was thrown about a prisoner's neck and he was hauled aloft—instead of being dropped in the normal way to break his neck—to strangle slowly.

For three sleepless days Eyre prowled the coast, satisfying himself that the rebellion which had ravaged St. Thomas was not spreading to nearby parishes, and when he returned to the scene of the major uprising and saw that each morning the courts-martial were hanging dozens of black prisoners with never a one found innocent, he was able to tell Croome: "We've broken the back of the rebellion. You stay here with the troops and see that the pacification continues." With that, he boarded the chartered French vessel and returned to Kingston, from where he immediately sent a report to London that he had contained the rebellion with a minimum loss of white lives and without having to throw all of Jamaica into convulsions by imposing martial law generally. When he finally fell into bed, he felt justified in believing that he had acted swiftly and in the great tradition of British colonial governors; indeed, he was so pleased with his behavior that he got out of bed and added a postscript to his report: "By stern and prompt action against the queen's foes, I believe I have averted another Indian Mutiny or a Haiti-type uprising."

For eleven hours Eyre lay in bed almost motionless, as if savoring the sleep of a hero who had behaved well in a major crisis, but when he woke his mouth felt ashen, for he knew that he had fallen far short of a real victory. Where is George Gordon? he asked himself, for the instigator of the rebellion had disappeared. No, he's too clever to show up in St. Thomas, because he knows I'd hang him if I caught him. In the silent speculation that followed, the governor never once considered that Gordon might not have been at the scene of the murders and that he was not involved, either directly or indirectly. To Eyre, Gordon was responsible for everything: He must have given the orders that launched the riot, and for it he must hang. His obsession was so all-consuming that he did not bother to consider what grounds could be used for hanging Gordon or even in what civil court the infuriating preacher could be tried. No civilian court in Kingston would condemn the man, for the very good reason that no valid charges could be brought against him in normal procedure. He had murdered no one. He had not taken up arms against the queen. There was no proof that he had incited the riots, beyond his open dissatisfaction with the queen's letter. And not even the most prejudiced witness could claim that she or he had seen Gordon in St. Thomas during the rioting or the weeks prior. But Eyre knew that if the Baptist preacher could be lured into going to St. Thomas, the courtmartial could grab him, and would not be constrained by any niceties of logic or legal tradition.

Now Eyre vowed: I will find Gordon and take him to St. Thomas; but no one could inform him as to where the archcriminal was: My God! Has he fled the island? Has he escaped the wrath due him?

For two days Eyre fumed, telling his subordinates: "I must have that criminal! Find him! Find him!" But Gordon could not be found and Eyre could not sleep, for the vision of Preacher Gordon standing on a gallows with a rope around his neck tormented his hours. His frustration in not being able to haul the man to justice infuriated him, and he roared at his underlings: "Find that man. Track him down," but not even spies among the black population knew where he was. Summoning the local custos, he stormed: "Sign a warrant for his arrest," and this was done, but it accomplished nothing, so his anger continued to seethe.

Then suddenly, on the morning of the third day, George William Gordon, still looking like a contentious preacher, walked calmly into Kingston's army headquarters and said quietly: "I think you may be looking for me. I am Reverend Gordon."

The astonished officer called for his commander, who gasped, then rushed to Eyre's office to inform him Gordon had been taken.

Suppressing his excitement, Eyre said: "This is very fortunate, we were looking for him," and when he was allowed to see the prisoner, he told Gordon, in a low, controlled voice: "You must come with me . . . to St. Thomas-in-the-East." Bowing slightly, Gordon repeated what he had been telling his black and colored friends during his days of hiding: "If I go before a military court-martial, it will be to my death," and Eyre said through gritting teeth: "Perhaps."

The ship *Wolverine* was scheduled to sail within the hour, but it was delayed because an agitated man with the highest credentials burst into Eyre's office, dusty and near exhaustion, with the cry: "Oh, sir! You must not send him to St. Thomas. You really mustn't!" and since the governor had to pay attention to this particular speaker, the delivery of Gordon to certain death was delayed.

On the morning almost a week before, when Jason Pembroke was commissioned to use his family's honored name to prevent the wild Maroons from joining the rebellious blacks, he entered upon an adventure which seemed an evocation of some earlier century. After a determined ride he left the Kingston area and entered turbulent St. Thomas-in-the East, and as soon as he approached Monklands, the settlement farthest west, he saw signs of upheaval, and a white planter who recognized him shouted: "Go farther at your own peril!"

"Government business," Jason shouted back as he headed resolutely for the Blue Mountains. They might not have been impressive in comparison with the Himalayas or Andes, but they were much higher than anything in Great Britain, reaching up at times to more than six thousand feet, deeply ravined and tree-covered. When he had traveled halfway to the east coast he turned his horse sharply to the north, up a rugged path containing a few slave shacks perched at lonely spots. Again he was warned, this time by blacks: "Here no more, massa! Yonder big trouble—Maroons."

"It's them I seek," he cried back, whereupon the blacks said: "Not go, massa, soon you hear horns," and not long after he passed the last shack in the ravine he was following, he heard that deep-throated mournful sound which terrified Jamaicans: the pulsating moan of three or four great horns sounded in unison, the lonely cry of the Maroons, those runaway slaves who had persisted in the mountains of Jamaica, living their own untrammeled lives for the past two hundred years. Laws did not affect them. Police never dared enter their mountain, and even well-trained army troops preferred not to engage these formidable warriors. No white man could even guess how they lived. Coming down from their mountain now and then to work for wages, tilling their fields and engaging in small-scale raids, but retreating quickly to their hidden lairs, they made do.

Their horns were fashioned from various materials: treasured seashells passed from father to son, horns from cattle taken in raids, curious instruments made from wood. Whatever they used, sometimes simply manipulating the human voice, they achieved fearful effects, for the sound of the Maroon horns signified trouble, meant that the mountain blacks were once more on a rampage.

But in recent years it meant primarily trouble for other blacks, rarely for white men, because as happened repeatedly in other parts of the world, like Panamá and Brazil, in which renegade slaves fled to the jungle to gain their freedom, they saw other blacks as their major enemy, people never to be trusted. The Maroons had gained their greatest concessions from white men by serving as human bloodhounds—tracking, capturing and returning valuable runaway slaves—but they had also admitted slaves to their brotherhood, especially black women, to keep their own numbers strong.

They were redoubtable warriors who had been able to defend themselves for more than two centuries, keeping alive traditions inherited from Africa and posing a kind of mythic background to Jamaican life. They understood English but preferred their own indecipherable patois rich in African words, and they were extremely black in a way that made their visages terrifying to a white man. Not one white person in ten on the island had ever seen a Maroon, but everyone had been aware since childhood of their presence—"Be quiet or the Maroon will grab you"—and it was into the fastness of their hideaways that Pembroke now proposed to penetrate.

As he moved higher into the mountains he became aware that the Maroons had spotted him, for he heard first one mournful horn in the far distance, then another, but remembering his brave ancestor Sir Hugh, who had been the principal agent in pacifying the Maroons, he plunged ahead, hoping that he would be allowed at least one moment to identify himself to someone who would remember favorably the Pembroke name. It was risky and he knew it, so when the path grew steeper, as if in approach to where the Maroons had their remote dwellings, he dismounted and walked close to the right flank of his horse so as to protect himself from at least one side.

Then he began calling out: "Pembroke coming!" and repeating this at intervals while the sounding of the horns intensified.

As he approached the crest of a slight hill he was startled by two black men who suddenly leaped in front of his horse, each grabbing the reins with one hand while threatening him with a club held in the other. "No! Stop!" he shouted as they brought the clubs close to his head.

These men were not savages from some jungle. They wore tattered trousers and torn shirts, and were clean-shaven. Pembroke, aware that what he did in these first moments might determine whether he lived or not, allowed them to take his horse, made no gesture that could be interpreted as unfriendly, and repeated over and over: "Pembroke your friend. Pembroke your friend." The men, making nothing of this, looked at each other as if to ask: "What shall we do with this one? He seems brave." They must have reached some unspoken decision, for one man led the horse forward while the other guarded Pembroke with his club as they started up the remaining portion of the climb.

Quickly they came to a village of sorts surrounded by small cleared fields, which their women tilled. The twenty-odd houses were little more than rude shacks, but a larger one in the center was sheathed in metal roofing and obviously housed the chief, an older black whose ancestors had fled to this mountain from the fields in 1657, two years after they had been landed as slaves by Sir William Penn, the British admiral who had captured the island from the Spanish. When the chief saw this white man coming toward him, his first inclination was to have him either slain for his impudence or thrown off the mountain, his horse being kept behind as a treasure, but Jason, hoping to prevent either of those misadventures, began talking swiftly, trusting that someone nearby would understand the force of what he was saying: "I am Pembroke. Same Pembroke who brought you peace, long ago."

The words had a magical effect, for the Maroon leader caught his breath, came forward to inspect the visitor, and then embraced him: "We know Pembroke. Many years. Good man. Trusted man." Extending his right hand, he said: "I am Colonel Seymour . . . in charge here."

When Jason saluted as if the man were a real colonel, the latter called for a rough-hewn bench, placed it alongside his own, and invited Jason to join him. After some pleasantries, Jason broached the purpose of his visit: "Big trouble Morant Bay."

"We know."

"Former slaves killing and being killed."

"He told us," the colonel said, pointing to one of his men who had slipped into Morant Bay as soon as the rioting started to observe what was happening and what effect it might have on the Maroon settlements in the mountains.

"Governor, big man, he send me to ask you not to join the rioting."

"I know governor. Name Eyre. Pretty good man. What he promise us, we stay out?"

"Horses. Like that one. Maybe more bullets for your guns."

After protracted dickering, the colonel astonished Jason by saying firmly: "We just about ready to march to Morant . . ."

"Oh no!" Paul pleaded, desperation almost checking his words. "If you join the rioters . . ."

"We not join them," the colonel said. "We kill them."

"No! No!" Jason pleaded. "Don't kill them. Don't kill the blacks. Don't kill anybody."

"Former slaves no good. They defeat you buckra, quick soon they go after us. We kill them first." And no urgent plea that Jason could utter had any effect on the colonel, who had decided long before Jason's arrival that the best interests of the Maroons would be served if they stormed into the troubled area and killed the black rioters.

With a speed that astonished Pembroke, Colonel Seymour signaled for the horns to resume blowing, and within minutes an expeditionary force consisting of some two hundred black men from various villages assembled, bringing with them a surprising number of good horses. Ordering the men who held Jason's horse to return it to him, Colonel Seymour said: "You ride, too. Speak the officers what we do." As Jason started for his horse, reluctant to participate in what might become a fearsome raid, he heard Seymour say: "Battle over, you can leave," and he deemed it wise to go along.

Moving back down the mountain trail at a clip which made Jason gasp, the Maroon cavalry reached the main road, and there they turned east toward the settled areas where rioting had taken place. In the first half-hour of the charge Pembroke learned what character this expedition was going to take, for when they reached the black village of Conari, named for some ancient African settlement, Seymour divided his force into two groups, one to encircle the place, the other to dash in with flaming brands to set all huts afire. As the terrified occupants ran out to escape immolation, he shouted: "Kill! Kill!" and everyone was chased down through the smoke. Men, women and children alike were slain by clubs and long cane knives if they were caught, by masterly gunfire in the middle of their backs if they tried to run. None survived.

"Seymour," Jason cried as the murder continued in a second village the riders encountered, "no more killing!" But the colonel harshly ignored this plea: "Niggers no good. Kill all," and he encouraged his Maroons to annihilate any blacks they came upon. Women and children were burned alive in their flaming shacks or shot as they tried to escape, and in this way the Maroons approached the principal town of Morant Bay.

There, fortunately, an army man, Colonel Hobbs, was in command, and he, anticipating the great confusion that would result if the Maroons were allowed into the town already beset by riots and hangings, had drawn his soldiers into a line to prevent the savage mountain men from entering. Undaunted, Colonel Seymour turned and led his marauders toward other rural areas where they could rampage at will. Pembroke, left behind and awed by the storm he had let loose and its fiery results in death and destruction, told Hobbs: "I came here on orders from the governor. To try to persuade the Maroons not to join the black rioters. I never dreamed they'd assassinate them."

Hobbs waved his left hand as if dismissing the dead bodies: "Forget them. They're rebellious niggers and there'll be hundreds more dead before we get through." Then he turned his horse northward and said: "Before you head back for Kingston you might like to see one of our courts-martial in operation," and he led the way to an improvised grass-walled shack in which three very young army and navy officers were conducting that day's trials.

A group of twenty-seven black men and two women stood shackled in one corner of the room guarded by armed sailors with dogs. The trial took exactly nine minutes, with the president of the court, an army man in his early twenties, asking: "What are the charges against these criminals?" Pembroke supposed that since Hobbs was senior officer present, he would object to this terribly pejorative implication that the accused were already criminals before the evidence was in. But then he discovered that there was to be no evidence. A white man told the court: "These were all involved in the rebellion."

"Even the women?"

"Yes."

"Verdict?" the judge asked his two fellow officials, and they said: "Guilty," whereupon the judge handed down his sentence: "Hang the men. Seventy-five lashes for the women," and the twenty-seven men were led out to be hanged. There were, however, spaces on the suspended beam for only twenty ropes, so the sergeant in charge, without consulting the court, shot the others, moving from one pinioned man to the next and firing a pistol through the head, then kicking the body aside as the corpse fell.

In a sense those seven were lucky, for the improvised mode of hanging allowed for no sudden drop to break the neck. The men were hauled aloft, kicking and struggling and slowly strangling, until the sergeant shouted: "Pull those men's legs!" and soldiers moved forward to lift the almost dead bodies slightly, then jerk them down with as much force as could be applied in that unsatisfactory way. Since this accomplished little, most of the men continued to strangle and gyrate on their ropes until the sergeant, in disgust, moved along the line shooting at them upward from the point of the chin through the head.

Pembroke was sickened by this brutality performed in the name of Governor Eyre and Queen Victoria, but it was what happened to the two women prisoners that made him realize the awful things a military court restrained by no law was capable of doing. The two women were stripped from the waist down, thrown on the ground with buttocks uncovered, and given twenty-five lashes each on the bare skin, not with an ordinary whip but with a cat-o'-nine-tails into which strong wires had been woven. The sailors given the task of whipping the women seemed to enjoy it, for they struck with such force that by the end of the fifth application of this almost deadly instrument, the flesh along the women's backsides and legs was raw and bleeding. Young soldiers watching the beatings counted out the strokes in a chorus, and at the end of the first twenty-five lashes the beatings stopped, with the women almost unconscious from the pain.

But that was far from the end of their punishment, for after they were revived by water thrown in their faces, they were again thrown onto the ground and another twenty-five were applied with increasing vigor by the energetic sailors, who were applauded by the counting soldiers. Again Jason expected Hobbs to intervene, but the latter stood near the two women, a smile on his face, fists clenched, and counting as the blows fell.

When the fiftieth lash tore at the shredding skin, the beating stopped, and Jason felt impelled to protest: "Colonel Hobbs, stop this cruelty, please."

"You heard the verdict. Guilty of rebellion. You heard the sentence," and he watched smiling as the women were thrown to the ground for the third time, with the dreadful metal-clothed cats cutting into their bloodied flesh. Only with supreme self-control did Pembroke refrain from leaping to their defense, and this was fortunate for him, for had he tried to make any move of compassion in this frenzied atmosphere of revenge, the young military men present, who saw nothing wrong with the punishment, might have turned on him and killed him.

When the hideous performance ended, with the flayed women unconscious beside the seven men who had been shot and below the dangling legs of the twenty who had been hanged, Pembroke wanted to flee, but as he prepared to ride back to Kingston, fifteen more accused were led into the shack where the same impartial court awaited them. At this moment, Hobbs said something which spurred Jason into precipitate action, regardless of the consequences: "Good news just in from Kingston. They've caught that bastard Gordon, and Governor Eyre is sending him over to us for trial."

As soon as he heard this wretched news, Jason realized how improper it was, and wishing to dissociate himself from the murderous Hobbs, he quietly slipped away and galloped eastward, hoping to persuade Governor Eyre to countermand what he knew to be a misguided order.

By dint of forced riding on a horse already tired, Jason reached Eyre's Kingston residence before the decision to ship Gordon to a St. Thomas court-martial had been put into effect, and breaking unannounced into Eyre's office, he blurted out: "Governor, for the love of God and mercy, do not send George Gordon to a court-martial in St. Thomas-in-the-East. They've gone crazy over there."

"They're doing their duty," Eyre said sternly, holding himself erect and speaking with controlled force. "Those who rebelled against the queen must pay the price."

"But the court's behavior is inhuman. Lashing women with wire bands in the cats."

"Women are often the worst offenders. They should be hanged also."

"Governor Eyre, I reached the Maroons. Kept them from joining the riots on the side of the blacks."

"Sterling job, Jason. Dangerous, too."

"The Maroons went on a rampage against the blacks. Killing, burning. Women and children."

"When a man like Gordon launches a rebellion, he should anticipate consequences."

"But he was not in St. Thomas. He played no role in starting the
riot."

Governor Eyre was so infuriated by this defense of the man he
was determined to hang that he almost dismissed Pembroke, but the
young man's gallantry in going alone into Maroon territory warranted approval, and Eyre had to bestow it: "You've behaved like a
true Englishman, Pembroke. Duty called and you answered."

"Now it's my duty, Governor, to tell you one basic truth. Everything you've done so far, every action you've taken has been impeccable. Governorship at its best. The rioting has been brought under
control. Island-wide disturbance has been avoided."

"Thank you. I tried my best . . . against great difficulties, I must
say. They all wanted me to declare martial law throughout the island."

"Thank God, you didn't. And now you must halt it where it does
exist."

Eyre could hardly bear to listen to such advice: "Gordon has
done a terrible wrong in starting this rebellion. Punishment must
continue as a lesson to rebels and he must bear his share."

"But you can't send him to St. Thomas. That's judicial murder."

"He must learn his lesson."

With anguish in his voice, Pembroke begged: "Governor Eyre, all
you've done so far bears the mark of greatness. But if you do this to
Gordon, and keep the courts-martial operating, you run a terrible
risk. You will be seen as having corrupted the channels of justice. England could well condemn you."

The words stung, for they touched upon the weakness of Eyre's
position, his lust for personal revenge so strong that he was willing to
ignore the traditions of English justice. He knew that Gordon was
not legally responsible for the rioting, which he termed rebellion. He
knew that a civil court in Kingston would never convict the preacher,
or hang him if it did. And worst of all, he was fully aware that he had
no authority to kidnap Gordon from civil law in Kingston and throw
him into the hands of a court-martial which had no authority over
him, an act equivalent to murder. But his smoldering animosity
toward this difficult man was so great that in his self-defense he made
an appalling admission: "I have always detested George Gordon. A
man of color marrying a white woman to gain advantages. A Baptist

sectarian always denigrating our national religion. And worst of all, an unlettered peasant daring to ridicule our queen."

"I don't believe he ever did," Pembroke said. "He merely protested the silly letter released in her name," but Eyre insisted: "He spat upon her letter," and when Jason again corrected: "Some foolish women did, not he," Eyre snapped: "He encouraged it and must pay the penalty. Come, we're sailing to St. Thomas today."

"Governor, I must protest again. You do this at great risk to your reputation. All honest men, Governor, will see that your actions are illegal and colored by a desire for personal vengeance. For the sake of your honorable name, do not do this thing."

Eyre could not be deterred. George Gordon, a frail bookish man in steel-rimmed glasses, was marched in handcuffs to the waiting *Wolverine;* Eyre came aboard attended by Pembroke, who still hoped to dissuade the governor from committing a hateful deed, and the fatal journey to St. Thomas-in-the-East began. But the short sea passage was like something from an ancient drama in which gods and nature conspired against an evil act, for a great storm arose, buffeting the ship for three days and nights and delaying Governor Eyre from delivering the preacher to the waiting court-martial. During this turbulence Pembroke had a last opportunity to talk with Gordon, who said with a surprising calmness. "I shall be hanged tomorrow, and Jamaica will never forget that day, for it will be murder."

When the storm abated, the preacher was led ashore under a naval guard and marched through the streets to where the court was sitting, and as he went, soldiers and sailors, convinced of his guilt, hurled epithets at him, and some cried: "Here comes Parson Gordon on his way to be hanged," while others shouted: "I'd love to give you a taste of the cat before you die, you traitor!" The mood was so savage that one reporter noted accurately: "Doubtless, if the blue jackets had been left to exercise their own will, he would have been torn to pieces alive."

In the improvised shed from which so many had been dragged to be hanged, the court-martial consisted of two young naval officers and one army man even younger. They had no concept of what jurisdiction was nor whether they had any authority to pass judgment on a man who had not been in St. Thomas, and certainly no idea whatever as to what constituted admissible evidence. They had been ordered to mete out justice to criminals, and they had no trouble in recognizing Parson Gordon as the principal instigator of the riots, because they were told that was what he had been.

There was evidence: letters written to the court from persons elsewhere in the island who were not present to be cross-questioned. Several people said they were sure Gordon had been responsible for the rebellion, and very damaging evidence was brought forth that he had scorned The Queen's Advice. The Morant Bay postmistress testified that since she always read whatever material came through her office in printed or open form, she could state positively that Gordon had mailed subversive literature, though what it was precisely she could not remember.

The young judge allowed Gordon to make a statement in his defense, but it contained only what the preacher had always said to Pembroke and others of his friends, that he wanted to help the citizens of Jamaica better their lot. The three judges paid little attention to his rambling and had no difficulty in finding him guilty, or in sentencing him to be hanged.

The trial was held on Saturday afternoon, and because the officer who would carry out the sentence felt it might be improper to hang a clergyman on a Sunday, the execution was deferred till Monday morning. It rained Sunday night, and on Monday heavy clouds, fringed by the sun which hid behind them, darkened the stone archway from which the rope was suspended. The preacher stood on a wooden plank, totally pinioned lest he try to escape, and when that plank was suddenly withdrawn he plunged to his slow, strangling death. Governor Eyre had been avenged for the insults he imagined that Gordon had heaped upon him.

Jason Pembroke, now anxious to return to Trevelyan, hoped that with the hanging of Gordon, martial law throughout St. Thomas would be terminated and that the various courts-martial, over which no one had any control would be dissolved, but neither of these desired orders was given. Instead, Governor Eyre assigned him to serve with that Colonel Hobbs he had met while with the Maroons. Hobbs, who had seen action overseas, especially at the siege of Sebastopol in the Crimean War, was an easy man for ordinary soldiers to like, for he treated his men well and obeyed a keen sense of military duty. Jason, aware that the rebellion, if it was one, expected Hobbs to exert stern discipline, keep his youthful charges under control, and report that military rule, at least in his quarter, should be ended, there being no signs of any further disturbance.

But Jason's analysis was flawed, for the real horror of martial law had not yet shown its cruel face. The Maroons, considering themselves free to loot and burn, shot nearly two hundred blacks, rejoicing as if engaged in a jolly hunting party. Colonel Hobbs' men specialized in shooting any blacks they saw on remote hillsides, competing among themselves as to who could kill at the greatest distance. When Jason protested these barbarities, Hobbs showed him the letter from the island headquarters under which he served:

> *Push on. Colonel Hole is doing splendid service, shooting every black man who cannot account for himself, sixty during one march. Colonel Nelson is hanging like fun. I hope you will not bring in any prisoners. Do punish the blackguards well.*

That, of course, was license for extermination, and Hobbs discharged his assignment with exuberance, finding special delight in hanging men or lashing women if it was said of them: "That one scorned the queen." He could not tolerate the thought that a black had cast aspersions on the queen, and his eyes glazed over when Jason argued: "Hobbs, can't you see that their protest was not disrespect for the queen?"

"How could that be?"

"They were unwilling to believe that she could have dismissed them so coldly, for they love her." Hobbs, eyes still glazed, rasped: "You heard. They laughed at her Advice. Hang them."

Jason could never anticipate what Hobbs might do next. Once along a distant road they came upon a black man who could have had no connection with the rioting, but when Hobbs heard that the man's name was Arthur Wellington and he was reputed to be an obeah man, a sorcerer, he fell into a maniacal rage: "How dare a nigger take the name of a great man like the duke! How dare he claim to have strange powers! I'll teach him!" and he had Wellington tethered to a tree on the far side of a gully. Then, ordering all blacks from nearby to watch, he had his men line up and fire from a distance of more than four hundred yards. Several of the bullets struck the tethered man, killing him, whereupon Hobbs shouted to the watchers: "What mystical powers does he have now?" and they were impressed with the superiority of the white man's gun over the black man's powers.

One soldier serving with Hobbs showed Jason the letter he was sending his parents in England:

I tell you we have never had so much fun. We leave no man or woman or child if they be black. We shoot them all, sometimes a hundred a day. Some we put aside to have sport with. We tie them to a tree, give them a hundred lashes, then drag them to the ships and hang them from the yardarm. I do believe we average fifty to sixty hanged every day. Such sport.

Pembroke, revolted by such excess, begged Hobbs to halt the killing, but the honored veteran of the Crimea, a man of proved valor, seemed to have turned into a frenzied savage, for all he would respond was: "It's like India . . . colored men rising against white. And it cannot be permitted."

While Pembroke was going through the agony of seeing Englishmen run wild, his cousin Oliver was having a much different reaction to martial law. He was serving as second-in-command to a certified military hero, Gordon Dewberry Ramsay, who had galloped in the lead during the charge of the Light Brigade at Balaklava and won England's highest honor for doing so, the Victoria Cross. He served in Jamaica as a police inspector, and because he was a hearty type, Croome worked well with him, assisting in the floggings, the shootings and the hangings. Like Ramsay, he believed that the honor of the white man had been traduced by the blacks, that Baptists had scorned the established church, and that almost every black had insulted the queen. Under those circumstances, mercy was unwarranted and almost any punishment that Ramsay meted out was justified.

Ramsay, carrying a small stick like a baton, would march through a village and peremptorily order his men: "Give that one a dozen," whereupon the metaled cat would be applied on the spot. Several times he growled: "That one looks a bad lot. Give him a score," and the man would be thrashed.

On one occasion he was watching the application of fifty lashes to a thin black man who had given no offense, when at the forty-seventh blow the man grimaced from the unbearable pain. In a rage Ramsay shouted: "That man bared his teeth at me. Take him down and hang him."

Croome saw nothing wrong in these excesses, for no matter what

preposterous act of revenge Ramsay engaged in, like the hanging of
scores without even the pretense of a trial, he approved, for as he told
Ramsay repeatedly: "They took arms against the queen. They deserve whatever you give them," and he applauded when any black
men who seemed to have an ugly countenance received proper punishment. "That one looks an evil fellow," Ramsay would cry, pointing
with his baton. "Hang him."

Jason Pembroke, having witnessed Hobbs behaving no better,
had at least questioned his mental stability, but Oliver Croome saw
nothing wrong with what Ramsay was doing, and even helped him
rampage through St. Thomas dispensing blind revenge. Once as the
pair watched a black woman receiving a hundred strokes of the cat,
Ramsay said: "She was heard by three different people to speak ill of
The Queen's Advice," and Croome said· "You do well to halt such
treason."

An admiring newspaperman who traveled for some days with
Ramsay and Croome wrote:

> These stalwarts, who are protecting the safety of all white
> men and women in the island, have with them a huge sailor
> from one of the ships who is a master-hand at flogging. Every
> stroke he applies lands with a resounding "Whoosh" and a
> dozen from his mighty right arm equal twoscore from some-
> one else. I saw him give seventy of his best to one man, and
> when he was finished, the criminal could barely stand erect,
> and a man near me said: "He'll go bent for life."

Of the routine hangings, Hobbs and Ramsay accounted for about
two hundred.

On the last day of October 1865, Governor Eyre, a humane man
at heart and unaware of the terrible havoc Hobbs and Ramsay had
been creating, ended martial law except for those already under arrest, and what was more important, granted a general amnesty. Then,
to demonstrate what a perceptive political leader he was, on 8 November he persuaded the inept Legislative Assembly, which had
proved itself powerless to halt the rebellion, to abolish itself, thus
terminating self-rule in Jamaica and reinstituting it as a Crown Colony to be governed by edict from London.

This move was enthusiastically approved throughout the island.
Laudatory editorials appeared in the press extolling both his heroism
and sagacity, and testimonials were offered by the score. As the year

ended with Jamaica under rule by the crown, the killings were forgotten and an honorable peace settled over the island, so that Eyre could reasonably claim, as he did, that his bold and forthright action, his prompt termination of military rule, and his attention to the welfare of all classes in Jamaica had brought the island a tranquillity it had not known for years. With the troublemaker Gordon disposed of, he could, with confidence, look forward to a rule of twenty more productive years, secure in the love of his people, who regarded him as a true hero. But even as he voiced this hope when alone, for he thought of himself as a modest man, a storm was brewing in Great Britain which would toss him about in its violent eddies, making him for three years one of the most noted men in the realm.

It was remarkable that grisly events in a remote corner of an island in the Caribbean should have disrupted the headquarters of empire, but Jamaica was no ordinary colony. For two centuries it had been a source not only of sugar fortunes but also of political power. Selfish laws bulled through by its members of Parliament had been a prime cause of the American Revolution, so that what happened on its great plantations had always been a matter of concern in London.

Now the most ugly rumors were flashing through Great Britain. "Nigger uprising in the colonies!" screamed some, while others muttered: "An English governor has been behaving as if it were 1766 on some savage island!" And before the year was out, the battle lines in Britain had formed dramatically. In sturdy, unwavering support of Eyre were five of the nation's greatest writers: Thomas Carlyle, the moralist who scorned niggers; John Ruskin, the popular aesthete; Charles Dickens, read by everyone; Charles Kingsley, who preached "manly Christianity" and wrote enormously popular novels; and above all, Alfred Tennyson, the wildly acclaimed poet laureate. These five formed a kind of patriotic-sentimental battalion around Eyre's heroic name, winning the publicity battles and defending to the bitter end Eyre's right to shoot down niggers if for any reason they took arms against whites. They had been terrified by the implications of the Indian Mutiny and deemed Eyre's actions to prevent a recurrence in Jamaica not only proper but also rather restrained. They saw him not as a chance hero but as a protector of the white race against a possibly resurgent black, and it was intolerable to them to hear others charge that he had been imprudent in declaring martial law or administering it. All five of these great authors agreed that the blacks had got only what they deserved.

But there was another group of British leaders, more sober and less sentimental, who deplored Eyre's behavior on a distant island far from the scrutiny of Parliament, and again some of the greatest names rallied to this version of the cause: Charles Darwin, the geneticist; Herbert Spencer, the moral philosopher; Thomas Huxley, the scientist; John Bright, the powerful Quaker reformer; and again above all, John Stuart Mill, perhaps the wisest and most brilliant man in the world at that time. These men, always brooding about the problems of right and wrong, believed that for Great Britain to condone Governor Eyre's frenzied behavior in the remote parish of St. Thomas-in-the-East was to imperil the security of the empire, and they were determined that he be brought before the bar of justice to give an account of himself. They interpreted his cruelty against blacks as a frightening throwback to the days of slavery, a last-gasp attempt of wealthy landowners to protect their interests, and an affront to all decent Christians and lovers of liberty.

Neither side was noted for restraint or its willingness to accept compromise.

The field was set for a fierce battle between two groups of men who evaluated the future in drastically different ways. The writers wanted to recapture the glories of the past or at least hold on to what remnants still existed throughout the empire; the scientists hoped to get on with building a new and better world. The writers put loyalty to the crown above everything; the scientists, loyalty to reason and inevitable development. The writers were committed to the defense of the white man in his benevolent rule over others; the scientists, to that fraternity of peoples which alone, they believed, could build the future. And in a curious way, each group was ardently loyal to the concept of British Empire, the writers holding that it could be preserved only by the bold actions of governors like Eyre, the scientists arguing that a few more governors like him would destroy any chance of keeping it together.

It was an honorable debate focused on the dishonorable behavior of men like Hobbs and Ramsay, a gigantic intellectual and moral confrontation centered upon a relatively minor historical figure like Eyre. Eventually it involved newspapers, orations in Parliament, the bold intercession of Britain's greatest jurists, and even the columns of *Punch,* which chimed in early with clever rhymes proving that they, like most of the establishment, were solidly behind Eyre:

> *Does human kindness drain its cup*
> *For black and whitey-brown,*
> *That still you cry the darkey up,*
> *And bawl the white man down?*

> *That every question, fairly tried,*
> *Two sides must have, is true;*
> *If this one have its sooty side,*
> *It has its white side too.*

People in all corners of the British Isles found themselves either supporting Eyre or condemning him, but there was also another topic of singular importance agitating the public. Britain in these years was struggling to pass a Reform Bill which would, at long last, award the smaller cities their proper share of the vote, which meant taking parliamentary seats from Conservative rural areas and turning them over to Liberal urban ones. Leaders of the anti-Eyre group, Mill and Bright in particular, were vigorous advocates of this reform, while pro-Eyre men were against it. However, attention at the moment focused not on Parliament but on what had happened in St. Thomas-in-the-East, and as in the 1760s when Jamaican planters dominated British politics, the descendants of those men now played an important role in British history.

On a sunny day in early 1866, a ruddy-faced Oliver Croome left the mansion in London's Cavendish Square which his sugar-rich ancestors had erected when they bought their seats in Parliament, and he was astonished to see coming from the Pembroke mansion on the opposite side of the square his cousin, the bearded, able Jason. Rushing over to him, Oliver cried with delight: "Jason! What brings you here?" and under the trees the two men who had worked so long and so well together revealed the surprising developments that had brought them by different paths to London.

Oliver spoke first: "When the committee of the world's best writers was put together to defend Governor Eyre against his enemies, and they're a nasty lot, the members asked him: 'Who can we bring up from Jamaica to counter the lies the others are telling?' and Eyre said I knew the facts better than most, and here I am, all expenses paid, though I'd have been proud to come on me own . . . to save the man's reputation."

Jason bowed his head, looked at his knuckles, and said quietly: "Sorry to tell you, Oliver, but the men who're determined to drag Eyre into court asked me to come help them. Miserable business."

To hide his shock, Oliver asked: "Didja bring your wife with you from Jamaica?"

"No, Beth said she'd heard enough of Eyre and his problems."

"Nell didn't want to come for the same reason," and Jason consoled his fellow bachelor: "We won't be here long."

Oliver generously proposed that his cousin stay with him: "Save time and trouble." But Jason had a good excuse for not accepting: "Mill has cramped rooms and likes to hold the meetings of our committee in my quarters. There is ample space," and the two parted, vowing not to let the Eyre business affect their personal relationship. Croome, from his side of the square, watched as the moral giants opposed to Eyre assembled in the Pembroke mansion, and thought: What an ugly group of self-righteous men, not a smile in the lot.

In any group of which John Stuart Mill was a member, he was the automatic chairman to whom others deferred, an icy intellect, a man carved from marble. On this day he was tardy, and in his absence John Bright sat with Jason between the two mammoth statues which had graced this room since the 1760s: *Venus Resisting the Advances of Mars* and *Victory Rewarding Heroism.* At first Bright sat facing the *Venus,* but her voluptuous curves so disturbed his Quaker austerity that he said: "Better, I think, if I exchange chairs with thee, Jason," but now he faced a blatant glorification of heroism, and this too he found intolerable: "Reminds one of Carlyle's nonsense, heroes and all that. Let us sit over here," and having found escape from the oppressive statues, he asked: "I suppose thee knows, Pembroke, that our Mill is a prodigious man?"

"I've seen he commands attention."

"But has thee heard of his schooling?" When Jason shook his head, Bright said with obvious enthusiasm and envy: "Never was he allowed to attend a day of school or university."

"Why not?"

"His father, an extraordinary man of forceful character, considered the boy too promising to be directed by ordinary teaching. 'I will educate him,' he said, and at three John had mastered Greek. At six he had read most of the easy works of the Greek authors like Herodotus and Xenophon and had launched into Plato. At eight he began his study of Latin and mastered Euclid. At eleven he started writing his own history of Rome, an excellent, mature work which he completed at twelve. From there on, it was the solid filling in of empty spots, all known knowledge of humankind, especially mathematics, science, French, German, everything."

"And it didn't turn him sour?"

"The contrary. His father wouldn't allow that. Took him on holiday journeys, gave him joyous books to read, introduced him to men of substance, anything to forge him into a man of learning and judgment. In my efforts for others, I've known many of the fine men of this world, and the best rate four to his ten. I myself rate three."

"What impressed me," Jason said, "was that when he learned I was from Jamaica, he hurried forward, sat me down beside him, and said, staring at me: 'What we desperately need is the truth. They tell me you were there, in all parts. What happened? Not what you heard, only what you saw.' "

"What did you tell him?"

"I said that the official report said that four hundred and thirty-nine people had been murdered, six hundred had been whipped, and a thousand homes had been burnt. He asked: 'But what really happened?' and I said: 'I saw at least six hundred dead, many killed in far corners by Maroons, bodies that could never be counted. I myself saw more than three hundred whipped, about half of them women. And since I passed at least a thousand destroyed houses, the real number must be twice that.' "

"And what did he say?"

"He put his hands to his head for some moments, then looked at me and said in that grave voice: 'Terrible carnage. Terrible wrong.' "

Now Mill came into the room like a cold, clear moon rising suddenly in autumn. Seeing Bright, he hastened to him: "Good friend, we've taken one step forward in the Eyre matter. We've forced the courts to issue warrants of murder against two of the officers who conducted those infamous courts-martial." This brought cheers from the others, except Bright, who pointed out the nagging fact: "But Eyre himself still escapes us, does he not?"

"He does," Mill said with distaste. "Fled to Market Drayton, a rural town northwest of Birmingham, where the London courts can't reach." Then he added, with obvious determination: "But we shall smoke him out. Governor Eyre will pay for his crimes, for we shall never rest."

Cries of *Hear! Hear!* greeted this reaffirmation of war, and Jason thought: How much he sounds like Eyre hounding Gordon. But then Mill began to speak in a more gentle voice, and for the first time Pembroke had a chance to hear this sixty-year-old oracle expound the wisdom for which he was famous. Totally bald and clean-shaven except for sideburns that framed his chiseled Roman face, he spoke deliberately as if calculating the precise weight of each word: "I have been much impressed by the reflections of a German scientist versed in the workings of the human mind, and he has led me to speculate on the error which trapped Eyre into persecuting Gordon, ignoring law and propriety and the tenets of military justice. The professor coined a new word for this affliction, *monomania,* built of two fine Greek words: *mono,* meaning *alone* or *one,* and *mania,* which of course is madness. Eyre is a classic example of the aberration. He was driven by one compulsion: vengeance on Gordon, and when we prove that in court, he . . . is . . . doomed."

"Can we lure him out of Market Drayton?" Bright asked, and Mill said: "If not, we shall carry our fight to him there, in his court-yard," to which Bright, a veteran brawler in the rugged alleyways of public opinion, warned: "The rustic justices of Market Drayton will not be much concerned about what happened in Jamaica, but they'll be most concerned about our hectoring a decent man who was trying only to do his duty."

In some perplexity Jason listened as these bulldogs of justice ended the meeting. He, like Mill, was determined to see Eyre chastised publicly lest this man of flawed character become a national hero, but he wanted to go only so far. He was willing to throw words at the man but not legal sanctions, and this confusion led him to reflect: When Oliver and I came to London, it was for five or six months at most. The other day I heard a lawyer say that if a trial is held, it might take three years. I must have Beth by my side."

Upon consulting with Croome, he found him of like mind, so they dispatched urgent notes to Jamaica: "Please hurry up to London. We need you," and when the women arrived to take charge of the mansions, Cavendish Square resembled the old days when the families spent nine months of each year in London.

At the end of the first week, Nell Croome read the signs: "Beth, our men are planning to stay here not for months but for years," and Beth replied: "The better for us. I love our house here," and she began to serve as hostess for the meetings of John Stuart Mill's committee, whose program was "Governor Eyre to the gallows for murder."

The closeness of the two wives encouraged Croome to believe that he had a chance of weaning his cousin away from the Mill madness and over to the side of responsible patriots defending Eyre: "You simply must meet our men, Jason. They're the backbone of Britain, and right now I'm taking you to see the best of the bunch, Thomas Carlyle. He'll straighten you out."

Jason said: "It might be improper for me to meet him under false colors, as it were. I am against Eyre, you know," and Oliver said: "You won't be after today," and Jason went with him, for he did want to see this formidable man whose writings recommending that slavery be reestablished had so astounded him, and who now fought so stubbornly to defend Eyre. They drove to a modest house in London where a man of smallish height greeted them in the very heavy Scottish tweed suit he preferred, his head of thick hair trimmed just above his eyebrows, his graying beard and mustache somewhat unkempt, but his deep-set eyes flashing with that intelligence which amazed his readers.

Recognizing Croome as one of his adherents in the Eyre case, Carlyle extended his hand, then asked: "Is this young man also one of us?" and Croome lied: "He is. And I brought him to fortify his commitment." At this, Carlyle invited them to join him in his study; as he led the way, they passed Mrs. Carlyle, who without any introduction said almost casually: "So you're the men who are going to protect dear Governor Eyre from the niggers?"

"Yes," Croome said eagerly, and she said: "Fight the good fight, young men. Evil spirits are afoot."

When the three were comfortably seated, Carlyle gave an animated account of his recent efforts on behalf of Eyre, ending with the exciting news: "The Earl of Cardigan, hero of *Charge of the Light Brigade*—excellent poem that, by our friend Tennyson—has come over to our side. Gallant fellow, the public loves him and will listen."

His razor-sharp, steel-hardened mind moved from one topic to another, and when Jason made bold to ask: "Do you still maintain the ideas you expressed in your essay on niggers?" he growled: "More than ever since the rebellion in your Jamaica," and before Jason could

protest, he added: "If you read my essay closely, written in 1848 or
'49 if I remember correctly, you'll find that I anticipated almost everything that happened. Quashee, not satisfied with free pumpkins to
his heart's desire, started a rebellion against law and order and paid
the price. We must alert all Britain to the dangers involved if the per-
secution of Eyre for having done his duty succeeds," and Jason noticed that Carlyle, as a devoted Scot, never spoke of England.

As Carlyle ticked off the charges being made by John Stuart Mill
and his committee, whom he termed "lunatic" and "corrupt," he became fiery in his denunciation: "They seem not to realize it! They're
threatening the very existence of the empire, all the good work our
men have done in civilizing the savages, all to protect lazy Quashee so
he can eat more pumpkins."

Then, before either of his visitors could interrupt, he proceeded
to lecture them on the realities of Britain's position: "All sensible men
during the troubled years just past supported the Southern side in the
American rebellion, for it represented stability and strength of character. Those not concerned about the ultimate freedom of their nation or mankind favored the North. Same factors operate in the Eyre
case. All who love decency and moral force defend Eyre. Those who
care not for the continuity of empire attack him." Jason was eager to
challenge this, but the dour Scotsman thundered on, his beard almost sparking with the fire his words carried: "And mind you this,
young men. Trouble's brewing in Europe, and if the sad day ever
comes when Britain aligns herself with France against Germany, the
empire is doomed."

"Why?" Jason asked, and Carlyle snapped his reply: "Because
Germany represents manly behavior, the highest aspirations of na-
tionhood, France the pusillanimous female meanderings."

"Then why is France a nation and Germany not?"

"Pitiful leadership. But with our strong men coming onto the
scene, real heroes in the ancient sense of that word, Germany will
reign supreme on the Continent, and we must support her and ally
with her." He also gave it as his opinion that it would not be until well
into the next century that any country in Europe would have to take
the United States seriously: "They lack strong men. Lincoln was a
disaster."

Then abruptly he turned to Eyre: "We shall see to it, if we all
work properly, that not a strand of his handsome black hair shall be
touched by the dogs baying in the alleyways. He behaved like a man

of character, reminding Quashee that there is more to life than eating pumpkins in the indolent shade of some tree. Work, work is what saves a man, and we have work to do, honest man's work, in holding off those fools who would attack a man for having done his duty."

"How will you defend him against the charge that he sanctioned brutality?" Jason asked, and Carlyle glowered at him, an intense man afire with righteousness: "In the long run of history and in the defense of human progress, young man, do not brood sentimentally over the fate of Quashee and a few of his pumpkin-eating friends. We are fighting for salvation, Eyre was fighting for it too, the salvation of the human race. Quashee has nothing to do with that, he will never make any contribution to it. Eyre contributed a great deal in pacifying Jamaica. Forget Quashee. Defend Eyre."

When his voice rose, reiterating his tirade against Quashee, Croome broke into applause: "Sir, you make the truth so explicit!" but Jason thought: What was that word Mill used to define blind rage? Monomania? Isn't Carlyle an example of it too?

On the ride home Croome misinterpreted his cousin's perplexed silence as proof that Carlyle's forceful logic had changed Jason's view of Eyre, and he believed that if his cousin would now experience the persuasive power of the governor's principal defender, Alfred Tennyson, he would be converted. To that end he directed his driver to stop by the house in which the great poet was staying during meetings of the Eyre committee, and there he scratched a note on the back of an envelope, asking the butler at the door if it might be delivered to Mr. Tennyson.

"Highly irregular," the man said stiffly, but Croome persisted: "We're members of his committee, you know." The man closed the door in their faces, but not before saying: "I'll ask." And in this way the two cousins from Jamaica worked their way in to see the most famous poet of his time.

They found him a tall, languid man dressed in formal black, with a heavy beard that covered most of his face, a very high forehead leading almost to baldness except that what hair he had was kept very long, almost obscuring his proper white collar. But his distinguishing mark was one which visitors never forgot, an unusually strong nose framed between a pair of deep-set eyes that seemed anguished and saddened by their view of the world. In every outward aspect, he was a poet in the grand visual tradition of Byron, Shelley and especially Keats.

"You do me honor," he said in a resonant voice, "you Two Gentlemen from Jamaica."

"You may remember me," Croome said. "On your committee. Very strong for Governor Eyre."

"No need to remind me, because I remember well in the last century the important role played in this city and in Parliament by your ancestor, gruff old Pentheny Croome." Then, turning gently toward Jason, he asked: "And would I be wrong in presuming that this young man's name is Pembroke? Two Peas in a Pod they were called in the old days."

"How could you know that?" Jason asked in amazement, and Tennyson replied: "I know much about the old days . . . the gallant fighters for what side was right . . . ancestors of those who are fighting the good fight today." He said this in a rather high, wavering voice.

Inviting them to sit, he called for tea, and as it was being served, he pointed to one cup that had been left empty: "Fortunate you came when you did. The Earl of Cardigan is stopping by, and you must meet him, the great hero of the charge at Balaklava, a veritable lion in defense of Eyre," and with the utterance of that name his voice lowered, became more grave and sharpened.

"We have much work to do, gentlemen. John Stuart Mill and his scientists are mounting a formidable assault on the splendid man we must defend," but holding his principal comments until Cardigan arrived, he turned to Jason and asked: "In Jamaica, did you get a good supply of books?"

"Oh yes! I remember so well that exciting day when the first copy of *Locksley Hall* arrived. I must have been no more than fourteen and Mother thought it too complex for me, but I read it anyway, and tears came when I realized that he was not going to win the girl he loved."

"It is good to know tears when you are very young and trying to sort out the world, and also when you're very old and realize what you've missed. But no tears in the middle years. Then there's work to be done, and a man must be a man."

"When I was older I became fascinated by one of your most powerful lines: 'Better fifty years of Europe than a cycle of Cathay.'"

"You have a good ear. That was effective, because it makes an important point with clarity, yet in simple words that can be easily comprehended."

"The line often came to haunt me when I was trying to decide, like your hero, whether to live in London like my grandparents or in Jamaica like Father and Mother."

"See! Life imitates art. The problem arises in every generation, where to apply one's talents."

"But did you honestly mean that fifty years in Luxembourg, say, was better than a thousand years in China and Japan?"

"Unfair! Unfair! I never mentioned Luxembourg, which I'm sure is an attractive place. But are fifty years in the Europe of Paris, Berlin, Rome and London more meaningful to the human race than a cycle of China and Japan? Yes, a thousand times yes, because the great work of the world has been performed here, the worthy ideas hammered out, and very little of significance has been contributed by Asia." He said this with great firmness, then added: "Of course, in the future, as exchange between various parts of the world improves, we may expect this to change. Even India, under our tutelage, will undoubtedly develop the capacity to make contributions, but for the present I will stand by the line you find troublesome."

This speculation ended when the butler announced the arrival of one of the flamboyant men of the age, the resplendent Earl of Cardigan, a lean, handsome man, approaching seventy but with a sure step, a head of gold-streaked white hair, dramatic sideburns, clean dimpled chin and a gargantuan mustache, heavy over the lip, majestic in its extended waxed tips that reached parallel to his ears. Wearing a neat, simple uniform decorated with only three of the two dozen medals he was entitled to show, and with a heavy leather belt encasing his slim waist, he was a fighting man to be admired, and he knew it.

Tennyson spoke first: "Ah, Cardigan, our strong right arm. These are two of our young friends from Jamaica. They know full details of the Eyre business and have come to help us protect our hero."

Cardigan, sitting primly with teacup balanced easily in his left hand, said in the mumbling, harrumphing manner he affected for dealing with the junior officers in the regiment whose colonelcy he had bought, and on which he spent a reputed ten thousand a year of his own money: "Damned poor business, hauling a governor up like this. He should have shot not four hundred of the black buggers but four thousand. Man is sent out to the ends of the world to govern, he's supposed to govern."

To Pembroke's surprise, it was Croome who objected, not on the question of the executions but on the phrase of "ends of the world" to describe Jamaica: "My lord, and begging your pardon, a hundred years ago the sugar planters of Jamaica controlled one-third of Parliament, and passed fine cautious laws."

"Gallant crew, I've heard. Where did they so lose their courage that they allowed their splendid governor to be so abused?"

Jason broke in with: "How does it feel, milord, to be the hero of a poem that everyone in the world is quoting, and with such admiration for both the poet and his subject?"

Cardigan, approving of both the idea and the gracious manner in which it was expressed, nodded first to Tennyson, then to Pembroke, and mumbled through his elegant mustache: "Man gives an artist something to work with, and if he's a genius, he does something with it, eh, Tennyson?" and he slapped the poet on the knee. Tennyson nodded.

"Are we making headway against those who would tear down the empire?" Cardigan asked, and Tennyson told the aging warrior: "We have thousands of men like these who agree with me. We'll give our lives rather than see Eyre abused, for we know we're fighting for the soul and future of England."

"Hear, hear!" Cardigan cried, banging his saucer and its cup on the table. "Day's past for allowing atheists like Mill and that Quaker Bright and Darwin, damn his heretical mind, to corrupt our government abroad. Damn me, you'd think we'd learn something from the Indian Mutiny—allow the little black ones to make one move on their own, they want to govern the world. You stop that nonsense with force, force I say," and all the teacups except Pembroke's rattled from the banging.

Then Tennyson spoke in a quieter tone: "His Lordship is correct. We cannot allow the lesser classes to dictate to those designated to govern. That way lies chaos. We must retain that hallowed discipline that allowed Cardigan here to lead his men into the mouths of the Russian guns, and encouraged his men to follow. When that spirit of nobility is lost in the world, the world is lost."

"What one must do, all nations, all times," Cardigan said, "is give manly men duties to do and support 'em when they do 'em. Eyre will not be persecuted so long as I have a right arm to defend him."

More gravely, Tennyson said: "Not fighting fire with fire, Cardigan. Fighting unreason with reason, an appeal to the everlasting qualities of patriotism, loyalty, love of queen. A return to the faith that made us great in the first place."

Cardigan rattled his saucer again, then asked: "What did you think of Charles Kingsley's suggestions that we ask the queen to elevate Eyre to the peerage? Suggested he be made an earl. I'd be proud to have him join me, very proud."

"We must not move too fast," Tennyson said. "Do nothing that might raise questions or ridicule. In private life Eyre is, after all, barely qualified to call himself a gentleman. An earldom? No, too soon. It would divert attention. Our task is to put out fires."

The rest of the afternoon was spent in devising strategies that would keep Governor Eyre out of the courts and out of jail, and in the discussion, Jason noted, the driving force was Tennyson, this almost effeminate poet who showed repeatedly, at difficult points, a courage to make decisions and the valor to execute them. "He sees himself," said Pembroke to his cousin, "as one of his embattled knights in one of his ancient lays. One goal, one path of honor, one right arm to strike the blow for justice. He will be formidable, and he will save Governor Eyre."

His chance meeting with Carlyle and Tennyson so disoriented Jason that on the drive back to Cavendish Square he listened attentively as Oliver tried to persuade him to abandon his allegiance to the men trying to persecute Eyre and join the vast majority of patriots who were defending him: "Jason, Eyre's one of us. He represents all that's good in England, all that's safe and proper—our church . . . our queen . . . How can you turn your back on everything the Pembrokes have stood for through the centuries? Eyre represents us, he defends us against the hordes . . . and we must rally round."

The hammering continued without respite, forcing Jason to question the propriety of heckling a man whom so many sensible people considered a wronged governor and a brave one. In an effort to defend himself he asked: "But the brutality during martial law? You saw Ramsay. I was with Hobbs. Those men, supposed to be officers, behaved like beasts."

"Jason! It was war. Black brutes against all we held dear. I saw no excess. Harsh punishment for evil acts, nothing more."

"You lack judgment if you saw no excess in Ramsay's behavior."

"But even if I grant that, it in no way touches the governor. He was not there. He did not condone their behavior. And certainly he did not order it."

"What was that again? He himself was not culpable? Not personally?"

"No! No! And he did terminate martial law as soon as possible. He stands guiltless, and you must call off your dogs."

They had reached Cavendish Square when Oliver made these final strong points, all of which Jason had to concede, and for some time they stood in the grassy area between their two houses while Oliver nailed down his persuasive reasoning: "A few blacks were killed after having murdered the queen's representatives. That and nothing more. Tomorrow you must go with me to Tennyson and inform him that you're joining his crusade to save an innocent man."

Bewildered, Jason crossed to his mansion where the gargantuan statues writhed in their marble agonies, and he sat in considerable confusion between them, knowing on the one hand that Governor Eyre had been morally responsible for a terrible chain of crimes, but knowing also that Oliver was right: Eyre had not ordered Hobbs and Ramsay to do the dreadful things they did, nor had he been present when they were carried out. "No court will convict him," he said to Mars and Venus. "Our effort to punish him is doomed."

This conclusion so distressed him that he left the mansion, whistled for a carriage, rode posthaste to the modest house where John Stuart Mill kept his headquarters during the battle for men's minds, and there blurted out his apprehensions: "Eyre cannot be held technically responsible for something he did not order or personally supervise. I do fear our effort will be fruitless."

The powerful intellect behaved as always when a problem was placed before it, pausing and evaluating relevant facts. Then the man with the placid face and endless brow asked quietly: "Now, friend Jason, what experience inspired this defeating conclusion?" and he listened intently as Pembroke described his discussions with Carlyle, Tennyson, the Earl of Cardigan and his cousin Oliver Croome.

At the end of the long report Mill sat silent, his fingers forming a cathedral at his waist, and finally he said in a steady voice, never betraying scorn or anger as he delivered his scathing denunciations: "Surely, Jason, you must know from what you've read and heard that Thomas Carlyle has a blemished mind which glories only in power and is incapable of pity, moral distinctions or the rights of the oppressed. No man who has written jocularly as he has about slavery and advocated our returning to it is a credible witness in dealing with Governor Eyre. To Carlyle, the man's grossest misbehavior becomes his badge of honor, solely because he acted in defense of what Carlyle calls 'the sacred obligation to law and order.' Whose law and order—his or humanity's?"

"But Tennyson was persuasive. You can't charge that immortal poet with playing the brute."

"A hundred years from now, Jason, Tennyson will be uncovered for what he is, a doddering old fellow in bedroom slippers who played the sycophant to anyone higher on the social scale than himself. His immortal poetry, as you call it, will be laughed at by those who know what real poetry is, the cry of a human heart. My father recommended that poets be barred from society because they made untruth and irrelevance palatable, deceiving the public with their wit and lack of brains. Tennyson with his sugary confections best exemplifies what my father despised. Do not take him as your moral guide in this troubled year when so much is coming to decision."

"The Earl of Cardigan said about the same as Tennyson—Eyre is to be commended, not condemned."

Upon hearing this dubious hero cited as an authority of anything, Mill leaned back, turned his face upward, closed his eyes and reflected for some moments: "How can I phrase this so as to do justice to the truth and to the present debate. I'll try." Opening his eyes, he twisted his head so as to face Pembroke, and said quietly: "Cardigan is an ass. And far from being a hero at Balaklava, he proved he was an ass, sacrificing his Light Brigade in his stupidity. And he is the perfect example of Carlyle's nonsense about heroes and hero worship. Heroes are usually counterfeit in their creation and preposterous in the adoration they receive, none more so than Cardigan."

"But he did lead his men personally, none braver than he, Tennyson said so."

"Jason, I shall give you Cardigan in a few sentences. Incredibly stupid in school. Was able to join a regiment only because he paid his way in. Bought the colonelcy, no military talent whatever. Ruled his officers like an insane tyrant, so wretched that most quit and one of his own men with spirit dueled the old fool in an effort to kill him. At Balaklava he and his equally stupid brother-in-law the Earl of Lucan got their orders from that classic incompetent Lord Raglan . . . all mixed up, and disaster followed. The three should have been court-martialed and shot; instead, a silly poem makes the worst offender a hero. Jason, I pray you, do not look to a ninny like Cardigan for guidance."

"Do you hold all members of the other side in contempt?"

"Charles Kingsley wants to have the queen create Eyre an earl? You really don't want me to comment on him, do you? I believe even Carlyle and Tennyson have begged him to remain mute, and not a moment too soon."

"Surely, Dickens . . ."

"A master storyteller whom time will not treat kindly. Can tug at the heartstrings, but no brain at all." He brought his fingertips to his lower lip, bowed his head in dismay, and then looked up with a rueful smile: "Our nation is not under good leadership these days." When Jason said nothing, Mill added, his voice growing ever more determined: "But we fight on many battlegrounds, Jason, and we lose individual skirmishes here and there, but in the long run we win the war. Our fight to bring Eyre to justice is a struggle we may lose, but in doing so, we shall educate the people in the greater questions of social justice, and it is our war for the reform of Parliament that we shall win. Great Britain will be a finer place when you and I are through."

"Then you're surrendering in the Governor Eyre case?"

The answer to this penetrating question came in a curious way, not in words but in actions, for a messenger from the rest of the Jamaica Committee broke in with startling news: "The magistrates of Market Drayton have refused to indict Governor Eyre! He goes free!"

Mill did not rise from his chair, nor did he speak until he had rung for a servant, who received instructions: "I think you had better speed about and assemble the others," and on that night of defeat, with Bright at his elbow and powerful men like Huxley and Darwin in support, Mill revealed his daring strategy: "English law allows any citizen who has been outraged by the refusal of ordinary channels to deal with an obnoxious case, especially where murder is concerned, to bring his own charges, which the courts must adjudge. Tomorrow I shall lodge a formal accusation of murder against Governor Eyre, and I shall take Jason Pembroke with me to establish a Jamaica connection."

Some of the members considered this so radical a move, and so likely to fail, that they dissociated themselves from the attempt, but the icy determination of Mill kept Jason and others in line, and early next morning Mill and he reported to legal authorities and took the first steps toward entering a charge of murder against the governor, thus throwing all of thoughtful Britain into a great debate.

It degenerated into a savage affair, with Carlyle tossing incendiary bombs of his turgid prose at anyone who spoke or acted against his hero, and Mill hanging on like a determined bulldog and infuriating the stable central portion of the population who resented any attack upon "a brave man what only done his duty." Jason, volunteering to handle the flood of letters that reached Mill, opened each week many that promised "to throw you out of Parliament come next election," and a regular two or three whose anonymous writers threatened to assassinate the austere philosopher.

One night, as Jason walked slowly back to Cavendish Square, he thought: I've watched three fine men trapped in the toils of their monomanias the way a peccary in some South American jungle is encoiled by a python. Eyre was so determined to punish Gordon that his judgment was affected. Carlyle is driven almost insane by his desire to establish Eyre as a hero and to protect him against all charges. And Mill, in his cold way, sees himself as an avenging angel . . . Then Jason broke into a laugh: And the Church of England zealots see the whole affair as proper punishment for the Baptist nonconformists. A crazy world.

But it was not until he reached his door and turned to look at the other Jamaican mansion facing his that he appreciated how painfully this affair had separated the families: There's Oliver and Nell in their lonely hall, there's Beth and me in ours, and that's insupportable. And despite the late hour, he determined to have a talk with his cousin. Quickly he went across the square and banged on Oliver's door until a light showed, and when the butler asked in sleepy tones: "What's this?" he brushed his way in and ran up the stairs. He found Oliver and Nell in their bedroom, exhausted by hours of rushing about London, drumming up support for Eyre.

"Jason!" Oliver said, startled at this sudden appearance. "What brings you here?"

"My committee is haling Governor Eyre into court . . . Charge? Murder."

"Oh my God!" Like a tense spring uncoiling, Oliver was out of bed. "This is terrible. Are your people out of their minds? Can't they see that all England is against them?"

"Mill says that doesn't signify. He's out to establish a principle."

"Let him write a book, not destroy a good man." Gripping his cousin by the arm, he said with great fervor: "And he is a good man, Jason, misguided in details perhaps, but damned good."

"I'm beginning to see that. Mill forced me to lodge the complaint, but I will refuse to testify against the governor. Tell him that."

"You shall tell him," and calling to Nell to bring him his trousers, he joined his cousin in the square, then waited while Jason ran to inform Beth that he would be away for a bit longer.

"Doing what?" she pleaded, and he kissed her: "I've a job to do. An error to correct," and he hurried to the cab which his cousin had waiting. Through the London night they sped to the modest house into which Eyre had moved from his sanctuary in Market Drayton. There they wakened him, and in his nightclothes he sat with them and listened quietly as Jason spoke: "I've supported Mill and his men because, as I warned you in Kingston, I felt you were persecuting poor Gordon for solely personal reasons. Many have abused you for that. But I cannot stand by and see a loyal public servant charged with murder because of atrocities committed by his half-crazed subordinates when he was in no way involved."

The gaunt hero of Australian exploration, in only his early fifties but his life already ruined, nodded deferentially to the young man who had in recent years been his enemy. His hair was still a solid black, but his copious beard now showed flecks of white and his once-fierce eyes had lost their ardor: "Thank you, Pembroke, for your gentlemanly support. I shall stand trial and testify as to my motives. But I assure you of this. I have never wavered in my belief that the English people and their splendid courts of law will in the end vindicate me as a civil servant who faced a cruel crisis and handled it as best he could. Do I repent the cruelties that others perpetrated during my proclamation of martial law? Of course. But do I repent of anything I myself did to save Jamaica for the empire? Never. Never." Thanking Croome for having brought him the news, he nodded gravely to Pembroke and went off to bed.

Mill had his way, for in response to the pressures he exerted, a London court charged Eyre with murder—and a shudder passed through the population. Threats against Mill's own life tripled, but before the case could come to trial, court officials decided in private consultation that since a somewhat similar case involving the military officers who had conducted the Jamaican courts-martial had been thrown out for lack of merit, the charges against Eyre were also invalid. He was set free, with all charges permanently dropped, to the delight of the cheering mobs who had rallied to his defense. Twice Mill had tried to send Eyre to jail and twice he had failed.

When Jason hurried to Mill's quarters to report the news, he saw the great leader at his best and worst. When Mill learned that he had lost again, he showed neither rage nor passive disappointment: "The courts have spoken and all must abide." But then, his brow darkening and his fists clenching: "*Those* courts have spoken. But there are other courts, and to them we shall drag him."

"Oh, sir! You're not going to go through this again?"

"I have determined that Eyre shall be punished, humiliated in public for the great wrong he did to the concept of just colonial government," and like a dog gnawing at a bone, he immediately started proceedings to have Eyre hauled into another court, in another jurisdiction to face a completely new set of charges. Reluctantly, the court ordered Eyre to stand trial once again, this time for high crimes and misdemeanors. A date was set to begin, 2 June 1868, almost three years after the riots and the courts-martial, but an impassioned defense lawyer asked members of the preliminary grand jury to "put yourselves in Eyre's place," and consider what steps a man facing a wild rebellion might do to save his island, his empire and the honor of his queen. Public observers in the courtroom cheered, and early next morning the jury announced that all charges were dismissed. At long last Eyre was really a free man, and at the next election John Stuart Mill would be thrown out of Parliament.

He did not brood about his defeat. When he learned that his young supporter Jason Pembroke and his wife were heading back to Jamaica, he stopped by their mansion to say farewell. Seated in the reception room in which the Pembrokes of 1760 had helped frame the good laws that determined the future of Great Britain, he looked with quiet amusement at Hester Pembroke's massive statues, and said: "Jason, we've lost every battle, you and I. We've allowed a great scoundrel to slip through our net unpunished. I'm about to lose my seat in Parliament, while Carlyle and Tennyson and Cardigan reign triumphant. And you slink back to Jamaica having accomplished nothing, so far as your public can see. But in reality, my young friend, you and I have achieved a tremendous victory. In the future, tin-soldier colonial governors will think twice before throwing their islands into martial law or allowing their underlings to terrorize people of a darker skin. Reform of Parliament has passed. Britain will be a better place for our efforts." Poking with his stick at the contorted figure of Mars wrestling with Venus, he confessed: "Had the jury found Eyre guilty of murder, as it should have, I would have been first in line to plead for clemency and a full pardon. It was the idea of the thing that mattered, the establishing of a principle."

Jason, confused by what he had witnessed in the past three years, asked: "Professor Mill, about that interesting word you used. Do you think your hounding of Governor Eyre was an example of monomania?"

Mill, appreciating the acuity of the question, allowed a smile to touch his icy countenance and said: "When the other fellow does it, we call it monomania. When I do it, we describe it as unwavering adherence to principle."

As he rose to go, he brought his stick down on one of the huge statues and said gruffly: "Get that monstrosity out of your home, Jason. Leave such outmoded images to Tennyson and Carlyle."

Jason took his advice. On his last day in London he arranged for stone-cutters to segment the statues, haul them out of the mansion, and reassemble them in a park attached to a zoo.

The final word on these hectic events was one which, had it been anticipated, might have saved Jamaica its travail and Great Britain the bitterness of its inflamed debate. Not long after the turbulence at St. Thomas-in-the-East, both Colonel Hobbs, the laughing monster with whom Pembroke had served, and Police Inspector Ramsay, whose savage behavior Croome approved, committed suicide, the first by shooting himself, the second by leaping off a steamship in midocean. Competent medical experts judged that the men had already been insane when performing their atrocities but that no one had noticed, because when martial law rages, insanity becomes the norm.

XII

LETTERS OF INTRODUCTION

O N 8 JANUARY 1938, DAN GROSS, EDITOR IN CHIEF OF THE *Detroit Chronicle,* saw on the Associated Press ticker a throwaway color item which could have been of interest to only a few American editors but which excited him enormously, for it fit like a searched-for piece in one of his jigsaw puzzles.

The *Chronicle* faced a unique problem. Because of the meandering way in which the international border separating Canada from the United States twisted and turned as it picked its path through the Great Lakes system, at this point Canada lay well south of the United States. This made Detroiters refer to the important Canadian city of Windsor as "our southern suburb," and Detroit newspapers which circulated widely there were forever trying to develop stories attractive to their Canadian readers.

The item which excited Gross read:

> Today the King of England nominated the famous cricket captain Lord Basil Wrentham to be his next governor general of the island of All Saints in the Leeward Islands of the Caribbean West Indies. It is presumed that the appointment will be well received by All Saints, since Lord Wrentham led the first English cricket team ever to play on that island, where he

was extremely popular because of the gracious manner in which he accepted the only loss suffered by a first-class English team in the West Indies up to then. England won the series, three matches to one, but the stunning islanders' victory is remembered on All Saints as an historic event. The new governor general will take the oath of office on 10 February 1938.

Tearing the item from the long roll of paper coming from the teletype, Gross hurried to a small bookcase in which he kept those reference books which enabled him to command much of the world's knowledge: a thesaurus, two big atlases, a French dictionary for use with Canadian material, and a most valuable book with a grease-marked, tattered jacket, Ploctz's *A Manual of Universal History.* Turning to the index, which he had learned to use with precision, he found that a suspicion awakened by the teletype item was confirmed. In 1763, at the Treaty of Paris, which ended what was known in Europe as the "Seven Years' War" and in North America as the "French and Indian War," an unbelievable set of options was seriously debated among the major powers: Should Great Britain receive all of Canada or the tiny Caribbean island of All Saints? Yes, there was the astonishing fact, but what to do about it?

Gross had on his staff an earnest young reporter named Millard McKay who had done graduate work at Columbia University's School of Journalism, and who showed solid, if somewhat unimaginative, talent but improved each month he was with the paper. He would in time, thought Gross, become a mainstay of the *Chronicle,* a man who could be relied upon to cover acceptably whatever topic he was assigned.

After watching him during his first year, Gross learned that McKay shared a weakness common to young men educated at East Coast universities and with a love of books: he wished ardently that he had been born an Englishman, with access to London theaters and a summer home in the Thomas Hardy countryside or perhaps the Lake District made famous by poets. Although he had not yet been able to visit England, he had picked up from his professors a touch of an Oxford accent, and was appalled when anyone suggested he might be Irish. "No," he would say firmly. "Actually, I'm English. Mother's name was Cottsfield." On starting a new life in Detroit, he had considered changing his name to Malcolm Cottsfield, which he thought more genteel and English, but he found the legal requirements so complicated and expensive that he backed off.

Mr. Gross had once asked him: "How did you generate this great love for things English?" and he told an unlikely story: "I grew up in a village of three hundred in the Pine Barrens of southern New Jersey, and they can be very barren. Got a scholarship to Rutgers University in northern Jersey and fell under the spell of a professor who'd been a Rhodes scholar. He lived and died for England, and I took three courses with him. He made us write long papers on various aspects of English life, and he threw the topics at us arbitrarily. I got 'How the English Parliament Functions' one term, 'Six English Novelists from Thomas Hardy to Greene' the next, and believe it or not, for the third course I wrote on 'English County Cricket.' When you study that way, you learn something."

When the copyboy called "Mr. Gross wants to see you," McKay immediately thought: What have I done wrong? But a rapid inventory of his recent stories produced none that were vulnerable, so he assumed he was about to receive a new assignment, and with restrained confidence he entered the editor's office, where the teletype fragment was thrust into his hands.

"You're an English-history buff," Gross said. "Any idea about the significance of this?"

Millard studied the elements in the story and found nothing that related to his rather wide knowledge of English history and custom. Wrentham was not a name that had played any significant role in English history, and although he knew how cricket was played, he could see no special significance in that brief reference. "I'm afraid it escapes me," he had to say.

"I wouldn't expect you to understand my next question. But does the date when Wrentham is supposed to arrive in All Saints, February tenth, ring any bell?"

"No."

"How about the Treaty of Paris?"

"Mr. Gross, you're throwing puzzles at me."

"I sure am," and with a chuckle Gross passed across his desk the Ploetz manual. "Look up the Treaty of Paris, 1763."

And when Millard did, he saw that astonishing entry regarding the complex treaty that ended the long wars in Europe and the lesser skirmishes in the Caribbean. France confirmed that it already had plans for ceding the Louisiana Territory to Spain, England gave Guadeloupe and Martinique to France, Spain gave Florida to England, and then came the provision that stirred Gross's imagination: "France and England both wanted the strategic island of All Saints in the Caribbean, but neither wanted Canada. English admirals argued that their fleets simply must have the vital island, key to the Caribbean and South America, and they saw no loss in throwing a bleak northern wilderness like Canada to the French, but they did not get their way. Britain got Canada, France got All Saints, which Britain would grab back at the first opportunity, so that poor France was cheated of everything."

"I never knew that!" Millard cried. "All of Canada in exchange for one little island!"

"And note the date: ten February 1763. Lord what's-his-name assumes command in All Saints on that anniversary."

"You want me to draft an article about this, for our Canadian readers?"

"Much more. I want to do this right. You get yourself down to All Saints, look the place over, and give us a long, thoughtful article or maybe a series, comparing All Saints today with Canada. Give our Canadian friends a good laugh."

From his bookcase he took an almanac. "Yes, here is it. Canada, 3,851,790 square miles; All Saints, 303. Population: Canada, 11,120,000; All Saints, 29,779. Keep those figures in mind and give us a rattling good yarn." He stopped, leaned across his desk, and asked: "You know Canada, don't you?"

"Yes, sir. I visited Calgary for the Stampede. From Winnipeg to Nova Scotia, I know rather well."

"Good. Bone up. Catch a train for Miami tonight, and you have maybe a week and a half before His Lordship reaches the island. Stay as long as needed, but this is a work trip, not a paid vacation."

As soon as McKay left Mr. Gross's office he headed for the *Chronicle* library, where he took down *Burke's Peerage,* to learn that the Wrenthams had started their climb to noble status in the mid-1600s, when a member of their family in Barbados was knighted as Sir Geoffrey because he defended the royal prerogatives of King Charles against the radical partisans of Oliver Cromwell. Some years later he was elevated to the peerage as Lord Wrentham for his daring sail westward from Barbados in a frail ship with sixty-one Englishmen, to land on the bleak eastern shore of All Saints Island, held by the French. In heroic fashion Sir Geoffrey led his men across the mountains and down to the bay, where the French had established a town. Falling upon the settlement by surprise, Wrentham drove the French into western headlands, from which they evacuated the island.

The third Lord Wrentham left the Caribbean and returned to England, where he performed such valiant services for the crown that he won significant promotion to Earl of Gore, a title which had since passed in orderly fashion to seven Wrentham inheritors.

The various Earls of Gore accomplished little of merit except the cultivation of their huge sugar estates on Barbados and All Saints, from which as absentee landlords, they garnered vast fortunes, to be spent ostentatiously in London. One of their minor grandsons, Alistair Wrentham, did return to the Caribbean as a first lieutenant aboard H.M.S. *Boreas* with the great Horatio Nelson, and served with him again at Trafalgar. For his heroism, he had later been commissioned admiral of the Caribbean fleet, in which capacity he gained several resounding victories over the French.

McKay, who relished the intricate rules governing English titles, learned from his swift scanning of *Burke's* that whoever was Earl of Gore also held the subsidiary title, Lord Wrentham. Millard mused: But the news clip said Lord Basil Wrentham. Whenever they use the first name, it means he's not next in line. Means he's a younger son called Lord as courtesy. Title dies with him. Lord Basil can never become Earl of Gore unless his older brother dies. But . . . even on those restricted terms, it would be nice to be a lord.

In his research he discovered an attractive story, which he planned to use in his first article, as to how All Saints got its name:

Because Columbus had a difficult time in his 1492 voyage of discovery, with only three small ships, people today suppose that he had the same limitations on his subsequent voyages. Not so! On his second trip in 1493 he led a veritable flotilla of seventeen ships, some of them quite large, and whereas the first crossing from the Canaries took five long weeks plus two days, they made it this time in an easy uneventful three weeks.

One of the ships bettered even that remarkable speed. A large new caravel, which had been christened *Todos Los Santos,* had as its navigator a learned Italian priest called Fra Benedetto, who was so skilled at gauging winds and currents that he prevailed upon his captain to follow a more southerly course than that being pursued by the main fleet.

Columbus with his sixteen ships would sail between the small eastern islands and enter the Caribbean on 3 November 1493, but *Todos Los Santos* would enter somewhat to the south two days earlier, then sail north to rejoin, and as the days of October waned, Fra Benedetto had a happy conceit: Would it not be a mark of God's favor if His ship *Todos Los Santos* were to make landfall at some new island on the very day of All Saints, November 1?

Fra Benedetto's calculations satisfied him that on All Saints Day, following the traditional eve of lost wanderers, souls and goblins, landfall would have to be close ahead. He posted special lookouts to watch for it, but the whole day and evening passed with no islands sighted. Shortly before midnight Fra Benedetto toppled the hourglass to return more sand to the top section, which gave him additional time for sighting land before All Saints Day had passed. Now he stalked the deck himself, anxiously looking for land, and fifteen minutes into his borrowed hour, a lad at the forward lookout spotted what he took to be a flickering light. The crew was alerted, and as the moon came out from behind a cloud, it illuminated the two majestic peaks which were later named by French occupants as Morne Jour and Morne Soir.

"We have found our new island!" Fra Benedetto cried as he danced about the ship. "And Todos Los Santos shall be its name."

In the early 1500s the Spaniards made four half-hearted attempts to wrest the island from the fierce Caribs, but were ignominiously repulsed by those fighting terrors. Then the English tried three times, with no better results. But in 1671 the English succeeded, to be promptly ousted by the French. In the following hundred and seventy-four years the ownership of this desirable isle changed hands eighteen times: Carib, Spanish, French, English, Dutch. Thirteen of these changes were the result of military action: the English trying to force their way ashore against the French; the Dutch blasting the English; the Caribs revolting against the Dutch; the French gaining substantial control and making it a French island. Five of the changes resulted not from any action in the Caribbean but rather from treaties arranged in Europe, when Caribbean islands were moved like pawns on a chessboard. All Saints figured in eleven of these treaties, and there were many who felt then or who still feel that the final disposition—British since 1814—placed All Saints in the wrong hands. It should have been French.

And in a small book which Millard grabbed at the last moment, he discovered the most intriguing fact of all: "Through all these varied shifts of ownership, a minor branch of the Wrentham family stubbornly stayed on All Saints, some of the members growing darker generation by generation as their parents mingled with black slaves. But regardless of their color, they were all distantly related to the Earl of Gore."

Before hurrying home to pack, McKay proved what a prudent young man he was by returning to Dan Gross's office to explain a problem: "Sir, this is an English colony, and I had it drummed into me by my professors who studied at Oxford: 'Never barge into any English social group without being fortified with letters of introduction establishing who you are and verifying your character.' Could you please write me such letters?"

"No! First of all, it's a British colony, not English. And you know our rules. We kowtow to no one, seek no extra privileges. You arrive in All Saints like an ordinary tourist. See things fresh and unbiased."

"Of course I know the accurate name has been Great Britain since 1603, but English sounds better, and I do know that in an English colony, letters . . ."

"No letters. Do it our way."

McKay entered All Saints by the most beautiful approach in the Caribbean: on an early sun-drenched morning he stood in the bow of his ship and watched two lovely peaks loom out of the sea. "That's Morne Jour to the north," a fellow traveler explained, "Morne Soir to the south."

"I don't know that word *morne*," Millard said, and the man replied: "Hill, I guess. All the place names here are French."

"I'm sure they would be," McKay said. "Seeing that the island was French longer than it's been English."

The traveler, an Englishman, did not like this extension of his friendly remarks and moved away, leaving McKay alone as the ship passed between two rocky pillars guarding the entrance to Baie de Soleil. But then McKay overheard him pointing out the glories of this entrance to another passenger: "Pointes Nord and Sud," he said, pronouncing the French with a flair.

Now McKay saw the wonder of this approach to a tropical island, for the two protecting rocks were so placed that any view of the sea behind was cut off. "We're in Baie de Soleil," the traveler exulted nearby. "The Bay of the Sun, and look at that sun!"

Dead ahead at the far end of the *baie,* perched on a rise which ensured a commanding view, stood the colonial settlement of Bristol Town, a congregation of two- and three-story white, gray and ocher houses, none dominating the others. "How harmonious!" McKay exclaimed, but the Englishman did not hear, for his eyes were fixed upon a stately structure that occupied the top of a small hill behind the town. Protected by tall trees, the rambling house looked cool, aloof and quietly efficient.

"Government House," the man said, turning toward McKay, and the reverential way in which he uttered these words evoked the grandeur of the British Empire. "Bristol Town may be one of the smallest capital cities of the empire, but it's one of the most memorable." The forcefulness of his speech carried an implied warning: "The names on the land and the heritage of the people who occupy it may be French, but the government is British . . . and don't you forget it."

The dock at Bristol was bustling, with scores of black stevedores moving at a slow, steady pace as they unloaded the ship and brought the passengers' luggage ashore. "Hey, hey!" McKay shouted at a man who was starting to walk off with two suitcases. "Those are mine!"

"I know, Mr. McKay. We be expectin' you," and then Millard saw that the man was wearing a badge indicating he was from the Belgrave Hotel. "Just follow me," and with delightful, dodging assurance, he darted into the traffic that crowded the dock area. He was headed for a ramshackle three-story building protected by verandas on each floor, and since these were held aloft by numerous slim wooden poles, the hotel displayed a fairy-tale elegance, even if it was a bit seedy. A man could grow fond of a place like this, Millard thought.

But as they were about to enter the dark interior, McKay suddenly turned to the porter: "Can't I register later? Just stow my luggage somewhere. I'd like to start seeing the town right away." Almost as if he expected to hear this, the porter said: "I take care everything.

You wait here," and when he came back, he grasped Millard by the arm and proceeded to lead him along the main street: "You come me, I show you best part Bristol Town."

Hurrying him along, the porter took McKay to a nondescript one-story building that could have housed a cheap restaurant but which turned out to be the Waterloo, a convivial bar with half a dozen old-style pedestal tables, where patrons lounged over their morning drink. The owner, who stood smiling behind his bar, was clearly a mulatto, but not an especially dark one. Half the patrons were mulatto but lighter than he, half were noticeably darker. The two waiters were very black, with no visible admixture of white blood. McKay was the only white there. It was an amazing congregation, assembled by chance and an instructive introduction to an island where a man's skin color was all-important.

The owner, an amiable, hefty man in his forties, winked at McKay's porter, indicating: There'll be a tip for you, bringing this customer to my bar.

The porter nudged McKay: "Waterloo owned by this nice man. His name Bart Wrentham, but they calls him Black Bart, famous pirate." He backed away, grinning broadly to make sure that he was remembered as the one who had delivered this customer.

"And your name?" Black Bart Wrentham asked with the easy familiarity of a bartender who wished to keep every customer at ease.

McKay gave his name, and added, so that his intentions should be understood from the start: "Newspaperman. Detroit."

Upon hearing these words, Wrentham's manner became even more genial, for he knew the value of having his bar mentioned in American newspapers. McKay became not an ordinary tourist but a most important visitor whose introduction to the island merited careful orchestration. Besides, as a man of color whose forebears had lived on the island for nearly three hundred years, Bart had certain strong attitudes that he wanted an American writer to understand. So, moving closer to where McKay stood, he leaned expansively on his side of the bar and said, in beautiful English with a lilting island accent: "Any new arrival brought to my establishment by Hippolyte gets a Tropical Bouquet."

McKay was captured by the free drink—a rum swizzle, decorated with three island flowers and a wedge of pineapple—the atmosphere of the place, and the intriguing discovery that the owner's name was the same as that of the incoming governor general: "You have a memorable name, same as the new head man."

"The English side of my ancestors came here . . ."

"I know," McKay broke in with one of the most productive interruptions he would make in his career as a newsman. "Your people came over from Barbados in 1662 with Sir Geoffrey Wrentham." He smiled at the man, who stood mouth open to find that this American had paid All Saints the respect of having studied its history. Slapping the bar resoundingly, the owner shouted to one of the waiters: "Give this learned American another free Tropical Bouquet! But leave out the pineapple, it costs money." More important, he left the bar and came around one end to lead McKay with his new drink to a table.

"Now, tell me," he said conspiratorially as he sat beside McKay, "what are you really here for?"

McKay evaded the question by taking a long swig: "You make good drinks."

"We try," Wrentham said, moving closer and staring directly into McKay's eyes. "Now answer my question." His words conveyed a challenge which Millard met by leaning back, revolving his glass, and saying carefully: "I work for the *Chronicle*, one of the better papers of our Midwest. Large readership in Canada." He returned to his drink to allow those facts to sink in.

"Quite clear. You're down here to report on the installation of our new Gee-Gee."

"Is that what you call your governor?"

When Wrentham heard the question he sucked in his breath, uttered a clicking sound, and said: "It's not easy to explain, unless you know the islands. As a Crown Colony, we're entitled to a governor. On other islands they call the governor 'H.E.,' His Excellency. Our governor has control over half a dozen other islands, so he is the governor general, and we abbreviate that to 'G-G' or 'Gee-Gee'— that's how we always write it, even in the paper. You should do the same in the article I'm sure you'll be writing."

McKay pointed his right forefinger as if firing a pistol: "You're a sharp fellow, Wrentham."

"Call me Bart." The easy way Wrentham handled his introduction, plus his obvious intelligence, made McKay think he might be a profitable informant, so he told him: "When I left Detroit on this assignment I asked my boss for letters of introduction, but he said that on our paper, we didn't do it that way. Told me to go down and dive into the swim. Your bar is my first dive."

Wrentham leaned back, studied the young newsman, and tapped the table twice, as if to signify that he had made up his mind: "You free?"

"I haven't checked in yet."

"Hippolyte took care of that. You ready for a spin?"

"I'd like that," and the two went out to where the bar owner had parked his 1932 left-hand-drive Chevrolet coupé. "Hop in. We'll do the north circle. It always refreshes me to see the beauty of my island." And he drove rather fast to the east, leaving the town by a twisting road that climbed through wooded land to a prominence from which they could look out upon the dark, surly Atlantic Ocean.

"My ancestors landed on that dangerous beach down there, Baie du Mort. I suppose you know French."

"Since I do a lot of my reporting in Canada, I'd better. Bay of Death."

For the balance of the twelve-mile drive north the two men talked of scenery, but Millard had a strong suspicion that this was not the purpose of the trip. "Our island isn't fine level land like most of Barbados. Didn't permit big sugar plantations like Jamaica. But once you treat this soil respectfully, it treats you the same way. We never starved."

When the road started west, toward the Caribbean, Wrentham said: "We should get a picnic," and he drove into the quaint, sleepy town of Tudor, where a shopkeeper, also named Wrentham and much darker than Bart, put together a large bag of groceries for the construction of a rural feast. "Better give us something to drink," Bart said, and his distant cousin responded with two bottles of English beer and a can of American fruit juice.

With this comforting cargo the sightseers headed due west across the top of All Saints, and McKay, in the right-hand seat, enjoyed this calmer view of the Atlantic but still had no clue as to why Wrentham had taken him upon such a long journey. It could not be from mere kindness. When they were well west of Tudor, the man began describing with a mix of bitterness and amusement the social structure of his island, and it became obvious that he had much he yearned to say, especially to a writer from America. He began disarmingly: "You must understand, Mr. Detroit, that almost everyone on this island will hate you, just a little."

"I've given no offense."

"Ah, but you're an American. And so was she."

"Who?"

"Wally Simpson. We love royalty on this island—all of us, regardless of color. And we adored King Edward. He was such a glorious young fellow when he visited us as Prince of Wales. If you look in a hundred of our homes like those over there, you'll find sixty or seventy with a chromo portrait of Edward. We can never forgive your Mrs. Simpson for having knocked him off our throne."

"I always supposed he knocked himself off." The words were scarcely out when Wrentham slowed the car and turned to warn his guest: "You'd be well advised not to voice an opinion like that in All Saints. You'll find all doors closed against you, because his memory is revered."

"I apologize."

"You should. Your tantalizing witch almost destroyed an empire."

Several moments of silence followed this surprising outburst, but it was soon clear that Bart had other things on his mind that he wanted to talk about, for he grasped the steering wheel with both hands, leaned forward far over it till his head almost touched the windshield, and said in conciliatory tones: "Even though your left-hand drive is a mite inconvenient, an American car is superior."

"Is it difficult?" Millard asked. "I mean, driving from the wrong side, as it were?" and Wrentham said with the pleasing lyrical intonation that was special to the Caribbean: "Indeed, it is most difficult because the driver cannot see all that ought to be seen, but it's worth it to have a fine car that holds the road and turns so easily."

Having rebroken the ice, he began the lecture to which everything up to now had been a prelude: "You may not use my name in your dispatches, but you can refer to me as a well-informed businessman of color. At the last census, All Saints had a population of twenty-nine thousand stacked in hundreds of different social levels, each determined by color. I am one level higher in scale than a man one shade darker than me. And I am certainly one level lower than the man who is a touch lighter in coloring. And remember, it's only the color of the *face* that counts, not how it looks down here," and he slapped his belly.

"But for your purposes, there are only a dozen levels that matter. At the exalted top: anyone born pure-white in England with a title or close claim to one. That is, the Gee-Gee and his circle of intimates. In a million years no man with my coloring will attain that Valhalla. Second level, anyone who can prove he comes from a good county family in England. No Scots nor Welsh need apply."

"What do you mean by 'good county family'?"

"No one knows scientifically, but everyone knows operationally."

"For example?"

"Daughter of a well-respected clergyman, but never a Baptist or a Methodist. Son of an official who conducted himself well. 'Good county family'—with us that explains everything."

Millard asked five or six rapid-fire questions which proved that from his college courses he understood the niceties of English rural life, and after fielding them, Wrentham continued: "The women who determine who fits in where socially keep the county group rather small, but then comes the rather large third level to which you might aspire if you immigrated here, behaved yourself, and had voted Republican in America. It includes all the whites of respectable reputation, especially the French farming families who have been here longer than any of us English.

"But then the separation becomes brutal. Remorseless, like the swath of the reaper's scythe. Level four, the ladies and gentlemen of color, spelled our way c-o-l-o-u-r. Light skin, much lighter than mine. Been to Oxford, maybe. Or the London School of Economics. Or Harvard. Serve in the gommint."

"The what?"

"The *gommint*. You better learn that word. We all say it that way, even the Gee-Gee. What you colonials call government. On an island like All Saints, the gommint is all-powerful, and the top officials of color are entitled to membership in this exalted level four, also a few substantial businessmen, some wealthy widows, and now and then someone difficult to justify. But of one thing you can be certain, Mr. Detroit. Their color will be much lighter than mine. That's the badge of honor."

Wrentham's disgust with the system he was describing was obvious, though he was able to talk of it with some levity. "Levels five, six and seven are all lighter than me . . . and keep that in mind," he said, "because I am an eight," which he then described as "hardworking men and women who save their money, send their children to school and know how to use a knife and fork."

"But if you're relegated to level eight, how did you acquire such an elegant vocabulary?" asked McKay, and Bart chuckled: "Man, we have schools. Wonderful dedicated teachers who love every inch of England, every word Shakespeare ever wrote. I've never read an American book, if there are any, but Walter Scott and Charles Dickens and Jane Austen . . . yes, yes!"

There were, he said, about six levels for those of mixed color darker than his own, and now he was approaching the sharpest line of all: "Below them is nothing. The blacks with heavy lips, fine teeth and no education—slaves, perpetual slaves."

"What if a black man were to immigrate here from, say, Carolina? Or a Hindu from India?"

"If he's black, he's black."

"Can he never aspire to entering the higher groups? Where you people of lighter skin come to rest?"

Wrentham drove in silence, ignoring this ugly question, then said: "Mr. Newspaperman, we're soon going to be at Cap Galant, where you will see the great beauty of our island. And there on the blanket I always carry in my Chevrolet, we shall spread our picnic, your first in the Caribbean, so we must make it unforgettable."

But before spreading the picnic he wanted to share the basic rule of All Saints, the one that all young people understood: "It will also explain things if you decide to visit the other Caribbean islands. A young colored man of promise simply must, if he wants to get ahead, marry a girl with lighter skin. He will fight, lie, steal, and murder to achieve this. And the colored girl of great beauty who wants to make something of herself, she must marry a man with skin even lighter than hers. And it is watching what happens in this whirligig impasse that produces the hilarity of Caribbean life, and the tragedies, and the suicides."

After a short run to the southwest, away from the Atlantic, they came to a small elevated peninsula jutting due westward and commanding an incomparable view. To the north, the distant ocean, to the east the slopes of Morne Jour reaching almost four thousand feet into the cloudless sky, to the south a perfect little bay with an arc of light sand, and best of all, to the west the quiet blue Caribbean spreading all the way to the Maya ruins of Cozumel.

"Which view is your favorite?" Millard asked, and Wrentham replied: "It's all so grand, I can never decide," and it was obvious that he was proud of this belvedere.

While he spread his blanket and laid out the delicacies he had purchased at Tudor, Millard looked about the area atop the cap and down into the cove that housed the beach. What he saw confirmed Bart's analysis of his island, for although he saw some eight or nine groups picnicking, each was off to itself and severely restricted in color. Whites ate with whites, light coloreds with their like, and rowdy blacks sang with their own kind. The beautiful cap and its beach were in no way segregated; anyone could eat anywhere, but he had better eat with his own color.

Wrentham had placed the blanket so that his American guest could lean comfortably against a rather large rock, and as the two men drank beer, munched sandwiches and nibbled at fine English biscuits and tartlets, Bart resumed his instruction: "On the hill behind Gommint House, which I'm sure you saw from your ship, there's a building of no great distinction surrounded by tennis courts, bowling greens and croquet lawns. That's The Club, and it is severely restricted to an all-white membership. Most of the people in levels one through three, including especially the French . . . Incidentally, the French speak little French. Their names announce them, not their verb forms. What was I saying?"

"Membership in The Club."

"Well now. Suppose for a moment that you did emigrate here. Satisfied the paperwork and all that. You behave yourself. Pay your bills. Act with respect toward your superiors. You could still fail to be accepted."

"Why?"

"You're not English. And you are American. And that means you've got to be an uncultivated boor."

"So I'll never see this glorious club?"

"Of course you will! You can be invited there, but to be an actual member, never."

"Is it pretty posh?"

"Heavens, no! Dues are minimal. Décor is deplorable, I'm told. I've never been allowed in, you understand. But I'm told its attraction is that it's like a cocoon or a womb. Your own kind of people. Your own color."

"Who runs it?"

"The women, fiercely. The wives of the senior officials, aided, of course, by Major Leckey. He's in charge of seeing that it remains pure."

"Who's he?"

"The Gee-Gee's aide-de-camp. Been here for years. Had a fine reputation in India, good regiment and all that. Major Devon Leckey. And if he takes a dislike to you, or if his madam, Pamela, does, you might as well pack up and leave, because he and the divine Pam rule the roost."

"How?"

"They more or less determine what group you fit into. What affairs it would be proper to invite you to. Who would be urged to attend if your daughter gets married on the island."

"An ugly type?"

"No, no! The Leckeys are the salt of the English earth. He didn't get three medals and a mention in dispatches because he's a dolt. He can trounce you at tennis, that I'll wager." He hesitated, took a large bite of sausage roll, then summarized his reaction to the ineffable major: "I find it difficult to like men who are a stone and half underweight and who have all their hair the color it was twenty years ago." Then he added a note of serious caution: "If you want to see All Saints at its best, you must build a bridge to Major Leckey. If you do, all doors will be opened invitations to Gommint House, dance at The Club, the interviews you seek. If you don't . . . Siberia!"

"And how do I build that bridge?"

"I'll tell you, old chap, it won't be easy and I'm not teasing. Our tourist ships drop off scores of Americans and Canadians like you . . . often people of considerable wealth and power back home. Here they're boors. Refuse to do things the British way, try to muscle their way in. And all they get is rebuffs. Major Leckey and his wife refuse even to see them. They never get to see Gee-Gee. And they go home cursing All Saints as an unfriendly place where the blacks are abused. That's what'll happen to you, old chap, if you hang around with the likes of me and don't get friendly with the Leckeys."

"And how do I do that?"

"You follow the traditions, long ingrained, of the British colony. You go to Gommint House before nightfall on the day of your arrival and sign the visitors' book, to let the officials know you're in town and are paying your proper respects. Then you present your credentials to assure people that you're who you say you are and that someone in the echelon higher than yourself back home is vouching for you. Then you retire to your hotel room, behave yourself in public at meals, and wait."

"Would my being seen in your saloon be a help or a hindrance?"

Wrentham laughed. "You're a bright lad, McKay. It would alert those who matter that you're no better than a seven or eight despite your white skin."

"But if I do the things you suggested, would I be accepted in, say, level three?"

"Laddie! The government of this island is not stupid. They seek good reports in American newspapers. To augment tourism, if nothing else. You behave yourself, Major Leckey will be falling all over you. But not if you try to bull yourself in. Try that and you're cut off, like a dead limb."

"But if I reported that snobbery in my articles?"

"You'd never do that, laddie. Because you're part of the system. I can see from our brief conversation that you're prime club material. You already enjoy this island more than I do."

A light-skinned couple who had been picnicking not far away recognized Wrentham and walked slowly over: "Hullo, Bart, shall we be seeing you at The Tennis tonight?"

"Of course. Save me a place at your table. This is my friend just in from America, Mr. Detroit Newspaperman."

The greetings were cordial, with the woman saying: "If we can do anything to help while you're here, call upon us. Roger has the importing business not far from Bart's Waterloo."

When they were gone, Millard asked: "What's this with tennis? You have lighted courts for night play, or what?"

"Now we come to the next part of the analysis. The Tennis, just that, nothing more to the name, is for light-colored blacks what The Club is for the whites. It's a rather nice building facing Anse de Jour, and its membership is just as exclusive in its way as The Club's. Even men and women of real accomplishment will never be eligible for The Club because their skins are . . . well . . ." He pointed to his face and laughed: "I didn't go to university in England, but many young fellows like me do. If they're good at sports, which most of them are, they're feted in Britain. Membership in good clubs, invited everywhere, move in exciting circles. If they can write stories, they become popular literary figures. Four years, maybe five, of living at the heart of empire. Then bang! Party's over. Back on the boat they come to All Saints, and when they step onto our dock, Cinderella's ball ends. They're colored again. And although they can get good jobs in government, and they do, they can never, never, join The Club where the real leaders celebrate at night, or even attend a ball there as guests. But they can join The Tennis."

Saying no more, he gathered the remnants of the picnic, threw the rubbish in a green-painted oil drum placed for such purpose, and started the drive down the western half of the island. As McKay watched the Caribbean, a sea of splendor in this latitude, his eye caught a sight which would enthrall him as long as he was in the islands: a hedge of low shrubs whose big copious leaves were multicolored, six blazingly different leaves to one stem, five radically different colors to each leaf.

"What's that magnificent thing?" he cried, and Wrentham replied: "Croton, symbol of the Caribbean. One central stalk, many contrasting colors," and Millard said: "A man could grow to love an oceanfront highway decorated with such flowers."

Ten miles of croton along the road brought them to the golden beach of Anse de Jour, and to The Tennis. As they passed the low, beautifully landscaped building Wrentham said: "It's better kept, really, than The Club. But that's as it should be. Its job is to hide a lot of heartache."

"That's two clubs, highly restricted," Millard said. "Where are the clubs for the bulk of the population?"

"What do you think my Waterloo is? That's where those who can't get into the other two can meet and have fun. You'll be welcomed at the Waterloo. And you'll be able to find many of the people you'd like to meet."

"But the real blacks? The ones you called slaves? Where do they meet?"

"On the waterfront. There's a bar called Tonton's."

"Four clubs, then. Would I be welcomed in Tennis and Tonton's?"

"You'd need an invitation to The Tennis. And I wouldn't just drift into Tonton's. They're proud, and they might think you were slumming."

As they returned to the Waterloo, where McKay invited his host to tea and little cakes, which many of the multicolored were having English-style, the reporter asked: "Is it necessary on an island with such a small population to have this rigorous caste system?" and Bart replied: "We want it that way. Each group is most determined to protect its own little corner of strength." He hesitated, then added: "Of course, citizens in the French islands don't feel it so necessary, nor the

Dutch, nor the Brazilians, nor, in some ways, the Spanish. But we're an *English* island, not a British one, and we're jealous of our English heritage." As Millard rose to check into his hotel finally, Wrentham said: "And we're the ones, all of us of whatever color, who preserve it."

McKay had been on the island seven hours without seeing the inside of his hotel, and he did not know what to expect. But when he pushed open the two swinging half-doors of the Belgrave and looked into the archaic lobby, the spacious dining room with its teakwood chairs and the lovely porch beyond with wicker furniture and a broad view of the Baie de Soleil, he cried aloud: "They employed Joseph Conrad and Somerset Maugham to decorate this place!" and he knew then that he would spend happy and profitable hours beneath the seven big fans that rotated slowly to keep the air fresh without cooling the food on the linen-clad tables laid with glistening silver.

The light-colored girl at the desk said with a soft island lilt: "Mr. McKay, your Hippolyte has taken your bags to room six, which has one of our best views down the *baie.*"

Room 6 had not only a superb view of the *baie* but also a glimpse of the Caribbean beyond; a black maid with an immense smile came to tell him she had unpacked his bags and that he would find his shirts here and his socks there. She said: "My duty, mastuh, to see you happy. Ring bell, tell me when you want hot water in your bath."

"Is the water in the tap good to drink?"

"Good me, maybe not you. I bring bottles."

He asked her when dinner was served, and she said: "Eight o'clock prompt, sir. Very punctual."

After a hot bath and a short nap, McKay sat on his veranda with a tall drink as he watched the tropical sun descend with a crash into the *baie:* Three weeks of evenings like this, All Saints will look better and better.

When he went down to the dining room he found it much more animated than before; now a flurry of barefooted black waiters in semi-military green uniforms moved studiously about the room, handing incoming diners big printed menus. The fare seemed to be the typical heavy English food that a small country inn north of London might provide, day after day throughout the year. Little concession was made to the fact that All Saints was in the tropics and that the waters nearby teemed with fish. Wondering where an island without much agriculture got its supply of beef and pork and lamb, Millard settled upon a roast chicken with stuffing. Looking up from the menu, he became aware that a fine-looking, well-dressed young man of very light coloring—perhaps a level four, McKay thought—was studying him intently, and the concentration continued until McKay grew embarrassed. But then the man got up from his table and went out to the hotel desk, obviously making inquiries as to who the newcomer might be.

Returning to the dining area, he came directly to McKay's table, to say in a carefully cultivated English accent: "I say! You must excuse my rudeness, but aren't you McKay, the man I've been looking for?" He coughed modestly, and added: "And I should think you might have been looking for me."

McKay rose, extended his hand, and said: "Millard McKay, *Detroit Chronicle.*"

"I know. Please be seated. I'm Etienne Boncour. Jeweler and chairman of the Tourist Board. It's my job to greet writers like you. To facilitate whatever it is you came to do. For we appreciate the value of your visit."

"Won't you join me?"

"Oh no, I mustn't intrude on a guest. But I'd be most gratified, really I would, if you'd join me over there." Then, realizing that this must also be intrusive, he laughed appealingly and said: "I mean, since we are in the same business, more or less." When McKay looked puzzled, as if unable to see how the jewelry business and newspaper work could be related, the young man said: "I mean, I'm often engaged in writing publicity for our island, and you write too."

The explanation was so gracious and so obviously well intended that McKay could not resist. Picking up his napkin, he moved to the other table, where he said: "I've pretty well decided on the chicken, but tell me, where does your island get all the meat on this menu? The beef and pork?"

"Refrigerator ships from Miami, but forget the beef and chicken. The chef always keeps a fish or two which he'll fix for special customers. That's what I'm having, and if you'd like, I'll alert him to cook up one of his bigger ones."

"I would like that," and while they waited for the sea bass baked in fennel, Boncour said: "Don't let my accent confuse you. I'm part of the French contingent on All Saints. Been here since 1620 or thereabouts. Family's never left. But I did go to Durham in England for my education."

"Jewelry store, Tourist Board . . ."

"And member of the Gee-Gee's Executive Council. That's the most fun."

"How did all that happen?"

"The business? My grandfather started it when tourists began to arrive. The education? I did well in school and won a rather substantial bursary. The council? In the old days, only white men of impeccable background and usually born in Britain. Recently the authorities have been reaching out to a few men of color, and I'm one of that lucky breed!" And McKay thought: I was right. He is a four.

"Does your council have any real power? Or is it what we call 'window dressing'?"

"Nice question. Let's say we're made to think we have power, but actually, Gee-Gee decides things pretty much as he wishes." Then, fearing that this might appear in print, he corrected himself: "There's a breath of freedom blowing in from the sea. We're terribly anxious to see how our new Gee-Gee responds to it."

"Hope the food comes soon. I'm starved," McKay said. Boncour glanced at his watch, and this led to a whole new path of conversation, for McKay asked: "Is that a Rolex you're wearing?" and when the jeweler nodded, McKay said like an admiring schoolboy: "I've never seen one. Just the ads in glossy magazines," and Boncour slipped the watch from his wrist and handed it over.

McKay was fascinated by the sharp styling, the reassuring heaviness of the watch: "Feels as if it could run for a hundred years."

"I've never heard them claim that."

"Since I saw my first good Swiss watch at age fourteen . . . in a Canadian shop . . . I've wanted one. But they're murderously expensive, aren't they? Cheapest Rolex I ever saw was ninety-five dollars, American."

"The one I'm wearing"—it had a solid-gold case—"sells retail for many times that," Boncour said. "I don't own it. Just wear it now and then to be sure it's working."

"What does an ordinary Rolex, the kind I might buy if I had the money . . ." Millard began, but Boncour hushed him: "Mr. McKay, I didn't visit your table to peddle watches. But if you stop by the shop in the morning, of your own volition, it could be that I might surprise you."

When the fish arrived, with a crisped skin and decoration of fennel, Boncour ordered a bottle of wine, and it became a gala dinner, with Boncour describing the island as if it were an entirely different place from the narrowly restricted one that Wrentham had talked of that afternoon: "There is great freedom of spirit here. Much human happiness."

After the fish had been consumed, McKay summoned the courage to ask: "Does a man like you, well educated, familiar with European countries and customs . . . do you experience any discrimination?" Immediately he added: "I'm a newspaperman, you know. But I'll not quote you."

"No censorship here."

"On the other Caribbean islands?" McKay asked, and Boncour replied: "All the English islands are pretty much the same. I have two other stores, you know. Barbados and Trinidad. Not much difference." Then he added: "In the islands where I have my shops, everyone knows my views. Of course there's discrimination, but it's tempered with decency. And the whites are sensible enough to offer us concessions, tiny perhaps in your view, in ours very significant."

"Like what?"

"Let's put it this way. The supreme social accolade open to us non-whites is to be invited to Gommint House. Major Leckey calls you on the phone and you tremble, thinking that maybe lowly you is going to be invited, and he says in his crisp, hesitant voice: 'That you, Boncour? Good. Leckey here. Could you possibly break free and come to a little reception Gee-Gee is holding, Thursday at dusk? Good.'"

"Then what happens?"

"I rustle out and get my hair cut, ask my maid to press my white suit, and up I go to Gommint House, where I see that I am one of only seven men of color, and I am, to put it frankly, elated that I have been allowed entrance to the Holy of Holies. And Gee-Gee, at least the last one we've had, is no fool, for lost in the middle of the crowd will be one jet-black man, to prove that Gommint House is available to all."

Then the light touch vanished, as Boncour said slowly and softly: "But when the gala ends, the taxis arrive to carry the important white people over to The Club for their dinner. The colored in their family cars ride out to The Tennis for their dinner. I come to the Waterloo, while the lone black man stops off at Tonton's, where his mates josh him enviously for having played the swell."

All Saints, like Trinidad and others, was a Crown Colony, and no one on the island was likely to forget it. It had never had an island legislature such as Barbados or Jamaica had enjoyed, although Jamaica had lost its government after the Governor Eyre disaster, and had reverted to Crown Colony status. All Saints did have two small advisory bodies to which whites and browns aspired, but since the island belonged in theory to the crown, ultimate power rested with the monarch's representative, the governor general. If he was prudent, he listened to his advisers and tried to avoid acting contrary to their strongly held convictions, but he knew and they knew that when push came to shove, he pushed with sufficient power to nullify their shoving.

Common sense prevented the system from becoming a tyranny, and cooperation between the Executive Council, comprised of mostly white appointed officials, and the Legislative Council of twelve, including five elected members, served to maintain an illusion that the general populace had some say in the government.

Etienne Boncour was one of the five elected members; officially he represented Bristol Town's business community, but emotionally he was known as one of the three members who had strong ties with the French component. In any important vote he and the other two Frenchmen were smothered by what was called "the alliance of proper Englishmen," a situation that generated no ill will, for as one Englishman growled at The Club: "Our French? They've jolly well been proper Englishmen for the last hundred years."

In the morning, but not too early, lest he betray his eagerness, Millard strolled over to Boncour's jewelry shop to see, as he told the owner, "what the story is on these Rolexes." The story was shocking. A solid-gold Rolex could cost upward of $2,500, an honest one in a lesser metal but with all the features, $125, but after Millard had inspected the less-expensive ones, realizing that he could not afford even them, Boncour amused him by producing, from a case in another part of the shop, a rather good-looking copy made in Hong Kong, indistinguishable from a real Rolex but priced at $17:50.

"Amazing," Millard said. "How do you tell the difference?"

"The copy falls apart in three months. The real one lasts forever."

And it was then that McKay discovered one of the secrets of doing business in the Caribbean: Boncour's shop had exquisite jewelry and gifts for sale to the island's white trade, but also hordes of low-cost imitations for tourists, local blacks and sailors off passing ships.

At this point Boncour was called away by an entering customer, and Millard was left alone to study the shop. Before he could see beyond the high-priced display cases and the low, he was distracted by the two golden-skinned girls who tended the shop, and they were so refreshing, so graceful with flowers in their hair, that he thought: It's not fair to young unmarried Englishmen to have girls as beautiful as that around, and of the wrong color.

When Boncour returned he said seriously: "I know what it is to want a really good watch. That's how I got into the business. I have a Rolex here, not new, but nearly so. Man brought it in to be fixed, and he may have stolen it, because two weeks later he was murdered. The police and I advertised everywhere, even on other islands, but I never found the owner. I want to get rid of it. I want my expenses for the replacement parts I had to send for and the advertising. I'll let you take it off my hands for thirty-two dollars."

Millard stepped back and looked at Boncour. As a newspaperman in Detroit he had investigated every kind of scam: the supposed millionaire who had died intestate in the Nevada gold fields, the bait-and-switch sales, the cruel deception in which widows deposited their savings. He not only knew the old angles, but he had also learned to be on the alert for those new tricks which had not surfaced before.

"That's a good watch. Worth a lot more than thirty-two dollars."

"Right on both counts."

"But I'd want police clearance on it before I could be interested."

To McKay's surprise, Boncour said: "You'd certainly get it! I want a record too . . . of having cleared up the case," and, pocketing the watch and some papers relating to it, he led McKay to the police station, which could have been a fake, except that it had a permanent sign outside and two uniformed officers behind the desk.

"The chief in?" Boncour asked, and one of the desk men indicated with his shoulder that the inner door was open. Inside, McKay faced a colored police sergeant in a natty twill uniform, who asked jovially: "Who's done what?"

Boncour spoke, placing watch and papers on the desk: "It's that watch the murdered man left. I have about thirty-two dollars in it, new parts and those advertisements. Mr. McKay, newspaperman from Detroit, needs a watch and is willing to pay the thirty-two dollars."

"So what do you want?"

"Police verification that I didn't steal it. A receipt so that Mr. McKay can take it back with him to the States."

"Why haven't you looked for a buyer here?"

"Thirty-two dollars is a lot of money for most of my customers. And it is essentially a used watch."

The sergeant shuffled the papers on his desk and was about to sign the prepared receipt, when he looked past Boncour and McKay and cried with huge affection: "Sir Benny! Come in!" and into the office came a most unusual man. He was jet-black, about five feet six, slightly chubby, beautifully relaxed and wreathed in an ingratiating smile.

Nodding graciously when introduced to McKay, the man greeted Boncour and the sergeant as old friends, then said in a low, soft voice with an impeccable English accent: "Sergeant, I've got to tell you before you go any further, my sister found the wheelbarrow."

The sergeant laughed: "I told you she would." Then turning to McKay, he said: "This criminal type is Sir Benny Castain."

McKay, thinking *Sir* Benny to be one of those calypso singers who favored names like *Lord* Invader or *Emperor* Divine, made a tremendous gaffe: "Have you recorded any of your songs?"

"No, no!" the station sergeant laughed. "He's a real knight. Sword of the King himself. Our greatest cricketer, batsman and/or bowler."

"He wouldn't know about cricket," Sir Benny said apologetically, but Millard corrected him: "Indeed I do. Don Bradman. Douglas Jardine."

The three island men gaped, and Sir Benny asked: "Now, how does an American know those names?"

"At Rutgers University, near New York, there were always West Indians playing cricket in some park. I read about it in a book by Neville Cardus. Part of my course in English."

"I cannot believe this!" Sir Benny said, and the men sat down while the sergeant recalled the glory of All Saints' cricket: "Lord Basil Wrentham, him who's to serve as our new Gee-Gee, brought a first-rate English team to the West Indies, 1932 it may have been. Four matches. They won handily in Jamaica, had a better challenge in Trinidad, and won again by a big margin in Barbados. We'd never had a topnotch international match in All Saints, but for that occasion we'd built a new oval, sodded it well, and could offer a first-class pitch.

"Great excitement when the ship brought the two teams over from Barbados. The English players, so white-skinned, so gentlemanly, won all hearts as they trooped off the ship behind Lord Basil and Douglas Jardine, both men tall and imperial. Then the great batsmen, Patsy Hendren and Walter Hammond. And the bowlers, Leslie Ames and Bill Voce." As he uttered each of the revered names, the other two islanders nodded approvingly. "That really was a great team," Boncour said, but Sir Benny said quietly: "You forget the best bowler of them all, got me three times before the game at All Saints, Hedley Verity," and the others agreed.

The sergeant, eager for this interested American to understand the greatness of Sir Benny, began to recite the details of that memorable four-day match. But as he started, McKay had a happy inspiration: "Why don't we all go over to the Waterloo and discuss this? Drinks are on me." The men instantly agreed. Leaving the police station, the sergeant said to McKay: "Don't forget your watch," and Boncour nodded: "It's yours now."

At the Waterloo, Bart Wrentham greeted them with enthusiasm, bowed to Sir Benny, and asked if he might join them. McKay said: "Yes, if you'll send out for the kind of picnic we had yesterday," and he handed Wrentham some pound notes. "You buy the food," Bart said. "I'll treat for the beer," and shortly he was back with another feast.

"England batted first," the sergeant resumed. "Brutal. Scored 352, with the loss of only six wickets." Turning to McKay, he asked: "You know what 'declaring' means?"

"Yes. If England already has 352 runs, a huge lead, they figure they'll be able to get your team out quickly and then make you follow on—that is, go right back in and do so poorly that your combined score will be less than 352. So with England batting only once, they swamp you and win the match, 352 to something like maybe 207. Great victory."

"Amazing," Sir Benny said. "Never thought to see an American who understands cricket."

"Lord Basil had made a daring gamble on behalf of England's team," the sergeant said, "but he stood to win, because our side didn't have great batsmen." He paused, and everyone looked at Sir Benny, who smiled smugly as he recalled yet again that glorious day. "But Lord Basil hadn't counted on this fellow here. He was plain Benny Castain then, grandson of a former slave, but a lad with a good education obtained in our schools. I shall never forget him coming out to bat. Not big. Not powerful. Two of our wickets down for a total of only 29, and England with that formidable 352. But Benny dug in, knocked the ball all over the oval, never saw such an innings. Finally clean bowled by Verity yet again, but he had put 139 on the board, and England was nervous, I can tell you that, when our innings ended at 291. Any desire to make us follow on was lost, thanks to Benny."

Then Bart Wrentham interrupted: "There were eighteen or more of us colored Wrenthams in the oval next day, and the rest were like me. Immensely proud that a white Wrentham was captain of the all-England team, but also excited that our crowd had put up such a fine showing against the best."

"Did you think," McKay asked, "that All Saints had a chance of winning?"

"Wait, wait! This wasn't an All Saints team. It was players from all our islands. Benny here was the only All Saints man. And having inflamed his home island with his batting, he now took to bowling, and when England's great batsmen came out, Hammond and Hendren and Jardine, they weren't so cocky, because they knew they had to put a lot of runs on the board to make their side safe. Had to have maybe 250 more, something like that."

The sergeant wanted the honor of reporting Sir Benny's immortal bowling that afternoon: "He had a mix of three, a fast ball, a right-arm chinaman, and a googly, and believe it or not, he put down seven of England's greatest batsmen for a total of only 57 runs. The fourth day of the match ended with the score England 409, West Indies 291, but with a fighting chance to overtake.

"I cannot tell you how we felt that night, here in All Saints. I had to get up five times to pee, and at dawn I was still awake. That day, at eleven in the morning, I think the entire population of All Saints was at the oval or near it. When play started, England had three more batsmen, but this tremendous fellow"—and he patted Sir Benny's knee—"dismissed them for only 21 additional runs. England 430, West Indies 291."

Now Bart spoke, slowly and reverently, for he was dealing with one of the spiritual climaxes of his island: "We opened our last innings against the great English bowlers needing 140 to win, and we gasped in anguish when the two V's, Voce and Verity, took five of our wickets for only 41 runs. Defeat loomed, but then Benny took over. Defending his wicket as never before, and punishing every loose ball that was bowled to him, he scored two sixes and thirteen fours. Never had we seen a West Indian punish English bowlers as he did that day, and in the late stages of the game, when it was obvious that we had a fighting chance to win the match, that damned Hedley Verity bowled Benny again. Stunned silence."

The men paused to recall that tremendous moment in their island's history, then Wrentham said quietly: "But our other batsmen picked up the challenge . . ." Here his voice rose to a roar, and he banged the table with his fist: "And we won! We had beaten England." On impulse, both Boncour and the sergeant rose and embraced Sir Benny, the black man who had brought black majesty to their island.

"The part I remember best," Wrentham said, "was when the players left the pitch. Lord Basil sought out Benny, threw his long right arm over his shoulder, and walked out of the oval with him." He stopped, looked at McKay, and said: "I predict he will be a very popular Gee-Gee."

Much could be learned about life in a British Crown Colony by observing the social laws governing Lord Wrentham's XI, as the English cricket team was invariably called, since Wrentham had picked his men and assumed responsibility for their pay, which amounted to about $700 American per man for the entire tour, plus steamboat fare and meals.

Of course, only the professional cricketers received pay, for the team was rigidly divided between *gentlemen,* that is, amateurs of good family, and *players,* professionals, who played for a living. The distinction between them was rigid: On the passage over, gentlemen sailed first class, players second. At clubhouses there was one entrance for gentlemen, another for players. A gentleman was referred to by his initials and last name, such as W. H. B. Wickham, and addressed deferentially as "sir," a player would be known and addressed simply by his last name, rarely even with the prefix "Mr."

At evening functions the team also divided, gentlemen often attending parties given by county families, the players dining at their hotel, with the senior professional carving the joint and serving the junior man last. But such distinctions were so ingrained that they were taken for granted and caused little rancor.

There were other minor refinements, like that between capped and uncapped members. Anyone who had been selected for his nation's test team was awarded a "cap," and professionals who were uncapped were unlikely to address directly a gentleman who had a cap. But it was a remarkable tribute to the pragmatic nature of Englishmen that these caste differences never impeded play on the field. Cricket was at the same time both the custodian of social principles and the arena in which men met as equals. A professional bowler who took the wicket of the finest gentleman batsman of the opposing team might well be roundly applauded . . . by both teams.

The day came when blacks thronged the streets, shouting: "The Gee-Gee, he ship in the *baie!*" and when the vessel from Southampton edged into the dock, McKay was there to watch the arrival of the new governor general, and he observed the present incumbent, a tall, slim, good-looking regimental officer in his sixties, waiting in the island's only Rolls-Royce, an impressive Silver Ghost. Now the crowd cheered, for at the top of the gangway Lord Basil Wrentham appeared, almost a twin of the man waiting in the Rolls: tall, underweight, austere, with a military bearing and a haughty manner. They must have a factory somewhere in England where they punch out these cookies to impress the colonies, McKay thought.

The new Gee-Gee stood very erect, saluted the ship he was leaving, and came imperially down the gangway, but he did not go to the waiting Rolls; he merely bowed to his predecessor, acknowledged the salutes of the guard, and looked inquisitively about the crowd. Then, having located what he sought, he moved briskly forward, ignoring everyone until he stood face-to-face with Sir Benny Castain. Throwing his arms wide, he embraced the chubby black man as he had done years ago at the end of that resplendent afternoon. "I guess there must be something extra about cricket that they don't tell you in books," McKay said aloud as he watched, but he could hardly hear his own words, for the crowd was cheering wildly.

On the third day after Lord Wrentham's arrival, the text of Millard McKay's first article reached All Saints from Detroit, creating a favorable stir. The author, after explaining that in 1763 many thoughtful Englishmen had advocated keeping All Saints and giving Canada away, described the island as it existed today, and he painted a loving, faithful portrait. Anyone familiar with All Saints would have to acknowledge that McKay had spotted the foibles, recognized the merits, and understood the role of a man's skin coloration in determining his social level.

People who had read the abbreviated excerpts that appeared in the *All Saints Journal,* courtesy of the Associated Press, nodded approvingly to McKay as he passed them in the streets, and since Bristol Town had a population of only six thousand, everyone soon knew who McKay was and what he had said. The passage most frequently commented upon was one he had worded carefully, relying upon data provided by Bart Wrentham and Etienne Boncour:

All Saints has, according to latest count, a population of 29,779, and if a visitor frequents only the top government offices, called gommint here, he gets the impression that they're all white. If you stay in the shops on the main streets, you think everyone is very lightly colored. And if you move about the back streets and the countryside, you'd swear All Saints was all black, and I mean very black, just out of Africa.

The best estimates this reporter has heard divide the population this way. Whites, including both English and French, about nine hundred. Coloreds about seven thousand. Blacks, the rest, about twenty-two thousand. So this is a black island, but sometimes a whole day passes without a visitor being aware of it.

It's the second category that provides confusion, because it contains many attractive, well-dressed, well-educated men and women who in the United States or Canada would pass for white . . . no question about it. But here everyone knows to the nth degree what his neighbors' antecedents are, and one thirty-second of black blood marks a man or woman as colored.

What happens is that when some especially talented All Saints man wants to enter the white world or some beautiful young woman wants to marry into a higher social circle, they emigrate to another island where they can start afresh. Of course, later on, rumor follows them and the truth becomes known, but by then a new status has been achieved.

So All Saints contains a score of delightful newcomers from Barbados, Jamaica and Trinidad who fill lively spots in the island social life, but of whom people whisper. And at the tenuous dividing line between black and colored, there is the same kind of maneuverability, and the visitor is told that sometimes a girl who is now known as colored will go to extreme lengths to prevent her new friends from meeting her sister, who may be many shades darker than she.

This harsh, but accurate, summary of how one's skin color determined status was alleviated by McKay's rhapsodic description of the island's rich natural beauties, including croton, and an affectionate account of Sir Benny Castain's old cricketing relationship with the newly appointed governor general. The article ended: "So if you're contemplating a vacation on some Caribbean island this winter, try All Saints. It could be close to the best."

Both Etienne Boncour and Bart Wrentham were pleased with McKay's report and told him so. Bart said gruffly: "Flattering but not excessively groveling," and Boncour assured him: "Gommint is delighted. When the Gee-Gee read it he said: 'Well, we're off to a good start,' but Major Leckey warned him: 'He wrote that before you got here. Let's wait. He's an American and we've been burned by them before.'"

There was a cryptic English couple staying at the Belgrave who took a more circumspect view of both McKay and his article. The Ponsfords, a married pair in their late fifties from one of the fashionable suburbs of London, had sailed to All Saints on the same ship that brought Lord Wrentham and his daughter Delia. Being rigorously proper, they did not impose upon His Lordship while aboard ship, but upon landing in All Saints they immediately hired a taxi, rode to Government House, and signed the book. In due course Major Leckey had called to invite them to afternoon tea, where they told Lord Wrentham and his daughter that they had shared the steamer with them but had not wanted to intrude upon their privacy. The courtesy was appreciated, and Major Leckey himself assumed responsibility for delivering their other letters of introduction to the proper authorities, so that within a few days the Ponsfords were moving within what was called "the cream of All Saints," that restricted circle of Britons from good families who ran the island. After his five weeks on the island, McKay had met none of that group.

The Ponsfords knew who McKay was and what he had written, but they would never approach him during his working day, for they had not been introduced. McKay could not decipher who they were or what business they were engaged in, for they kept rigidly to themselves, and it was not until Boncour was taking lunch at the Belgrave and saw the Ponsfords at their table and McKay at his that a meeting came about. Boncour made bold to tell the Ponsfords: "I think you might enjoy meeting that chap over there," and they allowed Boncour to bring McKay to their table. Having made the introduction, Boncour returned to his lunch, and Millard was left with a rather chilly pair who had not liked what they deemed the flippancy of his Detroit articles and said so.

"I could see no justification," Mr. Ponsford said with august condescension, "why one would feel obligated to stress the dark side of the island."

McKay was astonished. "I didn't think I did," and Mrs. Ponsford, a well-preserved and neatly coiffed woman with an aquiline nose that seemed always on the point of sniffing, explained: "You are harping on the fact that All Saints is mostly black."

"But it is!" McKay said, with obvious desire to stress the truth. "Just look about you."

"If it is," Mr. Ponsford said in his bank-manager manner, "it's unfortunate and should not be broadcast to the world. Excellent men and women with the best intentions govern this island, and they deserve every support we can give them."

"There is nothing finer, I told my husband the other day, than to see a distinguished man like Lord Basil riding through the streets in his Rolls-Royce, symbol of all that's good and right in the British Empire."

McKay, suppressing a smile, said to himself: I've got to remember that one, and thought: People make fun of Americans abroad, and I guess we can be pretty bad, but it takes an English couple like this insufferable pair to be really obnoxious. However, aware that he might have to share the dining room with them for several weeks, he turned to Mrs. Ponsford and asked: "Then what about the colored who fill so many of the spots here in Bristol Town? Dare I speak about them?"

"In time, as they educate themselves and move upward in the social scale," Mr. Ponsford said magisterially, "they'll become more and more like white people. They've already earned three places on the Executive Council."

"Will their skins become lighter as this progression upward is made?" McKay asked with no touch of sarcasm, and Mrs. Ponsford said: "Isn't that how it's already happening? I was told just yesterday that of the three mulatto men on the council each was three-quarters white."

"You'd expect nothing less," her husband said, but the pair were interrupted before they could explain further their interpretation of All Saints life by a handsome young Englishman in a trim off-white suit which displayed his slim, athletic bearing. He had neatly trimmed blond hair and the professional smile of one accustomed to greeting people.

"This is Major Leckey," Mrs. Ponsford said approvingly. "The governor general's invaluable factotum. This is Mr. McKay, who wrote about your island for the newspaper back in the States."

The next moment would be forever etched on Millard's mind: Major Leckey, who had known from the moment of McKay's arrival who and what he was but who felt honor-bound to ignore him until he presented his credentials properly, turned his head slightly away from looking at the Ponsfords, and gave the American interloper a brief, icy smile of semirecognition. Then, without offering to shake hands, he resumed conversation with the English couple, whom he had come to escort to an afternoon affair at Government House. In a flash they were gone, all three of them, and no one bothered to excuse himself to McKay.

He met Leckey again the next day at Boncour's jewelry store, and since Etienne was occupied with a woman tourist from England, the two men had to stand awkwardly almost side by side, but again the major studiously refused to recognize him. Only when another customer bumped into them, did they have to acknowledge each other. Major Leckey gave McKay a withered smile, to which McKay responded with the slightest possible nod, involving no shoulder movement. McKay felt that warfare between them had been declared.

It did not enflame at that moment, because Leckey had come to the shop on a more important matter. "I was told," he said to Boncour, in crisp and somewhat superior tones, as if he were slumming, "that the Honorable Delia would be awaiting me here."

"She's not been in," Boncour said, and McKay, whose senses were sharp, thought he detected in Boncour's manner an unusual level of excitement when speaking about the Gee-Gee's daughter. Then he saw why, for into the shop came a young woman of twenty-two who absolutely filled it with her radiance. She wore one of those flimsy lace and tulle dresses in which the starch of the latter held in fine form the soft fabric of the former. The lace was stark-white, the tulle had a touch of yellow, and their colors blended to make a gentle symphony that matched the cool beauty of the young woman who wore them.

She had a head of golden hair that was not completely tamed—obviously she did not want it whipped into set patterns—and it formed a kind of frame for a face that was larger than one might have expected, larger in each dimension and wonderfully composed, so that she seemed always to be smiling in quiet amusement at the follies of the world about her. She had large eyes which sparkled, a generous mouth and a way of tilting her impressive head that made her seem about to speak in a kindly manner to anyone at whom she looked. She was so much the acme of the young English gentlewoman of her period that one could not avoid asking two questions: "Why isn't she married?" and "Why in the world did her father bring her to a place like All Saints?"

"Yes! Miss Wrentham," Boncour cried as he hurried forward to attend her. "I have three to show you," and he was about to bring forth a tray of small bejeweled items when Major Leckey interrupted: "Delia, I'm most sorry, but your father's waiting, and he sent me to fetch you." With that, making no apologies to either Boncour or McKay, he whisked her out of the shop and into his waiting chauffeured car.

When she was gone, leaving an echoing void behind, McKay whistled to break the tension: "I never thought that daughters of Gee-Gees looked like that," and for a few moments the two men discussed her appearance and her manner. Boncour said: "She came in unannounced last week, as nice a customer as we ever meet. No frills, no demands, just sensible questions about some small items for what she called a charm bracelet."

"And what's that?"

"Started in France, I think. A silver or gold bracelet in links, and into each you attach . . ." Turning slightly, he called: "Irene, show him those pictures." A pretty girl with very light skin brought from the rear a London magazine in which there were photographs of charm bracelets, lovely delicate things if the attached items were kept small enough, rather gauche if they were too big or lacking in style. But after looking briefly at the bracelets, McKay leafed ahead and whistled: "Hey, look at this!" and the girl who had fetched the magazine said: "Yes indeed! No wonder Lord Basil hurried her out here."

The story, provocatively illustrated, told of the Honorable Delia Wrentham's escapade with an older married man and implied former misbehavior with several young Oxford and Cambridge chaps. The young lady who had brought the magazine from the rear of the store seemed to be an expert on the Honorable Delia, and said saucily without being asked: "Her father whisked her out here not a minute too soon. You ask me, he accepted the appointment to this sorry little post so's he'd have a place to cool her off."

McKay's jaw dropped. He had not expected a colored clerk to speak so freely and so boldly, but a moment's reflection set him straight: Hell, it's girls like these salesladies who set the patterns. They are the islands. And he asked the girl a chain of questions, learning from her that the Honorable Delia was one of the lights of the London social whirl, "a damned fine lass, if you ask me, and a great help to her widowed father, who overlooks her sporting behavior. He adores her, the stories say. And one look at her tells why."

In the days that followed, everything on All Saints seemed to focus on Sir Basil and his lively daughter. Talk at the Waterloo centered on little else, and at the Belgrave the American McKay was discovering a topic about which the Ponsfords were eager to talk: the history of the English Wrenthams and especially the doings of the Earl of Gore and his immediate family. Mrs. Ponsford said: "Very distinguished. They go back a long distance in our history. Famous for producing beautiful daughters."

"The Gee-Gee's Delia must be one of the best," McKay said, and both Ponsfords agreed.

Once the ice was broken, McKay found the couple to be rather interesting, solid middle-class Englishmen who adored their betters. They are stuffy, he told himself. I suppose they were trained that way, but once you discount it, they're not bad. However, he still wondered what they were doing in All Saints, but they surrendered no clues.

He was beginning to like them because they were willing, at meals which he took at their table increasingly, to talk about the Wrenthams: "Actually, we knew Lord Basil's father, before he inherited the earldom. Fine, outgoing man, very good on a horse."

"What was he like?"

"Understand, when he became the earl we didn't see him anymore. We're not members of those exalted circles."

McKay, eager to penetrate the cloak of reticence in which the couple had clothed themselves, asked with the double impertinence of both an American and a newspaperman: "What did you do . . . in private life . . . before you retired?"

Mr. Ponsford flinched at such a direct question; one did not ask questions like that in English society, but his increasing respect for McKay's sincerity and honesty encouraged him to respond: "Marine insurance, in a small company . . ." to which his wife added with obvious pride: "But by the time he retired . . . of course, he didn't need to retire, actually, because by then he owned the company, and a larger one in Liverpool."

"What do you make of the Gee-Gee's daughter?"

"She's a darling," Mrs. Ponsford said, but her husband was more cautious: "That one gives her father real headaches," and there the opening conversation about Delia ended, because Major Leckey appeared in gray tropical dress and topee to lead an excursion of the Ponsfords, the Gee-Gee and his daughter to a picnic at Cap Galant. When McKay heard this, he started to inform the Ponsfords that he had been picnicking at Cap Galant . . . But before he could finish, Leckey moved them off, for to him McKay without letters of introduction was still a non-person.

In the next days McKay interrogated the Ponsfords, Bart and Etienne about the Honorable Delia, and acquired a bit of information. Bart told him: "Lord Wrentham, the real one that is, heir to the earldom, was said to be quite upset by his niece's behavior. Delia wouldn't listen to Lady Gore, and only a sharp rebuke from His Lordship himself caused her to break off with a German colonel she had taken a liking to. She's twenty-two, you know. Has a mind of her own."

A man at a nearby table said: "The affair with the German colonel is supposed to have come close to tragedy," and McKay asked, his voice betraying his surprise at such a statement: "What kind of tragedy could a girl her age stumble into?"

The man volunteered no explanation, so taking his leave, McKay said: "I want the jeweler to engrave my initials on the Rolex he sold me the other day," and he walked to Boncour's shop, only to find that by the happiest coincidence Delia herself was there to finish the business she had started when Major Leckey had so imperiously dragged her away on her earlier visit.

"Hullo," she said breezily as McKay looked over her shoulder at the items she had selected for her charm bracelet. "I'm Delia Wrentham and you're . . . I know who you are. You wrote that article about us."

She had pretty well selected the little charms she wanted when the door to the shop slammed open, Major Leckey strode in, took her by the arm, and led her away without speaking a word to anyone. McKay, looking at Boncour when this happened, saw that he flushed as if he had been struck, and Millard could make nothing of the incident until the talkative salesgirl who had shown him the magazine whispered, when Boncour was attending to another customer: "She comes in here all the time."

When McKay's second article reached the islands, it made him a hero, for in it he had written with delicate charm of the social life on All Saints, with a most ingratiating portrait of the new Gee-Gee and his style. The Honorable Delia came off as a gift to any island she chose to occupy, and her father was presented as incredibly straight and stuffy by American or Canadian standards, but just about what the island needed according to British custom. McKay also offered ingratiating pen portraits of The Club, The Tennis, the Waterloo and Tonton's, inviting each reader to decide at what level he would fit should he visit the island.

Some English cynics asked: "How dare he write about The Club and The Tennis, seeing he's never been invited to either?" but they had to acknowledge that he had a right to describe the Waterloo and Tonton's, since he hung out at the former and had twice patronized the latter with Sir Benny Castain. The Ponsfords asked sharply: "How'd you know about The Club?" to which they'd already been invited on several occasions, and he gave the reporter's favorite explanation: "I'm a good listener."

"You must go there one day," they said sincerely, and he replied: "I'd like that."

The second article attracted such favorable attention at Government House that it became preposterous for Major Leckey to ignore its author any longer. But the long-overdue invitation came not from Leckey but from a more surprising source: "Hello, is this the American writer McKay? Good. Governor General here. I've been reading your reports, McKay. Jolly fine. We appreciate what you say about our island, warts and all. I'm giving a different kind of reception

Thursday at six. Could you find it possible to join us? Good, good. An invitation will be forthcoming."

The Gee-Gee was no fool. His long association with reporters who covered cricket matches and those who dealt in politics had taught him how valuable a newspaper story could sometimes be, and he suspected that his forthcoming reception would be worth an entire article in McKay's paper.

On a lovely Thursday night in early March 1938, Lord Basil Wrentham, the governor general of All Saints, the British island in the Caribbean, invited to his home for a gala celebration all the other Wrenthams on the island. Thirty-nine had been found who could come, men like Black Bart Wrentham, the owner of the Waterloo, women like Nancy Wrentham, who served as head night nurse in the charity ward at the hospital. They came in all kinds of dress, had all shades of coloring. Only two were white, a husband and wife who ran a farm near Anse du Soir, and well over half were decidedly dark, running to nearly black, so diluted had the noble Wrentham blood become.

But they were a sterling group, men and women whose ancestors had experienced the full triumph and tragedy of this island. Four had been in jail, and Major Leckey had made this known to the Gee-Gee, who said: "They aren't in jail now." The food served was a little more solid than usual, the drinks much weaker, but the same band played as for the all-white receptions and the floral decorations were just as carefully positioned about the big rooms. Lord Basil met everyone, greeted each as his cousin, and made the evening a true reunion.

Half a dozen members from each of the other All Saints social groups had also been invited: white business leaders, Sir Benny Castain, light-colored merchants and politicos like Etienne Boncour. The Gee-Gee took special pains to introduce McKay in the various rooms, telling his guests: "We're honored to have this distinguished American writer visiting our island and sharing with his readers some of the truths about us." As they passed from one room to another he whispered: "I'm having a small supper at The Club after we break and I'd be delighted if you could join us."

The evening should have been an unqualified success, for even Major Leckey, knowing that he must follow the Gee-Gee's lead, came up to welcome McKay as if they were established friends. But as he and McKay walked together, almost arm in arm, toward another room, they came upon an alcove and froze. There the Honorable Delia was embracing the jeweler Etienne Boncour with an almost animal passion.

In that one instant each pair saw the other, their eyes meeting, their voices unable to form words. Then Leckey gripped McKay's arm and hurried him along to another room. Neither spoke. Neither would ever refer to the incident. But each knew that what they had seen carried a terrible significance: for Major Leckey because the scene struck at the very fabric of the social order in All Saints; for Millard McKay because he was a practiced newsman, but also because he had himself fallen in love with Delia Wrentham.

The supper at The Club was a tense business—Delia, Leckey and McKay had to share the same table for twelve, with Lord Basil at the head, yet they could barely look at one another. Etienne Boncour, as a man of color, was ineligible to dine at The Club, of course, even if the Gee-Gee's daughter was infatuated with him.

Several of the older guests stopped by to congratulate McKay on his second article: "Much better than the first with all that white and black nonsense." One husband and wife asked: "Is The Club pretty much as you imagined it?" McKay ignored the barb and smiled: "It's a haven. A wonderful, tropical haven," and he pointed to the luxurious flowers.

He went to bed that night impressed by Lord Wrentham's imaginative gesture in bringing his island relatives together, but disturbed by his daughter's brazen lovemaking with Boncour. As he twisted back and forth, unable to sleep, he began to see the affair as any ordinary newsman would: She's a spoiled bitch. Been kicking up her heels all over Europe. Got in the habit, so when she hits an end of the world, like All Saints, she simply has to look around for any man who is remotely eligible. Hell, it could be anyone. This won't last long. She'll move on to another man in a short while, just like she did in England. And with that, he fell asleep without having given a thought as to how he was going to report this heartwarming reunion of the island Wrenthams.

Four days later, as he was finishing a lonely lunch, the Ponsfords came in for their own very late meal, and after taking a seat at a table somewhat removed from McKay's, Mrs. Ponsford slipped quietly over to speak with her American friend: "Make no gesture. Say nothing. But Delia Wrentham is going to drive by that front door shortly in a Government House car. You're to be waiting."

His heart thumping, he walked nonchalantly from the dining room, stood behind some shrubs where he would not be noticed, and waited for this bewitching woman. What could be the meaning of her summons? Why would the granddaughter of an earl seek him out? He had not even begun to frame the possibilities when a small English MG pulled up and he ran out to hop in.

"I need your help," she said tersely as the car leaped forward.

To McKay's surprise, she headed for the southeast corner of Bristol Town and the famous mountain road that first climbed up in a series of very tight turns, then dropped down in a chain of frightening hairpins downhill to the oceanfront town of Ely. Delia drove the straight-ahead portions connecting the seven turns at high speed, then, as the next hairpin approached, she slammed on the brakes and screamed half-sideways round the corner. McKay, sitting in what was for him the wrong side of the front seat, was terrified.

It was, he later said, "the worst ten miles I've ever ridden," but when he became accustomed to it, he had time, especially during the straightaways to think: This is great! I'm heading to an unknown destination with a titled Englishwoman, and a knockout! High adventure for a Detroit newspaperman educated at Rutgers, and he laughed at himself for feeling like a freshman.

Finally he asked, "Where are we going?" and she said: "You'll see." He did not venture even a guess as to what was happening.

He had half expected her to stop in Ely, a town he had wanted to see for its snug harbor on the Atlantic, but she roared through its narrow streets, rousting chickens and terrifying citizens. "Slow down, killer!" he cried. "This is a town." But she ignored him, exiting by a narrow southern trail that ran along the cliffs overlooking the ocean.

After a breathtaking ride they reached the top of a long descent at the foot of which lay the colorful and isolated town of York, a big village, really, strung out along the two sides of Marigot Baie, a starkly handsome indentation from the Atlantic. He had read that in hurricane season York sometimes absorbed a good deal of punishment, for great waves came storming into the enclosed *baie* and tumbled helter-skelter onto the roads and houses at lower levels. But a few days of sunshine usually dried out the damage and York resumed its quiet ways.

"What are we doing in York?" McKay asked, but Delia merely

fluffed out her hair with her right hand, then patted him on the knee with her left and assured him: "You'll see."

She was adorable, there was no other word McKay could think of as she sped them to the south arm of the *baie* where the island road ended. Darting impatiently from one cul-de-sac to the next, she found herself hitting dead ends repeatedly, and was forced at last to halt the car, summon a black peasant to her window, and ask almost petulantly: "Where's the road to Cap d'Enfer?" and he explained what she already knew: "There be no road, ma'am, just a path."

"I know," she snapped. "But where is the path?"

He showed her the almost invisible exit from the paved streets of the town to an earthen trail which would have been appropriate for cattle but not for a car accustomed to well-kept highways. But the man wanted to be helpful, so he assured Delia: "You drive slow, strong car, you get there fine." She thanked him with a huge, warm smile and took off down the dusty trail at a speed much greater than he would have advised.

Now McKay insisted that he be taken into her confidence: "Tell me what we're doing or I'm getting out."

"Not likely!" she said half scornfully. "You jump out of this car at this speed and you'll be a dead pigeon."

"Does it have to do with what Leckey and I came upon the other night?"

"Let's just say you're my alibi." She flushed, turned her eyes from the path, gave him an almost anguished look of appreciation, and said almost tearfully: "You know what that bastard Leckey's done? Because Etienne dared to kiss a white girl, he's been dismissed from the council, lost his job with the Tourist Board, and his jewelry business is already beginning to suffer!"

"I can't believe it. What a rotten deal . . ."

She leaned forward over the wheel as if to distance herself from McKay, then said in sincere frustration: "Have you ever reflected that in London, Etienne would be a sensation with those good looks, those manners, his solid education? The man's a find. In Paris he'd be the king of the Left Bank. But here in All Saints . . ."

"Or in Detroit," McKay added.

When she tried to respond, her voice caught and she had to bite her lower lip, a pouting action which made her even more desirable, so much so that McKay reached over impulsively and kissed her. She had apparently been in such a situation often before, because she said easily: "You do that again, buster, you'll wreck this car," then, to restore his confidence, she patted him on the leg again and whispered: "But I appreciate the vote of confidence."

"Okay, so now tell me."

Slowing the car to avoid the deep cuts which made the road perilous, she said: "I've never been down this way . . ." Then bluntly: "I need assistance from someone I can trust."

As she maneuvered the car deftly around the holes, McKay said: "You seem like the last girl in the world who needs assistance," and she laughed in agreement: "But I do need your secrecy. I trust you, Millard. I have to."

Now even this fragmentary trail ended, but off to the left continued a mere footpath leading to Cap d'Enfer, Cape of Hell, the rocky southeast tip of the island where in the old days sailing boats had frequently come to grief. Driving gingerly along the edge of a deep cliff, Delia, with a slow, sure hand, slowed the car to a walk, and at last they reached the tip end of the land, and there Etienne Boncour stood waiting beside his blue Ford pickup.

Delia leaped from the driver's seat and dashed across the somber headland to embrace Etienne and lead him behind the pile of rocks which marked the end of the island. There they remained for more than an hour while McKay tormented himself with imaginings of what they were doing. When they reappeared, Etienne more handsome than ever, she a windblown beauty standing out against the turbulent Atlantic, they formed a magnificent pair, and McKay was proud that he had been allowed to know each of them.

From the back of her MG, Delia produced a surprise hamper, the wicker kind that makes English and French open-air picnics extra delectable, as if demonstrating that the person who assembled the picnic had done so with proper seriousness. It was a sad feast they shared there at the end of the world, with a cliff for a table and an angry ocean for a tapestry, these three distraught strangers: a headstrong English girl rejecting womanly restraints, a fine young island man striving to find his precise plan in the world of shifting definitions, and a brash but perceptive American intruder, inheritor of English value systems respectful of island traditions. Proof of the confusion in which they found themselves came in the fact that each of them merely toyed with the good food that Delia had brought and stared disconsolately at the dark ocean to the east.

"How did Leckey acquire the power to discipline you, Etienne?"

McKay asked as a reporter, but Delia forestalled any answer: "We didn't come here to give you material for an article, Millard."

Boncour, however, wanted to explain: "Leckey acted only as he's done for the past nine years. Anything, even the most trivial, if it threatens the governor general's office in any way, he must stamp out. This island is on the brink of black-white trouble, all the Caribbean islands are, believe me. I see it when I travel to my other shops."

"Even Barbados?" McKay asked, and Etienne snapped: "Especially Barbados. But in All Saints, we're going to evade *that* trouble by bringing blacks and coloreds into full political partnership. Maybe even real self-government . . . earlier than you'd think."

"I believe you're right," Delia said. "And from things I've seen my father do, like that Wrentham gala . . ." She stopped, placed her arm about Boncour's shoulder, and quietly continued: "The night you and I were found out . . ." She did not complete her thought about her father.

"So," Boncour resumed, "if the daughter of our Gee-Gee and an island man of color were to become items of gossip . . ." He made a slashing motion with the edge of his hand: "Chop him off." He then looked at Delia and kissed her: "Or chop her off, if necessary. You're in as much trouble as I am, Lady Delia."

"I learned that during the trouble in Germany. Both sides were willing to throw little Delia overboard." She rose, walked to the edge of the cap and tried to toss stones into the ocean, but they fell short.

For the next half-hour they talked of many things, and then Millard said: "I'd love to extend my stay, maybe I could wire the boss, asking him to allow me to take my vacation here in All Saints. I've grown to love this island . . . people like you . . . scenes like this."

"Why don't you?" Delia asked. "You could write a book about us."

"It would take lots more knowledge than I have . . ."

"But Etienne and I would provide all your spadework. He knows All Saints, I know the government of British colonies."

McKay looked at them, this handsome pair of people who had become so important to him: "The much bigger question is—what are you going to do?"

Without hesitation Delia said: "If this were France and we were going to live in France, we could get married, now. But in English territory . . ." She turned to McKay, placing her hand in his: "If we lived in Detroit, would it be any easier?"

"You'd be ostracized. My paper wouldn't even run an article about your wedding. Too inflammatory."

"What's inflammatory?" she asked with snappish irritation.

"Black and white. Nobody's ready for that yet."

"But this man is *not* black. Look at him. He's damned near as white as you are."

"Does Major Leckey think so? That's what really matters."

When the time came to leave this tiny sanctuary, Delia jumped into Boncour's truck, tossed her keys to McKay, and said: "I'll pick it up at the Belgrave," but Etienne would have none of that. He knew she needed to be protected from herself, and said: "Delia, you must ride with him," and he made her leave his car.

He also insisted that she and McKay start off first: "I'll follow long after and enter York through a different side road, one not often used. If Major Leckey does have spies watching you, I'll fool them." Of course, Delia roared back into York with her dust and noise only alerting everyone to her presence, and McKay's cry "Don't drive like a damned fool" merely encouraged her to drive faster.

When McKay submitted his third long article, a tough assessment of Britain's future in her smaller islands like All Saints, his editor in Detroit assumed that he would be sailing home promptly, but McKay had become so emotionally involved with the probable fate of Delia and Etienne, with the success or failure of Lord Wrentham and Major Leckey, with the fortunes of his two dark friends Bart Wrentham and cricketer Sir Benny, and yes, even with what might happen to those formless Ponsfords, that he wired his paper for permission to take his 1938 vacation early, in All Saints, and Gross replied that since his articles had done so much good for circulation in Canada, the publisher wanted him to take a reporting trip to Barbados or Trinidad or both, and on regular salary, not vacation.

He replied SAILING TRINIDAD THEN BARBADOS TONIGHT, and he sought out Etienne at his jewelry store and then Delia at Gommint House to explain his absence and to wish them well. As he was about to leave the Belgrave he encountered Major Leckey coming to escort him to the ship: "McKay, we've been immensely pleased with your stories. Remarkable that an American could penetrate our mysteries so accurately. Gee-Gee sends his regards."

As they walked together toward the interisland ship, they were overtaken by Boncour heading the same way to meet an important customer from another island and, repeating his farewell, McKay said, in formal style to mask his close friendship with the man: "Good luck in your various projects, Mr. Boncour," and the major said stiffly, without bothering to look at the jeweler: "Evening, Boncour." After Etienne had hurried past, Leckey rebuked McKay as if the American were a newcomer who planned to settle in All Saints: "You must never refer to a man like that as *Mister*. He's in trade." When Millard asked what that meant, Leckey explained: "Among the upper classes on any British island there are two kinds of men, sharply divided, gentlemen and those in trade. You can meet the latter politically and in business, but never socially."

"What does that mean to a man like Boncour who's in trade?"

"If he does very well indeed, there's always the chance his daughter will marry a gentleman. Then, depending upon her father's habits . . ." He waved his right hand nebulously. "He could very well be accepted in the better circles and in his later years even become known as a gentleman . . . if his trade earns him a respectable fortune."

"Then Boncour has a chance?" McKay asked.

"Not that one. I'm afraid he's blotted his copybook."

At the ship, Leckey said with great sincerity: "When you're through with Barbados and Trinidad, come back here. We've grown fond of you, really." And then he cried: "Goodness, look who's come down!" It was the governor general and his daughter Delia, and they repeated what the major had said: "We'd like you to come back."

McKay spent six days in Trinidad, where his ship stopped first, and where he found so much strange and exciting material that he produced not one but two articles for his newspaper. For example, he had not known before that Trinidad contained so many Indians, that it was in some ways more a colonial adjunct of India than of England: "Hindus and Muslims, who were imported into Trinidad in the last century to work the great sugar plantations, perpetuate the tensions they experienced in their homeland, but in future, if they conciliate their differences, they can be expected to exert a new and vibrant political force in the island."

His second article dealt with Trinidad's proximity to Venezuela: "Actually, this island is a geographical extension of Venezuela, and only imperial Spain's indifference allowed it to slip very late into British hands. Since the island has copious oil deposits, we can expect

Venezuela at some point in the future to lay claim to it, especially if Trinidad gains its independence from Great Britain and then fumbles its freedom, for trained observers are certain that the moment chaos rules in this island, Venezuela will intervene." That information stunned many readers, even most Canadians.

But it was McKay's obvious affection for the clean orderliness of Barbados that shone through his opening article on that island: "At various periods in history the United States has speculated about occupying this or that Caribbean island: Cuba, Santo Domingo, the Virgin Islands, Nicaragua on the mainland or Haiti? We'd have been much smarter not to have conducted negotiations with any of that group. What we should have done in the early days is purchase Barbados from Great Britain. We'd have had a paradise, self-sustaining too. We still ought to think about it."

He filed that story on Wednesday, and on Thursday night he called Detroit: KILL WEDNESDAY STORY. HELL BROKE LOOSE BARBADOS. WILL FILE. And early next morning he filed the first of six long accounts of the race riots that had suddenly erupted on seemingly peaceful Barbados and various other British islands in the Caribbean including Jamaica. The condescending type of paternalism he had witnessed on All Saints had finally become so galling to the blacks that they could no longer tolerate it, and in wild anger and resentment, mobs coursed through the towns and villages while smaller bands tried to burn plantations. On Barbados it was a savage uprising, resulting in many deaths, and McKay's previous experiences in All Saints enabled him to write perceptively about the background causes.

As soon as Dan Gross in Detroit read McKay's dispatches he realized they were an international scoop, so he placed them on the Associated Press wire, which assured the articles nationwide and even worldwide attention. With those chance articles, McKay became a national figure, and others beside his own editor began to view his work favorably.

When the Barbados riots subsided, he looked at the island dispassionately, and wrote a beautiful *mea culpa:* "Because I had been allowed to see good colonial government in All Saints, and reasonable advances toward some kind of self-government in Trinidad, I thought I understood the islands. And certainly when I first saw the peaceful, almost tranquil beauty of Barbados, I was ready to write a prose poem about its irresistible charm. What I had not seen, nor understood if I did see it, was the deep, grinding hatred many blacks have for the system which had kept them in a kind of spiritual bondage. I am sorry if I misled my readers. I am overjoyed that peace has been restored to these admirable islands. And I hope the governments will begin to correct old wrongs."

Six days later, when his homeward bound ship put in to Baie de Soleil, All Saints still slumbered in the sun as if no uprisings had occurred throughout the other islands. Here was peace. Here was British colonial government at its best, and as the manifold beauties of the *baie* revealed themselves once more he realized that his affections were permanently tied to this island. When he reached the Belgrave he actually ran forward to greet the Ponsfords, whom he had once considered to be impossible. As soon as his bags were deposited in his room, he hurried off to the Waterloo, where Black Bart left the bar to embrace him and listen to his adventures during the riots.

Then, in a much more sober attitude, he walked slowly toward Etienne Boncour's jewelry store, where he found the fastidious Frenchman, as he was usually called, eager to talk. They went into a back room, where they could have privacy, and shared confidences. McKay had little news to offer, since Boncour had branch stores in both Barbados and Trinidad, but the Frenchman had much to confide: "Delia's seriously talking about marrying me and setting up our household on another island. Keep this shop operating, because it's the moneymaker. She thinks we could have a good life."

"And what do you think?"

Boncour smiled gently and held out his hands palms up: "Impossible. She once told me she was a child of Europe."

"She told me the same thing." McKay stopped. "You know, Etienne, I was very fond of that young woman. Still am."

"Who wouldn't be? She seems to have broken hearts around the compass points."

"So what's going to happen?"

Boncour stiffened, as if harsh decisions had firmed his backbone: "One cannot say. One simply cannot say, but one thing's certain. That girl could not exist, not happily, on a small British island."

It was that statement which preoccupied McKay for the following day: Interesting. To me and the other Americans, they're Caribbean islands. To Delia and Etienne and the other Englishmen, they're the British West Indies, as if the French islands didn't exist. But then his thoughts turned to the greater anomaly: Even the Dutch own islands here. Who's missing? The real owners, the Spaniards. Wouldn't it be richly rewarding if one of the big islands were honestly and totally Spanish, so we could observe what might have been accomplished under that governance? And even though he knew little of Spain or the Spanish heritage, he lamented the loss.

This momentary sentimentalism over vanished Spanish grandeur did not mask his great pleasure at being safe within the security of All Saints: Actually, I like everything about this island except Major Leckey and the heavy food. Upon reflection, one of the things he liked most was the efficient way in which the Gee-Gee governed: Like at the cricket field the other day. He appeared for practice in his old all-England blazer, chased ground balls that black players hit, then took his turn at bat and swiped two or three out toward the boundary. Players and casual spectators alike, they loved it. They felt he was one of them.

McKay also appreciated the clever tricks by which Lord Basil made blacks feel welcome at all his functions, save meals at Gommint House or soirees at The Club. He showed no personal animus toward blacks and preached to his white associates that the time was coming when blacks would have to be admitted into governing circles. But he also sternly upheld the dignity of his office, and he never looked better than when he rode in full uniform in the rear seat of his Rolls-Royce, nodding grandly and finally stepping forth in full authority and austerity to open a new school or dedicate the wing of a hospital. McKay had never before seen a British governor in action, and he was impressed: Maintains a more believable image of noble rule than, say, the governor of South Dakota.

On the first full day after his return a pleasant surprise awaited him, for Delia stopped by the Belgrave in her MG to invite him on a circuit of the north, and when they reached that incomparable picnic ground at Cap Galant and lazed in the April sun, he felt it appropriate to broach the critical question: "Delia, if marriage to Boncour is impossible on this island . . . ?"

"Who said so?"

"He did. He's not stupid."

"He should let me make my own decisions."

"Why couldn't you two marry and live on Barbados?"

She laughed almost insolently. "Have you ever been to Barbados?"

"I just came back. You know that."

"But did you realize when you were there that it's little more than half the size of this island?"

"But before the rioting the life was so . . . well, attractive . . . reassuring."

She became angry: "McKay, you fool! You've had a great time here, a genial reception in Barbados. But on either island, have you ever met a black family? I mean the people who work the fields, who make up four-fifths of the population. As they say in the cinema: 'Son, you ain't seen nothin' yet!' So don't ask me to live on Barbados."

He reflected on this as he watched her throwing the tag ends of her picnic back into the hamper, then said: "You seem to make everything a matter of race."

She laughed. "Don't you realize, Millard, that every human relationship on this island *is* a matter of race? Suppose you ask one of Etienne's pretty-clerks for a dinner date, it becomes an affair of state—she asks: 'Where will we dine? I have to be careful of where I am seen with a white man.' Why do you think I took you all the way out to Cap d'Enfer?"

"I've been wondering."

"For one thing, I'd never driven the road before, didn't know the way. But the main reason was to protect *Etienne* from being seen with *me*."

He could not accept that nonsensical rationalization: "Don't con me, Delia. On the way back you wanted to ride in his car . . . let everyone see you."

"That was on the way back. Love sets you free sometimes. You don't give a damn." She stared at the sea, then added: "Like that time with the German colonel. I could have got myself killed."

"Were you afraid?"

"No!" she cried with great emphasis. "I don't give a damn about myself. Never have. Ask my father, he's nursed me through enough scrapes."

"So back to my question: 'What'll happen to Boncour?' " and she replied: "Sooner or later we shall hurt each other terribly. He knows that, but we also know that the game's worth the risk. To live totally, that's everything." Abruptly halting her foreboding, she looked intently at McKay and repeated: "To live, that's what it's all about, isn't it?" and she jumped into the car.

As they sped south, accompanied by breathtaking vistas of the

Caribbean, its wave tips flashing in sunlight, and by hedges of croton that lined the roadway, McKay thought: This must be one of the loveliest roadways of the world and Delia one of the most glamorous women. But both are in jeopardy. The riots in Barbados proved how precarious stability can be. And Delia! What in hell will happen to this marvelous sprite? She's mercury, slipping now this way, now that, and always evading your grasp.

Impulsively he cried: "Delia, what's going to happen to you? Trouble wherever you go, so far as I can learn. Near-tragedy in Germany, in Malta, here in All Saints. One of these days your luck will run out."

She leaned over and kissed him lightly: "You're sweet to care. But really, does it matter?" and the extraordinary way in which she looked sideways at him as she spoke made him think: My God! She's letting me know she wouldn't mind if I wanted to make love to her, too. In great confusion he scrunched over into the far corner of the front seat, interlocked his knuckles in a grasp so tight they turned white, and said softly: "Delia, you know I've fallen in love with you."

"That's sweet," she said, almost flippantly, as if the avowal merited no deeper consideration.

"And I most desperately want you to do the right thing." Realizing that this must sound juvenile, he lamely added a cliché that made things even worse: "I want you to find happiness."

Dismissing him as she would have an attractive child, she teased: "McKay! You're talking like my maiden aunt! The one who moped her life away by dreaming of the grocer's boy she fell in love with," and there ended the serious discussion he had attempted to inaugurate.

When they reached Bristol Town she delivered him to the Belgrave, where they found Major Leckey, obviously outraged, awaiting them: "Really, Delia, you must keep us advised as to where you're going. An important visitor has come to Government House. Your father . . ."

"Well, here I am. Let's go."

"Not in those clothes. It's the German ambassador. Came from Barbados in that Royal Navy vessel you saw in the *baie* . . . if you bothered to look." And off they went, with Leckey driving very fast in his large car and Delia following a few yards behind in her small one.

When McKay came down for dinner, he found the Ponsfords

most eager to have him at their table, for they were brimming with astonishing news: "The German government has asked formal permission for one of their great battle cruisers, the *Graf Spee,* to put into Baie de Soleil. Courtesy visit during a training exercise in the South Atlantic."

"Permission granted?"

"Of course. Our relations with Germany have never been better. We hear there's to be a pact of mutual friendship with Italy, too, so the people of ill will who've been trying to keep our nations apart have lost out."

McKay had been vaguely aware that the various nations in Europe were having their differences and that harsh words had been voiced about Adolf Hitler, but in the areas west of Detroit, which contained many Americans of German descent, those rumors were derided. He was also aware, but in only the roughest terms, that since his departure from Detroit, Germany and Austria had united under some kind of agreement, but he had been led to believe, from the scraps of information he had available, that it was generally held to be a move toward peace in that part of the world.

Both Ponsfords were of that opinion: "We cannot abide the French. Hitler may have his faults, but the Jews did nearly overrun both Germany and Austria." Mr. Ponsford said: "I for one would be delighted to see the *Graf Spee* in the harbor. The Germans may be our allies one of these days, and I'd like to see what they'd bring into the partnership."

It was about quarter to nine that night when McKay was summoned to the phone. "Hullo, McKay? Leckey here. The Gee-Gee wants to know if you can join us and a few men? . . . Yes, right now. . . . Good! I'll fetch you, but would you be considerate and be waiting outside?"

When he was ushered into Lord Wrentham's study, he found four island men, all white, sitting with Wrentham and a ramrod-stiff European in his mid-forties: "Ambassador Freundlich, this is the distinguished American correspondent from the very part of the United States you were asking about. I wanted you two to meet. Exchange of ideas and all that."

The questioning did not touch that subject, because when the ambassador learned that McKay had just returned from Barbados, he wanted to know what the riots on that island had signified, but a swift glance from the Gee-Gee warned McKay not to discuss that embarrassment to British rule, so McKay gave only a casual explanation. The discussion was amiable, far-ranging, and, under the Gee-Gee's diplomatic guidance, never improperly intrusive.

The Gee-Gee seemed eager to introduce his daughter and ordered Leckey: "See if Delia can instruct the servants to fetch us some coffee." When she appeared, radiant in a charming pastel frock, leading two black servants who passed the cups and the biscuits, she seemed the epitome of the well-bred English lass of twenty-two whose anxious parents were beginning to seek a husband, but as she passed McKay with her coffee, she gave him a sly wink.

He used this break as an opportunity to ask, as he always felt honor-bound to do: "Am I allowed to wire Detroit, before it happens, that the *Graf Spee* will be paying a visit here?"

Lord Wrentham answered: "It was the ambassador's suggestion that you be invited, late though it was."

McKay said: "I think these courtesy visits are a great idea. Builds friendships." He stopped, aware that he was being somewhat more effusive than the occasion warranted, but then Major Leckey broke in with his own effusion: "You know, I'm sure, that in English the ambassador's name means *friendship*. May that be a good omen!" And a toast was drunk.

It was agreed that all would be at the dock at ten in the morning when the great German cruiser would maneuver slowly and majestically between the guardian rocks protecting the *baie*. Cheers echoed and salutes were fired as the mighty ship edged up to the dock, but McKay did not participate in the noisy celebration, because Bart Wrentham, who served in the island's volunteer marine rescue department, was whispering in his ear: "That's no cruiser. That's a bloody pocket battleship." And indeed the vessel was immense, with its batteries of guns pointing in different directions.

The *Graf Spee* was under the command of Captain Vreimark, who was piped ashore in stiff glory, saluting his quarterdeck as he left and all the island officials as they waited in formal ranks to greet him. He was especially gracious to Lord Wrentham, whom he had met once in Germany and to whom he introduced a young German civilian who served in some unspecified capacity aboard the *Spee:* "Excellency, I have the honor to introduce a most valued member of our visit, Baron Siegfried Sterner." The baron stepped smartly forward, clicked his heels, saluted, and said in flawless English: "I bring you personal greetings, milord, from my former tennis partner, Baron

Gottfried von Cramm, who stayed with you one year when he played in the finals at Wimbledon."

"Ah, yes! He was with us three years. Reached the finals every year, but had bad luck. Last time he lost to an American, Don Budge."

"He sends his best." Then, seeing Delia in the second row and assuming that she was the governor's daughter, he paused to acknowledge her with a bow, which she returned. Passing along, he came to Major Leckey, whom he recognized as the governor's aide-de-camp by the handsome gold aiguillette he wore suspended from his shoulder. Saluting with a pronounced snap of the hand and click of heel, he said: "Would you be so kind as to deliver this letter of introduction?" Even though Leckey knew that the baron was treating him insolently, he had to accept the letter, and when he glanced at it he saw that it was addressed to "Fräulein the Honorable Delia Wrentham" and a seal indicated that it came from Baron Gottfried von Cramm.

The eight days in the spring of 1938 that the *Graf Spee* remained at All Saints wound up the three most memorable events of recent island history: the visit of the Prince of Wales in 1929, the match with Lord Wrentham's cricket eleven in 1932, and now the monstrous presence of this great, sleek blue-gray warship. It made earlier visits by puny little British destroyers, which had once seemed so powerful, almost laughable.

On Thursday anyone on the island who cared to do so was invited to come aboard, and several thousand did. By means of ropes carefully strung and wooden stanchions properly placed, the islanders were led about the ship, but any so-called "military secrets" they were permitted to see could just as easily have been obtained from a picture postcard. But McKay observed that the Germans cleverly and unostentatiously provided three different tours for the visitors. White people were quietly diverted here and there; they were taken to see officers' quarters and part of the bridge. Coloreds were led down other lanes, and they saw enlisted quarters and some of the smaller guns, while persons obviously black were taken on long, winding tours that showed them almost nothing they could not have seen from the dock.

When McKay sought out an officer who spoke English to ask

about this, the German said frankly: "They're animals. I don't see how you English can breathe on an island so crowded with them."

"I'm American," McKay said, and the officer smiled: "Then you know what I mean."

On four successive nights there were festive dinners. The Gee-Gee invited the principal officers to Government House for a flower-strewn reception, followed by a sit-down dinner for twenty, and at both affairs three men stood out as the acme of their professions: Lord Wrentham, tall, slim, straight and very handsome in his formal attire with the three colorful ribbons signifying the honors he had been awarded; Captain Vreimark, the prototypical German naval officer, with a chestful of decorations testifying to his years of service with the fleet; Baron Sterner, young, good-looking, and crisp in formal wear with one ribbon over his left breast. Of the three, thought McKay, the Englishman was most impressive, and on the next night, when the officers of the *Spee* entertained aboard their ship, the Gee-Gee positively scintillated, for when he appeared in the dress uniform of one of the great British regiments, he was a most dazzling figure.

On the third night the civilian officials of All Saints entertained the Germans with a gracious buffet and island music, but the fourth afternoon and evening were best of all, for then a long entourage of island cars of every vintage carried the German officers north to the old town of Tudor, where a rural reception was held, with speeches and music, after which everyone rode on to Cap Galant, where tents had been erected to protect them against rain and where a typical island picnic was held, with entertainment by four calypso singers who happened to be visiting from Trinidad. Those Germans who understood English were not at ease with the flippant social and political observations of the uninhibited calypso men. "Such would never be allowed in Germany," an officer told McKay. "I can assure you of that."

It was during these dreamlike days that McKay first noticed that Delia alternately appeared and vanished, and since he knew no one in the official party whom he could ask about this, he had to fall back on the Ponsfords, who loved the tittle-tattle about their betters that so mesmerized the English middle classes. Mrs. Ponsford, adopting a conspiratorial manner as she shared a cold lunch with McKay, confided: "She's seeing that handsome young baron at every opportunity, and I do believe she spent the night with him aboard the ship once or twice."

"Do we know anything about him?" McKay asked, as if he were her worried uncle. "I mean, really?"

"Oh, he's impeccable," Mr. Ponsford said, for he was as much a gossip as his wife. "I understand the Gee-Gee checked by cabling the Foreign Office."

"Speaking about cables, what can I tell my paper about the purpose of this visit of the *Spee*? Seems most unusual."

"They're doing what we call 'showing the flag.' Herr Hitler wants it known that he has a ship like the *Spee*."

"You think the Gee-Gee is sending signals home about this huge thing?"

"I'm sure of it. He's no fool."

"If he's so smart, what's he doing about his daughter and that phony baron?"

Mrs. Ponsford laughed to see her American friend so upset about the German: "He's no phony, as you call it. He's a very real baron from a distinguished Prussian military family. But that's not what you asked. The Gee-Gee? I think he must be gratified to learn that his very lovely daughter isn't going to marry an island colored man or an American."

Mr. Ponsford weighed in with a heavy-handed joke: "And he wouldn't be able to tell you which would be worse."

Seeking comfort in his unease, McKay went along to Boncour's shop, where, in the Frenchman's absence, he thought seriously for the first time about what Delia had said that day at Cap Galant: "Suppose you invited one of Boncour's beautiful clerks to a dinner date . . ." Looking suddenly at the two girls, slim and lithe and graced by the warmest smiles, he realized how easy it would be to fall under their spell, and how difficult it would be to do anything about it. Indeed, where could he take them to dinner, in what social circles would they move? And these two girls were almost white. What if he were to remain in All Saints and fall in love with one of those lovely creatures several shades darker than Black Bart? Now, that would pose a real problem.

When Boncour returned from a meeting aboard the *Spee* with German officers who sought to buy watches at a discount, the goal of sailors of all nations, he was in no mood for gossip or frivolous chatter. Leading McKay to his back office, which was as neat and clean as the rest of his operation, he slumped in a chair, looked up helplessly, and said without being questioned: "McKay, she's making

a terrible mistake. An Englishwoman in the heart of German Na-
zism . . ."

"He's a country gentleman, no cartoon Nazi. Her father cabled
the Foreign Office for his credentials."

Boncour looked up in surprise: "Don't you realize what he is on
that battleship? He's the Nazi gauleiter . . ."

"He's what?"

"Gauleiter. Block captain to check on the crew . . . see that they
obey Hitler's orders."

"You're crazy."

"McKay, she's about to marry him. They were talking about it
on the ship. Maybe a big military wedding, Captain Vreimark offici-
ating."

"Oh." There was no exclamation point at the end of this word as
McKay pronounced it; it was the grunt of a man who had been
punched heavily in the stomach by a superior foe. He was involved in
matters about which he had little knowledge and over which he had
no control. "Hadn't we better speak to Delia about this? Frankly, all
cards on the table?"

"She's coming here. To say goodbye." The two young men sat in
silence. They were honestly thinking beyond themselves and of the
damaging mistake Delia could be making.

And then they heard her swinging into the store and asking
brightly: "Where's Etienne?" and when the girls told her, she made
her way into the back office: "Oh, there you both are! How terribly
convenient."

Boncour refused to accept her banter. "Delia, you mustn't marry
that German. He's a professional Nazi. Your life among his gang
would be hell . . ."

She stiffened, glared at the two men—lover and admirer—and
decided to put an end to this nonsense: "Siegfried is exactly what he
seems to be. A loyal official of the new German government."

"Seems to be?" McKay blurted out. "Nobody knows who in hell
he is, or what he's doing aboard that ship."

But it was sagacious Boncour, educated in England, who saw
things most clearly: "Delia, can't you see what's bound to happen?
Hitler and Great Britain, they've got to fall out sooner or later."

Their argument sounded hollow because all three, Delia, Etienne
and Millard, saw the absurdity of this situation—that an ordinary
colored man on a small island should be competing for the love of a

titled Englishwoman against a German baron who was obviously in favor with the leader of his nation. The combat was too unfair, and for that matter, McKay's chances wouldn't be much better: he would be a provincial American scribbler trying to muscle his way into a fine family above his station.

It was so preposterous that McKay could not avoid laughing, but Boncour was beyond that, for he was fighting for a life: "Delia, for God's sake, don't do this reckless thing . . ."

He had used the wrong word. "Reckless?" Her voice rose: "I've been reckless all my life and it's brought me what I want—excitement and joy. I'm not going to change now."

"But not with an official in the Nazi party. Someday we will be at war with Germany."

"Are you out of your mind? That's twice you've said that. Germany and Britain have signed a nonaggression pact, and I want to be part of the union." She moved nervously about the cramped office, then faced McKay, as if she had no further use for Boncour: "When I first went to Germany, I was thrilled at the vitality, the new world a-borning. Someone has called it 'The Wave of the Future,' and I do believe that."

Boncour started to rebut, for he did most desperately wish to save this wonderful woman, but she cut him off: "I've got to go. I wanted you two to hear it from me, direct. Yes, Siegfried and I are getting married. Day after tomorrow, on the *Spee*."

She kissed McKay on the cheek and tried to do the same with Boncour, but he turned away, so, as if to make him more miserable, she added: "And for our honeymoon we fly to Brazil!"

The wedding took place at five in the evening of the day prior to the *Spee*'s departure. On the quarterdeck a kind of chapel decorated with hundreds of island flowers had been erected, and within its sanctuary stood Captain Vreimark, more stern and erect than ever in his full-dress uniform. At his side were three junior officers, also solemn and very military, and beyond them sat the island band augmented by musicians from the *Spee*. Under a battery of big guns, Delia in a flowing pastel gown waited with her father in full uniform.

As the band played Mendelssohn and the lovely bride moved forward on her father's arm to meet Baron Sterner, McKay could not help thinking: What will happen to her? Should be fascinating to watch. But only then did he realize that the man who loved her most was not present. Etienne, humiliated by his dismissal from the Executive Council and the loss of his Tourist Board position, had been unwilling to parade his lowered status before the leading citizens of the island who knew of his chastisement. Where he was McKay did not know, but he was sure that Etienne was alone drinking bitter tea.

The bride and her handsome father swept past, paused to collect the baron, dressed in a military uniform, and all moved before Captain Vreimark, who greeted them, read a short ritual in German and then in English, and pronounced them man and wife. As guests lined up to sign the document attesting to the marriage, Delia spotted McKay and asked Major Leckey to fetch him: "Please, please, Millard, you sign too and let me know all is forgiven."

"You have my blessing," he said, and as the sun set over the glorious bay, with the two rocky pillars protecting its entrance, he had a brief feeling that perhaps Delia was right: Maybe the visit of this ship does signal a union between Germany and Great Britain. He did not know enough recent history to appreciate how unlikely that was, but he still voiced the hope as a blessing for Delia. She was an exceptional person, he had fallen in love with her and would never deny it. He was disgusted that she had chosen the German baron, but he had lost and he would neither grieve nor allow his loss to gnaw at him.

Because no woman could be allowed to sail aboard a German warship, the bridal party and many townspeople drove out to the improvised seaplane ramp at Anse du Soir, where a big, lumbering Pan American flying boat had delayed its schedule so as to carry the bridal couple to Rio. The band played a Hawaiian farewell song, "Aloha Oe," Captain Vreimark and Lord Basil saluted, Delia kissed everyone, and Baron Sterner looked pleased at having married the granddaughter of an English earl. McKay, still regretting that Etienne Boncour had not come to say farewell, waved at Delia as she boarded the plane and whispered to himself: "Good luck, sea sprite. You splashed your way into my heart," and suddenly he broke away from the noisy party, for tears were threatening to flood his eyes.

When he returned to the Belgrave for a late dinner, he was on his way to his room on the second floor to wash up, when he heard muffled voices as he passed the Ponsfords' door. Since he did not recognize them, he suspected that something might be amiss, and impulsively he tried to shove the door open, but it was locked from the inside, so with a rush of his shoulder he banged his way in, only to find himself facing Major Leckey, still in uniform, Mr. Ponsford and Mrs. Ponsford, who was holding a revolver pointed right at

McKay's head. Along two walls forming a corner were ranged the elements of a compact high-powered radio at which sat a colored man he had never seen before. An authoritative voice in London was issuing directions which McKay could not understand.

"Close the door," Major Leckey said with crisp authority.

"What is this?"

"Shut up!" Mrs. Ponsford snapped, her lips taut, her gun still pointed unflinchingly at McKay.

Then, slowly, as he caught fragments of what was being sent and received, he deduced that pompous but subservient Major Leckey was heading a secret island apparatus which was reporting directly to similar intelligence agencies in London. For some reason Leckey and his team found it necessary to bypass the Gee-Gee and his official shortwave radio.

Now, from words that were dropped, it became obvious that the Ponsfords, tested agents from years back and with experience in different countries, had been sent from headquarters to reinforce Leckey's operation, and the fact that they had fooled McKay so completely was proof that they had fooled others as well.

Mouth agape, he stared at the Ponsfords, piecing together the hints they had revealed concerning their mission but which he had failed to detect or evaluate: They did say they'd been friends of the Earl of Gore. Probably that's why they were sent on his trail. They seemed to have a complete dossier on Delia, and I should have wondered why they'd have taken the trouble. And once they learned I was a newspaperman, they went out of their way to convince me that they were vaudeville silly-ass Englishmen. They kept turning up at all the right spots. I feel damned stupid, with her pointing that gun at me, after the way I dismissed her as a gossip.

"Tell them," Leckey was saying to the man at the dials, "that we shall be sending them military details as soon as our man gets here. In the meantime, Mrs. Ponsford, since our Delia will probably turn up somewhere as a German agent, will you give headquarters the details of that obscene wedding?" Handing her revolver over to her husband, who kept it pointed at McKay, she delivered an icy, matter-of-fact report: "Delia behaved much as she did in Malta last year, but this time she messed around with a respectable local mulatto shopkeeper, practically ruining him, and perhaps at her father's suggestion, she took pains to bedazzle a simple-minded American journalist in hopes of coloring his reports in Hitler's favor. Tonight she married your well-vetted Baron Sterner, one-time tennis partner of that other German baron, the respectable one, Gottfried von Cramm, who has displayed gestures of friendship toward Great Britain."

Turning the microphone back, she reached for her gun and resumed guarding McKay, but the transmission was interrupted by the breathless arrival of Leckey's man, who had been surveying and photographing the *Graf Spee*. It was Bart Wrentham from the Waterloo, and when he saw McKay with the gun pointed at this head, he blurted out: "What in hell is he doing here?"

"He stumbled in," Leckey said crisply, "and we can't allow him to stumble out until the *Spee* has sailed."

Paying no further attention to his friend, Black Bart went to the transmitter and told the operator: "Get me Brazil," and for about ten minutes he provided an agent of the British admiralty with a professional assessment of the pocket battleship. Then Leckey took over, speaking to London: "Why did the *Graf Spee* make this extraordinary visit? From things Captain Vreimark said accidentally, but so that we would be sure to hear them, they wanted our governor general to report favorably on German-British friendship. And since they had to know that some group like ours would be trying to determine the capacity of their ship, they invited us to roam around it. They wanted to scare us and for us to scare you. Their game succeeded. It is indeed a formidable ship."

McKay was fascinated by what he was hearing, but he was not yet prepared for what Leckey reported next: "Lord Wrentham is a total prisoner of their propaganda. He extols Hitler, says he's watched the Nazi rise to power, and now believes he's unstoppable. He tries to convince any official visitor that Germany is destined to rule Central Europe and more. He despises France and holds America in contempt, but he's smart enough to coddle naïve American journalists and mask his convictions from them. We know he is an ass, but a dangerous one because people like him so much. All Saints is a good place to keep him isolated from the European capitals, but he must be continuously watched."

Having submitted their reports, the five plotters quickly disassembled their radio and packed its various parts in a surprisingly small set of hand-held grips. Then Leckey turned to the Ponsfords and asked: "What are we going to do with him?"

"He's heard too much," Mr. Ponsford warned. "And he is a newspaperman."

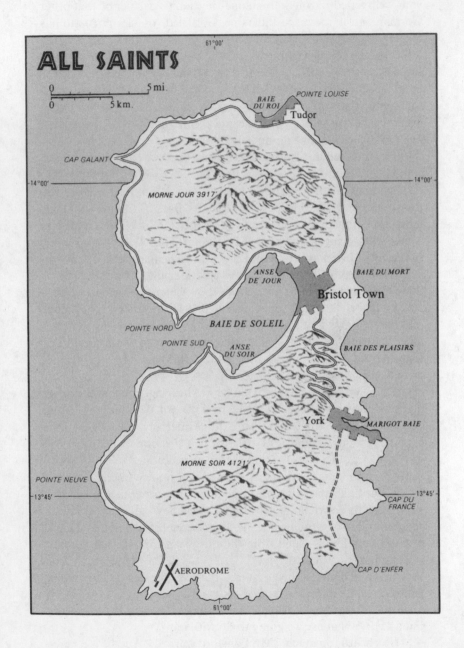

ALL SAINTS

0 ——————— 5 mi.
0 ——————— 5 km.

61°00'

BAIE DU ROI
POINTE LOUISE
Tudor

CAP GALANT

14°00'

MORNE JOUR 3917'

ANSE DE JOUR

BAIE DU MORT

Bristol Town

POINTE NORD

BAIE DE SOLEIL

POINTE SUD

ANSE DU SOIR

BAIE DES PLAISIRS

York

MARIGOT BAIE

MORNE SOIR 4121'

POINTE NEUVE

13°45'

CAP DU FRANCE

CAP D'ENFER

AERODROME

61°00'

"What are you recommending? That we shoot him?"

"Under other circumstances, yes. Certainly we can't let him run to his typewriter with what he's heard."

Black Bart said: "I've found him to be honest. Look at his articles."

"Yes," Leckey said, staring contemptuously at McKay. "Do look at them. Sycophantic. Falls in love with a bitch like Delia, writes poems of praise."

"So what are we going to do?" Mr. Ponsford asked, and Leckey said: "We've got to keep him here until the *Graf Spee* is on its way to Brazil. And we must keep Lord Wrentham thinking that his close association with the German ambassador went unnoticed." Finally speaking directly to McKay, he said: "So you stay in this room, guarded, until morning. Then we'll decide." Turning now to Mrs. Ponsford and her revolver, he asked: "Can you guard him till morning?" and she nodded.

So the four men, Leckey, Ponsford, Black Bart and the radioman, left the room, taking their radio gear to some other hiding spot, and were seen no more that night.

Without flinching, Mrs. Ponsford held the gun on McKay, rebuffing his attempts to engage her in revealing conversation. Once she observed: "This may seem a dirty business, but the enemy is unspeakable."

"Then you think there'll be war with Germany?"

"Don't you? After what you saw with the *Spee*?"

"Would you shoot me if I tried to bolt?"

"Try me."

He did not speak again until he had to go to the bathroom, and she said: "Go ahead," but she followed him into the little room, saying: "No escaping out the window like they do in the flicks." After a while he protested: "It's not possible for a man to urinate with a woman standing behind him with a pistol to his head," and she said: "Keep trying."

Soon thereafter she suggested: "Try it sitting down," and while he perched on the stool she ran water noisily in the basin, and this encouraged him to override his inhibitions.

Toward morning he asked: "Why did you put on such an English garden-party act with me?" and she said: "From the first I suspected we might want to use you. I acted the way you expected me to. Encouraged you to accept me."

"But why does Leckey play the fool?" and she explained: "For the last eight years he's had one of the world's most difficult jobs. Keeping tabs on real fools. If he ever stopped acting his role for one minute, they might trap him."

"Is he in charge of your group?" and she replied: "I won't tell you. Bart at the Waterloo could be, or my husband, or me."

"But Leckey gives the orders," and she said: "He seems to. Maybe that's the secret of his long success."

When dawn in the east reflected on Pointes Nord and Sud, Major Leckey and Bart returned and told Mrs. Ponsford: "Get some sleep," and she handed the revolver to Bart.

She fell asleep in minutes, and Leckey asked McKay: "Under what arrangements can we let you live?" and it was Bart who offered the workable suggestion: "He might be made to understand that his America is going to be at war with Hitler just as soon as we are. If he understood that, we could get him to swear that he'd write nothing about tonight . . . or our stupid Gee-Gee . . . or the Nazi gauleiter Sterner."

"Would you accept his word? On a matter of such vital importance?"

"I think we have to."

"Will you give us such assurance, McKay?" Before Millard could answer, Leckey said: "Before you swear to a promise you can't keep, remember, if you double-cross us, we have people like the Ponsfords who will quietly slip into Detroit one afternoon, and you'll have a nasty accident."

"I think I'm piecing the bits together," McKay said. "I'm not sure you're right about Germany, but I'm sure you think so." He licked his dry lips and said: "I give you my word."

"Nothing about the Gee-Gee being a German accomplice, whether he knows it or not? Nothing about Baron Sterner? Nothing about our radio? Nothing about me or Bart, since we have to remain here?"

A harsh agreement was reached, covering each incident in the All Saints case, with McKay swearing that he would forget every significant aspect of the battleship's visit and in no way imperil the cover of Leckey, Bart Wrentham or the Ponsfords. But these matters were eclipsed by the echoes of a loud fracas on the street below. They hurried out into the sunrise . . . to find a crowd gathering at Etienne Boncour's jewelry shop. "What's happening?" Leckey snapped, and two women, shaken with horror, pointed dumbly at the store entrance.

Pushing their way through the muttering crowd, the two men entered the beautifully organized shop, its gleaming counters neatly aligned. But when they looked at the display case that housed the expensive Rolex watches, they saw draped across it, arms and legs grotesquely extended, the inert body of the shop's owner. Etienne Boncour had shot himself through the head, and his body had pitched forward with such force that it had shattered the glass case.

McKay was stricken by the appalling sight of his dead friend, but Major Leckey took only one hasty professional look, then quickly assumed his aide-de-camp pose. Waving his hand sideways to disperse the gawking onlookers, he snapped out a chain of orders: "Be about your business. Go, go! Leave a path there!" and he pushed people back to make way for the converted truck that edged its way in to remove the dead body to the morgue.

XIII

THE SCHOLAR

A T FIFTY-ONE, MICHAEL CARMODY WAS BEGINNING TO WON-
der if he would ever find in his classes the brilliant kind of lad
who makes teaching bearable.

"None so far," he groaned one Monday morning as he reported
early for the weekly grind. "Acceptable students, yes, but never that
flaming talent bursting free to remind you of young Raphael or Mo-
zart. P'raps they don't make 'em anymore."

An Irish immigrant to Trinidad, Michael Carmody was an instructor at Queen's Own College in the pleasant town of Tunapuna,
some eight miles east of the capital of Port of Spain.

Queen's Own, in the British fashion, was called a college (in other
parts of the world it would be called a high school), the supposition
being that if a bright lad wanted to move ahead to advance his education, he would next attend a university. The educational standard
was high and top graduates had no difficulty in either winning bursaries to the best universities in Great Britain or doing well when they
got there, so Carmody kept hoping that one day there would come
wandering into his room a future Isaac Newton.

That Monday in 1970, as he reached his desk and dumped on it
the books he had taken home with him on Friday, he saw awaiting
him a sheet of white paper containing only the words *Master Car-*

mody. Lifting it, he found attached to it a second sheet of fourteen lines of poetry arranged in the classical form of the sonnet. Taking his chair and leaning back, feet on the desk, he read the sonnet, looked up at the ceiling and said: "Well now!"

In the few minutes before the students entered he read the poem again, and thought: This has to be Banarjee, and he visualized the timid Indian boy, fifteen years old, thin as an ebony wand, with dark complexion, a mass of almost shining black hair, and luminescent eyes that he seemed afraid to show in public. Ranjit Banarjee was unusually shy, especially with girls, and although he gave every evidence of possessing a mind of surprising capacity and range, he excelled in none of the traditional subjects. Classified by his teachers as "a difficult lad but never disruptive," he moved quietly through the school system, always keeping somewhat apart from the other students—a Hindu in a Catholic school, an Indian among blacks and mestizos.

The bell signaling the opening of school rang and the delightful young people of Trinidad streamed into the room, all boys, since this was a segregated Catholic college, established in the years when the island had been Spanish. The complete range of color was represented, from blackest black of the Negroes whose ancestors had been slaves, to the half-black, half-white of the mestizos, the light browns of the Hindus and Muslims, to the delicate tans of the Spanish and French families with black infusions at some distant time, and on to the whites like Carmody who had come mainly from the British Isles, and relatively recently. As they came rollicking into his room he thought: A tropical bouquet, and how much more refreshing than the sea of pasty white that used to greet me in Dublin.

When his students came to attention he said, holding the two pages aloft in his left hand: "This morning we start with a surprise, and a most pleasant one I can assure you. When I came to work this morning I found a poem waiting on my desk. From the way it is laid out, can you tell me what kind of poem it is?" One boy called out: "A sonnet," and Carmody asked: "How do you know?" and the boy said: "Eight lines at top, six at bottom."

"Good, and the poem is good too," and with that, he began in a rich Irish brogue intended for the recitation of poetry:

> *"When the immortal caravels passed through*
> *That splendid crescent of the Carib isles,*

They left the grim Atlantic and the crew
Cheered as they burst into a sea of smiles.
The waves were gentler here, the breezes soft,
The sun irradiated all the sea.
Bright-colored birds sang as they soared aloft
To celebrate this subtle victory.

"It was strange treasure that he found this day,
Columbus of the never-bending mind:
Not gold or silver or the facile kind
Sought by his queen, who lusted for Cathay.
He found new lands of ordinary clay
Two continents of hope for all mankind."

Betraying his delight with the sonnet, Carmody said quietly: "I'm sure we can guess who wrote these lovely words," and almost automatically the boys turned to look at Ranjit Banarjee, whose embarrassment showed as he enjoyed the fruits of authorship.

"Yes," Carmody said, "our fledgling poet is Ranjit, a quiet lad whose waters run deep," and the class applauded, but he stopped them with a surprising discussion that none who heard it would ever forget: "There's a great deal wrong with this poem, and in our enthusiasm we must not overlook the errors. Let's look at the octet first."

But after a long discussion of the rules of sonnet writing, Carmody stopped abruptly, placed his hands flat on his desk, and leaned forward: "Students, what have I just been engaging in?" When no one spoke, for they had not understood what point their teacher was trying to make with his harsh criticism, Ranjit said in a low voice: "Pedantry."

"Yes!" Carmody cried, bringing his hands down on his desk with an invigorating slap. "Pedantry. Remember what we said about Beckmesser in *Die Meistersinger*? Victor, what was it?"

"He knew all the rules for writing a song but never how to write one."

"Yes! Our Ranjit has broken all the rules, but he has written a perfectly lovely little sonnet immortalizing a great explorer." He smiled approvingly at Ranjit, then concluded: "And I, who know all the rules for sonnet making, could never in a hundred years compose a decent one. Ranjit, you're a poet and I'm not."

• • •

Having at last identified a possible genius, Carmody decided to strike fast and hard, and that afternoon he asked Ranjit to remain behind as the other boys thundered off to the cricket field: "Ranjit, you're a quiet lad, but one with great potential. What course in life do you intend following as you grow up?"

Innocently, the Indian boy looked up at this master he had grown to respect, and said: "I don't know."

This irritated Carmody, who banged his desk: "Dammit, lad, you've got to put your mind to something, don't you? Time's wasting. Look at Dawson. He wants to be a medic, and by the end of next year he'll have finished, right here in Queen's, many of the courses he'll need for the first year of his university work. What will you have accomplished and in what direction are you heading?"

When Ranjit said defensively: "But I don't know. It's all so confusing," Carmody decided to take matters into his own hands. After gaining permission from the dean, he plopped the boy in his little Austin and drove to Port of Spain, asking Ranjit to direct him to his grandfather's Portugee Shop.

"My grandfather is Sirdar Banarjee. Sirdar is a traditional name in our family."

Sirdar was a bustling white-haired man who had kept his Portugee Shop focused on two essential services: providing cheap, well-made clothing for the locals and expensive trinkets for the tourists, with special emphasis on keeping both groups happy. Eagerly extending his hand, he said effusively: "Ranjit tells me you're his favorite master, a very intelligent man indeed, Trinity College in Dublin. Now, what can I do for you?"

"Could we please talk about your grandson?"

"What's he done wrong?" Sirdar asked, scowling at the boy.

"Nothing! Quite the contrary, he's done so many things right that I want to talk seriously about his future."

"Future? Here's his future," and he spread his arms outward to encompass his shop.

"Could we, perhaps, ask his mother to join us? These are matters of great importance, Mr. Banarjee."

"Matters of great importance are settled by men," he said, stressing the word, and he led Carmody and Ranjit into his cluttered office, where he said, with hands spread on his desk: "Now tell me the problem, and reasoning together like sensible men, we can solve it."

"Your grandson here is a boy of dormant ability."

"*Dormant* means *sleeping*?" When Carmody nodded, Sirdar cuffed his grandson: "Wake up!"

"It's really you, Mr. Banarjee, who must wake up."

"Me? You don't run a shop like this in Trinidad by sleeping."

"Where'd you get the name Portugee?" Carmody asked, seeking to placate the man.

"When the Indians came here in 1850 or thereabouts to work the cane fields, most of the shops were owned by Portugees, and since they had the reputation of offering the best bargains, anyone who started his shop, like my grandfather, called it a Portugee."

"Very practical, and now I want you to be practical."

"This is going to cost me money, isn't it?"

"Yes. I want you to send Ranjit on to the university. He deserves it."

"University? Where?"

"I feel sure he could win a bursary in almost any of the finest. You have a very intelligent grandson, Mr. Banarjee. He deserves an opportunity."

Carmody saw at once that he had used effective words: *bursary, intelligent, finest* and *opportunity*. The conversation had been elevated to a level that the grandfather recognized and appreciated.

"That word *bursary*. Does it mean what I think?"

"That the university will pay most of his fees? Yes."

"Like what university?"

"Cambridge, Oxford, our own Caribbean university in Jamaica."

For the first time Ranjit entered the conversation: "Columbia in New York."

Sirdar leaned back and smiled, first at Carmody, then at Ranjit: "You mean that this boy could go to those places?" and Carmody said with vigor: "Yes, if you help him financially, and if he directs all his efforts to accomplishing something specific."

"What's he failing in?" and when Carmody explained that in little things Ranjit was doing well but that in big ones like the direction of his life or preparation for some major contribution he was accomplishing nothing, the old shopkeeper showed no anger: "I've known for some time that Ranjit would never be satisfied with taking my place. I've laid other plans . . . one of his cousins who is working in a sugar mill. That boy has desire." Then he turned to Ranjit and said: "Time is a fleeting chariot across the sky. So quick it sets at dusk behind the clouds. Talk with Master Carmody. Find out what you can do, and if you really have promise, as the master says, we can find the money to help. Oxford! My goodness."

On the trip back to school Carmody spelled out the agenda: "You've proved you can write, but you haven't proved you can tackle a subject of some importance and stay with it. If you demonstrate that ability, I'm positive I can land you a major bursary, because remember this, Ranjit, all universities are searching for really bright boys. The average, they can get by the bushel."

"What do you want me to do?"

"I don't want you to do anything. I want you to settle upon some project of substance and show me what you can accomplish."

The boy did not answer, but four days later Carmody again found on his desk a single sheet of paper, once again labeled *Master Carmody*, but this time it covered a sheaf of nine pages. The general title of the essay was "Teachings of My Grandfather Sirdar," and before Carmody had read the fourth page, so Indian in subject, so mature in observation, he muttered: "He can do it. My God! This Indian boy out of nowhere can do it!"

Who are the Trinidad Indians? In 1845 the white plantation owners of Trinidad finally awakened to the harsh facts: "Because the Sentimentalists in England have outlawed slavery, we are allowed no more African Negroes, and the ones we already have prance around shouting: 'We're free! Work no more!'" So the owners sent ships to Calcutta to import huge numbers of Indian peasants, who, when they reached here, were described in whispers as "our light-skinned slaves" and treated that way.

My ancestor, the first Sirdar. In one of the ships bringing Hindus to Trinidad was a young man of clever mind and unknown caste. Seeing that the British owners of the ship needed someone to keep the Hindus in order, he announced himself as a former Sirdar of distinguished caste, a kind of general manager of everything, and he made himself so helpful that those in command accepted him as their Sirdar, and he liked the title so much he kept it, and we Banarjees have used it ever since. Late in life, when his Portugee Shop was making lots of money, he provided his grandchildren a statement which they treasured but kept secret: "My name was not Banarjee. My caste was the lowest. I did not come from Calcutta. And I learned French when I was exiled to Reunion." And my grandfather told me that when he heard our first Sirdar, his grandfather, tell the story, the old man ended: "And I'm the best trader ever to reach Trinidad, no matter what color."

Carmody was delighted to think that in two paragraphs Ranjit had succintly defined his ancestry, but he was far more impressed by what the boy revealed about the Banarjees of this century.

Chooosing a wife: One of the first things my grandfather taught me was the importance of finding the right wife: "No Indian man can marry a black woman. It would be impossible." And in all the years since 1845, when the first Indians arrived in Trinidad until today, this has never happened among the Indians we know. But he said the same about Chinese women, and Portuguese, and especially white English or French women: "The Indian man can marry only the Indian woman. That is the one law before all others." And men like him have waited years to marry till proper Indian wives could be imported from India.

Jewels as a proof of love: Grandfather said that if an Indian really loved his wife, he gave her jewels to prove it. I found a diary of a French traveler who wrote in 1871 of my great-great-grandfather's wife: "In Port of Spain at the well-known Portugee Shop I met Madame Banarjee, a woman of great charm who wore on each arm some twelve or fourteen big bracelets of solid gold or silver. Around her neck she wore chains of the same metal on which hung large disks of silver embellished with precious stones from Brazil, while in her nose she wore an immense diamond. Her worth as she walked to greet me must have been tremendous."

How to treat grave robbers: When the wife of my great-great-grandfather died, he buried her wearing all her gold and silver, and an English official protested: "But you're throwing away a fortune," but he replied: "She brought me a fortune, and I would not like to see her in another world poorer than when she came to me." Three days later, when the police came to the Portugee Shop to inform him that grave robbers had dug into her coffin and taken all the precious metals and the jewels, he said: "They were hers. She spent them as she thought best." But when some of the jewels surfaced in the Trinidad bazaars sometime later, he made careful note of who had them and of how they had obtained them, and shortly after that several men were found dead . . . one by one.

Carmody read these glimpses into Indian life with growing interest, satisfied that Ranjit had not only a grasp of his heritage but also understood the fascinating complexities and contradictions of Trinidad life.

Muslims: In Trinidad three Indians out of four are Hindus, the others are Muslim, whom Hindus do not like. When you hear of an Indian husband who has cut off his wife's nose or ears, you can be sure it's a Muslim who has caught her looking at another man. He disfigures her so she'll not be pretty enough anymore to attract other men. Hindus act different. My grandfather's brother fancied that his wife was taking an undue interest in another man, and chopped her across the throat. When arrested for murder he could not understand what all the noise was about, and when the English judge ordered him to be hanged, he told the judge in a loud voice to go to hell. I think the Muslim way is better, for the husband still has his wife, nose or no nose, while my grandfather's brother lost his wife and his life, too.

Carmody was eager to see what Ranjit had to say about the Indians' capacity to excel in business regardless of where in the world they emigrated, and the boy did not disappoint:

Managing a shop: Grandfather told me: "Since white people have most of the money, you must be nice to them no matter what happens, no matter what complaints they make. If they say the cloth is no good, take it back. And keep on taking it back until they're satisfied. But remember that there aren't too many white people on the island, so you must also be attentive to the former slaves, because although they spend only pennies, if you can encourage enough people to spend their pennies, you can earn a lot of money. Muslims are never to be trusted, but their money is good. And people who get off the ships even for a few hours are to be treated with special care, for such people move about and tell others. And sometimes you'll get a letter from people you never saw, because you were nice to somebody who told them about us. And such letters often contain big orders." Grandfather has told me and all his grandchildren: "Integrity is everything. Live so that people speak of you as a man whose word is his bond of honor."

When Carmody read that excerpt he had to smile, because he had heard two lawyers and a judge affirm in his club that "Sirdar Banarjee is the biggest damned liar in Trinidad, with Tobago and Barbados thrown in." Another, overhearing this judgment, added from his table: "If Sirdar swears it's Thursday, check your calendar. It'll be Friday, but he'll say it's any other day of the week if that's to his advantage." Carmody was fascinated trying to guess what his star pupil would say about that.

Law: Since Indians in Trinidad have the bad reputation of being liars and in court to be perjurers, I wanted to know how my grandfather would explain this, and he told me: "They say that since we Hindus don't know the meaning of swearing on the Bible, we're all perjurers. It isn't that way. I know very well what it means, Ranjit. It means: 'God up in heaven is watching and listening and He wants me to tell the truth.' But the judge is down here and it's my job to tell him what he needs to give the right decision. You have to pick your way between these two persons sitting over you. And a good rule to follow is one I adopted years ago: 'Whatever is good for a member of the Banarjee family is good for the island of Trinidad,' and that helps me know what to say in court." Later he gave me a brief summary of his approach to the problem that the whites called perjury: "You give God what He expects and the judge what he needs."

Carmody found Ranjit's writing so capable and his sly comments so witty and mature, even though they may have been inadvertent, that he decided he must force the issue about the boy's ongoing education, so one afternoon when classes ended he invited Ranjit to accompany him on a hike into the hills above Tunapuna, and as they looked over the green fields of Trinidad he said: "Ranjit, with your grandfather willing to help pay for your education and me convinced that I can get you a bursary, you must make two big decisions. What university, and when you get there, what specialization? First the university, Oxford or Cambridge?"

"I might like to go to some good school in New York."

"That would be a mistake."

"Why?"

"You live in the Caribbean. Your future is in these English colonies— I mean nations— among leaders who've been educated in the English pattern."

"Maybe that pattern isn't so good anymore. Maybe I ought to go to Japan. Like all the Banarjees, I find languages easy."

The idea stunned Carmody. None of his friends in either Ireland or here on the islands had ever contemplated so much as a flying vacation to Japan, and now this youth, this hesitant boy, really, was talking of spending the formative years of his life there. It was preposterous.

"How about the University of the West Indies . . . in Jamaica . . . for your undergraduate work?" He stopped abruptly. "You *are* planning graduate work . . . to get your doctorate?"

"Well, if it worked out . . . maybe."

Irritated by the boy's indecision, Carmody asked gruffly: "How about U.W.I. to sort of feel your way about? You'll get top honors, I'm sure. And decide then where you wish to move on to. Oxford . . . I'm quite sure you'll be eligible . . . Maybe the London School of Economics if you have a political bent?"

"I still think I might want to go to Columbia in New York."

"Ranjit, as I've already told you, attending an American university won't help you if you want to make your life in what is essentially a British island." The boy said nothing, so Carmody said: "You must tell me what it is you want to be."

"A scholar. Like John Stuart Mill or John Dewey. I like knowing about things. Maybe I will study the history and the people of the Caribbean." Almost diffidently he added: "I can read French and Spanish."

Carmody contemplated this unexpected turn, and finally surrendered: "You could do well in such fields, Ranjit. You could pursue such studies and at the end find yourself qualified to go in either direction, writing or scholarship."

"Why do you always put writing first?"

"Because if a man has a chance to be a writer and turns it down, he's a damned fool." He stamped about kicking rocks, and came to rest facing Ranjit: "Have you read any of the Irish writers? Yeats, Synge, *Juno and the Paycock*? You must read them. They took an amorphous mass and turned it into a nation. Someone will do the same for the West Indies. It could be you."

"No, I'll be the one who gathers him the data."

"In that case, you really must spend your first three years at U.W.I. in Jamaica."

"Why?"

"Because you'll meet students from all the other islands. Learn from them the character of the Caribbean."

"Why should I do that?"

"Dammit!" Carmody stormed as he pitched rocks furiously into the valley below. "Don't act the indifferent fool. You said yourself you wanted to study about the Caribbean. The contribution you are ideally qualified to make focuses on this region. You're a Trinidadian, a native of a special island with special opportunities. You're an Indian with perspective on the British and French islands. You're a Hindu with your unique view of the other island religions. And you have been endowed with a rare sense of words and the English sentence. You have an obligation to more than yourself."

Before Ranjit could react, the emotional Irishman did something of which teachers are always aware but rarely reveal; he related the boy to himself: "It's not only your investment, Ranjit, it's mine too. A teacher finds a really promising student only once or twice in a long career. Many good, yes, but with a chance to be great . . . not often. You're my one chance. I've taught you, charted your progress, written letters to get you bursaries. And for what? So that you will be able to use your brains to the maximum for the rest of your life. You are not allowed to be indifferent, for I ride with you, to the heights or the depths. I've committed these years in Trinidad to you, and you must go forward, because you take me with you."

The statement so startled Ranjit, who had, up to this moment, never thought of himself as having any significance or the ability to make a contribution—had never, indeed, thought of himself as an adult doing anything—that he sat silent, hands clasped beneath his chin as he looked for the first time at his Trinidad, seeing the sugar fields on which his ancestors in the 1850s had toiled like slaves, and far in the southern distance, not discernible to the eye, the oil fields and the asphalt pits on which the island's riches depended. He caught a vision of himself as a kind of referee collecting data about this and the other islands and forming judgments about them, to be shared. In other words, he had been goaded into thinking of himself as a scholar.

"I will go to Jamaica," he said solemnly, "and make myself informed."

When Ranjit Banarjee, a precocious Hindu boy of fifteen, flew from Trinidad to Jamaica to enroll in the University of the West Indies, he was amazed at the distance between the two islands, more than a thousand miles, and when he studied the map of the Caribbean and found that Barbados far to the east was more than twelve hundred miles from Jamaica, he told an incoming freshman in the registration line: "Jamaica must have been the worst possible site for an island university," and the young man, a black from All Saints, replied jokingly: "Best location would have been my island, All Saints, but it's too small." Then he added: "Geography and history don't mix well in the Caribbean."

"What do you mean?" and the young black responded: "If Jamaica were a thousand miles farther east, where it's needed, everything would be all right."

Discussions like that occurred often during Ranjit's first Michaelmas term at the university. When he was not astonished by the wide variety of students—jet-black boys like the one from All Saints, Chinese from the western end of Jamaica, French speakers from the Dominican Republic, and eye-stopping girls of light color from Antigua and Barbados—he was surprised at how well educated they seemed to be. They behaved with a quiet confidence, as if they had come to Jamaica to learn something, and he told himself: I'll bet they were just as good at their books as I was, and his first days in class fortified that opinion.

These young people were able. They had all graduated from that commendable group of schools which England had scattered through her colonies, with each school likely to have one superb teacher like Mr. Carmody of Queen's Own. But Ranjit was also aware that U.W.I. had no students from Cuba, largest of the Caribbean islands, and apparently none from Guadeloupe or Martinique.

In those first days Ranjit identified no Indian students from the other islands and only two from Trinidad, so he was thrown in with a heady mix of young people from almost a score of different islands, and as he listened to their talk he began to acquire that sense of the Caribbean which would become his distinguishing mark. If a young man with a heavy Dutch accent said that he was from Aruba, Ranjit wanted to know all about that island and how it related to the other Dutch islands of the group, Curaçao and Bonaire. He was fascinated to learn that Aruba had a language of its own, Papiamento, comprised of borrowings from African slave speech, Dutch, English and a smattering of Spanish. "Less than a hundred thousand people in all the world speak it," the Aruba man said, "but we have newspapers printed in it."

But as Ranjit settled down for the three years of hard work—doing extra papers during vacations would enable him to graduate early—he found that the true excitement at U.W.I. was the faculty, who were so compelling that, as before, he was drawn to several different disciplines: anthropology, history, literature.

A Dr. Evelyn Baker, a white woman on loan from the University of Miami, was an inspired sociologist who had conducted field studies in four different islands while earning her doctorate at Columbia University in New York. She had an ecumenical grasp of the Caribbean that attracted Ranjit, who aspired one day to have the same. She was about forty years old, the author of two books on the islands, and a disciplinarian where term papers were concerned, for she taught as if every student facing her was destined to be either a sociologist or an anthropologist. Early on she recognized Ranjit's capacities, and paid such special attention to him that before the end of the first term she was satisfied that she had in this bright Indian boy a new cultural anthropologist for the area she had grown to love.

However, another teacher—Professor Philip Carpenter—a small, wiry, acidulous young Barbados scholar, a black man with his doctorate from the London School of Economics, that inspired breeding ground for colonial leaders, quickly recognized Ranjit as a young fellow ideally suited for historical studies: "I read your contribution to the anthology, Banarjee. Remarkable historical insight regarding the various Sirdars of your family. You could make a real contribution. History of the Indians in Trinidad . . . or the whole Caribbean. Why they prospered in Trinidad. Why they didn't in Jamaica." He walked about, then asked: "Were you Indians ever tried as field hands in Barbados? I really don't know. I wish you'd look into that, Banarjee. Give me a paper on it. We both need to know."

His most interesting professor was a black woman from Antigua who had taken her advanced degrees at the University of Chicago in Illinois and at Berkeley in California. An expert in the literature of colonial areas, Professor Aurelia Hammond had written on the religious writers of seventeenth-century New England and the early novelists of Australia. But her unique talent was that she could relate literature to reality, and place any colony, regardless of degree of servitude or freedom, in its exact developmental stage: "If you read what the dreamers and poets are saying, you know what's happening in the society," she told Ranjit. Contemptuous of much that she saw in the Caribbean, she was not averse to saying so: "Barbados and All Saints remain English colonies spiritually. Guadeloupe and Martinique should be ashamed of themselves for being tricked into thinking they're an indigenous part of metropolitan France. The Dominican Republic doesn't know what it thinks, and Haiti is a disgrace." She had high regard for Trinidad: "Its nice mix of African black, Indian Hindu and a few white businessmen has a good chance of creating a new prototype for the area," but her personal affection was saved for Jamaica: "You cannot imagine how exciting it was for me, a little black girl, coming from hidebound Antigua to this university and finding a creative environment in which music and art and politics and social change were all happening on an island bursting with energy and hope." Few who studied with her ever forgot her incandescent vision of the Caribbean.

Ranjit's education did not revolve solely about his professors; his fellow students were equally instructive, especially a Jamaican whose parents now worked in London: "They paid my way to go over last year. What a wonderful city! Hundreds of Trinidad Indians there, Ranjit. You'd be at home." He was so enchanted by the virtues of London that he wanted Ranjit to fly over in the coming vacation: "Once you see it, you'll make it your second home. As for me, soon as I get my degree, it's good old London for me."

Ranjit took his vacations seriously, as he did everything else, and to provide data for his essays he fanned out from Jamaica on cheap excursion airfares to a good mix of the Caribbean islands. He saw lovely Cozumel off the Yucatán coast but felt no affinity with the vanished Maya: "Egyptians are a lot more interesting, from what I've read." With two other young men from different islands, he took a quick trip to Haiti and was terrified by it, as were they: "It's so different from a well-ordered British island," one of his fellow travelers said, "Good God! They're living on earthen floors, one piece of furniture to a one-room shack for a family of eight." Any black or colored student from the other islands had to be perplexed as to why the Haitian blacks ruled their attractive country so poorly.

One of the best trips he took with the limited funds his grandfather was able to provide was a special air pilgrimage arranged for students by a Caribbean airline to seven different islands. He saw not only fascinating little islands like St. Martin, half-Dutch, half-French, but also the big French islands. Guadeloupe fascinated him. "It's two islands, really," the guide pointed out, "separated by a channel so narrow you could almost jump across." When the students convened at Basse-Terre to compare notes, an extremely attractive young woman from U.W.I. sat down beside Ranjit; he was delighted because he would never have made any approach on his own. He learned that she was Norma Wellington, niece of the medical doctor on St. Vincent, Church of England, and a premed student at U.W.I. who thought she might go on to the States for graduate work in hospital management. She had a sharp eye, evaluated different islands unemotionally, and displayed no nationalistic preference for her island over any other. She obviously found this young Hindu scholar interesting, or even exotic, for she conversed with him repeatedly on the tour.

Still very shy where girls were concerned, Ranjit found it difficult to engage in the normal chatter that young men his age employed when trying to impress their women friends, but once, as Norma and he were trudging along together on a quiet road in Grenada, he summoned courage to ask: "Norma, if you're so beautiful, why aren't you engaged . . . or something . . . or even married?" and she laughed easily: "Oh, Ranjit, I have so much to complete before that sort of stuff."

Interpreting this as a rebuff, when Norma had intended merely to say that she felt she must attend to her education first, he retreated from his burgeoning interest in girls and found solace instead in the work he was doing with his three professors.

Professor Hammond, the teacher of literature, told him: "You can write, young man. At least you know what a paragraph is, and that's more than I can say for most of my students." Dr. Baker, the sociologist from Miami, said: "Excellent perceptions, Mr. Banarjee. At some point in your education you might want to write more fully on the Barbados syndrome."

"What's that?" he asked, and she said: "The belief that if you wish strong enough, you halt the flow of change."

But it was Professor Carpenter who provided the immediate impetus to Ranjit's next concentrated work, for he gave an inspired lecture on a historical figure he termed "the most effective man the West Indies has so far produced and a principal architect of the American form of government." His lecture started with a dramatic account of a typical West Indian hurricane:

> "In 1755 there was born on the insignificant island of Nevis an illegitimate boy whose poor mother had a difficult time ensuring the protection of her family. Hoping to better her fortune, she moved to the Danish island of St. Croix, and there on the night of 31 August 1772, her son first experienced a major hurricane. Six days later he composed a remarkable account of the storm which was later published in the *Royal Danish American Gazette*."

Without revealing who the boy was, the professor read from the first paragraphs of the letter, pointing out that the writing was concise and the scientific data accurate. Only then did he disclose who the author was: "Alexander Hamilton wrote this account when he was either seventeen or fifteen, for throughout his life he lied about his age." And with that, he launched a scathing denunciation of the presumptuously long middle section of the letter.

> "Let's say we accept his claim and grant that he was only fifteen. Imagine the pomposity of writing: 'My reflections and feelings on this frightful and melancholy occasion, are set forth in the following self-discourse.' And with that modest statement he proceeds to write eight paragraphs of the most overblown theocratic nonsense one will ever read. Let me give you some samples:

> "'Where now, oh! vile worm, is all thy boasted fortitude and resolution? Why dost thou tremble and stand aghast?'

> "'Oh! impotent and presumptuous fool! How durst thou offend Omnipotence, whose nod alone were sufficient to quell the destruction that hovers over thee or crush thee into atoms?'

" 'And Oh! thou wretch, look still a little further; see the gulph of eternal misery open. There mayest thou shortly plunge— the just reward of thy vileness.'

" 'But see, the Lord relents. He hears our prayer. The lightning ceases. The winds are appeased . . . Yet hold, Oh vain mortal! Check thy ill timed joy. Art thou so selfish to exult because thy lot is happy in a season of universal woe?' "

When he had the full attention of his students, he proceeded to the worst of Hamilton's effusions, passages which caused the students to break into laughter, but then he squelched them:

"It is the closing passages of this extraordinary letter which interest us, for they reveal like lanterns in the night the future politician and financial planner Hamilton. He utters a heart-felt cry on behalf of the poor who have been desolated by the storm and an appeal to people of wealth to contribute a fair portion of their goods to help the stricken. I am very proud of Hamilton when he cries: 'My heart bleeds but I have no power to solace. O ye, who revel in affluence, see the afflictions of humanity and bestow your superfluity to ease them.' Here Hamilton the man speaks, the future financial genius of a new nation. Tax the rich to succor the poor.

"But it's in the final paragraph that he really delights me. This lad of fifteen feels obliged to pass judgment on the governor of St. Croix, and we see the future politician displaying his capacity and willingness to intervene: 'Our general has issued several very salutary and humane regulations, and both in his publick and private measures, has shewn himself *the Man.*' There spoke the rigorous taskmaster of the early 1800s."

He ended his lecture with the information that Hamilton, as a result solely of having written this letter, was invited at the expense of older men who saw in him a touch of genius to come to their America, where he would receive a free education at a school in New Jersey and later at King's College in New York. With a flourish Professor Carpenter said: "So if you write good term papers, there's no telling what good things might happen," and his students applauded his bravura performance.

The story of Alexander Hamilton so inflamed Ranjit's imagination that for some days he moved about the pleasant campus of the university picturing himself at the heart of a hurricane whipping about Jamaica, and then as a colonel fighting alongside Lafayette and Kosciusko, and finally orating in Philadelphia at the Constitutional Convention and serving as the Minister for Finance who saved his fledgling nation.

But insistently in his daydreaming he came back to the famous Hurricane of 1772 and the boy Hamilton caught in the mighty whirl but still taking mental notes of what was happening, and the event became so vividly real that he dropped out of classes for a full week to compose a heroic poem of a hundred and sixty-eight twelve-syllable lines. When finished, he typed out three copies, delivering one to each of his professors, with the curt explanation: "I've been engaged. Please forgive my absence." And each of the three read his poem with the conviction that Ranjit had spent his arbitrary vacation working on ideas promulgated in his or her class:

TO ALEXANDER HAMILTON
STRUGGLING IN THE HURRICANE OF 1772

The hurricane that swept me from my island home
Was benedicted with no clever name like Bruce.
Its cognomen was Ridicule *or* Racial scorn,
Justice deferred, The death of hope *or* Poverty,
Those sinister arrangements that good nations make
To drive their favored sons to exile in strange lands . . .

The first fifty lines of his poem summarized the reasons why a man like Hamilton in his day, or Ranjit in his, would feel driven to emigrate; some of the reasons were fatuous, most were real and inescapable, and their impassioned recitation by this Indian lad from Trinidad demonstrated how much he had matured since leaving the relative calm of Michael Carmody's class at Queen's Own two years before.

The next sixty lines depicted the kind of Caribbean area that might have kept Hamilton at home, a utopian society in which the races and the social classes cooperated in managing their wealth in sugar, cotton and bananas without the necessity of calling upon Marxism to lead the way. And the last fifty-eight lines were sardonic explanations of why the necessary cooperation was not possible, not now, nor ever in the future.

In these closing lines he reviewed bitterly the poor performances of the leaders in the painful period of 1958–1961 when the British islands of the Caribbean came tantalizingly close to federation, only to be frustrated by the personal vanities of three men: Alexander Bustamante, the flamboyant Jamaican leader; Eric Williams, the vain and scholarly Trinidad spokesman; and the gentle old fellow from Barbados, Sir Grantley Adams, who accepted the prime ministership of a federation that no longer really existed, and who tried heroically but in vain to hold the fragments together. Ranjit's final lines were mournful:

> *The hurricane returns, the ship is driven far*
> *But who like Hamilton can find a fresh new land*
> *Which needs his talents and his vision of a world*
> *That could rebuild itself in discipline and hope?*

> *Today our exile is to lands worse than our own*
> *Where greed prevails, hate thrives, force rules,*
>   *and hope is flown.*

As Michael Carmody had done in Trinidad, Ranjit's three professors saw to it that his poem was read in various places, and recommended him for various fellowships. And then, just as in Hamilton's case, as if good actions as well as hurricanes repeat themselves, he received three offers of fellowships leading to the doctorate. And he had a choice of three different fields of specialization, depending upon which local professor had put in the recommendation to that particular university: Chicago wanted him for history, Iowa for writing, and Miami for sociology.

He oscillated among the three, inclining first this way, then another, but the first to be eliminated was the writing program, because he still felt that this was not his forte. Writing came easily to him, obviously, but not with the all-consuming force that he believed necessary to sustain a career in that calling. "I love words," he explained to his literature professor, who had arranged for the fellowship at Iowa, "but truly, I have no conviction," and from her long experience with Third World writing, she said in local lingo: "If you ain't got that fire in the gut, Ranjit, you ain't got nuttin', and she wished him well: "Maybe you have something even bigger, Ranjit. You have a burning integrity. Maybe that's what we need in the Caribbean more than anything else."

Now as his soul-awakening years at U.W.I. drew to a close in the final Trinity Term in the spring of 1973, with any decision regarding his future still floating aimlessly above the beautiful hills of Jamaica, he sought counsel from Norma Wellington: "What's to do? What would you do, Norma?" and they wandered over the low hills lying east of the campus, discussing her future and his. "I have this invitation to the best nursing school in the United States," she said, and he asked: "Why would they do that for a young woman from U.W.I.?" and she explained: "Because the American hospitals have found that girls from the Caribbean make the very best nurses in the world. Take away the Caribbean nurses, and half the hospitals in the eastern states would shut down." Then, aware of her own boastfulness, she added: "They want to train me for hospital administration. In Boston."

"Are you going to take it?"

"I really don't know. I'd not feel safe so far from home. Besides, there's that color problem in the States."

"Come on! You're as good-looking as Lena Horne. She's fought your battle for you."

"You always think in historico-sociologic terms, don't you."

"I do. I want to anticipate how the various mixes are going to work out."

"Dammit, Ranjit! You've got to make up your mind. Historical approach? Sociological?"

"I simply don't know."

With that melancholy kind of self-indulgence for which only the French word *tristesse* is appropriate, the two young people, a dark Hindu from Trinidad and a beautiful light-skinned girl from St. Vincent, strolled among the low hills that rimmed their university, each aware that with their graduation, even their ephemeral, barely stated friendship was ending. It would have been impossible for him to take a girl of color, no matter how lovely, back to his circle of Indian friends and family, especially since she was also an Anglican, while for her to take a Hindu, educated though he was, into her family would be equally unthinkable.

As they walked beneath tall trees, he asked with a sense of urgency: "Straight answer, Norma, if you were me, what would you do?" When she hesitated, he added: "You've known me for over a year."

"As between Chicago and Miami as universities, I'd take Chicago by a slight margin. Between them as cities, I'd choose Miami by a very wide margin."

"Why?" Ranjit asked, and her reply, which came in short clear sentences, revealed what many young islanders who had considered the subject believed: "Whether we approve or not, Miami is destined to be the ipso facto capital of the Caribbean. Our trade is with Miami, not with London. Our money comes from there. When islanders want first-class dental or medical service, we fly to Miami, we do our shopping there, and for our vacations we go there and not to Paris or London. To put it briefly, most of our workable ideas come from there, so if you have a chance to get your doctorate in Miami and don't grab it, you're not thinking straight." She hesitated, for what she had to say next was painful, especially for a young woman from an extremely British island like St. Vincent: "And most of all, I suppose, because inch by inch the Caribbean has to fall under American domination. Know the enemy. Go to Miami."

Abruptly she stopped walking, stood beside a tree, and looked at him: "It's awful, really, so goddamned awful."

"What do you mean?" Ranjit asked.

"I mean that you'll go to Miami, find a teaching job in the States and never come back to help Trinidad. And I'm worse, because I know better. I'll go to Boston, lead my class in nursing school, and get four job offers to help manage the best hospitals in the states. Maurice will work for DuPont in Delaware, never for some firm that needs him in Grenada." She looked away, and said softly: "The waste, the waste is so deplorable. Year by year the Caribbean is robbed of its best, and how in hell can a region survive if it allows that?"

When they returned to the campus, there was no sense of a tragic Romeo-and-Juliet parting; they were two sensible young people from the highest levels of Caribbean intelligence and deportment who understood that their two contrasting cultures would never mix, and there was no sense of loss about the impossibility. Norma appreciated the opportunity she'd had to probe the thinking of a Hindu, while Ranjit was grateful for this escape from the confinements imposed upon him in Trinidad, and when they parted back on the campus, they did not even kiss, for although Norma might have wanted to do so as her gesture of farewell, Ranjit was far too self-conscious.

Three days later he told her as they passed in the hall: "It's Miami," and he started to move on, but she reached out, grasped his arm, and said: "I'm really happy you chose Miami. It's where the action will center from here on. I envy you."

"Come down and see the place when it snows in Boston," he said, and she replied: "I just might do that."

But his departure from Jamaica was not destined to be as placid as that. Two days before he was scheduled to fly back to Trinidad before enrolling for a doctorate in sociology at the University of Miami, he was in the center of Kingston having a kind of farewell dinner at a low-class eating joint when a riot erupted. A gang of terrifying black men, with long streamers of braided hair reaching almost to their waists, roared through the streets shouting incomprehensible cries. Some carried machetes which they swung wildly. Others dashed up to any white tourists they spotted, shouting in their faces: "Go home, fat white pig!" and in the confusion Ranjit saw two white people, a man and a woman, fall to the street with blood gushing from their wounds.

At the height of the melee he thought of stepping forth to shout: "They've done nothing wrong," but he was deterred by fear of what the rampaging blacks with the terrifying visages might do to someone like him—a Hindu who had no privileged place in Jamaica and was disliked by many islanders, black or white.

So he stayed motionless at the door of the restaurant, trying to make himself invisible, and when the rioting passed to another part of town, the Jamaican students who had accompanied him to the restaurant explained: "They're bogus Rastafarians. Thugs frightening people." But next day when he flew homeward the Kingston paper carried bold headlines: FOUR SLAIN IN RASTA RIOTING.

Banarjee said years later: "When I got off the airplane in Miami for the fall semester, my lungs expanded, as if responding to the freedom in the air, the excitement. Those were the years when the free-wheeling Cuban émigrés were converting a sleepy playground for rich people into an international capital. Ah! It was so vital to be in Miami in those days."

Fortunately for Ranjit, when he deplaned at Miami a young black man who had sat next to him in the plane saw him casting about, not knowing where to go, and he called: "Hey, Jamaica! Looking for the university?" and when Ranjit nodded, he said: "Stay with me. My girlfriend has my car waiting." When they reached the sports car, Ranjit saw that the very attractive young woman waiting in the front seat was white, and he was surprised when she embraced his guide ardently, then slid over to let him take the wheel, saying gaily: "It's your car, mister." Then, turning back to face Ranjit, she explained: "When you can run the hundred in nine-four and catch a football over your left shoulder, admirers arrange for a car like this." Kissing the driver again, she added: "And Paul can do both."

Finally she asked: "And where are you headed?" and Ranjit replied: "Miami University."

Screaming in mock horror, she pointed at Ranjit and cried: "That's a no-no! You said the dirty words!" and she asked Paul to explain.

"Miami University is a nothing little place in Ohio. It produces football coaches. The University *of* Miami is down here in paradise, and it produces football players. And you get both arms broken if you ever call it by its old name, Suntan U."

"At the beginning," the girl added, "it was a school for rich kids who couldn't make it up North. All scuba diving and tennis. Scoffers dubbed it Suntan U. Now it's a great place. Fine professors, tough courses."

"What's your field?" Ranjit asked, surprised that she should be so knowledgeable, and she said: "History and philosophy. All A's and B's."

When Paul broke in to ask: "Where you gonna live, Jamaica?" Ranjit said: "I'm from Trinidad, and I haven't a clue," and the athlete explained: "Rule of thumb: Dixie Highway, otherwise known as U. S. 1, runs from Key West to the Canadian border in Maine. It divides the sheep from the goats, and you look like goats."

"Meaning?"

"If you have money and a car you live west of Dixie, on the campus, in a new dorm. If you have no money and no car, you huddle in a batch of crowded housing east of Dixie so you can walk to classes. I know a real great bunch of houses. Lots of Caribbean kids live there. You'd like it."

Ranjit found the university just as exciting as the city of Miami. It was in transition from having been Suntan U. to becoming a first-class center for studies in oceanography, medicine, law, music, Latin

American studies and general liberal arts. It was accumulating a major library and attracting energetic faculty members. It was not yet a Duke, but it was not an East Podunk State, either. And it was an ideal place for a bright student like Ranjit.

Although he was only eighteen when he began his studies for the doctorate, Ranjit was so naturally intelligent and so painstakingly organized that he sailed through his obligatory courses and quickly leaped headfirst into the most advanced work on campus. As before, at U.W.I., he had the advantage of working right through the calendar year—fall, winter, summer semesters—with no time out for vacations; students from the North groaned when the Miami summer approached with its fierce heat and wilting humidity, but Ranjit actually blossomed, as if his dark skin fended off the sun's rays. "It's simply that Miami in summer is so much cooler than Trinidad," he explained to other students, who stared at him, and one said: "Warmer than here? You must boil down there," and he said: "We do."

But the speed with which he was working and the approval he received from his professors were catapulting him toward a singular precipice over which foreign students often plunged. And Ranjit would have remained blissfully ignorant of the danger toward which he was galloping had he not been accosted one day in 1974 by a tall, cadaverous Ph.D. student from Pakistan who took him aside for a fatherly warning.

Mehmed Muhammad was in his mid-thirties, and for some time Ranjit had been vaguely aware of him puttering about the library, extremely deferential to anyone in authority and with a perpetual half-smile that could not be dislodged, regardless of the day's disaster. Ranjit supposed, from the man's name and origin, that he must be a Muslim Pakistani, and that was the case.

"I'm from Lahore. My late father was a moneylender in a small way." Speaking in a whispering, confidential voice, he added: "I had an uncle who paid for my first seven years at Miami. But he is dead now."

"You've been here seven years?"

"Yes. Let me see what immigration papers you have."

Ranjit produced an F-1 form he had acquired from the American Consulate in Trinidad that permitted him to visit America in a Non-Immigrant Status, meaning that he could not work or later count this time toward eligibility for citizenship. At the airport a Form I-94,

Duration of Status, had been stapled into his passport, warning Ranjit and any official who examined his credentials that his presence was valid only so long as his status as a student continued. And finally he had from the university an I-20 verifying that he was a legitimate student working for a degree, in his case a doctorate in sociology.

"Well, papers in good order, but, my friend, you're sitting on a time bomb."

"What do you mean?"

"Taken together, these papers mean only one thing. You're legally in the United States only so long as you maintain your student status. The minute that ends, out you go." He spoke in that beguiling Irish lilt that Indians and Muslims from the subcontinent had acquired centuries ago from the first teachers of English who came to India, a group of needy Irishmen; it was musical, Elizabethan in a way, and totally charming. "The problem is, my young friend, if you sprint through your courses the way you're going, in two years you'll have your doctorate, and then what? You lose your classification as a student and back you must go, to Trinidad." He shuddered. He had never seen Trinidad, knew little about it except that it was crowded with Hindus.

"But I want to go back," Ranjit said. "To work with my people." When he saw the look of astonishment on Muhammad's face, he asked naïvely: "Don't you want to go back to Pakistan?"

Mehmed looked at him as if he were an idiot child whose question was incomprehensible but forgivable. Very slowly he asked, while staring at his knuckles: "Who would go back to Pakistan if he could remain in the United States?"

"So why don't you stay here?" Ranjit asked, and Mehmed explained: "I want to. Ten thousand Pakistanis want to. But the minute I get my Ph.D., home I must go."

"Then why get it?" Ranjit asked, and he was astounded by the duplicity of Mehmed's answer: "I'm not going to get it. I'll complete all the course work, write about half my thesis, then switch my major to something else. Maybe your sociology."

"With your background, why not history?"

"Three years ago I was six weeks short of my Ph.D. in Asian history. Switched just in time to philosophy."

"You could stay here forever. Who pays for your registration, your room?"

"I have another uncle."

"Why do you do this?" and Mehmed replied: "Because sooner or later something will come up . . . a new law . . . an extension of privileges."

"Do you ever intend to go home?"

"America needs me, and believe me, Mr. Banarjee, when you're six weeks short of your Ph.D. and face the prospect of returning to Trinidad, you'll realize that America needs you, too."

Some weeks later, in the spring semester, he met Mehmed Muhammad again, and the Pakistani had good news: "I've been accepted in your department. Sociology of the Muslim-Hindu conflict. I could write my thesis this weekend if I had to."

"But how do you have the course work to qualify for such a switch?" and Mehmed said· "I spent seven years in the colleges and universities of Bombay. I have enough undergraduate courses to qualify me for graduate work in almost anything . . . even calculus."

In the summer of 1976, Ranjit interrupted his headlong drive for his Ph.D. to take an inexpensive Greyhound bus trip through the tier of American states fronting on Canada, and he was enraptured by Glacier National Park and the cool beauty of its mountains, but when a fellow traveler who enjoyed his company suggested they go into Canada to see that extension of the park which was supposed to be even more rugged, Ranjit drew back in visible fright.

"What's the matter?" the traveler asked, and Ranjit explained: "Once I get out of the States, I might have trouble getting back in."

"That makes sense. You being so dark, some horse's ass on the border would delight in holding you up. Well, it takes all kinds to make a world and the pluperfect horse's ass is never in short supply."

When they parted, Ranjit remained in the American half of the park, and as he trudged through the lower levels, looking up at the Rockies wearing their white bonnets, he realized for the first time how enamored of the United States he was becoming. He especially appreciated Miami and was now prepared to accept Norma Wellington's judgment. "It's the ipso facto capital of the Caribbean." He conceded that she had been correct when claiming that most of the workable ideas circulating in the Caribbean filtered through Miami, and he thought, somewhat ruefully: The Caribbean's a fine group of little islands. America's the real world. And now, for the first time, here among the towering Rockies, he actually contemplated remaining permanently in the States: Here's where the decisions will be made. Spain, England, France . . . all had their chance and failed to maintain supremacy. Now, for better or worse, it's America's turn. Then, cynically: It might last fifty years, or even seventy-five. After that? He shrugged.

When Ranjit returned to Miami in the fall, a new man determined to find a place for himself in America's academic life, he awakened to the fact that he was perilously close to obtaining his Ph.D. in sociology before he had nailed down an appointment to some American university faculty. His right to continue as a student imperiled, he hastily switched his field of concentration to history, and this time he did not take his required courses in a rush. He spread them out during four semesters and took long vacations in the summers, finding cheap excursions to places like Yellowstone and Grand Canyon. By spacing his work meticulously and spending cautiously the funds his grandfather sent him, he felt sure of at least three more years of student eligibility.

It was in a barbershop on Dixie Highway that his life both as a student and a human being took a dramatic turn in 1981. Having managed to delay his doctorate in history, he had slipped into the gratifying routine of the scholar, pecking away in the library, drafting a learned paper now and then, and serving as substitute without pay when his professors had to attend the yearly meetings of their specialty groups. It was quite obvious to him, and to many of his fellow students, that he knew far more about the subject matter of the various courses than the regular professors, and infinitely more of the subtle interrelationships between the various fields. Also, he had managed to soften his sharp Trinidadian pronunciation so that he was now completely understandable to his American students.

Ranjit had to wait while two Hispanic students had their interminable haircuts, and when he finally reached the chair the barber, a tall man who had migrated to Miami from somewhere in the North, was actually glad to see him. "Where you from, young feller? Some sunburnt country out there, I'm sure." When Ranjit said he was from Trinidad, the barber was delighted: "Isn't that where they have the lake of asphalt? My teacher in the sixth grade told us that, and us fellows who'd seen roads being built and knew what asphalt was thought she was a liar."

"That's Trinidad."

"Now, in Trinidad are they all your color?" From the way he

asked this, it was apparent that he had no prejudice. He was merely seeking friendly information.

"I'm a bit unusual. I'm a Hindu."

"Now wait! Aren't they from India? Cobras and Gandhi and all that?"

"You're right again." Ranjit was beginning to like the warmth and interest of this barber, but then the man said: "Well, I'm glad you're not another damned Cuban."

Ranjit froze, for life in his grandfather's Portugee Shop, where customers of all colors had to be treated with respect, had taught him tolerance. "I like Cubans," he said quietly.

"Hey there! So do I," the barber said with honest excitement. "They've remade Miami. Best thing that's happened to us is the Cubans."

"Then what did you mean?"

"Cubans as a group I like. Very much. But the individual Cuban gentleman sitting in my chair I dislike. Very much."

"What do you mean?" As Ranjit asked this question he was vaguely aware that another man had entered the barbershop to take his place in the line of ordinary chairs used by waiting customers, but what kind of man he was, Ranjit could not have said.

The barber resumed: "You come in here. A nice-looking Hindu. You say 'Elmer, give me a haircut,' and fifteen, twenty minutes later you get out of my chair and pay me. But you take a Cuban man, especially a young one, your age, more or less. He sits in my chair and spends maybe four minutes instructin' me in how to cut his hair. He wants this, he wants that." The barber mimicked a Cuban dialect; it was obvious that he had rehearsed his complaint against Cuban men.

Leaving Ranjit for a moment, he addressed the other men in the shop: "One of those Cuban fellows you just saw leavin' my shop, he instructed me for five, six minutes. It had to be just so. And when I showed him the mirror . . . stand back! It's always the same. 'Could you take a little off here? Just a little more off there? Taper the side just a touch.' He gives me ten more minutes of advice, and he stays in my chair at least thirty-five minutes. The last fifteen with the mirror in his hand, a little here, a little there. He doesn't want a haircut, he wants a masterpiece."

He stopped his imitation and addressed Ranjit in particular: "You know why he does this? Because to a Cuban young man of your age, the most important thing in the world is how he looks. Because he believes in the bottom of his heart, without the slightest doubt, that if I give him the world's perfect haircut at ten-thirty this morning, and he walks out smellin' great, some girl from the university driving a Cadillac convertible is goin' to see him, be swept off her feet, pull over to the curb, and ask sweetly: 'Hey. Can I drive you anywhere?' He'll get in the car, and his day, his entire life on earth will be changed for the better." With a flourish he finished Ranjit's haircut, allowed him a fleeting glance in the mirror, and said: "That's what one of my haircuts can do for a Cuban man. For a dumb slob like you, from God knows where, it's just a haircut. You were an ordinary jerk when you came in. You'll be an ordinary jerk when you leave," he said jokingly. "You expect no miracles."

As he brushed Ranjit with the whisk broom he said warmly: "But I will concede this. Fine-looking fellow like you, it would be nice if, when you stepped out there, a rich girl from the university came by in her Cadillac convertible, pulled over to the curb, and asked you to hop in. Because if you married her, you wouldn't have to go back to Trinidad when you finished your education here." Two of the listeners applauded as he concluded his monologue and he added: "Cubans in general, yes, yes! Cuban men in my chair, no, no!"

As Ranjit left the barbershop, heartened by the owner's jovial banter, the unknown man who had entered during his haircut rose and followed him out. The barber, unhappy at losing a customer, called: "Only two ahead of you," and as the door started to slam shut the man called in a husky, rasping voice far deeper than most: "I'll be back." And that was how Ranjit first encountered Gunter Hudak.

He was not a man to be taken lightly. About forty, with a hunched-up muscular torso, powerful-looking arms and a jowly dark face framed in very black hair that covered much of his forehead, he appeared to Ranjit to be a man accustomed to getting his own way.

Then came the rasping, ominous voice: "Could I speak with you a minute?"

In that first moment Ranjit knew that he ought to have nothing to do with this man, but he felt that he might be in greater danger if he rebuffed him, so in a weak voice he said: "Yes."

"Name's Gunter Hudak. Yours I know. Ranjit Banarjee, Jamaica and Trinidad."

"How could you know that?"

"It's my business. Whenever an alien graduate student working on a Ph.D. switches majors, people notice and they call me." He spoke in a conspiratorial tone, his accent indicating that he too might have been an alien.

"Mind if I walk with you, Ranjit?" Banarjee did mind, but he was afraid to admit it, so leechlike had the man become. "My business is to remind you how right that barber was when he told that story."

"I have nothing against Cubans."

"I mean the part where you would be saved from going back to Trinidad if some American girl fell in love with you and married you." Before Ranjit could protest, he rushed on: "She marries you. Perfectly legal. You acquire legal status as her immigrant husband. Now nobody can force you to leave the country. Six months she divorces you, and there you are, on your way to American citizenship." Maintaining hold of Ranjit's arm, he whispered: "All for a lousy five thousand dollars. American citizenship for life."

Ranjit brushed his hand away: "I'm not a fool," and in his rasping voice Hudak replied: "You are if you don't listen. Ask around the dorm. Ask how many young fellows like you have gained citizenship through marriage and divorce. The way I do it, foolproof." Before he left he thrust into Ranjit's pocket a slip of paper, then disappeared in the traffic along Dixie Highway. In the privacy of his room, Ranjit read the message: Gunter Hudak, 2119 San Diego, Coral Gables. It could be done for $4,000.

In the months that followed, Ranjit ran into Hudak about once every other week. On the occasions that Hudak spoke to him, always with the same low, rasping voice, he would say something ominous, like: "Good evening, Mr. Banarjee. I'm sure you heard about the three graduate students that were flown back to Iran last week. I-94 forms expired."

At the beginning of the semester in September 1981, his eighth year in Miami, Ranjit's attention was diverted from his own problems by a surprising announcement from his Pakistani fellow scholar, Mehmed Muhammad: "Wonderful news! The American government has just added mathematics teachers to the list of preferred occupations."

"What does that mean?"

"Well, the rule's been on the books for years. If you want to immigrate to the United States, no chance at all. Waiting list miles long.

But if you're a tailor and want to immigrate, the government says: 'Hooray! We need tailors,' and they embrace you. Actually seek you out, because in this country we don't produce enough tailors." Ranjit noticed that he was speaking of the United States as *we,* and that week Mehmed transferred his graduate credits to Georgia Tech, where he would start on a doctor of science degree. He told Ranjit: "With my credits from India, I'll apply for an accelerated course. Maybe one year I'll be admitted as a math teacher." And off he went.

When he was gone, Ranjit made cautious inquiries about the supposed exempt categories and learned that Mehmed was right. Tailors were needed, glassblowers for the making of scientific instruments and a whole mix of curious occupations, for none of which was he remotely qualified. That avenue to freedom was barred.

Refusing to think about Gunter Hudak's proposition, despite the fact that the man had lowered his price to three thousand, Ranjit spent the fall term in a kind of numbed euphoria. His work toward his history Ph.D. leaped ahead, and one of his essays on the Dutch experience with her Caribbean colonies had been accepted for publication in a learned journal in Amsterdam, causing an envious but generous young professor with his doctorate from Yale to say: "Banarjee, we ought to initiate a Doctor-of-Everything. You'd be the first to get one. How's the thesis coming?" and Ranjit was tempted to say: "It's safely slowed down, thank you."

Before Halloween, Mehmet was back on campus exhibiting the same excitement he had shown when leaving for Georgia Tech: "The most wonderful news, Ranjit. Mathematics was more difficult than I thought. Could have done it, of course, but not in one year. What do you think's happened?"

When Ranjit said: "Something promising, I'm sure," Mehmet rhapsodized: "More than promising. Salvation at hand, on a silver platter!"

"Tell me."

"The government has added a new category to its preferred occupations. Male nurses! Yes, a critical shortage. I've enrolled in the advanced program here on campus, and with my various credits . . . I've taken a lot of science in my day. They tell me I should get my certificate by June. And once I get that . . . bedpans, here I come!"

When Ranjit looked into the new ruling he found that male nurses really were in demand, but since he had no aptitude for such work, and he was getting periously close to his Ph.D. in history, he switched his field of concentration to philosophy, and just in time. Of course, this had been his major interest all the time, the study of mankind's permanent values and the ways in which people organize their thinking.

Relieved by the last-minute reprieve, he spent much of that year, 1981–1982, exploring the value systems of Miami, and as he came to understand the intricacies of the city, he gained added appreciation each day for the heroic adjustments it had made. A flood of Cubans had been digested with relative ease. They were now about to take over political control of the city and the state, too, no doubt, and some Anglos did not like this, but they were free to move to the expensive oceanfront communities to the north, like Palm Beach.

The crime rate disturbed him, and at one point as he was coming home from downtown Miami he laughed at himself: In Trinidad it irritated me when white people found it repugnant that Indians slashed people with knives, especially their wives, and here I am in Miami, finding it deplorable that Hispanic men so often kill their wives and their best friends with knives. *Plus ça change, plus c'est la même chose.* But he could never joke about the drug menace that threatened most aspects of life in southern Florida; he could not imagine willfully introducing into his body any destructive substance: nicotine, alcohol, addictive medicines, and certainly not drugs injected into the bloodstream.

So Miami had its dark side, but on balance it was a magical city, with its miles of alluring waterfront, its increasingly beautiful new high-rise buildings, and the permanent charm of Calle Ocho, as Eighth Street was now known, for here the full flavor of Caribbean life manifested itself in carnivals and celebrations and the daily expression of Hispanic life. "Not as good as the real carnival in Trinidad," he told friends, "but it will suffice."

But then the self-delusion had to stop. He was not at carnival in Miami; he was engaged in the hard-nosed task of getting a Ph.D. at the university, and there was talk in the school that graduate students who had been in residence beyond a reasonable number of years were going to be handed an ultimatum: "Finish your thesis and accept your degree, or get out," and he knew that the last two words really meant *get out of the country.* Since he had been on campus since 1973 and this was now 1984, he knew his days were numbered. Indeed, the university had already cracked down on Mehmed Muhammad, who had been in and out since 1967, a gaudy seventeen years, but he had once more evaded expulsion by enrolling in yet another exempted specialty, this time nursing. Mehmed was an enterprising fellow, for after having ingratiated himself with one of the staff doctors at the hospital where he had volunteered for preliminary nursing experience, he talked the man into lending him his car while the doctor was on duty, and invited Ranjit to share in one of the most civilized adventures Miami provided—watching ships head out to sea. The two men, with Mehmed at the wheel, started to drive the doctor's car smack into the turbulent traffic of Dixie Highway, one of the wildest city thoroughfares in America where young vacationers, irresponsible university students and anarchistic Cubans who thought a red light meant "Hurry up, and bang on through" drove at seventy miles per hour in the heart of populated districts.

"Do you know how to drive?" Ranjit asked, and Mehmed said: "I've watched others. I'm sure it's not too difficult."

"Have you a driver's license?"

"No, but who's going to stop us?" and with an aplomb that amazed Ranjit, the emaciated Pakistani headed right into the midst of Miami traffic, screamed Urdu curses at anyone who refused to get out of his way, and came miraculously to that magical spot where knowing spectators in parked cars assembled each Saturday afternoon at five to watch the great cruise ships of the various lines head out to sea on their way to visit the Caribbean islands.

There was no place in America that equaled this, for the channel was so unbelievably narrow that watchers on land could see clearly the faces lining the railings of the huge white ships as they steamed past, one after another in majestic line. Deep-throated ships' sirens blew, bands played, passengers cheered, spectators in the cars sounded their horns, and for the better part of an hour this unique parade continued. It enchanted Mehmed: "I could reach out and touch this next one," and Ranjit agreed that the illusion was startling.

"Ah, there they go!" Mehmed cried. "After I get my nursing certificate, I'll study to become a doctor, and then I'll apply for ship's doctor on this one coming along. 'Madame, I'm afraid your appendix has burst. Matter of life and death. I must operate immediately.' And the ship plunges this way and that, and maybe even the lights go out. Snip, snip. There goes the fatal appendix! Another life saved!"

Ranjit, despite his desire to remain in the United States, suffered a momentary pang of homesickness: "How I'd like to be aboard one of those ships. Jamaica, St. Vincent, Trinidad."

"Are the islands so lovely?"

"They are."

Impulsively, Mehmed leaped from the car, ran to the edge of the channel, and shouted to the last ship, only a few yards away in the channel: "Great ship! Stop! Stop! Take my friend Ranjit with you." And from the railing overhead passengers looked down and cheered the frantically waving Pakistani.

What Mehmed called remorseless destiny could no longer be avoided, so the mournful evening came, the time when Ranjit had to bite the bullet. Walking slowly along the streets east of Dixie Highway, he came at last to the address on the slip of paper he had kept in his wallet. Approaching 2119 San Diego from the opposite side of the street, he studied the ordinary two-storied house, imagined all sorts of ugly things happening inside, and was about to slink away when a firm hand grasped his right arm from behind: "Good evening, Mr. Banarjee. I've been waiting for you. Let's talk." It was Gunter Hudak.

He did not take Ranjit into his home, but maneuvered him down back streets to a Burger King restaurant on Maynada Street near the University of Miami. Without explaining his purpose in bringing Ranjit to this place, Hudak edged him into the line and trailed along as Ranjit approached the ordering counter, where a kindly woman in her late forties asked: "Yes? What will it be?" When Ranjit hesitated, Hudak said: "Whopper, fries and vanilla shake." For himself he ordered a smaller hamburger and a strawberry shake.

When they were perched on revolving stools bolted to the floor, Hudak said in his insinuating rasp: "My sister works here. Which one do you think she is?" and while Ranjit studied the group of girls putting out the prepared orders, one of them, perhaps at a signal from her brother, moved into a position from which she could clearly be seen by the customers.

As she stood in the clean, bright light she was a memorable young woman. Her age? No one could say. She was about the same height as Ranjit, had the slim figure of a nineteen-year-old, and an attractive face with regular features set in a frame of neat brown hair. But her face was disturbing as well as inviting, for it had an acquired hardness which could have belonged to a woman of forty; nevertheless, she was a young woman that any man would look at twice, and Ranjit did.

"I think that one," he said, and Hudak pressed his hand in congratulations: "You're right. She's the girl who wants to marry you," and now he flashed an open signal, whereupon his sister left her job of supervising the delivery of French fries to the pickup counter and walked primly and with purpose to where her brother sat with his new client. "Hello," she said as she approached Ranjit's stool, "I'm Molly," and she looked down at him with eyes that almost shouted: "My God! You're a sexy man!"

Ranjit, who had never before received such a glance, was too befuddled to speak, but she continued. "My brother tells me interesting things about you, Mr. Banarjee. It would not only be a pleasure, it would be very exciting. A Hindu prince. Elephants. Tigers. The Taj Mahal. It would be wonderful."

Awkwardly, Ranjit mumbled: "I'm far from a Hindu prince." Then he tried a clumsy joke: "And I'm far from India, too. A Portugee Shop in Trinidad."

"I'm sure that's a fine place," she said, and when the bell rang, indicating that fries were accumulating, she excused herself: "You know, around here people get fired if they don't do their job. Mr. Banarjee, I'd be honored." Since nothing had been said about what she would be doing to be so honored, Ranjit was left in the dark, but as soon as Gunter and he were back on the street, Hudak began to bore in: "Now, Banarjee, I know damned well you have to do something by the end of June. You can't switch majors again. And your thesis is finished. I know the girl who typed it. So this time you graduate, and it's back to good old Trinidad. Unless you marry Molly and follow the route we've discussed. It's foolproof, it's quick, and Molly and I can do our part for twenty-five hundred. Make up your mind. Now!"

He snapped out the command so forcefully that Ranjit was left with the feeling that he had no alternative, and in a floundering confusion he accepted the proposal. As soon as he agreed, Hudak became a tough, clever manager, for he took Ranjit to the Hudak home, introduced him to his parents, and said they would wait for Molly to come home from work. As soon as she appeared, her brother launched a training program: "Every word I say is crucial. From this night on, you two are to look and act as if you are in love. People we can later use as witnesses must see you together. Banarjee, you're to be in that Burger King five nights a week, mooning at her, walking her home. You are to stop under streetlights so that people can see you. Three times a week you come here for lunch. You go to the movies on Dixie Highway. You are deeply, passionately in love, and you show it."

He gave Ranjit additional instructions about laying a trail of paperwork at the university, meeting with his professors, a session with a religious counselor about the problems of a Hindu marrying a Catholic, two sessions with Molly's priest, the purchase of a ring with Molly present. Keep the dated receipt. He had, in his management of several former such marriages, acquired a great deal of experience, and he knew how to fabricate the evidence that the Banarjee-Hudak wedding was an act of pure love, and he knew how to direct his actors in creating and maintaining that illusion.

So for six weeks Ranjit lived in a double dream world. He allowed his doctorate in philosophy to gallop toward a successful conclusion and at the same time he conducted his courtship of Molly Hudak. The latter operation involved bizarre elements. Four or five nights a week he sat in the Burger King staring at her as if he loved her, and by the end of the second week he did, for she was a delectable lass and sometimes he imagined what joy it was going to be when they were husband and wife, if only briefly; he walked her home faithfully, but she never allowed him to kiss her; and when he produced the two thousand dollars on which they finally agreed, it was Gunter who grabbed it, not Molly, for as he explained: "Not even the faintest taint of money must touch you, Molly. They'll investigate every penny in your possession."

"Investigate?" Ranjit gasped, and Hudak explained: "Like you won't believe. They'll look into everything, like bloodhounds, but we know how to cover our tracks. From now on, you do as I say." He never said, as he must have been tempted to: "I know we can trust Molly. She's been down this road before. But you, you stupid Hindu, I'm worried whether you can stand up to it."

The awkward courtship ran its course, with Ranjit convincing spectators that he was not only in love, but gratified that a young woman so appealing should be interested in him; this required little acting, and the day came when the Hudaks, Ranjit Banarjee and Mehmed Muhammad as his scarecrow best man traipsed off to the courthouse in downtown Miami where a wedding was performed in a civil ceremony.

The rest of that day was a hell so awful that Ranjit in later years would try to believe it had never happened. The wedding couple reached the Hudak home at 2119 San Diego with considerable noise so that the neighbors could testify, if needed, that the newlyweds were indeed living together, and when the front door was closed, Gunter, in a roaring voice unlike any Ranjit had heard before—an ugly, hissing voice—laid down the rules.

"Banarjee, you have to live in this house till Molly files for divorce, but you sleep down in the cellar. You use the laundry tub for your bathroom. You do not eat with us, never, and if you ever so much as touch my sister, by God, I'll break both your legs above the knees. Do you understand?"

He had thrust his face so menacingly close to his terrified brother-in-law that Ranjit had to fall back a step, but Gunter pressed on: "Do you understand, you damned filthy Hindu? You touch my sister, I'll kill you."

Modern houses in Coral Gables have no cellars, for the land is so flat and near the ocean inlets that moisture would have filled their cellars with inches of brackish water. Since Hudak's old house had been built on a slight rise, the builder had risked a cellar, which was now musty and fetid. In it Gunter had arranged a wooden slab on which his mother had thrown two blankets to form an inadequate mattress, with another blanket for cover. There, without adequate ventilation, Ranjit would sleep. A rusted, zinc laundry tub with a cold-water spigot was his bath, and he was given a big tin can for a urinal and instructions to go to the bathroom elsewhere when he got the chance, and never, under any circumstances, to use the Hudaks'.

To complete his agony, he must appear at the Burger King at least five nights a week to walk his wife home after closing, and in some ways this was the cruelest part of his treatment, for he would perch on one of the stools, watch Molly as she performed her tasks, then wait for her to join him, a beautiful young woman, really, one whom any man could love, and walk home with her in silence, for she refused to speak with him. Once, in despair, as they walked along Dixie, with the university looming across the highway, he cried: "Molly, how did you ever get caught up in such a dirty racket?" but she refused to answer him. She must have informed her brother that her husband was growing difficult, for that night Gunter grabbed his brother-in-law by the throat and started banging his head against the living-room wall: "I warned you not ever to touch my sister," and Ranjit gasped: "I didn't," and Hudak stormed: "But you yelled at her. You ever do that again, I'll kill you."

Since this was the second time Gunter had made this threat, Ranjit had to take it seriously, and now when he went to sleep in the damp cellar he sprang awake at any unusual noise, for he feared, with reason, that the Hudaks might be coming down to murder him.

Ranjit was diverted from the horror in which he was living by the unexpected appearance in Miami of a trusted friend, who arrived, as friends often do, exactly when she was needed most, but also, as so often happens, at a decidedly embarrassing moment. It was the hospital administrator Norma Wellington, the clever woman from St. Vincent and U.W.I. She was now an American citizen, with her nursing degree from Boston and a responsible job in a medium-sized hospital in Chicago, and she had come to Miami as a member of a four-person committee to advise on the interrelationships among that city's many hospitals. Knowing that her friend Ranjit Banarjee was in residence, she tracked him down through the university and learned that he had a permanent carrel at the library in which he kept the stack of books he was currently using in pursuit of one of his various interests.

The little room had no phone, so a librarian led Norma to the door, and when it opened, revealing Ranjit seated among his piles of books, she cried in unaffected delight: "Ranjit, how wonderful." The passing years and the important position she occupied had matured her in ways he could not have anticipated, and when the librarian left and she sat alone with this man of about thirty, the differences between them became apparent. She was a mature adult who interacted each day with other adults as able as she, for she had accepted and absorbed the years as they came along, not fighting the inevitable, but not surrendering to it either. In Chicago her light-colored skin was neither a hindrance nor a help, but it had aided her to avoid slipping easily into romances with either her doctors or the male members of her staff. Norma Wellington was about as well adjusted as a young woman of twenty-nine from a tiny island like St. Vincent could be.

Ranjit, on the other hand, had always been a diffident fellow, withdrawn as a lad, shy when girls became important, and now totally disoriented because of his relationship with the horrible Hudaks. As he welcomed Norma he fumbled, and when he faced her he did not know how to begin to tell her about himself.

They talked casually for a while, and then, in subtle ways that neither of them could have explained, she dropped hints that her coming to Miami was not entirely for professional reasons. Her refreshing experiences in the free air of Chicago had eliminated most of the prejudices she had acquired on St. Vincent and Jamaica, and she no longer gave a whistle about the inherent differences between Hindus and Anglicans, between Indians and West Indians. At times, when she had been pressured by this man or that in Chicago, she had compared him with Ranjit Banarjee, always to Ranjit's advantage, for she remembered him as a scholar who honestly sought the truth, wherever it led, and who had a heart expansive enough to embrace the entire human race. He was a man of merit, and the more she had thought of him in those years of establishing herself, the more attractive he had become and the more she wanted to renew their acquaintanceship.

When her purpose was almost overtly exposed, Ranjit drew back in trembling fear: My God! She came here to see me. And she thought: I've come so far and he's still so shy, I really must say something. It was not clever what she said, but it was a statement from the heart of an extremely well-balanced young woman who had not endless years to waste: "I have so often wanted to see you, Ranjit. Those talks we had at U.W.I. . . . really, they were the best part of my education." When he said nothing, she forged ahead: "In those days I think you and I both thought that Hindu and Anglican . . . they were irreconcilable, but after working in Chicago . . ."

"Norma," he blurted out with his old ineptitude, "I'm married."

She hesitated just a moment, then quietly and adroitly called back her exploratory cavalry: "How wonderful, Ranjit! Could I invite the two of you to lunch?"

He did not have the courage to tell her of the disaster in which he was trapped, but the pathetic way in which he mumbled "Sorry, she's working" revealed so much that Norma thought: Poor Ranjit! Something terrible's happened. But she did not try to find out what. Instead, she retracted into her own shell and began to evaluate rather more favorably than before a young gynecologist from Iowa, but both she and Ranjit knew that a proposal of marriage had been offered and rejected.

Her trip to the university was not a complete waste however, because Ranjit, to escape from his deep embarrassment, thought of his Pakistani friend Mehmed Muhammad: "Norma! There's someone you must meet," and he sent a library assistant scurrying to the carrel which Mehmed had occupied for nineteen years. When the tall fellow came shuffling in wearing bedroom slippers, Ranjit cried: "Mehmed! A wonderful break for you. This is Dr. Norma Wellington, director of a major hospital in Chicago. Norma, this is my good and trusted friend Mehmed Muhammad, who is about to get his certification as a nurse . . . and he's going to be a very good one."

Norma and Mehmed hit it off, for within a few moments she had him catalogued: How often I've met you before. The perpetual scholar. Who knows how many years at the university? Unmarried, sympathetic, loving. Striving desperately to remain in America, and America needs you. To Mehmed she said: "How soon do you get your certification?" and he said: "June."

Ranjit, who was watching his two friends carefully, could not fail to see the kindly scorn in which Norma, a no-nonsense working girl, held Muhammad, the ineffectual wandering scholar, and as they spoke together a horrible thought assailed him: Dear God! Do people look at me that way? A quiet Hindu off to one side, offending no one, just puttering around year after year? His flow of rhetorical questions was broken when he heard Norma saying brightly: "Mr. Muhammad, we're always looking for reliable men like you," and Ranjit, to assist a friend who had helped him, chimed in: "You know, Norma, Mehmed's taken a lot of fine courses that don't show in his record," and she replied: "I'm sure."

That night Ranjit, his mind in a turmoil from Norma's visit, decided he simply could not go through the pretense of reporting to the Burger King to escort his wife home, but after starting twice to the Hudak house, he turned and went dutifully along Dixie Highway to his appointment, partly because he was afraid that Gunter might punch him in the head if he didn't but mostly because he was truly in love with Molly and wanted to be near her, no matter how badly she treated him.

He was about to enter the restaurant when he was confronted by a man who pushed him into the shadows so they could not be seen from the restaurant. He was a Hispanic—a dark, handsome fellow with a small mustache and darting eyes—perhaps thirty-five and somewhat taller than Ranjit. His English was good but marked with the delightful singing lilt that made even a menacing statement light and airy.

"Are you the Hindu they told me about?" he asked ominously.

"I am Indian, yes."

"So you're the one married to her this time?"

Although aware that his response might mean fearful trouble, Ranjit said weakly: "Yes."

"So you fell for it?" Ranjit was puzzled, and he recognized that this could be a trap. The man looked Cuban, but he could also be a paid informer for Immigration, so how to answer this question? He had no need to try to devise an adroit escape, for suddenly the man whipped out a long-bladed knife and held it to Ranjit's throat: "I'm her real husband. You touch her, I'll kill you for sure. Get your citizenship like the others. Get your divorce and get the hell out of Miami. Or . . ." and he pushed the knife closer.

"Who are you?" Ranjit asked when the knife was withdrawn, and the man said: "José Lopez, Nicaraguan. I got a good job, plenty money. And I want her back."

Terrified by the complexity of the jungle in which he was entrapped and convinced that his assailant meant it when he threatened death, Ranjit tried to warn Molly during the silent walk home: "He had a knife," but she said scornfully: "Oh, that one," and she would say no more, but when they reached the Hudak house, Ranjit warned Gunter: "Molly's real husband, the Nicaraguan, is making threats," and the mastermind of deception said: "We'd better move you out of here as fast as possible," so next morning Molly filed for divorce in the Miami courts on the grounds of cruelty.

His colleagues in the Miami office of the United States Immigration Service said of Larry Schwartz: "He may not be the brightest guy on our staff, but he does have that fantastic stomach." They referred to the exceptional skill Larry had in evaluating the paperwork in a marriage suspected of being a fraudulent attempt to bring an alien into the country: "I've seen him do it a dozen times. He studies the papers, spots the fraud, and looks up at me and says: 'Oooh! My stomach is as tight as a knot.' And nineteen times out of twenty, when he goes to work on the case he proves that it's . . . How does he phrase it? 'As phony as a Nevada mining certificate.' "

As Larry worked, he kept on his desk, facing him, a cardboard sign with three big numerals outlined in red: 31-323-41, and he used them to indoctrinate new agents assigned to the Miami office: "Whenever you're investigating a marriage that looks fraudulent, remember that thirty-one is the average number of other aliens he will be legally entitled to bring in once you let him in. So if he's illegal, do your country some good. Keep him out. The three twenty-three? That's the worst case in this office, and I was responsible. I had to give the green light to a guy who'd contracted a fake marriage. I knew it but I couldn't prove it. And that's how many he succeeded in slipping past us as he brought in his brothers and sisters and their wives and children till he had three hundred and twenty-three, an entire village."

But it was the last number, the 41, that caused the real knots in his stomach: "In this office, when we got our computer working, we identified eight women scattered around south Florida who had among them an average—an average, mind you—of forty-one fake marriages."

"How do you define *fake*?" agent in-training Joe Anderson asked, and Larry said: "Anytime an American woman who is a legal citizen of our country marries an alien man solely for the purpose of enabling him to get his Resident Alien Card, and without any intention of establishing an honest husband wife relationship . . . we label that a fake and take action."

"Why does she do it?" and Larry said: "Money. Going rate seems to be somewhere between five hundred dollars and five thousand dollars."

So when the clerk who had first spotted the probable fraud delivered to Schwartz the rather fat dossier on the Ranjit Banarjec-Molly Hudak marriage and pending divorce, Larry turned the papers with a practiced thumb and felt his stomach definitely tightening at several facts: "She's older than he is, and that's always a flag. But my God! She's nine years older. They're not only different religions, but she's a Catholic and he's a Hindu, and you can't get much further apart than that. Also, whenever you have a graduate student switching his major three times . . . What were his grades as an undergraduate? Almost straight A's? But of course it was probably one of those Mickey Mouse universities in the Caribbean. But you can be almost certain he's switching majors to *avoid* getting his Ph.D. How long's he been in graduate school—1973 through 1986? That's not an education, it's a career."

On and on he went through the papers until his stomach was so knotted that he marched in to his superior's office, tossed the dossier on the desk, and said: "Sam, it's as phony as a Nevada mining certificate." After a cursory look at the signals that Schwartz had marked, Sam said: "Go for it," and the probe was on.

Special agents on the trail of what they had good reason to suspect was a fraudulent marriage followed one of two traditional procedures, as Larry explained to newcomer Anderson: "Some prefer to drag the couple in, interrogate them, throw the fear of God into them, and trap them into disclosing the fraud. Not bad. Often works. But I prefer the second route. Leave the couple alone, but quietly check their behavior, their work habits, their religious attendance, the comments of their friends, everything. And you'd be surprised at the canvas you begin to paint with those individual brush strokes. By the time you're through, the word *Fraud* is written two feet high across your painting. Then you bring them in."

So in the summer of 1986, Larry Schwartz, thirty-four years old, and his assistant Joe Anderson, twenty-seven, began spending many hours in the vicinity of the university, Dixie Highway and the area in which Mr. and Mrs. Ranjit Banarjee claimed they were living. They were careful not to speak directly to any university officials lest they inadvertently alert Banarjee, who after all, was not really the target.

"It's not even the woman," Schwartz kept reminding Anderson, "even though she's probably pulled the trick three, four times." Clenching his fist, he hammered his desk: "It's the miserable pimp who arranges these deals. I want to get that swine." Then he relaxed and laughed: "As soon as I nail down for sure that it is that bastard Hudak . . ."

When from a distance he checked the Hudak house, a plain affair a few blocks from the university, he saw that the Indian did come and go, but Larry was more interested in another youngish man who seemed to have the run of the place, and he quietly checked with some of the neighbors: "I'm the census taker. How many live in your house? And in that house over there?"

"You mean where the Indian married the daughter? Five. Him, her, the parents and their son Gunt."

"Does Gunt have a steady job?"

"Never seems to keep one long."

When he and Anderson had made more than a dozen checks, finding no glaring discrepancies between the facts as he observed them and the documents which were supposed to support the marriage, Schwartz started dropping in at the Burger King where Molly worked, and the more he saw of her, the easier it was to believe the

Indian's claim that he had fallen in love with her while taking his supper at the fast-food place, for although her birth certificate proved that she was thirty-eight, she was an attractive, slim woman who could not have weighed more than a hundred and twelve. Besides, her green uniform and cocky little hat seemed to have been designed just to make her look attractive. She's no dog, Larry thought as he finished his hamburger and shake without looking at her again.

Larry Schwartz had been born in Boston and had worked the northern Immigration beats before winning an assignment to Florida, and he was so grateful for the hot weather and so fed up with the cold that he customarily wore a lightweight seersucker jacket, white shirt and no tie. This made him conspicuous in the Florida summer, but he was not comfortable without the coat, so when he had eaten at the Burger King three or four times, he failed to notice that while he was shadowing Molly, someone off to the side was shadowing him. It was Gunter Hudak, who had been alerted by his sister, who was far more clever than the men around her assumed. "Gunt, there's this guy in a seersucker jacket keeps coming in at night."

"Lots of people come in at night."

"But he's different."

However, when Gunter studied the stranger he concluded that he was just another customer who had no wife and frequented the Burger King because the salad bar was copious and inexpensive, and he convinced his sister to stop worrying about him.

Then, one evening when Schwartz and Gunter happened to be in the restaurant at the same time, a tall, good-looking Hispanic came in, ordered a hamburger, kept his eye on Molly, and waited till her stint ended. Then, as she came out in street clothes, he moved close, took her arm, and encouraged her to snuggle up, betraying in a dozen different gestures that they were lovers. Her brother had become alarmed the minute he saw José Lopez, the Nicaraguan to whom his sister was legally married, and immediately notified his gang, who had given Lopez strict orders, and a few dollars, to stay away from his wife until she received her divorce from the Hindu, and this bold intrusion imperiled their plans. But what had worried Hudak even more was what he saw happening inside the restaurant: the man in the seersucker suit was carefully watching the lovers and making notes. And as Schwartz left the Burger King, he was grabbed by two members of the Hudak gang, who punched him about the head, and one of the men snarled: "Now who in hell are you, mister?"

When he blurted out the answer he always gave: "Insurance adjuster," one of the thugs rifled his pockets while the other man held him. There was not a single card indicating that Larry was with Immigration, but there were two forms proving he was in insurance, so after giving him several more sound thumps they let him go. That night the same thugs waited till Molly reached home, intercepted her, took her for a drive in their car, and cursed her for having been seen with her husband. "The goddamned Indian's divorce papers ain't final yet."

She promised never to take such a chance again until the Immigration paperwork was completed, but two days later Mr. and Mrs. Ranjit Banarjee received a registered letter requiring them to report to the office of Investigator Larry Schwartz at Immigration headquarters, and that night Gunter Hudak began his intensive coaching.

"This is deadly serious," he said to the divorcing couple, and with the assistance of a member of his gang who had handled such situations in the past, he laid out his instructions: "You have filed for divorce, and that's what alerted the Feds. Our job is to prove that even though you're splitting now, you did enter into a legal marriage last year." His accomplice, an evil-looking man from the Gainesville area who had supervised numerous fake marriages for alien students at the University of Florida, warned: "You've got to make it sound real, and we're here to teach you how. Molly's been through this before, but you"—and he stared contemptuously at Ranjit—"can screw it up if you don't learn your lines." And from a grease-stained portfolio he produced a well-thumbed xerox of Title 8 of the Federal Criminal Code, Section 1325 (b), brutal in its clarity and threat:

> *Marriage Fraud:* Any individual who knowingly enters into a marriage for the purpose of evading any provision of the Immigration laws shall be imprisoned for not more than 5 years or fined not more than $250,000 or both.

When Ranjit realized he might be subject to a quarter-of-a-milliondollar fine, he cried pathetically: "Why did I ever get mixed up . . . ?" but he was not allowed to finish, for Gunter struck him across the lips and growled: "Shut up, you damned fool. You asked to do this. You paid me money to arrange it."

When Ranjit tried to claim ignorance of the law, Gunter hit him again and said: "You have to protect yourself, but you also have to protect your wife. Even more, you have to protect me. And if you make one mistake, you filthy Hindu, you are dead, because my neck is on the line."

Satisfied that Ranjit was properly impressed by the gravity of the situation, he became conciliatory: "We're going to be all right. We've been through this before and we know all the cons to beat the rap." He told them that Schwartz, whoever he was and "ten to one he's the guy in the seersucker," would interrogate them separately, Molly in one room, Ranjit in the other, "and we've learned just about what questions he'll ask to trap you. So memorize these answers." And from a paper his gang had used when preparing for past interrogations, he hammered into their heads the answers they must both give when describing their happy marriage.

"Did you sleep in the same bed? . . . Yes."

"Who slept on the right-hand side, looking down from the head board? . . . You," and he indicated Ranjit.

"Who went to bed first?" Again Ranjit.

"Did you use the same bathroom? . . . Yes. And I want Ranjit's toothbrush and shaving things in there tonight."

"How many people had dinner at the table, most nights? Five. Because he probably knows I live here."

"How many went to church on Sunday? Where?"

He drilled them on about sixty questions with which interrogators tried to trick couples they suspected of fraud, and when he felt that his sister and her Indian had their answers pat, he turned to the matter of the money.

"Did you give her any money?" he roared at Ranjit, who fumbled. "Listen, damn you! This Schwartz could be very rough. He's got a million tricks. Now, did you give her any money? The answer is No! No! No!"

"Did you give her a wedding ring? Yes! Yes! Yes! Where is it now? And you both say that she hocked it when we needed money for a suit for you—you damned dumb Indian." And he gave his sister a pawnbroker's receipt with an appropriate date. "It's effective if you cry when you say it, Molly, and you must look very ashamed, Hindu."

When he felt they could defend themselves he allowed them to go into Miami to face their ordeal with this Schwartz, whoever he was, and as soon as Molly entered his office she noticed the seersucker coat hanging on a rack, and Schwartz noticed that she noticed, so they started even, but not quite, because he did not separate them for the traditional private grilling her brother had anticipated. Instead, he sat them in comfortable chairs, then called out for Joe Anderson to come in.

"This is my man Joe. Now, Joe, I want you to tell these good people what you did this morning the minute you were sure that these two and her brother Gunter had left the house at 2119 San Diego in Coral Gables, not far from the university."

Joe, a hefty fellow who looked capable of defending himself if he stumbled into trouble, said: "I went to the front door, knocked, and showed the woman who answered the door this court order." He showed them the document, a search-and-seize order covering the premises at 2119 San Diego.

"And then what?" Schwartz asked, and Joe said: "I searched the place, as you directed."

"You mean the whole house?" and Joe said: "No, just the cellar, like you said."

The Banarjees gasped, Ranjit more than Molly, for when Schwartz said: "Tell them what you found, Joe," the latter went into another room and returned with the entire bed on which Ranjit had been sleeping since his marriage.

Then, with remorseless probing, Schwartz hammered at the now-confused couple and all of Gunter's careful coaching flew out the window, for Schwartz did not ask one of the anticipated questions. When he had them hopelessly bewildered and practically admitting that their marriage had been a fraud, he signaled Joe, who now brought in brother Gunter and one of the men who had participated in the assault on him, and from an entirely different set of papers he read the results of a longtime investigation of the racket that the Hudak family had been running.

Icily he ticked off details of the three earlier marriages Molly had contracted, the amounts of money exchanged and the disposition of the cases against the unfortunate aliens who had been involved. When the irrefutable facts were laid out, he told Gunter and his thug: "Don't ever slug a special agent in the mouth. There are harsh laws against that. It cost me three hundred and twenty dollars to get my teeth fixed. It's going to cost you and your buddy about fifteen years," and Gunter was led away by two policemen.

But even when Schwartz was satisfied that his case against the Hudaks was so tight that they would surely go to jail in a later trial, he wasn't so sure about Molly. "Look," he told his team, "since we deported her three illegal husbands, the only one we have to testify against her is her husband, who we know won't say a word."

"We have the Hindu," Joe said, but Schwartz cautioned: "That little fellow is starry-eyed. He still loves her . . . would never say a word against her."

Joe protested: "Boss, consider what she did to him. Never allowed him to kiss her. Made him sleep in the cellar. Had her brother beat him up at least twice. Mark my words, Banarjee will make her burn."

"I'm not so sure," Schwartz said, for his stomach was sending messages, and when Ranjit was summoned to a hearing two weeks later, he refused to testify against the woman he had considered his real wife.

"Dr. Banarjee," the Federal District judge said, "I want you to stand over here so we can talk, man to man." Ranjit stood before the bench, a frail Hindu in a JCPenney suit that didn't quite fit, and awaited the questions.

"Do you still claim that yours was a marriage for love, not money?"

"I do."

"And do you still love your wife?"

"I do."

"And if I order you to be deported, do you wish to be returned to Trinidad?"

"I do."

"You will be removed this day to the waiting area at the Krome Avenue Detention Center, from which, two days hence, you will be flown to the airport at Port of Spain, Trinidad. You may approach the bench." When Ranjit stood before him, he said so that others could not hear: "You seem a decent sort. I'm sorry you've treated the United States poorly and vice versa."

In October 1986 a disconsolate Ranjit Banarjee, his marriage having been annulled because of fraud, flew out of the United States in a dull, aching trance. As he took his seat in the British West Indies plane to Trinidad, the stewardess handed him a Miami newspaper with the screaming headline JEALOUS NICARAGUAN LOVER MURDERS BEAUTIFUL WAITRESS. There were the photographs, some grisly with blood, some taken years ago when Molly graduated from high school and was quite lovely. On the inside pages were two photographs of her husband but none of Gunter Hudak, the cause of the tragedy.

Fifteen, twenty times during the flight Ranjit reopened the paper to study the front page and pursue the story on the inside, and as the plane approached Port of Spain he asked the stewardess if he could please have the papers that the other passengers were leaving on their seats, and she helped him collect some. He folded them reverently, for they contained the only photographs he would ever have of a woman whom he had, in his hesitant way, loved.

In Trinidad his friends, knowing of his arrest but not of Molly's murder, received him with tears of gratitude over his having escaped a prison sentence in America. He had a full-fledged doctorate in philosophy from the University of Miami, but there were no openings at the main campus of the University of the West Indies, nor in its Trinidad branch, and his deportation from the States prevented him from ever returning there for a job. The local colleges, high schools really, judged him to be overqualified for their needs, so after sitting around in idleness for some months unable to find work of any kind, he flew back to Jamaica, asked that his credentials for graduate courses in history be transferred to the registrar at U.W.I., where he enrolled to take a second doctorate, this time in history, and although he seemed ill at ease when the course work started, for he was much older than the other students, he soon found his place and liked it.

He was referred to as Dr. Banarjee, and younger students who hoped to become scholars themselves deferred to him, but those in business or the sciences smiled at his overly courteous manner, his diffident way of avoiding direct confrontations, and his aroma, one might almost say, of bookishness.

Some students in the humanities who rather liked him were perplexed one day when, before the start of a class, he was handed a letter bearing quite a few stamps and readdressing labels. Ranjit took it, studied the writing on the front, and said clearly: "Well, well." But his hands trembled as he opened it, and when he finished reading, he remained erect in the sunlight, but all the bones seemed to melt within his body, and finally he accepted help from a younger student, who led him to a bench. There he sat, a tidy little fellow, determined not to weep despite the tears welling from his eyes.

The letter was from Norma Wellington, who informed him that she had recently married the head of surgery at her hospital in Chicago and was happily engaged in caring for his two children by a former wife, who had died of cancer. The letter rambled a bit, then got to the point: "Ranjit, I've heard of the disaster in Miami. Remember that those of us who knew you best love you for the trim little gentleman you are, and that I love you with particular warmth. Keep studying, and someday you'll share your great understanding with the world. Norma." There was a postscript: "Mehmed Muhammad is the sensation of our hospital and the entire staff is helping him get his citizenship."

When he returned to Trinidad with his second Ph.D. he frequented libraries, poked about old records of shipping firms that had imported slaves, and created a bit of stir when it became known that several different universities in Great Britain had inquired about hiring him as professor. He was interested, certainly, and three times he went through the hideous British ritual called "the short leet" in which the university announced the three or four finalists who were being considered for an appointment. Photographs of the scholars appeared in the newspapers of the university city, of course, and were mailed off to the hometowns of the competitors, so that Trinidad papers could announce proudly: RANJIT BANARJEE ON THE SHORT LEET AT SALISBURY.

Sadly, he never won an appointment, but despite his repeated failures, his Indian friends in Port of Spain greeted him with extra deference: "You must be proud, Ranjit. Salisbury, no less," and he would reply jokingly: "I'm beginning to feel like those Indian scholars in Bombay and Calcutta who write passionate letters to the editor and sign them: 'Ranjit Banarjee, M.A. Oxon (Failed).' They had been enrolled at Oxford, had tried and had gained prestige even in failure." Ranjit's ability to mask his disappointments in jokes at his own expense imbedded him more securely in Trinidad as "our scholar."

The one man who was not fooled by Ranjit's apparent indifference was his old master Michael Carmody, who came to him after each announcement that the appointment had gone to someone else: "It must be galling to go through that experience, but take heart. I read the other day that the world has more than a thousand good universities. One of them will want a real scholar like you," but Ranjit replied: "Most of them are in the United States, and even if they did want me, I wouldn't be allowed to go there."

It was Carmody who secretly went from one wealthy Indian trader to the next, saying: "It's shameful the way Trinidad treats this splendid man. His cousin gives him a niggardly allowance even though the Portugee Shop should be his, and the poor fellow can hardly afford a new suit. I want you to arrange with your friends for him to have a decent sum each month. And I will launch the fund with this two hundred pounds. In years to come, you'll be proud of this man, a great intellect."

He also talked them into gathering a fund which enabled the U.W.I. to publish in respectable format a collection of Ranjit's academic essays, including his long poem on Alexander Hamilton and the hurricane and his seminal essay "Indians in Trinidad."

It was the circulation of these works which encouraged Yale University to invite him to publish through its prestigious Press his important full-length study *Prospect for the Caribbean*. Of course, the book earned no money, so Ranjit continued to live off the largesse of his family plus such funds as Carmody could quietly provide. And occasionally some older American couple would debark from a cruise ship for a one-day visit to Trinidad and inquire in the Portugee Shop: "Would it be possible, do you think, for us to meet your distinguished scholar Dr. Banarjee?" When the clerk said: "He lives quite close, I'll just ring him up," Ranjit would hurry down, greet the professor from Harvard or Indiana or San Diego, and lead the pair to the old Banarjee house built by his ancestors. There he would serve limeades and pistachio nuts and hold discourse with his fellow scholars.

XIV

THE RASTA MAN

PEOPLE WHO SAW HIM APPROACH GASPED, AND ONE WOMAN stood stock-still and cried aloud: "Oh my God!" All moved aside to give him free passage, and well they might, for none had ever seen anything like him on All Saints Island.

He was about twenty-five years old, six feet two inches tall and thin as the legs of a stork. His clothes were sensational: on his head a floppy gold and green tam, on his feet big leather flats, like those of a Roman centurion, with thongs winding up his pant legs, which were a hideous purple, all emphasized by a very loose T-shirt bearing a likeness of Haile Selassie and, in bold, well-printed letters, three phrases: I-MAN RASTA, DEATH TO POPE and HELL DESTRUCTION AMERICA.

But what made him look really wild and fierce was his hair, for it had been neither cut nor combed during the past five or six years. Natural tangling, assisted by plasterings of mud, oil and chemicals, had caused it to fall in long matted strands, which had been separated and plaited into two- and three-foot lengths that fell almost to his waist like writhing vipers. By this device he had converted himself into a male Medusa, whose frightening appearance was magnified by a heavy, untrimmed beard, equally matted. In addition to all this, he had a fierce, penetrating gaze and very white, big teeth that gleamed through his half-open mouth. He looked terrifying.

Inside the All Saints airport he took from his only piece of luggage, a big shapeless canvas sack, his passport, which read: RAS-NEGUS GRIMBLE. BORN 1956, COCKPIT TOWN, JAMAICA. And as soon as an Immigration official saw this, he slipped into a back room to telephone the commissioner of police in Bristol Town: "Colonel Wrentham, a Jamaican Rastafarian has just landed. Papers in order. Headed your way on the airport bus."

Passengers carefully avoided the man as they took their seats, repulsed by his savage appearance and fetid smell, but once the bus started north along the beautiful shoreline with its constant view of the Caribbean, they attended more to the unparalleled landscape than to their Gorgon-like companion. He seemed not to realize that he had frightened most of them, and at one point he leaned across the aisle, looked straight at two middle-aged women from Miami, and gave them one of the warmest smiles they had ever seen—all flashing eyes and dazzling white teeth: "Sistas, I-man nebber see ocean like dat."

Although they could not fathom his words, they were encouraged by his friendly tone, and one of them asked: "Why do you do that to your hair?" and he replied, as if he had expected their question: "Dreadlocks." Indeed, his strings of hair were known in Jamaica as *dreads,* but again the word had no meaning for the women, who now asked: "Are you a preacher?" to which he replied: "I-man be servant Jah, name belong me Negus, same Ras-Tafari, King Ithiop, Lord Almighty, Lion Judah, Ruler all Afrika, Savior World, Death to Pope."

This was such a fusillade of ideas that the women could do no more than stare at the young man, but their curiosity had been aroused, and he was proving so congenial that they were emboldened to point to the messages on his shirt and ask: "Why do you want to kill the pope?" and he said, almost gently: "He-&-he Great Babylon, must be die, all men free."

"But why do you want to Hell Destruction America?" and he explained something that was of extreme importance to him, his face becoming grave as he said in a low, confidential voice: "America Great Babylon, Great Whore of World, Bible say so," and from the canvas sack that carried all his goods he produced a Bible, which he turned expertly to Revelation 14:8, reading in an apocalyptic voice which could be heard through the bus: " 'Babylon is fallen, is fallen, that great city, because she made all nations drink of the wine of the wrath of her fornication.' "

The words seemed to intoxicate him, and he got up, stalking through the bus, pointing at white people, and shouting in a demonic voice: "Pope be Babylon, America be Great Babylon, police, sheriff, judge be Babylon the Whore. All be destroyed Marcus Garvey Great Emperor Haile Selassie. Afrika rule all de world. Negus say so. I-&-I perish."

He seemed almost demented as he preached from his Revelation text, but having made his point about the destruction of the pope, America and the white race, he returned to his seat, leaned once more across the aisle, and whispered, with a smile so winning that it once again charmed the two women who a moment before had been terrified: "Sistas, Emperor Selassie, King of Judah, I-man save good people."

When the bus came to a halt in Bristol Town, the driver managed rather clumsily to obstruct any exit of passengers until the island's black commissioner of police, Colonel Thomas Wrentham, had time to leave his office and walk casually past the bus as if he had no interest in it whatever. But when Grimble descended with a half coconut shell dangling by a cord from his waist, a homemade lute under his arm and his neck in his hand, Colonel Wrentham positioned himself in such a way that the self-proclaimed Rastafarian had to pass near him.

"Hullo," the police officer said easily. "What brings you to All Saints?"

"I-man go here, go there, Jah direct."

"You have friends on the island?"

The newcomer, shaking his matted reptilian locks, smiled as if to embrace all the people on the island, and said: "I-&-I who love Jah, my friends."

"Good," Wrentham said, nodding to the young stranger as if the entire island welcomed him, but as soon as the Rastafarian had disappeared toward the little jungle of cheap waterfront shacks, he hurried back to his office, where he made several rushed telephone calls: "Tom, cable Jamaica. Ask them to send full details. Ras-Negus Grimble, age twenty-five, Cockpit Town." To a schoolteacher he said: "Can you come down to the police office right away? No, you're not in trouble, but I may be." And to the Church of England minister he said: "Canon Tarleton, could I borrow your wisdom and counsel for about an hour?"

When the teacher, the radioman and the minister assembled, the first a black islander, the other two white Englishmen, Wrentham started speaking without the usual courtesies: "I've got two problems on my hands, and I need your help for answers. What is your explanation of a Rastafarian? And how do I get rid of the one that just landed at the airport?"

"Is he from Jamaica?" the teacher asked.

"Yes. And he has a valid ticket on to Trinidad, I called the airline. It's an open date, so we may have him for some time."

The clergyman asked: "Is there any way you can move him on? I mean, off the island? We've learned that men like him always generate trouble."

For the moment Wrentham evaded the suggestion that the man be deported, for he did not wish to embroil the government in drawn-out legal maneuverings unless he had no choice. To gain time, he asked the schoolteacher: "They tell me that when you studied at the university you dug pretty deep into this Rastafarianism. Tell us how the damned thing got started."

"Simple, if I'm allowed to skip the nuances. In the 1920s a Jamaican black, Marcus Garvey, appeared as a kind of John the Baptist talking about the revival of the black race, the return of blacks to Africa and the impending triumph of Africa over all the white nations. Heady stuff. He went to America, got hold of a ship illegally and proposed sending all blacks back to Africa. Landed in the penitentiary for fraud . . . set black minds afire. My grandfather believed every word Garvey said, tried to lead a contingent of blacks back to Yoruba lands. He wound up in jail, too."

The commissioner nodded, then asked: "Where does Haile Selassie enter the picture? Wasn't he the emperor of Abyssinia?"

"Yes," the clergyman said. "Jamaicans call it by its Biblical name, Ethiopia. For some reason that's never been explained, except that the Bible is full of references to Ethiopia and one to the Lion of Judah, the emperor's appellation. . . . Anyway, the blacks in Jamaica generated the fantastic idea that Haile Selassie was the latest reincarnation of God. Jah is the name they use . . ."

"Haile Selassie is God?" the perplexed commissioner asked.

The clergyman hesitated: "I guess those who cannot read believe Selassie to be God. The more sophisticated hold him to be more like Jesus or Muhammad or Mary Baker Eddy, a favored recipient of holy power. But all believe that he's somehow a form of Jah who will lead blacks to world power."

"But Selassie's dead," Wrentham protested, and as soon as he uttered the words he looked appealingly to the others: "He did die, didn't he?"

"Yes," the teacher said. "About six years ago."

"Then why are these people so convinced that he will save them?"

His question, which he meant to be rhetorical, evoked a reply from the Church of England man: "Christians believe that Jesus long dead will do the same for them, and Muslims believe that Muhammad, dead well over a thousand years, will protect them. And I would think that Mormons and Christian Scientists have similar beliefs." Realizing that his words might seem blasphemous, he coughed and concluded rather lamely: "So the Rastafarians with their Negus . . ."

"What's that word mean?" Wrentham asked. "This young fellow calls himself Ras Negus Grimble."

The schoolteacher answered: "Means *king*. Selassie is often called simply Negus or The Negus." But then the clergyman resumed command of the discussion: "The Rastafarian movement is bewildering to some, comical to others, but to many of us in these islands it is deadly serious for several reasons. It preaches that blacks will one day take over the world and rectify old injustices to their race. It teaches that the pope must be destroyed."

"Why?"

"They say he represents and therefore commands the world power that oppressed them brutally in slavery days and more subtly now. And of course, the United States as the center of visible power in this part of the world—radio, television, autos, surplus foodstuffs—it too must be destroyed. Now, those targets are rather exotic, and the Rastas can't do much about them, but when they get to fooling around with their favorite anathema, Great Babylon, that's when you get into big trouble. For they have proclaimed that in addition to the pope and America, the police in the islands are Great Babylon which the Bible says must be destroyed."

They sat quietly for a while as each man recalled reports of incidents throughout the Caribbean in which black men, their minds addled by Babylon, had attacked individual policemen, or stations, or town halls, or other symbols of repressive power. Finally, Commissioner Wrentham asked: "What should our policy be? On this particular island, when so far as I know we have only this one visiting Rastafarian?"

The radioman, who had been silent up to now, said bluntly: "You can expect trouble. I've been in contact with men on other islands and they tell me the Rastas are a bad lot."

Colonel Wrentham was obviously perplexed: "Maybe I'd better seek him out tomorrow and order him off the island."

"Not too fast," the schoolteacher warned. "If he hasn't done anything wrong, he could sue us . . . and he would."

"What you'd better do," the clergyman said, "is consult the island's legal counsel." Then he added: "But in the meantime I'd watch the man closely."

"Thank you, gentlemen," the commissioner said graciously, but when they were gone he told his sergeant: "They didn't give me much usable advice."

Alone in his office, he telephoned the prime minister's legal adviser, who lit all kinds of signal fires: "Now look here, Wrentham! Last thing we want on this island is any kind of religious trouble. Don't, for God's sake, make a martyr of this Rasta. Hands off!"

"Can I keep him under close surveillance?"

"From a distance, yes. But religious dislocations we do not need. Be very careful."

When Commissioner Wrentham turned his police headquarters over to the two night men, he walked homeward with only a vague program for dealing with this Rastafarian: Treat him decently, but get him off the island.

Conforming to his nightly custom, he walked home by a path that took him past his father's famous café, the Waterloo, and he checked to see how his son, who now owned the place, was doing. When he became commissioner he had felt obligated to get rid of what was essentially a saloon, and Lincoln, thirty years old and named after the Liberator, had improved the place in many ways, making it even more attractive to tourists than it had been before. Thomas chuckled, recalling the troubles Black Bart had suffered on the island: He may have had no Rastafarian. They didn't exist in his day. But he sure had something worse . . . The story was part of family lore. Bart's own cousin, Governor Lord Basil Wrentham, was a bosom friend of the Germans. But Bart, helped by a clever little Englishman named Leckey, managed to tie Lord Basil's tail in a knot. The noble lord was too stupid ever to know what hit him.

The commissioner did not stop at the Waterloo, but through the window of the brightly lit café, he saw his son waving to him to let him know that all was well, and Wrentham waved back in acknowledgment.

When he reached home, a small house occupied by his three forebears for almost a century, he was disappointed to find that his daughter, Sally, a young woman of twenty-two, would not be sharing supper with him, for although he prized the efficient manner in which his son had taken charge of the café, he had always had a special affection for Sally. She was intelligent, had done so well in school that she could have gone to Oxford or Cambridge had she cared to spend the years in England, and possessed the lyric beauty of movement and appearance which made certain young women of the islands so compelling. She was, thought her father, a person of special merit, and he had begun to speculate on whom she might marry.

Her position in the prime minister's office, her good salary and her lively interest in political matters made her attractive to many young men; indeed, her would-be suitors ran the entire gamut, from a white Englishman who had come to All Saints to study its economy, through several shades of brown both lighter and darker than herself, and on to one very black chap who might prove the best of the lot. Even though the fact that color distinctions were now of diminished importance on All Saints, the commissioner, despite his modernism, was quietly proud of the fact that Sally was several shades lighter than he or his father. He would be interested to watch whom she settled upon, but he felt no concern, because almost anyone from the field, as he called the young fellows who buzzed around her, would be acceptable.

The caste system that had prevailed before World War II, when there were rigid delineations—aristocracy, good county families, all other whites, light-skinned browns, dark-skinned browns and blacks—had quietly evaporated with independence. London no longer sent out members of the nobility to serve as governors general, so this class had been eliminated. Families with county connections back in England still existed but played a much smaller role in social life, so the three former distinctions among the whites had coalesced into one: white.

It was practically the same with that difficult-to-categorize class, the browns. There were almost no situations in which light-skinned browns could lord it over dark-skinned ones, so the two phrases were rarely heard. On All Saints it was simply white, brown, black, and a visitor who knew nothing of past distinctions would be hard put to say, merely from watching the people of the island in action, which category was atop the heap. The governor general was still appointed by the queen, but now he was a native of All Saints and very black indeed. The prime minister, a new official, was elected and was, in the old determination, dark brown, while the third in command, the commissioner of police, was light.

"Where's Sally?" Wrentham asked the older woman who had looked after his house since the death of his wife, and she responded: "She say: 'Meetin' on de black agenda.'"

Thomas laughed, for in recent months Sally had been caught up with a feisty group of young people who were discussing a problem that concerned thoughtful people on all the Caribbean islands except Cuba: "How should the principle of negritude, the spiritual essence of being black, modify personal and political life in the Caribbean?"

The commissioner approved of his daughter's participation in these discussions, because both he and his father, Black Bart, had been resolute in their belief in black power and forthright in their application of it. The blacks and browns of All Saints still talked admiringly of the manner in which Bart had solved the problem of The Club, that ultra-exclusive gathering spot on the hill in back of Gommint House. Prior to 1957, when a restricted form of self-government was introduced, only whites were permitted to enter those sacred portals, and this exclusivity was not only understood by everyone but also generally approved: "Each man to his own group."

But when real self-government came in 1964, with a white governor general still representing the queen but a locally elected black prime minister in effectual charge, Black Bart decided that a change was in order. So, one April evening, as the remaining white establishment was gathering at The Club to discuss the latest improprieties of the newly positioned brown and black officeholders, Bart Wrentham, by then police chief of the island, rode up the hill in his old Chevrolet, walked ceremoniously into the meeting room, and announced in respectful tones: "I'm applying for membership." Some of the older members gasped at the insolence, but others clapped hands and half a dozen of the younger members invited Bart to the bar for a drink. The social revolution which so many on All Saints had feared occurred without one ugly word spoken or shouted in public.

As the first non-white member of The Club, Bart paid his dues regularly but never imposed himself on the membership except in those cases when as police chief he had to entertain dignitaries from other islands. Then he appeared neatly dressed in his quasimilitary uniform, introduced his guests to any who were in the bar, and had dinner quietly in a corner where he could discuss Caribbean problems in carefully modulated tones.

At Bart's death, The Club sent an official delegation of seven to his funeral, and in the elegies they spoke of him proudly as their first member of color and a man who had served both The Club and the island with distinction. His son Thomas, the present police chief, now called Commissioner, inherited his sensible attitudes toward relations between the races, and had passed them on to his children. Two days earlier, when his daughter had informed him that she planned to join the discussion group on negritude, he said: "Fine. Your grandfather wrestled with the problem when he lived in a Crown Colony with its rigid attitudes, and he taught me how to handle it in these years of independence. Your job is to be prepared for the future, for whatever changes are coming."

As Wrentham reflected on these matters while eating his supper alone, Sally was immersed in a tense meeting of her group, some sixteen of the brightest young officeholders, all brown or black, who were discussing the significance of a powerful book on the subject of negritude written by a fellow Caribbean, Frantz Fanon of Martinique. His great book, *Les Damnés de la Terre,* had been published in English under various titles, but the copy which the leader of tonight's discussion had acquired was called *The Wretched of the Earth,* and its mind-shattering call for social change had considerable application to black islands like All Saints.

But when the animated discussion was at its height a young brown woman named Laura Shaughnessy who worked in the governor general's office appeared belatedly, bringing with her the young white Englishman who had come out from London seven years ago as economic adviser to the island government. Some of the discussion group were disturbed that a white official had been inserted into their group, for they feared his presence might inhibit the free flow of ideas, but the young woman who had brought him allayed their fears: "This is Harry Keeler. You've seen him about the halls. I invited him because he had been a British official in Algiers during the troubles and witnessed the economic and social data on which Fanon based many of his concepts."

After that introduction, Keeler made a brief statement about his experiences in Algeria and Tunis during the anticolonial revolutions, and then submitted himself to questioning. He could see in the dark faces of his audience their intense interest in his generalizations, so he refused to water down or in any way soften his conclusions: "Negritude is a powerful unifying force when fighting to gain independence, but I doubt it provides much effective guidance when it comes to governing the territory you've won." When he was hammered on this conclusion, which most of his listeners did not want to hear, he stuck to his guns and reiterated his message that whereas Frantz Fanon would have been an admirable guide to browns and blacks of All Saints fifteen years ago, what they needed now was an understanding of how General Motors and Mitsubishi operated: "When your Caribbean islands rejected federation in 1962, I wept. It was your chance to build a viable union of all the big and little English-speaking islands, and you frittered it away. Problem now is to evolve some sensible alternative."

When this evoked a storm of comment, he listened attentively, made notes of the salient points, and then asked for the floor. He was careful to speak only as an economist and only on those matters about which he had acquired expert knowledge, but he ended forcefully: "I'm not sure you understand what I'm saying. We've allowed the discussion to become too adversarial. It shouldn't be that. Fifteen years ago on this island, I'd have been a follower of Frantz Fanon on one simple principle: 'It's high time!' You and I won that battle. I fought for it in an African country gaining its independence. But tonight it's an entirely different battle, and Frantz Fanon is too impractical to teach us about how to take our next steps."

His words were so judicious and so straightforward that when he finished, Sally Wrentham went up to him and said: "Mr. Keeler, you made great sense as a white man looking down from above. But how about us blacks who have to look up from below?" He noticed that although she could have been considered white in many societies he had known, she preferred to call herself black, a good sign in his opinion.

"Now wait a minute, Miss Wrentham. You're the police commissioner's daughter."

"I am."

"It seems to me," and he spoke with charming diffidence, as if he had no right to a strong opinion on something which concerned him intellectually and her emotionally, "that we must look neither from above or below, but from dead-eye level . . . at the reality." The idea was strong and expressed so cogently that Sally offered no response, so he added: "In the old days on All Saints men like me were up and blacks like you were down. Your question then would have been quite pertinent. But today I believe that on this island, there is no up or down . . . just level eyes sighting level horizons." With the fingers of his right hand he built an imaginary bridge from his level eyes to hers, and, gesturing, he touched her cheek . . . and an electric thrill passed between them.

On that evening throughout the world, as the sun drifted to sleep in the west, thousands of young unmarried men in a hundred different countries met socially in groups to talk with young unmarried women, and with reassuring frequency some man would see in a flash some woman of intelligence or understanding or sympathy or sheer attractiveness, and his breath would catch and he would find himself assailed by ideas which he had not entertained even ten minutes before, and everything would be changed.

"Your interest in these matters?" he began, and she stopped him: "My grandfather, Black Bart Wrentham they called him . . ."

"I know. He led the fight for independence. Sterling man I'm told."

"He really was. Struggled to build a profitable café, saloon if you will, and became the first police chief under independence. Powerful force, that one. Died Sir Bart Wrentham, because respect for his integrity reached even to London."

"You must be proud of being in that family."

"I am."

"And did you attend school in England?" The question had a chilling effect on Sally, for despite the best intention on Keeler's part when he asked it, the only interpretation she could give it was: Since you are obviously a first-class person, your parents must have saved enough money to send you to England for your education.

She was irritated and about to rebuke him, when the door to the meeting room burst open to admit two men. The first was about five feet six, very black, and well regarded on the island as a sensible master of bookkeeping techniques and budgetary controls, but on this night no one even greeted him, because in tow he had the Rastafarian from Jamaica with his frayed shirt proclaiming DEATH TO POPE, HELL DESTRUCTION AMERICA and his coconut shell clacking against his lute as he walked toward the group.

"This is my friend Ras-Negus Grimble," the accountant said, "with messages for us from Jamaica," and the parlor discussion of abstract negritude ceased, for here in the flesh was the epitome of one kind of real negritude.

Serene, his dreadlocks framing his bearded face, the newcomer flashed one of the most all-embracing smiles that Sally had ever seen, and said: "I Rasta Man come to help." His eyes swept about the room, and he added: "I-man come this I-land help I-&-I I-cover things to happen." When she, like all the other listeners, betrayed her inability to follow what he said, he lapsed into normal English, with a Jamaican lilt that was most agreeable: "I have come from Jamaica to help you discover and achieve whatever it is you think ought to happen."

"Who sent you?" someone asked, and Grimble lapsed into Rastafarian again: "I-man have vision. 'Seek out I-&-I belong All Saints bring I-vine help I-alogue.' I-man come."

"I think you better tell it straight," the questioner recommended, and the visitor complied: "I was I-rected, I mean directed, to come here and hold I-alogue with you."

"Do you mean *dialogue*?" a man in back asked, and with a big smile he replied: "Oh yes! I do."

"And what is your message?" a young woman asked, and after carefully placing his shell and lute on the floor, he pulled up a chair, sat gracefully upon it with his long thin legs wrapped around each other twice, a feat totally impossible for a fat man or for most of medium weight. Flashing once more his smile of embrace and forgiveness, he explained: "Rastafari is a belief in peace, in tranquillity, in love of all persons . . ."

"How about the pope?"

Without changing pace or expression, he concluded: ". . . except those of evil intent."

"We heard that in Jamaica, your people led riots, real violence."

Turning on his chair, he looked benignly at his accuser and said in low, gentle tones: "It was Babylon that abused us, never the other way."

"But don't you say that Babylon must be destroyed?"

"With love. The way Gandhi destroyed the Great Babylon that oppressed him."

Now Sally spoke: "Why do you say I so much—what does it mean?"

He turned almost a complete revolution on his chair, and for a long moment Grimble sat silent, twisting his legs tighter together and staring into Sally's eyes until she felt mesmerized by the floating beard, the green and gold beret and those dreadful snakelike braids reaching into his lap as he leaned forward. Then came the liquid, pacifying voice of a totally committed young man: "In Rastafari we use our own language. *I* is straight and tall and beautiful and strong and decent and clean. *You* is bent over and twisted and losing its way and ugly and straight in nothing. So the pure *I* is given to all human beings. I-man means me. If you were speaking, you would call yourself I-woman."

"But who is I-&-I?"

"You, those over there, all in this room, the whole world apart from me."

"I don't understand."

"So when Rasta Man want to say *you,* he do not separate himself from you. He mean that you and he are together, you and he and everyone else in this room, we are a team. So it has to be I-&-I, because in Rastafari all people are equal. You cannot exist without a part of him. Rasta Man cannot exist without all you people to help him fight his battles against darkness. It is I-&-I, always the immortal team."

Sally, shivering at the intensity of his reply, was relieved when another woman asked: "But I heard a lot of other *I*'s in what you said," and now he turned his searchlight gaze on her: "You must understand. We Rasta Men lead simple, pure lives. Only natural foods eaten from this coconut shell. No meat. Every cloth I wear must be handwoven of natural threads. Same with words. From any word with morally sinful elements or negative syllables, we knock out those elements and substitute I, which is clean and pure."

"How can a syllable be morally negative?"

Eagerly he leaned forward to explain this basic tenet of Rastafarianism: "Words with *ded,* like *dedicate,* mean dead. Life gone. Word must become I-dicate. Beautiful ideas like *divine* or *divide* one's goods, they have *die* in them. They have to be cleansed, become *I-vine* and *I-vide*."

"You mean you go right through the dictionary?"

"Yes, beautiful words like *sincere* and *sinews* must be cleaned up."

"Why?"

"They have in them the word *sin,* so they have to become *I-cere* and *I-news*. But words with *sin* which are ugly and cruel, like *sinister* and *sinking,* they stay that way. They warn the world of their evil intent."

"Conversation among your members must be rather painful," volunteered a black accountant standing next to Harry Keeler. The Rastafarian whipped around to address him, but he falsely assumed that the speaker had been the white man, the only one in the room. His manner when speaking to Keeler became even more preachy than before, and the light in the room was such that he assumed an almost Christ-like sanctity: "You make a profound observation, my friend. Speech with us is sometimes slow and painful, ideas half expressed, half understood. But we do not speak to conduct idle conversation. We speak to bare the soul, and such words have to be carefully chosen, carefully protected." Looking about the room, he launched into a kind of Rastafarian prayer, a chant of all the mnemonic words, with Haile Selassie's name recurring frequently and Negus and Jah and Lion of Judah, all embellished by a blizzard of I-words which he made stand out with grace, dignity and power.

Sally, who understood not a word, whispered to the woman standing next to her: "It's like Latin in the Catholic Mass. You're not expected to understand. Each religion has its own mystical language," but when he concluded, she raised her hand and asked: "Share with us, please, what you were saying," and he replied: "Exactly what I said in your language. That words are important and we must clean them up now and then . . . to keep them pure."

For the members of the group this verbal and visual introduction to the Rastafarians was a mind-expanding affair, but with an innate showmanship Grimble had saved his most powerful impact till last— and reaching down, he picked up his lute.

It was a wooden box, sealed except for an opening over which four strings passed. Its neck was a length of board imbedded with seven staples as frets, while a metal bar served as bridge. When plucked, it had a surprisingly good sound, and when the box was drummed on, it echoed deeply.

Sitting with his legs still intertwined, he strummed for a moment, then startled his audience with one of Bob Marley's most powerful chants, "Slave Driver," which spoke of days in Africa and nights aboard the slave ship. It was powerful music, even more powerful imagery, and before long he had these descendants of slaves chanting with him: "Slave driver, slave driver."

Although Sally was deeply moved by the powerful rhythms, the repeated phrases and the imagery of the natal jungle and the slave ship, she was too analytical a young woman to miss a salient fact about the Rastafarian's performance: That rascal has three complete modes of speech. Colorful Jamaican street language, Rastafarian glossolalia, and in these established songs, perfect English. And he switches from one to another almost automatically.

"Slave Driver" finished, the singer turned to one of Marley's most provocative hits, one composed by another man but preempted by Marley as his theme song, "Four Hundred Years." It had a haunting beat, an endless repetition of the title which referred to the years of slavery, and a summons to remember that servitude. Now everyone in the room, including Harry Keeler, who had always liked Marley's music, became a slave assigned to some sugar plantation.

The evening ended with a dozen young people clustered about Grimble, for he had reminded them with music and imagery that some years back he must have been like them, an ordinary black man with an ordinary name. Their questioning pinned him in so tight that Sally had no chance to bid him goodbye, but he was so tall that he was able to catch her eye, and they exchanged glances as she moved toward the exit.

There Harry Keeler waited, and as she neared he asked: "May I accompany you home?" and wanting to be freed of the Rastafarian mystique, she said almost gladly: "I'd like that."

As they walked through the lovely island night, with stars as brilliant as guide lights on distant ships, she said: "A remarkable performance. What do you think it meant?"

"I doubt that a white man is qualified to summarize."

"But you know the islands. You know revolutionary movements, Frantz Fanon and his breed."

"It's a powerful breed, a necessary one. If I were a young black—without a university education, that is—I do believe that Brother Grimble might exert a strong and perhaps constructive influence on me." He paused, then brought the evening together in a tight knot: "Blacks really are 'the dispossessed of the earth,' as Fanon claimed."

"So you think that Rastafarians . . . ?"

"Don't jump the gun. As a white junior official who wants to see his society held together, I also know that Rastafarians really do believe that the police are the Great Babylon." Turning to look at her lovely face, he warned: "I think I can predict that in the weeks ahead your father, as commissioner of police, is going to have a basketful of trouble."

Irritated by what she interpreted as a white putdown of a black idea, even though it was grotesque, she drew apart from him as they strolled. And in those moments these two might have been any couple of mixed color in any of the Caribbean islands: a very dark man wooing a Martinique girl of very light color who dreamed of bettering herself on the color scale, a man in Cuba whose family claimed with great vigor and invention that they stemmed in line directly from soldiers of Ponce de Leon who had brought their Spanish wives with them: "And never was intermarriage with black slaves allowed." They were also much like the hesitant Hindu lass on Trinidad who finds herself admired by a nearly white Church of England businessman in Port of Spain.

In All Saints that winter night it was Sally, the daughter of the commissioner of police, walking slowly with Harry, the promising young economist from England, who would be returning there one of these days with a universe of experience in Algeria, Ghana and the Caribbean. How valuable to world society he was as he strolled that night, how precious she was as the new Caribbean black who could accomplish almost anything in her island society. Two young people of immense value, restrained by inherited taboos but at the same time set free by recent revolutions, they walked for some moments in silence, and then her prejudice against an ancient enemy softened and she said, changing the subject: "Who do you think'll get the top appointment in the Tourist Board?" and he said quickly: "It better be somebody damn good. For the next dozen years this island sinks or swims depending on how it handles its tourism." He walked for several steps, then turned to face Sally: "Insist to your father that we can't afford to blow up over the Rastafarian. Remind him that some years ago the Rastas nearly destroyed Jamaican tourism. I saw figures which suggested that Jamaica lost millions of American dollars."

"Must we always sell our soul to the American cruise ships?"

"Correction. Not a single cruise ship that stops here is owned by the Americans. Great Britain, Holland, Swedes, French . . ."

"But it's the American tourist they bring, with his American dollars."

"Correction. With *her* American dollars."

"You're a clever lad, Keeler," she said, and he replied: "I try to be," and from his front window Police Commissioner Wrentham watched as his daughter kissed the young economist goodnight.

• • •

Harry Keeler was one of the only two leading citizens who were white, himself and Canon Essex Tarleton of the Church of England; all others, from the governor general on down, were either black or brown. Because he had enjoyed his earlier experience in Africa, Keeler found it easy to work under black leaders, and he encountered no difficulty in adjusting to their sometimes arbitrary ways. He never allowed them to dissuade him from a right decision, but he was considerate and willing to spend a good deal of time in explaining why this or that move ought to be avoided and a better plan adopted.

For example, his sometimes radical innovations regarding tourism had produced rather better results than he had predicted, and the island now had an airport capable of handling medium-sized jets, a first-class tourist hotel at spectacular Pointe Neuve on the new road in from the airport, and a set of some two dozen bed-and-breakfast places at York, which had never before shared in the tourist dollar because of a frightening mountain road which separated it from Bristol Town. Keeler had said: "Straighten the hairpins on that damned road, or announce publicly that you're going to let York starve." This had made him a hero in York, and many tourists reported their stay in the homes of ordinary black families along the shore of Marigot Baie was "the highlight of our trip, not only to All Saints but to the entire Caribbean." Such reports came, of course, from the hardier travelers; the others preferred the deluxe accommodations at Pointe Neuve.

Keeler was proud of his contributions to All Saints: "It's possibly the best-run black country on earth, and that includes everything in Africa." But whenever he indulged in this comparison he drew back for two reasons: "Country? Can an island with only a hundred and ten thousand people be called a country even if it is represented in the United Nations? And its present prosperity does hang on the nebulous thread of tourism." And success in tourism, as he knew, was mercurial. It required that rich Americans be kept happy.

That was the danger he had perceived that night when he met with the island's first Rastafarian: "Who can forget what happened in Jamaica when that gang with their hideous dreadlocks and their fierce animosity began to molest white women and elderly millionaires? Tourism was wiped out for years. Untold losses and a change in government. That sort of upheaval we cannot afford."

But even while these apprehensions worried him, he was experiencing a euphoria he had not known for years. Miss Sally Wrentham was proving to be as exciting intellectually as she was provocative physically; she had a sense of humor, a knowledge of her island's history, a judicious attitude toward race. She did not believe, as some on the island did, that blacks were somehow superior in their understanding of Caribbean problems, but she would never concede that they were inferior. The quiet, effective way in which her grandfather Black Bart and her father Thomas had manipulated their white superiors until total freedom was gained had so convincingly proved that blacks could run a country that she had never wanted to leave All Saints for either London or New York, and Keeler appreciated that firmness of mind.

Indeed, as he pursued his more or less serious courtship of Sally he told himself: I would be quite happy making my life here. Helping the island to self-sufficiency, and yes, stepping aside in later years when blacks I'd trained took over. And if I made that choice, what better than to have a superior woman like Sally for my wife?

Three solid reasons, which he did not need to review, made such conclusions viable. He had no yearning desire to return to the drab village on the edge of Yorkshire from which he had come; life there had been oppressive and hemmed in. His memories of his failed marriage to Elspeth were enough to make him groan at night when he recalled them, and he wished no repetition; on the day their divorce became final he felt as if a village cart had been hauled off his chest.

His third reason for feeling content on All Saints could be appreciated only by another Briton. In previous centuries and in the first half of this one, the various parts of the British Empire had been ruled by well-disciplined young Englishmen who had attended the best boarding schools and either Oxford or Cambridge. They were sent out to India or Africa or the Caribbean as young administrators, deigning to spend a few years bringing civilization to God's children before returning home to retired glory as Lord This or Sir That, or at least with a civil medal of some distinction. Young men of the middle or lower classes, who had edged their way into lesser English colleges known collectively as "the red-brick universities," or the Scottish universities, who wanted to serve overseas were eligible only for minor posts. So in those days the British presence was almost invariably represented by an Englishman of good family at the head of government, flanked by young aides of social background much like his, and supported by a corps of men like him who could rarely hope to attain any position of major leadership.

Great Britain suffered by adhering to this restrictive system. In India, of course, it worked, for there a succession of noble viceroys gave stable and sometimes brilliant leadership, but in lesser places like All Saints the posting of well-bred, inadequate men to positions of leadership often resulted in disaster. The last governor general was an example. Just before World War II the Colonial Office had said: "It's time to give good old Basil Wrentham something or other," and so they dispatched him to All Saints, where he marched ashore in solemn majesty with only three qualifications: he was so thin and erect that he epitomized the archetypal English governor general, he was a noted cricketer, and he was the second son of the Earl of Gore. He had been a social success and a political catastrophe, striving even as late as June 1939 to engineer a pact of some kind between Great Britain and Nazi Germany. His uncontrollable daughter, Delia, had married a German baron who later became the brutal gauleiter of a large section of Belgium, where the baron's abused subjects hanged him just before Christmas, 1945.

Keeler was one of the new postwar breed of British colonial officers; the son of lower-middle-class parents, educated in ordinary schools and a red-brick university, he had progressed because of natural ability and hard work, and he found life overseas so congenial that he had no desire to leave. Consequently, marriage with an island girl like Sally was not only acceptable, but almost inevitable; he'd experienced a wife who had little interest in anything but her husband's income and her own social triumphs.

As his studied courtship progressed, he found himself looking at Sally Wrentham as a possible wife-to-be. So on a Saturday morning he dressed in his best whites, drove to her house, and invited her to accompany him to the one-day cricket match in York at the far end of the mountain road. Her reply: "Can I pack a lunch?" His response: "That would be great," and off they sped in his Volkswagen.

He always enjoyed driving this scenic highway whose newly revealed beauty was the result of his headstrong effort, and he was delighted when Sally said: "You must be pleased that your new road works so well. They were really after your scalp there for a while."

"It's a road that was needed," he said as the vistas which his men had chopped through the forest revealed the distant Atlantic.

The cricket match had occasioned much comment, for it was Bristol Town versus The Rest, and although the capital eleven traditionally smothered the team composed of the best players from outlying parts of the island, this year it looked as if The Rest might have a chance. The town of Tudor in the north sent two brothers who had set records as bowlers, York had several strong bats, and there were also two really good cricketers from London on temporary duty installing a new radar at the All Saints airport playing for The Rest; it had been agreed that although they were citizens of England, they had been working during a prolonged stay on the island, and were thus eligible.

A one-day match posed special strategic problems. Team A could bat first starting at ten-thirty and score 300 runs in powerful but dilatory fashion before its tenth and final wicket fell, but then it would probably not have time to get all the batsmen of Team B out before the end of play at five-thirty, in which case the match, with Team A leading 316–57, would be declared a draw. Proper strategy would be for Team A to bat merrily, score about 190, declare their innings ended even though they still had four players eligible to bat, then try to get all ten batsmen of Team B out before five-thirty and before they could score 191. In that case, Team A would win. But if Team B, in its innings, belted the ball over the boundary with abandon and scored a surprising 191 before five-thirty, they won.

In no other game played throughout the world was strategy and taking bold chances so much a part of the contest as in cricket; American tourists, of whom there would be a busload coming over the mountain today, never appreciated the wonderful intricacies of the game and the way a clever captain would first use two fast bowlers to chop up the pitch, then slip in a new bowler with a googly or a left-handed chinaman to take advantage of the roughened turf to take the batsman's wicket. Nor could they see how adroitly the captain placed his nine fielders—not counting the bowler and the wicket keeper—so that one of his men was positioned right where the careless batsman was likely to pop up an easy catch.

If cricket had been a mania back in the early 1930s when Lord Wrentham's XI visited the Caribbean, it was now a compelling obsession. Part of the excitement of this day's struggle on the field at York grew out of the fact that several older men who would serve as selectors for the next West Indian team to play England would be watching carefully to see just how good the two brothers from Tudor were as bowlers and whether the well-regarded batsmen from York could defend themselves on a bumpy pitch. They would also be watching Harry Keeler, who had established himself as a superb fielder at silly mid-on and a reliable batsman against all but googlies; he was a white man, but he had turned in his British passport for an island one on the reasonable grounds that "if I'm to live here the rest of my life, I may as well do it right." This made him eligible to play on the West Indies team conscripted from all the islands. He was most eager to make the team, for although he did not wish to live in England, he would relish a return there as a test-team cricketer.

When Keeler and Sally turned off the mountain road and into town at a quarter to ten they saw that the tourist bus from Bristol Town had arrived as well as six other buses from the north end of the island and three from the airport. "I hope," he said to Sally as they parked their car, "that no airplane from Barbados arrives at one this afternoon in trouble and needing ground support."

Nothing in the British islands of the Caribbean was more important than cricket. Trinidad, Jamaica and Barbados might disagree on the economy, airfares between the islands, the management of their one university, and what taxes should be imposed on Trinidadian gasoline, but when the time came to build a West Indies team for a tour of England, India, Pakistan or Australia, all differences were submerged and funds were mysteriously found to pay for the trip. Local prejudices drove the islands apart, cricket bound them together.

Today's game was a brilliant affair, a sky-blue Saturday, with flowering trees in bloom, fruit abundant in the open marketplace, people of all complexions seated in the tiny stands or lying on the grass—and everyone caught up in the excitement of a one-day match. Cricket purists did not appreciate such condensed and often rowdy affairs; they preferred the more stately matches that covered two, three or even five consecutive days, for then captains could engage in intricate strategies, depending on weather forecasts and the likely effect on the condition of the pitch. In a series of five matches it was not uncommon for two or even four to end in draws. One of the beauties of cricket was to watch a resolute captain whose team faced almost certain defeat swing things about to deprive the enemy of a sure win by prolonging the battle until time ran out. In such circumstances, a draw was almost as good as a win and sometimes more exciting as men batted against the clock. A proper five-day match with a little rain to cause uncertainty was cricket at its best, but in the islands a rousing one-day struggle had equal merit but of a more noisy nature.

How stately the scene appeared when the eleven players from The Rest, who had won the toss and elected to bat last, strolled casually onto the field, their white cricket gear standing out against the carefully tended green playing area. The men, who represented eight or nine different gradations of color, were handsome, at ease, smiling at their friends in the crowd; but how the tension grew when the opening batsmen from Bristol Town, protected by heavy leg pads and batting gloves, strode out, bats dragging behind them, to make their stand against The Rest bowlers!

One of the two umpires was always Canon Essex Tarleton—with ruddy face, white hair and a rotund body that looked like a Toby jug. When he marched onto the field, with a dignified waddling pace, there was decorous clapping, for he was a much-loved figure who reminded them of John Bull, and of other aspects of England which they still treasured.

What made him especially memorable was his garb, for cricket umpires traditionally wore their trousers and white shirt under a linen duster that reached halfway down the calf, but the canon (an honorary but inaccurate title awarded him by his shipmates aboard a wartime cruiser) wore instead of the duster a heavy ribbed sweater made of natural wool from the Hebrides Islands off the coast of Scotland. As soon as the day heated, which was early in the West Indies, Tarleton removed his sweater and tied its arms in a tight knot about his ample belly, so that the bulk of the sweater covered his rear. Many photographs were taken of his umpiring, and most showed the heavy sweater drooping from his waist.

In cricket, at the climax of a close play, the umpire was not required to render a decision unless there was a formal appeal, and this took the form of a shouted question: "Howzzat?" There was difference of opinion as to whether the curious word meant "How was that?" or "How is that?" but when six or seven fielders shouted at the same time "Howzzat?" Canon Tarleton came into his glory, for he stood as tall as he could, stared at the supplicants, and delivered his judgment, which was never appealed. His word was law.

Keeler's side batted first, but neither he nor his fellow batsmen accomplished much. One of the Tudor bowlers tricked Harry with an off-breaking fast ball, which he popped up for an easy catch by silly mid-off for a score of only 13. Bristol Town was in poor shape at the lunch break, when Sally broke out a small feast which players from both teams shared in easy companionship. "I think we have you on the hip," one of the Tudor men warned Keeler. "They tell me those two chaps from the airport are powerful batsmen."

"We'll see," Harry replied. "And if it looks bad for us, Sally here will pray for rain." In that case, no matter how poorly Bristol Town did after the lunch break, the match would be a draw.

Bristol did quite poorly, the Tudor brothers proving that they were bowlers of almost test class, all out for 133, leaving The Rest with ample time to win.

They sent in a cautious batsman first, paired with one of the good players from York, and although the cautious man went down quickly, the more experienced player hit out strongly and scored well. But when the next batsman came in, one of the tragedies of cricket unfolded. To score a run, *both* batsmen had to run, at the same time, exchanging creases, and it sometimes happened that a poor batsman would be too daring in his decision. He would try to run when the odds were against him; his partner, starting out of his safe area just a little late, would be thrown out through no fault of his own. Cricket being a gentleman's game, the good batsman did not in this moment of frustration thump his inept partner over the head with his bat, but he would have been justified in doing so.

That is what happened: the poor batsman was safe, the good one out. So The Rest lost two wickets in a hurry, but then one of the radar men from the airport came to bat, and it was obvious after his first few runs that he had played a good deal of high-quality cricket in the English counties. He was good, and it looked as if he might notch a century when Harry Keeler made a remarkable play. The airport man hit a well-placed ground ball which rolled rapidly out toward the boundary. If it escaped the fielders, it would be a four, and even if someone from the Bristol Town side did run it down, two or perhaps three runs would be scored. So the batsman and his partner set out confidently, but Harry, running at startling speed, overtook the ball, reached down without stopping, grabbed it with one hand, and with unbroken motion threw it with great force right into the hands of the distant wicketkeeper, who deftly ticked the bails, the two wooden crosspieces atop the wicket, into the grass. The play was very close. Did the runner reach safety before the bails went flying, or had the ball beaten him? "Howzzat?" shouted the Bristol men, and Canon Tarleton stood impassive. Then, after a dramatic pause, he signaled the runner out. A cheer went up from both sides in tribute to Harry Keeler's mighty throw which had dismissed The Rest's leading scorer.

The play did not aid Bristol much, because the other airport man teamed up with a strong batsman from York, and runs were added at a pace that seemed to doom Bristol. Keeler came up with another dazzling defensive play, a falling dive parallel to the ground to make a one-handed catch off the York batsman, but another stubborn man took his place, and with help from the high-scoring airport man, The Rest scored the necessary 134 well before quitting time.

A visitor from Barbados, an elderly black man who had as a youth once toured England with Sir Benny Castain, took the trouble to find Keeler at the end of the match: "I'm John Gaveny, selector from Bridgetown, and I must say any team could use a world-class fielder like you," but before Harry could feel elation, Gaveny added: "That is, if he could be relied upon to put together twenty or thirty runs."

Harry and Sally were among the last of the Bristol Town contingent to leave York, and after darkness fell at a quarter past six like a curtain in a theater crashing down, they stopped at one of the niches carved in the side of the mountain for the passage of buses and kissed with some ardor. When they reached home, Sally said: "Come in and have supper with us," and they found that the housekeeper had waiting for them and the commissioner a bubbling stew made of island vegetables, potatoes brought by ship from Ireland and beef flown in from Miami. After asking how the game had gone, Commissioner Wrentham said: "Those brothers from Tudor, if they can master a change of pace, they'll be on the test team for sure," and Sally said: "If you'd seen Harry's defensive plays, you'd put him there too." After supper Wrentham said: "I have work at the station," and he left the young lovers alone, satisfied on all counts: he had raised a splendid daughter who was being courted by a man worthy of her.

But the courtship, so appropriate from every outside evaluation, did not go smoothly, because two weeks after the cricket match, Laura Shaughnessy, from the governor general's office, said to Sally: "Let's take tomorrow off. The Rastafarian wants to see the north end of the island, and I said I'd take him in my car."

For Sally, what had started as a casual excursion turned out to be a day of tremendous significance, when values were up for review. It would prove to be totally different from the genteel ride with the Englishman Keeler to the cricket game at York. That had been essentially a trip back to England, with a break for tea, and an almost fanatical observation of the little niceties of the game.

Today would be a harsh, almost brutal ride into the realities of a new black republic with its dominant African heritage extruding at a dozen unexpected points. Laura, several shades darker than Sally, drove her small car with Ras-Negus Grimble hunched up beside her in the front seat and Sally tightly packed into the rear.

The difference between the two excursions started immediately, for instead of taking the mountain road south, Laura headed north, and as soon as they left the town, the Rastafarian took command, as if he were a young king and they his concubines. What he wanted to see was the lay of the land, its capacity for agriculture, the crops it was already growing, and how the little farms that peppered this apparently empty part of the island were positioned. Twice he ordered Laura peremptorily: "Stop! I want to visit that farmer," and when he left the car to talk with the black people occupying the hut he spoke about crops with such obvious authority, that Sally thought: I'll bet his ancestors inspected their fields that way in Africa.

When they were about two miles south of Tudor, Sally accompanied him on a walking visit to a third farmer whose fields were off the road, and was amazed at the turn their conversation took. "Can you grow a good ganja on your back fields?"

"Never tried."

"If I brought you number-one seed, would you try?"

"How I gonna sell ganja, suppose I grow it?"

"Great Babylon Americans hungry for ganja. Very good price."

"We don't grow much here All Saints. Don't use it much."

"All that's going to change. Remember. I told you. Great God Haile Selassie say so."

On the short hop into Tudor, Sally asked: "Isn't ganja what is usually called marijuana?"

"Ganja is the sacred herb of Rastafari. Opens all doors."

In Tudor he was electric, moving about among black people, who were overwhelmed by his tremendous locks, his colorful shirt, the secure manner in which he conducted himself. Sally noticed that he tended to keep away from people of light color like herself; his message was for the black farmer, the black storekeeper, the woman who washed clothes, and it was always the same: "Black people gonna rise all over the Caribbean. God comin' back to earth in Ethiopia, reconquer the world for us."

When his listeners asked about the messages on his shirt, he pointed to the picture of Haile Selassie and told them: "Great ruler. He conquer all Africa." He told them that his lion was the one mentioned in the Bible: "Lion of Judah. Come to give us total power." He also explained that the pope in Rome would soon be destroyed because he was the spirit of Babylon, but the Great Babylon itself was America, which would also be destroyed. He further predicted that very painful punishments would soon overtake Queen Elizabeth II: "She the daughter Queen Elizabeth I, who send her captain, John Hawkins, to Africa to bring your mammies and daddies here as slaves."

When the people stopped to listen to his ranting, intermixed with long passages of incomprehensible Rastafarian jumble, he dropped his voice and ended with great seriousness: "America the Great Babylon overseas. Who the Great Babylon here All Saints? The police." Always when he said this, he stopped, stared at his listeners with a fierce glance, utilizing his height and the fearful appearance of his hair and beard to terrify them. Then he would drop his voice to a whisper: "Great Babylon must be destroyed. The Bible say so. Revelation."

And now he whipped out his Bible: "Chapter Eighteen, verse two, look at it, read it for yourself: 'And he cried mightily with a strong voice, saying, Babylon the great is fallen, is fallen and is become the habitation of devils . . .' And now read verse twenty-one: 'And a mighty angel took up a stone like a great millstone, and cast it into the sea, saying, Thus with violence shall that great city Babylon be thrown down, and shall be found no more at all.'"

Sally noticed that he always stopped short of calling for outright revolution or an attack on the police, but that was certainly the import of his words, and his listeners knew it. But when the tension was at its maximum, he became once more the gentle messenger she had seen that first night at the meeting. Then the warmth in his eyes and the reassurance in his placid face, framed as it was in his Christ-like beard, exuded love for all and an invitation to join his crusade to rescue the black people of this earth.

When townsmen invited Ras-Negus and his two companions to take lunch with them, everyone noticed that he picked out only certain foods, and before eating, placed them in his coconut shell. Aware of the interest, he explained: "No canned food. No meat. Only food as Jah sends it, fresh from field and tree. And no plates or metal

spoons. Only fingers as Jah gave them." It was sometimes rather trying to watch as he dipped his long, bony fingers into his bowl and
brought them dripping to his bearded lips.

As he ate he took the opportunity to explain to his host in the
gentlest terms the principles of Rastafari, and when one man asked:
"Is it true you have ganja as your sacred herb?" he replied: "It's the
herb Jah sent down to earth to make black people joyous. You smoke
ganja like Haile Selassie say, you catch a glimpse of heaven." And he
left the men bedazzled by his description of what life was going to be
like when Haile Selassie, as the seventy-second incarnation of the
Godhead, returned to take command of the hundred and forty-four
thousand who were to be saved.

On the way west toward Cap Galant, Ras-Negus spoke with quiet
fervor of Rastafarian principles: the concept that all women were
empresses, that children were one of the world's great blessings, that
good men and women ate only natural foods and not canned poisons
sent to the island in cargo ships owned by the Great Babylon in
Miami.

The drone of his subdued and pleasant voice almost put Sally to
sleep, but when, to keep herself awake, she asked: "Mr. Grimble . . ."
and he stopped her: "Not Mr. Grimble, Ras-Negus, John the Baptist
of the Leeward and Windward Islands."

"Ras-Negus, what was that hundred and forty-four thousand
saved you spoke about?" and for the first time when talking with her
directly he produced his small leatherbound Bible and flipped it open
exactly to Revelation, Chapter 14, from which he read in low and
gentle tones: "'And I looked, and, lo, a Lamb stood on the mount
Sion, and with him an hundred forty and four thousand, having his
Father's name written in their foreheads . . . These were redeemed
from among men, being the firstfruits unto God and to the Lamb.'"

Closing the Bible, he said, looking at Sally: "You and I should live
our lives so that we can be one of the hundred and forty-four thousand."

"You mean that of all the people on earth only . . . ?"

"Group by group. Of these Windward Islands, maybe only one
hundred and forty-four thousand saved."

"In America, which has a huge population?"

"None. It is Babylon."

When they reached Cap Galant they found that the government
had erected from stone and wood a spacious belvedere in which some

dozen separate groups were picnicking or simply resting to enjoy the noble scene. The appearance of Ras-Negus was so striking that he commanded attention, and soon had about him a small group of curiosity seekers who encouraged him to descant on the glories of Rastafarianism. But Sally noticed that with this audience he did not even mention let alone stress revolution, the supremacy of black over white, or the ritual use of ganja, and she realized that he was much more clever than she had thought, for he knew instinctively how to tailor his comments to his crowd. She had more respect for him when he spoke with blacks, because then he was more forthright. But regardless of his audience, in whatever he said he conveyed a tremendous sense of Africa, and Sally thought: This Rastafarian has never been there, but he exudes the smell of the great rivers, the sounds of the deep jungle and even the chattering of the many plumed birds. God, this man has made himself Africa!

After he had been orating for some time, a woman came up who had attended that first night meeting and asked him to expound on the curious Rastafarian vocabulary. This was apparently one of the aspects of Rastafari about which he considered himself an expert, for he declaimed wildly and sometimes with unintended humor about how the English language would be modified when the Rastas took over. Among his more memorable suggestions:

. . . "Politics is how the white man oppresses the blacks. We must call it by its right name, *polytricks*."

. . . "Understand is too beautiful a word to be harmed by the negative concept *under*. It must become *overstand*."

. . . "Divine has the noblest meaning, but it's damaged by that first part *die*. It has to become *I-vine,* throwing all the divinity on the I, the immortal me."

. . . "In Tudor just now I saw the new library. Marvelous place for children, but it corrupts them with false information in that first part *lie*. It has got to be *truthbrary*."

. . . "One of the best things a Rasta can be is dedicated. But the power of the word is killed by that first part, *dead*. We call it *livicated*."

On and on he went, as if he were playing a child's game, dissecting the language and substituting crazy corrections. When he saw picnickers eating the most totally satisfying food of the islands, a ripe mango with its rich-tasting fruit and golden juice: "Man-go, it means some good fellow is dying. We make our word *I-come.*"

Sally could not determine whether he was making any converts or not, but a remarkable event occurred which proved that he saw his visit to All Saints as a missionary journey, for he attacked his targets with a cleverly designed two-pronged assault: first he gathered them about him with a performance on his homemade musical instrument, singing in fine style one of Bob Marley's best songs, "One Love," then he carefully scrutinized their faces to see who might be open to his next approach. With a psychological insight that was extraordinary, he identified half a dozen young men who seemed susceptible to what he intended doing. With Sally and Laura following, he led his group to a secluded portion of the cap and there produced from his bag a supply of the best ganja leaves from the hill country of Jamaica.

Sally had never before seen the notorious herb, illegal on All Saints, and was surprised at how pleasantly aromatic it was in its natural state, but she was even more startled when she saw how Ras-Negus smoked it. From what she had read in *Time,* she had expected him to roll it into something like a cigarette, but he did not. Taking a strip of newspaper, he formed a generous cornucopia, small like a cigar at the mouth end, flaring out to a diameter of three inches at the far end. When he lit the weed and started smoking in deep drafts, he looked as if he were making music on old Triton's "wreathèd horn."

He inhaled deeply, closed his eyes, allowed a look of saintly benevolence to clothe his face, then passed the strange contraption to the man standing near him, who took four deep first-time puffs. Since the cornucopia contained an immense amount of ganja, some ten young men could share it, and now it came to Laura, driver of the car. She had apparently been introduced earlier to the herb by Ras-Negus, for she took the smoking paper, dragged on it expertly, sighed deeply, and held it out to Sally.

This posed a problem. Sally, as the daughter of the commissioner of police, was well aware that even the possession of marijuana on All Saints, let alone the actual smoking of it, was illegal, but her experiences on this crowded day had awakened in her such an interest in Rastafari as an authentic black religion that she was inclined to participate in all its rituals, so she accepted the ganja from Laura.

"You must take deep breaths," Ras-Negus directed, and when she did she felt the subtle smoke diffusing through her lungs and apparently her heart and head as well. Eight deep drags produced a positive euphoria, and once more she felt the sense of Africa.

It was late afternoon when they started the drive home, and

although Sally's mind was not entirely clear, it was apparent to her
that Laura was surprised when Ras-Negus climbed not into the front
seat with her but in the back with Sally. Once there, he lit another
ganja cigar, and soon the car was filled with the sweetish aroma and
Sally was being pressured to take one drag for every three or four that
he took. Laura, from the front seat, also asked for her share, and the
little car bounced merrily homeward.

Now Ras-Negus, in a grand euphoria, started finding in his Bible
random passages which more or less substantiated the teaching of
Rastafari. Again from Revelation came: " 'And one of the elders
saith unto me, Weep not: behold, the Lion of the tribe of Judah, the
Root of David, hath prevailed . . .' " He said that this proved that
Haile Selassie, who was a lineal descendant from King David, would
soon take over Africa.

"But he's dead," Sally protested, and he countered: "His spirit.
Not his followers, like you and me. Africa will be ours."

To prove his point, he turned to Psalm 68, where he read in verses
31 and 32: " 'Princes shall come out of Egypt; Ethiopia shall soon
stretch out her hands unto God. Sing unto God, ye kingdoms of the
earth . . .' " This clearly meant, he claimed, that Great Babylon
America would soon fall under the sway of Ethiopia.

On and on he went, galloping through the Bible to lift this arcane
morsel and that, but always he came back to Revelation: "Victory
over Great Babylon isn't going to be easy. Listen to Chapter Nineteen, verse nineteen: 'And I saw the beast, and the kings of the earth,
and their armies, gathered together to make war against him that sat
on the horse, and against his army.' " This seemed pretty nebulous to
Sally until he pulled from his leather bag a small photograph of Haile
Selassie perched on a white horse. This led him immediately to Chapter 20, verse II: " 'And I saw a great white throne, and him that sat on
it, from whose face the earth and heaven fled away . . .' "

Sally, in her gently muddled state, could not see the connection
between a white horse and a white throne, but apparently there was
one, for the concept inspired Grimble to lean his head back and recite
long passages from the Bible, none of them directly related to Rastafari but all of them wonderfully narcotic, and as she drifted under the
united spell of the magical words and seductive herbs, she realized
that Ras-Negus was fumbling under her dress and then with his own
trousers, but his words were so persuasive and his presence so commanding that she found no wish to resist, until she wakened to the

horrifying fact that this frightening man with the Medusa locks intended having sex with her right there in the cramped back seat of the moving car.

She did not scream, but she did try to push him away. However, he was too powerful, and forced her to keep her hand inside his baggy trousers until he gained partial satisfaction.

It was frightening but not repulsive, for his entire being —his deportment, his narcotic words, his sense of dedication—bespoke a world she had not known before, and his wild vitality gave substance to that pretty word she and her friends had discussed so glibly: *negritude*. Exhausted and bewildered as the effects of the ganja subsided, pressed into her corner of the car, she prayed that it might soon reach Bristol Town. When Laura stopped her car at the home of Commissioner Wrentham, Sally jumped out and ran inside as if she sought sanctuary, for here, in the persons of her able father and her sane brother, black Africa and white England did meet in a decent and agreed-upon harmony.

Sally was so shaken by her experience with the Rastafarian and his ganja that next day at noon she went to the small, neat rectory attached to the Church of England building and asked if she could speak with Canon Tarleton, and his white-haired wife said brightly: "That's what he's here for, my dear," and off she went to fetch him.

The Reverend Essex Tarleton had been only an average boy at school in England and not much better at the university. In divinity training it was obvious that he was never going to be among the leaders of his church nationwide. But all who knew him in those years were satisfied that he was a young fellow with a clear call to the ministry, and when, in 1939, he joined the navy as chaplain, they were pleased that he had found his niche. After serving at various bases and in several important warships, he was, after the war, assigned to a small church in Barbados, where for many years he was both happy and effective, but when the community grew, it required a younger and more energetic man, and he was shunted off to the less populous island of All Saints. Here he would end his ministry, a well-intentioned white man helping a black congregation establish its norms. On Saturdays he umpired cricket matches, on Sundays he preached, and on all days he held himself in readiness to consult with his parishioners. He would have been astounded had anyone pointed out that he was the kind of humble servant who had held the British Empire together and who now accounted for the fact that on islands like All Saints emotional ties still bound the newly freed young nations to England. They banked in London, sent their bright youths to English schools, and purchased their books and magazines from what even the most ardent black patriot still called "The Homeland." In cricket it was grand when some fine test team came from Australia or India, but people marked their calendars in gold when an English team arrived.

"And what brings you to my little room?" he asked Sally as he bustled in, offering her a glass of sherry.

She said she would like some, then explained that she was bewildered by Rastafarianism, and as soon as she said the word, he stopped pouring and said: "Yes, I know he's been doing a lot of talking, that fellow from Jamaica."

"He's certainly been talking to me, quite persuasively."

"Now, now, Sally! You're much too sensible to be taken in by that nonsense."

"But he quotes the Bible with such telling effect. Tell me, Canon, are the words of Revelation meaningful?"

Canon Tarleton sipped his sherry, then broke into robust laughter: "Sally, I'm going to answer your question with what might be called terrible frankness, but for God's sake, listen to me. The religious kooks and weirdos of this world, and I'm borrowing a wonderfully appropriate pair of words I picked up from a recent issue of *Time,* have used two books of the Bible for the last two thousand years to prove any confounded thing they wished. Daniel and Revelation! They do as much harm in the world as Jamaica rum and Holland gin."

"How do you mean?"

"They're apocalyptic. Inspired rantings. You and I this morning could dip into those two books and prove almost anything we wanted to." He reached for his Bible, showed her that he was opening it to Revelation, and read a farrago of words and symbols and sheer obfuscation: "Now tell me, pray what does that mean?" And very cleverly he began to assign arbitrary meanings to each of the words and symbols, until in the end he had proved, by juggling Revelation, that in the year 2007 Canada was going to invade both the United States and Mexico.

"Using Daniel and Revelation, you can prove anything." He rubbed his chin and chuckled at a preposterous scene he had witnessed: "When I was in Washington last year for the meeting of our church, I listened to this new crop of radio and television ministers. What clever men they are! How handsome they are on the telly! And half of them were ranting about some inscrutable passage in Revelation."

"Then what the Rastafarians say is all junk?"

"You used the word, I didn't. But without answering you, because it's never right for one religion to knock another, I'm going to look out the window and nod my head."

Sally, much relieved to hear her suspicions confirmed, changed the subject: "Would you please look at Numbers—Chapter Five, verse six. I memorized the place because when he read the passage, it did seem to me to justify the strange way he wears his hair. Tell me, Canon, have you ever seen this Rastafarian?"

"I have. The other night at dusk, and he scared me half to death." He was trying to find the passage, and when he did he said: "I'm afraid there's nothing here that says anything about hair."

"Try Chapter Six, verse five," she said. "I may have gotten it backward."

"Ah ha!" he chuckled. "This is the famous passage that rebellious young men in London used to convince their parents that long hair for men was ordered by the Bible. 'The vow . . . there shall no razor come upon his head . . . he shall be holy, and shall let the locks of the hair of his head grow.'" Closing the Bible, he turned to Sally and smiled: "That certainly justifies . . . What is it they call that infamous hair? Dreadlocks?"

"It seems to."

"Ah, but my dear young woman. You can go terribly wrong if you settle upon one short passage of our Bible for your sole instruction on anything. When the young mods, as they were called back home, threw that notorious passage at their elders, scholars in our church combed through their Bible to see what other firm instructions were given about men's hair, and in Leviticus, the great book of law, they found in Chapter Fourteen, verses eight and nine, these words: 'And he that is to be cleansed shall wash his clothes, and shave off all his hair, and wash himself in water, that he may be clean . . . he shall shave all his hair off his head and his beard and his eyebrows, even all his hair he shall shave off: and he shall wash his clothes . . .' Your Rastafarian could profit from those admonitions, especially the part about washing."

Sally reached for the Bible, read the passages, and smiled, but the canon was not finished: "But as so often happens with the Bible, it was stout old St. Paul who clinched the matter in First Corinthians, if I can find the passage that was widely circulated when long hair for men first hit the streets. Yes, Chapter Eleven, verse fourteen: 'Doth not even nature itself teach you, that, if a man have long hair, it is a shame unto him?'"

After Sally had had an opportunity to study that passage, the old clergyman said compassionately: "A minister my age has seen a dozen sects rise and fall, and those that rely on selected passages from Daniel and Revelation are the most pernicious. But their error is understandable. Men and women grow restless when faced by tough, tested teachings of Roman Catholics or American Baptists. People aren't ready to discipline themselves according to the truth that has been distilled over twenty centuries. So they construct their own apocalyptic religions, all fire and hell and golden chariots and a hundred and forty-four thousand of this and that, and I suppose that in the long run, they do no great harm. But in the short span, dear God, can they be destructive!"

As she was about to leave, he said: "I heard about his predictions on Ethiopia, and you can find passages which support his wild dreams, but in Zephaniah, a little-known book tucked away near the end of the Old Testament, the prophet takes care of your Rastafarian's Ethiopia: 'The Lord will be terrible unto them: for he will famish all the gods of the earth . . . Ye Ethiopians also, ye shall be slain by my sword.'"

When he led her to the door he said amiably: "Sally, you and I, using our scissors and paste, could construct a wonderful new religion, but we'd use only the noble parts, Deuteronomy, Psalms, St. Luke, the letters of St. Paul. But of course, such a religion has already been compiled for us. It's called Christianity."

In the weeks following the tour of the north part of the island, the Rastafarian became an object of suspicion in Bristol Town. Harry Keeler, in charge of the managerial aspects of tourism, was distraught when a rather fat white woman from New York who had come ashore from a Scandinavian cruise ship was physically abused on the street by a big black man, who shouted at her in a loud and menacing voice: "Go home, you big fat white pig." When she regained her balance and looked at him in bewilderment, he added: "We don't want you fat pigs on our island."

The incident caused an uproar, for everyone appreciated instantly the damage it might do their principal industry; and when news was rushed to Keeler's office, he jumped to the conclusion that the black offender must have been the Rastafarian. But the most casual interrogations proved that to be untrue; the assailant had been identified by several disgusted islanders, and he denied having any association with the Rastafarian.

Keeler swung into action immediately, and without seeking approval from anyone he hurried to the cruise ship, *Tropic Sands,* out of Oslo, to make profuse apologies to the captain, the cruise director and any of the other officials he could find: "This sort of thing does not happen on All Saints. It was a shameful aberration and will not be tolerated. Assure your people of that."

When an officer took him to the ship's infirmary, where the New York tourist was resting under mild sedation, he accomplished a great deal of good by making an on-the-spot decision. "Madam, I know how frightened you must have been. Yelled at and pushed by a strange man. I sympathize with you and I'm mortified, because we don't allow things like that on our island. Here's what I'm going to do to try to win your forgiveness. The people of this island will pay the entire cost of your boat trip, and since the *Tropic Sands* doesn't sail until eleven tonight, the governor general invites you to have dinner with him, you and a friend of your choosing, at Government House, seven sharp. I'll be here to fetch you in a taxi." Having made peace with the offended woman, he then doubled back to the captain, invited him to the dinner also, and hurried ashore to phone the governor general to advise him of what he had done, and to ask his apology for having made what Keeler called a "unilateral decision."

The dinner was a huge success. The woman turned out to be a Mrs. Gottwald who served as entertainment officer for a large synagogue in Brooklyn, and it had been she who had organized the Caribbean cruise aboard the *Tropic Sands* that had brought forty-seven passengers to the ship. Suddenly she became a person of great importance not only to the ship but also to the island, and she proved a well-informed talker.

"People like me," she explained, "and there are lots of us who determine where groups will go for their vacation, are *extremely . . .*" (she emphasized the word) "attentive to press reports. Those airplane hijackings absolutely killed the Mediterranean. We couldn't give our cruises away. Nobody goes to poor old Haiti anymore. The ugly troubles in Jamaica destroyed its tourism for a while, but now we're back. But we take our people only to the north coast of the island, never to a troubled town like Kingston."

Captain Bergstrom said: "It's becoming profitable for our shipping companies to buy or lease an unpopulated island, or a remote stretch of a troubled island like Haiti or Jamaica, and build our own little vacation dreamland. Walled in behind a palisade, you see only those blacks who are allowed in as part of the work force . . ."

The way he described this new development in tourism betrayed his low assessment of it, but it remained for Mrs. Gottwald to dismiss it as a solution to the problems of tourism: "I would never take my people to an isolated place like that. And my people wouldn't want to go. They want to see a marvelous mix like your fine main street. They want to meet black people and brown. Otherwise they'll stay home."

This occasioned favorable comment, especially from the black governor general, but then she added the warning that had to be attended to on any island that hoped to maintain its tourist trade: "I shall never forget what happened on St. Croix in the American Virgins some years ago. I had my group, sixty or seventy at that time, in St. Thomas that day and we were terrified when the news flashed along the waterfront and into the cruise ships docked there: Black hoodlums with machine guns attacked guests at the posh Rockefeller golf club on St. Croix. Dead bodies all over the place. It killed the Virgins for that season, and even now we can't sell day excursions to St. Croix."

Now the governor spoke: "I do hope, Mrs. Gottwald and Captain Bergstrom, that you can help us avoid inflammatory publicity." He had been a scholarship student at Oxford and spoke with one of the world's loveliest accents: pure Oxford softened by Caribbean sunshine. "Of course, if incidents like today's should be repeated, news would have to circulate, and we would be honor-bound to let that happen, even though we knew it would be damaging our island. But I give you my word that we're not going to let it happen again . . ."

Captain Bergstrom chuckled and raised his glass: "You have a tremendous advantage over us, Governor. Our big ships have to stop somewhere. With the Mediterranean closed and the Orient so far away, we're left with only three choice areas for the American travelers like Mrs. Gottwald and her group: Alaska in the summer, Mexico and the Panama Canal for the in-between season, and your Caribbean in the winter." Then he added ominously: "But if things get out of hand, if our travelers are abused when they come ashore, we drop your island, just like we've had to drop Haiti."

As the party broke up, the governor said: "Mr. Keeler, you did me a signal honor in bringing these two experts to dinner. I've learned a great deal. And I trust that you, as our expert, listened and will take steps to protect our visitors and our island's good name."

Next morning at seven, Keeler was in the office of Commissioner of Police Thomas Wrentham: "Have you arrested the culprit?"

"Easily."

"Anybody interrogated him?"

"I did."

"Results?"

"I suppose you want to know whether he had been in any way influenced by the Rastafarian."

"Exactly."

"If we can believe him, and I'm inclined to, he's never even seen the stranger."

"Was he high on marijuana?"

"Smoking it is not a big problem on this island, as you know."

"But with the Rastafarian preaching his doctrines, it's going to be."

"I agree, but in this case, probably no."

"Then why in the world would he attack a white woman and say the provocative things he did?"

Wrentham leaned back and reflected on this: "Sometimes it's in the air. Word from other islands, radio broadcasts about terrorism, an article in *Time* or *Newsweek* . . ."

"Or the visit of a Rastafarian," Keeler suggested, and the commissioner said: "Today, on an island like this, that's usually the case," and he took from a desk drawer a report forwarded to him by his opposite number in Jamaica: "Take a look," and Keeler read:

Further study of Ras-Negus Grimble's background reveals that his grandfather was an English sailor who jumped ship in Kingston in 1887 when he was about thirty-nine. Took up with a black woman and had three children. One grandson married a black and produced Hastings Grimble, known since the Haile Selassie business as Ras-Negus.

As a young man he fell under the spell of the famous Jamaican reggae singer Bob Marley and his group The Wailers. On several occasions he filled in as substitute singer but did not earn a permanent role. We have a strong suspicion that he provided the Marley team with its ganja and he seems to have masterminded a rather big operation wholesaling Jamaican marijuana to the United States market. Small, fast planes were known to have dropped down into the high valleys near his home village of Cockpit Town, but my men never apprehended either the plane crew or Grimble, who we were sure was supplying them.

We believe he left Jamaica for one simple reason: we were hot on his trail. If he's moved his operations to your island, watch out for heavy traffic in marijuana. But he also preaches racial warfare and we think he was behind some of the uglier incidents in our sad affair some years ago. Watch out.

As for his rather deep involvement in religious matters, our informants assure us he is sincere. He really believes that Haile Selassie is the incarnation of the Godhead and that soon the blacks will command all of Africa and most of the rest of the world.

Nota bene: He not only preaches but absolutely believes that police are the Great Babylon which must be destroyed. I cannot discover where he got this idea, but friends tell me it was from the book of Revelation in the Bible. Regardless, wherever he or his friends appear, the police can be certain they will have trouble. My advice: get him off your island.

When Keeler passed the papers back, Wrentham asked: "How does that strike you?" and the Englishman replied: "I'm scared on two counts. That incident yesterday with Mrs. Gottwald could have proved devastating to our tourism, and will if it's repeated. And I'm beginning to see intimations that the Rastafarian's evil hand is surfacing in many surprising areas."

"What should we do?"

"Deport him."

"That's not so easy. There are rules now. A judge would have to issue an order, and a black judge doesn't like to do that against a fellow black. Too reminiscent of the old days when whites said who could live where."

"Then let's see if we can establish any kind of relationship between the man yesterday and the Rastafarian. If we can, you go into court and ask for a deportation order, and have the judge summon me to confirm that our tourist industry might be shot to hell if he's allowed to run loose any longer. Or, if we find him connected in any way with ganja . . ."

Three months passed, during which neither Colonel Wrentham nor Harry Keeler was able to devise a tactic for handling the difficult Rastafarian they had on their hands. In the meantime, the problem had taken a dramatic turn into wholly new channels, and now both Canon Tarleton and his wife were involved. One Thursday morning in late March they were seated in their rectory trying in vain to comfort a young woman member of their church who was totally distraught. She was Laura Shaughnessy, the fine-looking granddaughter of an adventurous young Irishman who had come to the island in the last century, had quarreled with the Catholic priest and joined the Church of England, and had taken a black wife, producing a large brood of children and grandchildren who brought honor to his name.

A trusted employee in the governor's office, she had her pick of suitors, and the Tarletons sometimes discussed whom she might marry. Mrs. Tarleton felt that Laura was a bit too bold in accepting dates with the young officers from the cruise ships, on the logical grounds that "such affairs never lead to anything," but the canon defended her: "She's a lass, and a bonny one, who's trying to find her way. Watch, she'll marry the best young man in these parts," and when it became obvious that Harry Keeler might very well stay on the island, Tarleton predicted: "Don't be surprised if Laura grabs him. Perfect pair."

It hadn't happened, and now Laura sat before them in tears. She was pregnant, had no desire to marry the man involved, whoever he was, and was desolated by the options that faced her. But she had come to the right pair of people for counsel, because Mrs. Tarleton assured her: "First thing to remember above all else, God has always wanted you to have children, perhaps not in this way, but you are now engaged in a holy process, one of the most magnificent in the world, and you must find joy and fulfillment in it."

"But . . ."

"All that comes later, Laura. Believe me, and I speak as a woman with children and great-grandchildren of my own, that God smiles on you at this moment. You bring Him joy in being fruitful, and, Essex, I wonder if you would lead us in a few words of prayer?"

Joining hands with his wife and Laura, he prayed that God would bless the child in the womb and bring it to a productive life. He spoke of the joys of motherhood despite temporary difficulties, and he assured Laura that God, the Tarletons and all sensible people supported her at this moment. Then, still holding on to the young woman's hand, he said reassuringly: "You must understand, Laura, that my wife and I have held meetings like this many times in the past. This is not the end of the world. It's a problem to be faced, and like all such problems, there are reasonable solutions."

Together the Tarletons explained that she had several specific options. She could have the baby here in All Saints and let the scandal expire, as it would in a short time, but that might make it difficult for her to find a husband locally; in such cases the girls almost always had to marry down in the color hierarchy. "But they always find husbands if they're basically good girls," Mrs. Tarleton said, and her husband added: "And you are."

Or she could do what many had done in the past—leave All Saints right now, take a job, any job she could find, in Trinidad or Barbados or Jamaica, keep a very low profile, have her baby, put it up for adoption, and about two years thereafter come back home, marry and settle down. Mrs. Tarleton said: "You would not believe how many have done that, and three of them right now are leaders in our church. And do you know why? Because God blessed them from the start, just as He blesses you."

They explored other possibilities, but in the end the canon returned to the one that lay closest to his religious belief: "Beyond all doubt, Laura, the best route, the one that God has always wanted you to take, is to marry the young man and start a Christian . . ."

She cut him off: "Impossible."

"Why?" both Tarletons asked, and she said grimly: "Because he wouldn't marry me, and I would never marry him."

"Who is he? I'll talk to him."

"The Rastafarian."

"Oh my God!" Reverend Tarleton cried, for he had only yesterday received from the church in Jamaica a report on Ras-Negus Grimble, and the information still burned in his mind:

We're glad you asked for further information on your visitor. Some years ago he formed a fast friendship with our famous reggae singer Bob Marley and together they strung together several Bible texts like the fundamental one in Genesis: "Male and female created he them. And God blessed them, and God said unto them, Be fruitful, and multiply." Using such quotations, they constructed a doctrine which preached: "Rasta Man must have as many children as possible and he must help Rasta Woman do the same." It is known that Marley impregnated twelve different women. Your man, Ras-Negus Grimble, has done almost as well, for we know of eight children he has fathered without ever having been married. When challenged about this, he told one of our social workers in my presence: "God has directed me to have children. That's my job. Yours is to find ways to care for them."

Turning to his wife, he asked, "Should we show her the letter?" and she replied: "I do believe we must," so without comment he handed it to Laura and watched her handsome face as she read it, observing that her expression passed from shock to anger.

Then Laura slowly folded the letter neatly, used one corner to tap her front teeth, and very quietly asked: "As a man of God, where can you send me to have an abortion?"

Neither of the Tarletons drew back from the responsibility implied in this terrible question. Instead, the clergyman took Laura's hand and said: "It would be better, my beloved daughter, if you had the child. But twice in my ministry I have been forced to advise otherwise. Once when a girl was pregnant by her father, again when a child of fourteen was pregnant by her idiot brother. Today you are pregnant by the devil, and you must go to this address in Port of Spain, Trinidad, and now, let us pray."

This time they knelt, and he said simply: "God in heaven, who has watched this meeting from the start, forgive the three of us for departing from Thy teachings, but we are faced by wholly new problems and are honestly striving to do our best. Bless Thy servant Laura, who is a good woman and who has ahead of her a life of great potential contribution, and please bless my wife and me, for we did not seek this problem, nor did we resolve it carelessly."

As Laura rose to leave, both Tarletons kissed her, and he said: "If you should need airfare to Trinidad, we could help," but she said: "I can manage."

The presence of the Rastafarian posed a dilemma to another person—Lincoln Wrentham, eight years older than his sister Sally and proprietor of the Waterloo. During the first month of Grimble's stay in All Saints, Lincoln had been only vaguely aware of his presence. He had seen his tall and distinctive figure once or twice moving rather furtively about the back streets, and after the incident with the American tourist woman from the *Tropic Sands,* he heard that it might have been the Rastafarian's preaching that had triggered the affair. As a man whose business now depended in large part on a constant new supply of American travelers, he was so concerned that he sought a meeting with Harry Keeler, at which he demanded action: "You've got to do something about this fellow."

Harry nodded, but then pointed out: "Isn't that more your father's job than mine?" and Lincoln had to agree, so he went along to his father's office, and there he was pleased to learn that the police were keeping a sharp eye on the Jamaican. "Any agitation, troublemaking, off this island he goes," Commissioner Wrentham assured his son, and there the matter rested. But sometime later, while Lincoln was tending bar at his café, he overheard two patrons talking about the Rastafarian, and one said, "I think he's dating Sally from the prime minister's office," and Lincoln drew closer to eavesdrop, but the men did not refer to his sister again.

He was sufficiently disturbed to stop by his father's office to ask if he knew anything about Sally's possible involvement, and was told: "No, Sally's been going to different affairs, cricket matches and the like, with young Harry Keeler, and I'm very pleased about it. The Rastafarian? Sally's not the type to fool around with him."

And there Lincoln's investigation ended, but the confidence that he and his father expressed about Sally's level-headedness was ill placed, because at the very time they were talking she was deeply involved with Ras-Negus, not like her friend Laura Shaughnessy as a bed partner, but rather as one interested in probing the depth and significance of his vision about the future of the world's black people, and especially those in the Caribbean.

She met with him after work, sometimes talking till near midnight, at other times just closing her eyes and listening to his rendition of some Bob Marley reggae, with the booming of the empty box echoing in her ears as Ras-Negus thumped it. But almost always, whether the session had begun with talk or music, it ended with them chanting "Four Hundred Years." Regularly he tried to make love with her, but her earlier experience in the back of Laura's car had ended any involvement in that area. What attracted her and kept her coming back to argue with him was his extraordinary views about life in general, his conviction that blacks could run their own affairs, and his certainty that domination by the white race was at an end. His Jamaican experience had not allowed him to know that about half the world was neither Caribbean black nor English-American white, but an Asian yellow. Still, the intensity of his thought regarding the little world of the Caribbean gave him authority, and Sally wished to share in it.

She had been reared without racial or social prejudices. After all, her grandfather, Black Bart, had been knighted for his exceptional leadership during World War II and it was rumored that her father, the commissioner, was being touted as the next governor general, so she watched in her own family the liberation and acceptance of blacks and browns. But what they would do with their freedom was another matter, and of late she had often wondered whether a minute island such as All Saints with only a hundred and ten thousand people, fewer than a small American or British city, could exist for long unless it associated itself with eight or nine islands of similar size to form a federation. And if they did, which seemed highly unlikely, on what would they subsist? What industry could thrive in such a small arena, except perhaps tourism, and was that a viable base for a society?

These were heady questions, and one might have thought that she would have gone to her friend Harry Keeler for answers, but she did not for good reason: she had already talked with him about these matters, and whatever he said was strongly colored by England's empire experience, so that all she would be getting from him was standard white-man's thinking. Nor could she talk seriously with her father or brother, because they had been conscripted into a subtle continuance of the white man's rule, her father through his appointment to high office with a promise perhaps of a higher one and her brother through his reliance on tourists to keep his café profitable.

What she really wanted at this moment in her life was a solid six hours with Marcus Garvey, the wild black philosopher of Jamaica, but he was long since dead; or with Frantz Fanon, the equally wild leader from Martinique, but he also was dead. These men would have understood both where she stood at this point in her life and where she wanted to go, but their teachings did not give specific answers to that galaxy of new problems that had arisen since their deaths. In their place she had the Rastafarian, whose savage vitality provided a much lower level of intellectualism. She was more than aware that to compare him with either Garvey or Fanon was preposterous, but she also realized that there might be subtle truth in something he had once said: "I am John the Baptist of the Leeward and Windward Islands." She thought it doubtful that he could be the forerunner of any serious religious movement, but she was not so pessimistic about his ability to inspire political action or at least reassessment, and she needed to hear more of his thinking.

So without ever making a conscious choice, she began engaging in a tricky game, though she wasn't devious. During normal encounters at the office and in the ordinary social events that came along each week, she encouraged Harry Keeler, in whom she was so interested that she was seriously considering marriage, but late at night or on evenings when Harry was engaged in government business, she sought out the Rastafarian for more discussions. Repelling easily the sexual advances he kept making and letting him know exactly what her interests were, she found his reactions to island problems sensible and refreshing so long as they did not involve religion or sex.

One morning as she dressed she thought it would be profitable if she and Laura Shaughnessy invited Ras-Negus to tour the southern end of the island with them as he had the northern, but when she went to ask Laura to join her in extending the invitation, she learned that her friend had left the island on an extended visit to relatives in either Jamaica or Barbados.

When she drove around to pick up Grimble from the tiny house in which he was living with the family of one of his girl friends, she was astonished to discover that he did not know how to drive. To explain this deficiency he reverted to Jamaican street talk, and Sally thought: This touches him deeply. He's a child again.

"That time, long time, me no have nuttin'. Mudder, she work all time, no earn nuttin'. Me never get job drive car, never learn."

"That's all right," she told him. "I'll drive," and they set off for the new road connecting York to the airport, and on this stretch she had first to rebuff him sharply when he tried to work his way under her dress: "Save that for the others, Grimble!" Then she started the long conversation which would continue almost unbroken till they returned to Bristol Town.

"What do you think will happen to the Caribbean, Grimble?" When he started his reply by citing certain obscure passages in Revelation, she cut him short: "None of that nonsense! You and I both know that two hundred years from now America will be where it is and functioning one way or another, and some pope will be in place in Rome with more or less power. And our islands will still be here, populated mostly by blacks and untold numbers of Indians imported from Asia. What I want to know, Grimble, is what kind of world we blacks will have here?"

He protested almost petulantly: "I don't like Grimble. My name Ras-Negus."

She apologized: "I'm sorry, dear friend, A man is entitled to be called by what he prefers. But your predictions, please?"

"In old days lots of blacks from all islands go to work in Cuba cane fields, help build Panama Canal, go live in Central American jungles, cut logwood for dye, mahogany for build things. Most never come back. Later, same kind of men go New York, London, work strong, send much money home. But like others, they too never come back. Things in island stay in balance. Babies born, man go away, room for everyone. But now . . ,"

Sally asked: "Ras-Negus, how old are you?" and he replied: "Twenty-five," to which she said: "You're a bright, able fellow, I could see that from the first. In the times you were talking about, you'd have left Jamaica for the adventure in Panama or headed for London."

He agreed: "If they start something big in Brazil, I go tomorrow," but she would not accept this evasion: "There isn't going to be anything big in Brazil, or Cuba or America. And if there was, people from Central America would rush to grab the jobs."

"I think maybe you're right. London closed, too many out of work. Can't go Trinidad, they won't let."

"So what?"

"Bob Marley . . . Jesus Christ of the Caribbean. Great, great man. He go Africa . . ." and apparently memories of Marley seduced him back into a Jamaican street vocabulary which she could not follow, so after she protested, he said: "Very impressed. Great place, Africa. He tell me when he get back: 'Maybe better we all go Africa. Like Marcus Garvey say. I mean everybody in Jamaica. Just up and go.' I beginnin' to think same way."

"Have you any idea how many ships, big ones, it would take to move Jamaica to Africa?"

"Atom power, maybe nuclear power, it could be done."

When they reached the airport at the southern extremity of the island, she interrupted the dialogue with a suggestion he appreciated: "Let's go into the canteen and have something to eat," but when they sat down at the counter she was amazed when he ordered not only a meat sandwich, but a large bowl of chili, a helping of French fries and a slab of chocolate cake with a large glass of milk. "I thought you ate only natural foods," she chided, and he explained: "Festival with beautiful girl," but she noticed that he did move all the food into his coconut bowl before he ate. He made no effort to pay for what he called his festival, for as usual he had no money, but he ate as if famished, and when Sally could not finish her generous sandwich, he wolfed that down too.

On the drive north, they stopped again, at the deluxe hotel at Pointe Neuve, where she treated him to a lemon squash, and after that she returned to her earlier question: "So what's to become of us in the Caribbean?" and with all other options foreclosed, he said thoughtfully: "Population grow. That for sure. Then people go Trinidad whether they want us or not. Maybe Venezuela, Colombia too. Also Cuba for sure, maybe United States, like people from Haiti."

"Do you think those other countries will allow us in?" and he replied instantly: "They better. What choice they got?"

"I think you'll find they have many choices. Guns along the shore, for example."

"They might. But people tell me guns along Florida don't stop Cubans, Haitians."

"So what else did you and Bob Marley have in mind?"

"Marley no politician. He pure Rasta voice of Jah. That for sure."

"I still want to know, Ras-Negus, what else?"

As she asked this question they were driving slowly along the glorious foreshore of the Caribbean, with an entire world of sun and bending trees and sudden glimpses of Morne de Jour far to the north, and Grimble suddenly cried: "Our islands are too beautiful to lose!" And she noted that now he spoke perfect English.

"Of course," she bore in. "But what are we going to do to keep them?"

"You know anything about communism?"

"Not much, except that it doesn't seem to work too well in Cuba. Why?"

"I've been wondering. Maybe in our islands we need something different. Like sugar and tobacco in the past, even the things we do now, maybe they're gone . . . forever. Like bauxite in Jamaica. When I was a boy, all men in my village looked forward to jobs in bauxite mines, big ships coming to north shore Jamaica, loading our bauxite, carrying it to Philadelphia's big aluminum plants, make frying pans, all things. Now that's all gone. Suppose you're a farmer, you don't want bauxite work, you want to raise bananas on all the hillsides. In the old days big ships came to the same harbors as bauxite, Fyffe & Elder carrying our bananas to Liverpool, Marseilles. Now no more. In old days, everybody worked, everybody happy. Now it's all gone."

He raised his hands in a gesture of despair, then he twisted his lute and began to sing "Four Hundred Years," in which she joined. In this manner they came finally to that lovely pinnacle which housed Pointe Sud, one of the rocky guardians of the Baie de Soleil, from which they could see ships moving from the Caribbean into the *baie*, with handsome Bristol Town gleaming in the distance, the sunlit roof of Government House high on its hill and The Club just visible behind. It was a sight to gladden the heart of any All Saints man, and even a stranger from another island like Grimble could appreciate the unmatched grandeur of this scene.

When Sally pulled her car into a paved parking lot atop the pinnacle, from where they could see both the town to the east and the sea to the west, she asked, not having lost her train of thought: "If Cuban communism isn't the answer, and I'm afraid it isn't because the other islands are too small and too disjointed to work as a unit, what is?"

The Rasta Man had exhausted his alternatives—negritude, Rastafarianism, communism. He had nothing more to offer the Caribbean islands, whose populations were not yet capable of making choices in a complex modern world or of executing them if they did make them. No Caribbean citizens had trained themselves the way the Japanese had before they boldly cried: "We can build automobiles better than Detroit!" or like the Koreans of a decade later who shouted: "We can make steel better and cheaper than Japan." The Caribbean had no black industrialists or engineers capable of duplicating the way the Taiwanese had leaped into world competition to follow the two city-states Hong Kong and Singapore. Citizens of this golden sea were still rural practitioners, some of the most congenial in the world, but self-restricted to digging, cutting and hauling.

Sally, dismayed to see this striving man lost in his simplicities, tried to bring common sense into their discussion: "Could we serve as a kind of manufacturing area for big firms in Britain and America?"

"They're Babylon. They're to be destroyed."

Sally became furious, and showed it: "Grimble! For Christ's sake, stop that nonsense! Put your mind to work. Do you think we could attract manufacturing? Sewing clothes or putting machines together?"

"Jamaica had bauxite. They left. Now we have nothing!"

"But we have people. Very able people who could learn anything."

"We had bananas, but now with Fyffe & Elder gone, we have nothing."

She wondered if the Caribbean islands could develop high-technology assembly industries, employing women to operate the demanding machinery, but Ras-Negus said that the women he knew would not be content to work in closed-in spaces: "They like outdoors."

This contemptuous dismissal of her proposal angered Sally, and she said: "The women in Haiti make all the baseballs used in what they call the American big leagues. Why couldn't we promote some industry like that?"

"Proud black women won't slave for American white men. Never."

Then, like so many thoughtful people in the islands, she asked: "Can we expand our hotels and beach areas, and bring in really great numbers of tourists with their dollars and pounds and bolivars?"

He dismissed this bluntly: "Proud black men don't want to serve those big fat pigs . . ." and she exploded: "Damn you! Those were your words that crazy man shouted when he assaulted the Jewish woman. 'Big fat white pig.' You came to this island solely to make trouble, and you ought to be ashamed of yourself. I don't want to share anything with you anymore." Then she shouted: "If I told my father about this, he'd have you arrested." And she abruptly got out of the car.

Hesitantly he followed her onto the headland, where her temper subsided, and there she halted her interrogation, for she realized that it was getting nowhere; she had plumbed the depths of his understanding and found them extremely shallow, but as they sat together and as he began talking of the values he really cherished, she found that it was he who was attuned to the great, basic, primordial reality of the Caribbean isles, not she. Her concern was only with the current-day politics and economics of the immediate future; he was in some primitive way in touch with Africa, and the old-time sugar plantation, and the struggle for freedom, and the manifestations of negritude at a basic level which she could never attain. She realized that here in bright daylight with a clean breeze blowing in from the sea, she was in much the same condition as she had been in the back of Laura Shaughnessy's car that night when marijuana fumes filled the air. In her harsh analysis of Caribbean reality a few minutes ago, there had been at best a metallic reality; in the Rastafarian's words, there was a narcotic beauty, and she wondered if, through music and ganja and dreaming, he had not come closer to understanding their Caribbean than she.

He now spoke reflectively in a fearful mix of Rastafarian glossolalia, old African words and rearranged English, but she understood the message: "The people of the Caribbean are different. Their early life in Africa made them so, right from the beginning. Terrible years on the sugar plantations increased the difference between them and white people. We think different. We value different things. We live different. And we must make our living in different ways. The white man has nothing to teach us. We build a good life here, we find the money to buy his radios, his televisions, his Sony Betamaxes, his Toyotas."

"Everything you mentioned comes from Japan, not from white people."

Ras-Negus, always displeased when reality was thrust into his dreams, ignored this: "So we make our life simple, strictly black folk living and working with black folk, we unite all the islands, even Cuba and Martinique, and we tell the rest of the world: 'This our little world. We run it our way. Stay out!'"

And Sally had to ask the terrible, unanswerable question: "But where do we get the money to live?"

But he did have an answer and it astonished her, for it was delivered with such poetic force and such rich allusion that she had to grant that he believed it: "When we lived free in Africa, we existed, didn't we? When we came over in the dreadful slave ships, most of us survived, didn't we? And when our fathers worked like animals, dawn to dusk in the sugar fields, we managed to remain human beings, didn't we? How in hell do you think you and I would be here if our black ancestors didn't have a powerful will to live? I got that same will, Sally, and I think you do, too."

Then came the incandescent moment she would never forget, regardless of what happened to Ras-Negus and his confused dreams. An earlier group of visitors to this headland had held a picnic, and to toast their bread and heat water for their tea they had scoured the area for limbs and branches to build a small fire. Somebody had dragged in a piece of wood much too long to be fitted in the fire, and it had been left behind for Ras-Negus to find.

Realizing that his conversation with Sally had come to an end, he lifted the piece of wood almost automatically, hefted it several times, and found that although it was as narrow as a broomstick, in other respects it resembled a cricket bat; length, weight and general feel were right. After taking a few desultory swings, he assumed the proper stance of a batsman in his crease, and as he lashed out at imaginary balls—a spinner attacking his wicket, a googly in the grass, a body-line bumper of the kind the mighty Larwood used to throw, right at the batsman's head—he began to speak of the real West Indies: "I saw my first cricket match in Kingston. I was nine and an uncle took me to the Oval, and for the first time I saw the players in their clean whites, the umpire in his linen duster, the colorful crowd, and I was captured.

"You want to know what our islands are best at? Cricket. In 1975, when I was nineteen, they got all the top countries of the world together, those that played cricket, and they held a world championship series in England: Ceylon, New Zealand, Pakistan, South Africa, India, and especially the Big Three, Australia, England, us. Two brackets. One-day matches, knock-out rounds. And who do you think won? West Indies! Sore losers in London and Delhi and Sydney shouted: 'Freak! The wicket wasn't sound!' So they held the same championship matches in 1979, and who won this time, against the world's best? West Indies. Champions of the whole world, twice running."

Then, assuming the postures of the great batsmen, he reeled off the names revered by West Indian boys, and by their elders too: "Sir Frank Worrell, from my island, Jamaica, maybe the handsomest man who ever played the game. I have a photo of him leaving the field at Lords after having demolished the English bowling. Head high, bat trailing, confident smile, he was a young god.

"Then there was Sir Gary Sobers," and here he took a series of wild cuts at the invisible ball. "Termed by critics in all countries the greatest all-round cricketer there ever was. Fantastic batsman, great bowler, maybe best at fielding with those catlike moves. He came from Barbados and blazed himself into glory."

He stopped, broke into a smile, waved his bat a couple of times, and said: "And there was Sir Benny Castain of your island. He was the little round fellow that everybody loved. Used cricket as a key to men's hearts." He reflected on the impressive parade of world-class figures that had come from his little islands.

He spent the next minutes in a haunting ballet, swinging his bat in borrowed glory, reliving the time when his black fellows were champions of the world, and wondering when the days of glory would come again. Cars passing on the road stopped to watch this very tall Rastafarian in his green and gold tam, flying dreadlocks, hopping stenciled shirt and unkempt trousers as he epitomized in his dance the one sure thing in which his islands excelled. It was one of the passengers in these stopped cars who recognized Sally Wrentham sitting on a rock, watching the dance, and who hurried back to Bristol Town to inform her brother.

Halting his dance to the gods of cricket, Ras Negus said to Sally: "And remember, these were all black men, not white, who mastered a new game and quickly became champions. If we did it once, we can do it again. In whatever field is necessary. You want our women to learn what Japanese women know about making televisions? They can do it. We can do anything, we black people."

He danced away from her, still pretending that he was Sir Benny, but then he threw the bat away and went back to the car: "I mean it. You and I can do anything. Anything." Then he added: "You with brains must tell me what. I with heart will tell you how."

It was late when Sally delivered Ras-Negus to his digs and then headed for home. But when she reached her driveway, she was flagged down by a young woman who worked in her office and lived on her street: "I've been waiting for you, Sally."

"Went for a long drive. We stopped at Pointe Sud for a chat, then I dropped him off at his place."

"Who?"

"The Rastafarian. He has a world of ideas."

The woman frowned: "That's what I feared. Your brother was out asking about you. I told him I didn't know where you'd gone or with who. But later your father stopped by, and he looked pretty angry."

"What did you tell him?"

"The same." She hesitated a moment, then shrugged her shoulders as if she had reached a decision reluctantly: "I guess I'd better tell you, Sally."

"What? Were they real mad?"

"This is something else. It's about Laura."

"An accident?"

"No. It seems she went to Trinidad, not Barbados."

"Why would she tell a lie? What purpose?"

"To have an abortion."

"Oh my God, who's the father?"

"Your Rastafarian."

Sally gasped. Then words and images flashed through her mind in a storm, helter-skelter: Poor Laura . . . what a horrible break . . . should we take up a collection to help her . . . no wonder Linc and Father were mad if they thought . . . Poor Laura, couldn't she see what a pathetic substitute for a real man he is . . .

"Are you okay?" the young woman asked solicitously, and Sally replied, "I think I'll take a walk. Sort things out," and the woman said: "Good luck. When they questioned me they looked like a pair of sharks."

Because she needed time to bring the hurricane revelations about Laura into focus, Sally took a circuitous route, and as she walked slowly, head down, through the warm April night, she tried to bring some order to her vagrant thoughts, and her first focus had to be upon her friend: Poor Laura. We must do everything to help her. I wonder what she thought that evening on our trip back from the north when the Rasta climbed into the back seat of the car to make passes at me. Had she been pregnant already? Oh my God!

Then she could think of herself: He never got me involved . . . well, not really. I took care of that as soon as my head cleared. But if that's true, why did I seek him out today, want to talk with him? Because he has a vital message . . . I may not like it, and it may not pertain to me, but it could matter a lot to others.

Finally she reached the main point of her analysis: He sure knows what a black person is. He thinks like one. He has the vision, take it or leave it, he has it.

Suspicious of these easy conclusions, she realized they made her look too good. A young woman who thought as straight as she wanted to ought to be judicious, fair to others, and aware of great social and racial problems. But then two other thoughts surged to the fore, and when she grappled with them she did not look so saintly, and she knew it. Why, if she was as interested in Harry Keeler as she apparently was, had she bothered to fool around with the Rastafarian on any terms whatever? Was her relationship with the white man so weak or so fundamentally wrong that the intrusion of the first vital black man, regardless of his appearance, posed a threat? As she asked herself this, she turned a corner, and in the light of the rising moon could see in the distance the headland at Pointe Sud where Ras-Negus had danced in honor of his great cricketing heroes, and she halted for a while to catch her breath and try to get the two men into focus. She could not.

Her final question struck close to home. If she suspected that Ras-Negus had first brought the phrase *You big fat white pig* onto the island, passing it along to sympathetic listeners in the barrios at night, where it lodged in the brain of the man who attacked the New York woman, was she not obligated to report this fact to her father, who was responsible for the safety of the island, or to Harry Keeler, who had to protect the income which the tourists brought?

Biting her lower lip, she strode forward, willing to confront the expected assaults on her behavior, but as she turned a corner and saw her house looming in the shadows, with who knew what awaiting inside, she slowed perceptibly, took deep breaths, and whispered to herself: "Come on, ladybug. Fly away home. You sought this out. And now your house is on fire."

When she opened the door, no one shouted at her or demanded to know where she had been. Instead, she saw four extremely sober men gathered in the living room: her father and brother; Harry, her acknowledged gentleman friend; and Canon Tarleton, her clergyman. They rose as she came in, stood until she sat down and turned to look at her father, who said: "Sally, we've been terribly worried about you."

"I took a ride to the airport with the Rastafarian."

"We know. A person who saw you at Pointe Sud went to Lincoln's café and told him."

"It was just a ride. We had things to talk about."

"If you'd told us," Lincoln interrupted, "we could have warned you."

"About what?"

In reply her brother said: "Both Canon Tarleton and Father have received letters from Jamaica . . . about your Rastafarian."

"He's not *my* Rastafarian."

"Thank God for that," Lincoln said, and he indicated that his father should hand over his letter, the long one from the Jamaican police, detailing Ras-Negus' relation to the law, and when Sally finished reading she was shaken. Taken one by one, she could believe each of the legal accusations against Ras-Negus, for she'd had intimations which supported them, but she had never taken the time to tie one to the other until an unmistakable thread evolved. The Jamaican police had very carefully tied them together, and the result was ugly.

Seeing her shock, the men bore in with harsh and pertinent questions: "Have you ever seen him with ganja?" Yes, at Cap Galant. "Have you ever known him to speak to any All Saints person about ganja?" Yes, a farmer south of Tudor. At this information the two men of her family looked meaningfully at each other, and Lincoln said: "That's where we think the airstrip is." The next question came closer to home: "Did you ever hear him speak of the police as the 'Great Babylon'?" Yes, many times. "And did you ever hear him say that this particular Great Babylon must be destroyed?" Many times.

But when they asked: "Did you ever hear him say anything about starting trouble for the police on this island?" she kept silent, because she had felt that her suspicion about the phrase "you big fat white pig" was that and nothing more. A coincidence in five words was not sufficient to damn a man.

The questioning now took a more delicate turn, with Canon Tarleton participating. The men wanted to know the extent of her personal involvement with the Rastafarian, and at first she thought she could handle this by confessing that she found parts of his philosophy about the future of black people fresh and challenging, but they pressed on. What her brother really wanted to know was: "Were you and he in any way personally involved?"

She stiffened. Her brother's question was inept and she did not intend to submit herself to any kind of moral interrogation, and things might have become tense had not the phone jangled at this moment. It was for her father, and after only six or eight brief grunts of approval, with no words spoken, he jammed down the receiver, turned to his son, and said: "They've found the airstrip. Up toward

Tudor." Before he dashed out the door, taking Lincoln with him, the commissioner turned to the minister: "Tarleton, you'd better show her that other letter," and as the car roared off, the canon produced his letter from the minister in Jamaica regarding moral behavior and silently handed it over. As she read it, Keeler watched.

The ugly report—which explained Laura's pregnancy and her willingness to have a Trinidad abortion—had a dull, sickening effect on Sally. Reading it twice, underlining the crucial words with her right forefinger, she understood why these four men had been waiting for her when she returned from her ride.

"I'm damned sorry," Keeler said, moving his chair closer to hers. "I suppose you've heard about Laura Shaughnessy? I thought so."

After looking closely at the two white men who obviously wished her well, she said: "Let's get the facts straight. I had no amorous involvement with the Rastafarian, not in any way. He made approaches, two or three times, and I brushed him off for the clown he was." She stopped, aware that what she had just said was only partially true. Then she added: "But as I said before, I did find him intellectually stimulating. It could be he represents the future."

"God forbid," Canon Tarleton said, and then Sally leaned back, totally relaxed, and said almost wittily: "And as for the question that's really bothering you. No, I am not pregnant, and there's no way I could be."

The interrogation might have continued had not the phone rung again. Keeler answered it. This time it brought a crisp command: "Keeler? Lincoln here. North end of the island. We've found the ganja airstrip. Captured a two-seater plane. Pilots and the man tending the strip implicate the Rastafarian, so we've got to fan out and arrest that bounder. Now!"

Grabbing Sally by the wrist, Keeler said: "I'll need your help to track him down," and when she asked "Who?" he said: "Your Rasta Man," and they sped off to pick up three policemen to help in the search, but even with Sally's knowing guidance, they had no luck in finding him.

Like most clever marijuana smugglers, the brainy men who organize the routes and hire the operators, Grimble tried never to be tied physically to the operation. No policeman must ever see him at a secret airstrip or even close to an airplane, and he had learned never to sleep three nights in a row at any location, so when Sally led Keeler and the policemen to the shack at which she had deposited Ras-

Negus earlier that evening, they found nothing, for he had long since fled.

She remembered another house from which she had once picked him up for a night session of reggae and talk, but the people inside told the policemen: "We not see more than two weeks." She remembered one last house, but it was empty, and that exhausted her clues. The men up north had proof of the ganja smuggling, but the mastermind of the operation was hiding somewhere, laughing at the frustration of Great Babylon, but after more than an hour of going to the kinds of places in which Grimble might be hiding, a boy of ten told the police: "You seek man long hair? Maybe he be with Betsy Rose."

Betsy Rose was a woman from the British Virgins who had come to All Saints as a maid, and had fallen into trouble with her mistress because the master of the household delighted in sleeping with her. Betsy Rose had been kicked out, had drifted from one job to another, and had wound up the companion of a sailor who was not concerned about her male visitors. When the police stormed the house, they found her and the Rastafarian in bed.

At first, Keeler wanted to protect Sally from the ugly sight of rousting the Jamaican out, but then he had a stronger idea: "Maybe you ought to see your hero as he really is," and he took her inside to watch as the police hauled the long-legged Rasta Man out from beneath the covers and on to his feet. Naked, he looked as if he were all hair, for his dreadlocks reached to his waist.

It was a revolting sight, and Sally thought: So much for the inner soul of negritude. But as she watched him struggle to pull on his trousers while Keeler held his left arm, she felt a sense of pity for the confused fellow: Loud talker, sweet singer, but still he winds up captured by white authorities. Not much different from Africa four hundred years ago, and the lyrics of the Bob Marley song echoed in her mind.

When Keeler and Sally reported, alone, to the prime minister waiting at the police station, Keeler said: "Good news. We have the Rastafarian locked up."

"Where?"

"Stashed away in a shack out toward the Anse de Soir. What shall we do with him?"

After looking carefully about to ensure that no one could hear, the prime minister growled: "Best if we could shoot him . . . about six weeks from now when no one's noticing. But I'm sure there must be a better way. Any suggestions?"

Keeler said: "I'd say ship him off the island on the first plane out."

"Where to?"

"Anywhere."

"Good. Pay his fare and throw him on the plane."

Keeler said: "When he landed, the airline told us that he had a prepaid ticket to somewhere," and a sergeant broke in: "He did. But he cashed it in the first full day he was here. Absolutely broke."

"We'll have to buy him a ticket. Well worth the price," the prime minister said. "Will you men promise me that he has no broken bones? No conspicuous wounds?"

"None," a policeman assured him. "Clothes not even torn. Nothing."

"I trust you, but as he heads for the plane I want witnesses at the airport who can later testify in court, if he launches a case against us, that he left the island without a scar. Even safer if we have photographs." As he was about to leave for home and some sleep, he added: "Fetch Tarleton, and his wife too. Clergymen make impressive witnesses."

As soon as he was gone, Keeler sprang into action: "Sally, go home and bring your big camera," and when she returned she saw a waiting car that contained three policemen. As it prepared to drive away, Keeler came up in another car containing Canon Tarleton and his wife, and into it Sally climbed for the short ride out to the shack, where handcuffs were applied to the Rasta Man's wrists and ankles before he was dragged into the rear seat of the police car.

In Keeler's car the Tarletons had no idea of how the Rasta Man had been arrested, so they peppered Sally with questions. She said: "We went to three different shacks, but found nothing till a little boy told us that he might be at Betsy Rose's."

"Who's she?" Mrs. Tarleton asked from the back seat, and her husband replied: "An unfortunate woman fallen from grace."

"Were you pleased to capture such a rascal?" asked the canon's wife, and Sally was ashamed to reveal the details of the arrest: "High time he's thrown off this island," but then she was almost driven to add: "I did feel sorry for him when they locked him in handcuffs. He is a free spirit, you know."

"You sound as if you might have been in love with him," Mrs.

Tarleton said with the charming frankness that the wives of English churchmen often acquire, and Sally laughed: "Not now, not ever. He had interesting things to say that I think we'd all better listen to. But that was all."

Not satisfied with this evasive answer, Mrs. Tarleton asked Sally bluntly: "What ideas of the Rastafarian did you find acceptable?" and before answering, Sally pondered how best to share her perceptions. Then, satisfied with her strategy, she said: "Look, I'm the only black person in a car of whites. Just like it was a hundred years ago . . . Today it ought to be three of us blacks and you, Mrs. Tarleton." Someone gasped at her boldness.

"But since you three are such dear friends and such worthy people to have on the island, I'll answer your question, which otherwise I might have found quite condescending."

She explained that Ras-Negus, no matter how he behaved with women, spoke as an authentic black man, with all the limitations of education and knowledge of history that this implied. She granted that his messing around with the English language, creating words like *overstand* as superior to *understand* was childish, and that his acceptance of Haile Selassie as the seventy-something incarnation of the Lord was preposterous.

"What's left?" Mrs. Tarleton asked, and Sally replied: "He speaks to the frustrations of former slaves . . . which is what I am, and all the officers on our island. He speaks to our African heritage, which I feel very strongly sometimes, and to which good people like you never speak. With you it's all England, England . . . and what is there in England for us? And he speaks to that mystical word we're all trying to define and isolate, *negritude*. He taught me more about negritude in ten minutes than you three could in ten years, because he knows and you will never be allowed to know, regardless of how generous you are in your attempts to learn."

She noticed that the Tarletons in the back seat elected not to respond, but she also saw that Harry, next to her in the front seat, had grown tense and that his hands gripped the steering wheel too tightly, so she quietly slipped her hand onto his left knee, patted it, and smiled as if to reassure him that whereas he would never understand the things that Ras-Negus had known intuitively, he deserved merit for trying.

When they reached the airport she saw something which made her burst into laughter. Her father and her brother had brought the

Rastafarian to the departure lounge in a disguise which masked his membership in the Selassie sect. His long dreadlocks were massed atop his head and hidden beneath a turban which made him look like a proper Sikh. His beard was tucked into the top of a poncho, covering his Rastafarian shirt calling for death to the pope, and instead of leather sandals he wore a pair of immense, cheap white tennis shoes. Whatever dignity his junglelike Rastafarian costume had provided was smothered in this wealth of everyday fabric. More than anything else, he resembled a messy long-haired mongrel dog dragged in from a storm, and Sally thought: You sired eight children in Jamaica and probably two or more here, and look at you now.

But then she heard the loud laughter of the Tarletons and Keeler, and the knowledge that Ras-Negus would be leaving All Saints accompanied by the derisive jeers of white folks was more than she could bear. Determined to make a gesture that would shock her white friends into realizing that she remained loyal to black causes, she pushed past them, ran to the departure gate, threw her arms about the Rasta Man, and kissed him. "Thank you for what you shared with me," she whispered. Then she drew back to watch him as he lifted his canvas bag, tucked his lute under his arm, and followed like an obedient child as the policemen unlocked his handcuffs and escorted him to the outbound plane.

XV

TWINS

"**D**R. STEVE CALDERON? MIAMI? CHAIRMAN OF WIN WITH Reagan 1984? This is the White House calling. Please hold for the President."

"Who is it?" Kate asked, seeing the startled look on her husband's face, the nervous tapping of his fingers. Then, frowning: "Has the bank refused our request for a loan on the addition to the clinic?"

"Not even close—and you'll never guess in a hundred years," he said out of the corner of his mouth. Then he tensed, held the phone away from his ear for a brief moment, and they both heard the husky voice they knew so well from TV and radio: "Steve Calderon? I'm not going to pull the old politician's trick and say I remember you perfectly. But they tell me you did a great job for the party last time. Hope you'll give George Bush the same help this November."

"He'll carry Florida in a landslide. We Cubans know who helped us when we needed it."

"Dr. Calderon, some of us would like to have a meeting with you, tomorrow, my office, two in the afternoon."

"I can be there," Steve replied without hesitation. And then came the first of the warnings from the President: "Speak to no one about this. That's of utmost importance."

"Very good, sir. I shall speak to no one."

"Well?" Kate asked as soon as he hung up. "What's it all about?"

"You heard me. I'm to talk to no one . . ." And she said: "But I'm not just no one."

She was right, as she usually was. Although Steve was in his middle fifties, he was as much in love with Kate as he had been almost thirty years ago when they drove at midnight in a darkened car twenty miles west of Havana to catch the small boat in which they escaped from Castro's Cuba. She had been his support then, assuring him: "You'll find a job somewhere, Estéfano. The whole world needs doctors." And when at the last moment he had been overcome with fear, it was she who would not allow him to falter: "This boat! Crowded or not, this boat!" and it was almost as if she had willed the frail craft north to the Florida Keys and freedom.

Nor did her courage fail during those first terrible years in Miami when he had been unable to prove his credentials as a doctor; nurses found it easier to get accredited, so Kate, after establishing an excellent record for dependability and attention to detail, persuaded the hospital administrator to give her husband a janitorial job on her ward, and for three years he patiently wore blue workman's jeans and watched as young American men who knew far less than he made decisions that determined life or death. Since she earned more than he, she paid for the courses he had to take to demonstrate his ability to be a doctor, and ultimately she watched as he marched up to receive his American medical diploma.

When he opened his office on what was to become Calle Ocho, Southwest Eighth Street near midtown Miami, it was her money that paid the rent, and during the first three years she served as his assistant so they could save money, and she encouraged those bold steps which led to Steve's becoming head of his own clinic with four associates under him, and then officer of one of the first Cuban banks, and finally its president.

Her husband was by no means a passive agent in this spectacular achievement—they were both proof of what an educated Cuban couple could accomplish in a new world. He was an excellent doctor, with a reassuring appearance and manner: tall, slightly underweight, graying hair at the temples, with a winning smile and a habit of telling each patient in Spanish: "Now, Mrs. Espinosa, I'm not sure I know all the answers in your case, but I certainly know how to find out, and we'll see if we can't help you." He'd had such good results that patients spoke of him to their friends, and soon he started treating

Anglos as well and on some days his office was crowded with them.

Until Steve Calderon was forty-eight he had been both a first-class doctor and a bank official, but when one of the biggest banks bought out his small one at enormous profit to him, he became a full-time banker. Kate could afford to stop nursing, and now she served as vice-president at the bank in charge of enticing women in the Spanish community to become depositors. She was also supervising the building of the addition to the medical clinic in which her husband still had a financial but not an operating interest.

The Calderons were repeatedly and justly pointed out as exemplars of the relative speed with which the Cubans of the 1959 immigration established themselves in Florida life, and in their case, at the very top ranks, for Dr. Steve, as he was known, had made himself a major factor in Miami's social, business and political life. And since the Cubans were fiercely Republican in their sympathies, believing that John F. Kennedy and Jimmy Carter had let them down at moments of crisis and that Democrats in general were soft on communism if not in fact crypto-communists, the Calderons fell naturally into the Republican party, where both were figures of considerable importance, Kate serving as chairperson of Women for a Strong Republic and Steve as leader of Win with Reagan. Noticeably, neither organization used the word *Cuban* in its title, in order not to alienate the old-time Floridians who resented how effectively Cubans had changed the region from Democratic to Republican.

So when Kate stared with good-natured determination at her husband as he hung up the phone, and said: "Well?" she expected him to tell her what the President said but he parried: "You heard what I had to promise. I can speak to no one," and she maneuvered: "Tell me only one thing. Cuba?" and he said: "Since I don't know, I suppose I am allowed to make a guess. Probably."

Now she became alert, pressing, moving close to him and warning: "Steve, under no circumstance, I don't care what, must you have anything to do with the Cuban question. It's just too inflammatory," and after taking her hands in his, he said: "I know."

And he did, for if a chain of recent incidents had not reminded him of how dangerous it was, an ugly visit from the wild man Máximo Quiroz would.

The incidents were representative of the pressure under which the Miami Cuban community lived. When a high military officer in the Castro government defected by flying a small plane at great danger to himself from Cuba to Key West, the American government was delighted to have in their hands a man who might provide substantial information, but even before the cheering stopped, experts warned Washington: "Get him the hell out of Florida right away! His life's in danger! Those fanatics will argue: 'If he stayed with Castro this long, he must have been involved in the Bay of Pigs. Let's shoot the bastard!'" So the Cuban general was whisked out of Florida, and four days later the FBI learned that had he dared set foot in Miami, the Quiroz Group had planned to assassinate him.

Máximo Quiroz was a special problem to the Calderons, for back in 1898, when Cuba gained its independence from Spain, the great-grandfathers of Steve Calderon and Quiroz, who stemmed from the same family, formed a friendship which had extended and flourished in the next generations, so that when Steve and Máximo fled Cuba in 1959 it was as fellow freedom seekers, young men of high intelligence and determination. But in Miami, their lives had separated dramatically, for Steve and his wife had followed the path of total integration into the Miami elites, while Máximo had become the obstreperous leader of those Cubans who said in effect: "To hell with America and American ways, we want to get back to a free Cuba," and his determination was so profound that he was among the first to volunteer for the Bay of Pigs invasion and the last to retreat from that fiasco. The failure of this gallant but shamefully mismanaged mission so infuriated Quiroz that he became a monomaniac who would never rest until Cuba was liberated and Castro was dead. The FBI was wise to keep a close watch on him, for Cuban circles reported: "If any refugee in Miami can be expected to get in a little rubber boat, paddle back to Havana and try to assassinate Castro, it will be Máximo Quiroz."

As recently as July of this year, when handicapped children from Cuba were invited by good-hearted people to participate in the International Special Olympics held at Notre Dame, Quiroz organized a group of super-patriots to descend upon the airport to taunt the adorable lot of wide-eyed youngsters, creating an ugly fuss which alienated many. Sometimes his activities generated a popular response, as when, in late August, on the opening day of the big Pan-American games in Indianapolis, he had a low-flying crop-dusting plane fly overhead trailing behind it a long banner reading: "Cubans! Choose Freedom!" while on the ground his volunteers distributed thousands of handbills which explained in Spanish how any member of the huge Cuban delegation could defect and claim political asylum in the United States. Again the FBI kept close watch.

More disturbing to the Calderons was the case of the Cuban artist living in exile in Miami who was invited to show examples of his work at an exhibition in Havana displaying art from all the Hispanic countries of the Western Hemisphere. This fellow had the bad luck to win second prize, and at the distribution of medals and checks that went with them, he had been photographed with Castro, who had thrown one arm about his shoulder. After this picture appeared in Miami papers, someone set the artist's studio ablaze, and when the firemen reached the embers they found tacked on a nearby wall the warning: "Don't fraternize with tyrants!" Although it could not be proved, it was widely suspected that the arsonist had been Quiroz.

He was definitely not involved with the bombing of a tobacco shop selling Cuban cigars, for when that incident occurred he was agitating in Chicago, but even so, knowing Cubans along Calle Ocho whispered: "Quiroz must have done it by mail." As a member of the Hispanic community observed: "To Quiroz and his kind, if you're not in favor of dropping a nuclear bomb on Havana, you're a communist."

The Calderons, fully aware of these tensions, had during their stay in America followed one simple rule: "We're totally opposed to that fiend Castro and wish him monstrous bad luck, but we're willing to let him fester on his island." They never said a good word about Castro or the Democratic party, and thus kept their credentials clean, but they also never descended to the pathological hatred that spurred Quiroz to his outrageous acts, and although they were distantly related to him, they kept away from him. "Máximo has made himself judge and jury where Cuban orthodoxy is concerned," Kate had warned her husband during one outbreak of anti-Castro demonstrations, "so beware of him. Let him ride his horse, but let us go our own more sensible way."

On the evening before her husband's departure for Washington, she repeated her warning: "Steve, have nothing to do with anything Cuban. Leave Castro alone. Stick to your work here at home," and he agreed: "I'm as wary of Máximo as you are," and on that promise they went to sleep.

Early next day, a very hot morning in September, Kate drove Steve to the always-crowded Miami airport, where he caught an Eastern flight to Washington, and after a hurried lunch reported to the White House, where guards inspected him and his briefcase with special care. The President did not take part in the meeting, but he did spend several minutes greeting the participants, and to Calderon he said: "Yes! Now I remember. You chaired that big dinner in Miami, and I hope we can count on your cooperation again." With that he vanished, calling back over his shoulder: "See you when you're through."

The discussion involved only six people, two from State, two from the National Security Council, plus a junior member of the President's staff on political matters and Steve. His intuition had been correct, the subject was Cuba. Said the senior man from State: "We've heard persistent rumors from our friends in Latin America that Castro is keen to receive some gesture from us—economic loans, promise to relax policies. You name it, we don't know."

"But have *we* received such hints from him?" Steve asked, and one of the NSC men said: "Vague rumors. Nothing substantive."

The man from State resumed: "Putting it all together, we've concluded it might be proper to send him a quiet signal—nothing flashy, nothing to get in the evening news, just a sign to let him know we're in the same ballpark. He's a great baseball fan, you know," he chuckled at the aptness of his phrase.

"What did you have in mind?" Steve asked, and one of the NSC men took over: "Like Tom said, nothing spectacular," and he opened a folder containing a sheaf of papers. "Says here that you're a cousin of Roberto Calderón Amadór, one of Castro's advisers, and curiously, that you're also his brother-in-law."

"Right on both counts. His grandfather and mine were brothers, and we married twin sisters."

"Let me verify this," and he checked his papers: "Your wife, Caterina, is the twin sister of his wife, Plácida. Were you by chance married on the same day?"

"Two years apart. I was attracted to Kate because Plácida was so attractive. Great wife, each of them."

"So if you were just to mosey down to Cuba . . . to meet your cousin . . . so your wives could renew childhood associations . . ."

"It would look quite normal, wouldn't it?" the State Department man broke in.

"Yes, except that as you probably know, Roberto and I haven't seen each other since Kate and I left Cuba in '59. Why would I have this sudden outburst of interest?"

"That's where your wives come in. Sentiment. Old ties of a pair of twins. What could be more natural?" The men spent some time congratulating themselves on having found a perfect cover, but when one of the NSC people used it in conversation later, the head man from State cautioned: "Do not use that word. This is a cover for nothing. In fact, Dr. Calderon will be doing nothing, nothing at all."

"He's right!" the second State man added. "The word *cover* would be totally misleading," and the NSC man asked rather testily: "What, then?" The man from State elaborated: "Don't even use *excuse* for visiting. Perhaps it's best if you just say *reason* for visiting."

"And your reason for going," chimed in the second NSC man, "is to quietly, almost accidentally, let your influential cousin know that when you worked for Ronald Reagan in the 1984 campaign, blah-blah-blah, that if the time was ever going to be ripe for a softening of attitudes toward Cuba, blah-blah-blah, well, it could be right now."

Again the man from the State broke in: "And if, as would seem highly probable, you could get your cousin to introduce you to Castro . . . Well, it would be advantageous for us if you would be able to meet the man."

"What would I say to him?" Steve asked, whereupon the blah-blah man from the NSC jumped in with a warning: "Nothing definitive, because you know nothing definitive. Keep the conversation casual and say that from conversations you've had with Reagan's men in Washington, you gleaned the distinct impression that if there ever was a time, blah-blah-blah. Just that, nothing more, and add that would be undoubtedly true: 'Of course, nothing may come of the mood, and I may be overstressing it, blah-blah-blah.' But let it be known that you personally think there might be a good deal in it."

"Could there be?" Steve asked, and now the young man from the President's office, obviously opposed to this meeting and the proposals coming from it, felt compelled to come in, and he did so with cold force: "Understand, Dr. Calderon, there is no change of policy or attitude in the White House. We still see Fidel Castro as a communist menace and we deplore his involvement in Nicaragua. If you should meet him, you're obligated to make that clear."

"They're largely my views, too," Steve said, but the man from State said quietly: "Of course, we wouldn't be meeting with you if things at headquarters hadn't changed somewhat, isn't that right, Terrence?" and the President's man said: "Naturally. But I didn't want Dr. Calderon to go to Cuba with any Sunday-school impressions. Castro is still the enemy." The man from State had the last word: "If your signal gets through, don't be surprised if a couple of months from now your cousin Roberto comes to Miami so that his wife can visit yours and so that he can slip you a countersignal."

Steve, aware that these men were playing hardball and that collegial agreement had not been reached among them, felt he had to speak: "You're aware, of course, that for a Miami Cuban to have anything to do with either Castro or Cuba is dangerous? Tempers run high in Miami."

Three of the men considered this an overstatement and said so, but the two NSC men had had ample confirmation of Steve's point, and one conceded: "Dangerous, yes, but not fatal. Besides, there would be no reason for anyone in Miami to know that you were going."

Steve's legitimate fears were not dissipated by this easy assurance, since the man giving it did not know Miami, but when, at the close of the meeting, the President reappeared to ask: "Well, is it all set?" Steve felt impelled to say: "On track," and the last ten minutes were devoted to hard nose decisions about the logistics of his trip and a reminder that his commission was extremely limited: "You're to make contact with your cousin. Nothing more. But if *he* can work it for you to see Castro, grab the opportunity . . . but don't seem too eager."

On the flight home Steve reflected on his curious relationship with the United States, of which he was now a citizen, and particularly on his ambivalent position in Miami, capital of the Cuban immigration into the country. Within the first few weeks of Castro's takeover of the island, he had foreseen with considerable accuracy what must happen in Cuba, that the drift toward communism would be inescapable and irreversible. And he had also realized that in such a country, there would be no place for him; his tendencies were too strongly imbedded in freedom and democracy.

He and Kate had been among the first to leave Cuba, far ahead of the mass emigrations of 1961, and they had never regretted their early decision, for as Kate had said at the time: "Everyone in Cuba knows that your branch of the Calderons was always in favor of joining Cuba to the United States—since the 1880s to be accurate—so maybe we better go there, now, while we can still get out!"

From the moment they landed at Key West, both Calderons had

been satisfied with their choice, and even in the dark days when Steve could not become qualified as an American doctor, they had remained steadfast in their loyalty; they had been the first married couple in the initial group of immigrants to win American citizenship and had never once, not even in moments of understandable nostalgia, considered returning to Cuba. They never wasted time or imagination dreaming of the day when Castro died and all the Cubans in Miami would be free to flood back to the island; for them, Cuba was a historical fact, an island on which their ancestors had prospered for nearly five hundred years and on which they themselves had known great happiness, but it was part of the past now. It was a memory, not a magnet.

Two little prepositions, Steve mused. Maybe they summarize everything. Down there I always said: "I live *on* the island of Cuba." But up here I say: "I live *in* the United States." I've traded a colorful little island for a great continent, and when you make a switch of that dimension, your mind expands to meet the challenges of a bigger arena.

But he had never sought to deny his Cuban ancestry as some émigrés did, and in 1972 he had helped in the movement to make Miami's Dade County officially bilingual. But in 1980 outraged Anglo citizens, feeling themselves pushed against the wall by the flood of Cubans, launched a counterattack and made English the official language of the county, and "to hell with that Spanish jazz," as one proponent shouted.

Steve, unable to accept what he viewed as a grievous step backward, led a new fight to establish Miami as a bilingual city, and on the night his resolution passed by a large majority, making Miami conduct its business in both English and Spanish, he appointed a committee to suggest Spanish names for streets in the Little Havana area. The valiant way in which he fought to promote Hispanic interests made him a hero to the Cubans, even though he did lose a later fight to restore Dade County bilingualism.

He had endeared himself to the Anglos by stating in a press conference on the night English was voted back to preeminence: "The public has spoken. Let's accept the decision in the spirit of good fellowship and learn English as fast as possible." But then he added, with a wink into the television cameras: "Of course, anyone in this city who does speak Spanish will be at a tremendous advantage, because we all know that Miami is destined to become a Hispanic city."

He also displayed his knack for civic leadership when the blacks of Miami voiced their dismay at seeing the types of jobs they had traditionally held—janitors, night watchmen, warehousemen, helpers in stores— monopolized by better-educated Cuban immigrants, leaving the city's blacks unemployed and unemployable. When black leaders met with government officials to plead for fairer treatment, Calderon listened as one older man complained: "We blacks have been here in Florida for more than four hundred years, and in that time we reached certain agreements with the whites. Now, if we want to keep the jobs we've always had, we have to learn Spanish, and at our age we can't do that. Your people have stolen our city from us."

Alert to the dangers this impasse presented, Steve had immediately hired two black aides at his clinic, despite the fact that Hispanics could do the job better; even if the black aides proved superior, they would be almost fifty-percent worthless, since they would not be able to speak with the clinic patients, a majority of whom were Hispanic. He also spoke in public about the necessity of protecting black employment, and he persuaded a group of well-to-do Cuban professionals and businessmen to finance a night school at which blacks could learn Spanish, but this charitable idea was scrapped when black leaders protested: "See, it proves what we said. Miami is becoming a Spanish city, with no place for the black worker unless he learns their language." And then came the perpetual complaint: "And we've been here more than four hundred years."

Airplanes flying from Washington, D.C., to Florida customarily cut across Virginia to a spot near Wilmington, North Carolina, where they head into the Atlantic on a straight line over water to Miami, but Dr. Calderon didn't notice the beautiful view because he was lost in deep thought. He had great sympathy for the Miami blacks. Their world seemed to him to be shifting under their feet and they were having real trouble adjusting. But he had no sympathy for the Anglos who crybabied about the Cuban invasion. They had done damned little with their city while they monopolized it, in his opinion, and nine-tenths of the good things that had made Miami a metropolis in the last decades were due to his fellow Cubans.

He had contempt for those English-speaking citizens of the city who moved northward toward Palm Beach to escape the Cubans— "Hispanic Panic" it was called—and it betrayed the fact that these fleeing Anglos feared they might not be able to cope with the Spanish city Miami was destined to become: Nor do they like the idea that we're also now a Catholic city, and a Republican one to boot. In fact, they don't like anything about us and our new ways. And he shook his head in disgust when he recalled the offensive bumper sticker that appeared so frequently: "Will the last American leaving Miami please bring the flag?"

But then, hands folded across his seat belt, he reflected on how ambivalent he had become regarding some Cuban newcomers. He believed that the first flood of Cubans in 1959 and '61 brought some of the finest immigrants ever to reach America. For any nation to have received in a short time two groups of such admirable human material was a boon which rarely happens: Not one of our group unemployed. Not one with children lacking an education. And not one so far as I know without savings in the bank. He chuckled: And not one voting anything but straight Republican. We became self-respecting American citizens overnight, and it's ridiculous for the Anglos to reject us, because we're just like them.

Then he groaned. He couldn't blame the Anglos for despising those Mariel boatlift gangsters who came in 1980, when Castro emptied the Cuban jails and shipped north some 125,000 criminals. They've set Cuban progress in Miami back a dozen years. He stared bleakly down at the gray ocean, visualizing that second flood of Cuban immigrants—the drug smugglers and holdup artists, the car thieves and embezzlers . . . and the uneducated.

Reluctantly he admitted an ugly question which had been festering for some time: Is the real reason we despise the Mariel boatlift people because they're primarily black and we don't want the United States to discover that hordes of Cubans in this generation are black, not white like our first group of arrivals? It was a nagging problem, this race discrimination that had plagued Cuba for the last four hundred years; people who ran the hotels that tourists frequented in the good old days were white or nearly so. Also the people who governed, the diplomats who graced Paris and Washington, the millionaire sugar planters, all white. But the mass of people out in the fields, the mountains, the ones who did the work and threatened to become the majority, they were black, descendants of the slaves the sugar barons had imported from Africa. Cuba, he mused, top third white, bottom third black, middle third mixed. He grimaced: I never liked the blacks in Cuba and I don't like them here. They're rascals, and no wonder American citizens have begun to fear all Cubans. From reading newspaper accounts of Mariel crimes, you'd think the principal contribution we Cubans brought with us to Miami was public corruption, Spanish style.

Wincing, he thought of several recent headline cases. A big group of police officers, all white Hispanics, formed a cabal to commit a chain of horrendous crimes for money. Two Mariel Cubans operating an aluminum-siding firm did such a wretched job for an Anglo client that he demanded a rebate, which so angered the aluminum men that they stormed into the man's home, beat him up, then drove their car straight at the man's wife, crushing her left leg so badly that it had to be amputated. On and on went a litany of criminal behavior so offensive that he appreciated why Anglos had come to resent even well-behaved Cubans. To counteract such negative impressions, he had, with the help of other Cuban leaders, established an informal club called Dos Patrias, the name, Two Homelands, referring to the emotional home which the Cubans had left behind and the legal one to which they were committed for the rest of their lives. It was a club without rules, regular meetings or set membership, just a group of intelligent men who studied how their community was developing and who sought to keep it on the right track. All who attended were Hispanics, ninety-five-percent Cuban, and most were as enlightened as Calderon. They recognized two basics: Miami was destined to become a Hispanic city; and it would be a more vital society if the Anglos who built it could be persuaded to remain instead of running away to the wealthy settlements in the north. Most Patrias had developed pragmatic solutions to the problem: "If the rednecks who can't stand hearing a person speak Spanish get scared, encourage them to move out and to hell with 'em. Little lost. But we must do everything reasonable to keep the sensible ones, because them we need."

Patrias assumed responsibility for seeing that Miami remained a city in which Anglos could feel at home, and Steve said at the close of one meeting: "I see a city that'll be maybe three-fourths Hispanic, one-fourth black and Anglo, and to make good Anglos feel at ease in such a place isn't going to be easy."

Then Steve shivered, recalling the deplorable visit he'd recently had from the Hazlitts, and he wondered if the battle had not already been lost. Norman Hazlitt was the kind of man who graced any community in which he worked: unusually successful as a businessman, he had practiced good relations with labor, had been a major force in building a strong Presbyterian church, had served the Boy Scouts for decades, and helped keep the local Republican party alive in years when it won few elections. His wife, Clara, had been a principal fundraiser for Doctors Hospital and the financial angel for the Center for Abused Wives. Among the charities of Miami it was known that "if you can't get the money anywhere else, try the Hazlitts."

Three months ago Steve had become aware that the Hazlitts were becoming unhappy with the way the Cubans were taking over the community; they were especially ill at ease regarding the religious sect Santeria. The matter became public when a brash young Santeria minister bought a vacant house at the far edge of the district in which the Hazlitts and other millionaires lived, and there conducted lively services in which large groups of predominantly Mariel worshipers sang in beautiful harmony and prayed in the Catholic style, for they were tangentially a part of that faith as practiced in Cuba. Trouble arose because their rituals were also strongly influenced by ancient African voodoo rites, including specifically the climactic sacrifice of live chickens and other animals in a way that allowed the blood to spatter members of the congregation. This was not ritual sacrifice, in which a symbolic knife made a symbolic pass over the animal; it was the severing of a living neck and the gushing of hot blood.

Mrs. Hazlitt, as a member of the SPCA, was shocked when she learned that a church in her community was conducting such rituals, and with the assistance of like-minded Episcopal, Baptist and Presbyterian women, she tried to put a stop to what she and others termed "this savage display more appropriate to the jungle than to a civilized neighborhood."

In the public debate that followed, two unfortunate statements were made which put the Hazlitts quite at odds with the Cuban community. One of the Santeria worshipers had a son just graduated from law school who saw the vigorous attempts of the Anglo community to outlaw the blood sacrifice as an attack upon freedom of religion. With skill he invoked one law after another in defense of the sacrifices, treating the practices of the Santeria sect with all the high gravity that another might treat a more established religion like Catholicism or Mormonism. This so infuriated the Anglo women that Mrs. Hazlitt told the press: "But those are *real* religions," and this roused a storm from many who loudly claimed that Santeria was equally real.

The women then tried to invoke a zoning ordinance, but the young lawyer defeated them. They attempted to outlaw the sacrifices as a menace to health, but again he used the law to hold them off. They tried to call upon what they called a "higher law of common sense" but he produced two professors of religion who proved that every tenet of Santeria, and especially the blood sacrifices, came straight out of the Old Testament.

But the *coup de grâce* was administered by the young lawyer during an interview on the radio talk station WJNZ: "Catholics and Protestants eat the wafer and drink the wine and pretend that these are the sacrificed body and blood of Jesus. They're doing exactly what we do in Santeria, but we have the courage to really kill our chicken." After that, any reasonable debate became impossible, and when the ACLU entered the battle in defense of the new religion, the Hazlitts knew their side could not win.

However, one die-hard Protestant woman—not Mrs. Hazlitt, who knew better—fired a final salvo, and it was savage: "If the Santerias start their sacrifice with a pigeon and then a chicken, then a turkey and a goat, how soon do they start killing human beings?" As a shudder passed through the community at this intemperate and wildly inappropriate assault, the Hazlitts told each other: "Sanity has lost. Santeria has triumphed."

Two weeks ago this fine couple had come to the Calderon residence with doleful news: "We're leaving Miami. Can't take it anymore."

"Please, please!" Steve had begged. "Forget the Santerias. They're on the other side of town behaving themselves."

"We have forgotten them. But we began really to worry last week. The attempt to burn the television station."

"You mean the Frei case?" Steve asked, and he listened to a lava flow of bitter complaint, for this Noriberto Frei, a minor city employee determined to get ahead in a hurry, had finally exceeded the bounds of decency and reason.

He was an engaging young fellow, not among the first Cubans to arrive after Castro but not a Mariel man, either. Announcing himself as the holder of a Harvard degree in business administration (although he had never seen New England) and a world traveler (although he had never been north of South Carolina), he had become involved in one scam after another. His explanations were always both brazen and ingenious: "Yes, I used the initials CPA, but I never claimed I'd taken any exams. Yes, I've appointed nine of my relatives to high-paying jobs, but they tested out to be the best qualified. Yes, the man who built the condominium on land that had been zoned for single-family residential does allow me to use that big apartment on the twelfth floor, but there are no papers to prove that I actually own it. And now about that ninety-seven thousand dollars the papers claim is missing, I can explain . . ."

"It isn't the devilish things he's done," Norman Hazlitt said. "It's how your Cuban community has defended his performances . . . made a hero of him. You're sending a signal and we're receiving it loud and clear."

"It's been unfortunate," Calderon conceded.

Indeed it was. Noriberto Frei had, through his charm and fast talking, built himself a little empire, from which he exercised considerable power. But when he became embroiled in yet another scandal, a local television station presented a skit of Frei's escapades, with the question at the end: WHAT WILL HE DO NEXT?

"It was proper castigation of a scoundrel," Hazlitt said, and Steve agreed.

But on the same evening, after the skit was broadcast, hundreds of Frei supporters—all Cubans—marched on the offices of the offending station, branding the broadcasters communists, and would have set the place afire had not the police intervened.

"That was a deplorable action," Calderon admitted, but Mrs. Hazlitt added: "I sometimes think there must be a secret Cuban Ayatollah that no Anglo is ever allowed to see who orchestrates these scandals," and Calderon winced.

But that was not what the Hazlitts had come to complain about. Brandishing a copy of the day's paper, they pointed to a typical Miami photograph spread across the front page: a jubilant Nariberto Frei brandishing a victory glass of champagne with some two dozen cheering supporters, mostly Hispanic, toasting the fact that he had once again outsmarted the Anglos. "Seven times they've tried to get me," Frei was quoted, "but it's been nothing but a futile vendetta mounted by that damned station. Well, I've proved I'm here to stay."

"And he is," Hazlitt admitted. "He and his style of government have won. Victorious, he declares war on people like me. Shut up or get out."

Then Clara spoke, and as she did she placed her trembling hand on Steve Calderon's arm: "You better than most, Steven, know that Norman and I are not racists."

"Heavens, no! Who loaned me the money to get my clinic started?" He reached over to kiss her on the cheek, but this did not placate her: "I do so hate it when I enter a store I've patronized for forty years and find that the salesgirls not only can't speak English but insult me because I use it. I can no longer visit my longtime hairdresser because the new management hires only Cubans who speak no English. Wherever I go, it's the same." Turning to face Steve, she said accusingly: "Your people have stolen our city from us."

When he tried to reassure her that Miami needed the Hazlitts now more than ever, she clenched her fists and said: "It's no longer a matter of words. We're frightened . . . terrified. Tell him what happened two nights ago, Norman," and the financier related yet another distressing Miami story: "Clara and I were driving home on Dixie Highway, obeying the speed limit. An urgent driver behind us, wanting to pass, honked at us angrily, then took a wild chance and whizzed by on the right-hand shoulder, cursing at us as he went. But that put him behind a car even slower than ours, and now his honking displayed real fury. But this time there was no shoulder. Enraged, he rushed up behind the slow car, bumped it three times, then pulled up beside it at a traffic light. Saying nothing, he reached in his glove compartment, whipped out a revolver, and shot the slow driver dead . . . not eight feet from us."

Clara added: "Before we could do anything, the killer sped through the red light and was gone."

"Did you identify the car for the police?"

"We were afraid to. He might come back and kill us, too."

"Was he Hispanic?"

"He must have been." Before Steve could point out what a shameful assumption that was, Hazlitt said: "We sold the house this morning . . . closing out my partnerships as soon as possible."

"But where will you go?" Calderon asked plaintively, and they said: "Somewhere fresh and clean north of Palm Beach, where we'll build a wall around our home and hope to keep it protected during our lifetime, while the rest of south Florida becomes wholly Hispanic."

When Steve reported this development to his Patrias, several expressed regret at losing such estimable citizens, but some of the realists countered: "A classic case of Hispanic Panic. Let 'em go." Another said: "I'm sick and tired of hearing complaints against our use of Spanish. A man can spend a month along Calle Ocho and never need a word of English," to which Steve replied: "Tell your Cubans they'd better learn, or they'll be left behind as Miami grows."

There was, however, a problem of greater threat to the nation, as a political scientist, invited down from the university at Gainesville, explained to the Patrias one evening:

"I think we must expect at some future time another mass exodus from Cuba and certainly a huge influx from Central America, where the birth rate is simply running wild. So we're talking about maybe two or three hundred thousand new Hispanics, and they won't be already educated the way you gentlemen were. They'll be illiterates, many of them will be black, and they'll all want to settle in Miami.

"The great risk these people will pose is that they'll introduce into Miami life the political corruption that seems to infect all Hispanic government: bribery of officials, fraud in elections, nepotism in political appointments, and invariably putting the interests of one's family members ahead of the general welfare. These characteristics are already surfacing in Miami, and with a constant influx of new arrivals the problem will worsen.

"It's up to you leaders of the Hispanic community to ensure that this doesn't happen. Florida's politics must not become Latin-Americanized. The officials you elect to office must live not by traditions of Colombia, where they shoot judges they don't like, or Bolivia, where everything can be stolen, but by the traditions of reasonable honesty and responsibility on which the United States has relied for the past three centuries."

As the man spoke, Calderon was thinking of the recent scandals on Wall Street in which Anglos of supposed probity had stolen the investors of the nation blind, and he felt that the young man was overstating his case, but in the heated question period the speaker modified his views somewhat:

"For the present, Miami is getting horrendous adverse publicity as the crime capital of the nation, the gangsterism associated with cocaine accounting for most of it, and I would look for this to continue through the end of the century. But we must remember that Al Capone made Chicago a similar capital in his day and Chicago didn't suffer more than three or four decades. Neither will Miami.

"Turbulence comes with vitality, and Miami has a strong chance of being one of the most vital cities in the Western Hemisphere—playground of the North . . . capital of the Caribbean . . . magnet to all the South American nations . . . blessed with a multiracial society . . . and don't forget those hardworking Haitians. Its future is bright indeed."

Calderon's plane had now reached a point in Florida north of Palm Beach, and in the final moments of approach he thought exclusively of what lay ahead—a possible meeting with Fidel Castro. He knew that as long as his generation lived in south Florida, hatred for that evil man would never subside. Bay of Pigs veterans like Máximo Quiroz would keep the bitterness alive. But he also knew there was a greater reality—the rest of the United States was willing to let Castro run his course, to keep him isolated, and when he did go, to get on with the job of reconciliation with Cuba.

Then a sardonic thought brought a smile to his face: If Castro vanished tomorrow, I wonder if even Máximo and his henchmen would go back. They know how good they have it here in Miami and they're not about to give it up. Not more than two in a hundred would go back. Maybe two is a mite few. There is such a thing as homesickness. Then, as the plane swung into its landing pattern: Make it five in a hundred. But of the kids born here and educated in American schools and colleges, make it one in a hundred . . . at most.

But when he reached home the problem at hand assumed an entirely different coloration, for his wife met him at the door with news that several callers who would not give their names had wanted to speak with him, and even as she said the words the phone jangled, and when he answered, a voice he did not recognize said in a low growl: "Don't you dare go to Cuba." Obviously, someone in his Washington meeting that afternoon had warned someone in Miami that contacts were about to be made with Castro and that injurious concessions might result.

"Who was on the phone?" Kate asked, and he lied: "Someone seeking my help on a zoning variance." Then she shifted the conversation: "At your meeting in Washington? Cuba?" He nodded, and she reminded him of the promise he had made yesterday. But he made light of the matter, though in the end he had to confide: "Maybe a trip to visit your sister in Havana," and she kissed him: "Now that I could tolerate . . . if we keep politics out of it," and he agreed.

Then the phone rang again, and a much different voice, still unrecognizable, said darkly: "We're warning you, Calderon. Don't go to Cuba."

This time when he replaced the receiver his hands were shaking, and he shifted his body to prevent his wife from seeing. He was frightened, and he had a right to be, for ten years ago, in 1978, one of the finest doctors in his clinic, Fermin Sanchez, had organized a group of seventy-five exiles, who then flew to Havana to see Castro and discuss the possibility of normalizing relations between Cuba and the United States. Word of their meeting exploded through the refugee community, and shortly after the committee's return to Miami, two members were murdered, another had both legs blown off, six had their businesses dynamited, and all were threatened by savage but anonymous phone calls: "Traitor, you too will die."

Once Steve took a call intended for Dr. Sanchez: "Oh, Dr. Calderon! Tell Dr. Sanchez I'd like to keep seeing him, but I'm afraid they'll bomb your office while I'm there."

"Who told you that?"

"They telephoned."

In time the wrath diminished, but Steve knew that even he was held in suspicion because he employed Sanchez. Considerable pressure had been applied to make him fire the doctor, but he had refused and eventually the raging fires had subsided.

If ever two cities were destined to be interlocked, each complementing the other, they were Miami, perched at the tip of a great continent, striving to retain its Anglo-Saxon character, and Havana, located on the edge of a glorious island and determined to protect its Spanish heritage. Only two hundred and thirty-five miles apart, a distance which could be covered in less than forty minutes by a moderately fast plane, they should have enjoyed a symbiotic relationship of mutual reward, with the residents of Miami flying south not only for recreation but also for instruction in Caribbean life and Spanish ways, and the Cubans flying north for shopping, medical help and advanced education. But the Castro revolution dislocated arrangements and made intercourse between the two natural neighbors impossible, to the grave detriment of each.

In the summer of 1988, when normal travel between the two cities was forbidden, there were three ways by which an American could get to Cuba: he could fly to Mexico, quietly arrange a visa there, and hop a speedy flight to Havana; or he could fly to Montreal for the same kind of transaction; or in difficult and somewhat secret circumstances, he could report quietly to the Miami airport at midnight, with a U.S. Treasury Department clearance, for a charter flight that left each night of the week to transfer those passengers and goods which each nation recognized had to be exchanged. Scant public notice was taken of these flights, for each nation knew they were necessary.

For the flight of Dr. Calderon and his wife to Havana, the State Department had decided that secrecy could best be preserved by using the Canadian route. Fortunately, in late August a large medical meeting involving Canadian and American doctors was scheduled in Toronto, and it was arranged that a formal invitation would be issued to Calderon, and news of this was circulated among other Miami-area doctors who had also been invited. The Calderons would appear at the convention early, meet the maximum numbers of Floridians, attend sessions during the first two days, then quietly disappear, ostensibly for a motor trip through Nova Scotia.

But before the Calderons could put this plan into operation, Steve was visited at his banking headquarters by a man he really did not care to see but who was not entirely unexpected. He was a Cuban in his late forties, of medium size and very rugged, with dark black hair combed forward over his forehead and a pinched countenance fixed into a permanent scowl. He was Máximo Quiroz.

He was a principal adversary to the conciliatory Dos Patrias group that Calderon had organized to provide sober guidance to Miami's Cuban community, for Quiroz wanted to go the confrontational route in all affairs pertaining to Hispanics. He dreamed not only of invading Cuba but also of ousting all the Anglos from Miami: "I'll be glad when the last of them head north and leave the running of this city to those of us who know what's needed." Men like Calderon were fed up with Quiroz, seeing him as an irresponsible agitator indifferent to the turbulent consequences his acts might have.

Dr. Calderon tried to be understanding and patient: "Well, Máximo, old friend, what's new these days?"

"All bad. Russia moving in tons of weapons to the island, not even unpacking them, then straight off to Nicaragua." He complained that mixed signals from the American Congress meant that the contras, whom he supported passionately, were left bewildered.

"What did you find when you went to Honduras last month?" Calderon asked, and his question was not mere courteous conversation, for he too was an ardent supporter of the contras.

"Noble determination to regain their country. Confusion as to where the supplies were going to come from." He added that if Calderon was really interested, he, Máximo, could arrange meetings with the contra leadership, all of whom were living in Miami, but although Steve supported the contras emotionally and with cash contributions, he did not care to become too deeply involved.

"What brings you here this morning?" he asked, and Quiroz began a long review of the relationships between the Calderons and the Quiroz branch of the family: "Don't forget," he said in Spanish, for he had refused to become proficient in English, having expected all along that he would be returning to Cuba, "that your great-grandfather's name was Calderón y Quiroz and his mother was my great-grandfather's sister. We're related, you must remember, and it isn't proper for you to oppose the things I'm trying to do."

"What are you trying to do?" Steve interrupted, drawing an even deeper scowl.

"Regain Cuba, and if that's impossible because the Russians won't allow it, even when Castro's gone, to make a safe place for us here in Miami."

"Do you have to insult the Anglos to accomplish that?"

"Yes!" he said defiantly. "I can never forget how they insulted us when we came here in 1959. Their days are numbered."

Distressed by such talk, Calderon rose and began pacing about his office, then turned to face Quiroz: "Máximo, you're free to fight for a Cuba freed from Russian domination, but you mustn't ruin south Florida for those of us who're going to remain here for the rest of our lives." He stopped suddenly, stared at his cousin, and asked: "By the way, have you ever applied for American citizenship?"

"My home is down there."

"Then for heaven's sake, spend your efforts there. Don't wreck Miami for the rest of us."

"What am I doing to wreck . . . ?"

"Reopening that bilingual problem."

"Ah! Your wealthy Anglo friends better accept the fact, Miami is going to be a Spanish city. Not only Cubans coming in. All the extra people in Central America—*todas la gente en América Central—*

they'll be coming here to live, and they must be free to conduct their lives in Spanish."

"But, Máximo," Steve asked almost pleadingly, "don't you realize that such a campaign, all over again, will make the Anglos . . ."

"I want to make them eat dirt the way you and I had to when we came to their city."

"I never ate dirt," Steve insisted, but Quiroz raged: "Yes you did. Year after year, working as a janitor, but you refused to admit it!" and Steve saw that it was hopeless to use either truth or logic with this difficult man: "I don't know why I bother with you, Máximo," he said, and his visitor leered at him provocatively: "Yes you do. You listen to me because you know I'm a true Cuban patriot . . . a hero . . . a man who will lead us back to Cuba." Quiroz could afford to be arrogant because he knew that he was a reproach to those Americanized Cubans who were uneasy about adopting a new homeland and turning their backs on the old.

Some months ago the Patrias, aware that friction was increasing between Quiroz and Calderon, sent one of their most stable members to reason with Steve, and the man said:

"Quiroz is difficult, and I'm a member of Patrias because I don't like his extremist acts here in Miami, but he's also a man of noble courage. I know. When he came to me here in Miami back in 1961 and whispered: 'We're going to invade Cuba, kill that bastard Castro, and make our homeland free once more,' I jumped forward to help.

"He and I were first on the beach at Bay of Pigs, last to leave. Fact is, he stayed behind so long, still firing at the communists, that we were captured and thrown into big trucks, door bolted shut and shipped in disgrace to Havana for the Cubans to gloat over us."

At this point in his recollection of that catastrophe, and overwhelmed by what he must say next, the veteran of that bungled cause asked for a drink of water before concluding:

"The trip in that locked bus took eight hours, with the sun beating upon our roof, and before long men began to die of suffocation. It was now that Máximo proved his heroism, for he told us to scratch at the siding with our belt buckles, try to make a hole, and when an hour passed with no results he screamed: 'Scratch harder or die!' and he was the first to complete a hole, and the fresh air he brought us saved my life. Today Máximo lives for only one thing. To get back to Cuba and finish with Castro."

Quietly, Steve had asked: "Will any Miami Cubans join him?" and this sensible man had replied instantly: "Me and ten thousand like me."

So now, when Steve stared across his desk at Quiroz, he had to admit that the unpleasant fellow was a verifiable hero. He also knew that Máximo had come for some specific reason, so he asked: "Now what is it that you came to see me about?" and Quiroz realized that the time had come for a frank discussion. With his scowl newly intensified, he growled: "They tell me you're going down to see Castro."

Steve's strong inclination was to ask: "Who told you that?" but he did not wish to engage in a lying contest, so he replied truthfully: "I have no plans to visit Castro, none at all."

"Then why are you visiting Cuba?"

"Who said I was?"

"We know. We too have friends in high places who dream of freedom in Cuba."

"If I were going," Steve said, "I'd take my wife, and the purpose of the trip would be to see your cousin and mine, Roberto Calderón." He paused: "I'm sure you know that his wife and mine are twin sisters."

"I did know. But that can't be a reason for a man like you going back to Cuba. With your family record of always favoring the United States, Cuba would be crazy to let you in."

"Times change, Máximo."

"Not where Castro is concerned. Let me warn you, Estéfano, do not go to visit with that criminal in La Habana." The use of his Spanish name evoked so many pleasant memories to Steve that he rose, embraced his formidable cousin, and said: "One of these day, Máximo, we'll all go back to La Habana for a long visit. Things will change, believe me," and Quiroz, disarmed by this gesture of good will, said grudgingly: "For me it won't be a visit. Castro will be dead and I'll be going home to stay . . . in triumph." Then quickly he regained his composure: "Estéfano, I warn you. Do not go to Cuba. Do not make concessions to that murderer."

"I have no intention . . ."

"But you already have a ticket to Toronto. I know what happens in Toronto. You slip into Cuba that way."

Astonished by Máximo's knowledge of his movements, Steve said: "If you know so much, you must also know that I'm attending a medical meeting up there."

Rising and heading for the door, Quiroz growled: "Estéfano, if you go to Cuba and try to meet with Castro, you'll be in grave danger. I warn you, don't do it."

When Steve heard him clumping down the hallway, he leaned back in his chair and wondered who it could have been in that Washington meeting who had slipped the word south to his allies in Miami concerning the government's new strategies relating to Cuba, and his own involvement in those strategies.

In Toronto, Steve and Kate attended the medical meetings and he spoke twice from the floor in order to verify his presence. On the third day they rented a car, and not wishing to provide any possible verification of their trip to Cuba, allowed themselves to be seen heading east toward Nova Scotia, but when they were well on their way they deviated to Montreal, parked their car at the airport, and boarded a plane for Mexico, where they transferred to a much smaller plane which sped them swiftly to Havana.

On the bus ride into town there were enough seats so that the Calderons could each have a window, Kate in front, Steve right behind her, and their remarks passing back and forth attested to their continuing surprise: "It's sure cleaner than it used to be," Kate said, and Steve responded: "A lot fewer uniforms than we used to see in Batista's day."

She asked: "Where are the donkeys that once lined this road?" and he echoed: "And where are those shiny new American cars?"

It was a new Cuba, and in certain obvious ways a better one, but Steve was reluctant to voice any general approval: "We've got to remember, most any city in the world has made improvements over the past quarter of a century. No special credit to communism," the last observation being made in a whisper close to Kate's ear.

However, when they were actually in the city he was shocked to see two aspects which grieved him as the owner of several extremely trim buildings in Miami: the gruesome deterioration of entire rows of buildings falling into disrepair, and the failure of owners to cut the grass or clean the pavements before their homes or places of business: "This city is a dump. It needs a million gallons of paint."

Kate did not hear his complaints, for she was making her own assessments: "Look how everybody has decent clothes to wear. And the relaxed attitude of the faces. Doesn't look like a dictatorship," and Steve cautioned: "Wait till you see what's going on behind those smiles."

As the ride ended and they disembarked at the portals of a big hotel, they did not enter immediately but remained on the street as Steve told the porter in Spanish: "These five bags. We'll register in just a minute," and they breathed deeply in the soft tropic air. "Look," Kate cried. "No beggars." And when Steve commented on the lack of clutter in the streets it became obvious that these two homecomers were pleased, perhaps against their deep convictions, to see that their native land was doing moderately well.

Alone in their room, Steve looked approvingly at the festoon of flowers which awaited them, and said: "In a grudging way, I'm proud of the old place. Dump or not, it feels like home." Running to him with an embrace, Kate whispered: "I was wrong in advising you not to come. Seeing Havana again, what little we have so far, is thrilling. Let's surprise Plácida with a call right now telling them we're in town," and in the next three-quarters of an hour they learned something about Cuba, for the registering of a simple phone call became an act of high strategy. One did not merely pick up the phone and dial; one entered into negotiation with the operator, whose lines were perpetually busy, but after interminable delays the call did sometimes go through. After Kate's efforts finally succeeded they waited anxiously in their room, and with surprising speed came the call from within the hotel: "We're waiting in the lobby."

It was an emotional moment when the twins met, for in the long years since 1959 they had seen only photographs of each other, and both they and their husbands were amazed at how much alike they still looked. Reddish hair piled high, flashing white teeth, neither over nor under weight, and with the roguish good humor they had preserved through the vicissitudes of life, Plácida appeared an ideal Cuban wife, Kate a typical Miami Hispanic adjusted to American ways. They were a striking pair, and the mutual affection they displayed even in these first moments of reunion was so disarming that the husbands moved away to give them privacy to express their feelings.

Like their wives, each husband epitomized his country: Roberto as an important fifty-two-year-old Cuban officeholder, with clothes and appearance in the Spanish mode; Estéfano as any uprooted Cuban, Puerto Rican or Mexican who had attained eminence in some profession in the States. Each was honestly glad to see the other after such a long absence, but since Roberto as a member of the government had to be suspicious of Americans, he wanted specific information as to why his cousin had come south, and Estéfano gave three honest reasons: "To see you. To see the old sugar mill. But most of all, so that Caterina could visit with Plácida again," and these reasons satisfied Roberto, who cried: "You're to leave this hotel and move in with us," and his wife, hearing the invitation, reinforced it by saying: "I'll help Caterina pack and we'll go to our place immediately."

The old Calderón sugar mill west of the city had long since ceased functioning, and after the revolution of 1959 all the extensive lands had been expropriated and turned into small holdings for peasants. But Roberto, an ardent supporter of the revolution, had been allowed to retain four small stoneworkers' cottages interconnected by lovely arched cloisters such as one might see in a monastery. By adding a few low stone walls to bind the area together, various small patios had resulted, and these were kept filled with flowers, producing an effect which recalled old Spain, and this was not surprising, since families of pure Spanish blood had owned the great plantation for nearly five centuries.

The many small rooms had been decorated by Plácida Calderón in the old style, so that when Steve and his wife were led through the simple but charming house, he cried: "Hey! You've made the old place into a palace," and Kate ran to one of the smaller buildings, leaned against it, and cried: "Plácida! Remember? This is where Estéfano first kissed me, and you were so delighted when I told you."

In those lovely moments of recollection and reconciliation a change came over the Miami Calderons, and the cause was simple but pervasive, as Steve recognized: "It's good to be called Estéfano again, and to be reminded that my name is really Calderón with a heavy accent, and followed by my mother's name, Arévalo. It's almost as if I'd become a whole man again," and for the remainder of his stay on the island he would be a Cubano, wary, inquisitive, judgmental and keenly aware of his heritage, and he would pronounce the word in the strong old style, Koo-*bahn*-oh. Caterina, nodding as he spoke, for she had felt the same pleasure in hearing only Spanish, reminded him: "And it's La Habana."

They were interested and in a sense gratified to learn that in two of the small houses which comprised the compound seven members of the Cuban Calderón family had found permanent refuge, the husbands working for Roberto in his government office, the women helping Plácida in the charity work with which she was involved. It was a warm, loving center of mutual interests and the Miami Calderons were pleased to become a part of it. The next week was one of illumination, confusion and joy. The first came as a result of explorations made through the countryside in Roberto's Russian-made Lada coupe, which to Caterina seemed awkward and boxlike but to Estéfano rather sturdily engineered. They visited places the Miami Calderons had known years ago, and they couldn't help crying out "Look at it now!" over and over, reflecting surprise at either how much improved it was or how deteriorated. Often there was a pang of lost innocence when the twins visited together some spot which had once been of great importance to them—the home of a friend long dead or an uncle who had simply disappeared—and they stood clasping hands as they recalled those happier days when they were young and striving to solve the riddles of love and marriage and destiny.

In those far-off days they had all been staunchly Catholic, and one afternoon when the four were seated with their rum drinks in the far corner of one of the patios where the sun could not reach them, Caterina said: "I'm astonished, Plácida, to hear that you've strayed from our Catholic beginnings."

"Nobody in Cuba bothers much with Catholicism today," her sister said, "because on this island, the church never behaved well. Remember that horrible Father Oquende, always sucking up to the rich? Well, he and his kind are gone, and I say, 'Good riddance.'"

Caterina said: "Now that's funny. When a Cuban moves to Miami and is overawed by the Anglos, he or she becomes more Catholic than ever. Estéfano and I go to Mass every Sunday, but I think he does it mostly for business reasons. In Miami he'd be badly damaged if it was rumored that he was not a strong Catholic."

"Down here just the opposite. Roberto would be suspect within the party if he was seen attending Mass. Were you there when the pope visited Miami?"

"We were. A sensational rededication to the Catholic faith and in a strange way a reinforcement of Hispanic values. Estéfano and I were very proud to be chosen as leaders of the Cuban community to meet him." When Plácida sniffed, Estéfano asked with just a hint of irritation: "If Castro's revoked the church and the past, what do you believe in?" and Roberto replied with firmness: "We don't bother much about the past. We keep our eye on the future."

"And what's that future likely to be? Continued dependence on Russia?"

"Now wait, you two *norteamericanos.* You maintain a Caribbean pigsty on Puerto Rico and you encourage poor Haiti to fester in her wounds . . ."

"While Russia sends you guns? Who's the better for it?"

"You miss the whole point, Estéfano, you really do. Russia does send us some guns, and we appreciate them, but what's much more important, she sends us oil, and what's most important of all, she buys her sugar from us at three cents above world price, which is just enough to keep us prospering." Before Estéfano could respond, his cousin added: "If you Americans were clever, you'd buy Caribbean sugar at that price, and the entire area would blossom, as it did when our fathers were kids. But your sugarbeet states won't allow that, so you watch as the Caribbean islands, on your own doorstep, edge closer to revolution or ruin."

And so their discussions went. Estéfano raising questions, and in response, Roberto defending Castroism fiercely, then making a stronger accusation against the United States. Their conversation became an antiphonal dialogue between the two nations.

ESTÉFANO: What about the Cubans in Angola?

ROBERTO: They're fighting to defend the freedom of Portugal's former slaves. And what are your mercenaries doing in Nicaragua?

ESTÉFANO: What about diminished supplies of consumer goods under communism?

ROBERTO: You don't see any starving Cubans, and from what I read, I understand that twenty-five percent of Americans are suffering from inadequate diets because food is so expensive.

ESTÉFANO: What about the huge number of political prisoners Castro keeps in his jails?

ROBERTO: The United States and South Africa are the only so-called civilized nations that still execute people for minor offenses.

ESTÉFANO: When I left Cuba, there were half a dozen wonderful publications like the weekly *Bohemia* and the daily *Marina,* but now I can find only grubby communist propaganda sheets like *Granma.*

ROBERTO: We know the press in America is the tool of Wall Street, but we don't allow anything like that in Cuba. We revere free speech . . . to safeguard the revolution.

After a score of such inconclusive exchanges, the Miami couple returned to their rooms, where Estéfano said: "Boy, he's really swallowed the Castro line," and Caterina replied: "Maybe in this country that's the smart thing to do," but then she added: "I still like it here. This isn't Lower Slobovia, like our papers sometimes claim."

Some days later, during a picnic on a hillside overlooking La Habana, the two Calderón men became engaged in a discussion of America's protracted role in Cuban affairs, and Estéfano said: "When the Spanish were driven out of Cuba in the 1898 war, our grandfathers were divided. My grandfather wanted Cuba to become a state in the American union, yours became a fierce Cuban patriot."

"Like you and me today," Roberto said, and Estéfano agreed: "More or less, yes. I don't want Cuba to become one of our states, but I do want her to participate in American leadership in the Caribbean."

Suddenly Roberto began to laugh, and when Caterina asked: "What's so funny about that idea?" he explained: "I was remembering what your victorious general, Leonard Wood, who became provisional governor of Cuba, told us: 'Cuba can be made a vital part of the United States if it makes those changes that will produce a stable society. Old Spanish ways will have to be forsworn and honest American patterns adopted.' "

Estéfano said: "Don't laugh. I can remember being told that my grandfather said in 1929: 'Look around the Caribbean. Everybody with any sense wants to join the United States. We do. Santo Domingo does. A few people on Barbados have always wanted to and even the Mexicans in Yucatán have begged the Yankees to take over.' He said he was perplexed by America's reluctance to take command of the area, and when someone pointed out that the French islands might have something to say about that, he fumed: 'They don't matter.' "

Roberto, falling back on his fervid patriotism, declared: "Cuba is free and will always remain aloof from the United States. We're building a new world with new hopes. Estéfano! You would complete your life if you came down to help us."

The two men agreed to differ on such matters, and they applauded the way their beautiful wives reestablished the warm, laughing companionship they had shared as twins in the years prior to Caterina's flight.

One morning Plácida suggested: "You men go about your business. Caterina and I are heading into town." It was a trip into nostalgia, for the two women walked along the narrow streets they had known as schoolgirls, looking in windows as they had done then, coming suddenly upon this corner shop or that which they had patronized together a quarter of a century earlier, and in some fortunate cases even meeting personnel who had waited on them in the past. But what Caterina appreciated most were the unique smells of La Habana: roasting chicory, pineapples, the odor coming from a corner coffeeshop, the aroma of newly baked bread and the indescribable, friendly scent of the plain little drapery shop that sold cloth and needles. They were, she told her sister, smells to torment memory, and she was delighted to be recovering them.

As they moved rapidly through the familiar corridors of the old city where buildings seemed to meet overhead, pinching in the narrowed streets below, Caterina got the impression that the Cuba she had really known, the one that mattered, had changed in no important respect, except for the failure to repaint, and she was relieved to see this, because it testified to the endurance of human values regardless of the political structure in which they operated. But then she began to notice the changes which Castro had imposed upon his island: one newspaper where there used to be half a dozen, each of a different persuasion; bookstores with none of the American books one would normally have seen—they were replaced by books of Russian authorship and Russian concerns. The old levity of La Habana was gone, but so were the beggars and the hideously deformed cripples preying on public sympathy. The sense of relaxation was absent too, for Cuba was now an intense society. But what she missed most in the center of town were the concentrations of Americans who used to flood it when La Habana was known worldwide as a brothel for tourists, and in one narrow street which Caterina did not remember, Plácida said: "Before Castro, one unbroken chain of red-light houses," and Caterina asked: "What became of the girls?" and Plácida said: "Working in factories or driving worn-out tractors."

But willful adventures into nostalgia run the risk of backfiring, because sooner or later, at arbitrary and unexpected points, veils are lifted to reveal present reality. This happened with Caterina when her sister led her into Galiano, a street she had loved to visit with her mother. It had been the heart of La Habana, a beautiful, crowded thoroughfare famous for the decoration of its sidewalks: wavy green and yellow lines set permanently into the paving. Her mother used to protest: "Caterina, stop trying to follow the wavy lines! That way you bump into people coming the other way. Stay on your own side."

With sorrow she saw that since the revolution these lines, so poetic and reminiscent of colonial times, had been paved over with cement so dull and colorless that she cried: "Oh, Plácida! The song has vanished!" And then, as she looked about her on this famous street, once so filled with gaiety and alluring windows that showed fine goods from all corners of the world, she began to realize how impoverished the new Habana had become: "Where are the little stores that used to crowd this street? Those shops filled with lovely things we used to dream about?"

They were gone. Galiano, once the proudest street in Latin America, unequaled even in Mexico City and Buenos Aires, was now so bleak and cheerless that Caterina, close to tears, said: "Let's get away, Plácida. This emptiness tears at my heart," and they hurried to the famous corner where Galiano intersected with San Rafael, down which they strolled, but it too had been deprived of its once glittering shops, and it became obvious that modern La Habana had cruelly little to offer its citizens in consumer goods. Shop after shop had only the bleakest selection, if any, and when exciting word flashed through the area that "Sanchez has shoes!" Caterina watched as women ran toward the shop, only to find themselves at the far end of a line which ran sixty yards down San Rafael. Plácida said: "And when we reach the shop, we find that only one kind of shoe has come in, and that one in only four sizes."

"What do you do?" Caterina asked, and her sister replied: "We grab whatever's left, and if we can't wear them, too small, too large, we trade them with neighbors who may have something in our size."

Caterina stopped opposite the middle of the long line and asked: "You mean, the only way to get shoes is to wait in lines like this?" and her sister replied: "We're lucky that Sanchez has anything. If I had time, I'd get in line and buy whatever."

"Is this the same with all goods?"

"Yes. Severe rationing. I'm authorized to buy one pair of shoes a year . . . coupons . . . must sign the register." She hesitated, waited till Caterina had moved away from the line, and whispered: "For the past half-year, no toilet paper at all. No toothpaste. For two years, no women's makeup."

"But you're wearing some."

"We arrange for friends to smuggle it in when they visit us from Mexico. We hoard it. Cherish it."

"But you have toilet paper in our bathroom. How?" and the same explanation: "Mexico. Smuggled."

Caterina was so distressed by the speed at which these revelations were hitting her that she grasped her sister's arm and cried: "Let's get out of here!" and she darted across the street, with Plácida trying to keep up. Safe on the other side, the twins ducked into the huge store which had always been their favorite, Fin de Siglo—End of the Century—founded in the 1880s. But this, too, was a terrible mistake, for the great store, its several floors once crowded with booths and kiosks and counters stacked with merchandise from New York and London and Rio and Tokyo, now stood almost empty. Of the first twenty booths Caterina passed, sixteen were abandoned—absolutely nothing to sell—and each of the other four had only one item, of poor quality and in short supply.

"My God! What's happened?" Caterina cried, and Plácida said: "It's all like this," and when they visited two of the other floors, walking up, since neither the elevators nor the escalators worked, they found a repetition of what they had seen at the shoestore: at the rare counters which had something to sell, long lines of women holding coupons.

As they came to a booth that had hanging in neat display three colorful dresses for girls aged ten or eleven, Caterina proposed to buy one for the daughter of the maid who worked at Plácida's, but the saleslady rebuffed her doubly: "You cannot buy without a coupon, and anyway, these aren't for sale."

"Then why do you have them on display?" and the woman said: "To show you what we might have if a shipment ever comes in," and to the amazement of both the saleslady and Plácida, Caterina burst into tears. When they tried to console her, she whimpered: "A little girl of eleven! She's entitled to a pretty dress now and then. To remind her that she's a girl . . . to help her mature properly," and she covered her face for the little girls of Cuba who were being deprived of this essential experience.

However, the day was saved by Plácida, who said: "Let's see what they're doing in that store where Mama used to buy our dresses," and when the twins entered the once-prosperous store an older saleswoman who had been alerted by Plácida hurried forward to cry: "The Céspedes twins! Haven't seen you together for hens' ages," and she started showing them the few dresses her seamstresses had been able to produce from the limited supply of cloth available.

Caterina had no intention of purchasing a new dress of any kind, but as the four lovely frocks drifted by, edged in lace, they produced a narcotic effect. The saleswoman then showed them the dress about which Plácida had inquired on the phone, a flimsy tropical creation in a fawn color replete with Spanish-style decorations. Caterina was enchanted by it, and when the woman unveiled an identical copy for Plácida, they both cried: "Let's do it!" Like schoolgirls they hurried into dressing rooms, changed hastily, and came out looking like real twins. The dresses required only minor alterations, which the saleslady said could be completed in the time it would take them to have lunch, so they paid for the dresses and went off to a restaurant that they had first patronized when they were sixteen and on their own in the big city. Men had smiled at them that day, and also today—and the twins nodded graciously, accepting the compliments.

They had a lunch which reminded Caterina of her youth: a small bit of barbecued meat well roasted on one edge; a small helping of black beans and white rice; thick slices of plantain, the rough, sweet banana that is impossible to eat when raw, delicious when fried; a meager salad utilizing the few fruits available in Cuba and a Spanish flan rich in its topping of caramelized sugar.

"Ah!" Caterina sighed as the fine old flavors seduced her palate. "I wish I could lunch here every day," and it was that admission which set her sister's mind churning.

When they returned to the dress shop and tried on their new purchases, they stood before the mirror as almost identical images, and they seemed ten or fifteen years younger, even though each was the mother of three children and the grandmother of four, each an epitome of how delectable a Spanish woman could be when she aged gracefully and was illuminated by an elfin sense of humor. They were beautiful women in their new gowns, and they knew it.

Packing their purchases carefully, they returned to the mill, where it was arranged that at dinner Plácida would appear first in her new dress, and after it had been admired, Caterina would casually drift in, and they would stand together in the archway leading to one of the patios for their husbands' approval, and the scheme worked so perfectly that for an instant in the old mill the Céspedes twins were again nineteen and their husbands twenty-four. It was an exquisite moment, fully appreciated by all, and it paved the way for remarkable conversations that occurred in the two bedrooms that night, conversations which proved that one of the most persistent of Spanish traits still exerted its historic power.

In the bedroom of the Miami Calderons, Caterina said as she took off her new dress and hung it carefully on a hanger: "Wouldn't it be wonderful if Plácida and Roberto could join us in Miami?" and she began plotting devices that might be useful in finding them a rent-free house, a position for Roberto, and jobs for their children. "In a pinch," she said, "we could pay their way till Roberto landed something, and he's so smart it wouldn't take him long."

In a normal American family, a proposal by a wife that her husband assume financial responsibility for her sister's family could be relied upon to send the husband up the wall with the screaming meemies, but Estéfano, trained in Spanish ways, accepted it as almost inevitable, for he appreciated how important it was to keep a family together or to reassemble it if it had become separated. So without hesitation, he volunteered: "We could afford to stake them for a couple of years. But it would be easier if he spoke English."

In the bedroom of the Cuban Calderóns, at that moment Plácida was saying: "Roberto, it looks to me as if Estéfano, forget all his money, is homesick for Cuba. He'd like to come back, spend his last years with his family. I know Caterina would like it."

"How do you know that?"

"Something she said at lunch. Money and Miami glitter aren't the biggest things in her life, believe me."

"But what could we offer Estéfano?" and she said: "He could easily become a doctor in our medical system. He has both his old Cuban licenses and his new American ones, and his experience would be welcome."

"But would he give up his good life in Miami?"

"Yes, he would. And so would Caterina, that I know for sure. She misses me and the rest of her family."

In the discussions that night, and in the nights that followed, the Miami family never once considered that *they* should move to Cuba, nor did the Cuban Calderóns consider the possibility that *they* should move to America; but that the family ought to be united, one way or another, all agreed.

• • •

It started as a trick devised by Plácida to remind the Miami Calderons of their rich Cuban heritage, but it became a day of haunting, even obsessive, memories. "Let's take a look at what our family really was," she said one evening, and when the others agreed, with even Roberto saying: "I'll take a day off from headquarters," it was planned that the two couples would leave La Habana at dawn the next day and drive well west toward the historic Calderón coffee plantation called Molino de Flores, the Mill of Flowers.

The Miami Calderons had visited the old site once or twice before the revolution, but had forgotten both its majesty and its honored place in Cuban history. They were startled when they saw the vast ruins of the main house, which must have been glorious back in the 1840s when famous travelers from all over the world visited it. "It's large enough," Estéfano exclaimed, "to hide a football field." The series of seven majestic stone arches, each three stories high, were awesome even though some of the walls nearby had begun to crumble. A solemn grandeur clothed the place, and the Miami pair could believe it when Plácida said: "Sometimes four entire Calderón families lived here at the same time, which meant perhaps forty or fifty people inside the walls."

When they left the mighty ruins, as classically balanced in all façades as those of any French château, they wandered down to one of the glories of the old place: a series of six cisterns so huge that they could provide water for the entire coffee operation. Roberto said: "When I was a boy Father told me that one torrential rain during a summer hurricane would fill all the cisterns in an afternoon." When Caterina started to enter one of the giants he warned: "Bats nesting in there!" and she said: "They don't fly in daylight," but as soon as she entered the cistern she beat a hasty, laughing retreat: "They sure fly in dark caves!" and out came a whole flock of the creatures.

"There it is," Plácida said, pointing to a construction of some kind on a high hill west of the cisterns. "That's where it happened," and when they had climbed to a new level they saw the great, brooding place which on two successive days had played a crucial role in Cuban history.

Now the four later-day Calderóns faced remnants of an iron fence that had once enclosed a stupendous area in which, as Plácida said: "They played their game of life and death." This was the famous *barracón* of Molino de Flores, the prison enclosure in which slaves were domiciled for more than half a century after their fellows had been given freedom in the British islands, thirty agonizing years after slaves were freed in the United States. Here, within this enclosure, guarded by a massive front gate still standing, more than eight hundred Calderón slaves had lived at one time in conditions so terrible that in 1884, while the Spanish governors of Cuba were still arguing that freedom for slaves would mean the death of Cuba, the slaves in this *barracón* finally decided to rebel.

"All eight hundred of them," Plácida said, "came surging at this one gate that held them prisoner. But up in that tower"—and everyone looked at the sinister gun tower rising beside the formidable iron gate—"waited six of our men, each with four rifles, and slaves to reload them. As the rebels down here started toward the gate, the men up there fired right into their faces . . . gun after gun . . . each reloaded many times . . . constant gunfire until more than three dozen slaves lay slaughtered right where we stand."

"I never heard such a story," Caterina protested, but Roberto defended his wife: "After Castro brought us freedom, books were written. Old memories were recalled. In 1884, two years before the general end of Cuban slavery, our slaves ended theirs right here."

"But you said they were driven back . . . by gunfire from up there," and all stared at the malevolent tower, each cut stone still in place.

"Yes, that night they were killed. But in the morning the hero of our family, a young dreamer named Elizondo, who had taken no part in repelling them, startled everyone by coming here from the great house, climbing that tower, and staring down at the bodies still lying there, for the other slaves knew that if they approached the gate, they too would be shot. He kept staring for more than an hour, speaking to no one."

"What did he do?" Caterina asked, and her sister said very slowly and with obvious pride: "He climbed down from the tower, called for the chief guard who lived in the room over there, and said: 'Hand me your keys,' and when he had them he went to the gate, unlocked it, threw it open, and shouted to the slaves who were still afraid to approach the gates: 'You are slaves no more. You have earned your freedom. Come bury your dead!' And he strode away, leaving the gate of the *barracón* ajar. After that morning it was never locked again."

"Two years later," Roberto said, "all Cuba followed his example, but Elizondo paid a terrible price for his leadership. His bold action branded him a traitor to Spain, so that when trouble followed in the years prior to the big revolution of 1898, the one the *norteamericanos* became involved in, he was shot by Spanish officers who questioned his loyalty."

The second family spot to which Plácida led them was one with happier memories, for she took them back to an area which had served at the turn of the century as a rural retreat for wealthy families who found the sweltering heat of La Habana insufferable. El Cerro it was called, The Hill, because of the eminence on which it stood, and along its one thoroughfare had stretched some two miles of the most splendid summer homes the Caribbean could provide. Sometimes a dozen mansions stood cheek by jowl along one side of the road, facing fifteen, equally grand, on the other side, and each of the twenty-seven would be fronted by seven or eight or nine of the most handsome marble pillars imaginable. Travelers came from all parts of La Habana to see what a poet had called "the forest of marble trees protecting the hiding places of the great." One visitor from Spain, after riding past the line of mansions, said: "I care not who owns the sugar mills if I can have the monopoly of selling the pillars for their little palaces."

As young people, the present Calderóns had known El Cerro in the years when it was about to be abandoned, and they had been aware, even then, that some of the mansions had begun to decay, but only now did they realize how widespread the devastation had become. "Oh my God!" Plácida cried. "The Count of Zaragón would be appalled! Look at those two lions he was so proud of." There stood the lions which had once proclaimed his nobility, heads off, feet chipped and scarred, while the once fabulous house they were supposed to protect lay in ruins behind them.

"Oh! The Pérez Espinals! We played there. Look! The walls are collapsing!" And then Caterina pointed to where a mansion, once so stately, so filled with summer voices, had vanished, and the destruction was so great that she asked nervously: "What will we see when we reach our swans?" And she almost dreaded to approach the place once owned by the Calderóns. But Roberto, from his position at the wheel of their auto, reminded them: "Look at how many pillars are still standing! There's a lot left to this street," and he was right, for a stranger driving slowly down it would see hundreds upon hundreds of the noble marble pillars still standing in almost military array, still trying to guard houses, some of which had disappeared behind them.

At one set of ten particularly handsome pillars, Roberto halted the car and explained: "Even before the revolution of 1959, owners realized they could no longer afford to maintain these mansions, and since no one else had the money to take them over, they were left to go to ruin. Where one distinguished family used to live, now eighteen or twenty entire families crowded in, paid no rent, and allowed everything to go to hell. Look at them!" and where the houses still remained intact, Caterina and her husband could see evidence that many families had moved in as squatters and were tearing the few remains apart. But before anyone could comment, Plácida cried: "Our swans!" and there, on the right-hand side of the splendid old road, stood one of its more remarkable mansions, walls still good, pillars intact.

What made this place memorable was that between the pillars and around the entire base of the porch, stood wing-to-wing a collection of forty-eight cast-iron swans, each about three feet high, only a few inches wide but designed and painted in such a manner as to create an explosion in the eye. Each swan stood icily erect, wings folded, head and long beak pointed straight down and kept close to the body; in this posture they looked like handsome pencils. Each was painted in three colors: gold for the legs, stark white for the head and body, a brilliant red for the long beak.

That alone would have made the swans unforgettable, but around the legs of each bird, making three complete circuits, came crawling upward a deadly serpent painted an ominous black and so positioned that its lethal head, also painted red, was poised only a few inches below the beak of the swan. Thus the swans were engaged in forty-eight deadly battles with the serpents, and no one who saw this chain of engagements engulfing him from all sides could ever forget it.

"*Olé* for our swans!" Plácida cried as the Calderóns left the car to renew their acquaintanceship with their loyal birds. "Not one serpent has ever made its way into our mansion," Roberto boasted as he patted the down-cocked head of a swan. "Faithful to the death, but they couldn't protect the place from this," and he pointed to the area behind the pillars and the porch. There the Calderóns saw the door hanging limp from its hinges, the grand stairway in ruins, the interior doors behind which families in untold numbers now lived, the whole tragic affair which must soon collapse like its sister mansions along the way. Plácida, patting the swans she had loved so dearly as a child, whispered: "You served us so much better than we served you," and she hurried to the car, where she sat head down like her swans, unwilling to look any further at the ruin which had overtaken her childhood.

Perhaps it was because Roberto Calderón had lived for the past twenty-nine years under a dictatorship, but he was the first to detect that wherever he and his brother-in-law went they were being followed at a respectable distance by at least one car and sometimes two whose occupants were apparently spying on them, and this became so irritating that one morning as they were being trailed into La Habana he checked his Russian car to see if it had been obviously bugged, then asked: "Estéfano, are you here under secret orders? Or anything like that?"

"No! Why do you ask?" and his cousin replied: "Because that first car back there is from the office of your American representative, and the one behind him, unless I'm mistaken, is from our police." When they reached La Habana, the trailing cars followed until the Calderóns parked and walked to Roberto's office.

On their drive home they were again followed, but this time only by the police car, and this experience, repeated on subsequent days, encouraged the Calderóns to ventilate the questions which seemed to obsess all Miami Cubanos: "Tell us, Roberto, what's the state of civil liberties on this island?" and Roberto said quickly and with apparent conviction: "Exactly the same as in the States. We have courts and fine lawyers, newspapers, public debate. This is a free land."

But Estéfano felt that he must, at this point, reveal his true feelings about Cuba and its communist leadership: "No matter what you say, Roberto, to me, Castro will always be a monster and his movement a retreat from human decency. But I see the land of Cuba and people like you two as the permanent representatives of the island, so I do think that some kind of rapprochement must be engineered. I want to see the day when I can fly openly to La Habana and you can fly with me back to the States."

"You mean . . . to emigrate?" Roberto spoke with such strong accents of rejection that his cousin, realizing that this was not the proper time to pursue that delicate matter, made a hasty denial: "Oh no! I meant free travel back and forth," and when he uttered the magical words for which so many of the world's people yearn—"free travel"—each Calderón visualized what a rich experience it could be to journey easily and without visas between their lovely twin cities, Miami and La Habana.

Finally Estéfano said: "I do believe that if you Cubanos could see the benefits of democracy as they exist for all Cubanos in Miami, you'd change your policies down here." Roberto and his wife just laughed, and Plácida made what was for her an uncharacteristic political observation: "We think that one of these days the rest of the Caribbean will follow our route to strong socialist government. We feel sure Puerto Rico and Santo Domingo will join us, and then probably most of the rest. Jamaica almost did, some years ago."

This was too much for Estéfano: "Surely no nation in its right senses would elect to align with Castro, considering the conditions on this island."

"What do you mean by that?"

"I'll tell you exactly what I mean. A dictatorship that provides very few amenities for its people. Nothing in the stores. No toilet paper. No toothpaste. No dresses for little girls. No decent automobiles. No paint for the houses. No new buildings to replace the crumbling ones on El Cerro. And no freedom for the young men to do anything but fly to Angola and die in the jungle."

Plácida chose to respond, and she did so vigorously, drawing Estéfano's attention to an article in *Granma:* "It tells here of the experiences of a Cubano in Miami, minor health problem. Asthma attack. Listen to what doctors like you, Estéfano, do to the people of your country." And she read a horrendous account, fortified with photostats of the actual bills from doctors, consultants, nurses and diagnosticians totaling $7,800 for a two-night stay in a hospital for what was essentially a trivial matter. When hectored by the Cuban Calderóns, Estéfano as a doctor and Caterina as a nurse had to acknowledge the probable accuracy of the report.

"The man in the house at our corner," Plácida continued, "had to have major heart surgery. Nineteen days in hospital, emergency care. Total cost? Not one peso. Dental treatment for his wife? Not one peso. World's best health care for his three children. Not one peso." Sternly she concluded: "We may not have the white paint you keep lamenting about, but we have the best health care in the world and the best schools for our children, both free. And that means something."

All four Calderóns realized that their discussion had entered upon perilous ground, so Roberto, always the conciliator, diverted to a question which nagged him: "Take a refugee like our cousin Quiroz. No special skills as I remember him. How does he make a living in Miami?" and Estéfano explained: "You must understand one thing, Roberto. There's an immense amount of Cuban money flowing about our city. Some of it real income, like what my bank handles, some of it cocaine money. But it's there and it's available."

"But how does a worthless fellow like Quiroz get his share?"

"People who hate Castro, and that's ninety-nine percent of us, they see to it that fellows like Máximo are kept alive. They feel he's doing their work for them, keeping Castro off balance."

"Would he lead another Bay of Pigs invasion?"

"Tomorrow, if the American government would allow it."

This occasioned a long pause, after which Roberto said, surprisingly: "Estéfano, I do wish you'd break the careless habit of using the word *American* as if you had stolen it from the rest of us. Use *norteamericano,* because we Cubans and Mexicans and Uruguayans, we're also Americans."

Up till now—the beginning of their second week in Cuba—the visit had been what it was supposed to be, an amiable family reunion. But Estéfano had been nervous all along as to how he could approach Roberto about getting to see Castro. One night he said to Caterina: "I can't ask Roberto outright: 'Can I see your leader?' but you might drop a suggestion to your sister, something like: 'Any chance of seeing Castro? To confirm he really exists?'" but she replied: "I'd feel safer if we didn't see him at all. No rumors flying back to Miami."

But, finally, Estéfano did open the subject with Roberto, saying, rather casually: "While I'm here, I'd sure like to get to meet Castro," and his cousin replied: "I'll see what I can do to arrange it. He's pretty open to visitors." But then he went on to say that Castro had the habit of keeping people on the hook for days, then without warning sending for them at midnight for a talk that lasted till dawn. So night after night, Estéfano delayed going to bed early.

Then, on Tuesday night it happened. A senior official from Castro's office dropped by the sugar mill to inform Roberto that if he cared to bring his cousin to the presidential quarters at eleven that night, Fidel would be pleased to chat with him about Cuban affairs in Florida, and without betraying that he had been awaiting just such a summons, Estéfano said without undue eagerness: "I'd be honored to meet him."

Not knowing whether the invitation at that odd hour would include dinner, Estéfano informed Caterina of the impending visit and then ate lightly: "To protect myself either way. If there's to be a full dinner, I'll be able to cram it in. If not, I won't starve."

At ten-fifteen a chauffeured car accompanied by a police escort arrived, and as they sped through a lovely moonlit September evening, Estéfano assured his cousin: "Don't worry. I'll tell him exactly what I told you. I oppose his politics, but I do look forward to the day when there will be free exchange between our countries."

"I'm sure that's what he would like to hear."

"But on our terms, not his."

"For the past quarter of a century your country has been trying to dictate to him and you've always failed, miserably. Maybe it's time to try some other tactic," and Estéfano laughed: "Maybe, but not on your terms, either," and Roberto said as they approached the presidential palace: "Agreed."

It was made clear as the cousins entered the waiting area, a large and handsome hall, that Roberto's role would be limited to introducing his cousin and then withdrawing to await the end of the conference, and he was not surprised at the arrangement. Both men remained in the outer hall for about two hours, after which the door to Castro's quarters broke open with a bang and a huge bearded man in rumpled army fatigues slammed his way forward to extend both hands, one to Estéfano, one to Roberto: "Welcome to the honorable children of our great patriot Baltazar Calderón y Quiroz." With that, he took Estéfano warmly by the hand, leading him into his quarters and leaving Roberto in the outer hall.

With a wide swing of his big right foot, he slammed the door closed, indicated a chair for his American guest and fell easily into his own. He was full of restless energy, his agile mind leaping from one subject to another, his tireless hands waving a big unlit cigar as he talked.

"A temptation and an obligation," he said, indicating the cigar. "Doctors told me: 'Fidel, you'll die ten years too soon if you continue smoking,' so I quit. But then our cigar manufacturers reminded me: 'Fidel, you and your cigar are the best advertisement for Cuban cigars, and that's where our foreign exchange comes from. Please keep smoking.' So I obeyed both sets of advisers this way," and he jammed the big, cold cigar into the corner of his mouth.

They talked for five hours, barely interrupting for a meal of soup, chicken sandwiches and a remarkable sweet: "Do you, as a doctor, warn your patients against too much sugar, the way ours do?"

To Estéfano's surprise, he asked this and occasional other questions in English, and Estéfano answered in that language, but when he finished explaining that yes, when he was a practicing doctor he did warn his patients against sugar, Castro leaped from his chair, wagged an admonitory finger, and cried in Spanish: "Well, stop it! We Cubanos want you to eat as much sugar as possible, and buy it all from us."

When the serious conversation started, Estéfano was astounded at the breadth of Castro's knowledge of things American, but he was also aware that the dictator was hitting these topics to make himself seem an amiable fellow: The knowing baseball jargon "Why do the Red Sox always lose the big series?" The inside knowledge of American entertainment "How do they take it in Georgia, a Negro like Bill Cosby dominating television?" The awareness of intricate situations "How are the two Koreas handling the Olympics?" And a dozen little questions that quietly needled the Americans: "Did your government arrest any of those crazies who tried to tease our athletes into defecting at Indianapolis?"

Calderon, well aware that this pleasant chatter was preamble, waited for the politics to begin, and he was prepared when Castro shot out a barrage of questions regarding the attitude of Miami Cubanos on conditions in Haiti, Santo Domingo, Puerto Rico and Cuba itself. He was especially concerned with two problems on which he pressed Estéfano almost to the point of rudeness: "If Manley wins the forthcoming election in Jamaica, will that reawaken anti-Americanism on the island?" and "What do you hear in Miami about racial unrest in Trinidad, like what's been happening in Fiji?"

He also wanted to know how the Miami Cubanos had reacted to the American invasion of Grenada, and was not surprised to hear: "Among our people I heard not one adverse comment and a thousand cheers." But he was irritated to learn: "Most of us were convinced that communist Cubano infiltrators were about to take control of Grenada."

"Rubbish!" he said, using a Cuban word that could be translated more vulgarly. Then he leaned back, twisting his cigar between thumb and forefinger, summoned a waiter to bring more drinks, and asked: "Now, Dr. Calderón . . ." and Estéfano noticed that whenever he began the exploration of a new topic, he spoke formally, and invariably used the title *Doctor:* "Explain in careful terms, because I know you're informed on these matters, what does the word *Hispanic* mean in various parts of the United States," and Estéfano also noticed that when Castro rolled out those magnificent syllables *Los Estados Unidos,* he did so with a certain respect, as if honoring the size of his northerly neighbor if not its politics.

Now the two Cubans settled down to another hourlong discussion, with Estéfano reviewing various experiences he'd had with the Spanish-speaking peoples of America: "I've had to travel a lot as a Hispanic banking leader and chairman for the election and reelection of President Reagan." Here he broke into a quiet laugh: "The Anglo politicians running the campaign apparently said: 'Look, Calderon speaks Spanish. And he has a good blue suit. Let's use him widely to get the others lined up.' So they shipped me off to New York, California and Texas."

Castro leaned forward, eyes gleaming above his dark beard: "A disaster?"

"Worse. In New York it's all Puerto Ricans, and they have their own agenda, which is unique. I could hardly speak to them, and they certainly did not look to me for guidance. They were quite capable of providing their own."

"California?"

"I don't want to insult you, Señor Presidente, but out there those red-hot Mexicans hardly know that you're in command in Cuba. Couldn't care less, because they have their own problems with Mexico. My ideas of politics and theirs are as different as night and day. It was a total flop."

"Texas?"

"On the surface the same as California, but fundamentally a much different set of Mexicans. Especially in Los Angeles they're more sophisticated, have more political power. In Texas they're more the peasant type. About two generations behind the Californians, I'd say."

They spent a long time exploring the differences among the four basic Hispanic groups as Estéfano defined them: the Cubanos of Miami, the Puerto Ricans of New York, the sophisticated Mexicans of California and the sturdy peasants of Texas, and at the end

Estéfano hammered home one basic point: "Anyone who thinks he can lump them all together and form a cohesive Hispanic minority that he can shift this way or that is out of his mind." Here he stared hard at Castro and said: "Don't even try to go down that road. It won't work."

"All strongly Catholic?"

"Yes."

"All Republican?"

"I'm not sure about the Californians and Texans, but probably even them." Then he added a salient point: "Bear in mind one thing, Señor Presidente. The Cubanos you sent to Miami in that first batch were all educated, well-to-do, middle-of-the-road people. They've adjusted easily to American life. None were illiterate peasants." He hesitated, then added: "Sometimes in California and Texas, I found it difficult to believe that these people were Hispanics at all. They weren't like anyone I've ever known either here as a young man or in Florida later on."

It was now well past three in the morning, and Estéfano kept reminding himself that he must resist the blandishments of this extraordinary man: He's the man who stole my country, who murdered many of my friends, who kept others in hideous jails, and who has done everything possible to embarrass the United States and support her enemy, the Soviet Union. He had no love for Castro, nor even much respect, but he could feel the immense power of his charisma, and at one point when the dictator was being especially persuasive about never having had animosity toward the States, Calderon thought: Now I know how a bird feels when the cobra weaves its spell. This son-of-a-bitch is mesmerizing.

Then, at the end of a long oration about how the United States should conduct itself in Central America, Castro leaned forward, studied his guest, and asked in the most amiable voice possible: "Dr. Calderón, why did you feel that you, the son of patriots, had to leave Cuba?" and after a frank discussion of mixed signals and lost opportunities, Castro asked, at a quarter of four: "Under what terms would you come back?" and now Estéfano felt both free and obligated to make several points: "With a great-grandfather like old Baltazar Calderón, I will always love and cherish Cuba. It's in my blood. The fact that I fled proves I wasn't enthusiastic about your takeover, but as you probably know from the reports of your consuls, I've never been a rabid anti-Castroite. And I'm convinced that because your island is so close to the States, some kind of reconciliation must be reestablished, probably before the end of this century."

"Does anyone else in your country think so?"

"Some of my more sensible friends in Washington . . . the ones I worked with on Reagan's campaigns."

Castro, realizing from this one sentence the reason Calderon had been sent south, looked up at the ceiling and started waving his cigar. Then he said as if he hadn't heard what Estéfano had just revealed: "The doctors told me: 'If you stop smoking these things, you could live to see the end of the century.' "

"When were you born?"

"Nineteen twenty-seven."

"You're only five years older than I am, and I certainly expect to see it."

"So you do come here speaking for someone, Dr. Calderón?"

"My wife came here to visit with her twin sister. Emotional meeting, I can tell you."

"Roberto Calderón's a valuable man for us. Knows his way around." More cigar pirouettes, then: "You know, Doctor, if you ever wanted to come down here and start a really fine clinic—I've heard about the one you run in Miami—you'd be most welcome, and we'd provide the building."

"I'm honored."

"Tell me, if all restrictions were lifted tomorrow, and I mean all, what percentage of your Cubans would return to our island?"

"Of my original group, to visit the old scenes they love, ninety-eight percent. To remain here permanently and give up all the good things they've acquired in Florida, two percent."

"Of the Mariel group?"

"A larger percent, men eager to get back into the criminal action. But of course, you wouldn't want their kind."

"And the children born there?"

"Not one in ten thousand. High schools, television, their own crowd, shopping malls. Irresistible to young people."

"So they're a lost generation . . . for us, that is."

"I think so."

"You never really answered me. Under what terms would you and your wife come back?"

Estéfano pondered how to answer this question without giving offense, and finally said: "When a man breaks a bone, at first it looks as if it could never be remedied. But you immobilize it in a splint, let it knit, and six weeks later, a miracle! It's stronger than it was before, because the tiny bits of bone have interlocked with each other. It's the same with émigrés. In the first six months away from the homeland, desolation of spirit. But then the knitting begins, and pretty soon the bond to the new land is overwhelmingly powerful."

"In your case, too strong to be broken again?"

"Yes."

Castro placed his arm on Estéfano's shoulder and said, as he walked him to the door: "Tell the man who sent you that if amicable relations are ever reestablished between our countries, I'd be happy to have you as the first ambassador in La Habana."

On their last evening in Cuba the Miami Calderons felt obligated to discuss the inevitable Hispanic problem, and Caterina broached the subject: "You know, if you two should ever wish to come to America, get away from these tensions, Estéfano and I will be prepared, even honored, to find a place for you to live . . . help you and your children get established. We'd enjoy having them about us."

"We couldn't . . ."

Caterina broke into tears: "It's been so wonderful, being together again. We're a family, Plácida, and we should not be in separate places. Please, please, think about what I've just said. And remember, Estéfano feels the same way. You can stay with us . . . two years . . . three, until you get settled, isn't that right, Estéfano?"

"Roberto knows it is. We'd be overjoyed to have you with us again, and I don't mean only you two. Your children could build great lives for themselves in America, and we'd help them."

Plácida's response, however, was not to her sister's offer; instead, she placed her hand on Caterina's arm and said with deep emotion: "Yes, we must stay together, now that we've seen how wonderful it can be . . . But we should be here, where we all belong. And Roberto's been working on a few plans. We could easily let you have two of these little buildings, and El Lider Máximo stopped by my office today to confirm what he said the other night. You can have a clinic in downtown La Habana. Come back home, Estéfano, and join the building of your homeland."

By the time the two couples parted it was obvious that neither of the families would ever move, but both were sincerely convinced that in extending their invitations, they were acting solely in the interest of their loved ones. Estéfano and Caterina were certain that the Cuban Calderóns could find real happiness in the Miami they knew, while Roberto and his wife were equally sure that any self-respecting Cubano could find lasting happiness only in coming home and working for the revolution. And with these mutual convictions they went to bed.

But no one fell easily to sleep, and as Estéfano lay awake, trying to assess what was said during his extraordinary visit with Castro, he became aware that Caterina was sobbing, and when he tried to comfort her, she said: "I should never have come down here. In Miami, I could ignore how much I was missing her . . . and Roberto . . . and the children . . . and the old mill . . . and let's face it, Cuba." And then she added: "I'm a Cubana and I'm damned sick of supermarkets and television serials."

Homesick though they were, the Miami Calderons had to be cautious about their movements lest ill-wishers at home learn of Estéfano's visit to Cuba; they arranged a flight to Mexico City and a quick transfer to a jet which would deposit them at Miami International in late afternoon. At the Havana airport four of the gloomiest people in Cuba said goodbye, each realizing that this might be the last time they would ever meet on this earth—so close geographically to one another in the twin cities of Miami and La Habana, so terribly far apart in politics and the interpretation of the future. The farewells were muted, the two men engaging in formalities, while their wives stood apart, shedding hot tears of regret. Suddenly Estéfano burst out: "My God! They're a handsome pair of twins we married, Roberto," and the two men stared lovingly at these two women, so well preserved, so proud of their appearance and so similar in their attitudes toward family and social responsibilities. They were, Estéfano thought, two of the finest women of their age in the world and proof of what Cubanas could accomplish.

With tears in his own eyes, he kissed Plácida farewell, shook hands with Roberto, and said: "I hope we accomplished something," but he was not at all sure, and when the plane rose into the sky he hammered his right fist into the open palm of his other hand as he looked down upon that lovely land of Cuba, so abused by its Spanish colonial owners, so maltreated by that gang of thieving murderers who had presumed to govern it during its first half-century of independence, and so misled by the Castro revolution which inevitably followed. "Cuba! Cuba!" he said as the island slowly vanished from sight. "You deserved so much more than what you've been allowed to be."

While he was tormenting himself with such thoughts, Caterina kept staring down till the faint outline of the island vanished totally from view. Then she sighed, reached back to grip her husband's arm, and whispered: "You were so right in insisting that we come. What a noble city and how grand that old mill was." But later in the day when Miami came into view, she pressed his hand and said: "This is better," and both of them knew that down below waited the world they really wanted.

From his window Steve admired the glorious skyline with its towering skyscrapers of imaginative design lining the bay, the islands and the inland waterways, making it one of the most beautiful cities in America. Leaning forward, he said: "I know how Augustus felt when he cried: 'I found Rome a city of brick and shall leave it a city of marble.' We Cubanos found Miami a sleepy town of low, frightened buildings and we shall leave it a city of towers."

Proudly he pointed to the buildings his bank had helped finance with money earned and deposited by his Cuban associates. "That one, those two, the one over there. All since 1959. Just thirty years. It's been a miracle and I'm proud of it. Me leave Miami? Never," and Kate whispered: "Nor me." But then she added: "However, if things ever did open up, and George Bush felt grateful for your assistance this fall, it would be nice if he appointed you as his first American ambassador."

The last words had scarcely been uttered when she felt Steve's ironlike grip and heard his anguished whisper: "Don't even *think* a thing like that. If people knew there was even a possibility . . ."

When the plane landed almost secretly at a remote corner of Miami International, an ashen-faced assistant to Dr. Calderon met him with miserable news, which he delivered in a trembling voice: "Your new clinic building, the one that's half finished . . . they dynamited it last night . . . burned to the ground."

And in the rush to Calle Ocho a suspicious car tailed them, pulled up beside them at a traffic light, and pumped four bullets directly at the Calderons. They missed the doctor but hit his wife three times, and before the car could speed to the nearest hospital, she was dead.

XVI

THE GOLDEN SEA

ON A BRIGHT JANUARY MORNING IN 1989 THE STRANDS OF Theresa Vaval's life tangled together in riotous climax. She received her doctorate in social anthropology from Harvard; Wellesley confirmed that she had a professorial appointment there, with an implied promise of tenure track if she enhanced her scholarly reputation; her father, Hyacinthe Vaval, received notice that he and his family would be granted permanent residence in the United States, which they had entered seven years ago after temporary refuge in Canada; and Dennis Krey, professor of creative writing at Yale, had at last summoned up courage to inform his Concord, New Hampshire, parents that he and Tessa, as she was known to her college friends, were getting married. As if that wasn't enough, the Swedish Lines had phoned, offering her an opportunity to teach a course aboard one of their cruise ships, the S.S. *Galante,* set to sail from Cap-Haïtien, Haiti, on 30 January. One hundred and thirty-seven students had signed up for the three-credit, fourteen-day course, entitled "Cruise-and-Muse in Paradise." "We'll do the cruising, you do the musing," the Swedish Lines representative had joked, telling Theresa that she would be the most honored among six lecturers already signed up.

All these happenings simply could not be better, especially the one concerning her father, for he had been one of the fine men of Haiti, descendant of that General Vaval who had played such a major role in helping Toussaint L'Ouverture win Haiti's independence back in the 1790s. From that time on, the Vavals, through all their generations, had been defenders of Haitian freedom, often at great risk, and some had been publicly executed, but their courage never flagged. When Papa Doc Duvalier, Haiti's self-appointed President-for-Life, sent out his death squads, the Tontons Macoutes, to terrorize newspaper editors and writers in the 1970s, torturing many to death, Tessa remembered her father coming home and saying: "No hope. Last night they killed Editor Gambrelle. We're slipping out on the next ship that makes a run for it."

They had left Port-au-Prince in three different groups so as to escape notice by the deadly Macoutes, and reunited at the seaport of St.-Marc, where in what seemed to nine-year-old Thérèse, as she was then called in French, an insane decision, they boarded a small, leaky ship and in dark of night set out for the Atlantic. Those were days she wanted to forget but knew she must remember, for those experiences made Haitians unique. But her fiancé Dennis Krey had to probe many times before she was able to speak of them: "Four people crowded on deck where one should have been. Food and water gone. Those who died pitched overboard and we could see the sharks. My mother told me: 'If you keep your hand in the water, the shark will take it on his next trip.' Each evening when darkness came I was terrified, but Father told us in reassuring tones that masked his own terror: 'Remember that Vavak fled St. John in a rowboat lots smaller than this, and he made it.' We'd have fallen apart, all of us, except my father kept saying quietly: 'We will live. It would be cowardly to die,' and we survived.

"After eleven days on the water, a wonderful, beautiful Canadian ship picked us up, and it took us to Québec City, where everyone spoke French and there was food and hope."

She wondered if Dennis had told his parents this story, and if it would make any difference to them. The Kreys were traditional New Englanders and Tessa, of course, was black. She was, however, one of those spectacular young Haitian women of light-tan complexion and exquisitely graceful carriage who seem as if they had dropped by a café on some Parisian boulevard. She was tall, slim, and blessed with a broad, even countenance that broke into smiles at any excuse. She had never worried about what might become of her in the cold lands of Canada, because young men persistently tried to date her, and once she moved to Boston, she had been among the most popular girls at Radcliffe. It did not surprise her that Krey had wanted to marry her; three or four other white young men had wanted to do the same, for against a New England background she was spectacular: tall, sinewy, with that glorious sunrise face and flashing white teeth.

But when Krey's parents drove down to see her receive her graduate degree from Harvard and to attend their son's engagement party, Tessa anticipated antagonism. She knew they must have had more exalted plans for their son than marriage to a Haitian, but she was not prepared for the subtle ways in which the elder Kreys manifested their displeasure. Judge Adolphus Krey, a tall, austere man in his sixties, looked at her as if he were thinking: Regardless of this terrible mistake Dennis is making, we shall not disown him, for he is, after all, our son. And the chill that fell over the rest of that day intensified, until Tessa muttered to herself: "The whole damned lake is freezing over."

Mrs. Krey reacted somewhat differently. When she first saw Tessa she congealed so completely that she could scarcely thaw her lips for a limited smile, but when Dennis explained that Tessa's father, Hyacinthe Vaval, would not be able to join them for lunch, she became enthralled by the reason her son gave: "He was summoned to Washington by President Bush. The new administration believes he might be just the man to serve as president of Haiti, if peace ever returns to that stricken island."

"As president?" she asked, but Tessa dampened the emerging enthusiasm by saying: "He'd be crazy if he takes it. Probably be murdered like his great-great-grandfather who tried to govern in the last century."

Mrs. Krey, who interpreted the remark as flippancy, glared disapprovingly and warned her future daughter-in-law: "At Concord, you know, young wives from outside have to earn their way, as it were," and Tessa said, almost harshly: "But we won't be living in Concord. Dennis will be starting a new career at Trinity in Hartford and I'll be doing the same at Wellesley."

"But you will be spending your summers in Concord, I hope."

"Later, perhaps. At first, mostly in Europe . . . pursuing studies and the like." When Dennis verified their plans for the next few years, Judge Krey said stiffly: "We think it would be more prudent if our friends in Concord could see your wife . . . get accustomed to her."

The implications of this revealing statement were too harsh for Tessa to accept unchallenged, and with the roguish humor she often used to puncture such comments, she broke into a ravishing smile and said: "You remind me, you really do, of the Jewish boy at Harvard who called his mother in New York to tell her: 'Mom! Guess what! I'm marrying that cute Japanese girl you met at the Princeton game,' and after a pause his mother said: 'That's fine, son. When you bring her down you can have my big room on the second floor.' Delighted that his mother was taking it so well, he said: 'No, Mom, you don't have to go that far,' and she said: 'It'll be empty, because the minute you bring that tramp in our front door, I jump out the window . . . headfirst!' "

She allowed the awful silence that followed to hang in the air for about ten seconds, then laughed easily and placed her hand on Judge Krey's forearm: "Our marriage can't be as shattering as it must seem in Concord. Dennis and I will be living in communities that are long used to mixed couples like us. I think we represent the wave of the future . . . of little or no concern to others."

Judge Krey, resenting the familiarity of her touch, withdrew stiffly, marshaled his New England rectitude, and said: "Cambridge is not the world, thank heavens," and they moved on to the engagement lunch, which should have been a festive affair, considering the handsomeness of the intended groom and the beauty of the bride, but which was painfully strained. When the elder Kreys departed for their drive back to the security of Concord, they left no doubt about the chilly reception Tessa would face in that proper New England town. And Dennis added to her insecurity by saying, as soon as his parents departed: "You should never have told that joke about the Jewish boy and his Japanese bride. You should have foreseen that it would embarrass my folks."

Somewhat chastened, Tessa put her Ph.D. diploma away and plunged into preparations for the Caribbean cruise. Swedish officials of the line that operated the *Galante,* aware that in addition to her impressive scholarly credentials, she was black, had thought it an asset. They told her: "You're a fine-looking black scholar explaining the new black republics in what we're going to advertise as 'your sea.' And you have a marvelous French accent, don't lose it. That'll be a double asset."

It was providential that the tour would be starting at Cap-Haïtien, with passengers being flown in from three major airports, for that would provide her with an opportunity to go down to Port-au-Prince two weeks before embarking and see what changes had taken place since that dark night in 1973 when the Vaval family had scuttled out of St.-Marc for freedom in Canada. When she informed Dennis of her plans, he was not entirely pleased: "I did approve the idea of the cruise. Great chance to renew your contacts in the area, but I hoped we'd have the time to ourselves before the boat sailed," and she replied: "For a Haitian to know what's happening in Haiti is tremendously important. Anyway, we'll be married as planned in late June."

The flight from Boston to Port-au-Prince covered far more than space; for although she started out as a self-directed young woman of twenty-five with career and marriage well in hand, by the time she landed she was once more an awkward, spindly-legged child fleeing her homeland, not fully aware of how important a citizen her father was nor what a significant role her family had played in Haitian history. Later she had learned that in the mid-1800s one of her ancestors had served a three-year term as president, a responsible subsitute for the impossible generals, murderers and psychopaths who had run the black republic during its one hundred and eighty-five years of independence. His term had ended before a firing squad directed by the next group of generals waiting to take over, but his martyrdom continued to inspire hope that at some point Haiti would learn to govern itself. "The good President Vaval," he was referred to, and his grandson had been "that clever Vaval who held off the Yankees" when American troops invaded early in the 1900s and he governed for some twenty years.

She knew a great deal about the two Duvaliers who had murdered so many good men, and she remembered that her father had called their horrible Tontons Macoutes the "Nazis of the New World, worse maybe, for they killed and maimed their own people, not a so-called alien race." At home her family had drummed two lessons into her: "If the slave Vavak had not had the courage to flee St. John when he did, none of us would be alive today, and if we hadn't fled Haiti when we did, we'd also be dead."

She thus saw Haiti not only as a romantic island nation which as a child she had loved for its color and music and delightful people, but also as a forbidding prison from which only the lucky had escaped. In contrast, she now regarded Canada as one of the kindest nations on earth and the United States as the benefactor that had given her, practically free, her B.A., M.A., and Ph.D. She was therefore in the proper mindset to evaluate her natal land, and what she saw appalled her. The revolution of 1986, which had ousted Baby Doc Duvalier and his outrageous entourage of thieves and murderers, had produced no brave new leaders like her father, and the continuing disorientation showed no signs of ending.

In Port-au-Prince, which she found a miasma of hunger and futility, only one thing gave her hope: when she stopped to speak to young people, explaining who she was, most of them greeted her enthusiastically: "Oh, Thérèse, I do hope your father comes back to run for high office. We need his guidance and his courage." But these signs of hope were dashed when older and wiser people whispered: "If he can get a foothold in the States, Thérèse, warn him never to return. This place is beyond redemption." After a string of such dismal days she caught a rickety bus that carried her north and into the rural area where the Vavals had for many generations owned a prosperous farm. She remembered this farm—the fine house of the owners, the earthen-floored shacks of the peasants—and she was dismayed to find that no improvements had been made in her absence. The poor people of Haiti still lived like animals, miserably housed, poorly fed and clothed in rags.

When she went to the main house, she found that even now it had no electricity; it still used a hand pump for water; and the rooms which had provided comforts for her family of seven now contained five different families living like rabbits in a crowded warren. Perching disconsolately on a bench improvised from a flat board propped on rocks, she turned in all directions, surveying the miserable signs of life: dangling from a frayed clothesline, laundry that should have been thrown away fifty washings ago, junky bits of machinery, shacks that were about to collapse, women of thirty who slaved so unremittingly that they looked sixty. Poverty and despair now defined a nation that had once been one of the richest in the world.

Then, inescapably, came the terrible question which had been in her mind even before she started her tour of the Caribbean: If Haiti had been an independent, self-governing republic ruled only by blacks since 1804, and if it had achieved so pitifully little for its people, what did that say about the ability of blacks to govern? And as she sat among the dreams of her childhood, she felt overwhelmed by the reality around her. She stood up, clenching her fists, and shouted at the cloudless sky: "What in hell is wrong with my country?"

Her next two-minute self-lecture, as might be expected, was more academic: It could all be so different. Dear God, it could have been so much better. Suppose in 1920 you'd had three young people like me who attended a good Jesuit college in New England where they learned to think and act. And another three who enrolled in a strong liberal college in New York where they had sense and character knocked into them. And they'd come back to Haiti and put their talents to work. Goodness, they'd have cozened the United States and Canada into giving them millions of dollars. France would have helped out from pride, because we speak French. And Russia would have leaped in to prove it could do even more than the other nations. We'd have had roads and railroads and factories and colleges, and new methods of agriculture. We could have built a paradise here . . . Haiti, which was once so wonderful, could have been wonderful again!

In the days that followed her disastrous visit to her old home, she met several leaders in Port-au-Prince who remembered her father, and they were pleased to learn that she would be teaching at Wellesley: "Fine college, we're told. Excellent reputation." She did not inform them of her impending marriage to a white man from New Hampshire, for they would be smart enough to know that this implied some interesting conflicts. Instead, she interrogated them about the future of Haiti, and was delighted to hear them orate in their lovely mix of polished French and lowdown creole which could be so colorful and expressive. Their message was not heartening, for they saw little hope for their nation. "What do we make that the world wants?" one man asked rhetorically. "Only one thing. All the baseballs used by the American big leagues are sewn together here. If the Taiwanese ever learn to sew baseball covers, we'll perish."

They said that the political situation was so bleak that the patterns set in the last two hundred years were likely to continue: "One petty dictator after another, one general with a little more braid and less brain than his predecessor."

One knowledgeable fellow suggested that she hire a car and he and two friends who worked for the government would show her something of basic importance in the hills north of the city. When they were well into those once-forested mountains in which her ancestor General Vaval had so ably thwarted Napoleon's French invaders, this young man pointed to the terrible desolation that had overtaken rural Haiti, for as far into the distance as she could see, the hills and valleys were denuded of trees. Every square inch had been stripped clean by charcoal makers, and the bare and dusty slopes were devoid of any growing thing, not even seedlings to replace the lost grandeur.

"See how the gullies run toward the sea. Torrential rains roar down them, carrying the loam away."

"You're creating a desert," Tessa cried, almost in pain, and the men said: "Wrong. It's already been created, and with rain and wind behaving as they do, it may never be reversed."

She had brought with her the address of an uncle who had remained behind during the evacuation, and now she repacked her belongings and caught another fearfully overcrowded bus, which took her well to the north of St.-Marc, the seaport where Napoleon's Polish Battalion had massacred the remnants of a black regiment, and if she had been appalled at conditions in the village north of the capital, she was speechless when she saw how her relatives were living. They had none of the amenities of a town, none of the incidentals which make even a life of poverty endurable: they were living as so many Haitians did, in a shack that had only bare earth for a floor, two mattress-less beds laid flat on the earth, two unsteady chairs, a rickety table, some nails for hanging such clothes as the family had acquired. They were living, these descendants of generals and presidents who had served Haiti well, at about the level that their ancestor Vavak had lived two and a half centuries ago when a slave on the Danish island of St. John.

Seeing this incredible degradation, caused by the endless chain of dictators who made themselves wealthy and their people poor, she impulsively threw open her purse, took out the wallet in which she kept her money, and gave her relatives funds she had saved for the purchase of books at various island stopovers: "Please, Father would insist."

"How did you get so much money?" they asked, and she said: "In Canada everyone has a job. It's quite wonderful, really," and she explained that most nations in the world provided for their people: "First two years out of college I worked for the Peace Corps. In African nations . . . probably because I was black. First-rate experience, and frankly, wherever I have been, I never found a country as poor as Haiti."

This condemnation so moved her uncle that he went to a miserable wooden shelf he had nailed to the wall and brought back a big handsome book printed in France in vivid color: "Each of us had to buy six copies, very expensive," and when Tessa looked inside she saw a big photograph of Papa Doc, with the caption: "The revered head of the nation presents the true visage of Haiti: the dignity, the pride, the wisdom of the thinker, the force of the conqueror." But what made her really gag was a photograph of fifteen handsome young black men in sparkling blue uniforms which bore the insulting caption: "The revered Tontons Macoutes benevolently assume responsibility for the liberty we enjoy."

In trembling rage she slammed the disgraceful thing to the floor and kicked it into a corner, crying: "They murder not only people but also the truth, and there is no shame in them, damn them to eternal hell!"

"What can we do?" her uncle asked, and she had only one suggestion: "Get on a boat, any boat—the way your brother did, and get out of here."

"Too late," her uncle said, and she burst into tears, for she knew he was right. For this family it was too late.

For younger Haitians, there was still a chance, and they meant to claim it. One afternoon when she went into St.-Marc to buy her uncle some groceries she saw in the shallow bay a boat so pitifully small that she thought: It ought to be on a lake somewhere, not in the ocean. But when she passed it again at dusk, she watched about forty black people climb into that fragile thing and sail off into the Atlantic. Horrified by the thought that they might be trying to reach the United States in such a vessel, she walked along the shores asking questions, and learned that yes, these fugitives were risking their lives on the high seas in an overloaded boat with insufficient provisions rather than remain one more day in Haiti. She fell to her knees at the edge of the Caribbean and prayed: "Beloved God, send a boat from Canada to rescue them," and in that moment she ceased being a trendy intellectual from Cambridge drinking Perrier water for lunch and listening to Vivaldi and became once more a Haitian black woman struggling against all odds to keep her life together.

When, still brooding about the refugees in their tragic boat, she delivered the groceries to her uncle, she found that an extraordinary item of news had arrived by runner from a much smaller village, Du Mort, four miles back into the mountains: "A zombie, eleven years dead, has come back to life."

The word *zombie* irritated her, because in both Québec City and Boston well-intentioned friends, when they heard she came from Haiti, had pestered her about zombies, as if they were the major characteristic of her homeland. Most such questions she laughed off, but some were more serious, particularly at Harvard.

To these scholars she replied truthfully: "I've heard folk tales about zombies throughout my childhood. And I was terrified. A zombie, we were taught, is a dead person brought back to life and used thereafter as a slave in perpetuity." Asked if she had ever heard of a real, authenticated case she was always tempted to answer, with a touch of ridicule: "No! Did your family ever see one of the giants or elves they told you about?" But she refrained from a blanket denial because she had an Uncle René, shot later by the Tontons Macoutes, who swore that when he was a boy a zombie, dead for many days, had been brought back to life and had served as a slave to a wealthy family. But like always, this very circumstantial miracle had happened in another village farther on.

But now it was a village only four miles away, in the real year of 1989, and she could go and check out the preposterous story for herself. Enlisting one of the two taxis in the village, she took her notebook and kit of medicines and drove out to where the alleged zombie had been seen.

The village contained some thirty mud-floored shacks distributed around a handsome public square, one side of which was a colorful market with stalls occupied by sellers of meat and fish, vegetables, fruits, needlework and clay pots. Near the village pump squatted a young black woman, about twenty-eight, of presentable appearance and fine placid features—except that she was almost inanimate. Her eyes showed no recognition of things about her; she did not respond to questions; and if anyone approached her, she drew back in obvious terror. If any human being could be justly described as "the living dead," it was this unfortunate.

Tessa was immediately drawn to her. "Who is this person?" she asked about, and several bystanders were eager to provide answers and explanations: "Her name Lalique Hébert. Her tombstone at edge of village, over there." And Tessa was taken by villagers to the rude cemetery where a flat tombstone made of flaking cement showed clearly that interred below were the mortal remains of LALIQUE HÉBERT, 1961–1978.

When Tessa asked: "Is this the same person?" one of the bystanders cried vigorously: "Yes! Yes! I know her sister." And another said: "I knew her parents." And when the question became: "But did any of you attend her funeral?" someone replied: "Yes, that one helped carry her coffin." And a man of about fifty stepped forward, willing to be interrogated.

"You carried the coffin?"

"I did."

"Did you actually see the corpse?"

"We all did," and a group of women moved toward the grave to confirm that they had seen the girl Lalique Hébert in her coffin at her home and had then helped carry her here for burial.

"You're sure she was dead?"

"Yes! We saw. Doctor signed paper."

A quick check at the church registry showed that in June 1978 the girl Lalique Hébert, aged seventeen, daughter of Jules and Marie Hébert of this parish, had been buried, her death having been attested to by a Dr. Malárie two days prior.

"Where could I see Dr. Malárie?" Tessa asked, and the custodian of the records said: "Dead, three years ago."

So back she went to the square where Lalique was still squatting by the pump in a position which would have numbed the legs of an ordinary person. "Hello, Lalique." No response. "Lalique, look at me . . . I want to help you." Not even a glance upward. But then Tessa had a clever idea. "Lalique, do you remember when you were dead, in your coffin?"

Very slowly the impassive woman raised her handsome, placid face, dark as ebony, to look at her questioner, and at first her eyes were filled with terror, as if Tessa reminded her of some woman who had abused her during her eleven years of zombie existence, but when she saw in her slow dumb way that this woman was much younger and lacked the brutal sneer of her longtime mistress, terror fled, and she answered: "Long time in grave, men come, I rise." And with her arms extended upward, she rose to a standing position from which she looked directly into Tessa's eyes. Then she collapsed again into her squatting position, inanimate as before.

In some agitation Tessa looked about for someone to consult with, and two women moved toward her. "What are you going to do with this woman?" Tessa asked, and one said: "Nothing. She is dead. She come back. She live . . ." They both made vague gestures with their hands.

"Where did she sleep last night?" and she was answered in the same indefinite way: "Maybe sleep here. Maybe against that wall." When Tessa showed astonishment, one of the women explained: "Not good have zombie in village. She come for revenge, maybe. Someone here in bad trouble, maybe."

"What will happen?" and the women both spoke at once: "She try to stay, people drive her out."

"Where? Where will she go?" and the women, speaking for their entire village, said: "Who knows? Zombies go many places. They not need eat . . . sleep . . . think. Missy, they not like you and me."

Distraught, Tessa left the harsh, practical women and returned to Lalique: "I am your friend, Lalique. Can I take you somewhere, help you in any way?"

When the zombie did not even look at her, Tessa had no option but to return to her taxi, but as they neared her home village she thought of all her lonely and outcast days in Québec City when she had first arrived in that cold and seemingly hostile city, and she cried out: "Driver! Take me back!"

When she reached the market square she saw that Lalique had not moved from the pump, and running to her as if the zombie were a lost daughter, she reached down, clasped her hands, drew her reluctantly to her feet, and led her toward the taxi: "We're going home, Lalique," and when they were in the cab, she hugged the frightened woman to her and began to sing an old Haitian lullaby:

"Bird over the sea, ho-ho!
You here on my knee, ha-ha!
Bird into the tree, ho-ho!
You stung by the bee, ha-ha!"

And for the first time in many years, Lalique Hébert, the verifiable zombie, clung to another human being and fell asleep.

Early next morning Tessa was called to her village's public phone, and a man's voice asked with obvious concern: "You the young woman from Harvard? Yes? Is it true that you went to the village of Du Mort and brought a young woman known as a zombie home with you?" When Tessa said yes to each of his questions, he said: "I'm Dr. Briant from St.-Marc. I've been specializing in this zombie business for the government and I must see your Lalique right away."

"Come over. You know where my village is."

"I'll be right over. Don't let anyone harm that young woman."

"Would that be likely?"

In a short time Dr. Briant arrived, a dark-skinned medical doctor in his fifties, graduate of Howard University in Washington, D.C., and a big, enveloping kind of man: "I'm fascinated to hear that after eleven years a woman relatively young made her escape. Tell me— why did you feel it necessary to rescue her from her village? Can she communicate?"

"No. I think she may be feeble-minded."

"Don't say that," Briant snapped. "They say that about all these unfortunates," and when Tessa led him to Lalique, who had slept in a bed for the first time in years, he was gentle and reassuring: "Lalique, I am your friend. Would you like some salt?"

For that brief moment the zombie was much more animated than she had been with Tessa, and when the doctor took from his pocket a little box of salt and sifted some onto his palm, she buried her face in his hand and lapped the salt like a dog.

"Horrible folk custom. Anyone who gets hold of one of these unfortunates . . . belief is that if you deprive them of salt, they stay mesmerized. You want some more salt, Lalique?" and again she gulped down the precious substance which had been denied her for so long.

"Who's been keeping her prisoner?"

"We're never able to find out. Nor will we ever know who put her in this condition and buried her alive." After feeding Lalique a further carefully controlled ration of salt, he asked: "Then you saw her grave?" When Tessa nodded, he said: "We must go there at once. Photograph it with the gravedigger, if we can find him. And any witnesses."

The two young women climbed into Dr. Briant's wobbly old car, and he drove hurriedly the four miles to Du Mort, where he created a sensation when he stepped out of the car with his camera and quickly issued forceful instructions to the villagers: "Take me to the cemetery. Fetch me the gravedigger. Bring me the record book from the church so that I can photograph it in sunlight. And I want everyone who knew this young woman eleven years ago to line up. Mlle. Vaval, please take their names in order."

And in the next hour he produced, with closeup photographs of each narrator, a compelling visual and oral account of the 1978 zombification of the seventeen-year-old girl Lalique Hébert. Knowing from long experience what questions to ask, he unraveled the story: Lalique had been the second of three daughters, a strong-willed girl who wanted to leave Du Mort and go to Port-au-Prince and become a secretary. In a quarrel over a young man, she incurred the jealousy of her older sister and the downright animosity of her mother. "It must have been," an old woman confided, "her own mother and her sister who had her murdered. I helped dress the body for funeral."

Dr. Briant did not flinch: "I suppose they paid a voodoo bocor to kill her?" and two women confirmed this guess: "They did. He was not from this village but his magic was powerful."

He then wanted to talk with the gravedigger, who was now an old man but who remembered well the burial of the pretty girl: "June . . . maybe July? No big storms. I dug right where you see the tomb. You can read the name LALIQUE HÉBERT."

The old man had much more to say, because the return of a zombie to a community in which she had been buried was an exciting matter, but Dr. Briant cut him short: "So for this one you dug a very shallow grave . . . maybe eighteen inches?"

"Yes. How did you know?"

"Tell me, did you ever dig eighteen-inch graves before?"

"Once. For a man nobody liked."

"And what happened?"

The gravedigger looked about the cemetery he had served so long, and whispered: "You seem to know," and Briant said: "I do. But I want you to tell her," and the man said quietly to Tessa: "He became a zombie too." Dr. Briant turned to Lalique, standing motionless, expressionless beside her grave, and tried to make her realize what was happening: "This is it, Lalique. Can I read your name as I point to the letters?" Tessa turned Lalique to face her grave and even inclined her head to make her look at the grisly tomb, but she refused to do so. But then, with a gesture so sudden that both Tessa and Dr. Briant were startled, she clasped Tessa in a passionate embrace and cried in a wail that filled the cemetery: "Lalique, Lalique!"

On the drive home the two women rode in the back seat, and like before, the shivering zombie recalled from the dead clung to Tessa and fell immediately asleep.

• • •

Dr. Briant remained two days at the Vaval place, during which he made minor progress in bringing the zombie back to reality, but his reassuring words accomplished little in comparison to his salt. Deprived of it for years, she craved it more than food or sleep or love.

During the two days, Briant shared with Tessa his accumulated knowledge on the zombies of Haiti: "They're real. Your Lalique was murdered. In a manner of speaking, she was clinically dead, and the doctor must not be abused for having certified the fact. She was buried, as you have seen, and during the second night she was taken from her grave and brought back to life. She was then sold, by her mother and sister, I'm sure, to someone who kept her in a zombie state and used her as a slave. Somehow she escaped, and with sure instinct found her way back to her home village. And if you hadn't rescued her when you did, she might now be dead. Murdered for the second time. This time for real."

"I'm totally at a loss."

"Everything I've said is true. Verifiable. She's the fourth incontrovertible case I've had, but never before with such splendid photographs."

When Tessa asked how all this was possible, he said: "Let's walk along this country road. What I have to say will sound more plausible with the trees and the ancient fields about us."

There had always been in Haiti, he explained, native necromancers or priests or holy men, or what scientists accurately call shamans and what Haitians call bocors. One found them in many primitive societies, but in Haiti they seemed to have special power, for they inherited from canny old men who had practiced the art in Africa a knowledge of secret and powerful poisons and drugs which in combination had the capacity to induce in targeted human beings a suspension of life functions: "Like ether or chloroform, but more powerful and with even stranger consequences. What's in the mixture? I've worked on this for years, but have found only two bocors who would talk honestly with me, and I'm sure they've told me only part of their trickery."

He found a fallen tree and invited Tessa to sit with him: "I know they use powder obtained from the desiccated body of a bufo frog. I sent one to the medical laboratories at Johns Hopkins, and they reported: 'We've known about the bufo for decades. Favorite animal of poisoners, but your Haiti version is incredible. A virtual repository of at least sixteen intricate poisons.' And our bocors also use the blowfish, called by some the poisonous puffer. You may have read about it in Japan, where they call it the *fugu*. I'm told, but have never had it verified, that the bocors also have a fatal cucumber, plus a kind of pepper from the Orinoco and a particular snake from the Amazon jungles."

"Sounds like that mix would kill a horse."

"It would. But that's not the purpose. The bocor becomes highly skilled in administering just the right amount to throw his victim into a kind of suspended animation. The corpse is buried in all solemnity, and two days later, at dead of night, the bocor digs it up, stops feeding it salt, and has himself a zombie."

"Are the services of the bocor available to anyone?"

"That I don't know. In fact, there's a great deal I don't know. How frequently this happens, for example." Then his voice firmed, and he said with great resolution: "But that it's happening, in the year 1989, I have no doubt whatever," and from his wallet he took photographs of three living zombies who had been declared dead, were buried, and then dug up.

"They live with me in St.-Marc. Government pays for their keep. And it's important that your young woman Lalique come home with me. Government will demand it."

Tessa prodded: "I'm interested in the zombie-maker. How does he become one?"

"Like a bishop in the Catholic church, who can claim a straight line inheritance from Jesus Christ, he's a straight-line descendant of some notable native doctor in Africa. But he has to be extremely skilled in making nice distinctions. Too much of his magical powder, the target dies. Too little, the target does not pass into perfect suspension, comes awake too soon, suffocates in his grave. Just right," and he pointed to Lalique, who was again squatting in her old position against the trunk of a tree.

Apparently word of her discovery and whereabouts had reached the capital, for an urgent message had been delivered to Dr. Briant's office in St.-Marc and forwarded to Tessa's village: ACQUIRE GUARDIANSHIP LALIQUE HÉBERT IMMEDIATELY. MINIMUM PUBLICITY.

So that afternoon the bedazed young woman—normal girl for seventeen years, dead for two days, zombie for eleven years, normal again for the rest of her life—left Tessa's care. "It could be three or four years before she returns fully to life," Briant said as he helped

Lalique into his car. "Salt will help. Vitamins will be needed. Contact with others. A human life being reborn."

When the car disappeared, it left a bewildered Tessa Vaval. At Port-au-Prince she had been dismayed by the political corruption; at the villages to the north, by the unrelieved poverty and despair; and now, by the perpetual mysteries of her homeland. Haiti was an island not to be perceived from a distance nor understood by inquiring young men at Harvard. In fact, she was discovering, even a girl born on the island lost her intuitive comprehension if she moved to a foreign country and alien society: Heavens! I know nothing about Haiti. I've lied to others and myself about this island, and my ignorance terrifies me!

It was then that a crazy idea first tangled itself into her brain: Perhaps it would be better if I spent my life here, trying to make things better for others, trying to probe the mysteries of this place and maybe, in the future, writing about Haiti as generations of my family have experienced it.

For two days she wrestled with images that were more writhing and real than those of a boa constrictor: she was tormented by zombies and mountains denuded of trees and hordes of peasants living worse than slaves, for they had no food, and persistently she saw the unanswered question passing before her eyes in flaming red letters: "Is this what a black republic after nearly two centuries of self-rule comes to?" And she was so obsessed by these images that she went to St.-Marc, where she sought Dr. Briant and the three zombies who were domiciled with him. Overjoyed at seeing that Lalique after only these few days in his care was returning from the living dead, she threw herself on Briant's guidance and said: "I have this terrible compulsion to give it all up—appointment at Wellesley . . . certainly my marriage to the white fellow I'm engaged to. My life is here in the Haiti of my fathers." Trembling, she asked: "Would there be a place here, working with you on the abiding problems?"

She was fortunate in that she had come to the one man in Haiti best qualified to speak to the precise situation in which she found herself. "At about your age," he said quietly, "I faced the same dilemmas. Passed my medical exams, had a running start at a good job in the States, chucked it all because I was drawn back to Haiti. Wanted to save the world. Tried to open an advanced medical office in Port-au-Prince. Duvalier wouldn't permit it. His henchman controlled medicine on that level and they wanted no interference with new ideas from anyone like me. But I was filled with whatever it is that fills you when you're twenty-five. Besides, I knew Haiti needed what I had to give, so I forged ahead." He stopped, laughed at himself, and asked ruefully: "Dr. Vaval, have you ever been interrogated by the Tontons Macoutes? Seen your office smashed to bits? Been left flat in a corner bleeding and with your case records torn in bits and thrown over you like confetti?"

He led her to a kiosk, where they shared an iced drink as he concluded: "The Tontons are still with us. Same men, same mission, different name, and they still interrogate in the same manner. A young woman with your ideas, and your family name . . . in their hands you'd last ten minutes."

"How do *you* survive?" for she had seen that he was an exceptional man.

"I work things out. I have my clinic, pitiful though it is. I write my papers. *New England Medical Journal* is printing one on tropical diseases." He looked about. "And I keep taking my notes on zombies, and maybe twenty years from now when the Tontons wouldn't care, I'll publish them, probably in Germany." As placid as a man of fifty could be who had seen his life slip away, he said: "So, Madame Professor of the Caribbean, please go on to Cap-Haïtien and your ship . . ." Then his voice broke, and he looked wildly at her and screamed there in the sunlight: "And get the hell out of Haiti!"

The hundred and thirty-seven advanced college students who would be enrolling in the "Cruise-and-Muse" seminar had assembled two weeks earlier at classrooms in the University of Miami, where three able young assistant professors from different universities had given intensive instruction on the Caribbean and provided basic outlines and maps. They had now flown to Cap-Haïtien to board the Swedish *Galante,* and they had one free day for which Tessa was responsible.

When she met them—two-thirds white, one-third black, with representatives from six foreign nations—she experienced that reassuring sensation which good teachers encounter each September when they first see the young people they will be teaching through the coming year: They look so bright! So eager! Oh, if I can only send them forward! She thought that this one could become an editorial writer for *The New York Times,* that girl a doctor at Mass General, that one a surgeon in Chicago, and that saucy girl a political leader for sure. Then her enthusiasm sobered as she ended her speculation with the truths that have prevailed for millennia: If only they develop character, and use the brains they have, and somehow catch fire." Looking at their smiling faces from Colorado and Vermont and Oregon, she promised herself: If there's any tinder in any of them, I will set it ablaze.

Tessa had arranged for jeeps to carry them inland to that incredible mountain fortress built by one of Toussaint L'Ouverture's black generals, with whom her ancestor, César Vaval, had often served. Henri Christophe, a fiery individual with no training and assisted by no architect, had built in the early 1800s one of the brooding masterpieces of the world. She had to chuckle when they arrived there, for the local peasants had through the years been successful in stopping all governments from building a jeep road to the top; if you wanted to see Christophe's magical fortress atop its mountain, you climbed aboard one of their donkeys, and for a hefty fee rode up as their ancestors had done since 1820.

The painful ride was amply rewarded, for at a lofty altitude above the sea the students broke out of the jungle to see looming mysteriously above them a huge stone mass, frighteningly tall, with towers and ramparts soaring above them. When they had climbed laboriously to the top, Tessa said: "Probably the most impressive building ever erected by a black man with no white assistance." When a student spoiled the effectiveness of her statement by asking: "Erected to what purpose?" she had to reply: "No one ever knew . . . then or now."

Overawed by the power of this raw structure built by a black, she withdrew from the students to stand alone at the far end of the parapet, from where she could look down upon the green mystery of this unspoiled corner of Haiti. She felt a throbbing identification with this land and she could hear voices of Haitians she had met on this visit calling her by her real name, *Thérèse,* and it echoed in her brain in two syllables of enchanting beauty: Tay-rez!

Rejoining her students, she said hesitantly: "You've been calling me Dr. Theresa, but it's really Thérèse . . . more musical and feminine, don't you think?" and on the mountaintop they approved her rechristening.

• • •

When the newly reborn Thérèse returned to Cap-Haïtien she was confronted by a wrenching tragedy, for along the waterfront there was noisy commotion centering upon a United States Coast Guard cutter that was delivering to local authorities thirty-two of the forty or so would-be émigrés she had watched departing from St.-Marc. As she had foreseen, the leaky craft had proceeded only a few leagues northward when it began to sink, and as she moved among the survivors she heard their dismal story.

"Too many in the boat . . . waves washed over us . . . sharks followed . . ."

"The boat should never have been allowed out of St.-Marc harbor."

"We would all have perished if the Americans had not rescued us."

But Thérèse wondered if the word *rescue* was proper, for these unfortunates were now not only back in a place they had tried to flee but actually worse off, for they were on police lists as fugitives who had tried to leave Haiti. When she left them huddled on the docks she felt a great soul sickness, which prepared her for the humiliation she was about to experience.

When the time came to board the *Galante* she found that its Swedish crew had brought their ship not to Cap-Haïtien, a typical brawling black port, but to a tidy enclave some miles to the east where the company had leased a large tropical acreage of great beauty—low mountains, spacious white beaches—and had completely enclosed it with a sturdy fence running for thousands of yards. In the space thus protected from the general population of Haiti, the Swedes had constructed an almost flawless vacation spot which merited its name, Le Paradis. More than a hundred employees kept the beach spotless and the recreation areas free of debris. Neatly tended gardens were full of Caribbean flowers in profusion and trees swayed in trade winds as they displayed their luscious treasures: coconuts, breadfruit, mangoes, limes and papayas. For vacationing shoppers, clusters of neat kiosks with grass roofs were tucked beneath the trees, while in a cleared area seven green-topped tennis courts invited players, and a nine-hole golf course stood ready to test the ship's passengers with its tree-lined fairways and gleaming white sand bunkers. To complete the Eden-like quality of the retreat, a fair-sized stream of clear water wound through the enclave on its way to the Atlantic.

Nearly five hundred years ago, during their first voyage of discovery, the three caravels of Christopher Columbus had anchored off this spot for their crews to replenish their water barrels prior to the long run back to Spain, and the sailors had declared the place to be a "fair paradise gifted with all the fresh water and fruit we needed." And so it still was, Thérèse concluded when she finished inspecting the place, but one with an appalling flaw, which she identified for her students: "It's perfect, except that white people can come here from Cleveland and Phoenix, enjoy the tropics, see the beauties of Haiti, and escape coming into contact with the blacks who form the major population group of the Caribbean." She spoke with some bitterness of the clever way in which this paradise had insulated itself and its wealthy clients from the realities of Haiti, ugly though they might be: "Is this what the classic travelers of history sought?" she asked. "I mean the intrepid souls who went out from London and Paris and the German cities to explore strange lands and people equally strange? I think not. If this collection of tennis courts and golf links is indistinguishable from Shaker Heights or Westchester County, why should one bother . . . ?"

But she had to laugh when a young fellow from Tulsa broke in: "Not many coconut palms in Shaker Heights." Later, when officers from the *Galante* heard of her strictures, one of them asked to address the students: "Every criticism Dr. Vaval makes is both accurate and relevant. Our company would have saved both time and money if we could have continued to make our stops at Port-au-Prince. Interesting city. Challenging history. Good food and people worth visiting with."

"Then why did you abandon that stop?" a student asked, and he replied crisply: "A chain of compelling reasons, and as you evaluate them, wait for the last in line, because it's a blockbuster. First, crime in the city endangered our passengers' lives. Second, the economy was so debased that hordes of beggars trailed anyone who ventured ashore, especially our women tourists. It was at first intrusive, in the end alienating, because you could see that no matter how much alms you gave, your charity accomplished nothing. Third, the discrepancy between the affluence of our visiting passengers and the incredible poverty ashore made the Haitians envious and downright hostile." He paused and surveyed the students before offering his clinching argument: "And in recent years the adverse publicity on AIDS, which has been reported as flourishing in Haiti, scared the hell out of our passengers. For all these reasons people became afraid to visit Haiti, and when we continued to bring them here on our scheduled stop they told us frankly: 'If you insist on visiting Port-au-Prince, we won't travel with you.' Without speeches or committees they initiated a boycott, and we knew it would be folly to oppose it."

He then shared with the young people his conclusions about Caribbean travel, a subject upon which he was becoming one of the world's experts: "Many islands in this sea are kept alive only with the dollars which tourists inject into the economy. And these dollars can be earned easily and without any loss of self-respect, but they are terribly fragile. Had we Swedes not built Le Paradis up here and protected it from the disasters of Port-au-Prince, Haiti would have lost all her tourist dollars. Complete wipeout. As it is, our ships pour a steady stream of currency into this black republic, but we can do it only if we maintain that fence which Dr. Vaval rightly condemns." He stopped, looked directly at Thérèse, and said: "Young people, please look at the world as it is. Haiti has a choice: no fence and no dollars, or a fence which does little harm but earns a great many dollars." He then broke into a wide smile and said: "Dr. Vaval's job is to visualize a world in which fences are not permitted, and we wish her well. Mine is to utilize such fences as we must have, and take constant steps to get rid of them. At Paradis we're doing just that." But after he had gone, Thérèse told her young people: "That fence is a moral abomination, for it keeps rich people from observing the problems of the poor, and believe me, whenever that happens, anywhere in the world, trouble is brewing."

When the group finally boarded the *Galante*—18,000 tons, 550 feet long, 765 ordinary passengers, 137 students, 418 crew, with the officers all Swedish, dining-room and kitchen help exclusively Italian, deckhands Indonesian, with Chinese hidden below to tend the laundry—Thérèse realized what a small proportion of the ship was allotted to her "Cruise-and-Muse" group—just over fifteen percent. But they did add color, especially as they clustered about the pool. When older passengers assured Thérèse: "We're so fortunate to have young people sharing the cruise with us," she said to herself: These next two weeks could be just what I needed.

That night as she sat in her cabin trying to forget the ignominy of being part of a black nation which experienced travelers were afraid to explore, she was visited by several students, who told her: "Discussion group aft. Don't miss it. Topflight ideas get kicked around," and, eager to escape her gloomy meditation, she allowed them to take her to where one of the other instructors was helping his students acquire a balanced view of the Caribbean; the topic was music:

"The United States is no doubt fortunate in having off each coast a magnificent collection of islands, Hawaii on the west, the Caribbean lands on the east. Neither is superior to the other, for in a curious way each supplements the other, but there are significant differences. In the field of signature music, Hawaii wins hands down. What a gorgeous array of wonderful tunes. 'Aloha Oe,' 'The Wedding Song,' 'The War Chant,' 'Beyond the Reef.' Name your favorite. The contestants seem infinite. But the Caribbean suffers from a paucity of comparable tunes. What represents the area, really, insofar as the general public is concerned? 'Yellow Bird' is magnificent but very lonely on that banana tree. 'Island in the Sun' is haunting but thin. 'Mary Ann' is one of those throwaways, only seven notes, really, but captivating, and a few calypsos with limited staying power. And that's about it."

Sharp discussion followed, with some students championing the Rastafarian reggae of Jamaica and others citing certain merengues and zouks from the French islands, but before the night's concert began, the students had to agree with their instructor that whereas they could sing from memory a dozen Hawaiian tunes, hardly anyone could sing more than a few phrases from anything Caribbean.

And then, even as she agreed with the instructor, Thérèse was thrown completely off balance—touched close to the heart—by a song of the Caribbean. Professional singers of some merit were offering the usual fare of songs popular forty years past, when onto the stage came two distinctive figures, a slim young soprano with a golden complexion, a haunting smile and a strong but gentle voice, and a very tall baritone dressed in somber black and wearing a nineteenth-century top hat. His voice was resonant and powerful as he introduced their duet: "We bring you a song of the islands . . . of all islands . . . the island girl and the American missionary from Boston." And with that, a small orchestra of six musicians began playing for him, while a steel band of eleven hammered gasoline drums as an accompaniment for the soprano, and as a result of exquisite timing and altered rhythms the two songs merged into an evocative whole of the most enchanting intertwined beauty.

He sang in deep, powerful tones "The Battle Hymn of the Republic," while in notes of delicate harmony she sang "Yellow Bird," and from the moment they started, Thérèse said in a soft whisper: "Oh, this is something special," for both the singers and their words spoke directly to her condition:

> *"He is trampling out the vintage*
> *Yel . . . . low   bird*

> *"where the grapes of wrath are stored*
> *up   high   in   banana   tree"*

The contrasting appearance they created and the magical blending of their voices created in Thérèse exactly the impression the singers had intended: She's all the island people. He's all the European missionaries and governors. The rivalry never ends. But as she listened carefully to the words the man uttered, all fire and bombast and death, she was almost projected out of her seat: My God! That's Judge Adolphus Krey! And it's me he's lecturing to, the black island girl! And at that moment the transformation was complete: the thundering basso was her proposed father-in-law, the girl singer was she,

> *"He hath loosed the fateful lightning*
> *Yel . . . . low   bird*

> *"of his terrible swift sword*
> *you sit all alone like me"*

When the duet ended to thunderous applause, Thérèse was limp, but she had to smile when students assured her: "Your Caribbean has one good song!" Back in her cabin, with the images and sounds of the concert whirling in her head like an island hurricane, she knew she ought to write Dennis and share with him her Haiti experiences, but the implacable image of the elder Krey hurling the thunderbolts of the "Battle Hymn" as if he were protecting his son against island women was so overpowering that she could not write nor could she sleep.

Her mind was filled with haunting images that she could not exorcise: Lalique returning from the dead, Henri Christophe building that insane fortress instead of roads or schools, that despicable portrait of a leering, all-wise Papa Doc, and especially the look on her uncle's face when he said that it was too late to escape from the prison of poverty. When she had boarded the plane in Boston she had expected to breeze through Haiti, nodding to family and friends and leaving a modest gift of money here or there, and then to depart the same person as when she entered; she had not foreseen that Haiti was a place which tore at the soul, especially the soul of an educated black woman. Rising from her bed, she tried again to write to Dennis Krey, but again she failed, because a two-week stay in the dark fogs of Haiti had converted her into an entirely different woman, and to explain this in a letter of one or two pages was impossible.

In the morning when the *Galante* approached San Juan, the capital of Puerto Rico, Thérèse stood with her students as they heard the voices of some excited Borinqueños, as natives of the island were called, announce over the ship's bullhorn: "There on the headland, see it! El Morro fortress with its round tower set into the walls. We love to see that sight. It means we're coming home." There were several of these little masonry towers jutting out from vulnerable corners, and she was still gazing at them as they glowed in the gold of sunrise, when a harbor boat pulled up to the *Galante,* bringing an eager young man from the State Department, blue-linen tropical suit freshly pressed and subdued red tie double-passed to give the trim look at the collar that diplomats favor. When he debarked and clambered up the jury-rigged ladder, he hurried to the ship's elevator while the students tried to guess his mission.

"Must be coming to make a drug bust. One of the belowdecks crew."

"No, he's inviting the captain to tea at the governor's palace."

"Brain surgeon. Emergency operation. He came to fetch the patient."

They were surprised when he sought out Professor Vaval and introduced himself: "John Swayling, attached to the Columbus Quincentenary Commission. We've been awaiting you, eagerly, Dr. Vaval. We need your help . . . urgently."

"What's up, Doc?" an irreverent student asked, imitating Bugs Bunny. Thérèse smiled and said: "The Feds are after me. See something of significance when you go ashore," and with that, she and the State Department man hustled below, climbed down the rope-and-wire ladder leading to the harbor boat, and disappeared toward what the guide on the bullhorn was describing as "the old city."

On the way ashore, Mr. Swayling outlined the day: "We have representatives from some forty nations meeting here. To plan the five-hundredth anniversary of our boy Christopher. I use that slang term because everybody's claiming rights to the old fellow . . . and wants to dictate how he shall be celebrated."

"That could get sticky," Thérèse said. "Spain, Italy, Portugal, United States."

"Keep going! Like Mexico, Peru, Venezuela, not to mention Hispaniola, Jamaica and Puerto Rico."

"That could be a dogfight."

"It is."

"Speaking of Puerto Rico. What's the political sentiment on the island? Regarding future status?"

"We had another plebiscite . . . last in a long series . . . inconclusive as ever. Continue the Commonwealth status quo, forty-six percent. Enter the Union as the fifty-first state, forty-four percent. Complete freedom immediately, six percent."

"That's only ninety-six. What about the balance?"

"Who gives a damn? Four percent."

When they left the boat, Swayling had a car and driver waiting, and as they sped through the wakening city he said enthusiastically: "This is a gorgeous city. Wish I could be stationed here permanently."

"I know the rest of the Caribbean rather well. What's so great about this place?"

"The Spanish heritage. The grand old buildings. And the women." There was a moment of silence in which he obviously expected her to speak, and when she didn't, he added: "I've seen about two dozen I'd like to know better."

"Young women of color, perhaps?"

"Every color you could think of. Why do you ask?"

"Because I'm engaged to marry a young man just about your age, and white like you. I know problems do arise."

"I'm engaged to a white girl and problems arise there, too."

"Now, what about this conference?"

Before he could respond, the car swung onto a handsome boulevard lined with sturdy old buildings dating back to the fifteenth and sixteenth centuries, when Spain relied on the incredibly stout walls of El Morro to defend the galleons heading back to Sevilla with the treasure from Peru and Mexico: "Hawkins and Drake both tried to sail past that fort over there and failed. I know that Hawkins died in the attempt, and Drake may have received wounds from which he died shortly after. This was a tough nut to crack."

"The area looks so Spanish. Quite extraordinary," and the young man explained: "You've touched the dilemma of the island. As you can see, they want to erase all signs of American intervention. U.S. army barracks used to be over there, another big American building at this corner. All being torn down as if to eradicate any memory of American influence. Huge funds spent to restore this as a Spanish city."

"It was Spanish for much longer than it's been American," Thérèse said.

"Yes, but at the same time the Borinqueños want to be completely Spanish. You get no cachet whatever if you're American . . . only Spanish counts . . . What point was I making?"

"I think you're going to say that although they want to be Spanish emotionally, they want to be American economically."

"Exactly." And together they marveled at the brilliance with which this part of San Juan at least had been reconverted into a Spanish town, and such thoughts brought them to a discussion of the important task the American government had asked her to perform. "We hope, Dr. Vaval, that as a scholar of high caliber, you could represent us today with the black leaders who are going to be most vociferous."

"What's it about?"

"A hilarious contretemps, really, except that it's so damned important," but before he could elaborate they were at the entrance to Casa Blanca, the exquisite mansion long held by the descendants of Ponce de León, who represented the acme of Spanish society and influence. It was perched atop a small mound that commanded the beautiful bay, El Morro and the principal buildings of the colonial era. When Americans assumed ownership of the island in 1898 they chose Casa Blanca as the residence for their military commanders, but after 1967 all evidence that they had ever set foot in the place was obliterated, and Casa Blanca became once more a Spanish mansion.

It was a stunning building, with massive white walls, cool patios, windows guarded by beautifully carved wooden spindles and floors of dark blood-red tiles in various shapes. It was a noble house and it breathed Hispanic values, but Thérèse was not allowed to savor it, for even though it was now only seven in the morning, four representatives of the United States delegation were waiting to brief her on the day's events.

Said the chairman: "It would be amusing if it weren't so pathetic.

Spain and the United States will be putting up most of the money for the Columbus celebrations, which should be a glorious affair."

"Certainly, those two nations can't be feuding," Thérèse said, whereupon the delegates burst into laughter.

"Oh, you're so naïve you're wonderful. Spain and the U.S. are at each other's throats. Spain wants this to be a celebration of Spanish contributions to the New World."

"I see nothing wrong with that."

"But Congress, which designated the members of our delegation . . ."

"I thought you were our members."

"No, we're just the supporting staff. The members have gone home in a terrible huff."

"Why?"

"The Italian contingent in Congress, and it's powerful, sent down a delegation one-hundred-percent Italian. New York, Boston, Chicago, San Francisco, leader types, and they were determined to use the Columbus affair to prove that it was Italy that had found the New World and given it the big push toward a wonderful civilization. To hear their plans, there couldn't have been any Spaniards aboard the three ships."

"Did Columbus think of himself as Italian?"

"Never wrote a word in that language, so far as we can find. Operationally, pure Spaniard."

"So what happened?"

"The other nations, laughing disgracefully, would not allow the American Italians to be seated."

"Did that solve anything?"

"Well, it got rid of our delegation, and maybe the funds which Congress was prepared to authorize, but the Spanish-speaking nations said: 'Good riddance. We're not going to pervert history to please the American Congress.'"

"So the Spaniards won?"

"Not really, because when they started to take command, to make it a great Spanish fiesta celebrating the fact that Queen Isabella . . ."

A counselor to the mission, a distinguished scholar from Stanford, broke in: "The real trouble started with that unfortunate word *discovered.* Nations of Central and South America, especially Mexico and Peru, had sent Indian delegates, who cried: 'Hey, wait a minute! Nobody *discovered* anything, neither Italian or Spanish. We were already here and were doing rather well. Whoever Columbus might have been, he *visited* us, he didn't *discover* us. Let's celebrate this as an important visit.'"

"I see some merit in the argument," Thérèse said, and then, focusing his attention on her, the chairman said: "This is where you come in. Because after the Italians, the Spaniards and the local Indians had finished registering their claims, the black rulers of the Caribbean islands pointed out, quite correctly I believe, that in the Caribbean generally for the last three hundred years it's been the blacks who have really counted—grew the cane, made the sugar, distilled the rum, grew the tobacco and tended the cotton. They insisted: 'It should be a celebration of what the blacks of Africa have achieved in the islands Columbus found,' and since we had no black member of our group to talk with them, they ignored us."

It was now heading for eight-thirty, when the day's plenary session was to begin, and final instructions were heaped upon Thérèse, who said, in response to questions: "Yes, my ancestors were slaves on St. John and later heavily involved in Haiti's fight for freedom. You might say that had I been in attendance at the earlier sessions, I would have supported the black leaders."

"Excellent. Represent us as ably as you can."

"Specific instructions?"

"Fraternize, listen, encourage. And above all, let them know they have a friend in America. We hope you can help us salvage something out of this mess."

It was a day of tropical brilliance, spent in a house whose every aspect recalled those earlier days when men of good will had sat in this white house plotting steps to defeat English villains like Drake and Morgan, forestall Admiral Vernon at Cartagena, and import fresh supplies of slaves on the yearly commercial armada from Africa. There was not even a shadow across the tiled floor to remind anyone that American military officers from states like Kansas and New Hampshire had ever ruled Puerto Rico from these halls, or that the island was now an integral part of the United States. Here, Spain still ruled emotionally.

Thérèse felt that she was achieving little for her government because the delegates from the Caribbean islands spoke so often and so forcefully that she was required to say nothing, but members of the American team assured her: "Your presence is worth two battalions.

Word is circulating. They realize we cared enough to send for you. Sit with them at lunch and let them know your feelings."

She did so, and when she conversed with these intelligent men and women from Barbados and Antigua and Jamaica and Guadeloupe, she felt an affinity of interest and outlook that ran deep in their consciousness and hers. At several points she cried: "I know just what you mean!" and her enthusiasm was so real that they began to ask her what she did in the United States, and to her surprise she found herself talking about her appointment to Wellesley.

"Is that an important college?" a black from Trinidad asked, and a young woman from St. Kitts cried: "A university, and one of the best. In many respects equal to Yale."

Later Thérèse could not recall how she happened to reveal that she was engaged to a white man, but when a contentious delegate from St. Lucia asked: "Does that mean you'll be abandoning your black heritage?" she replied sharply: "The name of the course I'll be teaching is 'Black Societies in the Caribbean,' and it will draw me ever closer to you."

Late in the afternoon, after some prompting from her chairman, she asked for the floor, and said: "The United States would look with favor upon any kind of exhibition or celebration which would emphasize the considerable contribution to Caribbean culture, economics and government made by the African slaves and their descendants, of which I'm one."

The group then turned to the delicate problem of how it could best lure the American Italian delegation back to the conference without surrendering the meeting to them, but since Thérèse had to hurry back to the *Galante* before it sailed for the American Virgins, she did not learn whether this attempt at reconciliation worked or not.

That night the Swedish captain stepped before the screen prior to the start of the movie to announce: "We're sailing with an extraordinary group of lecturers, and if you four will join me, I'd like to make some fascinating introductions." When they stood self-consciously beside him, he said: "Professor Vaval is not only charming, as you've discovered, but she is also a distinguished Haitian. Her ancestor General Vaval helped defeat Napoleon, another served as president, another was a trusted leader under the Americans. You can believe what she says." He then moved Dr. Carlos Ledesma forward and said: "This fine scholar is not only one of the most brilliant men in Colombia, but also the descendant of a great Spanish leader who dueled for forty years or more with Sir Francis Drake and won more often than he lost. Other Ledesmas governed Cartagena, where we will end our cruise, with distinction, one of them being a hero of the battle against Old Grog Vernon that you'll be hearing about."

Now Senator Maxim Lanzerac of Guadeloupe stepped forward: "And this fine politician will within the next few days be telling you about a sweetheart of a fellow who came out from France with a neat little machine that chopped off people's heads, and one of the first to go was a Royalist called Lanzerac, ancestor of our speaker, who now strives to see that such things don't happen again." He ended with a graceful statement: "So we're not only sailing in the Caribbean, we're bringing it with us," and the voyage became doubly meaningful.

When the fourth lecturer joined the captain, Thérèse realized that she had not known he was aboard or in any way connected with the floating university. He was a white man, in his sixties, gray-haired, slightly stooped and with the relaxed, pleasant face of one who had never participated in the aggressiveness of either business or university life. He had apparently determined his level early in life and found satisfaction in it. "This is Master Michael Carmody, a distinguished scholar from Queen's Own College in Trinidad," the captain said, "and he will give a series of six lectures, four of them prior to our visit there. Listen attentively, for he will introduce us to his fascinating island, unique in the Caribbean, half blacks from Africa, half Indians from Asia."

As the speech ended, Thérèse moved across the salon to introduce herself to the new man, and when she heard his magical voice she said: "You must be Irish," and he replied: "Long ago."

"I hope you'll allow me to audit your lectures. I teach Caribbean history and my knowledge of Trinidad is inadequate."

"They're not lectures, really. Reflections, ruminations."

"That's where learning begins. The raw data about the island I already have, it's the ruminations and reflections that I need," and they spent the balance of the evening in the pleasant way that he, using an old English phrase, described as "discussing a rum punch."

Next day, Wednesday, February 1, was one of intense involvement for Thérèse, for as she left the ship in Charlotte Amalie, capital of the American Virgin Islands, a bicycle gang swooped down upon her and the lead man used his front wheel to shove her off balance, whereupon the second in line deftly reached out, grabbed her handbag from her arm, and made off with it. Her money and her wallet, though fortunately not her passport, were gone.

When fellow passengers who had seen the bold robbery helped her in reporting to a policeman, the latter shrugged: "It happens all the time. No way possible for us to halt it," but he did say: "Government has been begging the young hoods not to destroy our tourist business, and it's had some effect. Chances are the ones who grabbed your handbag, ma'am, will lift the money and throw your bag where we'll find it. If they do, we'll return it to your ship before you sail."

With that ugly introduction to the Virgins, she borrowed funds from a passenger who had joined a small group she was leading to the nearby island of St. John, where the Rockefellers had their huge resort, and they taxied to the other end of St. Thomas, the main island, where a ferry waited to take them the short distance to the smaller island.

There a memorable experience awaited, for another taxi took them to the north side of the island, where at considerable expense the government had excavated and restored some dozen major buildings of the old Danish sugar plantation at which Vavak the slave had labored. Lunaberg it had been called, and as Thérèse led her charges among the ruins she could recall the emotional stories of how the original Vavak had toiled here, watched the terrible executions of his fellow slaves, and run away to Haiti.

When she reached the top of the plateau where in the old days the main buildings had been concentrated, she felt as if she had known each mill and holding pit and storage barn personally, and with remarkable accuracy she explained to her group how sugar was produced, from the planting of the cane, to its cutting and grinding, then the collection of the rich juices and their progressive treatment until the two contrasting products resulted, muscovado for sugar, molasses for rum.

But that was not the end of the process, not by a long shot, and when her group was seated on benches which provided a good view of the hilltop, Thérèse spoke of the immense fortunes made by sugar planters in islands like Barbados, Jamaica, Guadeloupe and Haiti, of the way such owners lived in Paris and London and Copenhagen, and of the importance of sugar in the old days. But after these colorful details had been shared, she became serious and spoke of the hardships the slaves had endured to make this largesse possible, and when she explained in some detail their daily life, she chanced to point to the exact spot where her ancestor Vavak had had his mean little hut and from which he fled to freedom, two hundred and fifty-six years earlier. She made the slave experience so vivid that when she finished her prepared comments, her listeners kept her among the ruins for another half-hour, asking about the sugar culture of the islands, and it was then that she expressed for the first time a basic truth about the Caribbean. "The one crop we are expressly qualified to produce"—and she herself was not aware that she had used the pronoun *we* as if identifying herself personally with the islands—"is sugar. On all the islands that's the premier crop, sugar, sugar, sugar. Cuba, Haiti, Jamaica, Trinidad . . . all the rest. And what's happened? Why can't we sell our sugar anymore? Why are our fields left barren?"

The tourists guessed at half a dozen plausible explanations, none of them close to the mark: "German chemists, that's what killed our sugar industry," and being a born teacher, Thérèse invited her guests to unravel that conundrum. When they failed, she explained: "In the 1850s, I think it was, German chemists, clever lads, discovered that whereas you could make excellent sugar from cane, you could make it even better, and with much less trouble, from beets, not red beets that you pickle, but huge white things just crammed with sugar. There went our cash crop, and we've discovered nothing to replace it."

Some men in the group offered ingenious suggestions for new industries, but were told that most had been tried, disastrously, so as the discussion ended she offered her own solution: "The industrial nations of the world, but especially the United States, because these lands are at her doorstep, ought to band together to buy our sugar at just a little over world price. A few cents a pound would allow all the islands you'll be seeing to prosper . . . save them from revolution or worse."

"Does anyone pay that now?" a man asked, and she replied: "Russia buys from Cuba, a little over world, Cuba thrives. France does the same with her two big colonies, Guadeloupe and Martinique. But the United States refuses. Sugar-beet interests in states like Colorado won't allow it." She hesitated, then added: "So we stagger along toward a disaster whose timing we cannot predict, but whose coming is inevitable. We're a fleet of magnificent islands, lost in the sun."

But even as she uttered this doleful prediction she turned to go down from the plateau where Vavak had labored under those terrible laws of Denmark, and she saw to the north and east the wonderful little islands of the British Virgins, Great Thatch, Little Thatch, big Tortola and the rest, and she thought: Vavak must have seen them a thousand times and wondered what was over there, but they were never mentioned in our family. My God, they are magnificent, a chain of jewels, and as the Caribbean had a way of doing, the present beauty erased the old ugliness.

But not entirely, for when Thérèse's group piled into their taxis to catch the ferry that would take them back to St. Thomas and the *Galante,* they found themselves caught in another of the ugly cheats which irritate experienced Caribbean travelers and scare away the novices. Vavak's plantation, Lunaberg, was on the extreme northern edge of St. John, the ferry depot at the opposite end, and at the start of the trip the taxi drivers had agreed upon a price, fearfully high Thérèse thought, and everyone assumed it was for the round trip— ferry landing and back—but now the drivers carried the travelers to a way station far from the ferry, and said: "You get out here."

"But we want the ferry!" Thérèse protested, and they laughed: "Trip always ends here."

"How do we get back to the ferry?"

"He might do it," one of the men said, and pointed to a confederate, who said yes, he could deliver them to the ferry, three trips, twenty-seven dollars. Before they could protest this holdup, the three original drivers had fled, so that they had to pay the extra fee or miss the sailing of the cruise ship.

When the angry passengers reported their mistreatment to the ship's officers, one young Swede took them aside and said: "You'll find that sort of petty cheating wherever you go in the Caribbean. They want tourist dollars but they treat tourists like scum. By the way, Miss Vaval, the police did retrieve your handbag and papers." She was so relieved to have her cards back that she actually felt grateful toward the thieves: "It was decent of them to return my credit cards," and the officer said: "We have reason to believe the thief was the brother of the policeman. Small dark fellow with a mustache?" "Yes, I saw him clearly." Then the officer grinned: "When he grabs a handbag we always get the papers back. His brother sees to it. But beware, on other islands it can be much worse."

• • •

The three academic credits that students could acquire for "Cruise-and-Muse" were not easily won: in addition to the two weeks of classroom study at Miami, and the submission of a sixty-page report within a month after the end of the cruise, the students were given a long reading list by the six lecturers. For her reading list, Thérèse had assigned four nicely differentiated books chosen for high quality and familiarity with English: Germán Arciniegas' view of the Caribbean as seen in 1946 by a Spanish scholar, *Caribbean, Sea of the New World;* a recent Yale University publication, *Prospect for the Caribbean,* by a local specialist, Ranjit Banarjee from the University of the West Indies; Alec Waugh's 1955 saucy but instructive novel of Caribbean life, *Island in the Sun;* and a remarkable book which few today would otherwise know, *The English in the West Indies,* 1887, by one of the crustiest, most opinionated historians ever to lift a pen, James Anthony Froude. The literary executor and biographer of Thomas Carlyle, he had adopted that surly gentleman's near-Nazi inclinations and applied them sulfurously to the Caribbean.

"His opinions," Thérèse warned her students when placing copies of his book in the corner of the ship's library reserved for those taking the cruise for credit, "are outrageous, and some are downright infuriating, but it's refreshing to know what learned and cultured gentlemen thought of this part of the world back when quote 'things were so good' unquote. Read and enjoy, but please do not spit on his preposterous pages or throw the book overboard."

After such an introduction the students became immersed in Froude, and during the next few days Thérèse heard squeals of outrage as one student after another discovered the obiter dicta of brother Froude, who despised slaves, anyone with a drop of color in his blood, Catholics, Baptists, Indians from India, liberals, and with special venom, any Irishmen or Haitians. One student found what seemed to be Froude's leitmotif: "The English have proved that they can play a great and useful role as rulers over people who recognize their own inferiority."

When Michael Carmody heard the rumpus being made over Froude's hideous statements about the Irish, he asked one of the students: "How can a mere book create so much confusion?" and after he had looked into what Froude was saying, he asked: "What other books did your professor assign?" and was delighted to learn that she had selected a work by one of his former students. Seeking her out, he found Thérèse on the sun deck watching the sky, and asked: "May

I take this chair?" and she nodded. Seated beside her, he asked: "How did you learn of Ranjit Banarjee's study?" and she explained:

"Yale University plugged the book heavily among Caribbean scholars, and rightly so. It's a fine work, and I was looking for something by a Jamaican."

"He's Trinidadian."

"But I'm sure the blurb said University of the West Indies."

"It could just as properly have said University of Miami and reared in Trinidad."

"That must account for his breadth of vision. It's an eye-opening book for my young people."

"It is indeed. And when we make our stop in Trinidad for Carnaval, you must meet him."

"Where does he teach?" She noticed that when she asked this question, a slight frown skittered across Carmody's face, as if he had at some point been at odds with the author of the book. After some undue hesitation, the Irishman said: "It's quite unfathomable, really. He has no university affiliation."

"High school?"

"No, he's like so many Indian Ph.D.'s, especially in India— fabulously trained but unable to locate an opening." Thérèse saw that he obviously wanted to say more, and again she suspected that he had been in some way responsible for Banarjee's loss of a job or, even more ugly, had caught the Indian in some misbehavior that made him unemployable, but since Carmody seemed to have decided not to talk about it, she ended the conversation lamely: "Well, he's written the best book I've come across since Arciniegas' years ago."

As Carmody rose to leave, he said: "I must congratulate you. If a student digests your four books, she or he will have a good grasp of the Caribbean, but now I want to hear the French version of the story," and he invited her to accompany him to Senator Lanzerac's first lecture. The senator spoke formal English, but with a mesmerizing French accent which he used to maximum effect:

"First thing to know about my island, it has been French for many, many years, and is indeed two islands separated one from the other by an arm of the sea you can almost jump across. After three hundred years of colonial status, it became in 1946 a structural part of metropolitan France, with two senators and three deputies who meet in Paris with all the others who help rule France. Therefore, we are nothing like Barbados, Trinidad or Jamaica, who pertain to Great Britain in an emotional sense but who are not a functional part of that country. Nor are we like Puerto Rico, which is essentially a colony of the United States, nor like Cuba, which is a free, independent country on its own. We are unique.

"Now when I say *we,* I mean of course the two related islands, Martinique and Guadeloupe. They are gentlemen, we are businessmen, but we form a strong team."

A man who knew geography asked the question which must have been on many minds: "Why, if you were so close to Martinique and so affiliated, did you allow the island in the middle, Dominica, to remain in English hands?" Lanzerac chuckled and cried: "Ah ha! You're the one who asks the ugly question, and I'll give you the ugly answer.

"We tried many times to capture Dominica, and failed every time. Do you know why? Not that English arms were better than ours, but because the damned Carib Indians, fierce cannibals, ate our men every time we tried to land."

"How did the English manage?" the man persisted, and Lanzerac said: "Because the Caribs were sensible, like people today. They liked French cooking and they couldn't stand English."

A vacationing professor from Chicago asked: "I've read some fascinating accounts of this man Victor Hugues who seems to have invaded your island in the 1790s. Will you be telling us anything about him?"

"Indeed I shall. Early tomorrow, when we land at Point-à-Pitre, capital of the eastern island, I'll be giving a short talk there on the infamous Hugues, who chopped off the head of my ancestor Paul Lanzerac and did his best to do the same to his wife, Eugénie Lanzerac. In my family we have no love for Hugues, but his story is a gripping one and you may find it instructive."

Later, Thérèse sat with him at dinner, and asked: "Didn't this Hugues free the slaves on Guadeloupe?" and Lanzerac cried with some enthusiasm: "He certainly did! Celebrations. A new day in world history. 'I kill all the whites, free all the slaves.'"

"From my point of view," Thérèse said with a touch of humor, "he couldn't have been so bad," and Lanzerac agreed immediately: "Splendid fellow, on paper. Of course, when Napoleon decided to reimpose slavery, who was his loudest supporter?" He pointed a sardonic finger at Thérèse and supplied his own answer: "Your boy Hugues. And if I may use an Americanism to a fellow scholar . . . a real bastard."

The traditional Caribbean cruise ships, in order to save port fees, almost never remained in any harbor overnight; they left at dusk and spent the dark hours sailing to the next island. But since "Cruise-and-Muse" had scheduled several important seminars on French history and culture at Guadeloupe, the ship spent two days on Grande-Terre, and Lanzerac immediately did something which established the quality of the visit: he conducted his lectures in the open area about the kiosk at the center of the marvelous square in Point-à-Pitre, and as he spoke, surrounded by the handsome old houses in which his ancestors had lived, he made the wild days of Victor Hugues come alive: "In 1794 he erected his guillotine right there where you're standing. He dragged my famous Lanzerac forebear from that house there. In 1894 my grandfather was expelled from that other house when he married a young woman of color." Later a student reported to Thérèse: "A morning in the public square at Point-à-Pitre is worth a seminar in the library at Duke."

On the second evening she suggested that she and Senator Lanzerac hold a colloquy ashore for the students to which townspeople would also be invited, and since she spoke fluent French, he saw this as a fine opportunity to do some campaigning for the next election. So the parish hall was filled, with a bilingual islander translating in whispers for the students.

The forum provided Lanzerac with a springboard from which to glorify the Guadeloupean form of government: "If you take every governmental unit in the Caribbean today, and I mean even Venezuela and Colombia as well as the mixed-up Central American nations and Cuba, the best governed, it seems to me, are the French islands. Becoming a structural part of metropolitan France (in 1946), just as if we bordered on the Rhone, helped us work out some difficult economic problems. We also have developed pragmatic solutions to the race problem, and we enjoy an unfettered freedom. We have no religious riots, no turmoil in the streets."

"Can your young people get a good education here?" a student asked, and Lanzerac replied as elders had in Point-à-Pitre for the last two hundred years: "Our bright boys we send back to the metropolitan for their education. I got mine in a fine little mountain village on the Italian border, Barcelonnette, if you care to look it up."

"Why do that?" the interrogator pursued, and Lanzerac replied: "Because it binds us to France."

"But do you consider yourself French or Guadeloupean?" and he replied: "French. I'm a citizen of France." Then he smiled disarmingly: "Of course, if my grandfather hadn't married a very lovely creole girl with golden-colored skin, I'd not be able to get elected to the senate here."

Under heavy questioning from the students, he defended his thesis that the best run of the Caribbean islands, all criteria considered, were the French: "We have a style suited to islands . . . an inborn love of freedom but also a desire to make something of ourselves. We're pragmatic people. We handle race problems better than either the English or the Americans . . ."

"How about the Spanish?" someone asked, and he said, whimsically but truthfully: "The dear old Spaniards, they never handle anything well, race or anything else. They just go banging down the road of civilization like a car with one drooping fender. But dammit, they always seem to reach their destination at just about the same time that we and the English do."

He emphasized the point that others had made about the Caribbean: it would probably be better if all the islands had remained under one European ownership rather than falling into scattered hands as they did, but he conceded that because Spain had been so lax in her custodianship, the scattering of interests became inevitable.

Before this easy generalization became too attractive to the students, Thérèse raised a ticklish question: "Would one religion for the region have helped?" and he replied: "Yes. In the Caribbean, in Europe, in the world."

"The Catholic, perhaps?" and he said: "Especially the Catholic. By and large, it's the easiest religion for a nation-state to live with."

Thérèse pressed: "You refer to the great accomplishments in Haiti? It's Catholic," and Lanzerac replied, with an ingratiating Gallic shrug: "You win some, you lose some."

On the final morning the group rented horses, and Lanzerac and Thérèse led the students on a long canter to the east, following the paths taken by Paul Lanzerac and Solange Vauclain in 1794, before the terror broke, and they called to each other in French as Paul and

Solange must have done on their daring rides. The earth and the sky and the memories became so French that Thérèse was almost persuaded to believe that even though France had made a complete mess of Haiti, which still bore the scars of her mismanagement, it might truly have been better for the Caribbean if these civilized men and women had made all the islands integral parts of homeland France. But that night when they returned to the *Galante* she asked Lanzerac: "Have you ever heard about the terrible international debt that France hung around the neck of Haiti at the granting of independence in 1804?" and he said: "Never heard of it," and she said: "A Haitian historian told the truth: 'We spent most of our energy in the nineteenth century repaying France, and our nation fell so far behind in all social services that it could never catch up.'" And Lanzerac said: "When I get back to Paris, I'll ask for a report on that."

None of the students who spent those two days in old Point-à-Pitre would ever again feel that the Caribbean was a Spanish Lake, or an English one, either, for it also contained a powerful French coloring, which made it even more interesting.

As the *Galante* steamed south from Guadeloupe an informal committee of women students accosted Thérèse with a justified complaint: "Wherever we stop, the stories are about men. Your ancestor Vavak, the murderer Hugues. Weren't there any women on these islands?"

Thérèse thought it odd that the question should come at this propitious moment, for to the west, adorned in sunset glow, rose the majestic peaks of France's other island, Martinique, and she told the women: "Fetch the others and I'll tell you about two girls a little younger than you who went to visit a cave on that island in the 1770s." When some men students wandered by she invited them to listen, so as night fell, most of her class were either sitting cross-legged before her or lounging about the deck where they could hear.

"Two centuries ago on that island lived a daydreaming girl of noble ancestry with a name like a poem, Marie-Joséphe-Rose Tascher de la Pagerie, and she had as her bosom friend a girl who was an even more confirmed dreamer, Aimée Dubec de Rivery. One afternoon, summoning their courage, they climbed a hill near their homes to visit a sorceress who lived in a cave. It must have been a mysterious affair, with incantations and rituals calculated to impress young girls, but suddenly the sorceress stopped in midflight, stared in open-mouthed amazement at the two, and said in a powerful voice they had not heard before: 'You will each become a queen! You will live in palaces surrounded by a magnificent court. You will reign over entire nations and men will bow before you, because you will have majestic power.' The strange voice stopped. The sorceress resumed speaking as before, and when the girls asked what the interruption had been, she affected not to know what she had said, but she assured them: 'Whatever it was, it was the truth, for I did not say it. But since the ancient ones spoke through me, you can rely upon it.'

"As the impressionable girls returned to their homes, each looked at the other and burst out laughing: 'You a queen! Palaces and glittering festivities!' The idea was so ridiculous they told no one of their visit, but in the long years ahead, separated by thousands of miles, they must often have reflected on that strange session in the cave."

"What happened to them?"

"Does the name Beauharnais mean anything to you?" When no one responded, she said: "The Tascher girl married a handsome young nobleman, Alexandre de Beauharnais, when he visited the island, and he took her back to France. He didn't amount to much and was guillotined during the Revolution, leaving her a widow in perilous times."

"What happened?" one of the girls asked, and all leaned forward to hear the conclusion of this tantalizing story.

"She called herself Joséphine, became known in Paris, was thrown into prison, and was on the verge of being guillotined herself when she caught the eye of a young officer with a bright future. His name? Napoleon Bonaparte. He fell desperately in love with her, married her, and she became, as the cavewoman had predicted, his empress."

There was silence as the young people studied the gradually vanishing island. "And what of Aimée?"

"A French ship on which she was sailing in the Mediterranean was captured by Algerian pirates. She was whisked off to Constantinople and sold as a slave. One of the sultan's eunuchs, seeking replenishments for the royal harem, saw her, bought her for his master, and she was so entrancing, so wise and witty, that she made the sultan her emotional slave, and he made her the equivalent of his queen." When some of the young women gasped, Thérèse added: "Romantic things can happen on the islands . . . especially French islands."

One young woman, already beginning to dream, asked: "Could

what you've just told us possibly be true?" and Thérèse replied: "I'm like the old woman in the cave. Everything I said is true."

Almost as if the organizers of the trip wished the tourists to see in rapid sequence the best of the French followed by the best of the British, the *Galante* deviated slightly to visit next the placid, gentle island of Barbados, treasured by stormbound Canadians, who sent two or three big airplanes down to Bridgetown every day filled with tourists seeking respite from the rigors of Montreal, Ottawa and Toronto. As a representative of the Swedish Lines remarked to Thérèse: "If you closed Canadian airports for one week, Barbados would perish."

A special lecturer joined them for the next three-day leg of the journey. He was Major Reginald Oldmixon, descendant of a famous Royalist family who had led a minor uprising in favor of the Divine Right of Kings after the beheading of Charles I in 1649, and at his first session with the travelers he made his apologies: "Barbados has a black governor general, a fine black prime minister, a black chief law officer, and black heads of most of the departments. I'd probably do a more representative job if I were black, but I do like to talk, and my family has been on the island since before any part of the United States was settled, so I do know something about the jolly old place." He laughed and said: "And to make things perfectly clear, my immediate boss is a black who can beat me at tennis."

He proved a great hit with the younger passengers and especially with Thérèse's students, for he had a lively wit, an aptitude for making himself the butt of jokes, and an agenda which he jolly well intended to further: "My job is to make you interested in Barbados and to feel at ease on our glorious island. It's always been popularly known as Little England, and we're proud to confess that the name has been appropriately awarded. When the rascals in the homeland chopped off the head of our king, we on Barbados said: 'You can't do that!' and declared war on the whole empire, such as it was at the time. We still feel that way. If things go bonkers in England, you can always find refuge in Barbados. Population two hundred and sixty thousand, like a small American city, area a hundred and sixty-six square miles, about like one of your larger counties, quality of life, among the best in the world."

By the time the *Galante* reached Bridgetown, the pleasant port

on the western side of the island, nearly everyone aboard was prepared to like Barbados, and when the tour buses set forth with the
regular passengers, the occupants saw an island which in no way
disappointed. The transition from a sugar culture to one of mixed
enterprises had been easily, almost graciously made, and since Barbados had never had any spare land, when the end of slavery came,
there had been no hiding place for disgruntled free men to run to,
as there had been on the other islands; the blacks had to stay put
and work things out with their former masters. There had been the
standard uprisings, some of them quite vicious, but they had neither
lingered nor festered, so that in the end Barbados found itself with
about the best island relationships in the Caribbean.

"The secret," one black bus driver told his wide-eyed passengers
who were seeing a peaceful island at work, "is that each of us intends
one day to make his fortune and go live like a toff in England."
Proudly he added: "Besides, our little island has produced the greatest all-round cricket player the world has ever seen, the great Sir Gary
Sobers, and believe me, that counts for something."

Thérèse's students met with government officials in an instructive
seminar which told them much about the islands they had already
seen or would be seeing shortly. The two principal speakers were
Major Oldmixon and a black professor of history from the Barbados
branch of the University of the West Indies. Their topic? The abortive effort in 1958 to unite all the British islands in one grand con-
federation, with one citizenship, one money system, one federal
government and one common destiny. Oldmixon spoke first, and at
times he was so deeply moved by the tragedy in which he had participated, tears almost came to his eyes:

"Every Oldmixon of whom we have record for the past three
hundred and fifty years has been staunchly in favor of Federation for the various islands of the Caribbean belonging to
Great Britain, and we usually included land areas in the vicinity like British Guiana in South America and British Honduras in Central. In fact, one of my ancestors, Admiral Hector
Oldmixon back in Napoleon's time, was so enthusiastic about
it that he went so far as to capture the French island of Guadeloupe to make it eligible to join. He kept it, alas, for only a
few weeks.

"Through the years we had a score of abortive attempts to join the islands into one sensible Federation, and from the beginning it was clear that the three moving forces would have to be Barbados, Trinidad and Jamaica. Most money, most people, most advanced ideas and capabilities. So it became an infuriating three-way jigsaw puzzle. When Barbados and Jamaica agreed, Trinidad held back. And when Trinidad and Barbados saw eye to eye, Jamaica played hard to get. The little islands? They always dreamed of Federation and were willing to make real concessions to get it.

"Finally, in January 1958, everything came together, and believe it or not, under careful urging from Britain, Federation was authorized, a site for our capital was agreed upon, a fine location in Trinidad, and in March of that year elections were to be held, and the final distribution of seats indicates the relative importance of the islands: Jamaica, thirty-one, Trinidad, fifteen, Barbados, five. Great idea, grand potential, but I'll let Professor Charles tell you what happened."

The black professor told a dismal story, one of regional hope and national despair, in which the personal ambitions of a few exhibitionistic leaders destroyed the hopes of the many:

"In the end it came down to a clash between black leaders, both honors graduates from English universities: Manley, the strong man of Jamaica, Williams, the extremely vain man of Trinidad; and dear old Sir Grantley Adams of Barbados, always striving to make peace between the Big Two. Vanity, vanity! Reconciliation denied, wrong decisions pushed forward. Through all of 1958 this grand design that might have saved this corner of the world hung in the balance, but nevertheless, princess Margaret of England, the one who lost the man she loved, came out and inaugurated the Federation, with Major Oldmixon and me in the crowd cheering.

"What went wrong? For the most insane reasons in the world Manley threatened to take Jamaica out, so Williams had to respond by threatening to take out Trinidad. Our world was threatened, and by 1960 it was crumbling about our ears. People like Oldmixon and me battled to save the concept, but in September 1961, Jamaica held a plebiscite and the vote was two hundred fifty-six thousand get out, two hundred seventeen thousand stay in, and the whole castle of cards came drifting down."

Oldmixon coughed, then said: "Men like my family and his tried to get a Federation of Nine functioning, without Jamaica and Trinidad, but lacking mighty Jamaica, nothing was reasonably possible."

The professor also lamented the loss, but he did have other considerations: "Geography was so against us. If only God had placed that damned Jamaica farther east, it would be in the center of any federation. What's the problem? Jamaica's our biggest unit, and it's only six hundred miles from Miami but twelve hundred from Barbados, much farther than from New York to Kansas City. Maybe the essentials for a federation were never present, maybe these islands will never be able to confederate on anything."

"Could anyone else take the lead and organize the islands under some new banner?" a student asked, and he replied: "There has been some speculation. It is possible that Cuba will stabilize, say, by the year 2020 when Castro's gone, and by *stabilize* I mean in some form of economic and social pattern acceptable to all of us, and then take the lead in building a great hegemony that would take in everything in the area, including Venezuela, Columbia, Central America and Yucatán after Mexico falls apart, as it probably will."

Before anyone could react to this idea so repugnant to many, he added: "I believe Cuba could take over Hispaniola and Puerto Rico fairly easily, I should think, also Central America. The English and French islands later, but economics and proximity work wonders."

"Are you a Marxist?" one of the brighter students asked, and he laughed: "Oldmixon and I are known as reactionaries. But I do speculate about the movement of nations, the realignments, and I would strongly advise you to do the same, because then you will probably have anticipated the changes that arrive on your doorstep some September morning."

None of the students could visualize a Cuban hegemony spread over the Caribbean and its shores, but one young man asked: "Why not an American hegemony, with Miami as its focal point?" and the professor answered: "Young man, don't you ever study maps? Your idea came to me about forty years ago, and as you can see, I must have been pretty young then. But with an American leadership, we come to what might be called the Jamaica Impasse. Miami is so very far off to the west," and the young man proved his mettle by saying: "Professor, may I insult you?" and the black scholar chuckled: "My students do, why shouldn't you?" and the young fellow said: "Maybe you better look at your maps again. Miami is east of about half of Cuba and ideally situated in relation to Central America and the relevant shoreline of South."

The professor laughed, and said: "Let's talk north and south. Your Miami is totally out of the picture, but Cuba forms that huge northern boundary of the Caribbean," but the young man would not give in: "Like New York and Washington perched on the edge of their domains, or Sidney, Australia, on its. We have jet aircraft, you know," and the professor said: "I wish you'd transfer to my university."

When Thérèse said goodnight to her students on leaving Barbados, she warned them: "I'm going to call everyone a half-hour before dawn," and when there were moaning protests, she became impatient: "Young people! As soon as I saved a little money, I took the cheapest cruise available to the Caribbean. A room so small and far belowdecks, I was practically swimming with the sharks. It was sensible for me to rise early, and I learned that one of the glorious experiences of travel is to be in a small boat just before dawn as you approach a tropic island. Darkness everywhere but a sense that something lies ahead. Then a distant glimmer of light, a kind of throbbing in the air, and because it is in the tropics, where the sun rises and sets with a rush, not a lingering tease, here comes the great orb, all of a sudden. Light everywhere! And then, far ahead the outline of an island in the midst of a great ocean. More light, more island, and as your boat sweeps in you see the palm trees and the hills and the reassurances that people live there. Don't miss a thrill that may come only once in your lifetime."

"Is it as exciting as you say?" a girl asked, and Thérèse replied: "It's not an ordinary island, Marcia. It's All Saints. Nothing in the Caribbean to match the harbor you'll see tomorrow."

And next day, when, with shocking abruptness, a bronze sun leaped into the sky, the drowsy students saw with gasps of delight the two Pointes which guarded the bay, then the distant Mornes, the white beaches, and finally the red roofs and spires of Bristol Town, each in turn revealing its loveliness in such a perfect way that some of the young people would remember this dawn forever.

The highlights of the morning came by accident, for as the students piled ashore, a girl from the University of Indiana saw a tall, loping figure that she recognized from the books she'd read during the cruise, and with a wild yelp she shouted to those behind: "Hey, kids! That's got to be a Rastafarian!" and all rushed to speak with a gangling black man dressed in flowing garb topped by a gold and green tam-o-shanter from beneath which tumbled long strands of matted hair that covered his back and shoulders. "They're dreadlocks!" the girl shouted, and soon the students had surrounded the stranger who had come to the pier to do missionary work with just such tourists.

His name, he said, was Ras-Negus Grimble and he had come to All Saints from Jamaica some years ago: "First time I come here, gommint throw me out. But I like All Saints, much better than Jamaica. So I come back, promise to behave. Gommint here grow up, they able to accept me now." He spoke with a lovely soft accent, throwing in an occasional Rasta word that no one understood, and when the students saw Thérèse coming down the gangway, they called: "Professor! Over here," and as she joined them she said, for the man to hear: "I'm so glad you've met a Rastafarian. They're a big influence in Jamaica and I was afraid you'd miss them."

Since it was early morning, she invited the Rastafarian to join them for coffee or a drink of some kind, and when she asked where they might find light refreshment, he said: "All tourists go the Waterloo," and he led them to a kind of bar, where Thérèse cried with the pleasure of discovery: "Wrentham! I have a letter for Sir Lincoln Wrentham," and when she asked the proprietor where she might find him, a young good-looking black man said: "Let me have the letter. I'll have the boy run it up to Gommint House," and she said: "If I gave him a dollar, could he deliver these other two for me?" and the young man said: "One trip does all and there's no fee," so off went letters to Millard McKay, a well-known writer on Caribbean subjects, and Harry Keeler, an Englishman with a long affiliation in All Saints.

In the meantime the Rastafarian, at home with young people, had sent for his homemade lute, on which he was now playing songs written by the famous Jamaican reggae artist Bob Marley, and two students who had records back home by Marley asked if he would sing "Four Hundred Years," the song of slaves coming out of Africa to the Caribbean. Several black men lounging in the bar joined the informal concert, but Thérèse wanted her students to know more about Rastafarianism than its music, so she interrupted: "Mr. Grimble, will you explain to my young people something about your interesting religion?" and he asked: "Sister, do you know anything about us, yourself?" and she said primly: "I know a great deal, but it'll be so much more interesting if you tell us." Then she smiled: "Besides, all I know is what I read in books, and that could be wrong." He smiled back.

His story fascinated the Americans: Marcus Garvey and his vision of a return to Africa; the emperor Haile Selassie as the new incarnation of the Godhead come down to earth; the rituals, customs, the arcane language, the vision of a black hegemony in the Caribbean and the music. When he reached that point in his informal lecture he took up his lute again and sang some of the compelling protest songs, then asked the prettiest of Thérèse's girl students to sit by him as he switched to love songs, which he sang to her alone.

At this point a stately white man in his seventies entered the café and asked for a Professor Vaval, and Thérèse hurried to meet him: "Are you the writer Millard McKay?" and when he said he was, she led him to a chair among the students and told them: "This is the American whose books you've been reading. He came down here as a newspaperman, when?"

"From Detroit, 1938. Wrote a series of articles for my newspaper, first of their kind in America, and a New York publisher on vacation down here read them and invited me to put them together in a book, which did so well I moved here, married a local girl, and have made my living writing about the Caribbean ever since."

Thérèse said with obvious enthusiasm and respect: "Kids, this man is an object lesson. He wrote fifty, a hundred great articles, but one day he stumbled upon the one subject that matched his talents. And what do you think his world-famous essay dealt with?"

Their guesses pretty well covered the Caribbean, but failed to come even close: " 'How to Eat a Mango' swept across the world of magazines and books, and it could not have been funnier or more quotable or more accurate." McKay smiled benevolently, his white hair complementing his tanned skin, and she placed her hand in his and gave a brief résumé of his lucky one-shot: "He started out by telling the truth, that the Caribbean mango is probably the world's most tantalizing fruit, a little smaller than a cantaloupe, with a heavy skin in variegated colors, and an immense central pit. How many of you have ever tasted a mango? A kind of mix between pineapple and peach with just a hint of turpentine?"

Quite a few had, and the students could not fathom why she was making such a fuss about this particular fruit, but now she reached the heart of his essay: "Mr. McKay, as an American newspaperman, knew that he ought to eat this 'queen of fruits' he'd been given by his black housekeeper, but he didn't know how, and he tells of his disastrous adventures while trying to solve the problem, until his housekeeper rescued him. 'Take off your shirt,' she said, 'and your undershirt, and now lean way over the sink and go at it.' And he did, golden-yellow juice flowing down his chest and arms. But when he wrote about it, he described it as well worth the effort.'"

One of the men in the group asked the barkeeper: "You got any mangoes?" and the black man said: "Not the season," whereupon Thérèse laughed and turned to McKay: "What was it that your housekeeper said: 'Mangoes like sex, very messy . . . but what's better?' "

Thérèse left the students to have lunch with the other lecturers at Gommint House, and when she returned in early afternoon, her students were still in session with the Rastafarian Grimble and three of his dreadlocked acolytes, who were alternately preaching their religious doctrine, smoking ganja, and singing the songs of Jamaica. Nodding to them, Thérèse sat alone at the bar and nursed a Coca-Cola until Millard McKay returned to fetch her for tea at his place, and when she reached his pleasant cottage set amid flowers and overlooking the glorious bay, she was faintly surprised to find that he had a colored wife, lighter than herself and much older, but very charming. And inside waited the other man she wanted to see, the Englishman Harry Keeler, who worked for the island government, and his wife, Sally, who was also colored. "I hear you had lunch with my brother Lincoln," Mrs. Keeler said. "He's been made the Gee-Gee recently and loves the pomp."

After desultory conversation about the economic condition of the various islands—topic number one wherever one went, Thérèse concluded—she looked at the two couples and boldly asked: "From firsthand experience—are mixed marriages difficult?" To justify her prying, she added quickly: "I'm engaged to a white man, totally liberated, and I'd appreciate some pointers," and to each of her listeners in turn she flashed a beguiling smile.

They were eager to talk, all four of them, and Mrs. McKay said with humor: "To tell the truth, this American of mine fell in love with the island first, then me, but once he gave me the eye, I wouldn't let go," and Mrs. Keeler said: "This cautious Englishman brooded and tortured himself: 'Could I be happy married to a black?' so one night I pushed him and said: 'Jump in! The water's fine.' "

Then Mrs. McKay said: "When Millard and I were married, it was too soon. We were outcasts, but when his book did well and he had gained a bit of both fame and fortune, they rushed to accept us. After that, clear sailing." And Mrs. Keeler added: "I think we might have had it a wee bit easier here in All Saints than you would in the States. We're rather ahead of you, what with my brother as the Gee-Gee and all his cabinet black."

McKay, a wise man who had served as one of the prototypes for Alec Waugh's witty novel, asked: "Why do you ask these questions? You having doubts?" and Thérèse replied "No!" so quickly that they knew she had. They agreed that if both she and Dennis already had good teaching jobs, and they planned to live in the North, the prognosis for success was high. "As a matter of fact," Mrs. Keeler said, "I don't believe I know of a single case here on the island in which a mixed marriage has foundered because of race. It just doesn't happen," and Thérèse said: "Yes, but you've worked out the relationships. In the States, we haven't." And they agreed that this was true.

As she prepared to return to the ship she told her hosts how grateful she was for their having allowed her to burden them with her problems, and Harry Keeler replied: "In these matters the only sensible rule is, do what's burning you and to hell with the others."

When the laughter subsided, McKay was reluctant to let Thérèse go, and taking her aside, he said: "You're so fortunate to be on a ship that stops at Trinidad. Most don't, you know, and travelers to the Caribbean lose so much."

"The only reason we're stopping is that the line sold a lot of our students on the promise that they'd see Carnaval, which they tell us is pretty gorgeous."

"Ah, there's far more than Carnaval," the writer said. He was seventy-seven and eager to share meanings with anyone who evidenced a sincere interest in the part of the world he had made his own. Almost forcing her into a chair, he said: "My adult life started in Trinidad. I came to All Saints as a callow Detroit newspaperman, studied the island, loved its English ways, and concluded that I knew the Caribbean. Then I drifted down to Trinidad, by accident really, and the place blew me apart—its color . . . its Hindus . . . the magnificent poetry of its young women. I wrote a series of articles on it, and my editor cabled back: 'So you finally fell in love. Who is she?' He was right. She was one of those golden Trinidadians, walked like a poem, flashing eyes that were not afraid to stare at men, not at all. Three heroic days. I wanted to quit my job, stay in Trinidad forever, marry this heavenly young woman."

He sighed, and Thérèse, tremendously interested these days in who married whom, and how, asked, pointing to Mrs. McKay: "Apparently you didn't marry the girl?"

"No," he said ruefully as he laughed at himself. "I found she worked in a kind of massage parlor. Met men there and conducted her own lucrative business on the side. I was shattered. Flew to Barbados, found myself right in the midst of one hell of a revolution. Had I remained here on All Saints, I'd have become a sentimental old fool, a kind of self-made English remittance man."

"Harsh lessons, but you certainly learned something. Your books on the Caribbean are quite valuable."

"There's a chap in Trinidad who's better. I'm nineteenth century, he's twenty-first."

"Who's this genius?"

"Chap named Banarjee."

She gasped with the joy of mutual discovery: "I'm using his Yale book as a text aboard the *Galante*." Suddenly he grasped her hands with deep emotion: "It's so exciting to meet someone who's trying to push knowledge forward. Oh, I would love to be forty years old and teaching in some university. Your problem about marrying across color lines? Give it no thought. You've already won the ball game." He kissed her and said: "May God bless you."

As the *Galante* headed south for Carnaval in Trinidad, Thérèse's emotions were so incandescent and jumbled that as she walked the deck under the stars, she thought it apt that the ship was leaving the comfort and order of the French and British islands and heading for turbulent Trinidad and the old Spanish mainland at Cartagena, because her life seemed to be traveling a parallel course: I'm seeing the Caribbean in a totally different light. Before I understood it as a scholar. Now I feel it as a human being.

She had been profoundly impressed by some of the academic lectures, like Carmody's on the realities of life in Trinidad and the black professor's speculation that one day Cuba might extend her hegemony over the entire Caribbean. Also, her fresh rereading of Banarjee's Yale publication on the islands had startled her with its vivid depictions of Caribbean customs and values, and she remembered that both Carmody and McKay had praised the author for different reasons: If I'm going to be a real professor, I'd better meet that man, because he knows something I don't.

So next morning when the ship drew alongside the quay in Trinidad and students rushed off to plunge themselves into the riot of Carnaval, she lingered on deck, waiting for Michael Carmody, and when he appeared, she asked him, rather boldly: "Your man Banarjee. People seem to think highly of him. Any chance I could meet him?"

"Simplest thing. He was my student. Lives not far from here."

As they looked down upon the quay a horde of young islanders, boys and girls, all dressed alike in gold and blue festival uniforms of the most flamboyant design, thronged into the area prior to marching through the streets, and when they were joined by sixteen elders in gargantuan multicolored mechanically controlled costumes, confusion filled the place. Then, as the chaos intensified, a band of sixteen men playing tantalizing music on marimbas made from gasoline drums marched through, until, with one wild spasm, Trinidad's Carnaval exploded.

In a hesitant voice that betrayed her misgivings that she might not be able to see the scholar, Thérèse said: "I suppose he'll be involved with that riot down there," but Carmody reassured her: "I doubt that a man like him will be much concerned."

As they descended into the maelstrom they found themselves in the midst of two large groups of young people, one dressed like mice, the other like astronauts. "Who pays for these costumes?" Thérèse asked, and Carmody said: "The parents of the kids. This is Carnaval, once a year."

Thérèse, growing more and more attentive to the throbbing of the steel bands, could barely hear Carmody when he explained: "Dr. Banarjee lives in a famous old house. Owned by his people for more than a hundred years."

"Does he live with his family?"

"Odds and ends of people look after him. He's not married."

Something in the way the Irishman said this troubled Thérèse, and she stopped in the middle of the confusion and grasped Car-

mody's arm: "You're hiding something from me. Is he what the girls
in college called a weirdo? Or someone I should be afraid of?"

Carmody was astounded: "He's one of the finest, gentlest men in
the Caribbean. Almost a genius."

"If he's not a professor, how does he make his living?"

"This is his place—and by the way, it's usually referred to as the
Sirdar's House," Carmody said, glad to be able to avoid her question
and indicating a fine, haphazard old building. "A lot of Indians have
got their start in this one," and he climbed three steps to knock on the
door.

When the scholar appeared he looked like a man who had settled
into a groove in which he would remain for the rest of his life. In his
mid-thirties, he stood less straight than he had as a boy; he slouched
forward just a bit, like a man searching for something he had lost,
and the fires of youthful enthusiasm had definitely waned. His hair
was still a handsome black with no signs of gray, and when he smiled,
which he did perfunctorily, his teeth were as white as ever. He looked,
Thérèse thought when she first saw him, much like the deferential
Indian bookkeeper one reads about in English novels on India, and
she liked him.

Carmody spoke first: "Ranjit, I bring you a most intelligent
young woman, Dr. Thérèse Vaval, professor-to-be at Wellesley. She's
been using your Yale book as a text." But before Banarjee could acknowledge the introduction, she hastened to explain further the reason for the intrusion: "You're a major contributor to the subjects I'll
be teaching. Caribbean history, Caribbean thought. I'm Haitian, you
know."

Without a shred of envy, Banarjee clapped his hands and cried:
"You lucky, lucky woman! I've wanted to teach those subjects all my
life. Never got the chance."

It was such an honest cry that Thérèse said quickly: "But, Dr.
Banarjee, you teach all of us."

Pleased by such recognition from a fellow scholar, Ranjit broke
free from the reticence that usually imprisoned him, and with the
boyish enthusiasm that Indian men of all ages can occasionally display, he cried: "Mr. Carmody! Dr. Vaval! We shall mount a small
celebration of this propitious day," and he hustled about, bringing
them a pitcher of limeade and a deep saucer filled with pistachios.
Carmody would take none: "I promised I'd spend the day at my college. Paperwork. You must excuse me."

"You will be coming back to the ship?" Thérèse asked, for she had grown to like this sensible man.

"Of course! I'm responsible for two more lectures, and reporting the student's grades." As he departed he added: "I leave you in good hands."

When they were alone, Banarjee said: "Now, tell me, please, how did you ever get from Haiti to Cambridge, Massachusetts. To begin with, how did you escape the Tontons Macoutes?"

The words of her reply reverberated in the hot Trinidad air like the echoing of crystal bells, summarizing three centuries of Caribbean history: "We escaped perilously, in a small boat with insufficient food. We were picked up, far north, by a Canadian shipping vessel and deposited in Québec City. I was nine."

"Could your father have been Hyacinthe Vaval?"

"With scars."

Ranjit rose and saluted, then asked: "So you were a nine-year-old black Haitian girl in Québec City. How did you get to Cambridge?"

"Well, of course I already spoke French. And the Canadians, they have hearts of molten gold beneath those cold exteriors. They adopted me. My teachers . . ." She paused. "Each one should get a medal."

"I've had teachers like that," Banarjee said, and then he wanted to know about her advanced schooling, and she gave the answer that bright young people so often give: "My teachers wanted me to succeed. I was the only black girl they'd ever had with any promise. They wrote to Radcliffe."

Banarjee snapped his fingers: "With me, the same. At the little college here in Trinidad. At the islands' university in Jamaica."

With that beginning, the two scholars launched into a swift, impassioned exchange of ideas, concepts, guesses about the future of their islands, and the chances for Third World countries even to survive, let alone prosper. Each had command of the general knowledge that formed the groundwork of the other's understandings, and each respected the peculiar expertise in certain subjects that he or she did not have. Thérèse peppered him with questions about Trinidad and he sought specific details about the debacle on Haiti.

Without being asked, she told him of her remarkable experience with Lalique Hébert, the zombie, and he expressed no surprise. "'There are more things than are dreamt of in your philosophy, Horatio.'"

They slipped easily into a discussion of the recent political switches in both Jamaica and Trinidad, and Ranjit asked: "Will Haiti ever mend itself?" and Thérèse said frankly: "Father wants to return to try to salvage something . . ."

"And you?" She replied: "After two weeks on the island just now, I warned him not to go. You can survive only so many escapes in small boats with no shelter or food."

"Are the Macoutes still active?"

"They emerge in all nations, in varying forms. If good people don't stand guard . . ."

"Tell me, Dr. Vaval, how do you feel spiritually about turning your back on Haiti and taking refuge in the United States?"

She rose and walked about the veranda of this very pleasing house, then confessed: "I've had a testing time on this cruise . . . my islands . . . my culture . . . my people trapped in their tragic dead ends. I flew out of Miami a totally assimilated American, with a great job, unlimited future and . . ." She stopped in midsentence, for she did not care to tell this stranger: ". . . and a delightful man to marry." But she did finish with part of the truth: "However, two weeks in Haiti, seeing my people again and the terrible poverty . . ." She stopped abruptly and asked for a tissue, after which she asked: "Professor Banarjee, you know the Caribbean. How did the slaves in your Trinidad and my Haiti have the courage to remain alive? Or the ancient Indians?"

He said very quietly: "The Arawaks refused. They handled the Spaniard very simply. They died. Just died."

"I see no evidence that either your people or mine will be satisfied to do that. My God! To be a Haitian and to be alive, merely alive. That's an act of unbelievable courage." He had no comment, for her words cut like red-hot swords snatched from the forge; there had been days in America when he had not wanted to stay alive, but he had. Nor was it easy to accept the years when he had to swallow his pride and go out on the streets of Port of Spain, nodding to people who he knew had read accounts of his failures.

In that pregnant moment of silence, of perfect unspoken communication, each person knew that the time had come for someone to say: "Why don't we have dinner and view the great nonsense of Carnaval?" but she was restrained because not even now did women in the islands make such suggestions and certainly not in a strange country and within a society as alien as Banarjee's. And he could not for a most painful reason: he had no money, and the precious instant of recognition might have passed had he not confessed: "Dr. Vaval, I would be most honored if I could invite you to dinner on this festive night, but I have . . ." and she said far too quickly: "Doctor, that's not a problem. We'll go Dutch," and he had to confess: "The allowance my family . . ." He came so close to breaking down that he could not complete his sentence and explain that his meager allowance came at stated intervals and that . . .

With the graciousness that marked Haitians when dealing with people they respected, she said with no embarrassment: "Doctor, your writings have brought light to certain dark pools of my life. I would be deeply honored if you would show me the glories of what our guide said was 'one of the major celebrations in the world.'"

He nodded, and they left the house, went out into the streets and mingled with the riotous crowd, then found themselves seats at a moderately priced restaurant where they ate and drank and gawked at the passing throngs in their wildly expensive costumes and masks. When steel bands went by, he explained how the soft musical quality of the gasoline drums had been discovered only lately, during World War II.

She was delighted when a band came by as accompanists to a famous calypso singer, Lord of all Creation, who had merciless rhymes about Ronald Reagan, Margaret Thatcher, Mikhail Gorbachev and several local figures she did not recognize. But the highlight of the protracted evening came when they heard a familiar voice shouting above the babel: "Ranjit! Thérèse! I hoped I'd find you out enjoying the scene." It was Michael Carmody, back from his day's work at his college.

Ranjit desperately wanted to invite him to join them for a drink, but even as he hesitated, Thérèse quickly perceived what ought to be done, and said graciously: "Won't you honor us?" and she summoned a boy peddling drinks. A night of revelry had been launched.

Thérèse found that Carmody's predictions about Carnaval had not been exaggerated, for the brightly costumed marchers came by in thousands, the noise was deafening, the calypsos daring and funny, the steel bands throbbing with invitation to join the dancing, the food spicy and the rum drinks endless. Even Ranjit, usually abstemious, allowed his friends to buy him two tall punches made with fruit juices, soda water and a dollop of Trevelyan dark.

At four in the morning, when the strolling bands seemed to burst with refreshed energy, Carmody suggested above the noise: "Let's go aboard ship and put the celebration to bed with a sunrise breakfast on the top deck," and this they did, eating their eggs Benedict as they gazed down upon the revelers and listened to the wild music.

At nine in the morning the party broke up, and it was time for Banarjee to make his departure, but when Thérèse accompanied him to the gangway she said: "Let's sleep till one or two, then I'll stop by and we'll watch another night."

"I'd like that," Ranjit said, and they spent that afternoon on his veranda with limeades and intense, far-ranging discussions: the differences between the behaviors of the various occupying nations, the current role of Cuba and its Marxism, the unwillingness of the United States to provide area leadership, and the residual effect of slavery on today's blacks.

When Thérèse asked: "How did you happen to take two doctorates? I saw it in the biographical material for one of your essays," he avoided answering, for he felt she might disapprove of his and Muhammad's antics to escape getting their degrees too soon. Then the conversation focused on topic one in any serious Caribbean discussion. Thérèse posed it this way: "What can our magnificent islands do to earn a living?"

She pointed out that Jamaica had lost its bauxite industry and its farmers no longer had a market in Europe for their bananas. He touched on a more pressing situation: "The one crop we can produce better than any other, sugar, we are no longer allowed to grow. It's infuriating. The United States won't buy it, thereby driving the islands into bankruptcy, and we're right on her doorstep."

These two bright people, among the best informed in the Caribbean that afternoon, could envisage no solution to this basic problem, and Thérèse suggested: "Tourism will be able to keep a limited population afloat. The surplus will have to emigrate to England or the United States," and he said: "That won't be allowed for long," and they ended their discussion in a gray despair.

As night fell she invited him to join her for supper, and now Carnaval had a special significance, for their intense ventilation of problems had brought them closer together. She tried to avoid any fellow passengers from the *Galante* and was relieved when Carmody did not reappear. During one spell they became members of a noisy group of outrageously dressed blacks, and Thérèse allowed the men to swing her high in the air and kiss her when they put her down. At one corner a group of students dressed like Spanish conquistadors grabbed her arms and ran off with her, and as Ranjit watched her flying through the crowd, her light Haitian face radiant, he thought: Who could have predicted that on this night I would be out on the town with the most beautiful woman in Carnaval? And when the students brought her back he was pleased when she gripped his hands as if she had come home.

It was Carnaval, a mix of ancient African rites, the pre-Easter mysteries of the Catholic church, and the stately processions of old England. It was fiery music and soft singing, the throb of the steel band and the whine of Bob Marley's "Four Hundred Years," the food, the dancing, the drunkenness, the priests garbed in black looking on benevolently and the crews from three cruise ships raising hell and kissing the compliant girls. Carnaval in Trinidad! One sailor shouted: "It makes Mardi Gras in New Orleans look like a Sunday-school picnic," and Ranjit told him: "That goes for Calle Ocho in Miami, too."

The *Galante* was scheduled to sail at eight in the morning, and as the whistle began to sound its warning Thérèse said: "I must go," and then she betrayed the cry of her heart: "Dear God, I do not want to leave this island."

Ranjit, awakened as he had not been since the murder of Molly Hudak, tried to prolong the parting. He was no longer slouching, no longer apologetic. Standing very erect, he listened as she told him at the gangway: "Oh, Ranjit, it's been a magical two days. A seminar on the meaning of our sea," and with a boldness that surprised him he added: "And of our lives." Then the ship's deep-throated whistle sounded for the last time, and they parted.

The Swedish Lines, in planning this unusual seminar cruise, had made provisions for a leisurely run to the west following Trinidad, in order for the teachers to provide intensive instruction prior to the featured stop at Cartagena, which was intended not only to be the final stop of the cruise but also the historical highlight. The plan was a good one, and during the first day at sea a lot of work was done in lectures and discussions. One of Thérèse's students voiced the general opinion: "Whoever had the idea for this cruise came up with a winner."

On the evening before the *Galante* arrived at the historic harbor of Cartagena, Professor Ledesma gave the master lecture of the cruise. Using a set of evocative slides, he explained how his natal city had once been the queen of the Caribbean and how ships heavy with silver and gold had gathered in its spacious harbor preparing for the dangerous run to Havana and Sevilla. He spoke of the great men who had frequented this harbor in their ships of war: Drake, Morgan, Vernon, the fierce French pirates, Sir John Hawkins, maybe the best seaman of them all, and then he said: "But I want you especially to appreciate a tough little Spaniard who helped one of my ancestors defend Cartagena against a massive English armada."

First he used drawings of the 1741 period to show the awesome weight of the English invading force, then said: "Now you must imagine the two Spaniards who opposed this mighty fleet and army. My ancestor, Governor Ledesma, must have looked a good deal like me, so we can forget him. But he was assisted by a man no one should ever forget, Marine General Blas de Lezo, old in service . . . and what a service! Fought in twenty-three major naval engagements, always in the midst of the shooting. In a running fight off Gibraltar he lost his left leg. Off Toulon he was blinded in his left eye, and in a major battle defending Barcelona he gave up his right arm!" As the professor listed these dismemberments he used his left arm like a meat cleaver, and he was so dramatic, he himself became this crippled old man fighting to defend his city.

"Did he win?" a student asked, and Ledesma said: "You won't believe it, but with only a handful of men he held off the entire British armada. Kept the ships at anchor and wouldn't allow the English soldiers inside his city. Like they boast in boxing: 'They never laid a hand on him,' but that's not quite right. In the fighting he received two more major wounds, and our victory bells had scarcely stopped ringing when they resumed to toll his death."

When the lecture ended, students gathered about him for further interrogation and the conversations lasted till well past midnight, but in the morning Ledesma was down for an early breakfast, since he was to supervise what everyone hoped would be a gala day. The government of Colombia, damaged by reports of uncontrolled cocaine traffic in its inland cities, had made an extra effort to provide the *Galante* passengers, especially the students, with a memorable experience in Cartagena: small boats were made available for tours of the incomparable harbor; military helicopters stood by to enable geographers or historians to see the area as a whole, and Ledesma himself led walking tours of the ancient battlements upon which an earlier Ledesma had once accompanied Sir Francis Drake on midnight strolls.

Thérèse, who had no responsibilities this day, was among the first to take the helicopter ride, and the young naval officer serving as pilot invited her to occupy the seat beside him, from where she gained an incomparable appreciation of how this city had survived the many assaults made upon it. There below her was the glistening harbor with its two entrances, Boca Grande and Boca Chica, the former now marked by a roadway built upon the skeletons of the innumerable wrecks which had been sunk there in times past to prevent enemy ships from sneaking in. But what impressed her most was the view when the helicopter flew to the north, for then she saw that Cartagena really did sit upon an island, protected by swamp-ridden lands north and east, the Caribbean west and south, so that no enemy could easily assault it from any direction. It stood by itself, a walled city with a unique personality which had been neither destroyed nor altered by the floods of gold and silver that reached it from Porto Bello or by the heavy gunfire that came from British fleets. It was a free-standing city within a wall.

When the flight ended she wandered alone along the narrow streets of the old city, and as she threaded her way through what was little more than an alley, with the fronts of houses almost touching one another, she suddenly burst into the heart of a plaza so lovely that she exclaimed: "Oh, what a treasure!"

Two broad paths intersecting in the middle divided the plaza into four equal quarters, each with its own bubbling fountain, and in the center, where the paths met, rose a fine statue of Bolívar. The square was embraced on all sides by handsome buildings, each a different color, so that the effect was more of a fine painting than a work of architecture. Her first thought on finding herself at the heart of this walled-in excellence was: So formal compared to that great free square in Point-à-Pitre, this one so Spanish, that one so French, but each memorable.

Then at the shadowy end of the plaza she saw a majestic building that seemed to have been hiding like a master actor who wished to make an impressive entrance; tall and imposing like a church, its façade decorated with stately ornament and statuary, it breathed an air of mystery and power. When she crossed the plaza to inspect it, she found it to be the office from which officials of the Holy Inquisition had policed the religious orthodoxy and private morals of the city through the long years from 1610 to 1811, and she shivered to think of what anguish this building had witnessed.

But when she entered its forbidding doorway she learned that it was now a museum, and from its well-arranged and labeled displays she learned that in Cartagena the Inquisition had not run wild, for in the course of its long dictatorship, it had given death sentences to only five, which in those years would have been miraculously humane in an English or American county, and it burned alive only two of them, both renegade clerics.

Relieved to learn this, she was nevertheless saddened to read a detailed account of the first great auto-da-fé held in 1611 at which, during a vast celebration held in the plaza she had just left, nineteen men and women received notice of their punishments. With ominous frequency came the dreaded phrase "*a los remos de galera por vida sin sueldo*"—to the oars of a galley for life without pay. Often there was an order that the accused's distinctive prison garb, his *sambenito,* be labeled with his name and displayed in perpetuity in the local cathedral so that all might be reminded of that family's disgrace.

The nationality of the victims and the harsh nature of their sentences bespoke the religious hatreds which scarred all Spanish colonies: "Juan Mercader, a French peddler who was heard ridiculing a Papal Bull calling for a crusade; Marco Pacio, an Italian who claimed that breaking the sixth commandment is not a sin; Juan Albert, a German who also made fun of a Papal Bull." In Cartagena they had been suspicious of anyone who wasn't Spanish.

The crimes of native-born sinners were indicative of what the church had feared: for not believing in purgatory, for having entered a sixteen-year pact with a devil named Buciraco, for having told fortunes with beans, for conjuring evil spirits, and for raising the dead from their graves.

To read these mournful records made Thérèse wonder if there had ever been a chance for the elysium of which Senator Lanzerac had dreamed, "a Caribbean with one nation, one language, one religion." Would not resolute souls, she asked herself, have emerged to cry: "I'll tolerate this domination no longer!" with riots and revolutions resulting? So after a while we'd be right where we are today: many nations, many rules.

When she arrived back on the *Galante* she went directly to her cabin, propped on her knees the writing portfolio provided there and started a long-overdue letter to Dennis Krey in Concord. Actually, she started two, but her mind was so agitated by this day's experiences that she could not concentrate. Crumpling the would-be letters, she went on deck to seek out Professor Ledesma, and when she found him she said: "Could we take a walk before dinner? Weighty decisions."

"I've been waiting for an invitation like this since we boarded," and they were soon walking along the ramparts and down narrow alleyways toward the center of town, where she guided him to the central plaza which had impressed her so favorably. There, sitting on benches facing the majestic Inquisition building, Ledesma spoke of the imperishable values that nurture a society and keep it vital, and he told her that Spanishness was one of the world's permanent systems, like Islam and Christianity and Judaism, but when Thérèse asked: "Then why is Spanish culture in the Americas unable to produce stable civil governments?" he parried: "Stability is overrated. Vitality, movement, the enjoyment of each day, that's what really counts."

Unwilling to allow what she considered a misguided judgment to pass, Thérèse cried: "Professor Ledesma! This week gunmen from the Medellín cocaine cartel murdered two more judges in that city and three political leaders in Bogotá. Is that what you call the flowering of Spanish culture?"

Ledesma mumbled: "One of the judges was my cousin. I admit that these are terrible times, but isn't your America having its own problems?"

Eager to give this crucial discussion some substantial footing, she took from her handbag a small book that dealt philosophically with these matters: "Since this was written by an outstanding French scholar who was predisposed to neither the Spanish nor the English cause, we can expect impartiality." Translating from the French, she read:

> "'If either Sir Francis Drake in 1586 or Admiral Vernon in 1741 had pressed his advantage and not only captured Cartagena but taken permanent possession of it, the history of the Caribbean, Central America, South America and perhaps the entire world might have been radically altered. With the great harbor of Cartagena in English hands, the Spanish silver fleet from Peru would not have dared to transport its wealth to

Porto Bello, and with that umbilical cord severed, the one between Mexico and Havana would have become untenable. No
more galleons freighted with gold and silver would have made
their way across the Atlantic to Sevilla, and Spain's loosely
bound and chaotic empire in the New World would have
crumbled. In its place would have risen an orderly English
colonization, so that great land areas like Argentina, Chile
and Brazil would have evolved into stable nations like Canada, Australia and New Zealand, perhaps to the betterment
of the world.' "

Closing the book with precise movements, as if she were conducting
one of her seminars, she asked Ledesma: "Now, what do you and I,
as good Catholics, say to that?" and he replied with considerable
vigor: "English-style order in government is not the world's greatest
boon," and he continued in words that the first Ledesma in Cartagena might have used: "To see your family prosper, all members of it.
To know a religion which gives you solace. To feel your spirit free to
soar. To burst with poetic idealism, those are the abiding virtues." He
paused, stared at Thérèse, and asked: "Do people in Gary, Indiana,
have it as good as we do here in Cartagena?"

"You make a persuasive case for the elegance of Spanish custom," Thérèse said, "but not for Spanish government," and he bris-
tled: "You young scholars infected by English interpretations of
history should remember one basic fact. We Spaniards held the New
World from 1492 through 1898, when you stole Cuba and Puerto
Rico from us. Four glorious centuries of achievement. England held
her empire only from the 1630s to the 1950s, pitifully short in comparison. And you cowardly Americans have been afraid to assume
the burdens we laid down, so you have no right to lecture me. We
were the great successes. And we'll be so again one of these days. You
can rely on that."

Reluctant to proffer any further observations which might distress this elderly gentleman, she gazed about her at the handsome
plaza, and the sadness which comes with the passing of old values
assailed her, so that she dropped her head, a gesture which Ledesma
noticed immediately: "What is it, Dr. Vaval? What's happened to disarm you?" and she said: "This cruise. This intimate view of the sea in
which my people slaved and triumphed and knew despair. It's made
a violent impression on me."

"Disorientating?"

"Very."

"That's why we go on voyages. You'll sort it out." He stared at the lovely patterns made by the late-afternoon sun on the façade of the Inquisition building, then asked: "It's a personal problem—your fiancé, I suppose?"

"Yes. I'm on the verge of marrying a lifelong New Englander. But I feel a growing sense of doubt . . . I find it impossible even to write to him."

He bent way over and picked up some pebbles from the plaza, bouncing them up and down in his right hand. "My family has been on this spot for four and a half centuries, and it's an act of faith with us that never in that time were any of us charged with heresy or united in marriage with an Indian or a black. It's the way I was brought up, and believe me, if I had a son of marriageable age and you came around, I'd hustle him off to Salamanca for a graduate degree and a Spanish wife. That's the way we are."

"My family says the same about being African, but this light skin testifies they wavered somewhere." When she laughed at the preposterousness of her situation, he said: "Let's walk to the far end where the lookouts stood," and when they had climbed to that eminence he said: "Here we served in darkness, Miss Vaval, staring at the Caribbean, watching for the enemy or the pirates or the hurricane, and never for three years in a row were we able to relax in assumed safety. That's still the honorable task of a good man or woman. Man the watchtower, look for the enemy, and flash the signal. Not a bad assignment for a professor, either."

It was exciting, that time she spent with Professor Ledesma, and as he said farewell that evening, for the ship would leave the harbor early in the morning, she took his right hand in her two and brought it to her lips: "I'm so glad that it was this cruise that you elected to take," and in farewell he said: "Our first great Ledesma claimed that the Caribbean was a Spanish Lake. You've proved that a lot of good blacks have come in since then, but the color of the sea itself hasn't changed. It's still golden."

He was about to leave with those appropriate words hanging in the air, when she suddenly cried: "Professor, stay one moment. I want you to mail a letter for me," and she dashed to her cabin, grabbed paper, and scrawled: "Dear Dennis, It would be most improper for you to marry me, and entirely wrong for me to marry you. I've just discovered the world of which I'm a part, so goodbye, with love and regret. Thérèse."

During the swift passage back to Miami, Thérèse was so nervous and confused that she stayed by herself, avoiding even her students and sometimes standing at the rail for long spells, staring at her newly discovered Caribbean as if she were never again to see its glorious waves. Remembering the suspicions she'd had that night prior to her arrival at Trinidad, she thought: This amazing cruise really has been a turning point in my life. It introduced me to contemporary Haiti as it actually is, and gave me the courage to write the letter terminating my engagement to Dennis Krey. And now I'm on the eve of starting a new life at Wellesley. All were part of the watershed: I did the right things in the right way, so let them stand. But then her cockiness left her, for the real reason for her anxiety emerged as an image in the passing waves. It was Ranjit Banarjee's grave face surrounded by the vibrant scenes of Carnaval, and she whispered: "Finding him was like finding a cove of calm water after thrashing around in turbulent waves," and suddenly, exultant, she flung her arms wide as if to embrace the entire Caribbean: "You are my sea! Your people are my people!"

Then she heard a man's voice: "Talking to yourself?" It was Michael Carmody, and when she made no reply, he said: "Let's take these chairs, because we should talk. You're in trouble, Dr. Vaval. It's been obvious to anyone who watched you from the start of our trip."

"Who are you to presume . . . ?" she snapped. But she knew immediately that this was the wrong tack: "I'm sorry. For you this voyage has been a working vacation; for me, a leap into a maelstrom."

"No need to explain. From what I saw of Haiti, this trip must have started with a shock."

"It did," and he said quickly: "You're right. I was presumptuous, but you'll learn that teachers are that way when they fear time's running out."

"What does that mean?"

"I came to Trinidad when I was about your age, as penniless as you were when you landed in Canada. I've always spent my life, my dreams in Trinidad, always hoping I would come upon that one brilliant lad who would justify my sacrifices . . ."

"Teaching's never a sacrifice."

"Professor Vaval, you know that people like you and me could earn vastly superior sums if we applied our energy to business or law."

"Ah, but we're not interested solely in sums."

"You're so right, and it's good of you to voice it, because it makes what I have to say much easier." He brought his forefingers to his lips, hesitated, and said: "We search endlessly to uncover that one resplendent intellect, and you'll find that years will be wasted, and then you begin to despair . . ." He found it difficult to continue, but then words came in a rush: "For me, Ranjit Banarjee was that boy. Heavenly sonnets, essays of great brilliance, he had the world before him."

"If he was on the fast track like you say, how was he derailed?"

"In the development of that fantastically able brain, nothing went wrong. He grows better year by year. In his private life, everything."

"Do you care to tell me?"

He considered for some moments, then said: "No. But I will tell you this. The moment I heard you speak aboard the *Galante,* and learned that you were not married, I almost shouted: 'There's the one! She's the one that could do it!'"

Thérèse laughed, then explained: "Oh, Mr. Carmody, at college the girls used to sit around and tell gruesome case histories that always ended: 'So, girls, there it is. Never marry a moral cripple. Spend that little extra effort and find yourself a real man.'"

"Dr. Vaval, believe me, this man is no cripple. He needs to have his soul set free. Someone to help him become the man he could be."

Soberly she said: "I suppose you could say that of many men."

"He's different. He's worth it." While she was pondering this, he said rather boldly: "On the second night of Carnaval, when I saw you and Ranjit sitting together, you looked as if you, too, for the moment had been set free."

"You should have joined us."

"It was clear you wished to be alone. Now it's clear that you wish you were back in Trinidad."

Thérèse, biting her knuckles, stared at the Caribbean and its white wave tips dancing by in pirouetting joy, but she felt only sadness in leaving this sea of her choice. She would miss its golden grandeur and its varied people, especially the man in Trinidad who knew it even better than she. Then came the quiet voice of the college counselor, as if he were talking to a student having trouble with algebra, except that in this instance the trouble was with the student's heart:

"Dr. Vaval, since you're from Haiti, I must assume you're Catholic, and he's certainly a Hindu. As a Catholic myself, and immersed in Trinidad, I must in all decency warn you that such radical differences are almost irreconcilable. But yet, it seems to me, with you and Ranjit the similarities are much greater than the differences, are they not?" And she whispered: "Yes."

Carmody, sixty and aware that his years as a teacher were ending with the job undone—he had not got his one brilliant student properly started—took Thérèse's hands in his and said: "You too are growing older, my dear. Twenty-five doesn't last forever, and thirty-five brings panic in all of us, especially women. I've seen it. So two lives are at stake, his and yours . . . and I have the feeling that the peril is almost equally shared."

When she said nothing, but did leave her hands in his, he continued. "A college guidance teacher deals with two kinds of students, those who need to discover the fundamental truths for themselves, nudged by his quiet prodding, and those who need to be told in the simplest and sometimes most brutal terms: 'Francis Xavier, change your ways or I will throw you out of this college.'"

"And you think I'm the latter?"

"I know it. So I'm giving an order. When the *Galante* docks in Miami tomorrow, you and I will grab a taxi, rush right out to the airport, and catch the next plane back to Trinidad. You're needed there."

Alarmed by the impetuousness of the step she was about to take, she asked in a burst of anxiety: "Would I be insane if I did fly back . . . I've known him only two days?" and the older voice said quietly: "Love is the self-revelation of two souls. Sometimes it comes in a blinding moment in only one day, sometimes after a slow awakening of eleven years. God takes no cognizance of the timetable."

So next morning when the ship was safely moored, the two popular instructors bade their students farewell, caught a cab, and sped to Miami International.

When Thérèse Vaval walked up the steps of the Sirdar's House and knocked on the door, her first words were abrupt and intense: "I was drawn back by a thousand magnets, Ranjit. Your ideas, your potential, and above all, by the fact that you need me to unlock the frozen doors."

When he did not respond, she spoke of her own frozen doors, of her engagement to Dennis Krey and of her confusion in Haiti. By his quiet smile she knew that he guessed these to be peripheral reasons, so she told of her conversation with Carmody and his insistence that she fly back immediately, since the rest of her life was in jeopardy. Only then did he realize that she had been as wounded by life as he. There was silence for a moment. Then, clearing her throat, she said: "Now, Ranjit, tell me how it was with you."

Mustering his courage and licking his dry lips, he said: "When you sailed away at the end of Carnaval, I learned what torment was. I lingered at the dock till your ship was out of sight, mumbling to myself: 'There she goes. The one light in this world.' And when I thought that I would never see you again, I was disconsolate . . . books were tedious. It was then I discovered what love was."

"As the ship sailed I was feeling the same, Ranjit. But the questions remain: Who are you? Why are you here and alone?"

Fear almost paralyzed him as he wondered how much he should tell her, how much he dared tell without frightening her and driving her away again. Seeing no escape, he blurted out: "I had an overpowering desire to be a scholar in the States, but my permit to stay was running out. I had to do something. So I went to a man who made a business of arranging marriages for foreign students so they could get American citizenship . . . and I married his sister. But it turned out that she had a real husband, a Nicaraguan, and three earlier fake marriages . . . no divorces. It was shameful and I was part of it."

Thérèse shivered, wondering what was to come next, and the burst of revelation shattered the quiet room like the gusts of a hurricane: "A bed in the cellar . . . punched me . . . her husband with a knife at my throat . . . the Immigration hearing . . . the expulsion." When he saw she was numbed he stopped, rummaged among his notebooks, then held before her the front page of the Miami paper from the day of his deportation: JEALOUS NICARAGUAN LOVER MURDERS . . .

Now she asked only one question, but it was astonishingly blunt: "Is your banishment for life?" and he replied: "I think so," and she said firmly: "Well, I don't. And I shall devise some way to get you back into the States . . . permanently . . . and find you a job teaching!" Then, as if a dam had broken, she threw her hands over her face, and from the convulsions of her shoulders he knew that she was silently sobbing. Finally she dropped her hands and looked straight at him: "We've never even kissed . . . and here I am, proposing to you."

He did not, as an ordinary man would, rush to embrace her; instead, he stood fearfully apart and said in a low voice: "I was married to Molly Hudak for nearly two years and she allowed me to kiss her only once, at our wedding when the clerk said almost menacingly: 'Now you may kiss her.' Apparently I'm not the kissing kind."

This broke the spell, and she came toward him, arms held wide. But he drew back, hesitant, for there was one more thing he was bound in honor as a gentleman to do. Softly he asked: "Thérèse, will you marry me?" and then, moving forward evenly, they kissed, and she whispered: "We're children of the golden sea . . . its destiny and ours are linked . . . and together, you and I shall help it find its way."

FURTHER READING

A novel like this serves a commendable purpose if it encourages the reader to consult other books on the subject. The University of Miami, where I worked during the writing, has a library with a wealth of Caribbean material. No matter how obscure the subject on which I required information, the librarians invariably found the books I needed. From the hundreds I consulted, I recommend the following. Most of these titles, if not in your bookshop, should be available through your local public-library system.

Maya. To supplement my research on the ancient cities of the Yucatán Peninsula, I found *The Ancient Maya* by Sylvanus Morley (Stanford University Press, 1983) and *The Rise and Fall of Maya Civilization* by J. Eric Thompson (University of Oklahoma Press, 1966) to be particularly helpful.

Columbus. In his magisterial biography *Admiral of the Ocean Sea* (Little, Brown, 1942), Samuel Eliot Morrison summarizes standard views of the great discoverer. Salvador de Madariaga, in *Christopher Columbus* (Hollis & Carter, 1949), assaults the argument that Columbus was, in any way that mattered, an Italian and argues instead that he was probably a wandering Jew.

Spanish Caribbean. In *Caribbean Sea of the New World* (Alfred A. Knopf, 1946), Germán Arciniegas provides a brilliantly composed defense of Spain's accomplishments in the Caribbean. Strongly argued, rich in detail. On the stories of Cartagena, Eduardo LeMaitre's comprehensive *Historia General de Cartagena* has not yet been translated from the Spanish, but an abbreviated account in English does exist (no date, but 1980s) and is worth the search.

Pirates and Buccaneers. Nobody knows for sure the spelling of the man's name or his nationality, but in 1684, Alexander Esquemeling published in London a powerful, some say mendacious, personal reminiscence of Henry Morgan and other pirates, *The Bucaniers* [sic] *of America* (Scribner, 1898, reprint). In a modern work of great merit, Dudley Pope's *Harry Morgan's Way* (Alison Press, 1977) gives a less hysterical but more astonishing account of Morgan's exploits. And *The Sack of Panama* by Peter Earle (Viking Press, 1972) brilliantly re-creates Morgan's most memorable, indeed incredible, adventures.

Sugar and Slavery. Sugar and slavery will forever be linked as the glory and shame of the Caribbean Islands, and for this inexhaustible subject three books were particularly valuable: *Sugar and Slavery* by Richard B. Sheridan (Johns Hopkins University Press, 1974); *The Fall of the Planter Class in the British Caribbean* by Lowell J. Ragatz (Century, 1928); and *A Jamaican Plantation* by Michael Crayton and James Walvin (University of Toronto Press, 1970).

British Islands. Alec Waugh, elder brother of Evelyn, gives a fine portrait of an imaginary English colony in *Island in the Sun* (Farrar, Straus, 1955). The gallantry of the Cavaliers on Barbados in offering to fight the entire British Empire in defense of King Charles I is told by N. Davis in his *The Cavaliers and Roundheads of Barbados* (Argosy Press, 1887). James Anthony Froude's *The English in the West Indies* (Scribner, 1897) is probably the worst travel book written by any historian on any subject at any time. A boastful champion of white supremacy and a merciless reviler of blacks and Irishmen, the author reveals himself as such a consummate ass that the modern reader alternately shudders and guffaws.

The Seamen of England. If the battles for naval supremacy in Europe were rehearsed in the waters of the Caribbean, two English sailors contributed monumentally to the course of history. The exploits of Francis Drake are well recorded in *The Life of Francis Drake* by A. E. W. Mason (Hodder & Stoughton, 1941), and his major claim to fame in *The Defeat of the Spanish Armada* by Garrett Mattingly (Jonathan Cape, 1959). Chronicling the extraordinary career and unashamedly venal temperament of Horatio Nelson are *The Life of Nelson* by Robert Southey (Constable, 1916) and Carola Oman's classic *Nelson* (Doubleday, 1946).

The French Connections. Cuba's finest novelist, Alejo Carpentier, in his *Explosion in a Cathedral* (first published in Mexico in 1962 and now available in Penguin Books, 1971), gives a dramatic portrait of Victor Hugues, with a background prior to his "reign" in Guadeloupe much different from the one I offer. An excellent book.

Haiti. Haiti's fight for independence under a brilliant black general who outfoxed the French, the Spanish and the British is well told in *The Life of Toussaint L'Ouverture* by the Reverend John Beard (Ingram Cook, 1923). The subsequent pitiful course of that independence is well covered in *Black Democracy, The Story of Haiti* by H. P. Davis (Dial Press, 1928) and in *Haiti, the Politics of Squalor* by Robert I. Rotberg (Houghton Mifflin, 1921). I especially recommend the work of a brilliant Trinidad scholar, C. L. R. James, *The Black Jacobins* (Secker & Warburg, 1938).

Trinidad. The complexities of an island shared equally by ethnic heritages of Africa and India are well cited by Morton Klass in *East Indians in Trinidad* (Columbia University Press, 1961). Her emergence as an independent republic is ably reported by Donald Wood in *Trinidad in Transition* (Oxford University Press, 1968).

Jamaica. There is a wealth of material on Jamaica, written at all stages of her history. Oliver Cox's *Upgrading and Renewing the Historic City of Port Royal, Jamaica* (Shankland Cox, London, 1984) is an enchanting official report replete with maps and plans. Robert F. Marx's *Pirate Port, the Story of the Sunken City of Port Royal* (World Publishing, 1967) provides a capitulation of the basic facts. On the tragedy of the Morant Bay rebellion under the governorship of John Eyre, Australian apologist Geoffrey Dutton, in *The Hero as Murderer* (Collins, 1967), depicts Eyre as an unquestioned hero during his tenure in Australia and as the cool-headed savior of the white man in Jamaica. In *The Myth of Governor Eyre* (Woolf, 1933), Lord Olivier, a later governor of Jamaica, proves his predecessor to have been a bumptious fool. For current books on Jamaica generally, two contemporary Jamaicans have made excellent contributions. Sir Philip Sherlock's *West Indian Nation* (St. Martin's Press, 1973) and Clinton V. Black's *History of Jamaica* (Collins, 1961) pull no punches, albeit in their own gentlemanly fashion. Sherlock was personally most helpful in guiding me toward experts on many aspects of Jamaican life, past and present.

Cuba. Of many instructive books, I used three which pertained directly to my story. R. Hart Phillips' *Cuba, Island of Paradox* (McDowell, Obolensky, 1959) is the intimate report of steps leading to Castro's triumph, by the mother superior of newspaper correspondents. Carleton Beals's *The Crime of Cuba* (Lippincott, 1933) is the standard pre-Castro warning of a liberal observer. Tad Szulc and Karl E. Meyer's *The Cuban Invasion* (Praeger, 1962) is a gripping account of the Bay of Pigs disaster. Of the more formal histories, I profited from Jaime Suchlicki's *Cuba from Columbus to Castro* (Scribner, 1974).

Rastafarians. Two books attempt to explain the many confusing aspects of this mystifying religious movement. *Dread: The Rastafarians of Jamaica* by Joseph Owens (Sangster, Kingston, Jamaica, 1976) and *The Rastafarians* by Leonard E. Barrett (idem, 1977) are supplemented by a gripping biography of reggae star Bob Marley by Timothy White, *Catch a Fire* (Holt, Rinehart, Winston, 1983).

Cricket. The importance of the Caribbean's other main religion, cricket, is rarely appreciated by the outsiders, but I have not exaggerated its significance. From the score of technical treatises I recommend two delightful reads: C. L. R. James's *Beyond a Boundary* (Pantheon Books, 1984), a reminiscence of boyhood in Trinidad, and Frances Edmonds' *Another Bloody Tour: England in the West Indies 1986* (Kingswood, 1986), the irreverent report of an Englishwoman intellectual married to a professional cricketer. (England was massacred by the islanders, 5 matches to 0.)

Caribbean. I found that most islanders pronounce this Car-ib-*bee*-an, and dictionaries give that as preferred, with Ca-*rib*-ee-an in second place as acceptable. A wag explained: "The hoi polloi use the first, but intellectual snobs prefer the second." And so do I. I have been unable to pin down when the word was first used to designate the sea which now bears that name. We know for sure that this confusion started with the first Spaniards who saw that the all-important Isthmus of Panama ran not vertically north to south, as laymen would always believe, but horizontally east to west. This caused early mariners to refer to the Pacific Ocean as La Mar del Sur (South Sea) and the future Caribbean as La Mar del Norte (North Sea). Sir Francis Drake did not sail into the Pacific on his historic circumnavigation of the globe: he ventured into the South Sea, and this usage continued through the sixteenth century and probably into the seventeenth. Sir Henry Morgan and his pirates ravaged the North Sea, not the Caribbean, and I have seen maps printed as late as 1770 still using the older terminology. I would appreciate instruction clarifying this interesting geographical puzzle.

THE SETTING

971,400 square miles, of which land is only a small portion

ISLAND	SQUARE MILES	POPULATION	DENSITY	COMPARISON IN SIZE
All Saints	303	110,000	363	Madeira
Antigua	171	82,400	456	Seychelles
Anguilla	34	7,000	206	Ascension
Aruba	75	62,000	785	American Samoa
Barbados	166	254,000	1566	Isle of Wight
Bonaire	111	8,753	52	Kiska
Curaçao	171	147,388	1147	Seychelles
Cayman	118	18,000	101	Martha's Vineyard
Cuba	42,827	10,290,000	231	Pennsylvania
Dominica	290	87,000	279	Tonga
Dominican Republic	18,704	6,708,000	316	Vermont + NH
Grenada	133	104,000	837	Malta
Guadeloupe	687	335,000	463	Skye
Haiti	10,714	5,532,000	495	Maryland
Jamaica	4,244	2,365,000	533	Connecticut
Martinique	425	329,000	746	Okinawa
Monserrat	39	13,000	329	Ascension
Puerto Rico	3,435	3,300,000	951	Rhode Is. + DE
St. Eustatius	11	1,358	93	Diomede, Russian
St. Kitts-Nevis	104	46,500	510	Christmas
Saint-Martin (Fr)	21	12,000	571	Bermuda
St. Vincent	150	112,000	680	Kanaga-Lapak
Sint Maarten (D)	13	13,156	382	Diomede, Russian
Trinidad & Tobago	1,970	1,221,000	632	Balearics
Virgin Is. (Br)	59	12,000	203	Nantucket
Virgin Is. (US)	133	112,000	759	Amchitka
TOTAL	85,045*	31,282,555†		

* About same number of square miles as Minnesota (84,068)
†About same population as California, Oregon and Washington (32,598,000)

JAMES A. MICHENER, one of the world's most popular writers, was the author of the Pulitzer Prize–winning *Tales of the South Pacific,* the bestselling novels *Hawaii, Texas, Chesapeake, The Covenant,* and *Alaska,* and the memoir *The World Is My Home.* Michener served on the advisory council to NASA and the International Broadcast Board, which oversees the Voice of America. Among dozens of awards and honors, he received America's highest civilian award, the Presidential Medal of Freedom, in 1977, and an award from the President's Committee on the Arts and Humanities in 1983 for his commitment to art in America. Michener died in 1997 at the age of ninety.